I0784961

Guy de Maupassant

The Collected Novels of Guy De Maupassant

OK Publishing 2021

Guy de Maupassant
THE COLLECTED NOVELS OF GUY DE MAUPASSANT

Bel-Ami, A Life, Pierre and Jean, Strong as Death, Mont Oriol & Notre Coeur

Published by
MUSAICUM
Books

- Advanced Digital Solutions & High-Quality book Formatting -

musaicumbooks@okpublishing.info

2021 OK Publishing

ISBN 978-80-272-7478-9

Contents

A Life

I

The weather was most distressing. It had rained all night. The roaring of the overflowing gutters filled the deserted streets, in which the houses, like sponges, absorbed the humidity, which penetrating to the interior, made the walls sweat from cellar to garret. Jeanne had left the convent the day before, free for all time, ready to seize all the joys of life, of which she had dreamed so long. She was afraid her father would not set out for the new home in bad weather, and for the hundredth time since daybreak she examined the horizon. Then she noticed that she had omitted to put her calendar in her travelling bag. She took from the wall the little card which bore in golden figures the date of the current year, 1819. Then she marked with a pencil the first four columns, drawing a line through the name of each saint up to the 2d of May, the day that she left the convent. A voice outside the door called "Jeannette." Jeanne replied, "Come in, papa." And her father entered. Baron Simon-Jacques Le Perthuis des Vauds was a gentleman of the last century, eccentric and good. An enthusiastic disciple of Jean Jacques Rousseau, he had the tenderness of a lover for nature, in the fields, in the woods and in the animals. Of aristocratic birth, he hated instinctively the year 1793, but being a philosopher by temperament and liberal by education, he execrated tyranny with an inoffensive and declamatory hatred. His great strength and his great weakness was his kind-heartedness, which had not arms enough to caress, to give, to embrace; the benevolence of a god, that gave freely, without questioning; in a word, a kindness of inertia that became almost a vice. A man of theory, he thought out a plan of education for his daughter, to the end that she might become happy, good, upright and gentle. She had lived at home until the age of twelve, when, despite the tears of her mother, she was placed in the Convent of the Sacred Heart. He had kept her severely secluded, cloistered, in ignorance of the secrets of life. He wished the Sisters to restore her to him pure at seventeen years of age, so that he might imbue her mind with a sort of rational poetry, and by means of the fields, in the midst of the fruitful earth, unfold her soul, enlighten her ignorance through the aspect of love in nature, through the simple tenderness of the animals, through the placid laws of existence. She was leaving the convent radiant, full of the joy of life, ready for all the happiness, all the charming incidents which her mind had pictured in her idle hours and in the long, quiet nights. She was like a portrait by Veronese with her fair, glossy hair, which seemed to cast a radiance on her skin, a skin with the faintest tinge of pink, softened by a light velvety down which could be perceived when the sun kissed her cheek. Her eyes were an opaque blue, like those of Dutch porcelain figures. She had a tiny mole on her left nostril and another on the right of her chin. She was tall, well developed, with willowy figure. Her clear voice sounded at times a little too sharp, but her frank, sincere laugh spread joy around her. Often, with a familiar gesture, she would raise her hands to her temples as if to arrange her hair.

She ran to her father and embraced him warmly. "Well, are we going to start?" she said. He smiled, shook his head and said, pointing toward the window, "How can we travel in such weather?" But she implored in a cajoling and tender manner, "Oh, papa, do let us start. It will clear up in the afternoon." "But your mother will never consent to it." "Yes, I promise you that she will, I will arrange that." "If you succeed in persuading your mother, I am per-fectly willing." In a few moments she returned from her mother's room, shouting in a voice that could be heard all through the house, "Papa, papa, mamma is willing. Have the horses harnessed." The rain was not abating; one might almost have said that it was raining harder when the carriage drove up to the door. Jeanne was ready to step in when the baroness came downstairs, supported on one side by her husband and on the other by a tall housemaid, strong and strapping as a boy. She was a Norman woman of the country of Caux, who looked at least twenty, although she was but eighteen at the most. She was treated by the family as a second daughter, for she was Jeanne's foster sister. Her name was Rosalie, and her chief duty lay in guiding the steps of her mistress, who had grown enormous in the last few years and also had an affection of the heart, which kept her complaining continually. The baroness, gasping from over-exertion, finally reached the doorstep of the old residence, looked at the court where the water was streaming and remarked: "It really is not wise." Her husband, always pleasant, replied: "It was you who desired it, Madame Adelaide." He always preceded her pompous name of Adelaide with the title madame with an air of half respectful mockery. Madame mounted with difficulty into the carriage, causing all the springs to bend. The baron sat beside her, while Jeanne and Rosalie were seated opposite, with their backs to the horses. Ludivine, the cook, brought a heap of wraps to put over their knees and two baskets, which were placed under the seats; then she climbed on the box beside Father Simon, wrapping herself in a great rug which covered her completely. The porter and his wife came to bid them good-by as they closed the carriage door, taking the last orders about the trunks, which were to follow in a wagon. So they started. Father Simon, the coachman, with head bowed and back bent in the pouring rain, was completely covered by his box coat with its triple cape. The howling storm beat upon the carriage windows and inundated the highway.

They drove rapidly to the wharf and continued alongside the line of tall-masted vessels until they reached the boulevard of Mont Riboudet. Then they crossed the meadows, where from time to time a drowned willow, its branches drooping limply, could be faintly distinguished through the mist of rain. No one spoke. Their minds themselves seemed to be saturated with moisture like the earth.

The baroness leaned her head against the cushions and closed her eyes. The baron looked out with mournful eyes at the monotonous and drenched landscape. Rosalie, with a parcel on her knee, was dreaming in the dull reverie of a peasant. But Jeanne, under this downpour, felt herself revive like a plant that has been shut up and has just been restored to the air, and so great was her joy that, like foliage, it sheltered her heart from sadness. Although she did not speak, she longed to burst out singing, to reach out her hands to catch the rain that she might drink it. She enjoyed to the full being carried along rapidly by the horses, enjoyed gazing at the desolate landscape and feeling herself under shelter amid this general inundation. Beneath the pelting rain the gleaming backs of the two horses emitted a warm steam.

Little by little the baroness fell asleep, and presently began to snore sonorously. Her husband leaned over and placed in her hands a little leather pocketbook.

This awakened her, and she looked at the pocketbook with the stupid, sleepy look of one suddenly aroused. It fell off her lap and sprang open and gold and bank bills were scattered on the floor of the carriage. This roused her completely, and Jeanne gave vent to her mirth in a merry peal of girlish laughter.

The baron picked up the money and placed it on her knees. "This, my dear," he said, "is all that is left of my farm at Eletot. I have sold it — so as to be able to repair the 'Poplars,' where we shall often live in the future."

She counted six thousand four hundred francs and quietly put them in her pocket. This was the ninth of thirty-one farms that they had inherited which they had sold in this way. Nevertheless they still possessed about twenty thousand livres income annually in land rentals, which, with proper care, would have yielded about thirty thousand francs a year.

Living simply as they did, this income would have sufficed had there not been a bottomless hole always open in their house — kind-hearted generosity. It dried up the money in their hands as the sun dries the water in marshes. It flowed, fled, disappeared. How? No one knew. Frequently one would say to the other, "I don't know how it happens, but I have spent one hundred francs to-day, and I have bought nothing of any consequence." This faculty of giving was, however, one of the greatest pleasures of their life, and they all agreed on this point in a superb and touching manner.

Jeanne asked her father, "Is it beautiful now, my castle?" The baron replied, "You shall see, my little girl."

The storm began to abate. The vault of clouds seemed to rise and heighten and suddenly, through a rift, a long ray of sunshine fell upon the fields, and presently the clouds separated, showing the blue firmament, and then, like the tearing of a veil, the opening grew larger and the beautiful azure sky, clear and fathomless, spread over the world. A fresh and gentle breeze passed over the earth like a happy sigh, and as they passed beside gardens or woods they heard occasionally the bright chirp of a bird as he dried his wings.

Evening was approaching. Everyone in the carriage was asleep except Jeanne. They stopped to rest and feed the horses. The sun had set. In the distance bells were heard. They passed a little village as the inhabitants were lighting their lamps, and the sky became also illuminated by myriads of stars. Suddenly they saw behind a hill, through the branches of the fir trees, the moon rising, red and full as if it were torpid with sleep.

The air was so soft that the windows were not closed. Jeanne, exhausted with dreams and happy visions, was now asleep. Finally they stopped. Some men and women were standing before the carriage door with lanterns in their hands. They had arrived. Jeanne, suddenly awakened, was the first to jump out. Her father and Rosalie had practically to carry the baroness, who was groaning and continually repeating in a weak little voice, "Oh, my God, my poor children!" She refused all offers of refreshment, but went to bed and immediately fell asleep.

Jeanne and her father, the baron, took supper together. They were in perfect sympathy with each other. Later, seized with a childish joy, they started on a tour of inspection through the restored manor. It was one of those high and vast Norman residences that comprise both farmhouse and castle, built of white stone which had turned gray, large enough to contain a whole race of people.

An immense hall divided the house from front to rear and a staircase went up at either side of the entrance, meeting in a bridge on the first floor. The huge drawingroom was on the ground floor to the right and was hung with tapestries representing birds and foliage. All the furniture was covered with fine needlework tapestry illustrating La Fontaine's fables, and Jeanne was delighted at finding a chair she had loved as a child, which pictured the story of "The Fox and the Stork."

Beside the drawingroom were the library, full of old books, and two unused rooms; at the left was the diningroom, the laundry, the kitchen, *etc.*

A corridor divided the whole first floor, the doors of ten rooms opening into it. At the end, on the right, was Jeanne's room. She and her father went in. He had had it all newly done over, using the furniture and draperies that had been in the storeroom.

There were some very old Flemish tapestries, with their peculiar looking figures. At sight of her bed, the young girl uttered a scream of joy. Four large birds carved in oak, black from age and highly polished, bore up the bed and seemed to be its protectors. On the sides were carved two wide garlands of flowers and fruit, and four finely fluted columns, terminating in Corinthian capitals, supported a cornice of cupids with roses intertwined. The tester and the coverlet were of antique blue silk, embroidered in gold fleur de lys. When Jeanne had sufficiently admired it, she lifted up the candle to examine the tapestries and the allegories they represented. They were mostly conventional subjects, but the last hanging represented a drama. Near a rabbit, which was still nibbling, a young man lay stretched out, apparently dead. A young girl, gazing at him, was plunging a sword into her bosom, and the fruit of the tree had turned black. Jeanne gave up trying to divine the meaning underlying this picture, when she saw in the corner a tiny little animal which the rabbit, had he lived, could have swallowed like a blade of grass; and yet it was a lion. Then she recognized the story of "Pyramus and Thisbe," and though she smiled at the simplicity of the design, she felt happy to have in her room this love adventure which would continually speak to her of her cherished hopes, and every night this legendary love would hover about her dreams.

It struck eleven and the baron kissed Jeanne goodnight and retired to his room. Before retiring, Jeanne cast a last glance round her room and then regretfully extinguished the candle. Through her window she could see the bright moonlight bathing the trees and the wonderful landscape. Presently she arose, opened a window and looked out. The night was so clear that one could see as plainly as by daylight. She looked across the park with its two long avenues of very tall poplars that gave its name to the château and separated it from the two farms that belonged to it, one occupied by the Couillard family, the other by the Martins. Beyond the enclosure stretched a long, uncultivated plain, thickly overgrown with rushes, where the breeze whistled day and night. The land ended abruptly in a steep white cliff three hundred feet high, with its base in the ocean waves.

Jeanne looked out over the long, undulating surface that seemed to slumber beneath the heavens. All the fragrance of the earth was in the night air. The odor of jasmine rose from the lower windows, and light whiffs of briny air and of seaweed were wafted from the ocean.

Merely to breathe was enough for Jeanne, and the restful calm of the country was like a soothing bath. She felt as though her heart was expanding and she began dreaming of love. What was it? She did not know. She only knew that she would adore him with all her soul and that he would cherish her with all his strength. They would walk hand in hand on nights like this, hearing the beating of their hearts, mingling their love with the sweet simplicity of the summer nights in such close communion of thought that by the sole power of their tenderness they would easily penetrate each other's most secret thoughts. This would continue forever in the calm of an enduring affection. It seemed to her that she felt him there beside her. And an unusual sensation came over her. She remained long musing thus, when suddenly she thought she heard a footstep behind the house. "If it were he." But it passed on and she felt as if she had been deceived. The air became cooler. The day broke. Slowly bursting aside the gleaming clouds, touching with fire the trees, the plains, the ocean, all the horizon, the great flaming orb of the sun appeared.

Jeanne felt herself becoming mad with happiness. A delirious joy, an infinite tenderness at the splendor of nature overcame her fluttering heart. It was her sun, her dawn! The beginning of her life! Thoroughly fatigued at last, she flung herself down and slept till her father called her at eight o'clock. He walked into the room and proposed to show her the improvements of the castle, of her castle. The road, called the parish road, connecting the farms, joined the high road between Havre and Fécamp, a mile and a half further on.

Jeanne and the baron inspected everything and returned home for breakfast. When the meal was over, as the baroness had decided that she would rest, the baron proposed to Jeanne that they should go down to Yport. They started, and passing through the hamlet of Etouvent, where the poplars were, and going through the wooded slope by a winding valley leading down to the sea, they presently perceived the village of Yport. Women sat in their doorways mending linen; brown fish-nets were hanging against the doors of the huts, where an entire family lived in one room. It was a typical little French fishing village, with all its concomitant odors. To Jeanne it was all like a scene in a play. On turning a corner they saw before them the limitless blue ocean. They bought a brill from a fisherman and another sailor offered to take them out sailing, repeating his name, "Lastique, Joséphin Lastique," several times, that they might not forget it, and the baron promised to remember. They walked home, chattering like two children, carrying the big fish between them, Jeanne having pushed her father's walking cane through its gills.

II

A delightful life commenced for Jeanne, a life in the open air. She wandered along the roads, or into the little winding valleys, their sides covered with a fleece of gorse blossoms, the strong sweet odor of which intoxicated her like the bouquet of wine, while the distant sound of the waves rolling on the beach seemed like a billow rocking her spirit.

A love of solitude came upon her in the sweet freshness of this landscape and in the calm of the rounded horizon, and she would remain sitting so long on the hill tops that the wild rabbits would bound by her feet.

She planted memories everywhere, as seeds are cast upon the earth, memories whose roots hold till death. It seemed to Jeanne that she was casting a little of her heart into every fold of these valleys. She became infatuated with sea bathing. When she was well out from shore, she would float on her back, her arms crossed, her eyes lost in the profound blue of the sky which was cleft by the flight of a swallow, or the white silhouette of a seabird.

After these excursions she invariably came back to the castle pale with hunger, but light, alert, a smile on her lips and her eyes sparkling with happiness.

The baron on his part was planning great agricultural enterprises. Occasionally, also, he went out to sea with the sailors of Yport. On several occasions he went fishing for mackerel and, again, by moonlight, he would haul in the nets laid the night before. He loved to hear the masts creak, to breathe in the fresh and whistling gusts of wind that arose during the night; and after having tacked a long time to find the buoys, guiding himself by a peak of rocks, the roof of a belfry or the Fécamp lighthouse, he delighted to remain motionless beneath the first gleams of the rising sun which made the slimy backs of the large fan-shaped rays and the fat bellies of the turbots glisten on the deck of the boat.

At each meal he gave an enthusiastic account of his expeditions, and the baroness in her turn told how many times she had walked down the main avenue of poplars.

As she had been advised to take exercise she made a business of walking, beginning as soon as the air grew warm. Leaning upon Rosalie's arm and dragging her left foot, which was rather heavier than the right, she wandered interminably up and down from the house to the edge of the wood, sitting down for five minutes at either end. The walking was resumed in the afternoon. A physician, consulted ten years before, had spoken of hypertrophy because she had suffered from suffocation. Ever since, this word had been used to describe the ailment of the baroness. The baron would say "my wife's hypertrophy" and Jeanne "mamma's hypertrophy" as they would have spoken of her hat, her dress, or her umbrella. She had been very pretty in her youth and slim as a reed. Now she had grown older, stouter, but she still remained poetical, having always retained the impression of "Corinne," which she had read as a girl. She read all the sentimental love stories it was possible to collect, and her thoughts wandered among tender adventures in which she always figured as the heroine. Her new home was infinitely pleasing to her because it formed such a beautiful framework for the romance of her soul, the surrounding woods, the waste land, and the proximity of the ocean recalling to her mind the novels of Sir Walter Scott, which she had been devouring for some months. On rainy days she remained shut up in her room, sending Rosalie in a special manner for the drawer containing her "souvenirs," which meant to the baroness all her old private and family letters.

Occasionally, Jeanne replaced Rosalie in the walks with her mother, and she listened eagerly to the tales of the latter's childhood. The young girl saw herself in all these romantic stories, and was astonished at the similarity of ideas and desires; each heart imagines itself to have been the first to tremble at those very sensations that awakened the hearts of the first beings, and that will awaken the hearts of the last.

One afternoon as the baroness and Jeanne were resting on the beach at the end of the walk, a stout priest who was moving in their direction greeted them with a bow, while still at a distance. He bowed when within three feet and, assuming a smiling air, cried: "Well, Madame la Baronne, how are you?" It was the village priest. The baroness seldom went to church, though she liked priests, from a sort of religious instinct peculiar to women. She had, in fact, entirely forgotten the Abbé Picot, her priest, and blushed as she saw him. She made apologies for not having prepared for his visit, but the good man was not at all embarrassed. He looked at Jeanne, complimented her on her appearance and sat down, placing his three-cornered hat on his knees. He was very stout, very red, and perspired profusely. He drew from his pocket every moment an enormous checked handkerchief and passed it over his face and neck, but hardly was the task completed when necessity forced him to repeat the process. He was a typical country priest, talkative and kindly.

Presently the baron appeared. He was very friendly to the abbé and invited him to dinner. The priest was well versed in the art of being pleasant, thanks to the unconscious astuteness which the guiding of souls gives to the most mediocre of men who are called by the chance of events to exercise a power over their fellows. Toward dessert he became quite merry, with the gaiety that follows a pleasant meal, and as if struck by an idea he said: "I have a new parishioner whom I must present to you, Monsieur le Vicomte de Lamare." The baroness, who was at home in heraldry, inquired if he was of the family of Lamares of Eure. The priest answered, "Yes, madame, he is the son of Vicomte Jean de Lamare, who died last year." After this, the baroness, who loved the nobility above all other things, inquired the history of the young vicomte. He had paid his father's debts, sold the family castle, made his home on one of the three farms which he owned in the town of Etouvent. These estates brought him in an income of five or six thousand livres. The vicomte was economical and lived in this modest manner for two or three years, so that he might save enough to cut a figure in society, and to marry advantageously, without contracting debts or mortgaging his farms. The priest added, "He is a very charming young man, so steady and quiet, though there is very little to amuse him in the country." The baron said, "Bring him in to see us, Monsieur l'Abbé, it will be a distraction for him occasionally." After the coffee the baron and the priest took a turn about the grounds and then returned to say goodnight to the ladies.

III

The following Sunday the baroness and Jeanne went to mass, prompted by a feeling of respect for their pastor, and after service waited to see the priest and invite him to luncheon the following Thursday. He came out of the sacristy leaning familiarly on the arm of a tall young man. As soon as he perceived the ladies, he exclaimed:

"How fortunate! Allow me, baroness and *Mlle.* Jeanne, to present to you your neighbor, M. le Vicomte de Lamare."

The vicomte said he had long desired to make their acquaintance, and began to converse in a well-bred manner. He had a face of which women dream and that men dislike. His black, wavy hair shaded a smooth, sunburnt forehead, and two large straight eyebrows, that looked almost artificial, cast a deep and tender shadow over his dark eyes, the whites of which had a bluish tinge.

His long, thick eyelashes accentuated the passionate eloquence of his expression which wrought havoc in the drawingrooms of society, and made peasant girls carrying baskets turn round to look at him. The languorous fascination of his glance impressed one with the depth of his thoughts and lent weight to his slightest words. His beard, fine and glossy, concealed a somewhat heavy jaw.

Two days later, M. de Lamare made his first call, just as they were discussing the best place for a new rustic bench. The vicomte was consulted and agreed with the baroness, who differed from her husband.

M. de Lamare expatiated on the picturesqueness of the country and from time to time, as if by chance, his eyes met those of Jeanne, and she felt a strange sensation at the quickly averted glance which betrayed tender admiration and an awakened sympathy.

M. de Lamare's father, who had died the preceding year, had known an intimate friend of the baroness's father, M. Cultaux, and this fact led to an endless conversation about family, relations, dates, etc., and names heard in her childhood were recalled, and led to reminiscences.

The baron, whose nature was rather uncultivated, and whose beliefs and prejudices were not those of his class, knew little about the neighboring families, and inquired about them from the vicomte, who responded:

"Oh, there are very few of the nobility in the district," just as he might have said, "there are very few rabbits on the hills," and he began to particularize: There was the Marquis de Coutelier, a sort of leader of Norman aristocracy, Vicomte and Vicomtesse de Briseville, people of excellent stock, but living to themselves, and the Comte de Fourville, a kind of ogre, who was said to have made his wife die of sorrow, and who lived as a huntsman in his château of La

Vrillette, built on a pond. There were a few parvenus among them who had bought properties here and there, but the vicomte did not know them.

As he left, his last glance was for Jeanne, as if it were a special tender and cordial farewell. The baroness was delighted with him, and the baron said: "Yes, indeed, he is a gentleman." And he was invited to dinner the following week, and from that time came regularly.

He generally arrived about four o'clock in the afternoon, went to join the baroness in "her avenue," and offered her his arm while she took her "exercise," as she called her daily walks. When Jeanne was at home she would walk on the other side of her mother, supporting her, and all three would walk slowly back and forth from one end of the avenue to the other. He seldom addressed Jeanne directly, but his eye frequently met hers.

He went to Yport several times with Jeanne and the baron. One evening, when they were on the beach, Père Lastique accosted him, and without removing his pipe, the absence of which would possibly have been more remarkable than the loss of his nose, he said:

"With this wind, m'sieu le baron, we could easily go to Étretat and back tomorrow."

Jeanne clasped her hands imploringly:

"Oh, papa, let us do it!"

The baron turned to M. de Lamare:

"Will you join us, vicomte? We can take breakfast down there."

And the matter was decided at once. From daybreak Jeanne was up and waiting for her father, who dressed more slowly. They walked in the dew across the level and then through the wood vibrant with the singing of birds. The vicomte and Père Lastique were seated on a capstan.

Two other sailors helped to shove off the boat from shore, which was not easy on the shingly beach. Once the boat was afloat, they all took their seats, and the two sailors who remained on shore shoved it off. A light, steady breeze was blowing from the ocean and they hoisted the sail, veered a little, and then sailed along smoothly with scarcely any motion. To landward the high cliff at the right cast a shadow on the water at its base, and patches of sunlit grass here and there varied its monotonous whiteness. Yonder, behind them, brown sails were coming out of the white harbor of Fécamp, and ahead of them they saw a rock of curious shape, rounded, with gaps in it looking something like an immense elephant with its trunk in the water; it was the little port of Étretat.

Jeanne, a little dizzy from the motion of the waves, held the side of the boat with one hand as she looked out into the distance. It seemed to her as if only three things in the world were really beautiful: light, space, water.

No one spoke. Père Lastique, who was at the tiller, took a pull every now and then from a bottle hidden under the seat; and he smoked a short pipe which seemed inextinguishable, although he never seemed to relight it or refill it.

The baron, seated in the bow looked after the sail. Jeanne and the vicomte seemed a little embarrassed at being seated side by side. Some unknown power seemed to make their glances meet whenever they raised their eyes; between them there existed already that subtle and vague sympathy which arises so rapidly between two young people when the young man is good looking and the girl is pretty. They were happy in each other's society, perhaps because they were thinking of each other. The rising sun was beginning to pierce through the slight mist, and as its beams grew stronger, they were reflected on the smooth surface of the sea as in a mirror.

"How beautiful!" murmured Jeanne, with emotion.

"Beautiful indeed!" answered the vicomte. The serene beauty of the morning awakened an echo in their hearts.

And all at once they saw the great arches of Étretat, like two supports of a cliff standing in the sea high enough for vessels to pass under them; while a sharp-pointed white rock rose in front of the first arch. They reached shore, and the baron got out first to make fast the boat, while the vicomte lifted Jeanne ashore so that she should not wet her feet. Then they walked up the shingly beach side by side, and they overheard Père Lastique say to the baron, "My! but they would make a pretty couple!"

They took breakfast in a little inn near the beach, and while the ocean had lulled their thoughts and made them silent, the breakfast table had the opposite effect, and they chattered like children on a vacation. The slightest thing gave rise to laughter.

Père Lastique, on taking his place at table, carefully hid his lighted pipe in his cap. That made them laugh. A fly, attracted no doubt by his red nose, persistently alighted on it, and each time it did so they burst into laughter. Finally the old man could stand it no longer, and murmured: "It is devilishly persistent!" whereupon Jeanne and the vicomte laughed till they cried.

After breakfast Jeanne suggested that they should take a walk. The vicomte rose, but the baron preferred to bask in the sun on the beach.

"Go on, my children, you will find me here in an hour."

They walked straight ahead of them, passing by several cottages and finally by a small château resembling a large farm, and found themselves in an open valley that extended for some distance. They now had a wild longing to run at large in the fields. Jeanne seemed to have a humming in her ears from all the new and rapidly changing sensations she had experienced. The burning rays of the sun fell on them. On both sides of the road the crops were bending over from the heat. The grasshoppers, as numerous as the blades of grass, were uttering their thin, shrill cry.

Perceiving a wood a little further on to the right, they walked over to it. They saw a narrow path between two hedges shaded by tall trees which shut out the sun. A sort of moist freshness in the air was perceptible, giving them a sensation of chilliness. There was no grass, owing to the lack of sunlight, but the ground was covered with a carpet of moss.

"See, we can sit down there a little while," she said.

They sat down and looked about them at the numerous forms of life that were in the air and on the ground at their feet, for a ray of sunlight penetrating the dense foliage brought them into its light.

"How beautiful it is here! How lovely it is in the country! There are moments when I should like to be a fly or a butterfly and hide in the flowers," said Jeanne with emotion.

They spoke in low tones as one does in exchanging confidences, telling of their daily lives and of their tastes, and declaring that they were already disgusted with the world, tired of its useless monotony; it was always the same thing; there was no truth, no sincerity in it.

The world! She would gladly have made its acquaintance; but she felt convinced beforehand that it was not equal to a country life, and the more their hearts seemed to be in sympathy, the more ceremonious they became, the more frequently their glances met and blended smiling; and it seemed that a new feeling of benevolence was awakened in them, a wider affection, an interest in a thousand things of which they had never hitherto thought.

They wended their way back, but the baron had already set off on foot for the Chambre aux Demoiselles, a grotto in a cleft at the summit of one of the cliffs, and they waited for him at the inn. He did not return until five in the evening after a long walk along the cliffs.

They got into the boat, started off smoothly with the wind at their backs, scarcely seeming to make any headway. The breeze was irregular, at one moment filling the sail and then letting it flap idly along the mast. The sea seemed opaque and lifeless, and the sun was slowly approaching the horizon. The lulling motion of the sea had made them silent again. Presently Jeanne said, "How I should love to travel!"

"Yes, but it is tiresome to travel alone; there should be at least two, to exchange ideas," answered the vicomte. She reflected a moment.

"That is true — I like to walk alone, however — how pleasant it is to dream all alone — — "

He gazed at her intently.

"Two can dream as well as one."

She lowered her eyes. Was it a hint? Possibly. She looked out at the horizon as if to discover something beyond it, and then said slowly:

"I should like to go to Italy — and Greece — ah, yes, Greece — and to Corsica — it must be so wild and so beautiful!"

He preferred Switzerland on account of its chalets and its lakes.

"No," said she, "I like new countries like Corsica, or very old countries full of souvenirs, like Greece. It must be delightful to find the traces of those peoples whose history we have known since childhood, to see places where great deeds were accomplished."

The vicomte, less enthusiastic, exclaimed: "As for me, England attracts me very much; there is so much to be learned there."

Then they talked about the world in general, discussing the attractions of each country from the poles to the equator, enthusing over imaginary scenes and the peculiar manners of certain peoples like the Chinese and the Lapps; but they arrived at the conclusion that the most beautiful country in the world was France, with its temperate climate, cool in summer, mild in winter, its rich soil, its green forests, its worship of the fine arts which existed nowhere else since the glorious centuries of Athens. Then they were silent. The setting sun left a wide dazzling train of light which extended from the horizon to the edge of their boat. The wind subsided, the ripples disappeared, and the motionless sail was red in the light of the dying day. A limitless calm seemed to settle down on space and make a silence amid this conjunction of elements; and by degrees the sun slowly sank into the ocean.

Then a fresh breeze seemed to arise, a little shiver went over the surface of the water, as if the engulfed orb cast a sigh of satisfaction across the world. The twilight was short, night fell with its myriad stars. Père Lastique took the oars, and they saw that the sea was phosphorescent. Jeanne and the vicomte, side by side, watched the fitful gleams in the wake of the boat. They were hardly thinking, but simply gazing vaguely, breathing in the beauty of the evening in a state of delicious contentment; Jeanne had one hand on the seat and her neighbor's finger touched it as if by accident; she did not move; she was surprised, happy, though embarrassed at this slight contact.

When she reached home that evening and went to her room, she felt strangely disturbed, and so affected that the slightest thing impelled her to weep. She looked at her clock, imagining that the little bee on the pendulum was beating like a heart, the heart of a friend; that it was aware of her whole life, that with its quick, regular tickings it would accompany her whole life; and she stopped the golden fly to press a kiss on its wings. She would have kissed anything, no matter what. She remembered having hidden one of her old dolls of former days at the bottom of a drawer; she looked for it, took it out, and was delighted to see it again, as people are to see loved friends; and pressing it to her heart, she covered its painted cheeks and curly wig with kisses. And as she held it in her arms, she thought:

Can he be the husband promised through a thousand secret voices, whom a superlatively good Providence had thus thrown across her path? Was he, indeed, the being created for her — the being to whom she would devote her existence? Were they the two predestined beings whose affection, blending in one, would beget love?

She did not as yet feel that tumultuous emotion, that mad enchantment, those deep stirrings which she thought were essential to the tender passion; but it seemed to her she was beginning to fall in love, for she sometimes felt a sudden faintness when she thought of him, and she thought of him incessantly. His presence stirred her heart; she blushed and grew pale when their eyes met, and trembled at the sound of his voice.

From day to day the longing for love increased. She consulted the marguerites, the clouds, and coins which she tossed in the air.

One day her father said to her:

"Make yourself look pretty tomorrow morning."

"Why, papa?"

"That is a secret," he replied.

And when she came downstairs the following morning, looking fresh and sweet in a pretty light dress, she found the drawingroom table covered with boxes of bonbons, and on a chair an immense bouquet.

A covered wagon drove into the courtyard bearing the inscription, "Lerat, Confectioner, Fécamp; Wedding Breakfasts," and from the back of the wagon Ludivine and a kitchen helper were taking out large flat baskets which emitted an appetizing odor.

The Vicomte de Lamare appeared on the scene, his trousers were strapped down under his dainty boots of patent leather, which made his feet appear smaller. His long frock coat, tight at the waist line, was open at the bosom showing the lace of his ruffle, and a fine neckcloth wound several times round his neck obliged him to hold erect his handsome brown head, with its air of serious distinction. Jeanne, in astonishment, looked at him as though she had never seen him before. She thought he looked the grand seigneur from his head to his feet.

He bowed and said, smiling:

"Well, comrade, are you ready?"

"But what is it? What is going on?" she stammered.

"You will know presently," said the baron.

The carriage drove up to the door, and Madame Adelaide, in festal array, descended the staircase, leaning on the arm of Rosalie, who was so much affected at the sight of M. de Lamare's elegant appearance that the baron whispered:

"I say, vicomte, I think our maid admires you."

The vicomte blushed up to his ears, pretended not to have heard and, taking up the enormous bouquet, handed it to Jeanne. She accepted it, more astonished than ever. They all four got into the carriage, and Ludivine, who brought a cup of bouillon to the baroness to sustain her strength, said: "Truly, madame, one would say it was a wedding!"

They alighted as soon as they entered Yport, and as they walked through the village the sailors, in their new clothes, still showing the creases, came out of their homes, and shaking hands with the baron, followed the party as if it were a procession. The vicomte, who had offered his arm to Jeanne, walked with her at the head.

When they reached the church they stopped, and an acolyte appeared holding upright the large silver crucifix, followed by another boy in red and white, who bore a chalice containing holy water.

Then came three old cantors, one of them limping; then the trumpet ("serpent"), and last, the curé with his gold embroidered stole. He smiled and nodded a greeting; then, with his eyes half closed, his lips moving in prayer, his beretta well over his forehead, he followed his surpliced bodyguard, walking in the direction of the sea.

On the beach a crowd was standing around a new boat wreathed with flowers. Its mast, sail and ropes were covered with long streamers of ribbon that floated in the breeze, and the name, "Jeanne," was painted in gold letters on the stern.

Père Lastique, the proprietor of this boat, built with the baron's money, advanced to meet the procession. All the men, simultaneously, took off their hats, and a row of pious persons wearing long black cloaks falling in large folds from their shoulders, knelt down in a circle at sight of the crucifix.

The curé walked, with an acolyte on either side of him, to one end of the boat, while at the other end, the three old cantors, in their white surplices, with a serious air and their eyes fixed on the psalter, sang at the top of their voices in the clear morning air. Each time they stopped to take breath, the "serpent" continued its bellowing alone, and as he puffed out his cheeks the musician's little gray eyes disappeared, and the skin of his forehead and neck seemed to distend.

The motionless, transparent sea seemed to be taking part meditatively in the baptism of this boat, rolling its tiny waves, no higher than a finger, with the faint sound of a rake on the shingle. And the big white gulls, with their wings unfurled, circled about in the blue heavens, flying off and then coming back in a curve above the heads of the kneeling crowd, as if to see what they were doing.

The singing ceased after an Amen that lasted five minutes; and the priest, in an unctuous voice, murmured some Latin words, of which one could hear only the sonorous endings. He then walked round the boat, sprinkling it with holy water, and next began to murmur the

"Oremus," standing alongside the boat opposite the sponsors, who remained motionless, hand in hand.

The vicomte had the usual grave expression on his handsome face, but Jeanne, choking with a sudden emotion, and on the verge of fainting, began to tremble so violently that her teeth chattered. The dream that had haunted her for some time was suddenly beginning, as if in a kind of hallucination, to take the appearance of reality. They had spoken of a wedding, a priest was present, blessing them; men in surplices were singing psalms; was it not she whom they were giving in marriage?

Did her fingers send out an electric shock, did the emotion of her heart follow the course of her veins until it reached the heart of her companion? Did he understand, did he guess, was he, like herself, pervaded by a sort of intoxication of love? Or else, did he know by experience, alone, that no woman could resist him? She suddenly noticed that he was squeezing her hand, gently at first, and then tighter, tighter, till he almost crushed it. And without moving a muscle of his face, without anyone perceiving it, he said — yes, he certainly said:

"Oh, Jeanne, if you would consent, this would be our betrothal."

She lowered her head very slowly, perhaps meaning it for "yes." And the priest, who was still sprinkling the holy water, sprinkled some on their fingers.

The ceremony was over. The women rose. The return was unceremonious. The crucifix had lost its dignity in the hands of the acolyte, who walked rapidly, the crucifix swaying to right and left, or bending forward as though it would fall. The priest, who was not praying now, walked hurriedly behind them; the cantors and the musician with the "serpent" had disappeared by a narrow street, so as to get off their surplices without delay; and the sailors hurried along in groups. One thought prompted their haste, and made their mouths water.

A good breakfast was awaiting them at "The Poplars."

The large table was set in the courtyard, under the apple trees.

Sixty people sat down to table, sailors and peasants. The baroness in the middle, with a priest at either side of her, one from Yport, and the other belonging to "The Poplars." The baron seated opposite her on the other side of the table, the mayor on one side of him, and his wife, a thin peasant woman, already aging, who kept smiling and bowing to all around her, on the other.

Jeanne, seated beside her co-sponsor, was in a sea of happiness. She saw nothing, knew nothing, and remained silent, her mind bewildered with joy. Presently she said:

"What is your Christian name?"

"Julien," he replied. "Did you not know?"

But she made no reply, thinking to herself:

"How often I shall repeat that name!"

When the feast was over, the courtyard was given up to the sailors, and the others went over to the other side of the château. The baroness began to take her exercise, leaning on the arm of the baron and accompanied by the two priests. Jeanne and Julien went toward the wood and walked along one of the mossy paths. Suddenly seizing her hands, the vicomte said:

"Tell me, will you be my wife?"

She lowered her head, and as he stammered: "Answer me, I implore you!" she raised her eyes to his timidly, and he read his answer there.

IV

The baron, one morning, entered Jeanne's room before she was up, and sitting down at the foot of her bed, said:

"M. le Vicomte de Lamare has asked us for your hand in marriage."

She wanted to hide her face under the sheets.

Her father continued:

"We have postponed our answer for the present."

She gasped, choking with emotion. At the end of a minute the baron, smiling, added:

"We did not wish to do anything without consulting you. Your mother and I are not opposed to this marriage, but we would not seek to influence you. You are much richer than he is; but, when it is a question of the happiness of a life, one should not think too much about money. He has no relations left. If you marry him, then, it would be as if a son should come into our family; if it were anyone else, it would be you, our daughter, who would go among strangers. The young fellow pleases us. Would he please you?"

She stammered, blushing up to the roots of her hair:

"I am willing, papa."

And the father, looking into her eyes and still smiling, murmured:

"I half suspected it, young lady."

She lived till evening in a condition of exhilaration, not knowing what she was doing, mechanically thinking of one thing by mistake for another, and with a feeling of weariness, although she had not walked at all.

Toward six o'clock, as she was sitting with her mother under the plane tree, the vicomte appeared.

Jeanne's heart began to throb wildly. The young man approached them apparently without any emotion. When he was close beside them, he took the baroness' hand and kissed her fingers, then raising to his lips the trembling hand of the young girl, he imprinted upon it a long, tender and grateful kiss.

And the radiant season of betrothal commenced. They would chat together alone in the corner of the parlor, or else seated on the moss at the end of the wood overlooking the plain. Sometimes they walked in Little Mother's Avenue; he, talking of the future, she, with her eyes cast down, looking at the dusty footprints of the baroness.

Once the matter was decided, they desired to waste no time in preliminaries. It was, therefore, decided that the ceremony should take place in six weeks, on the fifteenth of August; and that the bride and groom should set out immediately on their wedding journey. Jeanne, on being consulted as to which country she would like to visit, decided on Corsica where they could be more alone than in the cities of Italy.

They awaited the moment appointed for their marriage without too great impatience, but enfolded, lost in a delicious affection, expressed in the exquisite charm of insignificant caresses, pressure of hands, long passionate glances in which their souls seemed to blend; and, vaguely tortured by an uncertain longing for they knew not what.

They decided to invite no one to the wedding except Aunt Lison, the baron's sister, who boarded in a convent at Versailles. After the death of their father, the baroness wished to keep her sister with her. But the old maid, possessed by the idea that she was in every one's way, was useless, and a nuisance, retired into one of those religious houses that rent apartments to people that live a sad and lonely existence. She came from time to time to pass a month or two with her family.

She was a little woman of few words, who always kept in the background, appeared only at mealtimes, and then retired to her room where she remained shut in.

She looked like a kind old lady, though she was only forty-two, and had a sad, gentle expression. She was never made much of by her family as a child, being neither pretty nor boisterous, she was never petted, and she would stay quietly and gently in a corner. She had been neglected ever since. As a young girl nobody paid any attention to her. She was something like a shadow, or a familiar object, a living piece of furniture that one is accustomed to see every day, but about which one does not trouble oneself.

Her sister, from long habit, looked upon her as a failure, an altogether insignificant being. They treated her with careless familiarity which concealed a sort of contemptuous kindness. She called herself Lise, and seemed embarrassed at this frivolous youthful name. When they saw that she probably would not marry, they changed it from Lise to Lison, and since Jeanne's birth, she had become "Aunt Lison," a poor relation, very neat, frightfully timid, even with her sister and her brother-in-law, who loved her, but with an uncertain affection verging on indifference, with an unconscious compassion and a natural benevolence.

Sometimes, when the baroness talked of far away things that happened in her youth, she would say, in order to fix a date: "It was the time that Lison had that attack."

They never said more than that; and this "attack" remained shrouded, as in a mist.

One evening, Lise, who was then twenty, had thrown herself into the water, no one knew why. Nothing in her life, her manner, gave any intimation of this seizure. They fished her out half dead, and her parents, raising their hands in horror, instead of seeking the mysterious cause of this action, had contented themselves with calling it "that attack," as if they were talking of the accident that happened to the horse "Coco," who had broken his leg a short time before in a ditch, and whom they had been obliged to kill.

From that time Lise, presently Lison, was considered feeble-minded. The gentle contempt which she inspired in her relations gradually made its way into the minds of all those who surrounded her. Little Jeanne herself, with the natural instinct of children, took no notice of her, never went up to kiss her goodnight, never went into her room. Good Rosalie, alone, who gave the room all the necessary attention, seemed to know where it was situated.

When Aunt Lison entered the diningroom for breakfast, the little one would go up to her from habit and hold up her forehead to be kissed; that was all.

If anyone wished to speak to her, they sent a servant to call her, and if she was not there, they did not bother about her, never thought of her, never thought of troubling themselves so much as to say: "Why, I have not seen Aunt Lison this morning!"

When they said "Aunt Lison," these two words awakened no feeling of affection in anyone's mind. It was as if one had said: "The coffee pot, or the sugar bowl."

She always walked with little, quick, silent steps, never made a noise, never knocking up against anything; and seemed to communicate to surrounding objects the faculty of not making any sound. Her hands seemed to be made of a kind of wadding, she handled everything so lightly and delicately.

She arrived about the middle of July, all upset at the idea of this marriage. She brought a quantity of presents which, as they came from her, remained almost unnoticed. On the following day they had forgotten she was there at all.

But an unusual emotion was seething in her mind, and she never took her eyes off the engaged couple. She interested herself in Jeanne's trousseau with a singular eagerness, a feverish activity, working like a simple seamstress in her room, where no one came to visit her.

She was continually presenting the baroness with handkerchiefs she had hemmed herself, towels on which she had embroidered a monogram, saying as she did so: "Is that all right, Adelaide?" And little mother, as she carelessly examined the objects, would reply: "Do not give yourself so much trouble, my poor Lison."

One evening, toward the end of the month, after an oppressively warm day, the moon rose on one of those clear, mild nights which seem to move, stir and affect one, apparently awakening all the secret poetry of one's soul. The gentle breath of the fields was wafted into the quiet drawingroom. The baroness and her husband were playing cards by the light of a lamp, and Aunt Lison was sitting beside them knitting; while the young people, leaning on the window sill, were gazing out at the moonlit garden.

The linden and the plane tree cast their shadows on the lawn which extended beyond it in the moonlight, as far as the dark wood. Attracted by the tender charm of the night, and by this misty illumination that lighted up the trees and the bushes, Jeanne turned toward her parents and said: "Little father, we are going to take a short stroll on the grass in front of the house."

The baron replied, without looking up: "Go, my children," and continued his game.

They went out and began to walk slowly along the moonlit lawn as far as the little wood at the end. The hour grew late and they did not think of going in. The baroness grew tired, and wishing to retire, she said:

"We must call the lovers in."

The baron cast a glance across the spacious garden where the two forms were wandering slowly.

"Let them alone," he said; "it is so delicious outside! Lison will wait for them, will you not, Lison?"

The old maid raised her troubled eyes and replied in her timid voice:

"Certainly, I will wait for them."

Little father gave his hand to the baroness, weary himself from the heat of the day.

"I am going to bed, too," he said, and went up with his wife.

Then Aunt Lison rose in her turn, and leaving on the arm of the chair her canvas with the wool and the knitting needles, she went over and leaned on the window sill and gazed out at the night.

The two lovers kept on walking back and forth between the house and the wood. They squeezed each other's fingers without speaking, as though they had left their bodies and formed part of this visible poetry that exhaled from the earth.

All at once Jeanne perceived, framed in the window, the silhouette of the aunt, outlined by the light of the lamp behind her.

"See," she said, "there is Aunt Lison looking at us."

The vicomte raised his head, and said in an indifferent tone without thinking:

"Yes, Aunt Lison is looking at us."

And they continued to dream, to walk slowly, and to love each other. But the dew was falling fast, and the dampness made them shiver a little.

"Let us go in now," said Jeanne. And they went into the house.

When they entered the drawingroom, Aunt Lison had gone back to her work. Her head was bent over her work, and her fingers were trembling as if she were very tired.

"It is time to go to bed, aunt," said Jeanne, approaching her.

Her aunt turned her head, and her eyes were red as if she had been crying. The young people did not notice it; but suddenly M. de Lamare perceived that Jeanne's thin shoes were covered with dew. He was worried, and asked tenderly:

"Are not your dear little feet cold?"

All at once the old lady's hands shook so violently that she let fall her knitting, and hiding her face in her hands, she began to sob convulsively.

The engaged couple looked at her in amazement, without moving. Suddenly Jeanne fell on her knees, and taking her aunt's hands away from her face, said in perplexity:

"Why, what is the matter, Aunt Lison?"

Then the poor woman, her voice full of tears, and her whole body shaking with sorrow, replied:

"It was when he asked you — are not your — your — dear little feet cold? — no one ever said such things to me — to me — never — never — —"

Jeanne, surprised and compassionate, could still hardly help laughing at the idea of an admirer showing tender solicitude for Lison; and the vicomte had turned away to conceal his mirth.

But the aunt suddenly rose, laying her ball of wool on the floor and her knitting in the chair, and fled to her room, feeling her way up the dark staircase.

Left alone, the young people looked at one another, amused and saddened. Jeanne murmured:

"Poor aunt!" Julien replied. "She must be a little crazy this evening."

They held each other's hands and presently, gently, very gently, they exchanged their first kiss, and by the following day had forgotten all about Aunt Lison's tears.

The two weeks preceding the wedding found Jeanne very calm, as though she were weary of tender emotions. She had no time for reflection on the morning of the eventful day. She was only conscious of a feeling as if her flesh, her bones and her blood had all melted beneath her skin, and on taking hold of anything, she noticed that her fingers trembled.

She did not regain her self-possession until she was in the chancel of the church during the marriage ceremony.

Married! So she was married! All that had occurred since daybreak seemed to her a dream, a waking dream. There are such moments, when all appears changed around us; even our motions seem to have a new meaning; even the hours of the day, which seem to be out of their usual time. She felt bewildered, above all else, bewildered. Last evening nothing had as yet been changed in her life; the constant hope of her life seemed only nearer, almost within reach. She had gone to rest a young girl; she was now a married woman. She had crossed that boundary that seems to conceal the future with all its joys, its dreams of happiness. She felt as though a door had opened in front of her; she was about to enter into the fulfillment of her expectations.

When they appeared on the threshold of the church after the ceremony, a terrific noise caused the bride to start in terror, and the baroness to scream; it was a rifle salute given by the peasants, and the firing did not cease until they reached "The Poplars."

After a collation served for the family, the family chaplain, and the priest from Yport, the mayor and the witnesses, who were some of the large farmers of the district, they all walked in the garden. On the other side of the château one could hear the boisterous mirth of the peasants, who were drinking cider beneath the apple trees. The whole countryside, dressed in their best, filled the courtyard.

Jeanne and Julien walked through the copse and then up the slope and, without speaking, gazed out at the sea. The air was cool, although it was the middle of August; the wind was from the north, and the sun blazed down unpityingly from the blue sky. The young people sought a more sheltered spot, and crossing the plain, they turned to the right, toward the rolling and wooded valley that leads to Yport. As soon as they reached the trees the air was still, and they left the road and took a narrow path beneath the trees, where they could scarcely walk abreast.

Jeanne felt an arm passed gently round her waist. She said nothing, her breath came quick, her heart beat fast. Some low branches caressed their hair, as they bent to pass under them. She picked a leaf; two ladybirds were concealed beneath it, like two delicate red shells.

"Look, a little family," she said innocently, and feeling a little more confidence.

Julien placed his mouth to her ear, and whispered: "This evening you will be my wife."

Although she had learned many things during her sojourn in the country, she dreamed of nothing as yet but the poetry of love, and was surprised. His wife? Was she not that already?

Then he began to kiss her temples and neck, little light kisses. Startled each time afresh by these masculine kisses to which she was not accustomed, she instinctively turned away her head to avoid them, though they delighted her. But they had come to the edge of the wood. She stopped, embarrassed at being so far from home. What would they think?

"Let us go home," she said.

He withdrew his arm from her waist, and as they turned round they stood face to face, so close that they could feel each other's breath on their faces. They gazed deep into one another's eyes with that gaze in which two souls seem to blend. They sought the impenetrable unknown of each other's being. They sought to fathom one another, mutely and persistently. What would they be to one another? What would this life be that they were about to begin together? What joys, what happiness, or what disillusions were they preparing in this long, indissoluble tête-à-tête of marriage? And it seemed to them as if they had never yet seen each other.

Suddenly, Julien, placing his two hands on his wife's shoulders, kissed her full on the lips as she had never before been kissed. The kiss, penetrating as it did her very blood and marrow, gave her such a mysterious shock that she pushed Julien wildly away with her two arms, almost falling backward as she did so.

"Let us go away, let us go away," she faltered.

He did not reply, but took both her hands and held them in his. They walked home in silence, and the rest of the afternoon seemed long. The dinner was simple and did not last long, contrary to the usual Norman custom. A sort of embarrassment seemed to paralyze the guests. The two priests, the mayor, and the four farmers invited, alone betrayed a little of that broad mirth that is supposed to accompany weddings.

They had apparently forgotten how to laugh, when a remark of the mayor's woke them up. It was about nine o'clock; coffee was about to be served. Outside, under the apple-trees of the first court, the bal champêtre was beginning, and through the open window one could see all that was going on. Lanterns, hung from the branches, gave the leaves a grayish green tint. Rustics and their partners danced in a circle shouting a wild dance tune to the feeble accompaniment of two violins and a clarinet, the players seated on a large table as a platform. The boisterous singing of the peasants at times completely drowned the instruments, and the feeble strains torn to tatters by the unrestrained voices seemed to fall from the air in shreds, in little fragments of scattered notes.

Two large barrels surrounded by flaming torches were tapped, and two servant maids were kept busy rinsing glasses and bowls in order to refill them at the tap whence flowed the red wine, or at the tap of the cider barrel. On the table were bread, sausages and cheese. Every one swallowed a mouthful from time to time, and beneath the roof of illuminated foliage this wholesome and boisterous fête made the melancholy watchers in the diningroom long to dance also, and to drink from one of those large barrels, while they munched a slice of bread and butter and a raw onion.

The mayor, who was beating time with his knife, cried: "By Jove, that is all right; it is like the wedding of Ganache."

A suppressed giggle was heard, but Abbé Picot, the natural enemy of civil authority, cried: "You mean of Cana." The other did not accept the correction. "No, monsieur le curé, I know what I am talking about; when I say Ganache, I mean Ganache."

They rose from table and went into the drawingroom, and then outside to mix with the merrymakers. The guests soon left.

They went into the house. They were surprised to see Madame Adelaide sobbing on Julien's shoulder. Her tears, noisy tears, as if blown out by a pair of bellows, seemed to come from her nose, her mouth and her eyes at the same time; and the young man, dumfounded, awkward, was supporting the heavy woman who had sunk into his arms to commend to his care her darling, her little one, her adored daughter.

The baron rushed toward them, saying: "Oh, no scenes, no tears, I beg of you," and, taking his wife to a chair, he made her sit down, while she wiped away her tears. Then, turning to Jeanne: "Come, little one, kiss your mother and go to bed."

What happened then? She could hardly have told, for she seemed to have lost her head, but she felt a shower of little grateful kisses on her lips.

Day dawned. Julien awoke, yawned, stretched, looked at his wife, smiled and asked: "Did you sleep well, darling?"

She noticed that he now said "thou," and she replied, bewildered, "Why, yes. And you?" "Oh, very well," he answered. And turning toward her, he kissed her and then began to chat quietly. He set before her plans of living, with the idea of economy, and this word occurring several times, astonished Jeanne. She listened without grasping the meaning of his words, looked at him, but was thinking of a thousand things that passed rapidly through her mind hardly leaving a trace.

The clock struck eight. "Come, we must get up," he said. "It would look ridiculous for us to be late." When he was dressed he assisted his wife with all the little details of her toilet, not allowing her to call Rosalie. As they left the room he stopped. "You know, when we are alone, we can now use 'thou,' but before your parents it is better to wait a while. It will be quite natural when we come back from our wedding journey."

She did not go down till luncheon was ready. The day passed like any ordinary day, as if nothing new had occurred. There was one man more in the house, that was all.

V

Four days later the travelling carriage arrived that was to take them to Marseilles.

After the first night Jeanne had become accustomed to Julien's kisses and caresses, although her repugnance to a closer intimacy had not diminished. She thought him handsome, she loved him. She again felt happy and cheerful.

The farewells were short and without sadness. The baroness alone seemed tearful. As the carriage was just starting she placed a purse, heavy as lead, in her daughter's hand, saying, "That is for your little expenses as a bride."

Jeanne thrust the purse in her pocket and the carriage started.

Toward evening Julien said: "How much money did your mother give you in that purse?"

She had not given it a thought, and she poured out the contents on her knees. A golden shower filled her lap: two thousand francs. She clapped her hands. "I shall commit all kinds of extravagance," she said as she replaced it in the purse.

After travelling eight days in terribly hot weather they reached Marseilles. The following day the Roi-Louis, a little mail steamer which went to Naples by way of Ajaccio, took them to Corsica.

Corsica! Its "maquis," its bandits, its mountains! The birthplace of Napoleon! It seemed to Jeanne that she was leaving real life to enter into a dream, although wide awake. Standing side by side on the bridge of the steamer, they looked at the cliffs of Provence as they passed swiftly by them. The calm sea of deep blue seemed petrified beneath the ardent rays of the sun.

"Do you remember our excursion in Père Lastique's boat?" said Jeanne.

Instead of replying, he gave her a hasty kiss on the ear.

The paddle-wheels struck the water, disturbing its torpor, and a long track of foam like the froth of champagne remained in the wake of the boat, reaching as far as the eye could see. Jeanne drank in with delight the odor of the salt mist that seemed to go to the very tips of her fingers. Everywhere the sea. But ahead of them there was something gray, not clearly defined in the early dawn; a sort of massing of strange-looking clouds, pointed, jagged, seemed to rest on the waters.

Presently it became clearer, its outline more distinct on the brightening sky; a large chain of mountains, peaked and weird, appeared. It was Corsica, covered with a light veil of mist. The sun rose behind it, outlining the jagged crests like black shadows. Then all the summits were bathed in light, while the rest of the island remained covered with mist.

The captain, a little sun-browned man, dried up, stunted, toughened and shrivelled by the harsh salt winds, appeared on the bridge and in a voice hoarse after twenty years of command and worn from shouting amid the storms, said to Jeanne:

"Do you perceive it, that odor?"

She certainly noticed a strong and peculiar odor of plants, a wild aromatic odor.

"That is Corsica that sends out that fragrance, madame," said the captain. "It is her peculiar odor of a pretty woman. After being away for twenty years, I should recognize it five miles out at sea. I belong to it. He, down there, at Saint Helena, he speaks of it always, it seems, of the odor of his native country. He belongs to my family."

And the captain, taking off his hat, saluted Corsica, saluted down yonder, across the ocean, the great captive emperor who belonged to his family.

Jeanne was so affected that she almost cried.

Then, pointing toward the horizon, the captain said: "Les Sanguinaires."

Julien was standing beside his wife, with his arm round her waist, and they both looked out into the distance to see what he was alluding to. They at length perceived some pyramidal rocks which the vessel rounded presently to enter an immense peaceful gulf surrounded by lofty summits, the base of which was covered with what looked like moss.

Pointing to this verdant growth, the captain said: "Le maquis."

As they proceeded on their course the circle of mountains appeared to close in behind the steamer, which moved along slowly in such a lake of transparent azure that one could sometimes see to the bottom.

The town suddenly appeared perfectly white at the end of the gulf, on the edge of the water, at the base of the mountains. Some little Italian boats were anchored in the dock. Four or five rowboats came up beside the Roi-Louis to get passengers.

Julien, who was collecting the baggage, asked his wife in a low tone: "Twenty sous is enough, is it not, to give to the porter?" For a week he had constantly asked the same question, which annoyed her each time. She replied somewhat impatiently: "When one is not sure of giving enough, one gives too much."

He was always disputing with the hotel proprietors, with the servants, the drivers, the vendors of all kinds, and when, by dint of bargaining, he had obtained a reduction in price, he would say to Jeanne as he rubbed his hands: "I do not like to be cheated."

She trembled whenever a bill came in, certain beforehand of the remarks that he would make about each item, humiliated at this bargaining, blushing up to the roots of her hair beneath the contemptuous glances of the servants as they looked after her husband, while they held in their hand the meagre tip.

He had a dispute with the boatmen who landed him.

The first tree Jeanne saw was a palm. They went to a great, empty hotel at the corner of an immense square and ordered breakfast.

After an hour's rest they arranged an itinerary for their trip, and at the end of three days spent in this little town, hidden at the end of the blue gulf, and hot as a furnace enclosed in its curtain of mountains, which keep every breath of air from it, they decided to hire some saddle horses, so as to be able to cross any difficult pass, and selected two little Corsican stallions with fiery eyes, thin and unwearying, and set out one morning at daybreak. A guide, mounted on a mule, accompanied them and carried the provisions, for inns are unknown in this wild country.

The road ran along the gulf and soon turned into a kind of valley, and on toward the high mountains. They frequently crossed the dry beds of torrents with only a tiny stream of water trickling under the stones, gurgling faintly like a wild animal in hiding.

The uncultivated country seemed perfectly barren. The sides of the hills were covered with tall weeds, yellow from the blazing sun. Sometimes they met a mountaineer, either on foot or mounted on a little horse, or astride a donkey about as big as a dog. They all carried a loaded rifle slung across their backs, old rusty weapons, but redoubtable in their hands.

The pungent odor of the aromatic herbs with which the island is overgrown seemed to make the air heavy. The road ascended gradually amid the long curves of the mountains. The red or blue granite peaks gave an appearance of fairyland to the wild landscape, and on the foothills immense forests of chestnut trees looked like green brush, compared with the elevations above them.

Sometimes the guide, reaching out his hand toward some of these heights, would repeat a name. Jeanne and Julien would look where he pointed, but see nothing, until at last they discovered something gray, like a mass of stones fallen from the summit. It was a little village, a hamlet of granite hanging there, fastened on like a veritable bird's nest and almost invisible on the huge mountain.

Walking their horses like this made Jeanne nervous. "Let us go faster," she said. And she whipped up her horse. Then, as she did not hear her husband following her, she turned round and laughed heartily as she saw him coming along, pale, and holding on to his horse's mane as it bounced him up and down. His very appearance of a "beau cavalier" made his awkwardness and timidity all the more comical.

They trotted along quietly. The road now ran between two interminable forests of brush, which covered the whole side of the mountain like a garment. This was the "Maquis," composed of scrub oak, juniper, arbutus, mastic, privet, gorse, laurel, myrtle and boxwood, intertwined with clematis, huge ferns, honeysuckle, cytisus, rosemary, lavender and brambles, which covered the sides of the mountain with an impenetrable fleece.

They were hungry. The guide rejoined them and led them to one of those charming springs so frequent in rocky countries, a tiny thread of iced water issuing from a little hole in the rock and flowing into a chestnut leaf that some passerby had placed there to guide the water into one's mouth.

Jeanne felt so happy that she could hardly restrain herself from screaming for joy.

They continued their journey and began to descend the slope winding round the Bay of Sagone. Toward evening they passed through Cargese, the Greek village founded by a colony of refugees who were driven from their country. Tall, beautiful girls, with rounded hips, long hands and slender waists, and singularly graceful, were grouped beside a fountain. Julien called out, "Good evening," and they replied in musical tones in the harmonious language of their own land.

When they reached Piana they had to beg for hospitality, as in ancient times and in desert lands. Jeanne trembled with joy as they waited for the door to be opened after Julien knocked. Oh, this was a journey worth while, with all the unexpected of unexplored paths.

It happened to be the home of a young couple. They received the travellers as the patriarchs must have received the guest sent by God. They had to sleep on a corn husk mattress in an old moldy house. The woodwork, all eaten by worms, overrun with long boring-worms, seemed to emit sounds, to be alive and to sigh.

They set off again at daybreak, and presently stopped before a forest, a veritable forest of purple granite. There were peaks, pillars, bell-towers, wondrous forms molded by age, the ravaging wind and the sea mist. As much as three hundred metres in height, slender, round, twisted, hooked, deformed, unexpected and fantastic, these amazing rocks looked like trees, plants, animals, monuments, men, monks in their garb, horned devils, gigantic birds, a whole population of monsters, a menagerie of nightmares petrified by the will of some eccentric divinity.

Jeanne had ceased talking, her heart was full. She took Julien's hand and squeezed it, overcome with a longing for love in presence of the beauty of nature.

Suddenly, as they emerged from this chaos, they saw before them another gulf, encircled by a wall of blood-red granite. And these red rocks were reflected in the blue waters.

"Oh, Julien!" faltered Jeanne, unable to speak for wonder and choking with her emotion. Two tears fell from her eyes. Julien gazed at her in astonishment and said:

"What is the matter, my pet?"

She wiped away her tears, smiled and replied in a rather shaky voice:

"Nothing — I am nervous — I do not know — it just came over me. I am so happy that the least thing affects me."

He could not understand these feminine attacks of "nerves," the shocks of these vibrant beings, excited at nothing, whom enthusiasm stirs as might a catastrophe, whom an imperceptible sensation completely upsets, driving them wild with joy or despair.

These tears seemed absurd to him, and thinking only of the bad road, he said:

"You would do better to watch your horse."

They descended an almost impassable path to the shore of the gulf, then turned to the right to ascend the gloomy Val d'Ota.

But the road was so bad that Julien proposed that they should go on foot. Jeanne was delighted. She was enchanted at the idea of walking, of being alone with him after her late emotion.

The guide went ahead with the mule and the horses and they walked slowly.

The mountain, cleft from top to bottom, spreads apart. The path lies in this breach, between two gigantic walls. A roaring torrent flows through the gorge. The air is icy, the granite looks black, and high above one the glimpse of blue sky astonishes and bewilders one.

A sudden noise made Jeanne start. She raised her eyes. An immense bird flew away from a hollow; it was an eagle. His spread wings seemed to brush the two walls of the gorge and he soared into the blue and disappeared.

Farther on there was a double gorge and the path lay between the two in abrupt zigzags. Jeanne, careless and happy, took the lead, the pebbles rolling away beneath her feet, fearlessly leaning over the abysses. Julien followed her, somewhat out of breath, his eyes on the ground for fear of becoming dizzy.

All at once the sun shone down on them, and it seemed as if they were leaving the infernal regions. They were thirsty, and following a track of moisture, they crossed a wilderness of stones and found a little spring conducted into a channel made of a piece of hollowed-out wood for the benefit of the goatherds. A carpet of moss covered the ground all round it, and Jeanne and Julien knelt down to drink.

As they were enjoying the fresh cold water, Julien tried to draw Jeanne away to tease her. She resisted and their lips met and parted, and the stream of cold water splashed their faces, their necks, their clothes and their hands, and their kisses mingled in the stream.

They were a long time reaching the summit of the declivity, as the road was so winding and uneven, and they did not reach Evisa until evening and the house of Paoli Palabretti, a relative of their guide.

He was a tall man, somewhat bent, with the mournful air of a consumptive. He took them to their room, a cheerless room of bare stone, but handsome for this country, where all elegance is ignored. He expressed in his language — the Corsican patois, a jumble of French and Italian — his pleasure at welcoming them, when a shrill voice interrupted him. A little swarthy woman, with large black eyes, a skin warmed by the sun, a slender waist, teeth always showing in a perpetual smile, darted forward, kissed Jeanne, shook Julien's hand and said: "Good-day, madame; good-day, monsieur; I hope you are well."

She took their hats, shawls, carrying all on one arm, for the other was in a sling, and then she made them all go outside, saying to her husband: "Go and take them for a walk until dinner time."

M. Palabretti obeyed at once and walked between the two young people as he showed them the village. He dragged his feet and his words, coughing frequently, and repeating at each attack of coughing:

"It is the air of the Val, which is cool, and has struck my chest."

He led them on a by-path beneath enormous chestnut trees. Suddenly he stopped and said in his monotonous voice: "It is here that my cousin, Jean Rinaldi, was killed by Mathieu Lori. See, I was there, close to Jean, when Mathieu appeared at ten paces from us. 'Jean,' he cried, 'do not go to Albertacce; do not go, Jean, or I will kill you. I warn you!'

"I took Jean's arm: 'Do not go there, Jean; he will do it.'

"It was about a girl whom they were both after, Paulina Sinacoupi.

"But Jean cried out: 'I am going, Mathieu; you will not be the one to prevent me.'

"Then Mathieu unslung his gun, and before I could adjust mine, he fired.

"Jean leaped two feet in the air, like a child skipping, yes, monsieur, and he fell back full on me, so that my gun went off and rolled as far as the big chestnut tree over yonder.

"Jean's mouth was wide open, but he did not utter a word; he was dead."

The young people gazed in amazement at the calm witness of this crime. Jeanne asked:

"And what became of the assassin?"

Paoli Palabretti had a long fit of coughing and then said:

"He escaped to the mountain. It was my brother who killed him the following year. You know, my brother, Philippi Palabretti, the bandit."

Jeanne shuddered.

"Your brother a bandit?"

With a gleam of pride in his eye, the calm Corsican replied:

"Yes, madame. He was celebrated, that one. He laid low six gendarmes. He died at the same time as Nicolas Morali, when they were trapped in the Niolo, after six days of fighting, and were about to die of hunger.

"The country is worth it," he added with a resigned air in the same tone in which he said: "It is the air of the Val, which is cool."

Then they went home to dinner, and the little Corsican woman behaved as if she had known them for twenty years.

But Jeanne was worried. When Julien again held her in his arms, would she experience the same strange and intense sensation that she had felt on the moss beside the spring? And when they were alone together that evening she trembled lest she should still be insensible to his kisses. But she was reassured, and this was her first night of love.

The next day, as they were about to set out, she decided that she would not leave this humble cottage, where it seemed as though a fresh happiness had begun for her.

She called her host's little wife into her room and, while making clear that she did not mean it as a present, she insisted, even with some annoyance, on sending her from Paris, as soon as she arrived, a remembrance, a remembrance to which she attached an almost superstitious significance.

The little Corsican refused for some time, not wishing to accept it. But at last she consented, saying:

"Well, then, send me a little pistol, a very small one."

Jeanne opened her eyes in astonishment. The other added in her ear, as one confides a sweet and intimate secret: "It is to kill my brother-in-law." And smiling, she hastily unwound the bandages around the helpless arm, and showing her firm, white skin with the scratch of a stiletto across it, now almost healed, she said: "If I had not been almost as strong as he is, he would have killed me. My husband is not jealous, he knows me; and, besides, he is ill, you know, and that quiets your blood. And, besides, madame, I am an honest woman; but my brother-in-law believes all that he hears. He is jealous for my husband and he will surely try it again. Then I shall have my little pistol; I shall be easy, and sure of my revenge."

Jeanne promised to send the weapon, kissed her new friend tenderly and they set out on their journey.

The rest of the trip was nothing but a dream, a continual series of embraces, an intoxication of caresses. She saw nothing, neither the landscape, nor the people, nor the places where they stopped. She saw nothing but Julien.

On arriving at Bastia, they had to pay the guide. Julien fumbled in his pockets. Not finding what he wanted, he said to Jeanne: "As you are not using your mother's two thousand francs, give them to me to carry. They will be safer in my belt, and it will avoid my having to make change."

She handed him her purse.

They went to Leghorn, visited Florence, Genoa and all the Cornici. They reached Marseilles on a morning when the north wind was blowing. Two months had elapsed since they left the "Poplars." It was now the 15th of October.

Jeanne, affected by the cold wind that seemed to come from yonder, from far-off Normandy, felt sad. Julien had, for some time, appeared changed, tired, indifferent, and she feared she knew not what.

They delayed their return home four days longer, not being able to make up their minds to leave this pleasant land of the sun. It seemed to her that she had come to an end of her happiness.

At length they left. They were to make all their purchases in Paris, prior to settling down for good at the "Poplars," and Jeanne looked forward to bringing back some treasures, thanks to her mother's present. But the first thing she thought of was the pistol promised to the little Corsican woman of Evisa.

The day after they arrived she said to Julien: "Dear, will you give me that money of mamma's? I want to make my purchases."

He turned toward her with a look of annoyance.

"How much do you want?"

"Why — whatever you please."

"I will give you a hundred francs," he replied, "but do not squander it."

She did not know what to say, amazed and confused. At length she faltered: "But — I — handed you the money to — — "

He did not give her time to finish.

"Yes, of course. Whether it is in my pocket or yours makes no difference from the moment that we have the same purse. I do not refuse you, do I, since I am giving you a hundred francs?"

She took the five gold pieces without saying a word, but she did not venture to ask for any more, and she bought nothing but the pistol.

Eight days later they set out for the "Poplars."

VI

The family and servants were awaiting them outside the white gate with brick supports. The post-chaise drew up and there were long and affectionate greetings. Little mother wept; Jeanne, affected, wiped away some tears; father nervously walked up and down.

Then, as the baggage was being unloaded, they told of their travels beside the parlor fire. Jeanne's words flowed freely, and everything was told, everything, in a half hour, except, perhaps, a few little details forgotten in this rapid account.

The young wife then went to undo her parcels. Rosalie, also greatly affected, assisted her. When this was finished and everything had been put away, the little maid left her mistress, and Jeanne, somewhat fatigued, sat down.

She asked herself what she was now going to do, seeking some occupation for her mind, some work for her hands. She did not care to go down again into the drawingroom, where her mother was asleep, and she thought she would take a walk. But the country seemed so sad that she felt a weight at her heart on only looking out of the window.

Then it came to her that she had no longer anything to do, never again anything to do. All her young life at the convent had been preoccupied with the future, busied with dreams. The constant excitement of hope filled her hours at that time, so that she was not aware of their flight. Then hardly had she left those austere walls, where her illusions had unfolded, than her expectations of love were at once realized. The longed-for lover, met, loved and married within a few weeks, as one marries on these sudden resolves, had carried her off in his arms, without giving her time for reflection.

But now the sweet reality of the first days was to become the everyday reality, which closed the door on vague hopes, on the enchanting worries of the unknown. Yes, there was nothing more to look forward to. And there was nothing more to do, today, tomorrow, never. She felt all this vaguely as a certain disillusion, a certain crumbling of her dreams.

She rose and leaned her forehead against the cold window panes.

Then, after gazing for some time at the sky across which dark clouds were passing, she decided to go out.

Was this the same country, the same grass, the same trees as in May? What had become of the sunlit cheerfulness of the leaves and the poetry of the green grass, where dandelions, poppies and moon daisies bloomed and where yellow butterflies fluttered as though held by invisible wires? And this intoxication of the air teeming with life, with fragrance, with fertilizing pollen, existed no longer!

The avenues, soaked by the constant autumnal downpours, were covered with a thick carpet of fallen leaves which extended beneath the shivering bareness of the almost leafless poplars. She went as far as the shrubbery. It was as sad as the chamber of a dying person. A green hedge which separated the little winding walks was bare of leaves. Little birds flew from place to place with a little chilly cry, seeking a shelter.

The thick curtain of elm trees that formed a protection against the sea wind, the lime tree and the plane tree with their crimson and yellow tints seemed clothed, the one in red velvet and the other in yellow silk.

Jeanne walked slowly up and down petite mère's avenue, alongside the Couillards' farm. Something weighed on her spirit like a presentiment of the long boredom of the monotonous life about to begin.

She seated herself on the bank where Julien had first told her of his love and remained there, dreaming, scarcely thinking, depressed to the very soul, longing to lie down, to sleep, in order to escape the dreariness of the day.

All at once she perceived a gull crossing the sky, carried away in a gust of wind, and she recalled the eagle she had seen down there in Corsica, in the gloomy vale of Ota. She felt a spasm at her heart as at the remembrance of something pleasant that is gone by, and she had a sudden vision of the beautiful island with its wild perfume, its sun that ripens oranges and lemons, its mountains with their rosy summits, its azure gulfs and its ravines through which the torrents flowed.

And the moist, severe landscape that surrounded her, with the falling leaves and the gray clouds blown along by the wind, enfolded her in such a heavy mantle of misery that she went back to the house to keep from sobbing.

Her mother was dozing in a torpid condition in front of the fire, accustomed to the melancholy of the long days, and not noticing it any longer. Her father and Julien had gone for a walk to talk about business matters. Night was coming on, filling the large drawingroom with gloom lighted by reflections of light from the fire.

The baron presently appeared, followed by Julien. As soon as the vicomte entered the room he rang the bell, saying: "Quick, quick, let us have some light! It is gloomy in here."

And he sat down before the fire. While his wet shoes were steaming in the warmth and the mud was drying on his soles, he rubbed his hands cheerfully as he said: "I think it is going to freeze; the sky is clearing in the north, and it is full moon tonight; we shall have a stinger tonight."

Then turning to his daughter: "Well, little one, are you glad to be back again in your own country, in your own home, with the old folks?"

This simple question upset Jeanne. She threw herself into her father's arms, her eyes full of tears, and kissed him nervously, as though asking pardon, for in spite of her honest attempt to be cheerful, she felt sad enough to give up altogether. She recalled the joy she had promised herself at seeing her parents again, and she was surprised at the coldness that seemed to numb her affection, just as if, after constantly thinking of those one loves, when at a distance and unable to see them at any moment, one should feel, on seeing them again, a sort of check of affection, until the bonds of their life in common had been renewed.

Dinner lasted a long time. No one spoke much. Julien appeared to have forgotten his wife.

In the drawingroom Jeanne sat before the fire in a drowsy condition, opposite little mother, who was sound asleep. Aroused by the voices of the men, Jeanne asked herself, as she tried to rouse herself, if she, too, was going to become a slave to this dreary lethargy of habit that nothing varies.

The baron approached the fire, and holding out his hands to the glowing flame, he said, smiling: "Ah, that burns finely this evening. It is freezing, children; it is freezing." Then, placing his hand on Jeanne's shoulder and pointing to the fire, he said: "See here, little daughter, that is the best thing in life, the hearth, the hearth, with one's own around one. Nothing else counts. But supposing we retire. You children must be tired out."

When she was in her room, Jeanne asked herself how she could feel so differently on returning a second time to the place that she thought she loved. Why did she feel as though she were wounded? Why did this house, this beloved country, all that hitherto had thrilled her with happiness, now appear so distressing?

Her eyes suddenly fell on her clock. The little bee was still swinging from left to right and from right to left with the same quick, continuous motion above the scarlet blossoms. All at once an impulse of tenderness moved her to tears at sight of this little piece of mechanism that seemed to be alive. She had not been so affected on kissing her father and mother. The heart has mysteries that no arguments can solve.

For the first time since her marriage she was alone, Julien, under pretext of fatigue, having taken another room.

She lay awake a long time, unaccustomed to being alone and disturbed by the bleak north wind which beat against the roof.

She was awakened the next morning by a bright light that flooded her room. She put on a dressing gown and ran to the window and opened it.

An icy breeze, sharp and bracing, streamed into the room, making her skin tingle and her eyes water. The sun appeared behind the trees on a crimson sky, and the earth, covered with frost and dry and hard, rang out beneath one's footsteps. In one night all the leaves had blown off the trees, and in the distance beyond the level ground was seen the long green line of water, covered with trails of white foam.

Jeanne dressed herself and went out, and for the sake of an object she went to call on the farmers.

The Martins held up their hands in surprise, and Mrs. Martin kissed her on both cheeks, and then they made her drink a glass of noyau. She then went to the other farm. The Couillards also were surprised. Mrs. Couillard pecked her on the ears and she had to drink a glass of cassis. Then she went home to breakfast.

The day went by like the previous day, cold instead of damp. And the other days of the week resembled these two days, and all the weeks of the month were like the first week.

Little by little, however, she ceased to regret far-off lands. The force of habit was covering her life with a layer of resignation similar to the limestone formation deposited on objects by certain springs. And a kind of interest for the thousand-and-one little insignificant things of daily life, a care for the simple, ordinary everyday occupations, awakened in her heart. A sort of pensive melancholy, a vague disenchantment with life was growing up in her mind. What did she lack? What did she want? She did not know. She had no worldly desires, no thirst for amusement, no longing for permissible pleasures. What then? Just as old furniture tarnishes in time, so everything was slowly becoming faded to her eyes, everything seemed to be fading, to be taking on pale, dreary shades.

Her relations with Julien had completely changed. He seemed to be quite different since they came back from their honeymoon, like an actor who has played his part and resumes his ordinary manner. He scarcely paid any attention to her or even spoke to her. All trace of love had suddenly disappeared, and he seldom came into her room at night.

He had taken charge of the money and of the house, changed the leases, worried the peasants, cut down expenses, and having adopted the costume of a gentleman farmer, he had lost his polish and elegance as a fiancé.

He always wore the same suit, although it was covered with spots. It was an old velveteen shooting jacket with brass buttons, that he had found among his former wardrobe, and with the carelessness that is frequent with those who no longer seek to please, he had given up shaving, and his long beard, badly cut, made an incredible change for the worse in his appearance. His hands were never cared for, and after each meal he drank four or five glasses of brandy.

Jeanne tried to remonstrate with him gently, but he had answered her so abruptly: "Won't you let me alone!" that she never ventured to give him any more advice.

She had adapted herself to these changes in a manner that surprised herself. He had become a stranger to her, a stranger whose mind and heart were closed to her. She constantly thought about it, asking herself how it was that after having met, loved, married in an impulse of affection, they should all at once find themselves almost as much strangers as though they had never shared the same room.

And how was it that she did not feel this neglect more deeply? Was this life? Had they deceived themselves? Did the future hold nothing further for her?

If Julien had remained handsome, carefully dressed, elegant, she might possibly have suffered more deeply.

It had been agreed that after the new year the young couple should remain alone and that the father and mother should go back to spend a few months at their house in Rouen. The young people were not to leave the "Poplars" that winter, so as to get thoroughly settled and to become accustomed to each other and to the place where all their life would be passed. They had a few neighbors to whom Julien would introduce his wife. These were the Brisevilles, the Colteliers and the Fourvilles.

But the young people could not begin to pay calls because they had not as yet been able to get a painter to alter the armorial bearings on the carriage.

The old family coach had been given up to his son-in-law by the baron, and nothing would have induced him to show himself at the neighboring châteaux if the coat-of-arms of the De Lamares were not quartered with those of the Le Perthuis des Vauds.

There was only one man in the district who made a specialty of heraldic designs, a painter of Bolbec, called Bataille, who was in demand at all the Norman castles in turn to make these precious designs on the doors of carriages.

At length one morning in December, just as they were finishing breakfast, they saw an individual open the gate and walk toward the house. He was carrying a box on his back. This was Bataille.

They offered him some breakfast, and, while he was eating, the baron and Julien made sketches of quarterings. The baroness, all upset as soon as these things were discussed, gave her opinion. And even Jeanne took part in the discussion, as though some mysterious interest had suddenly awakened in her.

Bataille, while eating, gave his ideas, at times taking the pencil and tracing a design, citing examples, describing all the aristocratic carriages in the countryside, and seemed to have brought with him in his ideas, even in his voice, a sort of atmosphere of aristocracy.

As soon as he had finished his coffee, they all went to the coach house. They took off the cover of the carriage and Bataille examined it. He then gravely gave his views as to the size he considered suitable for the design, and after an exchange of ideas, he set to work.

Notwithstanding the cold, the baroness had her chair brought out so as to watch him working, and then her foot-stove, for her feet were freezing. She then began to chat with the painter, on all the recent births, deaths and marriages of which she had not heard, thus adding to the genealogical tree which she carried in her memory.

Julien sat beside her, astride on a chair. He was smoking, spitting on the ground, listening and following with his glances the emblazoning of his rank.

Presently old Simon, who was on his way to the vegetable garden, his spade on his shoulder, stopped to look at the work; and as Bataille's arrival had become known at the two farms, the farmers' wives soon put in an appearance. They went into raptures, standing one at either side of the baroness, exclaiming: "My! it requires some cleverness all the same to fix up those things."

The two doors could not be finished before the next day about eleven o'clock. Every one was on hand; and they dragged the carriage outside so as to get a better view of it.

It was perfect. Bataille was complimented, and went off with his box on his back. They all agreed that the painter had great ability, and if circumstances had been favorable would doubtless have been a great artist.

Julien, by way of economy, had introduced great reforms which necessitated making some changes. The old coachman had been made gardener, Julien undertaking to drive himself, having sold the carriage horses to avoid buying feed for them. But as it was necessary to have some one to hold the horses when he and his wife got out of the carriage, he had made a little cow tender named Marius into a groom. Then in order to get some horses, he introduced a special clause into the Couillards' and Martins' leases, by which they were bound to supply a horse each, on a certain day every month, the date to be fixed by him; and this would exempt them from their tribute of poultry.

So the Couillards brought a big yellow horse, and the Martins a small white animal with long, unclipped coat, and the two were harnessed up together. Marius, buried in an old livery belonging to old Simon, led the carriage up to the front door.

Julien, looking clean and brushed up, looked a little like his former self; but his long beard gave him a common look in spite of all. He looked over the horses, the carriage, and the little groom, and seemed satisfied, the only really important thing to him being the newly painted escutcheon.

The baroness came down leaning on her husband's arm and got into the carriage. Then Jeanne appeared. She began to laugh at the horses, saying that the white one was the son of the yellow horse; then, perceiving Marius, his face buried under his hat with its cockade, his nose alone preventing it from covering his face altogether, his hands hidden in his long sleeves, and the tail of his coat forming a skirt round his legs, his feet encased in immense shoes showing in a comical manner beneath it, and then when he threw his head back so as to see, and lifted up his leg to walk as if he were crossing a river, she burst into a fit of uncontrollable laughter.

The baron turned round, glanced at the little bewildered groom and he, too, burst out laughing, calling to his wife: "Look at Ma-Ma-Marius! Is he not comical? Heavens, how funny he looks!"

The baroness, looking out of the carriage window, was also convulsed, so that the carriage shook on its springs.

But Julien, pale with anger, asked: "What makes you laugh like that? Are you crazy?"

Jeanne, quite convulsed and unable to stop laughing, sat down on the doorstep; the baron did the same, while, in the carriage, spasmodic sneezes, a sort of constant chuckling, told that the baroness was choking. Presently there was a motion beneath Marius' livery. He had, doubtless, understood the joke, for he was shaking with laughter beneath his hat.

Julien darted forward in exasperation. With a box on the ear he sent the boy's hat flying across the lawn; then, turning toward his father-in-law, he stammered in a voice trembling with rage: "It seems to me that you should be the last to laugh. We should not be where we are now if you had not wasted your money and ruined your property. Whose fault is it if you are ruined?"

The laughter ceased at once, and no one spoke. Jeanne, now ready to cry, got into the carriage and sat beside her mother. The baron, silent and astonished, took his place opposite the two ladies, and Julien sat on the box after lifting to the seat beside him the weeping boy, whose face was beginning to swell.

The road was dreary and appeared long. The occupants of the carriage were silent. All three sad and embarrassed, they would not acknowledge to one another what was occupying their thoughts. They felt that they could not talk on indifferent subjects while these thoughts had possession of them, and preferred to remain silent than to allude to this painful subject.

They drove past farmyards, the carriage jogging along unevenly with the ill-matched animals, putting to flight terrified black hens who plunged into the bushes and disappeared, occasionally followed by a barking wolf-hound.

At length they entered a wide avenue of pine trees, at the end of which was a white, closed gate. Marius ran to open it, and they drove in round an immense grass plot, and drew up before a high, spacious, sad-looking building with closed shutters.

The hall door opened abruptly, and an old, paralyzed servant wearing a black waistcoat with red stripes partially covered by his working apron slowly descended the slanting steps. He took the visitors' names and led them into an immense reception room, and opened with difficulty the Venetian blinds which were always kept closed. The furniture had covers on it, and the clock and candelabra were wrapped in white muslin. An atmosphere of mildew, an atmosphere of former days, damp and icy, seemed to permeate one's lungs, heart and skin with melancholy.

They all sat down and waited. They heard steps in the hall above them that betokened unaccustomed haste. The hosts were hurriedly dressing. The baroness, who was chilled, sneezed constantly. Julien paced up and down. Jeanne, despondent, sat beside her mother. The baron leaned against the marble mantelpiece with his head bent down.

Finally, one of the tall doors opened, and the Vicomte and Vicomtesse de Briseville appeared. They were both small, thin, vivacious, of no age in particular, ceremonious and embarrassed.

After the first greetings, there seemed to be nothing to say. So they began to congratulate each other for no special reason, and hoped that these friendly relations would be kept up. It was a treat to see people when one lived in the country the year round.

The icy atmosphere pierced to their bones and made their voices hoarse. The baroness was coughing now and had stopped sneezing. The baron thought it was time to leave. The Brisevilles said: "What, so soon? Stay a little longer." But Jeanne had risen in spite of Julien's signals, for he thought the visit too short.

They attempted to ring for the servant to order the carriage to the door, but the bell would not ring. The host started out himself to attend to it, but found that the horses had been put in the stable.

They had to wait. Every one tried to think of something to say. Jeanne, involuntarily shivering with cold, inquired what their hosts did to occupy themselves all the year round. The Brisevilles were much astonished; for they were always busy, either writing letters to their aristocratic relations, of whom they had a number scattered all over France, or attending to microscopic duties, as ceremonious to one another as though they were strangers, and talking grandiloquently of the most insignificant matters.

At last the carriage passed the windows with its ill-matched team. But Marius had disappeared. Thinking he was off duty until evening, he had doubtless gone for a walk.

Julien, perfectly furious, begged them to send him home on foot, and after a great many farewells on both sides, they set out for the "Poplars."

As soon as they were inside the carriage, Jeanne and her father, in spite of Julien's brutal behavior of the morning which still weighed on their minds, began to laugh at the gestures and intonations of the Brisevilles. The baron imitated the husband, and Jeanne the wife. But the baroness, a little touchy in these particulars, said: "You are wrong to ridicule them thus; they are people of excellent family." They were silent out of respect for little mother, but nevertheless, from time to time, Jeanne and her father began again. The baroness could not forbear smiling in her turn, but she repeated: "It is not nice to laugh at people who belong to our class."

Suddenly the carriage stopped, and Julien called out to someone behind it. Then Jeanne and the baron, leaning out, saw a singular creature that appeared to be rolling along toward them. His legs entangled in his flowing coattails, and blinded by his hat which kept falling over his face, shaking his sleeves like the sails of a windmill, and splashing into puddles of water, and stumbling against stones in the road, running and bounding, Marius was following the carriage as fast as his legs could carry him.

As soon as he caught up with it, Julien, leaning over, seized him by the collar of his coat, sat him down beside him, and letting go the reins, began to shower blows on the boy's hat, which sank down to his shoulders with the reverberations of a drum. The boy screamed, tried to get away, to jump from the carriage, while his master, holding him with one hand, continued beating him with the other.

Jeanne, dumfounded, stammered: "Father — oh, father!" And the baroness, wild with indignation, squeezed her husband's arm. "Stop him, Jack!" she exclaimed. The baron quickly lowered the front window, and seizing hold of his son-in-law's sleeve, he sputtered out in a voice trembling with rage: "Have you almost finished beating that child?"

Julien turned round in astonishment: "Don't you see what a condition his livery is in?"

But the baron, placing his head between them, said: "Well, what do I care? There is no need to be brutal like that!"

Julien got angry again: "Let me alone, please; this is not your affair!" And he was raising his hand again when his father-in-law caught hold of it and dragged it down so roughly that he knocked it against the wood of the seat, and he roared at him so loud: "If you do not stop, I shall get out, and I will see that you stop it, myself," that Julien calmed down at once, and shrugging his shoulders without replying, he whipped up the horses, who set out at a quick trot.

The two women, pale as death, did not stir, and one could hear distinctly the thumping of the baroness' heart.

At dinner Julien was more charming than usual, as though nothing had occurred. Jeanne, her father, and Madame Adelaide, pleased to see him so amiable, fell in with his mood, and when Jeanne mentioned the Brisevilles, he laughed at them himself, adding, however: "All the same, they have the grand air."

They made no more visits, each one fearing to revive the Marius episode. They decided, to send New Year's cards, and to wait until the first warm days of spring before paying any more calls.

At Christmas they invited the curé, the mayor and his wife to dinner, and again on New Year's Day. These were the only events that varied the monotony of their life. The baron and his wife were to leave "The Poplars" on the ninth of January. Jeanne wanted to keep them, but Julien did not acquiesce, and the baron sent for a post-chaise from Rouen, seeing his son-in-law's coolness.

The day before their departure, as it was a clear frost, Jeanne and her father decided to go to Yport, which they had not visited since her return from Corsica. They crossed the wood where she had strolled on her wedding-day, all wrapped up in the one whose lifelong companion she had become; the wood where she had received her first kiss, trembled at the first breath of love, had a presentiment of that sensual love of which she did not become aware until she was in the wild vale of Ota beside the spring where they mingled their kisses as they drank of its waters. The trees were now leafless, the climbing vines dead.

They entered the little village. The empty, silent streets smelled of the sea, of wrack, of fish. Huge brown nets were still hanging up to dry outside the houses, or stretched out on the shingle. The gray, cold sea, with its eternal roaring foam, was going out, uncovering the green rocks at the foot of the cliff toward Fécamp.

Jeanne and her father, motionless, watched the fishermen setting out in their boats in the dusk, as they did every night, risking their lives to keep from starving, and so poor, nevertheless, that they never tasted meat.

The baron, inspired at the sight of the ocean, murmured: "It is terrible, but it is beautiful. How magnificent this sea is on which the darkness is falling, and on which so many lives are in peril, is it not, Jeannette?"

She replied with a cold smile: "It is nothing to the Mediterranean."

Her father, indignant, exclaimed: "The Mediterranean! It is oil, sugar water, bluing water in a washtub. Look at this sea, how terrible it is with its crests of foam! And think of all those men who have set out on it, and who are already out of sight."

Jeanne assented with a sigh: "Yes, if you think so." But this name, "Mediterranean," had wrung her heart afresh, sending her thoughts back to those distant lands where her dreams lay buried.

Instead of returning home by the woods, they walked along the road, mounting the ascent slowly. They were silent, sad at the thought of the approaching separation. As they passed along beside the farmyards an odor of crushed apples, that smell of new cider which seems to pervade the atmosphere in this season all through Normandy, rose to their nostrils, or else a strong smell of the cow stables. A small lighted window at the end of the yard indicated the farmhouse.

It seemed to Jeanne that her mind was expanding, was beginning to understand the psychic meaning of things; and these little scattered gleams in the landscape gave her, all at once, a keen sense of the isolation of all human lives, a feeling that everything detaches, separates, draws one far away from the things they love.

She said, in a resigned tone: "Life is not always cheerful."

The baron sighed: "How can it be helped, daughter? We can do nothing."

The following day the baron and his wife went away, and Jeanne and Julien were left alone.

VII

Cards now became a distraction in the life of the young people. Every morning after breakfast, Julien would play several games of bezique with his wife, smoking and sipping brandy as he played. She would then go up to her room and sit down beside the window, and as the rain beat against the panes, or the wind shook the windows, she would embroider away steadily. Occasionally she would raise her eyes and look out at the gray sea which had white-caps on it. Then, after gazing listlessly for some time, she would resume her work.

She had nothing else to do, Julien having taken the entire management of the house, to satisfy his craving for authority and his craze for economy. He was parsimonious in the extreme, never gave any tips, cut down the food to the merest necessaries; and as Jeanne since her return had ordered the baker to make her a little Norman "galette" for breakfast, he had cut down this extra expense, and condemned her to eat toast.

She said nothing in order to avoid recriminations, arguments and quarrels; but she suffered keenly at each fresh manifestation of avarice on the part of her husband. It appeared to her low and odious, brought up as she had been in a family where money was never considered. How often had she not heard her mother say: "Why, money is made to be spent." Julien would now say: "Will you never become accustomed to not throwing money away?" And each time he deducted a few sous from some one's salary or on a note, he would say with a smile, as he slipped the change into his pocket: "Little streams make big rivers."

On certain days Jeanne would sit and dream. She would gradually cease sewing and, with her hands idle, and forgetting her surroundings, she would weave one of those romances of her girlhood and be lost in some enchanting adventure. But suddenly Julien's voice giving some orders to old Simon would snatch her abruptly from her dreams, and she would take up her work again, saying: "That is all over," and a tear would fall on her hands as she plied the needle.

Rosalie, formerly so cheerful and always singing, had changed. Her rounded cheeks had lost their color, and were now almost hollow, and sometimes had an earthy hue. Jeanne would frequently ask her: "Are you ill, my girl?" The little maid would reply: "No, madame," while her cheeks would redden slightly and she would retire hastily.

At the end of January the snow came. In one night the whole plain was covered and the trees next morning were white with icy foam.

On one of these mornings, Jeanne was sitting warming her feet before the fire in her room, while Rosalie, who had changed from day to day, was making the bed. Suddenly hearing behind her a kind of moan, Jeanne asked, without turning her head: "What is the matter?"

The maid replied as usual: "Nothing, madame"; but her voice was weak and trembling.

Jeanne's thoughts were on something else, when she noticed that the girl was not moving about the room. She called: "Rosalie!" Still no sound. Then, thinking she might have left the room, she cried in a louder tone: "Rosalie!" and she was reaching out her arm to ring the bell, when a deep moan close beside her made her start up with a shudder.

The little servant, her face livid, her eyes haggard, was seated on the floor, her legs stretched out, and her back leaning against the bed. Jeanne sprang toward her. "What is the matter with you — what is the matter?" she asked.

The girl did not reply, did not move. She stared vacantly at her mistress and gasped as though she were in terrible pain. Then, suddenly, she slid down on her back at full length, clenching her teeth to smother a cry of anguish.

Jeanne suddenly understood, and almost distracted, she ran to the head of the stairs, crying: "Julien, Julien!"

"What do you want?" he replied from below.

She hardly knew how to tell him. "It is Rosalie, who — — "

Julien rushed upstairs two steps at a time, and going abruptly into the room, he found the poor girl had just been delivered of a child. He looked round with a wicked look on his face, and pushing his terrified wife out of the room, exclaimed: "This is none of your affair. Go away. Send me Ludivine and old Simon."

Jeanne, trembling, descended to the kitchen, and then, not daring to go upstairs again, she went into the drawingroom, in which there had been no fire since her parents left, and anxiously awaited news.

She presently saw the manservant running out of the house. Five minutes later he returned with Widow Dentu, the nurse of the district.

Then there was a great commotion on the stairs as though they were carrying a wounded person, and Julien came in and told Jeanne that she might go back to her room.

She trembled as if she had witnessed some terrible accident. She sat down again before the fire, and asked: "How is she?"

Julien, preoccupied and nervous, was pacing up and down the room. He seemed to be getting angry, and did not reply at first. Then he stopped and said: "What do you intend to do with this girl?"

She did not understand, and looked at her husband. "Why, what do you mean? I do not know."

Then suddenly flying into a rage, he exclaimed: "We cannot keep a bastard in the house."

Jeanne was very much bewildered, and said at the end of a long silence: "But, my friend, perhaps we could put it out to nurse?"

He cut her short: "And who will pay the bill? You will, no doubt."

She reflected for some time, trying to find some way out of the difficulty; at length she said: "Why, the father will take care of it, of the child; and if he marries Rosalie, there will be no more difficulty."

Julien, as though his patience were exhausted, replied furiously: "The father! — the father! — do you know him — the father? No, is it not so? Well then — — ?"

Jeanne, much affected, became excited: "But you certainly would not let the girl go away like that. It would be cowardly! We will inquire the name of the man, and we will go and find him, and he will have to explain matters."

Julien had calmed down and resumed his pacing up and down. "My dear," he said, "she will not tell the name of the man; she will not tell you any more than she will tell me — and, if he does not want her?... We cannot, however, keep a woman and her illegitimate child under our roof, don't you understand?"

Jeanne, persistent, replied: "Then he must be a wretch, this man. But we must certainly find out who it is, and then he will have us to deal with."

Julien colored, became annoyed again, and said: "But — meanwhile — — ?"

She did not know what course to take, and asked: "What do you propose?"

"Oh, I? That's very simple. I would give her some money and send her to the devil with her brat."

The young wife, indignant, was disgusted with him. "That shall never be," she said. "She is my foster-sister, that girl; we grew up together. She has made a mistake, so much the worse; but I will not cast her out of doors on that account; and, if it is necessary, I will bring up the child."

Then Julien's wrath exploded: "And we should earn a fine reputation, we, with our name and our position! And they would say of us everywhere that we were protecting vice, harboring beggars; and decent people would never set their foot inside our doors. What are you thinking of? You must be crazy!"

She had remained quite calm. "I shall never cast off Rosalie; and if you do not wish her to stay, my mother will take her; and we shall surely succeed in finding out the name of the father of the child."

He left the room in exasperation, banging the door after him and exclaiming: "What stupid ideas women have!"

In the afternoon Jeanne went up to see the patient. The little maid, watched over by Widow Dentu, was lying still in her bed, her eyes wide open, while the nurse held the newborn babe in her arms.

As soon as Rosalie perceived her mistress, she began to sob, hiding her face in the covers and shaking with her sorrow. Jeanne wanted to kiss her, but she avoided it by keeping her face covered. But the nurse interfered, and drawing away the sheet, uncovered her face, and she let Jeanne kiss her, weeping still, but more quietly.

A meagre fire was burning in the grate; the room was cold; the child was crying. Jeanne did not dare to speak of the little one, for fear of another attack, and she took her maid's hand as she said mechanically: "It will not matter, it will not matter." The poor girl glanced furtively at the nurse, and trembled as the infant cried, and the remembrance of her sorrow came to her mind occasionally in a convulsive sob, while suppressed tears choked her.

Jeanne kissed her again, and murmured softly in her ear: "We will take good care of it, never fear, my girl." Then as she was beginning to cry again, Jeanne made her escape.

She came to see her every day, and each time Rosalie burst into tears at the sight of her mistress.

The child was put out to nurse at a neighbor's.

Julien, however, hardly spoke to his wife, as though he had nourished anger against her ever since she refused to send away the maid. He referred to the subject one day, but Jeanne took from her pocket a letter from the baroness asking them to send the girl to them at once if they would not keep her at the "Poplars." Julien, furious, cried: "Your mother is as foolish as you are!" but he did not insist any more.

Two weeks later the patient was able to get up and take up her work again.

One morning, Jeanne made her sit down and, taking her hands and looking steadfastly at her, she said:

"See here, my girl, tell me everything."

Rosalie began to tremble, and faltered:

"What, madame?"

"Whose is it, this child?"

The little maid was overcome with confusion, and she sought wildly to withdraw her hands so as to hide her face. But Jeanne kissed her in spite of herself, and consoled her, saying: "It is a misfortune, but cannot be helped, my girl. You were weak, but that happens to many others. If the father marries you, no one will think of it again."

Rosalie sighed as if she were suffering, and from time to time made an effort to disengage herself and run away.

Jeanne resumed: "I understand perfectly that you are ashamed; but you see that I am not angry, that I speak kindly to you. If I ask you the name of the man it is for your own good, for I feel from your grief that he has deserted you, and because I wish to prevent that. Julien will go and look for him, you see, and we will oblige him to marry you; and as we will employ you both, we will oblige him also to make you happy."

This time Rosalie gave such a jerk that she snatched her hands away from her mistress and ran off as if she were mad.

That evening at dinner Jeanne said to Julien: "I tried to persuade Rosalie to tell me the name of her betrayer. I did not succeed. You try to find out so that we can compel this miserable man to marry her."

But Julien became angry: "Oh! you know I do not wish to hear anything about it. You wish to keep this girl. Keep her, but do not bother me about her."

Since the girl's illness he appeared to be more irritable than ever; and he had got into the way of never speaking to his wife without shouting as if he were in a rage, while she, on the contrary, would lower her voice, be gentle and conciliating, to avoid all argument; but she often wept at night after she went to bed.

In spite of his constant irritability, her husband had become more affectionate than customary since their return.

Rosalie was soon quite well and less sad, although she appeared terrified, pursued by some unknown fear, and she ran away twice when Jeanne tried to question her again.

Julien all at once became more amiable, and the young wife, clinging to vain hopes, also became more cheerful. The thaw had not yet set in and a hard, smooth, glittering covering of snow extended over the landscape. Neither men nor animals were to be seen; only the chimneys of the cottages gave evidence of life in the smoke that ascended from them into the icy air.

One evening the thermometer fell still lower, and Julien, shivering as he left the table — for the diningroom was never properly heated, he was so economical with the wood — rubbed his hands, murmuring: "It will be warmer tonight, won't it, my dear?" He laughed with his jolly laugh of former days, and Jeanne threw her arms around his neck: "I do not feel well, dear; perhaps I shall be better tomorrow."

"As you wish, my dear. If you are ill you must take care of yourself." And they began to talk of other things.

She retired early. Julien, for a wonder, had a fire lighted in her room. As soon as he saw that it was burning brightly, he kissed his wife on the forehead and left the room.

The whole house seemed to be penetrated by the cold; the very walls seemed to be shivering, and Jeanne shivered in her bed. Twice she got up to put fresh logs on the fire and to look for dresses, skirts, and other garments which she piled on the bed. Nothing seemed to warm her; her feet were numbed and her lower limbs seemed to tingle, making her excessively nervous and restless.

Then her teeth began to chatter, her hands shook, there was a tightness in her chest, her heart began to beat with hard, dull pulsations, and at times seemed to stop beating, and she gasped for breath. A terrible apprehension seized her, while the cold seemed to penetrate to her marrow. She never had felt such a sensation, she had never seemed to lose her hold on life like this before, never been so near her last breath.

"I am going to die," she thought, "I am dying — — "

And filled with terror, she jumped out of bed, rang for Rosalie, waited, rang again, waited again, shivering and frozen.

The little maid did not come. She was doubtless asleep, that first, sound sleep that nothing can disturb. Jeanne, in despair, darted toward the stairs in her bare feet, and groping her way, she ascended the staircase quietly, found the door, opened it, and called, "Rosalie!" She went forward, stumbled against the bed, felt all over it with her hands and found that it was empty. It was empty and cold, and as if no one had slept there. Much surprised, she said: "What! Has she gone out in weather like this?"

But as her heart began to beat tumultuously till she seemed to be suffocating, she went downstairs again with trembling limbs in order to wake Julien. She rushed into his room filled with the idea that she was going to die, and longing to see him before she lost consciousness.

By the light of the dying embers she perceived Rosalie's head leaning on her husband's shoulder.

At the cry she gave they both started to their feet; she stood motionless for a second, horrified at this discovery, and then fled to her room; and when Julien, at his wit's end, called "Jeanne!" she was seized with an overmastering terror of seeing him, of hearing his voice, of listening to him explaining, lying, of meeting his gaze; and she darted toward the stairs again and went down.

She now ran along in the darkness, at the risk of falling downstairs, at the risk of breaking her neck on the stone floor of the hall. She rushed along, impelled by an imperious desire to flee, to know nothing about it, to see no one.

When she was at the bottom of the stairs she sat down on one of the steps, still in her night-dress, and in bare feet, and remained in a dazed condition. She heard Julien moving and walking about. She started to her feet in order to escape him. He was starting to come downstairs and called: "Listen, Jeanne!"

No, she would not listen nor let him touch her with the tips of his fingers; and she darted into the diningroom as if she were fleeing from an assassin. She looked for a door of escape, a hiding place, a dark corner, some way of avoiding him. She hid under the table. But he was already at the door, a candle in his hand, still calling: "Jeanne!" She started off again like a hare, darted into the kitchen, ran round it twice like a trapped animal, and as he came near her, she suddenly opened the door into the garden and darted out into the night.

The contact with the snow, into which she occasionally sank up to her knees, seemed to give her the energy of despair. She did not feel cold, although she had little on. She felt nothing, her body was so numbed from the emotion of her mind, and she ran along as white as the snow.

She followed the large avenue, crossed the wood, crossed the ditch, and started off across the plain.

There was no moon, the stars were shining like sparks of fire in the black sky; but the plain was light with a dull whiteness, and lay in infinite silence.

Jeanne walked quickly, hardly breathing, not knowing, not thinking of anything. She suddenly stopped on the edge of the cliff. She stopped short, instinctively, and crouched down, bereft of thought and of will power.

In the abyss before her the silent, invisible sea exhaled the salt odor of its wrack at low tide.

She remained thus some time, her mind as inert as her body; then, all at once, she began to tremble, to tremble violently, like a sail shaken by the wind. Her arms, her hands, her feet, impelled by an invisible force, throbbed, pulsated wildly, and her consciousness awakened abruptly, sharp and poignant.

Old memories passed before her mental vision: the sail with him in Père Lastique's boat, their conversation, his nascent love, the christening of the boat; then she went back, further back, to that night of dreams when she first came to the "Poplars." And now! And now! Oh, her life was shipwrecked, all joy was ended, all expectation at an end; and the frightful future full of torture, of deception, and of despair appeared before her. Better to die, it would all be over at once.

But a voice cried in the distance: "Here it is, here are her steps; quick, quick, this way!" It was Julien who was looking for her.

Oh! she did not wish to see him again. In the abyss down yonder before her she now heard a slight sound, the indistinct ripple of the waves over the rocks. She rose to her feet with the idea of throwing herself over the cliff and bidding life farewell. Like one in despair, she uttered the last word of the dying, the last word of the young soldier slain in battle: "Mother!"

All at once the thought of little mother came to her mind, she saw her sobbing, she saw her father on his knees before her mangled remains, and in a second she felt all the pain of their sorrow.

She sank down again into the snow; and when Julien and old Simon, followed by Marius, carrying a lantern, seized her arm to pull her back as she was so close to the brink, she made no attempt to escape.

She let them do as they would, for she could not stir. She felt that they were carrying her, and then that she was being put to bed and rubbed with hot cloths; then she became unconscious.

Then she had a nightmare, or was it a nightmare? She was in bed. It was broad daylight, but she could not get up. Why? She did not know. Then she heard a little noise on the floor, a sort of scratching, a rustling, and suddenly a mouse, a little gray mouse, ran quickly across the sheet. Another followed it, then a third, who ran toward her chest with his little, quick scamper. Jeanne was not afraid, and she reached out her hand to catch the animal, but could not catch it. Then other mice, ten, twenty, hundreds, thousands, rose up on all sides of her. They climbed the bedposts, ran up the tapestries, covered the bed completely. And soon they got beneath the covers; Jeanne felt them gliding over her skin, tickling her limbs, running up and down her body. She saw them running from the bottom of the bed to get into her neck under the sheets; and she tried to fight them off, throwing her hands out to try and catch them, but always finding them empty.

She was frantic, wanted to escape, screamed, and it seemed as if she were being held down, as if strong arms enfolded her and rendered her helpless; but she saw no one.

She had no idea of time. It must have been long, a very long time.

Then she awoke, weary, aching, but quiet. She felt weak, very weak. She opened her eyes and was not surprised to see little mother seated in her room with a man whom she did not know.

How old was she? She did not know, and thought she was a very little girl. She had no recollection of anything.

The big man said: "Why, she has regained consciousness." Little mother began to weep. Then the big man resumed: "Come, be calm, baroness; I can ensure her recovery now. But do not talk to her at all. Let her sleep, let her sleep."

Then it seemed to Jeanne that she remained in a state of exhaustion for a long time, overcome by a heavy sleep as soon as she tried to think; and she tried not to remember anything whatever, as though she had a vague fear that the reality might come back to her.

Once when she awoke she saw Julien, alone, standing beside her; and suddenly it all came back to her, as if the curtain which hid her past life had been raised.

She felt a horrible pain in her heart, and wanted to escape once more. She threw back the coverlets, jumped to the floor and fell down, her limbs being too weak to support her.

Julien sprang toward her, and she began to scream for him not to touch her. She writhed and rolled on the floor. The door opened. Aunt Lison came running in with Widow Dentu, then the baron, and finally little mother, puffing and distracted.

They put her back into bed, and she immediately closed her eyes, so as to escape talking and be able to think quietly.

Her mother and aunt watched over her anxiously, saying: "Do you hear us now, Jeanne, my little Jeanne?"

She pretended to be deaf, not to hear them, and did not answer. Night came on and the nurse took up her position beside the bed. She did not sleep; she kept trying to think of things that had escaped her memory as though there were holes in it, great white empty places where events had not been noted down.

Little by little she began to recall the facts, and she pondered over them steadily.

Little mother, Aunt Lison, the baron had come, so she must have been very ill. But Julien? What had he said? Did her parents know? And Rosalie, where was she? And what should she do? What should she do? An idea came to her — she would return to Rouen and live with father and little mother as in old days. She would be a widow; that's all.

Then she waited, listening to what was being said around her, understanding everything without letting them see it, rejoiced at her returning reason, patient and crafty.

That evening, at last, she found herself alone with the baroness and called to her in a low tone: "Little Mother!" Her own voice astonished her, it seemed strange. The baroness seized her hands: "My daughter, my darling Jeanne! My child, do you recognize me?"

"Yes, little mother, but you must not weep; we have a great deal to talk about. Did Julien tell you why I ran away in the snow?"

"Yes, my darling, you had a very dangerous fever."

"It was not that, mamma. I had the fever afterward; but did he tell you what gave me the fever and why I ran away?"

"No, my dearie."

"It was because I found Rosalie in his room."

Her mother thought she was delirious again and soothed her, saying: "Go to sleep, darling, calm yourself, try to sleep."

But Jeanne, persistent, continued: "I am quite sensible now, little mother. I am not talking wildly as I must have done these last days. I felt ill one night and I went to look for Julien. Rosalie was with him in his room. I did not know what I was doing, for sorrow, and I ran out into the snow to throw myself off the cliff."

But the baroness reiterated, "Yes, darling, you have been very ill, very ill."

"It is not that, mamma. I found Rosalie in with Julien, and I will not live with him any longer. You will take me back with you to Rouen to live as we used to do."

The baroness, whom the doctor had warned not to thwart Jeanne in any way, replied: "Yes, my darling."

But the invalid grew impatient: "I see that you do not believe me. Go and fetch little father, he will soon understand."

The baroness left the room and presently returned, leaning on her husband's arm. They sat down beside the bed and Jeanne began to talk. She told them all, quietly, in a weak voice, but clearly; all about Julien's peculiar character, his harshness, his avarice, and, finally, his infidelity.

When she had finished, the baron saw that she was not delirious, but he did not know what to think, what to determine, or what to answer. He took her hand, tenderly, as he used to do when he put her to sleep with stories, and said: "Listen, dearie, we must act with prudence. We must do nothing rash. Try to put up with your husband until we can come to some decision —promise me this?"

"I will try, but I will not stay here after I get well," she replied.

Then she added in a lower tone: "Where is Rosalie now?"

"You will not see her any more," replied the baron. But she persisted: "Where is she? I wish to know." Then he confessed that she had not left the house, but declared that she was going to leave.

On leaving the room the baron, filled with indignation and wounded in his feelings as a father, went to look for Julien, and said to him abruptly: "Sir, I have come to ask you for an explanation of your conduct toward my daughter. You have been unfaithful to her with your maid, which is a double insult."

Julien pretended to be innocent, denied everything positively, swore, took God as his witness. What proof had they? he asked. Was not Jeanne delirious? Had she not had brain fever? Had she not run out in the snow, in an attack of delirium, at the very beginning of her illness? And it was just at this time, when she was running about the house almost naked, that she pretends that she saw her maid in her husband's room!

And he grew angry, threatened a lawsuit, became furious. The baron, bewildered, made excuses, begged his pardon, and held out his loyal hand to Julien, who refused to take it.

When Jeanne heard what her husband had said, she did not show any annoyance, but replied: "He is lying, papa, but we shall end by convicting him."

For some days she remained taciturn and reserved, thinking over matters. The third morning she asked to see Rosalie. The baron refused to send her up, saying she had left. Jeanne persisted, saying: "Well, let some one go and fetch her."

She was beginning to get excited when the doctor came. They told him everything, so that he could form an opinion. But Jeanne suddenly burst into tears, her nerves all unstrung, and almost screamed: "I want Rosalie; I wish to see her!"

The doctor took hold of her hand and said in a low tone: "Calm yourself, madame; any emotion may lead to serious consequences, for you are enceinte."

She was dumfounded, as though she had received a blow; and it seemed to her that she felt the first stirrings of life within her. Then she was silent, not even listening to what was being said, absorbed in her own thoughts. She could not sleep that night for thinking of the new life that was developing in her, and was sad at the thought that it was Julien's child, and might resemble him. The following morning she sent for the baron. "Little father," she said, "my resolution is formed; I wish to know everything, and especially just now; you understand, I insist, and you know that you must not thwart me in my present condition. Listen! You must go and get M. le Curé. I need him here to keep Rosalie from telling a lie. Then, as soon as he comes, send him up to me, and you stay downstairs with little mother. And, above all things, see that Julien does not suspect anything."

An hour later the priest came, looking fatter than ever, and puffing like the baroness. He sat down in an armchair and began to joke, wiping his forehead as usual with his plaid handkerchief. "Well, baroness, I do not think we grow any thinner; I think we make a good pair." Then, turning toward the patient, he said: "Eh, what is this I hear, young lady, that we are soon to have a fresh baptism? Aha, it will not be a boat this time." And in a graver tone he added: "It will be a defender of the country; unless" — after a moment's reflection — it "should be the prospective mother of a family, like you, madame," bowing to the baroness.

The door at the end of the room opened and Rosalie appeared, beside herself, weeping, refusing to enter the room, clinging to the door frame, and being pushed forward by the baron. Quite out of patience, he thrust her into the room. She covered her face with her hands and remained standing there, sobbing.

Jeanne, as soon as she saw her, rose to a sitting posture, whiter than the sheets, and with her heart beating wildly. She could not speak, could hardly breathe. At length she said, in a voice broken with emotion: "I — I — will not — need — to question you. It — it is enough for me to see you thus — to — to see your — your shame in my presence."

After a pause, for she was out of breath, she continued: "I had M. le Curé come, so that it might be like a confession, you understand."

Rosalie, motionless, uttered little cries that were almost screams behind her hands.

The baron, whose anger was gaining ground, seized her arms, and snatching her hands from her face, he threw her on her knees beside the bed, saying: "Speak! Answer!"

She remained on the ground, in the position assigned to Magdalens, her cap awry, her apron on the floor, and her face again covered by her hands.

Then the priest said: "Come, my girl, listen to what is said to you, and reply. We do not want to harm you, but we want to know what occurred."

Jeanne, leaning over, looked at her and said: "Is it true that you were with Julien when I surprised you?"

Rosalie moaned through her fingers, "Yes, madame."

Then the baroness suddenly began to cry in a choking fashion, and her convulsive sobs accompanied those of Rosalie.

Jeanne, with her eyes fixed on the maid, said: "How long had this been going on?"

"Ever since he came here," faltered Rosalie.

Jeanne could not understand. "Ever since he came — then — ever since — ever since the spring?"

"Yes, madame."

"Ever since he came into this house?"

"Yes, madame."

And Jeanne, as if overflowing with questions, asked, speaking precipitately:

"But how did it happen? How did he approach you? How did he persuade you? What did he say? When, how did you ever yield to him? How could you ever have done it?"

Rosalie, removing her hands from her face, and overwhelmed also with a feverish desire to speak, said:

"How do I know, myself? It was the day he dined here for the first time, and he came up to my room. He had hidden himself in the loft. I did not dare to scream for fear of making a scandal. I no longer knew what I was doing. Then I said nothing because I liked him."

Then Jeanne exclaimed with almost a scream:

"But — your — your child — is his child?"

Rosalie sobbed.

"Yes, madame."

Then they were both silent. The only sound to be heard was the sobs of Rosalie and of the baroness.

Jeanne, quite overcome, felt her tears also beginning to flow; and they fell silently down her cheeks.

The maid's child had the same father, as her child! Her anger was at an end; she now was filled with a dreary, slow, profound and infinite despair. She presently resumed in a changed, tearful voice, the voice of a woman who has been crying:

"When we returned from — from down there — from our journey — when did he begin again?"

The little maid, who had sunk down on the floor, faltered: "The first evening."

Each word wrung Jeanne's heart. So on the very first night of their return to the "Poplars" he left her for this girl. That was why he wanted to sleep alone!

She now knew all she wanted to know, and exclaimed: "Go away, go away!" And as Rosalie, perfectly crushed, did not stir, Jeanne called to her father: "Take her away, carry her away!" The priest, who had said nothing as yet, thought that the moment had arrived for him to preach a little sermon.

"What you have done is very wrong, my daughter, very wrong, and God will not pardon you so easily. Consider the hell that awaits you if you do not always act right. Now that you have a child you must behave yourself. No doubt madame la baronne will do something for you, and we will find you a husband."

He would have continued speaking, but the baron, having again seized Rosalie by the shoulders, raised her from the floor and dragged her to the door, and threw her like a package into the corridor. As he turned back into the room, looking paler than his daughter, the priest resumed: "What can one do? They are all like that in the district. It is shocking, but cannot be helped, and then one must be a little indulgent toward the weaknesses of our nature. They never get married until they have become enceinte, never, madame." He added, smiling: "One might call it a local custom. So, you see, monsieur, your maid did as all the rest do."

But the baron, who was trembling with nervousness, interrupted him, saying, "She! what do I care about her! It is Julien with whom I am indignant. It is infamous, the way he has behaved, and I shall take my daughter away."

He walked up and down excitedly, becoming more and more exasperated: "It is infamous to have betrayed my child, infamous! He is a wretch, this man, a cad, a wretch! and I will tell him so. I will slap his face. I will give him a horsewhipping!"

The priest, who was slowly taking a pinch of snuff, seated beside the baroness still in tears, and endeavoring to fulfill his office of a peacemaker, said: "Come, monsieur le baron, between ourselves, he has done what every one else does. Do you know many husbands who are faithful?" And he added with a sly good humor: "Come now, I wager that you have had your turn. Your hand on your heart, am I right?" The baron had stopped in astonishment before the priest, who continued: "Why, yes, you did just as others did. Who knows if you did not make love to a little sugar plum like that? I tell you that every one does. Your wife was none the less happy, or less loved; am I not right?"

The baron had not stirred, he was much disturbed. What the priest said was true, and he had sinned as much as any one and had not hesitated when his wife's maids were in question. Was he a wretch on that account? Why should he judge Julien's conduct so severely when his own had not been above blame?

The baroness, still struggling with her sobs, smiled faintly at the recollection of her husband's escapades, for she belonged to the sentimental class for whom love adventures are a part of existence.

Jeanne, exhausted, lay with wide-open eyes, absorbed in painful reflection. Something Rosalie had said had wounded her as though an arrow had pierced her heart: "As for me, I said nothing, because I liked him."

She had liked him also, and that was the only reason why she had given herself, bound herself for life to him, why she had renounced everything else, all her cherished plans, all the unknown future. She had fallen into this marriage, into this hole without any edges by which one could climb out, into this wretchedness, this sadness, this despair, because, like Rosalie, she had liked him!

The door was pushed violently open and Julien appeared, with a furious expression on his face. He had caught sight of Rosalie moaning on the stairs, and suspected that something was up, that the maid had probably told all. The sight of the priest riveted him to the spot.

"Why, what's the matter?" he asked in a trembling but quiet tone.

The baron, so violent a short while ago, did not venture to speak, afraid of the priest's remarks, and of what his son-in-law might say in the same strain. Little mother was weeping more copiously than ever; but Jeanne had raised herself with her hands and looked, breathing quickly, at the one who had caused her such cruel sorrow. She stammered out: "The fact is, we know all, all your rascality since — since the day you first entered this house — we know that the child of this maid is your child, just as — as — mine is — they will be brothers." Overcome with sorrow at this thought, she buried herself in the sheets and wept bitterly.

Julien stood there gaping, not knowing what to say or do. The priest came to the rescue.

"Come, come, do not give way like that, my dear young lady, be sensible." He rose, approached the bed and placed his warm hand on the despairing girl's forehead. This seemed to soothe her strangely. She felt quieted, as if this strong peasant's hand, accustomed to the gesture of absolution, to kindly consolations, had conveyed by its touch some mysterious solace.

The good man, still standing, continued: "Madame, we must always forgive. A great sorrow has come to you; but God in His mercy has balanced it by a great happiness, since you will become a mother. This child will be your comfort. In his name I implore you, I adjure you to forgive M. Julien's error. It will be a new bond between you, a pledge of his future fidelity. Can you remain apart in your heart from him whose child you bear?"

She did not reply, crushed, mortified, exhausted as she was, without even strength for anger or resentment. Her nerves seemed relaxed, almost severed, she seemed to be scarcely alive.

The baroness, who seemed incapable of resentment, and whose mind was unequal to prolonged effort, murmured: "Come, come, Jeanne."

Then the priest took the hand of the young man and leading him up to the bed, he placed his hand in that of his wife, and gave it a little tap as though to unite them more closely. Then laying aside his professional tone and manner, he said with a satisfied air: "Well, now, that's done. Believe me, that is the best thing to do." The two hands, joined for a moment, separated immediately. Julien, not daring to kiss Jeanne, kissed his motherin-law on the forehead, turned on his heel, took the arm of the baron, who acquiesced, happy at heart that the thing had been settled thus, and they went out together to smoke a cigar.

The patient, overcome, dozed off, while the priest and little mother talked in a low tone.

The priest explained and propounded his ideas, to which the baroness assented by nodding her head. He said in conclusion: "Well, then, that is understood; you will give this girl the Barville farm, and I will undertake to find her a husband, a good, steady fellow. Oh! with a property worth twenty thousand francs we shall have no lack of suitors. There will be more than enough to choose from."

The baroness was smiling now, quite happy, with the remains of two tears that had dried on her cheeks.

She repeated: "That is settled. Barville is worth at least twenty thousand francs, but it will be settled on the child, the parents having the use of it during their lifetime."

The curé rose, shook little mother's hand, saying: "Do not disturb yourself, Madame la Baronne, do not disturb yourself; I know what an effort it is."

As he went out he met Aunt Lison coming to see her patient. She noticed nothing; they told her nothing; and she knew nothing, as usual.

VIII

Rosalie had left the house. Jeanne felt no joy at the thought of being a mother, she had had so much sorrow. She awaited the advent of her child without curiosity, still filled with the apprehension of unknown misfortunes.

A big woman, big as a house, had taken Rosalie's place and supported the baroness in her monotonous walks along her avenue. The baron gave his arm to Jeanne, who was now always ailing, while Aunt Lison, uneasy, and busied about the approaching event, held her other hand, bewildered at this mystery which she would never know.

They all walked along like this almost in silence for hours at a time, while Julien was riding about the country on horseback, having suddenly acquired this taste. Nothing ever came to disturb their dreary life. The baron, his wife, and the vicomte paid a visit to the Fourvilles, whom Julien seemed to be already well acquainted with, without one knowing just how. Another ceremonious visit was exchanged with the Brisevilles, who were still hidden in their manor house.

One afternoon, about four o'clock, two persons, a lady and gentleman on horseback, rode up into the courtyard of the château. Julien, greatly excited, ran up to Jeanne's room. "Quick, quick, come downstairs; here are the Fourvilles. They have just come as neighbors, knowing your condition. Tell them that I have gone out, but that I will be back. I will just go and make myself presentable."

Jeanne, much surprised, went downstairs. A pale, pretty young woman with a sad face, dreamy eyes, and lustreless, fair hair, looking as though the sunlight had never kissed it, quietly introduced her husband, a kind of giant, or ogre with a large red mustache. She added: "We have several times had the pleasure of meeting M. de Lamare. We heard from him how you were suffering, and we would not put off coming to see you as neighbors, without any ceremony. You see that we came on horseback. I also had the pleasure the other day of a visit from madame, your mother, and the baron."

She spoke with perfect ease, familiar but refined. Jeanne was charmed, and fell in love with her at once. "This is a friend," she thought.

The Comte de Fourville, on the contrary, seemed like a bear in the drawingroom. As soon as he was seated, he placed his hat on the chair next him, did not know what to do with his hands, placed them on his knees, then on the arms of the chair, and finally crossed his fingers as if in prayer.

Suddenly Julien entered the room. Jeanne was amazed and did not recognize him. He was shaved. He looked handsome, elegant, and attractive as on the day of their betrothal. He shook the comte's hairy paw, kissed the hand of the comtesse, whose ivory cheeks colored up slightly while her eyelids quivered.

He began to speak; he was charming as in former days. His large eyes, the mirrors of love, had become tender again. And his hair, lately so dull and unkempt, had regained its soft, glossy wave, with the use of a hairbrush and perfumed oil.

At the moment that the Fourvilles were taking their leave the comtesse, turning toward him, said: "Would you like to take a ride on Thursday, dear vicomte?"

As he bowed and murmured, "Why, certainly, madame," she took Jeanne's hand and said in a sympathetic and affectionate tone, with a cordial smile: "Oh! when you are well, we will all three gallop about the country. It will be delightful. What do you say?"

With an easy gesture she held up her riding skirt and then jumped into the saddle with the lightness of a bird, while her husband, after bowing awkwardly, mounted his big Norman steed. As they disappeared outside the gate, Julien, who seemed charmed, exclaimed: "What delightful people! those are friends who may be useful to us."

Jeanne, pleased also without knowing why, replied: "The little comtesse is charming, I feel that I shall love her, but the husband looks like a brute. Where did you meet them?"

He rubbed his hands together good humoredly. "I met them by chance at the Brisevilles'. The husband seems a little rough. He cares for nothing but hunting, but he is a real noble for all that."

The dinner was almost cheerful, as though some secret happiness had come into the house.

Nothing new happened until the latter days of July, when Jeanne was taken ill. As she seemed to grow worse, the doctor was sent for and at the first glance recognized the symptoms of a premature confinement.

Her sufferings presently abated a little, but she was filled with a terrible anguish, a despairing sinking, something like a presentiment, the mysterious touch of death. It is in these moments when it comes so near to us that its breath chills our hearts.

The room was full of people. Little mother, buried in an armchair, was choking with grief. The baron, his hands trembling, ran hither and thither, carrying things, consulting the doctor and losing his head. Julien paced up and down, looking concerned, but perfectly calm, and Widow Dentu stood at the foot of the bed with an appropriate expression, the expression of a woman of experience whom nothing astonishes. The cook, Ludivine, and Aunt Lison remained discreetly concealed behind the door of the lobby.

Toward morning Jeanne became worse, and as her involuntary screams escaped from between her closed teeth, she thought incessantly of Rosalie, who had not suffered, who had hardly moaned, who had borne her child without suffering and without difficulty, and in her wretched and troubled mind she continually compared their conditions and cursed God, whom she had formerly thought to be just. She rebelled at the wicked partiality of fate and at the wicked lies of those who preach justice and goodness.

At times her sufferings were so great that her mind was a blank. She had neither strength, life nor knowledge for anything but suffering.

All at once her sufferings ceased. The nurse and the doctor leaned over her and gave her all attention. Presently she heard a little cry and, in spite of her weakness, she unconsciously held out her arms. She was suddenly filled with joy, with a glimpse of a new-found happiness which had just unfolded. Her child was born, she was soothed, happy, happy as she never yet had been. Her heart and her body revived; she was now a mother. She felt that she was saved, secure from all despair, for she had here something to love.

From now on she had but one thought — her child. She was a fanatical mother, all the more intense because she had been deceived in her love, deceived in her hopes. She would sit whole days beside the window, rocking the little cradle.

The baron and little mother smiled at this excess of tenderness, but Julien, whose habitual routine had been interfered with and his overweening importance diminished by the arrival of this noisy and allpowerful tyrant, unconsciously jealous of this mite of a man who had usurped his place in the house, kept on saying angrily and impatiently: "How wearisome she is with her brat!"

She became so obsessed by this affection that she would pass the entire night beside the cradle, watching the child asleep. As she was becoming exhausted by this morbid life, taking no rest, growing weaker and thinner and beginning to cough, the doctor ordered the child to be taken from her. She got angry, wept, implored, but they were deaf to her entreaties. His nurse took him every evening, and each night his mother would rise, and in her bare feet go to the door, listen at the keyhole to see if he was sleeping quietly, did not wake up and wanted nothing.

Julien found her here one night when he came home late, after dining with the Fourvilles. After that they locked her in her room to oblige her to stay in bed.

The baptism took place at the end of August. The baron was godfather and Aunt Lison godmother. The child was named Pierre-Simon-Paul and called Paul for short.

At the beginning of September Aunt Lison left without any commotion. Her absence was as little felt as her presence.

One evening after dinner the priest appeared. He seemed embarrassed as if he were burdened by some mystery, and after some idle remarks, he asked the baroness and her husband to grant him a short interview in private.

They all three walked slowly down the long avenue, talking with animation, while Julien, who was alone with Jeanne, was astonished, disturbed and annoyed at this secret.

He accompanied the priest when he took his leave, and they went off together toward the church where the Angelus was ringing.

As it was cool, almost cold, the others went into the drawingroom. They were all dozing when Julien came in abruptly, his face red, looking very indignant.

From the door he called out to his parents-in-law, without remembering that Jeanne was there: "Are you crazy, for God's sake! to go and throw away twenty thousand francs on that girl?"

No one replied, they were so astonished. He continued, bellowing with rage: "How can one be so stupid as that? Do you wish to leave us without a sou?"

The baron, who had recovered his composure, attempted to stop him: "Keep still! Remember that you are speaking before your wife."

But Julien was trembling with excitement: "As if I cared; she knows all about it, anyway. It is robbing her."

Jeanne, bewildered, looked at him without understanding. She faltered: "What in the world is the matter?"

Julien then turned toward her, to try and get her on his side as a partner who has been cheated out of an unexpected fortune. He hurriedly told her about the conspiracy to marry off Rosalie and about the gift of the Barville property, which was worth at least twenty thousand francs. He said: "Your parents are crazy, my dear, crazy enough to be shut up! Twenty thousand francs! twenty thousand francs! Why, they have lost their heads! Twenty thousand francs for a bastard!"

Jeanne listened without emotion and without anger, astonished at her own calmness, indifferent now to everything but her own child.

The baron was raging, but could find nothing to say. He finally burst forth and, stamping his foot, exclaimed: "Think of what you are saying; it is disgusting. Whose fault was it if we had to give this girl-mother a dowry? Whose child is it? You would like to abandon it now!"

Julien, amazed at the baron's violence, looked at him fixedly. He then resumed in a calmer tone: "But fifteen hundred francs would be quite enough. They all have children before they are legally married. It makes no difference whose child it is, in any case. Instead of giving one of your farms, to the value of twenty thousand francs, in addition to making the world aware of what has happened, you should, to say the least, have had some regard for our name and our position."

He spoke in a severe tone like a man who stood on his rights and was convinced of the logic of his argument. The baron, disturbed at this unexpected discussion, stood there gaping at him. Julien then, seeing his advantage, concluded: "Happily, nothing has yet been settled. I know the young fellow who is going to marry her. He is an honest chap and we can make a satisfactory arrangement with him. I will take charge of the matter."

And he went out immediately, fearing no doubt to continue the discussion, and pleased that he had had the last word, a proof, he thought, that they acquiesced in his views.

As soon as he had left the room, however, the baron exclaimed: "Oh, that is going too far, much too far!"

But Jeanne, happening to look up at her father's bewildered face, began to laugh with her clear, ringing laugh of former days, when anything amused her. She said: "Father, father, did you hear the tone in which he said: 'Twenty thousand francs?'"

Little mother, whose mirth was as ready as her tears, as she recalled her son-in-law's angry expression, his indignant exclamations and his refusal to allow the girl whom he had led astray to be given money that did not belong to him, delighted also at Jeanne's mirth, gave way to little bursts of laughter till the tears came to her eyes. The baron caught the contagion, and all three laughed to kill themselves as they used to do in the good old days.

As soon as they quieted down a little Jeanne said: "How strange it is that all this does not affect me. I look upon him now as a stranger. I cannot believe that I am his wife. You see how I can laugh at his — his — want of delicacy."

And without knowing why they all three embraced each other, smiling and happy.

Two days later, after breakfast, just as Julien had started away from the house on horseback, a strapping young fellow from twenty-one to twenty-five years old, clad in a brand-new blue blouse with wide sleeves buttoning at the wrist, slyly jumped over the gate, as though he had been there awaiting his opportunity all the morning, crept along the Couillards' ditch, came round the château, and cautiously approached the baron and his wife, who were still sitting under the plane-tree.

He took off his cap and advanced, bowing in an awkward manner. As soon as he was close to them he said: "Your servant, Monsieur le Baron, madame and the company." Then, as no one replied, he said: "It is I, I am Desiré Lecocq."

As the name conveyed nothing to them, the baron asked, "What do you want?"

Then, altogether upset at the necessity of explaining himself, the young fellow stuttered out as he gazed alternately at his cap, which he held in his hands, and at the roof of the château: "It was M'sieu le Curé who said something to me about this matter — — " And then he stopped, fearing he might say too much and compromise his own interests.

The other, lowering his voice, blurted out: "That matter of your maid — Rosalie — — "

Jeanne, who had guessed what was coming, had risen and moved away with her infant in her arms.

"Come nearer," said the baron, pointing to the chair his daughter had just left. The peasant sat down, murmuring: "You are very good." Then he waited as though he had no more to say. After a long silence, he screwed up courage, and looking up at the sky, remarked: "There's fine weather for the time of year. But the earth will be none the better for it, as the seed is already sown." And then he was silent again.

The baron was growing impatient. He plunged right into the subject and said drily: "Then it is you who are going to marry Rosalie?"

The man at once became uneasy, his Norman caution being on the alert. He replied with more animation, but with a tinge of defiance: "That depends; perhaps yes, perhaps no; it depends."

The baron, annoyed at this hedging, exclaimed angrily: "Answer frankly, damn it! Was this what you came here for? Yes or no! Will you marry her? Yes or no!"

The bewildered man looked steadfastly at his feet: "If it is as M'sieu le Curé said, I will take her, but if it is as M'sieu Julien said, I will not take her."

"What did M. Julien tell you?"

"M'sieu Julien told me fifteen hundred francs and M'sieu le Curé told me that I should have twenty thousand. I will do it for twenty thousand, but I will not do it for fifteen hundred."

The baroness, who was buried in her easy chair, began to giggle at the anxious expression of the peasant, who, not understanding this frivolity, glanced at her angrily out of the corner of his eye and waited in silence.

The baron, who was embarrassed at this bargaining, cut it short by saying: "I told M. le Curé that you should have the Barville farm during your lifetime and that then it would revert to the child. It is worth twenty thousand francs. I do not go back on my word. Is it settled? Yes or no!"

The man smiled with a humble and satisfied expression, and suddenly becoming loquacious, said: "Oh, in that case, I will not say no. That was all that stood in my way. When M'sieu le Curé spoke to me, I was ready at once, by gosh! and I was very pleased to accommodate the baron who was giving me that. I said to myself, 'Is it not true that when people are willing to do each other favors, they can always find a way and can make it worth while?' But M'sieu

Julien came to see me, and it was only fifteen hundred francs. I said to myself: 'I must see about that,' and so I came here. That is not to say that I did not trust you, but I wanted to know. Short accounts make long friends. Is not that true, M'sieu le Baron?"

The baron interrupted him by asking, "When do you wish to get married?"

The man became timid again, very much embarrassed, and finally said, hesitatingly: "I will not do it until I get a little paper."

This time the baron got angry: "Doggone it! you will have the marriage contract. That is the best kind of paper."

But the peasant was stubborn: "Meanwhile I might take a little turn; it will not be dark for a while."

The baron rose to make an end of the matter: "Answer yes or no at once. If you do not wish her, say so; I have another suitor."

The fear of a rival terrified the crafty Norman. He suddenly made up his mind and held out his hand, as after buying a cow, saying: "Put it there, M'sieu le Baron; it is a bargain. Whoever draws back is a skunk!"

The baron shook his hand, then called out: "Ludivine!" The cook appeared at the window. "Bring us a bottle of wine." They clinked glasses to seal the matter and the young peasant went off with a light tread.

Nothing was said to Julien about this visit. The contract was drawn up with all secrecy and as soon as the banns were published the wedding took place one Monday morning.

A neighbor carried the child to church, walking behind the bride and groom, as a sure sign of good luck. And no one in all the district was surprised; they simply envied Desiré Lecocq. "He was born with a caul," they said, with a sly smile into which there entered no resentment.

Julien was terribly angry and made such a scene that his parents-in-law cut short their visit to the "Poplars." Jeanne was only moderately sad at their departure, for little Paul had become for her an inexhaustible source of happiness.

IX

As Jeanne's health was quite restored, they determined to go and return the Fourvilles' visit and also to call on the Marquis de Coutelier.

Julien had bought at a sale a new one-horse phaeton, so that they could go out twice a month. They set out one fine December morning, and after driving for two hours across the plains of Normandy, they began to descend a little slope into a little valley, the sides of which were wooded, while the valley itself was cultivated. After an abrupt turn in the valley they saw the Château of Vrillette, a wooded slope on one side of it and a large pond on the other, out of which rose one of its walls and which was bounded by a wood of tall pine trees that formed the other side of the valley.

Julien explained all the portions of the building to Jeanne, like one who knows his subject thoroughly, and went into raptures over its beauty, adding; "It is full of game, this country. The comte loves to hunt here. This is a true seignorial residence."

The hall door was opened and the pale comtesse appeared, coming forward to meet the visitors, all smiles, and wearing a long-trained dress, like a chatelaine of olden times. She looked a fitting lady of the lake, born to inhabit this fairy castle.

The comtesse took both Jeanne's hands, as if she had known her all her life, and made her sit down beside her in a low chair, while Julien, all of whose forgotten elegance seemed to have revived within the past five months, chatted and smiled quietly and familiarly.

The comtesse and he talked of their horseback rides. She was laughing at his manner of mounting a horse and called him "Le Chevalier Trébuche," and he smiled also, having nick-named her "The Amazon Queen." A gun fired beneath the windows caused Jeanne to give a little scream. It was the comte, who had killed a teal.

His wife called to him. A sound of oars was heard, a boat grinding against the stones, and he appeared, enormous, booted, followed by two drenched dogs of a ruddy color like himself, who lay down on the mat outside the door.

He seemed more at his ease in his own home, and was delighted to see his visitors. He put some wood on the fire, sent for madeira and biscuits and then exclaimed suddenly: "Why, you will take dinner with us, of course."

Jeanne, whose child was never out of her thoughts, declined. He insisted, and as she could not be persuaded, Julien made a gesture of annoyance. She feared to arouse his ugly, quarrelsome temper, and although she was very unhappy at the thought that she should not see Paul until the next day, she consented to stay.

The afternoon was delightful. They first visited the springs which bubbled up at the foot of a mossy rock and then took a row on the pond. At one end of the boat Julien and the comtesse, wrapped in shawls, were smiling happily like those who have nothing left to wish for.

A huge fire was blazing in the spacious reception room, which imparted a sense of warmth and contentment. The comte seized his wife in his arms and lifted her from the floor as though she had been a child and gave her a hearty kiss on each cheek, like a man satisfied with the world.

Jeanne, smiling, looked at this good giant whom one would have thought was an ogre at the very sight of his mustaches, and she thought: "How one may be deceived each day about everybody." Then, almost involuntarily, she glanced at Julien standing in the doorway, looking horribly pale and with his eyes fixed on the comte. She approached him and said in a low tone: "Are you ill? What is the matter with you?" He answered her angrily: "Nothing. Let me alone! I was cold."

When they went into the diningroom the count asked if he might let his dogs come in, and they settled themselves one on either side of their master.

After dinner, as Jeanne and Julien were preparing to leave, M. de Fourville kept them a little longer to look at some fishing by torchlight. When they finally set out, wrapped up in their cloaks and some rugs they had borrowed, Jeanne said almost involuntarily: "What a fine man that giant is!" Julien, who was driving, replied: "Yes, but he does not always restrain himself before company."

A week later they called on the Couteliers, who were supposed to be the chief noble family in the province. Their property of Remenil adjoined the large town of Cany. The new château built in the reign of Louis XIV. was hidden in a magnificent park enclosed by walls. The ruins of the old château could be seen on an eminence. They were ushered into a stately reception room by men servants in livery. In the middle of the room a sort of column held an immense bowl of Sèvres ware and on the pedestal of the column an autograph letter from the king, under glass, requested the Marquis Leopold-Hervé-Joseph-Germer de Varneville de Rollebosc de Coutelier to receive this present from his sovereign.

Jeanne and Julien were looking at this royal gift when the marquis and marquise entered the room.

They were very ceremonious people whose minds, sentiments and words seemed always to be on stilts. They spoke without waiting for an answer, smiling complacently, appearing always to be fulfilling the duty imposed on them by their position, of showing civilities to the inferior nobility of the region.

Jeanne and Julien, somewhat taken aback, endeavored to be agreeable, but although they felt too embarrassed to remain any longer, they did not know exactly how to take their leave. The marquise herself put an end to the visit naturally and simply by bringing the conversation to a close like a queen giving a dismissal.

On the way home Julien said: "If you like, we will make this our first and last call; the Fourvilles are good enough for me." Jeanne was of the same opinion. December passed slowly and the shut-in life began again as in the previous year. But Jeanne did not find it wearisome, as she was always taken up with Paul, whom Julien looked at askance, uneasy and annoyed. Often when the mother held the child in her arms, kissing it frantically as women do their children, she would hold it up to its father, saying: "Give him a kiss; one would suppose you did not love him." He would hardly touch with his lips the child's smooth forehead, walking all round it, as though he did not wish to touch the restless little fists. Then he would walk away abruptly as though from something distasteful.

The mayor, the doctor and the curé came to dinner occasionally, and sometimes it was the Fourvilles, with whom they were becoming more and more intimate. The comte appeared to worship Paul. He held him on his knees during the whole visit and sometimes during the whole afternoon, playing with him and amusing him and then kissing him tenderly as mothers do. He always lamented that he had no children of his own.

Comtesse Gilberte again mentioned the rides they all four were going to take together. Jeanne, a little weary of the monotonous days and nights, was quite happy in anticipation of these plans, and for a week amused herself making a riding habit.

They always set out two and two, the comtesse and Julien ahead, the count and Jeanne a hundred feet behind them, talking quietly, like good friends, for such they had become through the sympathy of their straightforward minds and simple hearts. The others often spoke in a low tone, sometimes bursting into laughter and looking quickly at each other, as though their eyes were expressing what they dared not utter. And they would suddenly set off at a gallop, impelled by a desire to flee, to get away, far away.

Then Gilberte would seem to be growing irritable. Her sharp voice, borne on the breeze, occasionally reached the ears of the loitering couple. The comte would smile and say to Jeanne: "She does not always get out of bed the right side, that wife of mine."

One evening as they were coming home the comtesse was teasing her mount, spurring it and then checking it abruptly. They heard Julien say several time: "Take care, take care; you will be thrown." "So much the worse," she replied; "it is none of your business," in a hard clear tone that resounded across the fields as though the words hung in the air.

The animal reared, plunged and champed the bit. The comte, uneasy, shouted: "Be careful, Gilberte!" Then, as if in defiance, with one of those impulses of a woman whom nothing can stop, she struck her horse brutally between the ears. The animal reared in anger, pawed the air with his front feet and, landing again on his feet, gave a bound and darted across the plain at full speed.

First it crossed the meadow, then plunging into a ploughed field kicked up the damp rich earth behind it, going so fast that one could hardly distinguish its rider. Julien remained transfixed with astonishment, calling out in despair: "Madame, madame!" but the comte was rather annoyed, and, bending forward on his heavy mount, he urged it forward and started out at such a pace, spurring it on with his voice, his gestures and the spur, that the huge horseman seemed to be carrying the heavy beast between his legs and to be lifting it up as if to fly. They went at incredible speed, straight ahead, and Jeanne saw the outline of the wife and of the husband fleeing getting smaller and disappearing in the distance, as if they were two birds pursuing each other to the verge of the horizon.

Julien, approaching Jeanne slowly, murmured angrily: "I think she is crazy to-day." And they set out together to follow their friends, who were now hidden by the rising ground.

At the end of about a quarter of an hour they saw them returning and presently joined them. The comte, perspiring, his face red, but smiling, happy and triumphant, was holding his wife's trembling horse in his iron grasp. Gilberte was pale, her face sad and drawn, and she was leaning one hand on her husband's shoulder as if she were going to faint. Jeanne understood now that the comte loved her madly.

After this the comtesse for some months seemed happier than she had ever been. She came to the "Poplars" more frequently, laughed continually and kissed Jeanne impulsively. One might have said that some mysterious charm had come into her life. Her husband was also quite happy and never took his eyes off her. He said to Jeanne one evening: "We are very happy just now. Gilberte has never been so nice as this. She never is out of humor, never gets angry. I feel that she loves me; until now I was not sure of it."

Julien also seemed changed, no longer impatient, as though the friendship between the two families had brought peace and happiness to both. The spring was singularly early and mild. Everything seemed to be coming to life beneath the quickening rays of the sun. Jeanne was vaguely troubled at this awakening of nature. Memories came to her of the early days of her love. Not that her love for Julien was renewed; that was over, over forever. But all her being, caressed by the breeze, filled with the fragrance of spring, was disturbed as though in response to some invisible and tender appeal. She loved to be alone, to give herself up in the sunlight to all kinds of vague and calm enjoyment which did not necessitate thinking.

One morning as she was in a reverie a vision came to her, a swift vision of the sunlit nook amid the dark foliage in the little wood near Étretat. It was there that she had for the first time trembled, when beside the young man who loved her then. It was there that he had uttered for the first time the timid desire of his heart. It was there that she thought that she had all at once reached the radiant future of her hopes. She wished to see this wood again, to make a sort of sentimental and superstitious pilgrimage, as though a return to this spot might somehow change the current of her life. Julien had been gone since daybreak, she knew not whither. She had the little white horse, which she sometimes rode, saddled, and she set out. It was one of those days when nothing seemed stirring, not a blade of grass, not a leaf. All seemed wrapped in a golden mist beneath the blazing sun. Jeanne walked her horse, soothed and happy.

She descended into the valley which leads to the sea, between the great arches in the cliff that are called the "Gates" of Étretat, and slowly reached the wood. The sunlight was streaming through the still scanty foliage. She wandered about the little paths, looking for the spot.

All at once, as she was going along one of the lower paths, she perceived at the farther end of it two horses tied to a tree and recognized them at once; they belonged to Gilberte and Julien. The loneliness of the place was beginning to be irksome to her, and she was pleased at this chance meeting, and whipped up her horse.

When she reached the two patient animals, who were probably accustomed to these long halts, she called. There was no reply. A woman's glove and two riding whips lay on the beaten-down grass. So they had no doubt sat down there awhile and then walked away leaving their horses tied.

She waited a quarter of an hour, twenty minutes, surprised, not understanding what could be keeping them. She had dismounted. She sat there, leaning against a tree trunk. Suddenly a thought came to her as she glanced again at the glove, the whips and the two horses left tied there, and she sprang to her saddle with an irresistible desire to make her escape.

She started off at a gallop for the "Poplars." She was turning things over in her mind, trying to reason, to put two and two together, to compare facts. How was it that she had not suspected this sooner? How was it that she had not noticed anything? How was it she had not guessed the reason of Julien's frequent absences, the renewal of his former attention to his appearance and the improvement in his temper? She now recalled Gilberte's nervous abruptness, her exaggerated affection and the kind of beaming happiness in which she seemed to exist latterly and that so pleased the comte.

She reined in her horse, as she wanted to think, and the quick pace disturbed her ideas.

As soon as the first emotion was over she became almost calm, without jealousy or hatred, but filled with contempt. She hardly gave Julien a thought; nothing he might do could astonish her. But the double treachery of the comtesse, her friend, disgusted her. Everyone, then, was treacherous, untruthful and false. And tears came to her eyes. One sometimes mourns lost illusions as deeply as one does the death of a friend.

She resolved, however, to act as though she knew nothing, to close the doors of her heart to all ordinary affection and to love no one but Paul and her parents and to endure other people with an undisturbed countenance.

As soon as she got home she ran to her son, carried him up to her room and kissed him passionately for an hour.

Julien came home to dinner, smiling and attentive, and appeared interested as he asked: "Are not father and little mother coming this year?"

She was so grateful to him for this little attention that she almost forgave him for the discovery she had made in the wood, and she was filled all of a sudden with an intense desire to see without delay the two beings in the world whom she loved next to Paul, and passed the whole evening writing to them to hasten their journey.

They promised to be there on the 20th of May and it was now the 7th.

She awaited their arrival with a growing impatience, as though she felt, in addition to her filial affection, the need of opening her heart to honest hearts, to talk with frankness to pure-minded people, devoid of all infamy, all of whose life, actions and thoughts had been upright at all times.

What she now felt was a sort of moral isolation, amid all this immorality, and, although she had learned suddenly to disseminate, although she received the comtesse with outstretched hand and smiling lips, she felt this consciousness of hollowness, this contempt for humanity increasing and enveloping her, and the petty gossip of the district gave her a still greater disgust, a still lower opinion of her fellow creatures.

The immorality of the peasants shocked her, and this warm spring seemed to stir the sap in human beings as well as in plants. Jeanne did not belong to the race of peasants who are dominated by their lower instincts. Julien one day awakened her aversion anew by telling her a coarse story that had been told to him and that he considered very amusing.

When the travelling carriage stopped at the door and the happy face of the baron appeared at the window Jeanne was stirred with so deep an emotion, such a tumultuous feeling of affection as she had never before experienced. But when she saw her mother she was shocked and almost fainted. The baroness, in six months, had aged ten years. Her heavy cheeks had grown flabby and purple, as though the blood were congested; her eyes were dim and she could no longer move about unless supported under each arm. Her breathing was difficult and wheezing and affected those near her with a painful sensation.

When Jeanne had taken them to their room, she retired to her own in order to have a good cry, as she was so upset. Then she went to look for her father, and throwing herself into his arms, she exclaimed, her eyes still full of tears: "Oh, how mother is changed! What is the matter with her? Tell me, what is the matter?" He was much surprised and replied: "Do you think so? What an idea! Why, no. I have never been away from her. I assure you that I do not think she looks ill. She always looks like that."

That evening Julien said to his wife: "Your mother is in a pretty bad way. I think she will not last long." And as Jeanne burst out sobbing, he became annoyed. "Come, I did not say there was no hope for her. You always exaggerate everything. She is changed, that's all. She is no longer young."

The baroness was not able to walk any distance and only went out for half an hour each day to take one turn in her avenue and then she would sit on the bench. And when she felt unequal to walking to the end of her avenue, she would say: "Let us stop; my hypertrophy is breaking my legs today." She hardly ever laughed now as she did the previous year at anything that amused her, but only smiled. As she could see to read excellently, she passed hours reading "Corinne" or Lamartine's "Meditations." Then she would ask for her drawer of "souvenirs," and emptying her cherished letters on her lap, she would place the drawer on a chair beside her and put back, one by one, her "relics," after she had slowly gone over them. And when she was alone, quite alone, she would kiss some of them, as one kisses in secret a lock of hair of a loved one passed away.

Sometimes Jeanne, coming in abruptly, would find her weeping and would exclaim: "What is the matter, little mother?" And the baroness, sighing deeply, would reply: "It is my 'relics' that make me cry. They stir remembrances that were so delightful and that are now past forever, and one is reminded of persons whom one had forgotten and recalls once more. You seem to see them, to hear them and it affects you strangely. You will feel this later."

When the baron happened to come in at such times he would say gently: "Jeanne, dearie, take my advice and burn your letters, all of them — your mother's, mine, everyone's. There is nothing more dreadful, when one is growing old, than to look back to one's youth." But Jeanne also kept her letters, was preparing a chest of "relics" in obedience to a sort of hereditary instinct of dreamy sentimentality, although she differed from her mother in every other way.

The baron was obliged to leave them some days later, as he had some business that called him away.

One afternoon Jeanne took Paul in her arms and went out for a walk. She was sitting on a bank, gazing at the infant, whom she seemed to be looking at for the first time. She could hardly imagine him grown up, walking with a steady step, with a beard on his face and talking in a big voice. She heard someone calling and raised her head. Marius came running toward her.

"Madame, Madame la Baronne is very bad!"

A cold chill seemed to run down her back as she started up and walked hurriedly toward the house.

As she approached she saw a number of persons grouped around the plane tree. She darted forward and saw her mother lying on the ground with two pillows under her head. Her face was black, her eyes closed and her breathing, which had been difficult for twenty years, now quite hushed. The nurse took the child out of Jeanne's arms and carried it off.

Jeanne, with drawn, anxious face, asked: "What happened? How did she come to fall? Go for the doctor, somebody." Turning round, she saw the old curé, who had heard of it in some way. He offered his services and began rolling up the sleeves of his cassock. But vinegar, eau de cologne and rubbing the invalid proved ineffectual.

"She should be undressed and put to bed," said the priest.

Joseph Couillard, the farmer, was there and old Simon and Ludivine. With the assistance of Abbé Picot, they tried to lift the baroness, but after an attempt were obliged to bring a large easy chair from the drawingroom and place her in it. In this way they managed to get her into the house and then upstairs, where they laid her on her bed.

Joseph Couillard set out in hot haste for the doctor. As the priest was going to get the holy oil, the nurse, who had "scented a death," as the servants say, and was on the spot, whispered to him: "Do not put yourself out, monsieur; she is dead. I know all about these things."

Jeanne, beside herself, entreated them to do something. The priest thought it best to pronounce the absolution.

They watched for two hours beside this lifeless, discolored body. Jeanne, on her knees, was sobbing in an agony of grief.

When the door opened and the doctor appeared, Jeanne darted toward him, stammering out what she knew of the accident, but seeing the nurse exchange a meaning glance with the doctor, she stopped to ask him: "Is it serious? Do you think it is serious?"

He said presently: "I am afraid — I am afraid — it is all over. Be brave, be brave."

Jeanne, extending her arms, threw herself on her mother's body. Julien just then came in. He stood there amazed, visibly annoyed, without any exclamation of sorrow, any appearance of grief, taken so unawares that he had not time to prepare a suitable expression of countenance. He muttered: "I was expecting it, I felt that the end was near." Then he took out his handkerchief, wiped his eyes, knelt down, crossed himself, and then rising to his feet, attempted to raise his wife. But she was clasping the dead body and kissing it, and it became necessary to carry her away. She appeared to be out of her mind.

At the end of an hour she was allowed to come back. There was no longer any hope. The room was arranged as a death chamber. Julien and the priest were talking in a low tone near the window. It was growing dark. The priest came over to Jeanne and took her hands, trying to console her. He spoke of the defunct, praised her in pious phrases and offered to pass the night in prayer beside the body.

But Jeanne refused, amid convulsive sobs. She wished to be alone, quite alone on this last night of farewell. Julien came forward: "But you must not do it; we will stay together." She shook her head, unable to speak. At last she said: "It is my mother, my mother. I wish to watch beside her alone." The doctor murmured: "Let her do as she pleases; the nurse can stay in the adjoining room."

The priest and Julien consented, more interested in their own rest. Then Abbé Picot knelt down in his turn, and as he rose and left the room, he said: "She was a saint" in the same tone as he said "Dominus vobiscum."

The vicomte in his ordinary tone then asked: "Are you not going to eat something?" Jeanne did not reply, not knowing he was speaking to her, and he repeated: "You had better eat something to keep up your stomach." She replied in a bewildered manner: "Send at once for papa." And he went out of the room to send someone on horseback to Rouen.

She remained plunged in a sort of motionless grief, seeing nothing, feeling nothing, understanding nothing. She only wanted to be alone. Julien came back. He had dined and he asked her again: "Won't you take something?" She shook her head. He sat down with an air of resignation rather than sadness, without speaking, and they both sat there silent, till at length Julien arose, and approaching Jeanne, said: "Would you like to stay alone now?" She took his hand impulsively and replied: "Oh, yes! leave me!"

He kissed her forehead, murmuring: "I will come in and see you from time to time." He went out with Widow Dentu, who rolled her easy chair into the next room.

Jeanne shut the door and opened the windows wide. She felt the soft breath from the mown hay that lay in the moonlight on the lawn. It seemed to harrow her feelings like an ironical remark.

She went back to the bed, took one of the cold, inert hands and looked at her mother earnestly. She seemed to be sleeping more peacefully than she had ever done, and the pale flame of the tapers which flickered at every breath made her face appear to be alive, as if she had stirred. Jeanne remembered all the little incidents of her childhood, the visits of little mother to the "parloir" of the convent, the manner in which she handed her a little paper bag of cakes, a multitude of little details, little acts, little caresses, words, intonations, familiar gestures, the creases at the corner of her eyes when she laughed, the big sigh she gave when she sat down.

And she stood there looking at her, repeating half mechanically: "She is dead," and all the horror of the word became real to her. It was mamma lying there — little mother — Mamma Adelaide who was dead. She would never move about again, nor speak, nor laugh, nor sit at dinner opposite little father. She would never again say: "Good-morning, Jeannette." She was dead!

And she fell on her knees in a paroxysm of despair, her hands clutching the sheet, her face buried in the covers as she cried in a heartrending tone: "Oh, mamma, my poor mamma!" Then feeling that she was losing her reason as she had done on the night when she fled across the snow, she rose and ran to the window to drink in the fresh air. The soothing calmness of the night entered her soul and she began to weep quietly.

Presently she turned back into the room and sat down again beside her mother. Other remembrances came to her: those of her own life — Rosalie, Gilberte, the bitter disillusions of her heart. Everything, then, was only misery, grief, unhappiness and death. Everyone tried to deceive, everyone lied, everyone made you suffer and weep. Where could one find a little rest and happiness? In another existence no doubt, when the soul is freed from the trials of earth. And she began to ponder on this insoluble mystery.

A tender and curious thought came to her mind. It was to read over in this last watch, as though they were a litany, the old letters that her mother loved. It seemed to her that she was about to perform a delicate and sacred duty which would give pleasure to little mother in the other world.

She rose, opened the writing desk and took from the lower drawer ten little packages of yellow letters, tied and arranged in order, side by side. She placed them all on the bed over her mother's heart from a sort of sentiment and began to read them. They were old letters that savored of a former century. The first began, "My dear little granddaughter," then again "My dear little girl," "My darling," "My dearest daughter," then "My dear child," "My dear Adelaide," "My dear daughter," according to the periods — childhood, youth or young womanhood. They were all full of little insignificant details and tender words, about a thousand little matters, those simple but important events of home life, so petty to outsiders: "Father has the grip; poor Hortense burnt her finger; the cat, 'Croquerat,' is dead; they have cut down the pine tree to the right of the gate; mother lost her prayerbook on the way home from church, she thinks it was stolen."

All these details affected her. They seemed like revelations, as though she had suddenly entered the past secret heart life of little mother. She looked at her lying there and suddenly began to read aloud, to read to the dead, as though to distract, to console her.

And the dead woman appeared to be pleased.

Jeanne tossed the letters as she read them to the foot of the bed. She untied another package. It was a new handwriting. She read: "I cannot do without your caresses. I love you so that I am almost crazy."

That was all; no signature.

She put back the letter without understanding its meaning. The address was certainly "Madame la Baronne Le Perthuis des Vauds."

Then she opened another: "Come this evening as soon as he goes out; we shall have an hour together. I worship you." In another: "I passed the night longing in vain for you, longing to look into your eyes, to press my lips to yours, and I am insane enough to throw myself from the window at the thought that you are another's...."

Jeanne was perfectly bewildered. What did that mean? To whom, for whom, from whom were these words of love?

She went on reading, coming across fresh impassioned declarations, appointments with warnings as to prudence, and always at the end the six words: "Be sure to burn this letter!"

At last she opened an ordinary note, accepting an invitation to dinner, but in the same handwriting and signed: "Paul d'Ennemare," whom the baron called, whenever he spoke of him, "My poor old Paul," and whose wife had been the baroness' dearest friend.

Then a suspicion, which immediately became a certainty, flashed across Jeanne's mind: He had been her mother's lover.

And, almost beside herself, she suddenly threw aside these infamous letters as she would have thrown off some venomous reptile and ran to the window and began to cry piteously. Then, collapsing, she sank down beside the wall, and hiding her face in the curtain so that no one should hear her, she sobbed bitterly as if in hopeless despair.

She would have remained thus probably all night, if she had not heard a noise in the adjoining room that made her start to her feet. It might be her father. And all the letters were lying on the floor! He would have to open only one of them to know all! Her father!

She darted into the other room and seizing the letters in handfuls, she threw them all into the fireplace, those of her grandparents as well as those of the lover; some that she had not looked at and some that had remained tied up in the drawers of the desk. She then took one of the tapers that burned beside the bed and set fire to this pile of letters. When they were reduced to ashes she went back to the open window, as though she no longer dared to sit beside the dead, and began to cry again with her face in her hands: "Oh, my poor mamma! oh, my poor mamma!"

The stars were paling. It was the cool hour that precedes the dawn. The moon was sinking on the horizon and turning the sea to mother of pearl. The recollection of the night she passed at the window when she first came to the "Poplars" came to Jeanne's mind. How far away it seemed, how everything was changed, how different the future now seemed!

The sky was becoming pink, a joyous, love-inspiring, enchanting pink. She looked at it in surprise, as at some phenomenon, this radiant break of day, and asked herself if it were possible that, on a planet where such dawns were found, there should be neither joy nor happiness.

A noise at the door made her start. It was Julien. "Well," he said, "are you not very tired?"

She murmured, "No," happy at being no longer alone. "Go and rest now," he said. She kissed her mother a long, sad kiss; then she went to her room.

The next day passed in the usual attentions to the dead. The baron arrived toward evening. He wept for some time.

The funeral took place the following day. After pressing a last kiss on her mother's icy forehead and seeing the coffin nailed down, Jeanne left the room. The invited guests would soon arrive.

Gilberte was the first to come, and she threw herself sobbing on her friend's shoulder. Women in black presently entered the room one after another, people whom Jeanne did not know. The Marquise de Coutelier and the Vicomtesse de Briseville embraced her. She suddenly saw Aunt Lison gliding in behind her. She turned round and kissed her tenderly.

Julien came in, dressed all in black, elegant, very important, pleased at seeing so many people. He asked his wife some question in a low tone and added confidentially: "All the nobility are here; it will be a fine affair." And he walked away, gravely bowing to the ladies. Aunt Lison and Comtesse Gilberte alone remained with Jeanne during the service for the dead. The comtesse kissed her repeatedly, exclaiming: "My poor dear, my poor dear!"

When Comte de Fourville came to fetch his wife he was also crying as though it were for his own mother.

X

The following days were very sad and dreary, as they always are when there has been a death in the house. And, in addition, Jeanne was crushed at the thought of what she had discovered; her last shred of confidence had been destroyed with the destruction of her faith. Little father, after a short stay, went away to try and distract his thoughts from his grief, and the large house, whose former masters were leaving it from time to time, resumed its usual calm and monotonous course.

Then Paul fell ill, and Jeanne was almost beside herself, not sleeping for ten days, and scarcely tasting food. He recovered, but she was haunted by the idea that he might die. Then what should she do? What would become of her? And there gradually stole into her heart the hope that she might have another child. She dreamed of it, became obsessed with the idea. She longed to realize her old dream of seeing two little children around her; a boy and a girl.

But since the affair of Rosalie she and Julien had lived apart. A reconciliation seemed impossible in their present situation. Julien loved some one else, she knew it; and the very thought of suffering his approach filled her with repugnance. She had no one left whom she could consult. She resolved to go and see Abbé Picot and tell him, under the seal of confession, all that weighed upon her mind in this matter.

He was reading from his breviary in his little garden planted with fruit trees when she arrived.

After a few minutes' conversation on indifferent matters, she faltered, her color rising: "I want to confess, Monsieur l'Abbé."

He looked at her in astonishment, as he pushed his spectacles back on his forehead; then he began to laugh. "You surely have no great sins on your conscience." This embarrassed her greatly, and she replied: "No, but I want to ask your advice on a subject that is so — so — so painful that I dare not mention it casually."

He at once laid aside his jovial manner and assumed his priestly attitude. "Well, my child, I will listen to you in the confessional; come along."

But she held back, undecided, restrained by a kind of scruple at speaking of these matters, of which she was half ashamed, in the seclusion of an empty church.

"Or else, no — Monsieur le Curé — I might — I might — if you wish, tell you now what brings me here. Let us go and sit over there, in your little arbor."

They walked toward it, and Jeanne tried to think how she could begin. They sat down in the arbor, and then, as if she were confessing herself, she said: "Father — — " then hesitated, and repeated: "Father — — " and was silent from emotion.

He waited, his hands crossed over his paunch. Seeing her embarrassment, he sought to encourage her: "Why, my daughter, one would suppose you were afraid; come, take courage."

She plucked up courage, like a coward who plunges headlong into danger. "Father, I should like to have another child." He did not reply, as he did not understand her. Then she explained, timid and unable to express herself clearly:

"I am all alone in life now; my father and my husband do not get along together; my mother is dead; and — and — — " she added with a shudder, "the other day I nearly lost my son! What would have become of me then?"

She was silent. The priest, bewildered, was gazing at her. "Come, get to the point of your subject."

"I want to have another child," she said. Then he smiled, accustomed to the coarse jokes of the peasants, who were not embarrassed in his presence, and he replied, with a sly motion of his head:

"Well, it seems to me that it depends only on yourself."

She raised her candid eyes to his face, and said, hesitating with confusion: "But — but — you understand that since — since — what you know about — about that maid — my husband and I have lived — have lived quite apart."

Accustomed to the promiscuity and undignified relations of the peasants, he was astonished at the revelation. All at once he thought he guessed at the young woman's real desire, and looking at her out of the corner of his eye, with a heart full of benevolence and of sympathy for her distress, he said: "Oh, I understand perfectly. I know that your widowhood must be irksome to you. You are young and in good health. It is natural, quite natural."

He smiled, bearing out his easygoing character of a country priest, and tapping Jeanne lightly on the hand, he said: "That is permissible, very permissible indeed, according to the commandments. You are married, are you not? Well, then, what is the harm?"

She, in her turn, had not understood his hidden meaning; but as soon as she saw through it, she blushed scarlet, shocked, and with tears in her eyes exclaimed: "Oh, Monsieur le Curé, what are you saying? What are you thinking of? I swear to you — I swear to you — — " And sobs choked her words.

He was surprised and sought to console her: "Come, I did not mean to hurt your feelings. I was only joking a little; there is no harm in that when one is decent. But you may rely on me, you may rely on me. I will see M. Julien."

She did not know what to say. She now wished to decline this intervention, which she thought clumsy and dangerous, but she did not dare to do so, and she went away hurriedly, faltering: "I am grateful to you, Monsieur le Curé."

A week passed. One day at dinner Julien looked at her with a peculiar expression, a certain smiling curve of the lips that she had noticed when he was teasing her. He was even almost ironically gallant toward her, and as they were walking after dinner in little mother's avenue, he said in a low tone: "We seem to have made up again."

She did not reply, but continued to look on the ground at a sort of track that was almost effaced now that the grass was sprouting anew. They were the footprints of the baroness, which were vanishing as does a memory. And Jeanne was plunged in sadness; she felt herself lost in life, far away from everyone.

"As for me, I ask nothing better. I was afraid of displeasing you," continued Julien.

The sun was going down, the air was mild. A longing to weep came over Jeanne, one of those needs of unbosoming oneself to a kindred spirit, of unbending and telling one's griefs. A sob rose in her throat; she opened her arms and fell on Julien's breast, and wept. He glanced down in surprise at her head, for he could not see her face which was hidden on his shoulder. He supposed that she still loved him, and placed a condescending kiss on the back of her head.

They entered the house and he followed her to her room. And thus they resumed their former relations, he, as a not unpleasant duty, and she, merely tolerating him.

She soon noticed, however, that his manner had changed, and one day with her lips to his, she murmured: "Why are you not the same as you used to be?"

"Because I do not want any more children," he said jokingly.

She started. "Why not?"

He appeared greatly surprised. "Eh, what's that you say? Are you crazy? No, indeed! One is enough, always crying and bothering everyone. Another baby! No, thank you!"

At the end of a month she told the news to everyone, far and wide, with the exception of Comtesse Gilberte, from reasons of modesty and delicacy.

What the priest had foreseen finally came to pass. She became enceinte. Then, filled with an unspeakable happiness, she locked her door every night when she retired, vowing herself from henceforth to eternal chastity, in gratitude to the vague divinity she adored.

She was now almost quite happy again. Her children would grow up and love her; she would grow old quietly, happy and contented, without troubling herself about her husband.

Toward the end of September, Abbé Picot called on a visit of ceremony to introduce his successor, a young priest, very thin, very short, with an emphatic way of talking, and with dark circles round his sunken eyes.

The old abbé had been appointed Dean of Goderville.

Jeanne was really sorry to lose the old man, who had been associated with all her recollections as a young woman. He had married her, baptized Paul, and buried the baroness. She could not imagine Étouvent without Abbé Picot and his paunch passing along by the farms, and she loved him because he was cheerful and natural.

But he did not seem very cheerful at the thought of his promotion. "It is a wrench, it is a wrench, madame la comtesse. I have been here for eighteen years. Oh, the place does not bring in much, and is not wealthy. The men have no more religion than they need, and the women, look you, the women have no morals. But nevertheless, I loved it."

The new curé appeared impatient, and said abruptly: "When I am here all that will have to be changed." He looked like an angry boy, thin and frail in his somewhat worn, though clean cassock.

Abbé Picot looked at him sideways, as he did when he was in a joking mood, and said: "You see, abbé, in order to prevent those happenings, you will have to chain up your parishioners; and even that would not be of much use." The little priest replied sharply: "We shall see." And the older man smiled as he took a pinch of snuff, and said: "Age will calm you down, abbé, and experience also. You will drive away from the church the remaining faithful ones, and that is all the good it will do. In this district they are religious, but pig-headed; be careful. Faith, when I see a girl come to confess who looks rather stout, I say to myself: 'She is bringing me a new parishioner,' and I try to get her married. You cannot prevent them from making mistakes; but you can go and look for the man, and prevent him from deserting the mother. Get them married, abbé, get them married, and do not trouble yourself about anything else."

"We think differently," said the young priest rudely; "it is useless to insist." And Abbé Picot once more began to regret his village, the sea which he saw from his parsonage, the little valleys where he walked while repeating his breviary, glancing up at the boats as they passed.

As the two priests took their leave, the old man kissed Jeanne, who was on the verge of tears.

A week later Abbé Tolbiac called again. He spoke of reforms which he intended to accomplish, as a prince might have done on taking possession of a kingdom. Then he requested the vicomtesse not to miss the service on Sunday, and to communicate a all the festivals. "You and I," he said, "we are at the head of the district; we must rule it and always set them an example to follow. We must be of one accord so that we may be powerful and respected. The church and the château in joining forces will make the peasants obey and fear us."

Jeanne's religion was all sentiment; she had all a woman's dream faith, and if she attended at all to her religious duties, it was from a habit acquired at the convent, the baron's advanced ideas having long since overthrown her convictions. Abbé Picot contented himself with what observances she gave him, and never blamed her. But his successor, not seeing her at mass the preceding Sunday, had come to call, uneasy and stern.

She did not wish to break with the parsonage, and promised, making up her mind to be assiduous in attendance the first few weeks, out of politeness.

Little by little, however, she got into the habit of going to church, and came under the influence of this delicate, upright and dictatorial abbé. A mystic, he appealed to her in his enthusiasm and zeal. He set in vibration in her soul the chord of religious poetry that all women possess. His unyielding austerity, his disgust for ordinary human interests, his love of God, his youthful and untutored inexperience, his harsh words, and his inflexible will, gave Jeanne an idea of the stuff martyrs were made of; and she let herself be carried away, all disillusioned as she was, by the fanaticism of this child, the minister of God.

He led her to Christ, the consoler, showing her how the joy of religion will calm all sorrow; and she knelt at the confessional, humbling herself, feeling herself small and weak in presence of this priest, who appeared to be about fifteen.

He was, however, very soon detested in all the countryside. Inflexibly severe toward himself, he was implacably intolerant toward others, and the one thing that especially roused his wrath and indignation was love. The young men and girls looked at each other slyly across the church, and the old peasants who liked to joke about such things disapproved his severity. All the parish was in a ferment. Soon the young men all stopped going to church.

The curé dined at the château every Thursday, and often came during the week to chat with his penitent. She became enthusiastic like himself, talked about spiritual matters, handling all the antique and complicated arsenal of religious controversy.

They walked together along the baroness' avenue, talking of Christ and the apostles, the Virgin Mary and the Fathers of the Church as though they were personally acquainted with them.

Julien treated the new priest with great respect, saying constantly: "That priest suits me, he does not back down." And he went to confession and communion, setting a fine example. He now went to the Fourvilles' nearly every day, gunning with the husband, who was never happy without him, and riding with the comtesse, in spite of rain and storm. The comte said: "They are crazy about riding, but it does my wife good."

The baron returned to the château about the middle of November. He was changed, aged, faded, filled with a deep sadness. And his love for his daughter seemed to have gained in strength, as if these few months of dreary solitude had aggravated his need of affection, confidence and tenderness. Jeanne did not tell him about her new ideas, and her friendship for the Abbé Tolbiac. The first time he saw the priest he conceived a great aversion to him. And when Jeanne asked him that evening how he liked him, he replied: "That man is an inquisitor! He must be very dangerous."

When he learned from the peasants, whose friend he was, of the harshness and violence of the young priest, of the kind of persecution which he carried on against all human and natural instincts, he developed a hatred toward him. He, himself, was one of the old race of natural philosophers who bowed the knee to a sort of pantheistic Divinity, and shrank from the catholic conception of a God with bourgeois instincts, Jesuitical wrath, and tyrannical revenge. To him reproduction was the great law of nature, and he began from farm to farm an ardent campaign against this intolerant priest, the persecutor of life.

Jeanne, very much worried, prayed to the Lord, entreated her father; but he always replied: "We must fight such men as that, it is our duty and our right. They are not human."

And he repeated, shaking his long white locks: "They are not human; they understand nothing, nothing, nothing. They are moving in a morbid dream; they are anti-physical." And he pronounced the word "anti-physical" as though it were a malediction.

The priest knew who his enemy was, but as he wished to remain ruler of the château and of Jeanne, he temporized, sure of final victory. He was also haunted by a fixed idea. He had discovered by chance the amours of Julien and Gilberte, and he desired to put a stop to them at all costs.

He came to see Jeanne one day and, after a long conversation on spiritual matters, he asked her to give her aid in helping him to fight, to put an end to the evil in her own family, in order to save two souls that were in danger.

She did not understand, and did not wish to know. He replied: "The hour has not arrived. I shall see you some other time." And he left abruptly.

The winter was coming to a close, a rotten winter, as they say in the country, damp and mild. The abbé called again some days later and hinted mysteriously at one of those shameless intrigues between persons whose conduct should be irreproachable. It was the duty, he said, of those who were aware of the facts to use every means to bring it to an end. He took Jeanne's hand and adjured her to open her eyes and understand and lend him her aid.

This time she understood, but she was silent, terrified at the thought of all that might result in the house that was now peaceful, and she pretended not to understand. Then he spoke out clearly.

She faltered: "What do you wish me to do, Monsieur l'Abbé?"

"Anything, rather than permit this infamy. Anything, I say. Leave him. Flee from this impure house!"

"But I have no money; and then I have no longer any courage; and, besides, how can I go without any proof? I have not the right to do so."

The priest arose trembling: "That is cowardice, madame; I am mistaken in you. You are unworthy of God's mercy!"

She fell on her knees: "Oh, I pray you not to leave me, tell me what to do!"

"Open M. de Fourville's eyes," he said abruptly. "It is his place to break up this intrigue."

This idea filled her with terror. "Why, he would kill them, Monsieur l'Abbé! And I should be guilty of denouncing them! Oh, never that, never!"

He raised his hand as if to curse her in his fury: "Remain in your shame and your crime; for you are more guilty than they are. You are the complaisant wife! There is nothing more for me to do here." And he went off so furious that he trembled all over.

She followed him, distracted and ready to do as he suggested. But he strode along rapidly, shaking his large blue umbrella in his rage. He perceived Julien standing outside the gate superintending the lopping of the trees, so he turned to the left to go across the Couillard farm, and he said: "Leave me alone, madame, I have nothing further to say to you."

Jeanne was entreating him to give her a few days for reflection, and then if he came back to the château she would tell him what she had done, and they could take counsel together.

Right in his road, in the middle of the farmyard, a group of children, those of the house and some neighbor's children, were standing around the kennel of Mirza, the dog, looking curiously at something with silent and concentrated attention. In the midst of them stood the baron, his hands behind his back, also looking on with curiosity. One would have taken him for a schoolmaster. When he saw the priest approaching, he moved away so as not to have to meet him and speak to him.

The priest did not call again; but the following Sunday from the pulpit he hurled imprecations, curses and threats against the château, anathematizing the baron, and making veiled allusions, but timidly, to Julien's latest intrigue. The vicomte was furious, but the dread of a shocking scandal kept him silent. At each service thereafter the priest declared his indignation, predicting the approach of the hour when God would smite all his enemies.

Julien wrote a firm, but respectful letter to the archbishop; the abbé was threatened with suspension. He was silent thereafter.

Gilberte and Julien now frequently met him during their rides reading his breviary, but they turned aside so as not to pass him by. Spring had come and reawakened their love. As the foliage was still sparse and the grass damp, they used to meet in a shepherd's movable hut that had been deserted since autumn. But one day when they were leaving it, they saw the Abbé Tolbiac, almost hidden in the sea rushes on the slope.

"We must leave our horses in the ravine," said Julien, "as they can be seen from a distance and would betray us." One evening as they were coming home together to La Vrillette, where they were to dine with the comte, they met the curé of Étouvent coming out of the château. He stepped to the side of the road to let them pass, and bowed without their eyes meeting. They were uneasy for a few moments, but soon forgot it.

One afternoon, Jeanne was reading beside the fire while a storm of wind was raging outside, when she suddenly perceived Comte Fourville coming on foot at such a pace that she thought some misfortune had happened.

She ran downstairs to meet him, and when she saw him she thought he must be crazy. He wore a large quilted cap that he wore only at home, his hunting jacket, and looked so pale that his red mustache, usually the color of his skin, now seemed like a flame. His eyes were haggard, rolling as though his mind were vacant.

He stammered: "My wife is here, is she not?" Jeanne, losing her presence of mind, replied: "Why, no, I have not seen her to-day."

He sat down as if his legs had given way. He then took off his cap and wiped his forehead with his handkerchief mechanically several times. Then starting up suddenly, he approached Jeanne, his hands stretched out, his mouth open, as if to speak, to confide some great sorrow to her. Then he stopped, looked at her fixedly and said as though he were wandering: "But it is your husband — you also — — " And he fled, going toward the sea.

Jeanne ran after him, calling him, imploring him to stop, her heart beating with apprehension as she thought: "He knows all! What will he do? Oh, if he only does not find them!"

But she could not come up to him, and he disregarded her appeals. He went straight ahead without hesitation, straight to his goal. He crossed the ditch, then, stalking through the sea rushes like a giant, he reached the cliff.

Jeanne, standing on the mound covered with trees, followed him with her eyes until he was out of sight. Then she went into the house, distracted with grief.

He had turned to the right and started to run. Threatening waves overspread the sea, big black clouds were scudding along madly, passing on and followed by others, each of them coming down in a furious downpour. The wind whistled, moaned, laid the grass and the young crops low and carried away big white birds that looked like specks of foam and bore them far into the land.

The hail which followed beat in the comte's face, filling his ears with noise and his heart with tumult.

Down yonder before him was the deep gorge of the Val de Vaucotte. There was nothing before him but a shepherd's hut beside a deserted sheep pasture. Two horses were tied to the shafts of the hut on wheels. What might not happen to one in such a tempest as this?

As soon as he saw them the comte crouched on the ground and crawled along on his hands and knees as far as the lonely hut and hid himself beneath the hut that he might not be seen through the cracks. The horses on seeing him became restive. He slowly cut their reins with the knife which he held open in his hand, and a sudden squall coming up, the animals fled, frightened at the hail which rattled on the sloping roof of the wooden hut and made it shake on its wheels.

The comte then kneeling upright, put his eye to the bottom of the door and looked inside. He did not stir; he seemed to be waiting.

A little time elapsed and then he suddenly rose to his feet, covered with mud from head to foot. He frantically pushed back the bolt which closed the hut on the outside, and seizing the shafts, he began to shake the hut as though he would break it to pieces. Then all at once he got between the shafts, bending his huge frame, and with a desperate effort dragged it along like an ox, panting as he went. He dragged it, with whoever was in it, toward the steep incline.

Those inside screamed and banged with their fists on the door, not understanding what was going on.

When he reached the top of the cliff he let go the fragile dwelling, which began to roll down the incline, going ever faster and faster, plunging, stumbling like an animal and striking the ground with its shafts.

An old beggar hidden in a ditch saw it flying over his head and heard frightful screams coming from the wooden box.

All at once a wheel was wrenched off and it fell on its side and began to roll like a ball, as a house torn from its foundations might roll from the summit of a mountain. Then, reaching the ledge of the last ravine, it described a circle, and, falling to the bottom, burst open as an egg might do. It was no sooner smashed on the stones than the old beggar, who had seen it going past, went down toward it slowly amid the rushes, and with the customary caution of a peasant, not daring to go directly to the shattered hut, he went to the nearest farm to tell of the accident.

They all ran to look at it and raised the wreck of the hut. They found two bodies, bruised, crushed and bleeding. The man's forehead was split open and his whole face crushed; the woman's jaw was hanging, dislocated in one of the jolts, and their shattered limbs were soft as pulp.

"What were they doing in that shanty?" said a woman.

The old beggar then said that they had apparently taken refuge in it to get out of the storm and that a furious squall must have blown the hut over the cliff. He said he had intended to take shelter there himself, when he saw the horses tied to it, and understood that some one else must be inside. "But for that," he added in a satisfied tone, "I might have rolled down in it." Some one remarked: "Would not that have been a good thing?"

The old man, in a furious rage, said: "Why would it have been a good thing? Because I am poor and they are rich! Look at them now." And trembling, ragged and dripping with rain, he pointed to the two dead bodies with his hooked stick and exclaimed: "We are all alike when we get to this."

The comte, as soon as he saw the hut rolling down the steep slope, ran off at full speed through the blinding storm. He ran in this way for several hours, taking short cuts, leaping across ditches, breaking through the hedges, and thus got back home at dusk, not knowing how himself.

The frightened servants were awaiting his return and told him that the two horses had returned riderless some little time before, that of Julien following the other one.

Then M. de Fourville reeled and in a choked voice said: "Something must have happened to them in this dreadful weather. Let every one help to look for them."

He started off himself, but he was no sooner out of sight than he concealed himself in a clump of bushes, watching the road along which she whom he even still loved with an almost savage passion was to return dead, dying or maybe crippled and disfigured forever.

And soon a carriole passed by carrying a strange burden.

It stopped at the château and passed through the gate. It was that, it was she. But a fearful anguish nailed him to the spot, a fear to know the worst, a dread of the truth, and he did not stir, hiding as a hare, starting at the least sound.

He waited thus an hour, two hours perhaps. The buggy did not come out. He concluded that his wife was expiring, and the thought of seeing her, of meeting her gaze filled him with so much horror that he suddenly feared to be discovered in his hiding place and of being compelled to return and be present at this agony, and he then fled into the thick of the wood. Then all of a sudden it occurred to him that she perhaps might be needing his care, that no one probably could properly attend to her. Then he returned on his tracks, running breathlessly.

On entering the château he met the gardener and called out to him, "Well?" The man did not dare answer him. Then M. de Fourville almost roared at him: "Is she dead?" and the servant stammered: "Yes, M. le Comte."

He experienced a feeling of immense relief. His blood seemed to cool and his nerves relax somewhat of their extreme tension, and he walked firmly up the steps of his great hallway.

The other wagon had reached "The Poplars." Jeanne saw it from afar. She descried the mattress; she guessed that a human form was lying upon it, and understood all. Her emotion was so vivid that she swooned and fell prostrate.

When she regained consciousness her father was holding her head and bathing her temples with vinegar. He said hesitatingly: "Do you know?" She murmured: "Yes, father." But when she attempted to rise she found herself unable to do so, so intense was her agony.

That very night she gave birth to a stillborn infant, a girl.

Jeanne saw nothing of the funeral of Julien; she knew nothing of it. She merely noticed at the end of a day or two that Aunt Lison was back, and in her feverish dreams which haunted her she persistently sought to recall when the old maiden lady had left "The Poplars," at what period and under what circumstances. She could not make this out, even in her lucid moments, but she was certain of having seen her subsequent to the death of "little mother."

XI

Jeanne did not leave her room for three months and was so wan and pale that no one thought she would recover. But she picked up by degrees. Little father and Aunt Lison never left her; they had both taken up their abode at "The Poplars." The shock of Julien's death had left her with a nervous malady. The slightest sound made her faint and she had long swoons from the most insignificant causes.

She had never asked the details of Julien's death. What did it matter to her? Did she not know enough already? Every one thought it was an accident, but she knew better, and she kept to herself this secret which tortured her: the knowledge of his infidelity and the remembrance of the abrupt and terrible visit of the comte on the day of the catastrophe.

And now she was filled with tender, sweet and melancholy recollections of the brief evidences of love shown her by her husband. She constantly thrilled at unexpected memories of him, and she seemed to see him as he was when they were betrothed and as she had known him in the hours passed beneath the sunlight in Corsica. All his faults diminished, all his harshness vanished, his very infidelities appeared less glaring in the widening separation of the closed tomb. And Jeanne, pervaded by a sort of posthumous gratitude for this man who had held her in his arms, forgave all the suffering he had caused her, to remember only moments of happiness they had passed together. Then, as time went on and month followed month, covering all her grief and reminiscences with forgetfulness, she devoted herself entirely to her son.

He became the idol, the one thought of the three beings who surrounded him, and he ruled as a despot. A kind of jealousy even arose among his slaves. Jeanne watched with anxiety the great kisses he gave his grandfather after a ride on his knee, and Aunt Lison, neglected by him as she had been by every one else and treated often like a servant by this little tyrant who could scarcely speak as yet, would go to her room and weep as she compared the slight affection he showed her with the kisses he gave his mother and the baron.

Two years passed quietly, and at the beginning of the third winter it was decided that they should go to Rouen to live until spring, and the whole family set out. But on their arrival in the old damp house, that had been shut up for some time, Paul had such a severe attack of bronchitis that his three relatives in despair declared that he could not do without the air of "The Poplars." They took him back there and he got well.

Then began a series of quiet, monotonous years. Always around the little one, they went into raptures at everything he did. His mother called him Poulet, and as he could not pronounce the word, he said "Pol," which amused them immensely, and the nickname of "Poulet" stuck to him.

The favorite occupation of his "three mothers," as the baron called his relatives, was to see how much he had grown, and for this purpose they made little notches in the casing of the drawingroom door, showing his progress from month to month. This ladder was called "Poulet's ladder," and was an important affair.

A new individual began to play a part in the affairs of the household — the dog "Massacre," who became Paul's inseparable companion.

Rare visits were exchanged with the Brisevilles and the Couteliers. The mayor and the doctor alone were regular visitors. Since the episode of the mother dog and the suspicion Jeanne had entertained of the priest on the occasion of the terrible death of the comtesse and Julien, Jeanne had not entered the church, angry with a divinity that could tolerate such ministers.

The church was deserted and the priest came to be looked on as a sorcerer because he had, so they said, driven out an evil spirit from a woman who was possessed, and although fearing him the peasants came to respect him for this occult power as well as for the unimpeachable austerity of his life.

When he met Jeanne he never spoke. This condition of affairs distressed Aunt Lison, and when she was alone, quite alone with Paul, she talked to him about God, telling him the wonderful stories of the early history of the world. But when she told him that he must love Him very much, the child would say: "Where is He, auntie?" "Up there," she would say, pointing to the sky; "up there, Poulet, but do not say so." She was afraid of the baron.

One day, however, Poulet said to her: "God is everywhere, but He is not in church." He had told his grandfather of his aunt's wonderful revelations.

When Paul was twelve years old a great difficulty arose on the subject of his first communion.

Lison came to Jeanne one morning and told her that the little fellow should no longer be kept without religious instruction and from his religious duties. His mother, troubled and undecided, hesitated, saying that there was time enough. But a month later, as she was returning a call at the Brisevilles', the comtesse asked her casually if Paul was going to make his first communion that year. Jeanne, unprepared for this, answered, "Yes," and this simple word decided her, and without saying a word to her father, she asked Aunt Lison to take the boy to the catechism class.

All went well for a month, but one day Paul came home with a hoarseness and the following day he coughed. On inquiry his mother learned that the priest had sent him to wait till the lesson was over at the door of the church, where there was a draught, because he had misbehaved. So she kept him at home and taught him herself. But the Abbé Tobiac, despite Aunt Lison's entreaties, refused to admit him as a communicant on the ground that he was not thoroughly taught.

The same thing occurred the following year, and the baron angrily swore that the child did not need to believe all that tomfoolery, so it was decided that he should be brought up as a Christian, but not as an active Catholic, and when he came of age he could believe as he pleased.

The Brisevilles ceased to call on her and Jeanne was surprised, knowing the punctiliousness of these neighbors in returning calls, but the Marquise de Coutelier haughtily told her the reason. Considering herself, in virtue of her husband's rank and fortune, a sort of queen of the Norman nobility, the marquise ruled as a queen, said what she thought, was gracious or the reverse as occasion demanded, admonishing, restoring to favor, congratulating whenever she saw fit. So when Jeanne came to see her, this lady, after a few chilling remarks, said drily: "Society is divided into two classes: those who believe in God and those who do not believe in Him. The former, even the humblest, are our friends, our equals; the latter are nothing to us."

Jeanne, perceiving the insinuation, replied: "But may one not believe in God without going to church?"

"No, madame," answered the marquise. "The faithful go to worship God in His church, just as one goes to see people in their homes."

Jeanne, hurt, replied: "God is everywhere, madame. As for me, who believes from the bottom of my heart in His goodness, I no longer feel His presence when certain priests come between Him and me."

The marquise rose. "The priest is the standard bearer of the Church, madame. Whoever does not follow the standard is opposed to Him and opposed to us."

Jeanne had risen in her turn and said, trembling: "You believe, madame, in a partisan God. I believe in the God of upright people." She bowed and took her leave.

The peasants also blamed her among themselves for not having let Poulet make his first communion. They themselves never attended service or took the sacrament unless it might be at Easter, according to the rule ordained by the Church; but for boys it was quite another thing, and they would have all shrunk in horror at the audacity of bringing up a child outside this recognized law, for religion is religion.

She saw how they felt and was indignant at heart at all these discriminations, all these compromises with conscience, this general fear of everything, the real cowardice of all hearts and the mask of respectability assumed in public.

The baron took charge of Paul's studies and made him study Latin, his mother merely saying: "Above all things, do not get over tired."

As soon as the boy was at liberty he went down to work in the garden with his mother and his aunt.

He now loved to dig in the ground, and all three planted young trees in the spring, sowed seed and watched it growing with the deepest interest, pruned branches and cut flowers for bouquets.

Poulet was almost fifteen, but was a mere child in intelligence, ignorant, silly, suppressed between petticoat government and this kind old man who belonged to another century.

One evening the baron spoke of college, and Jeanne at once began to sob. Aunt Lison timidly remained in a dark corner.

"Why does he need to know so much?" asked his mother. "We will make a gentleman farmer of him. He can cultivate his land, as many of the nobility do. He will live and grow old happily in this house, where we have lived before him and where we shall die. What more can one do?"

But the baron shook his head. "What would you say to him if he should say to you when he is twenty-five: 'I amount to nothing, I know nothing, all through your fault, the fault of your maternal selfishness. I feel that I am incapable of working, of making something of myself, and yet I was not intended for a secluded, simple life, lonely enough to kill one, to which I have been condemned by your shortsighted affection.'"

She was weeping and said entreatingly: "Tell me, Poulet, you will not reproach me for having loved you too well?" And the big boy, in surprise, promised that he never would. "Swear it," she said. "Yes, mamma." "You want to stay here, don't you?" "Yes, mamma."

Then the baron spoke up loud and decidedly: "Jeanne, you have no right to make disposition of this life. What you are doing is cowardly and almost criminal; you are sacrificing your child to your own private happiness."

She hid her face in her hands, sobbing convulsively, and stammered out amid her tears: "I have been so unhappy — so unhappy! Now, just as I am living peacefully with him, they want to take him away from me. What will become of me now — all by myself?" Her father rose and, sitting down beside her, put his arms round her. "And how about me, Jeanne?"

She put her arms suddenly round his neck, gave him a hearty kiss and with her voice full of tears, she said: "Yes, you are right perhaps, little father. I was foolish, but I have suffered so much. I am quite willing he should go to college."

And without knowing exactly what they were going to do with him, Poulet in his turn began to weep.

Then the three mothers began to kiss him and pet him and encourage him. When they retired to their rooms it was with a weight at their hearts, and they all wept, even the baron, who had restrained himself up to that.

It was decided that when the term began to put the young boy to school at Havre, and during the summer he was petted more than ever; his mother sighed often as she thought of the separation. She prepared his wardrobe as if he were going to undertake a ten years' voyage. One October morning, after a sleepless night, the two women and the baron got into the carriage with him and set out on their journey.

They had previously selected his place in the dormitory and his desk in the school room. Jeanne, aided by Aunt Lison, spent the whole day in arranging his clothes in his little wardrobe. As it did not hold a quarter of what they had brought, she went to look for the superintendent to ask for another. The treasurer was called, but he pointed out that all that amount of clothing would only be in the way and would never be needed, and he refused, on behalf of the directors, to let her have another chest of drawers. Jeanne, much annoyed, decided to hire a room in a small neighboring hotel, begging the proprietor to go himself and take Poulet whatever he required as soon as the boy asked for it.

They then took a walk on the pier to look at the ships coming and going. They went into a restaurant to dine, but they were none of them able to eat, and looked at one another with moistened eyes as the dishes were brought on and taken away almost untouched.

They now returned slowly toward the school. Boys of all ages were arriving from all quarters, accompanied by their families or by servants. Many of them were crying.

Jeanne held Poulet in a long embrace, while Aunt Lison remained in the background, her face hidden in her handkerchief. The baron, however, who was becoming affected, cut short the adieus by dragging his daughter away. They got into the carriage and went back through the darkness to "The Poplars," the silence being broken by an occasional sob.

Jeanne wept all the following day and on the day after drove to Havre in the phaeton. Poulet seemed to have become reconciled to the separation. For the first time in his life he now had playmates, and in his anxiety to join them he could scarcely sit still on his chair when his mother called. She continued her visits to him every other day and called to take him home on Sundays. Not knowing what to do with herself while school was in session until recreation time, she would remain sitting in the reception room, not having the strength or the courage to go very far from the school. The superintendent sent to ask her to come to his office and begged her not to come so frequently. She paid no attention to his request. He therefore informed her that if she continued to prevent her son from taking his recreation at the usual hours, obliging him to work without a change of occupation, they would be forced to send him back home again, and the baron was also notified to the same effect. She was consequently watched like a prisoner at "The Poplars."

She became restless and worried and would ramble about for whole days in the country, accompanied only by Massacre, dreaming as she walked along. Sometimes she would remain seated for a whole afternoon, looking out at the sea from the top of the cliff; at other times she would go down to Yport through the wood, going over the ground of her former walks, the memory of which haunted her. How long ago — how long ago it was — the time when she had gone over these same paths as a young girl, carried away by her dreams.

Poulet was not very industrious at school; he was kept two years in the fourth form. The third year's work was only tolerable and he had to begin the second over again, so that he was in rhetoric when he was twenty.

He was now a big, fair young man, with downy whiskers and a faint sign of a mustache. He now came home to "The Poplars" every Sunday, riding over in a couple of hours, his mother, Aunt Lison and the baron starting out early to go and meet him.

Although he was a head taller than his mother, she always treated him as though he were a child, and when he returned to school in the evening she would charge him anxiously not to go too fast and to think of his poor mother, who would break her heart if anything happened to him.

One Saturday morning she received a letter from Paul, saying that he would not be home on the following day because some friends had arranged an excursion and had invited him. She was tormented with anxiety all day Sunday, as though she dreaded some misfortune, and on Thursday, as she could endure it no longer, she set out for Havre.

He seemed to be changed, though she could not have told in what manner. He appeared excited and his voice seemed deeper. And suddenly, as though it were the most natural thing in the world, he said: "I say, mother, as long as you have come to-day, I want to tell you that I will not be at 'The Poplars' next Sunday, for we are going to have another excursion."

She was amazed, smothering, as if he had announced his departure for America. At last, recovering herself, she said: "Oh, Poulet, what is the matter with you? Tell me what is going on."

He began to laugh, and kissing her, replied: "Why, nothing, nothing, mamma. I am going to have a good time with my friends; I am just at that age."

She had nothing to say, but when she was alone in the carriage all manner of ideas came into her mind. She no longer recognized him, her Poulet, her little Poulet of former days. She felt for the first time that he was grown up, that he no longer belonged to her, that he was going to live his life without troubling himself about the old people. It seemed to her that one day had wrought this change in him. Was it possible that this was her son, her poor little boy who had helped her to replant the lettuce, this great big bearded youth who had a will of his own!

For three months Paul came home only occasionally, and always seemed impatient to get away again, trying to steal off an hour earlier each evening. Jeanne was alarmed, but the baron consoled her, saying: "Let him alone; the boy is twenty years old."

One morning, however, an old man, poorly dressed, inquired in German-French for "Madame la Vicomtesse," and after many ceremonious bows, he drew from his pocket a dilapidated pocketbook, saying: "Che un betit bapier bour fous," and unfolding as he handed it to her a piece of greasy paper. She read and reread it, looked at the Jew, read it over again and asked: "What does it mean?"

He obsequiously explained: "I will tell you. Your son needed a little money, and as I knew that you are a good mother, I lent him a trifle to help him out."

Jeanne was trembling. "But why did he not ask me?" The Jew explained at length that it was a question of a debt that must be paid before noon the following day; that Paul not being of age, no one would have lent him anything, and that his "honor would have been compromised" without this little service that he had rendered the young man.

Jeanne tried to call the baron, but had not the strength to rise, she was so overcome by emotion. At length she said to the usurer: "Would you have the kindness to ring the bell?"

He hesitated, fearing some trap, and then stammered out: "If I am intruding, I will call again." She shook her head in the negative. He then rang, and they waited in silence, sitting opposite each other.

When the baron came in he understood the situation at once. The note was for fifteen hundred francs. He paid one thousand, saying close to the man's face: "And on no account come back." The other thanked him and went his way.

The baron and Jeanne set out at once for Havre. On reaching the college they learned that Paul had not been there for a month. The principal had received four letters signed by Jeanne saying that his pupil was not well and then to tell how he was getting along. Each letter was accompanied by a doctor's certificate. They were, of course, all forged. They were all dumb-founded, and stood there looking at each other.

The principal, very much worried, took them to the commissary of police. Jeanne and her father stayed at a hotel that night. The following day the young man was found in the apartment of a courtesan of the town. His grandfather and mother took him back to "The Poplars" and not a word was exchanged between them during the whole journey.

A week later they discovered that he had contracted fifteen thousand francs' worth of debts within the last three months. His creditors had not come forward at first, knowing that he would soon be of age.

They entered into no discussion about it, hoping to win him back by gentleness. They gave him dainty food, petted him, spoiled him. It was spring and they hired a boat for him at Yport, in spite of Jeanne's fears, so that he might amuse himself on the water.

They would not let him have a horse, for fear he should ride to Havre.

He was there with nothing to do and became irritable and occasionally brutally so. The baron was worried at the discontinuance of his studies. Jeanne, distracted at the idea of a separation, asked herself what they could do with him.

One evening he did not come home. They learned that he had gone out in a boat with two sailors. His mother, beside herself with anxiety, went down to Yport without a hat in the dark.

Some men were on the beach, waiting for the boat to come in. There was a light on board an incoming boat, but Paul was not on board. He had made them take him to Havre.

The police sought him in vain; he could not be found. The woman with whom he had been found the first time had also disappeared without leaving any trace; her furniture was sold and her rent paid. In Paul's room at "The Poplars" were found two letters from this person, who seemed to be madly in love with him. She spoke of a voyage to England, having, she said, obtained the necessary funds.

The three dwellers in the château lived silently and drearily, their minds tortured by all kinds of suppositions. Jeanne's hair, which had become gray, now turned perfectly white. She asked in her innocence why fate had thus afflicted her.

She received a letter from the Abbé Tolbiac: "Madame, the hand of God is weighing heavily on you. You refused Him your child; He took him from you in His turn to cast him into the hands of a prostitute. Will not you open your eyes at this lesson from Heaven? God's mercy is infinite. Perhaps He may pardon you if you return and fall on your knees before Him. I am His humble servant. I will open to you the door of His dwelling when you come and knock at it."

She sat a long time with this letter on her lap. Perhaps it was true what the priest said. And all her religious doubts began to torment her conscience. And in her cowardly hesitation, which drives to church the doubting, the sorrowful, she went furtively one evening at twilight to the parsonage, and kneeling at the feet of the thin abbé, begged for absolution.

He promised her a conditional pardon, as God could not pour down all His favors on a roof that sheltered a man like the baron. "You will soon feel the effects of the divine mercy," he declared.

Two days later she did, indeed, receive a letter from her son, and in her discouragement and grief she looked upon this as the commencement of the consolation promised her by the abbé. The letter ran:

"My Dear Mamma: Do not be uneasy. I am in London, in good health, in very great need of money. We have not a sou left, and we do not have anything to eat some days. The one who is with me, and whom I love with all my heart, has spent all that she had so as not to leave me — five thousand francs — and you see that I am bound in honor to return her this sum in the first place. So I wish you would be kind enough to advance me fifteen thousand francs of papa's fortune, for I shall soon be of age. This will help me out of very serious difficulties.

"Good-by, my dear mamma. I embrace you with all my heart, and also grandfather and Aunt Lison. I hope to see you soon.

"Your son,

"Vicomte Paul de Lamare."

He had written to her! He had not forgotten her then. She did not care anything about his asking for money! She would send him some as long as he had none. What did money matter? He had written to her! And she ran, weeping for joy, to show this letter to the baron. Aunt Lison was called and read over word by word this paper that told of him. They discussed each sentence.

Jeanne, jumping from the most complete despair to a kind of intoxication of hope, took Paul's part. "He will come back, he will come back as he has written."

The baron, more calm, said: "All the same he left us for that creature, so he must love her better than us, as he did not hesitate about it."

A sudden and frightful pang struck Jeanne's heart, and immediately she was filled with hatred of this woman who had stolen her son from her, an unappeasable, savage hate, the hatred of a jealous mother. Until now all her thoughts had been given to Paul. She scarcely took into consideration that a girl had been the cause of his vagaries. But the baron's words had suddenly brought before her this rival, had revealed her fatal power, and she felt that between herself and this woman a struggle was about to begin, and she also felt that she would rather lose her son than share his affection with another. And all her joy was at an end.

They sent him the fifteen thousand francs and heard nothing more from him for five months.

Then a business man came to settle the details of Julien's inheritance. Jeanne and the baron handed over the accounts without any discussion, even giving up the interest that should come to his mother. When Paul came back to Paris he had a hundred and twenty thousand francs. He then wrote four letters in six months, giving his news in concise terms and ending the letters with coldly affectionate expressions. "I am working," he said; "I have obtained a position on the stock exchange. I hope to go and embrace you at 'The Poplars' some day, my dear parents."

He did not mention his companion, and this silence implied more than if he had filled four pages with news of her. Jeanne, in these cold letters, felt this woman in ambush, the implacable, eternal enemy of mothers, the courtesan.

The three lonely beings discussed the best plan to follow in order to rescue Paul, but could decide on nothing. A voyage to Paris? What good would it do?

"Let his passion exhaust itself. He will come back then of his own accord," said the baron.

Some time passed without any further news. But one morning they were terrified at the receipt of a despairing letter:

"My Poor Mamma: I am lost. There is nothing left for me to do but to blow out my brains unless you come to my aid. A speculation that gave every prospect of success has fallen through, and I am eighty-five thousand dollars in debt. I shall be dishonored if I do not pay up — ruined — and it will henceforth be impossible for me to do anything. I am lost. I repeat that I would rather blow out my brains than undergo this disgrace. I should have done so already, probably, but for the encouragement of a woman of whom I never speak to you, and who is my providence.

"I embrace you from the bottom of my heart, my dear mamma — perhaps for the last time. Good-by.

"Paul."

A package of business papers accompanying the letter gave the details of the failure.

The baron answered by return mail that they would see what could be done. Then he set out for Havre to get advice and he mortgaged some property to raise the money which was sent to Paul.

The young man wrote three letters full of the most heartfelt thanks and passionate affection, saying he was coming home at once to see his dear parents.

But he did not come.

A whole year passed. Jeanne and the baron were about to set out for Paris to try and make a last effort, when they received a line to say that he was in London again, setting an enterprise on foot in connection with steamboats under the name of "Paul de Lamare & Co." He wrote: "This will give me an assured fortune, and perhaps great wealth, and I am risking nothing. You can see at once what a splendid thing it is. When I see you again I shall have a fine position in society. There is nothing but business these days to help you out of difficulties."

Three months later the steamboat company failed and the manager was being sought for on account of certain irregularities in business methods. Jeanne had a nervous attack that lasted several hours and then she took to her bed.

The baron again went to Havre to make inquiries, saw some lawyers, some business men, some solicitors and bailiffs and found that the liabilities of the De Lamare concern were two hundred and thirty-five thousand francs, and he once more mortgaged some property. The château of "The Poplars" and the two farms and all that went with them were mortgaged for a large sum.

One evening as he was arranging the final details in the office of a business man, he fell over on the floor with a stroke of apoplexy.

A man was sent on horseback to notify Jeanne, but when she arrived he was dead.

She took his body back to "The Poplars," so overcome that her grief was numbness rather than despair.

Abbé Tolbiac refused to permit the body to be brought to the church, despite the distracted entreaties of the two women. The baron was interred at twilight without any religious ceremony.

Paul learned of the event through one of the men who was settling up his affairs. He was still in hiding in England. He wrote to make excuses for not having come home, saying that he had learned of his grandfather's death too late. "However, now that you have helped me out of my difficulties, my dear mamma, I shall go back to France and hope to embrace you soon."

Jeanne was so crushed in spirit that she appeared not to understand anything. Toward the end of the winter Aunt Lison, who was now sixty-eight, had an attack of bronchitis that developed into pneumonia, and she died quietly, murmuring with her last breath: "My poor little Jeanne, I will ask God to take pity on you."

Jeanne followed her to the grave, and as the earth fell on her coffin she sank to the ground, wishing that she might die also, so as not to suffer, to think. A strong peasant woman lifted her up and carried her away as if she had been a child.

When she reached the château Jeanne, who had spent the last five nights at Aunt Lison's bedside, allowed herself to be put to bed without resistance by this unknown peasant woman, who handled her with gentleness and firmness, and she fell asleep from exhaustion, overcome with weariness and suffering.

She awoke about the middle of the night. A night light was burning on the mantelpiece. A woman was asleep in her easy chair. Who was this woman? She did not recognize her, and leaning over the edge of her bed, she sought to examine her features by the dim light of the wick floating in oil in a tumbler of water.

It seemed to her that she had seen this face. But when, but where? The woman was sleeping peacefully, her head to one side and her cap on the floor. She might be about forty or forty-five. She was stout, with a high color, squarely built and powerful. Her large hands hung down at either side of the chair. Her hair was turning gray. Jeanne looked at her fixedly, her mind in the disturbed condition of one awaking from a feverish sleep after a great sorrow.

She had certainly seen this face! Was it in former days? Was it of late years? She could not tell, and the idea distressed her, upset her nerves. She rose noiselessly to take another look at the sleeping woman, walking over on tiptoe. It was the woman who had lifted her up in the cemetery and then put her to bed. She remembered this confusedly.

But had she met her elsewhere at some other time of her life or did she only imagine she recognized her amid the confused recollections of the day before? And how did she come to be there in her room and why?

The woman opened her eyes and, seeing Jeanne, she rose to her feet suddenly. They stood face to face, so close that they touched one another. The stranger said crossly: "What! are you up? You will be ill, getting up at this time of night. Go back to bed!"

"Who are you?" asked Jeanne.

But the woman, opening her arms, picked her up and carried her back to her bed with the strength of a man. And as she laid her down gently and drew the covers over her, she leaned over close to Jeanne and, weeping as she did so, she kissed her passionately on the cheeks, her hair, her eyes, the tears falling on her face as she stammered out: "My poor mistress, Mam'zelle Jeanne, my poor mistress, don't you recognize me?"

"Rosalie, my girl!" cried Jeanne, throwing her arms round her neck and hugging her as she kissed her, and they sobbed together, clasped in each other's arms.

Rosalie was the first to regain her calmness. "Come," she said, "you must be sensible and not catch cold." And she covered her up warm and straightened the pillow under her former mistress' head. The latter continued to sob, trembling all over at the recollections that were awakened in her mind. She finally inquired: "How did you come back, my poor girl?"

"Pardi! do you suppose I was going to leave you all alone like that, now?" replied Rosalie.

"Light a candle, so I may see you," said Jeanne. And when the candle was brought to the bedside they looked at each other for some time without speaking a word. Then Jeanne, holding out her hand to her former maid, murmured: "I should not have recognized you, my girl, you have changed greatly; did you know it? But not as much as I have." And Rosalie, looking at this white-haired woman, thin and faded, whom she had left a beautiful and fresh young woman, said: "That is true, you have changed, Madame Jeanne, and more than you should. But remember, however, that we have not seen each other for twenty-five years."

They were silent, thinking over the past. At length Jeanne said hesitatingly: "Have you been happy?"

Rosalie, fearful of awakening certain painful souvenirs, stammered out: "Why — yes — yes — madame. I have nothing much to complain of. I have been happier than you have — that is sure. There was only one thing that always weighed on my heart, and that was that I did not stay here — " And she stopped suddenly, sorry she had referred to that unintentionally. But Jeanne replied gently: "How could you help it, my girl? One cannot always do as they wish. You are a widow now, also, are you not?" Then her voice trembled with emotion as she said: "Have you other — other children?"

"No, madame."

"And he — your — your boy — what has become of him? Has he turned out well?"

"Yes, madame, he is a good boy and works industriously. He has been married for six months, and he can take my farm now, since I have come back to you."

Jeanne murmured in a trembling voice: "Then you will never leave me again, my girl?"

"No, indeed, madame, I have arranged all that."

Jeanne, in spite of herself, began to compare their lives, but without any bitterness, for she was now resigned to the unjust cruelty of fate. She said: "And your husband, how did he treat you?"

"Oh, he was a good man, madame, and not lazy; he knew how to make money. He died of consumption."

Then Jeanne, sitting up in bed, filled with a longing to know more, said: "Come, tell me everything, my girl, all about your life. It will do me good just now."

Rosalie, drawing up her chair, began to tell about herself, her home, her people, entering into those minute details dear to country people, describing her yard, laughing at some old recollection that reminded her of good times she had had, and raising her voice by degrees like a farmer's wife accustomed to command. She ended by saying: "Oh, I am well off now. I don't have to worry." Then she became confused again, and said in a lower tone: "It is to you that I owe it, anyhow; and you know I do not want any wages. No, indeed! No, indeed! And if you will not have it so, I will go."

Jeanne replied: "You do not mean that you are going to serve me for nothing?"

"Oh, yes, indeed, madame. Money! You give me money! Why, I have almost as much as you. Do you know what is left to you will all your jumble of mortgages and borrowing, and interests unpaid which are mounting up every year? Do you know? No, is it not so? Well, then, I can promise you that you have not even ten thousand francs income. Not ten thousand, do you understand? But I will settle all that for you, and very quickly."

She had begun talking loud again, carried away in her indignation at these interests left unpaid, at this threatening ruin. And as a faint, tender smile passed over the face of her mistress, she cried in a tone of annoyance: "You must not laugh, madame, for without money we are nothing but laborers."

Jeanne took hold of her hands and kept them in her own; then she said slowly, still full of the idea that haunted her: "Oh, I have had no luck. Everything has gone against me. Fate has a grudge against my life."

But Rosalie shook her head: "You must not say that, madame. You married badly, that's all. One should not marry like that, anyway, without knowing anything about one's intended."

And they went on talking about themselves just as two old friends might have done.

The sun rose while they were still talking.

XII

In a week's time Rosalie had taken absolute control of everything and everyone in the château. Jeanne was quite resigned and obeyed passively. Weak and dragging her feet as she walked, as little mother had formerly done, she went out walking leaning on Rosalie's arm, the latter lecturing her and consoling her with abrupt and tender words as they walked slowly along, treating her mistress as though she were a sick child.

They always talked of bygone days, Jeanne with tears in her throat, and Rosalie in the quiet tone of a phlegmatic peasant. The servant kept referring to the subject of unpaid interests; and at last requested Jeanne to give her up all the business papers that Jeanne, in her ignorance of money matters, was hiding from her, out of consideration for her son.

After that, for a week, Rosalie went to Fécamp every day to have matters explained to her by a lawyer whom she knew.

One evening, after having put her mistress to bed, she sat down by the bedside and said abruptly: "Now that you are settled quietly, madame, we will have a chat." And she told her exactly how matters stood.

When everything was settled, there would be about seven thousand francs of income left, no more.

"We cannot help it, my girl," said Jeanne. "I feel that I shall not make old bones, and there will be quite enough for me."

But Rosalie was annoyed: "For you, madame, it might be; but M. Paul — will you leave nothing for him?"

Jeanne shuddered. "I beg you not to mention him again. It hurts me too much to think about him."

"But I wish to speak about him, because you see you are not brave, Madame Jeanne. He does foolish things. Well! what of it? He will not do so always; and then he will marry and have children. He will need money to bring them up. Pay attention to me: you must sell 'The Poplars.'"

Jeanne sprang up in a sitting posture. "Sell 'The Poplars'! Do you mean it? Oh, never, never!"

But Rosalie was not disturbed. "I tell you that you will sell the place, madame, because it must be done." And then she explained her calculations, her plans, her reasons.

Once they had sold "The Poplars" and the two farms belonging to it to a buyer whom she had found, they would keep four farms situated at St. Leonard, which, free of all mortgage, would bring in an income of eight thousand three hundred francs. They would set aside thirteen hundred francs a year for repairs and for the upkeep of the property; there would then remain seven thousand francs, five thousand of which would cover the annual expenditures and the other two thousand would be put away for a rainy day.

She added: "All the rest has been squandered; there is an end of it. And then I am to keep the key, you understand. As for M. Paul, he will have nothing left, nothing; he would take your last sou from you."

Jeanne, who was weeping silently, murmured:

"But if he has nothing to eat?"

"He can come and eat with us if he is hungry. There will always be a bed and some stew for him. Do you believe he would have acted as he has done if you had not given him a sou in the first place?"

"But he was in debt, he would have been disgraced."

"When you have nothing left, will that prevent him from making fresh debts? You have paid his debts, that is all right; but you will not pay any more; it is I who am telling you this. Now goodnight, madame."

And she left the room.

Jeanne did not sleep, she was so upset at the idea of selling "The Poplars," of going away, of leaving this house to which all her life was linked.

When Rosalie came into the room next morning she said to her: "My poor girl, I never could make up my mind to go away from here."

But the servant grew angry: "It will have to be, however, madame; the lawyer will soon be here with the man who wants to buy the château. Otherwise, in four years you will not have a rap left."

Jeanne was crushed, and repeated: "I could not do it; I never could."

An hour later the postman brought her a letter from Paul asking for ten thousand francs. What should she do? At her wit's end, she consulted Rosalie, who threw up her hands, exclaiming: "What was I telling you, madame? Ah! You would have been in a nice fix, both of you, if I had not come back." And Jeanne, bending to her servant's will, wrote as follows to the young man:

"My Dear Son: I can do nothing more for you. You have ruined me; I am even obliged to sell 'The Poplars.' But never forget that I shall always have a home whenever you want to seek shelter with your old mother, to whom you have caused much suffering. Jeanne."

When the notary arrived with M. Jeoffrin, a retired sugar refiner, she received them herself, and invited them to look over the château.

A month later, she signed a deed of sale, and also bought herself a little cottage in the neighborhood of Goderville, on the high road to Montiviliers, in the hamlet of Batteville.

Then she walked up and down all alone until evening, in little mother's avenue, with a sore heart and troubled mind, bidding distracted and sobbing farewells to the landscape, the trees, the rustic bench under the plane tree, to all those things she knew so well and that seemed to have become part of her vision and her soul, the grove, the mound overlooking the plain, where she had so often sat, and from where she had seen the Comte de Fourville running toward the sea on that terrible day of Julian's death, to an old elm whose upper branches were missing, against which she had often leaned, and to all this familiar garden spot.

Rosalie came out and took her by the arm to make her come into the house.

A tall young peasant of twenty-five was waiting outside the door. He greeted her in a friendly manner as if he had known her for some time: "Good-morning, Madame Jeanne. I hope you are well. Mother told me to come and help you move. I would like to know what you are going to take away, seeing that I shall do it from time to time so as not to interfere with my farm work."

It was her maid's son, Julien's son, Paul's brother.

She felt as if her heart stopped beating; and yet she would have liked to embrace this young fellow.

She looked at him, trying to find some resemblance to her husband or to her son. He was ruddy, vigorous, with fair hair and his mother's blue eyes. And yet he looked like Julien. In what way? How? She could not have told, but there was something like him in the whole makeup of his face.

The young man resumed: "If you could show me at once, I should be much obliged."

But she had not yet decided what she was going to take with her, as her new home was very small; and she begged him to come back again at the end of the week.

She was now entirely occupied with getting ready to move, which brought a little variety into her very dreary and hopeless life. She went from room to room, picking out the furniture which recalled episodes in her life, old friends, as it were, who have a share in our life and almost of our being, whom we have known since childhood, and to which are linked our happy or sad recollections, dates in our history; silent companions of our sad or sombre hours, who have grown old and become worn at our side, their covers torn in places, their joints shaky, their color faded.

She selected them, one by one, sometimes hesitating and troubled, as if she were taking some important step, changing her mind every instant, weighing the merits of two easy chairs or of some old writing-desk and an old work table.

She opened the drawers, sought to recall things; then, when she had said to herself, "Yes, I will take this," the article was taken down into the diningroom.

She wished to keep all the furniture of her room, her bed, her tapestries, her clock, everything.

She took away some of the parlor chairs, those that she had loved as a little child; the fox and the stork, the fox and the crow, the ant and the grasshopper, and the melancholy heron.

Then, while wandering about in all the corners of this dwelling she was going to forsake, she went one day up into the loft, where she was filled with amazement; it was a chaos of articles of every kind, some broken, others tarnished only, others taken up there for no special reason probably, except that they were tired of them or that they had been replaced by others. She saw numberless knickknacks that she remembered, and that had disappeared suddenly, trifles that she had handled, those old little insignificant articles that she had seen every day without noticing, but which now, discovered in this loft, assumed an importance as of forgotten relics, of friends that she had found again.

She went from one to the other of them with a little pang, saying: "Why, it was I who broke that china cup a few evenings before my wedding. Ah! there is mother's little lantern and a cane that little father broke in trying to open the gate when the wood was swollen with the rain."

There were also a number of things that she did not remember that had belonged to her grandparents or to their parents, dusty things that appeared to be exiled in a period that is not their own, and that looked sad at their abandonment, and whose history, whose experiences no one knows, for they never saw those who chose them, bought them, owned them, and loved them; never knew the hands that had touched them familiarly, and the eyes that looked at them with delight.

Jeanne examined carefully three-legged chairs to see if they recalled any memories, a copper warming pan, a damaged foot stove that she thought she remembered, and a number of housekeeping utensils unfit for use.

She then put together all the things she wished to take, and going downstairs, sent Rosalie up to get them. The servant indignantly refused to bring down "that rubbish." But Jeanne, who had not much will left, held her own this time, and had to be obeyed.

One morning the young farmer, Julien's son, Denis Lecoq, came with his wagon for the first load. Rosalie went back with him in order to superintend the unloading and placing of furniture where it was to stand.

Rosalie had come back and was waiting for Jeanne, who had been out on the cliff. She was enchanted with the new house, declaring it was much more cheerful than this old box of a building, which was not even on the side of the road.

Jeanne wept all the evening.

Ever since they heard that the château was sold, the farmers were not more civil to her than necessary, calling her among themselves "the crazy woman," without knowing exactly why, but doubtless because they guessed with their animal instinct at her morbid and increasing sentimentality, at all the disturbance of her poor mind that had undergone so much sorrow.

The night before they left she chanced to go into the stable. A growl made her start. It was Massacre, whom she had hardly thought of for months. Blind and paralyzed, having reached a great age for an animal, he existed in a straw bed, taken care of by Ludivine, who never forgot him. She took him in her arms, kissed him, and carried him into the house. As big as a barrel, he could scarcely carry himself along on his stiff legs, and he barked like the wooden dogs that one gives to children.

The day of departure finally came. Jeanne had slept in Julien's old room, as hers was dismantled. She got up exhausted and short of breath as if she had been running. The carriage containing the trunks and the rest of the furniture was in the yard ready to start. Another two-wheeled vehicle was to take Jeanne and the servant. Old Simon and Ludivine were to stay until the arrival of a new proprietor, and then to go to some of their relations, Jeanne having provided a little income for them. They had also saved up some money, and being now very old and garrulous, they were not of much use in the house. Marius had long since married and left.

About eight o'clock it began to rain, a fine icy rain, driven by a light breeze. On the kitchen table, some cups of café au lait were steaming. Jeanne sat down and sipped hers, then rising, she said, "Come along."

She put on her hat and shawl, and while Rosalie was putting on her overshoes, she said in a choking voice: "Do you remember, my girl, how it rained when we left Rouen to come here?"

As she said this, she put her two hands to her breast and fell over on her back, unconscious. She remained thus over an hour, apparently dead. Then she opened her eyes and was seized with convulsions accompanied by floods of tears.

When she was a little calmer she was so weak that she could not stand up, and Rosalie, fearing another attack if they delayed their departure, went to look for her son. They took her up and carried her to the carriage, placed her on the wooden bench covered with leather; and the old servant got in beside her, wrapped her up with a big cloak, and holding an umbrella over her head, cried: "Quick, Denis, let us be off." The young man climbed up beside his mother and whipped up the horse, whose jerky pace made the two women bounce about vigorously.

As they turned the corner to enter the village, they saw some one stalking along the road; it was Abbé Tolbiac, who seemed to be watching for them to go by. He stopped to let the carriage pass. He was holding up his cassock with one hand, to keep it out of the mud, and his thin legs, encased in black stockings, ended in a pair of enormous muddy shoes.

Jeanne lowered her eyes so as not to meet his glance, and Rosalie, who had heard all about him, flew into a rage. "Peasant! Peasant!" she murmured; and then seizing her son's hand: "Give him a good slash with the whip."

But the young man, just as they were passing the priest, made the wheel of the wagon, which was going at full speed, sink into a rut, splashing the abbé with mud from head to foot.

Rosalie was delighted and turned round to shake her fist at him, while the priest was wiping off the mud with his big handkerchief.

All at once Jeanne exclaimed: "We have forgotten Massacre!" They stopped, and, getting down, Denis ran to fetch the dog, while Rosalie held the reins. He presently reappeared, carrying in his arms the shapeless and crippled animal, which he placed at the feet of the two women.

XIII

Two hours later the carriage stopped at a little brick house built in the middle of a lot planted with pear trees at the side of the high road.

Four trellised arbors covered with honeysuckle and clematis formed the four corners of the garden, which was divided into little beds of vegetables separated by narrow paths bordered with fruit trees.

A very high box hedge enclosed the whole property, which was separated by a field from the neighboring farm. There was a blacksmith's shop about a hundred feet further along the road. There were no other houses within three-quarters of a mile.

The house commanded a view of the level district of Caux, covered with farms surrounded by their four double rows of tall trees which enclosed the courtyard planted with apple trees.

As soon as they reached the house, Jeanne wanted to rest; but Rosalie would not allow her to do so for fear she would begin to think of the past.

The carpenter from Goderville was there, and they began at once to place the furniture that had already arrived while waiting for the last load. This required a good deal of thought and planning.

At the end of an hour the wagon appeared at the gate and had to be unloaded in the rain. When night fell the house was in utter disorder, with things piled up anyhow. Jeanne, tired out, fell asleep as soon as she got into bed.

She had no time to mourn for some days, as there was so much to be done. She even took a certain pleasure in making her new house look pretty, the thought that her son would come back there haunting her continually. The tapestries from her old room were hung in the diningroom, which also had to serve as a parlor; and she took special pains with one of the two rooms on the first floor, which she thought of as "Poulet's room."

She kept the other room herself, Rosalie sleeping above, next to the loft. The little house, furnished with care, was very pretty, and Jeanne was happy there at first, although she seemed to lack something, but she did not know what.

One morning the lawyer's clerk from Fécamp brought her three thousand six hundred francs, the price of the furniture left at "The Poplars," and valued by an upholsterer. She had a little thrill of pleasure at receiving this money, and as soon as the man had gone, she ran to put on her hat, so as to get to Goderville as quickly as possible to send Paul this unexpected sum.

But as she was hurrying along the high road she met Rosalie coming from market. The servant suspected something, without at once guessing the facts; and when she discovered them, for Jeanne could hide nothing from her, she placed her basket on the ground that she might get angry with more comfort.

She began to scold with her fists on her hips; then taking hold of her mistress with her right arm and taking her basket in her left, and still fuming, she continued on her way to the house.

As soon as they were in the house the servant asked to have the money handed over to her. Jeanne gave all but six hundred francs, which she held back; but Rosalie soon saw through her tricks, and she was obliged to hand it all over. However, she consented to her sending this amount to the young man.

A few days later he wrote: "You have rendered me a great service, my dear mother, for we were in the greatest distress."

Jeanne, however, could not get accustomed to Batteville. It seemed to her as if she could not breathe as she did formerly, that she was more lonely, more deserted, more lost than ever. She went out for a walk, got as far as the hamlet of Verneuil, came back by the Trois-Mares, came home, then suddenly wanted to start out again, as if she had forgotten to go to the very place she intended.

And every day she did the same thing without knowing why. But one evening a thought came to her unconsciously which revealed to her the secret of her restlessness. She said as she was sitting down to dinner: "Oh, how I long to see the sea!"

That was what she had missed so greatly, the sea, her big neighbor for twenty-five years, the sea with its salt air, its rages, its scolding voice, its strong breezes, the sea which she sought from her window at "The Poplars" every morning, whose air she breathed day and night, the sea which she felt close to her, which she had taken to loving unconsciously as she would a person.

Winter was approaching, and Jeanne felt herself overcome by an unconquerable discouragement. It was not one of those acute griefs which seemed to wring the heart, but a dreary, mournful sadness.

Nothing roused her. No one paid any attention to her. The high road before her door stretched to right and left with hardly any passersby. Occasionally a dogcart passed rapidly, driven by a red-faced man, with his blouse puffed out by the wind, making a sort of blue balloon; sometimes a slow-moving wagon, or else two peasants, a man and a woman, who came near, passed by, and disappeared in the distance.

As soon as the grass began to grow again, a young girl in a short skirt passed by the gate every morning with two thin cows who browsed along the side of the road. She came back every evening with the same sleepy face, making a step every ten minutes as she walked behind the animals.

Jeanne dreamed every night that she was still at "The Poplars." She seemed to be there with father and little mother, and sometimes even with Aunt Lison. She did over again things forgotten and done with, thought she was supporting Madame Adelaide in her walk along the avenue. And each awakening was attended with tears.

She thought continually of Paul, wondering what he was doing — how he was — whether he sometimes thought of her. As she walked slowly in the by-roads between the farms, she thought over all these things which tormented her, but above all else, she cherished an intense jealousy of the woman who had stolen her son from her. It was this hatred alone which prevented her from taking any steps, from going to look for him, to see him. It seemed to her that she saw that woman standing on the doorsill asking: "What do you want here, madame?" Her mother's pride revolted at the possibility of such a meeting. And her haughty pride of a good woman whose character is blameless made her all the more indignant at the cowardice of a man subjugated by an unworthy passion.

When autumn returned with its long rains, its gray sky, its dark clouds, such a weariness of this kind of life came over her that she determined to make a great effort to get her Poulet back; he must have got over his infatuation by this time.

She wrote him an imploring letter:

"My Dear Child: I am going to entreat you to come back to me. Remember that I am old and delicate, all alone the whole year round except for a servant maid. I am now living in a little house on the main road. It is very lonely, but if you were here all would be different for me. I have only you in the world, and I have not seen you for seven years! You were my life, my dream, my only hope, my one love, and you failed me, you deserted me!

"Oh, come back, my little Poulet — come and embrace me. Come back to your old mother, who holds out her despairing arms towards you.

"Jeanne."

He replied a few days later:

"My Dear Mother: I would ask nothing better than to go and see you, but I have not a penny. Send me some money and I will come. I wanted, in any case, to see you to talk to you about a plan that would make it possible for me to do as you ask.

"The disinterestedness and love of the one who has been my companion in the dark days through which I have passed can never be forgotten by me. It is not possible for me to remain any longer without publicly recognizing her love and her faithful devotion. She has very pleasing manners, which you would appreciate. She is also educated and reads a good deal. In fact, you cannot understand what she has been to me. I should be a brute if I did not show her my gratitude. I am going, therefore, to ask you to give me your permission to marry her. You will forgive all my follies and we will all live together in your new house.

"If you knew her you would at once give your consent. I can assure you that she is perfect and very distingué. You will love her, I am sure. As for me, I could not live without her.

"I shall expect your reply with impatience, my dear mother, and we both embrace you with all our heart.

"Your son,

"Vicomte Paul de Lamare."

Jeanne was crushed. She remained motionless, the letter on her lap, seeing through the cunning of this girl who had had such a hold on her son for so long, and had not let him come to see her once, biding her time until the despairing old mother could no longer resist the desire to clasp her son in her arms, and would weaken and grant all they asked.

And grief at Paul's persistent preference for this creature wrung her heart. She said: "He does not love me. He does not love me."

Rosalie just then entered the room. Jeanne faltered: "He wants to marry her now."

The maid was startled. "Oh, madame, you will not allow that. M. Paul must not pick up that rubbish."

And Jeanne, overcome with emotion, but indignant, replied: "Never that, my girl. And as he will not come here, I am going to see him, myself, and we shall see which of us will carry the day."

She wrote at once to Paul to prepare him for her visit, and to arrange to meet him elsewhere than in the house inhabited by that baggage.

While awaiting a reply she made her preparations for departure. Rosalie began to pack her mistress' clothes in an old trunk, but as she was folding a dress, one of those she had worn in the country, she exclaimed: "Why, you have nothing to put on your back. I will not allow you to go like that. You would be a disgrace to everyone; and the Parisian ladies would take you for a servant."

Jeanne let her have her own way, and the two women went together to Goderville to choose some material, which was given a dressmaker in the village. Then they went to the lawyer, M. Roussel, who spent a fortnight in the capital every year, in order to get some information; for Jeanne had not been in Paris for twenty-eight years.

He gave them lots of advice on how to avoid being run over, on methods of protecting yourself from thieves, advising her to sew her money up inside the lining of her coat, and to keep in her pocket only what she absolutely needed. He spoke at length about moderate priced restaurants, and mentioned two or three patronized by women, and told them that they might mention his name at the Hotel Normandie.

Jeanne had never yet seen the railroad, though trains had been running between Paris and Havre for six years, and were revolutionizing the whole country.

She received no answer from Paul, although she waited a week, then two weeks, going every morning to meet the postman, asking him hesitatingly: "Is there anything for me, Père Malandain?" And the man always replied in his hoarse voice: "Nothing again, my good lady."

It certainly must be this woman who was keeping Paul from writing.

Jeanne, therefore, determined to set out at once. She wanted to take Rosalie with her, but the maid refused for fear of increasing the expense of the journey. She did not allow her mistress to take more than three hundred francs, saying: "If you need more you can write to me and I will go to the lawyer and ask him to send it to you. If I give you any more, M. Paul will put it in his pocket."

One December morning Denis Lecoq came for them in his light wagon and took them to the station. Jeanne wept as she kissed Rosalie good-by, and got into the train. Rosalie was also affected and said: "Good-by, madame, bon voyage, and come back soon!"

"Good-by, my girl."

A whistle and the train was off, beginning slowly and gradually going with a speed that terrified Jeanne. In her compartment there were two gentlemen leaning back in the two corners of the carriage.

She looked at the country as they swept past, the trees, the farms, the villages, feeling herself carried into a new life, into a new world that was no longer the life of her tranquil youth and of her present monotonous existence.

She reached Paris that evening. A commissionaire took her trunk and she followed him in great fear, jostled by the crowd and not knowing how to make her way amid this mass of moving humanity, almost running to keep up with the man for fear of losing sight of him.

On reaching the hotel she said at the desk: "I was recommended here by M. Roussel."

The proprietress, an immense woman with a serious face, who was seated at the desk, inquired:

"Who is he — M. Roussel?"

Jeanne replied in amazement: "Why, he is the lawyer at Goderville, who stops here every year."

"That's very possible," said the big woman, "but I do not know him. Do you wish a room?"

"Yes, madame."

A boy took her satchel and led the way upstairs. She felt a pang at her heart. Sitting down at a little table she sent for some luncheon, as she had eaten nothing since daybreak. As she ate, she was thinking sadly of a thousand things, recalling her stay here on the return from her wedding journey, and the first indication of Julien's character betrayed while they were in Paris. But she was young then, and confident and brave. Now she felt old, embarrassed, even timid, weak and disturbed at trifles. When she had finished her luncheon she went over to the window and looked down on the street filled with people. She wished to go out, but was afraid to do so. She would surely get lost. She went to bed, but the noise, the feeling of being in a strange city, kept her awake. About two o'clock in the morning, just as she was dozing off, she heard a woman scream in an adjoining room; she sat up in bed and then she thought she heard a man laugh. As daylight dawned the thought of Paul came to her, and she dressed herself before it was light.

Paul lived in the Rue du Sauvage, in the old town. She wanted to go there on foot so as to carry out Rosalie's economical advice. The weather was delightful, the air cold enough to make her skin tingle. People were hurrying along the sidewalks. She walked as fast as she could, according to directions given her, along a street, at the end of which she was to turn to the right and then to the left, when she would come to a square where she must make fresh inquiries. She did not find the square, and went into a baker's to ask her way, and he directed her differently. She started off again, went astray, inquired her way again, and finally got lost completely.

Half crazy, she now walked at random. She had made up her mind to call a cab, when she caught sight of the Seine. She then walked along the quays.

After about an hour she found the Rue Sauvage, a sort of dark alley. She stopped at a door, so overcome that she could not move.

He was there, in that house — Poulet.

She felt her knees and hands trembling; but at last she entered the door, and walking along a passage, saw the janitor's quarters. She said, as she held out a piece of money: "Would you go up and tell M. Paul de Lamare that an old lady, a friend of his mother's, is downstairs, and wishes to see him?"

"He does not live here any longer, madame," replied the janitor.

A shudder went over her. She faltered:

"Oh! Where — where is he living now?"

"I do not know."

She grew dizzy as though she were about to fall over, and stood there for some moments without being able to speak. At length, with a great effort, she collected her senses and murmured:

"How long is it since he left?"

"About two weeks ago. They went off like that, one evening, and never came back. They were in debt everywhere in the neighborhood, so you can understand that they did not care to leave their address."

Jeanne saw lights before her eyes, flashes of flame, as though a gun had been fired off in front of her eyes. But she had one fixed idea in her mind, and that sustained her, and kept her outwardly calm and rational. She wished to find Poulet and know all about him.

"Then he said nothing when he was going away?"

"Nothing at all; they ran off to escape their debts, that's all."

"But he surely sends someone to get his mail."

"More frequently than I send it. He never got more than ten letters a year. I took one up to them, however, two days before they left."

That was probably her letter. She said abruptly: "Listen! I am his mother, his own mother, and I have come to look for him. Here are ten francs for you. If you can get any news or any particulars about him, come and see me at the Hotel Normandie, Rue du Havre, and I will pay you well."

"You may count on me, madame," he replied.

She left him and began to walk away without caring whither she went. She hurried along as though she were on some important business, knocking up against people with packages, crossing the streets without paying attention to the approaching vehicles, and being sworn at by the drivers, stumbling on the curb of the sidewalk, and tearing along straight ahead in utter despair.

All at once she found herself in a garden, and was so tired that she sat down on a bench to rest. She stayed there some time apparently, weeping without being conscious of it, for passersby stopped to look at her. Then she felt very cold, and rose to go on her way; but her legs would scarcely carry her, she was so weak and distressed.

She wanted to go into a restaurant and get a cup of bouillon, but a sort of shame, of fear, of modesty at her grief being observed held her back. She would pause at the door, look in, see all the people sitting at table eating, and would turn away, saying: "I will go into the next one." But she had not the courage.

Finally she went into a bakery and bought a crescent and ate it as she walked along. She was very thirsty, but did not know where to go to get something to drink, so did without it.

Presently she found herself in another garden surrounded by arcades. She recognized the Palais Royal. Being tired and warm, she sat down here for an hour or two.

A crowd of people came in, a well-dressed crowd, chatting, smiling, bowing to each other, that happy crowd of beautiful women and wealthy men who live only for dress and amusement. Jeanne felt bewildered in the midst of this brilliant assemblage, and got up to make her escape. But suddenly the thought came to her that she might meet Paul in this place; and she began to wander about, looking into the faces, going and coming incessantly with her quick step from one end of the garden to the other.

People turned round to look at her, others laughed as they pointed her out. She noticed it and fled, thinking that they were doubtless amused at her appearance and at her dress of green plaid, selected by Rosalie, and made according to her ideas by the dressmaker at Goderville.

She no longer dared even to ask her way of passersby, but at last she ventured to do so and found her way back to the hotel.

The following day she went to the police department to ask them to look for her child. They could promise her nothing, but said they would do all they could. She wandered about the streets hoping that she might come across him. And she felt more alone in this bustling crowd, more lost, more wretched than in the lonely country.

That evening when she came back to the hotel she was informed that a man had come to see her from M. Paul, and that he would come back again the following day. Her heart began to beat violently and she never closed her eyes that night. If it should be he! Yes, it assuredly was, although she would not have recognized him from the description they gave her.

About nine o'clock the following morning there was a knock at the door. She cried: "Come in!" ready to throw herself into certain outstretched arms. But an unknown person appeared; and while he excused himself for disturbing her, and explained his business, which was to collect a debt of Paul's, she felt the tears beginning to overflow, and wiped them away with her finger before they fell on her cheeks.

He had learned of her arrival through the janitor of the Rue Sauvage, and as he could not find the young man, he had come to see his mother. He handed her a paper, which she took without knowing what she was doing and read the figures — ninety francs — which she paid without a word.

She did not go out that day.

The next day other creditors came. She gave them all that she had left except twenty francs and then wrote to Rosalie to explain matters to her.

She passed her days wandering about, waiting for Rosalie's answer, not knowing what to do, how to kill the melancholy, interminable hours, having no one to whom she could say an affectionate word, no one who knew her sorrow. She now longed to return home to her little house at the side of the lonely high road. A few days before she thought she could not live there, she was so overcome with grief, and now she felt that she could never live anywhere else but there where her serious character had been formed.

One evening the letter at last came, enclosing two hundred francs. Rosalie wrote:

"Madame Jeanne: Come back at once, for I shall not send you any more. As for M. Paul, it is I who will go and get him when we know where he is.

"With respect, your servant,

"Rosalie."

Jeanne set out for Batteville one very cold, snowy morning.

XIV

Jeanne never went out now, never stirred about. She rose at the same hour every day, looked out at the weather and then went downstairs and sat before the parlor fire.

She would remain for days motionless, gazing into the fire, thinking of nothing in particular. It would grow dark before she stirred, except to put a fresh log on the fire. Rosalie would then bring in the lamp and exclaim: "Come, Madame Jeanne, you must stir about or you will have no appetite again this evening."

She lived over the past, haunted by memories of her early life and her wedding journey down yonder in Corsica. Forgotten landscapes in that isle now rose before her in the blaze of the fire, and she recalled all the little details, all the little incidents, the faces she had seen down there. The head of the guide, Jean Ravoli, haunted her, and she sometimes seemed to hear his voice.

Then she remembered the sweet years of Paul's childhood, when they planted salad together and when she knelt in the thick grass beside Aunt Lison, each trying what they could do to please the child, and her lips murmured: "Poulet, my little Poulet," as though she were talking to him. Stopping at this word, she would try to trace it, letter by letter, in space, sometimes for hours at a time, until she became confused and mixed up the letters and formed other words, and she became so nervous that she was almost crazy.

She had all the peculiarities of those who live a solitary life. The least thing out of its usual place irritated her.

Rosalie often obliged her to walk and took her on the high road, but at the end of twenty minutes she declared she could not take another step and sat down on the side of the road.

She soon became averse to all movement and stayed in bed as late as possible. Since her childhood she had retained one custom, that of rising the instant she had drunk her café au lait in the morning. But now she would lie down again and begin to dream, and as she was daily growing more lazy, Rosalie would come and oblige her to get up and almost force her to get dressed.

She seemed no longer to have any will power, and each time the maid asked her a question or wanted her advice or opinion she would say: "Do as you think best, my girl."

She imagined herself pursued by some persistent ill luck and was like an oriental fatalist, and having seen her dreams all fade away and her hopes crushed, she would sometimes hesitate a whole day or longer before undertaking the simplest thing, for fear she might be on the wrong road and it would turn out badly. She kept repeating: "Talk of bad luck — I have never had any luck in life."

Then Rosalie would say: "What would you do if you had to work for your living, if you were obliged to get up every morning at six o'clock to go out to your work? Many people have to do that, nevertheless, and when they grow too old they die of want."

Jeanne replied: "Remember that I am all alone; that my son has deserted me." And Rosalie would get very angry: "That's another thing! Well, how about the sons who are drafted into the army and those who go to America?"

America to her was an undefined country, where one went to make a fortune and whence one never returned. She continued: "There always comes a time when people have to part, for old people and young people are not made to live together." And she added fiercely: "Well, what would you say if he were dead?"

Jeanne had nothing more to say.

One day in spring she had gone up to the loft to look for something and by chance opened a box containing old calendars which had been preserved after the manner of some country folks.

She took them up and carried them downstairs. They were of all sizes, and she laid them out on the table in the parlor in regular order. Suddenly she spied the earliest, the one she had brought with her to "The Poplars." She gazed at it for some time, at the days crossed off by her the morning she left Rouen, the day after she left the convent, and she wept slow, sorrowful tears, the tears of an old woman at sight of her wretched life spread out before her on this table.

One morning the maid came into her room earlier than usual, and placing the bowl of café au lait on the little stand beside her bed, she said: "Come, drink it quickly. Denis is waiting for us at the door. We are going to 'The Poplars,' for I have something to attend to down there."

Jeanne dressed herself with trembling hands, almost fainting at the thought of seeing her dear home once more.

The sky was cloudless and the nag, who was inclined to be frisky, would suddenly start off at a gallop every now and then. As they entered the commune of Étouvent Jeanne's heart beat so that she could hardly breathe.

They unharnessed the horse at the Couillard place, and while Rosalie and her son were attending to their own affairs, the farmer and his wife offered to let Jeanne go over the chateau, as the proprietor was away and they had the keys.

She went off alone, and when she reached the side of the chateau from which there was a view of the sea she turned round to look. Nothing had changed on the outside. When she turned the heavy lock and went inside the first thing she did was to go up to her old room, which she did not recognize, as it had been newly papered and furnished. But the view from the window was the same, and she stood and gazed out at the landscape she had so loved.

She then wandered all over the house, walking quietly all alone in this silent abode as though it were a cemetery. All her life was buried here. She went down to the drawingroom, which was dark with its closed shutters. As her eyes became accustomed to the dim light she recognized some of the old hangings. Two easy chairs were drawn up before the fire, as if some one had just left them, and as Jeanne stood there, full of old memories, she suddenly seemed to see her father and mother sitting there, warming their feet at the fire.

She started back in terror and knocked up against the edge of the door, against which she leaned to support herself, still staring at the armchairs.

The vision had vanished.

She remained bewildered for some minutes. Then she slowly recovered her composure and started to run away, for fear she might become insane. She chanced to look at the door against which she had been leaning and saw there "Poulet's ladder."

All the little notches were there showing the age and growth of her child. Here was the baron's writing, then hers, a little smaller, and then Aunt Lison's rather shaky characters. And she seemed to see her boy of long ago with his fair hair standing before her, leaning his little forehead against the door while they measured his height.

And she kissed the edge of the door in a frenzy of affection.

But some one was calling her outside. It was Rosalie's voice: "Madame Jeanne, Madame Jeanne, they are waiting breakfast for you." She went out in a dream and understood nothing of what they were saying to her. She ate what they gave her, heard them talking, but about what she knew not, let them kiss her on the cheeks and kissed them in return and then got into the carriage.

When they lost sight of the château behind the tall trees she felt a wrench at her heart, convinced that she had bid a last farewell to her old home.

When they reached Batteville and just as she was going into her new house, she saw something white under the door. It was a letter that the postman had slipped under the door while she was out. She recognized Paul's writing and opened it, trembling with anxiety. He wrote:

"My Dear Mother: I have not written sooner because I did not wish you to make a useless journey to Paris when it was my place to go and see you. I am just now in great sorrow and in great straits. My wife is dying after giving birth to a little girl three days ago, and I have not one sou. I do not know what to do with the child, whom my janitor's wife is bringing up on the bottle as well as she can, but I fear I shall lose her. Could you not take charge of it? I absolutely do not know what to do, and I have no money to put her out to nurse. Answer by return mail.

"Your son, who loves you,

"Paul."

Jeanne sank into a chair and had scarcely strength to call Rosalie. When the maid came into the room they read the letter over together and then remained silent for some time, face to face.

At last Rosalie said: "I am going to fetch the little one, madame. We cannot leave it like that."

"Go, my girl," replied Jeanne.

Then they were silent until the maid said: "Put on your hat, madame, and we will go to Goderville to see the lawyer. If she is going to die, the other one, M. Paul must marry her for the little one's sake later on."

Jeanne, without replying, put on her hat. A deep, inexpressible joy filled her heart, a treacherous joy that she sought to hide at any cost, one of those things of which one is ashamed, although cherishing it in one's soul — her son's sweetheart was going to die.

The lawyer gave the servant minute instructions, making her repeat them several times. Then, sure that she could make no mistake, she said: "Do not be afraid. I will see to it now."

She set out for Paris that very night.

Jeanne passed two days in such a troubled condition that she could not think. The third morning she received merely a line from Rosalie saying she would be back on the evening train. That was all.

About three o'clock she drove in a neighbor's light wagon to the station at Beuzeville to meet Rosalie.

She stood on the platform, looking at the railroad track as it disappeared on the horizon. She looked at the clock. Ten minutes still — five minutes still — two minutes more. Then the hour of the train's arrival, but it was not in sight. Presently, however, she saw a cloud of white smoke and gradually it drew up in the station. She looked anxiously and at last perceived Rosalie carrying a sort of white bundle in her arms.

She wanted to go over toward her, but her knees seemed to grow weak and she was afraid of falling.

But the maid had seen her and came forward with her usual calm manner and said: "How do you do, madame? Here I am back again, but not without some difficulty."

"Well?" faltered Jeanne.

"Well," answered Rosalie, "she died last night. They were married and here is the little girl." And she held out the child, who could not be seen under her wraps.

Jeanne took it mechanically and they left the station and got into the carriage.

"M. Paul will come as soon as the funeral is over — tomorrow about this time, I believe," resumed Rosalie.

Jeanne murmured "Paul" and then was silent.

The wagon drove along rapidly, the peasant clacking his tongue to urge on the horse. Jeanne looked straight ahead of her into the clear sky through which the swallows darted in curves. Suddenly she felt a gentle warmth striking through to her skin; it was the warmth of the little being who was asleep on her lap.

Then she was overcome with an intense emotion, and uncovering gently the face of the sleeping infant, she raised it to her lips and kissed it passionately.

But Rosalie, happy though grumpy, stopped her; "Come, come, Madame Jeanne, stop that; you will make it cry."

And then she added, probably in answer to her own thoughts: "Life, after all, is not as good or as bad as we believe it to be."

Bel-Ami (The History of a Scoundrel)

When the cashier had given him the change out of his five francpiece, George Duroy left the restaurant.

As he had a good carriage, both naturally and from his military training, he drew himself up, twirled his moustache, and threw upon the lingering customers a rapid and sweeping glance — one of those glances which take in everything within their range like a casting net.

The women looked up at him in turn — three little work-girls, a middle-aged music mistress, disheveled, untidy, and wearing a bonnet always dusty and a dress always awry; and two shopkeepers' wives dining with their husbands — all regular customers at this slap-bang establishment.

When he was on the pavement outside, he stood still for a moment, asking himself what he should do. It was the 28th of June, and he had just three francs forty centimes in his pocket to carry him to the end of the month. This meant the option of two dinners without lunch or two lunches without dinner. He reflected that as the earlier repasts cost twenty sous apiece, and the latter thirty, he would, if he were content with the lunches, be one franc twenty centimes to the good, which would further represent two snacks of bread and sausage and two bocks of beer on the boulevards. This latter item was his greatest extravagance and his chief pleasure of a night; and he began to descend the Rue Notre-Dame de Lorette.

He walked as in the days when he had worn a hussar uniform, his chest thrown out and his legs slightly apart, as if he had just left the saddle, pushing his way through the crowded street, and shouldering folk to avoid having to step aside. He wore his somewhat shabby hat on one side, and brought his heels smartly down on the pavement. He seemed ever ready to defy somebody or something, the passersby, the houses, the whole city, retaining all the swagger of a dashing cavalryman in civil life.

Although wearing a sixty-franc suit, he was not devoid of a certain somewhat loud elegance. Tall, well-built, fair, with a curly moustache twisted up at the ends, bright blue eyes with small pupils, and reddish-brown hair curling naturally and parted in the middle, he bore a strong resemblance to the dare-devil of popular romances.

It was one of those summer evenings on which air seems to be lacking in Paris. The city, hot as an oven, seemed to swelter in the stifling night. The sewers breathed out their poisonous breath through their granite mouths, and the underground kitchens gave forth to the street through their windows the stench of dishwater and stale sauces.

The doorkeepers in their shirtsleeves sat astride straw-bottomed chairs within the carriage entrances to the houses, smoking their pipes, and the pedestrians walked with flagging steps, head bare, and hat in hand.

When George Duroy reached the boulevards he paused again, undecided as to what he should do. He now thought of going on to the Champs Elysées and the Avenue du Bois de Boulogne to seek a little fresh air under the trees, but another wish also assailed him, a desire for a love affair.

What shape would it take? He did not know, but he had been awaiting it for three months, night and day. Occasionally, thanks to his good looks and gallant bearing, he gleaned a few crumbs of love here and there, but he was always hoping for something further and better.

With empty pockets and hot blood, he kindled at the contact of the prowlers who murmur at street corners: "Will you come home with me, dear?" but he dared not follow them, not being able to pay them, and, besides, he was awaiting something else, less venally vulgar kisses.

He liked, however, the localities in which women of the town swarm — their balls, their cafés, and their streets. He liked to rub shoulders with them, speak to them, chaff them, inhale their strong perfumes, feel himself near them. They were women at any rate, women made for love. He did not despise them with the innate contempt of a wellborn man.

He turned towards the Madeleine, following the flux of the crowd which flowed along overcome by the heat. The chief cafés, filled with customers, were overflowing on to the pavement, and displayed their drinking public under the dazzling glare of their lit-up facias. In front of them, on little tables, square or round, were glasses holding fluids of every shade, red, yellow, green, brown, and inside the decanters glittered the large transparent cylinders of ice, serving to cool the bright, clear water. Duroy had slackened his pace, a longing to drink parched his throat.

A hot thirst, a summer evening's thirst assailed him, and he fancied the delightful sensation of cool drinks flowing across his palate. But if he only drank two bocks of beer in the evening, farewell to the slender supper of the morrow, and he was only too well acquainted with the hours of short commons at the end of the month.

He said to himself: "I must hold out till ten o'clock, and then I'll have my bock at the American café. Confound it, how thirsty I am though." And he scanned the men seated at the tables drinking, all the people who could quench their thirst as much as they pleased. He went on, passing in front of the cafés with a sprightly swaggering air, and guessing at a glance from their dress and bearing how much money each customer ought to have about him. Wrath against these men quietly sitting there rose up within him. If their pockets were rummaged, gold, silver, and coppers would be found in them. On an average each one must have at least two louis. There were certainly a hundred to a café, a hundred times two louis is four thousand francs. He murmured "the swine," as he walked gracefully past them. If he could have had hold of one of them at a nice dark corner he would have twisted his neck without scruple, as he used to do the country-folk's fowls on field-days.

And he recalled his two years in Africa and the way in which he used to pillage the Arabs when stationed at little outposts in the south. A bright and cruel smile flitted across his lips at the recollection of an escapade which had cost the lives of three men of the Ouled-Alane tribe, and had furnished him and his comrades with a score of fowls, a couple of sheep, some gold, and food for laughter for six months.

The culprits had never been found, and, what is more, they had hardly been looked for, the Arab being looked upon as somewhat in the light of the natural prey of the soldier.

In Paris it was another thing. One could not plunder prettily, sword by side and revolver in hand, far from civil authority. He felt in his heart all the instincts of a sub-officer let loose in a conquered country. He certainly regretted his two years in the desert. What a pity he had not stopped there. But, then, he had hoped something better in returning home. And now —ah! yes, it was very nice now, was it not?

He clicked his tongue as if to verify the parched state of his palate.

The crowd swept past him slowly, and he kept thinking. "Set of hogs — all these idiots have money in their waistcoat pockets." He pushed against people and softly whistled a lively tune. Gentlemen whom he thus elbowed turned grumbling, and women murmured: "What a brute!"

He passed the Vaudeville Theater and stopped before the American café, asking himself whether he should not take his bock, so greatly did thirst torture him. Before making up his mind, he glanced at the illuminated clock. It was a quarter past nine. He knew himself that as soon as the glassful of beer was before him he would gulp it down. What would he do then up to eleven o'clock?

He passed on. "I will go as far as the Madeleine," he said, "and walk back slowly."

As he reached the corner of the Palace de l'Opera, he passed a stout young fellow, whose face he vaguely recollected having seen somewhere. He began to follow him, turning over his recollections and repeating to himself half-aloud: "Where the deuce did I know that joker?"

He searched without being able to recollect, and then all at once, by a strange phenomenon of memory, the same man appeared to him thinner, younger, and clad in a hussar uniform. He exclaimed aloud: "What, Forestier!" and stepping out he tapped the other on the shoulder. The promenader turned round and looked at him, and then said: "What is it, sir?"

Duroy broke into a laugh. "Don't you know me?" said he.

"No."

"George Duroy, of the 6th Hussars."

Forestier held out his hands, exclaiming: "What, old fellow! How are you?"

"Very well, and you?"

"Oh, not very brilliant! Just fancy, I have a chest in brown paper now. I cough six months out of twelve, through a cold I caught at Bougival the year of my return to Paris, four years ago."

And Forestier, taking his old comrade's arm, spoke to him of his illness, related the consultations, opinions, and advice of the doctors, and the difficulty of following this advice in his position. He was told to spend the winter in the South, but how could he? He was married, and a journalist in a good position.

"I am political editor of the Vie Francaise. I write the proceedings in the Senate for the Salut, and from time to time literary criticisms for the Planète. That is so. I have made my way."

Duroy looked at him with surprise. He was greatly changed, matured. He had now the manner, bearing, and dress of a man in a good position and sure of himself, and the stomach of a man who dines well. Formerly he had been thin, slight, supple, heedless, brawling, noisy, and always ready for a spree. In three years Paris had turned him into someone quite different, stout and serious, and with some white hairs about his temples, though he was not more than twenty-seven.

Forestier asked: "Where are you going?"

Duroy answered: "Nowhere; I am just taking a stroll before turning in."

"Well, will you come with me to the Vie Francaise, where I have some proofs to correct, and then we will take a bock together?"

"All right."

They began to walk on, arm-in-arm, with that easy familiarity existing between schoolfellows and men in the same regiment.

"What are you doing in Paris?" asked Forestier.

Duroy shrugged his shoulders. "Simply starving. As soon as I finished my term of service I came here — to make a fortune, or rather for the sake of living in Paris; and for six months I have been a clerk in the offices of the Northern Railway at fifteen hundred francs a year, nothing more."

Forestier murmured: "Hang it, that's not much!"

"I should think not. But how can I get out of it? I am alone; I don't know anyone; I can get no one to recommend me. It is not goodwill that is lacking, but means."

His comrade scanned him from head to foot, like a practical man examining a subject, and then said, in a tone of conviction: "You see, my boy, everything depends upon assurance here. A clever fellow can more easily become a minister than an under-secretary. One must obtrude one's self on people; not ask things of them. But how the deuce is it that you could not get hold of anything better than a clerk's berth on the Northern Railway?"

Duroy replied: "I looked about everywhere, but could not find anything. But I have something in view just now; I have been offered a riding-master's place at Pellerin's. There I shall get three thousand francs at the lowest."

Forestier stopped short. "Don't do that; it is stupid, when you ought to be earning ten thousand francs. You would nip your future in the bud. In your office, at any rate, you are hidden; no one knows you; you can emerge from it if you are strong enough to make your way. But once a riding-master, and it is all over. It is as if you were head-waiter at a place where all Paris goes to dine. When once you have given riding lessons to people in society or to their children, they will never be able to look upon you as an equal."

He remained silent for a few moments, evidently reflecting, and then asked:

"Have you a bachelor's degree?"

"No; I failed to pass twice."

"That is no matter, as long as you studied for it. If anyone mentions Cicero or Tiberius, you know pretty well what they are talking about?"

"Yes; pretty well."

"Good; no one knows any more, with the exception of a score of idiots who have taken the trouble. It is not difficult to pass for being well informed; the great thing is not to be caught in some blunder. You can maneuver, avoid the difficulty, turn the obstacle, and floor others by means of a dictionary. Men are all as stupid as geese and ignorant as donkeys."

He spoke like a self-possessed blade who knows what life is, and smiled as he watched the crowd go by. But all at once he began to cough, and stopped again until the fit was over, adding, in a tone of discouragement: "Isn't it aggravating not to be able to get rid of this cough? And we are in the middle of summer. Oh! this winter I shall go and get cured at Mentone. Health before everything."

They halted on the Boulevard Poissonière before a large glass door, on the inner side of which an open newspaper was pasted. Three passersby had stopped and were reading it.

Above the door, stretched in large letters of flame, outlined by gas jets, the inscription La Vie Francaise. The pedestrians passing into the light shed by these three dazzling words suddenly appeared as visible as in broad daylight, then disappeared again into darkness.

Forestier pushed the door open, saying, "Come in." Duroy entered, ascended an ornate yet dirty staircase, visible from the street, passed through an anteroom where two messengers bowed to his companion, and reached a kind of waiting-room, shabby and dusty, upholstered in dirty green Utrecht velvet, covered with spots and stains, and worn in places as if mice had been gnawing it.

"Sit down," said Forestier. "I will be back in five minutes."

And he disappeared through one of the three doors opening into the room.

A strange, special, indescribable odor, the odor of a newspaper office, floated in the air of the room. Duroy remained motionless, slightly intimidated, above all surprised. From time to time folk passed hurriedly before him, coming in at one door and going out at another before he had time to look at them.

They were now young lads, with an appearance of haste, holding in their hand a sheet of paper which fluttered from the hurry of their progress; now compositors, whose white blouses, spotted with ink, revealed a clean shirt collar and cloth trousers like those of men of fashion, and who carefully carried strips of printed paper, fresh proofs damp from the press. Sometimes a gentleman entered rather too elegantly attired, his waist too tightly pinched by his frock-coat, his leg too well set off by the cut of his trousers, his foot squeezed into a shoe too pointed at the toe, some fashionable reporter bringing in the echoes of the evening.

Others, too, arrived, serious, important-looking men, wearing tall hats with flat brims, as if this shape distinguished them from the rest of mankind.

Forestier reappeared holding the arm of a tall, thin fellow, between thirty and forty years of age, in evening dress, very dark, with his moustache ends stiffened in sharp points, and an insolent and self-satisfied bearing.

Forestier said to him: "Good night, dear master."

The other shook hands with him, saying: "Good night, my dear fellow," and went downstairs whistling, with his cane under his arm.

Duroy asked: "Who is that?"

"Jacques Rival, you know, the celebrated descriptive writer, the duellist. He has just been correcting his proofs. Garin, Montel, and he are the three best descriptive writers, for facts and points, we have in Paris. He gets thirty thousand francs a year here for two articles a week."

As they were leaving they met a short, stout man, with long hair and untidy appearance, who was puffing as he came up the stairs.

Forestier bowed low to him. "Norbert de Varenne," said he, "the poet; the author of 'Les Soleils Morts'; another who gets long prices. Every tale he writes for us costs three hundred francs, and the longest do not run to two hundred lines. But let us turn into the Neapolitan café, I am beginning to choke with thirst."

As soon as they were seated at a table in the café, Forestier called for two bocks, and drank off his own at a single draught, while Duroy sipped his beer in slow mouthfuls, tasting it and relishing it like something rare and precious.

His companion was silent, and seemed to be reflecting. Suddenly he exclaimed: "Why don't you try journalism?"

The other looked at him in surprise, and then said: "But, you know, I have never written anything."

"Bah! everyone must begin. I could give you a job to hunt up information for me — to make calls and inquiries. You would have to start with two hundred and fifty francs a month and your cab hire. Shall I speak to the manager about it?"

"Certainly!"

"Very well, then, come and dine with me tomorrow. I shall only have five or six people — the governor, Monsieur Walter and his wife, Jacques Rival, and Norbert de Varenne, whom you have just seen, and a lady, a friend of my wife. Is it settled?"

Duroy hesitated, blushing and perplexed. At length he murmured: "You see, I have no clothes."

Forestier was astounded. "You have no dress clothes? Hang it all, they are indispensable, though. In Paris one would be better off without a bed than without a dress suit."

Then, suddenly feeling in his waistcoat pocket, he drew out some gold, took two louis, placed them in front of his old comrade, and said in a cordial and familiar tone: "You will pay me back when you can. Hire or arrange to pay by installments for the clothes you want, whichever you like, but come and dine with me tomorrow, halfpast seven, number seventeen Rue Fontaine."

Duroy, confused, picked up the money, stammering: "You are too good; I am very much obliged to you; you may be sure I shall not forget."

The other interrupted him. "All right. Another bock, eh? Waiter, two bocks."

Then, when they had drunk them, the journalist said: "Will you stroll about a bit for an hour?"

"Certainly."

And they set out again in the direction of the Madeleine.

"What shall we, do?" said Forestier. "They say that in Paris a lounger can always find something to amuse him, but it is not true. I, when I want to lounge about of an evening, never know where to go. A drive round the Bois de Boulogne is only amusing with a woman, and one has not always one to hand; the café concerts may please my chemist and his wife, but not me. Then what is there to do? Nothing. There ought to be a summer garden like the Parc Monceau, open at night, where one would hear very good music while sipping cool drinks under the trees. It should not be a pleasure resort, but a lounging place, with a high price for entrance in order to attract the fine ladies. One ought to be able to stroll along well-graveled walks lit up by electric light, and to sit down when one wished to hear the music near or at a distance. We had about the sort of thing formerly at Musard's, but with a smack of the low-class dancing-room, and too much dance music, not enough space, not enough shade, not enough gloom. It would want a very fine garden and a very extensive one. It would be delightful. Where shall we go?"

Duroy, rather perplexed, did not know what to say; at length he made up his mind. "I have never been in the Folies Bergère. I should not mind taking a look round there," he said.

"The Folies Bergère," exclaimed his companion, "the deuce; we shall roast there as in an oven. But, very well, then, it is always funny there."

And they turned on their heels to make their way to the Rue du Faubourg Montmartre.

The lit-up front of the establishment threw a bright light into the four streets which met in front of it. A string of cabs were waiting for the close of the performance.

Forestier was walking in when Duroy checked him.

"You are passing the pay-box," said he.

"I never pay," was the reply, in a tone of importance.

When he approached the check-takers they bowed, and one of them held out his hand. The journalist asked: "Have you a good box?"

"Certainly, Monsieur Forestier."

He took the ticket held out to him, pushed the padded door with its leather borders, and they found themselves in the auditorium.

Tobacco smoke slightly veiled like a faint mist the stage and the further side of the theater. Rising incessantly in thin white spirals from the cigars and pipes, this light fog ascended to the ceiling, and there, accumulating, formed under the dome above the crowded gallery a cloudy sky.

In the broad corridor leading to the circular promenade a group of women were awaiting newcomers in front of one of the bars, at which sat enthroned three painted and faded vendors of love and liquor.

The tall mirrors behind them reflected their backs and the faces of passersby.

Forestier pushed his way through the groups, advancing quickly with the air of a man entitled to consideration.

He went up to a box-keeper. "Box seventeen," said he.

"This way, sir."

And they were shut up in a little open box draped with red, and holding four chairs of the same color, so near to one another that one could scarcely slip between them. The two friends sat down. To the right, as to the left, following a long curved line, the two ends of which joined the proscenium, a row of similar cribs held people seated in like fashion, with only their heads and chests visible.

On the stage, three young fellows in fleshings, one tall, one of middle size, and one small, were executing feats in turn upon a trapeze.

The tall one first advanced with short, quick steps, smiling and waving his hand as though wafting a kiss.

The muscles of his arms and legs stood out under his tights. He expanded his chest to take off the effect of his too prominent stomach, and his face resembled that of a barber's block, for a careful parting divided his locks equally on the center of the skull. He gained the trapeze by a graceful bound, and, hanging by the hands, whirled round it like a wheel at full speed, or, with stiff arms and straightened body, held himself out horizontally in space.

Then he jumped down, saluted the audience again with a smile amidst the applause of the stalls, and went and leaned against the scenery, showing off the muscles of his legs at every step.

The second, shorter and more squarely built, advanced in turn, and went through the same performance, which the third also recommenced amidst most marked expressions of approval from the public.

But Duroy scarcely noticed the performance, and, with head averted, kept his eyes on the promenade behind him, full of men and prostitutes.

Said Forestier to him: "Look at the stalls; nothing but middle-class folk with their wives and children, good noodlepates who come to see the show. In the boxes, men about town, some artistes, some girls, good second-raters; and behind us, the strangest mixture in Paris. Who are these men? Watch them. There is something of everything, of every profession, and every caste; but blackguardism predominates. There are clerks of all kinds — bankers' clerks, government clerks, shopmen, reporters, ponces, officers in plain clothes, swells in evening dress, who have dined out, and have dropped in here on their way from the Opera to the Théatre des Italiens; and then again, too, quite a crowd of suspicious folk who defy analysis. As to the women, only one type, the girl who sups at the American café, the girl at one or two louis who looks out for foreigners at five louis, and lets her regular customers know when she is disengaged. We have known them for the last ten years; we see them every evening all the year round in the same places, except when they are making a hygienic sojourn at Saint Lazare or at Lourcine."

Duroy no longer heard him. One of these women was leaning against their box and looking at him. She was a stout brunette, her skin whitened with paint, her black eyes lengthened at the corners with pencil and shaded by enormous and artificial eyebrows. Her too exuberant bosom stretched the dark silk of her dress almost to bursting; and her painted lips, red as a fresh wound, gave her an aspect bestial, ardent, unnatural, but which, nevertheless, aroused desire.

She beckoned with her head one of the friends who was passing, a blonde with red hair, and stout, like herself, and said to her, in a voice loud enough to be heard: "There is a pretty fellow; if he would like to have me for ten louis I should not say no."

Forestier turned and tapped Duroy on the knee, with a smile. "That is meant for you; you are a success, my dear fellow. I congratulate you."

The ex-sub-officer blushed, and mechanically fingered the two pieces of gold in his waistcoat pocket.

The curtain had dropped, and the orchestra was now playing a waltz.

Duroy said: "Suppose we take a turn round the promenade."

"Just as you like."

They left their box, and were at once swept away by the throng of promenaders. Pushed, pressed, squeezed, shaken, they went on, having before their eyes a crowd of hats. The girls, in pairs, passed amidst this crowd of men, traversing it with facility, gliding between elbows, chests, and backs as if quite at home, perfectly at their ease, like fish in water, amidst this masculine flood.

Duroy, charmed, let himself be swept along, drinking in with intoxication the air vitiated by tobacco, the odor of humanity, and the perfumes of the hussies. But Forestier sweated, puffed, and coughed.

"Let us go into the garden," said he.

And turning to the left, they entered a kind of covered garden, cooled by two large and ugly fountains. Men and women were drinking at zinc tables placed beneath evergreen trees growing in boxes.

"Another bock, eh?" said Forestier.

"Willingly."

They sat down and watched the passing throng.

From time to time a woman would stop and ask, with stereotyped smile: "Are you going to stand me anything?"

And as Forestier answered: "A glass of water from the fountain," she would turn away, muttering: "Go on, you duffer."

But the stout brunette, who had been leaning, just before, against the box occupied by the two comrades, reappeared, walking proudly arm-in-arm with the stout blonde. They were really a fine pair of women, well matched.

She smiled on perceiving Duroy, as though their eyes had already told secrets, and, taking a chair, sat down quietly in face of him, and making her friend sit down, too, gave the order in a clear voice: "Waiter, two grenadines!"

Forestier, rather surprised, said: "You make yourself at home."

She replied: "It is your friend that captivates me. He is really a pretty fellow. I believe that I could make a fool of myself for his sake."

Duroy, intimidated, could find nothing to say. He twisted his curly moustache, smiling in a silly fashion. The waiter brought the drinks, which the women drank off at a draught; then they rose, and the brunette, with a friendly nod of the head, and a tap on the arm with her fan, said to Duroy: "Thanks, dear, you are not very talkative."

And they went off swaying their trains.

Forestier laughed. "I say, old fellow, you are very successful with the women. You must look after it. It may lead to something." He was silent for a moment, and then continued in the dreamy tone of men who think aloud: "It is through them, too, that one gets on quickest."

And as Duroy still smiled without replying, he asked: "Are you going to stop any longer? I have had enough of it. I am going home."

The other murmured: "Yes, I shall stay a little longer. It is not late."

Forestier rose. "Well, goodnight, then. Till tomorrow. Don't forget. Seventeen Rue Fontaine, at halfpast seven."

"That is settled. Till tomorrow. Thanks."

They shook hands, and the journalist walked away.

As soon as he had disappeared Duroy felt himself free, and again he joyfully felt the two pieces of gold in his pocket; then rising, he began to traverse the crowd, which he followed with his eyes.

He soon caught sight of the two women, the blonde and the brunette, who were still making their way, with their proud bearing of beggars, through the throng of men.

He went straight up to them, and when he was quite close he no longer dared to do anything.

The brunette said: "Have you found your tongue again?"

He stammered "By Jove!" without being able to say anything else.

The three stood together, checking the movement, the current of which swept round them. All at once she asked: "Will you come home with me?"

And he, quivering with desire, answered roughly: "Yes, but I have only a louis in my pocket."

She smiled indifferently. "It is all the same to me," and took his arm in token of possession.

As they went out he thought that with the other louis he could easily hire a suit of dress clothes for the next evening.

II

"Monsieur Forestier, if you please?"

"Third floor, the door on the left," the concierge had replied, in a voice the amiable tone of which betokened a certain consideration for the tenant, and George Duroy ascended the stairs.

He felt somewhat abashed, awkward, and ill at ease. He was wearing a dress suit for the first time in his life, and was uneasy about the general effect of his toilet. He felt it was altogether defective, from his boots, which were not of patent leather, though neat, for he was naturally smart about his foot-gear, to his shirt, which he had bought that very morning for four franc fifty centimes at the Masgasin du Louvre, and the limp front of which was already rumpled. His everyday shirts were all more or less damaged, so that he had not been able to make use of even the least worn of them.

His trousers, rather too loose, set off his leg badly, seeming to flap about the calf with that creased appearance which secondhand clothes present. The coat alone did not look bad, being by chance almost a perfect fit.

He was slowly ascending the stairs with beating heart and anxious mind, tortured above all by the fear of appearing ridiculous, when suddenly he saw in front of him a gentleman in full dress looking at him. They were so close to one another that Duroy took a step back and then remained stupefied; it was himself, reflected by a tall mirror on the first-floor landing. A thrill of pleasure shot through him to find himself so much more presentable than he had imagined.

Only having a small shaving-glass in his room, he had not been able to see himself all at once, and as he had only an imperfect glimpse of the various items of his improvised toilet, he had mentally exaggerated its imperfections, and harped to himself on the idea of appearing grotesque.

But on suddenly coming upon his reflection in the mirror, he had not even recognized himself; he had taken himself for someone else, for a gentleman whom at the first glance he had thought very well dressed and fashionable looking. And now, looking at himself carefully, he recognized that really the general effect was satisfactory.

He studied himself as actors do when learning their parts. He smiled, held out his hand, made gestures, expressed sentiments of astonishment, pleasure, and approbation, and essayed smiles and glances, with a view of displaying his gallantry towards the ladies, and making them understand that they were admired and desired.

A door opened somewhere. He was afraid of being caught, and hurried upstairs, filled with the fear of having been seen grimacing thus by one of his friend's guests.

On reaching the second story he noticed another mirror, and slackened his pace to view himself in it as he went by. His bearing seemed to him really graceful. He walked well. And now he was filled with an unbounded confidence in himself. Certainly he must be successful with such an appearance, his wish to succeed, his native resolution, and his independence of mind. He wanted to run, to jump, as he ascended the last flight of stairs. He stopped in front of the third mirror, twirled his moustache as he had a trick of doing, took off his hat to run his fingers through his hair, and muttered half-aloud as he often did: "What a capital notion." Then raising his hand to the bell handle, he rang.

The door opened almost at once, and he found himself face to face with a manservant out of livery, serious, clean-shaven, and so perfect in his get-up that Duroy became uneasy again without understanding the reason of his vague emotion, due, perhaps, to an unwitting comparison of the cut of their respective garments. The manservant, who had patent-leather shoes, asked, as he took the overcoat which Duroy had carried on his arm, to avoid exposing the stains on it: "Whom shall I announce?"

And he announced the name through a door with a looped-back draping leading into a drawingroom.

But Duroy, suddenly losing his assurance, felt himself breathless and paralyzed by terror. He was about to take his first step in the world he had looked forward to and longed for. He advanced, nevertheless. A fair young woman, quite alone, was standing awaiting him in a large room, well lit up and full of plants as a greenhouse.

He stopped short, quite disconcerted. Who was this lady who was smiling at him? Then he remembered that Forestier was married, and the thought that this pretty and elegant blonde must be his friend's wife completed his alarm.

He stammered: "Madame, I am — "

She held out her hand, saying: "I know, sir; Charles has told me of your meeting last evening, and I am very pleased that he had the idea of asking you to dine with us to-day."

He blushed up to his ears, not knowing what to say, and felt himself examined from head to foot, reckoned up, and judged.

He longed to excuse himself, to invent some pretext for explaining the deficiencies of his toilet, but he could not think of one, and did not dare touch on this difficult subject.

He sat down on an armchair she pointed out to him, and as he felt the soft and springy velvet-covered seat yield beneath his weight, as he felt himself, as it were, supported and clasped by the padded back and arms, it seemed to him that he was entering upon a new and enchanting life, that he was taking possession of something delightful, that he was becoming somebody, that he was saved, and he looked at Madame Forestier, whose eyes had not quitted him.

She was attired in a dress of pale blue cashmere, which set off the outline of her slender waist and full bust. Her arms and neck issued from a cloud of white lace, with which the bodice and short sleeves were trimmed, and her fair hair, dressed high, left a fringe of tiny curls at the nape of her neck.

Duroy recovered his assurance beneath her glance, which reminded him, without his knowing why, of that of the girl met overnight at the Folies Bergére. She had gray eyes, of a bluish gray, which imparted to them a strange expression; a thin nose, full lips, a rather fleshy chin, and irregular but inviting features, full of archness and charm. It was one of those faces, every trait of which reveals a special grace, and seems to have its meaning — every movement to say or to hide something. After a brief silence she asked: "Have you been long in Paris?"

He replied slowly, recovering his self-possession: "A few months only, Madame. I have a berth in one of the railway companies, but Forestier holds out the hope that I may, thanks to him, enter journalism."

She smiled more plainly and kindly, and murmured, lowering her voice: "Yes, I know."

The bell had rung again. The servant announced "Madame de Marelle."

This was a little brunette, who entered briskly, and seemed to be outlined — modeled, as it were — from head to foot in a dark dress made quite plainly. A red rose placed in her black hair caught the eye at once, and seemed to stamp her physiognomy, accentuate her character, and strike the sharp and lively note needed.

A little girl in short frocks followed her.

Madame Forestier darted forward, exclaiming: "Good evening, Clotilde."

"Good evening, Madeleine." They kissed one another, and then the child offered her forehead, with the assurance of a grown-up person, saying: "Good evening, cousin."

Madame Forestier kissed her, and then introduced them, saying: "Monsieur George Duroy, an old friend of Charles; Madame de Marelle, my friend, and in some degree my relation." She added: "You know we have no ceremonious affectation here. You quite understand, eh?"

The young man bowed.

The door opened again, and a short, stout gentleman appeared, having on his arm a tall, handsome woman, much younger than himself, and of distinguished appearance and grave bearing. They were Monsieur Walter, a Jew from the South of France, deputy, financier, capitalist, and manager of the Vie Francaise, and his wife, the daughter of Monsieur Basile-Ravalau, the banker.

Then came, one immediately after the other, Jacques Rival, very elegantly got up, and Norbert de Varenne, whose coat collar shone somewhat from the friction of the long locks falling on his shoulders and scattering over them a few specks of white scurf. His badly-tied cravat looked as if it had already done duty. He advanced with the air and graces of an old beau, and taking Madame Forestier's hand, printed a kiss on her wrist. As he bent forward his long hair spread like water over her bare arm.

Forestier entered in his turn, offering excuses for being late. He had been detained at the office of the paper by the Morel affair. Monsieur Morel, a Radical deputy, had just addressed a question to the Ministry respecting a vote of credit for the colonization of Algeria.

The servant announced: "Dinner is served, Madame," and they passed into the diningroom.

Duroy found himself seated between Madame de Marelle and her daughter. He again felt ill at ease, being afraid of making some mistake in the conventional handling of forks, spoons, and glasses. There were four of these, one of a faint blue tint. What could be meant to be drunk out of that?

Nothing was said while the soup was being consumed, and then Norbert de Varenne asked: "Have you read the Gauthier case? What a funny business it is."

After a discussion on this case of adultery, complicated with blackmailing, followed. They did not speak of it as the events recorded in newspapers are spoken of in private families, but as a disease is spoken of among doctors, or vegetables among market gardeners. They were neither shocked nor astonished at the facts, but sought out their hidden and secret motives with professional curiosity, and an utter indifference for the crime itself. They sought to clearly explain the origin of certain acts, to determine all the cerebral phenomena which had given birth to the drama, the scientific result due to an especial condition of mind. The women, too, were interested in this investigation. And other recent events were examined, commented upon, turned so as to show every side of them, and weighed correctly, with the practical glance, and from the especial standpoint of dealers in news, and vendors of the drama of life at so much a line, just as articles destined for sale are examined, turned over, and weighed by tradesmen.

Then it was a question of a duel, and Jacques Rival spoke. This was his business; no one else could handle it.

Duroy dared not put in a word. He glanced from time to time at his neighbor, whose full bosom captivated him. A diamond, suspended by a thread of gold, dangled from her ear like a drop of water that had rolled down it. From time to time she made an observation which always brought a smile to her hearers' lips. She had a quaint, pleasant wit, that of an experienced tomboy who views things with indifference and judges them with frivolous and benevolent skepticism.

Duroy sought in vain for some compliment to pay her, and, not finding one, occupied himself with her daughter, filling her glass, holding her plate, and helping her. The child, graver than her mother, thanked him in a serious tone and with a slight bow, saying: "You are very good, sir," and listened to her elders with an air of reflection.

The dinner was very good, and everyone was enraptured. Monsieur Walter ate like an ogre, hardly spoke, and glanced obliquely under his glasses at the dishes offered to him. Norbert de Varenne kept him company, and from time to time let drops of gravy fall on his shirt front. Forestier, silent and serious, watched everything, exchanging glances of intelligence with his wife, like confederates engaged together on a difficult task which is going on swimmingly.

Faces grew red, and voices rose, as from time to time the manservant murmured in the guests' ears: "Corton or Chateau-Laroze."

Duroy had found the Corton to his liking, and let his glass be filled every time. A delicious liveliness stole over him, a warm cheerfulness, that mounted from the stomach to the head, flowed through his limbs and penetrated him throughout. He felt himself wrapped in perfect comfort of life and thought, body and soul.

A longing to speak assailed him, to bring himself into notice, to be appreciated like these men, whose slightest words were relished.

But the conversation, which had been going on unchecked, linking ideas one to another, jumping from one topic to another at a chance word, a mere trifle, and skimming over a thousand matters, turned again on the great question put by Monsieur Morel in the Chamber respecting the colonization of Algeria.

Monsieur Walter, between two courses, made a few jests, for his wit was skeptical and broad. Forestier recited his next day's leader. Jacques Rival insisted on a military government with land grants to all officers after thirty years of colonial service.

"By this plan," he said, "you will create an energetic class of colonists, who will have already learned to love and understand the country, and will be acquainted with its language, and with all those grave local questions against which newcomers invariably run their heads."

Norbert de Varenne interrupted him with: "Yes; they will be acquainted with everything except agriculture. They will speak Arabic, but they will be ignorant how beetroot is planted out and wheat sown. They will be good at fencing, but very shaky as regards manures. On the contrary, this new land should be thrown entirely open to everyone. Intelligent men will achieve a position there; the others will go under. It is the social law."

A brief silence followed, and the listeners smiled at one another.

George Duroy opened his mouth, and said, feeling as much surprised at the sound of his own voice as if he had never heard himself speak: "What is most lacking there is good land. The really fertile estates cost as much as in France, and are bought up as investments by rich Parisians. The real colonists, the poor fellows who leave home for lack of bread, are forced into the desert, where nothing will grow for want of water."

Everyone looked at him, and he felt himself blushing.

Monsieur Walter asked: "Do you know Algeria, sir?"

George replied: "Yes, sir; I was there nearly two years and a half, and I was quartered in all three provinces."

Suddenly unmindful of the Morel question, Norbert de Varenne interrogated him respecting a detail of manners and customs of which he had been informed by an officer. It was with respect to the Mzab, that strange little Arab republic sprung up in the midst of the Sahara, in the driest part of that burning region.

Duroy had twice visited the Mzab, and he narrated some of the customs of this singular country, where drops of water are valued as gold; where every inhabitant is bound to discharge all public duties; and where commercial honesty is carried further than among civilized nations.

He spoke with a certain raciness excited by the wine and the desire to please, and told regimental yarns, incidents of Arab life and military adventure. He even hit on some telling phrases to depict these bare and yellow lands, eternally laid waste by the devouring fire of the sun.

All the women had their eyes turned upon him, and Madame Walter said, in her deliberate tones: "You could make a charming series of articles out of your recollections."

Then Walter looked at the young fellow over the glasses of his spectacles, as was his custom when he wanted to see anyone's face distinctly. He looked at the dishes underneath them.

Forestier seized the opportunity. "My dear sir, I had already spoken to you about Monsieur George Duroy, asking you to let me have him for my assistant in gleaning political topics. Since Marambot left us, I have no one to send in quest of urgent and confidential information, and the paper suffers from it."

Daddy Walter became serious, and pushed his spectacles upon his forehead, in order to look Duroy well in the face. Then he said: "It is true that Monsieur Duroy has evidently an original turn of thought. If he will come and have a chat with us tomorrow at three o'clock, we will settle the matter." Then, after a short silence, turning right round towards George, he added: "But write us a little fancy series of articles on Algeria at once. Relate your experiences, and mix up the colonization question with them as you did just now. They are facts, genuine facts, and I am sure they will greatly please our readers. But be quick. I must have the first article tomorrow or the day after, while the subject is being discussed in the Chamber, in order to catch the public."

Madame Walter added, with that serious grace which characterized everything she did, and which lent an air of favor to her words: "And you have a charming title, 'Recollections of a Chasseur d'Afrique.' Is it not so, Monsieur Norbert?"

The old poet, who had worn renown late in life, feared and hated newcomers. He replied dryly: "Yes, excellent, provided that the keynote be followed, for that is the great difficulty; the exact note, what in music is called the pitch."

Madame Forestier cast on Duroy a smiling and protective glance, the glance of a connoisseur, which seemed to say: "Yes, you will get on." Madame de Marelle had turned towards him several times, and the diamond in her ear quivered incessantly as though the drop of water was about to fall.

The little girl remained quiet and serious, her head bent over her plate.

But the servant passed round the table, filling the blue glasses with Johannisberg, and Forestier proposed a toast, drinking with a bow to Monsieur Walter: "Prosperity to the Vie Francaise."

Everyone bowed towards the proprietor, who smiled, and Duroy, intoxicated with success, emptied his glass at a draught. He would have emptied a whole barrel after the same fashion; it seemed to him that he could have eaten a bullock or strangled a lion. He felt a superhuman strength in his limbs, unconquerable resolution and unbounded hope in his mind. He was now at home among these people; he had just taken his position, won his place. His glance rested on their faces with a newborn assurance, and he ventured for the first time to address his neighbor. "You have the prettiest earrings I have ever seen, Madame."

She turned towards him with a smile. "It was an idea of my own to have the diamonds hung like that, just at the end of a thread. They really look like dewdrops, do they not?"

He murmured, ashamed of his own daring, and afraid of making a fool of himself:

"It is charming; but the ear, too, helps to set it off."

She thanked him with a look, one of those woman's looks that go straight to the heart. And as he turned his head he again met Madame Forestier's eye, always kindly, but now he thought sparkling with a livelier mirth, an archness, an encouragement.

All the men were now talking at once with gesticulations and raised voices. They were discussing the great project of the metropolitan railway. The subject was not exhausted till dessert was finished, everyone having a deal to say about the slowness of the methods of communication in Paris, the inconvenience of the tramway, the delays of omnibus traveling, and the rudeness of cabmen.

Then they left the diningroom to take coffee. Duroy, in jest, offered his arm to the little girl. She gravely thanked him, and rose on tiptoe in order to rest her hand on it.

On returning to the drawingroom he again experienced the sensation of entering a green-house. In each of the four corners of the room tall palms unfolded their elegantly shaped leaves, rising to the ceiling, and there spreading fountain-wise.

On each side of the fireplace were india-rubber plants like round columns, with their dark green leaves tapering one above the other; and on the piano two unknown shrubs covered with flowers, those of one all crimson and those of the other all white, had the appearance of artificial plants, looking too beautiful to be real.

The air was cool, and laden with a soft, vague perfume that could scarcely be defined. The young fellow, now more himself, considered the room more attentively. It was not large; nothing attracted attention with the exception of the shrubs, no bright color struck one, but one felt at one's ease in it; one felt soothed and refreshed, and, as it were, caressed by one's surroundings. The walls were covered with an old-fashioned stuff of faded violet, spotted with little flowers in yellow silk about the size of flies. Hangings of grayish-blue cloth, embroidered here and there with crimson poppies, draped the doorways, and the chairs of all shapes and sizes, scattered about the room, lounging chairs, easy chairs, ottomans, and stools, were upholstered in Louise Seize silk or Utrecht velvet, with a crimson pattern on a cream-colored ground.

"Do you take coffee, Monsieur Duroy?" and Madame Forestier held out a cup towards him with that smile which never left her lips.

"Thank you, Madame." He took the cup, and as he bent forward to take a lump of sugar from the sugar-basin carried by the little girl, Madame Forestier said to him in a low voice: "Pay attention to Madame Walter."

Then she drew back before he had time to answer a word.

He first drank off his coffee, which he was afraid of dropping onto the carpet; then, his mind more at ease, he sought for some excuse to approach the wife of his new governor, and begin a conversation. All at once he noticed that she was holding an empty cup in her hand, and as she was at some distance from a table, did not know where to put it. He darted forward with, "Allow me, Madame?"

"Thank you, sir."

He took away the cup and then returned.

"If you knew, Madame," he began, "the happy hours the Vie Francaise helped me to pass when I was away in the desert. It is really the only paper that is readable out of France, for it is more literary, wittier, and less monotonous than the others. There is something of everything in it."

She smiled with amiable indifference, and answered, seriously:

"Monsieur Walter has had a great deal of trouble to create a type of newspaper supplying the want of the day."

And they began to chat. He had an easy flow of commonplace conversation, a charm in his voice and look, and an irresistible seductiveness about his moustache. It curled coquettishly about his lips, reddish brown, with a paler tint about the ends. They chatted about Paris, its suburbs, the banks of the Seine, watering places, summer amusements, all the current topics on which one can prate to infinity without wearying oneself.

Then as Monsieur Norbert de Varenne approached with a liqueur glass in his hand, Duroy discreetly withdrew.

Madame de Marelle, who had been speaking with Madame Forestier, summoned him.

"Well, sir," she said, abruptly, "so you want to try your hand at journalism?"

He spoke vaguely of his prospects, and there recommenced with her the conversation he had just had with Madame Walter, but as he was now a better master of his subject, he showed his superiority in it, repeating as his own the things he had just heard. And he continually looked his companion in the eyes, as though to give deep meaning to what he was saying.

She, in her turn, related anecdotes with the easy flow of spirits of a woman who knows she is witty, and is always seeking to appear so, and becoming familiar, she laid her hand from time to time on his arm, and lowered her voice to make trifling remarks which thus assumed a character of intimacy. He was inwardly excited by her contact. He would have liked to have shown his devotion for her on the spot, to have defended her, shown her what he was worth, and his delay in his replies to her showed the preoccupation of his mind.

But suddenly, without any reason, Madame de Marelle called, "Laurine!" and the little girl came.

"Sit down here, child; you will catch cold near the window."

Duroy was seized with a wild longing to kiss the child. It was as though some part of the kiss would reach the mother.

He asked in a gallant, and at the same time fatherly, tone: "Will you allow me to kiss you, Mademoiselle?"

The child looked up at him in surprise.

"Answer, my dear," said Madame de Marelle, laughingly.

"Yes, sir, this time; but it will not do always."

Duroy, sitting down, lifted Laurine onto his knees and brushed the fine curly hair above her forehead with his lips.

Her mother was surprised. "What! she has not run away; it is astounding. Usually she will only let ladies kiss her. You are irresistible, Monsieur Duroy."

He blushed without answering, and gently jogged the little girl on his knee.

Madame Forestier drew near, and exclaimed, with astonishment: "What, Laurine tamed! What a miracle!"

Jacques Rival also came up, cigar in mouth, and Duroy rose to take leave, afraid of spoiling, by some unlucky remark, the work done, his task of conquest begun.

He bowed, softly pressed the little outstretched hands of the women, and then heartily shook those of the men. He noted that the hand of Jacques Rival, warm and dry, answered cordially to his grip; that of Norbert de Varenne, damp and cold, slipped through his fingers; that of Daddy Walter, cold and flabby, was without expression or energy; and that of Forestier was plump and moist. His friend said to him in a low tone, "Tomorrow, at three o'clock; do not forget."

"Oh! no; don't be afraid of that."

When he found himself once more on the stairs he felt a longing to run down them, so great was his joy, and he darted forward, going down two steps at a time, but suddenly he caught sight in a large mirror on the second-floor landing of a gentleman in a hurry, who was advancing briskly to meet him, and he stopped short, ashamed, as if he had been caught tripping. Then he looked at himself in the glass for some time, astonished at being really such a handsome fellow, smiled complacently, and taking leave of his reflection, bowed low to it as one bows to a personage of importance.

III

When George Duroy found himself in the street he hesitated as to what he should do. He wanted to run, to dream, to walk about thinking of the future as he breathed the soft night air, but the thought of the series of articles asked for by Daddy Walter haunted him, and he decided to go home at once and set to work.

He walked along quickly, reached the outer boulevards, and followed their line as far as the Rue Boursault, where he dwelt. The house, six stories high, was inhabited by a score of small households, tradespeople or workmen, and he experienced a sickening sensation of disgust, a longing to leave the place and live like well-to-do people in a clean dwelling, as he ascended the stairs, lighting himself with wax matches on his way up the dirty steps, littered with bits of paper, cigarette ends, and scraps of kitchen refuse. A stagnant stench of cooking, cesspools and humanity, a close smell of dirt and old walls, which no rush of air could have driven out of the building, filled it from top to bottom.

The young fellow's room, on the fifth floor, looked into a kind of abyss, the huge cutting of the Western Railway just above the outlet by the tunnel of the Batignolles station. Duroy opened his window and leaned against the rusty iron crossbar.

Below him, at the bottom of the dark hole, three motionless red lights resembled the eyes of huge wild animals, and further on a glimpse could be caught of others, and others again still further. Every moment whistles, prolonged or brief, pierced the silence of the night, some near at hand, others scarcely discernible, coming from a distance from the direction of Asnières. Their modulations were akin to those of the human voice. One of them came nearer and nearer, with its plaintive appeal growing louder and louder every moment, and soon a big yellow light appeared advancing with a loud noise, and Duroy watched the string of railway carriages swallowed up by the tunnel.

Then he said to himself: "Come, let's go to work."

He placed his light upon the table, but at the moment of commencing he found that he had only a quire of letter paper in the place. More the pity, but he would make use of it by opening out each sheet to its full extent. He dipped his pen in ink, and wrote at the head of the page, in his best hand, "Recollections of a Chasseur d'Afrique."

Then he tried to frame the opening sentence. He remained with his head on his hands and his eyes fixed on the white sheet spread out before him. What should he say? He could no longer recall anything of what he had been relating a little while back; not an anecdote, not a fact, nothing.

All at once the thought struck him: "I must begin with my departure."

And he wrote: "It was in 1874, about the middle of May, when France, in her exhaustion, was reposing after the catastrophe of the terrible year."

He stopped short, not knowing how to lead up to what should follow — his embarkation, his voyage, his first impressions.

After ten minutes' reflection, he resolved to put off the introductory slip till tomorrow, and to set to work at once to describe Algiers.

And he traced on his paper the words: "Algiers is a white city," without being able to state anything further. He recalled in his mind the pretty white city flowing down in a cascade of flat-roofed dwellings from the summit of its hills to the sea, but he could no longer find a word to express what he had seen and felt.

After a violent effort, he added: "It is partly inhabited by Arabs."

Then he threw down his pen and rose from his chair.

On his little iron bedstead, hollowed in the center by the pressure of his body, he saw his everyday garments cast down there, empty, worn, limp, ugly as the clothing at the morgue. On a straw-bottomed chair his tall hat, his only one, brim uppermost, seemed to be awaiting an alms.

The wall paper, gray with blue bouquets, showed as many stains as flowers, old suspicious-looking stains, the origin of which could not be defined; crushed insects or drops of oil; finger tips smeared with pomatum or soapy water scattered while washing. It smacked of shabby, genteel poverty, the poverty of a Paris lodging-house. Anger rose within him at the wretchedness of his mode of living. He said to himself that he must get out of it at once; that he must finish with this irksome existence the very next day.

A frantic desire of working having suddenly seized on him again, he sat down once more at the table, and began anew to seek for phrases to describe the strange and charming physiognomy of Algiers, that anteroom of vast and mysterious Africa; the Africa of wandering Arabs and unknown tribes of negroes; that unexplored Africa of which we are sometimes shown in public gardens the improbable-looking animals seemingly made to figure in fairy tales; the ostriches, those exaggerated fowls; the gazelles, those divine goats; the surprising and grotesque giraffes; the grave-looking camels, the monstrous hippopotomi, the shapeless rhinosceri, and the gorillas, those frightful-looking brothers of mankind.

He vaguely felt ideas occurring to him; he might perhaps have uttered them, but he could not put them into writing. And his impotence exasperated him, he got up again, his hands damp with perspiration, and his temples throbbing.

His eyes falling on his washing bill, brought up that evening by the concierge, he was suddenly seized with wild despair. All his joy vanishing in a twinkling, with his confidence in himself and his faith in the future. It was all up; he could not do anything, he would never be anybody; he felt played out, incapable, good for nothing, damned.

And he went and leaned out of the window again, just as a train issued from the tunnel with a loud and violent noise. It was going away, afar off, across the fields and plains towards the sea. And the recollection of his parents stirred in Duroy's breast. It would pass near them, that train, within a few leagues of their house. He saw it again, the little house at the entrance to the village of Canteleu, on the summit of the slope overlooking Rouen and the immense valley of the Seine.

His father and mother kept a little inn, a place where the tradesfolk of the suburbs of Rouen came out to lunch on Sunday at the sign of the Belle Vue. They had wanted to make a gentleman of their son, and had sent him to college. Having finished his studies, and been plowed for his bachelor's degree, he had entered on his military service with the intention of becoming an officer, a colonel, a general. But, disgusted with military life long before the completion of his five years' term of service, he had dreamed of making a fortune at Paris.

He came there at the expiration of his term of service, despite the entreaties of his father and mother, whose visions having evaporated, wanted now to have him at home with them. In his turn he hoped to achieve a future; he foresaw a triumph by means as yet vaguely defined in his mind, but which he felt sure he could scheme out and further.

He had had some successful love affairs in the regiment, some easy conquests, and even some adventures in a better class of society, having seduced a tax collector's daughter, who wanted to leave her home for his sake, and a lawyer's wife, who had tried to drown herself in despair at being abandoned.

His comrades used to say of him: "He is a sharp fellow, a deep one to get out of a scrape, a chap who knows which side his bread is buttered," and he had promised himself to act up to this character.

His conscience, Norman by birth, worn by the daily dealings of garrison life, rendered elastic by the examples of pillaging in Africa, illicit commissions, shaky dodges; spurred, too, by the notions of honor current in the army, military bravadoes, patriotic sentiments, the fine-sounding tales current among sub-officers, and the vain glory of the profession of arms, had become a kind of box of tricks in which something of everything was to be found.

But the wish to succeed reigned sovereign in it.

He had, without noticing it, began to dream again as he did every evening. He pictured to himself some splendid love adventure which should bring about all at once the realization of his hopes. He married the daughter of some banker or nobleman met with in the street, and captivated at the first glance.

The shrill whistle of a locomotive which, issuing from the tunnel like a big rabbit bolting out of its hole, and tearing at full speed along the rails towards the machine shed where it was to take its rest, awoke him from his dream.

Then, repossessed by the vague and joyful hope which ever haunted his mind, he wafted a kiss into the night, a kiss of love addressed to the vision of the woman he was awaiting, a kiss of desire addressed to the fortune he coveted. Then he closed his window and began to undress, murmuring:

"I shall feel in a better mood for it tomorrow. My thoughts are not clear tonight. Perhaps, too, I have had just a little too much to drink. One can't work well under those circumstances."

He got into bed, blew out his light, and went off to sleep almost immediately.

He awoke early, as one awakes on mornings of hope and trouble, and jumping out of bed, opened his window to drink a cup of fresh air, as he phrased it.

The houses of the Rue de Rome opposite, on the other side of the broad railway cutting, glittering in the rays of the rising sun, seemed to be painted with white light. Afar off on the right a glimpse was caught of the slopes of Argenteuil, the hills of Sannois, and the windmills of Orgemont through a light bluish mist; like a floating and transparent veil cast onto the horizon.

Duroy remained for some minutes gazing at the distant country side, and he murmured: "It would be devilish nice out there a day like this." Then he bethought himself that he must set to work, and that at once, and also send his concierge's lad, at a cost of ten sous, to the office to say that he was ill.

He sat down at his table, dipped his pen in the ink, leaned his forehead on his hand, and sought for ideas. All in vain, nothing came.

He was not discouraged, however. He thought, "Bah! I am not accustomed to it. It is a trade to be learned like all other trades. I must have some help the first time. I will go and find Forestier, who will give me a start for my article in ten minutes."

And he dressed himself.

When he got into the street he came to the conclusion that it was still too early to present himself at the residence of his friend, who must be a late sleeper. He therefore walked slowly along beneath the trees of the outer boulevards. It was not yet nine o'clock when he reached the Parc Monceau, fresh from its morning watering. Sitting down upon a bench he began to dream again. A well-dressed young man was walking up and down at a short distance, awaiting a woman, no doubt. Yes, she appeared, close veiled and quick stepping, and taking his arm, after a brief clasp of the hand, they walked away together.

A riotous need of love broke out in Duroy's heart, a need of amours at once distinguished and delicate. He rose and resumed his journey, thinking of Forestier. What luck the fellow had!

He reached the door at the moment his friend was coming out of it. "You here at this time of day. What do you want of me?"

Duroy, taken aback at meeting him thus, just as he was starting off, stammered: "You see, you see, I can't manage to write my article; you know the article Monsieur Walter asked me to write on Algeria. It is not very surprising, considering that I have never written anything. Practice is needed for that, as for everything else. I shall get used to it very quickly, I am sure, but I do not know how to set about beginning. I have plenty of ideas, but I cannot manage to express them."

He stopped, hesitatingly, and Forestier smiled somewhat slyly, saying: "I know what it is."

Duroy went on: "Yes, it must happen to everyone at the beginning. Well, I came, I came to ask you for a lift. In ten minutes you can give me a start, you can show me how to shape it. It will be a good lesson in style you will give me, and really without you I do not see how I can get on with it."

Forestier still smiled, and tapping his old comrade on the arm, said: "Go in and see my wife; she will settle your business quite as well as I could. I have trained her for that kind of work. I, myself, have not time this morning, or I would willingly have done it for you."

Duroy suddenly abashed, hesitated, feeling afraid.

"But I cannot call on her at this time of the day."

"Oh, yes; she is up. You will find her in my study arranging some notes for me."

Duroy refused to go upstairs, saying: "No, I can't think of such a thing."

Forestier took him by the shoulders, twisted him round on his heels, and pushing him towards the staircase, said: "Go along, you great donkey, when I tell you to. You are not going to oblige me to go up these flights of stairs again to introduce you and explain the fix you are in."

Then Duroy made up his mind. "Thanks, then, I will go up," he said. "I shall tell her that you forced me, positively forced me to come and see her."

"All right. She won't scratch your eyes out. Above all, do not forget our appointment for three o'clock."

"Oh! don't be afraid about that."

Forestier hastened off, and Duroy began to ascend the stairs slowly, step by step, thinking over what he should say, and feeling uneasy as to his probable reception.

The man servant, wearing a blue apron, and holding a broom in his hand, opened the door to him.

"Master is not at home," he said, without waiting to be spoken to.

Duroy persisted.

"Ask Madame Forestier," said he, "whether she will receive me, and tell her that I have come from her husband, whom I met in the street."

Then he waited while the man went away, returned, and opening the door on the right, said: "Madame will see you, sir."

She was seated in an office armchair in a small room, the walls of which were wholly hidden by books carefully ranged on shelves of black wood. The bindings, of various tints, red, yellow, green, violet, and blue, gave some color and liveliness to those monotonous lines of volumes.

She turned round, still smiling. She was wrapped in a white dressing gown, trimmed with lace, and as she held out her hand, displayed her bare arm in its wide sleeve.

"Already?" said she, and then added: "That is not meant for a reproach, but a simple question."

"Oh, madame, I did not want to come up, but your husband, whom I met at the bottom of the house, obliged me to. I am so confused that I dare not tell you what brings me."

She pointed to a chair, saying: "Sit down and tell me about it."

She was twirling a goose-quill between her fingers, and in front of her was a half-written page, interrupted by the young fellow's arrival. She seemed quite at home at this work table, as much at her ease as if in her drawingroom, engaged on everyday tasks. A faint perfume emanated from her dressing gown, the fresh perfume of a recent toilet. Duroy sought to divine, fancied he could trace, the outline of her plump, youthful figure through the soft material enveloping it.

She went on, as he did not reply: "Well, come tell me what is it."

He murmured, hesitatingly: "Well, you see — but I really dare not — I was working last night very late and quite early this morning on the article upon Algeria, upon which Monsieur Walter asked me to write, and I could not get on with it — I tore up all my attempts. I am not accustomed to this kind of work, and I came to ask Forestier to help me this once — "

She interrupted him, laughing heartily. "And he told you to come and see me? That is a nice thing."

"Yes, madame. He said that you will get me out of my difficulty better than himself, but I did not dare, I did not wish to — you understand."

She rose, saying: "It will be delightful to work in collaboration with you like that. I am charmed at the notion. Come, sit down in my place, for they know my handwriting at the office. And we will knock you off an article; oh, but a good one."

He sat down, took a pen, spread a sheet of paper before him, and waited.

Madame Forestier, standing by, watched him make these preparations, then took a cigarette from the mantelshelf, and lit it.

"I cannot work without smoking," said she. "Come, what are you going to say?"

He lifted his head towards her with astonishment.

"But that is just what I don't know, since it is that I came to see you about."

She replied: "Oh, I will put it in order for you. I will make the sauce, but then I want the materials of the dish."

He remained embarrassed before her. At length he said, hesitatingly: "I should like to relate my journey, then, from the beginning."

Then she sat down before him on the other side of the table, and looking him in the eyes:

"Well, tell it me first; for myself alone, you understand, slowly and without forgetting anything, and I will select what is to be used of it."

But as he did not know where to commence, she began to question him as a priest would have done in the confessional, putting precise questions which recalled to him forgotten details, people encountered and faces merely caught sight of.

When she had made him speak thus for about a quarter of an hour, she suddenly interrupted him with: "Now we will begin. In the first place, we will imagine that you are narrating your impressions to a friend, which will allow you to write a lot of tomfoolery, to make remarks of all kinds, to be natural and funny if we can. Begin:

"'My Dear Henry, — You want to know what Algeria is like, and you shall. I will send you, having nothing else to do in a little cabin of dried mud which serves me as a habitation, a kind of journal of my life, day by day, and hour by hour. It will be a little lively at times, more is the pity, but you are not obliged to show it to your lady friends.'"

She paused to relight her cigarette, which had gone out, and the faint creaking of the quill on the paper stopped, too.

"Let us continue," said she.

"Algeria is a great French country on the frontiers of the great unknown countries called the Desert, the Sahara, central Africa, etc., *etc.*

"Algiers is the door, the pretty white door of this strange continent.

"But it is first necessary to get to it, which is not a rosy job for everyone. I am, you know, an excellent horseman, since I break in the colonel's horses; but a man may be a very good rider and a very bad sailor. That is my case.

"You remember Surgeon-Major Simbretras, whom we used to call Old Ipecacuanha, and how, when we thought ourselves ripe for a twenty-four hours' stay in the infirmary, that blessed sojourning place, we used to go up before him.

"How he used to sit in his chair, with his fat legs in his red trousers, wide apart, his hands on his knees, and his elbows stuck, rolling his great eyes and gnawing his white moustache.

"You remember his favorite mode of treatment: 'This man's stomach is out of order. Give him a dose of emetic number three, according to my prescription, and then twelve hours off duty, and he will be all right.'

"It was a sovereign remedy that emetic — sovereign and irresistible. One swallowed it because one had to. Then when one had undergone the effects of Old Ipecacuanha's prescription, one enjoyed twelve well-earned hours' rest.

"Well, my dear fellow, to reach Africa, it is necessary to undergo for forty hours the effects of another kind of irresistible emetic, according to the prescription of the Compagnie Transatlantique."

She rubbed her hands, delighted with the idea.

She got up and walked about, after having lit another cigarette, and dictated as she puffed out little whiffs of smoke, which, issuing at first through a little round hole in the midst of her compressed lips, slowly evaporated, leaving in the air faint gray lines, a kind of transparent mist, like a spider's web. Sometimes with her open hand she would brush these light traces aside; at others she would cut them asunder with her forefinger, and then watch with serious attention the two halves of the almost impenetrable vapor slowly disappear.

Duroy, with his eyes, followed all her gestures, her attitudes, the movements of her form and features — busied with this vague pastime which did not preoccupy her thoughts.

She now imagined the incidents of the journey, sketched traveling companions invented by herself, and a love affair with the wife of a captain of infantry on her way to join her husband.

Then, sitting down again, she questioned Duroy on the topography of Algeria, of which she was absolutely ignorant. In ten minutes she knew as much about it as he did, and she dictated a little chapter of political and colonial geography to coach the reader up in such matters and prepare him to understand the serious questions which were to be brought forward in the following articles. She continued by a trip into the provinces of Oran, a fantastic trip, in which it was, above all, a question of women, Moorish, Jewish, and Spanish.

"That is what interests most," she said.

She wound up by a sojourn at Saïda, at the foot of the great tablelands; and by a pretty little intrigue between the sub-officer, George Duroy, and a Spanish work-girl employed at the alfa factory at Ain el Hadjar. She described their rendezvous at night amidst the bare, stony hills, with jackals, hyenas, and Arab dogs yelling, barking and howling among the rocks.

And she gleefully uttered the words: "To be continued." Then rising, she added: "That is how one writes an article, my dear sir. Sign it, if you please."

He hesitated.

"But sign it, I tell you."

Then he began to laugh, and wrote at the bottom of the page, "George Duroy."

She went on smoking as she walked up and down; and he still kept looking at her, unable to find anything to say to thank her, happy to be with her, filled with gratitude, and with the sensual pleasure of this newborn intimacy. It seemed to him that everything surrounding him was part of her, everything down to the walls covered with books. The chairs, the furniture, the air in which the perfume of tobacco was floating, had something special, nice, sweet, and charming, which emanated from her.

Suddenly she asked: "What do you think of my friend, Madame de Marelle?"

He was surprised, and answered: "I think — I think — her very charming."

"Is it not so?"

"Yes, certainly."

He longed to add: "But not so much as yourself," but dared not.

She resumed: "And if you only knew how funny, original, and intelligent she is. She is a Bohemian — a true Bohemian. That is why her husband scarcely cares for her. He only sees her defects, and does not appreciate her good qualities."

Duroy felt stupefied at learning that Madame de Marelle was married, and yet it was only natural that she should be.

He said: "Oh, she is married, then! And what is her husband?"

Madame Forestier gently shrugged her shoulders, and raised her eyebrows, with a gesture of incomprehensible meaning.

"Oh! he is an inspector on the Northern Railway. He spends eight days out of the month in Paris. What his wife calls 'obligatory service,' or 'weekly duty,' or 'holy week.' When you know her better you will see how nice and bright she is. Go and call on her one of these days."

Duroy no longer thought of leaving. It seemed to him that he was going to stop for ever; that he was at home.

But the door opened noiselessly, and a tall gentleman entered without being announced. He stopped short on seeing a stranger. Madame Forestier seemed troubled for a moment; then she said in natural tones, though a slight rosy flush had risen to her cheeks:

"Come in, my dear sir. I must introduce one of Charles' old friends, Monsieur George Duroy, a future journalist." Then in another tone, she added: "Our best and most intimate friend, the Count de Vaudrec."

The two men bowed, looking each other in the eyes, and Duroy at once took his leave.

There was no attempt to detain him. He stammered a few thanks, grasped the outstretched hand of Madame Forestier, bowed again to the newcomer, who preserved the cold, grave air of a man of position, and went out quite disturbed, as if he had made a fool of himself.

On finding himself once more in the street, he felt sad and uneasy, haunted by the vague idea of some hidden vexation. He walked on, asking himself whence came this sudden melancholy. He could not tell, but the stern face of the Count de Vaudrec, already somewhat aged, with gray hair, and the calmly insolent look of a very wealthy man, constantly recurred to his recollection. He noted that the arrival of this unknown, breaking off a charming tête-à-tête, had produced in him that chilly, despairing sensation that a word overheard, a trifle noticed, the least thing suffices sometimes to bring about. It seemed to him, too, that this man, without his being able to guess why, had been displeased at finding him there.

He had nothing more to do till three o'clock, and it was not yet noon. He had still six francs fifty centimes in his pocket, and he went and lunched at a Bouillon Duval. Then he prowled about the boulevard, and as three o'clock struck, ascended the staircase, in itself an advertisement, of the Vie Francaise.

The messengers-in-waiting were seated with folded arms on a bench, while at a kind of desk a doorkeeper was sorting the correspondence that had just arrived. The entire get-up of the place, intended to impress visitors, was perfect. Everyone had the appearance, bearing, dignity, and smartness suitable to the anteroom of a large newspaper.

"Monsieur Walter, if you please?" inquired Duroy.

"The manager is engaged, sir," replied the doorkeeper. "Will you take a seat, sir?" and he indicated the waiting-room, already full of people.

There were men grave, important-looking, and decorated; and men without visible linen, whose frock-coats, buttoned up to the chin, bore upon the breast stains recalling the outlines of continents and seas on geographical maps. There were three women among them. One of them was pretty, smiling, and decked out, and had the air of a gay woman; her neighbor, with a wrinkled, tragic countenance, decked out also, but in more severe fashion, had about her something worn and artificial which old actresses generally have; a kind of false youth, like a scent of stale love. The third woman, in mourning, sat in a corner, with the air of a desolate widow. Duroy thought that she had come to ask for charity.

However, no one was ushered into the room beyond, and more than twenty minutes had elapsed.

Duroy was seized with an idea, and going back to the doorkeeper, said: "Monsieur Walter made an appointment for me to call on him here at three o'clock. At all events, see whether my friend, Monsieur Forestier, is here."

He was at once ushered along a lengthy passage, which brought him to a large room where four gentlemen were writing at a large green-covered table.

Forestier standing before the fireplace was smoking a cigarette and playing at cup and ball. He was very clever at this, and kept spiking the huge ball of yellow boxwood on the wooden point. He was counting "Twenty-two, twenty-three, twenty-four, twenty-five."

"Twenty-six," said Duroy.

His friend raised his eyes without interrupting the regular movement of his arm, saying: "Oh! here you are, then. Yesterday I landed the ball fifty-seven times right off. There is only Saint-Potin who can beat me at it among those here. Have you seen the governor? There is nothing funnier than to see that old tubby Norbert playing at cup and ball. He opens his mouth as if he was going to swallow the ball every time."

One of the others turned round towards him, saying: "I say, Forestier, I know of one for sale, a beauty in West Indian wood; it is said to have belonged to the Queen of Spain. They want sixty francs for it. Not dear."

Forestier asked: "Where does it hang out?"

And as he had missed his thirty-seventh shot, he opened a cupboard in which Duroy saw a score of magnificent cups and balls, arranged and numbered like a collection of art objects. Then having put back the one he had been using in its usual place, he repeated: "Where does this gem hang out?"

The journalist replied: "At a box-office keeper's of the Vaudeville. I will bring it you tomorrow, if you like."

"All right. If it is really a good one I will take it; one can never have too many." Then turning to Duroy he added: "Come with me. I will take you in to see the governor; otherwise you might be getting mouldy here till seven in the evening."

They recrossed the waiting-room, in which the same people were waiting in the same order. As soon as Forestier appeared the young woman and the old actress, rising quickly, came up to him. He took them aside one after the other into the bay of the window, and although they took care to talk in low tones, Duroy noticed that they were on familiar terms.

Then, having passed through two padded doors, they entered the manager's room. The conference which had been going on for an hour or so was nothing more than a game at ecarté with some of the gentlemen with the flat brimmed hats whom Duroy had noticed the night before.

Monsieur Walter dealt and played with concentrated attention and crafty movements, while his adversary threw down, picked up, and handled the light bits of colored pasteboard with the swiftness, skill, and grace of a practiced player. Norbert de Varenne, seated in the managerial armchair, was writing an article. Jacques Rival, stretched at full length on a couch, was smoking a cigar with his eyes closed.

The room smelled close, with that blended odor of leather-covered furniture, stale tobacco, and printing-ink peculiar to editors' rooms and familiar to all journalists. Upon the black wood table, inlaid with brass, lay an incredible pile of papers, letters, cards, newspapers, magazines, bills, and printed matter of every description.

Forestier shook hands with the punters standing behind the card players, and without saying a word watched the progress of the game; then, as soon as Daddy Walter had won, he said: "Here is my friend, Duroy."

The manager glanced sharply at the young fellow over the glasses of his spectacles, and said: "Have you brought my article? It would go very well to-day with the Morel debate."

Duroy took the sheets of paper folded in four from his pocket, saying: "Here it is sir."

The manager seemed pleased, and remarked, with a smile: "Very good, very good. You are a man of your word. You must look through this for me, Forestier."

But Forestier hastened to reply: "It is not worth while, Monsieur Walter. I did it with him to give him a lesson in the tricks of the trade. It is very well done."

And the manager, who was gathering up the cards dealt by a tall, thin gentleman, a deputy belonging to the Left Center, remarked with indifference: "All right, then."

Forestier, however, did not let him begin the new game, but stooping, murmured in his ear: "You know you promised me to take on Duroy to replace Marambot. Shall I engage him on the same terms?"

"Yes, certainly."

Taking his friend's arm, the journalist led him away, while Monsieur Walter resumed the game.

Norbert de Varenne had not lifted his head; he did not appear to have seen or recognized Duroy. Jacques Rival, on the contrary, had taken his hand with the marked and demonstrative energy of a comrade who may be reckoned upon in the case of any little difficulty.

They passed through the waiting-room again, and as everyone looked at them, Forestier said to the youngest of the women, in a tone loud enough to be heard by the rest: "The manager will see you directly. He is just now engaged with two members of the Budget Committee."

Then he passed swiftly on, with an air of hurry and importance, as though about to draft at once an article of the utmost weight.

As soon as they were back in the reporters' room Forestier at once took up his cup and ball, and as he began to play with it again, said to Duroy, breaking his sentences in order to count: "You will come here every day at three o'clock, and I will tell you the places you are to go to, either during the day or in the evening, or the next morning — one — I will give you, first of all, a letter of introduction to the head of the First Department of the Préfecture of Police — two — who will put you in communication with one of his clerks. You will settle with him about all the important information — three — from the Préfecture, official and quasi-official information, you know. In all matters of detail you will apply to Saint-Potin, who is up in the work — four — You can see him by-and-by, or tomorrow. You must, above all, cultivate the knack of dragging information out of men I send you to see — five — and to get in everywhere, in spite of closed doors — six — You will have for this a salary of two hundred francs a month, with two sous a line for the paragraphs you glean — seven — and two sous a line for all articles written by you to order on different subjects — eight."

Then he gave himself up entirely to his occupation, and went on slowly counting: "Nine, ten, eleven, twelve, thirteen." He missed the fourteenth, and swore, "Damn that thirteen, it always brings me bad luck. I shall die on the thirteenth of some month, I am certain."

One of his colleagues who had finished his work also took a cup and ball from the cupboard. He was a little man, who looked like a boy, although he was really five-and-thirty. Several other journalists having come in, went one after the other and got out the toy belonging to each of them. Soon there were six standing side by side, with their backs to the wall, swinging into the air, with even and regular motion, the balls of red, yellow, and black, according to the wood they were made of. And a match having begun, the two who were still working got up to act as umpires. Forestier won by eleven points. Then the little man, with the juvenile aspect, who had lost, rang for the messenger, and gave the order, "Nine bocks." And they began to play again pending the arrival of these refreshments.

Duroy drank a glass of beer with his new comrades, and then said to his friend: "What am I to do now?"

"I have nothing for you to-day. You can go if you want to."

"And our — our — article, will it go in tonight?"

"Yes, but do not bother yourself about it; I will correct the proofs. Write the continuation for tomorrow, and come here at three o'clock, the same as to-day."

Duroy having shaken hands with everyone, without even knowing their names, went down the magnificent staircase with a light heart and high spirits.

IV

George Duroy slept badly, so excited was he by the wish to see his article in print. He was up as soon as it was daylight, and was prowling about the streets long before the hour at which the porters from the newspaper offices run with their papers from kiosque to kiosque. He went on to the Saint Lazare terminus, knowing that the Vie Francaise would be delivered there before it reached his own district. As he was still too early, he wandered up and down on the footpath.

He witnessed the arrival of the newspaper vendor who opened her glass shop, and then saw a man bearing on his head a pile of papers. He rushed forward. There were the Figaro, the Gil Blas, the Gaulois, the Evenement, and two or three morning journals, but the Vie Francaise was not among them. Fear seized him. Suppose the "Recollections of a Chasseur d'Afrique" had been kept over for the next day, or that by chance they had not at the last moment seemed suitable to Daddy Walter.

Turning back to the kiosque, he saw that the paper was on sale without his having seen it brought there. He darted forward, unfolded it, after having thrown down the three sous, and ran through the headings of the articles on the first page. Nothing. His heart began to beat, and he experienced strong emotion on reading at the foot of a column in large letters, "George Duroy." It was in; what happiness!

He began to walk along unconsciously, the paper in his hand and his hat on one side of his head, with a longing to stop the passersby in order to say to them: "Buy this, buy this, there is an article by me in it." He would have liked to have bellowed with all the power of his lungs, like some vendors of papers at night on the boulevards, "Read the Vie Francaise; read George Duroy's article, 'Recollections of a Chasseur d'Afrique.'" And suddenly he felt a wish to read this article himself, read it in a public place, a café, in sight of all. He looked about for some establishment already filled with customers. He had to walk in search of one for some time. He sat down at last in front of a kind of wine shop, where several customers were already installed, and asked for a glass of rum, as he would have asked for one of absinthe, without thinking of the time. Then he cried: "Waiter, bring me the Vie Francaise."

A man in a white apron stepped up, saying: "We have not got it, sir; we only take in the Rappel, the Siecle, the Lanierne, and the Petit Parisien."

"What a den!" exclaimed Duroy, in a tone of anger and disgust. "Here, go and buy it for me."

The waiter hastened to do so, and brought back the paper. Duroy began to read his article, and several times said aloud: "Very good, very well put," to attract the attention of his neighbors, and inspire them with the wish to know what there was in this sheet. Then, on going away, he left it on the table. The master of the place, noticing this, called him back, saying: "Sir, sir, you are forgetting your paper."

And Duroy replied: "I will leave it to you. I have finished with it. There is a very interesting article in it this morning."

He did not indicate the article, but he noticed as he went away one of his neighbors take the Vie Francaise up from the table on which he had left it.

He thought: "What shall I do now?" And he decided to go to his office, take his month's salary, and tender his resignation. He felt a thrill of anticipatory pleasure at the thought of the faces that would be pulled up by the chief of his room and his colleagues. The notion of the bewilderment of the chief above all charmed him.

He walked slowly, so as not to get there too early, the cashier's office not opening before ten o'clock.

His office was a large, gloomy room, in which gas had to be kept burning almost all day long in winter. It looked into a narrow courtyard, with other offices on the further side of it. There were eight clerks there, besides a sub-chief hidden behind a screen in one corner.

Duroy first went to get the hundred and eighteen francs twenty-five centimes enclosed in a yellow envelope, and placed in the drawer of the clerk entrusted with such payments, and then, with a conquering air, entered the large room in which he had already spent so many days.

As soon as he came in the sub-chief, Monsieur Potel, called out to him: "Ah! it is you, Monsieur Duroy? The chief has already asked for you several times. You know that he will not allow anyone to plead illness two days running without a doctor's certificate."

Duroy, who was standing in the middle of the room preparing his sensational effect, replied in a loud voice:

"I don't care a damn whether he does or not."

There was a movement of stupefaction among the clerks, and Monsieur Potel's features showed affrightedly over the screen which shut him up as in a box. He barricaded himself behind it for fear of draughts, for he was rheumatic, but had pierced a couple of holes through the paper to keep an eye on his staff. A pin might have been heard to fall. At length the sub-chief said, hesitatingly: "You said?"

"I said that I don't care a damn about it. I have only called to-day to tender my resignation. I am engaged on the staff of the Vie Francaise at five hundred francs a month, and extra pay for all I write. Indeed, I made my début this morning."

He had promised himself to spin out his enjoyment, but had not been able to resist the temptation of letting it all out at once.

The effect, too, was overwhelming. No one stirred.

Duroy went on: "I will go and inform Monsieur Perthuis, and then come and wish you goodbye."

And he went out in search of the chief, who exclaimed, on seeing him: "Ah, here you are. You know that I won't have — "

His late subordinate cut him short with: "It's not worth while yelling like that."

Monsieur Perthuis, a stout man, as red as a turkey cock, was choked with bewilderment.

Duroy continued: "I have had enough of this crib. I made my début this morning in journalism, where I am assured of a very good position. I have the honor to bid you good-day." And he went out. He was avenged.

As he promised, he went and shook hands with his old colleagues, who scarcely dared to speak to him, for fear of compromising themselves, for they had overheard his conversation with the chief, the door having remained open.

He found himself in the street again, with his salary in his pocket. He stood himself a substantial breakfast at a good but cheap restaurant he was acquainted with, and having again purchased the Vie Francaise, and left it on the table, went into several shops, where he bought some trifles, solely for the sake of ordering them to be sent home, and giving his name: "George Duroy," with the addition, "I am the editor of the Vie Francaise."

Then he gave the name of the street and the number, taking care to add: "Leave it with the doorkeeper."

As he had still some time to spare he went into the shop of a lithographer, who executed visiting cards at a moment's notice before the eyes of passersby, and had a hundred, bearing his new occupation under his name, printed off while he waited.

Then he went to the office of the paper.

Forestier received him loftily, as one receives a subordinate. "Ah! here you are. Good. I have several things for you to attend to. Just wait ten minutes. I will just finish what I am about."

And he went on with a letter he was writing.

At the other end of the large table a fat, bald little man, with a very pale, puffy face, and a white and shining head, was writing, with his nose on the paper owing to extreme shortsightedness. Forestier said to him: "I say, Saint-Potin, when are you going to interview those people?"

"At four o'clock."

"Will you take young Duroy here with you, and let him into the way of doing it?"

"All right."

Then turning to his friend, Forestier added: "Have you brought the continuation of the Algerian article? The opening this morning was very successful."

Duroy, taken aback, stammered: "No. I thought I should have time this afternoon. I had heaps of things to do. I was not able."

The other shrugged his shoulders with a dissatisfied air. "If you are not more exact than that you will spoil your future. Daddy Walter was reckoning on your copy. I will tell him it will be ready tomorrow. If you think you are to be paid for doing nothing you are mistaken."

Then, after a short silence, he added: "One must strike the iron while it is hot, or the deuce is in it."

Saint-Potin rose, saying: "I am ready."

Then Forestier, leaning back in his chair, assumed a serious attitude in order to give his instructions, and turning to Duroy, said: "This is what it is. Within the last two days the Chinese General, Li Theng Fao, has arrived at the Hotel Continental, and the Rajah Taposahib Ramaderao Pali at the Hotel Bristol. You will go and interview them." Turning to Saint-Potin, he continued: "Don't forget the main points I told you of. Ask the General and the Rajah their opinion upon the action of England in the East, their ideas upon her system of colonization and domination, and their hopes respecting the intervention of Europe, and especially of France." He was silent for a moment, and then added in a theatrical aside: "It will be most interesting to our readers to learn at the same time what is thought in China and India upon these matters which so forcibly occupy public attention at this moment." He continued, for the benefit of Duroy: "Watch how Saint-Potin sets to work; he is a capital reporter; and try to learn the trick of pumping a man in five minutes."

Then he gravely resumed his writing, with the evident intention of defining their relative positions, and putting his old comrade and present colleague in his proper place.

As soon as they had crossed the threshold Saint-Potin began to laugh, and said to Duroy: "There's a fluffer for you. He tried to fluff even us. One would really think he took us for his readers."

They reached the boulevard, and the reporter observed: "Will you have a drink?"

"Certainly. It is awfully hot."

They turned into a café and ordered cooling drinks. Saint-Potin began to talk. He talked about the paper and everyone connected with it with an abundance of astonishing details.

"The governor? A regular Jew? And you know, nothing can alter a Jew. What a breed!" And he instanced some astounding traits of avariciousness peculiar to the children of Israel, economies of ten centimes, petty bargaining, shameful reductions asked for and obtained, all the ways of a usurer and pawnbroker.

"And yet with all this, a good fellow who believes in nothing and does everyone. His paper, which is Governmental, Catholic, Liberal, Republican, Orleanist, pay your money and take your choice, was only started to help him in his speculations on the Bourse, and bolster up his other schemes. At that game he is very clever, and nets millions through companies without four sous of genuine capital."

He went on, addressing Duroy as "My dear fellow."

"And he says things worthy of Balzac, the old shark. Fancy, the other day I was in his room with that old tub Norbert, and that Don Quixote Rival, when Montelin, our business manager, came in with his morocco bill-case, that bill-case that everyone in Paris knows, under his arm. Walter raised his head and asked: 'What news?' Montelin answered simply: 'I have just paid the sixteen thousand francs we owed the paper maker.' The governor gave a jump, an astonishing jump. 'What do you mean?' said he. 'I have just paid Monsieur Privas,' replied Montelin. 'But you are mad.' 'Why?' 'Why — why — why — ' he took off his spectacles and wiped them. Then he smiled with that queer smile that flits across his fat cheeks whenever he is going to say something deep or smart, and went on in a mocking and derisive tone, 'Why? Because we could have obtained a reduction of from four to five thousand francs.' Montelin replied, in astonishment: 'But, sir, all the accounts were correct, checked by me and passed by yourself.' Then the governor, quite serious again, observed: 'What a fool you are. Don't you know, Monsieur Montelin, that one should always let one's debts mount up, in order to offer a composition?'"

And Saint-Potin added, with a knowing shake of his head, "Eh! isn't that worthy of Balzac?"

Duroy had not read Balzac, but he replied, "By Jove! yes."

Then the reporter spoke of Madame Walter, an old goose; of Norbert de Varenne, an old failure; of Rival, a copy of Fervacques. Next he came to Forestier. "As to him, he has been lucky in marrying his wife, that is all."

Duroy asked: "What is his wife, really?"

Saint-Potin rubbed his hands. "Oh! a deep one, a smart woman. She was the mistress of an old rake named Vaudrec, the Count de Vaudrec, who gave her a dowry and married her off."

Duroy suddenly felt a cold shiver run through him, a tingling of the nerves, a longing to smack this gabbler on the face. But he merely interrupted him by asking:

"And your name is Saint-Potin?"

The other replied, simply enough:

"No, my name is Thomas. It is in the office that they have nicknamed me Saint-Potin."

Duroy, as he paid for the drinks, observed: "But it seems to me that time is getting on, and that we have two noble foreigners to call on."

Saint-Potin began to laugh. "You are still green. So you fancy I am going to ask the Chinese and the Hindoo what they think of England? As if I did not know better than themselves what they ought to think in order to please the readers of the Vie Francaise. I have already interviewed five hundred of these Chinese, Persians, Hindoos, Chilians, Japanese, and others. They all reply the same, according to me. I have only to take my article on the last comer and copy it word for word. What has to be changed, though, is their appearance, their name, their title, their age, and their suite. Oh! on that point it does not do to make a mistake, for I should be snapped up sharp by the Figaro or the Gaulois. But on these matters the hall porters at the Hotel Bristol and the Hotel Continental will put me right in five minutes. We will smoke a cigar as we walk there. Five francs cab hire to charge to the paper. That is how one sets about it, my dear fellow, when one is practically inclined."

"It must be worth something decent to be a reporter under these circumstances," said Duroy.

The journalist replied mysteriously: "Yes, but nothing pays so well as paragraphs, on account of the veiled advertisements."

They had got up and were passing down the boulevards towards the Madeleine. Saint-Potin suddenly observed to his companion: "You know if you have anything else to do, I shall not need you in any way."

Duroy shook hands and left him. The notion of the article to be written that evening worried him, and he began to think. He stored his mind with ideas, reflections, opinions, and anecdotes as he walked along, and went as far as the end of the Avenue des Champs Elysées, where only a few strollers were to be seen, the heat having caused Paris to be evacuated.

Having dined at a wine shop near the Arc de Triomphe, he walked slowly home along the outer boulevards and sat down at his table to work. But as soon as he had the sheet of blank paper before his eyes, all the materials that he had accumulated fled from his mind as though his brain had evaporated. He tried to seize on fragments of his recollections and to retain them, but they escaped him as fast as he laid hold of them, or else they rushed on him altogether pellmell, and he did not know how to clothe and present them, nor which one to begin with.

After an hour of attempts and five sheets of paper blackened by opening phrases that had no continuation, he said to himself: "I am not yet well enough up in the business. I must have another lesson." And all at once the prospect of another morning's work with Madame Forestier, the hope of another long and intimate tête-à-tête so cordial and so pleasant, made him quiver with desire. He went to bed in a hurry, almost afraid now of setting to work again and succeeding all at once.

He did not get up the next day till somewhat late, putting off and tasting in advance the pleasure of this visit.

It was past ten when he rang his friend's bell.

The manservant replied: "Master is engaged at his work."

Duroy had not thought that the husband might be at home. He insisted, however, saying: "Tell him that I have called on a matter requiring immediate attention."

After waiting five minutes he was shown into the study in which he had passed such a pleasant morning. In the chair he had occupied Forestier was now seated writing, in a dressing-gown and slippers and with a little Scotch bonnet on his head, while his wife in the same white gown leant against the mantelpiece and dictated, cigarette in mouth.

Duroy, halting on the threshold, murmured: "I really beg your pardon; I am afraid I am disturbing you."

His friend, turning his face towards him — an angry face, too — growled: "What is it you want now? Be quick; we are pressed for time."

The intruder, taken back, stammered: "It is nothing; I beg your pardon."

But Forestier, growing angry, exclaimed: "Come, hang it all, don't waste time about it; you have not forced your way in just for the sake of wishing us good-morning, I suppose?"

Then Duroy, greatly perturbed, made up his mind. "No — you see — the fact is — I can't quite manage my article — and you were — so — so kind last time — that I hoped — that I ventured to come — "

Forestier cut him short. "You have a pretty cheek. So you think I am going to do your work, and that all you have to do is to call on the cashier at the end of the month to draw your screw? No, that is too good."

The young woman went on smoking without saying a word, smiling with a vague smile, which seemed like an amiable mask, concealing the irony of her thoughts.

Duroy, colored up, stammered: "Excuse me — I fancied — I thought — " then suddenly, and in a clear voice, he went on: "I beg your pardon a thousand times, Madame, while again thanking you most sincerely for the charming article you produced for me yesterday." He bowed, remarked to Charles: "I shall be at the office at three," and went out.

He walked home rapidly, grumbling: "Well, I will do it all alone, and they shall see — "

Scarcely had he got in than, excited by anger, he began to write. He continued the adventure began by Madame Forestier, heaping up details of catch-penny romance, surprising incidents, and inflated descriptions, with the style of a schoolboy and the phraseology of the barrack-room. Within an hour he had finished an article which was a chaos of nonsense, and took it with every assurance to the Vie Francaise.

The first person he met was Saint-Potin, who, grasping his hand with the energy of an accomplice, said: "You have read my interview with the Chinese and the Hindoo? Isn't it funny? It has amused everyone. And I did not even get a glimpse of them."

Duroy, who had not read anything, at once took up the paper and ran his eye over a long article headed: "India and China," while the reporter pointed out the most interesting passages.

Forestier came in puffing, in a hurry, with a busy air, saying:

"Good; I want both of you."

And he mentioned a number of items of political information that would have to be obtained that very afternoon.

Duroy held out his article.

"Here is the continuation about Algeria."

"Very good; hand it over; and I will give it to the governor."

That was all.

Saint-Potin led away his new colleague, and when they were in the passage, he said to him: "Have you seen the cashier?"

"No; why?"

"Why? To draw your money. You see you should always draw a month in advance. One never knows what may happen."

"But — I ask for nothing better."

"I will introduce you to the cashier. He will make no difficulty about it. They pay up well here."

Duroy went and drew his two hundred francs, with twenty-eight more for his article of the day before, which, added to what remained of his salary from the railway company, gave him three hundred and forty francs in his pocket. He had never owned such a sum, and thought himself possessed of wealth for an indefinite period.

Saint-Potin then took him to have a gossip in the offices of four or five rival papers, hoping that the news he was entrusted to obtain had already been gleaned by others, and that he should be able to draw it out of them — thanks to the flow and artfulness of his conversation.

When evening had come, Duroy, who had nothing more to do, thought of going again to the Folies Bergères, and putting a bold face on, he went up to the box office.

"I am George Duroy, on the staff of the Vie Francaise. I came here the other day with Monsieur Forestier, who promised me to see about my being put on the free list; I do not know whether he has thought of it."

The list was referred to. His name was not entered.

However, the box office-keeper, a very affable man, at once said: "Pray, go in all the same, sir, and write yourself to the manager, who, I am sure, will pay attention to your letter."

He went in and almost immediately met Rachel, the woman he had gone off with the first evening. She came up to him, saying: "Good evening, ducky. Are you quite well?"

"Very well, thanks — and you?"

"I am all right. Do you know, I have dreamed of you twice since last time?"

Duroy smiled, feeling flattered. "Ah! and what does that mean?"

"It means that you pleased me, you old dear, and that we will begin again whenever you please."

"To-day, if you like."

"Yes, I am quite willing."

"Good, but — " He hesitated, a little ashamed of what he was going to do. "The fact is that this time I have not a penny; I have just come from the club, where I have dropped everything."

She looked him full in the eyes, scenting a lie with the instinct and habit of a girl accustomed to the tricks and bargainings of men, and remarked: "Bosh! That is not a nice sort of thing to try on me."

He smiled in an embarrassed way. "If you will take ten francs, it is all I have left."

She murmured, with the disinterestedness of a courtesan gratifying a fancy: "What you please, my lady; I only want you."

And lifting her charming eyes towards the young man's moustache, she took his arm and leant lovingly upon it.

"Let us go and have a grenadine first of all," she remarked. "And then we will take a stroll together. I should like to go to the opera like this, with you, to show you off. And we will go home early, eh?"

He lay late at this girl's place. It was broad day when he left, and the notion occurred to him to buy the Vie Francaise. He opened the paper with feverish hand. His article was not there, and he stood on the footpath, anxiously running his eye down the printed columns with the hope of at length finding what he was in search of. A weight suddenly oppressed his heart, for after the fatigue of a night of love, this vexation came upon him with the weight of a disaster.

He reached home and went to sleep in his clothes on the bed.

Entering the office some hours later, he went on to see Monsieur Walter.

"I was surprised at not seeing my second article on Algeria in the paper this morning, sir," said he.

The manager raised his head, and replied in a dry tone: "I gave it to your friend Forestier, and asked him to read it through. He did not think it up to the mark; you must rewrite it."

Duroy, in a rage, went out without saying a word, and abruptly entering his old comrade's room, said:

"Why didn't you let my article go in this morning?"

The journalist was smoking a cigarette with his back almost on the seat of his armchair and his feet on the table, his heels soiling an article already commenced. He said slowly, in a bored and distant voice, as though speaking from the depths of a hole: "The governor thought it poor, and told me to give it back to you to do over again. There it is." And he pointed out the slips flattened out under a paperweight.

Duroy, abashed, could find nothing to say in reply, and as he was putting his prose into his pocket, Forestier went on: "To-day you must first of all go to the Préfecture." And he proceeded to give a list of business errands and items of news to be attended to.

Duroy went off without having been able to find the cutting remark he wanted to. He brought back his article the next day. It was returned to him again. Having rewritten it a third time, and finding it still refused, he understood that he was trying to go ahead too fast, and that Forestier's hand alone could help him on his way. He did not therefore say anything more about the "Recollections of a Chasseur d'Afrique," promising himself to be supple and cunning since it was needful, and while awaiting something better to zealously discharge his duties as a reporter.

He learned to know the way behind the scenes in theatrical and political life; the waiting-rooms of statesmen and the lobby of the Chamber of Deputies; the important countenances of permanent secretaries, and the grim looks of sleepy ushers. He had continual relations with ministers, doorkeepers, generals, police agents, princes, bullies, courtesans, ambassadors, bishops, panders, adventurers, men of fashion, card-sharpers, cab drivers, waiters, and many others, having become the interested yet indifferent friend of all these; confounding them together in his estimation, measuring them with the same measure, judging them with the same eye, though having to see them every day at every hour, without any transition, and to speak with them all on the same business of his own. He compared himself to a man who had to drink off samples of every kind of wine one after the other, and who would soon be unable to tell Château Margaux from Argenteuil.

He became in a short time a remarkable reporter, certain of his information, artful, swift, subtle, a real find for the paper, as was observed by Daddy Walter, who knew what newspaper men were. However, as he got only centimes a line in addition to his monthly screw of two hundred francs, and as life on the boulevards and in cafés and restaurants is costly, he never had a halfpenny, and was disgusted with his poverty. There is some knack to be got hold of, he thought, seeing some of his fellows with their pockets full of money without ever being able to understand what secret methods they could make use of to procure this abundance. He enviously suspected unknown and suspicious transactions, services rendered, a whole system of contraband accepted and agreed to. But it was necessary that he should penetrate the mystery, enter into the tacit partnership, make himself one with the comrades who were sharing without him.

And he often thought of an evening, as he watched the trains go by from his window, of the steps he ought to take.

V

Two months had gone by, September was at hand, and the rapid fortune which Duroy had hoped for seemed to him slow in coming. He was, above all, uneasy at the mediocrity of his position, and did not see by what path he could scale the heights on the summit of which one finds respect, power, and money. He felt shut up in the mediocre calling of a reporter, so walled in as to be unable to get out of it. He was appreciated, but estimated in accordance with his position. Even Forestier, to whom he rendered a thousand services, no longer invited him to dinner, and treated him in every way as an inferior, though still accosting him as a friend.

From time to time, it is true, Duroy, seizing an opportunity, got in a short article, and having acquired through his paragraphs a mastery over his pen, and a tact which was lacking to him when he wrote his second article on Algeria, no longer ran any risk of having his descriptive efforts refused. But from this to writing leaders according to his fancy, or dealing with political questions with authority, there was as great a difference as driving in the Bois de Boulogne as a coachman, and as the owner of an equipage. That which humiliated him above everything was to see the door of society closed to him, to have no equal relations with it, not to be able to penetrate into the intimacy of its women, although several well-known actresses had occasionally received him with an interested familiarity.

He knew, moreover, from experience that all the sex, ladies or actresses, felt a singular attraction towards him, an instantaneous sympathy, and he experienced the impatience of a hobbled horse at not knowing those whom his future may depend on.

He had often thought of calling on Madame Forestier, but the recollection of their last meeting checked and humiliated him; and besides, he was awaiting an invitation to do so from her husband. Then the recollection of Madame de Marelle occurred to him, and recalling that she had asked him to come and see her, he called one afternoon when he had nothing to do.

"I am always at home till three o'clock," she had said.

He rang at the bell of her residence, a fourth floor in the Rue de Verneuil, at halfpast two.

At the sound of the bell a servant opened the door, an untidy girl, who tied her cap strings as she replied: "Yes, Madame is at home, but I don't know whether she is up."

And she pushed open the drawingroom door, which was ajar. Duroy went in. The room was fairly large, scantily furnished and neglected looking. The chairs, worn and old, were arranged along the walls, as placed by the servant, for there was nothing to reveal the tasty care of the woman who loves her home. Four indifferent pictures, representing a boat on a stream, a ship at sea, a mill on a plain, and a woodcutter in a wood, hung in the center of the four walls by cords of unequal length, and all four on one side. It could be divined that they had been dangling thus askew ever so long before indifferent eyes.

Duroy sat down immediately. He waited a long time. Then a door opened, and Madame de Marelle hastened in, wearing a Japanese morning gown of rose-colored silk embroidered with yellow landscapes, blue flowers, and white birds.

"Fancy! I was still in bed!" she exclaimed. "How good of you to come and see me! I had made up my mind that you had forgotten me."

She held out both her hands with a delighted air, and Duroy, whom the commonplace appearance of the room had put at his ease, kissed one, as he had seen Norbert de Varenne do.

She begged him to sit down, and then scanning him from head to foot, said: "How you have altered! You have improved in looks. Paris has done you good. Come, tell me the news."

And they began to gossip at once, as if they had been old acquaintances, feeling an instantaneous familiarity spring up between them; feeling one of those mutual currents of confidence, intimacy, and affection, which, in five minutes, make two beings of the same breed and character good friends.

Suddenly, Madame de Marelle exclaimed in astonishment: "It is funny how I get on with you. It seems to me as though I had known you for ten years. We shall become good friends, no doubt. Would you like it?"

He answered: "Certainly," with a smile which said still more.

He thought her very tempting in her soft and bright-hued gown, less refined and delicate than the other in her white one, but more exciting and spicy. When he was beside Madame Forestier, with her continual and gracious smile which attracted and checked at the same time; which seemed to say: "You please me," and also "Take care," and of which the real meaning was never clear, he felt above all the wish to lie down at her feet, or to kiss the lace bordering of her bodice, and slowly inhale the warm and perfumed atmosphere that must issue from it. With Madame de Marelle he felt within him a more definite, a more brutal desire — a desire that made his fingers quiver in presence of the rounded outlines of the light silk.

She went on talking, scattering in each phrase that ready wit of which she had acquired the habit just as a workman acquires the knack needed to accomplish a task reputed difficult, and at which other folk are astonished. He listened, thinking: "All this is worth remembering. A man could write charming articles of Paris gossip by getting her to chat over the events of the day."

Some one tapped softly, very softly, at the door by which she had entered, and she called out: "You can come in, pet."

Her little girl made her appearance, walked straight up to Duroy, and held out her hand to him. The astonished mother murmured: "But this is a complete conquest. I no longer recognize her."

The young fellow, having kissed the child, made her sit down beside him, and with a serious manner asked her pleasant questions as to what she had been doing since they last met. She replied, in her little flute-like voice, with her grave and grown-up air.

The clock struck three, and the journalist arose.

"Come often," said Madame de Marelle, "and we will chat as we have done to-day; it will always give me pleasure. But how is it one no longer sees you at the Forestiers?" He replied: "Oh! for no reason. I have been very busy. I hope to meet you there again one of these days."

He went out, his heart full of hope, though without knowing why.

He did not speak to Forestier of this visit. But he retained the recollection of it the following days, and more than the recollection — a sensation of the unreal yet persistent presence of this woman. It seemed to him that he had carried away something of her, the reflection of her form in his eyes, and the smack of her moral self in his heart. He remained under the haunted influence of her image, as it happens sometimes when we have passed pleasant hours with some one.

He paid a second visit a few days later.

The maid ushered him into the drawingroom, and Laurine at once appeared. She held out no longer her hand, but her forehead, and said: "Mamma has told me to request you to wait for her. She will be a quarter-of-an-hour, because she is not dressed yet. I will keep you company."

Duroy, who was amused by the ceremonious manners of the little girl, replied: "Certainly, Mademoiselle. I shall be delighted to pass a quarter-of-an-hour with you, but I warn you that for my part I am not at all serious, and that I play all day long, so I suggest a game at touch."

The girl was astonished; then she smiled as a woman would have done at this idea, which shocked her a little as well as astonished her, and murmured: "Rooms are not meant to be played in."

He said: "It is all the same to me. I play everywhere. Come, catch me."

And he began to go round the table, exciting her to pursue him, while she came after him, smiling with a species of polite condescension, and sometimes extending her hand to touch him, but without ever giving way so far as to run. He stopped, stooped down, and when she drew near with her little hesitating steps, sprung up in the air like a jack-in-the-box, and then bounded with a single stride to the other end of the diningroom. She thought it funny, ended by laughing, and becoming aroused, began to trot after him, giving little gleeful yet timid cries when she thought she had him. He shifted the chairs and used them as obstacles, forcing her to go round and round one of them for a minute at a time, and then leaving that one to seize upon another. Laurine ran now, giving herself wholly up to the charm of this new game, and with flushed face, rushed forward with the bound of a delighted child at each of the flights, the tricks, the feints of her companion. Suddenly, just as she thought she had got him, he seized her in his arms, and lifting her to the ceiling, exclaimed: "Touch."

The delighted girl wriggled her legs to escape, and laughed with all her heart.

Madame de Marelle came in at that moment, and was amazed. "What, Laurine, Laurine, playing! You are a sorcerer, sir."

He put down the little girl, kissed her mother's hand, and they sat down with the child between them. They began to chat, but Laurine, usually so silent, kept talking all the while, and had to be sent to her room. She obeyed without a word, but with tears in her eyes.

As soon as they were alone, Madame de Marelle lowered her voice. "You do not know, but I have a grand scheme, and I have thought of you. This is it. As I dine every week at the Forestiers, I return their hospitality from time to time at some restaurant. I do not like to entertain company at home, my household is not arranged for that, and besides, I do not understand anything about domestic affairs, anything about the kitchen, anything at all. I like to live anyhow. So I entertain them now and then at a restaurant, but it is not very lively when there are only three, and my own acquaintances scarcely go well with them. I tell you all this in order to explain a somewhat irregular invitation. You understand, do you not, that I want you to make one of us on Saturday at the Café Riche, at halfpast seven. You know the place?"

He accepted with pleasure, and she went on: "There will be only us four. These little outings are very amusing to us women who are not accustomed to them."

She was wearing a dark brown dress, which showed off the lines of her waist, her hips, her bosom, and her arm in a coquettishly provocative way. Duroy felt confusedly astonished at the lack of harmony between this carefully refined elegance and her evident carelessness as regarded her dwelling. All that clothed her body, all that closely and directly touched her flesh was fine and delicate, but that which surrounded her did not matter to her.

He left her, retaining, as before, the sense of her continued presence in species of hallucination of the senses. And he awaited the day of the dinner with growing impatience.

Having hired, for the second time, a dress suit — his funds not yet allowing him to buy one — he arrived first at the rendezvous, a few minutes before the time. He was ushered up to the second story, and into a small private diningroom hung with red and white, its single window opening into the boulevard. A square table, laid for four, displaying its white cloth, so shining that it seemed to be varnished, and the glasses and the silver glittered brightly in the light of the twelve candles of two tall candelabra. Without was a broad patch of light green, due to the leaves of a tree lit up by the bright light from the diningrooms.

Duroy sat down in a low armchair, upholstered in red to match the hangings on the walls. The worn springs yielding beneath him caused him to feel as though sinking into a hole. He heard throughout the huge house a confused murmur, the murmur of a large restaurant, made up of the clattering of glass and silver, the hurried steps of the waiters, deadened by the carpets in the passages, and the opening of doors letting out the sound of voices from the numerous private rooms in which people were dining. Forestier came in and shook hands with him, with a cordial familiarity which he never displayed at the offices of the Vie Francaise.

"The ladies are coming together," said he; "these little dinners are very pleasant."

Then he glanced at the table, turned a gas jet that was feebly burning completely off, closed one sash of the window on account of the draught, and chose a sheltered place for himself, with a remark: "I must be careful; I have been better for a month, and now I am queer again these last few days. I must have caught cold on Tuesday, coming out of the theater."

The door was opened, and, followed by a waiter, the two ladies appeared, veiled, muffled, reserved, with that charmingly mysterious bearing they assume in such places, where the surroundings are suspicious.

As Duroy bowed to Madame Forestier she scolded him for not having come to see her again; then she added with a smile, in the direction of her friend: "I know what it is; you prefer Madame de Marelle, you can find time to visit her."

They sat down to table, and the waiter having handed the wine card to Forestier, Madame de Marelle exclaimed: "Give these gentlemen whatever they like, but for us iced champagne, the best, sweet champagne, mind — nothing else." And the man having withdrawn, she added with an excited laugh: "I am going to get tipsy this evening; we will have a spree — a regular spree."

Forestier, who did not seem to have heard, said: "Would you mind the window being closed? My chest has been rather queer the last few days."

"No, not at all."

He pushed too the sash left open, and returned to his place with a reassured and tranquil countenance. His wife said nothing. Seemingly lost in thought, and with her eyes lowered towards the table, she smiled at the glasses with that vague smile which seemed always to promise and never to grant.

The Ostend oysters were brought in, tiny and plump like little ears enclosed in shells, and melting between the tongue and the palate like salt bonbons. Then, after the soup, was served a trout as rose-tinted as a young girl, and the guests began to talk.

They spoke at first of a current scandal; the story of a lady of position, surprised by one of her husband's friends supping in a private room with a foreign prince. Forestier laughed a great deal at the adventure; the two ladies declared that the indiscreet gossip was nothing less than a blackguard and a coward. Duroy was of their opinion, and loudly proclaimed that it is the duty of a man in these matters, whether he be actor, confidant, or simple spectator, to be silent as the grave. He added: "How full life would be of pleasant things if we could reckon upon the absolute discretion of one another. That which often, almost always, checks women is the fear of the secret being revealed. Come, is it not true?" he continued. "How many are there who would yield to a sudden desire, the caprice of an hour, a passing fancy, did they not fear to pay for a short-lived and fleeting pleasure by an irremediable scandal and painful tears?"

He spoke with catching conviction, as though pleading a cause, his own cause, as though he had said: "It is not with me that one would have to dread such dangers. Try me and see."

They both looked at him approvingly, holding that he spoke rightly and justly, confessing by their friendly silence that their flexible morality as Parisians would not have held out long before the certainty of secrecy. And Forestier, leaning back in his place on the divan, one leg bent under him, and his napkin thrust into his waistcoat, suddenly said with the satisfied laugh of a skeptic: "The deuce! yes, they would all go in for it if they were certain of silence. Poor husbands!"

And they began to talk of love. Without admitting it to be eternal, Duroy understood it as lasting, creating a bond, a tender friendship, a confidence. The union of the senses was only a seal to the union of hearts. But he was angry at the outrageous jealousies, melodramatic scenes, and unpleasantness which almost always accompany ruptures.

When he ceased speaking, Madame de Marelle replied: "Yes, it is the only pleasant thing in life, and we often spoil it by preposterous unreasonableness."

Madame Forestier, who was toying with her knife, added: "Yes — yes — it is pleasant to be loved."

And she seemed to be carrying her dream further, to be thinking things that she dared not give words to.

As the first entreé was slow in coming, they sipped from time to time a mouthful of champagne, and nibbled bits of crust. And the idea of love, entering into them, slowly intoxicated their souls, as the bright wine, rolling drop by drop down their throats, fired their blood and perturbed their minds.

The waiter brought in some lamb cutlets, delicate and tender, upon a thick bed of asparagus tips.

"Ah! this is good," exclaimed Forestier; and they ate slowly, savoring the delicate meat and vegetables as smooth as cream.

Duroy resumed: "For my part, when I love a woman everything else in the world disappears." He said this in a tone of conviction.

Madame Forestier murmured, with her let-me-alone air:

"There is no happiness comparable to that of the first hand-clasp, when the one asks, 'Do you love me?' and the other replies, 'Yes.'"

Madame de Marelle, who had just tossed a fresh glass of champagne off at a draught, said gayly, as she put down her glass: "For my part, I am not so Platonic."

And all began to smile with kindling eyes at these words.

Forestier, stretched out in his seat on the divan, opened his arms, rested them on the cushions, and said in a serious tone: "This frankness does you honor, and proves that you are a practical woman. But may one ask you what is the opinion of Monsieur de Marelle?"

She shrugged her shoulders slightly, with infinite and prolonged disdain; and then in a decided tone remarked: "Monsieur de Marelle has no opinions on this point. He only has — abstentions."

And the conversation, descending from the elevated theories, concerning love, strayed into the flowery garden of polished blackguardism. It was the moment of clever double meanings; veils raised by words, as petticoats are lifted by the wind; tricks of language; clever disguised audacities; sentences which reveal nude images in covered phrases; which cause the vision of all that may not be said to flit rapidly before the eye and the mind, and allow the well-bred people the enjoyment of a kind of subtle and mysterious love, a species of impure mental contact, due to the simultaneous evocation of secret, shameful, and longed-for pleasures. The roast, consisting of partridges flanked by quails, had been served; then a dish of green peas, and then a terrine of foie gras, accompanied by a curly-leaved salad, filling a salad bowl as though with green foam. They had partaken of all these things without tasting them, without knowing, solely taken up by what they were talking of, plunged as it were in a bath of love.

The two ladies were now going it strongly in their remarks. Madame de Marelle, with a native audacity which resembled a direct provocation, and Madame Forestier with a charming reserve, a modesty in her tone, voice, smile, and bearing that underlined while seeming to soften the bold remarks falling from her lips. Forestier, leaning quite back on the cushions, laughed, drank and ate without leaving off, and sometimes threw in a word so risque or so crude that the ladies, somewhat shocked by its appearance, and for appearance sake, put on a little air of embarrassment that lasted two or three seconds. When he had given vent to something a little too coarse, he added: "You are going ahead nicely, my children. If you go on like that you will end by making fools of yourselves."

Dessert came, and then coffee; and the liquors poured a yet warmer dose of commotion into the excited minds.

As she had announced on sitting down to table, Madame de Marelle was intoxicated, and acknowledged it in the lively and graceful rabble of a woman emphasizing, in order to amuse her guests, a very real commencement of drunkenness.

Madame Forestier was silent now, perhaps out of prudence, and Duroy, feeling himself too much excited not to be in danger of compromising himself, maintained a prudent reserve.

Cigarettes were lit, and all at once Forestier began to cough. It was a terrible fit, that seemed to tear his chest, and with red face and forehead damp with perspiration, he choked behind his napkin. When the fit was over he growled angrily: "These feeds are very bad for me; they are ridiculous." All his good humor had vanished before his terror of the illness that haunted his thoughts. "Let us go home," said he.

Madame de Marelle rang for the waiter, and asked for the bill. It was brought almost immediately. She tried to read it, but the figures danced before her eyes, and she passed it to Duroy, saying: "Here, pay for me; I can't see, I am too tipsy."

And at the same time she threw him her purse. The bill amounted to one hundred and thirty francs. Duroy checked it, and then handed over two notes and received back the change, saying in a low tone: "What shall I give the waiter?"

"What you like; I do not know."

He put five francs on the salver, and handed back the purse, saying: "Shall I see you to your door?"

"Certainly. I am incapable of finding my way home."

They shook hands with the Forestiers, and Duroy found himself alone with Madame de Marelle in a cab. He felt her close to him, so close, in this dark box, suddenly lit up for a moment by the lamps on the sidewalk. He felt through his sleeve the warmth of her shoulder, and he could find nothing to say to her, absolutely nothing, his mind being paralyzed by the imperative desire to seize her in his arms.

"If I dared to, what would she do?" he thought. The recollection of all the things uttered during dinner emboldened him, but the fear of scandal restrained him at the same time.

Nor did she say anything either, but remained motionless in her corner. He would have thought that she was asleep if he had not seen her eyes glitter every time that a ray of light entered the carriage.

"What was she thinking?" He felt that he must not speak, that a word, a single word, breaking this silence would destroy his chance; yet courage failed him, the courage needed for abrupt and brutal action. All at once he felt her foot move. She had made a movement, a quick, nervous movement of impatience, perhaps of appeal. This almost imperceptible gesture caused a thrill to run through him from head to foot, and he threw himself upon her, seeking her mouth with his lips, her form with his hands.

But the cab having shortly stopped before the house in which she resided, Duroy, surprised, had no time to seek passionate phrases to thank her, and express his grateful love. However, stunned by what had taken place, she did not rise, she did not stir. Then he was afraid that the driver might suspect something, and got out first to help her to alight.

At length she got out of the cab, staggering and without saying a word. He rang the bell, and as the door opened, said, tremblingly: "When shall I see you again?"

She murmured so softly that he scarcely heard it: "Come and lunch with me tomorrow." And she disappeared in the entry, pushed to the heavy door, which closed with a noise like that of a cannon. He gave the driver five francs, and began to walk along with rapid and triumphant steps, and heart overflowing with joy.

He had won at last — a married woman, a lady. How easy and unexpected it had all been. He had fancied up till then that to assail and conquer one of these so greatly longed-for beings, infinite pains, interminable expectations, a skillful siege carried on by means of gallant attentions, words of love, sighs, and gifts were needed. And, lo! suddenly, at the faintest attack, the first whom he had encountered had yielded to him so quickly that he was stupefied at it.

"She was tipsy," he thought; "tomorrow it will be another story. She will meet me with tears." This notion disturbed him, but he added: "Well, so much the worse. Now I have her, I mean to keep her."

He was somewhat agitated the next day as he ascended Madame de Marelle's staircase. How would she receive him? And suppose she would not receive him at all? Suppose she had forbidden them to admit him? Suppose she had said — but, no, she could not have said anything without letting the whole truth be guessed. So he was master of the situation.

The little servant opened the door. She wore her usual expression. He felt reassured, as if he had anticipated her displaying a troubled countenance, and asked: "Is your mistress quite well?"

She replied: "Oh! yes, sir, the same as usual," and showed him into the drawingroom.

He went straight to the chimney-glass to ascertain the state of his hair and his toilet, and was arranging his necktie before it, when he saw in it the young woman watching him as she stood at the door leading from her room. He pretended not to have noticed her, and the pair looked at one another for a few moments in the glass, observing and watching before finding themselves face to face. He turned round. She had not moved, and seemed to be waiting. He darted forward, stammering: "My darling! my darling!"

She opened her arms and fell upon his breast; then having lifted her head towards him, their lips met in a long kiss.

He thought: "It is easier than I should have imagined. It is all going on very well."

And their lips separating, he smiled without saying a word, while striving to throw a world of love into his looks. She, too, smiled, with that smile by which women show their desire, their consent, their wish to yield themselves, and murmured: "We are alone. I have sent Laurine to lunch with one of her young friends."

He sighed as he kissed her. "Thanks, I will worship you."

Then she took his arm, as if he had been her husband, to go to the sofa, on which they sat down side by side. He wanted to start a clever and attractive chat, but not being able to do so to his liking, stammered: "Then you are not too angry with me?"

She put her hand on his mouth, saying "Be quiet."

They sat in silence, looking into one another's eyes, with burning fingers interlaced.

"How I did long for you!" said he.

She repeated: "Be quiet."

They heard the servant arranging the table in the adjoining diningroom, and he rose, saying: "I must not remain so close to you. I shall lose my head."

The door opened, and the servant announced that lunch was ready. Duroy gravely offered his arm.

They lunched face to face, looking at one another and constantly smiling, solely taken up by themselves, and enveloped in the sweet enchantment of a growing love. They ate, without knowing what. He felt a foot, a little foot, straying under the table. He took it between his own and kept it there, squeezing it with all his might. The servant came and went, bringing and taking away the dishes with a careless air, without seeming to notice anything.

When they had finished they returned to the drawingroom, and resumed their place on the sofa, side by side. Little by little he pressed up against her, striving to take her in his arms. But she calmly repulsed him, saying: "Take care; someone may come in."

He murmured: "When can I see you quite alone, to tell you how I love you?"

She leant over towards him and whispered: "I will come and pay you a visit one of these days."

He felt himself redden. "You know — you know — my place is very small."

She smiled: "That does not matter. It is you I shall call to see, and not your rooms."

Then he pressed her to know when she would come. She named a day in the latter half of the week. He begged of her to advance the date in broken sentences, playing with and squeezing her hands, with glittering eyes, and flushed face, heated and torn by desire, that imperious desire which follows tête-à-tête repasts. She was amazed to see him implore her with such ardor, and yielded a day from time to time. But he kept repeating: "Tomorrow, only say tomorrow."

She consented at length. "Yes, tomorrow; at five o'clock."

He gave a long sigh of joy, and they then chatted almost quietly with an air of intimacy, as though they had known one another twenty years. The sound of the door bell made them start, and with a bound they separated to a distance. She murmured: "It must be Laurine."

The child made her appearance, stopped short in amazement, and then ran to Duroy, clapping her hands with pleasure at seeing him, and exclaiming: "Ah! pretty boy."

Madame de Marelle began to laugh. "What! Pretty boy! Laurine has baptized you. It's a nice little nickname for you, and I will call you Pretty-boy, too."

He had taken the little girl on his knee, and he had to play with her at all the games he had taught her. He rose to take his leave at twenty minutes to three to go to the office of the paper, and on the staircase, through the half-closed door, he still whispered: "Tomorrow, at five."

She answered "Yes," with a smile, and disappeared.

As soon as he had got through his day's work, he speculated how he should arrange his room to receive his mistress, and hide as far as possible the poverty of the place. He was struck by the idea of pinning a lot of Japanese trifles on the walls, and he bought for five francs quite a collection of little fans and screens, with which he hid the most obvious of the marks on the wall paper. He pasted on the window panes transparent pictures representing boats floating down rivers, flocks of birds flying across rosy skies, multicolored ladies on balconies, and processions of little black men over plains covered with snow. His room, just big enough to sleep and sit down in, soon looked like the inside of a Chinese lantern. He thought the effect satisfactory, and passed the evening in pasting on the ceiling birds that he had cut from the colored sheets remaining over. Then he went to bed, lulled by the whistle of the trains.

He went home early the next day, carrying a paper bag of cakes and a bottle of Madeira, purchased at the grocer's. He had to go out again to buy two plates and two glasses, and arranged this collation on his dressing-table, the dirty wood of which was covered by a napkin, the jug and basin being hidden away beneath it.

Then he waited.

She came at about a quarter-past five; and, attracted by the bright colors of the pictures, exclaimed: "Dear me, yours is a nice place. But there are a lot of people about on the staircase."

He had clasped her in his arms, and was eagerly kissing the hair between her forehead and her bonnet through her veil.

An hour and a half later he escorted her back to the cab-stand in the Rue de Rome. When she was in the carriage he murmured: "Tuesday at the same time?"

She replied: "Tuesday at the same time." And as it had grown dark, she drew his head into the carriage and kissed him on the lips. Then the driver, having whipped up his beast, she exclaimed: "Goodbye, Pretty-boy," and the old vehicle started at the weary trot of its old white horse.

For three weeks Duroy received Madame de Marelle in this way every two or three days, now in the evening and now in the morning. While he was expecting her one afternoon, a loud uproar on the stairs drew him to the door. A child was crying. A man's angry voice shouted: "What is that little devil howling about now?" The yelling and exasperated voice of a woman replied: "It is that dirty hussy who comes to see the penny-a-liner upstairs; she has upset Nicholas on the landing. As if dabs like that, who pay no attention to children on the staircase, should be allowed here."

Duroy drew back, distracted, for he could hear the rapid rustling of skirts and a hurried step ascending from the story just beneath him. There was soon a knock at the door, which he had reclosed. He opened it, and Madame de Marelle rushed into the room, terrified and breathless, stammering: "Did you hear?"

He pretended to know nothing. "No; what?"

"How they have insulted me."

"Who? Who?"

"The blackguards who live down below."

"But, surely not; what does it all mean, tell me?"

She began to sob, without being able to utter a word. He had to take off her bonnet, undo her dress, lay her on the bed, moisten her forehead with a wet towel. She was choking, and then when her emotion was somewhat abated, all her wrathful indignation broke out. She wanted him to go down at once, to thrash them, to kill them.

He repeated: "But they are only workpeople, low creatures. Just remember that it would lead to a police court, that you might be recognized, arrested, ruined. One cannot lower one's self to have anything to do with such people."

She passed on to another idea. "What shall we do now? For my part, I cannot come here again."

He replied: "It is very simple; I will move."

She murmured: "Yes, but that will take some time." Then all at once she framed a plan, and reassured, added softly: "No, listen, I know what to do; let me act, do not trouble yourself about anything. I will send you a telegram tomorrow morning."

She smiled now, delighted with her plan, which she would not reveal, and indulged in a thousand follies. She was very agitated, however, as she went downstairs, leaning with all her weight on her lover's arm, her legs trembled so beneath her. They did not meet anyone, though.

As he usually got up late, he was still in bed the next day, when, about eleven o'clock, the telegraph messenger brought him the promised telegram. He opened it and read:

"Meet me at five; 127, Rue de Constantinople. Rooms hired by Madame Duroy. — Clo."

At five o'clock to the minute he entered the doorkeeper's lodge of a large furnished house, and asked: "It is here that Madame Duroy has taken rooms, is it not?"

"Yes, sir."

"Will you show me to them, if you please."

The man, doubtless used to delicate situations in which prudence is necessary, looked him straight in the eyes, and then, selecting one of the long range of keys, said: "You are Monsieur Duroy?"

"Yes, certainly."

The man opened the door of a small suite of rooms on the ground floor in front of the lodge. The sitting-room, with a tolerably fresh wall-paper of floral design, and a carpet so thin that the boards of the floor could be felt through it, had mahogany furniture, upholstered in green rep with a yellow pattern. The bedroom was so small that the bed three-parts filled it. It occupied the further end, stretching from one wall to the other — the large bed of a furnished lodging-house, shrouded in heavy blue curtains also of rep, and covered with an eiderdown quilt of red silk stained with suspicious-looking spots.

Duroy, uneasy and displeased, thought: "This place will cost, Lord knows how much. I shall have to borrow again. It is idiotic what she has done."

The door opened, and Clotilde came in like a whirlwind, with outstretched arms and rustling skirts. She was delighted. "Isn't it nice, eh, isn't it nice? And on the ground floor, too; no stairs to go up. One could get in and out of the windows without the doorkeeper seeing one. How we will love one another here!"

He kissed her coldly, not daring to put the question that rose to his lips. She had placed a large parcel on the little round table in the middle of the room. She opened it, and took out a cake of soap, a bottle of scent, a sponge, a box of hairpins, a buttonhook, and a small pair of curling tongs to set right her fringe, which she got out of curl every time. And she played at moving in, seeking a place for everything, and derived great amusement from it.

She kept on chattering as she opened the drawers. "I must bring a little linen, so as to be able to make a change if necessary. It will be very convenient. If I get wet, for instance, while I am out, I can run in here to dry myself. We shall each have one key, beside the one left with the doorkeeper in case we forget it. I have taken the place for three months, in your name, of course, since I could not give my own."

Then he said: "You will let me know when the rent is to be paid."

She replied, simply: "But it is paid, dear."

"Then I owe it to you."

"No, no, my dear; it does not concern you at all; this is a little fancy of my own."

He seemed annoyed: "Oh, no, indeed; I can't allow that."

She came to him in a supplicating way, and placing her hands on his shoulders, said: "I beg of you, George; it will give me so much pleasure to feel that our little nest here is mine — all my own. You cannot be annoyed at that. How can you? I wanted to contribute that much towards our loves. Say you agree, Georgy; say you agree."

She implored him with looks, lips, the whole of her being. He held out, refusing with an irritated air, and then he yielded, thinking that, after all, it was fair. And when she had gone, he murmured, rubbing his hands, and without seeking in the depths of his heart whence the opinion came on that occasion: "She is very nice."

He received, a few days later, another telegram running thus: "My husband returns tonight, after six weeks' inspection, so we shall have a week off. What a bore, darling. — Clo."

Duroy felt astounded. He had really lost all idea of her being married. But here was a man whose face he would have liked to see just once, in order to know him. He patiently awaited the husband's departure, but he passed two evenings at the Folies Bergère, which wound up with Rachel.

Then one morning came a fresh telegram: "To-day at five. — Clo."

They both arrived at the meeting-place before the time. She threw herself into his arms with an outburst of passion, and kissed him all over the face, and then said: "If you like, when we have loved one another a great deal, you shall take me to dinner somewhere. I have kept myself disengaged."

It was at the beginning of the month, and although his salary was long since drawn in advance, and he lived from day to day upon money gleaned on every side, Duroy happened to be in funds, and was pleased at the opportunity of spending something upon her, so he replied: "Yes, darling, wherever you like."

They started off, therefore, at about seven, and gained the outer boulevards. She leaned closely against him, and whispered in his ear: "If you only knew how pleased I am to walk out on your arm; how I love to feel you beside me."

He said: "Would you like to go to Père Lathuile's?"

"Oh, no, it is too swell. I should like something funny, out of the way! a restaurant that shopmen and work-girls go to. I adore dining at a country inn. Oh! if we only had been able to go into the country."

As he knew nothing of the kind in the neighborhood, they wandered along the boulevard, and ended by going into a wine-shop where there was a diningroom. She had seen through the window two bareheaded girls seated at tables with two soldiers. Three cabdrivers were dining at the further end of the long and narrow room, and an individual impossible to classify under any calling was smoking, stretched on a chair, with his legs stuck out in front of him, his hands in the waistband of his trousers, and his head thrown back over the top bar. His jacket was a museum of stains, and in his swollen pockets could be noted the neck of a bottle, a piece of bread, a parcel wrapped up in a newspaper, and a dangling piece of string. He had thick, tangled, curly hair, gray with scurf, and his cap was on the floor under his chair.

The entrance of Clotilde created a sensation, due to the elegance of her toilet. The couples ceased whispering together, the three cabdrivers left off arguing, and the man who was smoking, having taken his pipe from his mouth and spat in front of him, turned his head slightly to look.

Madame de Marelle murmured: "It is very nice; we shall be very comfortable here. Another time I will dress like a work-girl." And she sat down, without embarrassment or disgust, before the wooden table, polished by the fat of dishes, washed by spilt liquors, and cleaned by a wisp of the waiter's napkin. Duroy, somewhat ill at ease, and slightly ashamed, sought a peg to hang his tall hat on. Not finding one, he put it on a chair.

They had a ragout, a slice of melon, and a salad. Clotilde repeated: "I delight in this. I have low tastes. I like this better than the Café Anglais." Then she added: "If you want to give me complete enjoyment, you will take me to a dancing place. I know a very funny one close by called the Reine Blanche."

Duroy, surprised at this, asked: "Whoever took you there?"

He looked at her and saw her blush, somewhat disturbed, as though this sudden question had aroused within her some delicate recollections. After one of these feminine hesitations, so short that they can scarcely be guessed, she replied: "A friend of mine," and then, after a brief silence, added, "who is dead." And she cast down her eyes with a very natural sadness.

Duroy, for the first time, thought of all that he did not know as regarded the past life of this woman. Certainly she already had lovers, but of what kind, in what class of society? A vague jealousy, a species of enmity awoke within him; an enmity against all that he did not know, all that had not belonged to him. He looked at her, irritated at the mystery wrapped up within that pretty, silent head, which was thinking, perhaps, at that very moment, of the other, the others, regretfully. How he would have liked to have looked into her recollections — to have known all.

She repeated: "Will you take me to the Reine Blanche? That will be a perfect treat."

He thought: "What matters the past? I am very foolish to bother about it," and smilingly replied: "Certainly, darling."

When they were in the street she resumed, in that low and mysterious tone in which confidences are made: "I dared not ask you this until now, but you cannot imagine how I love these escapades in places ladies do not go to. During the carnival I will dress up as a schoolboy. I make such a capital boy."

When they entered the ballroom she clung close to him, gazing with delighted eyes on the girls and the bullies, and from time to time, as though to reassure herself as regards any possible danger, saying, as she noticed some serious and motionless municipal guard: "That is a strong-looking fellow." In a quarter of an hour she had had enough of it and he escorted her home.

Then began quite a series of excursions in all the queer places where the common people amuse themselves, and Duroy discovered in his mistress quite a liking for this vagabondage of students bent on a spree. She came to their meeting-place in a cotton frock and with a servant's cap — a theatrical servant's cap — on her head; and despite the elegant and studied simplicity of her toilet, retained her rings, her bracelets, and her diamond earrings, saying, when he begged her to remove them: "Bah! they will think they are paste."

She thought she was admirably disguised, and although she was really only concealed after the fashion of an ostrich, she went into the most ill-famed drinking places. She wanted Duroy to dress himself like a workman, but he resisted, and retained his correct attire, without even consenting to exchange his tall hat for one of soft felt. She was consoled for this obstinacy on his part by the reflection that she would be taken for a chambermaid engaged in a love affair with a gentleman, and thought this delightful. In this guise they went into popular wine-shops, and sat down on rickety chairs at old wooden tables in smoke-filled rooms. A cloud of strong tobacco smoke, with which still blended the smell of fish fried at dinner time, filled the room; men in blouses shouted at one another as they tossed off nips of spirits; and the astonished waiter would stare at this strange couple as he placed before them two cherry brandies. She — trembling, fearsome, yet charmed — began to sip the red liquid, looking round her with uneasy and kindling eye. Each cherry swallowed gave her the sensation of a sin committed, each drop of burning liquor flowing down her throat gave her the pleasure of a naughty and forbidden joy.

Then she would say, "Let us go," and they would leave. She would pass rapidly, with bent head and the short steps of an actress leaving the stage, among the drinkers, who, with their elbows on the tables, watched her go by with suspicious and dissatisfied glances; and when she had crossed the threshold would give a deep sigh, as if she had just escaped some terrible danger.

Sometimes she asked Duroy, with a shudder: "If I were insulted in these places, what would you do?"

He would answer, with a swaggering air: "Take your part, by Jove!"

And she would clasp his arm with happiness, with, perhaps, a vague wish to be insulted and defended, to see men fight on her account, even such men as those, with her lover.

But these excursions taking place two or three times a week began to weary Duroy, who had great difficulty, besides, for some time past, in procuring the ten francs necessary for the cake and the drinks. He now lived very hardly and with more difficulty than when he was a clerk in the Northern Railway; for having spent lavishly during his first month of journalism, in the constant hope of gaining large sums of money in a day or two, he had exhausted all his resources and all means of procuring money. A very simple method, that of borrowing from the cashier, was very soon exhausted; and he already owed the paper four months' salary, besides six hundred francs advanced on his lineage account. He owed, besides, a hundred francs to Forestier, three hundred to Jacques Rival, who was free-handed with his money; and he was also eaten up by a number of small debts of from five francs to twenty. Saint-Potin, consulted as to the means of raising another hundred francs, had discovered no expedient, although a man of inventive mind, and Duroy was exasperated at this poverty, of which he was more sensible now than formerly, since he had more wants. A sullen rage against everyone smouldered within him, with an ever-increasing irritation, which manifested itself at every moment on the most futile pretexts. He sometimes asked himself how he could have spent an average of a thousand francs a month, without any excess and the gratification of any extravagant fancy, and he found that, by adding a lunch at eight francs to a dinner at twelve, partaken of in some large café on the boulevards, he at once came to a louis, which, added to ten francs pocket-money — that pocket-money that melts away, one does not know how — makes a total of thirty francs. But thirty francs a day is nine hundred francs at the end of the month. And he did not reckon in the cost of clothes, boots, linen, washing, *etc.*

So on the 14th December he found himself without a sou in his pocket, and without a notion in his mind how to get any money. He went, as he had often done of old, without lunch, and passed the afternoon working at the newspaper office, angry and preoccupied. About four o'clock he received a telegram from his mistress, running: "Shall we dine together, and have a lark afterwards?"

He at once replied: "Cannot dine." Then he reflected that he would be very stupid to deprive himself of the pleasant moments she might afford him, and added: "But will wait at nine at our place." And having sent one of the messengers with this, to save the cost of a telegram, he began to reflect what he should do to procure himself a dinner.

At seven o'clock he had not yet hit upon anything and a terrible hunger assailed him. Then he had recourse to the stratagem of a despairing man. He let all his colleagues depart, one after the other, and when he was alone rang sharply. Monsieur Walter's messenger, left in charge of the offices, came in. Duroy was standing feeling in his pockets, and said in an abrupt voice: "Foucart, I have left my purse at home, and I have to go and dine at the Luxembourg. Lend me fifty sous for my cab."

The man took three francs from his waistcoat pocket and said: "Do you want any more, sir?"

"No, no, that will be enough. Thanks."

And having seized on the coins, Duroy ran downstairs and dined at a slap-bank, to which he drifted on his days of poverty.

At nine o'clock he was awaiting his mistress, with his feet on the fender, in the little sitting-room. She came in, lively and animated, brisked up by the keen air of the street. "If you like," said she, "we will first go for a stroll, and then come home here at eleven. The weather is splendid for walking."

He replied, in a grumbling tone: "Why go out? We are very comfortable here."

She said, without taking off her bonnet: "If you knew, the moonlight is beautiful. It is splendid walking about tonight."

"Perhaps so, but I do not care for walking about!"

He had said this in an angry fashion. She was struck and hurt by it, and asked: "What is the matter with you? Why do you go on in this way? I should like to go for a stroll, and I don't see how that can vex you."

He got up in a rage. "It does not vex me. It is a bother, that is all."

She was one of those sort of women whom resistance irritates and impoliteness exasperates, and she said disdainfully and with angry calm: "I am not accustomed to be spoken to like that. I will go alone, then. Goodbye."

He understood that it was serious, and darting towards her, seized her hands and kissed them, saying: "Forgive me, darling, forgive me. I am very nervous this evening, very irritable. I have had vexations and annoyances, you know — matters of business."

She replied, somewhat softened, but not calmed down: "That does not concern me, and I will not bear the consequences of your ill-temper."

He took her in his arms, and drew her towards the couch.

"Listen, darling, I did not want to hurt you; I was not thinking of what I was saying."

He had forced her to sit down, and, kneeling before her, went on: "Have you forgiven me? Tell me you have forgiven me?"

She murmured, coldly: "Very well, but do not do so again;" and rising, she added: "Now let us go for a stroll."

He had remained at her feet, with his arms clasped about her hips, and stammered: "Stay here, I beg of you. Grant me this much. I should so like to keep you here this evening all to myself, here by the fire. Say yes, I beg of you, say yes."

She answered plainly and firmly: "No, I want to go out, and I am not going to give way to your fancies."

He persisted. "I beg of you, I have a reason, a very serious reason."

She said again: "No; and if you won't go out with me, I shall go. Goodbye."

She had freed herself with a jerk, and gained the door. He ran towards her, and clasped her in his arms, crying:

"Listen, Clo, my little Clo; listen, grant me this much."

She shook her head without replying, avoiding his kisses, and striving to escape from his grasp and go.

He stammered: "Clo, my little Clo, I have a reason."

She stopped, and looking him full in the face, said: "You are lying. What is it?"

He blushed not knowing what to say, and she went on in an indignant tone: "You see very well that you are lying, you low brute." And with an angry gesture and tears in her eyes, she escaped him.

He again caught her by the shoulders, and, in despair, ready to acknowledge anything in order to avoid a rupture, he said, in a despairing tone: "I have not a sou. That's what it all means." She stopped short, and looking into his eyes to read the truth in them, said: "You say?"

He had flushed to the roots of his hair. "I say that I have not a sou. Do you understand? Not twenty sous, not ten, not enough to pay for a glass of cassis in the café we may go into. You force me to confess what I am ashamed of. It was, however, impossible for me to go out with you, and when we were seated with refreshments in front of us to tell you quietly that I could not pay for them."

She was still looking him in the face. "It is true, then?"

In a moment he had turned out all his pockets, those of his trousers, coat, and waistcoat, and murmured: "There, are you satisfied now?"

Suddenly opening her arms, in an outburst of passion, she threw them around his neck, crying: "Oh, my poor darling, my poor darling, if I had only known. How did it happen?"

She made him sit down, and sat down herself on his knees; then, with her arm round his neck, kissing him every moment on his moustache, his mouth, his eyes, she obliged him to tell her how this misfortune had come about.

He invented a touching story. He had been obliged to come to the assistance of his father, who found himself in difficulties. He had not only handed over to him all his savings, but had even incurred heavy debts on his behalf. He added: "I shall be pinched to the last degree for at least six months, for I have exhausted all my resources. So much the worse; there are crises in every life. Money, after all, is not worth troubling about."

She whispered: "I will lend you some; will you let me?"

He answered, with dignity: "You are very kind, pet; but do not think of that, I beg of you. You would hurt my feelings."

She was silent, and then clasping him in her arms, murmured: "You will never know how much I love you."

It was one of their most pleasant evenings.

As she was leaving, she remarked, smilingly: "How nice it is when one is in your position to find money you had forgotten in your pocket — a coin that had worked its way between the stuff and the lining."

He replied, in a tone of conviction: "Ah, yes, that it is."

She insisted on walking home, under the pretense that the moon was beautiful and went into ecstasies over it. It was a cold, still night at the beginning of winter. Pedestrians and horses went by quickly, spurred by a sharp frost. Heels rang on the pavement. As she left him she said: "Shall we meet again the day after tomorrow?"

"Certainly."

"At the same time?"

"The same time."

"Goodbye, dearest." And they kissed lovingly.

Then he walked home swiftly, asking himself what plan he could hit on the morrow to get out of his difficulty. But as he opened the door of his room, and fumbled in his waistcoat pocket for a match, he was stupefied to find a coin under his fingers. As soon as he had a light he hastened to examine it. It was a louis. He thought he must be mad. He turned it over and over, seeking by what miracle it could have found its way there. It could not, however, have fallen from heaven into his pocket.

Then all at once he guessed, and an angry indignation awoke within him. His mistress had spoken of money slipping into the lining, and being found in times of poverty. It was she who had tendered him this alms. How shameful! He swore: "Ah! I'll talk to her the day after tomorrow. She shall have a nice time over it."

And he went to bed, his heart filled with anger and humiliation.

He woke late. He was hungry. He tried to go to sleep again, in order not to get up till two o'clock, and then said to himself: "That will not forward matters. I must end by finding some money." Then he went out, hoping that an idea might occur to him in the street. It did not; but at every restaurant he passed a longing to eat made his mouth water. As by noon he had failed to hit on any plan, he suddenly made up his mind: "I will lunch out of Clotilde's twenty francs. That won't hinder me from paying them back tomorrow."

He, therefore, lunched for two francs fifty centimes. On reaching the office he also gave three francs to the messenger, saying: "Here, Foucart, here is the money you lent me last night for my cab."

He worked till seven o'clock. Then he went and dined taking another three francs. The two evening bocks brought the expenditure of the day up to nine francs thirty centimes. But as he could not re-establish a credit or create fresh resources in twenty-four hours, he borrowed another six francs fifty centimes the next day from the twenty he was going to return that very evening, so that he came to keep his appointment with just four francs twenty centimes in his pocket.

He was in a deuce of a temper, and promised himself that he would pretty soon explain things. He would say to his mistress: "You know, I found the twenty francs you slipped into my pocket the other day. I cannot give them back to you now, because my situation is unaltered, and I have not had time to occupy myself with money matters. But I will give them to you the next time we meet."

She arrived, loving, eager, full of alarm. How would he receive her? She kissed him persistently to avoid an explanation at the outset.

He said to himself: "It will be time enough to enter on the matter by-and-by. I will find an opportunity of doing so."

He did not find the opportunity, and said nothing, shirking before the difficulty of opening this delicate subject. She did not speak of going out, and was in every way charming. They separated about midnight, after making an appointment for the Wednesday of the following week, for Madame de Marelle was engaged to dine out several days in succession.

The next day, as Duroy, on paying for his breakfast, felt for the four coins that ought to be remaining to him, he perceived that they were five, and one of them a gold one. At the outset he thought that he had received it by mistake in his change the day before, then he understood it, and his heart throbbed with humiliation at this persistent charity. How he now regretted not having said anything! If he had spoken energetically this would not have happened.

For four days he made efforts, as numerous as they were fruitless, to raise five louis, and spent Clotilde's second one. She managed, although he had said to her savagely, "Don't play that joke of the other evening's again, or I shall get angry," to slip another twenty francs into his trouser pockets the first time they met. When he found them he swore bitterly, and transferred them to his waistcoat to have them under his hand, for he had not a rap. He appeased his conscience by this argument: "I will give it all back to her in a lump. After all, it is only borrowed money."

At length the cashier of the paper agreed, on his desperate appeals, to let him have five francs daily. It was just enough to live upon, but not enough to repay sixty francs with. But as Clotilde was again seized by her passion for nocturnal excursions in all the suspicious localities in Paris, he ended by not being unbearably annoyed to find a yellow boy in one of his pockets, once even in his boot, and another time in his watch-case, after their adventurous excursions. Since she had wishes which he could not for the moment gratify himself, was it not natural that she should pay for them rather than go without them? He kept an account, too, of all he received in this way, in order to return it to her some day.

One evening she said to him: "Would you believe that I have never been to the Folies-Bergère? Will you take me there?"

He hesitated a moment, afraid of meeting Rachel. Then he thought: "Bah! I am not married, after all. If that girl sees me she will understand the state of things, and will not speak to me. Besides, we will have a box."

Another reason helped his decision. He was well pleased of this opportunity of offering Madame de Marelle a box at the theater without its costing anything. It was a kind of compensation.

He left her in the cab while he got the order for the box, in order that she might not see it offered him, and then came to fetch her. They went in, and were received with bows by the acting manager. An immense crowd filled the lounge, and they had great difficulty in making their way through the swarm of men and women. At length they reached the box and settled themselves in it, shut in between the motionless orchestra and the eddy of the gallery. But Madame de Marelle rarely glanced at the stage. Wholly taken up with the women promenading behind her back, she constantly turned round to look at them, with a longing to touch them, to feel their bodices, their skirts, their hair, to know what these creatures were made of.

Suddenly she said: "There is a stout, dark girl who keeps watching us all the time. I thought just now that she was going to speak to us. Did you notice her?"

He answered: "No, you must be mistaken." But he had already noticed her for some time back. It was Rachel who was prowling about in their neighborhood, with anger in her eyes and hard words upon her lips.

Duroy had brushed against her in making his way through the crowd, and she had whispered, "Good evening," with a wink which signified, "I understand." But he had not replied to this mark of attention for fear of being seen by his mistress, and he had passed on coldly, with haughty look and disdainful lip. The woman, whom unconscious jealousy already assailed, turned back, brushed against him again, and said in louder tones: "Good evening, George." He had not answered even then. Then she made up her mind to be recognized and bowed to, and she kept continually passing in the rear of the box, awaiting a favorable moment.

As soon as she saw that Madame de Marelle was looking at her she touched Duroy's shoulder, saying: "Good evening, are you quite well?"

He did not turn round, and she went on: "What, have you grown deaf since Thursday?" He did not reply, affecting a contempt which would not allow him to compromise himself even by a word with this slut.

She began to laugh an angry laugh, and said: "So you are dumb, then? Perhaps the lady has bitten your tongue off?"

He made an angry movement, and exclaimed, in an exasperated tone: "What do you mean by speaking to me? Be off, or I will have you locked up."

Then, with fiery eye and swelling bosom, she screeched out: "So that's it, is it? Ah! you lout. When a man sleeps with a woman the least he can do is to nod to her. It is no reason because you are with someone else that you should cut me to-day. If you had only nodded to me when I passed you just now, I should have left you alone. But you wanted to do the grand. I'll pay you out! Ah, so you won't say good evening when you meet me!"

She would have gone on for a long time, but Madame de Marelle had opened the door of the box and fled through the crowd, blindly seeking the way out. Duroy started off in her rear and strove to catch her up, while Rachel, seeing them flee, yelled triumphantly: "Stop her, she has stolen my sweetheart."

People began to laugh. Two gentlemen for fun seized the fugitive by the shoulders and sought to bring her back, trying, too, to kiss her. But Duroy, having caught her up, freed her forcibly and led her away into the street. She jumped into an empty cab standing at the door. He jumped in after her, and when the driver asked, "Where to, sir?" replied, "Wherever you like."

The cab slowly moved off, jolting over the paving stones. Clotilde, seized by a kind of hysterical attack, sat choking and gasping with her hands covering her face, and Duroy neither knew what to do nor what to say. At last, as he heard her sobbing, he stammered out: "Clo, my dear little Clo, just listen, let me explain. It is not my fault. I used to know that woman, some time ago, you know—"

She suddenly took her hands from her face, and overcome by the wrath of a loving and deceitful woman, a furious wrath that enabled her to recover her speech, she pantingly jerked out, in rapid and broken sentences: "Oh! —you wretch —you wretch —what a scoundrel you are —can it be possible? How shameful —O Lord —how shameful!" Then, getting angrier and angrier as her ideas grew clearer and arguments suggested themselves to her, she went on: "It was with my money you paid her, wasn't it? And I was giving him money —for that creature. Oh, the scoundrel!" She seemed for a few minutes to be seeking some stronger expression that would not come, and then all at once she spat out, as it were, the words: "Oh! you swine — you swine —you swine —you paid her with my money —you swine —you swine!" She could not think of anything else, and kept repeating, "You swine, you swine!"

Suddenly she leant out of the window, and catching the driver by the sleeve, cried, "Stop," and opening the door, sprang out.

George wanted to follow, but she cried, "I won't have you get out," in such loud tones that the passersby began to gather about her, and Duroy did not move for fear of a scandal. She took her purse from her pocket and looked for some change by the light of the cab lantern, then taking two francs fifty centimes she put them in the driver's hand, saying, in ringing tones: "There is your fare —I pay you, now take this blackguard to the Rue Boursault, Batignolles."

Mirth was aroused in the group surrounding her. A gentleman said: "Well done, little woman," and a young rapscallion standing close to the cab thrust his head into the open door and sang out, in shrill tones, "Goodnight, lovey!" Then the cab started off again, followed by a burst of laughter.

VI

George Duroy woke up chapfallen the next morning.

He dressed himself slowly, and then sat down at his window and began to reflect. He felt a kind of aching sensation all over, just as though he had received a drubbing over night. At last the necessity of finding some money spurred him up, and he went first to Forestier.

His friend received him in his study with his feet on the fender.

"What has brought you out so early?" said he.

"A very serious matter, a debt of honor."

"At play?"

He hesitated a moment, and then said: "At play."

"Heavy?"

"Five hundred francs."

He only owed two hundred and eighty.

Forestier, skeptical on the point, inquired: "Whom do you owe it to?"

Duroy could not answer right off. "To — to — a Monsieur de Carleville."

"Ah! and where does he live?"

"At — at — "

Forestier began to laugh. "Number ought, Nowhere Street, eh? I know that gentleman, my dear fellow. If you want twenty francs, I have still that much at your service, but no more."

Duroy took the offered louis. Then he went from door to door among the people he knew, and wound up by having collected at about five o'clock the sum of eighty francs. And he still needed two hundred more; he made up his mind, and keeping for himself what he had thus gleaned, murmured: "Bah! I am not going to put myself out for that cat. I will pay her when I can."

For a fortnight he lived regularly, economically, and chastely, his mind filled with energetic resolves. Then he was seized with a strong longing for love. It seemed to him that several years had passed since he last clasped a woman in his arms, and like the sailor who goes wild on seeing land, every passing petticoat made him quiver. So he went one evening to the Folies Bergère in the hope of finding Rachel. He caught sight of her indeed, directly he entered, for she scarcely went elsewhere, and went up to her smiling with outstretched hand. But she merely looked him down from head to foot, saying: "What do you want with me?"

He tried to laugh it off with, "Come, don't be stuck-up."

She turned on her heels, saying: "I don't associate with ponces."

She had picked out the bitterest insult. He felt the blood rush to his face, and went home alone.

Forestier, ill, weak, always coughing, led him a hard life at the paper, and seemed to rack his brain to find him tiresome jobs. One day, even, in a moment of nervous irritation, and after a long fit of coughing, as Duroy had not brought him a piece of information he wanted, he growled out: "Confound it! you are a bigger fool than I thought."

The other almost struck him, but restrained himself, and went away muttering: "I'll manage to pay you out some day." An idea shot through his mind, and he added: "I will make a cuckold of you, old fellow!" And he took himself off, rubbing his hands, delighted at this project.

He resolved to set about it the very next day. He paid Madame Forestier a visit as a reconnaissance. He found her lying at full length on a couch, reading a book. She held out her hand without rising, merely turning her head, and said: "Good-day, Pretty-boy!"

He felt as though he had received a blow. "Why do you call me that?" he said.

She replied, with a smile: "I saw Madame de Marelle the other day, and learned how you had been baptized at her place."

He felt reassured by her amiable air. Besides, what was there for him to be afraid of?

She resumed: "You spoil her. As to me, people come to see me when they think of it — the thirty-second of the month, or something like it."

He sat down near her, and regarded her with a new species of curiosity, the curiosity of the amateur who is bargain-hunting. She was charming, a soft and tender blonde, made for caresses, and he thought: "She is better than the other, certainly." He did not doubt his success, it seemed to him that he had only to stretch out his hand and take her, as one gathers a fruit.

He said, resolutely: "I did not come to see you, because it was better so."

She asked, without understanding: "What? Why?"

"No, not at all."

"Because I am in love with you; oh! only a little, and I do not want to be head over ears."

She seemed neither astonished, nor shocked, nor flattered; she went on smiling the same indifferent smile, and replied with the same tranquillity: "Oh! you can come all the same. No one is in love with me long."

He was surprised, more by the tone than by the words, and asked: "Why not?"

"Because it is useless. I let this be understood at once. If you had told me of your fear before, I should have reassured you, and invited you, on the contrary, to come as often as possible."

He exclaimed, in a pathetic tone: "Can we command our feelings?"

She turned towards him: "My dear friend, for me a man in love is struck off the list of the living. He becomes idiotic, and not only idiotic, but dangerous. I cease all intimate relations with people who are in love with me, or who pretend to be so — because they bore me, in the first place; and, secondly, because they are as much objects of suspicion to me as a mad dog, which may have a fit of biting. I therefore put them into a kind of moral quarantine until their illness is over. Do not forget this. I know very well that in your case love is only a species of appetite, while with me it would be, on the contrary, a kind of — of — of communion of souls, which does not enter into a man's religion. You understand its letter, and its spirit. But look me well in the face." She no longer smiled. Her face was calm and cold, and she continued, emphatically: "I will never, never be your mistress; you understand. It is therefore absolutely useless, it would even be hurtful, for you to persist in this desire. And now that the operation is over, will you agree to be friends — good friends — real friends, I mean, without any mental reservation."

He had understood that any attempt would be useless in face of this irrevocable sentence. He made up his mind at once, frankly, and, delighted at being able to secure this ally in the battle of life, held out both hands, saying: "I am yours, madame, as you will."

She read the sincerity of his intention in his voice, and gave him her hands. He kissed them both, one after the other, and then said simply, as he raised his head: "Ah, if I had found a woman like you, how gladly I would have married her."

She was touched this time — soothed by this phrase, as women are by the compliments which reach their hearts, and she gave him one of those rapid and grateful looks which make us their slaves. Then, as he could find no change of subject to renew the conversation, she said softly, laying her finger on his arm: "And I am going to play my part of a friend at once. You are clumsy." She hesitated a moment, and then asked: "May I speak plainly?"

"Yes."

"Quite plainly?"

"Quite."

"Well, go and see Madame Walter, who greatly appreciates you, and do your best to please her. You will find a place there for your compliments, although she is virtuous, you understand me, perfectly virtuous. Oh! there is no hope of — of poaching there, either. You may find something better, though, by showing yourself. I know that you still hold an inferior position on the paper. But do not be afraid, they receive all their staff with the same kindness. Go there — believe me."

He said, with a smile: "Thanks, you are an angel, a guardian angel."

They spoke of one thing and another. He stayed for some time, wishing to prove that he took pleasure in being with her, and on leaving, remarked: "It is understood, then, that we are friends?"

"It is."

As he had noted the effect of the compliment he had paid her shortly before, he seconded it by adding: "And if ever you become a widow, I enter the lists."

Then he hurried away, so as not to give her time to get angry.

A visit to Madame Walter was rather awkward for Duroy, for he had not been authorized to call, and he did not want to commit a blunder. The governor displayed some good will towards him, appreciated his services, and employed him by preference on difficult jobs, so why should he not profit by this favor to enter the house? One day, then, having risen early, he went to the market while the morning sales were in progress, and for ten francs obtained a score of splendid pears. Having carefully packed them in a hamper to make it appear that they had come from a distance, he left them with the doorkeeper at Madame Walter's with his card, on which he had written: "George Duroy begs Madame Walter to accept a little fruit which he received this morning from Normandy."

He found the next morning, among his letters at the office, an envelope in reply, containing the card of Madame Walter, who "thanked Monsieur George Duroy, and was at home every Saturday."

On the following Saturday he called. Monsieur Walter occupied, on the Boulevard Malesherbes, a double house, which belonged to him, and of which a part was let off, in the economical way of practical people. A single doorkeeper, quartered between the two carriage entrances, opened the door for both landlord and tenant, and imparted to each of the entrances an air of wealth by his get-up like a beadle, his big calves in white stockings, and his coat with gilt buttons and scarlet facings. The reception-rooms were on the first floor, preceded by an anteroom hung with tapestry, and shut in by curtains over the doorways. Two footmen were dozing on benches. One of them took Duroy's overcoat and the other relieved him of his cane, opened the door, advanced a few steps in front of the visitor, and then drawing aside, let him pass, calling out his name, into an empty room.

The young fellow, somewhat embarrassed, looked round on all sides when he perceived in a glass some people sitting down who seemed very far off. He was at sea at first as to the direction in which they were, the mirror having deceived his eyes. Then he passed through two empty drawingrooms and reached a small boudoir hung with blue silk, where four ladies were chatting round a table bearing cups of tea. Despite the assurance he had acquired in course of his Parisian life, and above all in his career as a reporter, which constantly brought him into contact with important personages, Duroy felt somewhat intimidated by the get-up of the entrance and the passage through the deserted drawingroom. He stammered: "Madame, I have ventured," as his eyes sought the mistress of the house.

She held out her hand, which he took with a bow, and having remarked: "You are very kind sir, to call and see me," she pointed to a chair, in seeking to sit down in which he almost fell, having thought it much higher.

They had become silent. One of the ladies began to talk again. It was a question of the frost, which was becoming sharper, though not enough, however, to check the epidemic of typhoid fever, nor to allow skating. Every one gave her opinion on this advent of frost in Paris, then they expressed their preference for the different seasons with all the trivial reasons that lie about in people's minds like dust in rooms. The faint noise made by a door caused Duroy to turn his head, and he saw in a glass a stout lady approaching. As soon as she made her appearance in the boudoir one of the other visitors rose, shook hands and left, and the young fellow followed her black back glittering with jet through the drawingrooms with his eyes. When the agitation due to this change had subsided they spoke without transition of the Morocco question and the war in the East and also of the difficulties of England in South Africa. These ladies discussed these matters from memory, as if they had been reciting passages from a fashionable play, frequently rehearsed.

A fresh arrival took place, that of a little curly-headed blonde, which brought about the departure of a tall, thin lady of middle age. They now spoke of the chance Monsieur Linet had of getting into the Academie-Francaise. The newcomer formerly believed that he would be beaten by Monsieur Cabanon-Lebas, the author of the fine dramatic adaption of Don Quixote in verse.

"You know it is to be played at the Odeon next winter?"

"Really, I shall certainly go and see such a very excellent literary effort."

Madame Walter answered gracefully with calm indifference, without ever hesitating as to what she should say, her mind being always made up beforehand. But she saw that night was coming on, and rang for the lamps, while listening to the conversation that trickled on like a stream of honey, and thinking that she had forgotten to call on the stationer about the invitation cards for her next dinner. She was a little too stout, though still beautiful, at the dangerous age when the general break-up is at hand. She preserved herself by dint of care, hygienic precautions, and salves for the skin. She seemed discreet in all matters; moderate and reasonable; one of those women whose mind is correctly laid out like a French garden. One walks through it with surprise, but experiencing a certain charm. She had keen, discreet, and sound sense, that stood her instead of fancy, generosity, and affection, together with a calm kindness for everybody and everything.

She noted that Duroy had not said anything, that he had not been spoken to, and that he seemed slightly ill at ease; and as the ladies had not yet quitted the Academy, that favorite subject always occupying them some time, she said: "And you who should be better informed than any one, Monsieur Duroy, who is your favorite?"

He replied unhesitatingly: "In this matter, madame, I should never consider the merit, always disputable, of the candidates, but their age and their state of health. I should not ask about their credentials, but their disease. I should not seek to learn whether they have made a metrical translation of Lope de Vega, but I should take care to obtain information as to the state of their liver, their heart, their lungs, and their spinal marrow. For me a good hypertrophy, a good aneurism, and above all, a good beginning of locomotor ataxy, would be a hundred times more valuable than forty volumes of disgressions on the idea of patriotism as embodied in barbaric poetry."

An astonished silence followed this opinion, and Madame Walter asked with a smile: "But why?"

He replied: "Because I never seek aught else than the pleasure that any one can give the ladies. But, Madame, the Academy only has any real interest for you when an Academician dies. The more of them die the happier you must be. But in order that they may die quickly they must be elected sick and old." As they still remained somewhat surprised, he continued. "Besides, I am like you, and I like to read of the death of an Academician. I at once ask myself: 'Who will replace him?' And I draw up my list. It is a game, a very pretty little game that is played in all Parisian salons at each decease of one of the Immortals, the game of 'Death and the Forty Fogies.'"

The ladies, still slightly disconcerted, began however, to smile, so true were his remarks. He concluded, as he rose: "It is you who really elect them, ladies, and you only elect them to see them die. Choose them old, therefore, very old; as old as possible, and do not trouble yourselves about anything else."

He then retired very gracefully. As soon as he was gone, one of the ladies said: "He is very funny, that young fellow. Who is he?"

Madame Walter replied: "One of the staff of our paper, who does not do much yet; but I feel sure that he will get on."

Duroy strode gayly down the Boulevard Malesherbes, content with his exit, and murmuring: "A capital start."

He made it up with Rachel that evening.

The following week two things happened to him. He was appointed chief reporter and invited to dinner at Madame Walter's. He saw at once a connection between these things. The Vie Francaise was before everything a financial paper, the head of it being a financier, to whom the press and the position of a deputy served as levers. Making use of every cordiality as a weapon, he had always worked under the smiling mask of a good fellow; but he only employed men whom he had sounded, tried, and proved; whom he knew to be crafty, bold, and supple. Duroy, appointed chief of the reporting staff, seemed to him a valuable fellow.

This duty had been filled up till then by the chief sub-editor, Monsieur Boisrenard, an old journalist, as correct, punctual, and scrupulous as a clerk. In course of thirty years he had been sub-editor of eleven different papers, without in any way modifying his way of thinking or acting. He passed from one office to another as one changes one's restaurant, scarcely noticing that the cookery was not quite the same. Political and religious opinions were foreign to him. He was devoted to his paper, whatever it might be, well up in his work, and valuable from his experience. He worked like a blind man who sees nothing, like a deaf man who hears nothing, and like a dumb man who never speaks of anything. He had, however, a strong instinct of professional loyalty, and would not stoop to aught he did not think honest and right from the special point of view of his business.

Monsieur Walter, who thoroughly appreciated him, had however, often wished for another man to whom to entrust the "Echoes," which he held to be the very marrow of the paper. It is through them that rumors are set afloat and the public and the funds influenced. It is necessary to know how to slip the all-important matter, rather hinted at than said right out, in between the description of two fashionable entertainments, without appearing to intend it. It is necessary to imply a thing by judicious reservations; let what is desired be guessed at; contradict in such a fashion as to confirm, or affirm in such a way that no one shall believe the statement. It is necessary that in the "Echoes" everyone shall find every day at least one line of interest, in order that every one may read them. Every one must be thought of, all classes, all professions, Paris and the provinces, the army and the art world, the clergy and the university, the bar and the world of gallantry. The man who has the conduct of them, and who commands an army of reporters, must be always on the alert and always on his guard; mistrustful, farseeing, cunning, alert, and supple; armed with every kind of cunning, and gifted with an infallible knack of spotting false news at the first glance, of judging which is good to announce and good to hide, of divining what will catch the public, and of putting it forward in such a way as to double its effect.

Monsieur Boisrenard, who had in his favor the skill acquired by long habit, nevertheless lacked mastery and dash; he lacked, above all, the native cunning needed to put forth day by day the secret ideas of the manager. Duroy could do it to perfection, and was an admirable addition to the staff. The wire-pullers and real editors of the Vie Francaise were half a dozen deputies, interested in all the speculations brought out or backed up by the manager. They were known in the Chamber as "Walter's gang," and envied because they gained money with him and through him. Forestier, the political editor, was only the man of straw of these men of business, the worker-out of ideas suggested by them. They prompted his leaders, which he always wrote at home, so as to do so in quiet, he said. But in order to give the paper a literary and truly Parisian smack, the services of two celebrated writers in different styles had been secured — Jacques Rival, a descriptive writer, and Norbert de Varenne, a poet and story-writer. To these had been added, at a cheap rate, theatrical, musical and art critics, a law reporter, and a sporting reporter, from the mercenary tribe of all-round pressmen. Two ladies, "Pink Domino" and "Lily Fingers," sent in fashion articles, and dealt with questions of dress, etiquette, and society.

Duroy was in all the joy of his appointment as chief of the "Echoes" when he received a printed card on which he read: "Monsieur and Madame Walter request the pleasure of Monsieur Geo. Duroy's company at dinner, on Thursday, January 20." This new mark of favor following on the other filled him with such joy that he kissed the invitation as he would have done a love letter. Then he went in search of the cashier to deal with the important question of money. A chief of the reporting staff on a Paris paper generally has his budget out of which he pays his reporters for the intelligence, important or trifling, brought in by them, as gardeners bring in their fruits to a dealer. Twelve hundred francs a month were allotted at the outset to Duroy, who proposed to himself to retain a considerable share of it. The cashier, on his pressing instances, ended by advancing him four hundred francs. He had at first the intention of sending Madame de Marelle the two hundred and eighty francs he owed her, but he almost immediately reflected that he would only have a hundred and twenty left, a sum utterly insufficient to carry on his new duties in suitable fashion, and so put off this resolution to a future day.

During a couple of days he was engaged in settling down, for he had inherited a special table and a set of pigeon holes in the large room serving for the whole of the staff. He occupied one end of the room, while Boisrenard, whose head, black as a crow's, despite his age, was always bent over a sheet of paper, had the other. The long table in the middle belonged to the staff. Generally it served them to sit on, either with their legs dangling over the edges, or squatted like tailors in the center. Sometimes five or six would be sitting on it in that fashion, perseveringly playing cup and ball. Duroy had ended by having a taste for this amusement, and was beginning to get expert at it, under the guidance, and thanks to the advice of Saint-Potin. Forestier, grown worse, had lent him his fine cup and ball in West Indian wood, the last he had bought, and which he found rather too heavy for him, and Duroy swung with vigorous arm the big black ball at the end of its string, counting quickly to himself: "One — two — three — four — five — six." It happened precisely that for the first time he spiked the ball twenty times running, the very day that he was to dine at Madame Walter's. "A good day," he thought, "I am successful in everything." For skill at cup and ball really conferred a kind of superiority in the office of the Vie Francaise.

He left the office early to have time to dress, and was going up the Rue de Londres when he saw, trotting along in front of him, a little woman whose figure recalled that of Madame de Marelle. He felt his cheeks flush, and his heart began to beat. He crossed the road to get a view of her. She stopped, in order to cross over, too. He had made a mistake, and breathed again. He had often asked how he ought to behave if he met her face to face. Should he bow, or should he seem not to have seen her. "I should not see her," he thought.

It was cold; the gutters were frozen, and the pavement dry and gray in the gaslight. When he got home he thought: "I must change my lodgings; this is no longer good enough for me." He felt nervous and lively, capable of anything; and he said aloud, as he walked from his bed to the window: "It is fortune at last — it is fortune! I must write to father." From time to time he wrote to his father, and the letter always brought happiness to the little Norman inn by the roadside, at the summit of the slope overlooking Rouen and the broad valley of the Seine. From time to time, too, he received a blue envelope, addressed in a large, shaky hand, and read the same unvarying lines at the beginning of the paternal epistle. "My Dear Son: This leaves your mother and myself in good health. There is not much news here. I must tell you, however," *etc.* In his heart he retained a feeling of interest for the village matters, for the news of the neighbours, and the condition of the crops.

He repeated to himself, as he tied his white tie before his little looking-glass: "I must write to father tomorrow. Wouldn't the old fellow be staggered if he could see me this evening in the house I am going to? By Jove! I am going to have such a dinner as he never tasted." And he suddenly saw the dark kitchen behind the empty café; the copper stewpans casting their yellow reflections on the wall; the cat on the hearth, with her nose to the fire, in sphinxlike attitude; the wooden table, greasy with time and spilt liquids, a soup tureen smoking upon it, and a lighted candle between two plates. He saw them, too — his father and mother, two slow-moving peasants, eating their soup. He knew the smallest wrinkles on their old faces, the slightest movements of their arms and heads. He knew even what they talked about every evening as they sat at supper. He thought, too: "I must really go and see them;" but his toilet being ended, he blew out his light and went downstairs.

As he passed along the outer boulevard girls accosted him from time to time. He replied, as he pulled away his arm: "Go to the devil!" with a violent disdain, as though they had insulted him. What did they take him for? Could not these hussies tell what a man was? The sensation of his dress coat, put on in order to go to dinner with such well-known and important people, inspired him with the sentiment of a new impersonality — the sense of having become another man, a man in society, genuine society.

He entered the anteroom, lit by tall bronze candelabra, with confidence, and handed in easy fashion his cane and overcoat to two valets who approached. All the drawingrooms were lit up. Madame Walter received her guests in the second, the largest. She welcomed him with a charming smile, and he shook hands with two gentlemen who had arrived before him — Monsieur Firmin and Monsieur Laroche-Mathieu, deputies, and anonymous editors of the Vie Francaise. Monsieur Laroche-Mathieu had a special authority at the paper, due to a great influence he enjoyed in the Chamber. No one doubted his being a minister some day. Then came the Forestiers; the wife in pink, and looking charming. Duroy was stupefied to see her on terms of intimacy with the two deputies. She chatted in low tones beside the fireplace, for more than five minutes, with Monsieur Laroche-Mathieu. Charles seemed worn out. He had grown much thinner during the past month, and coughed incessantly as he repeated: "I must make up my mind to finish the winter in the south." Norbert de Varenne and Jacques Rival made their appearance together. Then a door having opened at the further end of the room, Monsieur Walter came in with two tall young girls, of from sixteen to eighteen, one ugly and the other pretty.

Duroy knew that the governor was the father of a family; but he was struck with astonishment. He had never thought of his daughters, save as one thinks of distant countries which one will never see. And then he had fancied them quite young, and here they were grown-up women. They held out their hands to him after being introduced, and then went and sat down at a little table, without doubt reserved to them, at which they began to turn over a number of reels of silk in a work-basket. They were still awaiting someone, and all were silent with that sense of oppression, preceding dinners, between people who do not find themselves in the same mental atmosphere after the different occupations of the day.

Duroy having, for want of occupation, raised his eyes towards the wall, Monsieur Walter called to him from a distance, with an evident wish to show off his property: "Are you looking at my pictures? I will show them to you," and he took a lamp, so that the details might be distinguished.

"Here we have landscapes," said he.

In the center of the wall was a large canvas by Guillemet, a bit of the Normandy coast under a lowering sky. Below it a wood, by Harpignies, and a plain in Algeria, by Guillemet, with a camel on the horizon, a tall camel with long legs, like some strange monument. Monsieur Walter passed on to the next wall, and announced in a grave tone, like a master of the ceremonies: "High Art." There were four: "A Hospital Visit," by Gervex; "A Harvester," by Bastien-Lepage; "A Widow," by Bouguereau; and "An Execution," by Jean Paul Laurens. The last work represented a Vendean priest shot against the wall of his church by a detachment of Blues. A smile flitted across the governor's grave countenance as he indicated the next wall. "Here the fanciful school." First came a little canvas by Jean Beraud, entitled, "Above and Below." It was a pretty Parisian mounting to the roof of a tramcar in motion. Her head appeared on a level with the top, and the gentlemen on the seats viewed with satisfaction the pretty face approaching them, while those standing on the platform below considered the young woman's legs with a different expression of envy and desire. Monsieur Walter held the lamp at arm's length, and repeated, with a sly laugh: "It is funny, isn't it?" Then he lit up "A Rescue," by Lambert. In the middle of a table a kitten, squatted on its haunches, was watching with astonishment and perplexity a fly drowning in a glass of water. It had its paw raised ready to fish out the insect with a rapid sweep of it. But it had not quite made up its mind. It hesitated. What would it do? Then the governor showed a Detaille, "The Lesson," which represented a soldier in a barrack-room teaching a poodle to play the drum, and said: "That is very witty."

Duroy laughed a laugh of approbation, and exclaimed: "It is charming, charm — " He stopped short on hearing behind him the voice of Madame de Marelle, who had just come in.

The governor continued to light up the pictures as he explained them. He now showed a watercolor by Maurice Leloir, "The Obstacle." It was a sedan chair checked on its way, the street being blocked by a fight between two laborers, two fellows struggling like Hercules. From out of the window of the chair peered the head of a charming woman, who watched without impatience, without alarm, and with a certain admiration, the combat of these two brutes. Monsieur Walter continued: "I have others in the adjoining rooms, but they are by less known men. I buy of the young artists now, the very young ones, and hang their works in the more private rooms until they become known." He then went on in a low tone: "Now is the time to buy! The painters are all dying of hunger! They have not a sou, not a sou!"

But Duroy saw nothing, and heard without understanding. Madame de Marelle was there behind him. What ought he to do? If he spoke to her, might she not turn her back on him, or treat him with insolence? If he did not approach her, what would people think? He said to himself: "I will gain time, at any rate." He was so moved that for a moment he thought of feigning a sudden illness, which would allow him to withdraw. The examination of the walls was over. The governor went to put down his lamp and welcome the last comer, while Duroy began to re-examine the pictures as if he could not tire of admiring them. He was quite upset. What should he do? Madame Forestier called to him: "Monsieur Duroy." He went to her. It was to speak to him of a friend of hers who was about to give a fête, and who would like to have a line to that effect in the Vie Francaise. He gasped out: "Certainly, Madame, certainly."

Madame de Marelle was now quite close to him. He dared not turn round to go away. All at once he thought he was going mad; she had said aloud: "Good evening, Pretty-boy. So you no longer recognize me."

He rapidly turned on his heels. She stood before him smiling, her eyes beaming with sprightliness and affection, and held out her hand. He took it tremblingly, still fearing some trick, some perfidy. She added, calmly: "What has become of you? One no longer sees anything of you."

He stammered, without being able to recover his coolness: "I have a great deal to do, Madame, a great deal to do. Monsieur Walter has entrusted me with new duties which give me a great deal of occupation."

She replied, still looking him in the face, but without his being able to discover anything save good will in her glance: "I know it. But that is no reason for forgetting your friends."

They were separated by a lady who came in, with red arms and red face, a stout lady in a very low dress, got up with pretentiousness, and walking so heavily that one guessed by her motions the size and weight of her legs. As she seemed to be treated with great attention, Duroy asked Madame Forestier: "Who is that lady?"

"The Viscomtesse de Percemur, who signs her articles 'Lily Fingers.'"

He was astounded, and seized on by an inclination to laugh.

"'Lily Fingers!' 'Lily Fingers!' and I imagined her young like yourself. So that is 'Lily Fingers.' That is very funny, very funny."

A servant appeared in the doorway and announced dinner. The dinner was commonplace and lively, one of those dinners at which people talk about everything, without saying anything. Duroy found himself between the elder daughter of the master of the house, the ugly one, Mademoiselle Rose and Madame de Marelle. The neighborhood of the latter made him feel very ill at ease, although she seemed very much at her ease, and chatted with her usual vivacity. He was troubled at first, constrained, hesitating, like a musician who has lost the keynote. By degrees, however, he recovered his assurance, and their eyes continually meeting questioned one another, exchanging looks in an intimate, almost sensual, fashion as of old. All at once he thought he felt something brush against his foot under the table. He softly pushed forward his leg and encountered that of his neighbor, which did not shrink from the contact. They did not speak, each being at that moment turned towards their neighbor. Duroy, his heart beating, pushed a little harder with his knee. A slight pressure replied to him. Then he understood that their loves were beginning anew. What did they say then? Not much, but their lips quivered every time that they looked at one another.

The young fellow, however, wishing to do the amiable to his employer's daughter, spoke to her from time to time. She replied as the mother would have done, never hesitating as to what she should say. On the right of Monsieur Walter the Viscomtesse de Percemur gave herself the airs of a princess, and Duroy, amused at watching her, said in a low voice to Madame de Marelle. "Do you know the other, the one who signs herself 'Pink Domino'?"

"Yes, very well, the Baroness de Livar."

"Is she of the same breed?"

"No, but quite as funny. A tall, dried-up woman of sixty, false curls, projecting teeth, ideas dating from the Restoration, and toilets of the same epoch."

"Where did they unearth these literary phenomena?"

"The scattered waifs of the nobility are always sheltered by enriched cits."

"No other reason?"

"None."

Then a political discussion began between the master of the house, the two deputies, Norbert de Varenne, and Jacques Rival, and lasted till dessert.

When they returned to the drawingroom, Duroy again approached Madame de Marelle, and looking her in the eyes, said: "Shall I see you home tonight?"

"No."

"Why not?"

"Because Monsieur Laroche Mathieu, who is my neighbor, drops me at my door every time I dine here."

"When shall I see you?"

"Come and lunch with me tomorrow."

And they separated without saying anything more.

Duroy did not remain late, finding the evening dull. As he went downstairs he overtook Norbert de Varenne, who was also leaving. The old poet took him by the arm. No longer having to fear any rivalry as regards the paper, their work being essentially different, he now manifested a fatherly kindness towards the young fellow.

"Well, will you walk home a bit of my way with me?" said he.

"With pleasure, my dear master," replied Duroy.

And they went out, walking slowly along the Boulevard Malesherbes. Paris was almost deserted that night — a cold night — one of those nights that seem vaster, as it were, than others, when the stars seem higher above, and the air seems to bear on its icy breath something coming from further than even the stars. The two men did not speak at first. Then Duroy, in order to say something, remarked: "Monsieur Laroche Mathieu seems very intelligent and well informed."

The old poet murmured: "Do you think so?"

The young fellow, surprised at this remark, hesitated in replying: "Yes; besides, he passes for one of the most capable men in the Chamber."

"It is possible. In the kingdom of the blind the one-eyed man is king. All these people are commonplace because their mind is shut in between two walls, money and politics. They are dullards, my dear fellow, with whom it is impossible to talk about anything we care for. Their minds are at the bottom mud, or rather sewage; like the Seine Asnières. Ah! how difficult it is to find a man with breadth of thought, one who causes you the same sensation as the breeze from across the broad ocean one breathes on the seashore. I have known some such; they are dead."

Norbert de Varenne spoke with a clear but restrained voice, which would have rung out in the silence of the night had he given it rein. He seemed excited and sad, and went on: "What matter, besides, a little more or less talent, since all must come to an end."

He was silent, and Duroy, who felt light hearted that evening, said with a smile: "You are gloomy to-day, dear master."

The poet replied: "I am always so, my lad, so will you be in a few years. Life is a hill. As long as one is climbing up one looks towards the summit and is happy, but when one reaches the top one suddenly perceives the descent before one, and its bottom, which is death. One climbs up slowly, but one goes down quickly. At your age a man is happy. He hopes for many things, which, by the way, never come to pass. At mine, one no longer expects anything — but death."

Duroy began to laugh: "You make me shudder all over."

Norbert de Varenne went on: "No, you do not understand me now, but later on you will remember what I am saying to you at this moment. A day comes, and it comes early for many, when there is an end to mirth, for behind everything one looks at one sees death. You do not even understand the word. At your age it means nothing; at mine it is terrible. Yes, one understands it all at once, one does not know how or why, and then everything in life changes its aspect. For fifteen years I have felt death assail me as if I bore within me some gnawing beast. I have felt myself decaying little by little, month by month, hour by hour, like a house crumbling to ruin. Death has disfigured me so completely that I do not recognize myself. I have no longer anything about me of myself — of the fresh, strong man I was at thirty. I have seen death whiten my black hairs, and with what skillful and spiteful slowness. Death has taken my firm skin, my muscles, my teeth, my whole body of old, only leaving me a despairing soul, soon to be taken too. Every step brings me nearer to death, every moment, every breath hastens his odious work. To breathe, sleep, drink, eat, work, dream, everything we do is to die. To live, in short, is to die. I now see death so near that I often want to stretch my arms to push it back. I see it everywhere. The insects crushed on the path, the falling leaves, the white hair in a friend's head, rend my heart and cry to me, "Behold it!" It spoils for me all I do, all I see, all that I eat and drink, all that I love; the bright moonlight, the sunrise, the broad ocean, the noble rivers, and the soft summer evening air so sweet to breathe."

He walked on slowly, dreaming aloud, almost forgetting that he had a listener: "And no one ever returns — never. The model of a statue may be preserved, but my body, my face, my thoughts, my desires will never reappear again. And yet millions of beings will be born with a nose, eyes, forehead, cheeks, and mouth like me, and also a soul like me, without my ever returning, without even anything recognizable of me appearing in these countless different beings. What can we cling to? What can we believe in? All religions are stupid, with their puerile morality and their egoistical promises, monstrously absurd. Death alone is certain."

He stopped, reflected for a few moments, and then, with a look of resignation, said: "I am a lost creature. I have neither father nor mother, nor sister nor brother; no wife, no children, no God."

He added, after a pause: "I have only verse."

They reached the Pont de la Concorde, crossed it in silence, and walked past the Palais Bourbon. Norbert de Varenne began to speak again, saying: "Marry, my friend; you do not know what it is to live alone at my age. Solitude now fills me with horrible agony — solitude at home by the fireside of a night. It is so profound, so sad; the silence of the room in which one dwells alone. It is not alone silence about the body, but silence about the soul; and when the furniture creaks I shudder to the heart, for no sound but is unexpected in my gloomy dwelling." He was silent again for a moment, and then added: "When one is old it is well, all the same, to have children."

They had got half way down the Rue de Bourgoyne. The poet halted in front of a tall house, rang the bell, shook Duroy by the hand, and said: "Forget all this old man's doddering, youngster, and live as befits your age. Goodnight."

And he disappeared in the dark passage.

Duroy resumed his route with a pain at his heart. It seemed to him as though he had been shown a hole filled with bones, an unavoidable gulf into which all must fall one day. He muttered: "By Jove, it can't be very lively in his place. I should not care for a front seat to see the procession of his thoughts go by. The deuce, no."

But having paused to allow a perfumed lady, alighting from her carriage and entering her house, to pass before him, he drew in with eager breath the scent of vervain and orris root floating in the air. His lungs and heart throbbed suddenly with hope and joy, and the recollection of Madame de Marelle, whom he was to see the next day, assailed him from head to foot. All smiled on him, life welcomed him with kindness. How sweet was the realization of hopes!

He fell asleep, intoxicated with this idea, and rose early to take a stroll down the Avenue du Bois de Boulogne before keeping his appointment. The wind having changed, the weather had grown milder during the night, and it was as warm and as sunny as in April. All the frequenters of the Bois had sallied out that morning, yielding to the summons of a bright, clear day. Duroy walked along slowly. He passed the Arc de Triomphe, and went along the main avenue. He watched the people on horseback, ladies and gentlemen, trotting and galloping, the rich folk of the world, and scarcely envied them now. He knew them almost all by name — knew the amount of their fortune, and the secret history of their life, his duties having made him a kind of directory of the celebrities and the scandals of Paris.

Ladies rode past, slender, and sharply outlined in the dark cloth of their habits, with that proud and unassailable air many women have on horseback, and Duroy amused himself by murmuring the names, titles, and qualities of the lovers whom they had had, or who were attributed to them. Sometimes, instead of saying "Baron de Tanquelot," "Prince de la Tour-Enguerrand," he murmured "Lesbian fashion, Louise Michot of the Vaudeville, Rose Marquetin of the Opera."

The game greatly amused him, as if he had verified, beneath grave outward appearances, the deep, eternal infamy of mankind, and as if this had excited, rejoiced, and consoled him. Then he said aloud: "Set of hypocrites!" and sought out with his eye the horsemen concerning whom the worst tales were current. He saw many, suspected of cheating at play, for whom their clubs were, at all events, their chief, their sole source of livelihood, a suspicious one, at any rate. Others, very celebrated, lived only, it was well known, on the income of their wives; others, again, it was affirmed, on that of their mistresses. Many had paid their debts, an honorable action, without it ever being guessed whence the money had come — a very equivocal mystery. He saw financiers whose immense fortune had had its origin in a theft, and who were received everywhere, even in the most noble houses; then men so respected that the lower middle-class took off their hats on their passage, but whose shameless speculations in connection with great national enterprises were a mystery for none of those really acquainted with the inner side of things. All had a haughty look, a proud lip, an insolent eye. Duroy still laughed, repeating: "A fine lot; a lot of blackguards, of sharpers."

But a pretty little open carriage passed, drawn by two white ponies with flowing manes and tails, and driven by a pretty fair girl, a well-known courtesan, who had two grooms seated behind her. Duroy halted with a desire to applaud this mushroom of love, who displayed so boldly at this place and time set apart for aristocratic hypocrites the dashing luxury earned between her sheets. He felt, perhaps vaguely, that there was something in common between them — a tie of nature, that they were of the same race, the same spirit, and that his success would be achieved by daring steps of the same kind. He walked back more slowly, his heart aglow with satisfaction, and arrived a little in advance of the time at the door of his former mistress.

She received him with proffered lips, as though no rupture had taken place, and she even forgot for a few moments the prudence that made her opposed to all caresses at her home. Then she said, as she kissed the ends of his moustache: "You don't know what a vexation has happened to me, darling? I was hoping for a nice honeymoon, and here is my husband home for six weeks. He has obtained leave. But I won't remain six weeks without seeing you, especially after our little tiff, and this is how I have arranged matters. You are to come and dine with us on Monday. I have already spoken to him about you, and I will introduce you."

Duroy hesitated, somewhat perplexed, never yet having found himself face to face with a man whose wife he had enjoyed. He was afraid lest something might betray him — a slight embarrassment, a look, no matter what. He stammered out: "No, I would rather not make your husband's acquaintance."

She insisted, very much astonished, standing before him with wide open, wondering eyes. "But why? What a funny thing. It happens every day. I should not have thought you such a goose."

He was hurt, and said: "Very well, I will come to dinner on Monday."

She went on: "In order that it may seem more natural I will ask the Forestiers, though I really do not like entertaining people at home."

Until Monday Duroy scarcely thought any more about the interview, but on mounting the stairs at Madame de Marelle's he felt strangely uneasy, not that it was so repugnant to him to take her husband's hand, to drink his wine, and eat his bread, but because he felt afraid of something without knowing what. He was shown into the drawingroom and waited as usual. Soon the door of the inner room opened, and he saw a tall, white-bearded man, wearing the ribbon of the Legion of Honor, grave and correct, who advanced towards him with punctilious politeness, saying: "My wife has often spoken to me of you, sir, and I am delighted to make your acquaintance."

Duroy stepped forward, seeking to impart to his face a look of expressive cordiality, and grasped his host's hand with exaggerated energy. Then, having sat down, he could find nothing to say.

Monsieur de Marelle placed a log upon the fire, and inquired: "Have you been long engaged in journalism?"

"Only a few months."

"Ah! you have got on quickly?"

"Yes, fairly so," and he began to chat at random, without thinking very much about what he was saying, talking of all the trifles customary among men who do not know one another. He was growing seasoned now, and thought the situation a very amusing one. He looked at Monsieur de Marelle's serious and respectable face, with a temptation to laugh, as he thought: "I have cuckolded you, old fellow, I have cuckolded you." A vicious, inward satisfaction stole over him — the satisfaction of a thief who has been successful, and is not even suspected — a delicious, roguish joy. He suddenly longed to be the friend of this man, to win his confidence, to get him to relate the secrets of his life.

Madame de Marelle came in suddenly, and having taken them in with a smiling and impenetrable glance, went toward Duroy, who dared not, in the presence of her husband, kiss her hand as he always did. She was calm, and lighthearted as a person accustomed to everything, finding this meeting simple and natural in her frank and native trickery. Laurine appeared, and went and held up her forehead to George more quietly than usual, her father's presence intimidating her. Her mother said to her: "Well, you don't call him Pretty-boy to-day." And the child blushed as if a serious indiscretion had been committed, a thing that ought not to have been mentioned, revealed, an intimate and, so to say, guilty secret of her heart laid bare.

When the Forestiers arrived, all were alarmed at the condition of Charles. He had grown frightfully thin and pale within a week, and coughed incessantly. He stated, besides, that he was leaving for Cannes on the following Thursday, by the doctor's imperative orders. They left early, and Duroy said, shaking his head: "I think he is very bad. He will never make old bones."

Madame de Marelle said, calmly: "Oh! he is done for. There is a man who was lucky in finding the wife he did."

Duroy asked: "Does she help him much?"

"She does everything. She is acquainted with everything that is going on; she knows everyone without seeming to go and see anybody; she obtains what she wants as she likes. Oh! she is keen, clever, and intriguing as no one else is. She is a treasure for anyone wanting to get on."

George said: "She will marry again very quickly, no doubt?"

Madame de Marelle replied: "Yes. I should not be surprised if she had some one already in her eye — a deputy, unless, indeed, he objects — for — for — there may be serious — moral — obstacles. But then — I don't really know."

Monsieur de Marelle grumbled with slow impatience: "You are always suspecting a number of things that I do not like. Do not let us meddle with the affairs of others. Our conscience is enough to guide us. That should be a rule with everyone."

Duroy withdrew, uneasy at heart, and with his mind full of vague plans. The next day he paid a visit to the Forestiers, and found them finishing their packing up. Charles, stretched on a sofa, exaggerated his difficulty of breathing, and repeated: "I ought to have been off a month ago."

Then he gave George a series of recommendations concerning the paper, although everything had been agreed upon and settled with Monsieur Walter. As George left, he energetically squeezed his old comrade's hand, saying: "Well, old fellow, we shall have you back soon." But as Madame Forestier was showing him out, he said to her, quickly: "You have not forgotten our agreement? We are friends and allies, are we not? So if you have need of me, for no matter what, do not hesitate. Send a letter or a telegram, and I will obey."

She murmured: "Thanks, I will not forget." And her eye, too, said "Thanks," in a deeper and tenderer fashion.

As Duroy went downstairs, he met slowly coming up Monsieur de Vaudrec, whom he had met there once before. The Count appeared sad, at this departure, perhaps. Wishing to show his good breeding, the journalist eagerly bowed. The other returned the salutation courteously, but in a somewhat dignified manner.

The Forestiers left on Thursday evening.

VII

Charles's absence gave Duroy increased importance in the editorial department of the Vie Francaise. He signed several leaders besides his "Echoes," for the governor insisted on everyone assuming the responsibility of his "copy." He became engaged in several newspaper controversies, in which he acquitted himself creditably, and his constant relations with different statesmen were gradually preparing him to become in his turn a clever and perspicuous political editor. There was only one cloud on his horizon. It came from a little freelance newspaper, which continually assailed him, or rather in him assailed the chief writer of "Echoes" in the Vie Francaise, the chief of "Monsieur Walter's startlers," as it was put by the anonymous writer of the Plume. Day by day cutting paragraphs, insinuations of every kind, appeared in it.

One day Jacques Rival said to Duroy: "You are very patient."

Duroy replied: "What can I do, there is no direct attack?"

But one afternoon, as he entered the editor's room, Boisrenard held out the current number of the Plume, saying: "Here's another spiteful dig at you."

"Ah! what about?"

"Oh! a mere nothing — the arrest of a Madame Aubert by the police."

George took the paper, and read, under the heading, "Duroy's Latest":

"The illustrious reporter of the Vie Francaise to-day informs us that Madame Aubert, whose arrest by a police agent belonging to the odious brigade des mœurs we announced, exists only in our imagination. Now the person in question lives at 18 Rue de l'Ecureuil, Montmartre. We understand only too well, however, the interest the agents of Walter's bank have in supporting those of the Prefect of Police, who tolerates their commerce. As to the reporter of whom it is a question, he would do better to give us one of those good sensational bits of news of which he has the secret — news of deaths contradicted the following day, news of battles which have never taken place, announcements of important utterances by sovereigns who have not said anything — all the news, in short, which constitutes Walter's profits, or even one of those little indiscretions concerning entertainments given by would-be fashionable ladies, or the excellence of certain articles of consumption which are of such resource to some of our compeers."

The young fellow was more astonished than annoyed, only understanding that there was something very disagreeable for him in all this.

Boisrenard went on: "Who gave you this 'Echo'?"

Duroy thought for a moment, having forgotten. Then all at once the recollection occurred to him, "Saint-Potin." He re-read the paragraph in the Plume and reddened, roused by the accusation of venality. He exclaimed: "What! do they mean to assert that I am paid — "

Boisrenard interrupted him: "They do, though. It is very annoying for you. The governor is very strict about that sort of thing. It might happen so often in the 'Echoes.'"

Saint-Potin came in at that moment. Duroy hastened to him. "Have you seen the paragraph in the Plume?"

"Yes, and I have just come from Madame Aubert. She does exist, but she was not arrested. That much of the report has no foundation."

Duroy hastened to the room of the governor, whom he found somewhat cool, and with a look of suspicion in his eye. After having listened to the statement of the case, Monsieur Walter said: "Go and see the woman yourself, and contradict the paragraph in such terms as will put a stop to such things being written about you any more. I mean the latter part of the paragraph. It is very annoying for the paper, for yourself, and for me. A journalist should no more be suspected than Cæsar's wife."

Duroy got into a cab, with Saint-Potin as his guide, and called out to the driver: "Number 18 Rue de l'Ecureuil, Montmartre."

It was a huge house, in which they had to go up six flights of stairs. An old woman in a woolen jacket opened the door to them. "What is it you want with me now?" said she, on catching sight of Saint-Potin.

He replied: "I have brought this gentleman, who is an inspector of police, and who would like to hear your story."

Then she let him in, saying: "Two more have been here since you, for some paper or other, I don't know which," and turning towards Duroy, added: "So this gentleman wants to know about it?"

"Yes. Were you arrested by an agent des mœurs?"

She lifted her arms into the air. "Never in my life, sir, never in my life. This is what it is all about. I have a butcher who sells good meat, but who gives bad weight. I have often noticed it without saying anything; but the other day, when I asked him for two pounds of chops, as I had my daughter and my son-in-law to dinner, I caught him weighing in bits of trimmings — trimmings of chops, it is true, but not of mine. I could have made a stew of them, it is true, as well, but when I ask for chops it is not to get other people's trimmings. I refused to take them, and he calls me an old shark. I called him an old rogue, and from one thing to another we picked up such a row that there were over a hundred people round the shop, some of them laughing fit to split. So that at last a police agent came up and asked us to settle it before the commissary. We went, and he dismissed the case. Since then I get my meat elsewhere, and don't even pass his door, in order to avoid his slanders."

She ceased talking, and Duroy asked: "Is that all?"

"It is the whole truth, sir," and having offered him a glass of cordial, which he declined, the old woman insisted on the short weight of the butcher being spoken of in the report.

On his return to the office, Duroy wrote his reply:

"An anonymous scribbler in the Plume seeks to pick a quarrel with me on the subject of an old woman whom he states was arrested by an agent des mœurs, which fact I deny. I have myself seen Madame Aubert — who is at least sixty years of age — and she told me in detail her quarrel with the butcher over the weighing of some chops, which led to an explanation before the commissary of police. This is the whole truth. As to the other insinuations of the writer in the Plume, I despise them. Besides, a man does not reply to such things when they are written under a mask.

"George Duroy."

Monsieur Walter and Jacques Rival, who had come in, thought this note satisfactory, and it was settled that it should go in at once.

Duroy went home early, somewhat agitated and slightly uneasy. What reply would the other man make? Who was he? Why this brutal attack? With the brusque manners of journalists this affair might go very far. He slept badly. When he read his reply in the paper next morning, it seemed to him more aggressive in print than in manuscript. He might, it seemed to him, have softened certain phrases. He felt feverish all day, and slept badly again at night. He rose at dawn to get the number of the Plume that must contain a reply to him.

The weather had turned cold again, it was freezing hard. The gutters, frozen while still flowing, showed like two ribbons of ice alongside the pavement. The morning papers had not yet come in, and Duroy recalled the day of his first article, "The Recollections of a Chasseur d'Afrique." His hands and feet getting numbed, grew painful, especially the tips of his fingers, and he began to trot round the glazed kiosque in which the newspaper seller, squatting over her foot warmer, only showed through the little window a red nose and a pair of cheeks to match in a woolen hood. At length the newspaper porter passed the expected parcel through the opening, and the woman held out to Duroy an unfolded copy of the Plume.

He glanced through it in search of his name, and at first saw nothing. He was breathing again, when he saw between two dashes:

"Monsieur Duroy, of the Vie Francaise, contradicts us, and in contradicting us, lies. He admits, however, that there is a Madame Aubert, and that an agent took her before the commissary of police. It only remains, therefore, to add two words, 'des mœurs,' after the word 'agent,' and he is right. But the conscience of certain journalists is on a level with their talent. And I sign,

"Louis Langremont."

George's heart began to beat violently, and he went home to dress without being too well aware of what he was doing. So he had been insulted, and in such a way that no hesitation was possible. And why? For nothing at all. On account of an old woman who had quarreled with her butcher.

He dressed quickly and went to see Monsieur Walter, although it was barely eight o'clock. Monsieur Walter, already up, was reading the Plume. "Well," said he, with a grave face, on seeing Duroy, "you cannot draw back now." The young fellow did not answer, and the other went on: "Go at once and see Rival, who will act for you."

Duroy stammered a few vague words, and went out in quest of the descriptive writer, who was still asleep. He jumped out of bed, and, having read the paragraph, said: "By Jove, you must go out. Whom do you think of for the other second?"

"I really don't know."

"Boisrenard? What do you think?"

"Yes. Boisrenard."

"Are you a good swordsman?"

"Not at all."

"The devil! And with the pistol?"

"I can shoot a little."

"Good. You shall practice while I look after everything else. Wait for me a moment."

He went into his dressing-room, and soon reappeared washed, shaved, correct-looking.

"Come with me," said he.

He lived on the ground floor of a small house, and he led Duroy to the cellar, an enormous cellar, converted into a fencing-room and shooting gallery, all the openings on the street being closed. After having lit a row of gas jets running the whole length of a second cellar, at the end of which was an iron man painted red and blue; he placed on a table two pairs of breech-loading pistols, and began to give the word of command in a sharp tone, as though on the ground: "Ready? Fire — one — two — three."

Duroy, dumbfounded, obeyed, raising his arm, aiming and firing, and as he often hit the mark fair on the body, having frequently made use of an old horse pistol of his father's when a boy, against the birds, Jacques Rival, well satisfied, exclaimed: "Good — very good — very good — you will do — you will do."

Then he left George, saying: "Go on shooting till noon; here is plenty of ammunition, don't be afraid to use it. I will come back to take you to lunch and tell you how things are going."

Left to himself, Duroy fired a few more shots, and then sat down and began to reflect. How absurd these things were, all the same! What did a duel prove? Was a rascal less of a rascal after going out? What did an honest man, who had been insulted, gain by risking his life against a scoundrel? And his mind, gloomily inclined, recalled the words of Norbert de Varenne.

Then he felt thirsty, and having heard the sound of water dropping behind him, found that there was a hydrant serving as a douche bath, and drank from the nozzle of the hose. Then he began to think again. It was gloomy in this cellar, as gloomy as a tomb. The dull and distant rolling of vehicles sounded like the rumblings of a far-off storm. What o'clock could it be? The hours passed by there as they must pass in prisons, without anything to indicate or mark them save the visits of the warder. He waited a long time. Then all at once he heard footsteps and voices, and Jacques Rival reappeared, accompanied by Boisrenard. He called out as soon as he saw Duroy: "It's all settled."

The latter thought the matter terminated by a letter of apology, his heart beat, and he stammered: "Ah! thanks."

The descriptive writer continued: "That fellow Langremont is very square; he accepted all our conditions. Twenty-five paces, one shot, at the word of command raising the pistol. The hand is much steadier that way than bringing it down. See here, Boisrenard, what I told you."

And taking a pistol he began to fire, pointed out how much better one kept the line by raising the arm. Then he said: "Now let's go and lunch; it is past twelve o'clock."

They went to a neighboring restaurant. Duroy scarcely spoke. He ate in order not to appear afraid, and then, in course of the afternoon, accompanied Boisrenard to the office, where he got through his work in an abstracted and mechanical fashion. They thought him plucky. Jacques Rival dropped in in the course of the afternoon, and it was settled that his seconds should call for him in a landau at seven o'clock the next morning, and drive to the Bois de Vesinet, where the meeting was to take place. All this had been done so unexpectedly, without his taking part in it, without his saying a word, without his giving his opinion, without accepting or refusing, and with such rapidity, too, that he was bewildered, scared, and scarcely able to understand what was going on.

He found himself at home at nine o'clock, after having dined with Boisrenard, who, out of self-devotion, had not left him all day. As soon as he was alone he strode quickly up and down his room for several minutes. He was too uneasy to think about anything. One solitary idea filled his mind, that of a duel on the morrow, without this idea awakening in him anything else save a powerful emotion. He had been a soldier, he had been engaged with the Arabs, without much danger to himself though, any more than when one hunts a wild boar.

To reckon things up, he had done his duty. He had shown himself what he should be. He would be talked of, approved of, and congratulated. Then he said aloud, as one does under powerful impressions: "What a brute of a fellow."

He sat down and began to reflect. He had thrown upon his little table one of his adversary's cards, given him by Rival in order to retain his address. He read, as he had already done a score of times during the day: "Louis Langremont, 176 Rue Montmartre." Nothing more. He examined these assembled letters, which seemed to him mysterious and full of some disturbing import. Louis Langremont. Who was this man? What was his age, his height, his appearance? Was it not disgusting that a stranger, an unknown, should thus come and suddenly disturb one's existence without cause and from sheer caprice, on account of an old woman who had had a quarrel with her butcher. He again repeated aloud: "What a brute."

And he stood lost in thought, his eyes fixed on the card. Anger was aroused in him against this bit of paper, an anger with which was blended a strange sense of uneasiness. What a stupid business it was. He took a pair of nail scissors which were lying about, and stuck their points into the printed name, as though he was stabbing someone. So he was to fight, and with pistols. Why had he not chosen swords? He would have got off with a prick in the hand or arm, while with the pistols one never knew the possible result. He said: "Come, I must keep my pluck up."

The sound of his own voice made him shudder, and he glanced about him. He began to feel very nervous. He drank a glass of water and went to bed.

As soon as he was in bed he blew out his candle and closed his eyes. He was warm between the sheets, though it was very cold in his room, but he could not manage to doze off. He turned over and over, remained five minutes on his back, then lay on his left side, then rolled on the right. He was still thirsty, and got up to drink. Then a sense of uneasiness assailed him. Was he going to be afraid? Why did his heart beat wildly at each well-known sound in the room? When his clock was going to strike, the faint squeak of the lever made him jump, and he had to open his mouth for some moments in order to breathe, so oppressed did he feel. He began to reason philosophically on the possibility of his being afraid.

No, certainly he would not be afraid, now he had made up his mind to go through with it to the end, since he was firmly decided to fight and not to tremble. But he felt so deeply moved that he asked himself: "Can one be afraid in spite of one's self?" This doubt assailed him. If some power stronger than his will overcame it, what would happen? Yes, what would happen? Certainly he would go on the ground, since he meant to. But suppose he shook? suppose he fainted? And he thought of his position, his reputation, his future.

A strange need of getting up to look at himself in the glass suddenly seized him. He relit the candle. When he saw his face so reflected, he scarcely recognized himself, and it seemed to him that he had never seen himself before. His eyes appeared enormous, and he was pale; yes, he was certainly pale, very pale. Suddenly the thought shot through his mind: "By this time tomorrow I may be dead." And his heart began to beat again furiously. He turned towards his bed, and distinctly saw himself stretched on his back between the same sheets as he had just left. He had the hollow cheeks of the dead, and the whiteness of those hands that no longer move. Then he grew afraid of his bed, and in order to see it no longer he opened the window to look out. An icy coldness assailed him from head to foot, and he drew back breathless.

The thought occurred to him to make a fire. He built it up slowly, without looking around. His hands shook slightly with a kind of nervous tremor when he touched anything. His head wandered, his disjointed, drifting thoughts became fleeting and painful, an intoxication invaded his mind as though he had been drinking. And he kept asking himself: "What shall I do? What will become of me?"

He began to walk up and down, repeating mechanically: "I must pull myself together. I must pull myself together." Then he added: "I will write to my parents, in case of accident." He sat down again, took some notepaper, and wrote: "Dear papa, dear mamma." Then, thinking these words rather too familiar under such tragic circumstances, he tore up the first sheet, and began anew, "My dear father, my dear mother, I am to fight a duel at daybreak, and as it might happen that — " He did not dare write the rest, and sprang up with a jump. He was now crushed by one besetting idea. He was going to fight a duel. He could no longer avoid it. What was the matter with him, then? He meant to fight, his mind was firmly made up to do so, and yet it seemed to him that, despite every effort of will, he could not retain strength enough to go to the place appointed for the meeting. From time to time his teeth absolutely chattered, and he asked himself: "Has my adversary been out before? Is he a frequenter of the shooting galleries? Is he known and classed as a shot?" He had never heard his name mentioned. And yet, if this man was not a remarkably good pistol shot, he would scarcely have accepted that dangerous weapon without discussion or hesitation.

Then Duroy pictured to himself their meeting, his own attitude, and the bearing of his opponent. He wearied himself in imagining the slightest details of the duel, and all at once saw in front of him the little round black hole in the barrel from which the ball was about to issue. He was suddenly seized with a fit of terrible despair. His whole body quivered, shaken by short, sharp shudderings. He clenched his teeth to avoid crying out, and was assailed by a wild desire to roll on the ground, to tear something to pieces, to bite. But he caught sight of a glass on the mantelpiece, and remembered that there was in the cupboard a bottle of brandy almost full, for he had kept up a military habit of a morning dram. He seized the bottle and greedily drank from its mouth in long gulps. He only put it down when his breath failed him. It was a third empty. A warmth like that of flame soon kindled within his body, and spreading through his limbs, buoyed up his mind by deadening his thoughts. He said to himself: "I have hit upon the right plan." And as his skin now seemed burning he reopened the window.

Day was breaking, calm and icy cold. On high the stars seemed dying away in the brightening sky, and in the deep cutting of the railway, the red, green, and white signal lamps were paling. The first locomotives were leaving the engine shed, and went off whistling, to be coupled to the first trains. Others, in the distance, gave vent to shrill and repeated screeches, their awakening cries, like cocks of the country. Duroy thought: "Perhaps I shall never see all this again." But as he felt that he was going again to be moved by the prospect of his own fate, he fought against it strongly, saying: "Come, I must not think of anything till the moment of the meeting; it is the only way to keep up my pluck."

And he set about his toilet. He had another moment of weakness while shaving, in thinking that it was perhaps the last time he should see his face. But he swallowed another mouthful of brandy, and finished dressing. The hour which followed was difficult to get through. He walked up and down, trying to keep from thinking. When he heard a knock at the door he almost dropped, so violent was the shock to him. It was his seconds. Already!

They were wrapped up in furs, and Rival, after shaking his principal's hand, said: "It is as cold as Siberia." Then he added: "Well, how goes it?"

"Very well."

"You are quite steady?"

"Quite."

"That's it; we shall get on all right. Have you had something to eat and drink?"

"Yes; I don't need anything."

Boisrenard, in honor of the occasion, sported a foreign order, yellow and green, that Duroy had never seen him display before.

They went downstairs. A gentleman was awaiting them in the carriage. Rival introduced him as "Doctor Le Brument." Duroy shook hands, saying, "I am very much obliged to you," and sought to take his place on the front seat. He sat down on something hard that made him spring up again, as though impelled by a spring. It was the pistol case.

Rival observed: "No, the back seat for the doctor and the principal, the back seat."

Duroy ended by understanding him, and sank down beside the doctor. The two seconds got in in their turn, and the driver started. He knew where to go. But the pistol case was in the way of everyone, above all of Duroy, who would have preferred it out of sight. They tried to put it at the back of the seat and it hurt their own; they stuck it upright between Rival and Boisrenard, and it kept falling all the time. They finished by stowing it away under their feet. Conversation languished, although the doctor related some anecdotes. Rival alone replied to him. Duroy would have liked to have given a proof of presence of mind, but he was afraid of losing the thread of his ideas, of showing the troubled state of his mind, and was haunted, too, by the disturbing fear of beginning to tremble.

The carriage was soon right out in the country. It was about nine o'clock. It was one of those sharp winter mornings when everything is as bright and brittle as glass. The trees, coated with hoar frost, seemed to have been sweating ice; the earth rang under a footstep, the dry air carried the slightest sound to a distance, the blue sky seemed to shine like a mirror, and the sun, dazzling and cold itself, shed upon the frozen universe rays which did not warm anything.

Rival observed to Duroy: "I got the pistols at Gastine Renette's. He loaded them himself. The box is sealed. We shall toss up, besides, whether we use them or those of our adversary."

Duroy mechanically replied: "I am very much obliged to you."

Then Rival gave him a series of circumstantial recommendations, for he was anxious that his principal should not make any mistake. He emphasized each point several times, saying: "When they say, 'Are you ready, gentlemen?' you must answer 'Yes' in a loud tone. When they give the word 'Fire!' you must raise your arm quickly, and you must fire before they have finished counting 'One, two, three.'"

And Duroy kept on repeating to himself: "When they give the word to fire, I must raise my arm. When they give the word to fire, I must raise my arm." He learnt it as children learn their lessons, by murmuring them to satiety in order to fix them on their minds. "When they give the word to fire, I must raise my arm."

The carriage entered a wood, turned down an avenue on the right, and then to the right again. Rival suddenly opened the door to cry to the driver: "That way, down the narrow road." The carriage turned into a rutty road between two copses, in which dead leaves fringed with ice were quivering. Duroy was still murmuring: "When they give the word to fire, I must raise my arm." And he thought how a carriage accident would settle the whole affair. "Oh! if they could only upset, what luck; if he could only break a leg."

But he caught sight, at the further side of a clearing, of another carriage drawn up, and four gentlemen stamping to keep their feet warm, and he was obliged to open his mouth, so difficult did his breathing become.

The seconds got out first, and then the doctor and the principal. Rival had taken the pistol-case and walked away with Boisrenard to meet two of the strangers who came towards them. Duroy watched them salute one another ceremoniously, and then walk up and down the clearing, looking now on the ground and now at the trees, as though they were looking for something that had fallen down or might fly away. Then they measured off a certain number of paces, and with great difficulty stuck two walking sticks into the frozen ground. They then reassembled in a group and went through the action of tossing, like children playing heads or tails.

Doctor Le Brument said to Duroy: "Do you feel all right? Do you want anything?"

"No, nothing, thanks."

It seemed to him that he was mad, that he was asleep, that he was dreaming, that supernatural influences enveloped him. Was he afraid? Perhaps. But he did not know. Everything about him had altered.

Jacques Rival returned, and announced in low tones of satisfaction: "It is all ready. Luck has favored us as regards the pistols."

That, so far as Duroy was concerned, was a matter of profound indifference.

They took off his overcoat, which he let them do mechanically. They felt the breast-pocket of his frock-coat to make certain that he had no pocketbook or papers likely to deaden a ball. He kept repeating to himself like a prayer: "When the word is given to fire, I must raise my arm."

They led him up to one of the sticks stuck in the ground and handed him his pistol. Then he saw a man standing just in front of him — a short, stout, bald-headed man, wearing spectacles. It was his adversary. He saw him very plainly, but he could only think: "When the word to fire is given, I must raise my arm and fire at once."

A voice rang out in the deep silence, a voice that seemed to come from a great distance, saying: "Are you ready, gentlemen?"

George exclaimed "Yes."

The same voice gave the word "Fire!"

He heard nothing more, he saw nothing more, he took note of nothing more, he only knew that he raised his arm, pressing strongly on the trigger. And he heard nothing. But he saw all at once a little smoke at the end of his pistol barrel, and as the man in front of him still stood in the same position, he perceived, too, a little cloud of smoke drifting off over his head.

They had both fired. It was over.

His seconds and the doctor touched him, felt him and unbuttoned his clothes, asking, anxiously: "Are you hit?"

He replied at haphazard: "No, I do not think so."

Langremont, too, was as unhurt as his enemy, and Jacques Rival murmured in a discontented tone: "It is always so with those damned pistols; you either miss or kill. What a filthy weapon."

Duroy did not move, paralyzed by surprise and joy. It was over. They had to take away his weapon, which he still had clenched in his hand. It seemed to him now that he could have done battle with the whole world. It was over. What happiness! He felt suddenly brave enough to defy no matter whom.

The whole of the seconds conversed together for a few moments, making an appointment to draw up their report of the proceedings in the course of the day. Then they got into the carriage again, and the driver, who was laughing on the box, started off, cracking his whip. They breakfasted together on the boulevards, and in chatting over the event, Duroy narrated his impressions. "I felt quite unconcerned, quite. You must, besides, have seen it yourself."

Rival replied: "Yes, you bore yourself very well."

When the report was drawn up it was handed to Duroy, who was to insert it in the paper. He was astonished to read that he had exchanged a couple of shots with Monsieur Louis Langremont, and rather uneasily interrogated Rival, saying: "But we only fired once."

The other smiled. "Yes, one shot apiece, that makes a couple of shots."

Duroy, deeming the explanation satisfactory, did not persist. Daddy Walter embraced him, saying: "Bravo, bravo, you have defended the colors of Vie Francaise; bravo!"

George showed himself in the course of the evening at the principal newspaper offices, and at the chief cafés on the boulevards. He twice encountered his adversary, who was also showing himself. They did not bow to one another. If one of them had been wounded they would have shaken hands. Each of them, moreover, swore with conviction that he had heard the whistling of the other's bullet.

The next day, at about eleven, Duroy received a telegram. "Awfully alarmed. Come at once. Rue de Constantinople. — Clo."

He hastened to their meeting-place, and she threw herself into his arms, smothering him with kisses.

"Oh, my darling! if you only knew what I felt when I saw the papers this morning. Oh, tell me all about it! I want to know everything."

He had to give minute details. She said: "What a dreadful night you must have passed before the duel."

"No, I slept very well."

"I should not have closed an eye. And on the ground — tell me all that happened."

He gave a dramatic account. "When we were face to face with one another at twenty paces, only four times the length of this room, Jacques, after asking if we were ready, gave the word 'Fire.' I raised my arm at once, keeping a good line, but I made the mistake of trying to aim at the head. I had a pistol with an unusually stiff pull, and I am accustomed to very easy ones, so that the resistance of the trigger caused me to fire too high. No matter, it could not have gone very far off him. He shoots well, too, the rascal. His bullet skimmed by my temple. I felt the wind of it."

She was sitting on his knees, and holding him in her arms as though to share his dangers. She murmured: "Oh, my poor darling! my poor darling!"

When he had finished his narration, she said: "Do you know, I cannot live without you. I must see you, and with my husband in Paris it is not easy. Often I could find an hour in the morning before you were up to run in and kiss you, but I won't enter that awful house of yours. What is to be done?"

He suddenly had an inspiration, and asked: "What is the rent here?"

"A hundred francs a month."

"Well, I will take the rooms over on my own account, and live here altogether. Mine are no longer good enough for my new position."

She reflected a few moments, and then said: "No, I won't have that."

He was astonished, and asked: "Why not?"

"Because I won't."

"That is not a reason. These rooms suit me very well. I am here, and shall remain here. Besides," he added, with a laugh, "they are taken in my name."

But she kept on refusing, "No, no, I won't have it."

"Why not, then?"

Then she whispered tenderly: "Because you would bring women here, and I won't have it."

He grew indignant. "Never. I can promise you that."

"No, you will bring them all the same."

"I swear I won't."

"Truly?"

"Truly, on my word of honor. This is our place, our very own."

She clasped him to her in an outburst of love, exclaiming: "Very well, then, darling. But you know if you once deceive me, only once, it will be all over between us, all over for ever."

He swore again with many protestations, and it was agreed that he should install himself there that very day, so that she could look in on him as she passed the door. Then she said: "In any case, come and dine with us on Sunday. My husband thinks you are charming."

He was flattered "Really!"

"Yes, you have captivated him. And then, listen, you have told me that you were brought up in a country-house."

"Yes; why?"

"Then you must know something about agriculture?"

"Yes."

"Well, talk to him about gardening and the crops. He is very fond of that sort of thing."

"Good; I will not forget."

She left him, after kissing him to an indefinite extent, the duel having stimulated her affection.

Duroy thought, as he made his way to the office, "What a strange being. What a feather brain. Can one tell what she wants and what she cares for? And what a strange household. What fanciful being arranged the union of that old man and this madcap? What made the inspector marry this giddy girl? A mystery. Who knows? Love, perhaps." And he concluded: "After all, she is a very nice little mistress, and I should be a very big fool to let her slip away from me."

VIII

His duel had given Duroy a position among the leader-writers of the Vie Francaise, but as he had great difficulty in finding ideas, he made a specialty of declamatory articles on the decadence of morality, the lowering of the standard of character, the weakening of the patriotic fiber and the anemia of French honor. He had discovered the word anemia, and was very proud of it. And when Madame de Marelle, filled with that skeptical, mocking, and incredulous spirit characteristic of the Parisian, laughed at his tirades, which she demolished with an epigram, he replied with a smile: "Bah! this sort of thing will give me a good reputation later on."

He now resided in the Rue de Constantinople, whither he had shifted his portmanteau, his hairbrush, his razor, and his soap, which was what his moving amounted to. Twice or thrice a week she would call before he was up, undress in a twinkling, and slip into bed, shivering from the cold prevailing out of doors. As a set off, Duroy dined every Thursday at her residence, and paid court to her husband by talking agriculture with him. As he was himself fond of everything relating to the cultivation of the soil, they sometimes both grew so interested in the subject of their conversation that they quite forgot the wife dozing on the sofa. Laurine would also go to sleep, now on the knee of her father and now on that of Pretty-boy. And when the journalist had left, Monsieur de Marelle never failed to assert, in that doctrinal tone in which he said the least thing: "That young fellow is really very pleasant company, he has a well-informed mind."

February was drawing to a close. One began to smell the violets in the street, as one passed the barrows of the flower-sellers of a morning. Duroy was living beneath a sky without a cloud.

One night, on returning home, he found a letter that had been slipped under his door. He glanced at the post-mark, and read "Cannes." Having opened it, he read:

"Villa Jolie, Cannes.

"Dear Sir and Friend, — You told me, did you not, that I could reckon upon you for anything? Well, I have a very painful service to ask of you; it is to come and help me, so that I may not be left alone during the last moments of Charles, who is dying. He may not last out the week, as the doctor has forewarned me, although he has not yet taken to his bed. I have no longer strength nor courage to witness this hourly death, and I think with terror of those last moments which are drawing near. I can only ask such a service of you, as my husband has no relatives. You were his comrade; he opened the door of the paper to you. Come, I beg of you; I have no one else to ask.

"Believe me, your very sincere friend,

"Madeleine Forestier."

A strange feeling filled George's heart, a sense of freedom and of a space opening before him, and he murmured: "To be sure, I'll go. Poor Charles! What are we, after all?"

The governor, to whom he read the letter, grumblingly granted permission, repeating: "But be back soon, you are indispensable to us."

George left for Cannes next day by the seven o'clock express, after letting the Marelles know of his departure by a telegram. He arrived the following evening about four o'clock. A commissionaire guided him to the Villa Jolie, built halfway up the slope of the pine forest clothed with white houses, which extends from Cannes to the Golfe Juan. The house — small, low, and in the Italian style — was built beside the road which winds zig-zag fashion up through the trees, revealing a succession of charming views at every turning it makes.

The man servant opened the door, and exclaimed: "Oh! Sir, madame is expecting you most impatiently."

"How is your master?" inquired Duroy.

"Not at all well, sir. He cannot last much longer."

The drawingroom, into which George was shown, was hung with pink and blue chintz. The tall and wide windows overlooked the town and the sea. Duroy muttered: "By Jove, this is nice and swell for a country house. Where the deuce do they get the money from?"

The rustle of a dress made him turn round. Madame Forestier held out both hands to him. "How good of you to come, how good of you to come," said she.

And suddenly she kissed him on the cheek. Then they looked at one another. She was somewhat paler and thinner, but still fresh-complexioned, and perhaps still prettier for her additional delicacy. She murmured: "He is dreadful, do you know; he knows that he is doomed, and he leads me a fearful life. But where is your portmanteau?"

"I have left it at the station, not knowing what hotel you would like me to stop at in order to be near you."

She hesitated a moment, and then said: "You must stay here. Besides, your room is all ready. He might die at any moment, and if it were to happen during the night I should be alone. I will send for your luggage."

He bowed, saying: "As you please."

"Now let us go upstairs," she said.

He followed her. She opened a door on the first floor, and Duroy saw, wrapped in rugs and seated in an armchair near the window, a kind of living corpse, livid even under the red light of the setting sun, and looking towards him. He scarcely recognized, but rather guessed, that it was his friend. The room reeked of fever, medicated drinks, ether, tar, the nameless and oppressive odor of a consumptive's sick room. Forestier held out his hand slowly and with difficulty. "So here you are; you have come to see me die, then! Thanks."

Duroy affected to laugh. "To see you die? That would not be a very amusing sight, and I should not select such an occasion to visit Cannes. I came to give you a look in, and to rest myself a bit."

Forestier murmured, "Sit down," and then bent his head, as though lost in painful thoughts. He breathed hurriedly and pantingly, and from time to time gave a kind of groan, as if he wanted to remind the others how ill he was.

Seeing that he would not speak, his wife came and leaned against the windowsill, and indicating the view with a motion of her head, said, "Look! Is not that beautiful?"

Before them the hillside, dotted with villas, sloped downwards towards the town, which stretched in a half-circle along the shore with its head to the right in the direction of the pier, overlooked by the old city surmounted by its belfry, and its feet to the left towards the point of La Croisette, facing the Isles of Lerins. These two islands appeared like two green spots amidst the blue water. They seemed to be floating on it like two huge green leaves, so low and flat did they appear from this height. Afar off, bounding the view on the other side of the bay, beyond the pier and the belfry, a long succession of blue hills showed up against a dazzling sky, their strange and picturesque line of summits now rounded, now forked, now pointed, ending with a huge pyramidal mountain, its foot in the sea itself.

Madame Forestier pointed it out, saying: "This is L'Estherel."

The void beyond the dark hill tops was red, a glowing red that the eye would not fear, and Duroy, despite himself, felt the majesty of the close of the day. He murmured, finding no other term strong enough to express his admiration, "It is stunning."

Forestier raised his head, and turning to his wife, said: "Let me have some fresh air."

"Pray, be careful," was her reply. "It is late, and the sun is setting; you will catch a fresh cold, and you know how bad that is for you."

He made a feverish and feeble movement with his right hand that was almost meant for a blow, and murmured with a look of anger, the grin of a dying man that showed all the thinness of his lips, the hollowness of the cheeks, and the prominence of all the bones of the face: "I tell you I am stifling. What does it matter to you whether I die a day sooner or a day later, since I am done for?"

She opened the window quite wide. The air that entered surprised all three like a caress. It was a soft, warm breeze, a breeze of spring, already laden with the scents of the odoriferous shrubs and flowers which sprang up along this shore. A powerful scent of turpentine and the harsh savor of the eucalyptus could be distinguished.

Forestier drank it in with short and fevered gasps. He clutched the arm of his chair with his nails, and said in low, hissing, and savage tones: "Shut the window. It hurts me; I would rather die in a cellar."

His wife slowly closed the window, and then looked out in space, her forehead against the pane. Duroy, feeling very ill at ease, would have liked to have chatted with the invalid and reassured him. But he could think of nothing to comfort him. At length he said: "Then you have not got any better since you have been here?"

Forestier shrugged his shoulders with low-spirited impatience. "You see very well I have not," he replied, and again lowered his head.

Duroy went on: "Hang it all, it is ever so much nicer here than in Paris. We are still in the middle of winter there. It snows, it freezes, it rains, and it is dark enough for the lamps to be lit at three in the afternoon."

"Anything new at the paper?" asked Forestier.

"Nothing. They have taken on young Lacrin, who has left the Voltaire, to do your work, but he is not up to it. It is time that you came back."

The invalid muttered: "I — I shall do all my work six feet under the sod now."

This fixed idea recurred like a knell apropos of everything, continually cropping up in every idea, every sentence. There was a long silence, a deep and painful silence. The glow of the sunset was slowly fading, and the mountains were growing black against the red sky, which was getting duller. A colored shadow, a commencement of night, which yet retained the glow of an expiring furnace, stole into the room and seemed to tinge the furniture, the walls, the hangings, with mingled tints of sable and crimson. The chimney-glass, reflecting the horizon, seemed like a patch of blood. Madame Forestier did not stir, but remained standing with her back to the room, her face to the window pane.

Forestier began to speak in a broken, breathless voice, heartrending to listen to. "How many more sunsets shall I see? Eight, ten, fifteen, or twenty, perhaps thirty — no more. You have time before you; for me it is all over. And it will go on all the same, after I am gone, as if I was still here." He was silent for a few moments, and then continued: "All that I see reminds me that in a few days I shall see it no more. It is horrible. I shall see nothing — nothing of all that exists; not the smallest things one makes use of — the plates, the glasses, the beds in which one rests so comfortably, the carriages. How nice it is to drive out of an evening! How fond I was of all those things!"

He nervously moved the fingers of both hands, as though playing the piano on the arms of his chair. Each of his silences was more painful than his words, so evident was it that his thoughts must be fearful. Duroy suddenly recalled what Norbert de Varenne had said to him some weeks before, "I now see death so near that I often want to stretch out my arms to put it back. I see it everywhere. The insects crushed on the path, the falling leaves, the white hair in a friend's beard, rend my heart and cry to me, 'Behold!'"

He had not understood all this on that occasion; now, seeing Forestier, he did. An unknown pain assailed him, as if he himself was sensible of the presence of death, hideous death, hard by, within reach of his hand, on the chair in which his friend lay gasping. He longed to get up, to go away, to fly, to return to Paris at once. Oh! if he had known he would not have come.

Darkness had now spread over the room, like premature mourning for the dying man. The window alone remained still visible, showing, within the lighter square formed by it, the motionless outline of the young wife.

Forestier remarked, with irritation, "Well, are they going to bring in the lamp tonight? This is what they call looking after an invalid."

The shadow outlined against the window panes disappeared, and the sound of an electric bell rang through the house. A servant shortly entered and placed a lamp on the mantelpiece. Madame Forestier said to her husband, "Will you go to bed, or would you rather come down to dinner?"

He murmured: "I will come down."

Waiting for this meal kept them all three sitting still for nearly an hour, only uttering from time to time some needless commonplace remark, as if there had been some danger, some mysterious danger in letting silence endure too long, in letting the air congeal in this room where death was prowling.

At length dinner was announced. The meal seemed interminable to Duroy. They did not speak, but ate noiselessly, and then crumbled their bread with their fingers. The man servant who waited upon them went to and fro without the sound of his footsteps being heard, for as the creak of a boot-sole irritated Charles, he wore list slippers. The harsh tick of a wooden clock alone disturbed the calm with its mechanical and regular sound.

As soon as dinner was over Duroy, on the plea of fatigue, retired to his room, and leaning on the windowsill watched the full moon, in the midst of the sky like an immense lamp, casting its cold gleam upon the white walls of the villas, and scattering over the sea a soft and moving dappled light. He strove to find some reason to justify a swift departure, inventing plans, telegrams he was to receive, a recall from Monsieur Walter.

But his resolves to fly appeared more difficult to realize on awakening the next morning. Madame Forestier would not be taken in by his devices, and he would lose by his cowardice all the benefit of his self-devotion. He said to himself: "Bah! it is awkward; well so much the worse, there must be unpleasant situations in life, and, besides, it will perhaps be soon over."

It was a bright day, one of those bright Southern days that make the heart feel light, and Duroy walked down to the sea, thinking that it would be soon enough to see Forestier some time in course of the afternoon. When he returned to lunch, the servant remarked, "Master has already asked for you two or three times, sir. Will you please step up to his room, sir?"

He went upstairs. Forestier appeared to be dozing in his armchair. His wife was reading, stretched out on the sofa.

The invalid raised his head, and Duroy said, "Well, how do you feel? You seem quite fresh this morning."

"Yes, I am better, I have recovered some of my strength. Get through your lunch with Madeleine as soon as you can, for we are going out for a drive."

As soon as she was alone with Duroy, the young wife said to him, "There, to-day he thinks he is all right again. He has been making plans all the morning. We are going to the Golfe Juan now to buy some pottery for our rooms in Paris. He is determined to go out, but I am horribly afraid of some mishap. He cannot bear the shaking of the drive."

When the landau arrived, Forestier came down stairs a step at a time, supported by his servant. But as soon as he caught sight of the carriage, he ordered the hood to be taken off. His wife opposed this, saying, "You will catch cold. It is madness."

He persisted, repeating, "Oh, I am much better. I feel it."

They passed at first along some of those shady roads, bordered by gardens, which cause Cannes to resemble a kind of English Park, and then reached the highway to Antibes, running along the seashore. Forestier acted as guide. He had already pointed out the villa of the Court de Paris, and now indicated others. He was lively, with the forced and feeble gayety of a doomed man. He lifted his finger, no longer having strength to stretch out his arm, and said, "There is the Ile Sainte Marguerite, and the chateau from which Bazaine escaped. How they did humbug us over that matter!"

Then regimental recollections recurred to him, and he mentioned various officers whose names recalled incidents to them. But all at once, the road making a turn, they caught sight of the whole of the Golfe Juan, with the white village in the curve of the bay, and the point of Antibes at the further side of it. Forestier, suddenly seized upon by childish glee, exclaimed, "Ah! the squadron, you will see the squadron."

Indeed they could perceive, in the middle of the broad bay, half-a-dozen large ships resembling rocks covered with leafless trees. They were huge, strange, misshapen, with excrescences, turrets, rams, burying themselves in the water as though to take root beneath the waves. One could scarcely imagine how they could stir or move about, they seemed so heavy and so firmly fixed to the bottom. A floating battery, circular and high out of water, resembling the lighthouses that are built on shoals. A tall three-master passed near them, with all its white sails set. It looked graceful and pretty beside these iron war monsters squatted on the water. Forestier tried to make them out. He pointed out the Colbert, the Suffren, the Admiral Duperre, the Redoubtable, the Devastation, and then checking himself, added, "No I made a mistake; that one is the Devastation."

They arrived opposite a species of large pavilion, on the front of which was the inscription, "Art Pottery of the Golfe Juan," and the carriage, driving up the sweep, stopped before the door. Forestier wanted to buy a couple of vases for his study. As he felt unequal to getting out of the carriage, specimens were brought out to him one after the other. He was a long time in making a choice, and consulted his wife and Duroy.

"You know," he said, "it is for the cabinet at the end of the study. Sitting in my chair, I have it before my eyes all the time. I want an antique form, a Greek outline." He examined the specimens, had others brought, and then turned again to the first ones. At length he made up his mind, and having paid, insisted upon the articles being sent on at once. "I shall be going back to Paris in a few days," he said.

They drove home, but as they skirted the bay a rush of cold air from one of the valleys suddenly met them, and the invalid began to cough. It was nothing at first, but it augmented and became an unbroken fit of coughing, and then a kind of gasping hiccough.

Forestier was choking, and every time he tried to draw breath the cough seemed to rend his chest. Nothing would soothe or check it. He had to be borne from the carriage to his room, and Duroy, who supported his legs, felt the jerking of his feet at each convulsion of his lungs. The warmth of the bed did not check the attack, which lasted till midnight, when, at length, narcotics lulled its deadly spasm. The sick man remained till morning sitting up in his bed, with his eyes open.

The first words he uttered were to ask for the barber, for he insisted on being shaved every morning. He got up for this operation, but had to be helped back into bed at once, and his breathing grew so short, so hard, and so difficult, that Madame Forestier, in alarm, had Duroy, who had just turned in, roused up again in order to beg him to go for the doctor.

He came back almost immediately with Dr. Gavaut, who prescribed a soothing drink and gave some advice; but when the journalist saw him to the door, in order to ask his real opinion, he said, "It is the end. He will be dead tomorrow morning. Break it to his poor wife, and send for a priest. I, for my part, can do nothing more. I am, however, entirely at your service."

Duroy sent for Madame Forestier. "He is dying," said he. "The doctor advises a priest being sent for. What would you like done?"

She hesitated for some time, and then, in slow tones, as though she had calculated everything, replied, "Yes, that will be best — in many respects. I will break it to him — tell him the vicar wants to see him, or something or other; I really don't know what. You would be very kind if you would go and find a priest for me and pick one out. Choose one who won't raise too many difficulties over the business. One who will be satisfied with confession, and will let us off with the rest of it all."

The young fellow returned with a complaisant old ecclesiastic, who accommodated himself to the state of affairs. As soon as he had gone into the dying man's room, Madame Forestier came out of it, and sat down with Duroy in the one adjoining.

"It has quite upset him," said she. "When I spoke to him about a priest his face assumed a frightful expression as if he had felt the breath — the breath of — you know. He understood that it was all over at last, and that his hours were numbered." She was very pale as she continued, "I shall never forget the expression of his face. He certainly saw death face to face at that moment. He saw him."

They could hear the priest, who spoke in somewhat loud tones, being slightly deaf, and who was saying, "No, no; you are not so bad as all that. You are ill, but in no danger. And the proof is that I have called in as a friend as a neighbor."

They could not make out Forestier's reply, but the old man went on, "No, I will not ask you to communicate. We will talk of that when you are better. If you wish to profit by my visit — to confess, for instance — I ask nothing better. I am a shepherd, you know, and seize on every occasion to bring a lamb back to the fold."

A long silence followed. Forestier must have been speaking in a faint voice. Then all at once the priest uttered in a different tone, the tone of one officiating at the altar. "The mercy of God is infinite. Repeat the Comfiteor, my son. You have perhaps forgotten it; I will help you. Repeat after me: 'Comfiteor Deo omnipotenti — Beata Maria semper virgini.'"

He paused from time to time to allow the dying man to catch him up. Then he said, "And now confess."

The young wife and Duroy sat still seized on by a strange uneasiness, stirred by anxious expectation. The invalid had murmured something. The priest repeated, "You have given way to guilty pleasures — of what kind, my son?"

Madeleine rose and said, "Let us go down into the garden for a short time. We must not listen to his secrets."

And they went and sat down on a bench before the door beneath a rose tree in bloom, and beside a bed of pinks, which shed their soft and powerful perfume abroad in the pure air. Duroy, after a few moments' silence, inquired, "Shall you be long before you return to Paris?"

"Oh, no," she replied. "As soon as it is all over I shall go back there."

"Within ten days?"

"Yes, at the most."

"He has no relations, then?"

"None except cousins. His father and mother died when he was quite young."

They both watched a butterfly sipping existence from the pinks, passing from one to another with a soft flutter of his wings, which continued to flap slowly when he alighted on a flower. They remained silent for a considerable time.

The servant came to inform them that "the priest had finished," and they went upstairs together.

Forestier seemed to have grown still thinner since the day before. The priest held out his hand to him, saying, "Good-day, my son, I shall call in again tomorrow morning," and took his departure.

As soon as he had left the room the dying man, who was panting for breath, strove to hold out his two hands to his wife, and gasped, "Save me — save me, darling, I don't want to die — I don't want to die. Oh! save me — tell me what I had better do; send for the doctor. I will take whatever you like. I won't die — I won't die."

He wept. Big tears streamed from his eyes down his fleshless cheeks, and the corners of his mouth contracted like those of a vexed child. Then his hands, falling back on the bed clothes, began a slow, regular, and continuous movement, as though trying to pick something off the sheet.

His wife, who began to cry too, said: "No, no, it is nothing. It is only a passing attack, you will be better tomorrow, you tired yourself too much going out yesterday."

Forestier's breathing was shorter than that of a dog who has been running, so quick that it could not be counted, so faint that it could scarcely be heard.

He kept repeating: "I don't want to die. Oh! God — God — God; what is to become of me? I shall no longer see anything — anything any more. Oh! God."

He saw before him some hideous thing invisible to the others, and his staring eyes reflected the terror it inspired. His two hands continued their horrible and wearisome action. All at once he started with a sharp shudder that could be seen to thrill the whole of his body, and jerked out the words, "The graveyard — I — Oh! God."

He said no more, but lay motionless, haggard and panting.

Time sped on, noon struck by the clock of a neighboring convent. Duroy left the room to eat a mouthful or two. He came back an hour later. Madame Forestier refused to take anything. The invalid had not stirred. He still continued to draw his thin fingers along the sheet as though to pull it up over his face.

His wife was seated in an armchair at the foot of the bed. Duroy took another beside her, and they waited in silence. A nurse had come, sent in by the doctor, and was dozing near the window.

Duroy himself was beginning to doze off when he felt that something was happening. He opened his eyes just in time to see Forestier close his, like two lights dying out. A faint rattle stirred in the throat of the dying man, and two streaks of blood appeared at the corners of his mouth, and then flowed down into his shirt. His hands ceased their hideous motion. He had ceased to breathe.

His wife understood this, and uttering a kind of shriek, she fell on her knees sobbing, with her face buried in the bedclothes. George, surprised and scared, mechanically made the sign of the cross. The nurse awakened, drew near the bed. "It is all over," said she.

Duroy, who was recovering his self-possession, murmured, with a sigh of relief: "It was sooner over than I thought for."

When the first shock was over and the first tears shed, they had to busy themselves with all the cares and all the necessary steps a dead man exacts. Duroy was running about till nightfall. He was very hungry when he got back. Madame Forestier ate a little, and then they both installed themselves in the chamber of death to watch the body. Two candles burned on the night-table beside a plate filled with holy water, in which lay a sprig of mimosa, for they had not been able to get the necessary twig of consecrated box.

They were alone, the young man and the young wife, beside him who was no more. They sat without speaking, thinking and watching.

George, whom the darkness rendered uneasy in presence of the corpse, kept his eyes on this persistently. His eye and his mind were both attracted and fascinated by this fleshless visage, which the vacillating light caused to appear yet more hollow. That was his friend Charles Forestier, who was chatting with him only the day before! What a strange and fearful thing was this end of a human being! Oh! how he recalled the words of Norbert de Varenne haunted by the fear of death: "No one ever comes back." Millions on millions would be born almost identical, with eyes, a nose, a mouth, a skull and a mind within it, without he who lay there on the bed ever reappearing again.

For some years he had lived, eaten, laughed, loved, hoped like all the world. And it was all over for him all over for ever. Life; a few days, and then nothing. One is born, one grows up, one is happy, one waits, and then one dies. Farewell, man or woman, you will not return again to earth. Plants, beast, men, stars, worlds, all spring to life, and then die to be transformed anew. But never one of them comes back — insect, man, nor planet.

A huge, confused, and crushing sense of terror weighed down the soul of Duroy, the terror of that boundless and inevitable annihilation destroying all existence. He already bowed his head before its menace. He thought of the flies who live a few hours, the beasts who live a few days, the men who live a few years, the worlds which live a few centuries. What was the difference between one and the other? A few more days' dawn that was all.

He turned away his eyes in order no longer to have the corpse before them. Madame Forestier, with bent head, seemed also absorbed in painful thoughts. Her fair hair showed so prettily with her pale face, that a feeling, sweet as the touch of hope flitted through the young fellow's breast. Why grieve when he had still so many years before him? And he began to observe her. Lost in thought she did not notice him. He said to himself, "That, though, is the only good thing in life, to love, to hold the woman one loves in one's arms. That is the limit of human happiness."

What luck the dead man had had to meet such an intelligent and charming companion! How had they become acquainted? How ever had she agreed on her part to marry that poor and commonplace young fellow? How had she succeeded in making someone of him? Then he thought of all the hidden mysteries of people's lives. He remembered what had been whispered about the Count de Vaudrec, who had dowered and married her off it was said.

What would she do now? Whom would she marry? A deputy, as Madame de Marelle fancied, or some young fellow with a future before him, a higher class Forestier? Had she any projects, any plans, any settled ideas? How he would have liked to know that. But why this anxiety as to what she would do? He asked himself this, and perceived that his uneasiness was due to one of those half-formed and secret ideas which one hides from even one's self, and only discovers when fathoming one's self to the very bottom.

Yes, why should he not attempt this conquest himself? How strong and redoubtable he would be with her beside him!

How quick, and far, and surely he would fly! And why should he not succeed too? He felt that he pleased her, that she had for him more than mere sympathy; in fact, one of those affections which spring up between two kindred spirits and which partake as much of silent seduction as of a species of mute complicity. She knew him to be intelligent, resolute, and tenacious, she would have confidence in him.

Had she not sent for him under the present grave circumstances? And why had she summoned him? Ought he not to see in this a kind of choice, a species of confession. If she had thought of him just at the moment she was about to become a widow, it was perhaps that she had thought of one who was again to become her companion and ally? An impatient desire to know this, to question her, to learn her intentions, assailed him. He would have to leave on the next day but one, as he could not remain alone with her in the house. So it was necessary to be quick, it was necessary before returning to Paris to become acquainted, cleverly and delicately, with her projects, and not to allow her to go back on them, to yield perhaps to the solicitations of another, and pledge herself irrevocably.

The silence in the room was intense, nothing was audible save the regular and metallic tick of the pendulum of the clock on the mantelpiece.

He murmured: "You must be very tired?"

She replied: "Yes; but I am, above all, overwhelmed."

The sound of their own voices startled them, ringing strangely in this gloomy room, and they suddenly glanced at the dead man's face as though they expected to see it move on hearing them, as it had done some hours before.

Duroy resumed: "Oh! it is a heavy blow for you, and such a complete change in your existence, a shock to your heart and your whole life."

She gave a long sigh, without replying, and he continued, "It is so painful for a young woman to find herself alone as you will be."

He paused, but she said nothing, and he again went on, "At all events, you know the compact entered into between us. You can make what use of me you will. I belong to you."

She held out her hand, giving him at the same time one of those sweet, sad looks which stir us to the very marrow.

"Thank you, you are very kind," she said. "If I dared, and if I could do anything for you, I, too, should say, 'You may count upon me.'"

He had taken the proffered hand and kept it clasped in his, with a burning desire to kiss it. He made up his mind to this at last, and slowly raising it to his mouth, held the delicate skin, warm, slightly feverish and perfumed, to his lips for some time. Then, when he felt that his friendly caress was on the point of becoming too prolonged, he let fall the little hand. It sank back gently onto the knee of its mistress, who said, gravely: "Yes, I shall be very lonely, but I shall strive to be brave."

He did not know how to give her to understand that he would be happy, very happy, to have her for his wife in his turn. Certainly he could not tell her so at that hour, in that place, before that corpse; yet he might, it seemed to him, hit upon one of those ambiguous, decorous, and complicated phrases which have a hidden meaning under their words, and which express all one wants to by their studied reticence. But the corpse incommoded him, the stiffened corpse stretched out before them, and which he felt between them. For some time past, too, he fancied he detected in the close atmosphere of the room a suspicious odor, a fœtid breath exhaling from the decomposing chest, the first whiff of carrion which the dead lying on their bed throw out to the relatives watching them, and with which they soon fill the hollow of their coffin.

"Cannot we open the window a little?" said Duroy. "It seems to me that the air is tainted."

"Yes," she replied, "I have just noticed it, too."

He went to the window and opened it. All the perfumed freshness of night flowed in, agitating the flame of the two lighted candles beside the bed. The moon was shedding, as on the former evening, her full mellow light upon the white walls of the villas and the broad glittering expanse of the sea. Duroy, drawing in the air to the full depth of his lungs, felt himself suddenly seized with hope, and, as it were buoyed up by the approach of happiness. He turned round, saying: "Come and get a little fresh air. It is delightful."

She came quietly, and leant on the windowsill beside him. Then he murmured in a low tone: "Listen to me, and try to understand what I want to tell you. Above all, do not be indignant at my speaking to you of such a matter at such a moment, for I shall leave you the day after tomorrow, and when you return to Paris it may be too late. I am only a poor devil without fortune, and with a position yet to make, as you know. But I have a firm will, some brains I believe, and I am well on the right track. With a man who has made his position, one knows what one gets; with one who is starting, one never knows where he may finish. So much the worse, or so much the better. In short, I told you one day at your house that my brightest dream would have been to have married a woman like you. I repeat this wish to you now. Do not answer, let me continue. It is not a proposal I am making to you. The time and place would render that odious. I wish only not to leave you ignorant that you can make me happy with a word; that you can make me either a friend and brother, or a husband, at your will; that my heart and myself are yours. I do not want you to answer me now. I do not want us to speak any more about the matter here. When we meet again in Paris you will let me know what you have resolved upon. Until then, not a word. Is it not so?" He had uttered all this without looking at her, as though scattering his words abroad in the night before him. She seemed not to have heard them, so motionless had she remained, looking also straight before her with a fixed and vague stare at the vast landscape lit up by the moon. They remained for some time side by side, elbow touching elbow, silent and reflecting. Then she murmured: "It is rather cold," and turning round, returned towards the bed.

He followed her. When he drew near he recognized that Forestier's body was really beginning to smell, and drew his chair to a distance, for he could not have stood this odor of putrefaction long. He said: "He must be put in a coffin the first thing in the morning."

"Yes, yes, it is arranged," she replied. "The undertaker will be here at eight o'clock."

Duroy having sighed out the words, "Poor fellow," she, too, gave a long sigh of heartrending resignation.

They did not look at the body so often now, already accustomed to the idea of it, and beginning to mentally consent to the decease which but a short time back had shocked and angered them — them who were mortals, too. They no longer spoke, continuing to keep watch in befitting fashion without going to sleep. But towards midnight Duroy dozed off the first. When he woke up he saw that Madame Forestier was also slumbering, and having shifted to a more comfortable position, he reclosed his eyes, growling: "Confound it all, it is more comfortable between the sheets all the same."

A sudden noise made him start up. The nurse was entering the room. It was broad daylight. The young wife in the armchair in front of him seemed as surprised as himself. She was somewhat pale, but still pretty, fresh-looking, and nice, in spite of this night passed in a chair.

Then, having glanced at the corpse, Duroy started and exclaimed: "Oh, his beard!" The beard had grown in a few hours on this decomposing flesh as much as it would have in several days on a living face. And they stood scared by this life continuing in death, as though in presence of some fearful prodigy, some supernatural threat of resurrection, one of these startling and abnormal events which upset and confound the mind.

They both went and lay down until eleven o'clock. Then they placed Charles in his coffin, and at once felt relieved and soothed. They had sat down face to face at lunch with an aroused desire to speak of the livelier and more consolatory matters, to return to the things of life again, since they had done with the dead. Through the wide-open window the soft warmth of spring flowed in, bearing the perfumed breath of the bed of pinks in bloom before the door.

Madame Forestier suggested a stroll in the garden to Duroy, and they began to walk slowly round the little lawn, inhaling with pleasure the balmy air, laden with the scent of pine and eucalyptus. Suddenly she began to speak, without turning her head towards him, as he had done during the night upstairs. She uttered her words slowly, in a low and serious voice.

"Look here, my dear friend, I have deeply reflected already on what you proposed to me, and I do not want you to go away without an answer. Besides, I am neither going to say yes nor no.

We will wait, we will see, we will know one another better. Reflect, too, on your side. Do not give way to impulse. But if I speak to you of this before even poor Charles is lowered into the tomb, it is because it is necessary, after what you have said to me, that you should thoroughly understand what sort of woman I am, in order that you may no longer cherish the wish you expressed to me, in case you are not of a — of a — disposition to comprehend and bear with me. Understand me well. Marriage for me is not a charm, but a partnership. I mean to be free, perfectly free as to my ways, my acts, my going and coming. I could neither tolerate supervision, nor jealousy, nor arguments as to my behavior. I should undertake, be it understood, never to compromise the name of the man who takes me as his wife, never to render him hateful and ridiculous. But this man must also undertake to see in me an equal, an ally, and not an inferior or an obedient and submissive wife. My notions, I know, are not those of every one, but I shall not change them. There you are. I will also add, do not answer me; it would be useless and unsuitable. We shall see one another again, and shall perhaps speak of all this again later on. Now, go for a stroll. I shall return to watch beside him. Till this evening."

He printed a long kiss on her hand, and went away without uttering a word. That evening they only saw one another at dinnertime. Then they retired to their rooms, both exhausted with fatigue.

Charles Forestier was buried the next day, without any funeral display, in the cemetery at Cannes. George Duroy wished to take the Paris express, which passed through the town at halfpast one.

Madame Forestier drove with him to the station. They walked quietly up and down the platform pending the time for his departure, speaking of trivial matters.

The train rolled into the station. The journalist took his seat, and then got out again to have a few more moments' conversation with her, suddenly seized as he was with sadness and a strong regret at leaving her, as though he were about to lose her for ever.

A porter shouted, "Take your seats for Marseilles, Lyons, and Paris." Duroy got in and leant out of the window to say a few more words. The engine whistled, and the train began to move slowly on.

The young fellow, leaning out of the carriage, watched the woman standing still on the platform and following him with her eyes. Suddenly, as he was about to lose sight of her, he put his hand to his mouth and threw a kiss towards her. She returned it with a discreet and hesitating gesture.

IX

George Duroy had returned to all his old habits.

Installed at present in the little ground-floor suite of rooms in the Rue de Constantinople, he lived soberly, like a man preparing a new existence for himself.

Madame Forestier had not yet returned. She was lingering at Cannes. He received a letter from her merely announcing her return about the middle of April, without a word of allusion to their farewell. He was waiting, his mind was thoroughly made up now to employ every means in order to marry her, if she seemed to hesitate. But he had faith in his luck, confidence in that power of seduction which he felt within him, a vague and irresistible power which all women felt the influence of.

A short note informed him that the decisive hour was about to strike: "I am in Paris. Come and see me. — Madeleine Forestier."

Nothing more. He received it by the nine o'clock post. He arrived at her residence at three on the same day. She held out both hands to him smiling with her pleasant smile, and they looked into one another's eyes for a few seconds. Then she said: "How good you were to come to me there under those terrible circumstances."

"I should have done anything you told me to," he replied.

And they sat down. She asked the news, inquired about the Walters, about all the staff, about the paper. She had often thought about the paper.

"I miss that a great deal," she said, "really a very great deal. I had become at heart a journalist. What would you, I love the profession?"

Then she paused. He thought he understood, he thought he divined in her smile, in the tone of her voice, in her words themselves a kind of invitation, and although he had promised to himself not to precipitate matters, he stammered out: "Well, then — why — why should you not resume — this occupation — under — under the name of Duroy?"

She suddenly became serious again, and placing her hand on his arm, murmured: "Do not let us speak of that yet a while."

But he divined that she accepted, and falling at her knees began to passionately kiss her hands, repeating: "Thanks, thanks; oh, how I love you!"

She rose. He did so, too, and noted that she was very pale. Then he understood that he had pleased her, for a long time past, perhaps, and as they found themselves face to face, he clasped her to him and printed a long, tender, and decorous kiss on her forehead. When she had freed herself, slipping through his arms, she said in a serious tone: "Listen, I have not yet made up my mind to anything. However, it may be — yes. But you must promise me the most absolute secrecy till I give you leave to speak."

He swore this, and left, his heart overflowing with joy.

He was from that time forward very discreet as regards the visits he paid her, and did not ask for any more definite consent on her part, for she had a way of speaking of the future, of saying "by-and-by," and of shaping plans in which these two lives were blended, which answered him better and more delicately than a formal acceptation.

Duroy worked hard and spent little, trying to save money so as not to be without a penny at the date fixed for his marriage, and becoming as close as he had been prodigal. The summer went by, and then the autumn, without anyone suspecting anything, for they met very little, and only in the most natural way in the world.

One evening, Madeleine, looking him straight in the eyes said: "You have not yet announced our intentions to Madame de Marelle?"

"No, dear, having promised you to be secret, I have not opened my mouth to a living soul."

"Well, it is about time to tell her. I will undertake to inform the Walters. You will do so this week, will you not?"

He blushed as he said: "Yes, tomorrow."

She had turned away her eyes in order not to notice his confusion, and said: "If you like we will be married in the beginning of May. That will be a very good time."

"I obey you in all things with joy."

"The tenth of May, which is a Saturday, will suit me very nicely, for it is my birthday."

"Very well, the tenth of May."

"Your parents live near Rouen, do they not? You have told me so, at least."

"Yes, near Rouen, at Canteleu."

"What are they?"

"They are — they are small annuitants."

"Ah! I should very much like to know them."

He hesitated, greatly perplexed, and said: "But, you see, they are — " Then making up his mind, like a really clever man, he went on: "My dear, they are mere country folk, innkeepers, who have pinched themselves to the utmost to enable me to pursue my studies. For my part, I am not ashamed of them, but their — simplicity — their rustic manners — might, perhaps, render you uncomfortable."

She smiled, delightfully, her face lit up with gentle kindness as she replied: "No. I shall be very fond of them. We will go and see them. I want to. I will speak of this to you again. I, too, am a daughter of poor people, but I have lost my parents. I have no longer anyone in the world." She held out her hand to him as she added: "But you."

He felt softened, moved, overcome, as he had been by no other woman.

"I had thought about one matter," she continued, "but it is rather difficult to explain."

"What is it?" he asked.

"Well, it is this, my dear boy, I am like all women, I have my weaknesses, my pettinesses. I love all that glitters, that catches the ear. I should have so delighted to have borne a noble name. Could you not, on the occasion of your marriage, ennoble yourself a little?"

She had blushed in her turn, as if she had proposed something indelicate.

He replied simply enough: "I have often thought about it, but it did not seem to me so easy."

"Why so?"

He began to laugh, saying: "Because I was afraid of making myself look ridiculous."

She shrugged her shoulders. "Not at all, not at all Every one does it, and nobody laughs. Separate your name in two — Du Roy. That looks very well."

He replied at once like a man who understands the matter in question: "No, that will not do at all. It is too simple, too common, too well-known. I had thought of taking the name of my native place, as a literary pseudonym at first, then of adding it to my own by degrees, and then, later on, of even cutting my name in two, as you suggest."

"Your native place is Canteleu?" she queried.

"Yes."

She hesitated, saying: "No, I do not like the termination. Come, cannot we modify this word Canteleu a little?"

She had taken up a pen from the table, and was scribbling names and studying their physiognomy. All at once she exclaimed: "There, there it is!" and held out to him a paper, on which read — "Madame Duroy de Cantel."

He reflected a few moments, and then said gravely: "Yes, that does very well."

She was delighted, and kept repeating "Duroy de Cantel, Duroy de Cantel, Madame Duroy de Cantel. It is capital, capital." She went on with an air of conviction: "And you will see how easy it is to get everyone to accept it. But one must know how to seize the opportunity, for it will be too late afterwards. You must from tomorrow sign your descriptive articles D. de Cantel, and your 'Echoes' simply Duroy. It is done every day in the press, and no one will be astonished to see you take a pseudonym. At the moment of our marriage we can modify it yet a little more, and tell our friends that you had given up the 'Du' out of modesty on account of your position, or even say nothing about it. What is your father's Christian name?"

"Alexander."

She murmured: "Alexander, Alexander," two or three times, listening to the sonorous roll of the syllables, and then wrote on a blank sheet of paper:

"Monsieur and Madame Alexander Du Roy de Cantel have the honor to inform you of the marriage of Monsieur George Du Roy de Cantel, their son, to Madame Madeleine Forestier." She looked at her writing, holding it at a distance, charmed by the effect, and said: "With a little method we can manage whatever we wish."

When he found himself once more in the street, firmly resolved to call himself in future Du Roy, and even Du Roy de Cantel, it seemed to him that he had acquired fresh importance. He walked with more swagger, his head higher, his moustache fiercer, as a gentleman should walk. He felt in himself a species of joyous desire to say to the passersby: "My name is Du Roy de Cantel."

But scarcely had he got home than the thought of Madame de Marelle made him feel uneasy, and he wrote to her at once to ask her to make an appointment for the next day.

"It will be a tough job," he thought. "I must look out for squalls."

Then he made up his mind for it, with the native carelessness which caused him to slur over the disagreeable side of life, and began to write a fancy article on the fresh taxes needed in order to make the Budget balance. He set down in this the nobiliary "De" at a hundred francs a year, and titles, from baron to prince, at from five hundred to five thousand francs. And he signed it "D. de Cantel."

He received a telegram from his mistress next morning saying that she would call at one o'clock. He waited for her somewhat feverishly, his mind made up to bring things to a point at once, to say everything right out, and then, when the first emotion had subsided, to argue cleverly in order to prove to her that he could not remain a bachelor for ever, and that as Monsieur de Marelle insisted on living, he had been obliged to think of another than herself as his legitimate companion. He felt moved, though, and when he heard her ring his heart began to beat.

She threw herself into his arms, exclaiming: "Good morning, Pretty-boy." Then, finding his embrace cold, looked at him, and said: "What is the matter with you?"

"Sit down," he said, "we have to talk seriously."

She sat down without taking her bonnet off, only turning back her veil, and waited.

He had lowered his eyes, and was preparing the beginning of his speech. He commenced in a low tone of voice: "My dear one, you see me very uneasy, very sad, and very much embarrassed at what I have to admit to you. I love you dearly. I really love you from the bottom of my heart, so that the fear of causing you pain afflicts me more than even the news I am going to tell you."

She grew pale, felt herself tremble, and stammered out: "What is the matter? Tell me at once."

He said in sad but resolute tones, with that feigned dejection which we make use of to announce fortunate misfortunes: "I am going to be married."

She gave the sigh of a woman who is about to faint, a painful sigh from the very depths of her bosom, and then began to choke and gasp without being able to speak.

Seeing that she did not say anything, he continued: "You cannot imagine how much I suffered before coming to this resolution. But I have neither position nor money. I am alone, lost in Paris. I needed beside me someone who above all would be an adviser, a consoler, and a stay. It is a partner, an ally, that I have sought, and that I have found."

He was silent, hoping that she would reply, expecting furious rage, violence, and insults. She had placed one hand on her heart as though to restrain its throbbings, and continued to draw her breath by painful efforts, which made her bosom heave spasmodically and her head nod to and fro. He took her other hand, which was resting on the arm of the chair, but she snatched it away abruptly. Then she murmured, as though in a state of stupefaction: "Oh, my God!"

He knelt down before her, without daring to touch her, however, and more deeply moved by this silence than he would have been by a fit of anger, stammered out: "Clo! my darling Clo! just consider my situation, consider what I am. Oh! if I had been able to marry you, what happiness it would have been. But you are married. What could I do? Come, think of it, now. I must take a place in society, and I cannot do it so long as I have not a home. If you only knew. There are days when I have felt a longing to kill your husband."

He spoke in his soft, subdued, seductive voice, a voice which entered the ear like music. He saw two tears slowly gather in the fixed and staring eyes of his mistress and then roll down her cheeks, while two more were already formed on the eyelids.

He murmured: "Do not cry, Clo; do not cry, I beg of you. You rend my very heart."

Then she made an effort, a strong effort, to be proud and dignified, and asked, in the quivering tone of a woman about to burst into sobs: "Who is it?"

He hesitated a moment, and then understanding that he must, said:

"Madeleine Forestier."

Madame de Marelle shuddered all over, and remained silent, so deep in thought that she seemed to have forgotten that he was at her feet. And two transparent drops kept continually forming in her eyes, falling and forming again.

She rose. Duroy guessed that she was going away without saying a word, without reproach or forgiveness, and he felt hurt and humiliated to the bottom of his soul. Wishing to stay her, he threw his arms about the skirt of her dress, clasping through the stuff her rounded legs, which he felt stiffen in resistance. He implored her, saying: "I beg of you, do not go away like that."

Then she looked down on him from above with that moistened and despairing eye, at once so charming and so sad, which shows all the grief of a woman's heart, and gasped out: "I — I have nothing to say. I have nothing to do with it. You — you are right. You — you have chosen well."

And, freeing herself by a backward movement, she left the room without his trying to detain her further.

Left to himself, he rose as bewildered as if he had received a blow on the head. Then, making up his mind, he muttered: "Well, so much the worse or the better. It is over, and without a scene; I prefer that," and relieved from an immense weight, suddenly feeling himself free, delivered, at ease as to his future life, he began to spar at the wall, hitting out with his fists in a kind of intoxication of strength and triumph, as if he had been fighting Fate.

When Madame Forestier asked: "Have you told Madame de Marelle?" he quietly answered, "Yes."

She scanned him closely with her bright eyes, saying: "And did it not cause her any emotion?"

"No, not at all. She thought it, on the contrary, a very good idea."

The news was soon known. Some were astonished, others asserted that they had foreseen it; others, again, smiled, and let it be understood that they were not surprised.

The young man who now signed his descriptive articles D. de Cantel, his "Echoes" Duroy, and the political articles which he was beginning to write from time to time Du Roy, passed half his time with his betrothed, who treated him with a fraternal familiarity into which, however, entered a real but hidden love, a species of desire concealed as a weakness. She had decided that the marriage should be quite private, only the witnesses being present, and that they should leave the same evening for Rouen. They would go the next day to see the journalist's parents, and remain with them some days. Duroy had striven to get her to renounce this project, but not having been able to do so, had ended by giving in to it.

So the tenth of May having come, the newly-married couple, having considered the religious ceremony useless since they had not invited anyone, returned to finish packing their boxes after a brief visit to the Town Hall. They took, at the Saint Lazare terminus, the six o'clock train, which bore them away towards Normandy. They had scarcely exchanged twenty words up to the time that they found themselves alone in the railway carriage. As soon as they felt themselves under way, they looked at one another and began to laugh, to hide a certain feeling of awkwardness which they did not want to manifest.

The train slowly passed through the long station of Batignolles, and then crossed the mangy-looking plain extending from the fortifications to the Seine. Duroy and his wife from time to time made a few idle remarks, and then turned again towards the windows. When they crossed the bridge of Asniéres, a feeling of greater liveliness was aroused in them at the sight of the river covered with boats, fishermen, and oarsmen. The sun, a bright May sun, shed its slanting rays upon the craft and upon the smooth stream, which seemed motionless, without current or eddy, checked, as it were, beneath the heat and brightness of the declining day. A sailing boat in the middle of the river having spread two large triangular sails of snowy canvas, wing and wing, to catch the faintest puffs of wind, looked like an immense bird preparing to take flight.

Duroy murmured: "I adore the neighborhood of Paris. I have memories of dinners which I reckon among the pleasantest in my life."

"And the boats," she replied. "How nice it is to glide along at sunset."

Then they became silent, as though afraid to continue their outpourings as to their past life, and remained so, already enjoying, perhaps, the poesy of regret.

Duroy, seated face to face with his wife, took her hand and slowly kissed it. "When we get back again," said he, "we will go and dine sometimes at Chatou."

She murmured: "We shall have so many things to do," in a tone of voice that seemed to imply, "The agreeable must be sacrificed to the useful."

He still held her hand, asking himself with some uneasiness by what transition he should reach the caressing stage. He would not have felt uneasy in the same way in presence of the ignorance of a young girl, but the lively and artful intelligence he felt existed in Madeleine, rendered his attitude an embarrassed one. He was afraid of appearing stupid to her, too timid or too brutal, too slow or too prompt. He kept pressing her hand gently, without her making any response to this appeal. At length he said: "It seems to me very funny for you to be my wife."

She seemed surprised as she said: "Why so?"

"I do not know. It seems strange to me. I want to kiss you, and I feel astonished at having the right to do so."

She calmly held out her cheek to him, which he kissed as he would have kissed that of a sister.

He continued: "The first time I saw you — you remember the dinner Forestier invited me to — I thought, 'Hang it all, if I could only find a wife like that.' Well, it's done. I have one."

She said, in a low tone: "That is very nice," and looked him straight in the face, shrewdly, and with smiling eyes.

He reflected, "I am too cold. I am stupid. I ought to get along quicker than this," and asked: "How did you make Forestier's acquaintance?"

She replied, with provoking archness: "Are we going to Rouen to talk about him?"

He reddened, saying: "I am a fool. But you frighten me a great deal."

She was delighted, saying: "I — impossible! How is it?"

He had seated himself close beside her. She suddenly exclaimed: "Oh! a stag."

The train was passing through the forest of Saint Germaine, and she had seen a frightened deer clear one of the paths at a bound. Duroy, leaning forward as she looked out of the open window, printed a long kiss, a lover's kiss, among the hair on her neck. She remained still for a few seconds, and then, raising her head, said: "You are tickling me. Leave off."

But he would not go away, but kept on pressing his curly moustache against her white skin in a long and thrilling caress.

She shook herself, saying: "Do leave off."

He had taken her head in his right hand, passed around her, and turned it towards him. Then he darted on her mouth like a hawk on its prey. She struggled, repulsed him, tried to free herself. She succeeded at last, and repeated: "Do leave off."

He remained seated, very red and chilled by this sensible remark; then, having recovered more self-possession, he said, with some liveliness: "Very well, I will wait, but I shan't be able to say a dozen words till we get to Rouen. And remember that we are only passing through Poissy."

"I will do the talking then," she said, and sat down quietly beside him.

She spoke with precision of what they would do on their return. They must keep on the suite of apartments that she had resided in with her first husband, and Duroy would also inherit the duties and salary of Forestier at the Vie Francaise. Before their union, besides, she had planned out, with the certainty of a man of business, all the financial details of their household. They had married under a settlement preserving to each of them their respective estates, and every incident that might arise — death, divorce, the birth of one or more children — was duly provided for. The young fellow contributed a capital of four thousand francs, he said, but of that sum he had borrowed fifteen hundred. The rest was due to savings effected during the year in view of the event. Her contribution was forty thousand francs, which she said had been left her by Forestier.

She returned to him as a subject of conversation. "He was a very steady, economical, hard-working fellow. He would have made a fortune in a very short time."

Duroy no longer listened, wholly absorbed by other thoughts. She stopped from time to time to follow out some inward train of ideas, and then went on: "In three or four years you can be easily earning thirty to forty thousand francs a year. That is what Charles would have had if he had lived."

George, who began to find the lecture rather a long one, replied: "I thought we were not going to Rouen to talk about him."

She gave him a slight tap on the cheek, saying, with a laugh: "That is so. I am in the wrong."

He made a show of sitting with his hands on his knees like a very good boy.

"You look very like a simpleton like that," said she.

He replied: "That is my part, of which, by the way, you reminded me just now, and I shall continue to play it."

"Why?" she asked.

"Because it is you who take management of the household, and even of me. That, indeed, concerns you, as being a widow."

She was amazed, saying: "What do you really mean?"

"That you have an experience that should enlighten my ignorance, and matrimonial practice that should polish up my bachelor innocence, that's all."

"That is too much," she exclaimed.

He replied: "That is so. I don't know anything about ladies; no, and you know all about gentlemen, for you are a widow. You must undertake my education — this evening — and you can begin at once if you like."

She exclaimed, very much amused: "Oh, indeed, if you reckon on me for that!"

He repeated, in the tone of a school boy stumbling through his lesson: "Yes, I do. I reckon that you will give me solid information — in twenty lessons. Ten for the elements, reading and grammar; ten for finishing accomplishments. I don't know anything myself."

She exclaimed, highly amused: "You goose."

He replied: "If that is the familiar tone you take, I will follow your example, and tell you, darling, that I adore you more and more every moment, and that I find Rouen a very long way off."

He spoke now with a theatrical intonation and with a series of changes of facial expression, which amused his companion, accustomed to the ways of literary Bohemia. She glanced at him out of the corner of her eye, finding him really charming, and experiencing the longing we have to pluck a fruit from the tree at once, and the check of reason which advises us to wait till dinner to eat it at the proper time. Then she observed, blushing somewhat at the thoughts which assailed her: "My dear little pupil, trust my experience, my great experience. Kisses in a railway train are not worth anything. They only upset one." Then she blushed still more as she murmured: "One should never eat one's corn in the ear."

He chuckled, kindling at the double meanings from her pretty mouth, and made the sign of the cross, with a movement of the lips, as though murmuring a prayer, adding aloud: "I have placed myself under the protection of St. Anthony, patron-saint of temptations. Now I am adamant."

Night was stealing gently on, wrapping in its transparent shadow, like a fine gauze, the broad landscape stretching away to the right. The train was running along the Seine, and the young couple began to watch the crimson reflections on the surface of the river, winding like a broad strip of polished metal alongside the line, patches fallen from the sky, which the departing sun had kindled into flame. These reflections slowly died out, grew deeper, faded sadly. The landscape became dark with that sinister thrill, that deathlike quiver, which each twilight causes to pass over the earth. This evening gloom, entering the open window, penetrated the two souls, but lately so lively, of the now silent pair.

They had drawn more closely together to watch the dying day. At Nantes the railway people had lit the little oil lamp, which shed its yellow, trembling light upon the drab cloth of the cushions. Duroy passed his arms round the waist of his wife, and clasped her to him. His recent keen desire had become a softened one, a longing for consoling little caresses, such as we lull children with.

He murmured softly: "I shall love you very dearly, my little Made."

The softness of his voice stirred the young wife, and caused a rapid thrill to run through her. She offered her mouth, bending towards him, for he was resting his cheek upon the warm pillow of her bosom, until the whistle of the train announced that they were nearing a station. She remarked, flattening the ruffled locks about her forehead with the tips of her fingers: "It was very silly. We are quite childish."

But he was kissing her hands in turn with feverish rapidity, and replied: "I adore you, my little Made."

Until they reached Rouen they remained almost motionless, cheek against cheek, their eyes turned to the window, through which, from time to time, the lights of houses could be seen in the darkness, satisfied with feeling themselves so close to one another, and with the growing anticipation of a freer and more intimate embrace.

They put up at a hotel overlooking the quay, and went to bed after a very hurried supper.

The chambermaid aroused them next morning as it was striking eight. When they had drank the cup of tea she had placed on the night-table, Duroy looked at his wife, then suddenly, with the joyful impulse of the fortunate man who has just found a treasure, he clasped her in his arms, exclaiming: "My little Made, I am sure that I love you ever so much, ever so much, ever so much."

She smiled with her confident and satisfied smile, and murmured, as she returned his kisses: "And I too — perhaps."

But he still felt uneasy about the visit of his parents. He had already forewarned his wife, had prepared and lectured her, but he thought fit to do so again.

"You know," he said, "they are only rustics — country rustics, not theatrical ones."

She laughed.

"But I know that: you have told me so often enough. Come, get up and let me get up."

He jumped out of bed, and said, as he drew on his socks:

"We shall be very uncomfortable there, very uncomfortable. There is only an old straw palliasse in my room. Spring mattresses are unknown at Canteleu."

She seemed delighted.

"So much the better. It will be delightful to sleep badly — beside — beside you, and to be woke up by the crowing of the cocks."

She had put on her dressing-gown — a white flannel dressing-gown — which Duroy at once recognized. The sight of it was unpleasant to him. Why? His wife had, he was aware, a round dozen of these morning garments. She could not destroy her trousseau in order to buy a new one. No matter, he would have preferred that her bed-linen, her night-linen, her underclothing were not the same she had made use of with the other. It seemed to him that the soft, warm stuff must have retained something from its contact with Forestier.

He walked to the window, lighting a cigarette. The sight of the port, the broad stream covered with vessels with tapering spars, the steamers noisily unloading alongside the quay, stirred him, although he had been acquainted with it all for a long time past, and he exclaimed: "By Jove! it is a fine sight."

Madeleine approached, and placing both hands on one of her husband's shoulders, leaned against him with careless grace, charmed and delighted. She kept repeating: "Oh! how pretty, how pretty. I did not know that there were so many ships as that."

They started an hour later, for they were to lunch with the old people, who had been forewarned some days beforehand. A rusty open carriage bore them along with a noise of jolting ironmongery. They followed a long and rather ugly boulevard, passed between some fields through which flowed a stream, and began to ascend the slope. Madeleine, somewhat fatigued, had dozed off beneath the penetrating caress of the sun, which warmed her delightfully as she lay stretched back in the old carriage as though in a bath of light and country air.

Her husband awoke her, saying: "Look!"

They had halted two-thirds of the way up the slope, at a spot famous for the view, and to which all tourists drive. They overlooked the long and broad valley through which the bright river flowed in sweeping curves. It could be caught sight of in the distance, dotted with numerous islands, and describing a wide sweep before flowing through Rouen. Then the town appeared on the right bank, slightly veiled in the morning mist, but with rays of sunlight falling on its roofs; its thousand squat or pointed spires, light, fragile-looking, wrought like gigantic jewels; its round or square towers topped with heraldic crowns; its belfries; the numerous Gothic summits of its churches, overtopped by the sharp spire of the cathedral, that surprising spike of bronze — strange, ugly, and out of all proportion, the tallest in the world. Facing it, on the other side of the river, rose the factory chimneys of the suburb of Saint Serves — tall, round, and broadening at their summit. More numerous than their sister spires, they reared even in the distant country, their tall brick columns, and vomited into the blue sky their black and coaly breath. Highest of all, as high as the second of the summits reared by human labor, the pyramid of Cheops, almost level with its proud companion the cathedral spire, the great steam-pump of La Foudre seemed the queen of the busy, smoking factories, as the other was the queen of the sacred edifices. Further on, beyond the workmen's town, stretched a forest of pines, and the Seine, having passed between the two divisions of the city, continued its way, skirting a tall rolling slope, wooded at the summit, and showing here and there its bare bone of white stone. Then the river disappeared on the horizon, after again describing a long sweeping curve. Ships could be seen ascending and descending the stream, towed by tugs as big as flies and belching forth thick smoke. Islands were stretched along the water in a line, one close to the other, or with wide intervals between them, like the unequal beads of a verdant rosary.

The driver waited until the travelers' ecstasies were over. He knew from experience the duration of the admiration of all the breed of tourists. But when he started again Duroy suddenly caught sight of two old people advancing towards them some hundreds of yards further on, and jumped out, exclaiming: "There they are. I recognize them."

There were two country-folk, a man and a woman, walking with irregular steps, rolling in their gait, and sometimes knocking their shoulders together. The man was short and strongly built, high colored and inclined to stoutness, but powerful, despite his years. The woman was tall, spare, bent, careworn, the real hard-working countrywoman who has toiled afield from childhood, and has never had time to amuse herself, while her husband has been joking and drinking with the customers. Madeleine had also alighted from the carriage, and she watched these two poor creatures coming towards them with a pain at her heart, a sadness she had not anticipated. They had not recognized their son in this fine gentleman and would never have guessed this handsome lady in the light dress to be their daughter-in-law. They were walking on quickly and in silence to meet their long-looked-for boy, without noticing these city folk followed by their carriage.

They passed by when George, who was laughing, cried out: "Good-day, Daddy Duroy!"

They both stopped short, amazed at first, then stupefied with surprise. The old woman recovered herself first, and stammered, without advancing a step: "Is't thou, boy?"

The young fellow answered: "Yes, it is I, mother," and stepping up to her, kissed her on both cheeks with a son's hearty smack. Then he rubbed noses with his father, who had taken off his cap, a very tall, black silk cap, made Rouen fashion, like those worn by cattle dealers.

Then George said: "This is my wife," and the two country people looked at Madeleine. They looked at her as one looks at a phenomenon, with an uneasy fear, united in the father with a species of approving satisfaction, in the mother with a kind of jealous enmity.

The man, who was of a joyous nature and inspired by a loveliness born of sweet cider and alcohol, grew bolder, and asked, with a twinkle in the corner of his eyes: "I may kiss her all the same?"

"Certainly," replied his son, and Madeleine, ill at ease, held out both cheeks to the sounding smacks of the rustic, who then wiped his lips with the back of his hand. The old woman, in her turn, kissed her daughter-in-law with a hostile reserve. No, this was not the daughter-in-law of her dreams; the plump, fresh housewife, rosy-cheeked as an apple, and round as a brood mare. She looked like a hussy, the fine lady with her furbelows and her musk. For the old girl all perfumes were musk.

They set out again, walking behind the carriage which bore the trunk of the newly-wedded pair. The old fellow took his son by the arm, and keeping him a little in the rear of the others, asked with interest: "Well, how goes business, lad?"

"Pretty fair."

"So much the better. Has thy wife any money?"

"Forty thousand francs," answered George.

His father gave vent to an admiring whistle, and could only murmur, "Dang it!" so overcome was he by the mention of the sum. Then he added, in a tone of serious conviction: "Dang it all, she's a fine woman!" For he found her to his taste, and he had passed for a good judge in his day.

Madeleine and her motherin-law were walking side by side without exchanging a word. The two men rejoined them. They reached the village, a little roadside village formed of half-a-score houses on each side of the highway, cottages and farm buildings, the former of brick and the latter of clay, these covered with thatch and those with slates. Father Duroy's tavern, "The Bellevue," a bit of a house consisting of a ground floor and a garret, stood at the beginning of the village to the left. A pine branch above the door indicated, in ancient fashion, that thirsty folk could enter.

The things were laid for lunch, in the common room of the tavern, on two tables placed together and covered with two napkins. A neighbor, come in to help to serve the lunch, bowed low on seeing such a fine lady appear; and then, recognizing George, exclaimed: "Good Lord! is that the youngster?"

He replied gayly: "Yes, it is I, Mother Brulin," and kissed her as he had kissed his father and mother. Then turning to his wife, he said: "Come into our room and take your hat off."

He ushered her through a door to the right into a cold-looking room with tiled floor, whitewashed walls, and a bed with white cotton curtains. A crucifix above a holy-water stoup, and two colored pictures, one representing Paul and Virginia under a blue palm tree, and the other Napoleon the First on a yellow horse, were the only ornaments of this clean and dispiriting apartment.

As soon as they were alone he kissed Madeleine, saying: "Thanks, Made. I am glad to see the old folks again. When one is in Paris one does not think about it; but when one meets again, it gives one pleasure all the same."

But his father, thumbing the partition with his fist, cried out: "Come along, come along, the soup is ready," and they had to sit down to table.

It was a long, countrified repast, with a succession of ill-assorted dishes, a sausage after a leg of mutton, and an omelette after a sausage. Father Duroy, excited by cider and some glasses of wine, turned on the tap of his choicest jokes — those he reserved for great occasions of festivity, smutty adventures that had happened, as he maintained, to friends of his. George, who knew all these stories, laughed, nevertheless, intoxicated by his native air, seized on by the innate love of one's birthplace and of spots familiar from childhood, by all the sensations and recollections once more renewed, by all the objects of yore seen again once more; by trifles, such as the mark of a knife on a door, a broken chair recalling some pretty event, the smell of the soil, the breath of the neighboring forest, the odors of the dwelling, the gutter, the dunghill.

Mother Duroy did not speak, but remained sad and grim, watching her daughter-in-law out of the corner of her eye, with hatred awakened in her heart — the hatred of an old toiler, an old rustic with fingers worn and limbs bent by hard work — for the city madame, who inspired her with the repulsion of an accursed creature, an impure being, created for idleness and sin. She kept getting up every moment to fetch the dishes or fill the glasses with cider, sharp and yellow from the decanter, or sweet, red, and frothing from the bottles, the corks of which popped like those of ginger beer.

Madeleine scarcely ate or spoke. She wore her wonted smile upon her lips, but it was a sad and resigned one. She was downcast. Why? She had wanted to come. She had not been unaware that she was going among country folk — poor country folk. What had she fancied them to be — she, who did not usually dream? Did she know herself? Do not women always hope for something that is not? Had she fancied them more poetical? No; but perhaps better informed, more noble, more affectionate, more ornamental. Yet she did not want them high-bred, like those in novels. Whence came it, then, that they shocked her by a thousand trifling, imperceptible details, by a thousand indefinable coarsenesses, by their very nature as rustics, by their words, their gestures, and their mirth? She recalled her own mother, of whom she never spoke to anyone — a governess, brought up at Saint Denis — seduced, and died from poverty and grief when she, Madeleine, was twelve years old. An unknown hand had had her brought up. Her father, no doubt. Who was he? She did not exactly know, although she had vague suspicions.

The lunch still dragged on. Customers were now coming in and shaking hands with the father, uttering exclamations of wonderment on seeing his son, and slyly winking as they scanned the young wife out of the corner of their eye, which was as much as to say: "Hang it all, she's not a duffer, George Duroy's wife." Others, less intimate, sat down at the wooden tables, calling for "A pot," "A jugful," "Two brandies," "A raspail," and began to play at dominoes, noisily rattling the little bits of black and white bone. Mother Duroy kept passing to and fro, serving the customers, with her melancholy air, taking money, and wiping the tables with the corner of her blue apron.

The smoke of clay pipes and sou cigars filled the room. Madeleine began to cough, and said: "Suppose we go out; I cannot stand it."

They had not quite finished, and old Duroy was annoyed at this. Then she got up and went and sat on a chair outside the door, while her father-in-law and her husband were finishing their coffee and their nip of brandy.

George soon rejoined her. "Shall we stroll down as far as the Seine?" said he.

She consented with pleasure, saying: "Oh, yes; let us go."

They descended the slope, hired a boat at Croisset, and passed the rest of the afternoon drowsily moored under the willows alongside an island, soothed to slumber by the soft spring weather, and rocked by the wavelets of the river. Then they went back at nightfall.

The evening's repast, eaten by the light of a tallow candle, was still more painful for Madeleine than that of the morning. Father Duroy, who was half drunk, no longer spoke. The mother maintained her dogged manner. The wretched light cast upon the gray walls the shadows of heads with enormous noses and exaggerated movements. A great hand was seen to raise a pitchfork to a mouth opening like a dragon's maw whenever any one of them, turning a little, presented a profile to the yellow, flickering flame.

As soon as dinner was over, Madeleine drew her husband out of the house, in order not to stay in this gloomy room, always reeking with an acrid smell of old pipes and spilt liquor. As soon as they were outside, he said: "You are tired of it already."

She began to protest, but he stopped her, saying: "No, I saw it very plainly. If you like, we will leave tomorrow."

"Very well," she murmured.

They strolled gently onward. It was a mild night, the deep, all-embracing shadow of which seemed filled with faint murmurings, rustlings, and breathings. They had entered a narrow path, overshadowed by tall trees, and running between two belts of underwood of impenetrable blackness.

"Where are we?" asked she.

"In the forest," he replied.

"Is it a large one?"

"Very large; one of the largest in France."

An odor of earth, trees, and moss — that fresh yet old scent of the woods, made up of the sap of bursting buds and the dead and moldering foliage of the thickets, seemed to linger in the path. Raising her head, Madeleine could see the stars through the tree-tops; and although no breeze stirred the boughs, she could yet feel around her the vague quivering of this ocean of leaves. A strange thrill shot through her soul and fleeted across her skin — a strange pain gripped her at the heart. Why, she did not understand. But it seemed to her that she was lost, engulfed, surrounded by perils, abandoned by everyone; alone, alone in the world beneath this living vault quivering there above her.

She murmured: "I am rather frightened. I should like to go back."

"Well, let us do so."

"And — we will leave for Paris tomorrow?"

"Yes, tomorrow."

"Tomorrow morning?"

"Tomorrow morning, if you like."

They returned home. The old folks had gone to bed. She slept badly, continually aroused by all the country sounds so new to her — the cry of the screech owl, the grunting of a pig in a sty adjoining the house, and the noise of a cock who kept on crowing from midnight. She was up and ready to start at daybreak.

When George announced to his parents that he was going back they were both astonished; then they understood the origin of his wish.

The father merely said: "Shall I see you again soon?"

"Yes, in the course of the summer."

"So much the better."

The old woman growled: "I hope you won't regret what you have done."

He left them two hundred francs as a present to assuage their discontent, and the carriage, which a boy had been sent in quest of, having made its appearance at about ten o'clock, the newly-married couple embraced the old country folk and started off once more.

As they were descending the hill Duroy began to laugh.

"There," he said, "I had warned you. I ought not to have introduced you to Monsieur and Madame du Roy de Cantel, Senior."

She began to laugh, too, and replied: "I am delighted now. They are good folk, whom I am beginning to like very well. I will send them some presents from Paris." Then she murmured: "Du Roy de Cantel, you will see that no one will be astonished at the terms of the notification of our marriage. We will say that we have been staying for a week with your parents on their estate." And bending towards him she kissed the tip of his moustache, saying: "Good morning, George."

He replied: "Good morning, Made," as he passed an arm around her waist.

In the valley below they could see the broad river like a ribbon of silver unrolled beneath the morning sun, the factory chimneys belching forth their clouds of smoke into the sky, and the pointed spires rising above the old town.

X

The Du Roys had been back in Paris a couple of days, and the journalist had taken up his old work pending the moment when he should definitely assume Forestier's duties, and give himself wholly up to politics. He was going home that evening to his predecessor's abode to dinner, with a light heart and a keen desire to embrace his wife, whose physical attractions and imperceptible domination exercised a powerful impulse over him. Passing by a florist's at the bottom of the Rue Notre Dame de Lorette, he was struck by the notion of buying a bouquet for Madeleine, and chose a large bunch of half-open roses, a very bundle of perfumed buds.

At each story of his new staircase he eyed himself complacently in the mirrors, the sight of which continually recalled to him his first visit to the house. He rang the bell, having forgotten his key, and the same manservant, whom he had also kept on by his wife's advice, opened the door.

"Has your mistress come home?" asked George.

"Yes, sir."

But on passing through the diningroom he was greatly surprised to find the table laid for three, and the hangings of the drawingroom door being looped up, saw Madeleine arranging in a vase on the mantelpiece a bunch of roses exactly similar to his own. He was vexed and displeased; it was as though he had been robbed of his idea, his mark of attention, and all the pleasure he anticipated from it.

"You have invited some one to dinner, then?" he inquired, as he entered the room.

She answered without turning round, and while continuing to arrange the flowers: "Yes, and no. It is my old friend, the Count de Vaudrec, who has been accustomed to dine here every Monday, and who has come as usual."

George murmured: "Ah! very good."

He remained standing behind her, bouquet in hand, with a longing to hide it or throw it away. He said, however: "I have brought you some roses."

She turned round suddenly, smiling, and exclaimed: "Ah! how nice of you to have thought of that."

And she held out her arms and lips to him with an outburst of joy so real that he felt consoled. She took the flowers, smelt them, and with the liveliness of a delighted child, placed them in the vase that remained empty opposite the other. Then she murmured, as she viewed the result: "How glad I am. My mantelpiece is furnished now." She added almost immediately, in a tone of conviction: "You know Vaudrec is awfully nice; you will be friends with him at once."

A ring announced the Count. He entered quietly, and quite at his ease, as though at home. After having gallantly kissed the young wife's fingers, he turned to the husband and cordially held out his hand, saying: "How goes it, my dear Du Roy?"

It was no longer his former stiff and starched bearing, but an affable one, showing that the situation was no longer the same. The journalist, surprised, strove to make himself agreeable in response to these advances. It might have been believed within five minutes that they had known and loved one another for ten years past.

Then Madeleine, whose face was radiant, said: "I will leave you together, I must give a look to my dinner." And she went out, followed by a glance from both men. When she returned she found them talking theatricals apropos of a new piece, and so thoroughly of the same opinion that a species of rapid friendship awoke in their eyes at the discovery of this absolute identity of ideas.

The dinner was delightful, so intimate and cordial, and the Count stayed on quite late, so comfortable did he feel in this nice little new household.

As soon as he had left Madeleine said to her husband: "Is he not perfect? He gains in every way by being known. He is a true friend — safe, devoted, faithful. Ah, without him — "

She did not finish the sentence, and George replied: "Yes, I find him very agreeable. I think that we shall get on very well together."

She resumed: "You do not know, but we have some work to do together before going to bed. I had not time to speak to you about it before dinner, because Vaudrec came in at once. I have had some important news, news from Morocco. It was Laroche-Mathieu, the deputy, the future minister, who brought it to me. We must work up an important article, a sensational one. I have the facts and figures. We will set to work at once. Bring the lamp."

He took it, and they passed into the study. The same books were ranged in the bookcase, which now bore on its summit the three vases bought at the Golfe Juan by Forestier on the eve of his death. Under the table the dead man's mat awaited the feet of Du Roy, who, on sitting down, took up an ivory penholder slightly gnawed at the end by the other's teeth. Madeleine leant against the mantelpiece, and having lit a cigarette related her news, and then explained her notions and the plan of the article she meditated. He listened attentively, scribbling notes as he did so, and when she had finished, raised objections, took up the question again, enlarged its bearing, and sketched in turn, not the plan of an article, but of a campaign against the existing Ministry. This attack would be its commencement. His wife had left off smoking, so strongly was her interest aroused, so vast was the vision that opened before her as she followed out George's train of thought.

She murmured, from time to time: "Yes, yes; that is very good. That is capital. That is very clever."

And when he had finished speaking in turn, she said: "Now let us write."

But he always found it hard to make a start, and with difficulty sought his expressions. Then she came gently, and, leaning over his shoulder, began to whisper sentences in his ear. From time to time she would hesitate, and ask: "Is that what you want to say?"

He answered: "Yes, exactly."

She had piercing shafts, the poisoned shafts of a woman, to wound the head of the Cabinet, and she blended jests about his face with others respecting his policy in a curious fashion, that made one laugh, and, at the same time, impressed one by their truth of observation.

Du Roy from time to time added a few lines which widened and strengthened the range of attack. He understood, too, the art of perfidious insinuation, which he had learned in sharpening up his "Echoes"; and when a fact put forward as certain by Madeleine appeared doubtful or compromising, he excelled in allowing it to be divined and in impressing it upon the mind more strongly than if he had affirmed it. When their article was finished, George read it aloud. They both thought it excellent, and smiled, delighted and surprised, as if they had just mutually revealed themselves to one another. They gazed into the depths of one another's eyes with yearnings of love and admiration, and they embraced one another with an ardor communicated from their minds to their bodies.

Du Roy took up the lamp again. "And now to bye-bye," said he, with a kindling glance.

She replied: "Go first, sir, since you light the way."

He went first, and she followed him into their bedroom, tickling his neck to make him go quicker, for he could not stand that.

The article appeared with the signature of George Duroy de Cantel, and caused a great sensation. There was an excitement about it in the Chamber. Daddy Walter congratulated the author, and entrusted him with the political editorship of the Vie Francaise. The "Echoes" fell again to Boisrenard.

Then there began in the paper a violent and cleverly conducted campaign against the Ministry. The attack, now ironical, now serious, now jesting, and now virulent, but always skillful and based on facts, was delivered with a certitude and continuity which astonished everyone. Other papers continually cited the Vie Francaise, taking whole passages from it, and those in office asked themselves whether they could not gag this unknown and inveterate foe with the gift of a prefecture.

Du Roy became a political celebrity. He felt his influence increasing by the pressure of hands and the lifting of hats. His wife, too, filled him with stupefaction and admiration by the ingenuity of her mind, the value of her information, and the number of her acquaintances. Continually he would find in his drawingroom, on returning home, a senator, a deputy, a magistrate, a general, who treated Madeleine as an old friend, with serious familiarity. Where had she met all these people? In society, so she said. But how had she been able to gain their confidence and their affection? He could not understand it.

"She would make a terrible diplomatist," he thought.

She often came in late at meal times, out of breath, flushed, quivering, and before even taking off her veil would say: "I have something good to-day. Fancy, the Minister of Justice has just appointed two magistrates who formed a part of the mixed commission. We will give him a dose he will not forget in a hurry."

And they would give the minister a dose, and another the next day, and a third the day after. The deputy, Laroche-Mathieu, who dined at the Rue Fontaine every Tuesday, after the Count de Vaudrec, who began the week, would shake the hands of husband and wife with demonstrations of extreme joy. He never ceased repeating: "By Jove, what a campaign! If we don't succeed after all?"

He hoped, indeed, to succeed in getting hold of the portfolio of foreign affairs, which he had had in view for a long time.

He was one of those many-faced politicians, without strong convictions, without great abilities, without boldness, and without any depth of knowledge, a provincial barrister, a local dandy, preserving a cunning balance between all parties, a species of Republican Jesuit and Liberal mushroom of uncertain character, such as spring up by hundreds on the popular dunghill of universal suffrage. His village machiavelism caused him to be reckoned able among his colleagues, among all the adventurers and abortions who are made deputies. He was sufficiently well-dressed, correct, familiar, and amiable to succeed. He had his successes in society, in the mixed, perturbed, and somewhat rough society of the high functionaries of the day. It was said everywhere of him: "Laroche will be a minister," and he believed more firmly than anyone else that he would be. He was one of the chief shareholders in Daddy Walter's paper, and his colleague and partner in many financial schemes.

Du Roy backed him up with confidence and with vague hopes as to the future. He was, besides, only continuing the work begun by Forestier, to whom Laroche-Mathieu had promised the Cross of the Legion of Honor when the day of triumph should come. The decoration would adorn the breast of Madeleine's second husband, that was all. Nothing was changed in the main.

It was seen so well that nothing was changed that Du Roy's comrades organized a joke against him, at which he was beginning to grow angry. They no longer called him anything but Forestier. As soon as he entered the office some one would call out: "I say, Forestier."

He would pretend not to hear, and would look for the letters in his pigeon-holes. The voice would resume in louder tones, "Hi! Forestier." Some stifled laughs would be heard, and as Du Roy was entering the manager's room, the comrade who had called out would stop him, saying: "Oh, I beg your pardon, it is you I want to speak to. It is stupid, but I am always mixing you up with poor Charles. It is because your articles are so infernally like his. Everyone is taken in by them."

Du Roy would not answer, but he was inwardly furious, and a sullen wrath sprang up in him against the dead man. Daddy Walter himself had declared, when astonishment was expressed at the flagrant similarity in style and inspiration between the leaders of the new political editor and his predecessor: "Yes, it is Forestier, but a fuller, stronger, more manly Forestier."

Another time Du Roy, opening by chance the cupboard in which the cup and balls were kept, had found all those of his predecessor with crape round the handles, and his own, the one he had made use of when he practiced under the direction of Saint-Potin, ornamented with a pink ribbon. All had been arranged on the same shelf according to size, and a card like those in museums bore the inscription: "The Forestier-Du Roy (late Forestier and Co.) Collection." He quietly closed the cupboard, saying, in tones loud enough to be heard: "There are fools and envious people everywhere."

But he was wounded in his pride, wounded in his vanity, that touchy pride and vanity of the writer, which produce the nervous susceptibility ever on the alert, equally in the reporter and the genial poet. The word "Forestier" made his ears tingle. He dreaded to hear it, and felt himself redden when he did so. This name was to him a biting jest, more than a jest, almost an insult. It said to him: "It is your wife who does your work, as she did that of the other. You would be nothing without her."

He admitted that Forestier would have been no one without Madeleine; but as to himself, come now!

Then, at home, the haunting impression continued. It was the whole place now that recalled the dead man to him, the whole of the furniture, the whole of the knicknacks, everything he laid hands on. He had scarcely thought of this at the outset, but the joke devised by his comrades had caused a kind of mental wound, which a number of trifles, unnoticed up to the present, now served to envenom. He could not take up anything without at once fancying he saw the hand of Charles upon it. He only looked at it and made use of things the latter had made use of formerly; things that he had purchased, liked, and enjoyed. And George began even to grow irritated at the thought of the bygone relations between his friend and his wife. He was sometimes astonished at this revolt of his heart, which he did not understand, and said to himself, "How the deuce is it? I am not jealous of Madeleine's friends. I am never uneasy about what she is up to. She goes in and out as she chooses, and yet the recollection of that brute of a Charles puts me in a rage." He added, "At the bottom, he was only an idiot, and it is that, no doubt, that wounds me. I am vexed that Madeleine could have married such a fool." And he kept continually repeating, "How is it that she could have stomached such a donkey for a single moment?"

His rancor was daily increased by a thousand insignificant details, which stung him like pin pricks, by the incessant reminders of the other arising out of a word from Madeleine, from the manservant, from the waiting-maid.

One evening Du Roy, who liked sweet dishes, said, "How is it we never have sweets at dinner?"

His wife replied, cheerfully, "That is quite true. I never think about them. It is all through Charles, who hated — "

He cut her short in a fit of impatience he was unable to control, exclaiming, "Hang it all! I am sick of Charles. It is always Charles here and Charles there, Charles liked this and Charles liked that. Since Charles is dead, for goodness sake leave him in peace."

Madeleine looked at her husband in amazement, without being able to understand his sudden anger. Then, as she was sharp, she guessed what was going on within him; this slow working of posthumous jealousy, swollen every moment by all that recalled the other. She thought it puerile, may be, but was flattered by it, and did not reply.

He was vexed with himself at this irritation, which he had not been able to conceal. As they were writing after dinner an article for the next day, his feet got entangled in the foot mat. He kicked it aside, and said with a laugh:

"Charles was always chilly about the feet, I suppose?"

She replied, also laughing: "Oh! he lived in mortal fear of catching cold; his chest was very weak."

Du Roy replied grimly: "He has given us a proof of that." Then kissing his wife's hand, he added gallantly: "Luckily for me."

But on going to bed, still haunted by the same idea, he asked: "Did Charles wear nightcaps for fear of the draughts?"

She entered into the joke, and replied: "No; only a silk handkerchief tied round his head."

George shrugged his shoulders, and observed, with contempt, "What a baby."

From that time forward Charles became for him an object of continual conversation. He dragged him in on all possible occasions, speaking of him as "Poor Charles," with an air of infinite pity. When he returned home from the office, where he had been accosted twice or thrice as Forestier, he avenged himself by bitter railleries against the dead man in his tomb. He recalled his defects, his absurdities, his littleness, enumerating them with enjoyment, developing and augmenting them as though he had wished to combat the influence of a dreaded rival over the heart of his wife. He would say, "I say, Made, do you remember the day when that duffer Forestier tried to prove to us that stout men were stronger than spare ones?"

Then he sought to learn a number of private and secret details respecting the departed, which his wife, ill at ease, refused to tell him. But he obstinately persisted, saying, "Come, now, tell me all about it. He must have been very comical at such a time?"

She murmured, "Oh! do leave him alone."

But he went on, "No, but tell me now, he must have been a duffer to sleep with?" And he always wound up with, "What a donkey he was."

One evening, towards the end of June, as he was smoking a cigarette at the window, the fineness of the evening inspired him with a wish for a drive, and he said, "Made, shall we go as far as the Bois de Boulogne?"

"Certainly."

They took an open carriage and drove up the Champs Elysées, and then along the main avenue of the Bois de Boulogne. It was a breezeless night, one of those stifling nights when the overheated air of Paris fills the chest like the breath of a furnace. A host of carriages bore along beneath the trees a whole population of lovers. They came one behind the other in an unbroken line. George and Madeleine amused themselves with watching all these couples, the woman in summer toilet and the man darkly outlined beside her. It was a huge flood of lovers towards the Bois, beneath the starry and heated sky. No sound was heard save the dull rumble of wheels. They kept passing by, two by two in each vehicle, leaning back on the seat, silent, clasped one against the other, lost in dreams of desire, quivering with the anticipation of coming caresses. The warm shadow seemed full of kisses. A sense of spreading lust rendered the air heavier and more suffocating. All the couples, intoxicated with the same idea, the same ardor, shed a fever about them.

George and Madeleine felt the contagion. They clasped hands without a word, oppressed by the heaviness of the atmosphere and the emotion that assailed them. As they reached the turning which follows the line of the fortification, they kissed one another, and she stammered somewhat confusedly, "We are as great babies as on the way to Rouen."

The great flood of vehicles divided at the entrance of the wood. On the road to the lake, which the young couple were following, they were now thinner, but the dark shadow of the trees, the air freshened by the leaves and by the dampness arising from the streamlets that could be heard flowing beneath them, and the coolness of the vast nocturnal vault bedecked with stars, gave to the kisses of the perambulating pairs a more penetrating charm.

George murmured, "Dear little Made," as he pressed her to him.

"Do you remember the forest close to your home, how gloomy it was?" said she. "It seemed to me that it was full of horrible creatures, and that there was no end to it, while here it is delightful. One feels caresses in the breeze, and I know that Sevres lies on the other side of the wood."

He replied, "Oh! in the forest at home there was nothing but deer, foxes, and wild boars, and here and there the hut of a forester."

This word, akin to the dead man's name, issuing from his mouth, surprised him just as if some one had shouted it out to him from the depths of a thicket, and he became suddenly silent, assailed anew by the strange and persistent uneasiness, and gnawing, invincible, jealous irritation that had been spoiling his existence for some time past. After a minute or so, he asked: "Did you ever come here like this of an evening with Charles?"

"Yes, often," she answered.

And all of a sudden he was seized with a wish to return home, a nervous desire that gripped him at the heart. But the image of Forestier had returned to his mind and possessed and laid hold of him. He could no longer speak or think of anything else and said in a spiteful tone, "I say, Made?"

"Yes, dear."

"Did you ever cuckold poor Charles?"

She murmured disdainfully, "How stupid you are with your stock joke."

But he would not abandon the idea.

"Come, Made, dear, be frank and acknowledge it. You cuckolded him, eh? Come, admit that you cuckolded him?"

She was silent, shocked as all women are by this expression.

He went on obstinately, "Hang it all, if ever anyone had the head for a cuckold it was he. Oh! yes. It would please me to know that he was one. What a fine head for horns." He felt that she was smiling at some recollection, perhaps, and persisted, saying, "Come out with it. What does it matter? It would be very comical to admit that you had deceived him, to me."

He was indeed quivering with hope and desire that Charles, the hateful Charles, the detested dead, had borne this shameful ridicule. And yet — yet — another emotion, less definite. "My dear little Made, tell me, I beg of you. He deserved it. You would have been wrong not to have given him a pair of horns. Come, Made, confess."

She now, no doubt, found this persistence amusing, for she was laughing a series of short, jerky laughs.

He had put his lips close to his wife's ear and whispered: "Come, come, confess."

She jerked herself away, and said, abruptly: "You are crazy. As if one answered such questions."

She said this in so singular a tone that a cold shiver ran through her husband's veins, and he remained dumbfounded, scared, almost breathless, as though from some mental shock.

The carriage was now passing along the lake, on which the sky seemed to have scattered its stars. Two swans, vaguely outlined, were swimming slowly, scarcely visible in the shadow. George called out to the driver: "Turn back!" and the carriage returned, meeting the others going at a walk, with their lanterns gleaming like eyes in the night.

What a strange manner in which she had said it. Was it a confession? Du Roy kept asking himself. And the almost certainty that she had deceived her first husband now drove him wild with rage. He longed to beat her, to strangle her, to tear her hair out. Oh, if she had only replied: "But darling, if I had deceived him, it would have been with yourself," how he would have kissed, clasped, worshiped her.

He sat still, his arms crossed, his eyes turned skyward, his mind too agitated to think as yet. He only felt within him the rancor fermenting and the anger swelling which lurk at the heart of all mankind in presence of the caprices of feminine desire. He felt for the first time that vague anguish of the husband who suspects. He was jealous at last, jealous on behalf of the dead, jealous on Forestier's account, jealous in a strange and poignant fashion, into which there suddenly entered a hatred of Madeleine. Since she had deceived the other, how could he have confidence in her himself? Then by degrees his mind became calmer, and bearing up against his pain, he thought: "All women are prostitutes. We must make use of them, and not give them anything of ourselves." The bitterness in his heart rose to his lips in words of contempt and disgust. He repeated to himself: "The victory in this world is to the strong. One must be strong. One must be above all prejudices."

The carriage was going faster. It repassed the fortifications. Du Roy saw before him a reddish light in the sky like the glow of an immense forge, and heard a vast, confused, continuous rumor, made up of countless different sounds, the breath of Paris panting this summer night like an exhausted giant.

George reflected: "I should be very stupid to fret about it. Everyone for himself. Fortune favors the bold. Egotism is everything. Egotism as regards ambition and fortune is better than egotism as regards woman and love."

The Arc de Triomphe appeared at the entrance to the city on its two tall supports like a species of shapeless giant ready to start off and march down the broad avenue open before him. George and Madeleine found themselves once more in the stream of carriages bearing homeward and bedwards the same silent and interlaced couples. It seemed that the whole of humanity was passing by intoxicated with joy, pleasure, and happiness. The young wife, who had divined something of what was passing through her husband's mind, said, in her soft voice: "What are you thinking of, dear? You have not said a word for the last half hour."

He answered, sneeringly: "I was thinking of all these fools cuddling one another, and saying to myself that there is something else to do in life."

She murmured: "Yes, but it is nice sometimes."

"It is nice — when one has nothing better to do."

George's thoughts were still hard at it, stripping life of its poesy in a kind of spiteful anger. "I should be very foolish to trouble myself, to deprive myself of anything whatever, to worry as I have done for some time past." Forestier's image crossed his mind without causing any irritation. It seemed to him that they had just been reconciled, that they had become friends again. He wanted to cry out: "Good evening, old fellow."

Madeleine, to whom this silence was irksome, said: "Suppose we have an ice at Tortoni's before we go in."

He glanced at her sideways. Her fine profile was lit up by the bright light from the row of gas jets of a café. He thought, "She is pretty. Well, so much the better. Jack is as good as his master, my dear. But if ever they catch me worrying again about you, it will be hot at the

North Pole." Then he replied aloud: "Certainly, my dear," and in order that she should not guess anything, he kissed her.

It seemed to the young wife that her husband's lips were frozen. He smiled, however, with his wonted smile, as he gave her his hand to alight in front of the café.

XI

On reaching the office next day, Du Roy sought out Boisrenard.

"My dear fellow," said he, "I have a service to ask of you. It has been thought funny for some time past to call me Forestier. I begin to find it very stupid. Will you have the kindness to quietly let our friends know that I will smack the face of the first that starts the joke again? It will be for them to reflect whether it is worth risking a sword thrust for. I address myself to you because you are a calm-minded fellow, who can hinder matters from coming to painful extremities, and also because you were my second."

Boisrenard undertook the commission. Du Roy went out on business, and returned an hour later. No one called him Forestier.

When he reached home he heard ladies' voices in the drawingroom, and asked, "Who is there?"

"Madame Walter and Madame de Marelle," replied the servant.

His heart beat fast for a moment, and then he said to himself, "Well, let's see," and opened the door.

Clotilde was beside the fireplace, full in a ray of light from the window. It seemed to George that she grew slightly paler on perceiving him. Having first bowed to Madame Walter and her two daughters, seated like two sentinels on each side of their mother, he turned towards his late mistress. She held out her hand, and he took it and pressed it meaningly, as though to say, "I still love you." She responded to this pressure.

He inquired: "How have you been during the century that has elapsed since our last meeting?"

She replied with perfect ease: "Quite well; and you, Pretty-boy?" and turning to Madeleine, added: "You will allow me to call him Pretty-boy still?"

"Certainly, dear; I will allow whatever you please."

A shade of irony seemed hidden in these words.

Madame Walter spoke of an entertainment that was going to be given by Jacques Rival at his residence, a grand assault-at-arms, at which ladies of fashion were to be present, saying: "It will be very interesting. But I am so vexed we have no one to take us there, my husband being obliged to be away at that time."

Du Roy at once offered his services. She accepted, saying: "My daughters and I will be very much obliged to you."

He looked at the younger daughter, and thought: "She is not at all bad looking, this little Susan; not at all." She resembled a fair, fragile doll, too short but slender, with a small waist and fairly developed hips and bust, a face like a miniature, grayish-blue, enamel-like eyes, which seemed shaded by a careful yet fanciful painter, a polished, colorless skin, too white and too smooth, and fluffy, curly hair, in a charming aureola, like, indeed the hair of the pretty and expensive dolls we see in the arms of children much smaller than their plaything.

The elder sister, Rose, was ugly, dull-looking, and insignificant; one of those girls whom you do not notice, do not speak to, and do not talk about.

The mother rose, and, turning to George, said:

"Then I may reckon upon you for next Thursday, two o'clock?"

"You may reckon upon me, madame," he replied.

As soon as she had taken her departure, Madame de Marelle rose in turn, saying: "Good afternoon, Pretty-boy."

It was she who then clasped his hand firmly and for some time, and he felt moved by this silent avowal, struck again with a sudden caprice for this good-natured little, respectable Bohemian of a woman, who really loved him, perhaps.

As soon as he was alone with his wife, Madeleine broke out into a laugh, a frank, gay laugh, and, looking him fair in the face, said, "You know that Madame Walter is smitten with you."

"Nonsense," he answered, incredulously.

"It is so, I tell you; she spoke to me about you with wild enthusiasm. It is strange on her part. She would like to find two husbands such as you for her daughters. Fortunately, as regards her such things are of no moment."

He did not understand what she meant, and inquired, "How of no moment?"

She replied with the conviction of a woman certain of the soundness of her judgment, "Oh! Madame Walter is one of those who have never even had a whisper about them, never, you know, never. She is unassailable in every respect. Her husband you know as well as I do. But with her it is quite another thing. She has suffered enough through marrying a Jew, but she has remained faithful to him. She is an honest woman."

Du Roy was surprised. "I thought her a Jewess, too," said he.

"She, not at all. She is a lady patroness of all the good works of the Church of Madeleine. Her marriage, even, was celebrated religiously. I do not know whether there was a dummy baptism as regards the governor, or whether the Church winked at it."

George murmured: "Ah! so she fancied me."

"Positively and thoroughly. If you were not bespoken, I should advise you to ask for the hand of — Susan, eh? rather than that of Rose."

He replied, twisting his moustache: "Hum; their mother is not yet out of date."

Madeleine, somewhat out of patience, answered:

"Their mother! I wish you may get her, dear. But I am not alarmed on that score. It is not at her age that a woman is guilty of a first fault. One must set about it earlier."

George was reflecting: "If it were true, though, that I could have married Susan." Then he shrugged his shoulders. "Bah! it is absurd. As if her father would have ever have accepted me as a suitor."

He promised himself, though, to keep a more careful watch in the future over Madame Walter's bearing towards him, without asking whether he might ever derive any advantage from this. All the evening he was haunted by the recollection of his love passages with Clotilde, recollections at once tender and sensual. He recalled her drolleries, her pretty ways, and their adventures together. He repeated to himself, "She is really very charming. Yes, I will go and see her tomorrow."

As soon as he had lunched the next morning he indeed set out for the Rue de Verneuil. The same servant opened the door, and with the familiarity of servants of the middle-class, asked: "Are you quite well, sir?"

"Yes, thanks, my girl," he replied, and entered the drawingroom, in which an unskilled hand could be heard practicing scales on the piano. It was Laurine. He thought that she would throw her arms round his neck. But she rose gravely, bowed ceremoniously like a grown-up person, and withdrew with dignity. She had so much the bearing of an insulted woman that he remained in surprise. Her mother came in, and he took and kissed her hands.

"How I have thought of you," said he.

"And I," she replied.

They sat down and smiled at one another, looking into each other's eyes with a longing to kiss.

"My dear little Clo, I do love you."

"I love you, too."

"Then — then — you have not been so very angry with me?"

"Yes, and no. It hurt me a great deal, but I understood your reasons, and said to myself, 'He will come back to me some fine day or other.'"

"I dared not come back. I asked myself how I should be received. I did not dare, but I dearly wanted to. By the way, tell me what is the matter with Laurine. She scarcely said good-morning to me, and went out looking furious."

"I do not know. But we cannot speak of you to her since your marriage. I really believe she is jealous."

"Nonsense."

"It is so, dear. She no longer calls you Pretty-boy, but Monsieur Forestier."

Du Roy reddened, and then drawing close to her said:

"Kiss me."

She did so.

"Where can we meet again?" said he.

"Rue de Constantinople."

"Ah! the rooms are not let, then?"

"No, I kept them on."

"You kept them on?"

"Yes, I thought you would come back again."

A gush of joyful pride swelled his bosom. She loved him then, this woman, with a real, deep, constant love.

He murmured, "I love you," and then inquired, "Is your husband quite well?"

"Yes, very well. He has been spending a month at home, and was off again the day before yesterday."

Du Roy could not help laughing. "How lucky," said he.

She replied simply: "Yes, it is very lucky. But, all the same, he is not troublesome when he is here. You know that."

"That is true. Besides, he is a very nice fellow."

"And you," she asked, "how do you like your new life?"

"Not much one way or the other. My wife is a companion, a partner."

"Nothing more?"

"Nothing more. As to the heart — "

"I understand. She is pretty, though."

"Yes, but I do not put myself out about her."

He drew closer to Clotilde, and whispered. "When shall we see one another again?"

"Tomorrow, if you like."

"Yes, tomorrow at two o'clock."

"Two o'clock."

He rose to take leave, and then stammered, with some embarrassment: "You know I shall take on the rooms in the Rue de Constantinople myself. I mean it. A nice thing for the rent to be paid by you."

It was she who kissed his hands adoringly, murmuring: "Do as you like. It is enough for me to have kept them for us to meet again there."

Du Roy went away, his soul filled with satisfaction. As he passed by a photographer's, the portrait of a tall woman with large eyes reminded him of Madame Walter. "All the same," he said to himself, "she must be still worth looking at. How is it that I never noticed it? I want to see how she will receive me on Thursday?"

He rubbed his hands as he walked along with secret pleasure, the pleasure of success in every shape, the egotistical joy of the clever man who is successful, the subtle pleasure made up of flattered vanity and satisfied sensuality conferred by woman's affection.

On the Thursday he said to Madeleine: "Are you not coming to the assault-at-arms at Rival's?"

"No. It would not interest me. I shall go to the Chamber of Deputies."

He went to call for Madame Walter in an open landau, for the weather was delightful. He experienced a surprise on seeing her, so handsome and young-looking did he find her. She wore a light-colored dress, the somewhat open bodice of which allowed the fullness of her bosom to be divined beneath the blonde lace. She had never seemed to him so well-looking. He thought her really desirable. She wore her calm and ladylike manner, a certain matronly bearing that caused her to pass almost unnoticed before the eyes of gallants. She scarcely spoke besides, save on well-known, suitable, and respectable topics, her ideas being proper, methodical, well ordered, and void of all extravagance.

Her daughter, Susan, in pink, looked like a newly-varnished Watteau, while her elder sister seemed the governess entrusted with the care of this pretty doll of a girl.

Before Rival's door a line of carriages were drawn up. Du Roy offered Madame Walter his arm, and they went in.

The assault-at-arms was given under the patronage of the wives of all the senators and deputies connected with the Vie Francaise, for the benefit of the orphans of the Sixth Arrondissement of Paris. Madame Walter had promised to come with her daughters, while refusing the position of lady patroness, for she only aided with her name works undertaken by the clergy. Not that she was very devout, but her marriage with a Jew obliged her, in her own opinion, to observe a certain religious attitude, and the gathering organized by the journalist had a species of Republican import that might be construed as anti-clerical.

In papers of every shade of opinion, during the past three weeks, paragraphs had appeared such as: "Our eminent colleague, Jacques Rival, has conceived the idea, as ingenious as it is generous, of organizing for the benefit of the orphans of the Sixth Arrondissement of Paris a grand assault-at-arms in the pretty fencing-room attached to his apartments. The invitations will be sent out by Mesdames Laloigue, Remontel, and Rissolin, wives of the senators bearing these names, and by Mesdames Laroche-Mathieu, Percerol, and Firmin, wives of the well-known deputies. A collection will take place during the interval, and the amount will at once be placed in the hands of the mayor of the Sixth Arrondissement, or of his representative."

It was a gigantic advertisement that the clever journalist had devised to his own advantage.

Jacques Rival received all-comers in the hall of his dwelling, where a refreshment buffet had been fitted up, the cost of which was to be deducted from the receipts. He indicated with an amiable gesture the little staircase leading to the cellar, saying: "Downstairs, ladies, downstairs; the assault will take place in the basement."

He darted forward to meet the wife of the manager, and then shaking Du Roy by the hand, said: "How are you, Pretty-boy?"

His friend was surprised, and exclaimed: "Who told you that — "

Rival interrupted him with: "Madame Walter, here, who thinks the nickname a very nice one."

Madame Walter blushed, saying: "Yes, I will admit that, if I knew you better, I would do like little Laurine and call you Pretty-boy, too. The name suits you very well."

Du Roy laughed, as he replied: "But I beg of you, madame, to do so."

She had lowered her eyes, and remarked: "No. We are not sufficiently intimate."

He murmured: "Will you allow me the hope that we shall be more so?"

"Well, we will see then," said she.

He drew on one side to let her precede him at the beginning of the narrow stairs lit by a gas jet. The abrupt transition from daylight to this yellow gleam had something depressing about it. A cellar-like odor rose up this winding staircase, a smell of damp heat and of moldy walls wiped down for the occasion, and also whiffs of incense recalling sacred offices and feminine emanations of vervain, orris root, and violets. A loud murmur of voices and the quivering thrill of an agitated crowd could also be heard down this hole.

The entire cellar was lit up by wreaths of gas jets and Chinese lanterns hidden in the foliage, masking the walls of stone. Nothing could be seen but green boughs. The ceiling was ornamented with ferns, the ground hidden by flowers and leaves. This was thought charming, and a delightful triumph of imagination. In the small cellar, at the end, was a platform for the fencers, between two rows of chairs for the judges. In the remaining space the front seats, ranged by tens to the right and to the left, would accommodate about two hundred people. Four hundred had been invited.

In front of the platform young fellows in fencing costume, with long limbs, erect figures, and moustaches curled up at the ends, were already showing themselves off to the spectators. People were pointing them out as notabilities of the art, professionals, and amateurs. Around them were chatting old and young gentlemen in frock coats, who bore a family resemblance to the fencers in fighting array. They were also seeking to be seen, recognized, and spoken of, being masters of the sword out of uniform, experts on foil play. Almost all the seats were occupied by ladies, who kept up a loud rustling of garments and a continuous murmur of voices. They were fanning themselves as though at a theater, for it was already as hot as an oven in this leafy grotto. A joker kept crying from time to time: "Orgeat, lemonade, beer."

Madame Walter and her daughters reached the seats reserved for them in the front row. Du Roy, having installed them there, was about to quit them, saying: "I am obliged to leave you; we men must not collar the seats."

But Madame Walter remarked, in a hesitating tone: "I should very much like to have you with us all the same. You can tell me the names of the fencers. Come, if you stand close to the end of the seat you will not be in anyone's way." She looked at him with her large mild eyes, and persisted, saying: "Come, stay with us, Monsieur — Pretty-boy. We have need of you."

He replied: "I will obey with pleasure, madame."

On all sides could be heard the remark: "It is very funny, this cellar; very pretty, too."

George knew it well, this vault. He recalled the morning he had passed there on the eve of his duel, alone in front of the little white carton target that had glared at him from the depths of the inner cellar like a huge and terrible eye.

The voice of Jacques Rival sounded from the staircase: "Just about to begin, ladies." And six gentlemen, in very tight-fitting clothes, to set off their chests, mounted the platform, and took their seats on the chairs reserved for the judges. Their names flew about. General de Reynaldi, the president, a short man, with heavy moustaches; the painter, Joséphin Roudet, a tall, ball-headed man, with a long beard; Matthéo de Ujar, Simon Ramoncel, Pierre de Carvin, three fashionable-looking young fellows; and Gaspard Merleron, a master. Two placards were hung up on the two sides of the vault. That on the right was inscribed "M. Crévecœur," and that on the left "M. Plumeau."

They were two professors, two good second-class masters. They made their appearance, both sparely built, with military air and somewhat stiff movements. Having gone through the salute with automatic action, they began to attack one another, resembling in their white costumes of leather and duck, two soldier pierrots fighting for fun. From time to time the word "Touched" was heard, and the six judges nodded with the air of connoisseurs. The public saw nothing but two living marionettes moving about and extending their arms; they understood nothing, but they were satisfied. These two men seemed to them, however, not over graceful, and vaguely ridiculous. They reminded them of the wooden wrestlers sold on the boulevards at the New Year's Fair.

The first couple of fencers were succeeded by Monsieur Planton and Monsieur Carapin, a civilian master and a military one. Monsieur Planton was very little, and Monsieur Carapin immensely stout. One would have thought that the first thrust would have reduced his volume like that of a balloon. People laughed. Monsieur Planton skipped about like a monkey: Monsieur Carapin, only moved his arm, the rest of his frame being paralyzed by fat. He lunged every five minutes with such heaviness and such effort that it seemed to need the most energetic resolution on his part to accomplish it, and then had great difficulty in recovering himself. The connoisseurs pronounced his play very steady and close, and the confiding public appreciated it as such.

Then came Monsieur Porion and Monsieur Lapalme, a master and an amateur, who gave way to exaggerated gymnastics; charging furiously at one another, obliging the judges to scuttle off with their chairs, crossing and recrossing from one end of the platform to the other, one advancing and the other retreating, with vigorous and comic leaps and bounds. They indulged in little jumps backwards that made the ladies laugh, and long springs forward that caused them some emotion. This galloping assault was aptly criticized by some young rascal, who sang out: "Don't burst yourselves over it; it is a time job!" The spectators, shocked at this want of taste, cried "Ssh!" The judgment of the experts was passed around. The fencers had shown much vigor, and played somewhat loosely.

The first half of the entertainment was concluded by a very fine bout between Jacques Rival and the celebrated Belgian professor, Lebegue. Rival greatly pleased the ladies. He was really a handsome fellow, well made, supple, agile, and more graceful than any of those who had preceded him. He brought, even into his way of standing on guard and lunging, a certain fashionable elegance which pleased people, and contrasted with the energetic, but more commonplace style of his adversary. "One can perceive the well-bred man at once," was the remark. He scored the last hit, and was applauded.

But for some minutes past a singular noise on the floor above had disturbed the spectators. It was a loud trampling, accompanied by noisy laughter. The two hundred guests who had not been able to get down into the cellar were no doubt amusing themselves in their own way. On the narrow, winding staircase fifty men were packed. The heat down below was getting terrible. Cries of "More air," "Something to drink," were heard. The same joker kept on yelping in a shrill tone that rose above the murmur of conversation, "Orgeat, lemonade, beer." Rival made his appearance, very flushed, and still in his fencing costume. "I will have some refreshments brought," said he, and made his way to the staircase. But all communication with the ground floor was cut off. It would have been as easy to have pierced the ceiling as to have traversed the human wall piled up on the stairs.

Rival called out: "Send down some ices for the ladies." Fifty voices called out: "Some ices!" A tray at length made its appearance. But it only bore empty glasses, the refreshments having been snatched on the way.

A loud voice shouted: "We are suffocating down here. Get it over and let us be off." Another cried out: "The collection." And the whole of the public, gasping, but good-humored all the same, repeated: "The collection, the collection."

Six ladies began to pass along between the seats, and the sound of money falling into the collecting-bags could be heard.

Du Roy pointed out the celebrities to Madame Walter. There were men of fashion and journalists, those attached to the great newspapers, the old-established newspapers, which looked down upon the Vie Francaise with a certain reserve, the fruit of their experience. They had witnessed the death of so many of these politico-financial sheets, offspring of a suspicious partnership, and crushed by the fall of a ministry. There were also painters and sculptors, who are generally men with a taste for sport; a poet who was also a member of the Academy, and who was pointed out generally, and a number of distinguished foreigners.

Someone called out: "Good-day, my dear fellow." It was the Count de Vaudrec. Making his excuses to the ladies, Du Roy hastened to shake hands with him. On returning, he remarked: "What a charming fellow Vaudrec is! How thoroughly blood tells in him."

Madame Walter did not reply. She was somewhat fatigued, and her bosom rose with an effort every time she drew breath, which caught the eye of Du Roy. From time to time he caught her glance, a troubled, hesitating glance, which lighted upon him, and was at once averted, and he said to himself: "Eh! what! Have I caught her, too?"

The ladies who had been collecting passed to their seats, their bags full of gold and silver, and a fresh placard was hung in front of the platform, announcing a "surprising novelty." The judges resumed their seats, and the public waited expectantly.

Two women appeared, foil in hand and in fencing costume; dark tights, a very short petticoat halfway to the knee, and a plastron so padded above the bosom that it obliged them to keep their heads well up. They were both young and pretty. They smiled as they saluted the spectators, and were loudly applauded. They fell on guard, amidst murmured gallantries and whispered jokes. An amiable smile graced the lips of the judges, who approved the hits with a low "bravo." The public warmly appreciated this bout, and testified this much to the two combatants, who kindled desire among the men and awakened among the women the native taste of the Parisian for graceful indecency, naughty elegance, music hall singers, and couplets from operettas. Every time that one of the fencers lunged a thrill of pleasure ran through the public. The one who turned her back to the seats, a plump back, caused eyes and mouths to open, and it was not the play of her wrist that was most closely scanned. They were frantically applauded.

A bout with swords followed, but no one looked at it, for the attention of all was occupied by what was going on overhead. For some minutes they had heard the noise of furniture being dragged across the floor, as though moving was in progress. Then all at once the notes of a piano were heard, and the rhythmic beat of feet moving in cadence was distinctly audible. The people above had treated themselves to a dance to make up for not being able to see anything. A loud laugh broke out at first among the public in the fencing saloon, and then a wish for a dance being aroused among the ladies, they ceased to pay attention to what was taking place on the platform, and began to chatter out loud. This notion of a ball got up by the late-comers struck them as comical. They must be amusing themselves nicely, and it must be much better up there.

But two new combatants had saluted each other and fell on guard in such masterly style that all eyes followed their movements. They lunged and recovered themselves with such easy grace, such measured strength, such certainty, such sobriety in action, such correctness in attitude, such measure in their play, that even the ignorant were surprised and charmed. Their calm promptness, their skilled suppleness, their rapid motions, so nicely timed that they appeared slow, attracted and captivated the eye by their power of perfection. The public felt that they were looking at something good and rare; that two great artists in their own profession were showing them their best, all of skill, cunning, thought-out science and physical ability that it was possible for two masters to put forth. No one spoke now, so closely were they watched. Then, when they shook hands after the last hit, shouts of bravoes broke out. People stamped and yelled. Everyone knew their names — they were Sergent and Ravignac.

The excitable grew quarrelsome. Men looked at their neighbors with longings for a row. They would have challenged one another on account of a smile. Those who had never held a foil in their hand sketched attacks and parries with their canes.

But by degrees the crowd worked up the little staircase. At last they would be able to get something to drink. There was an outburst of indignation when they found that those who had got up the ball had stripped the refreshment buffet, and had then gone away declaring that it was very impolite to bring together two hundred people and not show them anything. There was not a cake, not a drop of champagne, syrup, or beer left; not a sweetmeat, not a fruit — nothing. They had sacked, pillaged, swept away everything. These details were related by the servants, who pulled long faces to hide their impulse to laugh right out. "The ladies were worse than the gentlemen," they asserted, "and ate and drank enough to make themselves ill." It was like the story of the survivors after the sack of a captured town.

There was nothing left but to depart. Gentlemen openly regretted the twenty francs given at the collection; they were indignant that those upstairs should have feasted without paying anything. The lady patronesses had collected upwards of three thousand francs. All expenses paid, there remained two hundred and twenty for the orphans of the Sixth Arrondissement.

Du Roy, escorting the Walter family, waited for his landau. As he drove back with them, seated in face of Madame Walter, he again caught her caressing and fugitive glance, which seemed uneasy. He thought: "Hang it all! I fancy she is nibbling," and smiled to recognize that he was really very lucky as regarded women, for Madame de Marelle, since the recommencement of their amour, seemed frantically in love with him.

He returned home joyously. Madeleine was waiting for him in the drawingroom.

"I have some news," said she. "The Morocco business is getting into a complication. France may very likely send out an expeditionary force within a few months. At all events, the opportunity will be taken of it to upset the Ministry, and Laroche-Mathieu will profit by this to get hold of the portfolio of foreign affairs."

Du Roy, to tease his wife, pretended not to believe anything of the kind. They would never be mad enough to recommence the Tunisian bungle over again. But she shrugged her shoulders impatiently, saying: "But I tell you yes, I tell you yes. You don't understand that it is a matter of money. Now-a-days, in political complications we must not ask: 'Who is the woman?' but 'What is the business?'"

He murmured "Bah!" in a contemptuous tone, in order to excite her, and she, growing irritated, exclaimed: "You are just as stupid as Forestier."

She wished to wound him, and expected an outburst of anger. But he smiled, and replied: "As that cuckold of a Forestier?"

She was shocked, and murmured: "Oh, George!"

He wore an insolent and chaffing air as he said: "Well, what? Did you not admit to me the other evening that Forestier was a cuckold?" And he added: "Poor devil!" in a tone of pity.

Madeleine turned her back on him, disdaining to answer; and then, after a moment's silence, resumed: "We shall have visitors on Tuesday. Madame Laroche-Mathieu is coming to dinner with the Viscountess de Percemur. Will you invite Rival and Norbert de Varenne? I will call tomorrow and ask Madame Walter and Madame de Marelle. Perhaps we shall have Madame Rissolin, too."

For some time past she had been strengthening her connections, making use of her husband's political influence to attract to her house, willy-nilly, the wives of the senators and deputies who had need of the support of the Vie Francaise.

George replied: "Very well. I will see about Rival and Norbert."

He was satisfied, and rubbed his hands, for he had found a good trick to annoy his wife and gratify the obscure rancor, the undefined and gnawing jealousy born in him since their drive in the Bois. He would never speak of Forestier again without calling him cuckold. He felt very well that this would end by enraging Madeleine. And half a score of times, in the course of the evening, he found means to mention with ironical good humor the name of "that cuckold of a Forestier." He was no longer angry with the dead! he was avenging him.

His wife pretended not to notice it, and remained smilingly indifferent.

The next day, as she was to go and invite Madame Walter, he resolved to forestall her, in order to catch the latter alone, and see if she really cared for him. It amused and flattered him. And then — why not — if it were possible?

He arrived at the Boulevard Malesherbes about two, and was shown into the drawingroom, where he waited till Madame Walter made her appearance, her hand outstretched with pleased eagerness, saying: "What good wind brings you hither?"

"No good wind, but the wish to see you. Some power has brought me here, I do not know why, for I have nothing to say to you. I came, here I am; will you forgive me this early visit and the frankness of this explanation?"

He uttered this in a gallant and jesting tone, with a smile on his lips. She was astonished, and colored somewhat, stammering: "But really — I do not understand — you surprise me."

He observed: "It is a declaration made to a lively tune, in order not to alarm you."

They had sat down in front of one another. She took the matter pleasantly, saying: "A serious declaration?"

"Yes. For a long time I have been wanting to utter it — for a very long time. But I dared not. They say you are so strict, so rigid."

She had recovered her assurance, and observed: "Why to-day, then?"

"I do not know." Then lowering his voice he added: "Or rather, because I have been thinking of nothing but you since yesterday."

She stammered, growing suddenly pale: "Come, enough of nonsense; let us speak of something else."

But he had fallen at her feet so suddenly that she was frightened. She tried to rise, but he kept her seated by the strength of his arms passed round her waist, and repeated in a voice of passion: "Yes, it is true that I have loved you madly for a long time past. Do not answer me. What would you have? I am mad. I love you. Oh! if you knew how I love you!"

She was suffocating, gasping, and strove to speak, without being able to utter a word. She pushed him away with her two hands, having seized him by the hair to hinder the approach of the mouth that she felt coming towards her own. She kept turning her head from right to left and from left to right with a rapid motion, closing her eyes, in order no longer to see him. He touched her through her dress, handled her, pressed her, and she almost fainted under his strong and rude caress. He rose suddenly and sought to clasp her to him, but, free for a moment, she had managed to escape by throwing herself back, and she now fled from behind one chair to another. He felt that pursuit was ridiculous, and he fell into a chair, his face hidden by his hands, feigning convulsive sobs. Then he got up, exclaimed "Farewell, farewell," and rushed away.

He quietly took his stick in the hall and gained the street, saying to himself: "By Jove, I believe it is all right there." And he went into a telegraph office to send a wire to Clotilde, making an appointment for the next day.

On returning home at his usual time, he said to his wife: "Well, have you secured all the people for your dinner?"

She answered: "Yes, there is only Madame Walter, who is not quite sure whether she will be free to come. She hesitated and talked about I don't know what — an engagement, her conscience. In short, she seemed very strange. No matter, I hope she will come all the same."

He shrugged his shoulders, saying: "Oh, yes, she'll come."

He was not certain, however, and remained anxious until the day of the dinner. That very morning Madeleine received a note from her: "I have managed to get free from my engagements with great difficulty, and shall be with you this evening. But my husband cannot accompany me."

Du Roy thought: "I did very well indeed not to go back. She has calmed down. Attention."

He, however, awaited her appearance with some slight uneasiness. She came, very calm, rather cool, and slightly haughty. He became humble, discreet, and submissive. Madame Laroche-Mathieu and Madame Rissolin accompanied their husbands. The Viscountess de Percemur talked society. Madame de Marelle looked charming in a strangely fanciful toilet, a species of Spanish costume in black and yellow, which set off her neat figure, her bosom, her rounded arms, and her bird-like head.

Du Roy had Madame Walter on his right hand, and during dinner only spoke to her on serious topics, and with an exaggerated respect. From time to time he glanced at Clotilde. "She is really prettier and fresher looking than ever," he thought. Then his eyes returned to his wife, whom he found not bad-looking either, although he retained towards her a hidden, tenacious, and evil anger.

But Madame Walter excited him by the difficulty of victory and by that novelty always desired by man. She wanted to return home early. "I will escort you," said he.

She refused, but he persisted, saying: "Why will not you permit me? You will wound me keenly. Do not let me think that you have not forgiven me. You see how quiet I am."

She answered: "But you cannot abandon your guests like that."

He smiled. "But I shall only be away twenty minutes. They will not even notice it. If you refuse you will cut me to the heart."

She murmured: "Well, then I agree."

But as soon as they were in the carriage he seized her hand, and, kissing it passionately, exclaimed: "I love you, I love you. Let me tell you that much. I will not touch you. I only want to repeat to you that I love you."

She stammered: "Oh! after what you promised me! This is wrong, very wrong."

He appeared to make a great effort, and then resumed in a restrained tone: "There, you see how I master myself. And yet — But let me only tell you that I love you, and repeat it to you every day; yes, let me come to your house and kneel down for five minutes at your feet to utter those three words while gazing on your beloved face."

She had yielded her hand to him, and replied pantingly: "No, I cannot, I will not. Think of what would be said, of the servants, of my daughters. No, no, it is impossible."

He went on: "I can no longer live without seeing you. Whether at your house or elsewhere, I must see you, if only for a moment, every day, to touch your hand, to breathe the air stirred by your dress, to gaze on the outline of your form, and on your great calm eyes that madden me."

She listened, quivering, to this commonplace love-song, and stammered: "No, it is out of the question."

He whispered in her ear, understanding that he must capture her by degrees, this simple woman, that he must get her to make appointments with him, where she would at first, where he wished afterwards. "Listen, I must see you; I shall wait for you at your door like a beggar; but I will see you, I will see you tomorrow."

She repeated: "No, do not come. I shall not receive you. Think of my daughters."

"Then tell me where I shall meet you — in the street, no matter where, at whatever hour you like, provided I see you. I will bow to you; I will say 'I love you,' and I will go away."

She hesitated, bewildered. And as the brougham entered the gateway of her residence she murmured hurriedly: "Well, then, I shall be at the Church of the Trinity tomorrow at halfpast three." Then, having alighted, she said to her coachman: "Drive Monsieur Du Roy back to his house."

As he reentered his home, his wife said: "Where did you get to?"

He replied, in a low tone: "I went to the telegraph office to send off a message."

Madame de Marelle approached them. "You will see me home, Pretty-boy?" said she. "You know I only came such a distance to dinner on that condition." And turning to Madeleine, she added: "You are not jealous?"

Madame Du Roy answered slowly: "Not over much."

The guests were taking their leave. Madame Laroche-Mathieu looked like a housemaid from the country. She was the daughter of a notary, and had been married to the deputy when he was only a barrister of small standing. Madame Rissolin, old and stuck-up, gave one the idea of a midwife whose fashionable education had been acquired through a circulating library. The Viscountess de Percemur looked down upon them. Her "Lily Fingers" touched these vulgar hands with repugnance.

Clotilde, wrapped in lace, said to Madeleine as she went out: "Your dinner was perfection. In a little while you will have the leading political drawingroom in Paris."

As soon as she was alone with George she clasped him in her arms, exclaiming: "Oh, my darling Pretty-boy, I love you more and more every day!"

XII

The Place de la Trinité lay, almost deserted, under a dazzling July sun. An oppressive heat was crushing Paris. It was as though the upper air, scorched and deadened, had fallen upon the city — a thick, burning air that pained the chests inhaling it. The fountains in front of the church fell lazily. They seemed weary of flowing, tired out, limp, too; and the water of the basins, in which leaves and bits of paper were floating, looked greenish, thick and glaucous. A dog having jumped over the stone rim, was bathing in the dubious fluid. A few people, seated on the benches of the little circular garden skirting the front of the church, watched the animal curiously.

Du Roy pulled out his watch. It was only three o'clock. He was half an hour too soon. He laughed as he thought of this appointment. "Churches serve for anything as far as she is concerned," said he to himself. "They console her for having married a Jew, enable her to assume an attitude of protestation in the world of politics and a respectable one in that of fashion, and serve as a shelter to her gallant rendezvous. So much for the habit of making use of religion as an umbrella. If it is fine it is a walking stick; if sunshiny, a parasol; if it rains, a shelter; and if one does not go out, why, one leaves it in the hall. And there are hundreds like that who care for God about as much as a cherry stone, but who will not hear him spoken against. If it were suggested to them to go to a hotel, they would think it infamous, but it seems to them quite simple to make love at the foot of the altar."

He walked slowly along the edge of the fountain, and then again looked at the church clock, which was two minutes faster than his watch. It was five minutes past three. He thought that he would be more comfortable inside, and entered the church. The coolness of a cellar assailed him, he breathed it with pleasure, and then took a turn round the nave to reconnoiter the place. Other regular footsteps, sometimes halting and then beginning anew, replied from the further end of the vast pile to the sound of his own, which rang sonorously beneath the vaulted roof. A curiosity to know who this other promenader was seized him. It was a stout, bald-headed gentleman who was strolling about with his nose in the air, and his hat behind his back. Here and there an old woman was praying, her face hidden in her hands. A sensation of solitude and rest stole over the mind. The light, softened by the stained-glass windows, was refreshing to the eyes. Du Roy thought that it was "deucedly comfortable" inside there.

He returned towards the door and again looked at his watch. It was still only a quarter-past three. He sat down at the entrance to the main aisle, regretting that one could not smoke a cigarette. The slow footsteps of the stout gentleman could still be heard at the further end of the church, near the choir.

Someone came in, and George turned sharply round. It was a poor woman in a woolen skirt, who fell on her knees close to the first chair, and remained motionless, with clasped hands, her eyes turned to heaven, her soul absorbed in prayer. Du Roy watched her with interest, asking himself what grief, what pain, what despair could have crushed her heart. She was worn out by poverty, it was plain. She had, perhaps, too, a husband who was beating her to death, or a dying child. He murmured mentally: "Poor creatures. How some of them do suffer." Anger rose up in him against pitiless Nature. Then he reflected that these poor wretches believed, at any rate, that they were taken into consideration up above, and that they were duly entered in the registers of heaven with a debtor and creditor balance. Up above! And Du Roy, whom the silence of the church inclined to sweeping reflections, judging creation at a bound, muttered contemptuously: "What bosh all that sort of thing is!"

The rustle of a dress made him start. It was she.

He rose, and advanced quickly. She did not hold out her hand, but murmured in a low voice: "I have only a few moments. I must get back home. Kneel down near me, so that we may not be noticed." And she advanced up the aisle, seeking a safe and suitable spot, like a woman well acquainted with the place. Her face was hidden by a thick veil, and she walked with careful footsteps that could scarcely be heard.

When she reached the choir she turned, and muttered, in that mysterious tone of voice we always assume in church: "The side aisles will be better. We are too much in view here."

She bowed low to the high altar, turned to the right, and returned a little way towards the entrance; then, making up her mind, she took a chair and knelt down. George took possession of the next one to her, and as soon as they were in an attitude of prayer, began: "Thanks; oh, thanks; I adore you! I should like to be always telling you so, to tell you how I began to love you, how I was captivated the first time I saw you. Will you allow me some day to open my heart to tell you all this?"

She listened to him in an attitude of deep meditation, as if she heard nothing. She replied between her fingers: "I am mad to allow you to speak to me like this, mad to have come here, mad to do what I am doing, mad to let you believe that — that — this adventure can have any issue. Forget all this; you must, and never speak to me again of it."

She paused. He strove to find an answer, decisive and passionate words, but not being able to join action to words, was partially paralyzed. He replied: "I expect nothing, I hope for nothing.

I love you. Whatever you may do, I will repeat it to you so often, with such power and ardor, that you will end by understanding it. I want to make my love penetrate you, to pour it into your soul, word by word, hour by hour, day by day, so that at length it impregnates you like a liquid, falling drop by drop; softens you, mollifies you, and obliges you later on to reply to me: 'I love you, too.'"

He felt her shoulder trembling against him and her bosom throbbing, and she stammered, abruptly: "I love you, too!"

He started as though he had received a blow, and sighed: "Good God."

She replied, in panting tones: "Ought I to have told you that? I feel I am guilty and contemptible. I, who have two daughters, but I cannot help it, I cannot help it. I could not have believed, I should never have thought — but it is stronger than I. Listen, listen: I have never loved anyone but you; I swear it. And I have loved you for a year past in secret, in my secret heart. Oh! I have suffered and struggled till I can do so no more. I love you."

She was weeping, with her hands crossed in front of her face, and her whole frame was quivering, shaken by the violence of her emotion.

George murmured: "Give me your hand, that I may touch it, that I may press it."

She slowly withdrew her hand from her face. He saw her cheek quite wet and a tear ready to fall on her lashes. He had taken her hand and was pressing it, saying: "Oh, how I should like to drink your tears!"

She said, in a low and broken voice, which resembled a moan: "Do not take advantage of me; I am lost."

He felt an impulse to smile. How could he take advantage of her in that place? He placed the hand he held upon his heart, saying: "Do you feel it beat?" For he had come to the end of his passionate phrases.

For some moments past the regular footsteps of the promenader had been coming nearer. He had gone the round of the altars, and was now, for the second time at least, coming down the little aisle on the right. When Madame Walter heard him close to the pillar which hid her, she snatched her fingers from George's grasp, and again hid her face. And both remained motionless, kneeling as though they had been addressing fervent supplications to heaven together. The stout gentleman passed close to them, cast an indifferent look upon them, and walked away to the lower end of the church, still holding his hat behind his back.

Du Roy, who was thinking of obtaining an appointment elsewhere than at the Church of the Trinity, murmured: "Where shall I see you tomorrow?"

She did not answer. She seemed lifeless — turned into a statue of prayer. He went on: "Tomorrow, will you let me meet you in the Parc Monseau?"

She turned towards him her again uncovered face, a livid face, contracted by fearful suffering, and in a jerky voice ejaculated: "Leave me, leave me now; go away, go away, only for five minutes! I suffer too much beside you. I want to pray, and I cannot. Go away, let me pray alone for five minutes. I cannot. Let me implore God to pardon me — to save me. Leave me for five minutes."

Her face was so upset, so full of pain, that he rose without saying a word, and then, after a little hesitation, asked: "Shall I come back presently?"

She gave a nod, which meant, "Yes, presently," and he walked away towards the choir. Then she strove to pray. She made a superhuman effort to invoke the Deity, and with quivering frame and bewildering soul appealed for mercy to heaven. She closed her eyes with rage, in order no longer to see him who just left her. She sought to drive him from her mind, she struggled against him, but instead of the celestial apparition awaited in the distress of her heart, she still perceived the young fellow's curly moustache. For a year past she had been struggling thus every day, every night, against the growing possession, against this image which haunted her dreams, haunted her flesh, and disturbed her nights. She felt caught like a beast in a net, bound, thrown into the arms of this man, who had vanquished, conquered her, simply by the hair on his lip and the color of his eyes. And now in this church, close to God, she felt still weaker, more abandoned, and more lost than at home. She could no longer pray, she could only think of him. She suffered already that he had quitted her. She struggled, however, despairingly, resisted, implored help with all the strength of her soul. She would liked to have died rather than fall thus, she who had never faltered in her duty. She murmured wild words of supplication, but she was listening to George's footsteps dying away in the distance.

She understood that it was all over, that the struggle was a useless one. She would not yield, however; and she was seized by one of those nervous crises that hurl women quivering, yelling, and writhing on the ground. She trembled in every limb, feeling that she was going to fall and roll among the chairs, uttering shrill cries. Someone approached with rapid steps. It was a priest. She rose and rushed towards him, holding out her clasped hands, and stammering: "Oh! save me, save me!"

He halted in surprise, saying: "What is it you wish, madame?"

"I want you to save me. Have pity on me. If you do not come to my assistance, I am lost."

He looked at her, asking himself whether she was not mad, and then said: "What can I do for you?"

He was a tall, and somewhat stout young man, with full, pendulous cheeks, dark, with a carefully shaven face, a good-looking city curate belonging to a wealthy district, and accustomed to rich penitents.

"Hear my confession, and advise me, sustain me, tell me what I am to do."

He replied: "I hear confessions every Saturday, from three to six o'clock."

Having seized his arm, she gripped it tightly as she repeated: "No, no, no; at once, at once! You must. He is here, in the church. He is waiting for me."

"Who is waiting for you?" asked the priest.

"A man who will ruin me, who will carry me off, if you do not save me. I cannot flee from him. I am too weak — too weak! Oh, so weak, so weak!" She fell at his feet sobbing: "Oh, have pity on me, father! Save me, in God's name, save me!"

She held him by his black gown lest he should escape, and he with uneasiness glanced around, lest some malevolent or devout eye should see this woman fallen at his feet. Understanding at length that he could not escape, he said: "Get up; I have the key of the confessional with me."

And fumbling in his pocket he drew out a ring full of keys, selected one, and walked rapidly towards the little wooden cabin, dust holes of the soul into which believers cast their sins. He entered the center door, which he closed behind him, and Madame Walter, throwing herself into the narrow recess at the side, stammered fervently, with a passionate burst of hope: "Bless me father, for I have sinned."

Du Roy, having taken a turn round the choir, was passing down the left aisle. He had got halfway when he met the stout, bald gentleman still walking quietly along, and said to himself: "What the deuce is that customer doing here?"

The promenader had also slackened his pace, and was looking at George with an evident wish to speak to him. When he came quite close he bowed, and said in a polite fashion: "I beg your pardon, sir, for troubling you, but can you tell me when this church was built?"

Du Roy replied: "Really, I am not quite certain. I think within the last twenty or five-and-twenty years. It is, besides, the first time I ever was inside it."

"It is the same with me. I have never seen it."

The journalist, whose interest was awakened, remarked: "It seems to me that you are going over it very carefully. You are studying it in detail."

The other replied, with resignation: "I am not examining it; I am waiting for my wife, who made an appointment with me here, and who is very much behind time." Then, after a few moments' silence, he added: "It is fearfully hot outside."

Du Roy looked at him, and all at once fancied that he resembled Forestier.

"You are from the country?" said he, inquiringly.

"Yes, from Rennes. And you, sir, is it out of curiosity that you entered this church?"

"No, I am expecting a lady," and bowing, the journalist walked away, with a smile on his lips.

Approaching the main entrance, he saw the poor woman still on her knees, and still praying. He thought: "By Jove! she keeps hard at it." He was no longer moved, and no longer pitied her.

He passed on, and began quietly to walk up the right-hand aisle to find Madame Walter again. He marked the place where he had left her from a distance, astonished at not seeing her. He thought he had made a mistake in the pillar; went on as far as the end one, and then returned. She had gone, then. He was surprised and enraged. Then he thought she might be looking for him, and made the circuit of the church again. Not finding her, he returned, and sat down on the chair she had occupied, hoping she would rejoin him there, and waited. Soon a low murmur of voices aroused his attention. He had not seen anyone in that part of the church. Whence came this whispering? He rose to see, and perceived in the adjacent chapel the doors of the confessional. The skirt of a dress issuing from one of these trailed on the pavement. He approached to examine the woman. He recognized her. She was confessing.

He felt a violent inclination to take her by the shoulders and to pull her out of the box. Then he thought: "Bah! it is the priest's turn now; it will be mine tomorrow." And he sat down quietly in front of the confessional, biding his time, and chuckling now over the adventure. He waited a long time. At length Madame Walter rose, turned round, saw him, and came up to him. Her expression was cold and severe, "Sir," said she, "I beg of you not to accompany me, not to follow me, and not to come to my house alone. You will not be received. Farewell."

And she walked away with a dignified bearing. He let her depart, for one of his principles was never to force matters. Then, as the priest, somewhat upset, issued in turn from his box, he walked up to him, and, looking him straight in the eyes, growled to his face: "If you did not wear a petticoat, what a smack you would get across your ugly chops." After which he turned on his heels and went out of the church, whistling between his teeth. Standing under the porch, the stout gentleman, with the hat on his head and his hands behind his back, tired of waiting, was scanning the broad squares and all the streets opening onto it. As Du Roy passed him they bowed to one another.

The journalist, finding himself at liberty, went to the office of the Vie Francaise. As soon as he entered he saw by the busy air of the messengers that something out of the common was happening, and at once went into the manager's room. Daddy Walter, in a state of nervous excitement, was standing up dictating an article in broken sentences; issuing orders to the reporters, who surrounded him, between two paragraphs; giving instructions to Boisrenard; and opening letters.

As Du Roy came in, the governor uttered a cry of joy: "Ah! how lucky; here is Pretty-boy!" He stopped short, somewhat confused, and excused himself: "I beg your pardon for speaking like that, but I am very much disturbed by certain events. And then I hear my wife and daughter speaking of you as Pretty-boy from morning till night, and have ended by falling into the habit myself. You are not offended?"

"Not at all!" said George, laughingly; "there is nothing in that nickname to displease me."

Daddy Walter went on: "Very well, then, I christen you Pretty-boy, like everyone else. Well, the fact is, great things are taking place. The Ministry has been overthrown by a vote of three hundred and ten to a hundred and two. Our prorogation is again postponed — postponed to the Greek calends, and here we are at the twenty-eighth of July. Spain is angry about the Morocco business, and it is that which has overthrown Durand de l'Aine and his following. We are right in the swim. Marrot is entrusted with the formation of a new Cabinet. He takes General Boutin d'Acre as minister of war, and our friend Laroche-Mathieu for foreign affairs. We are going to become an official organ. I am writing a leader, a simple declaration of our principles, pointing out the line to be followed by the Ministry." The old boy smiled, and continued: "The line they intend following, be it understood. But I want something interesting about Morocco; an actuality; a sensational article; something or other. Find one for me."

Du Roy reflected for a moment, and then replied: "I have the very thing for you. I will give you a study of the political situation of the whole of our African colony, with Tunis on the left, Algeria in the middle, and Morocco on the right; the history of the races inhabiting this vast extent of territory; and the narrative of an excursion on the frontier of Morocco to the great oasis of Figuig, where no European has penetrated, and which is the cause of the present conflict. Will that suit you?"

"Admirably!" exclaimed Daddy Walter. "And the title?"

"From Tunis to Tangiers."

"Splendid!"

Du Roy went off to search the files of the Vie Francaise for his first article, "The Recollections of a Chasseur d'Afrique," which, rebaptized, touched up, and modified, would do admirably, since it dealt with colonial policy, the Algerian population, and an excursion in the province of Oran. In three-quarters of an hour it was rewritten, touched up, and brought to date, with a flavor of realism, and praises of the new Cabinet. The manager, having read the article, said: "It is capital, capital, capital! You are an invaluable fellow. I congratulate you."

And Du Roy went home to dinner delighted with his day's work, despite the check at the Church of the Trinity, for he felt the battle won. His wife was anxiously waiting for him. She exclaimed, as soon as she saw him: "Do you know that Laroche-Mathieu is Minister for Foreign Affairs?"

"Yes; I have just written an article on Algeria, in connection with it."

"What?"

"You know, the first we wrote together, 'The Recollections of a Chasseur d'Afrique,' revised and corrected for the occasion."

She smiled, saying: "Ah, that is very good!" Then, after a few moments' reflection, she continued: "I was thinking — that continuation you were to have written then, and that you — put off. We might set to work on it now. It would make a nice series, and very appropriate to the situation."

He replied, sitting down to table: "Exactly, and there is nothing in the way of it now that cuckold of a Forestier is dead."

She said quietly, in a dry and hurt tone: "That joke is more than out of place, and I beg of you to put an end to it. It has lasted too long already."

He was about to make an ironical answer, when a telegram was brought him, containing these words: "I had lost my senses. Forgive me, and come at four o'clock tomorrow to the Parc Monceau."

He understood, and with heart suddenly filled with joy, he said to his wife, as he slipped the message into his pocket: "I will not do so any more, darling; it was stupid, I admit."

And he began his dinner. While eating he kept repeating to himself the words: "I had lost my senses. Forgive me, and come at four o'clock tomorrow to the Parc Monceau." So she was yielding. That meant: "I surrender, I am yours when you like and where you like." He began to laugh, and Madeleine asked: "What is it?"

"Nothing," he answered; "I was thinking of a priest I met just now, and who had a very comical mug."

Du Roy arrived to the time at the appointed place next day. On the benches of the park were seated citizens overcome by heat, and careless nurses, who seemed to be dreaming while their children were rolling on the gravel of the paths. He found Madame Walter in the little antique ruins from which a spring flows. She was walking round the little circle of columns with an uneasy and unhappy air. As soon as he had greeted her, she exclaimed: "What a number of people there are in the garden."

He seized the opportunity: "It is true; will you come somewhere else?"

"But where?"

"No matter where; in a cab, for instance. You can draw down the blind on your side, and you will be quite invisible."

"Yes, I prefer that; here I am dying with fear."

"Well, come and meet me in five minutes at the gate opening onto the outer boulevard. I will have a cab."

And he darted off.

As soon as she had rejoined him, and had carefully drawn down the blind on her side, she asked: "Where have you told the driver to take us?"

George replied: "Do not trouble yourself, he knows what to do."

He had given the man his address in the Rue de Constantinople.

She resumed: "You cannot imagine what I suffer on account of you, how I am tortured and tormented. Yesterday, in the church, I was cruel, but I wanted to flee from you at any cost. I was so afraid to find myself alone with you. Have you forgiven me?"

He squeezed her hands: "Yes, yes, what would I not forgive you, loving you as I do?"

She looked at him with a supplicating air: "Listen, you must promise to respect me — not to — not to — otherwise I cannot see you again."

He did not reply at once; he wore under his moustache that keen smile that disturbed women. He ended by murmuring: "I am your slave."

Then she began to tell him how she had perceived that she was in love with him on learning that he was going to marry Madeleine Forestier. She gave details, little details of dates and the like. Suddenly she paused. The cab had stopped. Du Roy opened the door.

"Where are we?" she asked.

"Get out and come into this house," he replied. "We shall be more at ease there."

"But where are we?"

"At my rooms," and here we will leave them to their tête-à-tête.

XIII

Autumn had come. The Du Roys had passed the whole of the summer in Paris, carrying on a vigorous campaign in the Vie Francaise during the short vacation of the deputies.

Although it was only the beginning of October, the Chambers were about to resume their sittings, for matters as regarded Morocco were becoming threatening. No one at the bottom believed in an expedition against Tangiers, although on the day of the prorogation of the Chamber, a deputy of the Right, Count de Lambert-Serrazin, in a witty speech, applauded even by the Center had offered to stake his moustache, after the example of a celebrated Viceroy of the Indies, against the whiskers of the President of the Council, that the new Cabinet could not help imitating the old one, and sending an army to Tangiers, as a pendant to that of Tunis, out of love of symmetry, as one puts two vases on a fireplace.

He had added: "Africa is indeed, a fireplace for France, gentleman — a fireplace which consumes our best wood; a fireplace with a strong draught, which is lit with bank notes. You have had the artistic fancy of ornamenting the left-hand corner with a Tunisian knickknack which had cost you dear. You will see that Monsieur Marrot will want to imitate his predecessor, and ornament the right-hand corner with one from Morocco."

This speech, which became famous, served as a peg for Du Roy for a half a score of articles upon the Algerian colony — indeed, for the entire series broken short off after his début on the paper. He had energetically supported the notion of a military expedition, although convinced that it would not take place. He had struck the chord of patriotism, and bombarded Spain with the entire arsenal of contemptuous arguments which we make use of against nations whose interests are contrary to our own. The Vie Francaise had gained considerable importance through its own connection with the party in office. It published political intelligence in advance of the most important papers, and hinted discreetly the intentions of its friends the Ministry, so that all the papers of Paris and the provinces took their news from it. It was quoted and feared, and people began to respect it. It was no longer the suspicious organ of a knot of political jugglers, but the acknowledged one of the Cabinet. Laroche-Mathieu was the soul of the paper, and Du Roy his mouthpiece. Daddy Walter, a silent member and a crafty manager, knowing when to keep in the background, was busying himself on the quiet, it is said, with an extensive transaction with some copper mines in Morocco.

Madeleine's drawingroom had been an influential center, in which several members of the Cabinet met every week. The President of the Council had even dined twice at her house, and the wives of the statesmen who had formerly hesitated to cross her threshold now boasted of being her friends, and paid her more visits than were returned by her. The Minister for Foreign Affairs reigned almost as a master in the household. He called at all hours, bringing dispatches, news, items of information, which he dictated either to the husband or the wife, as if they had been his secretaries.

When Du Roy, after the minister's departure, found himself alone with Madeleine, he would break out in a menacing tone with bitter insinuations against the goings-on of this common-place parvenu.

But she would shrug her shoulders contemptuously, repeating: "Do as much as he has done yourself. Become a minister, and you can have your own way. Till then, hold your tongue."

He twirled his moustache, looking at her askance: "People do not know of what I am capable," he said, "They will learn it, perhaps, some day."

She replied, philosophically: "Who lives long enough will see it."

The morning on which the Chambers reassembled the young wife, still in bed, was giving a thousand recommendations to her husband, who was dressing himself in order to lunch with M. Laroche-Mathieu, and receive his instructions prior to the sitting for the next day's political leader in the Vie Francaise, this leader being meant to be a kind of semi-official declaration of the real objects of the Cabinet.

Madeleine was saying: "Above all, do not forget to ask him whether General Belloncle is to be sent to Oran, as has been reported. That would mean a great deal."

George replied irritably: "But I know just as well as you what I have to do. Spare me your preaching."

She answered quietly: "My dear, you always forget half the commissions I entrust you with for the minister."

He growled: "He worries me to death, that minister of yours. He is a nincompoop."

She remarked quietly: "He is no more my minister than he is yours. He is more useful to you than to me."

He turned half round towards her, saying, sneeringly: "I beg your pardon, but he does not pay court to me."

She observed slowly: "Nor to me either; but he is making our fortune."

He was silent for a few moments, and then resumed: "If I had to make a choice among your admirers, I should still prefer that old fossil De Vaudrec. What has become of him, I have not seen him for a week?"

"He is unwell," replied she, unmoved. "He wrote to me that he was even obliged to keep his bed from an attack of gout. You ought to call and ask how he is. You know he likes you very well, and it would please him."

George said: "Yes, certainly; I will go some time to-day."

He had finished his toilet, and, hat on head, glanced at himself in the glass to see if he had neglected anything. Finding nothing, he came up to the bed and kissed his wife on the forehead, saying: "Goodbye, dear, I shall not be in before seven o'clock at the earliest."

And he went out. Monsieur Laroche-Mathieu was awaiting him, for he was lunching at ten o'clock that morning, the Council having to meet at noon, before the opening of Parliament. As soon as they were seated at table alone with the minister's private secretary, for Madame Laroche-Mathieu had been unwilling to change her own meal times, Du Roy spoke of his article, sketched out the line he proposed to take, consulting notes scribbled on visiting cards, and when he had finished, said: "Is there anything you think should be modified, my dear minister?"

"Very little, my dear fellow. You are perhaps a trifle too strongly affirmative as regards the Morocco business. Speak of the expedition as if it were going to take place; but, at the same time, letting it be understood that it will not take place, and that you do not believe in it in the least in the world. Write in such a way that the public can easily read between the lines that we are not going to poke our noses into that adventure."

"Quite so. I understand, and I will make myself thoroughly understood. My wife commissioned me to ask you, on this point, whether General Belloncle will be sent to Oran. After what you have said, I conclude he will not."

The statesman answered, "No."

Then they spoke of the coming session. Laroche-Mathieu began to spout, rehearsing the phrases that he was about to pour forth on his colleagues a few hours later. He waved his right hand, raising now his knife, now his fork, now a bit of bread, and without looking at anyone, addressing himself to the invisible assembly, he poured out his dulcet eloquence, the eloquence of a good-looking, dandified fellow. A tiny, twisted moustache curled up at its two ends above his lip like scorpion's tails, and his hair, anointed with brilliantine and parted in the middle, was puffed out like his temples, after the fashion of a provincial lady-killer. He was a little too stout, puffy, though still young, and his stomach stretched his waistcoat.

The private secretary ate and drank quietly, no doubt accustomed to these floods of loquacity; but Du Roy, whom jealousy of achieved success cut to the quick, thought: "Go on you proser. What idiots these political jokers are." And comparing his own worth to the frothy importance of the minister, he said to himself, "By Jove! if I had only a clear hundred thousand francs to offer myself as a candidate at home, near Rouen, and dish my sunning dullards of Normandy folk in their own sauce, what a statesman I should make beside these shortsighted rascals!"

Monsieur Laroche-Mathieu went on spouting until coffee was served; then, seeing that he was behind hand, he rang for his brougham, and holding out his hand to the journalist, said: "You quite understand, my dear fellow?"

"Perfectly, my dear minister; you may rely upon me."

And Du Roy strolled leisurely to the office to begin his article, for he had nothing to do till four o'clock. At four o'clock he was to meet, at the Rue de Constantinople, Madame de Marelle, whom he met there regularly twice a week — on Mondays and Fridays. But on reaching the office a telegram was handed to him. It was from Madame Walter, and ran as follows: "I must see you to-day. Most important. Expect me at two o'clock, Rue de Constantinople. Can render you a great service. Till death. — Virginie."

He began to swear: "Hang it all, what an infernal bore!" And seized with a fit of ill-temper, he went out again at once too irritated to work.

For six weeks he had been trying to break off with her, without being able to wear out her eager attachment. She had had, after her fall, a frightful fit of remorse, and in three successive rendezvous had overwhelmed her lover with reproaches and maledictions. Bored by these scenes and already tired of this mature and melodramatic conquest, he had simply kept away, hoping to put an end to the adventure in that way. But then she had distractedly clutched on to him, throwing herself into this amour as a man throws himself into a river with a stone about his neck. He had allowed himself to be recaptured out of weakness and consideration for her, and she had enwrapt him in an unbridled and fatiguing passion, persecuting him with her affection. She insisted on seeing him every day, summoning him at all hours to a hasty meeting at a street corner, at a shop, or in a public garden. She would then repeat to him in a few words, always the same, that she worshiped and idolized him, and leave him, vowing that she felt so happy to have seen him. She showed herself quite another creature than he had fancied her, striving to charm him with puerile glances, a childishness in love affairs ridiculous at her age. Having remained up till then strictly honest, virgin in heart, inaccessible to all sentiment, ignorant of sensuality, a strange outburst of youthful tenderness, of ardent, naive and tardy love, made up of unlooked-for outbursts, exclamations of a girl of sixteen, graces grown old without ever having been young, had taken place in this staid woman. She wrote him ten letters a day, maddeningly foolish letters, couched in a style at once poetic and ridiculous, full of the pet names of birds and beasts.

As soon as they found themselves alone together she would kiss him with the awkward prettiness of a great tomboy, pouting of the lips that were grotesque, and bounds that made her too full bosom shake beneath her bodice. He was above all, sickened with hearing her say, "My pet," "My doggie," "My jewel," "My birdie," "My treasure," "My own," "My precious," and to see her offer herself to him every time with a little comedy of infantile modesty, little movements of alarm that she thought pretty, and the tricks of a depraved schoolgirl. She would ask, "Whose mouth is this?" and when he did not reply "Mine," would persist till she made him grow pale with nervous irritability. She ought to have felt, it seemed to him, that in love extreme tact, skill, prudence, and exactness are requisite; that having given herself to him, she, a woman of mature years, the mother of a family, and holding a position in society, should yield herself gravely, with a kind of restrained eagerness, with tears, perhaps, but with those of Dido, not of Juliet.

She kept incessantly repeating to him, "How I love you, my little pet. Do you love me as well, baby?"

He could no longer bear to be called "my little pet," or "baby," without an inclination to call her "old girl."

She would say to him, "What madness of me to yield to you. But I do not regret it. It is so sweet to love."

All this seemed to George irritating from her mouth. She murmured, "It is so sweet to love," like the village maiden at a theater.

Then she exasperated him by the clumsiness of her caresses. Having become all at once sensual beneath the kisses of this young fellow who had so warmed her blood, she showed an unskilled ardor and a serious application that made Du Roy laugh and think of old men trying to learn to read. When she would have gripped him in her embrace, ardently gazing at him with the deep and terrible glance of certain aging women, splendid in their last loves, when she should have bitten him with silent and quivering mouth, crushing him beneath her warmth and weight, she would wriggle about like a girl, and lisp with the idea of being pleasant: "Me love 'ou so, ducky, me love 'ou so. Have nice lovey-lovey with 'ittle wifey."

He then would be seized with a wild desire to take his hat and rush out, slamming the door behind him.

They had frequently met at the outset at the Rue de Constantinople; but Du Roy, who dreaded a meeting there with Madame de Marelle, now found a thousand pretexts for refusing such appointments. He had then to call on her almost every day at her home, now to lunch, now to dinner. She squeezed his hand under the table, held out her mouth to him behind the doors. But he, for his part, took pleasure above all in playing with Susan, who amused him with her whimsicalities. In her doll-like frame was lodged an active, arch, sly, and startling wit, always ready to show itself off. She joked at everything and everybody with biting readiness. George stimulated her imagination, excited it to irony and they understood one another marvelously. She kept appealing to him every moment, "I say, Pretty-boy. Come here, Pretty-boy."

He would at once leave the mother and go to the daughter, who would whisper some bit of spitefulness, at which they would laugh heartily.

However, disgusted with the mother's love, he began to feel an insurmountable repugnance for her; he could no longer see, hear, or think of her without anger. He ceased, therefore, to visit her, to answer her letters, or to yield to her appeals. She understood at length that he no longer loved her, and suffered terribly. But she grew insatiable, kept watch on him, followed him, waited for him in a cab with the blinds drawn down, at the door of the office, at the door of his dwelling, in the streets through which she hoped he might pass. He longed to ill-treat her, swear at her, strike her, say to her plainly, "I have had enough of it, you worry my life out." But he observed some circumspection on account of the Vie Francaise, and strove by dint of coolness, harshness, tempered by attention, and even rude words at times, to make her understand that there must be an end to it. She strove, above all, to devise schemes to allure him to a meeting in the Rue de Constantinople, and he was in a perpetual state of alarm lest the two women should find themselves some day face to face at the door.

His affection for Madame de Marelle had, on the contrary, augmented during the summer. He called her his "young rascal," and she certainly charmed him. Their two natures had kindred links; they were both members of the adventurous race of vagabonds, those vagabonds in society who so strongly resemble, without being aware of it, the vagabonds of the highways. They had had a summer of delightful love-making, a summer of students on the spree, bolting off to lunch or dine at Argenteuil, Bougival, Maisons, or Poissy, and passing hours in a boat gathering flowers from the bank. She adored the fried fish served on the banks of the Seine, the stewed rabbits, the arbors in the tavern gardens, and the shouts of the boating men. He liked to start off with her on a bright day on a suburban line, and traverse the ugly environs of Paris, sprouting with tradesmen's hideous boxes, talking lively nonsense. And when he had to return to dine at Madame Walter's he hated the eager old mistress from the mere recollection of the young one whom he had left, and who had ravished his desires and harvested his ardor among the grass by the water side.

He had fancied himself at length pretty well rid of Madame Walter, to whom he had expressed, in a plain and almost brutal fashion, his intentions of breaking off with her, when he received at the office of the paper the telegram summoning him to meet her at two o'clock at the Rue de Constantinople. He re-read it as he walked along, "Must see you to-day. Most important. Expect me two o'clock, Rue de Constantinople. Can render you a great service. Till death. — Virginie."

He thought, "What does this old screech-owl want with me now? I wager she has nothing to tell me. She will only repeat that she adores me. Yet I must see what it means. She speaks of an important affair and a great service; perhaps it is so. And Clotilde, who is coming at four o'clock! I must get the first of the pair off by three at the latest. By Jove, provided they don't run up against one another! What bothers women are."

And he reflected that, after all, his own wife was the only one who never bothered him at all. She lived in her own way, and seemed to be very fond of him during the hours destined to love, for she would not admit that the unchangeable order of the ordinary occupations of life should be interfered with.

He walked slowly towards the rendezvous, mentally working himself up against Madame Walter. "Ah! I will just receive her nicely if she has nothing to tell me. Cambronne's language will be academical compared to mine. I will tell her that I will never set foot in her house again, to begin with."

He went in to wait for Madame Walter. She arrived almost immediately, and as soon as she caught sight of him, she exclaimed, "Ah, you have had my telegram! How fortunate."

He put on a grumpy expression, saying: "By Jove, yes; I found it at the office just as I was going to start off to the Chamber. What is it you want now?"

She had raised her veil to kiss him, and drew nearer with the timid and submissive air of an oft-beaten dog.

"How cruel you are towards me! How harshly you speak to me! What have I done to you? You cannot imagine how I suffer through you."

He growled: "Don't go on again in that style."

She was standing close to him, only waiting for a smile, a gesture, to throw herself into his arms, and murmured: "You should not have taken me to treat me thus, you should have left me sober-minded and happy as I was. Do you remember what you said to me in the church, and how you forced me into this house? And now, how do you speak to me? how do you receive me? Oh, God! oh, God! what pain you give me!"

He stamped his foot, and exclaimed, violently: "Ah, bosh! That's enough of it! I can't see you a moment without hearing all that foolery. One would really think that I had carried you off at twelve years of age, and that you were as ignorant as an angel. No, my dear, let us put things in their proper light; there was no seduction of a young girl in the business. You gave yourself to me at full years of discretion. I thank you. I am infinitely grateful to you, but I am not bound to be tied till death to your petticoat strings. You have a husband and I a wife. We are neither of us free. We indulged in a mutual caprice, and it is over."

"Oh, you are brutal, coarse, shameless," she said; "I was indeed no longer a young girl, but I had never loved, never faltered."

He cut her short with: "I know it. You have told me so twenty times. But you had had two children."

She drew back, exclaiming: "Oh, George, that is unworthy of you," and pressing her two hands to her heart, began to choke and sob.

When he saw the tears come he took his hat from the corner of the mantelpiece, saying: "Oh, you are going to cry, are you? Goodbye, then. So it was to show off in this way that you came here, eh?"

She had taken a step forward in order to bar the way, and quickly pulling out a handkerchief from her pocket, wiped her eyes with an abrupt movement. Her voice grew firmer by the effort of her will, as she said, in tones tremulous with pain, "No — I came to — to tell you some news — political news — to put you in the way of gaining fifty thousand francs — or even more — if you like."

He inquired, suddenly softening, "How so? What do you mean?"

"I caught, by chance, yesterday evening, some words between my husband and Laroche-Mathieu. They do not, besides, trouble themselves to hide much from me. But Walter recommended the Minister not to let you into the secret, as you would reveal everything."

Du Roy had put his hat down on a chair, and was waiting very attentively.

"What is up, then?" said he.

"They are going to take possession of Morocco."

"Nonsense! I lunched with Laroche-Mathieu, who almost dictated to me the intention of the Cabinet."

"No, darling, they are humbugging you, because they were afraid lest their plan should be known."

"Sit down," said George, and sat down himself in an armchair. Then she drew towards him a low stool, and sitting down on it between his knees, went on in a coaxing tone, "As I am always thinking about you, I pay attention now to everything that is whispered around me."

And she began quietly to explain to him how she had guessed for some time past that something was being hatched unknown to him; that they were making use of him, while dreading his cooperation. She said, "You know, when one is in love, one grows cunning."

At length, the day before, she had understood it all. It was a business transaction, a thumping affair, worked out on the quiet. She smiled now, happy in her dexterity, and grew excited, speaking like a financier's wife accustomed to see the market rigged, used to rises and falls that ruin, in two hours of speculation, thousands of little folk who have placed their savings in undertakings guaranteed by the names of men honored and respected in the world of politics of finance.

She repeated, "Oh, it is very smart what they have been up to! Very smart. It was Walter who did it all, though, and he knows all about such things. Really, it is a first-class job."

He grew impatient at these preliminaries, and exclaimed, "Come, tell me what it is at once."

"Well, then, this is what it is. The Tangiers expedition was decided upon between them on the day that Laroche-Mathieu took the ministry of foreign affairs, and little by little they have bought up the whole of the Morocco loan, which had fallen to sixty-four or sixty-five francs. They have bought it up very cleverly by means of shady brokers, who did not awaken any mistrust. They have even sold the Rothschilds, who grew astonished to find Morocco stock always asked for, and who were astonished by having agents pointed out to them — all lame ducks. That quieted the big financiers. And now the expedition is to take place, and as soon as we are there the French Government will guarantee the debt. Our friends will gain fifty or sixty millions. You understand the matter? You understand, too, how afraid they have been of everyone, of the slightest indiscretion?”

She had leaned her head against the young fellow’s waistcoat, and with her arms resting on his legs, pressed up against him, feeling that she was interesting him now, and ready to do anything for a caress, for a smile.

“You are quite certain?” he asked.

“I should think so,” she replied, with confidence.

“It is very smart indeed. As to that swine of a Laroche-Mathieu, just see if I don’t pay him out one of these days. Oh, the scoundrel, just let him look out for himself! He shall go through my hands.” Then he began to reflect, and went on, “We ought, though, to profit by all this.”

“You can still buy some of the loan,” said she; “it is only at seventy-two francs.”

He said, “Yes, but I have no money under my hand.”

She raised her eyes towards him, eyes full of entreaty, saying, “I have thought of that, darling, and if you were very nice, very nice, if you loved me a little, you would let me lend you some.”

He answered, abruptly and almost harshly, “As to that, no, indeed.”

She murmured, in an imploring voice: “Listen, there is something that you can do without borrowing money. I wanted to buy ten thousand francs’ worth of the loan to make a little nest-egg. Well, I will take twenty thousand, and you shall stand in for half. You understand that I am not going to hand the money over to Walter. So there is nothing to pay for the present. If it all succeeds, you gain seventy thousand francs. If not, you will owe me ten thousand, which you can pay when you please.”

He remarked, “No, I do not like such pains.”

Then she argued, in order to get him to make up his mind. She proved to him that he was really pledging his word for ten thousand francs, that he was running risks, and that she was not advancing him anything, since the actual outlay was made by Walter’s bank. She pointed out to him, besides, that it was he who had carried on in the Vie Francaise the whole of the political campaign that had rendered the scheme possible. He would be very foolish not to profit by it. He still hesitated, and she added, “But just reflect that in reality it is Walter who is advancing you these ten thousand Francs, and that you have rendered him services worth a great deal more than that.”

“Very well, then,” said he, “I will go halves with you. If we lose, I will repay you the ten thousand francs.”

She was so pleased that she rose, took his head in both her hands, and began to kiss him eagerly. He did not resist at first, but as she grew bolder, clasping him to her and devouring him with caresses, he reflected that the other would be there shortly, and that if he yielded he would lose time and exhaust in the arms of the old woman an ardor that he had better reserve for the young one. So he repulsed her gently, saying, “Come, be good now.”

She looked at him disconsolately, saying, “Oh, George, can’t I even kiss you?”

He replied, “No, not to-day. I have a headache, and it upsets me.”

She sat down again docilely between his knees, and asked, “Will you come and dine with us tomorrow? You would give me much pleasure.”

He hesitated, but dared not refuse, so said, “Certainly.”

“Thanks, darling.”

She rubbed her cheek slowly against his breast with a regular and coaxing movement, and one of her long black hairs caught in his waistcoat. She noticed it, and a wild idea crossed her mind, one of those superstitious notions which are often the whole of a woman’s reason. She began to twist this hair gently round a button. Then she fastened another hair to the next button, and a third to the next. One to every button. He would tear them out of her head presently when he rose, and hurt her. What happiness! And he would carry away something of her without knowing it; he would carry away a tiny lock of her hair which he had never yet asked for. It was a tie by which she attached him to her, a secret, invisible bond, a talisman she left with him. Without willing it he would think of her, dream of her, and perhaps love her a little more the next day.

He said, all at once, "I must leave you, because I am expected at the Chamber at the close of the sitting. I cannot miss attending to-day."

She sighed, "Already!" and then added, resignedly, "Go, dear, but you will come to dinner tomorrow."

And suddenly she drew aside. There was a short and sharp pain in her head, as though needles had been stuck into the skin. Her heart throbbed; she was pleased to have suffered a little by him. "Goodbye," said she.

He took her in his arms with a compassionate smile, and coldly kissed her eyes. But she, maddened by this contact, again murmured, "Already!" while her suppliant glance indicated the bedroom, the door of which was open.

He stepped away from her, and said in a hurried tone, "I must be off; I shall be late."

Then she held out her lips, which he barely brushed with his, and having handed her her parasol, which she was forgetting, he continued, "Come, come, we must be quick, it is past three o'clock."

She went out before him, saying, "Tomorrow, at seven," and he repeated, "Tomorrow, at seven."

They separated, she turning to the right and he to the left. Du Roy walked as far as the outer boulevard. Then he slowly strolled back along the Boulevard Malesherbes. Passing a pastry cook's, he noticed some marrons glaces in a glass jar, and thought, "I will take in a pound for Clotilde."

He bought a bag of these sweetmeats, which she was passionately fond of, and at four o'clock returned to wait for his young mistress. She was a little late, because her husband had come home for a week, and said, "Can you come and dine with us tomorrow? He will be so pleased to see you."

"No, I dine with the governor. We have a heap of political and financial matters to talk over."

She had taken off her bonnet, and was now laying aside her bodice, which was too tight for her. He pointed out the bag on the mantelshelf, saying, "I have bought you some marrons glaces."

She clapped her hands, exclaiming: "How nice; what a dear you are."

She took one, tasted them, and said: "They are delicious. I feel sure I shall not leave one of them." Then she added, looking at George with sensual merriment: "You flatter all my vices, then."

She slowly ate the sweetmeats, looking continually into the bag to see if there were any left. "There, sit down in the armchair," said she, "and I will squat down between your knees and nibble my bonbons. I shall be very comfortable."

He smiled, sat down, and took her between his knees, as he had had Madame Walter shortly before. She raised her head in order to speak to him, and said, with her mouth full: "Do you know, darling, I dreamt of you? I dreamt that we were both taking a long journey together on a camel. He had two humps, and we were each sitting astride on a hump, crossing the desert. We had taken some sandwiches in a piece of paper and some wine in a bottle, and were dining on our humps. But it annoyed me because we could not do anything else; we were too far off from one another, and I wanted to get down."

He answered: "I want to get down, too."

He laughed, amused at the story, and encouraged her to talk nonsense, to chatter, to indulge in all the child's play of conversation which lovers utter. The nonsense which he thought delightful in the mouth of Madame de Marelle would have exasperated him in that of Madame Walter. Clotilde, too, called him "My darling," "My pet," "My own." These words seemed sweet and caressing. Said by the other woman shortly before, they had irritated and sickened him. For words of love, which are always the same, take the flavor of the lips they come from.

But he was thinking, even while amusing himself with this nonsense, of the seventy thousand francs he was going to gain, and suddenly checked the gabble of his companion by two little taps with his finger on her head. "Listen, pet," said he.

"I am going to entrust you with a commission for your husband. Tell him from me to buy tomorrow ten thousand francs' worth of the Morocco loan, which is quoted at seventy-two, and I promise him that he will gain from sixty to eighty thousand francs before three months are over. Recommend the most positive silence to him. Tell him from me that the expedition to Tangiers is decided on, and that the French government will guarantee the debt of Morocco. But do not let anything out about it. It is a State secret that I am entrusting to you."

She listened to him seriously, and murmured: "Thank you, I will tell my husband this evening. You can reckon on him; he will not talk. He is a very safe man, and there is no danger."

But she had eaten all the sweetmeats. She crushed up the bag between her hands and flung it into the fireplace. Then she said, "Let us go to bed," and without getting up, began to unbutton George's waistcoat. All at once she stopped, and pulling out between two fingers a long hair, caught in a buttonhole, began to laugh. "There, you have brought away one of Madeleine's hairs. There is a faithful husband for you."

Then, becoming once more serious, she carefully examined on her head the almost imperceptible thread she had found, and murmured: "It is not Madeleine's, it is too dark."

He smiled, saying: "It is very likely one of the maid's."

But she was inspecting the waistcoat with the attention of a detective, and collected a second hair rolled round a button; then she perceived a third, and pale and somewhat trembling, exclaimed: "Oh, you have been sleeping with a woman who has wrapped her hair round all your buttons."

He was astonished, and gasped out: "No, you are mad."

All at once he remembered, understood it all, was uneasy at first, and then denied the charge with a chuckle, not vexed at the bottom that she should suspect him of other loves. She kept on searching, and still found hairs, which she rapidly untwisted and threw on the carpet. She had guessed matters with her artful woman's instinct, and stammered out, vexed, angry, and ready to cry: "She loves you, she does — and she wanted you to take away something belonging to her. Oh, what a traitor you are!" But all at once she gave a cry, a shrill cry of nervous joy. "Oh! oh! it is an old woman — here is a white hair. Ah, you go in for old women now! Do they pay you, eh — do they pay you? Ah, so you have come to old women, have you? Then you have no longer any need of me. Keep the other one."

She rose, ran to her bodice thrown onto a chair, and began hurriedly to put it on again. He sought to retain her, stammering confusedly: "But, no, Clo, you are silly. I do not know anything about it. Listen now — stay here. Come, now — stay here."

She repeated: "Keep your old woman — keep her. Have a ring made out of her hair — out of her white hair. You have enough of it for that."

With abrupt and swift movements she had dressed herself and put on her bonnet and veil, and when he sought to take hold of her, gave him a smack with all her strength. While he remained bewildered, she opened the door and fled.

As soon as he was alone he was seized with furious anger against that old hag of a Mother Walter. Ah, he would send her about her business, and pretty roughly, too! He bathed his reddened cheek and then went out, in turn meditating vengeance. This time he would not forgive her. Ah, no! He walked down as far as the boulevard, and sauntering along stopped in front of a jeweler's shop to look at a chronometer he had fancied for a long time back, and which was ticketed eighteen hundred francs. He thought all at once, with a thrill of joy at his heart, "If I gain my seventy thousand francs I can afford it."

And he began to think of all the things he would do with these seventy thousand francs. In the first place, he would get elected deputy. Then he would buy his chronometer, and would speculate on the Bourse, and would —

He did not want to go to the office, preferring to consult Madeleine before seeing Walter and writing his article, and started for home. He had reached the Rue Druot, when he stopped short. He had forgotten to ask after the Count de Vaudrec, who lived in the Chaussee d'Antin. He therefore turned back, still sauntering, thinking of a thousand things, mainly pleasant, of his coming fortune, and also of that scoundrel of a Laroche-Mathieu, and that old stickfast of a Madame Walter. He was not uneasy about the wrath of Clotilde, knowing very well that she forgave quickly.

He asked the doorkeeper of the house in which the Count de Vaudrec resided: "How is Monsieur de Vaudrec? I hear that he has been unwell these last few days."

The man replied: "The Count is very bad indeed, sir. They are afraid he will not live through the night; the gout has mounted to his heart."

Du Roy was so startled that he no longer knew what he ought to do. Vaudrec dying! Confused and disquieting ideas shot through his mind that he dared not even admit to himself. He stammered: "Thank you; I will call again," without knowing what he was saying.

Then he jumped into a cab and was driven home. His wife had come in. He went into her room breathless, and said at once: "Have you heard? Vaudrec is dying."

She was sitting down reading a letter. She raised her eyes, and repeating thrice: "Oh! what do you say, what do you say, what do you say?"

"I say that Vaudrec is dying from a fit of gout that has flown to the heart." Then he added: "What do you think of doing?"

She had risen livid, and with her cheeks shaken by a nervous quivering, then she began to cry terribly, hiding her face in her hands. She stood shaken by sobs and torn by grief. But suddenly she mastered her sorrow, and wiping her eyes, said: "I — I am going there — don't bother about me — I don't know when I shall be back — don't wait for me."

He replied: "Very well, dear." They shook hands, and she went off so hurriedly that she forgot her gloves.

George, having dined alone, began to write his article. He did so exactly in accordance with the minister's instructions, giving his readers to understand that the expedition to Morocco would not take place. Then he took it to the office, chatted for a few minutes with the governor, and went out smoking, lighthearted, though he knew not why. His wife had not come home, and he went to bed and fell asleep.

Madeleine came in towards midnight. George, suddenly roused, sat up in bed. "Well?" he asked.

He had never seen her so pale and so deeply moved. She murmured: "He is dead."

"Ah! — and he did not say anything?"

"Nothing. He had lost consciousness when I arrived."

George was thinking. Questions rose to his lips that he did not dare to put. "Come to bed," said he.

She undressed rapidly, and slipped into bed beside him, when he resumed: "Were there any relations present at his deathbed?"

"Only a nephew."

"Ah! Did he see this nephew often?"

"Never. They had not met for ten years."

"Had he any other relatives?"

"No, I do not think so."

"Then it is his nephew who will inherit?"

"I do not know."

"He was very well off, Vaudrec?"

"Yes, very well off."

"Do you know what his fortune was?"

"No, not exactly. One or two millions, perhaps."

He said no more. She blew out the light, and they remained stretched out, side by side, in the darkness — silent, wakeful, and reflecting. He no longer felt inclined for sleep. He now thought the seventy thousand francs promised by Madame Walter insignificant. Suddenly he fancied that Madeleine was crying. He inquired, in order to make certain: "Are you asleep?"

"No."

Her voice was tearful and quavering, and he said: "I forgot to tell you when I came in that your minister has let us in nicely."

"How so?"

He told her at length, with all details, the plan hatched between Laroche-Mathieu and Walter. When he had finished, she asked: "How do you know this?"

He replied: "You will excuse me not telling you. You have your means of information, which I do not seek to penetrate. I have mine, which I wish to keep to myself. I can, in any case, answer for the correctness of my information."

Then she murmured: "Yes, it is quite possible. I fancied they were up to something without us."

But George, who no longer felt sleepy, had drawn closer to his wife, and gently kissed her ear. She repulsed him sharply. "I beg of you to leave me alone. I am not in a mood to romp." He turned resignedly towards the wall, and having closed his eyes, ended by falling asleep.

XIV

The church was draped with black, and over the main entrance a huge scutcheon, surmounted by a coronet, announced to the passersby that a gentleman was being buried. The ceremony was just over, and those present at it were slowly dispersing, defiling past the coffin and the nephew of the Count de Vaudrec, who was shaking extended hands and returning bows. When George Du Roy and his wife came out of the church they began to walk homeward side by side, silent and preoccupied. At length George said, as though speaking to himself: "Really, it is very strange."

"What, dear?" asked Madeleine.

"That Vaudrec should not have left us anything."

She blushed suddenly, as though a rosy veil had been cast over her white skin, and said: "Why should he have left us anything? There was no reason for it." Then, after a few moments' silence, she went on: "There is perhaps a will in the hands of some notary. We know nothing as yet."

He reflected for a short time, and then murmured: "Yes, it is probable, for, after all, he was the most intimate friend of us both. He dined with us twice a week, called at all hours, and was at home at our place, quite at home in every respect. He loved you like a father, and had no children, no brothers and sisters, nothing but a nephew, and a nephew he never used to see. Yes, there must be a will. I do not care for much, only a remembrance to show that he thought of us, that he loved us, that he recognized the affection we felt for him. He certainly owed us some such mark of friendship."

She said in a pensive and indifferent manner: "It is possible, indeed, that there may be a will."

As they entered their rooms, the manservant handed a letter to Madeleine. She opened it, and then held it out to her husband. It ran as follows:

"Office of Maitre Lamaneur, Notary,
"17 Rue des Vosges.

"Madame: I have the honor to beg you to favor me with a call here on Tuesday, Wednesday, or Thursday between the hours of two and four, on business concerning you. — I am, *etc.* — Lamaneur."

George had reddened in turn. "That is what it must be," said he. "It is strange, though, that it is you who are summoned, and not myself, who am legally the head of the family."

She did not answer at once, but after a brief period of reflection, said: "Shall we go round there by and by?"

"Yes, certainly."

They set out as soon as they had lunched. When they entered Maitre Lamaneur's office, the head clerk rose with marked attention and ushered them in to his master. The notary was a round, little man, round all over. His head looked like a ball nailed onto another ball, which had legs so short that they almost resembled balls too. He bowed, pointed to two chairs, and turning towards Madeleine, said: "Madame, I have sent for you in order to acquaint you with the will of the Count de Vaudrec, in which you are interested."

George could not help muttering: "I thought so."

The notary went on: "I will read to you the document, which is very brief."

He took a paper from a box in front of him, and read as follows:

"I, the undersigned, Paul Emile Cyprien Gontran, Count de Vaudrec, being sound in body and mind, hereby express my last wishes. As death may overtake us at any moment, I wish, in provision of his attacks, to take the precaution of making my will, which will be placed in the hands of Maitre Lamaneur. Having no direct heirs, I leave the whole of my fortune, consisting of stock to the amount of six hundred thousand francs, and landed property worth about five hundred thousand francs, to Madame Claire Madeleine Du Roy without any charge or condition. I beg her to accept this gift of a departed friend as a proof of a deep, devoted, and respectful affection."

The notary added: "That is all. This document is dated last August, and replaces one of the same nature, written two years back, with the name of Madame Claire Madeleine Forestier. I have this first will, too, which would prove, in the case of opposition on the part of the family, that the wishes of Count de Vaudrec did not vary."

Madeleine, very pale, looked at her feet. George nervously twisted the end of his moustache between his fingers. The notary continued after a moment of silence: "It is, of course, understood, sir, that your wife cannot accept the legacy without your consent."

Du Roy rose and said, dryly: "I must ask time to reflect."

The notary, who was smiling, bowed, and said in an amiable tone: "I understand the scruples that cause you to hesitate, sir. I should say that the nephew of Monsieur de Vaudrec, who became acquainted this very morning with his uncle's last wishes, stated that he was prepared to respect them, provided the sum of a hundred thousand francs was allowed him. In my opinion the will is unattackable, but a lawsuit would cause a stir, which it may perhaps suit you to avoid. The world often judges things ill-naturedly. In any case, can you give me your answer on all these points before Saturday?"

George bowed, saying: "Yes, sir."

Then he bowed again ceremoniously, ushered out his wife, who had remained silent, and went out himself with so stiff an air that the notary no longer smiled.

As soon as they got home, Du Roy abruptly closed the door, and throwing his hat onto the bed, said: "You were Vaudrec's mistress."

Madeleine, who was taking off her veil, turned round with a start, exclaiming: "I? Oh!"

"Yes, you. A man does not leave the whole of his fortune to a woman, unless — "

She was trembling, and was unable to remove the pins fastening the transparent tissue. After a moment's reflection she stammered, in an agitated tone: "Come, come — you are mad — you are — you are. Did not you, yourself, just now have hopes that he would leave us something?"

George remained standing beside her, following all her emotions like a magistrate seeking to note the least faltering on the part of an accused. He said, laying stress on every word: "Yes, he might have left something to me, your husband — to me, his friend — you understand, but not to you — my wife. The distinction is capital, essential from the point of propriety and of public opinion."

Madeleine in turn looked at him fixedly in the eyes, in profound and singular fashion, as though seeking to read something there, as though trying to discover that unknown part of a human being which we never fathom, and of which we can scarcely even catch rapid glimpses in those moments of carelessness or inattention, which are like doors left open, giving onto the mysterious depths of the mind. She said slowly: "It seems to me, however, that a legacy of this importance would have been looked on as at least equally strange left to you."

He asked abruptly: "Why so?"

She said: "Because — " hesitated, and then continued: "Because you are my husband, and have only known him for a short time, after all — because I have been his friend for a very long while — and because his first will, made during Forestier's lifetime, was already in my favor."

George began to stride up and down. He said: "You cannot accept."

She replied in a tone of indifference: "Precisely so; then it is not worth while waiting till Saturday, we can let Maitre Lamaneur know at once."

He stopped short in front of her, and they again stood for some moments with their eyes riveted on one another, striving to fathom the impenetrable secret of their hearts, to cut down to the quick of their thoughts. They tried to see one another's conscience unveiled in an ardent and mute interrogation; the struggle of two beings who, living side by side, were always ignorant of one another, suspecting, sniffing round, watching, but never understanding one another to the muddy depths of their souls. And suddenly he murmured to her face, in a low voice: "Come, admit that you were De Vaudrec's mistress."

She shrugged her shoulders, saying: "You are ridiculous. Vaudrec was very fond of me, very — but there was nothing more — never."

He stamped his foot. "You lie. It is not possible."

She replied, quietly: "It is so, though."

He began to walk up and down again, and then, halting once more, said: "Explain, then, how he came to leave the whole of his fortune to you."

She did so in a careless and disinterested tone, saying: "It is quite simple. As you said just now, he had only ourselves for friends, or rather myself, for he has known me from a child. My mother was a companion at the house of some relatives of his. He was always coming here, and as he had no natural heirs he thought of me. That there was a little love for me in the matter is possible. But where is the woman who has not been loved thus? Why should not such secret, hidden affection have placed my name at the tip of his pen when he thought of expressing his last wishes? He brought me flowers every Monday. You were not at all astonished at that, and yet he did not bring you any, did he? Now he has given me his fortune for the same reason, and because he had no one to offer it to. It would have been, on the contrary, very surprising for him to have left it to you. Why should he have done so? What were you to him?"

She spoke so naturally and quietly that George hesitated. He said, however: "All the same, we cannot accept this inheritance under such conditions. The effect would be deplorable. All the world would believe it; all the world would gossip about it, and laugh at me. My fellow journalists are already only too disposed to feel jealous of me and to attack me. I should have, before anyone, a care for my honor and my reputation. It is impossible for me to allow my wife to accept a legacy of this kind from a man whom public report has already assigned to her as a lover. Forestier might perhaps have tolerated it, but not me."

She murmured, mildly: "Well, dear, do not let us accept it. It will be a million the less in our pockets, that is all."

He was still walking up and down, and began to think aloud, speaking for his wife's benefit without addressing himself directly to her: "Yes, a million, so much the worse. He did not understand, in making his will, what a fault in tact, what a breach of propriety he was committing. He did not see in what a false, a ridiculous position he would place me. Everything is a matter of detail in this life. He should have left me half; that would have settled everything."

He sat down, crossed his legs, and began to twist the end of his moustache, as he did in moments of boredom, uneasiness, and difficult reflection. Madeleine took up some embroidery at which she worked from time to time, and said, while selecting her wools: "I have only to hold my tongue. It is for you to reflect."

He was a long time without replying, and then said, hesitatingly: "The world will never understand that Vaudrec made you his sole heiress, and that I allowed it. To receive his fortune in that way would be an acknowledgment on your part of a guilty connection, and on mine of a shameful complaisance. Do you understand now how our acceptance of it would be interpreted? It would be necessary to find a side issue, some clever way of palliating matters. To let it go abroad, for instance, that he had divided the money between us, leaving half to the husband and half to the wife."

She observed: "I do not see how that can be done, since the will is plain."

"Oh, it is very simple. You could leave me half the inheritance by a deed of gift. We have no children, so it is feasible. In that way the mouth of public malevolence would be closed."

She replied, somewhat impatiently: "I do not see any the more how the mouth of public malevolence is to be closed, since the will is there, signed by Vaudrec?"

He said, angrily: "Have we any need to show it and to paste it up on all the walls? You are really stupid. We will say that the Count de Vaudrec left his fortune between us. That is all. But you cannot accept this legacy without my authorization. I will only give it on condition of a division, which will hinder me from becoming a laughing stock."

She looked at him again with a penetrating glance, and said: "As you like. I am agreeable."

Then he rose, and began to walk up and down again. He seemed to be hesitating anew, and now avoided his wife's penetrating glance. He was saying: "No, certainly not. Perhaps it would be better to give it up altogether. That is more worthy, more correct, more honorable. And yet by this plan nothing could be imagined against us — absolutely nothing. The most unscrupulous people could only admit things as they were." He paused in front of Madeleine. "Well, then, if you like, darling, I will go back alone to Maitre Lamaneur to explain matters to him and consult him. I will tell him of my scruples, and add that we have arrived at the notion of a division to prevent gossip. From the moment that I accept half this inheritance, it is plain that no one has the right to smile. It is equal to saying aloud: 'My wife accepts because I accept — I, her husband, the best judge of what she may do without compromising herself. Otherwise a scandal would have arisen.'"

Madeleine merely murmured: "Just as you like."

He went on with a flow of words: "Yes, it is all as clear as daylight with this arrangement of a division in two. We inherit from a friend who did not want to make any difference between us, any distinction; who did not wish to appear to say: 'I prefer one or the other after death, as I did during life.' He liked the wife best, be it understood, but in leaving the fortune equally to both, he wished plainly to express that his preference was purely platonic. And you may be sure that, if he had thought of it, that is what he would have done. He did not reflect. He did not foresee the consequences. As you said very appropriately just now, it was you to whom he offered flowers every week, it is to you he wished to leave his last remembrance, without taking into consideration that — "

She checked him, with a shade of irritation: "All right; I understand. You have no need to make so many explanations. Go to the notary's at once."

He stammered, reddening: "You are right. I am off."

He took his hat, and then, at the moment of going out, said: "I will try to settle the difficulty with the nephew for fifty thousand francs, eh?"

She replied, with dignity: "No. Give him the hundred thousand francs he asks. Take them from my share, if you like."

He muttered, shamefacedly: "Oh, no; we will share that. Giving up fifty thousand francs apiece, there still remains to us a clear million." He added: "Goodbye, then, for the present, Made." And he went off to explain to the notary the plan which he asserted had been imagined by his wife.

They signed the next day a deed of gift of five hundred thousand francs, which Madeleine Du Roy abandoned to her husband. On leaving the notary's office, as the day was fine, George suggested that they should walk as far as the boulevards. He showed himself pleasant and full of attention and affection. He laughed, pleased at everything, while she remained thoughtful and somewhat severe.

It was a somewhat cool autumn day. The people in the streets seemed in a hurry, and walked rapidly. Du Roy led his wife to the front of the shop in which he had so often gazed at the longed-for chronometer. "Shall I stand you some jewelry?" said he.

She replied, indifferently: "Just as you like."

They went in, and he asked: "What would you prefer — a necklace, a bracelet, or a pair of earrings?"

The sight of the trinkets in gold, and precious stones overcame her studied coolness, and she scanned with kindling and inquisitive eyes the glass cases filled with jewelry. And, suddenly moved by desire, said: "That is a very pretty bracelet."

It was a chain of quaint pattern, every link of which had a different stone set in it.

George inquired: "How much is this bracelet?"

"Three thousand francs, sir," replied the jeweler.

"If you will let me have it for two thousand five hundred, it is a bargain."

The man hesitated, and then replied: "No, sir; that is impossible."

Du Roy went on: "Come, you can throw in that chronometer for fifteen hundred; that will make four thousand, which I will pay at once. Is it agreed? If not, I will go somewhere else."

The jeweler, in a state of perplexity, ended by agreeing, saying: "Very good, sir."

And the journalist, after giving his address, added: "You will have the monogram, G. R. C., engraved on the chronometer under a baron's coronet."

Madeleine, surprised, began to smile, and when they went out, took his arm with a certain affection. She found him really clever and capable. Now that he had an income, he needed a title. It was quite right.

The jeweler bowed them out, saying: "You can depend upon me; it will be ready on Thursday, Baron."

They paused before the Vaudeville, at which a new piece was being played.

"If you like," said he, "we will go to the theater this evening. Let us see if we can have a box."

They took a box, and he continued: "Suppose we dine at a restaurant."

"Oh, yes; I should like that!"

He was as happy as a king, and sought what else they could do. "Suppose we go and ask Madame de Marelle to spend the evening with us. Her husband is at home, I hear, and I shall be delighted to see him."

They went there. George, who slightly dreaded the first meeting with his mistress, was not ill-pleased that his wife was present to prevent anything like an explanation. But Clotilde did not seem to remember anything against him, and even obliged her husband to accept the invitation.

The dinner was lovely, and the evening pleasant. George and Madeleine got home late. The gas was out, and to light them upstairs, the journalist struck a wax match from time to time. On reaching the first-floor landing the flame, suddenly starting forth as he struck, caused their two lit-up faces to show in the glass standing out against the darkness of the staircase. They resembled phantoms, appearing and ready to vanish into the night.

Du Roy raised his hand to light up their reflections, and said, with a laugh of triumph: "Behold the millionaires!"

XV

The conquest of Morocco had been accomplished two months back. France, mistress of Tangiers, held the whole of the African shore of the Mediterranean as far as Tripoli, and had guaranteed the debt of the newly annexed territory. It was said that two ministers had gained a score of millions over the business, and Laroche-Mathieu was almost openly named. As to Walter, no one in Paris was ignorant of the fact that he had brought down two birds with one stone, and made thirty or forty millions out of the loan and eight to ten millions out of the copper and iron mines, as well as out of a large stretch of territory bought for almost nothing prior to the conquest, and sold after the French occupation to companies formed to promote colonization. He had become in a few days one of the lords of creation, one of those omnipotent financiers more powerful than monarchs who cause heads to bow, mouths to stammer, and all that is base, cowardly, and envious, to well up from the depths of the human heart. He was no longer the Jew Walter, head of a shady bank, manager of a fishy paper, deputy suspected of illicit jobbery. He was Monsieur Walter, the wealthy Israelite.

He wished to show himself off. Aware of the monetary embarrassments of the Prince de Carlsbourg, who owned one of the finest mansions in the Rue de Faubourg, Saint Honoré, with a garden giving onto the Champs Elysées, he proposed to him to buy house and furniture, without shifting a stick, within twenty-four hours. He offered three millions, and the prince, tempted by the amount, accepted. The following day Walter installed himself in his new domicile. Then he had another idea, the idea of a conqueror who wishes to conquer Paris, the idea of a Bonaparte. The whole city was flocking at that moment to see a great painting by the Hungarian artist, Karl Marcowitch, exhibited at a dealer's named Jacques Lenoble, and representing Christ walking on the water. The art critics, filled with enthusiasm, declared the picture the most superb masterpiece of the century. Walter bought it for four hundred thousand francs, and took it away, thus cutting suddenly short a flow of public curiosity, and forcing the whole of Paris to speak of him in terms of envy, blame, or approbation. Then he had it announced in the papers that he would invite everyone known in Parisian society to view at his house some evening this triumph of the foreign master, in order that it might not be said that he had hidden away a work of art. His house would be open; let those who would, come. It would be enough to show at the door the letter of invitation.

This ran as follows: "Monsieur and Madame Walter beg of you to honor them with your company on December 30th, between 9 and 12 p. m., to view the picture by Karl Marcowitch, 'Jesus Walking on the Waters,' lit up by electric light." Then, as a postscript, in small letters: "Dancing after midnight." So those who wished to stay could, and out of these the Walters would recruit their future acquaintances. The others would view the picture, the mansion, and their owners with worldly curiosity, insolent and indifferent, and would then go away as they came. But Daddy Walter knew very well that they would return later on, as they had come to his Israelite brethren grown rich like himself. The first thing was that they should enter his house, all these titled paupers who were mentioned in the papers, and they would enter it to see the face of a man who had gained fifty millions in six weeks; they would enter it to see and note who else came there; they would also enter it because he had had the good taste and dexterity to summon them to admire a Christian picture at the home of a child of Israel. He seemed to say to them: "You see I have given five hundred thousand francs for the religious masterpiece of Marcowitch, 'Jesus Walking on the Waters.' And this masterpiece will always remain before my eyes in the house of the Jew, Walter."

In society there had been a great deal of talk over these invitations, which, after all, did not pledge one in any way. One could go there as one went to see watercolors at Monsieur Petit's. The Walters owned a masterpiece, and threw open their doors one evening so that everyone could admire it. Nothing could be better. The Vie Francaise for a fortnight past had published every morning a note on this coming event of the 30th December, and had striven to kindle public curiosity.

Du Roy was furious at the governor's triumph. He had thought himself rich with the five hundred thousand francs extorted from his wife, and now he held himself to be poor, fearfully poor, when comparing his modest fortune with the shower of millions that had fallen around him, without his being able to pick any of it up. His envious hatred waxed daily. He was angry with everyone — with the Walters, whom he had not been to see at their new home; with his wife, who, deceived by Laroche-Mathieu, had persuaded him not to invest in the Morocco loan; and, above all, with the minister who had tricked him, who had made use of him, and who dined at his table twice a week. George was his agent, his secretary, his mouthpiece, and when he was writing from his dictation felt wild longings to strangle this triumphant foe. As a minister, Laroche-Mathieu had shown modesty in mien, and in order to retain his portfolio, did not let it be seen that he was gorged with gold. But Du Roy felt the presence of this gold in the haughtier tone of the parvenu barrister, in his more insolent gestures, his more daring affirmation, his perfect self-confidence. Laroche-Mathieu now reigned in the Du Roy household, having taken the place and the days of the Count de Vaudrec, and spoke to the servants like a second master. George tolerated him with a quiver running through him like a dog who wants to bite, and dares not. But he was often harsh and brutal towards Madeleine, who shrugged her shoulders and treated him like a clumsy child. She was, besides, astonished at his continual ill-humor, and repeated: "I cannot make you out. You are always grumbling, and yet your position is a splendid one."

He would turn his back without replying.

He had declared at first that he would not go to the governor's entertainment, and that he would never more set foot in the house of that dirty Jew. For two months Madame Walter had been writing to him daily, begging him to come, to make an appointment with her whenever he liked, in order, she said, that she might hand over the seventy thousand francs she had gained for him. He did not reply, and threw these despairing letters into the fire. Not that he had renounced receiving his share of their profits, but he wanted to madden her, to treat her with contempt, to trample her under feet. She was too rich. He wanted to show his pride. The very day of the exhibition of the picture, as Madeleine pointed out to him that he was very wrong not to go, he replied: "Hold your tongue. I shall stay at home."

Then after dinner he suddenly said: "It will be better after all to undergo this affliction. Get dressed at once."

She was expecting this, and said: "I will be ready in a quarter of an hour." He dressed growling, and even in the cab he continued to spit out his spleen.

The courtyard of the Carlsbourg mansion was lit up by four electric lights, looking like four small bluish moons, one at each corner. A splendid carpet was laid down the high flight of steps, on each of which a footman in livery stood motionless as a statue.

Du Roy muttered: "Here's a fine show-off for you," and shrugged his shoulders, his heart contracted by jealousy.

His wife said: "Be quiet and do likewise."

They went in and handed their heavy outer garments to the footmen who advanced to meet them. Several ladies were also there with their husbands, freeing themselves from their furs. Murmurs of: "It is very beautiful, very beautiful," could be heard. The immense entrance hall was hung with tapestry, representing the adventures of Mars and Venus. To the right and left were the two branches of a colossal double staircase, which met on the first floor. The banisters were a marvel of wrought-iron work, the dull old gilding of which glittered with discreet luster beside the steps of pink marble. At the entrance to the reception-rooms two little girls, one in a pink folly costume, and the other in a blue one, offered a bouquet of flowers to each lady. This was held to be charming.

The reception-rooms were already crowded. Most of the ladies were in outdoor dress, show-ing that they came there as to any other exhibition. Those who intended remaining for the ball were bare armed and bare necked. Madame Walter, surrounded by her friends, was in the second room acknowledging the greetings of the visitors. Many of these did not know her, and walked about as though in a museum, without troubling themselves about the masters of the house.

When she perceived Du Roy she grew livid, and made a movement as though to advance towards him. Then she remained motionless, awaiting him. He greeted her ceremoniously, while Madeleine overwhelmed her with affection and compliments. Then George left his wife with her and lost himself in the crowd, to listen to the spiteful things that assuredly must be said.

Five reception-rooms opened one into the other, hung with costly stuffs, Italian embroideries, or oriental rugs of varying shades and styles, and bearing on their walls pictures by old masters. People stopped, above all, to admire a small room in the Louis XVI style, a kind of boudoir, lined with silk, with bouquets of roses on a pale blue ground. The furniture, of gilt wood, upholstered in the same material, was admirably finished.

George recognized some well-known people — the Duchess de Ferraciné, the Count and Countess de Ravenal, General Prince d'Andremont, the beautiful Marchioness des Dunes, and all those folk who are seen at first performances. He was suddenly seized by the arm, and a young and pleased voice murmured in his ear: "Ah! here you are at last, you naughty Pretty-boy. How is it one no longer sees you?"

It was Susan Walter, scanning him with her enamel-like eyes from beneath the curly cloud of her fair hair. He was delighted to see her again, and frankly pressed her hand. Then, excusing himself, he said: "I have not been able to come. I have had so much to do during the past two months that I have not been out at all."

She said, with her serious air: "That is wrong, very wrong. You have caused us a great deal of pain, for we adore you, mamma and I. As to myself, I cannot get on without you. When you are not here I am bored to death. You see I tell you so plainly, so that you may no longer have the right of disappearing like that. Give me your arm, I will show you 'Jesus Walking on the Waters' myself; it is right away at the end, beyond the conservatory. Papa had it put there so that they should be obliged to see everything before they could get to it. It is astonishing how he is showing off this place."

They went on quietly among the crowd. People turned round to look at this good-looking fellow and this charming little doll. A well-known painter said: "What a pretty pair. They go capitally together."

George thought: "If I had been really clever, this is the girl I should have married. It was possible. How is it I did not think of it? How did I come to take that other one? What a piece of stupidity. We always act too impetuously, and never reflect sufficiently."

And envy, bitter envy, sank drop by drop into his mind like a gall, embittering all his pleasures, and rendering existence hateful.

Susan was saying: "Oh! do come often, Pretty-boy; we will go in for all manner of things now, papa is so rich. We will amuse ourselves like madcaps."

He answered, still following up his idea: "Oh! you will marry now. You will marry some prince, a ruined one, and we shall scarcely see one another."

She exclaimed, frankly: "Oh! no, not yet. I want someone who pleases me, who pleases me a great deal, who pleases me altogether. I am rich enough for two."

He smiled with a haughty and ironical smile, and began to point out to her people that were passing, very noble folk who had sold their rusty titles to the daughters of financiers like herself, and who now lived with or away from their wives, but free, impudent, known, and respected. He concluded with: "I will not give you six months before you are caught with that same bait. You will be a marchioness, a duchess or a princess, and will look down on me from a very great height, miss."

She grew indignant, tapped him on the arm with her fan, and vowed that she would marry according to the dictates of her heart.

He sneered: "We shall see about all that, you are too rich."

She remarked: "But you, too, have come in for an inheritance."

He uttered in a tone of contempt: "Oh! not worth speaking about. Scarcely twenty thousand francs a year, not much in these days."

"But your wife has also inherited."

"Yes. A million between us. Forty thousand francs' income. We cannot even keep a carriage on it."

They had reached the last of the reception-rooms, and before them lay the conservatory — a huge winter garden full of tall, tropical trees, sheltering clumps of rare flowers. Penetrating beneath this somber greenery, through which the light streamed like a flood of silver, they breathed the warm odor of damp earth, and an air heavy with perfumes. It was a strange sensation, at once sweet, unwholesome, and pleasant, of a nature that was artificial, soft, and enervating. They walked on carpets exactly like moss, between two thick clumps of shrubs. All at once Du Roy noticed on his left, under a wide dome of palms, a broad basin of white marble, large enough to bathe in, and on the edge of which four large Delft swans poured forth water through their open beaks. The bottom of the basin was strewn with golden sand, and swimming about in it were some enormous goldfish, quaint Chinese monsters, with projecting eyes and scales edged with blue, mandarins of the waters, who recalled, thus suspended above this gold-colored ground, the embroideries of the Flowery Land. The journalist halted with beating heart. He said to himself: "Here is luxury. These are the houses in which one ought to live. Others have arrived at it. Why should not I?"

He thought of means of doing so; did not find them at once, and grew irritated at his powerlessness. His companion, somewhat thoughtful, did not speak. He looked at her in sidelong fashion, and again thought: "To marry this little puppet would suffice."

But Susan all at once seemed to wake up. "Attention!" said she; and pushing George through a group which barred their way, she made him turn sharply to the right.

In the midst of a thicket of strange plants, which extended in the air their quivering leaves, opening like hands with slender fingers, was seen the motionless figure of a man standing on the sea. The effect was surprising. The picture, the sides of which were hidden in the moving foliage, seemed a black spot upon a fantastic and striking horizon. It had to be carefully looked at in order to understand it. The frame cut the center of the ship in which were the apostles, scarcely lit up by the oblique rays from a lantern, the full light of which one of them, seated on the bulwarks, was casting upon the approaching Savior. Jesus was advancing with his foot upon a wave, which flattened itself submissively and caressingly beneath the divine tread. All was dark about him. Only the stars shone in the sky. The faces of the apostles, in the vague light of the lantern, seemed convulsed with surprise. It was a wonderful and unexpected work of a master; one of those works which agitate the mind and give you something to dream of for years. People who look at such things at the outset remain silent, and then go thoughtfully away, and only speak later on of the worth of the painting. Du Roy, having contemplated it for some time, said: "It is nice to be able to afford such trifles."

But as he was pushed against by others coming to see it, he went away, still keeping on his arm Susan's little hand, which he squeezed slightly. She said: "Would you like a glass of champagne? Come to the refreshment buffet. We shall find papa there."

And they slowly passed back through the saloons, in which the crowd was increasing, noisy and at home, the fashionable crowd of a public fête. George all at once thought he heard a voice say: "It is Laroche-Mathieu and Madame Du Roy." These words flitted past his ear like those distant sounds borne by the wind. Whence came they? He looked about on all sides, and indeed saw his wife passing by on the minister's arm. They were chatting intimately in a low tone, smiling, and with their eyes fixed on one another's. He fancied he noticed that people whispered as they looked at them, and he felt within him a stupid and brutal desire to spring upon them, these two creatures, and smite them down. She was making him ridiculous. He thought of Forestier. Perhaps they were saying: "That cuckold Du Roy." Who was she? A little parvenu sharp enough, but really not over-gifted with parts. People visited him because they feared him, because they felt his strength, but they must speak in unrestrained fashion of this little journalistic household. He would never make any great way with this woman, who would always render his home a suspected one, who would always compromise herself, whose very bearing betrayed the woman of intrigue. She would now be a cannon ball riveted to his ankle. Ah! if he had only known, if he had only guessed. What a bigger game he would have played. What a fine match he might have won with this little Susan for stakes. How was it he had been blind enough not to understand that?

They reached the diningroom — an immense apartment, with marble columns, and walls hung with old tapestry. Walter perceived his descriptive writer, and darted forward to take him by the hands. He was intoxicated with joy. "Have you seen everything? Have you shown him everything, Susan? What a lot of people, eh, Pretty-boy! Did you see the Prince de Guerche? He came and drank a glass of punch here just now," he exclaimed.

Then he darted towards the Senator Rissolin, who was towing along his wife, bewildered, and bedecked like a stall at a fair. A gentleman bowed to Susan, a tall, thin fellow, slightly bald, with yellow whiskers, and that air of good breeding which is everywhere recognizable. George heard his name mentioned, the Marquis de Cazolles, and became suddenly jealous of him. How long had she known him? Since her accession to wealth, no doubt. He divined a suitor.

He was taken by the arm. It was Norbert de Varenne. The old poet was airing his long hair and worn dress-coat with a weary and indifferent air. "This is what they call amusing themselves," said he. "By and by they will dance, and then they will go bed, and the little girls will be delighted. Have some champagne. It is capital."

He had a glass filled for himself, and bowing to Du Roy, who had taken another, said: "I drink to the triumph of wit over wealth." Then he added softly: "Not that wealth on the part of others hurts me; or that I am angry at it. But I protest on principle."

George no longer listened to him. He was looking for Susan, who had just disappeared with the Marquis de Cazolles, and abruptly quitting Norbert de Varenne, set out in pursuit of the young girl. A dense crowd in quest of refreshments checked him. When he at length made his way through it, he found himself face to face with the de Marelles. He was still in the habit of meeting the wife, but he had not for some time past met the husband, who seized both his hands, saying: "How can I thank you, my dear fellow, for the advice you gave me through Clotilde. I have gained close on a hundred thousand francs over the Morocco loan. It is to you I owe them. You are a valuable friend."

Several men turned round to look at the pretty and elegant brunette. Du Roy replied: "In exchange for that service, my dear fellow, I am going to take your wife, or rather to offer her my arm. Husband and wife are best apart, you know."

Monsieur de Marelle bowed, saying: "You are quite right. If I lose you, we will meet here in an hour."

"Exactly."

The pair plunged into the crowd, followed by the husband. Clotilde kept saying: "How lucky these Walters are! That is what it is to have business intelligence."

George replied: "Bah! Clever men always make a position one way or another."

She said: "Here are two girls who will have from twenty to thirty millions apiece. Without reckoning that Susan is pretty."

He said nothing. His own idea, coming from another's mouth, irritated him. She had not yet seen the picture of "Jesus Walking on the Water," and he proposed to take her to it. They amused themselves by talking scandal of the people they recognized, and making fun of those they did not. Saint-Potin passed by, bearing on the lapel of his coat a number of decorations, which greatly amused them. An ex-ambassador following him showed far fewer.

Du Roy remarked: "What a mixed salad of society."

Boisrenard, who shook hands with him, had also adorned his buttonhole with the green and yellow ribbon worn on the day of the duel. The Viscountess de Percemur, fat and bedecked, was chatting with a duke in the little Louis XVI boudoir.

George whispered: "An amorous tête-à-tête."

But on passing through the greenhouse, he noticed his wife seated beside Laroche-Mathieu, both almost hidden behind a clump of plants. They seemed to be asserting: "We have appointed a meeting here, a meeting in public. For we do not care a rap what people think."

Madame de Marelle agreed that the Jesus of Karl Marcowitch was astounding, and they retraced their steps. They had lost her husband. George inquired: "And Laurine, is she still angry with me?"

"Yes, still so as much as ever. She refuses to see you, and walks away when you are spoken of."

He did not reply. The sudden enmity of this little girl vexed and oppressed him. Susan seized on them as they passed through a doorway, exclaiming: "Ah! here you are. Well, Pretty-boy, you must remain alone. I am going to take away Clotilde to show her my room."

The two moved rapidly away, gliding through the throng with that undulating snake-like motion women know how to adopt in a crowd. Almost immediately a voice murmured: "George."

It was Madame Walter, who went on in a low tone: "Oh! how ferociously cruel you are. How you do make me suffer without reason. I told Susan to get your companion away in order to be able to say a word to you. Listen, I must speak to you this evening, I must, or you don't know what I will do. Go into the conservatory. You will find a door on the left leading into the garden. Follow the path in front of it. At the end of it you will find an arbor. Wait for me there in ten minutes' time. If you won't, I declare to you that I will create a scene here at once."

He replied loftily: "Very well. I will be at the spot you mention within ten minutes."

And they separated. But Jacques Rival almost made him behindhand. He had taken him by the arm and was telling him a lot of things in a very excited manner. He had no doubt come from the refreshment buffet. At length Du Roy left him in the hands of Monsieur de Marelle, whom he had come across, and bolted. He still had to take precautions not to be seen by his wife or Laroche-Mathieu. He succeeded, for they seemed deeply interested in something, and found himself in the garden. The cold air struck him like an ice bath. He thought: "Confound it, I shall catch cold," and tied his pocket-handkerchief round his neck. Then he slowly went along the walk, seeing his way with difficulty after coming out of the bright light of the reception-rooms. He could distinguish to the right and left leafless shrubs, the branches of which were quivering. Light filtered through their branches, coming from the windows of the mansion. He saw something white in the middle of the path in front of him, and Madame Walter, with bare arms and bosom, said in a quivering voice; "Ah here you are; you want to kill me, then?"

He answered quickly: "No melodramatics, I beg of you, or I shall bolt at once."

She had seized him round the neck, and with her lips close to his, said: "But what have I done to you? You are behaving towards me like a wretch. What have I done to you?"

He tried to repulse her. "You wound your hair round every one of my buttons the last time I saw you, and it almost brought about a rupture between my wife and myself."

She was surprised for a moment, and then, shaking her head, said: "Oh! your wife would not mind. It was one of your mistresses who had made a scene over it."

"I have no mistresses."

"Nonsense. But why do you no longer ever come to see me? Why do you refuse to come to dinner, even once a week, with me? What I suffer is fearful. I love you to that degree that I no longer have a thought that is not for you; that I see you continually before my eyes; that I can no longer say a word without being afraid of uttering your name. You cannot understand that, I know. It seems to me that I am seized in some one's clutches, tied up in a sack, I don't know what. Your remembrance, always with me, clutches my throat, tears my chest, breaks my legs so as to no longer leave me strength to walk. And I remain like an animal sitting all day on a chair thinking of you."

He looked at her with astonishment. She was no longer the big frolicsome tomboy he had known, but a bewildered despairing woman, capable of anything. A vague project, however, arose in his mind. He replied: "My dear, love is not eternal. We take and we leave one another. But when it drags on, as between us two, it becomes a terrible drag. I will have no more of it. That is the truth. However, if you can be reasonable, and receive and treat me as a friend, I will come as I used to. Do you feel capable of that?"

She placed her two bare arms on George's coat, and murmured: "I am capable of anything in order to see you."

"Then it is agreed on," said he; "we are friends, and nothing more."

She stammered: "It is agreed on;" and then, holding out her lips to him: "One more kiss; the last."

He refused gently, saying: "No, we must keep to our agreement."

She turned aside, wiping away a couple of tears, and then, drawing from her bosom a bundle of papers tied with pink silk ribbon, offered it to Du Roy, saying: "Here; it is your share of the profit in the Morocco affair. I was so pleased to have gained it for you. Here, take it."

He wanted to refuse, observing: "No, I will not take that money."

Then she grew indignant. "Ah! so you won't take it now. It is yours, yours, only. If you do not take it, I will throw it into the gutter. You won't act like that, George?"

He received the little bundle, and slipped it into his pocket.

"We must go in," said he, "you will catch cold."

She murmured: "So much the better, if I could die."

She took one of his hands, kissed it passionately, with rage and despair, and fled towards the mansion. He returned, quietly reflecting. Then he reentered the conservatory with haughty forehead and smiling lip. His wife and Laroche-Mathieu were no longer there. The crowd was thinning. It was becoming evident that they would not stay for the dance. He perceived Susan arm-in-arm with her sister. They both came towards him to ask him to dance the first quadrille with the Count de Latour Yvelin.

He was astonished, and asked: "Who is he, too?"

Susan answered maliciously: "A new friend of my sister's." Rose blushed, and murmured: "You are very spiteful, Susan; he is no more my friend than yours."

Susan smiled, saying: "Oh! I know all about it."

Rose annoyed, turned her back on them and went away. Du Roy familiarly took the elbow of the young girl left standing beside him, and said in his caressing voice: "Listen, my dear, you believe me to be your friend?"

"Yes, Pretty-boy."

"You have confidence in me?" "Quite."

"You remember what I said to you just now?"

"What about?"

"About your marriage, or rather about the man you are going to marry." "Yes."

"Well, then, you will promise me one thing?"

"Yes; but what is it?"

"To consult me every time that your hand is asked for, and not to accept anyone without taking my advice."

"Very well."

"And to keep this a secret between us two. Not a word of it to your father or your mother."

"Not a word."

"It is a promise, then?" "It is a promise."

Rival came up with a bustling air. "Mademoiselle, your papa wants you for the dance."

She said: "Come along, Pretty-boy."

But he refused, having made up his mind to leave at once, wishing to be alone in order to think. Too many new ideas had entered his mind, and he began to look for his wife. In a short time he saw her drinking chocolate at the buffet with two gentlemen unknown to him. She introduced her husband without mentioning their names to him. After a few moments, he said, "Shall we go?"

"When you like."

She took his arm, and they walked back through the reception-rooms, in which the public were growing few. She said: "Where is Madame Walter, I should like to wish her goodbye?"

"It is better not to. She would try to keep us for the ball, and I have had enough of this."

"That is so, you are quite right."

All the way home they were silent. But as soon as they were in their room Madeleine said smilingly, before even taking off her veil. "I have a surprise for you."

He growled ill-temperedly: "What is it?"

"Guess." "I will make no such effort."

"Well, the day after tomorrow is the first of January."

"Yes."

"The time for New Year's gifts."

"Yes."

"Here's one for you that Laroche-Mathieu gave me just now."

She gave him a little black box resembling a jewel-case. He opened it indifferently, and saw the cross of the Legion of Honor. He grew somewhat pale, then smiled, and said: "I should have preferred ten millions. That did not cost him much."

She had expected an outburst of joy, and was irritated at this coolness. "You are really incredible. Nothing satisfies you now," said she.

He replied, tranquilly: "That man is only paying his debt, and he still owes me a great deal."

She was astonished at his tone, and resumed: "It is though, a big thing at your age."

He remarked: "All things are relative. I could have something bigger now."

He had taken the case, and placing it on the mantelshelf, looked for some moments at the glittering star it contained. Then he closed it and went to bed, shrugging his shoulders.

The Journal Officiel of the first of January announced the nomination of Monsieur Prosper George Du Roy, journalist, to the dignity of chevalier of the Legion of Honor, for special services. The name was written in two words, which gave George more pleasure than the derivation itself.

An hour after having read this piece of news he received a note from Madame Walter begging him to come and dine with her that evening with his wife, to celebrate his new honors. He hesitated for a few moments, and then throwing this note, written in ambiguous terms, into the fire, said to Madeleine:

"We are going to dinner at the Walter's this evening."

She was astonished. "Why, I thought you never wanted to set foot in the house again."

He only remarked: "I have changed my mind."

When they arrived Madame Walter was alone in the little Louis XVI. boudoir she had adopted for the reception of personal friends. Dressed in black, she had powdered her hair, which rendered her charming. She had the air at a distance of an old woman, and close at hand, of a young one, and when one looked at her well, of a pretty snare for the eyes.

"You are in mourning?" inquired Madeleine.

She replied, sadly: "Yes, and no. I have not lost any relative. But I have reached the age when one wears the mourning of one's life. I wear it to-day to inaugurate it. In future I shall wear it in my heart."

Du Roy thought: "Will this resolution hold good?"

The dinner was somewhat dull. Susan alone chattered incessantly. Rose seemed preoccupied. The journalist was warmly congratulated. During the evening they strolled chatting through the saloons and the conservatory. As Du Roy was walking in the rear with Madame Walter, she checked him by the arm.

"Listen," said she, in a low voice, "I will never speak to you of anything again, never. But come and see me, George. It is impossible for me to live without you, impossible. It is indescribable torture. I feel you, I cherish you before my eyes, in my heart, all day and all night. It is as though you had caused me to drink a poison which was eating me away within. I cannot bear it, no, I cannot bear it. I am willing to be nothing but an old woman for you. I have made my hair white to show you so, but come here, only come here from time to time as a friend."

She had taken his hand and was squeezing it, crushing it, burying her nails in his flesh.

He answered, quietly: "It is understood, then. It is useless to speak of all that again. You see I came to-day at once on receiving your letter."

Walter, who had walked on in advance with his two daughters and Madeleine, was waiting for Du Roy beside the picture of "Jesus Walking on the Waters."

"Fancy," said he, laughing, "I found my wife yesterday on her knees before this picture, as if in a chapel. She was paying her devotions. How I did laugh."

Madame Walter replied in a firm voice — a voice thrilling with secret exultation: "It is that Christ who will save my soul. He gives me strength and courage every time I look at Him." And pausing in front of the Divinity standing amidst the waters, she murmured: "How handsome he is. How afraid of Him those men are, and yet how they love Him. Look at His head, His eyes — how simple yet how supernatural at the same time."

Susan exclaimed, "But He resembles you, Pretty-boy. I am sure He resembles you. If you had a beard, or if He was clean shaven, you would be both alike. Oh, but it is striking!"

She insisted on his standing beside the picture, and they all, indeed, recognized that the two faces resembled one another. Everyone was astonished. Walter thought it very singular. Madeleine, smiling, declared that Jesus had a more manly air. Madame Walter stood motionless, gazing fixedly at the face of her lover beside the face of Christ, and had become as white as her hair.

XVI

During the remainder of the winter the Du Roys often visited the Walters. George even dined there by himself continually, Madeleine saying she was tired, and preferring to remain at home. He had adopted Friday as a fixed day, and Madame Walter never invited anyone that evening; it belonged to Pretty-boy, to him alone. After dinner they played cards, and fed the goldfish, amusing themselves like a family circle. Several times behind a door or a clump of shrubs in the conservatory, Madame Walter had suddenly clasped George in her arms, and pressing him with all her strength to her breast, had whispered in his ear, "I love you, I love you till it is killing me." But he had always coldly repulsed her, replying, in a dry tone: "If you begin that business once again, I shall not come here any more."

Towards the end of March the marriage of the two sisters was all at once spoken about. Rose, it was said, was to marry the Count de Latour-Yvelin, and Susan the Marquis de Cazolles. These two gentlemen had become familiars of the household, those familiars to whom special favors and marked privileges are granted. George and Susan continued to live in a species of free and fraternal intimacy, romping for hours, making fun of everyone, and seeming greatly to enjoy one another's company. They had never spoken again of the possible marriage of the young girl, nor of the suitors who offered themselves.

The governor had brought George home to lunch one morning. Madame Walter was called away immediately after the repast to see one of the tradesmen, and the young fellow said to Susan: "Let us go and feed the goldfish."

They each took a piece of crumb of bread from the table and went into the conservatory. All along the marble brim cushions were left lying on the ground, so that one could kneel down round the basin, so as to be nearer the fish. They each took one of these, side by side, and bending over the water, began to throw in pellets of bread rolled between the fingers. The fish, as soon as they caught sight of them, flocked round, wagging their tails, waving their fins, rolling their great projecting eyes, turning round, diving to catch the bait as it sank, and coming up at once to ask for more. They had a funny action of the mouth, sudden and rapid movements, a strangely monstrous appearance, and against the sand of the bottom stood out a bright red, passing like flames through the transparent water, or showing, as soon as they halted, the blue edging to their scales. George and Susan saw their own faces looking up in the water, and smiled at them. All at once he said in a low voice: "It is not kind to hide things from me, Susan."

"What do you mean, Pretty-boy?" asked she.

"Don't you remember, what you promised me here on the evening of the fête?"

"No."

"To consult me every time your hand was asked for."

"Well?"

"Well, it has been asked for."

"By whom?"

"You know very well."

"No. I swear to you."

"Yes, you do. That great fop, the Marquis de Cazolles."

"He is not a fop, in the first place."

"It may be so, but he is stupid, ruined by play, and worn out by dissipation. It is really a nice match for you, so pretty, so fresh, and so intelligent."

She inquired, smiling: "What have you against him?"

"I, nothing."

"Yes, you have. He is not all that you say."

"Nonsense. He is a fool and an intriguer."

She turned round somewhat, leaving off looking into the water, and said: "Come, what is the matter with you?"

He said, as though a secret was being wrenched from the bottom of his heart: "I — I — am jealous of him."

She was slightly astonished, saying: "You?"

"Yes, I."

"Why so?"

"Because I am in love with you, and you know it very well, you naughty girl."

She said, in a severe tone: "You are mad, Pretty-boy."

He replied; "I know very well that I am mad. Ought I to have admitted that — I, a married man, to you, a young girl? I am more than mad, I am guilty. I have no possible hope, and the thought of that drives me out of my senses. And when I hear it said that you are going to be married, I have fits of rage enough to kill someone. You must forgive me this, Susan."

He was silent. The whole of the fish, to whom bread was no longer being thrown, were motionless, drawn up in line like English soldiers, and looking at the bent heads of those two who were no longer troubling themselves about them. The young girl murmured, half sadly, half gayly: "It is a pity that you are married. What would you? Nothing can be done. It is settled."

He turned suddenly towards her, and said right in her face: "If I were free, would you marry me?"

She replied, in a tone of sincerity: "Yes, Pretty-boy, I would marry you, for you please me far better than any of the others."

He rose, and stammered: "Thanks, thanks; do not say 'yes' to anyone yet, I beg of you; wait a little longer, I entreat you. Will you promise me this much?"

She murmured, somewhat uneasily, and without understanding what he wanted: "Yes, I promise you."

Du Roy threw the lump of bread he still held in his hand into the water, and fled as though he had lost his head, without wishing her goodbye. All the fish rushed eagerly at this lump of crumb, which floated, not having been kneaded in the fingers, and nibbled it with greedy mouths. They dragged it away to the other end of the basin, and forming a moving cluster, a kind of animated and twisting flower, a live flower fallen into the water head downwards.

Susan, surprised and uneasy, got up and returned slowly to the diningroom. The journalist had left.

He came home very calm, and as Madeleine was writing letters, said to her: "Are you going to dine at the Walters' on Friday? I am going."

She hesitated, and replied: "No. I do not feel very well. I would rather stay at home."

He remarked: "Just as you like."

Then he took his hat and went out again at once. For some time past he had been keeping watch over her, following her about, knowing all her movements. The hour he had been awaiting was at length at hand. He had not been deceived by the tone in which she had said: "I would rather stay at home."

He was very amiable towards her during the next few days. He even appeared lively, which was not usual, and she said: "You are growing quite nice again."

He dressed early on the Friday, in order to make some calls before going to the governor's, he said. He started just before six, after kissing his wife, and went and took a cab at the Place Notre Dame de Lorette. He said to the driver: "Pull up in front of No. 17, Rue Fontaine, and stay there till I tell you to go on again. Then drive to the Cock Pheasant restaurant in the Rue Lafayette."

The cab started at a slow trot, and Du Roy drew down the blinds. As soon as he was opposite the door he did not take his eyes off it. After waiting ten minutes he saw Madeleine come out and go in the direction of the outer boulevards. As soon as she had got far enough off he put his head through the window, and said to the driver: "Go on." The cab started again, and landed him in front of the Cock Pheasant, a well-known middle-class restaurant. George went into the main diningroom and ate slowly, looking at his watch from time to time. At halfpast seven, when he had finished his coffee, drank two liqueurs of brandy, and slowly smoked a good cigar, he went out, hailed another cab that was going by empty, and was driven to the Rue La Rochefoucauld. He ascended without making any inquiry of the doorkeeper, to the third story of the house he had told the man to drive to, and when a servant opened the door to him, said: "Monsieur Guibert de Lorme is at home, is he not?"

"Yes sir."

He was ushered into the drawingroom, where he waited for a few minutes. Then a gentleman came in, tall, and with a military bearing, gray-haired though still young, and wearing the ribbon of the Legion of Honor. Du Roy bowed, and said: "As I foresaw, Mr. Commissionary, my wife is now dining with her lover in the furnished rooms they have hired in the Rue des Martyrs."

The commissary of police bowed, saying: "I am at your service, sir."

George continued: "You have until nine o'clock, have you not? That limit of time passed, you can no longer enter a private dwelling to prove adultery."

"No, sir; seven o'clock in winter, nine o'clock from the 31st March. It is the 5th of April, so we have till nine o'clock.

"Very well, Mr. Commissionary, I have a cab downstairs; we can take the officers who will accompany you, and wait a little before the door. The later we arrive the best chance we have of catching them in the act."

"As you like, sir."

The commissary left the room, and then returned with an overcoat, hiding his tricolored sash. He drew back to let Du Roy pass out first. But the journalist, who was preoccupied, declined to do so, and kept saying: "After you, sir, after you."

The commissary said: "Go first, sir, I am at home."

George bowed, and passed out. They went first to the police office to pick up three officers in plain clothes who were awaiting them, for George had given notice during the day that the surprise would take place that evening. One of the men got on the box beside the driver. The other two entered the cab, which reached the Rue des Martyrs. Du Roy said: "I have a plan of the rooms. They are on the second floor. We shall first find a little anteroom, then a diningroom, then the bedroom. The three rooms open into one another. There is no way out to facilitate flight. There is a locksmith a little further on. He is holding himself in readiness to be called upon by you."

When they arrived opposite the house it was only a quarter past eight, and they waited in silence for more than twenty minutes. But when he saw the three quarters about to strike, George said: "Let us start now."

They went up the stairs without troubling themselves about the doorkeeper, who, indeed, did not notice them. One of the officers remained in the street to keep watch on the front door. The four men stopped at the second floor, and George put his ear to the door and then looked through the keyhole. He neither heard nor saw anything. He rang the bell.

The commissary said to the officers: "You will remain in readiness till called on."

And they waited. At the end of two or three minutes George again pulled the bell several times in succession. They noted a noise from the further end of the rooms, and then a slight step approached. Someone was coming to spy who was there. The journalist then rapped smartly on the panel of the door. A voice, a woman's voice, that an attempt was evidently being made to disguise asked: "Who is there?"

The commissary replied: "Open, in the name of the law."

The voice repeated: "Who are you?"

"I am the commissary of police. Open the door, or I will have it broken in."

The voice went on: "What do you want?"

Du Roy said: "It is I. It is useless to seek to escape."

The light steps, the tread of bare feet, was heard to withdraw, and then in a few seconds to return.

George said: "If you won't open, we will break in the door."

He grasped the handle, and pushed slowly with his shoulder. As there was no longer any reply, he suddenly gave such a violent and vigorous shock that the old lock gave way. The screws were torn out of the wood, and he almost fell over Madeleine, who was standing in the anteroom, clad in a chemise and petticoat, her hair down, her legs bare, and a candle in her hand.

He exclaimed: "It is she, we have them," and darted forward into the rooms. The commissary, having taken off his hat, followed him, and the startled woman came after, lighting the way. They crossed a drawingroom, the uncleaned table of which displayed the remnants of a repast — empty champagne bottles, an open pot of fatted goose liver, the body of a fowl, and some half-eaten bits of bread. Two plates piled on the sideboard were piled with oyster shells.

The bedroom seemed disordered, as though by a struggle. A dress was thrown over a chair, a pair of trousers hung astride the arm of another. Four boots, two large and two small, lay on their sides at the foot of the bed. It was the room of a house let out in furnished lodgings, with commonplace furniture, filled with that hateful and sickening smell of all such places, the odor of all the people who had slept or lived there a day or six months. A plate of cakes, a bottle of chartreuse, and two liqueur glasses, still half full, encumbered the mantelshelf. The upper part of the bronze clock was hidden by a man's hat.

The commissary turned round sharply, and looking Madeleine straight in the face, said: "You are Madame Claire Madeleine Du Roy, wife of Monsieur Prosper George Du Roy, journalist, here present?"

She uttered in a choking voice: "Yes, sir."

"What are you doing here?" She did not answer.

The commissary went on: "What are you doing here? I find you away from home, almost undressed, in furnished apartments. What did you come here for?" He waited for a few moments. Then, as she still remained silent, he continued: "Since you will not confess, madame, I shall be obliged to verify the state of things."

In the bed could be seen the outline of a form hidden beneath the clothes. The commissary approached and said: "Sir."

The man in bed did not stir. He seemed to have his back turned, and his head buried under a pillow. The commissary touched what seemed to be his shoulder, and said: "Sir, do not, I beg of you, force me to take action."

But the form still remained as motionless as a corpse. Du Roy, who had advanced quickly, seized the bedclothes, pulled them down, and tearing away the pillow, revealed the pale face of Monsieur Laroche-Mathieu. He bent over him, and, quivering with the desire to seize him by the throat and strangle him, said, between his clenched teeth: "Have at least the courage of your infamy."

The commissary again asked: "Who are you?"

The bewildered lover not replying, he continued: "I am a commissary of police, and I summon you to tell me your name."

George, who was quivering with brutal wrath, shouted: "Answer, you coward, or I will tell your name myself."

Then the man in the bed stammered: "Mr. Commissary, you ought not to allow me to be insulted by this person. Is it with you or with him that I have to do? Is it to you or to him that I have to answer?"

His mouth seemed to be dried up as he spoke.

The commissary replied: "With me, sir; with me alone. I ask you who you are?"

The other was silent. He held the sheet close up to his neck, and rolled his startled eyes. His little, curled-up moustache showed up black upon his blanched face.

The commissary continued: "You will not answer, eh? Then I shall be forced to arrest you. In any case, get up. I will question you when you are dressed."

The body wriggled in the bed, and the head murmured: "But I cannot, before you."

The commissary asked: "Why not?"

The other stammered: "Because I am — I am — quite naked."

Du Roy began to chuckle sneeringly, and picking up a shirt that had fallen onto the floor, threw it onto the bed, exclaiming: "Come, get up. Since you have undressed in my wife's presence, you can very well dress in mine."

Then he turned his back, and returned towards the fireplace. Madeleine had recovered all her coolness, and seeing that all was lost, was ready to dare anything. Her eyes glittered with bravado, and twisting up a piece of paper she lit, as though for a reception, the ten candles in the ugly candelabra, placed at the corners of the mantelshelf. Then, leaning against this, and holding out backwards to the dying fire one of her bare feet which she lifted up behind the petticoat, scarcely sticking to her hips, she took a cigarette from a pink paper case, lit it, and began to smoke. The commissary had returned towards her, pending that her accomplice got up.

She inquired insolently: "Do you often have such jobs as these, sir?"

He replied gravely: "As seldom as possible, madame."

She smiled in his face, saying: "I congratulate you; it is dirty work."

She affected not to look at or even to see her husband.

But the gentleman in the bed was dressing. He had put on his trousers, pulled on his boots, and now approached putting on his waistcoat. The commissary turned towards him, saying: "Now, sir, will you tell me who you are?"

He made no reply, and the official said: "I find myself obliged to arrest you."

Then the man exclaimed suddenly: "Do not lay hands on me. My person is inviolable."

Du Roy darted towards him as though to throw him down, and growled in his face: "Caught in the act, in the act. I can have you arrested if I choose; yes, I can." Then, in a ringing tone, he added: "This man is Laroche-Mathieu, Minister of Foreign Affairs."

The commissary drew back, stupefied, and stammered: "Really, sir, will you tell me who you are?"

The other had made up his mind, and said in forcible tones: "For once that scoundrel has not lied. I am, indeed, Laroche-Mathieu, the minister." Then, holding out his hand towards George's chest, in which a little bit of red ribbon showed itself, he added: "And that rascal wears on his coat the cross of honor which I gave him."

Du Roy had become livid. With a rapid movement he tore the bit of ribbon from his buttonhole, and, throwing it into the fireplace, exclaimed: "That is all that is fit for a decoration coming from a swine like you."

They were quite close, face to face, exasperated, their fists clenched, the one lean, with a flowing moustache, the other stout, with a twisted one. The commissary stepped rapidly between the pair, and pushing them apart with his hands, observed: "Gentlemen, you are forgetting yourselves; you are lacking in self-respect."

They became quiet and turned on their heels. Madeleine, motionless, was still smoking in silence.

The police official resumed: "Sir, I have found you alone with Madame Du Roy here, you in bed, she almost naked, with your clothes scattered about the room. This is legal evidence of adultery. You cannot deny this evidence. What have you to say for yourself?"

Laroche-Mathieu murmured: "I have nothing to say; do your duty."

The commissary addressed himself to Madeleine: "Do you admit, madame, that this gentleman is your lover?"

She said with a certain swagger: "I do not deny it; he is my lover."

"That is enough."

The commissary made some notes as to the condition and arrangement of the rooms. As he was finishing writing, the minister, who had finished dressing, and was waiting with his greatcoat over his arm and his hat in his hand, said: "Have you still need of me, sir? What am I to do? Can I withdraw?"

Du Roy turned towards him, and smiling insolently, said: "Why so? We have finished. You can go to bed again, sir; we will leave you alone." And placing a finger on the official's arm, he continued: "Let us retire, Mr. Commissary, we have nothing more to do in this place."

Somewhat surprised, the commissary followed, but on the threshold of the room George stopped to allow him to pass. The other declined, out of politeness. Du Roy persisted, saying: "Pass first, sir."

"After you, sir," replied the commissary.

The journalist bowed, and in a tone of ironical politeness, said: "It is your turn, sir; I am almost at home here."

Then he softly reclosed the door with an air of discretion.

An hour later George Du Roy entered the offices of the Vie Francaise. Monsieur Walter was already there, for he continued to manage and supervise with solicitude his paper, which had enormously increased in circulation, and greatly helped the schemes of his bank. The manager raised his head and said: "Ah! here you are. You look very strange. Why did you not come to dinner with us? What have you been up to?"

The young fellow, sure of his effect, said, emphasizing every word: "I have just upset the Minister of Foreign Affairs."

The other thought he was joking, and said: "Upset what?"

"I am going to turn out the Cabinet. That is all. It is quite time to get rid of that rubbish."

The old man thought that his leader-writer must be drunk. He murmured: "Come, you are talking nonsense."

"Not at all. I have just caught Monsieur Laroche-Mathieu committing adultery with my wife. The commissary of police has verified the fact. The minister is done for."

Walter, amazed, pushed his spectacles right back on his forehead, and said: "You are not joking?"

"Not at all. I am even going to write an article on it."

"But what do you want to do?"

"To upset that scoundrel, that wretch, that open evildoer." George placed his hat on an armchair, and added: "Woe to those who cross my path. I never forgive."

The manager still hesitated at understanding matters. He murmured: "But — your wife?"

"My application for a divorce will be lodged tomorrow morning. I shall send her back to the departed Forestier."

"You mean to get a divorce?"

"Yes. I was ridiculous. But I had to play the idiot in order to catch them. That's done. I am master of the situation."

Monsieur Walter could not get over it, and watched Du Roy with startling eyes, thinking: "Hang it, here is a fellow to be looked after."

George went on: "I am now free. I have some money. I shall offer myself as a candidate at the October elections for my native place, where I am well known. I could not take a position or make myself respected with that woman, who was suspected by every one. She had caught me like a fool, humbugged and ensnared me. But since I became alive to her little game I kept watch on her, the slut." He began to laugh, and added: "It was poor Forestier who was cuckold, a cuckold without imagining it, confiding and tranquil. Now I am free from the leprosy he left me. My hands are free. Now I shall get on." He had seated himself astride a chair, and repeated, as though thinking aloud, "I shall get on."

And Daddy Walter, still looking at him with unveiled eyes, his spectacles remaining pushed up on his forehead, said to himself: "Yes, he will get on, the rascal."

George rose. "I am going to write the article. It must be done discreetly. But you know it will be terrible for the minister. He has gone to smash. He cannot be picked up again. The Vie Francaise has no longer any interest to spare him."

The old fellow hesitated for a few moments, and then made up his mind. "Do so," said he; "so much the worse for those who get into such messes."

XVII

Three months had elapsed. Du Roy's divorce had just been granted. His wife had resumed the name of Forestier, and, as the Walters were to leave on the 15th of July for Trouville, it was decided that he and they should spend a day in the country together before they started. A Thursday was selected, and they started at nine in the morning in a large traveling landau with six places, drawn by four horses with postilions. They were going to lunch at the Pavilion Henri-Quatre at Saint Germain. Pretty-boy had asked to be the only man of the party, for he could not endure the presence of the Marquis de Cazolles. But at the last moment it was decided that the Count de Latour-Yvelin should be called for on the way. He had been told the day before.

The carriage passed up the Avenue of the Champs Elyseés at a swinging trot, and then traversed the Bois de Boulogne. It was splendid summer weather, not too warm. The swallows traced long sweeping lines across the blue sky that one fancied one could still see after they had passed. The three ladies occupied the back seat, the mother between her daughters, and the men were with their backs to the horses, Walter between the two guests. They crossed the Seine, skirted Mount Valerien, and gained Bougival in order to follow the river as far as Le Pecq.

The Count de Latour-Yvelin, a man advancing towards middle-age, with long, light whiskers, gazed tenderly at Rose. They had been engaged for a month. George, who was very pale, often looked at Susan, who was pale too. Their eyes often met, and seemed to concert something, to understand one another, to secretly exchange a thought, and then to flee one another. Madame Walter was quiet and happy.

The lunch was a long one. Before starting back for Paris, George suggested a turn on the terrace. They stopped at first to admire the view. All ranged themselves in a line along the parapet, and went into ecstasies over the far-stretching horizon. The Seine at the foot of a long hill flowed towards Maisons-Lafitte like an immense serpent stretched in the herbage. To the right, on the summit of the slope, the aqueduct of Marly showed against the skyline its outline, resembling that of a gigantic, long-legged caterpillar, and Marly was lost beneath it in a thick cluster of trees. On the immense plain extending in front of them, villages could be seen dotted. The pieces of water at Le Vesinet showed like clear spots amidst the thin foliage of the little forest. To the left, away in the distance, the pointed steeple of Sastrouville could be seen.

Walter said: "Such a panorama is not to be found anywhere in the world. There is not one to match it in Switzerland."

Then they began to walk on gently, to have a stroll and enjoy the prospect. George and Susan remained behind. As soon as they were a few paces off, he said to her in a low and restrained voice: "Susan, I adore you. I love you to madness."

She murmured: "So do I you, Pretty-boy."

He went on: "If I do not have you for my wife, I shall leave Paris and this country."

She replied: "Ask Papa for my hand. Perhaps he will consent."

He made a gesture of impatience. "No, I tell you for the twentieth time that is useless. The door of your house would be closed to me. I should be dismissed from the paper, and we should not be able even to see one another. That is a pretty result, at which I am sure to arrive by a formal demand for you. They have promised you to the Marquis de Cazolles. They hope that you will end by saying 'yes,' and they are waiting for that."

She asked: "What is to be done?"

He hesitated, glancing at her, sidelong fashion. "Do you love me enough to run a risk?"

She answered resolutely: "Yes."

"A great risk?"

"Yes."

"The greatest of risks?"

"Yes."

"Have you the courage to set your father and mother at defiance?"

"Yes."

"Really now?"

"Yes."

"Very well, there is one way and only one. The thing must come from you and not from me. You are a spoilt child; they let you say whatever you like, and they will not be too much astonished at an act of daring the more on your part. Listen, then. This evening, on reaching home, you must go to your mamma first, your mamma alone, and tell her you want to marry me. She will be greatly moved and very angry — "

Susan interrupted him with: "Oh, mamma will agree."

He went on quickly: "No, you do not know her. She will be more vexed and angrier than your father. You will see how she will refuse. But you must be firm, you must not give way, you must repeat that you want to marry me, and no one else. Will you do this?"

"I will."

"On leaving your mother you must tell your father the same thing in a very serious and decided manner."

"Yes, yes; and then?"

"And then it is that matters become serious. If you are determined, very determined — very, very determined to be my wife, my dear, dear little Susan — I will — run away with you."

She experienced a joyful shock, and almost clapped her hands. "Oh! how delightful. You will run away with me. When will you run away with me?"

All the old poetry of nocturnal elopements, post-chaises, country inns; all the charming adventures told in books, flashed through her mind, like an enchanting dream about to be realized. She repeated: "When will you run away with me?"

He replied, in low tones: "This evening — tonight."

She asked, quivering: "And where shall we go to?"

"That is my secret. Reflect on what you are doing. Remember that after such a flight you can only be my wife. It is the only way, but is — it is very dangerous — for you."

She declared: "I have made up my mind; where shall I rejoin you?"

"Can you get out of the hotel alone?"

"Yes. I know how to undo the little door."

"Well, when the doorkeeper has gone to bed, towards midnight, come and meet me on the Place de la Concorde. You will find me in a cab drawn up in front of the Ministry of Marine."

"I will come."

"Really?"

"Really."

He took her hand and pressed it. "Oh! how I love you. How good and brave you are! So you don't want to marry Monsieur de Cazolles?"

"Oh! no."

"Your father was very angry when you said no?"

"I should think so. He wanted to send me back to the convent."

"You see that it is necessary to be energetic."

"I will be so."

She looked at the vast horizon, her head full of the idea of being ran off with. She would go further than that with him. She would be ran away with. She was proud of it. She scarcely thought of her reputation — of what shame might befall her. Was she aware of it? Did she even suspect it?

Madame Walter, turning round, exclaimed: "Come along, little one. What are you doing with Pretty-boy?"

They rejoined the others and spoke of the seaside, where they would soon be. Then they returned home by way of Chatou, in order not to go over the same road twice. George no longer spoke. He reflected. If the little girl had a little courage, he was going to succeed at last. For three months he had been enveloping her in the irresistible net of his love. He was seducing, captivating, conquering her. He had made himself loved by her, as he knew how to make himself loved. He had captured her childish soul without difficulty. He had at first obtained of her that she should refuse Monsieur de Cazolles. He had just obtained that she would fly with him. For there was no other way. Madame Walter, he well understood, would never agree to give him her daughter. She still loved him; she would always love him with unmanageable violence. He restrained her by his studied coldness; but he felt that she was eaten up by hungry and impotent passion. He could never bend her. She would never allow him to have Susan. But once he had the girl away he would deal on a level footing with her father. Thinking of all this, he replied by broken phrases to the remarks addressed to him, and which he did not hear. He only seemed to come to himself when they returned to Paris.

Susan, too, was thinking, and the bells of the four horses rang in her ears, making her see endless miles of highway under eternal moonlight, gloomy forests traversed, wayside inns, and the hurry of the hostlers to change horses, for every one guesses that they are pursued.

When the landau entered the courtyard of the mansion, they wanted to keep George to dinner. He refused, and went home. After having eaten a little, he went through his papers as if about to start on a long journey. He burnt some compromising letters, hid others, and wrote to some friends. From time to time he looked at the clock, thinking: "Things must be getting warm there." And a sense of uneasiness gnawed at his heart. Suppose he was going to fail? But what could he fear? He could always get out of it. Yet it was a big game he was playing that evening.

He went out towards eleven o'clock, wandered about some time, took a cab, and had it drawn up in the Place de la Concorde, by the Ministry of Marine. From time to time he struck a match to see the time by his watch. When he saw midnight approaching, his impatience became feverish. Every moment he thrust his head out of the window to look. A distant clock struck twelve, then another nearer, then two together, then a last one, very far away. When the latter had ceased to sound, he thought: "It is all over. It is a failure. She won't come." He had made up his mind, however, to wait till daylight. In these matters one must be patient.

He heard the quarter strike, then the halfhour, then the quarter to, and all the clocks repeated "one," as they had announced midnight. He no longer expected her; he was merely remaining, racking his brain to divine what could have happened. All at once a woman's head was passed through the window, and asked: "Are you there, Pretty-boy?"

He started, almost choked with emotion, "Is that you, Susan?"

"Yes, it is I."

He could not manage to turn the handle quickly enough, and repeated: "Ah! it is you, it is you; come inside."

She came in and fell against him. He said, "Go on," to the driver, and the cab started.

She gasped, without saying a word.

He asked: "Well, how did it go off?"

She murmured, almost fainting: "Oh! it was terrible, above all with mamma."

He was uneasy and quivering. "Your mamma. What did she say? Tell me."

"Oh! it was awful. I went into her room and told her my little story that I had carefully prepared. She grew pale, and then she cried: 'Never, never.' I cried, I grew angry. I vowed I would marry no one but you. I thought that she was going to strike me. She went on just as if she were mad; she declared that I should be sent back to the convent the next day. I had never seen her like that — never. Then papa came in, hearing her shouting all her nonsense. He was not so angry as she was, but he declared that you were not a good enough match. As they had put me in a rage, too, I shouted louder than they did. And papa told me to leave the room, with a melodramatic air that did not suit him at all. This is what decided me to run off with you. Here I am. Where are we going to?"

He had passed his arm gently round her and was listening with all his ears, his heart throbbing, and a ravenous hatred awakening within him against these people. But he had got their daughter. They should just see.

He answered: "It is too late to catch a train, so this cab will take us to Sevres, where we shall pass the night. Tomorrow we shall start for La Roche-Guyon. It is a pretty village on the banks of the Seine, between Nantes and Bonnieres."

She murmured: "But I have no clothes. I have nothing."

He smiled carelessly: "Bah! we will arrange all that there."

The cab rolled along the street. George took one of the young girl's hands and began to kiss it slowly and with respect. He scarcely knew what to say to her, being scarcely accustomed to platonic love-making. But all at once he thought he noted that she was crying. He inquired, with alarm: "What is the matter with you, darling?"

She replied in tearful tones: "Poor mamma, she will not be able to sleep if she has found out my departure."

Her mother, indeed, was not asleep.

As soon as Susan had left the room, Madame Walter remained face to face with her husband. She asked, bewildered and cast down: "Good heavens! What is the meaning of this?"

Walter exclaimed furiously: "It means that that schemer has bewitched her. It is he who made her refuse Cazolles. He thinks her dowry worth trying for." He began to walk angrily up and down the room, and went on: "You were always luring him here, too, yourself; you flattered him, you cajoled him, you could not cosset him enough. It was Pretty-boy here, Pretty-boy there, from morning till night, and this is the return for it."

She murmured, livid: "I — I lured him?"

He shouted in her face: "Yes, you. You were all mad over him — Madame de Marelle, Susan, and the rest. Do you think I did not see that you could not pass a couple of days without having him here?"

She drew herself up tragically: "I will not allow you to speak to me like that. You forget that I was not brought up like you, behind a counter."

He stood for a moment stupefied, and then uttered a furious "Damn it all!" and rushed out, slamming the door after him. As soon as she was alone she went instinctively to the glass to see if anything was changed in her, so impossible and monstrous did what had happened appear. Susan in love with Pretty-boy, and Pretty-boy wanting to marry Susan! No, she was mistaken; it was not true. The girl had had a very natural fancy for this good-looking fellow; she had hoped that they would give him her for a husband, and had made her little scene because she wanted to have her own way. But he — he could not be an accomplice in that. She reflected, disturbed, as one in presence of great catastrophes. No, Pretty-boy could know nothing of Susan's prank.

She thought for a long time over the possible innocence or perfidy of this man. What a scoundrel, if he had prepared the blow! And what would happen! What dangers and tortures she foresaw. If he knew nothing, all could yet be arranged. They would travel about with Susan for six months, and it would be all over. But how could she meet him herself afterwards? For she still loved him. This passion had entered into her being like those arrowheads that cannot be withdrawn. To live without him was impossible. She might as well die.

Her thoughts wandered amidst these agonies and uncertainties. A pain began in her head; her ideas became painful and disturbed. She worried herself by trying to work things out; grew mad at not knowing. She looked at the clock; it was past one. She said to herself: "I cannot remain like this, I shall go mad. I must know. I will wake up Susan and question her."

She went barefooted, in order not to make a noise, and with a candle in her hand, towards her daughter's room. She opened the door softly, went in, and looked at the bed. She did not comprehend matters at first, and thought that the girl might still be arguing with her father. But all at once a horrible suspicion crossed her mind, and she rushed to her husband's room. She reached it in a bound, blanched and panting. He was in bed reading.

He asked, startled: "Well, what is it? What is the matter with you?"

She stammered: "Have you seen Susan?"

"I? No. Why?"

"She has — she has — gone! She is not in her room."

He sprang onto the carpet, thrust his feet into his slippers, and, with his shirt tails floating in the air, rushed in turn to his daughter's room. As soon as he saw it, he no longer retained any doubt. She had fled. He dropped into a chair and placed his lamp on the ground in front of him.

His wife had rejoined him, and stammered: "Well?"

He had no longer the strength to reply; he was no longer enraged, he only groaned: "It is done; he has got her. We are done for."

She did not understand, and said: "What do you mean? done for?"

"Yes, by Jove! He will certainly marry her now."

She gave a cry like that of a wild beast: "He, never! You must be mad!"

He replied, sadly: "It is no use howling. He has run away with her, he has dishonored her. The best thing is to give her to him. By setting to work in the right way no one will be aware of this escapade."

She repeated, shaken by terrible emotion: "Never, never; he shall never have Susan. I will never consent."

Walter murmured, dejectedly: "But he has got her. It is done. And he will keep her and hide her as long as we do not yield. So, to avoid scandal, we must give in at once."

His wife, torn by pangs she could not acknowledge, repeated: "No, no, I will never consent."

He said, growing impatient: "But there is no disputing about it. It must be done. Ah, the rascal, how he has done us! He is a sharp one. All the same, we might have made a far better choice as regards position, but not as regards intelligence and prospects. He will be a deputy and a minister."

Madame Walter declared, with savage energy: "I will never allow him to marry Susan. You understand — never."

He ended by getting angry and taking up, as a practical man, the cudgels on behalf of Pretty-boy. "Hold your tongue," said he. "I tell you again that it must be so; it absolutely must. And who knows? Perhaps we shall not regret it. With men of that stamp one never knows what may happen. You saw how he overthrew in three articles that fool of a Laroche-Mathieu, and how he did it with dignity, which was infernally difficult in his position as the husband. At all events, we shall see. It always comes to this, that we are nailed. We cannot get out of it."

She felt a longing to scream, to roll on the ground, to tear her hair out. She said at length, in exasperated tones: "He shall not have her. I won't have it."

Walter rose, picked up his lamp, and remarked: "There, you are stupid, just like all women. You never do anything except from passion. You do not know how to bend yourself to circumstances. You are stupid. I will tell you that he shall marry her. It must be."

He went out, shuffling along in his slippers. He traversed — a comical phantom in his nightshirt — the broad corridor of the huge slumbering house, and noiselessly reentered his room.

Madame Walter remained standing, torn by intolerable grief. She did not yet quite understand it. She was only conscious of suffering. Then it seemed to her that she could not remain there motionless till daylight. She felt within her a violent necessity of fleeing, of running away, of seeking help, of being succored. She sought whom she could summon to her. What man? She could not find one. A priest; yes, a priest! She would throw herself at his feet, acknowledge everything, confess her fault and her despair. He would understand that this wretch must not marry Susan, and would prevent it. She must have a priest at once. But where could she find one? Whither could she go? Yet she could not remain like that.

Then there passed before her eyes, like a vision, the calm figure of Jesus walking on the waters. She saw it as she saw it in the picture. So he was calling her. He was saying: "Come to me; come and kneel at my feet. I will console you, and inspire you with what should be done."

She took her candle, left the room, and went downstairs to the conservatory. The picture of Jesus was right at the end of it in a small drawingroom, shut off by a glass door, in order that the dampness of the soil should not damage the canvas. It formed a kind of chapel in a forest of strange trees. When Madame Walter entered the winter garden, never having seen it before save full of light, she was struck by its obscure profundity. The dense plants of the tropics made the atmosphere thick with their heavy breath; and the doors no longer being open, the air of this strange wood, enclosed beneath a glass roof, entered the chest with difficulty; intoxicated, caused pleasure and pain, and imparted a confused sensation of enervation, pleasure, and death. The poor woman walked slowly, oppressed by the shadows, amidst which appeared, by the flickering light of her candle, extravagant plants, recalling monsters, living creatures, hideous deformities. All at once she caught sight of the picture of Christ. She opened the door separating her from it, and fell on her knees. She prayed to him, wildly, at first, stammering forth words of true, passionate, and despairing invocations. Then, the ardor of her appeal slackening, she raised her eyes towards him, and was struck with anguish. He resembled Pretty-boy so strongly, in the trembling light of this solitary candle, lighting the picture from below, that it was no longer Christ — it was her lover who was looking at her. They were his eyes, his forehead, the expression of his face, his cold and haughty air.

She stammered: "Jesus, Jesus, Jesus!" and the name "George" rose to her lips. All at once she thought that at that very moment, perhaps, George had her daughter. He was alone with her somewhere. He with Susan! She repeated: "Jesus, Jesus!" but she was thinking of them — her daughter and her lover. They were alone in a room, and at night. She saw them. She saw them so plainly that they rose up before her in place of the picture. They were smiling at one another. They were embracing. She rose to go towards them, to take her daughter by the hair and tear her from his clasp. She would seize her by the throat and strangle her, this daughter whom she hated — this daughter who was joining herself to this man. She touched her; her hands encountered the canvas; she was pressing the feet of Christ. She uttered a loud cry and fell on her back. Her candle, overturned, went out.

What took place then? She dreamed for a long time wild, frightful dreams. George and Susan continually passed before her eyes, with Christ blessing their horrible loves. She felt vaguely that she was not in her room. She wished to rise and flee; she could not. A torpor had seized upon her, which fettered her limbs, and only left her mind on the alert, tortured by frightful and fantastic visions, lost in an unhealthy dream — the strange and sometimes fatal dream engendered in human minds by the soporific plants of the tropics, with their strange and oppressive perfumes.

The next morning Madame Walter was found stretched out senseless, almost asphyxiated before "Jesus Walking on the Waters." She was so ill that her life was feared for. She only fully recovered the use of her senses the following day. Then she began to weep. The disappearance of Susan was explained to the servants as due to her being suddenly sent back to the convent. And Monsieur Walter replied to a long letter of Du Roy by granting him his daughter's hand.

Pretty-boy had posted this letter at the moment of leaving Paris, for he had prepared it in advance the evening of his departure. He said in it, in respectful terms, that he had long loved the young girl; that there had never been any agreement between them; but that finding her come freely to him to say, "I wish to be your wife," he considered himself authorized in keeping her, even in hiding her, until he had obtained an answer from her parents, whose legal power had for him less weight than the wish of his betrothed. He demanded that Monsieur Walter should reply, "post restante," a friend being charged to forward the letter to him.

When he had obtained what he wished he brought back Susan to Paris, and sent her on to her parents, abstaining himself from appearing for some little time.

They had spent six days on the banks of the Seine at La Roche-Guyon.

The young girl had never enjoyed herself so much. She had played at pastoral life. As he passed her off as his sister, they lived in a free and chaste intimacy — a kind of loving friendship. He thought it a clever stroke to respect her. On the day after their arrival she had purchased some linen and some country-girl's clothes, and set to work fishing, with a huge straw hat, ornamented with wild flowers, on her head. She thought the country there delightful. There was an old tower and an old chateau, in which beautiful tapestry was shown.

George, dressed in a boating jersey, bought readymade from a local tradesman, escorted Susan, now on foot along the banks of the river, now in a boat. They kissed at every moment, she in all innocence, and he ready to succumb to temptation. But he was able to restrain himself; and when he said to her, "We will go back to Paris tomorrow; your father has granted me your hand," she murmured simply, "Already? It was so nice being your wife here."

XVIII

It was dark in the little suite of rooms in the Rue de Constantinople; for George Du Roy and Clotilde de Marelle, having met at the door, had gone in at once, and she had said to him, without giving him time to open the Venetian blinds: "So you are going to marry Susan Walter?"

He admitted it quietly, and added: "Did not you know it?"

She exclaimed, standing before him, furious and indignant:

"You are going to marry Susan Walter? That is too much of a good thing. For three months you have been humbugging in order to hide that from me. Everyone knew it but me. It was my husband who told me of it."

Du Roy began to laugh, though somewhat confused all the same; and having placed his hat on a corner of the mantelshelf, sat down in an armchair. She looked at him straight in the face, and said, in a low and irritated tone: "Ever since you left your wife you have been preparing this move, and you only kept me on as a mistress to fill up the interim nicely. What a rascal you are!"

He asked: "Why so? I had a wife who deceived me. I caught her, I obtained a divorce, and I am going to marry another. What could be simpler?"

She murmured, quivering: "Oh! how cunning and dangerous you are."

He began to smile again. "By Jove! Simpletons and fools are always someone's dupes."

But she continued to follow out her idea: "I ought to have divined your nature from the beginning. But no, I could not believe that you could be such a blackguard as that."

He assumed an air of dignity, saying: "I beg of you to pay attention to the words you are making use of."

His indignation revolted her. "What? You want me to put on gloves to talk to you now. You have behaved towards me like a vagabond ever since I have known you, and you want to make out that I am not to tell you so. You deceive everyone; you take advantage of everyone; you filch money and enjoyment wherever you can, and you want me to treat you as an honest man!"

He rose, and with quivering lip, said: "Be quiet, or I will turn you out of here."

She stammered: "Turn me out of here; turn me out of here! You will turn me out of here —you — you?" She could not speak for a moment for choking with anger, and then suddenly, as though the door of her wrath had been burst open, she broke out with: "Turn me out of here? You forget, then, that it is I who have paid for these rooms from the beginning. Ah, yes, you have certainly taken them on from time to time. But who first took them? I did. Who kept them on? I did. And you want to turn me out of here. Hold your tongue, you good-for-nothing fellow. Do you think I don't know you robbed Madeleine of half Vaudrec's money? Do you think I don't know how you slept with Susan to oblige her to marry you?"

He seized her by the shoulders, and, shaking her with both hands, exclaimed: "Don't speak of her, at any rate. I won't have it."

She screamed out: "You slept with her; I know you did."

He would have accepted no matter what, but this falsehood exasperated him. The truths she had told him to his face had caused thrills of anger to run through him, but this lie respecting the young girl who was going to be his wife, awakened in the palm of his hand a furious longing to strike her.

He repeated: "Be quiet — have a care — be quiet," and shook her as we shake a branch to make the fruit fall.

She yelled, with her hair coming down, her mouth wide open, her eyes aglow: "You slept with her!"

He let her go, and gave her such a smack on the face that she fell down beside the wall. But she turned towards him, and raising herself on her hands, once more shouted: "You slept with her!"

He rushed at her, and, holding her down, struck her as though striking a man. She left off shouting, and began to moan beneath his blows. She no longer stirred, but hid her face against the bottom of the wall and uttered plaintive cries. He left off beating her and rose up. Then he walked about the room a little to recover his coolness, and, an idea occurring to him, went into the bedroom, filled the basin with cold water, and dipped his head into it. Then he washed his hands and came back to see what she was doing, carefully wiping his fingers. She had not budged. She was still lying on the ground quietly weeping.

"Shall you have done grizzling soon?"

She did not answer. He stood in the middle of the room, feeling somewhat awkward and ashamed in the presence of the form stretched out before him. All at once he formed a resolution, and took his hat from the mantelshelf, saying: "Goodnight. Give the key to the doorkeeper when you leave. I shan't wait for your convenience."

He went out, closed the door, went to the doorkeeper's, and said: "Madame is still there. She will be leaving in a few minutes. Tell the landlord that I give notice to leave at the end of September. It is the 15th of August, so I am within the limits."

And he walked hastily away, for he had some pressing calls to make touching the purchase of the last wedding gifts.

The wedding was fixed for the 20th of October after the meeting of the Chambers. It was to take place at the Church of the Madeleine. There had been a great deal of gossip about it without anyone knowing the exact truth. Different tales were in circulation. It was whispered that an elopement had taken place, but no one was certain about anything. According to the servants, Madame Walter, who would no longer speak to her future son-in-law, had poisoned herself out of rage the very evening the match was decided on, after having taken her daughter off to a convent at midnight. She had been brought back almost dead. Certainly, she would never get over it. She had now the appearance of an old woman; her hair had become quite gray, and she had gone in for religion, taking the Sacrament every Sunday.

At the beginning of September the Vie Francaise announced that the Baron Du Roy de Cantel had become chief editor, Monsieur Walter retaining the title of manager. A battalion of well-known writers, reporters, political editors, art and theatrical critics, detached from old important papers by dint of monetary influence, were taken on. The old journalists, the serious and respectable ones, no longer shrugged their shoulders when speaking of the Vie Francaise. Rapid and complete success had wiped out the contempt of serious writers for the beginnings of this paper.

The marriage of its chief editor was what is styled a Parisian event, George Du Roy and the Walters having excited a great deal of curiosity for some time past. All the people who are written about in the papers promised themselves to be there.

The event took place on a bright autumn day.

At eight in the morning the sight of the staff of the Madeleine stretching a broad red carpet down the lofty flight of steps overlooking the Rue Royale caused passersby to pause, and announced to the people of Paris that an important ceremony was about to take place. The clerks on the way to their offices, the work-girls, the shopmen, paused, looked, and vaguely speculated about the rich folk who spent so much money over getting spliced. Towards ten o'clock idlers began to halt. They would remain for a few minutes, hoping that perhaps it would begin at once, and then moved away. At eleven squads of police arrived and set to work almost at once to make the crowd move on, groups forming every moment. The first guests soon made their appearance — those who wanted to be well placed for seeing everything. They took the chairs bordering the main aisles. By degrees came others, ladies in rustling silks, and serious-looking gentlemen, almost all bald, walking with well-bred air, and graver than usual in this locality.

The church slowly filled. A flood of sunlight entered by the huge doorway lit up the front row of guests. In the choir, which looked somewhat gloomy, the altar, laden with tapers, shed a yellow light, pale and humble in face of that of the main entrance. People recognized one another, beckoned to one another, and gathered in groups. The men of letters, less respectful than the men in society, chatted in low tones and looked at the ladies.

Norbert de Varenne, who was looking out for an acquaintance, perceived Jacques Rival near the center of the rows of chair, and joined him. "Well," said he, "the race is for the cunning."

The other, who was not envious, replied: "So much the better for him. His career is safe." And they began to point out the people they recognized.

"Do you know what became of his wife?" asked Rival.

The poet smiled. "Yes, and no. She is living in a very retired style, I am told, in the Montmartre district. But — there is a but — I have noticed for some time past in the Plume some political articles terribly like those of Forestier and Du Roy. They are by Jean Le Dal, a handsome, intelligent young fellow, of the same breed as our friend George, and who has made the acquaintance of his late wife. From whence I conclude that she had, and always will have, a fancy for beginners. She is, besides, rich. Vaudrec and Laroche-Mathieu were not assiduous visitors at the house for nothing."

Rival observed: "She is not bad looking, Madeleine. Very clever and very sharp. She must be charming on terms of intimacy. But, tell me, how is it that Du Roy comes to be married in church after a divorce?"

Norbert replied: "He is married in church because, in the eyes of the Church, he was not married before."

"How so?"

"Our friend, Pretty-boy, from indifference or economy, thought the registrar sufficient when marrying Madeleine Forestier. He therefore dispensed with the ecclesiastical benediction, which constituted in the eyes of Holy Mother Church a simple state of concubinage. Consequently he comes before her to-day as a bachelor, and she lends him all her pomp and ceremony, which will cost Daddy Walter a pretty penny."

The murmur of the augmented throng swelled beneath the vaulted room. Voices could be heard speaking almost out loud. People pointed out to one another celebrities who attitudinized, pleased to be seen, and carefully maintained the bearing adopted by them towards the public accustomed to exhibit themselves thus at all such gatherings, of which they were, it seemed to them, the indispensable ornaments.

Rival resumed: "Tell me, my dear fellow, you who go so often to the governor's, is it true that Du Roy and Madame Walter no longer speak to one another?"

"Never. She did not want to give him the girl. But he had a hold, it seems, on the father through skeletons in the house — skeletons connected with the Morocco business. He threatened the old man with frightful revelations. Walter recollected the example he made of Laroche-Mathieu, and gave in at once. But the mother, obstinate like all women, swore that she would never again speak a word to her son-in-law. She looks like a statue, a statue of Vengeance, and he is very uneasy at it, although he puts a good face on the matter, for he knows how to control himself, that fellow does."

Fellow-journalists came up and shook hands with them. Bits of political conversation could be caught. Vague as the sound of a distant sea, the noise of the crowd massed in front of the church entered the doorway with the sunlight, and rose up beneath the roof, above the more discreet murmur of the choicer public gathered within it.

All at once the beadle struck the pavement thrice with the butt of his halberd. Every one turned round with a prolonged rustling of skirts and a moving of chairs. The bride appeared on her father's arm in the bright light of the doorway.

She had still the air of a doll, a charming white doll crowned with orange flowers. She stood for a few moments on the threshold, then, when she made her first step up the aisle, the organ gave forth a powerful note, announcing the entrance of the bride in loud metallic tones. She advanced with bent head, but not timidly; vaguely moved, pretty, charming, a miniature bride. The women smiled and murmured as they watched her pass. The men muttered: "Exquisite! Adorable!" Monsieur Walter walked with exaggerated dignity, somewhat pale, and with his spectacles straight on his nose. Behind them four bridesmaids, all four dressed in pink, and all four pretty, formed the court of this gem of a queen. The groomsmen, carefully chosen to match, stepped as though trained by a ballet master. Madame Walter followed them, giving her arm to the father of her other son-in-law, the Marquis de Latour-Yvelin, aged seventy-two. She did not walk, she dragged herself along, ready to faint at each forward movement. It could be felt that her feet stuck to the flagstones, that her legs refused to advance, and that her heart was beating within her breast like an animal bounding to escape. She had grown thin. Her white hair made her face appear still more blanched and her cheeks hollower. She looked straight before her in order not to see any one — in order not to recall, perhaps, that which was torturing her.

Then George Du Roy appeared with an old lady unknown. He, too, kept his head up without turning aside his eyes, fixed and stern under his slightly bent brows. His moustache seemed to bristle on his lip. He was set down as a very good-looking fellow. He had a proud bearing, a good figure, and a straight leg. He wore his clothes well, the little red ribbon of the Legion of Honor showing like a drop of blood on his dress coat.

Then came the relations, Rose with the Senator Rissolin. She had been married six weeks. The Count de Latour-Yvelin accompanied by the Viscountess de Percemur. Finally, there was a strange procession of the friends and allies of Du Roy, whom he introduced to his new family; people known in the Parisian world, who became at once the intimates, and, if need be, the distant cousins of rich parvenus; gentlemen ruined, blemished; married, in some cases, which is worse. There were Monsieur de Belvigne, the Marquis de Banjolin, the Count and Countess de Ravenel, Prince Kravalow, the Chevalier, Valréali; then some guests of Walter's, the Prince de Guerche, the Duke and the Duchess de Ferraciné, the beautiful Marchioness des Dunes. Some of Madame Walter's relatives preserved a well-to-do, countrified appearance amidst the throng.

The organ was still playing, pouring forth through the immense building the sonorous and rhythmic accents of its glittering throats, which cry aloud unto heaven the joy or grief of mankind. The great doors were closed, and all at once it became as gloomy as if the sun had just been turned out.

Now, George was kneeling beside his wife in the choir, before the lit-up altar. The new Bishop of Tangiers, crozier in hand and miter on head, made his appearance from the vestry to join them together in the Eternal name. He put the customary questions, exchanged the rings, uttered the words that bind like chains, and addressed the newly-wedded couple a Christian allocution. He was a tall, stout man, one of those handsome prelates to whom a rounded belly lends dignity.

The sound of sobs caused several people to look round. Madame Walter was weeping, with her face buried in her hands. She had to give way. What could she have done else? But since the day when she had driven from her room her daughter on her return home, refusing to embrace her; since the day when she had said, in a low voice, to Du Roy, who had greeted her ceremoniously on again making his appearance: "You are the vilest creature I know of; never speak to me again, for I shall not answer you," she had been suffering intolerable and unappeasable tortures. She hated Susan with a keen hatred, made up of exasperated passion and heartrending jealousy, the strange jealousy of a mother and mistress — unacknowledgable, ferocious, burning like a new wound. And now a bishop was marrying them — her lover and her daughter — in a church, in presence of two thousand people, and before her. And she could say nothing. She could not hinder it. She could not cry out: "But that man belongs to me; he is my lover. This union you are blessing is infamous!"

Some ladies, touched at the sight, murmured: "How deeply the poor mother feels it!"

The bishop was declaiming: "You are among the fortunate ones of this world, among the wealthiest and most respected. You, sir, whom your talent raises above others; you who write, who teach, who advise, who guide the people, you who have a noble mission to fulfill, a noble example to set."

Du Roy listened, intoxicated with pride. A prelate of the Roman Catholic Church was speaking thus to him. And he felt behind him a crowd, an illustrious crowd, gathered on his account. It seemed to him that some power impelled and lifted him up. He was becoming one of the masters of the world — he, the son of two poor peasants at Canteleu. He saw them all at once in their humble wayside inn, at the summit of the slope overlooking the broad valley of Rouen, his father and mother, serving the country-folk of the district with drink, He had sent them five thousand francs on inheriting from the Count de Vaudrec. He would now send them fifty thousand, and they would buy a little estate. They would be satisfied and happy.

The bishop had finished his harangue. A priest, clad in a golden stole, ascended the steps of the altar, and the organ began anew to celebrate the glory of the newly-wedded couple. Now it gave forth long, loud notes, swelling like waves, so sonorous and powerful that it seemed as though they must lift and break through the roof to spend abroad into the sky. Their vibrating sound filled the church, causing body and spirit to thrill. Then all at once they grew calmer, and delicate notes floated through the air, little graceful, twittering notes, fluttering like birds; and suddenly again this coquettish music waxed once more, in turn becoming terrible in its strength and fullness, as if a grain of sand had transformed itself into a world. Then human voices rose, and were wafted over the bowed heads — Vauri and Landeck, of the Opera, were singing. The incense shed abroad a delicate odor, and the Divine Sacrifice was accomplished on the altar, to consecrate the triumph of the Baron George Du Roy!

Pretty-boy, on his knees beside Susan, had bowed his head. He felt at that moment almost a believer, almost religious; full of gratitude towards the divinity who had thus favored him, who treated him with such consideration. And without exactly knowing to whom he was addressing himself, he thanked him for his success.

When the ceremony was concluded he rose up, and giving his wife his arm, he passed into the vestry. Then began the interminable defiling past of the visitors. George, with wild joy, believed himself a king whom a nation had come to acclaim. He shook hands, stammered unmeaning remarks, bowed, and replied: "You are very good to say so."

All at once he caught sight of Madame de Marelle, and the recollection of all the kisses that he had given her, and that she had returned; the recollection of all their caresses, of her pretty ways, of the sound of her voice, of the taste of her lips, caused the desire to have her once more for his own to shoot through his veins. She was so pretty and elegant, with her boyish air and bright eyes. George thought to himself: "What a charming mistress, all the same."

She drew near, somewhat timid, somewhat uneasy, and held out her hand. He took it in his, and retained it. Then he felt the discreet appeal of a woman's fingers, the soft pressure that forgives and takes possession again. And for his own part, he squeezed it, that little hand, as though to say: "I still love you; I am yours."

Their eyes met, smiling, bright, full of love. She murmured in her pleasant voice: "I hope to have the pleasure of seeing you again soon, sir."

He replied, gayly: "Soon, madame."

She passed on. Other people were pushing forward. The crowd flowed by like a stream. At length it grew thinner. The last guests took leave.

George took Susan's arm in his to pass through the church again. It was full of people, for everyone had regained their seats in order to see them pass together. They went by slowly, with calm steps and uplifted heads, their eyes fixed on the wide sunlit space of the open door. He felt little quiverings run all over his skin those cold shivers caused by overpowering happiness. He saw no one. His thoughts were solely for himself. When he gained the threshold he saw the crowd collected — a dense, agitated crowd, gathered there on his account — on account of George Du Roy. The people of Paris were gazing at and envying him. Then, raising his eyes, he could see afar off, beyond the Palace de la Concorde, the Chamber of Deputies, and it seemed to him that he was going to make but one jump from the portico of the Madeleine to that of the Palais Bourbon.

He slowly descended the long flight of steps between two ranks of spectators. But he did not see them; his thoughts had now flown backwards, and before his eyes, dazzled by the brilliant sun, now floated the image of Madame de Marelle, readjusting before the glass the little curls on her temples, always disarranged when she rose.

Mont Oriol

I

THE first bathers, the early risers, who had already been at the water, were walking slowly, in pairs or alone, under the huge trees along the stream which rushes down the gorges of Enval.

Others arrived from the village, and entered the establishment in a hurried fashion. It was a spacious building, the ground floor being reserved for thermal treatment, while the first story served as a casino, café, and billiard-room. Since Doctor Bonnefille had discovered in the heart of Enval the great spring, baptized by him the Bonnefille Spring, some proprietors of the country and the surrounding neighborhood, timid speculators, had decided to erect in the midst of this superb glen of Auvergne, savage and gay withal, planted with walnut and giant chestnut trees, a vast house for every kind of use, serving equally for the purpose of cure and of pleasure, in which mineral waters, douches, and baths were sold below, and beer, liqueurs, and music above.

A portion of the ravine along the stream had been inclosed, to constitute the park indispensable to every spa; and three walks had been made, one nearly straight, and the other two zigzag. At the end of the first gushed out an artificial spring detached from the parent spring, and bubbling into a great basin of cement, sheltered by a straw roof, under the care of an impassive woman, whom everyone called "Marie" in a familiar sort of way. This calm Auvergnat, who wore a little cap always as white as snow, and a big apron, perfectly clean at all times, which concealed her working-dress, rose up slowly as soon as she saw a bather coming along the road in her direction.

The bather would smile with a melancholy air, drink the water, and return her the glass, saying, "Thanks, Marie." Then he would turn on his heel and walk away. And Marie sat down again on her straw chair to wait for the next comer.

They were not, however, very numerous. The Enval station had just been six years open for invalids, and scarcely could count more patients at the end of these six years than it had at the start. About fifty had come there, attracted more than anything else by the beauty of the district, by the charm of this little village lost under enormous trees, whose twisted trunks seemed as big as the houses, and by the reputation of the gorges at the end of this strange glen which opened on the great plain of Auvergne and ended abruptly at the foot of the high mountain bristling with craters of unknown age — a savage and magnificent crevasse, full of rocks fallen or threatening, from which rushed a stream that cascaded over giant stones, forming a little lake in front of each.

This thermal station had been brought to birth as they all are, with a pamphlet on the spring by Doctor Bonnefille. He opened with a eulogistic description, in a majestic and sentimental style, of the Alpine seductions of the neighborhood. He selected only adjectives which convey a vague sense of delightfulness and enjoyment — those which produce effect without committing the writer to any material statement. All the surroundings were picturesque, filled with splendid sites or landscapes whose graceful outlines aroused soft emotions. All the promenades in the vicinity possessed a remarkable originality, such as would strike the imagination of artists and tourists. Then abruptly, without any transition, he plunged into the therapeutic qualities of the Bonnefille Spring, bicarbonate, sodium, mixed, lithineous, ferruginous, et cetera, et cetera, capable of curing every disease. He had, moreover, enumerated them under this heading: Chronic affections or acute specially associated with Enval. And the list of affections associated with Enval was long — long and varied, consoling for invalids of every kind. The pamphlet concluded with some information of practical utility, the cost of lodgings, commodities, and hotels — for three hotels had sprung up simultaneously with the casino-medical establishment. These were the Hotel Splendid, quite new, built on the slope of the glen looking down on the baths; the Thermal Hotel, an old inn with a new coat of plaster; and the Hotel Vidaillet, formed very simply by the purchase of three adjoining houses, which had been altered so as to convert them into one.

Then, all at once, two new doctors had installed themselves in the locality one morning, without anyone well knowing how they came, for at spas doctors seem to dart up out of the springs, like gas-jets. These were Doctor Honorat, a native of Auvergne, and Doctor Latonne, of Paris. A fierce antagonism soon burst out between Doctor Latonne and Doctor Bonnefille, while Doctor Honorat, a big, clean-shaven man, smiling and pliant, stretched forth his right hand to the first, and his left hand to the second, and remained on good terms with both. But Doctor Bonnefille was master of the situation, with his title of Inspector of the Waters and of the thermal establishment of Enval-les-Bains.

This title was his strength and the establishment his chattel. There he spent his days, and even his nights, it was said. A hundred times, in the morning, he would go from his house which was quite near in the village to his consultation-study fixed at the right-hand side facing the entrance to the thermal baths. Lying in wait there, like a spider in his web, he watched the comings and goings of the invalids, inspecting his own patients with a severe eye and those of the other doctors with a look of fury. He questioned everybody almost in the style of a ship's captain, and he struck terror into newcomers, unless it happened that he made them smile.

This day, as he arrived with rapid steps, which made the big flaps of his old frock coat fly up like a pair of wings, he was stopped suddenly by a voice exclaiming: "Doctor!"

He turned round. His thin face, full of big ugly wrinkles, and looking quite black at the end with a grizzled beard rarely cut, made an effort to smile; and he took off the tall silk hat, shabby, stained, and greasy, that covered his thick pepper-and-salt head of hair — "pepper and soiled," as his rival, Doctor Latonne, put it. Then he advanced a step, made a bow, and murmured:

"Good morning, Marquis — are you quite well this morning?"

The Marquis de Ravenel, a little man well preserved, stretched out his hand to the doctor, as he replied:

"Very well, doctor, very well, or, at least, not ill. I am always suffering from my kidneys; but indeed I am better, much better; and I am as yet only at my tenth bath. Last year I did not obtain the effect until the sixteenth, you recollect?"

"Yes, perfectly."

"But it is not about this I want to talk to you. My daughter has arrived this morning, and I wish to have a chat with you about her case first of all, because my son-in-law, William Andermatt, the banker — "

"Yes, I know."

"My son-in-law has a letter of recommendation addressed to Doctor Latonne. As for me, I have no confidence except in you, and I beg of you to have the kindness to come up to the hotel before — you understand? I prefer to say things to you candidly. Are you free at the present moment?"

Doctor Bonnefille had put on his hat again, and looked excited and troubled. He answered at once:

"Yes, I shall be free immediately. Do you wish me to accompany you?"

"Why, certainly."

And, turning their backs on the establishment, they directed their steps up a circular walk leading to the door of the Hotel Splendid, built on the slope of the mountain so as to offer a view of it to travelers.

They made their way to the drawingroom in the first story adjoining the apartments occupied by the Ravenel and Andermatt families, and the Marquis left the doctor by himself while he went to look for his daughter.

He came back with her presently. She was a fair young woman, small, pale, very pretty, whose features seemed like those of a child, while her blue eyes, boldly fixed, cast on people a resolute look that gave an alluring impression of firmness and a peculiar charm to this refined and fascinating creature. There was not much the matter with her — vague languors, sadnesses, bursts of tears without apparent cause, angry fits for which there seemed no season, and lastly anæmia. She craved above all for a child, which had been vainly looked forward to since her marriage, more than two years before.

Doctor Bonnefille declared that the waters of Enval would be effectual, and proceeded forthwith to write a prescription. The doctor's prescriptions had always the formidable aspect of an indictment. On a big white sheet of paper such as schoolboys use, his directions exhibited themselves in numerous paragraphs of two or three lines each, in an irregular handwriting, bristling with letters resembling spikes. And the potions, the pills, the powders, which were to be taken fasting in the morning, at midday, and in the evening, followed in ferocious-looking characters. One of these prescriptions might read:

"Inasmuch as M. X. is affected with a chronic malady, incurable and mortal, he will take, first, sulphate of quinine, which will render him deaf, and will make him lose his memory; secondly, bromide of potassium, which will destroy his stomach, weaken all his faculties, cover him with pimples, and make his breath foul; thirdly, salicylate of soda, whose curative effects have not yet been proved, but which seems to lead to a terrible and speedy death the patient treated by this remedy. And concurrently, chloral, which causes insanity, and belladonna, which attacks the eyes; all vegetable solutions and all mineral compositions which corrupt the blood, corrode the organs, consume the bones, and destroy by medicine those whom disease has spared."

For a long time he went on writing on the front page and on the back, then signed it just as a judge might have signed a death-sentence.

The young woman, seated opposite to him, stared at him with an inclination to laugh that made the corners of her lips rise up.

When, with a low bow, he had taken himself off, she snatched up the paper blackened with ink, rolled it up into a ball, and flung it into the fire. Then, breaking into a hearty laugh, said:

"Oh! father, where did you discover this fossil? Why, he looks for all the world like an old-clothesman. Oh! how clever of you to dig up a physician that might have lived before the Revolution! Oh! how funny he is, aye, and dirty — ah, yes! dirty — I believe really he has stained my penholder."

The door opened, and M. Andermatt's voice was heard saying, "Come in, doctor."

And Doctor Latonne appeared. Erect, slender, circumspect, comparatively young, attired in a fashionable morning-coat, and holding in his hand the high silk hat which distinguishes the practicing doctor in the greater part of the thermal stations of Auvergne, the physician from Paris, without beard or mustache, resembled an actor who had retired into the country.

The Marquis, confounded, did not know what to say or do, while his daughter put her handkerchief to her mouth to keep herself from bursting out laughing in the newcomer's face. He bowed with an air of self-confidence, and at a sign from the young woman took a seat.

M. Andermatt, who followed him, minutely detailed for him his wife's condition, her illnesses, together with their accompanying symptoms, the opinions of the physicians consulted in Paris, and then his own opinion based on special grounds which he explained in technical language.

He was a man still quite youthful, a Jew, who devoted himself to financial transactions. He entered into all sorts of speculations, and displayed in all matters of business a subtlety of intellect, a rapidity of penetration, and a soundness of judgment that were perfectly marvelous. A little too stout already for his figure, which was not tall, chubby, bald, with an infantile expression, fat hands, and short thighs, he looked much too greasy to be quite healthy, and spoke with amazing facility.

By means of tact he had been able to form an alliance with the daughter of the Marquis de Ravenel with a view to extending his speculations into a sphere to which he did not belong. The Marquis, besides, possessed an income of about thirty thousand francs, and had only two children; but, when M. Andermatt married, though scarcely thirty years of age, he owned already five or six millions, and had sown enough to bring him in a harvest of ten or twelve. M. de Ravenel, a man of weak, irresolute, shifting, and undecided character, at first angrily repulsed the overtures made to him with respect to this union, and was indignant at the thought of seeing his daughter allied to an Israelite. Then, after six months' resistance, he gave way, under the pressure of accumulated wealth, on the condition that the children should be brought up in the Catholic religion.

But they waited for a long time and no offspring was yet announced. It was then that the Marquis, enchanted for the past two years with the waters of Enval, recalled to mind the fact that Doctor Bonnefille's pamphlet also promised the cure for sterility.

Accordingly, he sent for his daughter, whom his son-in-law accompanied, in order to install her and to intrust her, acting on the advice of his Paris physician, to the care of Doctor Latonne. Therefore, Andermatt, since his arrival, had gone to look for this practitioner, and went on enumerating the symptoms which presented themselves in his wife's case. He finished by mentioning how much he had been pained at finding his hopes of paternity unrealized.

Doctor Latonne allowed him to go on to the end; then, turning toward the young woman: "Have you anything to add, Madame?"

She replied gravely: "No, Monsieur, nothing at all." He went on: "In that case, I will trouble you to take off your traveling-dress and your corset, and to put on a simple white dressing-gown, all white."

She was astonished; he rapidly explained his system: "Good heavens, Madame, it is very simple. Formerly, the belief was that all diseases came from a poison in the blood or from an organic cause; to-day, we simply assume that, in many cases, and, above all, in your particular case, the uncertain ailments from which you suffer, and even certain serious troubles, very serious, mortal, may proceed only from the fact that some organ or other, having taken, under influences easy to determine, an abnormal development, to the detriment of the neighboring organs, destroys all the harmony, all the equilibrium of the human body, modifies or arrests its functions, and obstructs the play of all the other organs. A swelling of the stomach may be sufficient to make us believe in a disease of the heart, which, impeded in its movements, becomes violent, irregular, sometimes even intermittent. The dilatation of the liver or of certain glands may cause ravages which unobservant physicians attribute to a thousand different causes. Therefore, the first thing that we should do is to ascertain whether all the organs of a patient have their true compass and their normal position, for a very little thing is enough to upset a person's health. I am going, then, Madame, if you will allow me, to examine you with great care, and to mark out on your dressing-gown the limits, the dimensions, and the positions of your organs."

He had put down his hat on a chair, and he spoke in a facile manner. His large mouth, in opening and closing, made two deep hollows in his shaven cheeks, which gave him a certain ecclesiastical air.

Andermatt, delighted, exclaimed: "Capital, capital! That is very clever, very ingenious, very new, very modern."

"Very modern" in his mouth was the height of admiration.

The young woman, highly amused, rose and passed into her own apartment. She came back, after the lapse of a few minutes, in a white dressing-gown.

The physician made her lie down on a sofa, then, drawing from his pocket a pencil with three points, a black, a red, and a blue, he commenced to auscultate and to tap his new patient, riddling the dressing-gown all over with little dots of color by way of noting each observation.

She resembled, after a quarter of an hour of this work, a map indicating continents, seas, capes, rivers, kingdoms, and cities, and bearing the names of all these terrestrial divisions, for the doctor wrote on every line of demarcation two or three Latin words intelligible to himself alone.

Now, when he had listened to all the internal sounds in Madame Andermatt's body, and tapped on all the parts of her person that were irritated or hollow-sounding, he drew forth from his pocket a notebook of red leather with gold threads to fasten it, divided in alphabetical order, consulted the index, opened it, and wrote: "Observation 6347. — Madame A — , 21 years."

Then, collecting from her head to her feet the colored notes on her dressing-gown, and reading them as an Egyptologist deciphers hieroglyphics, he entered them in the notebook.

He observed, when he had finished: "Nothing disquieting, nothing abnormal, save a slight, a very slight deviation, which some thirty acidulated baths will cure. You will take furthermore three halfglasses of water each morning before noon. Nothing else I will come back to see you in four or five days." Then he rose, bowed, and went out with such promptitude that everyone remained stupefied at it. This abrupt style of departure was a part of his mannerism, his tact, his special stamp. He considered it very good form, and thought it made a great impression on the patient.

Madame Andermatt ran to look at herself in the glass, and, shaking all over with a joyous burst of childlike laughter, said:

"Oh! how amusing they are, how droll they are! Tell me, is there not one more left of them? I want to see him immediately! Will, go and find him for me! We must have the third one here — I want to see him."

Her husband, surprised, asked:

"How, a third, a third what?"

The Marquis deemed it advisable to explain, while offering excuses, for he was a little afraid of his son-in-law. He related, therefore, how Doctor Bonnefille had come to see himself, and how he had introduced him to Christiane, in order to ascertain his opinion, as he had great confidence in the experience of the old physician, who was a native of the district, and who had discovered the spring.

Andermatt shrugged his shoulders, and declared that Doctor Latonne alone would take care of his wife, so that the Marquis, very uneasy, began to reflect on the best course to take in order to arrange matters without offending his irascible physician.

Christiane asked: "Is Gontran here?" This was her brother.

Her father replied: "Yes, for the past four days, with a friend of his of whom he has often spoken, M. Paul Bretigny. They are making a tour together in Auvergne. They have come from Mont Doré and from Bourboule, and will be setting out for Cantal at the end of next week."

Then he asked the young woman whether she desired to rest till luncheon after the night in the train; but she had slept perfectly in the sleeping car, and only required an hour for her toilette, after which she wished to visit the village and the establishment.

Her father and her husband went back to their rooms to wait till she was ready. She soon came out to call them, and they descended together. She grew enthusiastic at first sight over the aspect of the village, built in the middle of a wood in a deep valley, which seemed hemmed in on every side by chestnut-trees lofty as mountains. These could be seen everywhere, springing up just as they chanced to have shot forth here and there in a century, in front of doorways, in the courtyards, in the streets. Then, again, there were fountains everywhere made of a great black stone standing upright pierced with a small aperture, through which dashed a streamlet of clear water that whirled about in a circle before it fell into the trough. A fresh odor of grass and of stables floated over those masses of verdure; and they saw the peasant women of Auvergne standing in front of their dwellings, spinning at their distaffs with lively movements of their fingers the black wool attached to their girdles. Their short petticoats showed their thin ankles covered with blue stockings, and the bodies of their dresses fastened over their shoulders with straps left exposed the linen sleeves of their chemises, out of which stretched their hard, dry arms and bony hands.

But, suddenly, queer lilting kind of music burst on the promenaders' ears. It was like a barrel-organ with piping sounds, a barrel-organ used up, broken-winded, invalided.

Christiane exclaimed: "What is that?"

Her father began to laugh: "It is the orchestra of the Casino. It takes four of them to make that noise." And he led her up to a red bill affixed to a corner of a farmhouse, on which appeared in black letters:

CASINO OF ENVAL

UNDER THE DIRECTION OF M. PETRUS MARTEL, OF THE ODEON.

Saturday, 6th of July.

GRAND CONCERT organized by the Maestro, Saint Landri, second grand prize winner at the Conservatoire.

The piano will be presided over by M. Javel, grand laureate of the Conservatoire.

Flute, M. Noirot, laureate of the Conservatoire. Double-bass, M. Nicordi, laureate of the Royal Academy of Brussels. After the Concert, grand representation of Lost in the Forest, a Comedy in one act, by M. Pointellet.

Characters:

Pierre de Lapointe — M. Petrus Martel, of the Odéon.

Oscar Leveillé — M. Petitnivelle, of the Vaudeville.

Jean — M. Lapalme, of the Grand Theater of Bordeaux.

Philippine — Mademoiselle Odelin, of the Odéon.

During the representation, the Orchestra will be likewise conducted by the Maestro, Saint Landri.

Christiane read this aloud, laughed, and was astonished.

Her father went on: "Oh! they will amuse you. Come and look at them."

They turned to the right, and entered the park. The bathers promenaded gravely, slowly, along the three walks. They drank their glasses of water, and then went away. Some of them, seated on benches, traced lines in the sand with the ends of their walking-sticks or their umbrellas. They did not talk, seemed not to think, scarcely to live, enervated, paralyzed by the ennui of the thermal station. Only the odd music of the orchestra broke the sweet silence as it leaped into the air, coming one knew not whence, produced one knew not how, passing under the foliage and appearing to stir up these melancholy walkers.

A voice cried: "Christiane!"

She turned round. It was her brother. He rushed toward her, embraced her, and, having pressed Andermatt's hand, took his sister by the arm, and drew her along with him, leaving his father and his brother-in-law in the rear.

They chatted. He was a tall, well-made young fellow, prone to laughter like her, lighthearted as the Marquis, indifferent to events, but always on the lookout for a thousand francs.

"I thought you were asleep," said he. "But for that I would have come to embrace you. And then Paul carried me off this morning to the chateau of Tournoel."

"Who is Paul? Oh, yes, your friend!"

"Paul Bretigny. It is true you don't know him. He is taking a bath at the present moment."

"He is a patient, then?"

"No, but he is curing himself, all the same. He is trying to get over a love episode."

"And so he's taking acidulated baths — they're called acidulated, are they not? — in order to restore himself."

"Yes. He's doing all I told him to do. Oh! he has been hit hard. He's a violent youth, terrible, and has been at death's door. He wanted to kill himself, too. It was an actress — a well-known actress. He was madly in love with her. And then she was not faithful to him, do you see? The result was a frightful drama. So I brought him away. He's going on better now, but he's still thinking about it."

She smiled for a moment, then, becoming grave, she returned:

"It will amuse me to see him."

For her, however, this thing, "Love," did not mean very much. She sometimes bestowed a thought on it, just as you think, when you are poor, now and then of a pearl necklace, of a diadem of brilliants, with a desire awakened in you for this thing — possible though far away. This fancy would come to her after reading some novel to kill time, without attaching to it, beyond that, any special importance. She had never dreamed about it much, having been born with a happy soul, tranquil and contented, and, although now two years and a half married, she had not yet awakened out of that sleep in which innocent young girls live, that sleep of the heart, of the mind, and of the senses, which, with some women, lasts until death. For her life was simple and good, without complications. She had never looked for the causes or the hidden meaning of things. She had lived on from day to day, slept soundly, dressed with taste, laughed, and felt satisfied. What more could she have asked for?

When Andermatt had been introduced to her as her future husband, she refused to wed him at first with a childish indignation at the idea of becoming the wife of a Jew. Her father and her brother, sharing her repugnance, replied with her and like her by formally declining the offer. Andermatt disappeared, acted as if he were dead, but, at the end of three months, had lent Gontran more than twenty thousand francs; and the Marquis, for other reasons, was beginning to change his opinion.

In the first place, he always on principle yielded when one persisted, through sheer egotistical desire not to be disturbed. His daughter used to say of him: "All papa's ideas are jumbled up together"; and this was true. Without opinions, without beliefs, he had only enthusiasms, which varied every moment. At one time, he would attach himself, with a transitory and poetic exaltation, to the old traditions of his race, and would long for a king, but an intellectual king, liberal, enlightened, marching along with the age. At another time, after he had read a book by Michelet or some democratic thinker, he would become a passionate advocate of human equality, of modern ideas, of the claims of the poor, the oppressed, and the suffering. He believed in everything, just as each thing harmonized with his passing moods; and, when his old friend, Madame Icardon, who, connected as she was with many Israelites, desired the marriage of Christiane and Andermatt, and began to preach in favor of it, she knew full well the kind of arguments with which she should attack him.

She pointed out to him that the Jewish race had arrived at the hour of vengeance. It had been a race crushed down as the French people had been before the Revolution, and was now going to oppress others by the power of gold. The Marquis, devoid of religious faith, but convinced that the idea of God was rather a legislative idea, which had more effect in keeping the foolish, the ignorant, and the timid in the right path than the simple notion of Justice, regarded dogmas with a respectful indifference, and held in equal and sincere esteem Confucius, Mohammed, and Jesus Christ. Accordingly, the fact that the latter was crucified did not at all present itself as an original wrongdoing but as a gross, political blunder. In consequence it only required a few weeks to make him admire the toil, hidden, incessant, and allpowerful, of the persecuted Jews everywhere. And, viewing with different eyes their brilliant triumph, he looked upon it as a just reparation for the indignities that so long had been heaped upon them. He saw them masters of kings, who are the masters of the people — sustaining thrones or allowing them to collapse, able to make a nation bankrupt as one might a wine-merchant, proud in the presence of princes who had grown humble, and casting their impure gold into the half-open purses of the most Catholic sovereigns, who thanked them by conferring on them titles of nobility and lines of railway. So he consented to the marriage of William Andermatt with Christiane de Ravenel.

As for Christiane, under the unconscious pressure of Madame Icardon, her mother's old companion, who had become her intimate adviser since the Marquise's death, a pressure to which was added that of her father and the interested indifference of her brother, she consented to marry this big, overrich youth, who was not ugly but scarcely pleased her, just as she would have consented to spend a summer in a disagreeable country.

She found him a good fellow, kind, not stupid, nice in intimate relations; but she frequently laughed at him along with Gontran, whose gratitude was of the perfidious order.

He would say to her: "Your husband is rosier and balder than ever. He looks like a sickly flower, or a sucking pig with its hair shaved off. Where does he get these colors?" —

She would reply: "I assure you I have nothing to do with it. There are days when I feel inclined to paste him on a box of sugarplums."

But they had arrived in front of the baths. Two men were seated on straw chairs with their backs to the wall, smoking their pipes, one at each side of the door.

Said Gontran: "Look, here are two good types. Watch the fellow at the right, the hunchback with the Greek cap! That's Père Printemps, an ex-jailer from Riom, who has become the guardian, almost the manager, of the Enval establishment. For him nothing is changed, and he governs the invalids just as he did his prisoners in former days. The bathers are always prisoners, their bathing-boxes are cells, the douche-room a black-hole, and the place where Doctor Bonnefille practices his stomach-washings with the aid of the Baraduc sounding-line a chamber of mysterious torture. He does not salute any of the men on the strength of the principle that all convicts are contemptible beings. He treats women with much more consideration, upon my honor — a consideration mingled with astonishment, for he had none of them under his control in the prison of Riom. That retreat being destined for males only, he has not yet got accustomed to talking to members of the fair sex. The other fellow is the cashier. I defy you to make him write your name. You are just going to see."

And Gontran, addressing the man at the left, slowly said:

"Monsieur Seminois, this is my sister, Madame Andermatt, who wants to subscribe for a dozen baths."

The cashier, very tall, very thin, with a poor appearance, rose up, went into his office, which exactly faced the study of the medical inspector, opened his book, and asked:

"What name?"

"Andermatt."

"What did you say?"

"Andermatt."

"How do you spell it?"

"A-n-d-e-r-m-a-t-t."

"All right."

And he slowly wrote it down. When he had finished, Gontran asked:

"Would you kindly read over my sister's name?"

"Yes, Monsieur! Madame Anterpat."

Christiane laughed till the tears came into her eyes, paid for her tickets, and then asked:

"What is it that one hears up there?"

Gontran took her arm in his. Two angry voices reached their ears on the stairs. They went up, opened a door, and saw a large coffee-room with a billiard table in the center. Two men in their shirtsleeves at opposite sides of the billiard-table, each with a cue in his hand, were furiously abusing one another.

"Eighteen!"

"Seventeen!"

"I tell you I'm eighteen."

"That's not true — you're only seventeen!"

It was the director of the Casino, M. Petrus Martel of the Odéon, who was playing his ordinary game with the comedian of his company, M. Lapalme of the Grand Theater of Bordeaux.

Petrus Martel, whose stomach, stout and inactive, swayed underneath his shirt above a pair of pantaloons fastened anyhow, after having been a strolling player in various places, had undertaken the directorship of the Casino of Enval, and spent his days in drinking the allowances intended for the bathers. He wore an immense mustache like a dragoon, which was steeped from morning till night in the froth of bocks and the sticky syrup of liqueurs, and he had aroused in the old comedian whom he had enlisted in his service an immoderate passion for billiards.

As soon as they got up in the morning, they proceeded to play a game, insulted and threatened one another, expunged the record, began over again, scarcely gave themselves time for breakfast, and could not tolerate two clients coming to drive them away from their green cloth.

They soon put everyone to flight, and did not find this sort of existence unpleasant, though Petrus Martel always found himself at the end of the season in a bankrupt condition.

The female attendant, overwhelmed, would have to look on all day at this endless game, listen to the interminable discussion, and carry from morning till night glasses of beer or halfglasses of brandy to the two indefatigable players.

But Gontran carried off his sister: "Come into the park. 'Tis fresher."

At the end of the establishment they suddenly perceived the orchestra under a Chinese kiosque. A fairhaired young man, frantically playing the violin, was conducting with movements of his head. His hair was shaking from one side to the other in the effort to keep time, and his entire torso bent forward and rose up again, swaying from left to right, like the stick of the leader of an orchestra. Facing him sat three strange-looking musicians. This was the maestro, Saint Landri.

He and his assistants — a pianist, whose instrument, mounted on rollers, was wheeled each morning from the vestibule of the baths to the kiosque; an enormous flautist, who presented the appearance of sucking a match while tickling it with his big swollen fingers, and a double-bass of consumptive aspect — produced with much fatigue this perfect imitation of a bad barrel-organ, which had astonished Christiane in the village street.

As she stopped to look at them, a gentleman saluted her brother.

"Good day, my dear Count."

"Good day, doctor."

And Gontran introduced them: "My sister — Doctor Honorat."

She could scarcely restrain her merriment at the sight of this third physician. The latter bowed and made some complimentary remark.

"I hope that Madame is not an invalid?"

"Yes — slightly."

He did not go farther with the matter, and changed the subject.

"You are aware, my dear Count, that you will shortly have one of the most interesting spectacles that could await you on your arrival in this district."

"What is it, pray, doctor?"

"Père Oriol is going to blast his hill. This is of no consequence to you, but for us it is a big event." And he proceeded to explain. "Père Oriol — the richest peasant in this part of the country — he is known to be worth over fifty thousand francs a year

— — owns all the vineyards along the plain up to the outlet of Enval. Now, just as you go out from the village at the division of the valley, rises a little mountain, or rather a high knoll, and on this knoll are the best vineyards of Père Oriol. In the midst of two of them, facing the road, at two paces from the stream, stands a gigantic stone, an elevation which has impeded the cultivation and put into the shade one entire side of the field, on which it looks down. For six years, Père Oriol has every week been announcing that he was going to blast his hill; but he has never made up his mind about it.

"Every time a country boy went to be a soldier, the old man would say to him: 'When you're coming home on furlough, bring me some powder for this rock of mine.' And all the young soldiers would bring back in their knapsacks some powder that they stole for Père Oriol's rock. He has a chest full of this powder, and yet the hill has not been blasted. At last, for a week past, he has been noticed scooping out the stone, with his son, big Jacques, surnamed Colosse, which in Auvergne is pronounced 'Coloche.' This very morning they filled with powder the empty belly of the enormous rock; then they stopped up the mouth of it, only letting in the fuse bought at the tobacconist's. In two hours' time they will set fire to it. Then, five or ten minutes afterward, it will go off, for the end of the fuse is pretty long."

Christiane was interested in this narrative, amused already at the idea of this explosion, finding here again a childish sport that pleased her simple heart. They had now reached the end of the park.

"Where do you go now?" she said.

Doctor Honorat replied: "To the End of the World, Madame; that is to say, into a gorge that has no outlet and which is celebrated in Auvergne. It is one of the loveliest natural curiosities in the district." But a bell rang behind them. Gontran cried: "Look here! breakfast-time already!"

They turned back. A tall, young man came up to meet them.

Gontran said: "My dear Christiane, let me introduce to you M. Paul Bretigny." Then, to his friend: "This is my sister, my dear boy."

She thought him ugly. He had black hair, close-cropped and straight, big, round eyes, with an expression that was almost hard, a head also quite round, very strong, one of those heads that make you think of cannonballs, herculean shoulders, a rather savage expression, heavy and brutish. But from his jacket, from his linen, from his skin perhaps, came a very subtle perfume, with which the young woman was not familiar, and she asked herself:

"I wonder what odor that is?"

He said to her: "You arrived this morning, Madame?" His voice was a little hollow.

She replied: "Yes, Monsieur."

But Gontran saw the Marquis and Andermatt making signals to them to come in quickly to breakfast.

Doctor Honorat took leave of them, asking as he left whether they really meant to go and see the hill blasted. Christiane declared that she would go; and, leaning on her brother's arm, she murmured as she dragged him along toward the hotel:

"I am as hungry as a wolf. I shall be very much ashamed to eat as much as I feel inclined before your friend."

II

THE breakfast was long, as the meals usually are at a table d'hôte. Christiane, who was not familiar with all the faces of those present, chatted with her father and her brother. Then she went up to her room to take a rest till the time for blasting the rock.

She was ready long before the hour fixed, and made the others start along with her so that they might not miss the explosion. Just outside the village, at the opening of the glen, stood, as they had heard, a high knoll, almost a mountain, which they proceeded to climb under a burning sun, following a little path through the vine-trees. When they reached the summit the young woman uttered a cry of astonishment at the sight of the immense horizon displayed before her eyes. In front of her stretched a limitless plain, which immediately gave her soul the sensation of an ocean. This plain, overhung by a veil of light blue vapor, extended as far as the most distant mountain-ridges, which were scarcely perceptible, some fifty or sixty kilometers away. And under the transparent haze of delicate fineness, which floated above this vast stretch, could be distinguished towns, villages, woods, vast yellow squares of ripe crops, vast green squares of herbage, factories with long, red chimneys and blackened steeples and sharp-pointed structures, with the solidified lava of dead volcanoes.

"Turn around," said her brother.

She turned around. And behind she saw the mountain, the huge mountain indented with craters. This was the entrance to the foundation on which Enval stood, a great expanse of greenness in which one could scarcely trace the hidden gash of the gorge. The trees in a waving mass scaled the high slope as far as the first crater and shut out the view of those beyond. But, as they were exactly on the line that separated the plains from the mountain, the latter stretched to the left toward Clermont-Ferrand, and, wandering away, unrolled over the blue sky their strange mutilated tops, like monstrous blotches —— extinct volcanoes, dead volcanoes. And yonder — over yonder, between two peaks — could be seen another, higher still, more distant still, round and majestic, and bearing on its highest pinnacle something of fantastic shape resembling a ruin. This was the Puy de Dome, the king of the mountains of Auvergne, strong and unwieldy, wearing on its head, like a crown placed thereon by the mightiest of peoples, the remains of a Roman temple.

Christiane exclaimed: "Oh! how happy I shall be here!"

And she felt herself happy already, penetrated by that sense of well-being which takes possession of the flesh and the heart, makes you breathe with ease, and renders you sprightly and active when you find yourself in a spot which enchants your eyes, charms and cheers you, seems to have been awaiting you, a spot for which you feel that you were born.

Some one called out to her: "Madame, Madame!" And, at some distance away, she saw Doctor Honorat, recognizable by his big hat. He rushed across to them, and conducted the family toward the opposite side of the hill, over a grassy slope beside a grove of young trees, where already some thirty persons were waiting, strangers and peasants mingled together.

Beneath their feet, the steep hillside descended toward the Riom road, overshadowed by willows that sheltered the shallow river; and in the midst of a vineyard at the edge of this stream rose a sharp-pointed rock before which two men on bended knees seemed to be praying. This was the scene of action.

The Oriols, father and son, were attaching the fuse. On the road, a crowd of curious spectators had stationed themselves, with a line of people lower down in front, among whom village brats were scampering about.

Doctor Honorat chose a convenient place for Christiane to sit down, and there she waited with a beating heart, as if she were going to see the entire population blown up along with the rock.

The Marquis, Andermatt, and Paul Bretigny lay down on the grass at the young woman's side, while Gontran remained standing. He said, in a bantering tone:

"My dear doctor, you must be much less busy than your brother-practitioners, who apparently have not an hour to spare to attend this little fête?" Honorat replied in a good-humored tone:

"I am not less busy; only my patients occupy less of my time. And again I prefer to amuse my patients rather than to physic them."

He had a quiet manner which greatly pleased Gontran. Other persons now arrived, fellow-guests at the table d'hôte — the ladies Paille, two widows, mother and daughter; the Monecus, father and daughter; and a very small, fat, man, who was puffing like a boiler that had burst, M. Aubry-Pasteur, an exengineer of mines, who had made a fortune in Russia.

M. Pasteur and the Marquis were on intimate terms. He seated himself with much difficulty after some preparatory movements, circumspect and cautious, which considerably amused Christiane. Gontran sauntered away from them, in order to have a look at the other persons whom curiosity had attracted toward the knoll.

Paul Bretigny pointed out to Christiane Andermatt the views, of which they could catch glimpses in the distance. First of all, Riom made a red patch with its row of tiles along the plain; then Ennezat, Maringues, Lezoux, a heap of villages scarcely distinguishable, which only broke the wide expanse of verdure with a somber indentation here and there, and, further down, away down below, at the base of the mountains, he pretended that he could trace out Thiers.

He said, in an animated fashion: "Look, look! Just in front of my finger, exactly in front of my finger. For my part, I can see it quite distinctly."

She could see nothing, but she was not surprised at his power of vision, for he looked like a bird of prey, with his round, piercing eyes, which appeared to be as powerful as telescopes. He went on:

"The Allier flows in front of us, in the middle of that plain, but it is impossible to perceive it. It is very far off, thirty kilometers from here."

She scarcely took the trouble to glance toward the place which he indicated, for she had riveted her eyes on the rock and given it her entire attention. She was saying to herself that presently this enormous stone would no longer exist, that it would disappear in powder, and she felt herself seized with a vague pity for the stone, the pity which a little girl would feel for a broken plaything. It had been there so long, this stone; and then it was imposing —— it had a picturesque look. The two men, who had by this time risen, were heaping up pebbles at the foot of it, and digging with the rapid movements of peasants working hurriedly.

The crowd gathered along the road, increasing every moment, had pushed forward to get a better view. The brats brushed against the two diggers, and kept rushing and capering round them like young animals in a state of delight; and from the elevated point at which Christiane was sitting, these people looked quite small, a crowd of insects, an anthill in confusion.

The buzz of voices ascended, now slight, scarcely noticeable, then more lively, a confused mixture of cries and human movements, but scattered through the air, evaporated already — a dust of sounds, as it were. On the knoll likewise the crowd was swelling in numbers, incessantly arriving from the village, and covering up the slope which looked down on the condemned rock.

They were distinguished from each other, as they gathered together, according to their hotels, their classes, their castes. The most clamorous portion of the assemblage was that of the actors and musicians, presided over and generaled by the conductor, Petrus Martel of the Odéon, who, under the circumstances, had given up his incessant game of billiards.

With a Panama flapping over his forehead, a black alpaca jacket covering his shoulders and allowing his big stomach to protrude in a semicircle, for he considered a waistcoat useless in the open country, the actor, with his thick mustache, assumed the airs of a commander-in-chief, and pointed out, explained, and criticised all the movements of the two Oriols. His subordinates, the comedian Lapalme, the young premier Petitnivelle, and the musicians, the maestro Saint Landri, the pianist Javel, the huge flautist Noirot, the double-bass Nicordi, gathered round him to listen. In front of them were seated three women, sheltered by three parasols, a white, a red, and a blue, which, under the sun of two o'clock, formed a strange and dazzling French flag. These were Mademoiselle Odelin, the young actress; her mother, — a mother that she had hired out, as Gontran put it, — and the female attendant of the coffee-room, three ladies who were habitual companions. The arrangement of these three parasols' so as to suit the national colors was an invention of Petrus Martel, who, having noticed at the commencement of the season the blue and the white in the hands of the ladies Odelin, had made a present of the red to the coffee-room attendant.

Quite close to them, another group excited interest and observation, that of the chefs and scullions of the hotels, to the number of eight, for there was a war of rivalry between the kitchen-folk, who had attired themselves in linen jackets to make an impression on the bystanders, extending even to the scullery-maids. Standing all in a group they let the crude light of day fall on their flat white caps, presenting, at the same time, the appearance of fantastic staff-officers of lancers and a deputation of cooks.

The Marquis asked Doctor Honorat: "Where do all these people come from? I never would have imagined Enval was so thickly populated!"

"Oh! they come from all parts, from Chatel-Guyon, from Tournoel, from La Roche-Pradière, from Saint-Hippolyte. For this affair has been talked of a long time in the country, and then Père Oriol is a celebrity, an important personage on account of his influence and his wealth, besides a true Auvergnat, remaining still a peasant, working himself, hoarding, piling up gold on gold, intelligent, full of ideas and plans for his children's future."

Gontran came back, excited, his eyes sparkling.

He said, in a low tone: "Paul, Paul, pray come along with me; I'm going to show you two pretty girls; yes, indeed, nice girls, you know!"

The other raised his head, and replied: "My dear fellow, I'm in very good quarters here; I'll not budge."

"You're wrong. They are charming!" Then, in a louder tone: "But the doctor is going to tell me who they are. Two little girls of eighteen or nineteen, rustic ladies, oddly dressed, with black silk dresses that have close-fitting sleeves, some kind of uniform dresses, convent-gowns — two brunettes — "Doctor Honorat interrupted him: "That's enough. They are Père Oriol's daughters, two pretty young girls indeed, educated at the Benedictine Convent at Clermont, and sure to make very good matches. They are two types, but simply types of our race, of the fine race of women of Auvergne, Marquis. I will show you these two little lasses — "

Gontran here slyly interposed: "You are the medical adviser of the Oriol family, doctor?"

The other appreciated this sly question, and simply responded with a "By Jove, I am!" uttered in atone of the utmost good-humor.

The young man went on: "How did you come to win the confidence of this rich patient?"

"By ordering him to drink a great deal of good wine." And he told a number of anecdotes about the Oriols. Moreover, he was distantly related to them, and had known them for a considerable time. The old fellow, the father, quite an original, was very proud of his wine; and above all he had one vine-garden, the produce of which was reserved for the use of the family, solely for the family and their guests. In certain years they happened to empty the casks filled with the growth of this aristocratic vineyard, but in other years they scarcely succeeded in doing so. About the month of May or June, when the father saw that it would be hard to drink all that was still left, he would proceed to encourage his big son, Colosse, and would repeat: "Come on, son, we must finish it." Then they would go on pouring down their throats pints of red wine from morning till night. Twenty times during every meal, the old chap would say in a grave tone, while he held the jug over his son's glass: "We must finish it." And, as all this liquor with its mixture of alcohol heated his blood and prevented him from sleeping, he would rise up in the middle of the night, draw on his breeches, light a lantern, wake up Colosse, and off they would go to the cellar, after snatching a crust of bread each out of the cupboard, in order to steep it in their glasses, filled up again and again out of the same cask. Then, when they had swallowed so much wine that they could feel it rolling about in their stomachs, the father would tap the resounding wood of the cask to find out whether the level of the liquor had gone down.

The Marquis asked: "Are these the same people that are working at the hillock?"

"Yes, yes, exactly."

Just at that moment the two men hurried off with giant strides from the rock charged with powder, and all the crowd that surrounded them down below began to run away like a retreating army. They fled in the direction of Riom and Enval, leaving behind them by itself the huge rock on the top of the hillock covered with thin grass and pebbles, for it divided the vineyard into two sections, and its immediate surroundings had not been grubbed up yet.

The crowd assembled on the slope above, now as dense as that below, waited in trembling expectancy; and the loud voice of Petrus Martel exclaimed:

"Attention! the fuse is lit!"

Christiane shivered at the thought of what was about to happen, but the doctor murmured behind her back:

"Ho! if they left there all the fuse I saw them buying, we'll have ten minutes of it!"

All eyes were fixed on the stone, and suddenly a dog, a little black dog, a kind of pug, was seen approaching it. He ran round it, began smelling, and no doubt, discovered a suspicious odor, for he commenced yelping as loudly as ever he could, his paws stiff, the hair on his back standing on end, his tail sticking out, and his ears erect.

A burst of laughter came from the spectators, a cruel burst of laughter; people expressed a hope that he would not keep riveted to the spot up to the time of the blast. Then voices called out to him to make him come back; some men whistled to him; they tried to hit him with stones to prevent him from going on the whole way. But the pug did not budge an inch, and kept barking furiously at the rock.

Christiane began to tremble. A horrible fear of seeing the animal disemboweled took possession of her; all her enjoyment was at an end. She cried repeatedly, with nerves unstrung, stammering, vibrating all over with anguish:

"Oh! good heavens! Oh! good heavens! it will be killed. I don't want to look at it! I don't want to look at it! I will not wait to see it! Come away!"

Paul Bretigny, who had been sitting by her side, arose, and, without saying one word, began to descend toward the hillock with all the speed of which his long legs were capable.

Cries of terror escaped from many lips; a panic agitated the crowd; and the pug, seeing this big man coming toward him, took refuge behind the rock. Paul pursued him; the dog ran off to the other side; and, for a minute or two, they kept rushing round the stone, now to right, now to left, as if they were playing a game of hide and seek. Seeing at last that he could not overtake the animal, the young man proceeded to reascend the slope, and the dog, seized once more with fury, renewed his barking.

Vociferations of anger greeted the return of the imprudent youth, who was quite out of breath, for people do not forgive those who excite terror in their breasts. Christiane v/as suffocating with emotion, her two hands pressed against her palpitating heart. She had lost her head so completely that she sobbed: "At least you are not hurt?" while Gontran cried angrily:

"He is mad, that idiot; he never does anything but tomfooleries of this kind. I never met a greater donkey!"

But the soil was now shaking; it rose in air. A formidable detonation made the entire country all around vibrate, and for a full minute thundered over the mountain, while all the echoes repeated it, like so many cannon-shots.

Christiane saw nothing but a shower of stones falling, and a high column of light clay sinking in a heap. And immediately afterward the crowd from above rushed down like a wave, uttering wild shouts. The battalion of kitchen-drudges came racing down in the direction of the knoll, leaving behind them the regiment of theatrical performers, who descended more slowly, with Petrus Martel at their head. The three parasols forming a tricolor were nearly carried away in this descent.

And all ran, men, women, peasants, and villagers. They could be seen falling, getting up again, starting on afresh, while in long procession the two streams of people, which had till now been kept back by fear, rolled along so as to knock against one another and get mixed up on the very spot where the explosion had taken place.

"Let us wait a while," said the Marquis, "till all this curiosity is satisfied, so that we may go and look in our turn."

The engineer, M. Aubry-Pasteur, who had just arisen with very great difficulty, replied:

"For my part, I am going back to the village by the footpaths. There is nothing further to keep me here."

He shook hands, bowed, and went away.

Doctor Honorat had disappeared. The party talked about him, and the Marquis said to his son:

"You have only known him three days, and all the time you have been laughing at him. You will end by offending him."

But Gontran shrugged his shoulders: "Oh! he's a wise man, a good sceptic, that doctor. I tell you in reply that he will not bother himself. When we are both alone together, he laughs at all the world and everything, commencing with his patients and his waters. I will give you a free thermal course if you ever see him annoyed by my nonsense."

Meanwhile, there was considerable agitation further down around the site of the vanished hillock. The enormous crowd, swelling, rising up, and sinking down like billows, broke out into exclamations, manifestly swayed by some emotion, some astonishing occurrence which nobody had foreseen. Andermatt, ever eager and inquisitive, was repeating:

"What is the matter with them now? What can be the matter with them?"

Gontran announced that he was going to find out, and walked off. Christiane, who had now sunk into a state of indifference, was reflecting that if the igniting substance had been only a little shorter, it would have been sufficient to have caused the death of their foolish companion or led to his being mutilated by the blasting of the rock, and all because she was afraid of a dog losing its life. She could not help thinking that he must, indeed, be very violent and passionate — this man — to expose himself to such a risk in this way without any good reason for it — simply owing to the fact that a woman who was a stranger to him had given expression to a desire.

People could be observed running along the road toward the village. The Marquis now asked, in his turn: "What is the matter with them?" And Andermatt, unable to stand it any longer, began to run down the side of the hill. Gontran, from below, made a sign to him to come on.

Paul Bretigny asked: "Will you take my arm, Madame?" She took his arm, which seemed to her as immovable as iron, and, as her feet glided along the warm grass, she leaned on it as she would have leaned on a baluster with a sense of absolute security. Gontran, who had just come back after making inquiries, exclaimed: "It is a spring. The explosion has made a spring gush out!"

And they fell in with the crowd. Then, the two young men, Paul and Gontran, moving on in front, scattered the spectators by jostling against them, and without paying any heed to their gruntings, opened a way for Christiane and her father. They walked through a chaos of sharp stones, broken, and blackened with powder, and arrived in front of a hole full of muddy water which bubbled up and then flowed away toward the river over the feet of the bystanders. Andermatt was there already, having effected a passage through the multitude by insinuating ways peculiar to himself, as Gontran used to say, and was watching with rapt attention the water escaping through the broken soil.

Doctor Honorat, facing him at the opposite side of the hole, was observing him with an air of mingled surprise and boredom.

Andermatt said to him: "It might be desirable to taste it; it is perhaps a mineral spring."

The physician returned: "No doubt it is mineral. There are any number of mineral waters here. There will soon be more springs than invalids."

The other in reply said: "But it is necessary to taste it."

The physician displayed little or no interest in the matter: "It is necessary at least to wait till we see whether it is clean."

And everyone wanted to see. Those in the second row pushed those in front almost into the muddy water. A child fell in, and caused a laugh. The Oriols, father and son, were there, contemplating gravely this unexpected phenomenon, not knowing yet what they ought to think about it. The father was a spare man, with a long, thin frame, and a bony head — the hard head of a beardless peasant; and the son, taller still, a giant, thin also, and wearing a mustache, had the look at the same time of a trooper and a vinedresser.

The bubblings of the water appeared to increase, its volume to grow larger, and it was beginning to get clearer. A movement took place among the people, and Doctor Latonne appeared with a glass in his hand. He perspired, panted, and stood quite stupefied at the sight of his brother-physician, Doctor Honorat, with one foot planted at the side of the newly discovered spring, like a general who has been the first to enter a fortress.

He asked, breathlessly: "Have you tasted it?"

"No, I am waiting to see whether 'tis clear." Then Doctor Latonne thrust his glass into it, and drank with that solemnity of visage which experts assume when tasting wines. After that, he exclaimed, "Excellent!" which in no way compromised him, and extending the glass toward his rival said: "Do you wish to taste it?"

But Doctor Honorat, decidedly, had no love for mineral waters, for he smilingly replied:

"Many thanks. 'Tis quite sufficient that you have appreciated it. I know the taste of them."

He did know the taste of them all, and he appreciated it, too, though in quite a different fashion. Then, turning toward Pére Oriol said:

"'Tisn't as good as your excellent vine-growth." The old man was flattered. Christiane had seen, enough, and wanted to go away. Her brother and Paul once more forced a path for her through the populace. She followed them, leaning on her father's arm. Suddenly she slipped and was near falling, and glancing down at her feet she saw that she had stepped on a piece of bleeding flesh, covered with black hairs and sticky with mud. It was a portion of the pug-dog, who had been mangled by the explosion and trampled underfoot by the crowd. She felt a choking sensation, and was so much moved that she could not restrain her tears. And she murmured, as she dried her eyes with her handkerchief: "Poor little animal! poor little animal!"

She wanted to know nothing more about it. She wished to go back, to shut herself up in her room. That day, which had begun so pleasantly, had ended sadly for her. Was it an omen? Her heart, shriveling up, beat with violent palpitations. They were now alone on the road, and in front of them they saw a tall hat and the two skirts of a frock-coat flapping like wings. It was Doctor Bonnefille, who had been the last to hear the news, and who was now rushing to the spot, glass in hand, like Doctor Latonne.

When he recognized the Marquis, he drew up. "What is this I hear, Marquis? They tell me it is a spring — a mineral spring?"

"Yes, my dear doctor."

"Abundant?"

"Why, yes."

"Is it true that — that they are there?"

Gontran replied with an air of gravity: "Why, yes, certainly; Doctor Latonne has even made the analysis already."

Then Doctor Bonnefille began to run, while Christiane, a little tickled and enlivened by his face, said: "Well, no, I am not going back yet to the hotel. Let us go and sit down in the park."

Andermatt had remained at the site of the knoll, watching the flowing of the water.

III

THE table d'hôte was noisy that evening at the Hotel Splendid. The blasting of the hillock and the discovery of the new spring gave a brisk impetus to conversation. The diners were not numerous, however, — — a score all told, — people usually taciturn and quiet, patients who, after having vainly tried all the well-known waters, had now turned to the new stations. At the end of the table occupied by the Ravenels and the Andermatts were, first, the Monecus, a little man with white hair and face and his daughter, a very pale, big girl, who sometimes rose up and went out in the middle of a meal, leaving her plate half full; fat M. Aubry-Pasteur, the exengineer; the Chaufours, a family in black, who might be met every day in the walks of the park behind a little vehicle which carried their deformed child, and the ladies Paille, mother and daughter, both of them widows, big and strong, strong everywhere, before and behind. "You may easily see," said Gontran, "that they ate up their husbands; that's how their stomachs got affected." It was, indeed, for a stomach affection that they had come to the station.

Further on, a man of extremely red complexion, brick-colored, M. Riquier, whose digestion was also very indifferent, and then other persons with bad complexions, travelers of that mute class who usually enter the diningrooms of hotels with slow steps, the wife in front, the husband behind, bow as soon as they have passed the door, and then take their seats with a timid and modest air.

All the other end of the table was empty, although the plates and the covers were laid there for the guests of the future.

Andermatt talked in an animated fashion. He had spent the afternoon chatting with Doctor Latonne, giving vent in a flood of words to vast schemes with reference to Enval. The doctor had enumerated to him, with burning conviction, the wonderful qualities of his water, far superior to those of Chatel-Guyon, whose reputation nevertheless had been definitely established for the last ten years. Then, at the right, they had that hole of a place, Royat, at the height of success, and at the left, that other hole, Chatel-Guyon, which had lately been set afloat. What could they not do with Enval, if they knew how to set about it properly?

He said, addressing the engineer: "Yes, Monsieur, there's where it all is, to know the way to set about it. It is all a matter of skill, of tact, of opportunism, and of audacity. In order to establish a spa, it is necessary to know how to launch it, nothing more, and in order to launch it, it is necessary to interest the great medical body of Paris in the matter. I, Monsieur, always succeed in what I undertake, because I always seek the practical method, the only one that should determine success in every particular case with which I occupy myself; and, as long as I have not discovered it, I do nothing — I wait. It is not enough to have the water, it is necessary to get people to drink it; and to get people to drink it, it is not enough to get it cried up as unrivaled in the newspapers and elsewhere; it is necessary to know how to get this discreetly said by the only men who have influence on the public that will drink it, on the invalids whom we require, on the peculiarly credulous public that pays for drugs — in short, by the physicians.

You can only address a Court of Justice through the mouths of advocates; it will only hear them, and understands only them. So you can only address the patient through the doctors — he listens only to them."

The Marquis, who greatly admired the practical common sense of his son-in-law, exclaimed:

"Ah! how true this is! Apart from this, my dear boy, you are unique for giving the right touch." Andermatt, who was excited, went on: "There is a fortune to be made here. The country is admirable, the climate excellent. One thing alone disturbs my mind — would we have water enough for a large establishment? — for things that are only half done always miscarry. We would require a very large establishment, and consequently a great deal of water, enough of water to supply two hundred baths at the same time, with a rapid and continuous current; and the new spring added to the old one, would not supply fifty, whatever Doctor Latonne may say about it — "

M. Aubry-Pasteur interrupted him. "Oh! as for water, I will give you as much as you want of it."

Andermatt was stupefied. "You?"

"Yes, I. That astonishes you? Let me explain myself. Last year, I was here about the same time as this year, for I really find myself improved by the Enval baths. Now one morning, I lay asleep in my own room, when a stout gentleman arrived. He was the president of the governing body of the establishment. He was in a state of great agitation, and the cause of it was this: the Bonnefille Spring had lowered so much that there were some apprehensions lest it might entirely disappear. Knowing that I was a mining engineer, he had come to ask me if I could not find a means of saving the establishment.

"I accordingly set about studying the geological system of the country. You know that in each stratum of the soil original disturbances have led to different changes and conditions in the surface of the ground. The question, therefore, was to discover how the mineral water came — by what fissures — and what were the direction, the origin, and the nature of these fissures. I first inspected the establishment with great care, and, noticing in a corner an old disused pipe of a bath, I observed that it was already almost stopped up with limestone. Now the water, by depositing the salts which it contained on the coatings of the ducts, had rapidly led to an obstruction of the passage. It would inevitably happen likewise in the natural passages in the soil, this soil being granitic. So it was that the Bonnefille Spring had stopped up. Nothing more. It was necessary to get at it again farther on.

"Most people would have searched above its original point of egress. As for me, after a month of study, observation, and reasoning, I sought for and found it fifty meters lower down. And this was the explanation of the matter: I told you before that it was first necessary to determine the origin, nature, and direction of the fissures in the granite which enabled the water to spring forth. It was easy for me to satisfy myself that these fissures ran from the plain toward the mountain and not from the mountain toward the plain, inclined like a roof undoubtedly, in consequence of a depression of this plain which in breaking up had carried along with it the primitive buttresses of the mountains. Accordingly, the water, in place of descending, rose up again between the different interstices of the granitic layers. And I then discovered the cause of this unexpected phenomenon.

"Formerly the Limagne, that vast expanse of sandy and argillaceous soil, of which you can scarcely see the limits, was on a level with the first tableland of the mountains; but owing to the geological character of its lower portions, it subsided, so as to tear away the edge of the mountain, as I explained to you a moment ago. Now this immense sinking produced, at the point of separating the earth and the granite, an immense barrier of clay of great depth and impenetrable by liquids. And this is what happens: The mineral water comes from the beds of old volcanoes. That which comes from the greatest distance gets cooled on its way, and rises up perfectly cold like ordinary springs; that which comes from the volcanic beds that are nearer gushes up still warm, at varying degrees of heat, according to the distance of the subterranean fire.

"Here is the course it pursues. It is expelled from some unknown depths, up to the moment when it meets the clay barrier of the Limagne. Not being able to pass through it, and pushed on by enormous pressure, it seeks a vent. Finding then the inclined gaps of granite, it gets in there, and reascends to the point at which they reach the level of the soil. Then, resuming its original direction, it again proceeds to flow toward the plain along the ordinary bed of the streams. I may add that we do not see the hundredth part of the mineral waters of these glens. We can only discover those whose point of egress is open. As for the others, arriving as they do at the side of the fissures in the granite under a thick layer of vegetable and cultivated soil, they are lost in the earth, which absorbs them.

"From this I draw the conclusion: first, that to have the water, it is sufficient to search by following the inclination and the direction of the superimposed strips of granite; secondly, that in order to preserve it, it is enough to prevent the fissures from being stopped up by calcareous deposits, that is to say, to maintain carefully the little artificial wells by digging; thirdly, that in order to obtain the adjoining spring, it is necessary to get at it by means of a practical sounding as far as the same fissure of granite below, and not above, it being well understood that you must place yourself at the side of the barrier of clay which forces the waters to reascend. From this point of view, the spring discovered to-day is admirably situated only some meters away from this barrier. If you want to set up a new establishment, it is here you should erect it."

When he ceased speaking, there was an interval of silence.

Andermatt, ravished, said merely: "That's it! When you see the curtain drawn, the entire mystery vanishes. You are a most valuable man, M. Aubry-Pasteur."

Besides him, the Marquis and Paul Bretigny alone had understood what he was talking about. Gontran had not heard a single word. The others, with their ears and mouths open, while the engineer was talking, were simply stupefied with amazement. The ladies Paille especially, being very religious women, asked themselves if this explanation of a phenomenon ordained by God and accomplished by mysterious means had not in it something profane. The mother thought she ought to say: "Providence is very wonderful." The ladies seated at the center of the table conveyed their approval by nods of the head, disturbed also by listening to these unintelligible remarks.

M. Riquier, the brick-colored man, observed: "They may well come from volcanoes or from the moon, these Enval waters — here have I been taking them ten days, and as yet I experience no effect from them!"

M. and Madame Chaufour protested in the name of their child, who was beginning to move the right leg, a thing that had not happened during the six years they had been nursing him.

Riquier replied: "That proves, by Jove, that we have not the same ailment; it doesn't prove that the Enval water cures affections of the stomach." He seemed in a rage, exasperated by this fresh, useless experiment.

But M. Monecu also spoke in the name of his daughter, declaring -that for the last eight days she was beginning to be able to retain food without being obliged to go out at every meal. And his big daughter blushed, with her nose in her plate. The ladies Paille likewise thought they had improved.

Then Riquier was vexed, and abruptly turning toward the two women said:

"Your stomachs are affected, Mesdames."

They replied together: "Why, yes, Monsieur. We can digest nothing."

He nearly leaped out of his chair, stammering: "You — you! Why, 'tis enough to look at you. Your stomachs are affected, Mesdames. That is to say, you eat too much."

Madame Paille, the mother, became very angry, and she retorted: "As for you, Monsieur, there is no doubt about it, you exhibit certainly the appearance of persons whose stomachs are destroyed. It has been well said that good stomachs make nice men."

A very thin, old lady, whose name was not known, said authoritatively: "I am sure everyone would find the waters of Enval better if the hotel chef would only bear in mind a little that he is cooking for invalids. Truly, he sends us up things that it is impossible to digest."

And suddenly the entire table agreed on the point, and indignation was expressed against the hotelkeeper, who served them with crayfish, porksteaks, salt eels, cabbage, yes, cabbage and sausages, all the most indigestible kinds of food in the world for persons for whom Doctors Bonnefille, Latonne, and Honorât had prescribed only white meats, lean and tender, fresh vegetables, and milk diet.

Riquier was shaking with fury: "Why should not the physicians inspect the table at thermal stations without leaving such an important thing as the selection of nutriment to the judgment of a brute? Thus, every day, they give us hard eggs, anchovies, and ham as side-dishes — "

M. Monecu interrupted him: "Oh! excuse me! My daughter can digest nothing well except ham, which, moreover has been prescribed for her by Mas-Roussel and Remusot."

Riquier exclaimed: "Ham! ham! why, that's poison, Monsieur."

And an interminable argument arose, which each day was taken up afresh, as to the classification of foods. Milk itself was discussed with passionate warmth. Riquier could not drink a glass of claret and milk without immediately suffering from indigestion.

Aubry-Pasteur, in answer to his remarks, irritated in his turn, observed that people questioned the properties of things which he adored:

"Why, gracious goodness, Monsieur, if you were attacked with dyspepsia and I with gastralgia, we would require food as different as the glass of the spectacles that suits shortsighted and long-sighted people, both of whom, however, have diseased eyes."

He added: "For my part I begin to choke when I swallow a glass of red wine, and I believe there is nothing worse for man than wine. All water-drinkers live a hundred years, while we — "

Gontran replied with a laugh: "Faith, without wine and without marriage, I would find life monotonous enough."

The ladies Paille lowered their eyes. They drank a considerable quantity of Bordeaux of the best quality without any water in it, and their double widowhood seemed to indicate that they had applied the same treatment to their husbands, the daughter being twenty-two and the mother scarcely forty.

But Andermatt, usually so chatty, remained taciturn and thoughtful. He suddenly asked Gontran: "Do you know where the Oriols live?"

"Yes, their house was pointed out to me a little while ago."

"Could you bring me there after dinner?"

"Certainly. It will even give me pleasure to accompany you. I shall not be sorry to have another look at the two lassies."

And, as soon as dinner was over, they went off, while Christiane, who was tired, went up with the Marquis and Paul Bretigny to spend the rest of the day in the drawingroom.

It was still broad daylight, for they dine early at thermal stations.

Andermatt took his brother-in-law's arm.

"My dear Gontran, if this old man is reasonable, and if the analysis realizes Doctor Latonne's expectations, I am probably going to try a big stroke of business here — a spa. I am going to start a spa!"

He stopped in the middle of the street, and seized his companion by both sides of his jacket.

"Ha! you don't understand, fellows like you, how amusing business is, not the business of merchants or traders, but big undertakings such as we go in for! Yes, my boy, when they are properly understood, we find in them everything that men care for — — they cover, at the same time, politics, war, diplomacy, everything, everything! It is necessary to be always searching, finding, inventing, to understand everything, to foresee everything, to combine everything, to dare everything. The great battle to-day is being fought by means of money. For my part, I see in the hundred-sou pieces raw recruits in red breeches, in the twenty-franc pieces very glittering lieutenants, captains in the notes for a hundred francs, and in those for a thousand I see generals. And I fight, by heavens! I fight from morning till night against all the world, with all the world. And this is how to live, how to live on a big scale, just as the mighty lived in days of yore. We are the mighty of to-day — there you are — the only true mighty ones!

"Stop, look at that village, that poor village! I will make a town of it, yes, I will, a lovely town full of big hotels which will be filled with visitors, with elevators, with servants, with carriages, a crowd of rich folk served by a crowd of poor; and all this because it pleased me one evening to fight with Royat, which is at the right, with Chatel-Guyon, which is at the left, with Mont Doré, La Bourboule, Châteauneuf, Saint Nectaire, which are behind us, with Vichy, which is facing us. And shall succeed because I have the means, the only means. I have seen it in one glance, just as a great general sees the weak side of an enemy. It is necessary too to know how to lead men, in our line of business, both to carry them along with us and to subjugate them.

"Good God! life becomes amusing when you can do such things. I have now three years of pleasure to look forward to with this town of mine. And then see what a chance it is to find this engineer, who told us such interesting things at dinner, most interesting things, my dear fellow. It is as clear as day, my system. Thanks to it, I can smash the old company, without even having any necessity of buying it up."

He then resumed his walk, and they quietly went up the road to the left in the direction of Chatel-Guyon."

Gontran presently observed: "When I am walking by my brother-in-law's side, I feel that the same noise disturbs his brain as that heard in the gambling rooms at Monte Carlo — that noise of gold moved about, shuffled, drawn away, raked off, lost or gained."

Andermatt did, indeed, suggest the idea of a strange human machine, constructed only for the purpose of calculating and debating about money, and mentally manipulating it. Moreover, he exhibited much vanity about his special knowledge of the world, and plumed himself on his power of estimating at one glance of his eye the actual value of anything whatever. Accordingly, he might be seen, wherever he happened to be, every moment taking up an article, examining it, turning it round, and declaring: "This is worth so much."

His wife and his brother-in-law, diverted by this mania, used to amuse themselves by deceiving him, exhibiting to him queer pieces of furniture and asking him to estimate them; and when he remained perplexed, at the sight of their unexpected finds, they would both burst out laughing like fools. Sometimes also, in the street at Paris, Gontran would stop in front of a warehouse and force him to make a calculation of an entire shop-window, or perhaps of a horse with a jolting vehicle, or else again of a luggage-van laden with household goods.

One evening, while seated at his sister's dinner-table before fashionable guests, he called on William to tell him what would be the approximate value of the Obelisk; then, when the other happened to name some figure, he would put the same question as to the Solferino Bridge, and the Arc de Triomphe de l'Etoile. And he gravely concluded: "You might write a very interesting work on the valuation of the principal monuments of the globe." Andermatt never got angry, and fell in with all his pleasantries, like a superior man sure of himself.

Gontran having asked one day: "And I — how much am I worth?" William declined to answer; then, as his brother-in-law persisted, saying: "Look here! If I should be captured by brigands, how much would you give to release me?" he replied at last: "Well, well, my dear fellow, I would give a bill." And his smile said so much that the other, a little disconcerted, did not press the matter further.

Andermatt, besides, was fond of artistic objects, and having fine taste and appreciating such things thoroughly, he skillfully collected them with that bloodhound's scent which he carried into all commercial transactions.

They had arrived in front of a house of a middle-class type. Gontran stopped him and said: "Here it is." An iron knocker hung over a heavy oaken door; they knocked, and a lean servant-maid came to open it.

The banker asked: "Monsieur Oriol?"

The woman said: "Come in."

They entered a kitchen, a big farm-kitchen, in which a little fire was still burning under a pot; then they were ushered into another part of the house, where the Oriol family was assembled.

The father was asleep, seated on one chair with his feet on another. The son, with both elbows on the table, was reading the "Petit Journal" with the spasmodic efforts of a feeble intellect always wandering; and the two girls, in the recess of the same window, were working at the same piece of tapestry, having begun it one at each end.

They were the first to rise, both at the same moment, astonished at this unexpected visit; then, big Jacques raised his head, a head congested by the pressure of his brain; then, at last, Père Oriol waked up, and took down his long legs from the second chair one after the other.

The room was bare, with whitewashed walls, a stone flooring, and furniture consisting of straw seats, a mahogany chest of drawers, four engravings by Epinal with glass over them, and big white curtains.

They were all staring at each other, and the servant-maid, with her petticoat raised up to her knees, was waiting at the door, riveted to the spot by curiosity.

Andermatt introduced himself, mentioning his name as well as that of his brother-in-law, Count de Ravenel, made a low bow to the two young girls, bending his head with extreme politeness, and then calmly seated himself, adding:

"Monsieur Oriol, I came to talk to you about a matter of business. Moreover, I will not take four roads to explain myself. See here. You have just discovered a spring on your property. The analysis of this water is to be made in a few days. If it is of no value, you will understand that I will have nothing to do with it; if, on the contrary, it fulfills my anticipations, I propose to buy from you this piece of ground, and all the lands around it. Think on this. No other person but myself could make you such an offer. The old company is nearly bankrupt; it will not, therefore, have the least notion of building a new establishment, and the ill success of this enterprise will not encourage fresh attempts. Don't give me an answer to-day. Consult your family. When the analysis is known you will fix your price. If it suits me, I will say 'yes'; if it does not suit me, I will say 'no.' I never haggle for my part."

The peasant, a man of business in his own way, and sharp as anyone could be, courteously replied that he would see about it, that he felt honored, that he would think it over — and then he offered them a glass of wine.

Andermatt made no objection, and, as the day was declining, Oriol said to his daughters, who had resumed their work, with their eyes lowered over the piece of tapestry: "Let us have some light, girls."

They both got up together, passed into an adjoining room, then came back, one carrying two lighted wax-candles, the other four wineglasses without stems, glasses such as the poor use. The wax-candles were fresh looking and were garnished with red paper — placed, no doubt, by way of ornament on the young girl's mantelpiece.

Then, Colosse rose up; for only the male members of the family visited the cellar. Andermatt had an idea. "It would give me great pleasure to see your cellar. You are the principal vinedresser of the district, and it must be a very fine one."

Oriol, touched to the heart, hastened to conduct them, and, taking up one of the wax-candles, led the way. They had to pass through the kitchen again, then they got into a court where the remnant of daylight that was left enabled them to discern empty casks standing on end, big stones of giant granite in a corner pierced with a hole in the middle, like the wheels of some antique car of colossal size, a dismounted winepress with wooden screws, its brown divisions rendered smooth by wear and tear, and glittering suddenly in the light thrown by the candle on the shadows that surrounded it. Close to it, the working implements of polished steel on the ground had the glitter of arms used in warfare. All these things gradually grew more distinct, as the old man drew nearer to them with the candle in his hand, making a shade of the other.

Already they got the smell of the wine, the pounded grapes drained dry. They arrived in front of a door fastened with two locks. Oriol opened it, and quickly raising the candle above his head vaguely pointed toward a long succession of barrels standing in a row, and having on their swelling flanks a second line of smaller casks. He showed them first of all that this cellar, all on one floor, sank right into the mountain, then he explained the contents of its different casks, the ages, the nature of the various vine-crops, and their merits; then, having reached the supply reserved for the family, he caressed the cask with his hand just as one might rub the crupper of a favorite horse, and in a proud tone said:

"You are going to taste this. There's not a wine bottled equal to it — not one, either at Bordeaux or elsewhere."

For he possessed the intense passion of countrymen for wine kept in a cask.

Colosse followed him, carrying a jug, stooped down, turned the cock of the funnel, while his father cautiously held the light for him, as though he were accomplishing some difficult task requiring minute attention. The candle's flame fell directly on their faces, the father's head like that of an old attorney, and the son's like that of a peasant soldier.

Andermatt murmured in Gontran's ear: "Hey, what a fine Teniers!"

The young man replied in a whisper: "I prefer the girls."

Then they went back into the house. It was necessary, it seemed, to drink this wine, to drink a great deal of it, in order to please the two Oriols.

The lassies had come across to the table where they continued their work as if there had been no visitors. Gontran kept incessantly staring at them, asking himself whether they were twins, so closely did they resemble one another. One of them, however, was plumper and smaller, while the other was more ladylike. Their hair, dark-brown rather than black, drawn over their temples in smooth bands, gleamed with every slight movement of their heads. They had the rather heavy jaw and forehead peculiar to the people of Auvergne, cheekbones some-what strongly marked, but charming mouths, ravishing eyes, with brows of rare neatness, and delightfully fresh complexions. One felt, on looking at them, that they had not been brought up in this house, but in a select boarding-school, in the convent to which the daughters of the aristocracy of Auvergne are sent, and that they had acquired there the well-bred manners of cultivated young ladies.

Meanwhile, Gontran, seized with disgust before this red glass in front of him, pressed Andermatt's foot to induce him to leave. At length he rose, and they both energetically grasped the hands of the two peasants; then they bowed once more ceremoniously, the young girls each responding with a slight nod, without again rising from their seats.

As soon as they had reached the village, Andermatt began talking again. —

"Hey, my dear boy, what an odd family! How manifest here is the transition from people in good society. A son's services are required to cultivate the vine so as to save the wages of a laborer, — stupid economy, — however, he discharges this function, and is one of the people. As for the girls, they are like girls of the better class — almost quite so already.

Let them only make good matches, and they would pass as well as any of the women of our own class, and even much better than most of them. I am as much gratified at seeing these people as a geologist would be at finding an animal of the tertiary period."

Gontran asked: "Which do you prefer?"

"Which? How, which? Which what?"

"Of the lassies?"

"Oh! upon my honor, I haven't an idea on the subject. I have not looked at them from the standpoint of comparison. But what difference can this make to you? You have no intention to carry off one of them?"

Gontran began to laugh: "Oh! no, but I am delighted to meet for once fresh women, really fresh, fresh as women never are with us. I like looking at them, just as you like looking at a Teniers. There is nothing pleases me so much as looking at a pretty girl, no matter where, no matter of what class. These are my objects of vertu. I don't collect them, but I admire them — I admire them passionately, artistically, my friend, in the spirit of a convinced and disinterested artist. What would you have? I love this! By the bye, could you lend me five thousand francs?"

The other stopped, and murmured an "Again!" energetically.

Gentran replied, with an air of simplicity: "Always!" Then they resumed their walk.

Andermatt then said: "What the devil do you do with the money?"

"I spend, it."

"Yes, but you spend it to excess."

"My dear friend, I like spending money as much as you like making it. Do you understand?"

"Very fine, but you don't make it."

"That's true. I know it. One can't have everything. You know how to make it, and, upon my word, you don't at all know how to spend it. Money appears to you no use except to get interest on it. I, on the other hand, don't know how to make it, but I know thoroughly how to spend it. It procures me a thousand things of which you don't know the name. We were cut out for brothers-in-law. We complete one another admirably."

Andermatt murmured: "What stuff! No, you sha'n't have five thousand francs, but I'll lend you fifteen hundred francs, because — because in a few days I shall, perhaps, have need of you."

Gontran rejoined: "Then I accept them on account." The other gave him a slap on the shoulder without saying anything by way of answer.

They reached the park, which was illuminated with lamps hung to the branches of the trees. The orchestra of the Casino was playing in slow time a classical piece that seemed to stagger along, full of breaks and silences, executed by the same four performers, exhausted with constant playing, morning and evening, in this solitude for the benefit of the leaves and the brook, with trying to produce the effect of twenty instruments, and tired also of never being fully paid at the end of the month. Petrus Martel always completed their remuneration, when it fell short, with hampers of wine or pints of liqueurs which the bathers might have left unconsumed.

Amid the noise of the concert could also be distinguished that of the billiard-table, the clicking of the balls and the voices calling out: "Twenty, twenty-one, twenty-two."

Andermatt and Gontran went in. M. Aubry-Pasteur and Doctor Honorat, by themselves, were drinking their coffee, at the side facing the musicians. Petrus Martel and Lapalme were playing their game with desperation; and the female attendant woke up to ask:

"What do these gentlemen wish to take?"

IV

PERE ORIOL and his son had remained for a long time chatting after the girls had gone to bed. Stirred up and excited by Andermatt's proposal, they were considering how they could inflame his desire more effectually without compromising their own interests. Like the cautious, practically-minded peasants that they were, they weighed nil the chances carefully, understanding very clearly that in a country in which mineral springs gushed out along all the streams, it was not advisable to repel by an exaggerated demand this unexpected enthusiast, the like of whom they might never find again. And at the same time it would not do either to leave entirely in his hands this spring, which might, some day, yield a flood of liquid money, Royat and Chatel-Guyon serving as a precedent for them.

Therefore, they asked themselves by what course of action they could kindle into frenzy the banker's ardor; they conjured up combinations of imaginary companies covering his offers, a succession of clumsy schemes, the defects of which they felt, without succeeding in inventing more ingenious ones. They slept badly; then, in the morning, the father, having awakened first, thought in his own mind that the spring might have disappeared during the night. It was possible, after all, that it might have gone as it had come, and reentered the earth, so that it could not be brought back. He got up in a state of unrest, seized with avaricious fear, shook his son, and told him about his alarm; and big Colosse, dragging his legs out of his coarse sheets, dressed himself in order to go out with his father, to make sure about the matter.

In any case, they would put the field and the spring in proper trim themselves, would carry off the stones, and make it nice and clean, like an animal that they wanted to sell. So they took their picks and their spades, and started for the spot side by side with great, swinging strides.

They looked at nothing as they walked on, their minds being preoccupied with the business, replying with only a single word to the "Good morning" of the neighbors and friends whom they chanced to meet. When they reached the Riom road they began to get agitated, peering into the distance to see whether they could observe the water bubbling up and glittering in the morning sun. The road was empty, white, and dusty, the river running beside it sheltered by willow-trees. Beneath one of the trees Oriol suddenly noticed two feet, then, having advanced three steps further, he recognized Père Clovis seated at the edge of the road, with his crutches lying beside him on the grass.

This was an old paralytic, well known in the district, where for the last ten years he had prowled about on his supports of stout oak, as he said himself, like a poor man made of stone.

Formerly a poacher in the woods and streams, often arrested and imprisoned, he had got rheumatic pains by his long watchings stretched on the moist grass and by his nocturnal fishings in the rivers, through which he used to wade up to his middle in water. Now he whined, and crawled about, like a crab that had lost its claws. He stumped along, dragging his right leg after him like a piece of ragged cloth. But the boys of the neighborhood, who used in foggy weather to run after the girls or the hares, declared that they used to meet Père Clovis, swiftfooted as a stag, and supple as an adder, under the bushes and in the glades, and that, in short, his rheumatism was only "a dodge on the gendarmes." Colosse, especially, insisted on maintaining that he had seen him, not once, but fifty times, straining his neck with his crutches under his arms.

And Père Oriol stopped in front of the old vagabond, his mind possessed by an idea which as yet was undefined, for the brain works slowly in the thick skulls of Auvergne. He said "Good morning" to him. The other responded "Good morning." Then they spoke about the weather, the ripening of the vine, and two or three other things; but, as Colosse had gone ahead, his father with long steps hastened to overtake him.

The spring was still flowing, clear by this time, and all the bottom of the hole was red, a fine, dark red, which had arisen from an abundant deposit of iron. The two men gazed at it with smiling faces, then they proceeded to clear the soil that surrounded it, and to carry off the stones of which they made a heap. And, having found the last remains of the dead dog, they buried them with jocose remarks. But all of a sudden Père Oriol let his spade fall. A roguish leer of delight and triumph wrinkled the corners of his leathery lips and the edges of his cunning eyes, and he said to his son: "Come on, till we see." The other obeyed. They got on the road once more, and retraced their steps. Père Clovis was still toasting his limbs and his crutches in the sun.

Oriol, drawing up before him, asked: "Do you want to earn a hundred-franc piece?"

The other cautiously refrained from answering.

The peasant said: "Hey! a hundred francs?" Thereupon the vagabond made up his mind, and murmured: "Of course, but what am I asked to do?"

"Well, father, here's what I want you to do." And he explained to the other at great length with tricky circumlocutions, easily understood hints, and innumerable repetitions, that, if he would consent to take a bath for an hour every day from ten to eleven in a hole which they, Colosse and he, intended to dig at the side of the spring, and to be cured at the end of a month, they would give him a hundred francs in cash.

The paralytic listened with a stupid air, and then said: "Since all the drugs haven't been able to help me, 'tisn't your water that'll cure me."

But Colosse suddenly got into a passion. "Come, my old play-actor, you're talking rubbish. I know what your disease is — don't tell me about it' What were you doing on Monday last in the Comberombe wood at eleven o'clock at night?"

The old fellow promptly answered: "That's not true."

But Colosse, firing up: "Isn't it true, you old blackguard, that you jumped over the ditch to Jean Cannezat and that you made your way along the Paulin chasm?"

The other energetically repeated: "It is not true!"

"Isn't it true that I called out to you: 'Oho, Clovis, the gendarmes!' and that you turned up the Moulinet road?"

"No, it is not."

Big Jacques, raging, almost menacing, exclaimed: "Ah! it's not true! Well, old three paws, listen! The next time I see you there in the wood at night or else in the water, I'll take a grip of you, as my legs are rather longer than your own, and I'll tie you up to some tree till morning, when we'll go and take you away, the whole village together — "

Père Oriol stopped his son; then, in a very wheedling tone: "Listen, Clovis! you can easily do the thing. We prepare a bath for you, Coloche and myself. You come there every day for a month. For that I give you, not one hundred, but two hundred francs. And then, listen! if you're cured at the end of the month, it will mean five hundred francs more. Understand clearly, five hundred in ready money, and two hundred more — that makes seven hundred. Therefore you get two hundred for taking a bath for a month and five hundred more for the curing. And listen again! Suppose the pains come back. If this happens you in the autumn, there will be nothing more for us to do, for the water will have none the less produced its effect!"

The old fellow coolly replied: "In that case I'm quite willing. If it won't succeed, we'll always see it." And the three men pressed one another's hands to seal the bargain they had concluded. Then, the two Oriols returned to their spring, in order to dig the bath for Père Clovis.

They had been working at it for a quarter of an hour, when they heard voices on the road. It was Andermatt and Doctor Latonne. The two peasants winked at one another, and ceased digging the soil.

The banker came across to them, and grasped their hands; then the entire four proceeded to fix their eyes on the water without uttering a word. It stirred about like water set in movement above a big fire, threw out bubbles and steam, then it flowed away in the direction of the brook through a tiny gutter which it had already traced out. Oriol, with a smile of pride on his lips, said suddenly: "Hey, that's iron, isn't it?"

In fact the bottom was now all red, and even the little pebbles which it washed as it flowed along seemed covered with a sort of purple mold.

Doctor Latonne replied: "Yes, but that is nothing to the purpose. We would require to know its other qualities."

The peasant observed: "Coloche and myself first drank a glass of it yesterday evening, and it has already made our bodies feel fresh. Isn't that true, son?"

The big youth replied in a tone of conviction: "Sure enough, it was very refreshing."

Andermatt remained motionless, his feet on the edge of the hole. He turned toward the physician: "We would want nearly six times this volume of water for what I would wish to do, would we not?"

"Yes, nearly."

"Do you think that we'll be able to get it?"

"Oh! as for me, I know nothing about it."

"See here! The purchase of the grounds can only be definitely effected after the soundings. It would be necessary, first of all, to have a promise of sale drawn up by a notary, once the analysis is known, but not to take effect unless the consecutive soundings give the results hoped for."

Père Oriol became restless. He did not understand. Andermatt thereupon explained to him the insufficiency of only one spring, and demonstrated to him that he could not purchase unless he found others. But he could not search for these other springs till after the signature of a promise of sale.

The two peasants appeared forthwith to be convinced that their fields contained as many springs as vine-stalks. It would be sufficient to dig for them — they would see, they would see.

Andermatt said simply: "Yes, we shall see."

But Père Oriol dipped his fingers in the water, and remarked: "Why, 'tis hot enough to boil an egg, much hotter than the Bonnefille one!"

Latonne in his turn steeped his fingers in it, and realized that this was possible.

The peasant went on: "And then it has more taste and a better taste; it hasn't a false taste, like the other. Oh! this one, I'll answer for it, is good!

I know the waters of the country for the fifty years that I've seen them flowing. I never seen a finer one than this, never, never!"

He remained silent for a few seconds, and then continued: "It is not in order to puff the water that I say this! — certainly not. I would like to make a trial of it before you, a fair trial, not what your chemists make, but a trial of it on a person who has a disease. I'll bet that it will cure a paralytic, this one, so hot is it and so good to taste — I'll make a bet on it!"

He appeared to be searching his brain, then cast a look at the tops of the neighboring mountains to see whether he could discover the paralytic that he required. Not having made the discovery, he lowered his eyes to the road.

Two hundred meters away from it, at the side of the road could be distinguished the two inert legs of the vagabond, whose body was hidden by the trunk of a willow tree.

Oriol placed his hand on his forehead as a shade, and said questioningly to his son: "That isn't Père Clovis over there still?"

Colosse laughingly replied: "Yes, yes. 'Tis he — he doesn't go as quick as a hare."

Then Oriol stepped over to Andermatt's side, and with an air of serious and deep conviction: "Look here, Monchieu! Listen to me. There's a paralytic over yonder, who is well known to the doctor, a genuine one, who hasn't been seen to make a single step for the last ten years. Isn't that so, doctor?"

Latonne returned: "Oh! if you cure that fellow, I would pay a franc a glass for your water!"

Then, turning toward Andermatt: "'Tis an old fellow suffering from rheumatic gout with a sort of spasmodic contraction of the left leg and a complete paralysis of the right; in fact, I believe, an incurable."

Oriol had allowed him to talk; he resumed in a deliberate fashion: "Well, doctor, would you like to make a trial of it on him for a month? I don't say that it will succeed, — I say nothing on the matter, — I only ask to have a trial made. Hold on! Coloche and myself are going to dig a hole for the stones — well, we'll make a hole for Cloviche; he'll remain an hour there every morning, and then we'll see — there!

— — we'll see."

The physician murmured: "You may try. I answer confidently that you will not succeed."

But Andermatt, beguiled by the prospect of an almost miraculous cure, gladly fell in with the peasant's suggestion; and the entire four directed their steps toward the vagabond, who, all this time, had been lying motionless in the sun. The old poacher, understanding the dodge, pretended to refuse, resisted for a long time, then allowed himself to be persuaded, on the condition that Andermatt would give him two francs a day for the hour which he would spend in the water.

So the matter was settled. It was even decided that, as soon as the hole was dug, Père Clovis should take his bath that very day. Andermatt would supply him with clothes to dress himself afterward, and the two Oriols would bring him a disused shepherd's hut, which was lying in their yard, so that the invalid might shut himself in there, and change his apparel.

Then the banker and the physician returned to the village. When they reached it, they parted, the doctor going to his own house for his consultations, and Andermatt hurrying to attend on his wife, who had to come to the establishment at half past nine o'clock.

She appeared almost immediately, dressed from head to foot in pink — with a pink hat, a pink parasol, and a pink complexion, she looked like an aurora, and she descended the steps of the hotel to avoid the turn of the road with the hopping movements of a bird, as it goes from stone to stone, without opening its wing. As soon as she saw her husband, she exclaimed:

"Oh! what a pretty country it is! I am quite delighted with it."

A few bathers wandering sadly through the little park in silence turned round as she passed by, and Petrus Martel, who was smoking his pipe in his shirtsleeves at the window of the billiard-room, called to his chum, Lapalme, sitting in a corner before a glass of white wine, and said, smacking the roof of his mouth with his tongue:

"Deuce take it, there's something sweet!" Christiane made her way into the establishment, bowed smilingly toward the cashier, who sat at the left of the entrance-door, and saluted the ex-jailer seated at the right with a "Good morning"; then, holding out a ticket to a bath-attendant dressed like the girl in the refreshment-room, followed her into a corridor facing the doors of the bathrooms. The lady was shown into one of them, rather large, with bare walls, furnished with a chair, a glass, and a shoe-horn, while a large oval orifice, coated, like the floor, with yellow cement, served the purposes of a bath.

The woman turned a cock like those used for making the street-gutters flow, and the water gushed through a little round grated aperture at the bottom of the bath so that it was soon full to the brim, and its overflow was diverted through a furrow sunk into the wall.

Christiane, having left her chambermaid at the hotel, declined the attendant's services in undressing, and remained there alone, saying that if she required anything, she would ring, and would do the same when she wanted her linen.

She slowly disrobed, watching as she did so the almost invisible movement of the wave gently stirring on the clear surface of the basin. When she had divested herself of all her clothing she dipped her foot in, and the pleasant warm sensation mounted to her throat; then she plunged into the tepid water first one leg, and after it the other, and sat down in the midst of this caressing heat, in this transparent bath, in this spring, which flowed over her, around her, covering her body with tiny globules all along her legs, all along her arms, and also all over her breasts. She noticed with surprise those particles of air innumerable and minute which clothed her from head to foot with an entire mail-suit of little pearls. And these pearls, so minute, flew off incessantly from her white flesh, and evaporated on the surface of the bath, driven on by others that sprung to life over her form. They sprung up over her skin, like light fruits incapable of being grasped yet charming, the fruits of this exquisite body rosy and fresh, which had generated those pearls in the water.

And Christiane felt herself so happy in it, so sweetly, so softly, so deliciously caressed and clasped by the restless wave, the living wave, the animated wave from the spring which gushed up from the depths of the basin under her legs and fled through the little opening toward the edge of the bath, that she would have liked to have remained there forever, without moving, almost without thinking. The sensation of a calm delight composed of rest and comfort, of tranquil dreamfulness, of health, of discreet joy, and silent gaiety, entered into her with the soothing warmth of this. And her spirit mused, vaguely lulled into repose by the gurgling of the overflow which was escaping — dreamed of what she would be doing by and by, of what she would be doing tomorrow, of promenades, of her father, of her husband, of her brother, and of that big boy who had made her feel slightly ill at ease since the adventure of the dog. She did not care for persons of violent tendencies.

No desire agitated her soul, calm as her heart in this grateful moist warmth, no desires save the shadowy hopes of a child, no desire of any other life, of emotion, or passion. She felt that it was well with her, and she was satisfied with the happiness of her lot.

She was suddenly startled — the door flew open; it was the Auvergnat carrying the linen. Twenty minutes had passed; it was already time for her to be dressed. It was almost a pang, almost a calamity, this awakening; she felt a longing to beg of the woman to give her a few minutes more; then she reflected that every day she would find again the same delight, and she regretfully left the bath to be wrapped in a white dressing-gown whose scorching heat felt somewhat unpleasant.

Just as she was going out, Doctor Bonnefille opened the door of his consultation-room and invited her to enter, bowing ceremoniously. He inquired about her health, felt her pulse, looked at her tongue, took note of her appetite and her digestion, asked her how she slept, and then accompanied her to the door, repeating:

"Come, come, that's right, that's right. My respects, if you please, to your father, one of the most distinguished men that I have met in my career."

At last, she got away, bored by these undesirable attentions, and at the door she saw the Marquis chatting with Andermatt, Gontran, and Paul Bretigny. Her husband, in whose head every new idea was continually buzzing, like a fly in a bottle, was relating the story of the paralytic, and wanted to go back to see whether the vagabond was taking his bath. They were about to go with him to the spot in order to please him. But Christiane very gently detained her brother, and, when they were a short distance away from the others:

"Tell me now! I wanted to talk to you about your friend; I must say I don't much care for him. Explain to me exactly what he is like."

And Gontran, who had known Paul for many years, told her about this passionate nature, uncouth, sincere, and kindly by starts. He was, according to Gontran, a clever young fellow, whose wild spirit impetuously flung itself into every new idea. Yielding to every impulse, unable to control or to direct his passions, or to fight against his feelings with the aid of reason, or to govern his life by a system based on settled convictions, he obeyed the promptings of his heart, whether they were virtuous or vicious, the moment that any desire, any thought, any emotion whatever, agitated his excitable nature.

He had already fought seven duels, as ready to insult people as to become their friend. He had been madly in love with women of every class, adored them with the same transports from the working-girl whom he picked up in the corner of some store to the actress whom he carried off, yes, carried off, on the night of a first performance, just as she was stepping into a vehicle on her way home, bearing her away in his arms in the midst of the astonished spectators, and pushing her into a carriage, which disappeared at a gallop before anyone could follow it or overtake it.

And Gontran concluded: "There you are! He is a good fellow, but a fool; very rich, moreover, and capable of anything, of anything at all, when he loses his head."

Christiane said: "What a strange perfume he carries about him! It is rather nice. What is it?"

Gontran answered: "I don't really know; he doesn't want to tell about it. I believe it comes from Russia. 'Tis the actress, his actress, she whom I cured him of this time, that gave it to him. Yes, indeed, it has a very pleasant odor."

They saw, on their way, a group of bathers and of peasants, for it was the custom every morning before breakfast to take a turn along the road.

Christiane and Gontran joined the Marquis, Andermatt, and Paul, and soon they beheld, in the place where the knoll had stood the day before, a queer-looking human head covered with a ragged felt hat, and wearing a big white beard, looking as if it had sprung up out of the ground, the head of a decapitated man, as it were, growing there like a plant. Around it, some vinedressers were looking on, amazed, impassive, the peasantry of Auvergne not being scoffers, while three tall gentlemen, visitors at second-class hotels, were laughing and joking.

Oriol and his son stood there contemplating the vagabond, who was steeped in his hole, sitting on a stone, with the water up to his chin. He might have been taken for a desperate criminal of olden times condemned to death for some unusual kind of sorcery; and he had not let go his crutches, which were by his sides in the water.

Andermatt kept repeating enthusiastically: "Bravo! bravo! there's an example which all the people in the country suffering from rheumatic pains should imitate."

And, bending toward the old man, he shouted at him as if he were deaf: "Do you feel well?"

The other, who seemed completely stupefied by this boiling water, replied: "It seems to me that I'm melting!"

But Père Oriol exclaimed: "The hotter it is, the more good it will do you."

A voice behind the Marquis said: "What is that?"

And M. Aubry-Pasteur, always puffing, stopped on his way back from his daily walk. Then Andermatt explained his experiment in curing. But the old man kept repeating: "Devil take it! how hot it is!" And he wanted to get out, asking some one to help him up. The banker succeeded eventually in calming him by promising him twenty sous more for each bath. The

spectators formed a circle round the hole, in which the dirty, grayish rags were soaking wherewith this old body was covered.

A voice said: "Nice meat for broth! I wouldn't care to make soup of it!"

Another rejoined: "The meat would scarcely agree with me!"

But the Marquis observed that the bubbles of carbonic acid seemed more numerous, larger,
and brighter in this new spring than in that of the baths.

The vagabond's rags were covered with them; and these bubbles rose to the surface in such
abundance that the water appeared to be crossed by innumerable little chains, by an infinity
of beads of exceedingly small, round diamonds, the strong midday sun making them as clear
as brilliants.

Then Aubry-Pasteur burst out laughing: "Egad," said he, "I must tell you what they do at
the establishment. You know they catch a spring like a bird in a kind of snare, or rather in a
bell. That's what they call coaxing it. Now last year here is what happened to the spring that
supplies the baths. The carbonic acid, lighter than water, was stored up to the top of the bell;
then, when it was collected there in a very large quantity, it was driven back into the ducts,
reascended in abundance into the baths, filled up the compartments, and all but suffocated the
invalids. We have had three accidents in the course of three months. Then they consulted me
again, and I invented a very simple apparatus consisting of two pipes which led off separately
the liquid and the gas in the bell in order to combine them afresh immediately under the bath,
and thus to reconstitute the water in its normal state while avoiding the dangerous excess of
carbonic acid. But my apparatus would have cost a thousand francs. Do you know what the
custodian does then? I give you a thousand guesses to find out. He bores a hole in the bell
to get rid of the gas, which flies out, you understand, so that they sell you acidulated baths
without any acid, or so little acid that it is not worth much. Whereas here, why just look!"

Everybody became indignant. They no longer laughed, and they cast envious looks toward
the paralytic. Every bather would gladly have seized a pickax to make another hole beside that
of the vagabond. But Andermatt took the engineer's arm, and they went off chatting together.
From time to time Aubry-Pasteur stopped, made a show of drawing lines with his walking-stick,
indicating certain points, and the banker wrote down notes in a memorandum-book.

Christiane and Paul Bretigny entered into conversation. He told her about his journey to
Auvergne, and all that he had seen and experienced. He loved the country, with those warm
instincts of his, with which always mingled an element of animality. He had a sensual love of
nature because it excited his blood, and made his nerves and organs quiver. He said: "For my
part, Madame, it seems to me as if I were open, so that everything enters into me, everything
passes through me, makes me weep or gnash my teeth. Look here! when I cast a glance at that
hillside facing us, that vast expanse of green, that race of trees clambering up the mountain,
I feel the entire wood in my eyes; it penetrates me, takes possession of me, runs through my
whole frame; and it seems to me also that I am devouring it, that it fills my being — I become
a wood myself!"

He laughed, while he told her this, strained his big, round eyes, now on the wood, now on
Christiane; and she, surprised, astonished, but easily impressed, felt herself devoured also, like
the wood, by his great avid glance.

Paul went on: "And if you only knew what delights I owe to my sense of smell. I drink in
this air through my nostrils. I become intoxicated with it; I live in it, and I feel that there is
within it everything — absolutely everything. What can be sweeter? It intoxicates one more
than wine; wine intoxicates the mind, but perfume intoxicates the imagination. With perfume
you taste the very essence, the pure essence of things and of the universe — you taste the flowers,
the trees, the grass of the fields; you can even distinguish the soul of the dwellings of olden
days which sleep in the old furniture, the old carpets, the old curtains. Listen! I am going
to tell you something.

"Did you notice, when first you came here, a delicious odor, to which no other odor can be compared — — so fine, so light, that it seems almost — how shall I express it? — an immaterial odor? You find it everywhere — you can seize it nowhere — you cannot discern where it comes from. Never, never has anything more divine than it arisen in my heart. Well, this is the odor of the vine in bloom. Ah! it has taken me four days to discover it. And is it not charming to think, Madame, that the vine-tree, which gives us wine, wine which only superior spirits can understand and relish, gives us, too, the most delicate and most exciting of perfumes, which only persons of the most refined sensibility can discover? And then do you recognize also the powerful smell of the chestnut-trees, the luscious savor of the acacias, the aroma of the mountains, and the grass, whose scent is so sweet, so sweet — sweeter than anyone imagines?"

She listened to these words of his in amazement, not that they were surprising so much as that they appeared so different in their nature from everything encompassing her every day. Her mind remained possessed, moved, and disturbed by them.

He kept talking uninterruptedly in a voice somewhat hollow but full of passion.

"And again, just think, do you not feel in the air, along the roads, when the day is hot, a slight savor of vanilla. Yes, am I not right? Well, that is — that is — but I dare not tell it to you!"

And now he broke into a great laugh, and waving his hand in front of him all of a sudden said: "Look there!"

A row of wagons laden with hay was coming up drawn by cows yoked in pairs. The slow-footed beasts, with their heads hung down, bent by the yoke, their horns fastened with pieces of wood, toiled painfully along; and under their skin, as it rose up and down, the bones of their legs could be seen moving. Before each team, a man in shirtsleeves, waistcoat, and black hat, was walking with a switch in his hand, directing the pace of the animals. From time to time the driver would turn round, and, without ever hitting, would barely touch the shoulder or the forehead of a cow who would blink her big, wandering eyes, and obey the motion of his arm. Christiane and Paul drew up to let them pass.

He said to her: "Do you feel it?"

She was amazed: "What then? That is the smell of the stable."

"Yes, it is the smell of the stable; and all these cows going along the roads — for they use no horses in this part of the country — scatter on their way that odor of the stable, which, mingled with the fine dust, gives to the wind a savor of vanilla."

Christiane, somewhat disgusted, murmured: "Oh!" He went on: "Excuse me, at that moment, I was analyzing it like a chemist. In any case, we are, Madame, in the most seductive country, the most delightful, the most restful, that I have ever seen — a country of the golden age. And the Limagne — oh! the Limagne! But I must not talk to you about it; I want to show it to you. You shall see for yourself."

The Marquis and Gontran came up to them. The Marquis passed his arm under that of his daughter, and, making her turn round and retrace her steps, in order to get back to the hotel for breakfast, he said: "Listen, young people! this concerns you all three. William, who goes mad when an idea comes into his head, dreams of nothing any longer but of building this new town of his, and he wants to win over to him the Oriol family. He is, therefore, anxious that Christiane should make the acquaintance of the two young girls, in order to see if they are 'possible.' But it is not necessary that the father should suspect our ruse. So I have got an idea; it is to organize a charitable fête. You, my dear, must go and see the curé; you will together hunt up two of his parishioners to make collections along with you. You understand what people you will get him to nominate, and he will invite them on his own responsibility. As for you, young men, you are going to get up a tombola at the Casino with the assistance of

Petrus Martel with his company and orchestra. And if the little Oriols are nice girls, as it is said they have been well brought up at the convent, Christiane will make a conquest of them."

V

For eight days, Christiane wholly occupied herself with preparations for this fete. The curé, indeed, was able to find no one among his female parishioners except the Oriol girls who could be deemed worthy of collecting along with the Marquis de Ravenel's daughter; and, happy at having the opportunity of making himself prominent, he took all the necessary steps, organized everything, regulated everything, and himself invited the young girls, as if the idea had originated with him.

The inhabitants were in a state of excitement, and the gloomy bathers, finding a new topic of conversation, entertained one another at the table d'hôte with various estimates as to the possible receipts from the two portions of the fête, the sacred and the profane.

The day opened finely. It was admirable summer weather, warm and clear, with bright sunshine in the open plain and a grateful shade under the village trees. The mass was fixed for nine o'clock — a quick mass with Church music. Christiane, who had arrived before the office, in order to inspect the ornamentation of the church with garlands of flowers that had been sent from Royat and Clermont-Ferrand, consented to walk behind it. The curé, Abbé Litre, followed her accompanied by the Oriol girls, and he introduced them to her. Christiane immediately invited the young girls to luncheon. They accepted her invitation with blushes and respectful bows.

The faithful were now making their appearance. Christiane and her girls sat down on three chairs of honor reserved for them at the side of the choir, facing three other chairs, which were occupied by young lads dressed in their Sunday clothes, sons of the mayor, of the deputy, and of a municipal councilor, selected to accompany the lady-collectors and to flatter the local authorities. Everything passed off well.

The office was short. The collection realized one hundred and ten francs, which, added to Andermatt's five hundred francs, the Marquis's fifty francs, and a hundred francs contributed by Paul Bretigny, made a total of seven hundred and sixty, an amount never before reached in the parish of Enval. Then, after the conclusion of the ceremony, the Oriol girls were brought to the hotel. They appeared to be a little abashed, without any display of awkwardness, however, and scarcely uttered one word, through modesty rather than through timidity. They sat down to luncheon at the table d'hôte, and pleased the merry all the men.

The elder the more serious of the pair, the younger the more sprightly, the elder better bred, in the commonplace acceptation of the word, the younger more pleasant, they yet resembled one another as closely as two sisters possibly could.

As soon as the meal was finished, they repaired to the Casino for the lottery-drawing at the tombola, which was fixed for two o'clock.

The park, already invaded by the mixed crowd of bathers and peasants, presented the aspect of an out landish fête.

Under their Chinese kiosque the musicians were executing a rural symphony, a work composed by Saint Landri himself. Paul, who accompanied Christiane, suddenly drew up:

"Look here!" said he, "that's pretty! He has some talent, that chap! With an orchestra, he could produce a fine effect."

Then he asked: "Are you fond of music, Madame?"

"Exceedingly."

"As for me, it overwhelms me. When I am listening to a work that I like, it seems to me first that the opening notes detach my skin from my flesh, melt it, dissolve it, cause it to disappear, and leave me like one flayed alive, under the combined attacks of the instruments. And in fact it is on my nerves that the orchestra is playing, on my nerves stripped bare, vibrating, trembling at every note.! hear it, the music, not merely with my ears, but with all the sensibility of my body quivering from head to foot. Nothing gives me such exquisite pleasure, or rather such exquisite happiness."

She smiled, and then said: "Your sensibilities are keen."

"By Jove, they are! What is the good of living if one has not keen sensibilities? I do not envy those people who wear over their hearts a tortoise's shell or a hippopotamus's hide. Those alone are happy who feel their sensations acutely, who receive them like shocks, and savor them like dainty morsels. For it is necessary to reason out all our emotions, joyous and sad, to be satiated with them, to be intoxicated with them to the most intense degree of bliss or the most extreme pitch of suffering."

She raised her eyes to look up at his face, with that sense of astonishment which she had experienced during the past eight days at all the things that he said. Indeed, during these eight days, this new friend — for, despite her repugnance toward him, on first acquaintance, he had in this short interval become her friend — was every moment shaking the tranquillity of her soul, and disturbing it as a pool of water is disturbed by flinging stones into it. And he flung stones, big stones, into this soul which had calmly slumbered until now.

Christiane's father, like all fathers, had always treated her as a little girl, to whom one ought not to say anything of a serious nature; her brother made her laugh rather than reflect; her husband did not consider it right for a man to speak of anything whatever to his wife outside the interests of their common life; and so she had hitherto lived perfectly contented, her mind steeped in a sweet torpor.

This newcomer opened her intellect with ideas which fell upon it like strokes of a hatchet. Moreover, he was one of those men who please women, all women, by his very nature, by the vibrating acuteness of his emotions. He knew how to talk to them, to tell them everything, and he made them understand everything. Incapable of continuous effort but extremely intelligent, always loving or hating passionately, speaking of everything with the ingenious ardor of a man fanatically convinced, variable as he was enthusiastic, he possessed to an excessive degree the true feminine temperament, the credulity, the charm, the mobility, the nervous sensibility of a woman, with the superior intellect, active, comprehensive, and penetrating, of a man.

Gontran came up to them in a hurry. "Come back," said he, "and give a look at the Honorât family."

They returned, and saw Doctor Honorât, accompanied by a fat, old woman in a blue dress, whose head looked like a nursery-garden, for every variety of plants and flowers were gathered together on her head.

Christiane asked in astonishment: "This is his wife, then? But she is fifteen years older than her husband."

"Yes, she is sixty-five — an old midwife whom he fell in love with between two confinements. This, however, is one of those households in which they are nagging at one another from morning till night."

They made their way toward the Casino, attracted by the exclamations of the crowd. On a large table, in front of the establishment, were displayed the lots of the tombola, which were drawn by Petrus Martel, assisted by Mademoiselle Odelin of the Odéon, a very small brunette, who also announced the numbers, with mountebank's tricks, which greatly diverted the spectators. The Marquis, accompanied by the Oriol girls and Andermatt, reappeared, and asked: "Are we to remain here? It is very noisy." —

They accordingly resolved to take a walk halfway up the hill on the road from Enval to La Roche-Pradière. In order to reach it, they first ascended, one behind the other, a narrow path through vine-trees. Christiane walked on in front with a light and rapid step. Since her arrival in this neighborhood, she felt as if she existed in a new sort of way, with an active sense of enjoyment and of vitality which she had never known before. Perhaps, the baths, by improving her health, and so ridding her of that slight disturbance of the vital organs which annoyed and saddened her without any apparent cause, disposed her to perceive and to relish everything more thoroughly. Perhaps she simply felt herself animated, lashed by the presence and by the ardor of spirit of that unknown youth who had taught her how to understand. She drew a long, deep breath, as she thought of all he had said to her about the perfumes that were scattered through the atmosphere. "It is true," she mused, "that he has shown me how to feel the air." And she found again all the odors, especially that of the vine, so light, so delicate, so fleeting.

She gained the level road, and they formed themselves into groups. Andermatt and Louise Oriol, the elder girl, started first side by side, chatting about the produce of lands in Auvergne. She knew, this Auvergnat, true daughter of her sire, endowed with the hereditary instinct, all the correct and practical details of agriculture, and she spoke about them in her grave tone, in the ladylike fashion, and with the careful pronunciation which they had taught her at the convent. While listening to her, he cast a side glance at her, every now and then, and thought this little girl quite charming with her gravity of manner and her mind so full already of practical knowledge. He occasionally repeated with some surprise: "What! is the land in the Limagne worth so much as thirty thousand francs for each hectare?"

"Yes, Monsieur, when it is planted with beautiful apple-trees, which supply dessert apples. It is our country which furnishes nearly all the fruit used in Paris."

Then, they turned back in order to make a more careful estimate of the Limagne, for from the road they were pursuing they could see, as far as their eyes could reach, the vast plain always covered with a light haze of blue vapor.

Christiane and Paul also halted in front of this immense veiled tract of country, so agreeable to the eye that they would have liked to remain there incessantly gazing at it. The road was bordered by enormous walnut-trees, the dense shade of which made the skin feel a refreshing sensation of coolness. It no longer ascended, but took a winding course halfway up on the slope of the hillside adorned lower down with a tapestry of vines, and then with short green herbage as far as the crest, which at this point looked rather steep.

Paul murmured: "Is it not lovely? Tell me, is it not lovely? And why does this landscape move me? Yes, why? It diffuses a charm so profound, so wide, that it penetrates to my very heart. It seems, as you gaze at this plain, that thought opens its wings, does it not? And it flies away, it soars, it passes on, it goes off there below, farther and farther, toward all the countries seen in dreams which we shall never see. Yes, see here, this is worthy of admiration because it is much more like a thing we dream of than a thing that we have seen."

She listened to him without saying anything, waiting, expectant, gathering up each of his words; and she felt herself affected without too well knowing how to explain her emotions. She caught glimpses, indeed, of other countries, blue countries, rose-hued countries, countries unlikely and marvelous, countries undiscoverable though ever sought for, which make us look upon all others as commonplace.

He went on: "Yes, it is lovely, because it is lovely. Other horizons are more striking but less harmonious. Ah! Madame, beauty, harmonious beauty! There is nothing but that in the world. Nothing exists but beauty. But how few understand it! The line of a body, of a statue, or of a mountain, the color of a painting or of that plain, the inexpressible something of the 'Joconde,' a phrase that bites you to the soul, that — nothing more — which makes an artist a creator just like God, which, therefore, distinguishes him among men. Wait! I am going to recite for you two stanzas of Baudelaire."

And he declaimed:

> "Whether you come from heaven or hell I do not care,
> O Beauty, monster of splendor and terror, yet sweet at the core,
> As long as your eye, your smile, your feet lay the infinite bare,
> Unveiling a world of love that I never have known before!
>
> "From Satan or God, what matter, whether angel or siren you be,
> What matter if you can give, enchanting, velvet-eyed fay,

Rhythm, perfume, and light, and be queen of the earth for me,
And make all things less hideous, and the sad moments fly away."

Christiane now was gazing at him, struck with wonder by his lyricism, questioning him with her eyes, not comprehending well what extraordinary meaning might be embodied in this poetry. He divined her thoughts, and was irritated at not having communicated his own enthusiasm to her, for he had recited those verses very effectively, and he resumed, with a shade of disdain:

"I am a fool to wish to force you to relish a poet of such subtle inspiration. A day will come, I hope, when you will feel those things just as I do. Women, endowed rather with intuition than comprehension, do not seize the secret and veiled purposes of art in the same way as if a sympathetic appeal had first been made to their minds."

And, with a bow, he added: "I will strive, Madame, to make this sympathetic appeal."

She did not think him impertinent, but fantastic; and moreover she did not seek any longer to understand, suddenly struck by a circumstance which she had not previously noticed: he was very elegant, though he was a little too tall and too strongly-built, with a gait so virile that one could not immediately perceive the studied refinement of his attire. And then his head had a certain brutishness about it, an incompleteness, which gave to his entire person a somewhat heavy aspect at first glance. But when one had got accustomed to his features, one found in them some charm, a charm powerful and fierce, which at moments became very pleasant according to the inflections of his voice, which always seemed veiled.

Christiane said to herself, as she observed for the first time what attention he had paid to his external appearance from head to foot: "Decidedly this is a man whose qualities must be discovered one by one."

But here Gontran came rushing toward them. He exclaimed: "Sister, I say, Christiane, wait!" And when he had overtaken them, he said to them, still laughing: "Oh! just come and listen to the younger Oriol girl! She is as droll as anything — she has wonderful wit. Papa has succeeded in putting her at her ease, and she has been telling us the most comical things in the world. Wait for them."

And they awaited the Marquis, who presently appeared with the younger of the two girls, Charlotte Oriol. She was relating with a childlike, knowing liveliness some village tales, accounts of rustic simplicity and roguery. And she imitated them with their slow movements, their grave remarks, their "fouchtras," their innumerable "bougrres," mimicking, in a fashion that made her pretty, sprightly face look charming, all the changes of their physiognomies. Her bright eyes sparkled; her rather large mouth was opened wide, displaying her white teeth; her nose, a little tip-tilted, gave her a humorous look; and she was fresh, with a flower's freshness that might make lips quiver with desire.

The Marquis, having spent nearly his entire life on his estate, in the family château where Christiane and Gontran had been brought up in the midst of rough, big Norman farmers who were occasionally invited to dine there, in accordance with custom, and whose children, companions of theirs from the period of their first communion, had been on terms of familiarity with them, knew how to talk to this little girl, already three-fourths a woman of the world, with a friendly candor which awakened at once in her a gay and self-confident assurance.

Andermatt and Louise returned after having walked as far as the village, which they did not care to enter. And they all sat down at the foot of a tree, on the grassy edge of a ditch. There they remained for a long time pleasantly chatting about everything and nothing in a torpor of languid ease. Now and then, a wagon would roll past, always drawn by the two cows whose heads were bent and twisted by the yoke, and always driven by a peasant with a shrunken frame and a big black hat on his head, guiding the animals with the end of his thin switch in the swaying style of the conductor of an orchestra.

The man would take off his hat, bowing to the Oriol girls, and they would reply with a familiar, "Good day," flung out by their fresh young voices.

Then, as the hour was growing late, they went back. As they drew near the park, Charlotte Oriol exclaimed: "Oh! the boree! the boree!" In fact, the boree was being danced to an old air well known in Auvergne.

There they were, male and female peasants stepping out, hopping, making courtesies, — turning and bowing to each other, — the women taking hold of their petticoats and lifting them up with two fingers of each hand, the men swinging their arms or holding them akimbo. The pleasant monotonous air was also dancing in the fresh evening wind; it was always the same refrain played in a very high note by the violin, and taken up in concert by the other instruments, giving a more rattling pace to the dance. And it was not unpleasant, this simple rustic music, lively and artless, keeping time as it did with this shambling country minuet.

The bathers, too, made an attempt to dance. Petrus Martel went skipping in front of little Odelin, who affected the style of a danseuse walking through a ballet, and the comic Lapalme mimicked a fantastic step round the attendant at the Casino, who seemed agitated by recollections of Bullier.

But suddenly Gontran saw Doctor Honorat dancing away with all his heart and all his limbs, and executing the classical boree like a true-blue native of Auvergne.

The orchestra became silent. All stopped. The doctor came over and bowed to the Marquis. He was wiping his forehead and puffing.

"'Tis good," said he, "to be young sometimes." Gontran laid his hand on the doctor's shoulder, and smiling with a mischievous air: "You never told me you were married."

The physician stopped wiping his face, and gravely responded: "Yes, I am, and marred."

"What do you say?"

"I say, married and marred. Never commit that folly, young man."

"Why?"

"Why! See here! I have been married now for twenty years, and haven't got used to it yet. Every evening, when I reach home, I say to myself, 'Hold hard! this old woman is still in my house! So then she'll never go away?'" Everyone began to laugh, so serious and convinced was his tone.

But the bells of the hotel were ringing for dinner. The fête was over. Louise and Charlotte were accompanied back to their father's house; and when their new friends had left them, they commenced talking about them. Everyone thought them charming, Andermatt alone preferred the elder girl.

The Marquis said: "How pliant the feminine nature is! The mere vicinity of the paternal gold, of which they do not even know the use, has made ladies of these country girls."

Christiane, having asked Paul Bretigny: "And you, which of them do you prefer?" he murmured:

"Oh! I? I have not even looked at them. It is not they whom I prefer."

He had spoken in a very low voice; and she made no reply.

VI

THE days that followed were charming for Christiane Andermatt. She lived, lighthearted, her soul full of joy. The morning bath was her first pleasure, a delicious pleasure that made the skin tingle, an exquisite half hour in the warm, flowing water, which disposed her to feel happy all day long. She was, indeed, happy in all her thoughts and in all her desires. The affection with which she felt herself surrounded and penetrated, the intoxication of youthful life throbbing in her veins, and then again this new environment, this superb country, made for daydreams and repose, wide and odorous, enveloping her like a great caress of nature, awakened in her fresh emotions. Everything that approached, everything that touched her, continued this sensation of the morning, this sensation of a tepid bath, of a great bath of happiness wherein she plunged herself body and soul.

Andermatt, who had to leave Enval for a fortnight or perhaps a month, had gone back to Paris, having previously reminded his wife to take good care that the paralytic should not discontinue his course of treatment. So each day, before breakfast, Christiane, her father, her brother, and Paul, went to look at what Gontran called "the poor man's soup." Other bathers came there also, and they formed a circular group around the hole, while chatting with the vagabond.

He was not better able to walk, he declared, but he had a feeling as if his legs were covered with ants; and he told how these ants ran up and down, climbing as far as his thighs, and then going back again to the tips of his toes. And even at night he felt these insects tickling and biting him, so that he was deprived of sleep.

All the visitors and the peasants, divided into two camps, that of the believers and that of the sceptics, were interested in this cure.

After breakfast, Christiane often went to look for the Oriol girls, so that they might take a walk with her. They were the only members of her own sex at the station to whom she could talk or with whom she could have friendly relations, sharing a little of her confidence and asking in return for some feminine sympathy. She had at once taken a liking for the grave common sense allied with amiability which the elder girl exhibited and still more for the spirit of sly humor possessed by the younger; and it was less to please her husband than for her own amusement that she now sought the friendship of the two sisters.

They used to set forth on excursions sometimes in a landau, an old traveling landau with six seats, got from a livery-man at Riom, and at other times on foot. They were especially fond of a little wild valley near Chatel-Guyon, leading toward the hermitage of Sans-Souci. Along the narrow road, which they slowly traversed, under the pine-trees, on the bank of the little river, they would saunter in pairs, each pair chatting together. At every stage along their track, where it was necessary to cross the stream, Paul and Gontran, standing on stepping-stones in the water, seized the women each with one arm, and carried them over with a jump, so as to deposit them at the opposite side. And each of these fordings changed the order of the pedestrians. Christiane went from one to another, but found the opportunity of remaining a little while alone with Paul Bretigny either in front or in the rear.

He had no longer the same ways while in her company as in the first days of their acquaintanceship; he was less disposed to laugh, less abrupt in manner, less like a comrade, but more respectful and attentive. Their conversations, however, assumed a tone of intimacy, and the things that concerned the heart held in them the foremost place. He talked to her about sentiment and love, like a man well versed in such subjects, who had sounded the depths of women's tenderness, and who owed to them as much happiness as suffering.

She, ravished and rather touched, urged him on to confidences with an ardent and artful curiosity. All that she knew of him awakened in her a keen desire to learn more, to penetrate in thought into one of those male existences of which she had got glimpses out of books, one of those existences full of tempests and mysteries of love. Yielding to her importunities, he told her each day a little more about his life, his adventures, and his griefs, with a warmth of language which his burning memories sometimes rendered impassioned, and which the desire to please made also seductive. He opened to her gaze a world till now unknown to her, found eloquent words to express the subtleties of desire and expectation, the ravages of growing hopes, the religion of flowers and bits of ribbons, all the little objects treasured up as sacred, the enervating effect of sudden doubts, the anguish of alarming conjectures, the tortures of jealousy, and the inexpressible frenzy of the first kiss.

And he knew how to describe all these things in a very seemly fashion, veiled, poetic, and captivating. Like all men who are perpetually haunted by desire and thoughts about woman he spoke discreetly of those whom he had loved with a fever that throbbed within him still. He recalled a thousand romantic incidents calculated to move the heart, a thousand delicate circumstances calculated to make tears gather in the eyes, and all those sweet futilities of gallantry which render amorous relationships between persons of refined souls and cultivated minds the most beautiful and most entrancing experiences that can be conceived.

All these disturbing and familiar chats, renewed each day and each day more prolonged, fell on Christiane's soul like grains cast into the earth. And the charm of this country spread wide around her, the odorous air, that blue Limagne, so vast that it seemed to make the spirit expand, those extinguished volcanoes on the mountain, furnaces of the antique world serving now only to warm springs for invalids, the cool shades, the rippling music of the streams as they rushed over the stones — all this, too, penetrated the heart and the flesh of the young woman, penetrated them and softened them like a soft shower of warm rain on soil that is yet virgin, a rain that will cause to bourgeon and blossom in it the flowers of which it had received the seed.

She was quite conscious that this youth was paying court to her a little, that he thought her pretty, even more than pretty; and the desire to please him spontaneously suggested to her a thousand inventions, at the same time designing and simple, to fascinate him and to make a conquest of him.

When he looked moved, she would abruptly leave him; when she anticipated some tender allusion on his lips, she would cast toward him, ere the words were finished, one of those swift, unfathomable glances which pierce men's hearts like fire. She would greet him with soft utterances, gentle movements of her head, dreamy gestures with her hands, or sad looks quickly changed into smiles, as if to show him, even when no words had been exchanged between them, that his efforts had not been in vain.

What did she desire? Nothing. What did she expect from all this? Nothing.

She amused herself with this solely because she was a woman, because she did not perceive the danger of it, because, without foreseeing anything, she wished to find out what he would do.

And then she had suddenly developed that native coquetry which lies hidden in the veins of all feminine beings. The slumbering, innocent child of yesterday had unexpectedly waked up, subtle and keen-witted, when facing this man who talked to her unceasingly about love. She divined the agitation that swept across his mind when he was by her side, she saw the increasing emotion that his face expressed, and she understood all the different intonations of his voice with that special intuition possessed by women who feel themselves solicited to love.

Other men had ere now paid attentions to her in the fashionable world without getting anything from her in return save the mockery of a playful young woman. Their commonplace flatteries diverted her; their looks of melancholy love filled her with merriment; and to all their manifestations of passion she responded only with derisive laughter. In the case of this man, however, she felt herself suddenly confronted with a seductive and dangerous adversary; and she had been changed into one of those clever creatures, instinctively clear-sighted, armed with audacity and coolness, who, so long as their hearts remain untrammeled, watch for, surprise, and draw men into the invisible net of sentiment.

As for him, he had, at first, thought her rather silly. Accustomed to women versed in intrigues, exercised in love just as an old soldier is in military maneuvers, skilled in all the wiles of gallantry and tenderness, he considered this simple heart commonplace, and treated it with a light disdain.

But, little by little, her ingenuousness had amused him, and then fascinated him; and yielding to his impressionable nature, he had begun to make her the object of his affectionate attentions. He knew full well that the best way to excite a pure soul was to talk incessantly about love, while exhibiting the appearance of thinking about others; and accordingly, humoring in a crafty fashion the dainty curiosity which he had aroused in her, he proceeded, under the pretense of confiding his secrets to her, to teach her what passion really meant, under the shadow of the wood.

He, too, found this play amusing, showed her, by all the little gallantries that men know how to display, the growing pleasure that he found in her society, and assumed the attitude of a lover without suspecting that he would become one in reality. And all this came about as naturally in the course of their protracted walks as it does to take a bath on a warm day, when you find yourself at the side of a river.

But, from the first moment when Christiane began to indulge in coquetry, from the time when she resorted to all the native skill of woman in beguiling men, when she conceived the thought of bringing this slave of passion to his knees, in the same way that she would have undertaken to win a game at croquet, he allowed himself to yield, this candid libertine, to the attack of this simpleton, and began to love her.

And now he became awkward, restless, nervous, and she treated him as a cat does a mouse. With another woman he would not have been embarrassed; he would have spoken out; he would have conquered by his irresistible ardor; with her he did not dare, so different did she seem from all those whom he had known. The others, in short, were women already singed by life, to whom everything might be said, with whom one could venture on the boldest appeals, murmuring close to their lips the trembling words which set the blood aflame. He knew his power, he felt that he was bound to triumph when he was able to communicate freely to the soul, the heart, the senses of her whom he loved, the impetuous desire by which he was ravaged.

With Christiane, he imagined himself by the side of a young girl, so great a novice did he consider her; and all his resources seemed paralyzed. And then he cared for her in a new sort of way, partly as a man cares for a child, and partly as he does for his betrothed. He desired her; and yet he was afraid of touching her, of soiling her, of withering her bloom. He had no longing to clasp her tightly in his arms, such as he had felt toward others, but rather to fall on his knees, to kiss her robe, and to touch gently with his lips, with an infinitely chaste and tender slowness, the little hairs about her temples, the corners of her mouth, and her eyes, her closed eyes, whose blue he could feel glancing out toward him, the charming glance awakened under the drooping lids. He would have liked to protect her against everyone and against everything, not to let her be elbowed by common people, gaze at ugly people, or go near unclean people. He would have liked to carry away the dirt of the street over which she walked, the pebbles on the roads, the brambles and the branches in the wood, to make all things easy and delicious around her, and to carry her always, so that she should never walk. And he felt annoyed because she had to talk to the other guests at the hotel, to eat the same food at the table d'hôte, and submit to all the disagreeable and inevitable little things that belong to everyday existence.

He knew not what to say to her so much were his thoughts absorbed by her; and his powerlessness to express the state of his heart, to accomplish any of the things that he wished to do, to testify to her the imperious need of devoting himself to her which burned in his veins, gave him some of the aspects of a chained wild beast, and, at the same time, made him feel a strange desire to break into sobs.

All this she perceived without completely understanding it, and felt amused by it with the malicious enjoyment of a coquette. When they had lingered behind the others, and she felt from his look that he was about to say something disquieting, she would abruptly begin to run, in order to overtake her father, and, when she got up to him, would exclaim: "Suppose we make a four-cornered game."

Four-cornered games served generally for the termination of the excursions. They looked out for a glade at the end of a wider road than usual, and they began to play like boys out for a walk.

The Oriol girls and Gontran himself took great delight in this amusement, which satisfied that incessant longing to run that is to be found in all young creatures. Paul Bretigny alone grumbled, beset by other thoughts; then, growing animated by degrees he would join in the game with more desperation than any of the others, in order to catch Christiane, to touch her, to place his hand abruptly on her shoulder or on her corsage.

The Marquis, whose indifferent and listless nature yielded in everything, as long as his rest was not disturbed, sat down at the foot of a tree, and watched his boarding-school at play, as he said. He thought this quiet life very agreeable, and the entire world perfect.

However, Paul's behavior soon alarmed Christiane. One day she even got afraid of him. One morning, they went with Gontran to the most remote part of the oddly-shaped gap which is called the End of the World. The gorge, becoming more and more narrow and winding, sank into the mountain. They climbed over enormous rocks; they crossed the little river by means of stepping-stones, and, having wheeled round a lofty crag more than fifty meters in height which entirely blocked up the cleft of the ravine, they found themselves in a kind of trench encompassed between two gigantic walls, bare as far as their summits, which were covered with trees and with verdure.

The stream formed a wide lake of bowl-like shape, and truly it was a wild-looking chasm, strange and unexpected, such as one meets more frequently in narratives than in nature. Now, on this day, Paul, gazing at the projections of the rocky eminence which barred them out from the road at the right where all pedestrians were compelled to halt, remarked that it bore traces of having been scaled. He said: "Why, we can go on farther."

Then, having clambered up the first ledge, not without difficulty, he exclaimed: "Oh! this is charming! a little grove in the water — come on, then!"

And, leaning backward, he drew Christiane up by the two hands, while Gontran, feeling his way, planted his feet on all the slight projections of the rock. The soil which had drifted down from the summit had formed on this ledge a savage and bushy garden, in which the stream ran across the roots. Another step, a little farther on, formed a new barrier of this granite corridor. They climbed it, too, —— then a third; and they found themselves at the foot of an impassable wall from which fell, straight and clear, a cascade twenty meters high into a deep basin hollowed out by it, and buried under bindweeds and branches.

The cleft of the mountain had become so narrow that the two men, clinging on by their hands, could touch its sides. Nothing further could be seen, save a line of sky; nothing could be heard save the murmur of the water. It might have been taken for one of those undiscoverable retreats in which the Latin poets were wont to conceal the antique nymphs. It seemed to Christiane as if she had just intruded on the chamber of a fay.

Paul Bretigny said nothing. Gontran exclaimed: "Oh! how nice it would be if a woman white and rosy-red were bathing in that water!"

They returned. The first two shelves were as easy to descend, but the third frightened Christiane, so high and straight was it, without any visible steps. Bretigny let himself slip down the rock; then, stretching out his two arms toward her, "Jump," said he.

She would not venture. Not that she was afraid of falling, but she felt afraid of him, afraid above all of his eyes. He gazed at her with the avidity of a famished beast, with a passion which had grown ferocious; and his two hands extended toward her had such an imperious attraction for her that she was suddenly terrified and seized with a mad longing to shriek, to run away, to climb up the mountain perpendicularly to escape this irresistible appeal.

Her brother standing up behind her, cried: "Go on then!" and pushed her forward. Feeling herself falling she shut her eyes, and, caught in a gentle but powerful clasp, she felt, without seeing it, all the huge body of the young man, whose panting warm breath passed over her face. Then, she found herself on her feet once more, smiling, now that her terror had vanished, while Gontran descended in his turn.

This emotion having rendered her prudent, she took care, for some days, not to be alone with Bretigny, who now seemed to be prowling round her like the wolf in the fable round a lamb.

But a grand excursion had been planned. They were to carry provisions in the landau with six seats, and go to dine with the Oriol girls on the border of the little lake of Tazenat, which in the language of the country was called the "gour" of Tazenat, and then return at night by moonlight. Accordingly, they started one afternoon of a day of burning heat, under a devouring sun, which made the granite of the mountain as hot as the floor of an oven.

The carriage ascended the mountain-side drawn by three horses, blowing, and covered with sweat. The coachman was nodding on his seat, his head hanging down; and at the side of the road ran legions of green lizards. The heated atmosphere seemed filled with an invisible and oppressive dust of fire. Sometimes it seemed hard, unyielding, dense, as they passed through it, sometimes it stirred about and sent across their faces ardent breaths of flame in which floated an odor of resin in the midst of the long pine-wood.

Nobody in the carriage uttered a word. The three ladies, at the lower end, closed their dazzled eyes, which they shaded with their red parasols. The Marquis and Gontran, their foreheads wrapped round with handkerchiefs, had fallen asleep. Paul was looking toward Christiane, who was also watching him from under her lowered eyelids. And the landau, sending up a column of smoking white dust, kept always toiling up this interminable ascent.

When it had reached the plateau, the coachman straightened himself up, the horses broke into a trot; and they drove through a beautiful, undulating country, thickly-wooded, cultivated, studded with villages and solitary houses here and there. In the distance, at the left, could be seen the great truncated summits of the volcanoes. The lake of Tazenat, which they were going to see, had been formed by the last crater in the mountain chain of Auvergne. After they had been driving for three hours, Paul said suddenly: "Look here, the lava-currents!"

Brown rocks, fantastically twisted, made cracks in the soil at the border of the road. At the right could be seen a mountain, snub-nosed in appearance, whose wide summit had a flat and hollow look. They took a path, which seemed to pass into it through a triangular cutting; and Christiane, who was standing erect, discovered all at once, in the midst of a vast deep crater, a lovely lake, bright and round, like a silver coin. The steep slopes of the mountain, wooded at the right and bare at the left, sank toward the water, which they surrounded with a high inclosure, regular in shape. And this placid water, level and glittering, like the surface of a medal, reflected the trees on one side, and on the other the barren slope, with a clearness so complete that the edges escaped one's attention, and the only thing one saw in this funnel, in whose center the blue sky was mirrored, was a transparent, bottomless opening, which seemed to pass right through the earth, pierced from end to end up to the other firmament.

The carriage could go no farther. They got down, and took a path through the wooded side winding round the lake, under the trees, halfway up the declivity of the mountain. This track, along which only the woodcutters passed, was as green as a prairie; and, through the branches, they could see the opposite side, and the water glittering at the bottom of this mountain-lake.

Then they reached, through an opening in the wood, the very edge of the water, where they sat down upon a sloping carpet of grass, overshadowed by oak-trees.

They all stretched themselves on the green turf with sensuous and exquisite delight. The men rolled themselves about in it, plunged their hands into it; while the women, softly lying down on their sides, placed their cheeks close to it, as if to seek there a refreshing caress.

After the heat of the road, it was one of those sweet sensations so deep and so grateful that they almost amount to pure happiness.

Then once more the Marquis went to sleep; Gontran speedily followed his example. Paul began chatting with Christiane and the two young girls. About what? About nothing in particular. From time to time, one of them gave utterance to some phrase; another replied after a minute's pause, and the lingering words seemed torpid in their mouths like the thoughts within their minds.

But, the coachman having brought across to them the hamper which contained the provisions, the Oriol girls, accustomed to domestic duties in their own house, and still clinging to their active habits, quickly proceeded to unpack it, and to prepare the dinner, of which the party would by and by partake on the grass.

Paul lay on his back beside Christiane, who was in a reverie. And he murmured, in so low a tone that she scarcely heard him, so low that his words just grazed her ear, like those confused sounds that are borne on by the wind: "These are the best days of my life."

Why did these vague words move her even to the bottom of her heart? Why did she feel herself suddenly touched by an emotion such as she had never experienced before?

She was gazing through the trees at a tiny house, a hut for persons engaged in hunting and fishing, so narrow that it could barely contain one small apartment. Paul followed the direction of her glance, and said:

"Have you ever thought, Madame, what days passed together in a hut like that might be for two persons who loved one another to distraction? They would be alone in the world, truly alone, face to face! And, if such a thing were possible, ought not one be ready to give up everything in order to realize it, so rare, unseizable, and short-lived is happiness? Do we find it in our everyday life? What more depressing than to rise up without any ardent hope, to go through the same duties dispassionately, to drink in moderation, to eat with discretion, and to sleep tranquilly like a mere animal?"

She kept, all the time, staring at the little house; and her heart swelled up, as if she were going to burst into tears; for, in one flash of thought, she divined intoxicating joys, of whose existence she had no conception till that moment.

Indeed, she was thinking how sweet it would be for two to be together in this tiny abode hidden under the trees, facing that plaything of a lake, that jewel of a lake, true mirror of love! One might feel happy with nobody near, without a neighbor, without one sound of life, alone with a lover, who would pass his hours kneeling at the feet of the adored one, looking up at her, while her gaze wandered toward the blue wave, and whispering tender words in her ear, while he kissed the tips of her fingers. They would live there, amid the silence, beneath the trees, at the bottom of that crater, which would hold all their passion, like the limpid, unfathomable water, in the embrace of its firm and regular inclosure, with no other horizon for their eyes save the round line of the mountain's sides, with no other horizon for their thoughts save the bliss of loving one another, with no other horizon for their desires save kisses lingering and endless.

Were there, then, people on the earth who could enjoy days like this? Yes, undoubtedly! And why not? Why had she not sooner known that such joys exist?

The girls announced that dinner was ready. It was six o'clock already. They roused up the Marquis and Gontran in order that they might squat in Turkish fashion a short distance off, with the plates glistening beside them in the grass. The two sisters kept waiting on them, and the heedless men did not gainsay them. They ate at their leisure, flinging the cast-off pieces and the bones of the chickens into the water. They had brought champagne with them; the sudden noise of the first cork jumping up produced a surprising effect on everyone, so unusual did it appear in this solitary spot.

The day was declining; the air became impregnated with a delicious coolness. As the evening stole on, a strange melancholy fell on the water that lay sleeping at the bottom of the crater. Just as the sun was about to disappear, the western sky burst out into flame, and the lake suddenly assumed the aspect of a basin of fire. Then, when the sun had gone to rest, the horizon becoming red like a brasier on the point of being extinguished, the lake looked like a basin of blood. And suddenly above the crest of mountain, the moon nearly at its full rose up all pale in the still, cloudless firmament. Then, as the shadows gradually spread over the earth, it ascended glittering and round above the crater which was round also. It looked as if it were going to let itself drop down into the chasm; and when it had risen far up into the sky, the lake had the aspect of a basin of silver. Then, on its surface, motionless all day long, trembling movements could now be seen sometimes slow and sometimes rapid. It seemed as if some spirits skimming just above the water were drawing across it invisible veils.

It was the big fish at the bottom, the venerable carp and the voracious pike, who had come up to enjoy themselves in the moonlight.

The Oriol girls had put back all the plates, dishes, and bottles into the hamper, which the coachman came to take away. They rose up to go.

As they were passing into the path under the trees, where rays of light fell, like a silver shower, through the leaves and glittered on the grass, Christiane, who was following the others with Paul in the rear, suddenly heard a panting voice saying close to her ear: "I love youl — I love you! — I love you!"

Her heart began to beat so wildly that she was near sinking to the ground, and felt as if she could not move her limbs. Still she walked on, like one distraught, ready to turn round, her arms hanging wide and her lips tightly drawn. He had by this time caught the edge of the little shawl which she had drawn over her shoulders, and was kissing it frantically. She continued walking with such tottering steps that she no longer could feel the soil beneath her feet.

And now she emerged from under the canopy of trees, and finding herself in the full glare of the moonlight, she got the better of her agitation with a desperate effort; but, before stepping into the landau and losing sight of the lake, she half turned round to throw a long kiss with both hands toward the water, which likewise embraced the man who was following her.

On the return journey, she remained inert both in soul and body, dizzy, cramped up, as if after a fall; and, the moment they reached the hotel, she quickly rushed up to her own apartment, where she locked herself in. Even when the door was bolted and the key turned in the lock, she pressed her hand on it again, so much did she feel herself pursued and desired. Then she remained trembling in the middle of the room, which was nearly quite dark and had an empty look. The wax-candle placed on the table cast on the walls the quivering shadows of the furniture and of the curtains. Christiane sank into an armchair. All her thoughts were rushing, leaping, flying away from her so that she found it impossible to seize them, to hold them, to link them together. She felt now ready to weep, without well knowing why, broken-hearted, wretched, abandoned, in this empty room, lost in existence, just as in a forest. Where was she going, what would she do?

Breathing with difficulty, she rose up, flung open the window and the shutters in front of it, and leaned on her elbows over the balcony. The air was refreshing. In the depths of the sky, wide and empty, too, the distant moon, solitary and sad, having ascended now into the blue heights of night, cast forth a hard, cold luster on the trees and on the mountains.

The entire country lay asleep. Only the light strain of Saint Landri's violin, which he played till a late hour every night, broke the deep silence of the valley with its melancholy music. Christiane scarcely heard it. It ceased, then began again — the shrill and dolorous cry of the thin fiddlestrings.

And that moon lost in a desert sky, that feeble sound lost in the silent night, filled her heart with such a sense of solitude that she burst into sobs. She trembled and quivered to the very marrow of her bones, shaken by anguish and by the shuddering sensations of people attacked by some formidable malady; for suddenly it dawned upon her mind that she, too, was all alone in existence.

She had never realized this until to-day, and now she felt it so vividly in the distress of her soul that she imagined she was going mad.

She had a father! a brother! a husband! She loved them still, and they loved her. And here she was all at once separated from them, she had become a stranger to them as if she scarcely knew them. The calm affection of her father, the friendly companionship of her brother, the cold tenderness of her husband, appeared to her nothing any longer, nothing any longer. Her husband! This, her husband, the rosy-cheeked man who was accustomed to say to her in a careless tone, "Are you going far, dear, this morning?" She belonged to him, to this man, body and soul, by the mere force of a contract. Was this possible? Ah! how lonely and lost she felt herself! She closed her eyes to look into her own mind, into the lowest depths of her thoughts.

And she could see, as she evoked them out of her inner consciousness the faces of all those who lived around her — her father, careless and tranquil, happy as long as nobody disturbed his repose; her brother, scoffing and sceptical; her husband moving about, his head full of figures, and with the announcement on his lips, "I have just done a fine stroke of business!" when he should have said, "I love you!"

Another man had murmured that word a little while ago, and it was still vibrating in her ear and in her heart. She could see him also, this other man, devouring her with his fixed look; and, if he had been near her at that moment, she would have flung herself into his arms!

VII

Christiane, who had not gone to I sleep till a very late hour, awoke as soon as the sun cast a flood of red light into her room through the window which she had left wide open. She glanced at her watch — it was five o'clock — and remained lying on her back deliciously in the warmth of the bed. It seemed to her, so active and full of joy did her soul feel, that a happiness, a great happiness, had come to her during the night. What was it? She sought to find out what it was; she sought to find out what was this new source of happiness which had thus penetrated her with delight. All her sadness of the night before had vanished, melted away, during sleep.

So Paul Bretigny loved her! How different he appeared to her from the first day! In spite of all the efforts of her memory, she could not bring back her first impression of him; she could not even recall to her mind the man introduced to her by her brother. He whom she knew to-day had retained nothing of the other, neither the face nor the bearing — nothing — — for his first image had passed, little by little, day by day, through all the slow modifications which take place in the soul with regard to a being who from a mere acquaintance has come to be a familiar friend and a beloved object. You take possession of him hour by hour without suspecting it; possession of his movements, of his attitudes, of his physical and moral characteristics. He enters into you, into your eyes and your heart, by his voice, by all his gestures, by what he says and by what he thinks. You absorb him; you comprehend him; you divine him in all the meanings of his smiles and of his words; it seems at last that he belongs entirely to you, so much do you love, unconsciously still, all that is his and all that comes from him.

Then, too, it is impossible to remember what this being was like — to your indifferent eyes — when first he presented himself to your gaze. So then Paul Bretigny loved her! Christiane experienced from this discovery neither fear nor anguish, but a profound tenderness, an immense joy, new and exquisite, of being loved — of knowing that she was loved.

She was, however, a little disturbed as to the attitude that he would assume toward her and that she should preserve toward him. But, as it was a matter of delicacy for her conscience even to think of these things, she ceased to think about them, trusting to her own tact and ingenuity to direct the course of events.

She descended at the usual hour, and found Paul smoking a cigarette before the door of the hotel. He bowed respectfully to her:

"Good day, Madame. You feel well this morning?"

"Very well, Monsieur. I slept very soundly."

And she put out her hand to him, fearing lest he might hold it in his too long. But he scarcely pressed it; and they began quietly chatting as if they had forgotten one another.

And the day passed off without anything being done by him to recall his ardent avowal of the night before. He remained, on the days that followed, quite as discreet and calm; and she placed confidence in him. He realized, she thought, that he would wound her by becoming bolder; and she hoped, she firmly believed, that they might be able to stop at this delightful halting-place of tenderness, where they could love, while looking into the depths of one another's eyes, without remorse, inasmuch as they would be free from defilement. Nevertheless, she was careful never to wander out with him alone.

Now, one evening, the Saturday of the same week in which they had visited the lake of Tazenat, as they were returning to the hotel about ten o'clock, — the Marquis, Christiane, and Paul, — for they had left Gontran playing écarté with Aubrey and Riquier and Doctor Honorat in the great hall of the Casino, Bretigny exclaimed, as he watched the moon shining through the branches:

"How nice it would be to go and see the ruins of Tournoel on a night like this!"

At this thought alone, Christiane was filled with emotion, the moon and ruins having on her the same influence which they have on the souls of all women.

She pressed the Marquis's hands. "Oh! father dear, would you mind going there?"

He hesitated, being exceedingly anxious to go to bed.

She insisted: "Just think a moment, how beautiful Tournoel is even by day! You said yourself that you had never seen a ruin so picturesque, with that great tower above the château. What must it be at night!"

At last he consented: "Well, then, let us go! But we'll only look at it for five minutes, and then come back immediately. For my part, I want to be in bed at eleven o'clock."

"Yes, we will come back immediately. It takes * only twenty minutes to get there."

They set out all three, Christiane leaning on her father's arm, and Paul walking by her side.

He spoke of his travels in Switzerland, in Italy, in Sicily. He told what his impressions were in the presence of certain phenomena, his enthusiasm on seeing the summit of Monte Rosa, when the sun, rising on the horizon of this row of icy peaks, this congealed world of eternal snows, cast on each of those lofty mountain-tops a dazzling white radiance, and illumined them, like the pale beacon-lights that must shine down upon the kingdoms of the dead. Then he spoke of his emotion on the edge of the monstrous crater of Etna, when he felt himself, an imperceptible mite, many meters above the cloud line, having nothing any longer around him save the sea and the sky, the blue sea beneath, the blue sky above, and leaning over this dreadful chasm of the earth, whose breath stifled him. He enlarged the objects which he described in order to excite the young woman; and, as she listened, she panted with visions she conjured up, by a flight of imagination, of those wonderful things that he had seen.

Suddenly, at a turn of the road, they discovered Tournoel. The ancient château, standing on a mountain peak, overlooked by its high and narrow tower, letting in the light through its chinks, and dismantled by time and by the wars of bygone days, traced, upon a sky of phantoms, its huge silhouette of a fantastic manor-house.

They stopped, all three surprised. The Marquis said, at length: "Indeed, it is impressive — like a dream of Gustave Doré realized. Let us sit down for five minutes."

And he sat down on the sloping grass.

But Christiane, wild with enthusiasm, exclaimed: "Oh! father, let us go on farther! It is so beautiful! so beautiful! Let us walk to the foot, I beg of you!" This time the Marquis refused: "No, my darling, I have walked enough; I can't go any farther. If you want to see it more closely, go on there with M. Bretigny. I will wait here for you."

Paul asked: "Will you come, Madame?"

She hesitated, seized by two apprehensions, that of finding herself alone with him, and that of wounding an honest man by having the appearance of suspecting him.

The Marquis repeated: "Go on! Go on! I will wait for you."

Then she took it for granted that her father would remain within reach of their voices, and she said resolutely: "Let us go on, Monsieur."

But scarcely had she walked on for some minutes when she felt herself possessed by a poignant emotion, by a vague, mysterious fear — fear of the ruin, fear of the night, fear of this man. Suddenly she felt her legs trembling under her, just as she felt the other night by the lake of Tazenat; they refused to bear her any further, bent under her, appeared to be sinking into the soil, where her feet remained fixed when she strove to raise them.

A large chestnut-tree, planted close to the path they had been pursuing, sheltered one side of a meadow. Christiane, out of breath just as if she had been running, let herself sink against the trunk. And she stammered: "I shall remain here — we can see very well."

Paul sat down beside her. She heard his heart beating with great emotional throbs. He said, after a brief silence: "Do you believe that we have had a previous life?"

She murmured, without having well understood his question: "I don't know. I have never thought on it."

He went on: "But I believe it — at moments — or rather I feel it. As being is composed of a soul and a body, which seem distinct, but are, without doubt, only one whole of the same nature, it must reappear when the elements which have originally formed it find themselves together for the second time. It is not the same individual assuredly, but it is the same man who comes back when a body like the previous form finds itself inhabited by a soul like that which animated him formerly. Well, I, tonight, feel sure, Madame, that I lived in that chateau, that I possessed it that I fought there, that I defended it. I recognized it — it was mine, I am certain of it!

And I am also certain that I loved there a woman who resembled you, and who, like you, bore the name of Christiane. I am so certain of it that I seem to see you still calling me from the top of that tower.

"Search your memory! recall it to your mind! There is a wood at the back, which descends into a deep valley. We have often walked there. You had light robes in the summer evenings, and I wore heavy armor, which clanked beneath the trees. You do not recollect? Look back, then, Christiane! Why, your name is as familiar to me as those we hear in childhood! Were we to inspect carefully all the stones of this fortress, we should find it there carved by my hand in days of yore! I declare to you that I recognize my dwelling-place, my country, just as I recognized you, you, the first time I saw you!"

He spoke in an exalted tone of conviction, poetically intoxicated by contact with this Woman, and by the night, by the moon, and by the ruin.

He abruptly flung himself on his knees before Christiane, and, in a trembling voice said: "Let me adore you still since I have found you again! Here have I been searching for you a long time!"

She wanted to rise and to go away, to join her father, but she had not the strength; she had not the courage, held back, paralyzed by a burning desire to listen to him still, to hear those ravishing words entering her heart. She felt herself carried away in a dream, in the dream always hoped for, so sweet, so poetic, full of rays of moonlight and lays of love.

He had seized her hands, and was kissing the ends of her finger-nails, murmuring:

"Christiane — Christiane — take me — kill me! I love you, Christiane!"

She felt him quivering, shuddering at her feet. And now he kissed her knees, while his chest heaved with sobs. She was afraid that he was going mad, and started up to make her escape. But he had risen more quickly, and seizing her in his arms he pressed his mouth against hers.

Then, without a cry, without revolt, without resistance, she let herself sink back on the grass, as if this caress, by breaking her will, had crushed her physical power to struggle. And he possessed her with as much ease as if he were culling a ripe fruit.

But scarcely had he loosened his clasp when she rose up distracted, and rushed away shuddering and icy-cold all of a sudden, like one who had just fallen into the water. He overtook her with a few strides, and caught her by the arm, whispering: "Christiane, Christiane! Be on your guard with your father!"

She walked on without answering, without turning round, going straight before her with stiff, jerky steps. He followed her now without venturing to speak to her.

As soon as the Marquis saw them, he rose up: "Hurry," said he; "I was beginning to get cold. These things are very fine to look at, but bad for one undergoing thermal treatmentl."

Christiane pressed herself close to her father's side, as if to appeal to him for protection and take refuge in his tenderness.

As soon as she had reentered her apartment, she undressed herself in a few seconds and buried herself in her bed, hiding her head under the clothes; then she wept. She wept with her face pressed against the pillow for a long, long time, inert, annihilated. She did not think, she did not suffer, she did not regret. She wept without thinking, without reflecting, without knowing why. She wept instinctively as one sings when one feels gay. Then, when her tears were exhausted, overwhelmed, paralyzed with sobbing, she fell asleep from fatigue and lassitude.

She was awakened by light taps at the door of her room, which looked out on the drawingroom. It was broad daylight, as it was nine o'clock.

"Come in," she cried.

And her husband presented himself, joyous, animated, wearing a traveling-cap and carrying by his side his little money-bag, which he was never without while on a journey.

He exclaimed: "What? You were sleeping still, my dear! And I had to awaken you. There you are! I arrived without announcing myself. I hope you are going on well. It is superb weather in Paris."

And having taken off his cap, he advanced to embrace her. She drew herself away toward the wall, seized by a wild fear, by a nervous dread of this little man, with his smug, rosy countenance, who had stretched out his lips toward her.

Then, abruptly, she offered him her forehead, while she closed her eyes. He planted there a chaste kiss, and asked: "Will you allow me to wash in your dressing-room? As no one attended on me to-day, my room was not prepared."

She stammered: "Why, certainly."

And he disappeared through a door at the end of the bed.

She heard him moving about, splashing, snorting; then he cried: "What news here? For my part, I have splendid news. The analysis of the water has given unexpected results. We can cure at least three times more patients than they can at Royat. It is superb!"

She was sitting in the bed, suffocating, her brain overwrought by this unforeseen return, which hurt her like a physical pain and gripped her like a pang of remorse. He reappeared, self-satisfied, spreading around him a strong odor of verbena. Then he sat down familiarly at the foot of the bed, and asked: "And the paralytic? How is he going on? Is he beginning to walk? It is not possible that he is not cured with what we found in the water!"

She had forgotten all about it for several days, and she faltered: "Why, I — I believe he is beginning to walk better. Besides, I have not seen him this week. I — I am a little unwell."

He looked at her with interest, and returned: "It is true, you are a little pale. All the same, it becomes you very well. You look charming thus — quite charming."

And he drew nearer, and bending toward her was about to pass one arm into the bed under her waist.

But she made such a backward movement of terror that he remained stupefied, with his hands extended and his mouth held toward her. Then he asked: "What's the matter with you nowadays? One cannot touch you any longer. I assure you I do not intend to hurt you."

And he pressed close to her eagerly, with a glow of sudden desire in his eyes. Then she stammered: "No — let me be — let me be! The fact is, I believe — I believe I am pregnant!"

She had said this, maddened by the mental agony she was enduring, without thinking about her words, to avoid his touch, just as she would have said: "I have leprosy, or the plague."

He grew pale in his turn, moved by a profound joy; and he merely murmured: "Already!" He yearned now to embrace her a long time, softly, tenderly, as a happy and grateful father. Then, he was seized with uneasiness.

"Is it possible? — What? — Are you sure? — So soon?"

She replied: "Yes — it is possible!"

Then he jumped about the room, and rubbing his hands, exclaimed: "Christi! Christi! What a happy day!"

There was another tap at the door. Andermatt opened it, and a chambermaid said to him: "Doctor Latonne would like to speak to Monsieur immediately."

"All right. Bring him into our drawingroom.

I am going there."

He hurried away to the adjoining apartment. The doctor presently appeared. His face had a solemn look, and his manner was starched and cold. He bowed, touched the hand which the banker, a little surprised, held toward him, took a seat, and explained in the tone of a second in an affair of honor: "A very disagreeable matter has arisen with reference to me, my dear Monsieur, and, in order to explain my conduct, I must give you an account of it. When you did me the honor to call me in to see Madame Andermatt, I hastened to come at the appointed hour; now it has transpired that, a few minutes before me, my brother-physician, the medical inspector, who, no doubt, inspires more confidence in the lady, had been sent for, owing to the attentions of the Marquis de Ravenel.

"The result of this is that, having been the second to see her I create the impression of having taken by a trick from Doctor Bonnefille a patient who already belonged to him — I create the impression of having committed an indelicate act, one unbecoming and unjustifiable from one member of the profession toward another. Now it is necessary for us to carry, Monsieur, into the exercise of our art certain precautions and unusual tact in order to avoid every collision which might lead to grave consequences. Doctor Bonnefille, having been apprised of my visit here, believing me capable of this want of delicacy, appearances being in fact against me, has spoken about me in such terms that, were it not for his age, I would have found myself compelled to demand an explanation from him. There remains for me only one thing to do, in order to exculpate myself in his eyes, and in the eyes of the entire medical body of the country, and that is to cease, to my great regret, to give my professional attentions to your wife, and to make the entire truth about this matter known, begging of you in the meantime to accept my excuses." Andermatt replied with embarrassment:

"I understand perfectly well, doctor, the difficult situation in which you find yourself. The fault is not mine or my wife's, but that of my father-in-law, who called in M. Bonnefille without giving us notice. Could I not go to look for your brother-doctor, and tell him? — "

Doctor Latonne interrupted him: "It is useless, my dear Monsieur. There is here a question of dignity and professional honor, which I am bound to respect before everything, and, in spite of my lively regrets — "

Andermatt, in his turn, interrupted him. The rich man, the man who pays, who buys a prescription for five, ten, twenty, or forty francs, as he does a box of matches for three sous, to whom everything should belong by the power of his purse, and who only appreciates beings and objects in virtue of an assimilation of their value with that of money, of a relation, rapid and direct, established between coined metal and everything else in the world, was irritated at the presumption of this vendor of remedies on paper. He said in a stiff tone:

"Be it so, doctor. Let us stop where we are. But I trust for your own sake that this step may not have a damaging influence on your career. We shall see, indeed, which of us two shall have the most to suffer from your decision."

The physician, offended, rose up and bowing with the utmost politeness, said: "I have no doubt, Monsieur, it is I who will suffer. That which I have done to-day is very painful to me from every point of view. But I never hesitate between my interests and my conscience."

And he went out. As he emerged through the open door, he knocked against the Marquis, who was entering, with a letter in his hand. And M. de Ravenel exclaimed, as soon as he was alone with his son-in-law: "Look here, my dear fellow! this is a very troublesome thing, which has happened me through your fault. Doctor Bonnefille, hurt by the circumstance that you sent for his brother-physician to see Christiane, has written me a note couched in very dry language informing me that I cannot count any longer on his professional services."

Thereupon, Andermatt got quite annoyed. He walked up and down, excited himself by talking, gesticulated, full of harmless and noisy anger, that kind of anger which is never taken seriously. He went on arguing in a loud voice. Whose fault was it, after all? That of the Marquis alone, who had called in that pack-ass Bonnefille without giving any notice of the fact to him, though he had, thanks to his Paris physician, been informed as to the relative value of the three charlatans at Enval! And then what business had the Marquis to consult a doctor, behind the back of the husband, the husband who was the only judge, the only person responsible for his wife's health? In short, it was the same thing day after day with everything! People did nothing but stupid things around him, nothing but stupid things! He repeated it incessantly; but he was only crying in the desert, nobody understood, nobody put faith in his experience, until it was too late.

And he said, "My physician,"

"My experience," with the authoritative tone of a man who has possession of unique things. In his mouth the possessive pronouns had the sonorous ring of metals. And when he pronounced the words "My wife," one felt very clearly that the Marquis had no longer any rights with regard to his daughter since Andermatt had married her, to marry and to buy having the same meaning in the latter's mind.

Gontran came in, at the most lively stage of the discussion, and seated himself in an armchair with a smile of gaiety on his lips. He said nothing, but listened, exceedingly amused. When the banker stopped talking, having fairly exhausted his breath, his brother-in-law raised his hand, exclaiming:

"I request permission to speak. Here are both of you without physicians, isn't that so? Well, I propose my candidate, Doctor Honorat, the only one who has formed an exact and unshaken opinion on the water of Enval. He makes people drink it, but he would not drink it himself for all the world. Do you wish me to go and look for him? I will take the negotiations on myself."

It was the only thing to do, and they begged of Gontran to send for him immediately. The Marquis, filled with anxiety at the idea of a change of regimen and of nursing wanted to know immediately the opinion of this new physician; and Andermatt desired no less eagerly to consult him on Christiane's behalf.

She heard their voices through the door without listening to their words or understanding what they were talking about. As soon as her husband had left her, she had risen from the bed, as if from a dangerous spot, and hurriedly dressed herself, without the assistance of the chambermaid, shaken by all these occurrences.

The world appeared to her to have changed around her, her former life seemed to have vanished since last night, and people themselves looked quite different.

The voice of Andermatt was raised once more: "Hallo, my dear Bretigny, how are you getting on?"

He no longer used the word "Monsieur." Another voice could be heard saying in reply: "Why, quite well, my dear Andermatt. You only arrived, I suppose, this morning?"

Christiane, who was in the act of raising her hair over her temples, stopped with a choking sensation, her arms in the air. Through the partition, she fancied she could see them grasping one another's hands. She sat down, no longer able to hold herself erect; and her hair, rolling down, fell over her shoulders.

It was Paul who was speaking now, and she shivered from head to foot at every word that came from his mouth. Each word, whose meaning she did not seize, fell and sounded on her heart like a hammer striking a bell.

Suddenly, she articulated in almost a loud tone: "But I love him! — I love him!" as though she were affirming something new and surprising, which saved her, which consoled her, which proclaimed her innocence before the tribunal of her conscience. A sudden energy made her rise up; in one second, her resolution was taken. And she proceeded to rearrange her hair, murmuring: "I have a lover, that is all. I have a lover." Then, in order to fortify herself still more, in order to get rid of all mental distress, she determined there and then, with a burning faith, to love him to distraction, to give up to him her life, her happiness, to sacrifice everything for him, in accordance with the moral exaltation of hearts conquered but still scrupulous, that believe themselves to be purified by devotedness and sincerity.

And, from behind the wall which separated them, she threw out kisses to him. It was over; she abandoned herself to him, without reserve, as she might have offered herself to a god. The child already coquettish and artful, but still timid, still trembling, had suddenly died within her; and the woman was born, ready for passion, the woman resolute, tenacious, announced only up to this time by the energy hidden in her blue eye, which gave an air of courage and almost of bravado to her dainty white face.

She heard the door opening, and did not turn round, divining that it was her husband, without seeing him, as though a new sense, almost an instinct, had just been generated in her also.

He asked: "Will you be soon ready? We are all going presently to the paralytic's bath, to see if he is really getting better."

She replied calmly: "Yes, my dear Will, in five minutes."

But Gontran, returning to the drawingroom, was calling back Andermatt.

"Just imagine," said he; "I met that idiot Honorat in the park, and he, too, refuses to attend you for fear of the others. He talks of professional etiquette, deference, usages. One would imagine that he creates the impression of — in short, he is a fool, like his two brother-physicians. Certainly, I thought he was less of an ape than that."

The Marquis remained overwhelmed. The idea of taking the waters without a physician, of bathing for five minutes longer than necessary, of drinking one glass less than he ought, tortured him with apprehension, for he believed all the doses, the hours, and the phases of the treatment, to be regulated by a law of nature, which had made provision for invalids in causing the flow of those mineral springs, all whose mysterious secrets the doctors knew, like priests inspired and learned.

He exclaimed: "So then we must die here — we may perish like dogs, without any of these gentlemen putting himself about!"

And rage took possession of him, the rage egotistical and unreasoning of a man whose health is endangered.

"Have they any right to do this, since they pay for a license like grocers, these blackguards? We ought to have the power of forcing them to attend people, as trains can be forced to take all passengers. I am going to write to the newspapers to draw attention to the matter."

He walked about, in a state of excitement; and he went on, turning toward his son:

"Listen! It will be necessary to send for one to Royat or Clermont. We can't remain in this state." Gontran replied, laughing: "But those of Clermont and of Royat are not well acquainted with the liquid of Enval, which has not the same special action as their water on the digestive system and on the circulatory apparatus. And then, be sure, they won't come any more than the others in order to avoid the appearance of taking the bread out of their brother-doctors' mouths."

The Marquis, quite scared, faltered: "But what, then, is to become of us?"

Andermatt snatched up his hat, saying: "Let me settle it, and I'll answer for it that we'll have the entire three of them this evening — you understand clearly, the — entire — three — at our knees. Let us go now and see the paralytic."

He cried: "Are you ready, Christiane?"

She appeared at the door, very pale, with a look of determination. Having embraced her father and her brother, she turned toward Paul, and extended her hand toward him. He took it, with downcast eyes, quivering with emotion. As the Marquis, Andermatt, and Gontran had gone on before, chatting, and without minding them, she said, in a firm voice, fixing on the young man a tender and decided glance: "I belong to you, body and soul. Do with me henceforth what you please." Then she walked on, without giving him an opportunity of replying.

As they drew near the Oriols' spring, they perceived, like an enormous mushroom, the hat of Père Clovis, who was sleeping beneath the rays of the sun, in the warm water at the bottom of the hole. He now spent the entire morning there, having got accustomed to this boiling water which made him, he said, more lively than a yearling.

Andermatt woke him up: "Well, my fine fellow, you are going on better?"

When he had recognized his patron, the old fellow made a grimace of satisfaction: "Yes, yes, I am going on — I am going on as well as you please."

"Are you beginning to walk?"

"Like a rabbit, Mochieu — like a rabbit. I will dance a boree with my sweetheart on the first Sunday of the month."

Andermatt felt his heart beating; he repeated: "It is true, then, that you are walking?"

Père Clovis ceased jesting. "Oh! not very much, not very much. No matter — I'm getting on — I'm getting on!"

Then the banker wanted to see at once how the vagabond walked. He kept rushing about the hole, got agitated, gave orders, as if he were going to float again a ship that had foundered.

"Look here, Gontran! you take the right arm. You, Bretigny, the left arm. I am going to keep up his back. Come on! together! — one — two — three! My dear father-in-law, draw the leg toward you — no, the other, the one that's in the water. Quick, pray! I can't hold out longer. There we are — one, two — there! — ouf!"

They had put the old trickster sitting on the ground; and he allowed them to do it with a jeering look, without in any way assisting their efforts.

Then they raised him up again, and set him on his legs, giving him his crutches, which he used like walking-sticks; and he began to step out, bent double, dragging his feet after him, whining and blowing. He advanced in the fashion of a slug, and left behind him a long trail of water on the white dust of the road.

Andermatt, in a state of enthusiasm, clapped his hands, crying out as people do at theaters when applauding the actors: "Bravo, bravo, admirable, bravo!!!"

Then, as the old fellow seemed exhausted, he rushed forward to hold him up, seized him in his arms, although his clothes were streaming, and he kept repeating:

"Enough, don't fatigue yourself! We are going to put you back into your bath."

And Père Clovis was plunged once more into his hole by the four men who caught him by his four limbs and carried him carefully like a fragile and precious object.

Then, the paralytic observed in a tone of conviction: "It is good water, all the same, good water that hasn't an equal. It is worth a treasure, water like that!"

Andermatt turned round suddenly toward his father-in-law: "Don't keep breakfast waiting for me.

I am going to the Oriols', and I don't know when I'll be free. It is necessary not to let these things drag!"

And he set forth in a hurry, almost running, and twirling his stick about like a man bewitched.

The others sat down under the willows, at the side of the road, opposite Père Clovis's hole.

Christiane, at Paul's side, saw in front of her the high knoll from which she had seen the rock blown up.

She had been up there that day, scarcely a month ago. She had been sitting on that russet grass. One month! Only one month! She recalled the most trifling details, the tricolored parasols, the scullions, the slightest things said by each of them! And the dog, the poor dog crushed by the explosion! And that big youth, then a stranger to her, who had rushed forward at one word uttered by her lips in order to save the animal. To-day, he was her lover! her lover! So then she had a lover! She was his mistress — his mistress! She repeated this word in the recesses of her consciousness — his mistress! What a strange word! This man, sitting by her side, whose hand she saw tearing up one by one blades of grass, close to her dress, which he was seeking to touch, this man was now bound to her flesh and to his heart, by that mysterious chain, buried in secrecy and mystery, which nature has stretched between woman and man.

With that voice of thought, that mute voice which seems to speak so loudly in the silence of troubled souls, she incessantly repeated to herself: "I am his mistress! his mistress!" How strange, how unforeseen, a thing this was!

"Do I love him?" She cast a rapid glance at him. Their eyes met, and she felt herself so much caressed by the passionate look with which he covered her, that she trembled from head to foot. She felt a longing now, a wild, irresistible longing, to take that hand which was toying with the grass, and to press it very tightly in order to convey to him all that may be said by a clasp. She let her own hand slip along her dress down to the grass, then laid it there motionless, with the fingers spread wide. Then she saw the other come softly toward it like an amorous animal seeking his companion. It came nearer and nearer; and their little fingers touched. They grazed one another at the ends gently, barely, lost one another and found one another again, like lips meeting. But this imperceptible caress, this slight contact entered into her being so violently that she felt herself growing faint as if he were once more straining her between his arms.

And she suddenly understood how a woman can belong to some man, how she no longer is anything under the love that possesses her, how that other being takes her body and soul, flesh, thought, will, blood, nerves, — all, all, all that is in her, — just as a huge bird of prey with large wings swoops down on a wren.

The Marquis and Gontran talked about the future station, themselves won over by Will's enthusiasm. And they spoke of the banker's merits, the clearness of his mind, the sureness of his judgment, the certainty of his system of speculation, the boldness of his operations, and the regularity of his character. Father-in-law and brother-in-law, in the face of this probable success, of which they felt certain, were in agreement, and congratulated one another on this alliance.

Christiane and Paul did not seem to hear, so much occupied were they with each other.

The Marquis said to his daughter: "Hey! darling, you may perhaps one day be one of the richest women in France, and people will talk of you as they do about the Rothschilds. Will has truly a remarkable, very remarkable — a great intelligence."

But a morose and whimsical jealousy entered all at once into Paul's heart.

"Let me alone now," said he, "I know it, the intelligence of all those engaged in stirring up business. They have only one thing in their heads — money! All the thoughts that we bestow on beautiful things, all the actions that we waste on our caprices, all the hours which we fling away for our distractions, all the strength that we squander on our pleasures, all the ardor and the power which love, divine love, takes from us, they employ in seeking for gold, in thinking of gold, in amassing gold!

The man of intelligence lives for all the great disinterested tendernesses, the arts, love, science, travels, books; and, if he seeks money, it is because this facilitates the true pleasures of intellect and even the happiness of the heart! But they — they have nothing in their minds or their hearts but this ignoble taste for traffic! They resemble men of worth, these skimmers of life, just as much as the picture-dealer resembles the painter, as the publisher resembles the writer, as the theatrical manager resembles the dramatic poet."

He suddenly became silent, realizing that he had allowed himself to be carried away, and in a calmer voice he went on: "I don't say that of Andermatt, whom I consider a charming man. I like him a great deal, because he is a hundred times superior to all the others."

Christiane had withdrawn her hand. Paul once more stopped talking. Gontran began to laugh; and, in his malicious voice, with which he ventured to say everything, in his hours of mocking and raillery:

"In any case, my dear fellow, these men have one rare merit: that is, to marry our sisters and to have rich daughters, who become our wives."

The Marquis, annoyed, rose up: "Oh! Gontran, you are perfectly revolting."

Paul thereupon turned toward Christiane, and murmured: "Would they know how to die for one woman, or even to give her all their fortune — all — without keeping anything?"

This meant so clearly: "All I have is yours, including my life," that she was touched, and she adopted this device in order to take his hands in hers:

"Rise, and lift me up. I am benumbed from not moving."

He stood erect, seized her by the wrists, and drawing her up placed her standing on the edge of the road close to his side. She saw his mouth articulating the words, "I love you," and she quickly turned aside, to avoid saying to him in reply three words which rose to her lips in spite of her, in a burst of passion which was drawing her toward him.

They returned to the hotel. The hour for the bath was passed. They awaited the breakfast-bell. It rang, but Andermatt did not make his appearance. After taking another turn in the park, they resolved to sit down to table. The meal, although a long one, was finished before the return of the banker. They went back to sit down under the trees. And the hours stole by, one after another; the sun glided over the leaves, bending toward the mountains; the day was ebbing toward its close; and yet Will did not present himself.

All at once, they saw him. He was walking quickly, his hat in his hand, wiping his forehead, his necktie on one side, his waistcoat half open, as if after a journey, after a struggle, after a terrible and prolonged effort.

As soon as he beheld his father-in-law, he exclaimed: "Victory! 'tis done! But what a day, my friends! Ah! the old fox, what trouble he gave me!"

And immediately he explained the steps he had taken and the obstacles he had met with.

Père Oriol had, at first, shown himself so unreasonable that Andermatt was breaking off the negotiations and going away. Then the peasant called him back. The old man pretended that he would not sell his lands but would assign them to the Company with the right to resume possession of them in case of ill success. In case of success, he demanded half the profits.

The banker had to demonstrate to him, with figures on paper and tracings to indicate the different bits of land, that the fields all together would not be worth more than forty-five thousand francs at the present hour, while the expenses of the Company would mount up at one swoop to a million.

But the Auvergnat replied that he expected to benefit by the enormously increased value that would be given to his property by the erection of the establishment and hotels, and to draw his interest in the undertaking in accordance with the acquired value and not the previous value.

Andermatt had then to represent to him that the risks should be proportionate with the possible gains, and to terrify him with the apprehension of the loss.

They accordingly arrived at this agreement: Père Oriol was to assign to the Company all the grounds stretching as far as the banks of the stream, that is to say, all those in which it appeared possible to find mineral water, and in addition the top of the knoll, in order to erect there a casino and a hotel, and some vine-plots on the slope which should be divided into lots and offered to the leading physicians of Paris.

The peasant, in return for this apportionment valued at two hundred and fifty thousand francs, that is, at about four times its value, would participate to the extent of a quarter in the profits of the Company. As there was very much more land, which he did not part with, round the future establishment, he was sure, in case of success, to realize a fortune by selling on reasonable terms these grounds, which would constitute, he said, the dowry of his daughters.

As soon as these conditions had been arrived at, Will had to carry the father and the son with him to the notary's office in order to have a promise of sale drawn up defeasible in the event of their not finding the necessary water. And the drawing up of the agreement, the discussion of every point, the indefinite repetition of the same arguments, the eternal commencement over again of the same contentions, had lasted all the afternoon.

At last the matter was concluded. The banker had got his station. But he repeated, devoured by a regret: "It will be necessary for me to confine myself to the water without thinking of the questions about the land. He has been cunning, the old ape."

Then he added: "Bah! I'll buy up the old Company, and it is on that I may speculate! No matter —— it is necessary that I should start this evening again for Paris."

The Marquis, astounded, cried out: "What? This evening?"

"Why, yes, my dear father-in-law, in order to get the definitive instrument prepared, while M. Aubry-Pasteur will be making excavations. It is necessary also that I should make arrangements to commence the works in a fortnight. I haven't an hour to lose. With regard to this, I must inform you that you are to constitute a portion of my board of directors in which I will need a strong majority. I give you ten shares. To you, Gontran, also I give ten shares." Gontran began to laugh: "Many thanks, my dear fellow. I sell them back to you. That makes five thousand francs you owe me."

But Andermatt no longer felt in a mood for joking, when dealing with business of so much importance. He resumed dryly: "If you are not serious, I will address myself to another person."

Gontran ceased laughing: "No, no, my good friend, you know that I have cleared off everything with you."

The banker turned toward Paul: "My dear Monsieur, will you render me a friendly service, that is, to accept also ten shares with the rank of director?" Paul, with a bow, replied: "You will permit me, Monsieur, not to accept this graceful offer, but to put a hundred thousand francs into the undertaking, which I consider a superb one. So then it is I who have to ask for a favor from you."

William, ravished, seized his hands. This confidence had conquered him. Besides he always experienced an irresistible desire to embrace persons who brought him money for his enterprises.

But Christiane crimsoned to her temples, pained, bruised. It seemed to her that she had just been bought and sold. If he had not loved her, would Paul have offered these hundred thousand francs to her husband? No, undoubtedly! He should not, at least, have entered into this transaction in her presence.

The dinner-bell rang. They reentered the hotel. As soon as they were seated at table, Madame Paille, the mother, asked Andermatt:

"So you are going to set up another establishment?"

The news had already gone through the entire district, was known to everyone, it put the bathers into a state of commotion.

William replied: "Good heavens, yes! The existing one is too defective!"

And turning round to M. Aubry-Pasteur: "You will excuse me, dear Monsieur, for speaking to you at dinner of a step which I wished to take with regard to you; but I am starting again for Paris, and time presses on me terribly. Will you consent to direct the work of excavation, in order to find a volume of superior water?"

The engineer, feeling flattered, accepted the office. In five minutes everything had been discussed and settled with the clearness and precision which Andermatt imported into all matters of business. Then they talked about the paralytic. He had been seen crossing the park in the afternoon with only one walking-stick, although that morning he had used two. The banker kept repeating: "This is a miracle, a real miracle. His cure proceeds with giant strides!" Paul, to please the husband, rejoined: "It is Père Clovis himself who walks with giant strides."

A laugh of approval ran round the table. Every eye was fixed on Will; every mouth complimented him.

The waiters of the restaurant made it their business to serve him the first, with a respectful deference, which disappeared from their faces as soon as they passed the dishes to the next guest.

One of them presented to him a card on a plate. He took it up, and read it, half aloud:

"Doctor Latonne of Paris would be happy if M. Andermatt would be kind enough to give him an interview of a few seconds before hit departure."

"Tell him in reply that I have no time, but that I will be back in eight or ten days."

At the same moment, a box of flowers sent by Doctor Honorat was presented to Christiane. Gontran laughed: "Père Bonnefille is a bad third," said he.

The dinner was nearly over. Andermatt was informed that his landau was waiting for him. He went up to look for his little bag; and when he came down again he saw half the village gathered in front of the door.

Petrus Martel came to grasp his hand, with the familiarity of a strolling actor, and murmured in his ear: "I shall have a proposal to make to you — something stunning — with reference to your undertaking."

Suddenly, Doctor Bonnefille appeared, hurrying in his usual fashion. He passed quite close to Will, and bowing very low to him as he would do to the Marquis, he said to him:

"A pleasant journey, Baron."

"That settles it!" murmured Gontran.

Andermatt, triumphant, swelling with joy and pride, pressed the hands extended toward him, thanked them, and kept repeating: "Au revoir!"

He was nearly forgetting to embrace his wife, so much was he thinking about other things. This indifference was a relief to her, and, when she saw the landau moving away on the darkening road, as the horses broke into a quick trot, it seemed to her that she had nothing more to fear from anyone for the rest of her life.

She spent the whole evening seated in front of the hotel, between her father and Paul Bretigny, Gontran having gone to the Casino, where he went every evening.

She did not want either to walk or to talk, and remained motionless, her hands clasped over her knees, her eyes lost in the darkness, languid and weak, a little restless and yet happy, scarcely thinking, not even dreaming, now and then struggling against a vague remorse, which she thrust away from her, always repeating to herself, "I love him! I love him!"

She went up to her apartment at an early hour, in order to be alone and to think. Seated in the depths of an armchair and covered with a dressing-gown which floated around her, she gazed at the stars through the window, which was left open; and in the frame of that window she evoked every minute the image of him who had conquered her. She saw him, kind, gentle, and powerful — so strong and so yielding in her presence. This man had taken herself to himself, — she felt it, — taken her forever. She was alone no longer; they were two, whose two hearts would henceforth form but one heart, whose two souls would henceforth form but one soul. Where was he? She knew not; but she knew full well that he was dreaming of her, just as she was thinking of him. At each throb of her heart she believed she heard another throb answering somewhere. She felt a desire wandering round her and fanning her cheek like a bird's wing. She felt it entering through that open window, this desire coming from him, this burning desire, which entreated her in the silence of the night.

How good it was, how sweet and refreshing to be loved! What joy to think of some one, with a longing in your eyes to weep, to weep with tenderness, and a longing also to open your arms, even without seeing him, in order to invite him to come, to stretch one's arms toward the image that presents itself, toward that kiss which your lover casts unceasingly from far or near, in the fever of his waiting.

And she stretched toward the stars her two white arms in the sleeves of her dressing-gown. Suddenly she uttered a cry. A great black shadow, striding over her balcony, had sprung up into her window.

She sprang wildly to her feet! It was he! And, without even reflecting that somebody might see them, she threw herself upon his breast.

VIII

THE absence of Andermatt was prolonged. M. Aubry-Pasteur got the soil dug up. He found, in addition, four springs, which supplied the new Company with more than twice as much water as they required. The entire district, driven crazy by these searches, by these discoveries, by the great news which circulated everywhere, by the prospects of a brilliant future, became agitated and enthusiastic, talked of nothing else, and thought of nothing else. The Marquis and Gontran themselves spent their days hanging round the workmen, who were boring through the veins of granite; and they listened with increasing interest to the explanations and the lectures of the engineer on the geological character of Auvergne. And Paul and Christiane loved one another freely, tranquilly, in absolute security, without anyone suspecting anything, without anyone thinking even of spying on them, for the attention, the curiosity, and the zeal of all around them were absorbed in the future station.

Christiane acted like a young girl under the intoxication of a first love. The first draught, the first kiss, had burned, had stunned her. She had swallowed the second very quickly, and had found it better, and now again and again she raised the intoxicating cup to her lips.

Since the night when Paul had broken into her apartment, she no longer took any heed of what was happening in the world. For her, time, events, beings, no longer had any existence; there was nothing else in life save one man, he whom she loved. Henceforth, her eyes saw only him, her mind thought only of him, her hopes were fixed on him alone. She lived, went from place to place, ate, dressed herself, seemed to listen and to reply, without consciousness or thought about what she was doing. No disquietude haunted her, for no misfortune could have fallen on her. She had become insensible to everything. No physical pain could have taken hold of her flesh, as love alone could, so as to make her shudder. No moral suffering could have taken hold of her soul, paralyzed by happiness. Moreover, he, loving her with the self-abandonment which he displayed in all his attachments, excited the young woman's tenderness to distraction.

Often, toward evening, when he knew that the Marquis and Gontran had gone to the springs, he would say, "Come and look at our heaven." He called a cluster of pine-trees growing on the hillside above even the gorges their heaven. They ascended to this spot through a little wood, along a steep path, to climb which took away Christiane's breath. As their time was limited, they proceeded rapidly, and, in order that she might not be too much fatigued, he put his arm round her waist and lifted her up. Placing one hand on his shoulder, she let herself be borne along; and, from time to time, she would throw herself on his neck and place her mouth against his lips. As they mounted higher, the air became keener; and, when they reached the cluster of pine-trees, the odor of the balsam refreshed them like a breath of the sea.

They sat down under the shadowy trees, she on a grassy knoll, and he lower down, at her feet. The wind in the stems sang that sweet chant of the pine-trees which is like a wail of sorrow; and the immense Limagne, with its unseen backgrounds steeped in fog, gave them a sensation exactly like that of the ocean. Yes, the sea was there in front of them, down below. They could have no doubt of it, for they felt its breath fanning their faces.

He talked to her in the coaxing tone that one uses toward a child.

"Give me your fingers and let me eat them — they are my bonbons, mine!"

He put them one after the other into his mouth, and seemed to be tasting them with gluttonous delight.

"Oh! how nice they are! — especially the little one. I have never eaten anything better than the little one."

Then he threw himself on his knees, placed his elbows on Christiane's lap, and murmured:

"'Liane,' are you looking at me?" He called her Liane because she entwined herself around him in order to embrace him the more closely, as a plant clings around a tree. "Look at me. I am going to enter your soul."

And they exchanged that immovable, persistent glance, which seems truly to make two beings mingle with one another!

"We can only love thoroughly by thus possessing one another," he said. "All the other things of love are but foul pleasures."

And, face to face, their breaths blending into one, they sought to see one another's images in the depths of their eyes.

He murmured: "I love you, Liane. I see your adored heart."

She replied: "I, too, Paul, see your heart!"

And, indeed, they did see one another even to the depths of their hearts and souls, for there was no longer in their hearts and souls anything but a mad transport of love for one another.

He said: "Liane, your eye is like the sky. It is blue, with so many reflections, with so much clearness. It seems to me that I see swallow's passing through them — these, no doubt, must be your thoughts."

And when they had thus contemplated one another for a long, long time, they drew nearer still to one another, and embraced softly with little jerks, gazing once more into each other's eyes between each kiss. Sometimes he would take her in his arms, and carry her, while he ran along the stream, which glided toward the gorges of Enval, before dashing itself into them. It was a narrow glen, where meadows and woods alternated. Paul rushed over the grass, and now and then he would raise her up high with his powerful wrists, and exclaim: "Liane, let us fly away." And with this yearning to fly away, love, their impassioned love, filled them, harassing, incessant, sorrowful. And everything around them whetted this desire of their souls, the light atmosphere — a bird's atmosphere, he said — and the vast blue horizon, in which they both would fain have taken wing, holding each other by the hand, so as to disappear above the boundless plain when the night spread its shadows across it. They would have flown thus across the hazy evening sky, never to return. Where would they have gone? They knew not; but what a glorious dream! When he had got out of breath from running while carrying her in this way, he placed her sitting on a rock in order to kneel down before her; and, kissing her ankles, he adored her, murmuring infantile and tender words.

Had they been lovers in a city, their passion, no doubt, would have been different, more prudent, more sensual, less ethereal, and less romantic. But there, in that green country, whose horizon widened the flights of the soul, alone, without anything to distract them, to attenuate their instinct of awakened love, they had suddenly plunged into a passionately poetic attachment made up of ecstasy and frenzy. The surrounding scenery, the balmy air, the woods, the sweet perfume of the fields, played for them all day and all night the music of their love — music which excited them even to madness, as the sound of tambourines and of shrill flutes drives to acts of savage unreason the dervish who whirls round with fixed intent.

One evening, as they were returning to the hotel for dinner, the Marquis said to them, suddenly: "Andermatt is coming back in four days. Matters are all arranged. We are to leave the day after his return. We have been here a long time. We must not prolong mineral water seasons too much."

They were as much taken by surprise as if they had heard the end of the world announced, and during the meal neither of them uttered a word, so much were they thinking with astonishment of what was about to happen. So then they would, in a few days, be separated and would no longer be able to see one another freely. That appeared so impossible and so extraordinary to them that they could not realize it.

Andermatt did, in fact, come back at the end of the week. He had telegraphed in order that two landaus might be sent on to him to meet the first train.

Christiane, who had not slept, tormented as she was by a strange and new emotion, a sort of fear of her husband, a fear mingled with anger, with inexplicable contempt, and a desire to set him at defiance, had risen at daybreak, and was awaiting him. He appeared in the first carriage, accompanied by three gentlemen well attired but modest in demeanor. The second landau contained four others, who seemed persons of rank somewhat inferior to the first. The Marquis and Gontran were astonished. The latter asked: "Who are these people?"

Andermatt replied: "My shareholders. We are going to establish the Company this very day, and to nominate the board of directors immediately."

He embraced his wife without speaking to her, and almost without looking at her, so preoccupied was he; and, turning toward the seven gentlemen, who were standing behind him, silent and respectful:

"Go and have breakfast, and take a walk," said he. "We'll meet again here at twelve o'clock."

They went off without saying anything, like soldiers obeying orders, and mounting the steps of the hotel one after another, they went in. Gontran, who had been watching them as they disappeared from view, asked in a very serious tone:

"Where did you find them, these 'supers' of yours?"

The banker smiled: "They are very well-to-do men, moneyed men, capitalists."

And, after a pause, he added, with a more significant smile: "They busy themselves about my affairs."

Then he repaired to the notary's office to read over again the documents, of which he had sent the originals, all prepared, some days before. There he found Doctor Latonne, with whom, moreover, he had been in correspondence, and they chatted for a long time in low tones, in a corner of the office, while the clerks' pens ran along the paper, with the buzzing noise of insects.

The meeting to establish the Company was fixed for two o'clock. The notary's study had been fitted up as if for a concert. Two rows of chairs were placed for the shareholders in front of the table, where Maître Alain was to take his seat beside his principal clerk. Maître Alain had put on his official garment in consideration of the importance of the business in hand. He was a very small man, a stuttering ball of white flesh.

Andermatt entered just as it struck two, accompanied by the Marquis, his brother-in-law, and Bretigny, and followed by the seven gentlemen, whom Gontran described as "supers." He had the air of a general. Père Oriol also made his appearance with Colosse by his side. He seemed uneasy, distrustful, as people always are when about to sign a document. The last to arrive was Doctor Latonne. He had made his peace with Andermatt by a complete submission preceded by excuses skillfully turned, and followed by an offer of his services without any reserve or restrictions.

Thereupon, the banker, feeling that he had Latonne in his power, promised him the post he longed for, of medical inspector of the new establishment.

When everyone was in the room, a profound silence reigned. The notary addressed the meeting: "Gentlemen, take your seats." He gave utterance to a few words more, which nobody could hear in the confusion caused by the moving about of the chairs.

Andermatt lifted up a chair, and placed it in front of his army, in order to keep his eye on all his supporters; then, when he was seated, he said:

"Messieurs, I need not enter into any explanations with you as to the motive that brings us together. We are going, first of all, to establish the new Company in which you have consented to become shareholders. It is my duty, however, to apprise you of a few details, which have caused us a little embarrassment. I have found it necessary, before even entering on the undertaking at all, to assure myself that we could obtain the required authority for the creation of a new establishment of public utility. This assurance I have got. What remains to be done with respect to this, I will make it my business to do. I have the Minister's promise. But another point demands my attention. We are going, Messieurs, to enter on a struggle with the old Company of the Enval waters. We shall come forth victorious in this struggle, victorious and enriched, you may be certain; but, just as in the days of old, a war cry was necessary for the combatants, we, combatants in the modern battle, require a name for our station, a name sonorous, attractive, well fashioned for advertising purposes, which strikes the ear like the note of a clarion, and penetrates the ear like a flash of lightning. Now, Messieurs, we are in Enval, and we can not unbaptize this district. One resource only is left to us. To designate our establishment, our establishment alone, by a new appellation.

"Here is what I propose to you: If our bathhouse is to be at the foot of the knoll, of which M. Oriol, here present, is the proprietor, our future Casino will be erected on the summit of this same knoll. We may, therefore, say that this knoll, this mountain — — for it is a mountain, a little mountain — furnishes the site of our establishment, inasmuch as we have the foot and the top of it. Is it not, therefore, natural to call our baths the Baths of Mont Oriol, and to attach to this station, which will become one of the most important in the entire world, the name of the original proprietor? Render to Cæsar what belongs to Cæsar.

"And observe, Messieurs, that this is an excellent vocable. People will talk of the Mont Oriol' as they talk of 'the Mont Doré.' It fixes itself on the eye and in the ear; we can see it well; we can hear it well; it abides in us — Mont Oriol! — Mont Oriol! — The baths of Mont Oriol!"

And Andermatt made this word ring, flung it out like a ball, listening to the echo of it. He went on, repeating imaginary dialogues: "'You are going to the baths of Mont Oriol?'

"'Yes, Madame. People say they are perfect, these waters of Mont Oriol.'

"'Excellent, indeed. Besides, Mont Oriol is a delightful district.'"

And he smiled, assumed the air of people chatting to one another, altered his voice to indicate when the lady was speaking, saluted with the hand when representing the gentleman.

Then he resumed, in his natural voice: "Has anyone an objection to offer?"

The shareholders answered in chorus: "No, none."

All the "supers" applauded. Père Oriol, moved, flattered, conquered, overcome by the deep-rooted pride of an upstart peasant, began to smile while he twisted his hat about between his hands, and he made a sign of assent with his head in spite of him, a movement which revealed his satisfaction, and which Andermatt observed without pretending to see it. Colosse remained impassive, but was quite as much satisfied as his father.

Then Andermatt said to the notary: "Kindly read the instrument whereby the Company is incorporated, Maître Alain."

And he resumed his seat. The notary said to his clerk: "Go on, Marinet."

Marinet, a wretched consumptive creature, coughed, and with the intonations of a preacher, and an attempt at declamation, began to enumerate the statutes relating to the incorporation of an anonymous Company, called the Company of the Thermal Establishment of Mont Oriol at Enval with a capital of two millions.

Père Oriol interrupted him: "A moment, a moment," said he. And he drew forth from his pocket a few sheets of greasy paper, which during the past eight days had passed through the hands of all the notaries and all the men of business of the department. It was a copy of the statutes which his son and himself by this time were beginning to know by heart. Then, he slowly fixed his spectacles on his nose, raised up his head, looked out for the exact point where he could easily distinguish the letters, and said in a tone of command:

"Go on from that place, Marinet."

Colosse, having got close to his chair, also kept his eye on the paper along with his father.

And Marinet commenced over again. Then old Oriol, bewildered by the double task of listening and reading at the same time, tortured by the apprehension of a word being changed, beset also by the desire to see whether Andermatt was making some sign to the notary, did not allow a single line to be got through without stopping ten times the clerk whose elocutionary efforts he interrupted.

He kept repeating: "What did you say? What did you say there? I didn't understand — not so quick!" Then turning aside a little toward his son: "What place is he at, Coloche?"

Coloche, more self-controlled, replied: "It's all right, father — let him go on — it's all right."

The peasant was still distrustful. With the end of his crooked finger he went on tracing on the paper the words as they were read out, muttering them between his lips; but he could not fix his attention at the same time on both matters. When he listened, he did not read, and he did not hear when he was reading. And he puffed as if he had been climbing a mountain; he perspired as if he had been digging his vinefields under a midday sun, and from time to time, he asked for a few minutes' rest to wipe his forehead and to take breath, like a man fighting a duel.

Andermatt, losing patience, stamped with his foot on the ground. Gontran, having noticed on a table the "Moniteur du Puy-de-Dome," had taken it up and was running his eye over it, and Paul, astride on his chair, with downcast eyes and an anxious heart, was reflecting that this little man, rosy and corpulent, sitting in front of him, was going to carry off, next day, the woman whom he loved with all his soul, Christiane, his Christiane, his fair Christiane, who was his, his entirely, nothing to anyone save him. And he asked himself whether he was not going to carry her off this very evening.

The seven gentlemen remained serious and tranquil.

At the end of an hour, it was finished. The deed was signed. The notary made out certificates for the payments on the shares. On being appealed to, the cashier, M. Abraham Levy, declared that he had received the necessary deposits. Then the company, from that moment legally constituted, was announced to be gathered together in general assembly, all the shareholders being in attendance, for the appointment of a board of directors and the election of their chairman.

All the votes with the exception of two, were recorded in favor of Andermatt's election to the post of chairman. The two dissentients — the old peasant and his son — had nominated Oriol. Bretigny was appointed commissioner of superintendence. Then, the Board, consisting of MM. Andermatt, the Marquis and the Count de Ravenel, Bretigny, the Oriols, father and son, Doctor Latonne, Abraham Levy, and Simon Zidler, begged of the remaining shareholders to withdraw, as well as the notary and his clerk, in order that they, as the governing body, might determine on the first resolutions, and settle the most important points.

Andermatt rose up again: "Messieurs, we are entering on the vital question, that of success, which we must win at any cost.

"It is with mineral waters as with everything. It is necessary to get them talked about a great deal, and continually, so that invalids may drink them.

"The great modern question, Messieurs, is that of advertising. It is the god of commerce and of contemporary industry. Without advertising there is no security. The art of advertising, moreover, is difficult, complicated, and demands a considerable amount of tact. The first persons who resorted to this new expedient employed it rudely, attracting attention by noise, by beating the big drum, and letting off cannon-shots. Mangin, Messieurs, was only a forerunner.

To-day, clamor is regarded with suspicion, showy placards cause a smile, the crying out of names in the streets awakens distrust rather than curiosity. And yet it is necessary to attract public attention, and after having fixed it, it is necessary to produce conviction. The art, therefore, consists in discovering the means, the only means which can succeed, having in our possession something that we desire to sell. We, Messieurs, for our part, desire to sell water. It is by the physicians that we are to get the better of the invalids.

"The most celebrated physicians, Messieurs, are men like ourselves — who have weaknesses like us. I do not mean to convey that we can corrupt them. The reputation of the illustrious masters, whose assistance we require, places them above all suspicion of venality. But what man is there that cannot be won over by going properly to work with him? There are also women who cannot be purchased. These it is necessary to fascinate.

"Here, then, Messieurs, is the proposition which I am going to make to you, after having discussed it at great length with Doctor Latonne:

"We have, in the first place, classified in three leading groups the maladies submitted for our treatment. These are, first, rheumatism in all its forms, skin-disease, arthritis, gout, and so forth; secondly, affections of the stomach, of the intestines and of the liver; thirdly, all the disorders arising from disturbed circulation, for it is indisputable that our acidulated baths have an admirable effect on the circulation.

"Moreover, Messieurs, the marvelous cure of Père Clovis promises us miracles. Accordingly, when we have to deal with maladies which these waters are calculated to cure, we are about to make to the principal physicians who attend patients for such diseases the following proposition: 'Messieurs,' we shall say to them, 'come and see, come and see with your own eyes; follow your patients; we offer you hospitality. 'The country is magnificent; you require a rest after your severe labors during the winter — come! And come not to our houses, worthy professors, but to your own, for we offer you a cottage, which will belong to you, if you choose, on exceptional conditions.'"

Andermatt took breath, and went on in a more subdued tone:

"Here is how I have tried to work out this idea. We have selected six lots of land of a thousand meters each. On each of these six lots, the Bernese 'Chalets Mobiles' Company undertakes to fix one of their model buildings. We shall place gratuitously these dwellings, as elegant as they are comfortable, at the disposal of our physicians. If they are pleased with them, they need only buy the houses from the Bernese Company; as for the grounds, we shall assign them to the physicians, who are to pay us back — in invalids. Therefore, Messieurs, we obtain these multiplied advantages of covering our property with charming villas which cost us nothing, of attracting thither the leading physicians of the world and their legion of clients, and above all of convincing the eminent doctors who will very rapidly become proprietors in the district of the efficacy of our waters. As to all the negotiations necessary to bring about these results I take them upon myself, Messieurs; and I will do so, not as a speculator but as a man of the world."

Père Oriol interrupted him. The parsimony which he shared with the peasantry of Auvergne made him object to this gratuitous assignment of land.

Andermatt was inspired with a burst of eloquence. He compared the agriculturist on a large scale who casts his seed in handfuls into the teeming soil with the rapacious peasant who counts the grains and never gets more than half a harvest.

Then, as Oriol, annoyed by this language, persisted in his objections, the banker made his board divide, and shut the old man's mouth with six votes against two.

He next opened a large morocco portfolio and took out of it plans of the new establishment — the hotel and the Casino — as well as the estimates, and the most economical methods of procuring materials, which had been all prepared by the contractors, so that they might be approved of and signed before the end of the meeting. The works should be commenced by the beginning of the week after next.

The two Oriols alone wanted to investigate and discuss matters. But Andermatt, becoming irritated, said to them: "Did I ask you for money? No! Then give me peace! And, if you are not satisfied, we'll take another division on it."

Thereupon, they signed along with the remaining members of the Board; and the meeting terminated.

All the inhabitants of the place were waiting to see them going out, so intense was the excitement. The people bowed respectfully to them. As the two peasants were about to return home, Andermatt said to them:

"Do not forget that we are all dining together at the hotel. And bring your girls; I have brought them presents from Paris."

They were to meet at seven o'clock in the drawingroom of the Hotel Splendid.

It was a magnificent dinner to which the banker had invited the principal bathers and the authorities of the village. Christiane, who was the hostess, had the curé at her right, and the mayor at her left.

The conversation was all about the future establishment and the prospects of the district. The two Oriol girls had found under their napkins two caskets containing two bracelets of pearls and emeralds, and wild with delight, they talked as they had never done before with Gontran sitting between them. The elder girl herself laughed with all her heart at the jokes of the young man, who became animated, while he talked to them, and in his own mind formed about them those masculine judgments, those judgments daring and secret, which are generated in the flesh and in the mind, at the sight of every pretty woman.

Paul did not eat, and did not open his lips. It seemed to him that his life was going to end tonight. Suddenly he remembered that just a month had glided away, day by day, since the open-air dinner by the lake of Tazenat. He had in his soul that vague sense of pain caused rather by presentiments than by grief, known to lovers alone, that sense of pain which makes the heart so heavy, the nerves so vibrating that the slightest noise makes us pant, and the mind so wretchedly sad that everything we hear assumes a somber hue so as to correspond with the fixed idea.

As soon as they had quitted the table, he went to join Christiane in the drawingroom.

"I must see you this evening," he said, "presently, immediately, since I no longer can tell when we may be able to meet. Are you aware that it is just a month to-day?"

She replied: "I know it."

He went on: "Listen! I am going to wait for you on the road to La Roche Pradière, in front of the village, close to the chestnut-trees. Nobody will notice your absence at the time. Come quickly in order to bid me adieu, since tomorrow we part."

She murmured: "I'll be there in a quarter of an hour."

And he went out to avoid being in the midst of this crowd which exasperated him.

He took the path through the vineyards which they had followed one day — the day when they had gazed together at the Limagne for the first time. And soon he was on the highroad. He was alone, and he felt alone, alone in the world. The immense, invisible plain increased still more this sense of isolation. He stopped in the very spot where they had seated themselves on the occasion when he recited Baudelaire's lines on Beauty. How far away it was already! And, hour by hour, he retraced in his memory all that had since taken place. Never had he been so happy, never! Never had he loved so distractedly, and at the same time so chastely, so devotedly. And he recalled that evening by the "gour" of Tazenat, only a month from to-day — the cool wood mellowed with a pale luster, the little lake of silver, and the big fishes that skimmed along its surface; and their return, when he saw her walking in front of him with light and shadow falling on her in turn, the moon's rays playing on her hair, on her shoulders, and on her arms through the leaves of the trees. These were the sweetest hours he had tasted in his life. He turned round to ascertain whether she might not have arrived. He did not see her, but he perceived the moon, which appeared at the horizon. The same moon which had risen for his first declaration of love had risen now for his first adieu.

A shiver ran through his body, an icy shiver. The autumn had come — the autumn that precedes the winter. He had not till now felt this first touch of cold, which pierced his frame suddenly like a menace of misfortune.

The white road, full of dust, stretched in front of him, like a river between its banks. A form at that moment rose up at the turn of the road. He recognized her at once; and he waited for her without flinching, trembling with the mysterious bliss of feeling her drawing near, of seeing her coming toward him, for him.

She walked with lingering steps, without venturing to call out to him, uneasy at not finding him yet, for he remained concealed under a tree, and disturbed by the deep silence, by the clear solitude of the earth and sky. And, before her, her shadow advanced, black and gigantic, some distance away from her, appearing to carry toward him something of her, before herself.

Christiane stopped, and the shadow remained also motionless, lying down, fallen on the road.

Paul quickly took a few steps forward as far as the place where the form of the head rounded itself on her path. Then, as if he wanted to lose no portion of her, he sank on his knees, and prostrating himself, placed his mouth on the edge of the dark silhouette. Just as a thirsty dog drinks crawling on his belly in a spring he began to kiss the dust passionately, following the outlines of the beloved shadow. In this way, he moved toward her on his hands and knees, covering with caresses the lines of her body, as if to gather up with his lips the obscure image, dear because it was hers, that lay spread along the ground.

She, surprised, a little frightened even, waited till he was at her feet before she had the courage to speak to him; then, when he had lifted up his head, still remaining on his knees, but now straining her with both arms, she asked:

"What is the matter with you, tonight?"

He replied: "Liane, I am going to lose you."

She thrust all her fingers into the thick hair of her lover, and, bending down, held back his forehead in order to kiss his eyes.

"Why lose me?" said she, smiling, full of confidence.

"Because we are going to separate tomorrow."

"We separate? For a very short time, darling."

"One never knows. We shall not again find days like those that we passed here."

"We shall have others which will be as lovely." She raised him up, drew him under the tree, where he had been awaiting her, made him sit down close to her, but lower down, so that she might have her hand constantly in his hair; and she talked in a serious strain, like a thoughtful, ardent, and resolute woman, who loves, who has already provided against everything, who instinctively knows what must be done, who has made up her mind for everything.

"Listen, my darling. I am very free at Paris. William never bothers himself about me. His business concerns are enough for him. Therefore, as you are not married, I will go to see you. I will go to see you every day, sometimes in the morning before breakfast, sometimes in the evening, on account of the servants, who might chatter if I went out at the same hour. We can meet as often as here, even more than here, for we shall not have to fear inquisitive persons."

But he repeated with his head on her knees, and her waist tightly clasped: "Liane, Liane, I am going to lose you!"

She became impatient at this unreasonable grief, at this childish grief in this vigorous frame, while she, so fragile compared with him, was yet so sure of herself, so sure that nothing could part them.

He murmured: "If you wished it, Liane, we might fly off together, we might go far away, into a beautiful country full of flowers where we could love one another. Say, do you wish that we should go off together this evening — are you willing?"

But she shrugged her shoulders, a little nervous, a little dissatisfied, at his not having listened to her, for this was not the time for dreams and soft puerilities. It was necessary now for them to show themselves energetic and prudent, and to find out a way in which they could continue to love one another without rousing suspicion.

She said in reply: "Listen, darling! we must thoroughly understand our position, and commit no mistakes or imprudences. First of all, are you sure about your servants? The thing to be most feared is lest some one should give information or write an anonymous letter to my husband. Of his own accord, he will guess nothing. I know William well." This name, twice repeated, all at once had an irritating effect on Paul's nerves. He said: "Oh! don't speak to me about him this evening."

She was astonished: "Why? It is quite necessary, however. Oh! I assure you that he has scarcely anything to do with me."

She had divined his thoughts. An obscure jealousy, as yet unconscious, was awakened within him. And suddenly, sinking on his knees and seizing her hands:

"Listen, Liane! What terms are you on with him?"

"Why — why — very good!"

"Yes, I know. But listen — understand me clearly. He is — he is your husband, in fact — and — and — you don't know how much I have been brooding over this for some time past — how much it torments, tortures me. You know what I mean. Tell me!"

She hesitated a few seconds, then in a flash she realized his entire meaning, and with an outburst of indignant candor:

"Oh! my darling! — can you — can you think such a thing? Oh! I am yours — do you understand? — yours alone — since I love you — oh! Paul!"

He let his head sink on the young woman's lap, and in a very soft voices, said:

"But! — after all, Liane, you know he is your husband. What will you do? Have you thought of that? Tell me! What will you do this evening or tomorrow? For you cannot — always, always say 'No' to him!"

She murmured, speaking also in a very low tone: "I have pretended to be enceinte, and — and that is enough for him. Oh! there is scarcely anything between us — Come! say no more about this, my darling. You don't know how this" wounds me. Trust me, since I love you!"

He did not move, breathing hard and kissing her dress, while she caressed his face with her amorous, dainty fingers.

But, all of a sudden, she said: "We must go back, for they will notice that we are both absent." They embraced each other, clinging for a long time to one another in a clasp that might well have crushed their bones.

Then she rushed away so as to be back first and to enter the hotel quickly, while he watched her departing and vanishing from his sight, oppressed with sadness, as if all his happiness and all his hopes had taken flight along with her.

IX

THE station of Enval could hardly be recognized on the first of July of the following year. On the summit of the knoll, standing between the two outlets of the valley, rose a building in the Moorish style of architecture, bearing on its front the word "Casino" in letters of gold.

A little wood had been utilized for the purpose of creating a small park on the slope facing the Limagne. Lower down, among the vines, six chalets here and there showed their façades of polished wood.

On the slope facing the south, an immense structure was visible at a distance to travelers, who perceived it on their way from Riom.

This was the Grand Hotel of Mont Oriol. And exactly below it, at the very foot of the hill, a square house, simpler and more spacious, surrounded by a garden, through which ran the rivulet which flowed down from the gorges, offered to invalids the miraculous cure promised by a pamphlet of Doctor Latonne.

On the façade could be read: "Thermal baths of Mont Oriol." Then, on the right wing, in smaller letters: " Hydropathy. — Stomach-washing. — Piscina with running water." And, on the left wing: "Medical institute of automatic gymnastics."

All this was white, with a fresh whiteness, shining and crude. Workmen were still occupied in completing it — house-painters, plumbers, and laborers employed in digging, although the establishment had already been a month open.

Its success, moreover, had since the start, surpassed the hopes of its founders. Three great physicians, three celebrities, Professor Mas-Roussel, Professor Cloche, and Professor Remusot, had taken the new station under their patronage, and consented to sojourn for sometime in the villas of the Bernese "Chalets Mobiles" Company, placed at their disposal by the Board intrusted with the management of the waters.

Under their influence a crowd of invalids flocked to the place. The Grand Hotel of Mont Oriol was full.

Although the baths had commenced working since the first days of June, the official opening of the station had been postponed till the first of July, in order to attract a great number of people. The fête was to commence at three o'clock with the ceremony of blessing the springs; and in the evening, a magnificent performance, followed by fireworks and a ball, would bring together all the bathers of the place, as well as those of the adjoining stations, and the principal inhabitants of Clermont-Ferrand and Riom.

The Casino on the summit of the hill was hidden from view by the flags. Nothing could be seen any longer but blue, red, white, yellow, a kind of dense and palpitating cloud; while from the tops of the gigantic masts planted along the walks in the park, huge oriflammes curled themselves in the blue sky with serpentine windings.

M. Petrus Martel, who had been appointed conductor of this new Casino, seemed to think that under this cloud of flags he had become the allpowerful captain of some fantastic ship; and he gave orders to the white-aproned waiters with the resounding and terrible voice which admirals need in order to exercise command under fire. His vibrating words, borne on by the wind, were heard even in the village.

Andermatt, out of breath already, appeared on the terrace. Petrus Martel advanced to meet him and bowed to him in a lordly fashion.

"Everything is going on well?" inquired the banker.

"Everything is going on well, my dear President."

"If anyone wants me, I am to be found in the medical inspector's study. We have a meeting this morning."

And he went down the hill again. In front of the door of the thermal establishment, the overseer and the cashier, carried off also from the other Company, which had become the rival Company, but doomed without a possible contest, rushed forward to meet their master. The ex-jailer made a military salute. The other bent his head like a poor person receiving alms. Andermatt asked:

"Is the inspector here?"

The overseer replied: "Yes, Monsieur le President, all the gentlemen have arrived."

The banker passed through the vestibule, in the midst of bathers and respectful waiters, turned to the right, opened a door, and found in a spacious apartment of serious aspect, full of books and busts of men of science, all the members of the Board at present in Enval assembled: his father-in-law the Marquis, and his brother-in-law Gontran, the Oriols, father and son, who had almost been transformed into gentlemen wearing frock-coats of such length that — — with their own tallness, they looked like advertisements for a mourning-warehouse — Paul Bretigny, and Doctor Latonne.

After some rapid handshaking, they took their seats, and Andermatt commenced to address them:

"It remains for us to regulate an important matter, the naming of the springs. On this subject I differ entirely in opinion from the inspector. The doctor proposes to give to our three principal springs the names of the three leaders of the medical profession who are here. Assuredly, there would in this be a flattery which might touch them and win them over to us still more. But be sure, Messieurs, that it would alienate from us forever those among their distinguished professional brethren who have not yet responded to our invitation, and whom we should convince, at the cost of our best efforts and of every sacrifice, of the sovereign efficacy of our waters. Yes, Messieurs, human nature is unchangeable; it is necessary to know it and to make use of it. Never would Professors Plantureau, De Larenard, and Pascalis, to refer only to these three specialists in affections of the stomach and intestines, send their patients to be cured by the water of the Mas-Roussel Spring, the Cloche Spring, or the Remusot Spring. For these patients and the entire public would in that case be somewhat disposed to believe that it was by Professors Remusot, Cloche, and Mas-Roussel that our water and all its therapeutic properties had been discovered. There is no doubt, Messieurs, that the name of Gubler, with which the original spring at Chatel-Guyon was baptized, for a long time prejudiced against these waters, to-day in a prosperous condition, a section, at least, of the great physicians, who might have patronized it from the start.

"I accordingly propose to give quite simply the name of my wife to the spring first discovered and the names of the Mademoiselles Oriol to the other two. We shall thus have the Christiane, the Louise, and the Charlotte Springs. This suits very well; it is very nice. What do you say to it?"

His suggestion was adopted even by Doctor Latonne, who added: "We might then beg of MM. Mas-Roussel, Cloche, and Remusot to be godfathers and to offer their arms to the god-mothers."

"Excellent, excellent," said Andermatt. "I am hurrying to meet them. And they will consent. I may answer for them — they will consent. Let us, therefore, reassemble at three o'clock in the church where the procession is to be formed."

And he went off at a running pace. The Marquis and Gontran followed him almost immediately. The Oriols, father and son, with tall hats on their heads, hastened to walk in their turn side by side, grave looking and all in black, on the white road; and Doctor Latonne said to Paul, who had only arrived the previous evening, to be present at the fête:

"I have detained you, Monsieur, in order to show you a thing from which I expect marvelous results. It is my medical institute of automatic gymnastics." He took him by the arm, and led him in. But they had scarcely reached the vestibule when a waiter at the baths stopped the doctor:

"M. Riquier is waiting for his wash."

Doctor Latonne had, last year, spoken disparagingly of the stomach washings, extolled and practiced by Doctor Bonnefille, in the establishment of which he was inspector. But time had modified his opinion, and the Baraduc probe had become the great instrument of torture of the new inspector, who plunged it with an infantile delight into every gullet.

He inquired of Paul Bretigny: "Have you ever seen this little operation?"

The other replied: "No, never."

"Come on then, my dear fellow — it is very curious."

They entered the shower-bath room, where M. Riquier, the brick-colored man, who was this year trying the newly discovered springs, as he had tried, every summer, every fresh station, was waiting in a wooden armchair.

Like some executed criminal of olden times, he was squeezed and choked up in a kind of straight waistcoat of oilcloth, which was intended to preserve his clothes from stains and splashes; and he had the wretched, restless, and pained look of patients on whom a surgeon is about to operate.

As soon as the doctor appeared, the waiter took up a long tube, which had three divisions near the middle, and which had the appearance of a thin serpent with a double tail. Then the man fixed one of the ends to the extremity of a little cock communicating with the spring. The second was let fall into a glass receiver, into which would be presently discharged the liquids rejected by the patient's stomach; and the medical inspector, seizing with a steady hand the third arm of this conduit-pipe, drew it, with an air of amiability, toward M. Riquier's jaw, passed it into his mouth, and guiding it dexterously, slipped it into his throat, driving it in more and more with the thumb and index-finger, in a gracious and benevolent fashion, repeating:

"Very good! very good! very good! That will do, that will do; that will do; that will do exactly!" M. Riquier, with staring eyes, purple cheeks, lips covered with foam, panted for breath, gasped as if ha were suffocating, and had agonizing fits of coughing; and, clutching the arms of the chair, he made terrible efforts to get rid of that beastly india-rubber which was penetrating into his body.

When he had swallowed about a foot and a halt of it, the doctor said: "We are at the bottom. Turn it on!"

The attendant thereupon turned on the cock, and soon the patient's stomach became visibly swollen, having been filled up gradually with the warm water of the spring.

"Cough," said the physician, "cough, in order to facilitate the descent."

In place of coughing, the poor man had a rattling in the throat, and shaken with convulsions, he looked as if his eyes were going to jump out of his head.

Then suddenly a light gurgling could be heard on the ground close to the armchair. The spout of the tube with the two passages had at last begun to work; and the stomach now emptied itself into this glass receiver where the doctor searched eagerly for the indications of catarrh and the recognizable traces of imperfect digestion.

"You are not to eat any more green peas," said he, "or salad. Oh! no salad! You cannot digest it at all. No more strawberries either! I have already repeated to you ten times, no strawberries!"

M. Riquier seemed raging with anger. He excited himself now without being able to utter a word on account of this tube, which stopped up his throat. But when, the washing having been finished, the doctor had delicately drawn out the probe from his interior, he exclaimed:

"Is it my fault if I am eating every day filth that ruins my health? Isn't it you that should watch the meals supplied by your hotelkeeper? I have come to your new cook-shop because they used to poison me at the old one with abominable food, and I am worse than ever in your big barrack of a Mont Oriol inn, upon my honor!"

The doctor had to appease him, and promised over and over again to have the invalids' food at the table d'hote submitted beforehand to his inspection. Then, he took Paul Bretigny's arm again, and said as he led him away:

"Here are the extremely rational principles on which I have established my special treatment by the self-moving gymnastics, which we are going to inspect. You know my system of organo-metric medicine, don't you? I maintain that a great portion of our maladies entirely proceed from the excessive development of some one organ which encroaches on a neighboring organ, impedes its functions, and, in a little while, destroys the general harmony of the body, whence arise the most serious disturbances.

"Now, the exercise is, along with the shower-bath and the thermal treatment, one of the most powerful means of restoring the equilibrium and bringing back the encroaching parts to their normal proportions.

"But how are we to determine the man to make the exercise? There is not merely the act of walking, of mounting on horseback, of swimming or rowing — a considerable physical effort. There is also and above all a moral effort. It is the mind which determines, draws along, and sustains the body. The men of energy are men of movement. Now energy is in the soul and not in the muscles. The body obeys the vigorous will.

"It is not necessary to think, my dear friend, of giving courage to the cowardly or resolution to the weak. But we can do something else, we can do more — we can suppress mental energy, suppress moral effort and leave only physical subsisting. This moral effort, I replace with advantage by a foreign and purely mechanical force. Do you understand? No, not very well. Let us go in."

He opened a door leading into a large apartment, in which were ranged fantastic looking instruments, big armchairs with wooden legs, horses made of rough deal, articulated boards, and movable bars stretched in front of chairs fixed in the ground. And all these objects were connected with complicated machinery, which was set in motion by turning handles.

The doctor went on: "Look here. We have four principal kinds of exercise. These are walking, equitation, swimming, and rowing. Each of these exercises develops different members, acts in a special fashion. Now, we have them here — the entire four — — produced by artificial means. All you have to do is to let yourself act, while thinking of nothing, and you can run, mount on horseback, swim, or row for an hour, without the mind taking any part — the slightest part in the world — in this entirely muscular work."

At that moment, M. Aubry-Pasteur entered, followed by a man whose tucked-up sleeves displayed the vigorous biceps on each arm. The engineer was as fat as ever. He was walking with his legs spread Wide apart and his arms held out from his body, While he panted for breath.

The doctor said: "You will understand by looking on at it yourself."

And addressing his patient: "Well, my dear Monsieur, what are we going to do to-day? Walking or equitation?"

M. Aubry-Pasteur, who pressed Paul's hand, replied: "I would like a little walking seated; that fatigues me less."

M. Latonne continued: "We have, in fact, walking seated and walking erect. Walking erect, while more efficacious, is rather painful. I procure it by means of pedals on which you mount and which set your legs in motion while you maintain your equilibrium by clinging to rings fastened to the wall. But here is an example of walking while seated."

The engineer had fallen back into a rocking armchair, and he placed his legs in the wooden legs with movable joints attached to this seat. His thighs, calves, and ankles were strapped down in such a way that he was unable to make any voluntary movement; then, the man with the tucked-up sleeves, seizing the handle, turned it round with all his strength. The armchair, at first, swayed to and fro like a hammock; then, suddenly, the patient's legs went out, stretching forward and bending back, advancing and returning, with extreme speed.

"He is running," said the doctor, who then gave the order: "Quietly! Go at a walking pace."

The man, turning the handle more slowly, caused the fat engineer to do the sitting walk in a more moderate fashion, which ludicrously distorted all the movements of his body.

Two other patients next made their appearance, both of them enormous, and followed also by two attendants with naked arms.

They were hoisted upon wooden horses, which, set in motion, began immediately to jump along the room, shaking their riders in an abominable manner.

"Gallop!" cried the doctor. And the artificial animals, rushing like waves and capsizing like ships, fatigued the two patients so much that they began to scream out together in a panting and pitiful tone:

"Enough! enough! I can't stand it any longer! Enough!"

The physician said in a tone of command: "Stop!" He then added: "Take breath for a little while. You will go on again in five minutes."

Paul Bretigny, who was choking with suppressed laughter, drew attention to the fact that the riders were not warm, while the handle-turners were perspiring.

"If you inverted the rôles," said he, "would it not be better?"

The doctor gravely replied: "Oh! not at all, my dear friend. We must not confound exercise and fatigue. The movement of the man who is turning the wheel is injurious, while the movement of the walker or the rider is beneficial."

But Paul noticed a lady's saddle.

"Yes," said the physician; "the evening is reserved for the other sex. The men are no longer admitted after twelve o'clock. Come, then, and look at the dry swimming."

A system of movable little boards screwed together at their ends and at their centers, stretched out in lozenge-shape or closing into squares, like that children's game which carries along soldiers who are spurred on, permitted three swimmers to be garroted and mangled at the same time.

The doctor said: "I need not extol to you the benefits of dry swimming, which does not moisten the body except by perspiration, and consequently does not expose our imaginary bather to any danger of rheumatism."

But a waiter, with a card in his hand, came to look for the doctor.

"The Duc de Ramas, my dear friend. I must leave you. Excuse me."

Paul, left there alone, turned round. The two cavaliers were trotting afresh. M. Aubry-Pasteur was walking still; and the three natives of Auvergne, with their arms all but broken and their backs cracking with thus shaking the patients on whom they were operating, were quite out of breath. They looked as if they were grinding coffee.

When he had reached the open air, Bretigny saw Doctor Honorât watching, along with his wife, the preparations for the fête. They began to chat, gazing at the flags which crowned the hill with a kind of halo.

"Is it at the church the procession is to be formed?" the physician asked his wife.

"It is at the church."

"At three o'clock?"

"At three o'clock."

"The professors will be there?"

"Yes, they will accompany the lady-sponsors." The next persons to stop were the ladies Paille. Then, came the Monecus, father and daughter. But as he was going to breakfast alone with his friend Gontran at the Casino Café, he slowly made his way up to it. Paul, who had arrived the night before, had not had an interview with his comrade for the past month; and he was longing to tell him many boulevard stories — stories about gay women and houses of pleasure.

They remained chattering away till half past two when Petrus Martel came to inform them that people were on their way to the church.

"Let us go and look for Christiane," said Gontran.

"Let us go," returned Paul.

They found her standing on the steps of the new hotel. She had the hollow cheeks and the swarthy complexion of pregnant women; and her figure indicated a near accouchement.

"I was waiting for you," she said. "William is gone on before us. He has so many things to do to-day."

She cast toward Paul Bretigny a glance full of tenderness, and took his arm. They went quietly on their way, avoiding the stones.

She kept repeating: "How heavy I am! How heavy I am! I am no longer able to walk. I am so much afraid of falling!"

He did not reply, and carefully held her up, without seeking to meet her eyes which she turned toward him incessantly.

In front of the church, a dense crowd was awaiting them.

Andermatt cried: "At last! at last! Come, make haste. See, this is the order: two choir-boys, two chanters in surplices, the cross, the holy water, the priest, then Christiane with Professor Cloche, Mademoiselle Louise with Professor Remusot, and Mademoiselle Charlotte with Professor Mas-Roussel. Next come the members of the Board, the medical body, then the public. This is understood. Forward!"

The ecclesiastical staff thereupon left the church, taking their places at the head of the procession. Then a tall gentleman with white hair brushed back over his ears, the typical "scientist," in accordance with the academic form, approached Madame Andermatt, and saluted her with a low bow.

When he had straightened himself up again, with his head uncovered, in order to display his beautiful, scientific head, and his hat resting on his thigh with an imposing air as if he had learned to walk at the Comédie Française, and to show the people his rosette of officer of the Legion of Honor, too big for a modest man.

He began to talk: "Your husband, Madame, has been speaking to me about you just now, and about your condition which gives rise to some affectionate disquietude. He has told me about your doubts and your hesitations as to the probable moment of your delivery."

She reddened to the temples, and she murmured: "Yes, I believed that I would be a mother a very long time before the event. Now I can't tell either — I can't tell either — "

She faltered in a state of utter confusion.

A voice from behind them said: "This station has a very great future before it. I have already obtained surprising effects."

It was Professor Remusot addressing his companion, Louise Oriol. This gentleman was small, with yellow, unkempt hair, and a frock-coat badly cut, the dirty look of a slovenly savant.

Professor Mas-Roussel, who gave his arm to Charlotte Oriol, was a handsome physician, without beard or mustache, smiling, well-groomed, hardly turning gray as yet, a little fleshy, and, with his smooth, clean-shaven face, resembling neither a priest nor an actor, as was the case with Doctor Latonne.

Next came the members of the Board, with Andermatt at their head, and the tall hats of old Oriol and his son towering above them.

Behind them came another row of tall hats, the medical body of Enval, among whom Doctor Bonnefille was not included, his place, indeed, being taken by two new physicians, Doctor Black, a very short old man almost a dwarf, whose excessive piety had surprised the whole district since the day of his arrival; then a very good-looking young fellow, very much given to flirtation, and wearing a small hat, Doctor Mazelli, an Italian attached to the person of the Duc de Ramas — others said, to the person of the Duchesse.

And behind them could be seen the public, a flood of people — bathers, peasants, and inhabitants of the adjoining towns.

The ceremony of blessing the springs was very short. The Abbé Litre sprinkled them one after the other with holy water, which made Doctor Honorât say that he was going to give them new properties with chloride of sodium. Then all the persons specially invited entered the large reading-room, where a collation had been served.

Paul said to Gontran: "How pretty the little Oriol girls have become!"

"They are charming, my dear fellow."

"You have not seen M. le President?" suddenly inquired the ex-jailer overseer.

"Yes, he is over there, in the corner."

"Père Clovis is gathering a big crowd in front of the door."

Already, while moving in the direction of the springs for the purpose of having them blessed, the entire procession had filed off in front of the old invalid, cured the year before, and now again more paralyzed than ever. He would stop the visitors on the road and the last-comers as a matter of choice, in order to tell them his story:

"These waters here, you see, are no good — they cure, 'tis true, but you relapse again afterward, and after this relapse you're half a corpse. As for me, my legs were better before, and here I am now with my arms gone in consequence of the cure. And my legs, they're iron, but iron that you have to cut before it bends."

Andermatt, filled with vexation, had tried to prosecute him in a court of justice and to get him sent to jail for having depreciated the waters of Mont Oriol and having attempted extortion. But he had not succeeded in obtaining a conviction or in shutting the old fellow's mouth.

The moment he was informed that the old vagabond was babbling before the door of the establishment, he rushed out to make Clovis keep silent.

At the side of the highroad, in the center of an excited crowd, he heard angry voices. People pressed forward to listen and to see. Some ladies asked: "What is this?" Some men replied: "'Tis an invalid, whom the waters here have finished." Others believed that an infant had just been squashed. It was also said that a poor woman had got an attack of epilepsy.

Andermatt broke through the crowd, as he knew how to do, by violently pushing his little round stomach between the stomachs of other people. "It proves," Gontran remarked, "the superiority of balls to points."

Père Clovis, sitting on the ditch, whined about his pains, recounted his sufferings in a sniveling tone, while standing in front of him, and separating him from the public, the Oriols, father and son, exasperated, were hurling insults and threats at him as loudly as ever they could.

"That's not true," cried Colosse. "This fellow is a liar, a sham, a poacher, who runs all night through the wood."

But the old fellow, without getting excited, kept reiterating in a high, piercing voice which was heard above the vociferations of the two Oriols: "They've killed me, my good monchieus, they've killed me with their water. They bathed me in it by force last year. And here I am at this moment — here I am!" Andermatt imposed silence on all, and stooping toward the impotent man, said to him, looking into the depths of his eyes: "If you are worse, it is your own fault, mind. If you listen to me, I undertake to cure you, I do, with fifteen or twenty baths at most. Come and look me up at the establishment in an hour, when the people have all gone away, my good father. In the meantime, hold your tongue."

The old fellow had understood. He became silent, then, after a pause, he answered: "I'm always willing to give it a fair trial. You'll see."

Andermatt caught the two Oriols by the arms and quickly dragged them away; while Père Clovis remained stretched on the grass between his crutches, at the side of the road, blinking his eyes under the rays of the sun.

The puzzled crowd kept pressing round him. Some gentlemen questioned him, but he did not reply, as though he had not heard or understood; and as this curiosity, futile just now, ended by fatiguing him, he began to sing, bareheaded, in a voice as false as it was shrill, an interminable ditty in an unintelligible dialect.

The crowd ebbed away gradually. Only a few children remained standing a long time in front of him, with their fingers in their noses, contemplating him.

Christiane, exceedingly tired, had gone in to take a rest. Paul and Gontran walked about through the new park in the midst of the visitors. Suddenly they saw the company of players, who had also deserted the old Casino, to attach themselves to the growing fortunes of the new.

Mademoiselle Odelin, who had become quite fashionable, was leaning as she walked on the arm of her mother, who had assumed an air of importance. M. Petitnivelle, of the Vaudeville, appeared very attentive to these ladies, who followed M. Lapalme of the Grand Theater of Bordeaux, arguing with the musicians just as of old, the maestro Saint Landri, the pianist Javel, the flautist Noirot, and the double-bass Nicordi.

On perceiving Paul and Gontran, Saint Landri rushed toward them. He had, during the winter, got a very small musical composition performed in a very small out-of-the-way theater; but the newspapers had spoken of him with a certain favor, and he now treated Massenet, Beyer, and Gounod contemptuously.

He stretched forth both hands with an outburst of friendly regard, and immediately proceeded to repeat what he had been saying to those gentlemen of the orchestra over whom he was the conductor.

"Yes, my dear friend, it is finished, finished, finished, the hackneyed style of the old school. The melodists have had their day. This is what people cannot understand. Music is a new art, melody is its first lisping. The ignorant ear loves the burden of a song. It takes a child's pleasure, a savage's pleasure in it. I may add that the ears of the people or of the ingenuous public, the simple ears, will always love little songs, airs, in a word. It is an amusement similar to that in which the frequenters of café concerts indulge. I am going to make use of a comparison in order to make myself understood. The eye of the rustic loves crude colors and glaring pictures; the eye of the intelligent representative of the middle class who is not artistic loves shades benevolently pretentious and affecting subjects; but the artistic eye, the refined eye, loves, understands, and distinguishes the imperceptible modulations of a single tone, the mysterious harmonies of light touches invisible to most people.

"It is the same with literature. Doorkeepers like romances of adventure, the middle class like novels which appeal to the feelings; while the real lovers of literature care only for the artistic books which are incomprehensible to the others. When an ordinary citizen talks music to me I feel a longing to kill him. And when it is at the opera, I. ask him: 'Are you capable of telling me whether the third violin has made a false note in the overture of the third act? No. Then be silent. You have no ear. The man who does not understand, at the same time, the whole and all the instruments separately in an orchestra has no ear, and is no musician. There you are! Good night!'"

He turned round on his heel, and resumed: "For an artist all music is in a chord. Ah! my friend, certain chords madden me, cause a flood of inexpressible happiness to penetrate all my flesh. I have to-day an ear so well exercised, so finished, so matured, that I end by liking even certain false chords, just like a virtuoso whose fully-developed taste amounts to a form of depravity. I am beginning to be a vitiated person who seeks for extreme sensations of hearing. Yes, my friends, certain false notes. What delights! What perverse and profound delights! How this moves, how it shakes the nerves! how it scratches the ear — how it scratches! how it scratches!"

He rubbed his hands together rapturously, and he hummed: "You shall hear my opera — my opera — my opera. You shall hear my opera."

Gontran said: "You are composing an opera?"

"Yes, I have finished it." But the commanding voice of Petrus Martel resounded:

"You understand perfectly! A yellow rocket, and off you go!"

He was giving orders for the fireworks. They joined him, and he explained his arrangements by showing with his outstretched arm, as if he were threatening a hostile fleet, stakes of white wood on the mountain above the gorge, on the opposite side of the valley.

"It is over there that they are to be shot out. I told my pyrotechnist to be at his post at half past eight. The very moment the spectacle is over, I will give the signal from here by a yellow rocket, and then he will illuminate the opening piece."

The Marquis made his appearance: "I am going to drink a glass of water," he said.

Paul and Gontran accompanied him, and again descended the hill. On reaching the establishment, they saw Père Clovis, who had got there, sustained by the two Oriols, followed by Andermatt and by the doctor, and making, every time he trailed his legs on the ground, contortions suggestive of extreme pain.

"Let us go in," said Gontran, "this will be funny."

The paralytic was placed sitting in an armchair. Then Andermatt said to him: "Here is what I propose, old cheat that you are. You are going to be cured immediately by taking two baths a day. And the moment you walk you'll have two hundred francs."

The paralytic began to groan: "My legs, they are iron, my good Monchieu!"

Andermatt made him hold his tongue, and went on: "Now, listen! You shall again have two hundred francs every year up to the time of your death — — you understand — up to the time of your death, if you continue to experience the salutary effect of our waters."

The old fellow was in a state of perplexity. The continuous cure was opposed to his plan of action. He asked in a hesitating tone: "But when — when it is closed up — this box of yours — if this should take hold of me again — I can do nothing then — I — — seeing that it will be shut up — your water — "

Doctor Latonne interrupted him, and, turning toward Andermatt, said: "Excellent! excellent! We'll cure him every year. This will be even better, and will show the necessity of annual treatment, the indispensability of returning hither. Excellent — this is perfectly clear!"

But the old man repeated afresh: "It will not suit this time, my good Monchieu. My legs, they're iron, iron in bars."

A new idea sprang up in the doctor's mind: "If I got him to try a course of seated walking," he said, "I might hasten the effect of the waters considerably. It is an experiment worth trying."

"Excellent idea," returned Andermatt, adding: "Now, Père Clovis, take yourself off, and don't forget our agreement."

The old fellow went away still groaning; and, when evening came on, all the directors of Mont Oriol came back to dine, for the theatrical representation was announced to take place at half past seven.

The great hall of the new Casino was the place where they were to dine. It was capable of holding a thousand persons.

At seven o'clock the visitors who had not numbered seats presented themselves. At half past seven the hall was filled, and the curtain was raised for the performance of a vaudeville in two acts, which preceded Saint Landri's operetta, interpreted by vocalists from Vichy, who had given their services for the occasion.

Christiane in the front row, between her brother and her husband, suffered a great deal from the heat. Every moment she repeated: "I feel quite exhausted! I feel quite exhausted!"

After the vaudeville, as the operetta was opening, she was becoming ill, and turning round to her husband, said: "My dear Will, I shall have to leave. I am suffocating!"

The banker was annoyed. He was desirous above everything in the world that this fête should be a success, from start to finish, without a single hitch. He replied:

"Make every effort to hold out. I beg of you to do so! Your departure would upset everything. You would have to pass through the entire hall!"

But Gontran, who was sitting along with Paul behind her, had overheard. He leaned toward his sister: "You are too warm?" said he.

"Yes, I am suffocating."

"Good. Stay! You are going to have a laugh." There was a window near. He slipped toward it, got upon a chair, and jumped out without attracting hardly any notice. Then he entered the café, which was perfectly empty, stretched his hand out under the bar where he had seen Petrus Martel conceal the signal-rocket, and, having filched it, he ran off to hide himself under a group of trees, and then set it on fire. The swift yellow sheaf flew up toward the clouds, describing a curve, and casting across the sky a long shower of flame-drops. Almost instantaneously a terrible detonation burst forth over the neighboring mountain, and a cluster of stars sent flying sparks through the darkness of the night.

Somebody exclaimed in the hall where the spectators were gathered, and where at the moment Saint Landri's chords were quivering: "They're letting off the fireworks!"

The spectators who were nearest to the door abruptly rose to their feet to make sure about it, and went out with light steps. All the rest turned their eyes toward the windows, but saw nothing, for they were looking at the Limagne. People kept asking: "Is it true? Is it true?"

The impatient assembly got excited, hungering above everything for simple amusements. A voice from outside announced: "It is true! The firework's are let off!"

Then, in a second everyone in the hall was standing up. They rushed toward the door; they jostled against each other; they yelled at those who obstructed their egress: "Hurry on! hurry on!"

The entire audience, in a short time, had emerged into the park. Saint Landri alone, in a state of exasperation continued beating time in front of his distracted orchestra. Meanwhile, fiery suns succeeded Roman candles in the midst of detonations.

Suddenly, a formidable voice sent forth thrice this wild exclamation: "Stop, in God's name! Stop, in God's name! Stop, in God's name!"

And, as an immense Bengal fire next illuminated the mountain and lighted up in red to the right and blue to the left, the enormous rocks and trees, Petrus Martel could be seen standing on one of the vases of imitation marble that decorated the terrace of the Casino, bareheaded, with his arms in the air, gesticulating and howling.

Then, the great illumination being extinguished, nothing could be seen any longer save the real stars. But immediately another rocket shot up, and Petrus Martel, jumping on the ground, exclaimed: "What a disaster! what a disaster! My God, what a disaster!"

And he passed through the crowd with tragic gestures, with blows of his fist in the empty air, furious stampings of his feet, always repeating: "What a disaster! My God, what a disaster!"

Christiane had taken Paul's arm to get a seat in the open air, and kept looking with delight at the rockets which ascended into the sky.

Her brother came up to her suddenly, and said: "Hey, is it a success? Do you think it is funny?" She murmured: "What, it is you?"

"Why, yes, it is I. Is it good, hey?"

She began to laugh, finding it really amusing. But Andermatt arrived in a state of great mental distress. He did not understand how such a blow could have come. The rocket had been stolen from the bar to give the signal agreed upon. Such an infamy could only have been perpetrated by some emissary of the old Company, some agent of Doctor Bonnefille!

And he repeated: "'Tis maddening, positively maddening. Here are fireworks worth two thousand three hundred francs destroyed, entirely destroyed!" Gontran replied: "No, my dear fellow, on a proper calculation, the loss does not mount up to more than a quarter; let us put it at a third, if you like; say seven hundred and sixty-six francs. Your guests will, therefore, have enjoyed fifteen hundred and thirty-four francs' worth of rockets. This truly is not bad."

The banker's anger turned against his brother-in-law. He caught him roughly by the arm: "Gontran, I want to talk seriously to you. Since I have a hold of you, let us take a turn in the walks. Besides, I have five minutes to spare."

Then, turning toward Christiane: "I place you in charge of our friend Bretigny, my dear; but don't remain a long time out — take care of yourself. You might catch cold, you know. Be careful! careful!"

She murmured: "Never fear, dear."

So Andermatt carried off Gontran. When they were alone, at a little distance from the crowd, the banker stopped: "My dear fellow, 'tis about your financial position that I want to talk."

"About my financial position?"

"Yes, you know it well, your financial position."

"No. But you ought to know it for me, since you lent money to me."

"Well, yes, I do know it, and 'tis for that reason I want to talk to you."

"It seems to me, to say the least of it, that the moment is ill chosen — in the midst of a display of fireworks!"

"The moment, on the contrary, is very well chosen. I am not talking to you in the midst of a display of fireworks, but before a ball."

"Before a ball? I don't understand."

"Well, you are going to understand. Here is your position: you have nothing except debts; and you'll never have anything but debts."

Gontran gravely replied: "You tell me that a little bluntly."

"Yes, because it is necessary. Listen to me! You have eaten up the share which came to you as a fortune from your mother. Let us say no more about that."

"Let us say no more about it."

"As for your father, he possesses a yearly income of thirty thousand francs, say, a capital of about eight hundred thousand francs. Your share, later on, will, therefore, be four hundred thousand francs. Now you owe me — me, personally — one hundred and ninety thousand francs. You owe money besides to usurers."

Gontran muttered in a haughty tone: "Say, to Jews."

"Be it so, to Jews, although among the number there is a churchwarden from Saint Sulpice who made use of a priest as an intermediary between himself and you — but I will not cavil about such trifles. You owe, then, to various usurers, Israelites or Catholics, nearly as much. Let us put it at a hundred and fifty thousand at the lowest estimate. This makes a total of three hundred and forty thousand francs, on which you are paying interest, always borrowing, except with regard to mine, which you do not pay."

"That's right," said Gontran.

"So then, you have nothing more left."

"Nothing, indeed — except my brother-in-law."

"Except your brother-in-law, who has had enough of lending money to you."

"What then?"

"What then, my dear fellow? The poorest peasant living in one of these huts is richer than you."

"Exactly — and next?"

"Next — next — ? If your father were to die tomorrow, you would no longer have any resource to get bread — to get bread, mind you — except to take a post as a clerk in my house. And this again would only be a means of disguising the pension which I should be allowing you."

Gontran, in a tone of irritation, said: "My dear William, these things bore me. I know them, besides, just as well as you do, and, I repeat, the moment is ill chosen to remind me about them — with — with so little diplomacy."

"Allow me, let me finish. You can only extricate yourself from it by a marriage. Now, you are a wretched match, in spite of your name, which sounds well without being illustrious. In short, it is not one of those which an heiress, even a Jewish one, buys with a fortune. Therefore, we must find you a wife acceptable and rich — which is not very easy — "Gontran interrupted him: "Give her name at once — — that is the best way."

"Be it so — one of Père Oriol's daughters, whichever you prefer. And this is why I wanted to talk to you before the ball."

"And now explain yourself at greate" length," returned Gontran, coldly.

"It is very simple. You see the success I have obtained at the start with this station. Now if I had in my hands, or rather if we had in our hands all the land which this cunning peasant has kept for himself, I could turn it into gold. To speak only of the vineyards which lie between the establishment and the hotel and between the hotel and the Casino, I would pay a million francs for them tomorrow — I, Andermatt. Now, these vineyards and others all round the knoll will be the dowries of these girls. The father told me so again a short time since, not without an object, perhaps. Well, if you were willing, we could do a big stroke of business there, the two of us."

Gontran muttered, with a thoughtful air: "'Tis possible. I'll think over it."

"Do think over it, my dear boy, and don't forget that I never speak of things that are not very sure, or without having given matters every consideration, and realized all the possible consequences and all the decided advantages."

But Gontran, lifting up his arm, as if he had suddenly forgotten all that his brother-in-law had been saying to him: "Look! How beautiful that is!"

The bunch of rockets flamed up, in imitation of a burning palace on which a blazing flag had inscribed on it "Mont Oriol" in letters of fire perfectly red and, right opposite to it, above the plain, the moon, red also, seemed to have come out to contemplate this spectacle. Then, when the palace, after it had been burning for some minutes, exploded like a ship which is blown up, flinging toward the wide heavens fantastic stars which burst in their turn, the moon remained all alone, calm and round, on the horizon.

The public applauded wildly, exclaiming: "Hurrah! Bravo! bravo!"

Andermatt, all of a sudden, said: "Let us go and open the ball, my dear boy. Are you willing to dance the first quadrille face to face with me?"

"Why, certainly, my dear brother-in-law."

"Who have you thought of asking to dance with you? As for me, I have bespoken the Duchesse de Ramas."

Gontran answered in a tone of indifference: "I will ask Charlotte Oriol."

They reascended. As they passed in front of the spot where Christiane was resting with Paul Bretigny, they did not notice the pair. William murmured: "She has followed my advice. She went home to go to bed. She was quite tired out to-day." And he advanced toward the ballroom which the attendants had been getting ready during the fireworks.

But Christiane had not returned to her room, as her husband supposed. As soon as she realized that she was alone with Paul she said to him in a very low tone, while she pressed his hand:

"So then you came. I was waiting for you for the past month. Every morning I kept asking myself, 'Shall I see him to-day?' and every night I kept saying to myself, 'It will be tomorrow then.' Why have you delayed so long, my love?"

He replied with some embarrassment: "I had matters to engage my attention — business."

She leaned toward him, murmuring: "It was not right to leave me here alone with them, especially in my state."

He moved his chair a little away from her.

"Be careful! We might be seen. These rockets light up the whole country around."

She scarcely bestowed a thought on it; she said: "I love you so much!" Then, with sudden starts of joy: "Ah! how happy I feel, how happy I feel at finding that we are once more together, here! Are you thinking about it? What joy, Paul! How we are going to love one another again!"

She sighed, and her voice was so weak that it seemed a mere breath.

"I feel a foolish longing to embrace you, but it is foolish — there! — foolish. It is such a long time since I saw you!"

Then, suddenly, with the fierce energy of an impassioned woman, to whom everything should give way: "Listen! I want — you understand — I want to go with you immediately to the place where we said adieu to one another last year! You remember well, on the road from La Roche Pradière?"

He replied, stupefied: "But this is senseless! You cannot walk farther. You have been stand-ing all day. This is senseless; I will not allow it."

She had risen to her feet, and she said: "I am determined on it! If you do not accompany me, I'll go alone!"

And pointing out to him the moon which had risen: "See here! It was an evening just like this! Do you remember how you kissed my shadow?"

He held her back: "Christiane — listen — this is ridiculous — Christiane!"

She did not reply, and walked toward the descent leading to the vineyards. He knew that calm will which nothing could divert from its purpose, the graceful obstinacy of these blue eyes, of that little forehead of a fair woman that could not be stopped; and he took her arm to sustain her on her way. "Supposing we are seen, Christiane?"

"You did not say that to me last year. And then, everyone is at the fete. We'll be back before our absence can be noticed."

It was soon necessary to ascend by the stony path. She panted, leaning with her whole weight on him, and at every step she said:

"It is good, it is good, to suffer thus!"

He stopped, wishing to bring her back. But she would not listen to him.

"No, no. I am happy. You don't understand this, you. Listen! I feel it leaping in me — our child — — your child — what happiness. Give me your hand."

She did not realize that he — this man — was one of the race of lovers who are not of the race of fathers. Since he discovered that she was pregnant, he kept away from her, and was disgusted with her, in spite of himself. He had often in bygone days said that a woman who has performed the function of reproduction is no longer worthy of love. What raised him to a high pitch of tenderness was that soaring of two hearts toward an inaccessible ideal, that entwining of two souls which are immaterial — all those artificial and unreal elements which poets have associated with this passion. In the physical woman he adored the Venus whose sacred side must always preserve the pure form of sterility. The idea of a little creature which owed its birth to him, a human larva stirring in that body defiled by it and already grown ugly, inspired him with an almost unconquerable repugnance. Maternity had made this woman a brute. She was no longer the exceptional being adored and dreamed about, but the animal that reproduces its species. And even a material disgust was mingled in him with these loathings of his mind.

How could she have felt or divined this — she whom each movement of the child she yearned for attached the more closely to her lover? This man whom she adored, whom she had every day loved a little more since the moment of their first kiss, had not only penetrated to the bottom of her heart, but had given her the proof that he had also entered into the very depths of her flesh, that he had sown his own life there, that he was going to come forth from her, again becoming quite small. Yes, she carried him there under her crossed hands, himself, her good, her dear, her tenderly beloved one, springing up again in her womb by the mystery of nature. And she loved him doubly, now that she had him in two forms — the big, and the little one as yet unknown, the one whom she saw, touched, embraced, and could hear speaking to her, and the one whom she could up to this only feel stirring under her skin. They had by this time reached the road.

"You were waiting for me over there that evening," said she. And she held her lips out to him.

He kissed them, without replying, with a cold kiss.

She murmured for the second time: "Do you remember how you embraced me on the ground. We were like this — look!"

And in the hope that he would begin it all over again she commenced running to get some distance away from him. Then she stopped, out of breath, and waited, standing in the middle of the road. But the moon, which lengthened out her profile on the ground, traced there the protuberance of her swollen figure. And Paul, beholding at his feet the shadow of her pregnancy, remained unmoved at sight of it, wounded in his pcetic sense with shame, exasperated that she was not able to share his feelings or divine his thoughts, that she had not sufficient coquetry, tact, and feminine delicacy to understand all the shades which give such a different complexion to circumstances; and he said to her with impatience in his voice:

"Look here, Christiane! This child's play is ridiculous."

She came back to him moved, saddened, with outstretched arms, and, flinging herself on his breast:

"Ah! you love me less. I feel it! I am sure of it!"

He took pity on her, and, encircling her head with his arms, he imprinted two long sweet kisses on her eyes.

Then in silence they retraced their steps. He could find nothing to say to her; and, as she leaned on him, exhausted by fatigue, he quickened his pace so that he might no longer feel against his side the touch of this enlarged figure. When they were near the hotel, they separated, and she went up to her own apartment.

The orchestra at the Casino was playing dance-music; and Paul went to look at the ball. It was a waltz; and they were all waltzing — Doctor Latonne with the younger Madame Paille, Andermatt with Louise Oriol, handsome Doctor Mazelli with the Duchesse de Ramas, and Gontran with Charlotte Oriol. He was whispering in her ear in that tender fashion which denotes a courtship begun; and she was smiling behind her fan, blushing, and apparently delighted.

Paul heard a voice saying behind him: "Look here! look here at M. de Ravenel whispering gallantries to my fair patient."

He added, after a pause: "And there is a pearl, good, gay, simple, devoted, upright, you know, an excellent creature. She is worth ten of the elder sister. I have known them since their childhood — these little girls. And yet the father prefers the elder one, because she is more — more like him — more of a peasant — less upright — more thrifty — more cunning — — and more — more jealous. Ah! she is a good girl, all the same. I would not like to say anything bad of her; but, in spite of myself, I compare them, you understand — and, after having compared them, I judge them — there you are!"

The waltz was coming to an end; Gontran went to join his friend, and, perceiving the doctor:

"Ah! tell me now — there appears to me to be a remarkable increase in the medical body at Enval. We have a Doctor Mazelli who waltzes to perfection and an old little Doctor Black who seems on very good terms with Heaven."

But Doctor Honorat was discreet. He did not like to sit in judgment on his professional brethren.

X

THE burning question now was that of the physicians at Enval. They had suddenly made themselves the masters of the district, and absorbed all the attention and all the enthusiasm of the inhabitants. Formerly the springs flowed under the authority of Doctor Bonnefille alone, in the midst of the harmless animosities of restless Doctor Latonne and placid Doctor Honorat.

Now, it was a very different thing. Since the success planned during the winter by Andermatt had quite taken definite shape, thanks to the powerful cooperation of Professors Cloche, Mas-Roussel, and Remusot, who had each brought there a contingent of two or three hundred patients at least, Doctor Latonne, inspector of the new establishment, had become a big personage, specially patronized by Professor Mas-Roussel, whose pupil he had been, and whose deportment and gestures he imitated.

Docter Bonnefille was scarcely ever talked about any longer. Furious, exasperated, railing against Mont Oriol, the old physician remained the whole day in the old establishment with a few old patients who had kept faithful to him.

In the minds of some invalids, indeed, he was the only person that understood the true properties of the waters; he possessed, so to speak, their secret, since he had officially administered them from the time the station was first established.

Doctor Honorat barely managed to retain his practice among the natives of Auvergne. With the moderate income he derived from this source he contented himself, keeping on good terms with everybody, and consoled himself by much preferring cards and wine to medicine. He did not, however, go quite so far as to love his professional brethren.

Doctor Latonne would, therefore, have continued to be the great soothsayer of Mont Oriol, if one morning there had not appeared a very small man, nearly a dwarf, whose big head sunk between his shoulders, big round eyes, and big hands combined to produce a very odd-looking individual. This new physician, M. Black, introduced into the district by Professor Remusot immediately excited attention by his excessive devotion. Nearly every morning, between two visits, he went into a church for a few minutes, and he received communion nearly every Sunday. The curé soon got him some patients, old maids, poor people whom he attended for nothing, pious ladies who asked the advice of their spiritual director before calling on a man of science, whose sentiments, reserve, and professional modesty, they wished to know before everything else.

Then, one day, the arrival of the Princess de Maldebourg, an old German Highness, was announced — — a very fervent Catholic, who on the very evening when she first appeared in the district, sent for Doctor Black on the recommendation of a Roman cardinal. From that moment he was the fashion. It was good taste, good form, the correct thing, to be attended by him. He was the only doctor, it was said, who was a perfect gentleman — the only one in whom a woman could repose absolute confidence.

And from morning till evening this little man with the bulldog's head, who always spoke in a subdued tone in every corner with everybody, might be seen rushing from one hotel to the other. He appeared to have important secrets to confide or to receive, for he could constantly be met holding long mysterious conferences in the lobbies with the masters of the hotels, with his patients' chambermaids, with anyone who was brought into contact with the invalids. As soon as he saw any lady of his acquaintance in the street, he went straight up to her with his short, quick step, and immediately began to mumble fresh and minute directions, after the fashion of a priest at confession.

The old women especially adored him. He would listen to their stories to the end without interrupting them, took note of all their observations, all their questions, and all their wishes.

He increased or diminished each day the proportion of water to be consumed by his patients, which made them feel perfect confidence in the care taken of them by him.

"We stopped yesterday at two glasses and three-quarters," he would say; "well, to-day we shall only take two glasses and a half, and tomorrow three glasses. Don't forget! Tomorrow, three glasses.

I am very, very particular about it!"

And all the patients were convinced that he was very particular about it, indeed.

In order not to forget these figures and fractions of figures, he wrote them down in a memorandum-book, in order that he might never make a mistake. For the patient does not pardon a mistake of a single halfglass. He regulated and modified with equal minuteness the duration of the daily baths in virtue of principles known only to himself.

Doctor Latonne, jealous and exasperated, disdainfully shrugged his shoulders, and declared: "This is a swindler!" His hatred against Doctor Black had even led him occasionally to run down the mineral waters. "Since we can scarcely tell how they act, It is quite impossible to prescribe every day modifications of the dose, which any therapeutic law cannot regulate. Proceedings of this kind do the greatest injury to medicine."

Doctor Honorat contented himself with smiling. He always took care" to forget, five minutes after a consultation, the number of glasses which he had ordered. "Two more or less," said he to Gontran in his hours of gaiety, "there is only the spring to take notice of it; and yet this scarcely incommodes it!" The only wicked pleasantry that he permitted himself on his religious brother-physician consisted in describing him as "the doctor of the Holy Sitting-Bath." His jealousy was of the prudent, sly, and tranquil kind.

He added sometimes: "Oh, as for him, he knows the patient thoroughly; and this is often better than to know the disease!"

But lo! there arrived one morning at the hotel of Mont Oriol a noble Spanish family, the Duke and Duchess of Ramas-Aldavarra, who brought with her her own physician, an Italian, Doctor Mazelli from Milan. He was a man of thirty, a tall, thin, very handsome young fellow, wearing only mustaches. From the first evening, he made a conquest of the table d'hote, for the Duke, a melancholy man, attacked with monstrous obesity, had a horror of isolation, and desired to take his meals in the same diningroom as the other patients. Doctor Mazelli already knew by their names almost all the frequenters of the hotel; he had a kindly word for every man, a compliment for every woman, a smile even for every servant.

Placed at the right-hand side of the Duchess, a beautiful woman of between thirty-five and forty, with a pale complexion, black eyes, blue-black hair, he would say to her as each dish came round:

"Very little," or else, "No, not this," or else, "Yes, take some of that." And he would himself pour out the liquid which she was to drink with very great care, measuring exactly the proportions of wine and water which he mingled.

He also regulated the Duke's food, but with visible carelessness. The patient, however, took no heed of his advice, devoured everything with bestial voracity, drank at every meal two decanters of pure wine, then went tumbling about in a chaise for air in front of the hotel, and began whining with pain and groaning over his bad digestion.

After the first dinner, Doctor Mazelli, who had judged and weighed all around him with a single glance, went to join Gontran, who was smoking a cigar on the terrace of the Casino, told his name, and began to chat. At the end of an hour, they were on intimate terms. Next day, he got himself introduced to Christiane just as she was leaving the bath, won her goodwill after ten minutes' conversation, and brought her that very day into contact with the Duchess, who no longer cared for solitude.

He kept watch over everything in the abode of the Spaniards, gave excellent advice to the chef about cooking, excellent hints to the chambermaid on the hygiene of the head in order to preserve in her mistress's hair its luster, its superb shade, and its abundance, very useful information to the coachman about veterinary medicine; and he knew how to make the hours swift and light, to invent distractions, and to pick up in the hotels casual acquaintances but always prudently chosen.

The Duchess said to Christiane, when speaking of him: "He is a wonderful man, dear Madame. He knows everything; he does everything. It is to him that I owe my figure."

"How, your figure?"

"Yes, I was beginning to grow fat, and he saved me with his regimen and his liqueurs."

Moreover, Mazelli knew how to make medicine itself interesting; he spoke about it with such ease, with such gaiety, and with a sort of light scepticism which helped to convince his listeners of his superiority.

"'Tis very simple," said he; "I don't believe in remedies — or rather I hardly believe in them. The old-fashioned medicine started with this principle — that there is a remedy for everything. God, they believe, in His divine bounty, has created drugs for all maladies, only He has left to men, through malice, perhaps, the trouble of discovering these drugs. Now, men have discovered an incalculable number of them without ever knowing exactly what disease each of them is suited for. In reality there are no remedies; there are only maladies. When a malady declares itself, it is necessary to interrupt its course, according to some, to precipitate it, according to others, by some means or another. Each school extols its own method. In the same case, we see the most antagonistic systems employed, and the most opposed kinds of medicine — ice by one and extreme heat by the other, dieting by this doctor and forced nourishment by that. I am not speaking of the innumerable poisonous products extracted from minerals or vegetables, which chemistry procures for us. All this acts, 'tis true, but nobody knows how. Sometimes it succeeds, and sometimes it kills."

And, with much liveliness, he pointed out the impossibility of certainty, the absence of all scientific basis as long as organic chemistry, biological chemistry had not become the starting-point of a new medicine. He related anecdotes, monstrous errors of the greatest physicians, and proved the insanity and the falsity of their pretended science.

"Make the body discharge its functions," said he. "Make the skin, the muscles, all the organs, and, above all, the stomach, which is the foster-father of the entire machine, its regulator and life-warehouse, discharge their functions."

He asserted that, if he liked, by nothing save regimen, he could make people gay or sad, capable of physical work or intellectual work, according to the nature of the diet which he imposed on them. He could even act on the faculties of the brain, on the memory, the imagination, on all the manifestations of intelligence. And he ended jocosely with these words:

"For my part, I nurse my patients with massage and curaçoa."

He attributed marvelous results to massage, and spoke of the Dutchman Hamstrang as of a god performing miracles. Then, showing his delicate white hands:

"With those, you might resuscitate the dead." And the Duchess added: "The fact is that he performs massage to perfection."

He also lauded alcoholic beverages, in small proportions to excite the stomach at certain moments; and he composed mixtures, cleverly prepared, which the Duchess had to drink, at fixed hours, either before or after her meals.

He might have been seen each morning entering the Casino Café about half past nine and asking for his bottles. They were brought to him fastened with little silver locks of which he had the key. He would pour out a little of one, a little of another, slowly into a very pretty blue glass, which a very correct footman held up respectfully.

Then the doctor would give directions: "See! Bring this to the Duchess in her bath, to drink it, before she dresses herself, when coming out of the water."

And when anyone asked him through curiosity: "What have you put into it?" he would answer: "Nothing but refined aniseed-cordial, very pure curaçoa, and excellent bitters,"

This handsome doctor, in a few days, became the center of attraction for all the invalids. And every sort of device was resorted to, in order to attract a few opinions from him.

When he was passing along through the walks in the park, at the hour of promenade, one heard nothing but that exclamation of "Doctor" on all the chairs where sat the beautiful women, the young women, who were resting themselves a little between two glasses of the Christiane Spring. Then, when he stopped with a smile on his lip, they would draw him aside for some minutes into the little path beside the river. At first, they talked about one thing or another; then discreetly, skillfully, coquettishly, they came to the question of health, but in an indifferent fashion as if they were touching on sundry topics.

For this medical man was not at the disposal of the public. He was not paid by them, and people could not get him to visit them at their own houses. He belonged to the Duchess, only to the Duchess. This situation even stimulated people's efforts, and provoked their desires. And, as it was whispered positively that the Duchess was jealous, very jealous, there was a desperate struggle between all these ladies to get advice from the handsome Italian doctor. He gave it without forcing them to entreat him very strenuously.

Then, among the women whom he had favored with his advice arose an interchange of intimate confidences, in order to give clear proof of nis solicitude.

"Oh! my dear, he asked me questions — but such questions!"

"Very indiscreet?"

"Oh! indiscreet! Say frightful. I actually did not know what answers to give him. He wanted to know things — but such things!"

"It was the same way with me. He questioned me a great deal about my husband!"

"And me, also — together with details so — so personal! These questions are very embarrassing. However, we understand perfectly well that it is necessary to ask them."

"Oh! of course. Health depends on these minute details. As for me, he promised to perform massage on me at Paris this winter. I have great need of it to supplement the treatment here."

"Tell me, my dear, what do you intend to do in return? He cannot take fees."

"Good heavens! my idea was to present him with a scarf-pin. He must be fond of them, for he has already two or three very nice ones."

"Oh! how you embarrass me! The same notion was in my head. In that case I'll give him a ring." And they concocted surprises in order to please him, thought of ingenious presents in order to touch him, graceful pleasantries in order to fascinate him. He became the "talk of the day," the great subject of conversation, the sole object of public attention, till the news spread that Count Gontran de Ravenel was paying his addresses to Charlotte Oriol with a view to marrying her. And this at once led to a fresh outburst of deafening clamor in Enval.

Since the evening when he had opened with her the inaugural ball at the Casino, Gontran had tied himself to the young girl's skirts. He publicly showed her all those little attentions of men who want to please without hiding their object; and their ordinary relations assumed at the same time a character of gallantry, playful and natural, which seemed likely to lead to love.

They saw one another nearly every day, for the two girls had conceived feelings of strong friendship toward Christiane, into which, no doubt, there entered a considerable element of gratified vanity. Gontran suddenly showed a disposition to remain constantly at his sister's side; and he began to organize parties for the morning and entertainments for the evening, which greatly astonished Christiane and Paul. Then they noticed that he was devoting himself to Charlotte; he gaily teased her, paid her compliments without appearing to do so, and manifested toward her in a thousand ways that tender care which tends to unite two beings in bonds of affection. The young girl, already accustomed to the free and familiar manners of this gay Parisian youth, did not at first see anything remarkable in these attentions; and, abandoning herself to the impulses of her honest and confiding heart, she began to laugh and enjoy herself with him as she might have done with a brother.

Now, she had returned home with her elder sister, after an evening party at which Gontran had several times attempted to kiss her in consequence of forfeits due by her in a game of "fly-pigeon," when Louise, who had appeared anxious and nervous for some time past, said to her in an abrupt tone:

"You would do well to be a little careful about your deportment. M. Gontran is not a suitable companion for you."

"Not a suitable companion? What has he done?"

"You know well what I mean — don't play the ninny! In the way you're going on, you would soon compromise yourself; and if you don't know how to watch over your conduct, it is my business to see after it."

Charlotte, confused, and filled with shame, faltered: "But I don't know — I assure you — I have seen nothing — "

Her sister sharply interrupted her: "Listen! Things must not go on this way. If he wants to marry you, it is for papa — for papa to consider the matter and to give an answer; but, if he only wants to trifle with you, he must desist at once!"

Then, suddenly, Charlotte got annoyed without knowing why or with what. She was indignant at her sister having taken it on herself to direct her actions and to reprimand her; and, in a trembling voice, and with tears in her eyes, she told her that she should not have interfered in what did not concern her. She stammered in her exasperation, divining by a vague but unerring instinct the jealousy that had been aroused in the embittered heart of Louise.

They parted without embracing one another, and Charlotte wept when she got into bed, as she thought over things that she had never foreseen or suspected.

Gradually her tears ceased to flow, and she began to reflect. It was true, nevertheless, that Gontran's demeanor toward her had altered. She had enjoyed his acquaintance hitherto without understanding him. She understood him now. At every turn he kept repeating to her pretty compliments full of delicate flattery. On one occasion he had kissed her hand. What were his intentions? She pleased him, but to what extent? Was it possible by any chance that he desired to marry her? And all at once she imagined that she could hear somewhere in the air, in the silent night through whose empty spaces her dreams were flitting, a voice exclaiming, "Comtesse de Ravenel." —

The emotion was so vivid that she sat up in the bed; then, with her naked feet, she felt for her slippers under the chair over which she had thrown her clothes, and she went to open the window without consciousness of what she was doing, in order to find space for her hopes. She could hear what they were saying in the room below stairs, and Colosse's voice was raised: "Let it alone! let it alone! There will be time enough to see to it. Father will arrange that. There is no harm up to this. 'Tis father that will do the thing."

She noticed that the window in front of the house, just below that at which she was standing, was still lighted up. She asked herself: "Who is there now? What are they talking about?" A shadow passed over the luminous wall. It was her sister. So then, she had not yet gone to bed. Why? But the light was presently extinguished; and Charlotte began to think about other things that were agitating her heart.

She could not go to sleep now. Did he love her? Oh! no; not yet. But he might love her, since she had caught his fancy. And if he came to love her much, desperately, as people love in society, he would certainly marry her.

Born in a house of vinedressers, she had preserved, although educated in the young ladies' convent at Clermont, the modesty and humility of a peasant girl. She used to think that she might marry a notary, perhaps, or a barrister or a doctor; but the ambition to become a real lady of high social position, with a title of nobility attached to her name had never entered her mind. Even when she had just finished the perusal of some love-story, and was musing over the glimpse presented to her of such a charming prospect for a few minutes, it would speedily Vanish from her soul just as chimeras vanish. Now, here was this unforeseen, inconceivable thing, which had been suddenly conjured up by some words of her sister, apparently drawing near her after the fashion of a ship's sail driven onward by the wind.

Every time she drew breath, she kept repeating with her lips: "Comtesse de Ravenel." And the shades of her dark eyelashes, as they closed in the night, were illuminated with visions. She saw beautiful drawingrooms brilliantly lighted up, beautiful women greeting her with smiles, beautiful carriages waiting before the steps of a chateau, and grand servants in livery bowing as she passed.

She felt heated in her bed; her heart was beating. She rose up a second time in order to drink a glass of water, and to remain standing in her bare feet for a few moments on the cold floor of her apartment.

Then, somewhat calmed, she ended by falling asleep. But she awakened at dawn, so much had the agitation of her heart passed into her veins.

She felt ashamed of her little room with its white walls, washed with water by a rustic glazier, her poor cotton curtains, and some straw-chairs which never quitted their place at the two corners of her chest of drawers.

She realized that she was a peasant in the midst of these rude articles of furniture which bespoke her origin. She felt herself lowly, unworthy of this handsome, mocking young fellow, whose fair hair and laughing face had floated before her eyes, had disappeared from her vision and then come back, had gradually engrossed her thoughts, and had already found a place in her heart.

Then she jumped out of bed and ran to look for her glass, her little toilette-glass, as large as the center of a plate; after that, she got into bed again, her mirror between her hands; and she looked at her face surrounded by her hair which hung loose on the white background of the pillow.

Presently she laid down on the bedclothes the little piece of glass which reflected her lineaments, and she thought how difficult it would be for such an alliance to take place, so great was the distance between them. Thereupon a feeling of vexation seized her by the throat. But immediately afterward she gazed at her image, once more smiling at herself in order to look nice, and, as she considered herself pretty, the difficulties disappeared.

When she went down to breakfast, her sister, who wore a look of irritation, asked her:

"What do you propose to do to-day?"

Charlotte replied unhesitatingly: "Are we not going in the carriage to Royat with Madame Andermatt?"

Louise returned: "You are going alone, then; but you might do something better, after what I said to you last night."

The younger sister interrupted her: "I don't ask for your advice — mind your own business!"

And they did not speak to one another again.

Père Oriol and Jacques came in, and took their seats at the table. The old man asked almost immediately: "What are you doing to-day, girls?" Charlotte said without giving her sister time to answer: "As for me, I am going to Royat with Madame Andermatt."

The two men eyed her with an air of satisfaction; and the father muttered with that engaging smile which he could put on when discussing any business of a profitable character: "That's good! that's good!"

She was more surprised at this secret complacency which she observed in their entire bearing than at the visible anger of Louise; and she asked herself, in a somewhat disturbed frame of mind: "Can they have been talking this over all together?" As soon as the meal was over, she went up again to her room, put on her hat, seized her parasol, threw a light cloak over her arm, and she went off in the direction of the hotel, for they were to start at half past one.

Christiane expressed her astonishment at finding that Louise had not come.

Charlotte felt herself flushing as she replied: "She is a little fatigued; I believe she has a headache."

And they stepped into the landau, the big landau with six seats, which they always used. The Marquis and his daughter remained at the lower end, while the Oriol girl found herself seated at the opposite side between the two young men.

They passed in front of Tournoel; they proceeded along the foot of the mountain, by a beautiful winding road, under the walnut and chestnut-trees. Charlotte several times felt conscious that Gontran was pressing close up to her, but was too prudent to take offense at it. As he sat at her right-hand side, he spoke with his face close to her cheek; and she did not venture to turn round to answer him, through fear of touching his mouth, which she felt already on her lips, and also through fear of his eyes, whose glance would have unnerved her.

He whispered in her ear gallant absurdities, laughable fooleries, agreeable and well-turned compliments.

Christiane scarcely uttered a word, heavy and sick from her pregnancy. And Paul appeared sad, preoccupied. The Marquis alone chatted without unrest or anxiety, in the sprightly, graceful style of a selfish old nobleman.

They got down at the park of Royat to listen to the music, and Gontran, offering Charlotte his arm, set forth with her in front. The army of bathers, on the chairs, around the kiosk, where the leader of the orchestra was keeping time with the brass instruments and the violins, watched the promenaders filing past. The women exhibited their dresses by stretching out their legs as far as the bars of the chairs in front of them, and their dainty summer headgear made them look more fascinating.

Charlotte and Gontran sauntered through the midst of the people who occupied the seats, looking out for faces of a comic type to find materials for their pleasantries.

Every moment he heard some one saying behind them: "Look there! what a pretty girl!" He felt flattered, and asked himself whether they took her for his sister, his wife, or his mistress.

Christiane, seated between her father and Paul, saw them passing several times, and thinking they exhibited too much youthful frivolity, she called them over to her to soberize them. But they paid no attention to her, and went on vagabondizing through the crowd, enjoying themselves with their whole hearts.

She said in a whisper to Paul Bretigny: "He will finish by compromising her. It will be necessary that we should speak to him this evening when he comes back."

Paul replied: "I had already thought about it. You are quite right."

They went to dine in one of the restaurants of Clermont-Ferrand, those of Royat being no good, according to the Marquis, who was a gourmand, and they returned at nightfall.

Charlotte had become serious, Gontran having strongly pressed her hand, while presenting her gloves to her, before she quitted the table. Her young girl's conscience was suddenly troubled. This was an avowal! an advance! an impropriety! What ought she to do? Speak to him? but about what? To be offended would be ridiculous. There was need of so much tact in these circumstances. But by doing nothing, by saying nothing, she produced the impression of accepting his advances, of becoming his accomplice, of answering "yes" to this pressure of the hand.

And she weighed the situation, accusing herself of having been too gay and too familiar at Royat, thinking just now that her sister was right, that she was compromised, lost! The carriage rolled along the road. Paul and Gontran smoked in silence; the Marquis slept; Christiane gazed at the stars; and Charlotte found it hard to keep back her tears — for she had swallowed three glasses of champagne.

When they had got back, Christiane said to her father: "As it is dark, you have to see this young girl home."

The Marquis, without delay, offered her his arm, and went off with her.

Paul laid his hands on Gontran's shoulders, and whispered in his ear: "Come and have five minutes' talk with your sister and myself."

And they went up to the little drawingroom communicating with the apartments of Andermatt and his wife.

When they were seated, Christiane said: "Listen! M. Paul and I want to give you a good lecture."

"A good lecture! But about what? I'm as wise as an image for want of opportunities."

"Don't trifle! You are doing a very imprudent and very dangerous thing without thinking on it. You are compromising this young girl."

He appeared much astonished. "Who is that? Charlotte?"

"Yes, Charlotte!"

"I'm compromising Charlotte? — I?"

"Yes, you are compromising her. Everyone here is talking about it, and this evening again in the park at Royat you have been very — very light. Isn't that so, Bretigny?"

Paul answered: "Yes, Madame, I entirely share your sentiments."

Gontran turned his chair around, bestrode it like a horse, took a fresh cigar, lighted it, then burst out laughing.

"Ha! so then I am compromising Charlotte Oriol?" He waited a few seconds to see the effect of his words, then added: "And who told you I did not intend to marry her?"

Christiane gave a start of amazement.

"Marry her? You? Why, you're mad!"

"Why so?"

"That — that little peasant girl!"

"Tra! la! la! Prejudices! Is it from your husband you learned them?"

As she made no response to this direct argument, he went on, putting both questions and answers himself:

"Is she pretty? — Yes! Is she well educated? — Yes! And more ingenuous, more simple, and more honest than girls in good society. She knows as much as another, for she can speak both English and the language of Auvergne — that makes two foreign languages. She will be as rich as any heiress of the Faubourg Saint-Germain — as it was formerly called (they are now going to christen it Faubourg Sainte-Deche) — and finally, if she is a peasant's daughter, she'll be only all the more healthy to present me with fine children. Enough!"

As he had always the appearance of laughing and jesting, Christiane asked hesitatingly: "Come! are you speaking seriously?"

"Faith, I am! She is charming, this little girl! She has a good heart and a pretty face, a genial character and a good temper, rosy cheeks, bright eyes, white teeth, ruby lips, and flowing tresses, glossy, thick, and full of soft folds. And then her vinedressing father will be as rich as Croesus, thanks to your husband, my dear sister. What more do you want? The daughter of a peasant! Well, is not the daughter of a peasant as good as any of those moneylenders' daughters who pay such high prices for dukes with doubtful titles, or any of the daughters born of aristocratic prostitution whom the Empire has given us, or any of the daughters with double sires whom we meet in society? Why, if I did marry this girl I should be doing the first wise and rational act of my life!"

Christiane reflected, then, all of a sudden, convinced, overcome, delighted, she exclaimed:

"Why, all you have said is true! It is quite true, quite right! So then you are going to marry her, my little Gontran?"

It was he who now sought to moderate her ardor. "Not so quick — not so quick — let me reflect in my turn. I only declare that, if I did marry her, I would be doing the first wise and rational act of my life. That does not go so far as saying that I will marry her; but I am thinking over it; I am studying her, I am paying her a little attention to see if I can like her sufficiently. In short, I don't answer 'yes' or 'no,' but it is nearer to 'yes' than to 'no.'"

Christiane turned toward Paul: "What do you think of it, Monsieur Bretigny?"

She called him at one time Monsieur Bretigny, and at another time Bretigny only.

He, always fascinated by the things in which he imagined he saw an element of greatness, by unequal matches which seemed to him to exhibit generosity, by all the sentimental parade in which the human heart masks itself, replied: "For my part I think he is right in this. If he likes her, let him marry her; he could not find better."

But, the Marquis and Andermatt having returned, they had to talk about other subjects; and the two young men went to the Casino to see whether the gaming-room was still open.

From that day forth Christiane and Paul appeared to favor Gontran's open courtship of Charlotte.

The young girl was more frequently invited to the hotel by Christiane, and was treated in fact as if she were already a member of the family. She saw all this clearly, understood it, and was quite delighted at it. Her little head throbbed like a drum, and went building fantastic castles in Spain. Gontran, in the meantime had said nothing definite to her; but his demeanor, all his words, the tone that he assumed with her, his more serious air of gallantry, the caress of his glance seemed every day to keep repeating to her: "I have chosen you; you are to be my wife."

And the tone of sweet affection, of discreet selfsurrender, of chaste reserve which she now adopted toward him, seemed to give this answer: "I know it, and I'll say 'yes' whenever you ask for my hand."

In the young girl's family, the matter was discussed in confidential whispers. Louise scarcely opened her lips now except to annoy her with hurtful allusions, with sharp and sarcastic remarks. Père Oriol and Jacques appeared to be content.

She did not ask herself, all the same, whether she loved this good-looking suitor, whose wife she was, no doubt, destined to become. She liked him, she was constantly thinking about him; she considered him handsome, witty, elegant — she was speculating, above all, on what she would do when she was married to him.

In Enval people had forgotten the malignant rivalries of the physicians and the proprietors of springs, the theories as to the supposed attachment of the Duchess de Ramas for her doctor, all the scandals that flow along with the waters of thermal stations, in order to occupy their minds entirely with this extraordinary circumstance — that Count Gontran de Ravenel was going to marry the younger of the Oriol girls.

When Gontran thought the moment had arrived, taking Andermatt by the arm, one morning, as they were rising from the breakfast-table, he said to him: "My dear fellow, strike while the iron is hot! Here is the exact state of affairs: The little one is waiting for me to propose, without my having committed myself at all; but, you may be quite certain she will not refuse me. It is necessary to sound her father about it in such a way as to promote, at the same time, your interests and mine."

Andermatt replied: "Make your mind easy. I'll take that on myself. I am going to sound him this very day without compromising you and without thrusting you forward; and when the situation is perfectly clear, I'll talk about it."

"Capital!"

Then, after a few moments' silence, Gontran added: "Hold on! This is perhaps my last day of bachelorhood. I am going on to Royat, where I saw some acquaintances of mine the other day. I'll be back tonight, and I'll tap at your door to know the result."

He saddled his horse, and proceeded along by the mountain, inhaling the pure, genial air, and sometimes starting into a gallop to feel the keen caress of the breeze brushing the fresh skin of his cheek and tickling his mustache.

The evening-party at Royat was a jolly affair. He met some of his friends there who had brought girls along with them. They lingered a long time at supper; he returned home at a very late hour. Everyone had gone to bed in the hotel of Mont Oriol when Gontran went to tap at Andermatt's door. There was no answer at first; then, as the knocking became much louder, a hoarse voice, the voice of one disturbed while asleep, grunted from within: "Who's there?"

"'Tis I, Gontran."

"Wait — I'm opening the door."

Andermatt appeared in his nightshirt, with puffed-up face, bristling chin, and a silk handkerchief tied round his head. Then he got back into bed, sat down in it, and with his hands stretched over the sheets:

"Well, my dear fellow, this won't do me. Here is how matters stand: I have sounded this old fox Oriol, without mentioning you, referring merely to a certain friend of mine — I have perhaps allowed him to suppose that the person I meant was Paul Bretigny — as a suitable match for one of his daughters, and I asked what dowry he would give her. He answered me by asking in his turn what were the young man's means; and I fixed the amount at three hundred thousand francs with expectations."

"But I have nothing," muttered Gontran.

"I am lending you the money, my dear fellow. If we work this business between us, your lands would yield me enough to reimburse me."

Gontran sneered: "All right. I'll have the woman and you the money."

But Andermatt got quite annoyed. "If I am to interest myself in your affairs in order that you might insult me, there's an end of it — let us say no more about it!"

Gontran apologized: "Don't get vexed, my dear fellow, and excuse me! I know that you are a very honest man of irreproachable loyalty in matters of business. I would not ask you for the price of a drink if I were your coachman; but I would intrust my fortune to you if I were a millionaire."

William, less excited, rejoined: "We'll return presently to that subject. Let us first dispose of the principal question. The old man was not taken in by my wiles, and said to me in reply: 'It depends on which of them is the girl you're talking about. If 'tis Louise, the elder one, here's her dowry.' And he enumerated for me all the lands that are around the establishment, those which are between the baths and the hotel and between the hotel and the Casino, all those, in short, which are indispensable to us, those which have for me an inestimable value. He gives, on the contrary, to the younger girl the other side of the mountain, which will be worth as much money later on, no doubt, but which is worth nothing to me. I tried in every possible way to make him modify their partition and invert the lots. I was only knocking my head against the obstinacy of a mule. He will not change; he has fixed his resolution. Reflect — what do you think of it?"

Gontran, much troubled, much perplexed, replied: "What do you think of it yourself? Do you believe that he was thinking of me in thus distributing the shares in the land?"

"I haven't a doubt of it. The clown said to himself: 'As he likes the younger one, let us take care of the bag.' He hopes to give you his daughter while keeping his best lands. And again perhaps his object is to give the advantage to the elder girl. He prefers her — who knows? — she is more like himself — she is more cunning — more artful — more practical. I believe she is a strapping lass, this one — for my part, if I were in your place, I would change my stick from one shoulder to the other."

But Gontran, stunned, began muttering: "The devil! the devil! the devil! And Charlotte's lands — you don't want them?"

Andermatt exclaimed: "I — no — a thousand times, no! I want those which are close to my baths, my hotel, and my Casino. It is very simple, I wouldn't give anything for the others, which could only be sold, at a later period, in small lots to private individuals."

Gontran kept still repeating: "The devil! the devil! the devil! here's a plaguy business! So then you advise me?"

"I don't advise you at all. I think you would do well to reflect before deciding between the two sisters."

"Yes — yes — that's true — I will reflect — I am going to sleep first — that brings counsel."

He rose up; Andermatt held him back.

"Excuse me, my dear boy! — a word or two on another matter. I may not appear to understand, but I understand very well the allusions with which you sting me incessantly, and I don't want any more of them. You reproach me with being a Jew — that is to say, with making money, with being avaricious, with being a speculator, so as to come close to sheer swindling. Now, my friend, I spend my life in lending you this money that I make — not without trouble — — or rather in giving it to you. However, let that be! But there is one point that I don't admit! No, I am not avaricious. The proof of it is that I have made presents to your sister, presents of twenty thousand francs at a time, that I gave your father a Theodore Rousseau worth ten thousand francs, to which he took a fancy, and that I presented you, when you were coming here, with the horse on which you rode a little while ago to Royat. In what then am I avaricious? In not letting myself be robbed. And we are all like that among my race, and we are right, Monsieur. I want to say it to you once for all. We are regarded as misers because we know the exact value of things. For you a piano is a piano, a chair is a chair, a pair of trousers is a pair of trousers. For us also, but it represents, at the same time, a value, a mercantile value appreciable and precise, which a practical man should estimate with a single glance, not through stinginess, but in order not to countenance fraud. What would you say if a tobacconist asked you four sous for a postage-stamp or for a box of wax-matches? You would go to look for a policeman, Monsieur, for one sou, yes, for one sou — so indignant would you be! And that because you knew, by chance, the value of these two articles. Well, as for me, I know the value of all salable articles; and that indignation which would take possession of you, if you were asked four sous for a postage-stamp, I experience when I am asked twenty francs for an umbrella which is worth fifteen! I protest against the established theft, ceaseless and abominable, of merchants, servants, and coachmen. I protest against the commercial dishonesty of all your race which despises us. I give the price of a drink which I am bound to give for a service rendered, and not that which as the result of a whim you fling away without knowing why, and which ranges from five to a hundred sous according to the caprice of your temper! Do you understand?" Gontran had risen by this time, and smiling with that refined irony which came happily from his lips: "Yes, my dear fellow, I understand, and you are perfectly right, and so much the more right because my grandfather, the old Marquis de Ravenel, scarcely left anything to my poor father in consequence of the bad habit which he had of never picking up the change handed to him by the shopkeepers when he was paying for any article whatsoever. He thought that unworthy of a gentleman, and always gave the round sum and the entire coin."

And Gontran went out with a self-satisfied air.

XI

THEY were just ready to go in to dinner, on the following day, in the Private diningroom of the Andermatt and Ravenel families, when Gontran opened the door announcing the "Mesdemoiselles Oriol."

They entered, with an air of constraint, pushed forward by Gontran, who laughed while he explained:

"Here they are! I have carried them both off through the middle of the street. Moreover, it excited public attention. I brought them here by force to you because I want to explain myself to Madame Louise, and could not do so in the open air."

He took from them their hats and their parasols, which they were still carrying, as they had been on their way back from a promenade, made them sit down, embraced his sister, pressed the hands of his father, of his brother-in-law, and of Paul, and then, approaching Louise Oriol once more, said:

"Here now, Mademoiselle, kindly tell me what you have against me for some time past?"

She seemed scared, like a bird caught in a net, and carried away by the hunter.

"Why, nothing, Monsieur, nothing at all! What has made you believe that?"

"Oh! everything, Mademoiselle, everything at all! You no longer come here — you no longer come in the Noah's Ark [so he had baptized the big landau]. You assume a harsh tone whenever I meet you and when I speak to you."

"Why, no, Monsieur, I assure you!"

"Why, yes, Mam'zelle, I declare to you! In any case, I don't want this to continue, and I am going to make peace with you this very day. Oh! you know I am obstinate. There's no use in your looking black at me. I'll know easily how to get the better of your hoity-toity airs, and make you be nice toward your sister, who is an angel of grace."

It was announced that dinner was ready; and they made their way to the diningroom. Gontran took Louise's arm in his. He was exceedingly attentive to her and to her sister, dividing his compliments between them with admirable tact, and remarking to the younger girl: "As for you, you are a comrade of ours — I am going to neglect you for a few days. One goes to less expense for friends than for strangers, you are aware."

And he said to the elder: "As for you, I want to bewitch you, Mademoiselle, and I warn you as a loyal foe! I will even make love to you. Ha! you are blushing — that's a good sign. You'll see that I am very nice, when I take pains about it. Isn't that so, Mademoiselle Charlotte?"

And they were both, indeed, blushing, and Louise stammered with her serious air: "Oh! Monsieur, how foolish you are!"

He replied: "Bah! you will hear many things said by others by and by in society, when you are married, which will not be long. 'Tis then they will really pay you compliments."

Christiane and Paul Bretigny expressed their approval of his action in having brought back Louise Oriol; the Marquis smiled, amused by these childish affectations. Andermatt was thinking: "He's no fool, the sly dog." And Gontran, irritated by the part which he was compelled to play, drawn by his senses toward Charlotte and by his interests toward Louise, muttered between his teeth with a sly smile in her direction: "Ah! your rascal of a father thought to play a trick fupon me; but I am going to carry it with a high hand over you, my lassie, and you will see whether I won't go about it the right way!"

And he compared the two, inspecting them one after the other. Certainly, he liked the younger more; she was more amusing, more lively, with her nose tilted slightly, her bright eyes, her straight forehead, and her beautiful teeth a little too prominent in a mouth which was somewhat too wide.

However, the other was pretty, too, colder, less gay. She would never be lively or charming in the intimate relations of life; but when at the opening of a ball "the Comtesse de Ravenel" would be announced, she could carry her title well — better perhaps than her younger sister, when she got a little accustomed to it, and had mingled with persons of high birth. No matter; he was annoyed. He was full of spite against the father and the brother also, and he promised himself that he would pay them off afterward for his mischance when he was the master. When they returned to the drawingroom, he got Louise to read the cards, as she was skilled in foretelling the future. The Marquis, Andermatt, and Charlotte listened attentively, attracted, in spite of themselves, by the mystery of the unknown, by the possibility of the improbable, by that invincible credulity with reference to the marvelous which haunts man, and often disturbs the strongest minds in the presence of the silly inventions of charlatans.

Paul and Christiane chatted in the recess of an open window. For some time past she had been miserable, feeling that she was no longer loved in the same fashion; and their misunderstanding as lovers was every day accentuated by their mutual error. She had suspected this unfortunate state of things for the first time on the evening of the fete when she brought Paul along the road. But while she understood that he had no longer the same tenderness in his look, the same caress in his voice, the same passionate anxiety about her as in the days of their early love, she had not been able to divine the cause of this change.

It had existed for a long time now, ever since the day when she had said to him with a look of happiness on reaching their daily meeting-place: "You know, I believe I am really enceinte." He had felt at that moment an unpleasant little shiver running all over his skin. Then at each of their meetings she would talk to him about her condition, which made her heart dance with joy; but this preoccupation with a matter which he regarded as vexatious, ugly, and unclean clashed with his devoted exaltation about the idol that he had adored. At a later stage, when he saw her altered, thin, her cheeks hollow, her complexion yellow, he thought that she might have spared him that spectacle, and might have vanished for a few months from his sight, to reappear afterward fresher and prettier than ever, thus knowing how to make him forget this accident, or perhaps knowing how to unite to her coquettish fascinations as a mistress, another charm, the thoughtful reserve of a young mother, who only allows her baby to be seen at a distance covered up in red ribbons.

She had, besides, a rare opportunity of displaying that tact which he expected of her by spending the summer apart from him at Mont Oriol, and leaving him in Paris so that he might not see her robbed of her freshness and beauty. He had fondly hoped that she might have understood him.

But, immediately on reaching Auvergne, she had appealed to him in incessant and despairing letters so numerous and so urgent that he had come to her through weakness, through pity. And now she was boring him to death with her ungracious and lugubrious tenderness; and he felt an extreme longing to get away from her, to see no more of her, to listen no longer to her talk about love, so irritating and out of place. He would have liked to tell her plainly all that he had in his mind, to point out to her how unskillful and foolish she showed herself; but he could not bring himself to do this, and he dared not take his departure. As a result he could not restrain himself from testifying his impatience with her in bitter and hurtful words.

She was stung by them the more because, every day more ill, more heavy, tormented by all the sufferings of pregnant women, she had more need than ever of being consoled, fondled, encompassed with affection. She loved him with that utter abandonment of body and soul, of her entire being, which sometimes renders love a sacrifice without reservations and without bounds. She no longer looked upon herself as his mistress, but as his wife, his companion, his devotee, his worshiper, his prostrate slave, his chattel. For her there seemed no further need of any gallantry, coquetry, constant desire to please, or fresh indulgence between them, since she belonged to him entirely, since they were linked together by that chain so sweet and so strong — the child which would soon be born. When they were alone at the window, she renewed her tender lamentation: "Paul, my dear Paul, tell me, do you love me as much as ever?"

"Yes, certainly! Come now, you keep repeating this every day — it will end by becoming monotonous."

"Pardon me. It is because I find it impossible to believe it any longer, and I want you to reassure me; I want to hear you saying it to me forever that word which is so sweet; and, as you don't repeat it to me so often as you used to do, I am compelled to ask for it, to implore it, to beg for it from you."

"Well, yes, I love you! But let us talk of something else, I entreat of you."

"Ah! how hard you are!"

"Why, no! I am not hard. Only — only you do not understand — you do not understand that — ""Oh! yes! I understand well that you no longer love me. If you knew how I am suffering!"

"Come, Christiane, I beg of you not to make me nervous. If you knew yourself how awkward what you are now doing is!"

"Ah! if you loved me, you would not talk to me in this way."

"But, deuce take it! if I did not love you, I would not have come."

"Listen. You belong to me now. You are mine; I am yours. There is between us that tie of a budding life which nothing can break; but will you promise me that, if one day, you should come 'to love me no more, you will tell me so?"

"Yes, I do promise you."

"You swear it to me?"

"I swear it to you."

"But then, all the same, we would remain friends, would we not?"

"Certainly, let us remain friends."

"On the day when you no longer regard me with love you'll come to find me and you'll say to me: 'My little Christiane, I am very fond of you, but it is not the same thing any more. Let us be friends, there! nothing but friends.'"

"That is understood; I promise it to you."

"You swear it to me?"

"I swear it to you."

"No matter, it would cause me great grief. How you adored me last year!"

A voice called out behind them: "The Duchess de Ramas-Aldavarra."

She had come as a neighbor, for Christiane held receptions each day for the principal bathers, just as princes hold receptions in their kingdoms.

Doctor Mazelli followed the lovely Spaniard with a smiling and submissive air. The two women pressed one another's hands, sat down, and commenced to chat.

Andermatt called Paul across to him: "My dear friend come here! Mademoiselle Oriol reads the cards splendidly; she has told me some astonishing things! " He took Paul by the arm, and added: "What an odd being you are! At Paris, we never saw you, even once a month, in spite of the entreaties of my wife. Here it required fifteen letters to get you to come. And since you have come, one would think you are losing a million a day, you look so disconsolate. Come, are you hearing any matter that ruffles you? We might be able to assist you. You should tell us about it."

"Nothing at all, my dear fellow. If I haven't visited you more frequently in Paris — 'tis because at Paris, you understand — "

"Perfectly — I grasp your meaning. But here, at least, you ought to be in good spirits. I am preparing for you two or three fêtes, which will, I am sure, be very successful."

"Madame Barre and Professor Cloche" were announced. He entered with his daughter, a young widow, red-haired and bold-faced. Then, almost in the same breath, the manservant called out: "Professor Mas-Roussel."

His wife accompanied him, pale, worn, with flat headbands drawn over her temples.

Professor Remusot had left the day before, after having, it was said, purchased his chalet on exceptionally favorable conditions.

The two other doctors would have liked to know what these conditions were, but Andermatt merely said in reply to them: "Oh! we have made little advantageous arrangements for everybody. If you desired to follow his example, we might see our way to a mutual understanding — we might see our way. When you have made up your mind, you can let me know, and then we'll talk about it."

Doctor Latonne appeared in his turn, then Doctor Honorât, without his wife, whom he did not bring with him. A din of voices now filled the drawingroom, the loud buzz of conversation. Gontran never left Louise Oriol's side, put his head over her shoulder in addressing her, and said with a laugh every now and again to whoever was passing near him: "This is an enemy of whom I am making a conquest."

Mazelli took a seat beside Professor Cloche's daughter. For some days he had been constantly following her about; and she had received his advances with provoking audacity.

The Duchess, who kept him well in view, appeared irritated and trembling. Suddenly she rose, crossed the drawingroom, and interrupted her doctor's confidential chat with the pretty red-haired widow, saying: "Come, Mazelli, we are going to retire. I feel rather ill at ease."

As soon as they had gone out, Christiane drew close to Paul's side, and said to him: "Poor woman! she must suffer so much!"

He asked heedlessly: "Who, pray?"

"The Duchess! You don't see how jealous she is." He replied abruptly: "If you begin to groan over everything you can lay hold of now, you'll have no end of weeping."

She turned away, ready, indeed, to shed tears, so cruel did she find him, and, sitting down near Charlotte Oriol, who was all alone in a dazed condition, unable to comprehend the meaning of Gontran's conduct, she said to the young girl, without letting the latter realize what her words conveyed: "There are days when one would like to be dead."

Andermatt, in the midst of the doctors, was relating the extraordinary case of Père Clovis, whose legs were beginning to come to life again. He appeared so thoroughly convinced that nobody could doubt his good faith.

Since he had seen through the trick of the peasants and the paralytic, understood that he had let himself be duped and persuaded, the year before, through the sheer desire to believe in the efficacy of the waters with which he had been bitten, since, above all, he had not been able to free himself, without paying, from the formidable complaints of the old man, he had converted it into a strong advertisement, and worked it wonderfully well.

Mazelli had just come back, after having accompanied his patient to her own apartments.

Gontran caught hold of his arm: "Tell me your opinion, my good doctor. Which of the Oriol girls do you prefer?"

The handsome physician whispered in his ear: "The younger one, to love; the elder one, to marry."

"Look at that! We are exactly of the same way of thinking. I am delighted at it!"

Then, going over to his sister, who was still talking to Charlotte: "You are not aware of it? I have made up my mind that we are to visit the Puy de la Nugère on Thursday. It is the finest crater of the chain. Everyone consents. It is a settled thing." Christiane murmured with an air of indifference: "I consent to anything you like."

But Professor Cloche, followed by his daughter, was about to take his leave, and Mazelli, offering to see them home, started off behind the young widow. In five minutes, everyone had left, for Christiane went to bed at eleven o'clock. The Marquis, Paul, and Gontran accompanied the Oriol girls. Gontran and Louise walked in front, and Bretigny, some paces behind them, felt Charlotte's arm trembling a little as it leaned on his.

They separated with the agreement: "On Thursday at eleven for breakfast at the hotel!"

On their way back they met Andermatt, detained in a corner of the park by Professor Mas-Roussel, who was saying to him: "Well, if it does not put you about, I'll come and have a chat with you tomorrow morning about that little business of the chalet." William joined the young men to go in with them, and, drawing himself up to his brother-in-law's ear, said: "My best compliments, my dear boy! You have acted your part admirably."

Gontran, for the past two years, had been harassed by pecuniary embarrassments which had spoiled his existence. So long as he was spending the share which came to him from his mother, he had allowed his life to pass in that carelessness and indifference which he inherited from his father, in the midst of those young men, rich, blasé, and corrupted, whose doings we read about every morning in the newspapers, who belong to the world of fashion but mingle in it very little, preferring the society of women of easy virtue and purchasable hearts.

There were a dozen of them in the same set, who were to be found every night at the same café on the boulevard between midnight and three o'clock in the morning. Very well dressed, always in black coats and white waistcoats, wearing shirt-buttons worth twenty louis changed every month, and bought in one of the principal jewelers' shops, they lived careless of everything, save amusing themselves, picking up women, making them a subject of talk, and getting money by every possible means.

As the only things they had any knowledge of were the scandals of the night before, the echoes of alcoves and stables, duels and stories about gambling transactions, the entire horizon of their thoughts was shut in by these barriers. They had had all the women who were for sale in the market of gallantry, had passed them through their hands, given them up, exchanged them with one another, and talked among themselves as to their erotic qualities as they might have talked about the qualities of race-horses. They also associated with people of rank whose voluptuous habits excited comment and whose women nearly all kept up intrigues which were matters of notoriety, under the eyes of husbands indifferent or averted or closed or devoid of perception; and they passed judgment on these women as on the others, forming much the same estimate about them, save that they made a slight distinction on the grounds of birth and social position.

By dint of resorting to dodges to get the money necessary for the life which they led, outwitting usurers, borrowing on all sides, putting off tradesmen, laughing in the faces of their tailors when presented with a big bill every six months, listening to girls telling about the infamies they perpetrated in order to gratify their feminine greed, seeing systematic cheating at clubs, knowing and feeling that they were individually robbed by everyone, by servants, merchants, keepers of big restaurants and others, becoming acquainted with certain sharp practices and shady transactions in which they themselves had a hand in order to knock out a few Louis, their moral sense had become blunted, used up, and their sole point of honor consisted in fighting duels when they realized that they were suspected of all the things of which they were either capable or actually guilty.

Everyone of these young roués, after some years of this existence, ended with a rich marriage, or a scandal, or a suicide, or a mysterious disappearance as complete as death. But they put their principal reliance on the rich marriage. Some trusted to their families to procure such a thing for them; others looked out themselves for it without letting it be noticed; and they had lists of heiresses just as people have lists of houses for sale. They kept their eyes fixed especially on the exotics, the Americans of the north and of the south, whom they dazzled by their "chic," by their reputation as fast men, by talk about their successes, and by the elegance of their persons. And their tradesmen also placed reliance on the rich marriage.

But this hunt after the girl with a fortune was bound to be protracted. In any case it involved inquiries, the trouble of winning a female heart, fatigues, visits, all that exercise of energy of which Gontran, careless by nature, remained utterly incapable. For a long time past, he had been saying to himself, feeling each day more keenly the unpleasantness of impecuniosity: "I must, for all that, think over it." But he did not think over it, and so he found nothing. He had been reduced to the ingenious pursuit of paltry sums, to all the questionable steps of people at the end of their resources, and, to crown all, to long sojourns in the family, when Andermatt had suddenly suggested to him the idea of marrying one of the Oriol girls.

He had, at first, said nothing through prudence, although the young girl appeared to him, at first blush, too much beneath him for him to consent to such an unequal match. But a few minutes' reflection had very speedily modified his view; and he forthwith made up his mind to make love to her in a bantering sort of way — the love-making of a spa — which would not compromise him, and would permit him to back out of it.

Thoroughly acquainted with his brother-in-law's character, he knew that this proposition must have been cogitated for a long time, and weighed and matured by him — that she meant to him a valuable prize such as it would be hard to find elsewhere.

It would cost him no trouble but that of stooping down and picking up a pretty girl, for he liked the younger sister very much, and he had often said to himself that she would be nice to associate with later on. He had accordingly selected Charlotte Oriol; and in a little time would have brought matters to the point when a regular proposal might have been made to her.

Now, as the father was bestowing on his other daughter the dowry coveted by Andermatt, Gontran had either to renounce this union or turn round to the elder sister. He felt intense dissatisfaction with this state of affairs and he had been thinking in his first moments of vexation of sending his brother-in-law to the devil and remaining a bachelor until a fresh opportunity arose. But just at that very time he found himself quite cleaned out, so that he had to ask, for his play at the Casino, a sum of twenty-five louis from Paul, after many similar loans, which he had never paid back. And again, he would have to look for a rich wife, find her, and captivate her, while without any change of place, with only a few days of attention and gallantry, he could capture the elder of the Oriol girls just as he had been able to make a conquest of the younger. In this way he would make sure in his brother-in-law of a banker whom he might render always responsible, on whom he might cast endless reproaches, and whose cash-box would always be open for him.

As for his wife, he could bring her to Paris, and there introduce her into society as the daughter of Andermatt's partner. Moreover, she bore the name of the spa, to which he would never bring her back!

Never! never! in virtue of the natural law that streams do not return to their sources. She had a nice face and figure, sufficiently distinguished already to become entirely so, sufficiently intelligent to understand the ways of society, to hold her own in it, to make a good show in it, and even to do him honor. People would say: "This joker here has married a lovely girl, at whom he looks as if he were not making a bad joke of it." And he would not make a bad joke of it, in fact, for he counted on resuming by her side his bachelor existence with the money in his pockets.

So he turned toward Louise Oriol, and, taking advantage of the jealousy awakened in the skittish heart of the young girl, without being aware of it, had excited in her a coquetry which had hitherto slumbered, and a vague desire to take away from her sister this handsome lover whom people addressed as "Monsieur le Comte."

She had not said this in her own mind. She had neither thought it out nor contrived it, being surprised at their being thrown together and going off in one another's company. But when she saw him assiduous and gallant toward her, she felt from his demeanor, from his glances, and his entire attitude, that he was not enamored of Charlotte, and without trying to see beyond that, she was in a happy, joyous, almost triumphant frame of mind as she lay down to sleep.

They hesitated for a long time on the following Thursday before starting for the Puy de la Nugère. The gloomy sky and the heavy atmosphere made them anticipate rain. But Gontran insisted so strongly on going that he carried the waverers along with him. The breakfast was a melancholy affair. Christiane and Paul had quarreled the night before, without apparent cause. Andermatt was afraid that Gontran's marriage might not take place, for Père Oriol had, that very morning, spoken of him in equivocal terms. Gontran, on being informed of this, got angry and made up his mind that he would succeed. Charlotte, foreseeing her sister's triumph, without at all understanding this transfer of Gontran's affections, strongly desired to remain in the village. With some difficulty they prevailed on her to come.

Accordingly the Noah's Ark carried its full number of ordinary passengers in the direction of the high plateau which looks down on Volvic. Louise Oriol, suddenly becoming loquacious, acted as their guide along the road. She explained how the stone of Volvic, which is nothing else but the lava-current of the surrounding peaks, had helped to build all the churches and all the houses in the district — a circumstance which gives to the towns in Auvergne the dark and charred-looking aspect that they present.

She pointed out the yards where this stone was cut, showed them the molten rock that was worked as a quarry, from which was extracted the rough lava, and made them view with admiration, standing on a hilltop and bending over Volvic, the immense black Virgin who protects the town. Then they ascended toward the upper plateau, embossed with extinct volcanoes. The horses went at a walking pace over the long and toilsome road. Their path was bordered with beautiful green woods, and nobody talked any longer.

Christiane was thinking about Tazenat. It was the same carriage; they were the same persons; but their hearts were no longer the same. Everything seemed as it had been — and yet? and yet? What then had happened? Almost nothing. A little love the more on her part! A little love the less on his! Almost nothing — the invisible rent which weariness makes in an intimate attachment — oh! almost nothing — and the look in the changed eyes, because the same eyes no longer saw the same faces in the same way. What is this but a look? Almost nothing!

The coachman drew up, and said: "It is here, at the right, through that path in the wood. You have only to follow it in order to get there.

All descended, save the Marquis, who thought the weather too warm. Louise and Gontran went on in front, and Charlotte remained behind with Paul and Christiane, who found difficulty in walking. The path appeared to them long, right through the wood; then they reached a crest covered with tall grass which led by a steep ascent to the sides of the old crater. Louise and Gontran, halting when they got to the top, both looking tall and slender, had the appearance of standing in the clouds. When the others had come up with them, Paul Bretigny's enthusiastic soul was inflamed with poetic rapture.

Around them, behind them, to right, to left, they were surrounded by strange cones, decapitated, some shooting forth, others crushed into a mass, but all preserving their fantastic physiognomy of dead volcanoes. These heavy fragments of mountains with flat summits rose from south to west along an im mense plateau of desolate appearance, which, itself a thousand meters above the Limagne, looked down upon it, as far as the eye could reach, toward the east and the north, on to the invisible horizon, always veiled, always blue.

The Puy de Dome, at the right, towered above all its fellows, with from seventy to eighty craters now gone to sleep. Further on were the Puy de Gravenoire, the Puy de Crouel, the Puy de la Pedge, the Puy de Sault, the Puy de Noschamps, the Puy de la Vache. Nearer, were the Puy de Come, the Puy de Jumes, the Puy de Tressoux, the Puy de Louchadière ——a vast cemetery of volcanoes.

The young men gazed at the scene in amazement. At their feet opened the first crater of La Nugère, a deep grassy basin at the bottom of which could be seen three enormous blocks of brown lava, lifted up with the monster's last puff and then sunk once more into his throat as he expired, remaining there from century to century forever.

Gontran exclaimed: "As for me, I am going down to the bottom. I want to see how they give up the ghost — creatures of this sort. Come along, Mesdemoiselles, for a little run down the slope." And seizing Louise's arm, he dragged her after him. Charlotte followed them, running after them. Then, all of a sudden, she stopped, watched them as they flew along, jumping with their arms linked, and, turning back abruptly, she reascended toward Christiane and Paul, who were seated on the grass at the top of the declivity. When she reached them, she fell upon her knees, and, hiding her face in the young girl's robe she wore, she burst out sobbing.

Christiane, who understood what was the matter, and whom all the sorrows of others had, for some time past, pierced like wounds inflicted upon herself, flung her arms around the girl's neck, and, moved also by her tears, murmured: "Poor little thing! poor little thing!" The girl kept crying incessantly, and with her hands dropping listlessly to the ground, she tore up the grass unconscious of what she was doing.

Bretigny had risen up in order to avoid the appearance of having observed her, but this misery endured by a young girl, this distress of an innocent creature, filled him suddenly with indignation against Gontran. He, whom Christiane's deep anguish only exasperated, was touched to the bottom of his heart by a girl's first disillusion.

He came back, and kneeling down in his turn, in order to speak to her, said: "Come, calm yourself, I beg of you. They are going to return presently. They must not see you crying."

She sprang to her feet, scared by this idea that her sister might find her with tears in her eyes. Her throat remained choking with sobs, which she held back, which she swallowed down, which she sent back into her heart, filling it with more poignant grief. She faltered: "Yes — yes — it is over — it is nothing — it is over. Look here! It cannot be noticed now. Isn't that so? It cannot be noticed now."

Christiane wiped her cheeks with her handkerchief, then passed it also across her own. She said to Paul:

"Go, pray, and see what they are doing. We cannot see them any longer. They have disappeared under the blocks of lava. I will look after this little one, and console her."

Bretigny had again stood up, and in a trembling voice, said: "I am going there — and I'll bring them back, but it will be my affair — your brother — this very day — and he shall give me an explanation of his unjustifiable conduct, after what he said to us the other day." He began to descend, running toward the center of the crater.

Gontran, hurrying Louise along, had pulled her with all his strength over the steep side of the chasm, in order to hold her up, to sustain her, to put her out of breath, to make her dizzy, and to frighten her. She, carried along by his wild rush, attempted to stop him, gasping: "Oh! not so quickly — I'm going to fall — why, you're mad — I'm going to fall!"

They knocked against the blocks of lava, and remained standing up, both breathless. Then they walked round the crater staring at the big gaps which formed below a kind of cavern, with a double outlet.

When at the end of its life, the volcano had cast out this last mouthful of foam, unable to shoot it up to the sky as in former times, he had spat it forth, so that, thick and half-cooled, it fixed itself upon his dying lips.

"We must enter under there," said Gontran. And he pushed the young girl before him. Then, when they were in the grotto, he said: "Well, Mademoiselle, this is the moment to make a declaration to you." She was stupefied: "A declaration — to me!"

"Why, yes, in four words — I find you charming!': "It is to my sister you should say that!"

"Oh! you know well that I am not making a declaration to your sister."

"Come, now!"

"Look here! you would not be a woman if you did not understand that I have paid attentions to her to see what you would think of it! — and what looks you gave me on account of it. Why, you looked daggers at me! Oh! I'm quite satisfied. So then I have tried to prove to you, by all the consideration in my power, how much I thought about you." Nobody had ever before talked to her in this way. She felt confused and delighted, her heart full of joy and pride. He went on: "I know well that I have been nasty toward your little sister. So much the worse. She is not deceived by it, never fear. You see how she remained on the hillside, how she was not inclined to follow us. Oh! she understands! she understands!"

He had caught hold of one of Louise Oriol's hands, and he kissed the ends of her fingers softly, gallantly, murmuring: "How nice you are! How nice you are!"

She, leaning against the wall of lava, heard his heart beating with emotion without uttering a word. The thought, the sole thought, which floated in her agitated mind, was one of triumph; she had got the better of her sister! But a shadow appeared at the entrance to the grotto. Paul Bretigny was looking at them. Gontran, in a natural fashion, let fall the little hand which he had been raising to his lips, and said: "Hallo! you here? Are you alone?"

"Yes. We were surprised to see you disappearing down here."

"Oh! well, let us go back. We were looking at this. Isn't it rather curious?"

Louise, flushed up to her temples, went out first, and began to reascend the slope, followed by the two young men, who were talking behind in a low tone.

Christiane and Charlotte saw them approaching, and awaited them with clasped hands.

They went back to the carriage in which the Marquis had remained, and the Noah's Ark set out again for Enval.

Suddenly, in the midst of a little forest of pine-trees the landau stopped, and the coachman began to swear. An old dead ass blocked the way.

Everyone wanted to look at it, and they got down off the carriage. He lay stretched on the blackened dust, himself discolored, and so lean that his worn skin at the places where the bones projected seemed as if it would have been burst through if the animal had not breathed forth his last sigh. The entire carcass outlined itself under the gnawed hair of his sides, and his head looked enormous — a poor-looking head, with the eyes closed, tranquil now on its bed of broken stones, so tranquil, so calm in death, that it appeared happy and surprised at this new-found rest. His big ears, now relaxed, lay like rags. Two raw wounds on his knees told how often he had fallen that very day before sinking down for the last time; and another wound on the side showed the place where his master, for years and years, had been pricking him with an iron spike attached to the end of a stick, to hasten his slow pace.

The coachman, having caught its hind legs, dragged it toward a ditch, and the neck was strained as if the dead brute were going to bray once more, to give vent to a last complaint. When this was done, the man, in a rage, muttered: "What brutes, to leave this in the middle of the road!"

No other person had said a word; they again stepped into the carriage. Christiane, heart-broken, crushed, saw all the miserable life of this animal ended thus at the side of the road: the merry little donkey with his big head, in which glittered-a pair of big eyes, comical and good-tempered, with his rough hair and his long ears, gamboling about, still free, close to his mother's legs; then the first cart; the first uphill journey; the first blows; and, after that, the ceaseless and terrible walking along interminable roads, the overpowering heat of the sun, and nothing for food save a little straw, a little hay, or some branches, while all along the hard roads there was the temptation of the green meadows.

And then, again, as age came upon him, the iron spike replacing the pliant switch; and the frightful martyrdom of the animal, worn out, bereft of breath, bruised, always dragging after it excessive loads, and suffering in all its limbs, in all its old body, shabby as a beggar's cart. And then the death, the beneficent death, three paces away from the grass of the ditch, to which a man, passing by, drags it with oaths, in order to clear the road.

Christiane, for the first time, understood the wretchedness of enslaved creatures; and death appeared to her also a very good thing at times.

Suddenly they passed by a little cart, which a man nearly naked, a woman in tatters, and a lean dog were dragging along, exhausted by fatigue. The occupants of the carriage noticed that they were sweating and panting. The dog, with his tongue out, fleshless and mangy, was fastened between the wheels. There were in this cart pieces of wood picked up everywhere, stolen, no doubt, roots, stumps, broken branches, which seemed to hide other things; then over these branches rags, and on these rags a child, nothing but a head starting out through gray old scraps of cloth, a round ball with two eyes, a nose, and a mouth!

This was a family, a human family! The ass had succumbed to fatigue, and the man, without pity for his dead servant, without pushing it even into the rut, had left it in the open road, in front of any vehicles which might be coming up. Then, yoking himself in his turn with his wife in the empty shafts, they proceeded to drag it along as the beast had dragged it a short time before. They were going on. Where? To do what? Had they even a few sous? That cart — would they be dragging it forever, not being in a position to buy another animal? What would they live on? Where would they stop? They would probably die as their donkey had died.

Were they married, these beggars, or merely living together? And their child would do the same as they did, this little brute as yet unformed, concealed under sordid wrappings. Christiane was thinking on all these things; and new sensations rose up in the depths of her pitying soul. She had a glimpse of the misery of the poor.

Gontran said, all of a sudden: "I don't know why, but I would think it a delicious thing if we were all to dine together this evening at the Café Anglais. It would give me pleasure to have a look at the boulevard."

And the Marquis muttered: "Bah! we are well enough here. The new hotel is much better than the old one."

They passed in front of Tournoel. A recollection of the spot made Christiane's heart palpitate, as she recognized a certain chestnut-tree. She glanced toward Paul, who had closed his eyes, so that he did not see her meek, appealing face.

Soon they perceived two men before the carriage, two vinedressers returning from work carrying their rakes on their shoulders, and walking with the long, weary steps of laborers. The Oriol girls reddened to their very temples. It was their father and their brother, who had gone back to their vinelands as in former times, and passed their days sweating over the soil which they had enriched, and bent double, with their buttocks in the air, kept toiling at it from morning until evening, while the fine frock-coats, carefully folded up, were at rest in the chest of drawers, and the tall hats in a press.

The two peasants bowed with a friendly smile, while everyone in the landau waved a hand in response to their "Good evening."

When they got back, just as Gontran was stepping out of the Ark to go up to the Casino, Bretigny accompanied him, and stopping on the first steps, said:

"Listen, my friend! What you're doing is not right, and I've promised your sister to speak to you about it."

"To speak about what?"

"About the way you have been acting during the last few days."

Gontran had resumed his impertinent air.

"Acting? Toward whom?"

"Toward this girl whom you are meanly jilting."

"Do you think so?"

"Yes, I do think so — and I am right in thinking so."

"Bah! you are becoming very scrupulous on the subject of jilting."

"Ah, my friend, 'tis not a question of a loose woman here, but of a young girl."

"I know that perfectly; therefore, I have not seduced her. The difference is very marked."

They went on walking together side by side. Gontran's demeanor exasperated Paul, who replied:

"If I were not your friend, I would say some very severe things to you."

"And for my part I would not permit you to say them."

"Look here, listen to me, my friend! This young girl excites my pity. She was weeping a little while ago."

"Bah! she was weeping! Why, that's a compliment to me!"

"Come, don't trifle! What do you mean to do?"

"I? Nothing!"

"Just consider! You have gone so far with her that you have compromised her. The other day you told your sister and me that you were thinking of marrying her."

Gontran stopped in his walk, and in that mocking tone through which a menace showed itself:

"My sister and you would do better not to bother yourselves about other people's love affairs. I told you that this girl pleases me well enough, and that if I happened to marry her, I would be doing a wise and reasonable act. That's all. Now it turns out that to-day I like the elder girl better. I have changed my mind. That's a thing that happens to everyone."

Then, looking him full in the face: "What is it that you do yourself when you cease to care about a woman? Do you look after her?"

Paul Bretigny, astonished, sought to penetrate the profound meaning, the hidden sense, of these words. A little feverishness also mounted into his brain. He said in a violent tone:

"I tell you again this is not a question of a hussy or a married woman, but of a young girl whom you have deceived, if not by promises, at least by your advances. That is not, mark you, the part of a man of honor! — or of an honest man!"

Gontran, pale, his voice quivering, interrupted him: "Hold your tongue! You have already said too much — and I have listened to too much of this. In my turn, if I were not your friend I — I might show you that I have a short temper. Another word, and there is an end of everything between us forever!"

Then, slowly weighing his words, and flinging them in Paul's face, he said: "I have no explanations to offer you — I might rather have to demand them from you. There is a certain kind of indelicacy of which it is not the part of a man of honor or of an honest man to be guilty — which might take many forms — from which friendship ought to keep certain people — and which love does not excuse."

All of a sudden, changing his tone, and almost jesting, he added:

"As for this little Charlotte, if she excites your pity, and if you like her, take her, and marry her. Marriage is often a solution of difficult cases. It is a solution, and a stronghold, in which one may barricade himself against desperate obstacles. She is pretty and rich! It would be very desirable for you to finish with an accident like this! — it would be amusing for us to marry here, the same day, for I certainly will marry the elder one. I tell it to you as a secret, and don't repeat it as yet. Now don't forget that you have less right than anyone else yourself ever to talk about integrity in matters of sentiment, and scruples of affection. And now go and look after your own affairs. I am going to look after mine. Good night!"

And suddenly turning off in another direction, he went down toward the village. Paul Bretigny, with doubts in his mind and uneasiness in his heart, returned with lingering steps to the hotel of Mont Oriol.

He tried to understand thoroughly, to recall each word, in order to determine its meaning, and he was amazed at the secret byways, shameful and unfit to be spoken of, which may be hidden in certain souls.

When Christiane asked him: "What reply did you get from Gontran?"

He faltered: "My God! he — he prefers the elder, just now. I believe he even intends to marry her — and in answer to my rather sharp reproaches he shut my mouth by allusions that are — disquieting to both of us."

Christiane sank into a chair, murmuring: "Oh! my God! my God!"

But, as Gontran had just come in, for the bell had rung for dinner, he kissed her gaily on the forehead, asking: "Well, little sister, how do you feel now? You are not too tired?"

Then he pressed Paul's hand, and, turning toward Andermatt, who had come in after him:

"I say, pearl of brothers-in-law, of husbands, and of friends, can you tell me exactly what an old ass dead on a road is worth?"

XII

Andermatt and Doctor Latonne were walking in front of the Casino on a terrace adorned with vases made of imitation marble.

"He no longer salutes me," the doctor was saying, referring to his brother-physician Bonnefille. "He is over there in his pit, like a wild-boar. I believe he would poison our springs, if he could!"

Andermatt, with his hands behind his back and his hat — a small round hat of gray felt — thrown back over his neck, so as to let the baldness above his forehead be seen, was deeply plunged in thought. At length he said:

"Oh! in three months the Company will have knuckled under. We might buy it over at ten thousand francs. It is that wretched Bonnefille who is exciting them against me, and who makes them fancy that I will give way. But he is mistaken."

The new inspector returned: "You are aware that they have shut up their Casino since yesterday. They have no one any longer."

"Yes, I am aware of it; but we have not enough of people here ourselves. They stick in too much at the hotels; and people get bored in the hotels, my dear fellow. It is necessary to amuse the bathers, to distract them, to make them think the season too short. Those staying at our Mont Oriol hotel come every evening, because they are quite near, but the others hesitate and remain in their abodes. It is a question of routes — nothing else. Success always depends on certain imperceptible causes which we ought to know how to discover. It is necessary that the routes leading to a place of recreation should be a source of recreation in themselves, the commencement of the pleasure which one will be enjoying presently.

"The ways which lead to this place are bad, stony, hard; they cause fatigue. When a route which goes to any place, to which one has a vague desire of paying a visit, is pleasant, wide, and full of shade in the daytime, easy and not too steep at night, one selects it naturally in preference to others. If you knew how the body preserves the recollection of a thousand things which the mind has not taken the trouble to retain! I believe this is how the memory of animals is constructed. Have you felt too hot when repairing to such a place? Have you tired your feet on badly broken stones? Have you found an ascent too rough, even while you were thinking of something else? If so, you will experience invincible repugnance to revisiting that spot. You were chatting with a friend; you took no notice of the slight annoyances of the journey; you were looking at nothing, remarking notice; but your legs, your muscles, your lungs, your whole body have not forgotten, and they say to the mind, when it wants to take them along the same route: 'No, I won't go; I have suffered too much there.' And the mind yields to this refusal without disputing it, submitting to this mute language of the companions who carry it along.

"So then, we want fine pathways, which comes back to saying that I require the bits of ground belonging to that donkey of a Père Oriol. But patience! Ha! with reference to that point, Mas-Roussel has become the proprietor of his own chalet on the same conditions as Remusot.

It is a trifling sacrifice for which he will amply indemnify us. Try, therefore, to find out exactly what are Cloche's intentions."

"He'll do just the same thing as the others," said the physician. "But there is something else, of which I have been thinking for the last few days, and which we have completely forgotten — it is the meteorological bulletin."

"What meteorological bulletin?"

"In the big Parisian newspapers. It is indispensable, this is! It is necessary that the temperature of a thermal station should be better, less variable, more uniformly mild than that of the neighboring and rival stations. You subscribe to the meteorological bulletin in the leading organs of opinion, and I will send every evening by telegraph the atmospheric situation.

I will do it in such a way that the average arrived at when the year is at an end may be higher than the best mean temperatures of the surrounding stations. The first thing that meets our eyes when we open the big newspapers are the temperatures of Vichy, of Royat, of Mont Doré, of Chatel-Guyon, and other places during the summer season, and, during the winter season, the temperatures of Cannes, Mentone, Nice, Saint Raphael. It is necessary that the weather should always be hot and always fine in these places, in order that the Parisian might say: 'Christi! how lucky the people are who go down there!'"

Andermatt exclaimed: "Upon my honor, you're right. Why have I never thought of that? I will attend to it this very day. With regard to useful things, have you written to Professors Larenard and Pascalis? There are two men I would like very much to have here."

"Unapproachable, my dear President — unless — unless they are satisfied of themselves after many trials that our waters are of a superior character. But, as far as they are concerned, you will accomplish nothing by persuasion — by anticipation."

They passed by Paul and Gontran, who had come to take coffee after luncheon. Other bathers made their appearance, especially men, for the women, on rising from the table, always went up to their rooms for an hour or two. Petrus Martel was looking after his waiters, and crying out: "A kummel, a nip of brandy, a glass of aniseed cordial," in the same rolling, deep voice which he would assume an hour later while conducting rehearsals, and giving the keynote to the young première.

Andermatt stopped a few moments for a short chat with the two young men; then he resumed his promenade by the side of the inspector.

Gontran, with legs crossed and folded arms, lolling in his chair, with the nape of his neck against the back of it, and his eyes and his cigar facing the sky, was puffing in a state of absolute contentment.

Suddenly, he asked: "'Would you mind taking a turn, presently, in the valley of Sans-Souci? The girls will be there."

Paul hesitated; then, after some reflection: "Yes, I am quite willing." Then he added: "Is your affair progressing?"

"Egad, it is! Oh! I have a hold of her. She won't escape me now."

Gontran had, by this time, taken his friend into his confidence, and told him, day by day, how he was going on and how much ground he had gained. He even got him to be present, as a confederate, at his appointments, for he had managed to obtain appointments with Louise Oriol by a little bit of ingenuity.

After their promenade at the Puy de la Nugère, Christiane put an end to these excursions by not going out at all, and so rendered it more and more difficult for the lovers to meet. Her brother, put out at first by this attitude on her part, bethought him of some means of extricating himself from this predicament. Accustomed to Parisian morals, according to which women are regarded by men of his stamp as game, the chase of which is often no easy one, he had in former days made use of many artifices in order to gain access to those for whom he had conceived a passion. He knew better than anyone else how to make use of pimps, to discover those who were accommodating through interested motives, and to determine with a single glance the men or women who were disposed to aid him in his designs.

The unconscious support of Christiane having suddenly been withdrawn from him, he had looked about him for the requisite connecting link, the "pliant nature," as he expressed it himself, whereby he could replace his sister; and his choice speedily fixed itself on Doctor Honorat's wife. Many reasons pointed at her as a suitable person. In the first place, her husband, closely associated with the Oriols, had been for the past twenty years attending this family. He had been present at the birth of the children, had dined with them every Sunday, and had entertained them at his own table every Tuesday. His wife, a fat old woman of the lower-middle class, trying to pass as a lady, full of pretension, easy to overcome through her vanity, was sure to lend both hands to every desire of the Comte de Ravenel, whose brother-in-law owned the establishment of Mont Oriol.

Besides, Gontran, who was a good judge of a go-between, had satisfied himself that this woman was naturally well adapted for the part, by merely seeing her walking through the street.

"She has the physique," was his reflection, "and when one has the physique for an employment, one has the soul required for it, too!"

Accordingly, he made his way into her abode, one day, after having accompanied her husband to his own door. He sat down, chatted, complimented the lady, and, when the dinner-bell rang, he said, as he rose up: "You have a very savory smell here. You cook better than they do at the hotel."

Madame Honorat, swelling with pride, faltered: "Good heavens! if I might make so bold — if I might make so bold, Monsieur le Comte, as — "

"If you might make so bold as what, dear Madame?"

"As to ask you to share our humble meal." "Faith — faith, I would say 'yes.'"

The doctor, ill at ease, muttered: "But we have nothing, nothing — soup, a joint of beef, and a chicken, that's all!"

Gontran laughed: "Thai's quite enough for me. I accept the invitation."

And he dined at the Honorat household. The fat woman rose up, went to take the dishes out of the servant-maid's hands, in order that the latter might not spill the sauce over the tablecloth, and, in spite of her husband's impatience, insisted on attending at table herself.

The Comte congratulated her on the excellence of the cooking, on the good house she kept, on her attention to the duties of hospitality, and he left her inflamed with enthusiasm.

He returned to leave his card, accepted a fresh invitation, and thenceforth made his way constantly to Madame Honorat's house, to which the Oriol girls had paid visits frequently also for many years as neighbors and friends.

So then he spent hours there, in the midst of the three ladies, attentive to both sisters, but accentuating clearly, from day to day, his marked preference for Louise.

The jealousy that had sprung up between the girls since the time when he had begun to make love to Charlotte had assumed an aspect of spiteful hostility on the side of the elder girl and of disdain on the side of the younger. Louise, with her reserved air, imported into her reticences and her demure ways in Gontran's society much more coquetry and encouragement than the other had formerly shown with all her free and joyous unconstraint. Charlotte, wounded to the quick, concealed through pride the pain that she endured, pretended not to see or hear anything of what was happening around her, and continued her visits to Madame Honorat's house with a beautiful appearance of indifference to all these lovers' meetings. She would not remain behind at her own abode lest people might think that her heart was sore, that she was weeping, that she was making way for her sister.

Gontran, too proud of his achievement to throw a veil over it, could not keep himself from talking about it to Paul. And Paul, thinking it amusing, began to laugh. He had, besides, since the first equivocal remarks of his friend, resolved not to interfere in his affairs, and he often asked himself with uneasiness: "Can it be possible that he knows something about Christiane and me?"

He knew Gontran too well not to believe him capable of shutting his eyes to an intrigue on the part of his sister. But then, why did he not let it be understood sooner that he guessed it or was aware of it? Gontran was, in fact, one of those in whose opinion every woman in society ought to have a lover or lovers, one of those for whom the family is merely a society of mutual help, for whom morality is an attitude that is indispensable in order to veil the different appetites which nature has implanted in us, and for whom worldly honor is a front behind which amiable vices should be hidden. Moreover, if he had egged on his dear sister to marry Andermatt was it not with the vague, if not clearly-defined, idea that this Jew might be utilized, in every way, by all the family? — and he would probably have despised Christiane for being faithful to this husband of convenience, of utility, just as much as he would have despised himself for not borrowing freely from his brother-in-law's purse.

Paul pondered over all this, and it disturbed his modern Don Quixote's soul, which, in any event, was disposed toward compromise. He had, therefore, become very reserved with this enigmatic friend of his. When, accordingly, Gontran told him the use that he was making of Madame Honorat, Bretigny burst out laughing; and he had even, for some time past, allowed himself to be brought to that lady's house, and found great pleasure in chatting with Charlotte there.

The doctor's wife lent herself, with the best grace in the world, to the part she was made to play, and offered them tea about five o'clock, like the Parisian ladies, with little cakes manufactured by her own hands. On the first occasion when Paul made his way into this household, she welcomed him as if he were an old friend, made him sit down, removed his hat herself, in spite of his protests, and placed it beside the clock upon the mantelpiece. Then, eager, bustling, going from one to the other, tremendously big and fat, she asked:

"Do you feel inclined for a little dinner?"

Gontran told funny stories, joked, and laughed quite at his ease. Then, he took Louise into the recess of a window under the troubled eyes of Charlotte.

Madame Honorat, who sat chatting with Paul, said to him in a maternal tone:

"These dear children, they come here to have a few minutes' conversation with one another. 'Tis very innocent — isn't it, Monsieur Bretigny?"

"Oh! very innocent, Madame!"

When he came the next time, she familiarly addressed him as "Monsieur Paul," treating him more or less as a crony.

And from that time forth, Gontran told him, with a sort of teasing liveliness, all about the complaisant behavior of the doctor's wife, to whom he had said, the evening before: "Why do you never go out for a walk along the Sans-Souci road?"

"But we will go, M. le Comte — we will go." "Say, tomorrow about three o'clock."

"Tomorrow, about three o'clock, M. le Comte." And Gontran explained to Paul: "You understand that in this drawingroom, I cannot say anything of a very confidential nature to the elder girl before the younger. But in the wood I can go on before or remain behind with Louise. So then you will come?"

"Yes, I have no objection."

"Let us go on then."

And they rose up, and set forth at a leisurely pace along the highroad; then, having passed through La Roche Pradière, they turned to the left and descended into the wooded glen in the midst of tangled brushwood. When they had passed the little river, they sat down at the side of the path and waited.

The three ladies soon arrived, walking in single file, Louise in front, and Madame Honorat in the rear.

They exhibited surprise on both sides at having met in this way. Gontran exclaimed: "Well, now, what a good idea this was of yours to come along here!" The doctor's wife replied: "Yes, the idea was mine."

They continued their walk. Louise and Gontran gradually quickened their steps, went on in advance, and rambled so far together that they disappeared from view at a turn of the narrow path.

The fat lady, who was breathing hard, murmured, as she cast an indulgent eye in their direction: "Bah! they're young — they have legs. As for me, I can't keep up with them."

Charlotte exclaimed: "Wait! I'm going to call them back!"

She was rushing away. The doctor's wife held her back: "Don't interfere with them, child, if they want to chat! It would not be nice to disturb them. They will come back all right by themselves."

And she sat down on the grass, under the shade of a pine-tree, fanning herself with her pocket-handkerchief. Charlotte cast a look of distress toward Paul, a look imploring and sorrowful.

He understood, and said: "Well, Mademoiselle, we are going to let Madame take a rest, and we'll both go and overtake your sister."

She answered impetuously: "Oh, yes, Monsieur." Madame Honorat made no objection: "Go, my children, go. As for me, I'll wait for you here. Don't be too long."

And they started off in their turn. They walked quickly at first, as they could see no sign of the two others, and hoped to come up with them; then, after a few minutes, it struck them that Louise and Gontran might have turned off to the right or to the left through the wood, and Charlotte began to call them in a trembling and undecided voice. There was no response. She exclaimed: "Oh! good heavens, where can they be?"

Paul felt himself overcome once more by that profound pity, by that sympathetic tenderness toward her which had previously taken possession of him on the edge of the crater of La Nugère.

He did not know what to say to this afflicted young creature. He felt a longing, a paternal and passionate longing to take her in his arms, to embrace her, to find sweet and consoling words with which to soothe her. But what words?

She looked about on every side, searched the branches with wild glances, listening to the faintest sounds, murmuring: "I think that they are here — No, there — Do you hear nothing?"

"No, Mademoiselle, I don't hear anything. The best thing we can do is to wait here."

"Oh! heavens, no. We must find them!"

He hesitated for a few seconds, and then said to her in a low tone: "This, then, causes you much pain?"

She raised toward his her eyes, in which there was a look of wild alarm, while the gathering tears filled them with a transparent watery mist, as yet held back by the lids, over which drooped the long, brown lashes. She strove to speak, but could not, and did not venture to open her lips. But her heart swollen, choked with grief, was yearning to pour itself out.

He went on: "So then you loved him very much. He is not worthy of your love. Take heart!"

She could not restrain herself any longer, and hiding with her hands the tears that now gushed forth from her eyes, she sobbed: "No! — no! — I do not love him — he — it is too base to have acted as he did. He made a fool of me — it is too base — too cowardly — but, all the same, it does pain me — a great deal — for it is hard — very hard — oh! yes. But what grieves me most is that my sister — my sister does not care for me any longer — she who has been even more wicked than he was! I feel that she no longer cares for me — not a bit — that she hates me —— I have only her — I have no one else — and I, I have done nothing!"

He only saw her ear and her neck with its young flesh sinking into the collar of her dress under the light material she wore till it was lost in the curves of her bust. And he felt himself overpowered with compassion, with sympathy, carried away by that impetuous desire of self-devotion which got the better of him every time that a woman touched his heart. And that heart of his, responsive to outbursts of enthusiasm, was excited by this innocent sorrow, agitating, ingenuous, and cruelly charming.

He stretched forth his hand toward her with an unstudied movement such as one might use in order to caress, to calm a child, and he drew it round her waist from behind over her shoulder. Then he felt her heart beating with rapid throbs, as he might have heard the little heart of a bird that he had caught. And this beating, continuous, precipitate, sent a thrill all over his arm into his heart, accelerating its movements. And he felt those quick heart-beats coming from her and penetrating him through his flesh, his muscles, and his nerves, so that between them there was now only one heart wounded by the same pain, agitated by the same palpitation, living the same life, like clocks connected by a string at some distance from one another and made to keep time together second by second.

But suddenly she uncovered her flushed face, still tear-dimmed, quickly wiped it, and said:

"Come, I ought not to have spoken to you about this. I am foolish. Let us go back at once to Madame Honorat, and forget. Do you promise me?"

"I do promise you."

She gave him her hand. "I have confidence in you. I believe you are very honest!"

They turned back. He lifted her up in crossing the stream, just as he had lifted up Christiane, the year before. How often had he passed along this path with her in the days when he adored her! He reflected, wondering at his own changed feelings: "How short a time this passion lasted!"

Charlotte, laying a finger on his arm, murmured: "Madame Honorat is asleep. Let us sit down without making a noise."

Madame Honorat was, indeed, slumbering, with her back to a pine-tree, her handkerchief over her face and her hands crossed over her stomach. They seated themselves a few paces away from her, and refrained from speaking in order not to awaken her. Then the stillness of the wood was so profound that it became as painful to them as actual suffering. Nothing could be heard save the water gurgling over the stones, a little lower down, then those imperceptible quiverings of insects passing by, those light buzzings of flies or of other living creatures whose movements made the dead leaves flutter.

Where then were Louise and Gontran? What were they doing? All at once, the sound of their voices reached them from a distance. They were returning. Madame Honorat woke up and looked astonished.

"What! you are here again! I did not notice you coming back. And the others, have you found them?"

Paul replied: "There they are! They are coming."

They recognized Gontran's laughter. This laughter relieved Charlotte from a crushing weight, which had oppressed her mind — she could not have explained why.

They were soon able to distinguish the pair. Gontran had almost broken into a running pace, dragging by the arm the young girl, who was quite flushed. And, even before they had come up, so great a hurry was he in to tell his story, he shouted:

"You don't know what we surprised. I give you a thousand guesses to discover it! The handsome Doctor Mazelli along with the daughter of the illustrious Professor Cloche, as Will would say, the pretty widow with the red hair. Oh! yes, indeed — surprised, you understand? He was embracing her, the scamp. Oh! yes — oh! yes."

Madame Honorat, at this immoderate display of gaiety, made a dignified movement:

"Oh! M. le Comte, think of these young ladies!"

Gontran made a respectful obeisance.

"You are perfectly right, dear Madame, to recall me to the proprieties. All your inspirations are excellent."

Then, in order that they might not be all seen going back together, the two young men bowed to the ladies, and returned through the wood to the village.

"Well?" asked Paul.

"Well, I told her that I adored her and that I would be delighted to marry her."

"And she said?"

"She said, with charming discretion, 'That concerns my father. It is to him that I will give my answer.'"

"So then you are going to — "

"To intrust my ambassador Andermatt at once with the official application. And if the old boor makes any row about it, I'll compromise his daughter with a splash."

And, as Andermatt was again engaged in conversation with Doctor Latonne on the terrace of the Casino, Gontran stopped here, and immediately made his brother-in-law acquainted with the situation.

Paul went off along the road to Riom. He wanted to be alone so much did he find himself invaded by that agitation of the entire mind and body into which every meeting with a woman casts a man who is on the point of falling in love. For some time past he had felt, without quite realizing it, the penetrating and youthful fascination of this forsaken girl. He found her so nice, so good, so simple, so upright, so innocent, that from the first he had been moved by compassion for her, by that tender compassion with which the sorrows of women always inspire us. Then, when he had seen her frequently, he had allowed to bud forth in his heart that grain, that tiny grain, of tenderness which they sow in us so quickly, and which grows to such a height. And now, for the last hour especially, he was beginning to feel himself possessed, to feel within him that constant presence of the absent which is the first sign of love. He proceeded along the road, haunted by the remembrance of her glance, by the sound of her voice, by the way in which she smiled or wept, by the gait with which she walked, even by the color and the flutter of her dress. And he said to himself:

"I believe I am bitten. I know it. It is annoying, this! The best thing, perhaps, would be to go back to Paris. Deuce take it, it is a young girl! However, I can't make her my mistress."

Then, he began dreaming about it, just as he had dreamed about Christiane, the year before. How different was this one, too, from all the women he had hitherto known, born and brought up in the city, different even from those young maidens sophisticated from their childhood by the coquetry of their mothers or the coquetry which shows itself in the streets. There was in her none of the artificiality of the woman prepared for seduction, nothing studied in her words, nothing conventional in her actions, nothing deceitful in her looks. Not only was she a being fresh and pure, but she came of a primitive race; she was a true daughter of the soil at the moment when she was about to be transformed into a woman of the city.

And he felt himself stirred up, pleading for her against that vague resistance which still struggled in his breast. The forms of heroines in sentimental novels passed before his mind's eye — the creations of Walter Scott, of Dickens, and of George Sand, exciting the more his imagination, always goaded by ideal pictures of women.

Gontran passed judgment on him thus: "Paul! he is a pack-horse with a Cupid on his back. When he flings one on the ground, another jumps up in its place." But Bretigny saw that night was falling. He had been a long time walking. He returned to the village.

As he was passing in front of the new baths, he saw Andermatt and the two Oriols surveying and measuring the vineflelds; and he knew from their gestures that they were disputing in an excited fashion.

An hour afterward, Will, entering the drawingroom, where the entire family had assembled, said to the Marquis: "My dear father-in-law, I have to inform you that your son Gontran is going to marry, in six weeks or two months, Mademoiselle Louise Oriol."

M. de Ravenel was startled: "Gontran? You 'say?"

"I say that he is going to marry in six weeks or two months, with your consent, Mademoiselle Louise Oriol, who will be very rich."

Thereupon the Marquis said simply: "Good heavens! if he likes it, I have no objection."

And the banker related how he had dealt with the old countryman. As soon as he had learned from the Comte that the young girl would consent, he wanted to obtain, at one interview, the vinedresser's assent without giving him time to prepare any of his dodges. He accordingly hurried to Oriol's house, and found him making up his accounts with great difficulty, assisted by Colosse, who was adding figures together with his fingers.

Seating himself: "I would like to drink of your excellent wine," said he.

When big Colosse had returned with the glasses and the jug brimming over, he asked whether Mademoiselle Louise had come home; then he begged of them to send for her. When she stood facing him, he rose, and, making her a low bow:

"Mademoiselle, will you regard me at this moment as a friend to whom one may say everything? Is it not so? Well, I am charged with a very delicate mission with reference to you. My brother-in-law, Comte Raoul-Olivier-Gontran de Ravenel, is smitten with you — a thing for which I commend him — and he has commissioned me to ask you, in the presence of your family, whether you will consent to become his wife."

Taken by surprise in this way, she turned toward her father her eyes, which betrayed her confusion. And Père Oriol, scared, looked at his son, his usual counselor, while Colosse looked at Andermatt, who went on, with a certain amount of pomposity:

"You understand, Mademoiselle, that I am only intrusted with this mission on the terms of an immediate reply being given to my brother-in-law. He is quite conscious of the fact that you may not care for him, and in that case he will quit this neighborhood tomorrow, never to come back to it again. I am aware, besides, that you know him sufficiently to say to me, a simple intermediary, 'I consent,' or 'I do not consent.'"

She hung down her head, and, blushing, but resolute, she faltered: "I consent, Monsieur."

Then she fled so quickly that she knocked herself against the door as she went out.

Thereupon, Andermatt sat down, and, pouring out a glass of wine after the fashion of peasants:

"Now we are going to talk about business," said he. And, without admitting the possibility even of hesitation, he attacked the question of the dowry, relying on the declarations made to him by the vinedresser three months before. He estimated at three hundred thousand francs, in addition to expectations, the actual fortune of Gontran, and he let it be understood that if a man like the Comte de Ravenel consented to ask for the hand of Oriol's daughter, a very charming young lady in other respects, it was unquestionable that the girl's family were bound to show their appreciation of this honor by a sacrifice of money.

Then the countryman, much disconcerted, but flattered — almost disarmed, tried to make a fight for his property. The discussion was a long one. An admission on Andermatt's part had, however, rendered it easy from the start:

"We don't ask for ready money nor for bills — nothing but the lands, those which you have already indicated as forming Mademoiselle Louise's dowry, in addition to some others which I am going to point you."

The prospect of not having to pay money, that money slowly heaped together, brought into the house franc after franc, sou after sou, that good money, white or yellow, worn by the hands, the purses, the pockets, the tables of cafés, the deep drawers of old presses, that money in whose ring was told the history of so many troubles, cares, fatigues, labors, so sweet to the heart, to the eyes, to the fingers of the peasant, dearer than the cow, than the vine, than the field, than the house, that money harder to part with sometimes than life itself — the prospect of not seeing it go v/ith the girl brought on immediately a great calm, a desire to conciliate, a secret but restrained joy, in the souls of the father and the son.

They continued the discussion, however, in order to keep a few more acres of soil. On the table was spread out a minute plan of Mont Oriol; and they marked one by one with a cross the portions assigned to Louise. It took an hour for Andermatt to secure the last two pieces. Then, in order that there might not be any deceit on one side or the other, they went over all the places on the plan. After that, they identified carefully all the slices designated by crosses, and marked them afresh.

But Andermatt got uneasy, suspecting that the two Oriols were capable of denying, at their next interview, a part of the grants to which they had consented and would seek to take back ends of vinefields, corners useful for his project; and he thought of a practical and certain means of giving definiteness to the agreement.

An idea crossed his mind, made him smile at first, then appeared to him excellent, although singular.

"If you like," said he, "we'll write it all out so as not to forget it later on."

And as they were entering the village, he stopped before a tobacconist's shop to buy two stamped sheets of paper. He knew that the list of lands drawn up on these leaves with their legal aspect would take an almost inviolable character in the peasant's eyes, for these leaves would represent the law, always invisible and menacing, vindicated by gendarmes, fines, and imprisonment.

Then he wrote on one sheet and copied on the other:

"In pursuance of the promise of marriage exchanged between Comte Gontran de Ravenel and Mademoiselle Louise Oriol, M. Oriol, Senior, surrenders as a dowry to his daughter the lands designated below — "

And he enumerated them minutely, with the figures attached to them in the register of lands for the district.

Then, having dated and signed the document, he made Père Oriol affix his signature, after the latter had exacted in turn a written statement of the intended husband's fortune, and he went back to the hotel with the document in his pocket.

Everyone laughed at his narrative and Gontran most of all. Then the Marquis said to his son with a lofty air of dignity: "We shall both go this evening to pay a visit to this family, and I shall myself renew the application previously made by my son-in-law in order that it may be more regular."

XIII

GONTRAN made an admirable fiance, as I courteous as he was assiduous. With the aid of Andermatt's purse, he made presents to everyone; and he constantly visited the young girl, either at her own house, or that of Madame Honorat. Paul nearly always accompanied him now, in order to have the opportunity of meeting Charlotte, saying to himself, after each visit, that he would see her no more. She had bravely resigned herself to her sister's marriage, and she referred to it with apparent unconcern, as if it did not cause her the slightest anxiety. Her character alone seemed a little altered, more sedate, less open. While Gontran was talking soft nothings to Louise in a half-whisper in a corner, Bretigny conversed with her in a serious fashion, and allowed himself to be slowly vanquished, allowed this fresh love to inundate his soul like a flowing tide. He knew what was happening to him, and gave himself up to it, thinking: "Bah! when the moment arrives. I will make my escape — that's all."

When he left her, he would go up to see Christiane, who now lay from morning till night stretched on a long chair. At the door, he could not help feeling nervous and irritated, prepared beforehand for those light quarrels to which weariness gives birth. All that she said, all that she was thinking of, annoyed him, even ere she had opened her lips. Her appearance of suffering, her resigned attitude, her looks of reproach and of supplication, made words of anger rise to his lips, which he repressed through good-breeding; and, even when by her side, he kept before his mind the constant memory, the fixed image, of the young girl whom he had just quitted.

As Christiane, tormented with seeing so little of him, overwhelmed him with questions as to how he spent his days, he invented stories, to which she listened attentively, seeking to find out whether he was thinking of some other woman. The powerlessness which she felt in herself to keep a hold on this man, the powerlessness to pour into him a little of that love with which she was tortured, the physical powerlessness to fascinate him still, to give herself to him, to win him back by caresses, since she could not regain him by the tender intimacies of love, made her suspect the worst, without knowing on what to fix her fears.

She vaguely realized that some danger was lowering over her, some great unknown danger. And she was filled with undefined jealousy, jealousy of everything — of women whom she saw passing by her window, and whom she thought charming, without even having any proof that Bretigny had ever spoken to them.

She asked of him: "Have you noticed a very pretty woman, a brunette, rather tall, whom I saw a little while ago, and who must have arrived here within the past few days?"

When he replied, "No, I don't know her," she at once jumped to the conclusion that he was lying, turned pale, and went on: "But it is not possible that you have not seen her. She appears to me very beautiful."

He was astonished at her persistency. "I assure you I have not seen her. I'll try to come across her."

She thought: "Surely it must be she!" She felt persuaded, too, on certain days, that he was hiding some intrigue in the locality, that he had sent for his mistress, an actress perhaps. And she questioned everybody, her father, her brother, and her husband, about all the women young and desirable, whom they observed in the neighborhood of Enval. If only she could have walked about, and seen for herself, she might have reassured herself a little; but the almost complete loss of motion which her condition forced upon her now made her endure an intolerable martyrdom.

When she spoke to Paul, the tone of her voice alone revealed her anguish, and intensified his nervous impatience with this love, which for him was at an end. He could no longer talk quietly about anything with her save the approaching marriage of Gontran, a subject which enabled him to pronounce Charlotte's name, and to give vent to his thoughts aloud about the young girl. And it was a mysterious source of delight to him even to hear Christiane articulating that name, praising the grace and all the qualities of this little maiden, compassionating her, regretting that her brother should have sacrificed her, and expressing a desire that some man, some noble heart, should appreciate her, love her, and marry her.

He said: "Oh! yes, Gontran acted foolishly there. She is perfectly charming, that young girl."

Christiane, without any misgiving, echoed: "Perfectly charming. She is a pearl! a piece of perfection!"

Never had she thought that a man like Paul could love a little maid like this, or that he would be likely to marry her. She had no apprehensions save of his mistresses. And it was a singular phenomenon of the heart that praise of Charlotte from Christiane's lips assumed in his eyes an extreme value, excited his love, whetted his desire, and surrounded the young girl with an irresistible attraction.

Now, one day, when he called at Madame Honorat's house to meet there the Oriol girls, they found Doctor Mazelli installed there as if he was at home. He stretched forth both hands to the two young men, with that Italian smile of his, which seemed to give away his entire heart with every word and every movement.

Gontran and he were linked by a friendship at once familiar and futile, made up of secret affinities, of hidden likenesses, of a sort of confederacy of instincts, rather than any real affection or confidence.

The Comte asked: "What about your little blonde of the Sans-Souci wood?"

The Italian smiled: "Bah! we are on terms of indifference toward one another. She is one of those women who offer everything and give nothing."

And they began to chat. The handsome physician performed certain offices for the young girls, especially for Charlotte. When addressing women, he manifested a perpetual adoration in his voice, his gestures, and his looks. His entire person, from head to foot, said to them, "I love you" with an eloquence in his attitude which never failed to win their favor. He displayed the graces of an actress, the light pirouettes of a danseuse, the supple movements of a juggler, an entire science of seduction natural and acquired, of which he constantly made use.

Paul, when returning to the hotel with Gontran, exclaimed in a tone of sullen vexation: "What does this charlatan come to that house for?"

The Comte replied quietly: "How can you ever tell when dealing with such adventurers? These sort of people slip in everywhere. This fellow must be tired of his vagabond existence, and of giving way to every caprice of his Spaniard, of whom he is rather the valet than the physician — and perhaps something more. He is looking about him. Professor Cloche's daughter was a good catch — he has failed with her, he says. The second of the Oriol girls would not be less valuable to him. He is making the attempt, feeling his way, smelling about, sounding. He would become co-proprietor of the waters, would try to knock over that idiot, Latonne, would in any case get an excellent practice here every summer for himself, which would last him over the winter. Faith! this is his plan exactly — no doubt of it!"

A dull rage, a jealous animosity, was aroused in Paul's heart. A voice exclaimed: "Hey! hey!" It was Mazelli, who had overtaken them. Bretigny said to him, with aggressive irony: "Where are you rushing so quickly, doctor? One would say that you were pursuing fortune." The Italian smiled, and, without stopping, but skipping backward, he plunged, with a mimic's graceful movement, his hands into his two pockets, quickly turned them out and showed them, both empty, holding them wide between two fingers by the ends of the seams. Then he said: "I have not got hold of it yet." And, turning on his toes, he rushed away like a man in a great hurry.

They found him again several times, on the following days, at Doctor Honorat's house, where he made himself useful to the three ladies by a thousand graceful little services, by the same clever tactics which he had no doubt adopted when dealing with the Duchess. He knew how to do everything to perfection, from paying compliments to making macaroni. He was, moreover, an excellent cook, and protecting himself from stains by means of a servant's blue apron, and wearing a chef's cap made of paper on his head, while he sang Neapolitan ditties in Italian, he did the work of a scullion, without appearing a bit ridiculous, amusing and fascinating everybody, down to the half-witted housekeeper, who said of him: "He is a marvel!"

His plans were soon obvious, and Paul no longer had any doubt that he was trying to get Charlotte to fall in love with him. He seemed to be succeeding in this. He was so profuse of flattery, so eager, so artful in striving to please, that the young girl's face had, when she looked at him, that air of contentment which indicates that the heart is gratified.

Paul, in his turn, without being even able to account to himself for his conduct, assumed the attitude of a lover, and set himself up as a rival. When he saw the doctor with Charlotte, he would come on the scene, and, with his more direct manner, exert himself to win the young girl's affections. He showed himself straigthforward and sympathetic, fraternal, devoted, repeating to her, with the sincerity of a friend, in a tone so frank that one could scarcely see in it an avowal of love: "I am very fond of you; cheer up!"

Mazelli, astonished at this unexpected rivalry, had recourse to all his powers of captivation; and, when Bretigny, bitten with jealousy, that naïve jealousy which takes possession of a man when he is dealing with any woman, even without being in love with her, provided only he has taken a fancy to her — when, filled with this natural violence, he became aggressive and haughty, the other, more pliant, always master of himself, replied with sly allusions, witticisms, well-turned and mocking compliments.

It was a daily warfare which they both waged fiercely, without either of them perhaps having a well-defined object in view. They did not want to give way, like two dogs who have gained a grip of the same quarry.

Charlotte had recovered her good humor, but along with it she now exhibited a more biting waggery, a certain sphinxlike attitude, less candor in her smile and in her glance. One would have said that Gontran's desertion had educated her, prepared her for possible deceptions, disciplined, and armed her.

She played off her two admirers against one another in a sly and dexterous fashion, saying to each of them what she thought necessary, without letting the one fall foul of the other, without ever letting the one suppose that she preferred the other, laughing slightly at each of them in turn in the presence of his rival, leaving them an equal match without appearing even to take either of them seriously. But all this was done simply, in the manner of a schoolgirl rather than in that of a coquette, with that mischievous air exhibited by young girls which sometimes renders them irresistible.

Mazelli, however, seemed suddenly to be having the advantage. He had apparently become more intimate with her, as if a secret understanding had been established between them. While talking to her, he played lightly with her parasol and with one of the ribbons of her dress, which appeared to Paul, as it were, an act of moral possession, and exasperated him so much that he longed to box the Italian's ears.

But, one day, at Père Oriol's house, while Bretigny was chatting with Louise and Gontran, and, at the same time, keeping his eye fixed on Mazelli, who was telling Charlotte in a subdued voice some things that made her smile, he suddenly saw her blush with such an appearance of embarrassment as to leave no doubt for one moment on his mind that the other had spoken of love. She had cast down her eyes, and ceased to smile, but still continued listening; and Paul, who felt disposed to make a scene, said to Gontran: "Will you have the goodness to come out with me for five minutes?"

The Comte made his excuses to his betrothed, and followed his friend.

When they were in the street, Paul exclaimed: "My dear fellow, this wretched Italian must, at any cost, be prevented from inveigling this girl, who is defenseless against him."

"What do you wish me to do?"

"To warn her of the fact that he is an adventurer."

"Hey, my dear boy, those things are no concern of mine."

"After all, she is to be your sister-in-law."

"Yes, but there is nothing to show me conclusively that Mazelli has guilty designs upon her. He exhibits the same gallantry toward all women, and he has never said or done anything improper."

"Well, if you don't want to take it on yourself, I'll do it, although it concerns me less assuredly than it does you."

"So then you are in love with Charlotte?"

"I? No — but I see clearly through this blackguard's game."

"My dear fellow, you are mixing yourself up in matters of a delicate nature, and — unless you are in love with Charlotte — "

"No — I am not in love with her — but I am hunting down imposters, that's what I mean!"

"May I ask what you intend to do?"

"To thrash this beggar."

"Good! the best way to make her fall in love with him. You fight with him, and whether he wounds you, or you wound him, he will become a hero in her eyes."

"What would you do then?"

"In your place?"

"In my place."

"I would speak to the girl as a friend. She has great confidence in you. Well, I would say to her simply in a few words what these hangers-on of society are. You know very well how to say these things. You possess an eloquent tongue. And I would make her understand, first, why he is attached to the Spaniard; secondly, why he attempted to lay siege to Professor Cloche's daughter; thirdly, why, not having succeeded in this effort, he is striving, in the last place, to make a conquest of Mademoiselle Charlotte Oriol."

"Why do you not do that, yourself, who will be her brother-in-law?"

"Because — because — on account of what passed between us — come! I can't."

"That's quite right. I am going to speak to her."

"Do you want me to procure for you a private conversation with her immediately?"

"Why, yes, assuredly."

"Good! Walk about for ten minutes. I am going to carry off Louise and Mazelli, and, when you come back, you will find the other alone."

Paul Bretigny rambled along the side of the Enval gorges, thinking over the best way of opening this difficult conversation.

He found Charlotte Oriol alone, indeed, on his return, in the cold, whitewashed parlor of the paternal abode; and he said to her, as he sat down beside her: "It is I, Mademoiselle, who asked Gontran to procure me this interview with you."

She looked at him with her clear eyes: "Why, pray?"

"Oh! it is not to pay you insipid compliments in the Italian fashion. It is to speak to you as a friend — — as a very devoted friend, who owes you good advice."

"Tell me what it is."

He took up the subject in a roundabout style, dwelt upon his own experience, and upon her inexperience, so as to lead gradually by discreet but explicit phrases to a reference to those adventurers who are everywhere going in quest of fortune, taking advantage with their professional skill of every ingenuous and good-natured being, man or woman, whose purses or hearts they explored.

She turned rather pale as she listened to him.

Then she said: "I understand and I don't understand. You are speaking of some one — of whom?"

"I am speaking of Doctor Mazelli."

Then, she lowered her eyes, and remained a few seconds without replying; after this, in a hesitating voice: "You are so frank that I will be the same with you. Since — since my sister's marriage has been arranged, I have become a little less — a little less stupid! Well, I had already suspected what you tell me — and I used to feel amused of my own accord at seeing him coming."

She raised her face to his as she spoke, and in her smile, in her arch look, in her little retroussé nose, in the moist and glittering brilliancy of her teeth which showed themselves between her lips, so much open-hearted gracefulness, sly gaiety, and charming frolicsomeness appeared that Bretigny felt himself drawn toward her by one of those tumultuous transports which flung him distracted with passion at the feet of the woman who was his latest love. And his heart exulted with joy because Mazelli had not been preferred to him. So then he had triumphed.

He asked: "You do not love him, then?"

"Whom? Mazelli?"

"Yes."

She looked at him with such a pained expression in her eyes that he felt thrown off his balance, and stammered, in a supplicating voice: "What? — you don't love — anyone?"

She replied, with a downward glance: "I don't know — I love people who love me."

He seized the young girl's two hands, all at once, and kissing them wildly in one of those moments of impulse in which the head loses its controlling power, and the words which rise to the lips come from the excited flesh rather than the wandering mind, he faltered:

"I! — I love you, my little Charlotte; yes, I love you!"

She quickly drew away one of her hands, and placed it on his mouth, murmuring: "Be silent! — be silent, I beg of you! It would cause me too much pain if this were another falsehood."

She stood erect; he rose up, caught her in his arms, and embraced her passionately.

A sudden noise parted them; Père Oriol had just come in, and he was gazing at them, quite scared. Then, he cried: "Ah! bougrrre! ah! bougrrre! ah! bougrrre of a savage!"

Charlotte had rushed out, and the two men remained face to face. After some seconds of agitation, Paul made an attempt to explain his position.

"My God! Monsieur — I have conducted myself — it is true — like a — "

But the old man would not listen to him. Anger, furious anger, had taken possession of him, and he advanced toward Bretigny, with clenched fists, repeating:

"Ah! bougrrre of a savage — "

Then, when they were nose to nose, he seized Paul by the collar with his knotted peasant's hands.

But the other, as tall, and strong with that superior strength acquired by the practice of athletics, freed himself with a single push from the countryman's grip, and, pushing him up against the wall:

"Listen, Père Oriol, this is not a matter for us to fight about, but to settle quietly. It is true, I was embracing your daughter. I swear to you that this is the first time — and I swear to you, too, that I desire to marry her."

The old man, whose physical excitement had subsided under the assault ot his adversary, but whose anger had not yet been calmed, stuttered:

"Ha! that's how it is! You want to steal my daughter; you want my money. Bougrrre of a deceiver!" Thereupon, he allowed all that was on his mind to escape from him in a heap of grumbling words. He found no consolation for the dowry promised with his elder girl, for his vinelands going into the hands of these Parisians. He now had his suspicions as to Gontran's want of money, Andermatt's craft, and, without forgetting the unexpected fortune which the banker brought him, he vented his bile and his secret rancor against those mischievous people who did not let him sleep any longer in peace.

One would have thought that his family and his friends were coming every night to plunder him, to rob him of everything, his lands, his springs, and his daughters. And he cast these reproaches into Paul's face, accusing him also of wanting to get hold of his property, of being a rogue, and of taking Charlotte in order to have his lands.

The other, soon losing all patience, shouted under his very nose: "Why, I am richer than you, you infernally currish old donkey. I would bring you money."

The old man listened in silence to these words, incredulous but vigilant, and then, in a milder tone, he renewed his complaints.

Paul then answered him and entered into explanations; and, believing that an obligation was imposed on him, owing to the circumstances under which he had been surprised, and for which he was solely responsible, he proposed to marry the girl without asking for any dowry.

Père Oriol shook his head and his ears, heard Paul reiterating his statements, but was unable to understand. To him this young man seemed still a pauper, a penniless wretch.

And, when Bretigny, exasperated, yelled, in his teeth: "Why, you old rascal, I have an income of more than a hundred and twenty thousand francs a year — do you understand? — three millions," the other suddenly asked: "Will you write that down on a piece of paper?"

"Yes, I will write it down!"

"And you'll sign it?"

"Yes, I will sign it."

"On a sheet of notary's paper?"

"Yes, certainly — on a sheet of notary's paper!" Thereupon, he rose up, opened a press, took out of it two leaves marked with the Government stamp, and, seeking for the undertaking which Andermatt, a few days before, had required from him, he drew up an odd promise of marriage, in which it was made a condition that the fiancé vouched for his being worth three millions; and, at the end of it Bretigny affixed his signature.

When Paul found himself in the open air once more, he felt as if the earth no longer turned round in the same way. So then, he was engaged, in spite of himself, in spite of her, by one of those accidents, by one of those tricks of circumstance, which shut out from you every point of escape. He muttered: "What madness!" Then he reflected: "Bah! I could not have found better perhaps in all the world!" And in his secret heart he rejoiced at this snare of destiny.

XIV

THE dawn of the following day brought bad news to Andermatt.

He learned on his arrival at the bath-establishment that M. Aubry-Pasteur had died during the night from an attack of apoplexy at the Hotel Splendid. In addition to the fact that the deceased was very useful to him on account of his vast scientific attainments, disinterested zeal, and attachment to the Mont Oriol station, which, in some measure, he looked upon as a daughter, it was much to be regretted that a patient who had come there to fight against a tendency toward congestion should have died exactly in this fashion, in the midst of his treatment, in the very height of the season, at the very moment when the rising spa was beginning to prove a success.

The banker, exceedingly annoyed, walked up and down in the study of the absent inspector, thinking of some device whereby this misfortune might be attributed to some other cause, such as an accident, a fall, a want of prudence, the rupture of an artery; and he impatiently awaited Doctor Latonne's arrival in order that the decease might be ingeniously certified without awakening any suspicion as to the initial cause of the fatality.

All at once, the medical inspector appeared on the scene, his face pale and indicative of extreme agitation; and, as soon as he had passed through the door, he asked: "Have you heard the lamentable news?"

"Yes, the death of M. Aubry-Pasteur."

"No, no, the flight of Doctor Mazelli with Professor Cloche's daughter."

Andermatt felt a shiver running along his skin.

"What? you tell me — "

"Oh! my dear manager, it is a frightful catastrophe, a crash!"

He sat down and wiped his forehead; then he related the facts as he got them from Petrus Martel, who had learned them directly through the professor's valet.

Mazelli had paid very marked attentions to the pretty red-haired widow, a coarse coquette, a wanton, whose first husband had succumbed to consumption, brought on, it was said, by excessive devotion to his matrimonial duties. But M. Cloche, having discovered the projects of the Italian physician, and not desiring this adventurer as a second son-in-law, violently turned him out of doors on surprising him kneeling at the widow's feet.

Mazelli, having been sent out by the door, soon reentered through the window by the silken ladder of lovers. Two versions of the affair were current. According to the first, he had rendered the professor's daughter mad with love and jealousy; according to the second, he had continued to see her secretly, while pretending to be devoting his attention to another woman; and ascertaining finally through his mistress that the professor remained inflexible, he had carried her off, the same night, rendering a marriage inevitable, in consequence of this scandal.

Doctor Latonne rose up and, leaning his back against the mantelpiece, while Andermatt, astounded, continued walking up and down, he exclaimed:

"A physician, Monsieur, a physician to do such a thing! — a doctor of medicine! — what an absence of character!"

Andermatt, completely crushed, appreciated the consequences, classified them, and weighed them, as one docs a sum in addition. They were: "First, the disagreeable report spreading over the neighboring spas and all the way to Paris. If, however, they went the right way about it, perhaps they could make use of this elopement as an advertisement. A fortnight's cchoes well written and prominently printed in the newspapers would strongly attract attention to Mont Oriol. Secondly: Professor Cloche's departure an irreparable loss. Thirdly: The departure of the Duchess and the Duke de Ramas-Aldavarra, a second inevitable loss without possible compensation. In short, Doctor Latonne was right. It was a frightful catastrophe."

Then, the banker, turning toward the physician: "You ought to go at once to the Hotel Splendid, and draw up the certificate of the death of Aubry-

Pasteur in such a way that no one could suspect it to be a case of congestion."

Doctor Latonne put on his hat; then just as he was leaving: "Ha! another rumor which is circulating! Is it true that your friend Paul Bretigny is going to marry Charlotte Oriol?"

Andermatt gave a start of astonishment. "Bretigny? Come now! — who told you that?"

"Why, as in the other case, Petrus Martel, who had it from Père Oriol himself."

"From Père Oriol?"

"Yes, from Père Oriol, who declared that his future son-in-law possessed a fortune of three millions." William did not know what to think. He muttered: "In point of fact, it is possible. He has been rather hot on her for some time past! But in that case the whole knoll is ours — the whole knoll! Oh! I must make certain of this immediately." And he went out after the doctor in order to meet Paul before breakfast.

As he was entering the hotel, he was informed that his wife had several times asked to see him. He found her still in bed, chatting with her father and with her brother, who was looking through the newspapers with a rapid and wandering glance. She felt poorly, very poorly, restless. She was afraid, without knowing why. And then an idea had come to her, and had for some days been growing stronger in her brain, as usually happens with pregnant women. She wanted to consult Doctor Black. From the effect of hearing around her some jokes at Doctor Latonne's expense, she had lost all confidence in him, and she wanted another opinion, that of Doctor Black, whose success was constantly increasing. Fears, all the fears, all the hauntings, by which women toward the close of pregnancy are besieged, now tortured her from morning until night. Since the night before, in consequence of a dream, she imagined that the Cæsarian operation might be necessary. And she was present in thought at this operation performed on herself. She saw herself lying on her back in a bed covered with blood, while something red was being taken away, which did not move, which did not cry, and which was dead! And for ten minutes she shut her eyes, in order to witness this over again, to be present once more at her horrible and painful punishment. She had, therefore, become impressed with the notion that Doctor Black alone could tell her the truth, and she wanted him at once; she required him to examine her immediately, immediately, immediately! Andermatt, greatly agitated, did not know what answer to give her.

"But my dear child, it is difficult, having regard to my relations with Latonne it is even impossible. Listen! an idea occurs to me: I will look up Professor Mas-Roussel, who is a hundred times better than Black. He will not refuse to come when I ask him."

But she persisted. She wanted Black, and no one else. She required to see him with his big bulldog's head beside her. It was a longing, a wild, superstitious desire. She considered it necessary for him to see her.

Then William attempted to change the current of her thoughts:

"You haven't heard how that intriguer Mazelli carried off Professor Cloche's daughter the other night.

They are gone away; nobody can tell where they levanted to. There's a nice story for you!"

She was propped up on her pillow, her eyes strained with grief, and she faltered: "Oh! the poor Duchess — the poor woman — how I pity her!" Her heart had long since learned to understand that other woman's heart, bruised and impassioned! She suffered from the same malady and wept the same tears. But she resumed: "Listen, Will! Go and find M. Black for me. I know I shall die unless he comes!"

Andermatt caught her hand, and tenderly kissed it: "Come, my little Christiane, be reasonable — understand."

He saw her eyes filled with tears, and, turning toward the Marquis:

"It is you that ought to do this, my dear father-in-law. As for me, I can't do it. Black comes here every day about one o'clock to see the Princess de Maldebourg. Stop him in the passage, and send him in to your daughter. You can easily wait an hour, can you not, Christiane?"

She consented to wait an hour, but refused to get up to breakfast with the men, who passed alone into the diningroom.

Paul was there already. Andermatt, when he saw him, exclaimed: "Ah! tell me now, what is it I have been told a little while ago? You are going to marry Charlotte Oriol? It is not true, is it?"

The young man replied in a low tone, casting a restless look toward the closed door: "Good God! it is true!" Nobody having been sure of it till now, the three stared at him in amazement.

William asked: "What came over you? With your fortune, to marry — to embarrass yourself with one woman, when you have the whole of them? And then, after all, the family leaves something to be desired in the matter of refinement. It is all very well for Gontran, who hasn't a sou!"

Bretigny began to laugh: "My father made a fortune out of flour; he was then a miller on a large scale. If you had known him, you might have said he lacked refinement. As for the young girl — "

Andermatt interrupted him: "Oh! perfect — charming — perfect — and you know — she will be as rich as yourself — if not more so. I answer for it — I — I answer for it!"

Gontran murmured: "Yes, this marriage interferes with nothing, and covers retreats. Only he was wrong in not giving us notice beforehand. How the devil was this business managed, my friend?"

Thereupon, Paul related all that had occurred with some slight modifications. He told about his hesitation, which he exaggerated, and his sudden determination on discovering from the young girl's own lips that she loved him. He described the unexpected entrance of Père Oriol, their quarrel, which he enlarged upon, the countryman's doubts concerning his fortune, and the incident of the stamped paper drawn by the old man out of the press.

Andermatt, laughing till the tears ran down his face, hit the table with his fist: "Ha! he did that over again, the stamped paper touch! It's my invention, that is!"

But Paul stammered, reddening a little: "Pray don't let your wife know about it yet. Owing to the terms which we are on at present, it is more suitable that I should announce it to her myself." Gontran eyed his friend with an odd, good-humored smile, which seemed to say: "This is quite right, all this, quite right! That's the way things ought to end, without noise, without scandals, without any dramatic situations."

He suggested: "If you like, my dear Paul, we'll go together, after dinner, when she's up, and you will inform her of your decision."

Their eyes met, fixed, full of unfathomable thoughts, then looked in another direction. And Paul replied with an air of indifference:

"Yes, willingly. We'll talk about this presently." A waiter from the hotel came to inform them that Doctor Black had just arrived for his visit to the Princess; and the Marquis forthwith went out to catch him in the passage. He explained the situation to the doctor, his son-in-law's embarrassment and his daughter's earnest wish, and he brought him in without resistance.

As soon as the little man with the big head had entered Christiane's apartment, she said: "Papa, leave us alone!" And the Marquis withdrew.

Thereupon, she enumerated her disquietudes, her terrors, her nightmares, in a low, sweet voice, as though she were at confession. And the physician listened to her like a priest, covering her sometimes with his big round eyes, showed his attention by a little nod of the head, murmured a "That's it," which seemed to mean, "I know your case at the end of my fingers, and I will cure you whenever I like."

When she had finished speaking, he began in his turn to question her with extreme minuteness of detail about her life, her habits, her course of diet, her treatment. At one moment he appeared to express approval with a gesture, at another to convey blame with an "Oh!" full of reservations. When she came to her great fear that the child was misplaced, he rose up, and with an ecclesiastical modesty, lightly passed his hand over the counterpane, and then remarked, "No, it's all right."

And she felt a longing to embrace him. What a good man this physician was!

He sat down at the table, took a sheet of paper, and wrote out the prescription. It was long, very long. Then he came back close to the bed, and, in an altered tone, clearly indicating that he had finished his professional and sacred duty, he began to chat. He had a deep, unctuous voice, the powerful voice of a thickset dwarf, and there were hidden questions in his most ordinary phrases. He talked about everything. Gontran's marriage seemed to interest him considerably. Then, with his ugly smile like that of an ill-shaped being:

"I have said nothing yet to you about M. Bretigny's marriage, although it cannot be a secret, for Père Oriol has told it to everybody."

A kind of fainting fit took possession of her, commencing at the end of her fingers, then invading her entire body — her arms, her breast, her stomach, her legs. She did not, however, quite understand; but a horrible fear of not learning the truth suddenly restored her powers of observation, and she faltered: "Ha! Père Oriol has told it to everybody?"

"Yes, yes. He was speaking to myself about it less than ten minutes ago. It appears that M. Bretigny is very rich, and that he has been in love with little Charlotte for some time past. Moreover, it is Madame Honorat who made these two matches. She lent her hands and her house for the meetings of the young people."

Christiane had closed her eyes. She had lost consciousness. In answer to the doctor's call, a chambermaid rushed in; then appeared the Marquis, Andermatt, and Gontran, who went to search for vinegar, ether, ice, twenty different things all equally useless. Suddenly, the young woman moved, opened her eyes, lifted up her arms, and uttered a heartrending cry, writhing in the bed. She tried to speak, and in a broken voice said:

"Oh! what pain I feel — my God! — what pain I feel — in my back — something is tearing me — Oh! my God!" And she broke out into fresh shrieks.

The symptoms of confinement were speedily recognized. Then Andermatt rushed off to find Doctor Latonne, and came upon him finishing his meal.

"Come on quickly — my wife has met with a mishap — hurry on!" Then he made use of a little deception, telling how Doctor Black had been found in the hotel at the moment of the first pains. Doctor Black himself confirmed this falsehood by saying to his brother-physician:

"I had just come to visit the Princess when I was informed that Madame Andermatt was taken ill. I hurried to her. It was time!"

But William, in a state of great excitement, his heart beating, his soul filled with alarm was all at once seized with doubts as to the competency of the two professional men, and he started off afresh, bareheaded, in order to run in the direction of Professor Mas-Roussel's house, and to entreat him to come. The professor consented to do so at once, buttoned on his frock-coat with the mechanical movement of a physician going out to pay a visit, and set forth with great, rapid strides, the eager strides of an eminent man whose presence may save a life.

When he arrived on the scene, the two other doctors, full of deference, consulted him with an air of humility, repeating together or nearly at the same time:

"Here is what has occurred, dear master. Don't you think, dear master? Isn't there reason to believe, dear master?"

Andermatt, in his turn, driven crazy with anguish at the moanings of his wife, harassed M. Mas-Roussel with questions, and also addressed him as "dear master" with wide-open mouth.

Christiane, almost naked in the presence of these men, no longer saw, noticed, or understood anything. She was suffering so dreadfully that everything else had vanished from her consciousness. It seemed to her that they were drawing from the tops of her hips along her side and her back a long saw, with blunt teeth, which was mangling her bones and muscles slowly and in an irregular fashion, with shakings, stoppages, and renewals of the operation, which became every moment more and more frightful.

When this torture abated for a few seconds, when the rendings of her body allowed her reason to come back, one thought then fixed itself in her soul, more cruel, more keen, more terrible, than her physical pain: "He was in love with another woman, and was going to marry her!"

And, in order to get rid of this pang, which was eating into her brain, she struggled to bring on once more the atrocious torment of her flesh; she shook her sides; she strained her back; and when the crisis returned again, she had, at least, lost all capacity for thought.

For fifteen hours she endured this martyrdom, so much bruised by suffering and despair that she longed to die, and strove to die in those spasms in which she writhed.

But, after a convulsion longer and more violent than the rest, it seemed to her that everything inside her body suddenly escaped from her. It was over; her pangs were assuaged, like the waves of the sea, when they are calmed; and the relief which she experienced was so intense that, for a time, even her grief became numbed. They spoke to her. She answered in a voice very weak, very low.

Suddenly, Andermatt stooped down, his face toward hers, and he said: "She will live — she is almost at the end of it. It is a girl!"

Christiane was only able to articulate: "Ah! my God!"

So then she had a child, a living child, who would grow big — a child of Paul! She felt a desire to cry out, all this fresh misfortune crushed her heart. She had a daughter. She did not want it! She would not look at it! She would never touch it!

They had laid her down again on the bed, taken care of her, tenderly embraced her. Who had done this? No doubt, her father and her husband. She could not tell. But he — where was he? What was he doing? How happy she would have felt at that moment, if only he still loved her!

The hours dragged along, following each other without any distinction between day and night so far as she was concerned, for she felt only this one thought burning into her soul: he loved another woman.

Then she said to herself all of a sudden: "What if it were false? Why should I not have known about his marriage sooner than this doctor?" After that, came the reflection that it had been kept hidden from her. Paul had taken care that she should not hear about it.

She glanced around her room to see who was there. A woman whom she did not know was keeping watch by her side, a woman of the people. She did not venture to question her. From whom, then, could she make inquiries about this matter?

The door was suddenly pushed open. Her husband entered on the tips of his toes. Seeing that her eyes were open, he came over to her.

"Are you better?"

"Yes, thanks."

"You frightened us very much since yesterday. But there is an end of the danger! By the bye, I am quite embarrassed about your case. I telegraphed to our friend, Madame Icardon, who was to have come to stay with you during your confinement, informing her about your premature illness, and imploring her to hasten down here. She is with her nephew, who has an attack of scarlet fever. You cannot, however, remain without anyone near you, without some woman who is a little — a little suitable for the purpose. Accordingly, a lady from the neighborhood has offered to nurse you, and to keep you company every day, and, faith, I have accepted the offer. It is Madame Honorat."

Christiane suddenly remembered Doctor Black's words. A start of fear shook her; and she groaned: "Oh! no — no — not she!"

William did not understand, and went on: "Listen, I know well that she is very common; but your brother has a great esteem for her; she has been of great service to him; and then it has been thrown out that she was originally a midwife, whom Honorat made the acquaintance of while attending a patient. If you take a strong dislike to her, I will send her away the next day. Let us try her at any rate. Let her come once or twice."

She remained silent, thinking. A craving to know, to know everything, entered into her, so violent that the hope of milking this woman chatter freely, of tearing from her one by one the words that would rend her own heart, now filled her with a yearning to reply: "Go, go, and look for her immediately — immediately. Go, pray!"

And to this irresistible desire to know was also superadded a strange longing to suffer more intensely, to roll herself about in her misery, as she might have rolled herself on thorns, the mysterious longing, morbid and feverish, of a martyr calling for fresh pain.

So she faltered: "Yes, I have no objection. Bring me Madame Honorat."

Then, suddenly, she felt that she could not wait any longer without making sure, quite sure, of this treason; and she asked William in a voice weak as a breath:

"Is it true that M. Bretigny is getting married?"

He replied calmly: "Yes, it is true. We would have told you before this if we could have talked with you."

She continued: "With Charlotte?"

"With Charlotte."

Now William had also a fixed idea himself which from this time forth never left him — his daughter, as yet barely alive, whom every moment he was going to look at. He felt indignant because Christiane's first words were not to ask for the baby; and in a tone of gentle reproach:

"Well, look here! you have not yet inquired about the little one. You are aware that she is going on very well?"

She trembled as if he had touched a living wound; but it was necessary for her to pass through all the stations of this Calvary.

"Bring her here," she said.

He vanished to the foot of the bed behind the curtain, then he came back, his face lighted up with pride and happiness, and holding in his hands, in an awkward fashion, a bundle of white linen.

He laid it down on the embroidered pillow close to the head of Christiane, who was choking with emotion, and he said: "Look here, see how lovely she is!"

She looked. He opened with two of his fingers the fine lace with which was hidden from view a little red face, so small, so red, with closed eyes, and mouth constantly moving.

And she thought, as she leaned over this beginning of being: "This is my daughter — Paul's daughter. Here then is what made me suffer so much. This — this — this is my daughter!"

Her repugnance toward the child, whose birth had so fiercely torn her poor heart and her tender woman's body had, all at once, disappeared; she now contemplated it with ardent and sorrowing curiosity, with profound astonishment, the astonishment of a being who sees her firstborn come forth from her.

Andermatt was waiting for her to caress it passionately. He was surprised and shocked, and asked: "Are you not going to kiss it?"

She stooped quite gently toward this little red forehead; and in proportion as she drew her lips closer to it, she felt them drawn, called by it. And when she had placed them upon it, when she touched it, a little moist, a little warm, warm with her own life, it seemed to her that she could not withdraw her lips from that infantile flesh, that she would leave them there forever.

Something grazed her cheek; it was her husband's beard as he bent forward to kiss her. And when he had pressed her a long time against himself with a grateful tenderness, he wanted, in his turn, to kiss his daughter, and with his outstretched mouth he gave it very soft little strokes on the nose.

Christiane, her heart shriveled up by this caress, gazed at both of them there by her side, at her daughter and at him — him!

He soon wanted to carry the infant back to its cradle.

"No," said she, "let me have it a few minutes longer, that I may feel it close to my face. Don't speak to me any more — don't move — leave us alone, and wait."

She passed one of her arms over the body hidden under the swaddling-clothes, put her forehead close to the little grinning face, shut her eyes, and no longer stirred, or thought about anything.

But, at the end of a few minutes, William softly touched her on the shoulder: "Come, my darling, you must be reasonable! No emotions, you know, no emotions!"

Thereupon, he bore away their little daughter, while the mother's eyes followed the child till it had disappeared behind the curtain of the bed.

After that, he came back to her: "Then it is understood that I am to bring Madame Honorat to you tomorrow morning, to keep you company?"

She replied in a firm tone: "Yes, my dear, you may send her to me — tomorrow morning."

And she stretched herself out in the bed, fatigued, worn out, perhaps a little less unhappy.

Her father and her brother came to see her in the evening, and told her news about the locality — the precipitate departure of Professor Cloche in search of his daughter, and the conjectures with reference to the Duchess de Ramas, who was no longer to be seen, and who was also supposed to have started on Mazelli's track. Gontran laughed at these adventures, and drew a comic moral from the occurrences:

"The history of those spas is incredible. They are the only fairylands left upon the earth! In two months more things happen in them than in the rest of the universe during the remainder of the year. One might say with truth that the springs are not mineralized but bewitched.

And it is everywhere the same, at Aix, Royat, Vichy, Luchon, and also at the sea-baths, at Dieppe, Étretat, Trouville, Biarritz, Cannes, and Nice. You meet there specimens of all kinds of people, of every social grade — admirable adventures, a mixture of races and people not to be found elsewhere, and marvelous incidents. Women play pranks there with facility and charming promptitude. At Paris one resists temptation — at the waters one falls; there you are! Some men find fortune at them, like Andermatt; others find death, like Aubry-Pasteur; others find worse even than that — and get married there — like myself and Paul. Isn't it queer and funny, this sort of thing? You have heard about Paul's intended marriage — have you not?"

She murmured: "Yes; William told me about it a little while ago."

Gontran went on: "He is right, quite right. She is a peasant's daughter. Well, what of that? She is better than an adventurer's daughter or a daughter who's too short. I knew Paul. He would have ended by marrying a streetwalker, provided she resisted him for six months. And to resist him it needed a jade or an innocent. He has lighted on the innocent. So much the better for him!"

Christiane listened, and every word, entering through her ears, went straight to her heart, and inflicted on her pain, horrible pain.

Closing her eyes, she said: "I am very tired. I would like to have a little rest."

They embraced her and went out.

She could not sleep, so wakeful was her mind, active and racked with harrowing thoughts. That idea that he no longer loved her at all became so intolerable that, were it not for the presence of this woman, this nurse nodding asleep in the armchair, she would have got up, opened the window, and flung herself out on the steps of the hotel. A very thin ray of moonlight penetrated through an opening in the curtains, and formed a round bright spot on the floor. She observed it; and in a moment a crowd of memories rushed together into her brain: the lake, the wood, that first "I love you," scarcely heard, so agitating, at Tournoel, and all their caresses, in the evening, beside the shadowy paths, and the road from La Roche Pradière.

Suddenly, she saw this white road, on a night when the heavens were filled with stars, and he, Paul, with his arm round a woman's waist, kissing her at every step they walked. It was Charlotte! He pressed her against him, smiled as he knew how to smile, murmured in her ear sweet words, such as he knew how to utter, then flung himself on his knees and kissed the ground in front of her, just as he had kissed it in front of herself! It was so hard, so hard for her to bear, that turning round and hiding her face in the pillow, she burst out sobbing. She almost shrieked, so much did despair rend her soul. Every beat of her heart, which jumped into her throat, which throbbed in her temples, sent forth from her one word — "Paul — Paul — Paul" — endlessly re-echoed. She stopped up her ears with her hands in order to hear nothing more, plunged her head under the sheets; but then his name sounded in the depths of her bosom with every pant of her tormented heart.

The nurse, waking up, asked of her: "Are you worse, Madame?"

Christiane turned round, her face covered with tears, and murmured: "No, I was asleep — I was dreaming — I was frightened."

Then, she begged of her to light two wax-candles, so that the ray of moonlight might be no longer visible. Toward morning, however, she slumbered.

She had been asleep for a few hours when Andermatt came in, bringing with him Madame Honorât. The fat lady, immediately adopting a familiar tone, questioned her like a doctor; then, satisfied with her answers, said: "Come, come! you're going on very nicely!" Then she took off her hat, her gloves, and her shawl, and, addressing the nurse: "You may go, my girl. You will come when we ring for you." Christiane, already inflamed with dislike to the woman, said to her husband: "Give me my daughter for a little while."

As on the previous day, William carried the child to her, tenderly embracing it as he did so, and placed it upon the pillow. And, as on the previous day, too, when she felt close to her cheek, through the wrappings, the heat of this little stranger's body, imprisoned in linen, she was suddenly penetrated with a grateful sense of peace.

Then, all at once, the baby began to cry, screaming out in a shrill and piercing voice. "She wants nursing," said Andermatt.

He rang, and the wet-nurse appeared, a big red woman, with a mouth like an ogress, full of large, shining teeth, which almost terrified Christiane. And from the open body of her dress she drew forth a breast, soft and heavy with milk. And when Christiane beheld her daughter drinking, she felt a longing to snatch away and take back the baby, moved by a certain sense of jealousy. Madame Honorat now gave directions to the wet-nurse, who went off, carrying the baby in her arms. Andermatt, in his turn, went out, and the two women were left alone together.

Christiane did not know how to speak of what tortured her soul, trembling lest she might give way to too much emotion, lose her head, burst into tears, and betray herself. But Madame Honorat began to babble of her own accord, without having been asked a single question. When she had related all the scandalous stories that were circulating through the neighborhood, she came to the Oriol family: "They are good people," said she, "very good people. If you had known the mother, what a worthy, brave woman she was! She was worth ten women, Madame. The girls take after her, for that matter." Then, as she was passing on to another topic, Christiane asked: "Which of the two do you prefer, Louise or Charlotte?"

"Oh! for my own part, Madame. I prefer Louise, your brother's intended wife; she is more sensible, more steady. She is a woman of order. But my husband likes the other better. Men you know, have tastes different from ours."

She ceased speaking. Christiane, whose strength was giving way, faltered: "My brother has often met his betrothed at your house."

"Oh! yes, Madame — I believe really every day. Everything was brought about at my house, everything! As for me, 1 let them talk, these young people, I understood the thing thoroughly. But what truly gave me pleasure was when I saw that M. Paul was getting smitten by the younger one."

Then, Christiane, in an almost inaudible voice: "Is he deeply in love with her?"

"Ah! Madame, is he in love with her? He had lost his head about her some time since. And then, when the Italian — he who ran off with Doctor Cloche's daughter — kept hanging about the girl a little, it was something worth seeing and watching —

I thought they were going to fight! Ah! if you had seen M. Paul's eyes. And he looked upon her as if she were a holy Virgin, nothing less — it's a pleasant thing to see people so much in love as that!"

Thereupon, Christiane asked her about all that had taken place in her presence, about all they had said, about all they had done, about their promenades in the glen of Sans-Souci, where he had so often told her of his love for her. She put unexpected questions, which astonished the fat lady, about matters that nobody would have dreamed of, for she was constantly making comparisons; she recalled a thousand details of what had occurred the year before, all Paul's delicate gallantries, his thoughtfulness about her, his ingenious devices to please her, all that display of charming attentions and tender anxieties which on the part of a man show an imperious desire to win a woman's affections; and she wanted to find out whether he had manifested the same affectionate interest toward the other, whether he had commenced afresh this siege of a soul with the same ardor, with the same enthusiasm, with the same irresistible passion.

And every time she recognized a little circumstance, a little trait, one of those nothings which cause such exquisite bliss, one of those disquieting surprises which cause the heart to beat fast, and of which Paul was so prodigal when he loved, Christiane, as she lay prostrate in the bed, gave utterance to a little "Ah!" expressive of keen suffering.

Amazed at this strange exclamation, Madame Honorat declared more emphatically: "Why, yes. 'Tis as I tell you, exactly as I tell you. I never saw a man so much in love!"

"Has he recited verses to her?"

"I believe so indeed, Madame, and very pretty ones, too!"

And, when they had relapsed into silence, nothing more could be heard save the monotonous and soothing song of the nurse as she rocked the baby to sleep in the adjoining room.

Steps were drawing near in the corridor outside. Doctors Mas-Roussel and Latonne had come to visit their patient. They found her agitated, not quite so well as she had been on the previous day.

When they had left, Andermatt opened the door again, and without coming in: "Doctor Black would like to see you. Will you see him?"

She exclaimed, as she raised herself up in the bed: "No — no — I will not — no!"

William came over to her, looking quite astounded: "But listen to me now — it would only be right — it is his due — you ought to!"

She looked, with her wide-open eyes and quivering lips, as if she had lost her reason. She kept repeating in a piercing voice, so loud that it must have penetrated through the walls: "No! — no! — never!" And then, no longer knowing what she said, and pointing with outstretched arm toward Madame Honorat, who was standing in the center of the apartment:

"I do not want her either! — send her away! — 1 don't want to see her! — send her away!"

Then he rushed to his wife's side, took her in his arms, and kissed her on the forehead: "My little Christiane, be calm! What is the matter with you?

— — come now, be calm!"

She had by this time lost the power of raising her voice. The tears gushed from her eyes.

"Send them all away," said she, "and remain alone with me!"

He went across, in a distracted frame of mind, to the doctor's wife, and gently pushing her toward the door: "Leave us for a few minutes, pray. It is the fever — the milk-fever. I will calm her. I will look for you again by and by."

When he came back to the bedside Christiane was lying down, weeping quietly, without moving in any way, quite prostrated.

And then, for the first time in his life, he, too, began to weep.

In fact, the milk-fever had broken out during the night, and delirium supervened. After some hours of extreme excitement, the recently delivered woman suddenly began to speak.

The Marquis and Andermatt, who had resolved to remain near her, and who passed the time playing cards, counting the tricks in hushed tones, imagined that she was calling them, and, rising up, approached the bed. She did not see them; she did not recognize them. Intensely pale, on her white pillow, with her fair tresses hanging loose over her shoulders, she was gazing, with her clear blue eyes, into that unknown, mysterious, and fantastic world, in which dwell the insane.

Her hands, stretched over the bedclothes, stirred now and then, agitated by rapid and involuntary movements, tremblings, and starts.

She did not, at first, appear to be talking to anyone, but to be seeing things and telling what she saw. And the things she said seemed disconnected, incomprehensible. She found a rock too high to jump off. She was afraid of a sprain, and then she was not on intimate terms enough with the man who reached out his arms toward her. Then she spoke about perfumes. She was apparently trying to remember some forgotten phrases. "What can be sweeter? This intoxicates one like wine — wine intoxicates the mind, but perfume intoxicates the imagination. With perfume you taste the very essence, the pure essence of things and of the universe — you taste the flowers — the trees — the grass of the fields — — you can even distinguish the soul of the dwellings of olden days which sleeps in the old furniture, the old carpets, and the old curtains." Then her face contracted as if she had undergone a long spell of fatigue. She was ascending a hillside slowly, heavily, and was saying to some one: "Oh! carry me once more, I beg of you. I am going to die here! I can walk no farther. Carry me as you did above the gorges. Do you remember? — how you loved me!" Then she uttered a cry of anguish — a look of horror came into her eyes. She saw in front of her a dead animal, and she was imploring to have it taken away without giving her pain. The Marquis said in a whisper to his son-in-law: "She is thinking about an ass that we came across on our way back from La Nugère." And now she was addressing this dead beast, consoling it, telling it that she, too, was very unhappy, because she had been abandoned.

Then, on a sudden, she refused to do something required of her. She cried: "Oh! no, not that! Oh! it is you, you who want me to drag this cart!" Then she panted, as if indeed she were dragging A vehicle along. She wept, moaned, uttered exclamations, and always, during a period of half an hour, she was climbing up this hillside, dragging after her with horrible efforts the ass's cart, beyond a doubt.

And some one was harshly beating her, for she said: "Oh! how you hurt me! At least, don't beat me! I will walk — but don't beat me any more, I entreat you! I'll do whatever you wish, but don't beat me any more!"

Then her anguish gradually abated, and all she did was to go on quietly talking in her incoherent fashion till daybreak. After that, she became drowsy, and ended by going to sleep.

Until the following day, however, her mental powers remained torpid, somewhat wavering, fleeting. She could not immediately find the words she wanted, and fatigued herself terribly in searching for them. But, after a night of rest, she completely regained possession of herself.

Nevertheless, she felt changed, as if this crisis had transformed her soul. She suffered less and thought more. The dreadful occurrences, really so recent, seemed to her to have receded into a past already far off; and she regarded them with a clearness of conception with which her mind had never been illuminated before. This light, which had suddenly dawned on her brain, and which comes to certain beings in certain hours of suffering, showed her life, men, things, the entire earth and all that it contains as she had never seen them before.

Then, more than on the evening when she had felt herself so much alone in the universe in her room, after her return from the lake of Tazenat, she looked upon herself as utterly abandoned in existence. She realized that all human beings walk along side by side in the midst of circumstances without anything ever truly uniting two persons together. She learned from the treason of him in whom she had reposed her entire confidence that the others, all the others, would never again be to her anything but indifferent neighbors in that journey short or long, sad or gay, that followed tomorrows no one could foresee.

She comprehended that even in the clasp of this man's arms, when she believed that she was intermingling with him, entering into him, when she believed that their flesh and their souls had become only one flesh and one soul, they had only drawn a little nearer to one another, so as to bring into contact the impenetrable envelopes in which mysterious nature has isolated and shut up each human creature. And she saw as well that nobody has ever been able, or ever will be able, to break through that invisible barrier which places living beings as far from each other as the stars of heaven. She divined the impotent effort, ceaseless since the first days of the world, the indefatigable effort of men and women to tear off the sheath in which their souls forever imprisoned, forever solitary, are struggling — an effort of arms, of lips, of eyes, of mouths, of trembling, naked flesh, an effort of love, which exhausts itself in kisses, to finish only by giving life to some other forlorn being.

Then an uncontrollable desire to gaze on her daughter took possession of her. She asked for it, and when it was brought to her, she begged to have it stripped, for as yet she only knew its face.

The wet-nurse thereupon unfastened the swaddling-clothes, and discovered the poor little body of the newborn infant agitated by those vague movements which life puts into these rough sketches of humanity. Christiane touched it with a timid, trembling hand, then wanted to kiss the stomach, the back, the legs, the feet, and then she stared at the child full of fantastic thoughts.

Two beings came together, loved one another with rapturous passion; and from their embrace, this being was born. It was he and she intermingled; until the death of this little child, it was he and she, living again both together; it was a little of him, and a little of her, with an unknown something which make it different from them. It reproduced them both in the form of its body as well as in that of its mind, in its features, its gestures, its eyes, its movements, its tastes, its passions, even in the sound of its voice and its gait in walking, and yet it would be a new being!

They were separated now — he and she — forever! Never again would their eyes blend in one of those outbursts of love which make the human race indestructible. And pressing the child against her heart, she murmured: "Adieu! adieu!" It was to him that she was saying "adieu" in her baby's ear, the brave and sorrowing "adieu" of a woman who would yet have much to suffer, always, it might be, but who would know how to hide her tears.

"Ha! ha!" cried William through the half-open door. "1 catch you there! Will you be good enough to give me back my daughter?"

Running toward the bed, he seized the little one in his hands already practiced in the art of handling it, and lifting it over his head, he went on repeating: "Good day, Mademoiselle Andermatt — good day, Mademoiselle Andermatt."

Christiane was thinking: "Here, then, is my husband!"

And she contemplated him, with eyes as astonished as if they were beholding him for the first time. This was he, the man who ought to be, according to human ideas of religion, of society, the other half of her — more than that, her master, the master of her days and of her nights, of her heart and of her body! She felt almost a desire to smile, so strange did this appear to her at the moment, for between her and him no bond could ever exist, none of those bonds alas! so quickly broken, but which seem eternal, ineffably sweet, almost divine.

No remorse even came to her for having deceived him, for having betrayed him. She was surprised at this, and asked herself why it was. Why? No doubt, there was too great a difference between them, they were too far removed from one another, of races too widely dissimilar. He did not understand her at all; she did not understand him at all. And yet he was good, devoted, complaisant.

But only perhaps beings of the same shape, of the same nature, of the same moral essence can feel themselves attached to one another by the sacred bond of voluntary duty.

They dressed the baby again. William sat down. "Listen, my darling," said he; "I don't venture to announce Doctor Black's visit to you, since you have been so nice toward myself. There is, however, one person whom I would very much like you to see — I mean Doctor Bonnefille."

Then, for the first time, she laughed, with a colorless sort of laugh, which fixed itself on her lips, without going near her heart; and she asked:

"Doctor Bonnefille! what a miracle! So then you are reconciled?"

"Why, yes! Listen! I am going to tell you, as a secret, a great bit of news. I have just bought up the old establishment. I have all the district now. Hey! what a victory. That poor Doctor Bonnefille knew it before anybody, be it understood. So then he has been sly. He came every day to obtain information as to how you were, leaving his card with a word of sympathy written on it. For my part, I responded to these advances with a single visit; and at present we are on excellent terms."

"Let him come," said Christiane, "whenever he likes. I will be glad to see him."

"Good. Thank you. I'll bring him here to you tomorrow morning. I need scarcely tell you that Paul is constantly asking me to convey to you a thousand compliments from him, and he inquires a great deal about the little one. He is very anxious to see her." In spite of her resolutions she felt a sense of oppression. She was able, however, to say: "You will thank him on my behalf."

Andermatt rejoined: "He was very uneasy to learn whether you had been told about his intended marriage. I informed him that you had; then he asked me several times what you thought about it."

She exerted her strength to the utmost, and felt able to murmur: "You will tell him that I entirely approve of it."

William, with cruel persistency, went on: "He wishes also to know for certain what name you mean to call your daughter. I told him we were hesitating between Marguerite and Genevieve."

"I have changed my mind," said she. "I intend to call her Arlette."

Formerly, in the early days of her pregnancy, she had discussed with Paul the name which they ought to select whether for a son or for a daughter; and for a daughter they had remained undecided between Genevieve and Marguerite. She no longer wanted these two names.

William repeated: "Arlette! Arlette! That's a very nice name —you are right. For my part, I would have liked to call her Christiane, like you. I adore that name —Christiane!"

She sighed deeply: "Oh! it forebodes too much suffering to bear the name of the Crucified."

He reddened, never having dreamed of this comparison, and rising up: "Besides, Arlette is very nice. By-bye, my darling."

As soon as he had left the room, she called the wet-nurse, and directed her for the future to place the cradle beside the bed.

When the little couch in the form of a wherry, always rocking, and carrying its white curtain like a sail on its mast of twisted copper, had been rolled close to the big bed, Christiane stretched out her hand to the sleeping infant, and she said in a very hushed voice: "Go by-bye, my baby! You will never find anyone who will love you as much as I."

She passed the next few days in a state of tranquil melancholy, thinking a great deal, building up within herself a resisting soul, an energetic heart, in order to resume her life again in a few weeks. Her chief occupation now consisted in gazing into the eyes of her child, seeking to surprise in them a first look, but only seeing there two little bluish caverns invariably turned toward the sunlight coming in through the window.

And she experienced a feeling of profound sadness as she reflected that these eyes now closed in sleep would look out on the world, as she herself had looked on it, through the illusion of those secret dreamings which make the souls of young women trustful and joyous. They would love all that she had loved, the beautiful bright days, the flowers, the wood, and alas! living beings too! They would, no doubt, love a man! They would carry in their depths his image, well known, cherished, would see it when he would be far away, would be inflamed on seeing him again. And then —and then they would learn to weep! Tears, horrible tears, would flow over these little cheeks. And the frightful sufferings of love betrayed would render them unrecognizable, those poor wandering eyes which would be blue.

And she wildly embraced the child, saying to it: "Love me alone, my child!"

At length, one day, Professor Mas-Roussel, who came every morning to see her, declared: "You can soon get up for a little, Madame."

Andermatt, when the physician had left, said to his wife: "It is very unfortunate that you are not quite well, for we have a very interesting experiment to-day at the establishment. Doctor Latonne has performed a real miracle with Père Clovis by subjecting him to his system of self-moving gymnastics. Just imagine! This old vagabond is now able to walk as well as anyone. The progress of the cure, moreover, is manifest after each exhibition!"

To please him, she asked: "And are you going to have a public exhibition?"

"Yes, and no. We are having an exhibition before the medical men and a few friends."

"At what hour?"

"Three o'clock."

"Will M. Bretigny be there?"

"Yes, yes. He promised me that he would come to it. From a medical point of view, it is exceedingly curious."

"Well," she said, "as I'll just have risen myself at that time, you will ask M. Bretigny to come and see me. He will keep me company while you are looking at the experiment."

"Yes, my darling."

"You won't forget?"

"No, no. Make your mind easy."

And he went off in search of those who were to witness the exhibition.

After having been imposed upon by the Oriols at the time of the first treatment of the paralytic, he had in his turn imposed upon the credulity of invalids —so easy to get the better of, when it is a question of curing. And now he imposed upon himself with the farce of this cure, talking about it so frequently, with so much ardor and such an air of conviction that it would have been hard to determine whether he believed or disbelieved in it.

About three o'clock, all the persons whom he had induced to attend found themselves gathered together before the door of the establishment, expecting Père Clovis's arrival. He made his appearance, leaning on two walking-sticks, always dragging his legs after him, and bowing politely to everyone as he passed.

The two Oriols followed him, together with the two young girls. Paul and Gontran accompanied their intended wives.

In the great hall where the articulated instruments were fixed, Doctor Latonne was waiting, and killed time by chatting with Andermatt and Doctor Honorat.

When he saw Père Clovis, a smile of delight passed over his clean-shaven lips. He asked: "Well! how are we going on to-day?"

"Oh! all right, all right."

Petrus Martel and Saint Landri presented themselves. They wanted to satisfy their minds. The first believed; the second doubted. Behind them, people saw with astonishment Doctor Bonnefille coming up, saluting his rival, and extending his hand toward Andermatt. Doctor Black was the last to arrive.

"Well, Messieurs and Mesdemoiselles," said Doctor Latonne, as he bowed to Louise and Charlotte Oriol, "you are going to witness a very curious phenomenon. Observe first, before the experiment, this worthy fellow walking a little, but very little. Can you walk without your sticks, Père Clovis?"

"Oh! no, Mochieu!"

"Good, then let us begin."

The old fellow was hoisted on the armchair; his legs were strapped to the movable feet of the sitting-machine; then, at the command of the inspector: "Go quietly!" the attendant, with bare arms, turned the handle.

Thereupon, the right knee of the vagabond was seen rising up, stretching out, bending, then moving forward again; after that, the left knee did the same; and Père Clovis, seized with a sudden delight, began to laugh, while he repeated with his head and his long, white beard all the movements imposed on his legs.

The four physicians and Andermatt, stooping over him, examined him with the gravity of augurs, while Colosse exchanged sly winks with the old chap.

As the door had been left open, other persons kept constantly crowding in, and convinced and anxious bathers pressed forward to behold the experiment.

"Quicker!" said Doctor Latonne; and, in obedience to his command, the man who worked the handle turned it with greater energy. The old fellow's legs began to go at a running pace, and he, seized with irresistible gaiety, like a child being tickled, laughed as loudly as ever he could, moving his head about wildly. And, in the midst of his peals of laughter, he kept repeating: "What a rigolo! what a rigolo!" having, no doubt, picked up this word from the mouth of some foreigner.

Colosse, in his turn, broke out, and, stamping on the ground with his foot and striking his thighs with his hands, he exclaimed: "Ha! bougrrre of a Cloviche! bougrrre of a Cloviche!"

"Enough!" was the inspector's next command.

The vagabond was unfastened, and the physicians drew apart in order to verify the result.

Then Père Clovis was seen rising from the armchair, stepping on the ground, and walking. He proceeded with short steps, it was true, quite bent, and grimacing from fatigue at every effort, but still he walked!

Doctor Bonnefille was the first to declare: "This is quite a remarkable case!" Doctor Black immediately improved upon his brother-physician. Doctor Honorat, alone, said nothing.

Gontran whispered in Paul's ear: "I don't understand. Look at their heads. Are they dupes or humbugs?"

But Andermatt was speaking. He told the history of this cure since the first day, the relapse, and the final recovery which was declared to be settled and absolute.

He gaily added: "If our patient goes back a little every winter, we'll cure him again every summer."

Then he pompously eulogized the waters of Mont Oriol, extolled their properties, all their properties: "For my own part," said he; "I have had a proof of their efficacy in the case of a being who is very dear to me; and, if my family is not extinct, it is to Mont Oriol that I will owe it."

But, all at once, he had a flash of recollection. He had promised his wife a visit from Paul Bretigny. He was filled with regret for his forgetfulness, as he was most anxious to gratify her every wish. Accordingly he glanced around him, espied Paul, and coming up to him: "My dear friend, I completely forgot to tell you that Christiane is expecting you at this moment."

Bretigny said falteringly: "Me — at this moment?"

"Yes, she has got up to-day; and she desires to see you before anyone. Hurry then as quickly as possible, and excuse me."

Paul directed his steps toward the hotel, his heart throbbing with emotion. On his way he met the Marquis de Ravenel, who said to him:

"My daughter is up, and is surprised at not having seen you yet."

He halted, however, on the first steps of the staircase in order to consider what he would say to her. How would she receive him? Would she be alone? If she spoke about his marriage, what reply should he make?

Since he had heard of her confinement, he could not think about her without groaning, so uneasy did he feel; and the thought of their first meeting, every time it floated through his mind, made him suddenly redden or grow pale with anguish. He had also thought with deep anxiety of this unknown child, of which he was the father; and he remained harassed by a desire to see it, mingled with a dread of looking at it. He felt himself sunk in one of those moral foulnesses which stain a man's conscience up to the hour of his death. But he feared above all the glance of this woman, for whom his love had been so fierce and so short-lived.

Would she meet him with reproaches, with tears, or with disdain? Would she receive him, only to drive him away?

And what attitude ought he to assume toward her? Humble, crushed, suppliant, or cold? Should he explain himself or should he listen without replying? Ought he to sit down or to remain standing?

And when the child was shown to him, what should he do? What should he say? With what feeling should he appear to be agitated?

Before the door he stopped again, and at the moment when he was on the point of ringing, he noticed that his hand was trembling. However, he placed his finger on the little ivory button, and he heard the sound of the electric bell coming from the interior of the apartment.

A female servant opened the door, and admitted him. And, at the drawingroom door, he saw Christiane, at the end of the second room, lying on her long chair with her eyes fixed upon him.

These two rooms seemed to him interminable as he was passing through them. He felt himself tottering. He was afraid of knocking against the seats, and he did not venture to look down toward his feet in order to avoid lowering his eyes. She did not make a single gesture, or utter a single word. She waited till he was close beside her. Her right hand remained stretched out over her robe and her left leaned over the side of the cradle, covered all round with its curtains.

When he was three paces away from her he stopped, not knowing what best to do. The chambermaid had closed the door after him.

They were alone!

Then, he felt a longing to sink upon his knees, and implore her pardon. But she slowly raised the hand which had rested on her robe, and, extending it slightly toward him, said, "Good day," in a grave tone.

He did not venture to touch her fingers, which, however, he brushed with his lips, while he bowed to her.

She added: "Sit down." And he sat down on a lower chair, close to her feet.

He felt that he ought to speak, but he could not find a word or an idea, and he dared not even look at her. However, he ended by stammering out: "Your husband forgot to let me know that you were waiting for me; but for that, I would have come sooner."

She replied: "Oh! it matters little, since we were bound to see one another again — a little sooner — — a little later!"

As she added nothing more, he hastened to say in an inquiring tone: "I hope you are getting on well by this time?"

"Thanks. As well as one can get on, after such shocks!"

She was very pale and thin, but prettier than before her confinement. Her eyes especially had gained a depth of expression which he had never seen in them before. They seemed to have acquired a darker shade, a blue less clear, less transparent, more intense. Her hands were so white that their flesh looked like that of a corpse.

She went on: "Those are hours very hard to live through. But, when one has suffered thus, one feels strong till the end of one's days."

Much affected, he murmured: "Yes; they are terrible experiences!"

She repeated, like an echo: "Terrible."

For some moments there had been light movements in the cradle — the all but imperceptible sounds of an infant awakening from sleep. Bretigny could not longer avert his gaze, preyed upon by a melancholy, morbid yearning which gradually grew stronger, tortured by the desire to behold what lived within there.

Then he observed that the curtains of the tiny bed were fastened from top to bottom with the gold pins which Christiane was accustomed to wear in her corsage. Often had he amused himself in bygone days by taking them out and pinning them again on the shoulders of his beloved, those fine pins with crescent-shaped heads. He understood what she meant; and a poignant emotion seized him, made him feel shriveled up before this barrier of golden spikes which forever separated him from this child.

A little cry, a shrill plaint arose in this white prison. Christiane quickly rocked the wherry, and in a rather abrupt tone:

"I must ask your pardon for allowing you so little time; but I must look after my daughter."

He rose, and once more kissed the hand which she extended toward him; and, as he was on the point of leaving, she said:

"I pray that you may be happy."

THE END

Notre Coeur – A Woman's Pastime

ONE day Massival, the celebrated composer of "Rebecca," who for fifteen years, now, had been known as "the young and illustrious master," said to his friend André Mariolle:

"Why is it that you have never secured a presentation to *Mme.* Michèle de Burne? Take my word for it, she is one of the most interesting women in new Paris."

"Because I do not feel myself at all adapted to her surroundings."

"You are wrong, my dear fellow. It is a house where there is a great deal of novelty and originality; it is wideawake and very artistic. There is excellent music, and the conversation is as good as in the best salons of the last century. You would be highly appreciated — in the first place because you play so well on the violin, then because you have been very favorably spoken of in the house, and finally because you have the reputation of being select in your choice of friends."

Flattered, but still maintaining his attitude of resistance, supposing, moreover, that this urgent invitation was not given without the young woman being aware of it, Mariolle ejaculated a "Bah! I shall not bother my head at all about it," in which, through the disdain that he intended to express, was evident his foregone acceptance.

Massival continued: "Would you like to have me present you some of these days? You are already known to her through all of us who are on terms of intimacy with her, for we talk about you often enough. She is a very pretty woman of twenty-eight abounding in intelligence, who will never take a second husband, for her first venture was a very unfortunate one. She has made her abode a rendezvous for agreeable men. There are not too many clubmen or society-men found there — just enough of them to give the proper effect. She will be delighted to have me introduce you."

Mariolle was vanquished; he replied: "Very well, then; one of these days."

At the beginning of the following week the musician came to his house and asked him: "Are you disengaged tomorrow?"

"Why, yes."

"Very well. I will take you to dine with Mme de Burne; she requested me to invite you. Besides, here is a line from her."

After a few seconds' reflection, for form's sake, Mariolle answered: "That is settled!"

André Mariolle was about thirty-seven years old, a bachelor without a profession, wealthy enough to live in accordance with his likings, to travel, and even to indulge himself in collecting modern paintings and ancient knickknacks. He had the reputation of being a man of intelligence, rather odd and unsociable, a little capricious and disdainful, who affected the hermit through pride rather than through timidity. Very talented and acute, but indolent, quick to grasp the meaning of things, and capable, perhaps, of accomplishing something great, he had contented himself with enjoying life as a spectator, or rather as a dilettante. Had he been poor, he would doubtless have turned out to be a remarkable or celebrated man; born with a good income, he was eternally reproaching himself that he could never be anything better than a nobody.

It is true that he had made more than one attempt in the direction of the arts, but they had lacked vigor. One had been in the direction of literature, by publishing a pleasing book of travels, abounding in incident and correct in style; one toward music by his violin-playing, in which he had gained, even among professional musicians, a respectable reputation; and, finally, one at sculpture, that art in which native aptitude and the faculty of rough-hewing striking and deceptive figures atone in the eyes of the ignorant for deficiencies in study and knowledge. His statuette in terra-cotta, "Masseur Tunisien," had even been moderately successful at the Salon of the preceding year. He was a remarkable horseman, and was also, it was said, an excellent fencer, although he never used the foils in public, owing, perhaps, to the same self-distrustful feeling which impelled him to absent himself from society resorts where serious rivalries were to be apprehended.

His friends appreciated him, however, and were unanimous in extolling his merits, perhaps for the reason that they had little to fear from him in the way of competition. It was said of him that in every case he was reliable, a devoted friend, extremely agreeable in manner, and very sympathetic in his personality.

Tall of stature, wearing his black beard short upon the cheeks and trained down to a fine point upon the chin, with hair that was beginning to turn gray but curled very prettily, he looked one straight in the face with a pair of clear, brown, piercing eyes in which lurked a shade of distrust and hardness.

Among his intimates he had an especial predilection for artists of every kind — among them Gaston de Lamarthe the novelist, Massival the musician, and the painters Jobin, Rivollet, De Mandol — who seemed to set a high value on his reason, his friendship, his intelligence, and even his judgment, although at bottom, with the vanity that is inseparable from success achieved, they set him down as a very agreeable and very intelligent man who had failed to score a success.

Mariolle's haughty reserve seemed to say: "I am nothing because I have not chosen to be anything." He lived within a narrow circle, therefore, disdaining gallantry and the great frequented salons, where others might have shone more brilliantly than he, and might have obliged him to take his place among the lay-figures of society. He visited only those houses where appreciation was extended to the solid qualities that he was unwilling to display; and though he had consented so readily to allow himself to be introduced to *Mme.* Michèle de Burne, the reason was that his best friends, those who everywhere proclaimed his hidden merits, were the intimates of this young woman.

She lived in a pretty entresol in the Rue du Général-Foy, behind the church of Saint Augustin. There were two rooms with an outlook on the street — the diningroom and a salon, the one in which she received her company indiscriminately — and two others that opened on a handsome garden of which the owner of the property had the enjoyment. Of the latter the first was a second salon of large dimensions, of greater length than width, with three windows opening on the trees, the leaves of which brushed against the awnings, a room which was embellished with furniture and ornaments exceptionally rare and simple, in the purest and soberest taste and of great value. The tables, the chairs, the little cupboards or étagères, the pictures, the fans and the porcelain figures beneath glass covers, the vases, the statuettes, the great clock fixed in the middle of a panel, the entire decoration of this young woman's apartment attracted and held attention by its shape, its age, or its elegance. To create for herself this home, of which she was almost as proud as she was of her own person, she had laid under contribution the knowledge, the friendship, the good nature, and the rummaging instinct of every artist of her acquaintance. She was rich and willing to pay well, and her friends had discovered for her many things, distinguished by originality, which the mere vulgar amateur would have passed by with contempt. Thus, with their assistance, she had furnished this dwelling, to which access was obtained with difficulty, and where she imagined that her friends received more pleasure and returned more gladly than elsewhere.

If was even a favorite hobby of hers to assert that the colors of the curtains and hangings, the comfort of the seats, the beauty of form, and the gracefulness of general effect are of as much avail to charm, captivate, and acclimatize the eye as are pretty smiles. Sympathetic or antipathetic rooms, she would say, whether rich or poor, attract, hold, or repel, just like the people who live in them. They awake the feelings or stifle them, warm or chill the mind, compel one to talk or be silent, make one sad or cheerful; in a word, they give every visitor an unaccountable desire to remain or to go away.

About the middle of this dimly lighted gallery a grand piano, standing between two jardinières filled with flowers, occupied the place of honor and dominated the room. Beyond this a lofty door with two leaves opened gave access to the bedroom, which in turn communicated with a dressing-room, also very large and elegant, hung with chintz like a drawingroom in summer, where Mme de Burne generally kept herself when she had no company.

Married to a well-mannered good-for-nothing, one of those domestic tyrants before whom everything must bend and yield, she had at first been very unhappy. For five years she had had to endure the unreasonable exactions, the harshness, the jealousy, even the violence of this intolerable master, and terrified, beside herself with astonishment, she had submitted without revolt to this revelation of married life, crushed as she was beneath the despotic and torturing will of the brutal man whose victim she had become.

He died one night, from an aneurism, as he was coming home, and when she saw the body of her husband brought in, covered with a sheet, unable to believe in the reality of this deliverance, she looked at his corpse with a deep feeling of repressed joy and a frightful dread lest she might show it.

Cheerful, independent, even exuberant by nature, very flexible and attractive, with bright flashes of wit such as are shown in some incomprehensible way in the intellects of certain little girls of Paris, who seem to have breathed from their earliest childhood the stimulating air of the boulevards — where every evening, through the open doors of the theaters, the applause or the hisses that greet the plays come forth, borne on the air — she nevertheless retained from her five years of servitude a strange timidity grafted upon her oldtime audacity, a great fear lest she might say too much, do too much, together with a burning desire for emancipation and a stern resolve never again to do anything to imperil her liberty.

Her husband, a man of the world, had trained her to receive like a mute slave, elegant, polite, and well dressed. The despot had numbered among his friends many artists, whom she had received with curiosity and listened to with delight, without ever daring to allow them to see how she understood and appreciated them.

When her period of mourning was ended she invited a few of them to dinner one evening. Two of them sent excuses; three accepted and were astonished to find a young woman of admirable intelligence and charming manners, who immediately put them at their ease and gracefully told them of the pleasure that they had afforded her in former days by coming to her house. From among her old acquaintances who had ignored her or failed to recognize her qualities she thus gradually made a selection according to her inclinations, and as a widow, an enfranchised woman, but one determined to maintain her good name, she began to receive all the most distinguished men of Paris whom she could bring together, with only a few women. The first to be admitted became her intimates, formed a nucleus, attracted others, and gave to the house the air of a small court, to which every habitué contributed either personal merit or a great name, for a few well-selected titles were mingled with the intelligence of the commonalty.

Her father, M. de Pradon, who occupied the apartment over hers, served as her chaperon and "sheep-dog." An old beau, very elegant and witty, and extremely attentive to his daughter, whom he treated rather as a lady acquaintance than as a daughter, he presided at the Thursday dinners that were quickly known and talked of in Paris, and to which invitations were much sought after. The requests for introductions and invitations came in shoals, were discussed, and very frequently rejected by a sort of vote of the inner council. Witty sayings that had their origin in this circle were quoted and obtained currency in the city. Actors, artists, and young poets made their débuts there, and received, as it were, the baptism of their future greatness. Longhaired geniuses, introduced by Gaston de Lamarthe, seated themselves at the piano and replaced the Hungarian violinists that Massival had presented, and foreign ballet-dancers gave the company a glimpse of their graceful steps before appearing at the Eden or the Folies-Bergères.

Mme de Burne, over whom her friends kept jealous watch and ward and to whom the recollection of her commerce with the world under the auspices of marital authority was loathsome, was sufficiently wise not to enlarge the circle of her acquaintance to too great an extent. Satisfied and at the same time terrified as to what might be said and thought of her, she abandoned herself to her somewhat Bohemian inclinations with consummate prudence. She valued her good name, and was fearful of any rashness that might jeopardize it; she never allowed her fancies to carry her beyond the bounds of propriety, was moderate in her audacity and careful that no liaison or small love affair should ever be imputed to her.

All her friends had made love to her, more or less; none of them had been successful. They confessed it, admitted it to each other with surprise, for men never acknowledge, and perhaps they are right, the power of resistance of a woman who is her own mistress. There was a story current about her. It was said that at the beginning of their married life her husband had exhibited such revolting brutality toward her that she had been forever cured of the love of men. Her friends would often discuss the case at length. They inevitably arrived at the conclusion that a young girl who has been brought up in the dream of future tenderness and the expectation of an awe-inspiring mystery must have all her ideas completely upset when her initiation into the new life is committed to a clown. That worldly philosopher, George de Maltry, would give a gentle sneer and add: "Her hour will strike; it always does for women like her, and the longer it is in coming the louder it strikes. With our friend's artistic tastes, she will wind up by falling in love with a singer or a pianist."

Gaston de Lamarthe's ideas upon the subject were quite different. As a novelist, observer, and psychologist, devoted to the study of the inhabitants of the world of fashion, of whom he drew ironical and lifelike portraits, he claimed to analyze and know women with infallible and unique penetration. He put Mme de Burne down among those flighty creatures of the time, the type of whom he had given in his interesting novel, "Une d'Elles." He had been the first to diagnose this new race of women, distracted by the nerves of reasoning, hysterical patients, drawn this way and that by a thousand contradictory whims which never ripen into desires, disillusioned of everything, without having enjoyed anything, thanks to the times, to the way of living, and to the modern novel, and who, destitute of all ardor and enthusiasm, seem to combine in their persons the capricious, spoiled child and the old, withered sceptic. But he, like the rest of them, had failed in his love-making.

For all the faithful of the group had in turn been lovers of Mme de Burne, and after the crisis had retained their tenderness and their emotion in different degrees. They had gradually come to form a sort of little church; she was its Madonna, of whom they conversed constantly among themselves, subject to her charm even when she was not present. They praised, extolled, criticised, or disparaged her, according as she had manifested irritation or gentleness, aversion or preference. They were continually displaying their jealousy of each other, played the spy on each other a little, and above all kept their ranks well closed up, so that no rival might get near her who could give them any cause for alarm.

These assiduous ones were few in number: Massival, Gaston de Lamarthe, big Fresnel, George de Maltry, a fashionable young philosopher, celebrated for his paradoxes, for his eloquent and involved erudition that was always up to date though incomprehensible even to the most impassioned of his female admirers, and for his clothes, which were selected with as much care as his theories. To this tried band she had added a few more men of the world who had a reputation for wit, the Comte de Marantin, the Baron de Gravil, and two or three others.

The two privileged characters of this chosen battalion seemed to be Massival and Lamarthe, who, it appears, had the gift of being always able to divert the young woman by their artistic unceremoniousness, their chaff, and the way they had of making fun of everybody, even of herself, a little, when she was in humor to tolerate it. The care, whether natural or assumed, however, that she took never to manifest a marked and prolonged predilection for any one of her admirers, the unconstrained air with which she practiced her coquetry and the real im-partiality with which she dispensed her favors maintained between them a friendship seasoned with hostility and an alertness of wit that made them entertaining.

One of them would sometimes play a trick on the others by presenting a friend; but as this friend was never a very celebrated or very interesting man, the rest would form a league against him and quickly send him away.

It was in this way that Massival brought his comrade André Mariolle to the house. A servant in black announced these names: "Monsieur Massival! Monsieur Mariolle!"

Beneath a great rumpled cloud of pink silk, a huge shade that was casting down upon a square table with a top of ancient marble the brilliant light of a lamp supported by a lofty column of gilded bronze, one woman's head and three men's heads were bent over an album that Lamarthe had brought in with him. Standing between them, the novelist was turning the leaves and explaining the pictures.

As they entered the room, one of the heads was turned toward them, and Mariolle, as he stepped forward, became conscious of a bright, blond face, rather tending to ruddiness, upon the temples of which the soft, fluffy locks of hair seemed to blaze with the flame of burning brushwood. The delicate retroussé nose imparted a smiling expression to this countenance, and the clean-cut mouth, the deep dimples in the cheeks, and the rather prominent cleft chin, gave it a mocking air, while the eyes, by a strange contrast, veiled it in melancholy. They were blue, of a dull, dead blue as if they had been washed out, scoured, used up, and in the center the black pupils shone, round and dilated. The strange and brilliant glances that they emitted seemed to tell of dreams of morphine, or perhaps, more simply, of the coquettish artifice of belladonna.

Mme de Burne arose, gave her hand, thanked and welcomed them.

"For a long time I have been begging my friends to bring you to my house," she said to Mariolle, "but I always have to tell these things over and over again in order to get them done."

She was tall, elegantly shaped, rather deliberate in her movements, modestly décolletée, scarcely showing \he tips of her handsome shoulders, the shoulders of a red-headed woman, that shone out marvelously under the light. And yet her hair was not red, but of the inexpressible color of certain dead leaves that have been burned by the frosts of autumn.

She presented M. Mariolle to her father, who bowed and shook hands.

The men were conversing familiarly together in three groups; they seemed to be at home, in a kind of club that they were accustomed to frequent, to which the presence of a woman imparted a note of refinement.

Big Fresnel was chatting with the Comte de Marantin. Fresnel's frequent visits to this house and the preference that Mme de Burne evinced for him shocked and often provoked her friends. Still young, but with the proportions of a drayman, always puffing and blowing, almost beard-less, his head lost in a vague cloud of light, soft hair, commonplace, tiresome, ridiculous, he certainly could have but one merit in the young woman's eyes, a merit that was displeasing to the others but indispensable to her, — that of loving her blindly. He had received the nickname of "The Seal." He was married, but never said anything about bringing his wife to the house. It was said that she was very jealous in her seclusion.

Lamarthe and Massival especially evinced their indignation at the evident sympathy of their friend for this windy person, and when they could no longer refrain from reproaching her with this reprehensible inclination, this selfish and vulgar liking, she would smile and answer:

"I love him as I would love a great, big, faithful dog."

George de Maltry was entertaining Gaston de Lamarthe with the most recent discovery, not yet fully developed, of the micro-biologists. M. de Maltry was expatiating on his theme with many subtle and far-reaching theories, and the novelist accepted them enthusiastically, with the facility with which men of letters receive and do not dispute everything that appears to them original and new.

The philosopher of "high life," fair, of the fairness of linen, slender and tall, was incased in a coat that fitted very closely about the hips. Above, his pale, intelligent face emerged from his white collar and was surmounted by smooth, blond hair, which had the appearance of being glued on.

As to Lamarthe, Gaston de Lamarthe, to whom the particle that divided his name had im-parted some of the pretensions of a gentleman and man of the world, he was first, last, and all the time a man of letters, a terrible and pitiless man of letters. Provided with an eye that gathered in images, attitudes, and gestures with the rapidity and accuracy of the photographer's camera, and endowed with penetration and the novelist's instinct, which were as innate in him as the faculty of scent is in a hound, he was busy from morning till night storing away im-pressions to be used afterward in his profession. With these two very simple senses, a distinct idea of form and an intuitive one of substance, he gave to his books, in which there appeared none of the ordinary aims of psychological writers, the color, the tone, the appearance, the movement of life itself.

Each one of his novels as it appeared excited in society curiosity, conjecture, merriment, or wrath, for there always seemed to be prominent persons to be recognized in them, only faintly disguised under a torn mask; and whenever he made his way through a crowded salon he left a wake of uneasiness behind him. Moreover, he had published a volume of personal recollections, in which he had given the portraits of many men and women of his acquaintance, without any clearly defined intention of unkindness, but with such precision and severity that they felt sore over it. Some one had applied to him the sobriquet, "Beware of your friends." He kept his secrets close-locked within his breast and was a puzzle to his intimates. He was reputed to have once passionately loved a woman who caused him much suffering, and it was said that after that he wreaked his vengeance upon others of her sex.

Massival and he understood each other very well, although the musician was of a very different disposition, more frank, more expansive, less harassed, perhaps, but manifestly more impressible. After two great successes — a piece performed at Brussels and afterward brought to Paris, where it was loudly applauded at the Opéra-Comique; then a second work that was received and interpreted at the Grand Opéra as soon as offered — he had yielded to that species of cessation of impulse that seems to smite the greater part of our contemporary artists like premature paralysis. They do not grow old, as their fathers did, in the midst of their renown and success, but seem threatened with impotence even when in the very prime of life. Lamarthe was accustomed to say: "At the present day there are in France only great men who have gone wrong."

Just at this time Massival seemed very much smitten with Mme de Burne, so that every eye was turned upon him when he kissed her hand with an air of adoration. He inquired:

"Are we late?"

She replied:

"No, I am still expecting the Baron de Gravil and the Marquise de Bratiane."

"Ah, the Marquise! What good luck! We shall have some music this evening, then."

"I hope so."

The two laggards made their appearance. The Marquise, a woman perhaps a little too diminutive, Italian by birth, of a lively disposition, with very black eyes and eyelashes, black eyebrows, and black hair to match, which grew so thick and so low down that she had no forehead to speak of, her eyes even being threatened with invasion, had the reputation of possessing the most remarkable voice of all the women in society.

The Baron, a very gentlemanly man, hollowchested and with a large head, was never really himself unless he had his violoncello in his hands. He was a passionate melomaniac, and only frequented those houses where music received its due share of honor.

Dinner was announced, and Mme de Burne, taking André Mariolle's arm, allowed her guests to precede her to the diningroom; then, as they were left together, the last ones in the drawingroom, just as she was about to follow the procession she cast upon him an oblique, swift glance from her pale eyes with their dusky pupils, in which he thought that he could perceive more complexity of thought and more curiosity of interest than pretty women generally bestow upon a strange gentleman when receiving him at dinner for the first time.

The dinner was monotonous and rather dull. Lamarthe was nervous, and seemed ill disposed toward everyone, not openly hostile, for he made a point of his good-breeding, but displaying that almost imperceptible bad humor that takes the life out of conversation. Massival, abstracted and preoccupied, ate little, and from time to time cast furtive glances at the mistress of the house, who seemed to be in any place rather than at her own table. Inattentive, responding to remarks with a smile and then allowing her face to settle back to its former intent expression, she appeared to be reflecting upon something that seemed greatly to preoccupy her, and to interest her that evening more than did her friends. Still she contributed her share to the conversation — very amply as regarded the Marquise and Mariolle, — but she did it from habit, from a sense of duty, visibly absent from herself and from her abode Fresnel and M. de Maltry disputed over contemporary poetry. Fresnel held the opinions upon poetry that are current among men of the world, and M. de Maltry the perceptions of the spinners of most complicated verse — verse that is incomprehensible to the general public.

Several times during the dinner Mariolle had again encountered the young woman's inquiring look, but more vague, less intent, less curious. The Marquise de Bratiane, the Comte de Marantin, and the Baron de Gravil were the only ones who kept up an uninterrupted conversation, and they had quantities of things to say.

After dinner, during the course of the evening, Massival, who had kept growing more and more melancholy, seated himself at the piano and struck a few notes, whereupon Mme de Burne appeared to awake and quickly organized a little concert, the numbers of which comprised the pieces that she was most fond of.

The Marquise was in voice, and, animated by Massival's presence, she sang like a real artist. The master accompanied her, with that dreamy look that he always assumed when he sat down to play. His long hair fell over the collar of his coat and mingled with his full, fine, shining, curling beard. Many women had been in love with him, and they still pursued him with their attentions, so it was said. Mme de Burne, sitting by the piano and listening with all her soul, seemed to be contemplating him and at the same time not to see him and Mariolle was a little jealous. He was not particularly jealous because of any relation that there was between her and him, but in presence of that look of a woman fixed so intently upon one of the Illustrious he felt himself humiliated in his masculine vanity by the consciousness of the rank that They bestow on us in proportion to the renown that we have gained. Often before this he had secretly suffered from contact with famous men whom he was accustomed to meet in the presence of those beings whose favor is by far the dearest reward of success.

About ten o'clock the Comtesse de Frémines and two Jewesses of the financial community arrived, one after the other. The talk was of a marriage that was on the carpet and a threatened divorce suit. Mariolle looked at Madame de Burne, who was now seated beneath a column that sustained a huge lamp. Her well-formed, tip-tilted nose, the dimples in her cheeks, and the little indentation that parted her chin gave her face the frolicsome expression of a child, although she was approaching her thirtieth year, and something in her glance that reminded one of a withering flower cast a shade of melancholy over her countenance. Beneath the light that streamed upon it her skin took on tones of blond velvet, while her hair actually seemed colored by the autumnal sun which dyes and scorches the dead leaves.

She was conscious of the masculine glance that was traveling toward her from the other end of the room, and presently she arose and went to him, smiling, as if in response to a summons from him.

"I am afraid you are somewhat bored," she said. "A person who has not got the run of a house is always bored."

He protested the contrary. She took a chair and seated herself by him, and at once the conversation began to be animated. It was instantaneous with both of them, like a fire that blazes up brightly as soon as a match is applied to it. It seemed as if they had imparted their sensations and their opinions to each other beforehand, as if a similarity of disposition and education, of tastes and inclinations, had predisposed them to a mutual understanding and fated them to meet.

Perhaps there may have been a little artfulness on the part of the young woman, but the delight that one feels in encountering one who is capable of listening, who can understand you and reply to you and whose answers give scope for your repartees, put Mariolle into a fine glow of spirits. Flattered, moreover, by the reception which she had accorded him, subjugated by the alluring favor that she displayed and by the charm which she knew how to use so adroitly in captivating men, he did his best to exhibit to her that shade of subdued but personal and delicate wit which, when people came to know him well, had gained for him so many and such warm friendships.

She suddenly said to him:

"Really, it is very pleasant to converse with you, Monsieur. I had been told that such was the case, however."

He was conscious that he was blushing, and replied at a venture:

"And I had been told, Madame, that you were — "

She interrupted him:

"Say a coquette. I am a good deal of a coquette with people whom I like. Everyone knows it, and I do not attempt to conceal it from myself, but you will see that I am very impartial in my coquetry, and this allows me to keep or to recall my friends without ever losing them, and to retain them all about me."

She said this with a sly air which was meant to say: "Be easy and don't be too presumptuous. Don't deceive yourself, for you will get nothing more, than the others."

He replied:

"That is what you might call warning your guests of the perils that await them here. Thank you, Madame: I greatly admire your mode of procedure."

She had opened the way for him to speak of herself, and he availed himself of it. He began by paying her compliments and found that she was fond of them; then he aroused her woman's curiosity by telling her what was said of her in the different houses that he frequented. She was rather uneasy and could not conceal her desire for further information, although she affected much indifference as to what might be thought of herself and her tastes. He drew for her a charming portrait of a superior, independent, intelligent, and attractive woman, who had surrounded herself with a court of eminent men and still retained her position as an accomplished member of society. She disclaimed his compliments with smiles, with little disclaimers of gratified egotism, all the while taking much pleasure in the details that he gave her, and in a playful tone kept constantly asking him for more, questioning him artfully, with a sensual appetite for flattery.

As he looked at her, he said to himself, "She is nothing but a child at heart, just like all the rest of them"; and he went on to finish a pretty speech in which he was commending her love for art, so rarely found among women. Then she assumed an air of mockery that he had not before suspected in her, that playfully tantalizing manner that seems inherent in the French. Mariolle had overdone his eulogy; she let him know that she was not a fool.

"Mon Dieu!" she said, "I will confess to you that I am not quite certain whether it is art or artists that I love."

He replied: "How could one love artists without being in love with art?"

"Because they are sometimes more comical than men of the world."

"Yes, but they have more unpleasant failings."

"That is true."

"Then you do not love music?"

She suddenly dropped her bantering tone. "Excuse me! I adore music; I think that I am more fond of it than of anything else. And yet Massival is convinced that I know nothing at all about it."

"Did he tell you so?"

"No, but he thinks so."

"How do you know?"

"Oh! we women guess at almost everything that we don't know."

"So Massival thinks that you know nothing of music?"

"I am sure of it. I can see it only by the way that he has of explaining things to me, by the way in which he underscores little niceties of expression, all the while saying to himself: 'That won't be of any use, but I do it because you are so nice.'"

"Still he has told me that you have the best music in your house of any in Paris, no matter whose the other may be."

"Yes, thanks to him."

"And literature, are you not fond of that?"

' "I am very fond of it; and I am even so audacious as to claim to have a very good perception of it, notwithstanding Lamarthe's opinion."

"Who also decides that you know nothing at all about it?"

"Of course."

"But who has not told you so in words, any more than the other."

"Pardon me; he is more outspoken. He asserts that certain women are capable of showing a very just and delicate perception of the sentiments that are expressed, of the truthfulness of the characters, of psychology in general, but that they are totally incapable of discerning the superiority that resides in his profession, its art. When he has once uttered this word, Art, all that is left one to do is to show him the door."

Mariolle smiled and asked:

"And you, Madame, what do you think of it?" She reflected for a few seconds, then looked him straight in the face to see if he was in a frame of mind to listen and to understand her.

"I believe that sentiment, you understand — sentiment — can make a woman's mind receptive of everything; only it is frequently the case that what enters does not remain there. Do you follow me?"

"No, not fully, Madame."

"Very well! To make us comprehensive to the same degree as you, our woman's nature must be appealed to before addressing our intelligence. We take no interest in what a man has not first made sympathetic to us, for we look at all things through the medium of sentiment. I do not say through the medium of love; no, — but of sentiment, which has shades, forms, and manifestations of every sort. Sentiment is something that belongs exclusively to our domain, which you men have no conception of, for it befogs you while it enlightens us. Oh! I know that all this is incomprehensible to you, the more the pity! In a word, if a man loves us and is agreeable to us, for it is indispensable that we should feel that we are loved in order to become capable of the effort — and if this man is a superior being, by taking a little pains he can make us feel, know, and possess everything, everything, I say, and at odd moments and by bits impart to us the whole of his intelligence. That is all often blotted out afterward; it disappears, dies out, for we are forgetful. Oh! we forget as the wind forgets the words that are spoken to it. We are intuitive and capable of enlightenment, but changeable, impressionable, readily swayed by our surroundings. If I could only tell you how many states of mind I pass through that make of me entirely different women, according to the weather, my health, what I may have been reading, what may have been said to me! Actually there are days when I have the feelings of an excellent mother without children, and others when I almost have those of a cocotte without lovers."

Greatly pleased, he asked: "Is it your opinion that intelligent women generally are gifted with this activity of thought?"

"Yes," she said. "Only they allow it to slumber, and then they have a life shaped for them which draws them in one direction or the other."

Again he questioned: "Then in your heart of hearts it is music that you prefer above all other distractions?"

"Yes! But what I was telling you just now is so true! I should certainly never have enjoyed it as I do enjoy it, adored it as I do adore it, had it not been for that angelic Massival. He seems to have given me the soul of the great masters by teaching me to play their works, of which I was passionately fond before. What a pity that he is married!"

She said these last words with a sprightly air, but so regretfully that they threw everything else into shadow, her theories upon women and her admiration for art.

Massival was, in fact, married. Before the days of his success he had contracted one of those unions that artists make and afterward trail after them through their renown until the day of their death. He never mentioned his wife's name, never presented her in society, which he frequented a great deal; and although he had three children the fact was scarcely known.

Mariolle laughed. She was decidedly nice, was this unconventional woman, pretty, and of a type not often met with. Without ever tiring, with a persistency that seemed in no wise embarrassing to her, he kept gazing upon that face, grave and gay and a little self-willed, with its audacious nose and its sensual coloring of a soft, warm blonde, warmed by the midsummer of a maturity so tender, so full, so sweet that she seemed to have reached the very year, the month, the minute of her perfect flowering. He wondered: "Is her complexion false?" And he looked for the faint telltale line, lighter or darker, at the roots of her hair, without being able to discover it.

Soft footsteps on the carpet behind him made him start and turn his head. It was two servants bringing in the tea-table. Over the blue flame of the little lamp the water bubbled gently in a great silver receptacle, as shining and complicated as a chemist's apparatus.

"Will you have a cup of tea?" she asked.

Upon his acceptance she arose, and with a firm step in which there was no undulation, but which was rather marked by stiffness, proceeded to the table where the water was simmering in the depths of the machine, surrounded by a little garden of cakes, pastry, candied fruits, and bonbons. Then, as her profile was presented in clear relief against the hangings of the salon, Mariolle observed the delicacy of her form and the thinness of her hips beneath the broad shoulders and the full chest that he had been admiring a moment before. As the train of her light dress unrolled and dragged behind her, seemingly prolonging upon the carpet a body that had no end, this blunt thought arose to his mind: "Behold, a siren! She is altogether promising." She was now going from one to another, offering her refreshments with gestures of exquisite grace. Mariolle was following her with his eyes; but Lamarthe, who was walking about with his cup in his hand, came up to him and said:

"Shall we go, you and I?"

"Yes, I think so."

"We will go at once, shall we not? I am tired."

"At once. Come."

They left the house. When they were in the street, the novelist asked:

"Are you going home or to the club?"

"I think that I will go and spend an hour at the club."

"At the Tambourins?"

"Yes."

"I will go as far as the door with you. Those places are tiresome to me; I never put my foot in them. I join them only because they enable me to economize in hack-hire."

They locked arms and went down the street toward Saint Augustin. They walked a little way in silence; then Mariolle said:

"What a singular woman! What do you think of her?"

Lamarthe began to laugh outright. "It is the commencement of the crisis," he said. "You will have to pass through it, just as we have all done. I have had the malady, but I am cured of it now. My dear friend, the crisis consists of her friends talking of nothing but of her when they are together, whenever they chance to meet, wherever they may happen to be."

"At all events, it is the first time in my case, and it is very natural for me to ask for information, since I scarcely know her."

"Let it be so, then; we will talk of her. Well, you are bound to fall in love with her. It is your fate, the lot that is shared by all."

"She is so very seductive, then?"

"Yes and no. Those who love the women of other days, women who have a heart and a soul, women of sensibility, the women of the old-fashioned novel, cannot endure her and execrate her to such a degree as to speak of her with ignominy. We, on the other hand, who are disposed to look favorably upon what is modern and fresh, are compelled to confess that she is delicious, provided always that we don't fall in love with her. And that is just exactly what everybody does. No one dies of the complaint, however; they do not even suffer very acutely, but they fume because she is not other than she is. You will have to go through it all if she takes the fancy; besides, she is already preparing to snap you up." Mariolle exclaimed, in response to his secret thought:

"Oh! I am only a chance acquaintance for her, and I imagine that she values acquaintances of all sorts and conditions."

"Yes, she values them, parbleu! and at the same time she laughs at them. The most celebrated, even the most distinguished, man will not darken her door ten times if he is not congenial to her, and she has formed a stupid attachment for that idiotic Fresnel, and that tiresome De Maltry. She inexcusably suffers herself to be carried away by those idiots, no one knows why; perhaps because she gets more amusement out of them than she does out of us, perhaps because their love for her is deeper; and there is nothing in the world that pleases a woman so much as to be loved like that."

And Lamarthe went on talking of her, analyzing her, pulling her to pieces, correcting himself only to contradict himself again, replying with unmistakable warmth and sincerity to Mariolle's questions, like a man who is deeply interested in his subject and carried away by it; a little at sea also, having his mind stored with observations that were true and deductions that were false. He said:

"She is not the only one, moreover; at this minute there are fifty women, if not more, who are like her. There is the little Frémines who was in her drawingroom just now; she is Mme de Burne's exact counterpart, save that she is more forward in her manners and married to an outlandish kind of fellow, the consequence of which is that her house is one of the most entertaining lunatic asylums in Paris. I go there a great deal."

Without noticing it, they had traversed the Boulevard Malesherbes, the Rue Royale, the Avenue des Champs-Élysées, and had reached the Arc de Triomphe, when Lamarthe suddenly pulled out his watch.

"My dear fellow," he said, "we have spent an hour and ten minutes in talking of her; that is sufficient for to-day. I will take some other occasion of seeing you to your club. Go home and go to bed; it is what I am going to do."

II

THE room was large and well lighted, the walls and ceiling hung with admirable hangings of chintz that a friend of hers in the diplomatic service had brought home and presented to her. The ground was yellow, as if it had been dipped in golden cream, and the designs of all colors, in which Persian green was predominant, represented fantastic buildings with curving roofs, about which monstrosities in the shape of beasts and birds were running and flying: lions wearing wigs, antelopes with extravagant horns, and birds of paradise.

The furniture was scanty. Upon three long tables with tops of green marble were arranged all the implements requisite for a pretty woman's toilette. Upon one of them, the central one, were the great basins of thick crystal; the second presented an array of bottles, boxes, and vases of all sizes, surmounted by silver caps bearing her arms and monogram; while on the third were displayed all the tools and appliances of modern coquetry, countless in number, designed to serve various complex and mysterious purposes. The room contained only two reclining chairs and a few low, soft, and luxurious seats, calculated to afford rest to weary limbs and to bodies relieved of the restraint of clothing.

Covering one entire side of the apartment was an immense mirror, composed of three panels. The two wings, playing on hinges, allowed the young woman to view herself at the same time in front, rear, and profile, to envelop herself in her own image. To the right, in a recess that was generally concealed by hanging draperies, was the bath, or rather a deep pool, reached by a descent of two steps. A bronze Love, a charming conception of the sculptor Prédolé, poured hot and cold water into it through the seashells with which he was playing. At the back of this alcove a Venetian mirror, composed of smaller mirrors inclined to each other at varying angles, ascended in a curved dome, shutting in and protecting the bath and its occupant, and reflecting them in each one of its many component parts. A little beyond the bath was her writing-desk, a plain and handsome piece of furniture of modern English manufacture, covered with a litter of papers, folded letters, little torn envelopes on which glittered gilt initials, for it was in this room that she passed her time and attended to her correspondence when she was alone.

Stretched at full length upon her reclining-chair, enveloped in a dressing-gown of Chinese silk, her bare arms — and beautiful, firm, supple arms they were — issuing forth fearlessly from out the wide folds of silk, her hair turned up and burdening the head with its masses of blond coils, Mme de Burne was indulging herself with a gentle reverie after the bath. The chambermaid knocked, then entered, bringing a letter. She took it, looked at the writing, tore it open, and read the first lines; then calmly said to the servant: "I will ring for you in an hour."

When she was alone she smiled with the delight of victory. The first words had sufficed to let her understand that at last she had received a declaration of love from Mariolle. He had held out much longer than she had thought he was capable of doing, for during the last three months she had been besieging him with such attentions, such display of grace and efforts to charm, as she had never hitherto employed for anyone. He had seemed to be distrustful and on his guard against her, against the bait of insatiable coquetry that she was continually dangling before his eyes.

It had required many a confidential conversation, into which she had thrown all the physical seduction of her being and all the captivating efforts of her mind, many an evening of music as well, when, seated before the piano that was ringing still, before the leaves of the scores that were full of the soul of the tuneful masters, they had both thrilled with the same emotion, before she at last beheld in his eyes that avowal of the vanquished man, the mendicant supplication of a love that can no longer be concealed. She knew all this so well, the rouée! Many and many a time, with feline cunning and inexhaustible curiosity, she had made this secret, torturing plea rise to the eyes of the men whom she had succeeded in beguiling. It afforded her so much amusement to feel that she was gaining them, little by little, that they were conquered, subjugated by her invincible woman's might, that she was for them the Only One, the sovereign Idol whose caprices must be obeyed.

It had all grown up within her almost imperceptibly, like the development of a hidden instinct, the instinct of war and conquest. Perhaps it was that a desire of retaliation had germinated in her heart during her years of married life, a dim longing to repay to men generally that measure of ill which she had received from one of them, to be in turn the strongest, to make stubborn wills bend before her, to crush resistance and to make others, as well as she, feel the keen edge of suffering. Above all else, however, she was a born coquette, and as soon as her way in life was clear before her she applied herself to pursuing and subjugating lovers, just as the hunter pursues the game, with no other end in view than the pleasure of seeing them fall before her.

And yet her heart was not eager for emotion, like that of a tender and sentimental woman; she did not seek a man's undivided love, nor did she look for happiness in passion. All that she needed was universal admiration, homage, prostrations, an incense-offering of tenderness. Whoever frequented her house had also to become the slave of her beauty, and no consideration of mere intellect could attach her for any length of time to those who would not yield to her coquetry, disdainful of the anxieties of love, their affections, perhaps, being placed elsewhere.

In order to retain her friendship it was indispensable to love her, but that point once reached she was infinitely nice, with unimaginable kindnesses and delightful attentions, designed to retain at her side those whom she had captivated. Those who were once enlisted in her regiment of adorers seemed to become her property by right of conquest. She ruled them with great skill and wisdom, according to their qualities and their defects and the nature of their jealousy. Those who sought to obtain too much she expelled forthwith, taking them back again afterward when they had become wiser, but imposing severe conditions. And to such an extent did this game of bewitchment amuse her, perverse woman that she was, that she found it as pleasurable to befool steady old gentlemen as to turn the heads of the young.

It might even have been said that she regulated her affection by the fervency of the ardor that she had inspired, and that big Fresnel, a dull, heavy companion who was of no imaginable benefit to her, retained her favor thanks to the mad passion by which she felt that he was possessed. She was not entirely indifferent to men's merits, either, and more than once had been conscious of the commencement of a liking that no one divined except herself, and which she quickly ended the moment it became dangerous.

Everyone who had approached her for the first time and warbled in her ear the fresh notes of his hymn of gallantry, disclosing to her the unknown quantity of his nature — artists more especially, who seemed to her to possess more subtile and more delicate shades of refined emotion — had for a time disquieted her, had awakened in her the intermittent dream of a grand passion and a long liaison. But swayed by prudent fears, irresolute, driven this way and that by her distrustful nature, she had always kept a strict watch upon herself until the moment she ceased to feel the influence of the latest lover.

And then she had the sceptical vision of the girl of the period, who would strip the greatest man of his prestige in the course of a few weeks. As soon as they were fully in her toils, and in the disorder of their heart had thrown aside their theatrical posturings and their parade manners, they were all alike in her eyes, poor creatures whom she could tyrannize over with her seductive powers. Finally, for a woman like her, perfect as she was, to attach herself to a man, what inestimable merits he would have had to possess!

She suffered much from ennui, however, and was without fondness for society, which she frequented for the sake of appearances, and the long, tedious evenings of which she endured with heavy eyelids and many a stifled yawn. She was amused only by its refined trivialities, by her own caprices and by her quickly changing curiosity for certain persons and certain things, attaching herself to it in such degree as to realize that she had been appreciated or admired and not enough to receive real pleasure from an affection or a liking — suffering from her nerves and not from her desires. She was without the absorbing preoccupations of ardent or simple souls, and passed her days in an ennui of gaieties, destitute of the simple faith that attends on happiness, constantly on the lookout for something to make the slow hours pass more quickly, and sinking with lassitude, while deeming herself contented.

She thought that she was contented because she was the most seductive and the most sought after of women. Proud of her attractiveness, the power of which she often made trial, in love with her own irregular, odd, and captivating beauty, convinced of the delicacy of her perceptions, which allowed her to divine and understand a thousand things that others were incapable of seeing, rejoicing in the wit that had been appreciated by so many superior men, and totally ignoring the limitations that bounded her intelligence, she looked upon herself as an almost unique being, a rare pearl set in the midst of this common, workaday world, which seemed to her slightly empty and monotonous because she was too good for it.

Not for an instant would she have suspected that in her unconscious self lay the cause of the melancholy from which she suffered so continuously. She laid the blame upon others and held them responsible for her ennui. If they were unable sufficiently to entertain and amuse or even impassion her, the reason was that they were deficient in agreeableness and possessed no real merit in her eyes. "Everyone," she would say with a little laugh, "is tiresome. The only endurable people are those who afford me pleasure, and that solely because they do afford me pleasure."

And the surest way of pleasing her was to tell her that there was no one like her. She was well aware that no success is attained without labor, and so she gave herself up, heart and soul, to her work of enticement, and found nothing that gave her greater enjoyment than to note the homage of the softening glance and of the heart, that unruly organ which she could cause to beat violently by the utterance of a word.

She had been greatly surprised by the trouble that she had had in subjugating André Mariolle, for she had been well aware, from the very first day, that she had found favor in his eyes. Then, little by little, she had fathomed his suspicious, secretly envious, extremely subtile, and concentrated disposition, and attacking him on his weak side, she had shown him so many attentions, had manifested such preference and natural sympathy for him, that he had finally surrendered.

Especially in the last month had she felt that he was her captive; he was agitated in her presence, now taciturn, now feverishly animated, but would make no avowal. Oh, avowals! She really did not care very much for them, for when they were too direct, too expressive, she found herself obliged to resort to severe measures. Twice she had even had to make a show of being angry and close her door to the offender. What she adored were delicate manifestations, semi-confidences, discreet allusions, a sort of moral getting-down-on-the-marrow-bones; and she really showed exceptional tact and address in extorting from her admirers this moderation in their expressions.

For a month past she had been watching and waiting to hear fall from Mariolle's lips the words, distinct or veiled, according to the nature of the man, which afford relief to the over-burdened heart.

He had said nothing, but he had written. It was a long letter: four pages! A thrill of satisfaction crept over her as she held it in her hands. She stretched herself at length upon her lounge so as to be more comfortable and kicked the little slippers from off her feet upon the carpet; then she proceeded to read. She met with a surprise. In serious terms he told her that he did not desire to suffer at her hands, and that he already knew her too well to consent to be her victim. With many compliments, in very polite words, which everywhere gave evidence of his repressed love, he let her know that he was apprised of her manner of treating men — that he, too, was in the toils, but that he would release himself from the servitude by taking himself off. He would just simply begin his vagabond life of other days over again. He would leave the country. It was a farewell, an eloquent and firm farewell.

Certainly it was a surprise as she read, re-read, and commenced to read again these four pages of prose that were so full of tender irritation and passion. She arose, put on her slippers, and began to walk up and down the room, her bare arms out of her turned-back sleeves, her hands thrust halfway into the little pockets of her dressing-gown, one of them holding the crumpled letter.

Taken all aback by this unforeseen declaration, she said to herself: "He writes very well, very well indeed; he is sincere, feeling, touching. He writes better than Lamarthe; there is nothing of the novel sticking out of his letter."

She felt like smoking, went to the table where the perfumes were and took a cigarette from a box of Dresden china; then, having lighted it, she approached the great mirror in which she saw three young women coming toward her in the three diversely inclined panels. When she was quite near she halted, made herself a little bow with a little smile, a friendly little nod of the head, as if to say: "Very pretty, very pretty." She inspected her eyes, looked at her teeth, raised her arms, placed her hands on her hips and turned her profile so as to behold her entire person in the three mirrors, bending her head slightly forward. She stood there amorously facing herself surrounded by the threefold reflection of her own being, which she thought was charming, filled with delight at sight of herself, engrossed by an egotistical and physical pleasure in presence of her own beauty, and enjoying it with a keen satisfaction that was almost as sensual as a man's.

Every day she surveyed herself in this manner, and her maid, who had often caught her at it, used to say, spitefully:

"Madame looks at herself so much that she will end up by wearing out all the looking-glasses in the house."

In this love of herself, however, lay all the secret of her charm and the influence that she exerted over men. Through admiring herself and tenderly loving the delicacy of her features and the elegance of her form, by constantly seeking for and finding means of showing them to the greatest advantage, through discovering imperceptible ways of rendering her gracefulness more graceful and her eyes more fascinating, through pursuing all the artifices that embellished her to her own vision, she had as a matter of course hit upon that which would most please others. Had she been more beautiful and careless of her beauty, she would not have possessed that attractiveness which drew to her everyone who had not from the beginning shown himself unassailable.

Wearying soon a little of standing thus, she spoke to her image that was smiling to her still, and her image in the threefold mirror moved its lips as if to echo: "We will see about it." Then she crossed the room and seated herself at her desk. Here is what she wrote:

"Dear Monsieur Mariolle: Come to see me tomorrow at four o'clock. I shall be alone, and hope to be able to reassure you as to the imaginary danger that alarms you.

"I subscribe myself your friend, and will prove to you that I am — — Michèle de Burne."

How plainly she dressed next day to receive André Mariolle's visit! A little gray dress, of a light gray bordering on lilac, melancholy as the dying day and quite unornamented, with a collar fitting closely to the neck, sleeves fitting closely to the arms, corsage fitting closely to the waist and bust, and skirt fitting closely to the hips and legs.

When he made his appearance, wearing rather a solemn face, she came forward to meet him, extending both her hands. He kissed them, then they seated themselves, and she allowed the silence to last a few moments in order to assure herself of his embarrassment.

He did not know what to say, and was waiting for her to speak. She made up her mind to do so.

"Well! let us come at once to the main question. What is the matter? Are you aware that you wrote me a very insolent letter?"

"I am very well aware of it, and I render my most sincere apology. I am, I have always been with everyone, excessively, brutally frank. I might have gone away without the unnecessary and insulting explanations that I addressed to you. I considered it more loyal to act in accordance with my nature and trust to your understanding, with which I am acquainted."

She resumed with an expression of pitying satisfaction:

"Come, come! What does all this folly mean?" He interrupted her: "I would prefer not to speak of it."

She answered warmly, without allowing him to proceed further:

"I invited you here to discuss it, and we will discuss it until you are quite convinced that you are not exposing yourself to any danger." She laughed like a little girl, and her dress, so closely resembling that of a boarding-school miss, gave her laughter a character of childish youth.

He hesitatingly said: "What I wrote you was the truth, the sincere truth, the terrifying truth." Resuming her seriousness, she rejoined: "I do not doubt you: all my friends travel that road. You also wrote that I am a fearful coquette. I admit it, but then no one ever dies of it; I do not even believe that they suffer a great deal. There is, indeed, what Lamarthe calls the crisis. You are in that stage now, but that passes over and subsides into — what shall I call it? — into the state of chronic love, which does no harm to a body, and which I keep simmering over a slow fire in all my friends, so that they may be very much attached, very devoted, very faithful to me. Am not I, also, sincere and frank and nice with you? Eh? Have you known many women who would dare to talk as I have talked to you?"

She had an air of such drollness, coupled with such decision, she was so unaffected and at the same time so alluring, that he could not help smiling in turn. "All your friends," he said, "are men who have often had their fingers burned in that fire, even before it was done at your hearth. Toasted and roasted already, it is easy for them to endure the oven in which you keep them; but for my part, I, Madame, have never passed through that experience, and I have felt for some time past that it would be a dreadful thing for me to give way to the sentiment that is growing and waxing in my heart."

Suddenly she became familiar, and bending a little toward him, her hands clasped over her knees: "Lister to me," she said, "I am in earnest. I hate to lose; friend for the sake of a fear that I regard as chimerical. You will be in love with me, perhaps, but the men of this generation do not love the women of to-day so violently as to do themselves any actual injury. You may believe me; I know them both." She was silent; then with the singular smile of a woman who utters a truth while she thinks she is telling a fib, she added: "Besides, I have not the necessary qualifications to make men love me madly; I am too modern. Come, I will be a friend to you, a real nice friend, for whom you will have affection, but nothing more, for I will see to it." She went on in a more serious tone: "In any case I give you fair warning that I am incapable of feeling a real passion for anyone, let him be who he may; you shall receive the same treatment as the others, you shall stand on an equal footing with the most favored, but never on any better; I abominate despotism and jealousy. I have had to endure everything from a husband, but from a friend, a simple friend, I do not choose to accept affectionate tyrannizings, which are the bane of all cordial relations. You see that I am just as nice as nice can be, that I talk to you like a comrade, that I conceal nothing from you. Are you willing loyally to accept the trial that I propose? If it does not work well, there will still be time enough for you to go away if the gravity of the situation demands it. A lover absent is a lover cured."

He looked at her, already vanquished by her voice, her gestures, all the intoxication of her person; and quite resigned to his fate, and thrilling through every fiber at the consciousness that she was sitting there beside him, he murmured:

"I accept, Madame, and if harm comes to me, so much the worse! I can afford to endure a little suffering for your sake."

She stopped him.

"Now let us say nothing more about it," she said; "let us never speak of it again." And she diverted the conversation to topics that might calm his agitation.

In an hour's time he took his leave; in torments, for he loved her; delighted, for she had asked and he had promised that he would not go away.

III

HE WAS in torments, for he loved her. Differing in this from the common run of lovers, in whose eyes the woman chosen of their heart appears surrounded by an aureole of perfection, his attachment for her had grown within him while studying her with the clairvoyant eyes of a suspicious and distrustful man who had never been entirely enslaved. His timid and sluggish but penetrating disposition, always standing on the defensive in life, had saved him from his passions. A few intrigues, two brief liaisons that had perished of ennui, and some mercenary loves that had been broken off from disgust, comprised the history of his heart. He regarded women as an object of utility for those who desire a well-kept house and a family, as an object of comparative pleasure to those who are in quest of the pastime of love.

Before he entered Mme de Burne's house his friends had confidentially warned him against her.

What he had learned of her interested, puzzled, and pleased him, but it was also rather distasteful to him. As a matter of principle he did not like those gamblers who never pay when they lose. After their first few meetings he had decided that she was very amusing, and that she possessed a special charm that had a contagion in it. The natural and artificial beauties of this charming, slender, blond person, who was neither fat nor lean, who was furnished with beautiful arms that seemed formed to attract and embrace, and with legs that one might imagine long and tapering, calculated for flight, like those of a gazelle, with feet so small that they would leave no trace, seemed to him to be a symbol of hopes that could never be realized.

He had experienced, moreover, in his conversation with her a pleasure that he had never thought of meeting with in the intercourse of fashionable society. Gifted with a wit that was full of familiar animation, unforeseen and mocking and of a caressing irony, she would, notwithstanding this, sometimes allow herself to be carried away by sentimental or intellectual influences, as if beneath her derisive gaiety there still lingered the secular shade of poetic tenderness drawn from some remote ancestress. These things combined to render her exquisite.

She petted him and made much of him, desirous of conquering him as she had conquered the others, and he visited her house as often as he could, drawn thither by his increasing need of seeing more of her. It was like a force emanating from her and taking possession of him, a force that lay in her charm, her look, her smile, her speech, a force that there was no resisting, although he frequently left her house provoked at something that she had said or done.

The more he felt working on him that indescribable influence with which a woman penetrates and subjugates us, the more clearly did he see through her, the more did he understand and suffer from her nature, which he devoutly wished was different. It was certainly true, however, that the very qualities which he disapproved of in her were the qualities that had drawn him toward her and captivated him, in spite of himself, in spite of his reason, and more, perhaps, than her real merits.

Her coquetry, with which she toyed, making no attempt at concealing it, as with a fan, open-ing and folding it in presence of everybody according as the men to whom she was talking were pleasing to her or the reverse; her way of taking nothing in earnest, which had seemed droll to him upon their first acquaintance, but now seemed threatening; her constant desire for distrac-tion, for novelty, which rested insatiable in her heart, always weary — all these things would so exasperate him that sometimes upon returning to his house he would resolve to make his visits to her more infrequent until such time as he might do away with them altogether. The very next day he would invent some pretext for going to see her. What he thought to impress upon himself, as he became more and more enamored, was the insecurity of this love and the certainty that he would have to suffer for it.

He was not blind; little by little he yielded to this sentiment, as a man drowns because his vessel has gone down under him and he is too far from the shore. He knew her as well as it was possible to know her, for his passion had served to make his mental vision abnormally clairvoy-ant, and he could not prevent his thoughts from going into indefinite speculations concerning her. With indefatigable perseverance, he was continually seeking to analyze and understand the obscure depths of this feminine soul, this incomprehensible mixture of bright intelligence and disenchantment, of sober reason and childish triviality, of apparent affection and fickleness, of all those ill-assorted inclinations that can be brought together and co-ordinated to form an unnatural, perplexing, and seductive being.

But why was it that she attracted him thus? He constantly asked himself this question, and was unable to find a satisfactory answer to it, for, with his reflective, observing, and proudly retiring nature, his logical course would have been to look in a woman for those old-fashioned and soothing attributes of tenderness and constancy which seem to offer the most reliable as-surance of happiness to a man. In her, however, he had encountered something that he had not expected to find, a sort of early vegetable of the human race, as it were, one of those creatures who are the beginning of a new generation, exciting one by their strange novelty, unlike any-thing that one has ever known before, and even in their imperfections awakening the dormant senses by a formidable power of attraction.

To the romantic and dreamily passionate women of the Restoration had succeeded the gay triflers of the imperial epoch, convinced that pleasure is a reality; and now, here there was afforded him a new development of this everlasting femininity, a woman of refinement, of in-determinate sensibility, restless, without fixed resolves, her feelings in constant turmoil, who seemed to have made it part of her experience to employ every narcotic that quiets the aching nerves: chloroform that stupefies, ether and morphine that excite to abnormal reverie, kill the senses, and deaden the emotions.

He relished in her that flavor of an artificial nature, the sole object of whose existence was to charm and allure. She was a rare and attractive bauble, exquisite and delicate, drawing men's eyes to her, causing the heart to throb, and desire to awake, as one's appetite is excited when he looks through the glass of the shop-window and beholds the dainty viands that have been prepared and arranged for the purpose of making him hunger for them.

When he was quite assured that he had started on his perilous descent toward the bottom of the gulf, he began to reflect with consternation upon the dangers of his infatuation. What would happen him? What would she do with him? Most assuredly she would do with him what she had done with everyone else: she would bring him to the point where a man follows a woman's capricious fancies as a dog follows his master's steps, and she would classify him among her collection of more or less illustrious favorites. Had she really played this game with all the others? Was there not one, not a single one, whom she had loved, if only for a month, a day, an hour, in one of those effusions of feeling that she had the faculty of repressing so readily? He talked with them interminably about her as they came forth, from her dinners, warmed by contact with her. He felt that they were all uneasy, dissatisfied, unstrung, like men whose dreams have failed of realization.

No, she had loved no one among these paraders before public curiosity. But he, who was a nullity in comparison with them, he, to whom it was not granted that heads should turn and wondering eyes be fixed on him when his name was mentioned in a crowd or in a salon, — what would he be for her? Nothing, nothing; a mere supernumerary upon her scene, a Monsieur, the sort of man that becomes a familiar, commonplace attendant upon a distinguished woman, useful to hold her bouquet, a man comparable to the common grade of wine that one drinks with water. Had he been a famous man he might have been willing to accept this rôle, which his celebrity would have made less humiliating; but unknown as he was, he would have none of it. So he wrote to bid her farewell.

When he received her brief answer he was moved by it as by the intelligence of some unexpected piece of good fortune, and when she had made him promise that he would not go away he was as delighted as a schoolboy released for a holiday.

Several days elapsed without bringing any fresh development to their relations, but when the calm that succeeds the storm had passed, he felt his longing for her increasing within him and burning him. He had promised that he would never again speak to her on the forbidden topic, but he had not promised that he would not write, and one night when he could not sleep, when she had taken possession of all his faculties in the restless vigil of his insomnia of love, he seated himself at his table, almost against his will, and set himself to put down his feelings and his sufferings upon fair, white paper. It was not a letter; it was an aggregation of notes, phrases, thoughts, throbs of moral anguish, transmuting themselves into words. It soothed him; it seemed to him to give him a little comfort in his suffering, and lying down upon his bed, he was at last able to obtain some sleep.

Upon awaking the next morning he read over these few pages and decided that they were sufficiently harrowing; then he inclosed and addressed them, kept them by him until evening, and mailed them very late so that she might receive them when she arose. He thought that she would not be alarmed by these innocent sheets of paper. The most timorous of women have an infinite kindness for a letter that speaks to them of a sincere love, and when these letters are written by a trembling hand, with tearful eyes and melancholy face, the power that they exercise over the female heart is unbounded.

He went to her house late that afternoon to see how she would receive him and what she would say to him. He found M. de Pradon there, smoking cigarettes and conversing with his daughter. He would often pass whole hours with her in this way, for his manner toward her was rather that of a gentleman visitor than of a father. She had brought into their relations and their affection a tinge of that homage of love which she bestowed upon herself and exacted from everyone else.

When she beheld Mariolle her face brightened with delight; she shook hands with him warmly and her smile, told him: "You have afforded me much pleasure."

Mariolle was in hopes that the father would go away soon, but M. de Pradon did not budge. Although he knew his daughter thoroughly, and for a long time past had placed the most implicit confidence in her as regarded her relations with men, he always kept an eye on her with a kind of curious, uneasy, somewhat marital attention. He wanted to know what chance of success there might be for this newly discovered friend, who he was, what he amounted to. Would he be a mere bird of passage, like so many others, or a permanent member of their usual circle?

He intrenched himself, therefore, and Mariolle immediately perceived that he was not to be dislodged. The visitor made up his mind accordingly, and even resolved to gain him over if it were possible, considering that his goodwill, or at any rate his neutrality, would be better than his hostility. He exerted himself and was brilliant and amusing, without any of the airs of a sighing lover. She said to herself contentedly: "He is not stupid; he acts his part in the comedy extremely well"; and M. de Pradon thought: "This is a very agreeable man, whose head my daughter does not seem to have turned."

When Mariolle decided that it was time for him to take his leave, he left them both delighted with him.

But he left that house with sorrow in his soul. In the presence of that woman he felt deeply the bondage in which she held him, realizing that it would be vain to knock at that heart, as a man imprisoned fruitlessly beats the iron door with his fist. He was well assured that he was entirely in her power, and he did not try to free himself. Such being the case, and as he could not avoid this fatality, he resolved that he would be patient, tenacious, cunning, dissembling, that he would conquer by address, by the homage that she was so greedy of, by the adoration that intoxicated her, by the voluntary servitude to which he would suffer himself to be reduced.

His letter had pleased her; he would write. He wrote. Almost every night, when he came home, at that hour when the mind, fresh from the influence of the day's occurrences, regards whatever interests or moves it with a sort of abnormally developed hallucination, he would seat himself at his table by his lamp and exalt his imagination by thoughts of her. The poetic germ, that so many indolent men suffer to perish within them from mere slothfulness, grew and throve under this regimen. He infused a feverish ardor into this task of literary tenderness by means of constantly writing the same thing, the same idea, that is, his love, in expressions that were ever renewed by the constantly fresh-springing, daily renewal of his desire. All through the long day he would seek for and find those irresistible words that stream from the brain like fiery sparks, compelled by the overexcited emotions. Thus he would breathe upon the fire of his own heart and kindle it into raging flames, for often love-letters contain more danger for him who writes than for her who receives them.

By keeping himself in this continuous state of effervescence, by heating his blood with words and peopling his brain with one solitary thought, his ideas gradually became confused as to the reality of this woman. He had ceased to entertain the opinion of her that he had first held, and now beheld her only through the medium of his own lyrical phrases, and all that he wrote of her night by night became to his heart so many gospel truths. This daily labor of idealization displayed her to him as in a dream. His former resistance melted away, moreover, in presence of the affection that Mme de Burne undeniably evinced for him. Although no word had passed between them at this time, she certainly showed a preference for him beyond others, and took no pains to conceal it from him. He therefore thought, with a kind of mad hope, that she might finally come to love him.

The fact was that the charm of those letters afforded her a complicated and naïve delight. No one had ever flattered and caressed her in that manner, with such mute reserve. No one had ever had the delicious idea of sending to her bedside, every morning, that feast of sentiment in paper wrapping that her maid presented to her on the little silver salver. And what made it all the dearer in her eyes was that he never mentioned it, that he seemed to be quite unaware of it himself, that when he visited her salon he was the most undemonstrative of her friends, that he never by word or look alluded to those showers of tenderness that he was secretly raining down upon her.

Of course she had had love-letters before that, but they had been pitched in a different key, had been less reserved, more pressing, more like a summons to surrender. For the three months that his "crisis" had lasted Lamarthe had dedicated to her a very nice correspondence from a much-smitten novelist who maunders in a literary way. She kept in her secretary, in a drawer specially allotted to them, these delicate and seductive epistles from a writer who had shown much feeling, who had caressed her with his pen up to the very day when he saw that he had no hope of success.

Mariolle's letters were quite different; they were so strong in their concentrated desire, so deep in the expression of their sincerity, so humble in their submissiveness, breathing a devotion that promised to be lasting, that she received and read them with a delight that no other writings could have afforded her.

It was natural that her friendly feeling for the man should increase under such conditions. She invited him to her house the more frequently because he displayed such entire reserve in his relations toward her, seeming not to have the slightest recollection in conversation with her that he had ever taken up a sheet of paper to tell her of his adoration. Moreover she looked upon the situation as an original one, worthy of being celebrated in a book; and in the depths of her satisfaction in having at her side a being who loved her thus, she experienced a sort of active fermentation of sympathy which caused her to measure him by a standard other than her usual one.

Up to the present time, notwithstanding the vanity of her coquetry she had been conscious of preoccupations that antagonized her in all the hearts that she had laid waste. She had not held undisputed sovereignty over them, she had found in them powerful interests that were entirely dissociated from her. Jealous of music in Massival's case, of literature in Lamarthe's, always jealous of something, discontented that she only obtained partial successes, powerless to drive all before her in the minds of these ambitious men, men of celebrity, or artists to whom their profession was a mistress from whom nobody could part them, she had now for the first time fallen in with one to whom she was all in all. Certainly big Fresnel, and he alone, loved her to the same degree. But then he was big Fresnel. She felt that it had never been granted her to exercise such complete dominion over anyone, and her selfish gratitude for the man who had afforded her this triumph displayed itself in manifestations of tenderness. She had need of him now; she had need of his presence, of his glance, of his subjection, of all this domesticity of love. If he flattered her vanity less than the others did, he flattered more those supreme exactions that sway coquettes body and soul — her pride and her instinct of domination, her strong instinct of feminine repose.

Like an invader she gradually assumed possession of his life by a series of small incursions that every day became more numerous. She got up fetes, theater-parties, and dinners at the restaurant, so that he might be of the party. She dragged him after her with the satisfaction of a conqueror; she could not dispense with his presence, or rather with the state of slavery to which he was reduced. He followed in her train, happy to feel himself thus petted, caressed by her eyes, her voice, by her every caprice, and he lived only in a continuous transport of love and longing that desolated and burned like a wasting fever.

IV

ONE day Mariolle had gone to her house. He was awaiting her, for she had not come in, although she had sent him a telegram to tell him that she wanted to see him that morning. Whenever he was alone in this drawingroom which it gave him such pleasure to enter and where everything was so charming to him, he nevertheless was conscious of an oppression of the heart, a slight feeling of affright and breathlessness that would not allow him to remain seated as long as she was not there. He walked about the room in joyful expectation, dashed by the fear that some unforeseen obstacle might intervene to detain her and cause their interview to go over until next day. His heart gave a hopeful bound when he heard a carriage draw up before the street door, and when the bell of the apartment rang he ceased to doubt.

She came in with her hat on, a thing which she was not accustomed to do, wearing a busy and satisfied look. "I have some news for you," she said.

"What is it, Madame?"

She looked at him and laughed. "Well! I am going to the country for a while."

Her words produced in him a quick, sharp shock of sorrow that was reflected upon his face. "Oh! and you tell me that as if you were glad of it!"

"Yes. Sit down and I will tell you all about it.

I don't know whether you are aware that M. Valsaci, my poor mother's brother, the engineer and bridge-builder, has a country-place at Avranches where he spends a portion of his time with his wife and children, for his business lies mostly in that neighborhood. We pay them a visit every summer. This year I said that I did not care to go, but he was greatly disappointed and made quite a time over it with papa. Speaking of scenes, I will tell you confidentially that papa is jealous of you and makes scenes with me, too; he says that I am entangling myself with you. You will have to come to see me less frequently. But don't let that trouble you; I will arrange matters. So papa gave me a scolding and made me promise to go to Avranches for a visit of ten days, perhaps twelve. We are to start Tuesday morning. What have you got to say about it?"

"I say that it breaks my heart."

"Is that all?"

"What more can I say? There is no way of preventing you from going."

"And nothing presents itself to you?"

"Why, no; I can't say that there does. And you?"

"I have an idea; it is this: Avranches is quite near Mont Saint-Michel. Have you ever been at Mont Saint-Michel?"

"No, Madame."

"Well, something will tell you next Friday that you want to go and see this wonder. You will leave the train at Avranches; on Friday evening at sunset, if you please, you will take a walk in the public garden that overlooks the bay. We will happen to meet there. Papa will grumble, but I don't care for that. I will make up a party to go and see the abbey next day, including all the family. You must be enthusiastic over it, and very charming, as you can be when you choose; be attentive to my aunt and gain her over, and invite us all to dine at the inn where we alight. We will sleep there, and will have all the next day to be together. You will return by way of Saint Malo, and a week later I shall be back in Paris. Isn't that an ingenious scheme? Am I not nice?"

With an outburst of grateful feeling, he murmured: "You are dearer to me than all the world."

"Hush!" said she.

They looked each other for a moment in the face. She smiled, conveying to him in that smile — very sincere and earnest it was, almost tender — all her gratitude, her thanks for his love, and her sympathy as well. He gazed upon her with eyes that seemed to devour her. He had an insane desire to throw himself down and grovel at her feet, to kiss the hem of her robe, to cry aloud and make her see what he knew not how to tell in words, what existed in all his form from head to feet, in every fiber of his body as well as in his heart, paining him inexpressibly because he could not display it — his love, his terrible and delicious love.

There was no need of words, however; she understood him, as the marksman instinctively feels that his ball has penetrated the bull's-eye of the target. Nothing any longer subsisted within this man, nothing, nothing but her image. He was hers more than she herself was her own. She was satisfied, and she thought he was charming.

She said to him, in high good-humor: "Then that is settled; the excursion is agreed on."

He answered in a voice that trembled with emotion: "Why, yes, Madame, it is agreed on."

There was another interval of silence. "I cannot let you stay any longer to-day," she said without further apology. "I only ran in to tell you what I have told you, since I am to start day after tomorrow. All my time will be occupied tomorrow, and I have still half-a-dozen things to attend to before dinnertime."

He arose at once, deeply troubled, for the sole desire of his heart was to be with her always; and having kissed her hands, went his way, sore at heart, but hopeful nevertheless.

The four intervening days were horribly long ones to him. He got through them somehow in Paris without seeing a soul, preferring silence to conversation, and solitude to the company of friends.

On Friday morning, therefore, he boarded the eight-o'clock express. The anticipation of the journey had made him feverish, and he had not slept a wink. The darkness of his room and its silence, broken only by the occasional rattling of some belated cab that served to remind him of his longing to be off, had weighed upon him all night long like a prison.

At the earliest ray of light that showed itself between his drawn curtains, the gray, sad light of early morning, he jumped from his bed, opened the window, and looked at the sky. He had been haunted by the fear that the weather might be unfavorable. It was clear. There was a light floating mist, presaging a warm day. He dressed more quickly than was needful, and in his consuming impatience to get out of doors and at last begin his journey he was ready two hours too soon, and nothing would do but his valet must go out and get a cab lest they should all be gone from the stand. As the vehicle jolted over the stones, its movements were so many shocks of happiness to him, but when he reached the Mont Parnasse station and found that he had fifty minutes to wait before the departure of the train, his spirits fell again.

There was a compartment disengaged; he took it so that he might be alone and give free course to his reveries. When at last he felt himself moving, hurrying along toward her, soothed by the gentle and rapid motion of the train, his eagerness, instead of being appeased, was still further excited, and he felt a desire, the unreasoning desire of a child, to push with all his strength against the partition in front of him, so as to accelerate their speed. For a long time, until midday, he remained in this condition of Waiting expectancy, but when they were past Argentan his eyes were gradually attracted to the window by the fresh verdure of the Norman landscape.

The train was passing through a wide, undulating region, intersected by valleys, where the peasant holdings, mostly in grass and apple-orchards, were shut in by great trees, the thick-leaved tops of which seemed to glow in the sunlight. It was late in July, that lusty season when this land, an abundant nurse, gives generously of its sap and life. In all the inclosures, separated from each other by these leafy walls, great light-colored oxen, cows whose flanks were striped with undefined figures of odd design, huge, red, wide-fronted bulls of proud and quarrelsome aspect, with their hanging dewlaps of hairy flesh, standing by the fences or lying down among the pasturage that stuffed their paunches, succeeded each other, until there seemed to be no end to them in this fresh, fertile land, the soil of which appeared to exude cider and fat sirloins. In every direction little streams were gliding in and out among the poplars, partially concealed by a thin screen of willows; brooks glittered for an instant among the herbage, disappearing only to show themselves again farther on, bathing all the scene in their vivifying coolness. Mariolle was charmed at the sight, and almost forgot his love for a moment in his rapid flight through this far-reaching park of apple-trees and flocks and herds.

When he had changed cars at Folligny station, however, he was again seized with an impatient longing to be at his destination, and during the last forty minutes he took out his watch twenty times. His head was constantly turned toward the window of the car, and at last, situated upon a hill of moderate height, he beheld the city where she was waiting for his coming. The train had been delayed, and now only an hour separated him from the moment when he was to come upon her, by chance, on the public promenade.

He was the only passenger that climbed into the hotel omnibus, which the horses began to drag up the steep road of Avranches with slow and reluctant steps. The houses crowning the heights gave to the place from a distance the appearance of a fortification. Seen close at hand it was an ancient and pretty Norman city, with small dwellings of regular and almost similar appearance built closely adjoining one another, giving an aspect of ancient pride and modern comfort, a feudal yet peasant-like air.

As soon as Mariolle had secured a room and thrown his valise into it, he inquired for the street that led to the Botanical Garden and started off in the direction indicated with rapid strides, although he was ahead of time. But he was in hopes that perhaps she also would be on hand early. When he reached the iron railings, he saw at a glance that the place was empty or nearly so. Only three old men were walking about in it, bourgeois to the manner born, who probably were in the habit of coming there daily to cheer their leisure by conversation, and a family of English children, lean-legged boys and girls, were playing about a fairhaired governess whose wandering looks showed that her thoughts were far away.

Mariolle walked straight ahead with beating heart, looking scrutinizingly up and down the intersecting paths. He came to a great alley of dark green elms which cut the garden in two portions crosswise and stretched away in its center, a dense vault of foliage; he passed through this, and all at once, coming to a terrace that commanded a view of the horizon, his thoughts suddenly ceased to dwell upon her whose influence had brought him hither.

From the foot of the elevation upon which he was standing spread an illimitable sandy plain that stretched away in the distance and blended with sea and sky. Through it rolled a stream, and beneath the azure, aflame with sunlight, pools of water dotted it with luminous sheets that seemed like orifices opening upon another sky beneath. In the midst of this yellow desert, still wet and glistening with the receding tide, at twelve or fifteen kilometers from the shore rose a pointed rock of monumental profile, like some fantastic pyramid, surmounted by a cathedral. Its only neighbor in these immense wastes was a low, round backed reef that the tide had left uncovered, squatting among the shifting ooze: the reef of Tombelaine. Farther still away, other submerged rocks showed their brown heads above the bluish line of the waves, and the eye, continuing to follow the horizon to the right, finally rested upon the vast green expanse of the Norman country lying beside this sandy waste, so densely covered with trees that it had the aspect of a limitless forest. It was all Nature offering herself to his vision at a single glance, in a single spot, in all her might and grandeur, in all her grace and freshness, and the eye turned from those woodland glimpses to the stern apparition of the granite mount, the hermit of the sands, rearing its strange Gothic form upon the far-reaching strand.

The strange pleasure which in other days had often made Mariolle thrill, in the presence of the surprises that unknown lands preserve to delight the eyes of travelers, now took such sudden possession of him that he remained motionless, his feelings softened and deeply moved, oblivious of his tortured heart. At the sound of a striking bell, however, he turned, suddenly repossessed by the eager hope that they were about to meet. The garden was still almost untenanted. The English children had gone; the three old men alone kept up their monotonous promenade. He came down and began to walk about like them.

Immediately — in a moment — she would be there. He would see her at the end of one of those roads that centered in this wondrous terrace. He would recognize her form, her step, then her face and her smile; he would soon be listening to her voice. What happiness! What delight! He felt that she was near him, somewhere, invisible as yet, but thinking of him, knowing that she was soon to see him again.

With difficulty he restrained himself from uttering a little cry. For there, down below, a blue sunshade, just the dome of a sunshade, was visible, gliding along beneath a clump of trees. It must be she; there could be no doubt of it. A little boy came in sight, driving a hoop before him; then two ladies, — he recognized her, — then two men: her father and another gentleman. She was all in blue, like the heavens in springtime. Yes, indeed! he recognized her, while as yet he could not distinguish her features; but he did not dare to go toward her, feeling that he would blush and stammer, that he would be unable to account for this chance meeting beneath M. de Pradon's suspicious glances.

He went forward to meet them, however, keeping his field-glass to his eye, apparently quite intent on scanning the horizon. She it was who addressed him first, not even taking the trouble to affect astonishment.

"Good day, M. Mariolle," she said. "Isn't it splendid?"

He was struck speechless by this reception, and knew not what tone to adopt in reply. Finally he stammered: "Ah, it is you, Madame; how glad I am to meet you! I wanted to see something of this delightful country."

She smiled as she replied: "And you selected the very time when I chanced to be here. That was extremely kind of you." Then she proceeded to make the necessary introductions. "This is M. Mariolle, one of my dearest friends; my aunt, *Mme.* Valsaci; my uncle, who builds bridges."

When salutations had been exchanged, M. de Pradon and the young man shook hands rather stiffly and the walk was continued.

She had made room for him between herself and her aunt, casting upon him a very rapid glance, one of those glances which seem to indicate a weakening determination.

"How do you like the country?" she asked.

"I think that I have never beheld anything more beautiful," he replied.

"Ah! if you had passed some days here, as I have just been doing, you would feel how it penetrates one. The impression that it leaves is beyond the power of expression. The advance and retreat of the sea upon the sands, that grand movement that is going on unceasingly, that twice a day floods all that you behold before you, and so swiftly that a horse galloping at top speed would scarce have time to escape before it — this wondrous spectacle that Heaven gratuitously displays before us, I declare to you that it makes me forgetful of myself. I no longer know myself. Am I not speaking the truth, aunt?"

Mme. Valsaci, an old, gray-haired woman, a lady of distinction in her province and the respected wife of an eminent engineer, a supercilious functionary who could not divest himself of the arrogance of the school, confessed that she had never seen her niece in such a state of enthusiasm. Then she added reflectively: "It is not surprising, however, when, like her, one has never seen any but theatrical scenery."

"But I go to Dieppe and Trouville almost every year."

The old lady began to laugh. "People only go to Dieppe and Trouville to see their friends. The sea is only there to serve as a cloak for their rendezvous." It was very simply said, perhaps without any concealed meaning.

People were streaming along toward the terrace, which seemed to draw them to it with an irresistible attraction. They came from every quarter of the garden, in spite of themselves, like round bodies rolling down a slope. The sinking sun seemed to be drawing a golden tissue of finest texture, transparent and ethereally light, behind the lofty silhouette of the abbey, which was growing darker and darker, like a gigantic shrine relieved against a veil of brightness. Mariolle, however, had eyes for nothing but the adored blond form walking at his side, wrapped in its cloud of blue. Never had he beheld her so seductive. She seemed to him to have changed, without his being able to specify in what the change consisted; she was bright with a brightness he had never seen before, which shone in her eyes and upon her flesh, her hair, and seemed to have penetrated her soul as well, a brightness emanating from this country, this sky, this sunlight, this verdure. Never had he known or loved her thus.

He walked at her side and could find no word to say to her. The rustle of her dress, the occasional touch of her arm, the meeting, so mutely eloquent, of their glances, completely overcame him. He felt as if they had annihilated his personality as a man — felt himself suddenly obliterated by contact with this woman, absorbed by her to such an extent as to be nothing; nothing but desire, nothing but appeal, nothing but adoration. She had consumed his being, as one burns a letter.

She saw it all very clearly, understood the full extent of her victory, and thrilled and deeply moved, feeling life throb within her, too, more keenly among these odors of the country and the sea, full of sunlight and of sap, she said to him: "I am so glad to see you!" Close upon this, she asked: "How long do you remain here?"

He replied: "Two days, if to-day counts for a day." Then, turning to the aunt: "Would *Mme.* Valsaci do me the honor to come and spend the day tomorrow at Mont Saint-Michel with her husband?"

Mme de Burne made answer for her relative: "I will not allow her to refuse, since we have been so fortunate as to meet you here."

The engineer's wife replied: "Yes, Monsieur, I accept very gladly, upon the condition that you come and dine with me this evening."

He bowed in assent. All at once there arose within him a feeling of delirious delight, such a joy as seizes you when news is brought that the desire of your life is attained. What had come to him? What new occurrence was there in his life? Nothing; and yet he felt himself carried away by the intoxication of an indefinable presentiment.

They walked upon the terrace for a long time, waiting for the sun to set, so as to witness until the very end the spectacle of the black and battlemented mount drawn in outline upon a horizon of flame. Their conversation now was upon ordinary topics, such as might be discussed in presence of a stranger, and from time to time Mme de Burne and Mariolle glanced at each other. Then they all returned to the villa, which stood just outside Avranches in a fine garden, overlooking the bay.

Wishing to be prudent, and a little disturbed, moreover, by M. de Pradon's cold and almost hostile attitude toward him, Mariolle withdrew at an early hour. When he took Mme de Burne's hand to raise it to his lips, she said to him twice in succession, with a peculiar accent: "Till tomorrow! Till tomorrow!"

As soon as he was gone M. and *Mme.* Valsaci, who had long since habituated themselves to country ways, proposed that they should go to bed.

"Go," said Mme de Burne. "I am going to take a walk in the garden."

"So am I," her father added.

She wrapped herself in a shawl and went out, and they began to walk side by side upon the white-sanded alleys which the full moon, streaming over lawn and shrubbery, illuminated as if they had been little winding rivers of silver.

After a silence that had lasted for quite a while, M. de Pradon said in a low voice: "My dear child, you will do me the justice to admit that I have never troubled you with my counsels?"

She felt what was coming, and was prepared to meet his attack. "Pardon me, papa," she said 'but you did give me one, at least."

"I did?"

"Yes, yes."

"A counsel relating to your way of life?"

"Yes; and a very bad one it was, too. And so, if you give me any more, I have made up my mind not to follow them."

"What was the advice that I gave you?"

"You advised me to marry M. de Burne. That goes to show that you are lacking in judgment, in clearness of insight, in acquaintance with mankind in general and with your daughter in particular."

"Yes I made a mistake on that occasion; but I am sure that I am right in the very paternal advice that I feel called upon to give you at the present juncture."

"Let me hear what it is. I will accept as much of it as the circumstances call for."

"You are on the point of entangling yourself." She laughed with a laugh that was rather too hearty, and completing the expression of his idea, said: "With M. Mariolle, doubtless?"

"With M. Mariolle."

"You forget," she rejoined, "the entanglements that I have already had with M. de Maltry, with M. Massival, with M. Gaston de Lamarthe, and a dozen others, of all of whom you have been jealous; for I never fall in with a man who is nice and willing to show a little devotion for me but all my flock flies into a rage, and you first of all, you whom nature has assigned to me as my noble father and general manager."

'No, no, that is not it," he replied with warmth; "you have never compromised your liberty with anyone. On the contrary you show a great deal of tact in your relations with your friends."

"My dear papa, I am no longer a child, and I promise you not to involve myself with M. Mariolle any more than I have done with the rest of them; you need have no fears. I admit, however, that it was at my invitation that he came here. I think that he is delightful, just as intelligent as his predecessors and less egotistical; and you thought so too, up to the time when you imagined that you had discovered that I was showing some small preference for him. Oh, you are not so sharp as you think you are! I know you, and I could say a great deal more on this head if I chose. As M. Mariolle was agreeable to me, then, I thought it would be very nice to make a pleasant excursion in his company, quite by chance, of course. It is a piece of stupidity to deprive ourselves of everything that can amuse us when there is no danger attending it. And I incur no danger of involving myself, since you are here."

She laughed openly as she finished, knowing well that every one of her words had told, that she had tied his tongue by the adroit imputation of a jealousy of Mariolle that she had suspected, that she had instinctively scented in him for a long time past, and she rejoiced over this discovery with a secret, audacious, unutterable coquetry. He maintained an embarrassed and irritated silence, feeling that she had divined some inexplicable spite underlying his paternal solicitude, the origin of which he himself did not care to investigate.

"There is no cause for alarm," she added. "It is quite natural to make an excursion to Mont Saint-Michel at this time of the year in company with you, my father, my uncle and aunt, and a friend. Besides no one will know it; and even if they do, what can they say against it? When we are back in Paris I will reduce this friend to the ranks again, to keep company with the others."

"Very well," he replied. "Let it be as if I had said nothing."

They took a few steps more; then M. de Pradon asked:

"Shall we return to the house? I am tired; I am going to bed."

"No; the night is so fine. I am going to walk awhile yet."

He murmured meaningly: "Do not go far away. One never knows what people may be around."

"Oh, I will be right here under the windows."

"Good night, then, my dear child."

He gave her a hasty kiss upon the forehead and went in. She took a seat a little way off upon a rustic bench that was set in the ground at the foot of a great oak. The night was warm, filled with odors from the fields and exhalations from the sea and misty light, for beneath the full moon shining brightly in the cloudless sky a fog had come up and covered the waters of the bay. Onward it slowly crept, like white smoke-wreaths, hiding from sight the beach that would soon be covered by the incoming tide.

Michèle de Burne, her hands clasped over her knees and her dreamy eyes gazing into space, sought to look into her heart through a mist that was as impenetrable and pale as that which lay upon the sands. How many times before this, seated before her mirror in her dressing-room at Paris, had she questioned herself:

"What do I love? What do I desire? What do I hope for? What am I?"

Apart from the pleasure of being beautiful, and the imperious necessity which she felt of pleasing, which really afforded her much delight, she had never been conscious of any appeal to her heart beyond some passing fancy that she had quickly put her foot upon. She was not ignorant of herself, for she had devoted too much of her time and attention to watching and studying her face and all her person not to have been observant of her feelings as well. Up to the present time she had contented herself with a vague interest in that which is the subject of emotion in others, but was powerless to impassion her, or capable at best of affording her a momentary distraction.

And yet, whenever she had felt a little warmer liking for anyone arising within her, whenever a rival had tried to take away from her a man whom she valued, and by arousing her feminine instincts had caused an innocuous fever of attachment to simmer gently in her veins, she had discovered that these false starts of love had caused her an emotion that was much deeper than the mere gratification of success. But it never lasted. Why? Perhaps because she was too clear-sighted; because she allowed herself to become wearied, disgusted. Everything that at first had pleased her in a man, everything that had animated, moved, and attracted her, soon appeared in her eyes commonplace and divested of its charm. They all resembled one another too closely, without ever being exactly similar, and none of them had yet presented himself to her endowed with the nature and the merits that were required to hold her liking sufficiently long to guide her heart into the path of love.

Why was this so? Was it their fault or was it hers? Were they wanting in the qualities which she was looking for, or was it she who was deficient in the attribute that makes one loved? Is love the result of meeting with a person whom one believes to have been created expressly for himself, or is it simply the result of having been born with the faculty of loving? At times it seemed to her that everyone's heart must be provided with arms, like the body, loving, outstretching arms to attract, embrace, and enfold, and that her heart had only eyes and nothing more.

Men, superior men, were often known to become madly infatuated with women who were unworthy of them, women without intelligence, without character, often without beauty. Why was this? Wherein lay the mystery? Was such a crisis in the existence of two beings not to be attributed solely to a providential meeting, but to a kind of seed that everyone carries about within him, and that puts forth its buds when least expected? She had been intrusted with confidences, she had surprised secrets, she had even beheld with her own eyes the swift trans-figuration that results from the breaking forth of this intoxication of the feelings, and she had reflected deeply upon it.

In society, in the unintermitting whirl of visiting and amusement, in all the small tomfoo-leries of fashionable existence by which the wealthy beguile their idle hours, a feeling of envious, jealous, and almost incredulous astonishment had sometimes been excited in her at the sight of men and women in whom some extraordinary change had incontestably taken place. The change might not be conspicuously manifest, but her watchful instinct felt it and divined it as the hound holds the scent of his game. Their faces, their smiles, their eyes especially would betray something that was beyond expression in words, an ecstasy, a delicious, serene delight, a joy of the soul made manifest in the body, illuming look and flesh.

Without being able to account for it she was displeased with them for this. Lovers had always been disagreeable objects to her, and she imagined that the deep and secret feeling of irritation inspired in her by the sight of people whose hearts were swayed by passion was simply disdain. She believed that she could recognize them with a readiness and an accuracy that were exceptional, and it was a fact that she had often divined and unraveled liaisons before society had even suspected their existence.

When she reflected upon all this, upon the fond folly that may be induced in woman by the contact of some neighboring existence, his aspect, his speech, his thought, the inexpress-ible something in the loved being that robs the heart of tranquillity, she decided that she was incapable of it. And yet, weary of everything, oppressed by ineffable yearnings, tormented by a haunting longing after change and some unknown state, feelings which were, perhaps, only the undeveloped movements of an undefined groping after affection, how often had she desired, with a secret shame that had its origin in her pride, to meet with a man, who, for a time, were it only for a few months, might by his sorceries raise her to an abnormally excited condition of mind and body — for it seemed to her that life must assume strange and attractive forms of ecstasy and delight during these emotional periods. Not only had she desired such an encounter, but she had even sought it a little — only a very little, however — with an indolent activity that never devoted itself for any length of time to one pursuit.

In all her inchoate attachments for the men called "superior," who had dazzled her for a few weeks, the short-lived effervescence of her heart had always died away in irremediable disap-pointment. She looked for too much from their dispositions, their characters, their delicacy, their renown, their merits. In the case of everyone of them she had been compelled to open her eyes to the fact that the defects of great men are often more prominent than their merits; that talent is a special gift, like a good digestion or good eyesight, an isolated gift to be exercised, and unconnected with the aggregate of personal charm that makes one's relations cordial and attractive.

Since she had known Mariolle, however, she was otherwise attached to him. But did she love him, did she love him with the love of woman for man? Without fame or prestige, he had conquered her affections by his devotedness, his tenderness, his intelligence, by all the real and unassuming attractions of his personality. He had conquered, for he was constantly present in her thoughts; unremittingly she longed for his society; in all the world there was no one more agreeable, more sympathetic, more indispensable to her. Could this be love?

She was not conscious of carrying in her soul that divine flame that everyone speaks of, but for the first time she was conscious of the existence there of a sincere wish to be something more to this man than merely a charming friend. Did she love him? Does love demand that a man appear endowed with exceptional attractions, that he be different from all the world and tower above it in the aureole that the heart places about its elect, or does it suffice that he find favor in your eyes, that he please you to that extent that you scarce know how to do without him?

In the latter event she loved him, or at any rate she was very near loving him. After having pondered deeply on the matter with concentrated attention, she at length answered herself: "Yes, I love him, but I am lacking in warmth; that is the defect of my nature."

Still, she had felt some warmth a little while before when she saw him coming toward her upon the terrace in the garden of Avranches. For the first time she had felt that inexpressible something that bears us, impels us, hurries us toward some one; she had experienced great pleasure in walking at his side, in having him near her, burning with love for her, as they watched the sun sinking behind the shadow of Mont Saint-Michel, like a vision in a legend. Was not love itself a kind of legend of the soul, in which some believe through instinct, and in which others sometimes also come to believe through stress of pondering over it? Would she end by believing in it? She had felt a strange, half-formed desire to recline her head upon the shoulder of this man, to be nearer to him, to seek that closer union that is never found, to give him what one offers vainly and always retains: the close intimacy with one's inner self.

Yes, she had experienced a feeling of warmth toward him, and she still felt it there at the bottom of her heart, at that very moment. Perhaps it would change to passion should she give way to it. She opposed too much resistance to men's powers of attraction; she reasoned on them, combated them too much. How sweet it would be to walk with him on an evening like this along the river-bank beneath the willows, and allow him to taste her lips from time to time in recompense of all the love he had given her!

A window in the villa was flung open. She turned her head. It was her father, who was doubtless looking to see if she were there. She called to him: "You are not asleep yet?"

He replied: "If you don't come in you will take cold."

She arose thereupon and went toward the house. When she was in her room she raised her curtains for another look at the mist over the bay, which was becoming whiter and whiter in the moonlight, and it seemed to her that the vapors in her heart were also clearing under the influence of her dawning tenderness.

For all that she slept soundly, and her maid had to awake her in the morning, for they were to make an early start, so as to have breakfast at the Mount.

A roomy wagonette drew up before the door. When she heard the rolling of the wheels upon the sand she went to her window and looked out, and the first thing that her eyes encountered was the face of André Mariolle who was looking for her. Her heart began to beat a little more rapidly. She was astonished and dejected as she reflected upon the strange and novel impression produced by this muscle, which palpitates and hurries the blood through the veins merely at the sight of some one. Again she asked herself, as she had done the previous night before going to sleep: "Can it be that I am about to love him?" Then when she was seated face to face with him her instinct told her how deeply he was smitten, how he was suffering with his love, and she felt as if she could open her arms to him and put up her mouth. They only exchanged a look, however, but it made him turn pale with delight.

The carriage rolled away. It was a bright summer morning; the air was filled with the melody of birds and everything seemed permeated by the spirit of youth. They descended the hill, crossed the river, and drove along a narrow, rough, stony road that set the travelers bumping upon their seats. Mme de Burne began to banter her uncle upon the condition of this road; that was enough to break the ice, and the brightness that pervaded the air seemed to be infused into the spirit of them all.

As they emerged from a little hamlet the bay suddenly presented itself again before them, not yellow as they had seen it the evening before, but sparkling with clear water which covered everything, sands, salt-meadows, and, as the coachman said, even the very road itself a little way further on. Then, for the space of an hour they allowed the horses to proceed at a walk, so as to give this inundation time to return to the deep.

The belts of elms and oaks that inclosed the farms among which they were now passing momentarily hid from their vision the profile of the abbey standing high upon its rock, now entirely surrounded by the sea; then all at once it was visible again between two farmyards, nearer, more huge, more astounding than ever. The sun cast ruddy tones upon the old crenelated granite church, perched on its rocky pedestal. Michèle de Burne and André Mariolle contemplated it, both mingling with the newborn or acutely sensitive disturbances of their hearts the poetry of the vision that greeted their eyes upon this rosy July morning.

The talk went on with easy friendliness. *Mme.* Valsaci told tragic tales of the coast, nocturnal dramas of the yielding sands devouring human life. M. Valsaci took up arms for the dike, so much abused by artists, and extolled it for the uninterrupted communication that it afforded with the Mount and for the reclaimed sand-hills, available at first for pasturage and afterward for cultivation.

Suddenly the wagonette came to a halt; the sea had invaded the road. It did not amount to much, only a film of water upon the stony way, but they knew that there might be sink-holes beneath, openings from which they might never emerge, so they had to wait. "It will go down very quickly," M. Valsaci declared, and he pointed with his finger to the road from which the thin sheet of water was already receding, seemingly absorbed by the earth or drawn away to some distant place by a powerful and mysterious force.

They got down from the carriage for a nearer look at this strange, swift, silent flight of tne sea, and followed it step by step. Now spots of green began to appear among the submerged vegetation, lightly stirred by the waves here and there, and these spots broadened, rounded themselves out and became islands. Quickly these islands assumed the appearance of continents, separated from each other by miniature oceans, and finally over the whole expanse of the bay it was a headlong flight of the waters retreating to their distant abode. It resembled nothing so much as a long silvery veil withdrawn from the surface of the earth, a great, torn, slashed veil, full of rents, which left exposed the wide meadows of short grass as it was pulled aside, but did not yet disclose the yellow sands that lay beyond.

They had climbed into the carriage again, and everyone was standing in order to obtain a better view. The road in front of them was drying and the horses were sent forward, but still at a walk, and as the rough places sometimes caused them to lose their equilibrium, André Mariolle suddenly felt Michèle de Burne's shoulder resting against his. At first he attributed this contact to the movement of the vehicle, but she did not stir from her position, and at every jolt of the wheels' a trembling started from the spot where she had placed herself and shook all his frame and laid waste his heart. He did not venture to look at the young woman, paralyzed as he was by this unhoped-for familiarity, and with a confusion in his brain such as arises from drunkenness, he said to himself: "Is this real? Can it be possible? Can it be that we are both losing our senses?"

The horses began to trot and they had to resume their seats. Then Mariolle felt some sudden, mysterious imperious necessity of showing himself attentive to M. de Pradon, and he began to devote himself to him with flattering courtesy. Almost as sensible to compliments as his daughter, the father allowed himself to be won over and soon his face was all smiles.

At last they had reached the causeway and were advancing rapidly toward the Mount, which reared its head among the sands at the point where the long, straight road ended. Pontorson river washed its left-hand slope, while, to the right, the pastures covered with short grass, which the coachman wrongly called "samphire," had given way to sand-hills that were still trickling with the water of the sea. The lofty monument now assumed more imposing dimensions upon the blue heavens, against which, very clear and distinct now in every slightest detail, its summit stood out in bold relief, with all its towers and belfries, bristling with grimacing gargoyles, heads of monstrous beings with which the faith and the terrors of our ancestors crowned their Gothic sanctuaries.

It was nearly one o'clock when they reached the inn, where breakfast had been ordered. The hostess had delayed the meal for prudential reasons; it was not ready. It was late, therefore, when they sat down at table and everyone was very hungry. Soon, however, the champagne restored their spirits. Everyone was in good humor, and there were two hearts that felt that they were on the verge of great happiness. At dessert, when the cheering effect of the wine that they had drunk and the pleasures of conversation had developed in their frames the feeling of well-being and contentment that sometimes warms us after a good meal, and inclines us to take a rosy view of everything, Mariolle suggested: "What do you say to staying over here until tomorrow? It would be so nice to look upon this scene by moonlight, and so pleasant to dine here together this evening!"

Mme de Burne gave her assent at once, and the two men also concurred. *Mme.* Valsaci alone hesitated, on account of the little boy that she had left at home, but her husband reassured her and reminded her that she had frequently remained away before; he at once sat down and dispatched a telegram to the governess. André Mariolle had flattered him by giving his approval to the causeway, expressing his judgment that it detracted far less than was generally reported from the picturesque effect of the Mount, thereby making himself persona grata to the engineer.

Upon rising from table they went to visit the monument, taking the road of the ramparts. The city, a collection of old houses dating back to the Middle Ages and rising in tiers one above the other upon the enormous mass of granite that is crowned by the abbey, is separated from the sands by a lofty crenelated wall. This wall winds about the city in its ascent with many a twist and turn, with abrupt angles and elbows and platforms and watchtowers, all forming so many surprises for the eye, which, at every turn, rests upon some new expanse of the far-reaching horizon. They were silent, for whether they had seen this marvelous edifice before or not, they were equally impressed by it, and the substantial breakfast that they had eaten, moreover, had made them short-winded. There it rose above them in the sky, a wondrous tangle of granite ornamentation, spires, belfries, arches thrown from one tower to another, a huge, light, fairylike lacework in stone, embroidered upon the azure of the heavens, from which the fantastic and bestial-faced array of gargoyles seemed to be preparing to detach themselves and wing their flight away. Upon the northern flank of the Mount, between the abbey and the sea, a wild and almost perpendicular descent that is called the Forest, because it is covered with ancient trees, began where the houses ended and formed a speck of dark green coloring upon the limitless expanse of yellow sands. Mme de Burne and Mariolle, who headed the little procession, stopped to enjoy the view. She leaned upon his arm, her senses steeped in a rapture such as she had never known before. With light steps she pursued her upward way, willing to keep on climbing forever in his company toward this fabric of a vision, or indeed toward any other end. She would have been glad that the steep way should never have an ending, for almost for the first time in her life she knew what it was to experience a plenitude of satisfaction.

"Heavens! how beautiful it is!" she murmured. Looking upon her, he answered: "I can think only of you."

She continued, with a smile: "I am not inclined to be very poetical, as a general thing, but this seems to me so beautiful that I am really moved."

He stammered: "I — I love you to distraction." He was conscious of a slight pressure of her arm, and they resumed the ascent.

They found a keeper awaiting them at the door of the abbey, and they entered by that superb staircase, between two massive towers, which leads to the Hall of the Guards. Then they went from hall to hall, from court to court, from dungeon to dungeon, listening, wondering, charmed with everything, admiring everything, the crypt, with its huge pillars, so beautiful in their massiveness, which sustains upon its sturdy arches all the weight of the choir of the church above, and all of the Wonder, an awe-inspiring edifice of three stories of Gothic monuments rising one above the other, the most extraordinary masterpiece of the monastic and military architecture of the Middle Ages.

Then they came to the cloisters. Their surprise was so great that they involuntarily came to a halt at sight of this square court inclosing the lightest, most graceful, most charming of colonnades to be seen in any cloisters in the world. For the entire length of the four galleries the slender shafts in double rows, surmounted by exquisite capitals, sustain a continuous garland of flowers and Gothic ornamentation of infinite variety and constantly changing design, the elegant and unaffected fancies of the simple-minded old artists who thus worked out their dreams in stone beneath the hammer.

Michèle de Burne and André Mariolle walked completely around the inclosure, very slowly, arm in arm, while the others, somewhat fatigued, stood near the door and admired from a distance.

"Heavens! what pleasure this affords me!" she said, coming to a stop.

"For my part, I neither know where I am nor what my eyes behold. I am conscious that you are at my side, and that is all."

Then smiling, she looked him in the face and murmured: "André!"

He saw that she was yielding. No further word was spoken, and they resumed their walk. The inspection of the edifice was continued, but they hardly had eyes to see anything.

Nevertheless their attention was attracted for the space of a moment by the airy bridge, seemingly of lace, inclosed within an arch thrown across space between two belfries, as if to afford a way to scale the clouds, and their amazement was still greater when they came to the "Madman's Path," a dizzy track, devoid of parapet, that encircles the farthest tower nearly at its summit.

"May we go up there?" she asked.

"It is forbidden," the guide replied.

She showed him a twenty-franc piece. All the members of the party, giddy at sight of the yawning gulf and the immensity of surrounding space, tried to dissuade her from the imprudent freak.

She asked Mariolle: "Will you go?"

He laughed: "I have been in more dangerous places than that." And paying no further attention to the others, they set out.

He went first along the narrow cornice that overhung the gulf, and she followed him, gliding along close to the wall with eyes downcast that she might not see the yawning void beneath, terrified now and almost ready to sink with fear, clinging to the hand that he held out to her; but she felt that he was strong, that there was no sign of weakening there, that he was sure of head and foot; and enraptured for all her fears, she said to herself: "Truly, this is a man." They were alone in space, at the height where the seabirds soar; they were contemplating the same horizon that the white-winged creatures are ceaselessly scouring in their flight as they explore it with their little yellow eyes.

Mariolle felt that she was trembling; he asked: "Do you feel dizzy?"

"A little," she replied in a low voice; "but in your company I fear nothing."

At this he drew near and sustained her by putting his arm about her, and this simple assistance inspired her with such courage that she ventured to raise her head and take a look at the distance. He was almost carrying her and she offered no resistance, enjoying the protection of those strong arms which thus enabled her to traverse the heavens, and she was grateful to him with a romantic, womanly gratitude that he did not mar their seagull flight by kisses.

When they had rejoined the others of the party, who were awaiting them with the greatest anxiety, M. de Pradon angrily said to his daughter: "Dieu! what a silly thing to do!"

She replied with conviction: "No, it was not, papa, since it was successfully accomplished. Nothing that succeeds is ever stupid."

He merely gave a shrug of the shoulders, and they descended the stairs. At the porter's lodge there was another stoppage to purchase photographs, and when they reached the inn it was nearly dinnertime. The hostess recommended a short walk upon the sands, so as to obtain a view of the Mount toward the open sea, in which direction, she said, it presented its most imposing aspect. Although they were all much fatigued, the band started out again and made the tour of the ramparts, picking their way among the treacherous downs, solid to the eye but yielding to the step, where the foot that was placed upon the pretty yellow carpet that was stretched beneath it and seemed solid would suddenly sink up to the calf in the deceitful golden ooze.

Seen from this point the abbey, all at once losing the cathedral-like appearance with which it astounded the beholder on the mainland, assumed, as if in menace of old Ocean, the martial appearance of a feudal manor, with its huge battlemented wall picturesquely pierced with loopholes and supported by gigantic buttresses that sank their Cyclopean stone foundations in the bosom of the fantastic mountain. Mme de Burne and André Mariolle, however, were now heedless of all that. They were thinking only of themselves, caught in the meshes of the net that they had set for each other, shut up within the walls of that prison to which no sound comes from the outer world, where the eye beholds only one being.

When they found themselves again seated before their well-filled plates, however, beneath the cheerful light of the lamps, they seemed to awake, and discovered that they were hungry, just like other mortals.

They remained a long time at table, and when the dinner was ended the moonlight was quite forgotten in the pleasure of conversation. There was no one, moreover, who had any desire to go out, and no one suggested it. The broad moon might shed her waves of poetic light down upon the little thin sheet of rising tide that was already creeping up the sands with the noise of a trickling stream, scarcely perceptible to the ear, but sinister and alarming; she might light up the ramparts that crept in spirals up the flanks of the Mount and illumine the romantic shadows of all the belfries of the old abbey, standing in its wondrous setting of a boundless bay, in the bosom of which were quiveringly reflected the lights that crawled along the downs — no one cared to see more.

It was not yet ten o'clock when *Mme.* Valsaci, overcome with sleep, spoke of going to bed, and her proposition was received without a dissenting voice. Bidding one another a cordial good night, each withdrew to his chamber.

André Mariolle knew well that he would not sleep; he therefore lighted his two candles and placed them on the mantelpiece, threw open his window, and looked out into the night.

All the strength of his body was giving way beneath the torture of an unavailing hope. He knew that she was there, close at hand, that there were only two doors between them, and yet it was almost as impossible to go to her as it would be to dam the tide that was coming in and submerging all the land. There was a cry in his throat that strove to liberate itself, and in his nerves such an unquenchable and futile torment of expectation that he asked himself what he was to do, unable as he was longer to endure the solitude of this evening of sterile happiness.

Gradually all the sounds had died away in the inn and in the single little winding street of the town. Mariolle still remained leaning upon his windowsill, conscious only that time was passing, contemplating the silvery sheet of the still rising tide and rejecting the idea of going to bed as if he had felt the undefined presentiment of some approaching, providential good fortune.

All at once it seemed to him that a hand was fumbling with the fastening of his door. He turned with a start: the door slowly opened and a woman entered the room, her head veiled in a cloud of white lace and her form enveloped in one of those great dressing-gowns that seem made of silk, cashmere, and snow. She closed the door carefully behind her; then, as if she had not seen him where he stood motionless — as if smitten with joy — in the bright square of moonlight of the window, she went straight to the mantelpiece and blew out the two candles.

V

THEY were to meet next morning in front of the inn to say goodbye to one another. André, the first one down, awaited her coming with a poignant feeling of mixed uneasiness and delight. What would she do? What would she be to him? What would become of her and of him? In what thrice-happy or terrible adventure had he engaged himself? She had it in her power to make of him what she would, a visionary, like an opium-eater, or a martyr, at her will. He paced to and fro beside the two carriages, for they were to separate, he, to continue the deception, ending his trip by way of Saint Malo, they returning to Avranches.

When would he see her again? Would she cut short her visit to her family, or would she delay her return? He was horribly afraid of what she would first say to him, how she would first look at him, for he had not seen her and they had scarcely spoken during their brief interview of the night be-

fore. There remained to Mariolle from that strange, fleeting interview the faint feeling of disappointment of the man who has been unable to reap all that harvest of love which he thought was ready for the sickle, and at the same time the intoxication of triumph and, resulting from that, the almost assured hope of finally making himself complete master of her affections.

He heard her voice and started; she was talking loudly, evidently irritated at some wish that her father had expressed, and when he beheld her standing at the foot of the staircase there was a little angry curl upon her lips that bespoke her impatience.

Mariolle took a couple of steps toward her; she saw him and smiled. Her eyes suddenly recovered their serenity and assumed an expression of kindliness which diffused itself over the other features, and she quickly and cordially extended to him her hand, as if in ratification of their new relations.

"So then, we are to separate?" she said to him.

"Alas! Madame, the thought makes me suffer more than I can tell."

"It will not be for long," she murmured. She saw M. de Pradon coming toward them, and added in a whisper: "Say that you are going to take a ten days' trip through Brittany, but do not take it."

Mme de Valsaci came running up in great excitement. "What is this that your father has been telling me — that you are going to leave us day after tomorrow? You were to stay until next Monday, at least."

Mme de Burne replied, with a suspicion of ill humor: "Papa is nothing but a bungler, who never knows enough to hold his tongue. The sea-air has given me, as it does every year, a very unpleasant neuralgia, and I did say something or other about going away so as not to have to be ill for a month. But this is no time for bothering over that."

Mariolle's coachman urged him to get into the carriage and be off, so that they might not miss the Pontorson train.

Mme de Burne asked: "And you, when do you expect to be back in Paris?"

He assumed an air of hesitancy: "Well, I can't say exactly; I want to see Saint Malo, Brest, Douarnenez, the Bay des Trépassés, Cape Raz, Audierne, Penmarch, Morbihan, all this celebrated portion of the Breton country, in a word. That will take me say — "after a silence devoted to feigned calculation, he exceeded her estimate — "fifteen or twenty days."

"That will be quite a trip," she laughingly said. "For my part, if my nerves trouble me as they did last night, I shall be at home before I am two days older."

His emotion was so great that he felt like exclaiming: "Thanks!" He contented himself with kissing, with a lover's kiss, the hand that she extended to him for the last time, and after a profuse exchange of thanks and compliments with the Valsacis and M. de Pradon, who seemed to be somewhat' reassured by the announcement of his projected trip, he climbed into his vehicle and drove off, turning his head for a parting look at her.

He made no stop on his journey back to Paris and was conscious of seeing nothing on the way. All night long he lay back in the corner of his compartment with eyes half closed and folded arms, his mind reverting to the occurrences of the last few hours, and all his thoughts concentrated upon the realization of his dream.

Immediately upon his arrival at his own abode, upon the cessation of the noise and bustle of travel, in the silence of the library where he generally passed his time, where he worked and wrote, and where he almost always felt himself possessed by a restful tranquillity in the friendly companionship of his books, his piano, and his violin, there now commenced in him that unending torment of impatient waiting which devours, as with a fever, insatiable hearts like his. He was surprised that he could apply himself to nothing, that nothing served to occupy his mind, that reading and music, the occupations that he generally employed to while away the idle moments of his life, were unavailing, not only to afford distraction to his thoughts, but even to give rest and quiet to his physical being, and he asked himself what he was to do to appease this new disturbance. An inexplicable physical need of motion seemed to have taken possession of him — of going forth and walking the streets, of constant movement, the crisis of that agitation that is imparted by the mind to the body and which is nothing more than an instinctive and unappeasable longing to seek and find some other being.

He put on his hat and overcoat, and as he was descending the stairs he asked himself: "In which direction shall I go?" Thereupon an idea occurred to him that he had not yet thought of: he must procure a pretty and secluded retreat to serve them as a trysting place.

He pursued his investigations in every quarter, ransacking streets, avenues, and boulevards, distrustfully examining concierges with their servile smiles, lodging-house keepers of suspicious appearance and apartments with doubtful furnishings, and at evening he returned to his house in a state of discouragement. At nine o'clock the next day he started out again, and at nightfall he finally succeeded in discovering at Auteuil, buried in a garden that had three exits, a lonely pavilion which an upholsterer in the neighborhood promised to render habitable in two days. He ordered what was necessary, selecting very plain furniture of varnished pine and thick carpets. A baker who lived near one of the garden gates had charge of the property, and an arrangement was completed with his wife whereby she was to care for the rooms, while a gardener of the quarter also took a contract for filling the beds with flowers.

All these arrangements kept him busy until it was eight o'clock, and when at last he got home, worn out with fatigue, he beheld with a beating heart a telegram lying on his desk. He opened it and read:

"I will be home tomorrow. Await instructions.

"MICHE."

He had not written to her yet, fearing that as she was soon to leave Avranches his letter might go astray, and as soon as he had dined he seated himself at his desk to lay before her what was passing in his mind. The task was a long and difficult one, for all the words and phrases that he could muster, and even his ideas, seemed to him weak, mediocre, and ridiculous vehicles in which to convey to her the delicacy and passionateness of his thanks.

The letter that he received from her upon waking next morning confirmed the statement that she would reach home that evening, and begged him not to make his presence known to anyone for a few days, in order that full belief might be accorded to the report that he was traveling. She also requested him to walk upon the terrace of the Tuileries garden that overlooks the Seine the following day at ten o'clock.

He was there an hour before the time appointed, and to kill time wandered about in the immense garden that was peopled only by a few early pedestrians, belated officeholders on their way to the public buildings on the left bank, clerks and toilers of every condition. It was a pleasure to him to watch the hurrying crowds driven by the necessity of earning their daily bread to brutalizing labors, and to compare his lot with theirs, on this spot, at the minute when he was awaiting his mistress — a queen among the queens of the earth. He felt himself so fortunate a being, so privileged, raised to such a height beyond their petty struggles, that he felt like giving thanks to the blue sky, for to him Providence was but a series of alternations of sunshine and of rain due to Chance, mysterious ruler over weather and over men.

When it wanted a few minutes of ten he ascended to the terrace and watched for her coming. "She will be late!" he thought. He had scarcely more than heard the clock in an adjacent building strike ten when he thought he saw her at a distance, coming through the garden with hurrying steps, like a working-woman in haste to reach her shop. "Can it indeed be she?" He recognized her step but was astonished by her changed appearance, so unassuming in a neat little toilette of dark colors. She was coming toward the stairs that led up to the terrace, however, in a bee-line, as if she had traveled that road many times before.

"Ah!" he said to himself, "she must be fond of this place and come to walk here sometimes." He watched her as she raised her dress to put her foot on the first step and then nimbly flew up the remaining ones, and as he eagerly stepped forward to meet her she said to him as he came near with a pleasant smile, in which there was a trace of uneasiness: "You are very imprudent! You must not show yourself like that; I saw you almost from the Rue de Rivoli. Come, we will go and take a seat on a bench yonder. There is where you must wait for me next time."

He could not help asking her: "So you come here often?"

"Yes, I have a great liking for this place, and as I am an early walker I come here for exercise and to look at the scenery, which is very pretty. And then one never meets anybody here, while the Bois is out of the question on just that account. But you must be careful not to give away my secret."

He laughed: "I shall not be very likely to do that." Discreetly taking her hand, a little hand that was hanging at her side conveniently concealed in the folds of her dress, he sighed: "How I love you! My heart was sick with waiting for you. Did you receive my letter?"

"Yes; I thank you for it. It was very touching."

"Then you have not become angry with me yet?"

"Why no! Why should I? You are just as nice as you can be."

He sought for ardent words, words that would vibrate with his emotion and his gratitude. As none came to him, and as he was too deeply moved to permit of the free expression of the thought that was within him, he simply said again: "How I love you!"

She said to him: "I brought you here because there are water and boats in this place as well as down yonder. It is not at all like what we saw down there; still it is not disagreeable."

They were sitting on a bench near the stone balustrade that runs along the river, almost alone, invisible from every quarter. The only living beings to be seen on the long terrace at that hour were two gardeners and three nursemaids. Carriages were rolling along the quay at their feet, but they could not see them; footsteps were resounding upon the adjacent sidewalk, over against the wall that sustained the promenade; and still unable to find words in which to express their thoughts, they let their gaze wander over the beautiful Parisian landscape that stretches from the île Saint-Louis and the towers of Notre-Dame to the heights of Meudon. She repeated her thought: "None the less, it is very pretty, isn't it?" But he was suddenly seized by the thrilling remembrance of their journey through space up on the summit of the abbey tower, and with a regretful feeling for the emotion that was past and gone, he said: "Oh, Madame, do you remember our escapade of the 'Madman's Path?'"

"Yes; but I am a little afraid now that I come to think of it when it is all over. Dieu! how my head would spin around if I had it to do over again! I was just drunk with the fresh air, the sunlight, and the sea. Look, my friend, what a magnificent view we have before us. How I do love Paris!"

He was surprised, having a confused feeling of missing something that had appeared in her down there in the country. He murmured: "It matters not to me where I am, so that I am only near you!"

Her only answer was a pressure of the hand. Inspired with greater happiness, perhaps, by this little signal than he would have been by a tender word, his heart relieved of the care that had oppressed it until now, he could at last find words to express his feelings. He told her, slowly, in words that were almost solemn, that he had given her his life forever that she might do with it what she would.

She was grateful; but like the child of modern scepticism that she was and willing captive of her iconoclastic irony, she smiled as she replied: "I would not make such a long engagement as that if I were you!"

He turned and faced her, and, looking her straight in the eyes with that penetrating look which is like a touch, repeated what he had just said at greater length, in a more ardent, more poetical form of expression. All that he had written in so many burning letters he now expressed with such a fervor of conviction that it seemed to her as she listened that she was sitting in a cloud of incense. She felt herself caressed in every fiber of her feminine nature by his adoring words more deeply than ever before.

When he had ended she simply said: "And I, too, love you dearly!"

They were still holding each other's hand, like young folks walking along a country road, and watching with vague eyes the little steamboats plying on the river. They were alone by themselves in Paris, in the great confused uproar, whether remote or near at hand, that surrounded them in this city full of all the life of all the world, more alone than they had been on the summit of their aerial tower, and for some seconds they were quite oblivious that there existed on earth any other beings but their two selves.

She was the first to recover the sensation of reality and of the flight of time. "Shall we see each other again tomorrow?" she said.

He reflected for an instant, and abashed by what he had in mind to ask of her: "Yes — yes — certainly," he replied. "But — shall we never meet in any other place? This place is unfrequented. Still — people may come here."

She hesitated. "You are right. Still it is necessary also that you should not show yourself for at least two weeks yet, so that people may think that you are away traveling. It will be very nice and mysterious for us to meet and no one know that you are in Paris. Meanwhile, however, I cannot receive you at my house, so — I don't see — "

He felt that he was blushing, and continued: "Neither can I ask you to come to my house. Is there nothing else — is there no other place?"

Being a woman of practical sense, logical and without false modesty, she was neither surprised nor shocked.

"Why, yes," she said, "only we must have time to think it over."

"I have thought it over."

"What! so soon?"

"Yes, Madame."

"Well?"

"Are you acquainted with the Rue des Vieux-Champs at Auteuil?"

"No."

"It runs into the Rue Tournemine and the Rue Jean-de-Saulge."

"Well?"

"In this street, or rather lane, there is a garden, and in this garden a pavilion that also communicates with the two streets that I mentioned."

"What next?"

"That pavilion awaits you."

She reflected, still with no appearance of embarrassment, and then asked two or three questions that were dictated by feminine prudence. His explanations seemed to be satisfactory, for she murmured as she arose:

"Well, I will go tomorrow."

"At what time?"

"Three o'clock."

"Seven is the number; I will be waiting for you behind the door. Do not forget. Give a knock as you pass."

"Yes, my friend. Adieu, till tomorrow."

"Till tomorrow, adieu. Thanks; I adore you." They had risen to their feet. "Do not come with me," she said. "Stay here for ten minutes, and when you leave go by the way of the quay."

"Adieu!"

"Adieu!"

She started off very rapidly, with such a modest, unassuming air, so hurriedly, that actually she might have been mistaken for one of Paris' pretty working-girls, who trot along the streets in the morning on the way to their honest labors.

He took a cab to Auteuil, tormented by the fear that the house might not be ready against the following day. He found it full of workmen, however; the hangings were all in place upon the walls, the carpets laid upon the floors. Everywhere there was a sound of pounding, hammering, beating, washing. In the garden, which was quite large and rather pretty, the remains of an ancient park, containing a few large old trees, a thick clump of shrubbery that stood for a forest, two green tables, two grassplots, and paths twisting about among the beds, the gardener of the vicinity had set out rose-trees, geraniums, pinks, reseda, and twenty other species of those plants, the growth of which is advanced or retarded by careful attention, so that a naked field may be transformed in a day into a blooming flower garden.

Mariolle was as delighted as if he had scored another success with his Michèle, and having exacted an oath from the upholsterer that all the furniture should be in place the next day before noon, he went off to various shops to buy some bric-à-brac and pictures for the adornment of the interior of this retreat. For the walls he selected some of those admirable photographs of celebrated pictures that are produced nowadays, for the tables and mantelshelves some rare pottery and a few of those familiar objects that women always like to have about them. In the course of the day he expended the income of three months, and he did it with great pleasure, reflecting that for the last ten years he had been living very economically, not from penuriousness, but because of the absence of expensive tastes, and this circumstance now allowed him to do things somewhat magnificently.

He returned to the pavilion early in the morning of the following day, presided over the arrival and placing of the furniture, climbed ladders and hung the pictures, burned perfumes and vaporized them upon the hangings and poured them over the carpets. In his feverish joy, in the excited rapture of all his being, it seemed to him that he had never in his life been engaged in such an engrossing, such a delightful labor. At every moment he looked to see what time it was, and calculated how long it would be before she would be there; he urged on the workmen, and stimulated his invention so to arrange the different objects that they might be displayed in their best light.

In his prudence he dismissed everyone before it was two o'clock, and then, as the minute-hand of the clock tardily made its last revolution around the dial, in the silence of that house where he was awaiting the greatest happiness that ever he could have wished for, alone with his reverie, going and coming from room to room, he passed the minutes until she should be there.

Finally he went out into the garden. The sunlight was streaming through the foliage upon the grass and falling with especially charming brilliancy upon a bed of roses. The very heavens were contributing their aid to embellish this trysting-place. Then he went and stood by the gate, partially opening it to look out from time to time for fear she might mistake the house.

Three o'clock rang out from some belfry, and forthwith the sounds were echoed from a dozen schools and factories. He stood waiting now with watch in hand, and gave a start of surprise when two little, light knocks were given against the door, to which his ear was closely applied, for he had heard no sound of footsteps in the street.

He opened: it was she. She looked about her with astonishment. First of all she examined with a distrustful glance the neighboring houses, but her inspection reassured her, for certainly she could have no acquaintances among the humble bourgeois who inhabited the quarter. Then she examined the garden with pleased curiosity, and finally placed the backs of her two hands, from which she had drawn her gloves, against her lover's mouth; then she took his arm. At every step she kept repeating: "My! how pretty it is! how unexpected! how attractive!" Catching sight of the rosebed that the sun was shining upon through the branches of the trees, she exclaimed: "Why, this is fairyland, my friend!"

She plucked a rose, kissed it, and placed it in her corsage. Then they entered the pavilion, and she seemed so pleased with everything that he felt like going down on his knees to her, although he may have felt at the bottom of his heart that perhaps she might as well have shown more attention to him and less to the surroundings. She looked about her with the pleasure of a child who has received a new plaything, and admired and appreciated the elegance of the place with the satisfaction of a connoisseur whose tastes have been gratified. She had feared that she was coming to some vulgar, commonplace resort, where the furniture and hangings had been contaminated by other rendezvous, whereas all this, on the contrary, was new, unforeseen, and alluring, prepared expressly for her, and must have cost a lot of money. Really he was perfect, this man. She turned to him and extended her arms, and their lips met in one of those long kisses that have the strange, twofold sensation of self-effacement and unadulterated bliss.

When, at the end of three hours, they were about to separate, they walked through the garden and seated themselves in a leafy arbor where no eye could reach them. André addressed her with an exuberance of feeling, as if she had been an idol that had come down for his sake from her sacred pedestal, and she listened to him with that fatigued languor which he had often seen reflected in her eyes after people had tired her by too long a visit. She continued affectionate, however, her face lighted up by a tender, slightly constrained smile, and she clasped the hand that she held in hers with a continuous pressure that perhaps was more studied than spontaneous.

She could not have been listening to him, for she interrupted one of his sentences to say: "Really, I must be going. I was to be at the Marquise de Bratiane's at six o'clock, and I shall be very late."

He conducted her to the gate by which she had obtained admission. They gave each other a parting kiss, and after a furtive glance up and down the street, she hurried away, keeping close to the walls.

When he was alone he felt within him that sudden void that is ever left by the disappearance of the woman whose kiss is still warm upon your lips, the queer little laceration of the heart that is caused by the sound of her retreating footsteps. It seemed to him that he was abandoned and alone, that he was never to see her again, and he betook himself to pacing the gravel-walks, reflecting upon this never-ceasing contrast between anticipation and realization. He remained there until it was dark, gradually becoming more tranquil and yielding himself more entirely to her influence, now that she was away, than if she had been there in his arms. Then he went home and dined without being conscious of what he was eating, and sat down to write to her.

The next day was a long one to him, and the evening seemed interminable. Why had she not answered his letter, why had she sent him no word? The morning of the second day he received a short telegram appointing another rendezvous at the same hour. The little blue envelope speedily cured him of the heartsickness of hope deferred from which he was beginning to suffer.

She came, as she had done before, punctual, smiling, and affectionate, and their second interview in the little house was in all respects similar to the first. André Mariolle, surprised at first and vaguely troubled that the ecstatic passion he had dreamed of had not made itself felt between them, but more and more overmastered by his senses, gradually forgot his visions of anticipation in the somewhat different happiness of possession. He was becoming attached to her by reason of her caresses, an invincible tie, the strongest tie of all, from which there is no deliverance when once it has fully possessed you and has penetrated through your flesh into your veins.

Twenty days rolled by, such sweet, fleeting days. It seemed to him that there was to be no end to it, that he was to live forever thus, nonexistent for all and living for her alone, and to his mental vision there presented itself the seductive dream of an unlimited continuance of this blissful, secret way of living.

She continued to make her visits at intervals of three days, offering no objections, attracted, it would seem, as much by the amusement she derived from their clandestine meetings — by the charm of the little house that had now been transformed into a conservatory of rare exotics and by the novelty of the situation, which could scarcely be called dangerous, since she was her own mistress, but still was full of mystery — as by the abject and constantly increasing tenderness of her lover.

At last there came a day when she said to him: " Now, my dear friend, you must show yourself in society again. You will come and pass the afternoon with me tomorrow. I have given out that you are at home again."

He was heartbroken. "Oh, why so soon?" he said.

"Because if it should leak out by any chance that you are in Paris your absence would be too inexplicable not to give rise to gossip."

He saw that she was right and promised that he would come to her house the next day. Then he asked her: "Do you receive tomorrow?"

"Yes," she replied. "It will be quite a little solemnity."

He did not like this intelligence. "Of what description is your solemnity?"

She laughed gleefully. "I have prevailed upon Massival, by means of the grossest sycophancy, to give a performance of his 'Dido,' which no one has heard yet. It is the poetry of antique love. Mme de Bratiane, who considered herself Massival's sole proprietor, is furious. She will be there, for she is to sing. Am I not a sly one?"

"Will there be many there?"

"Oh, no, only a few intimate friends. You know them nearly all."

"Won't you let me off? I am so happy in my solitude."

"Oh! no, my friend. You know that I count on you more than all the rest."

His heart gave a great thump. "Thank you," he said; "I will come."

VI

GOOD day, M. Mariolle."

Mariolle noticed that it was no longer the "dear friend" of Auteuil, and the clasp of the hand was a hurried one, the hasty pressure of a busy woman wholly engrossed in her social functions. As he entered the salon Mme de Burne was advancing to speak to the beautiful Mme le Prieur, whose sculpturesque form, and the audacious way that she had of dressing to display it, had caused her to be nicknamed, somewhat ironically, "The Goddess." She was the wife of a member of the Institute, of the section of Inscriptions and Belles-Lettres.

"Ah, Mariolle!" exclaimed Lamarthe, "where do you come from? We thought that you were dead."

"I have been making a trip through Finistère."

He was going on to relate his impressions when the novelist interrupted him: "Are you acquainted with the Baronne de Frémines?"

"Only by sight; but I have heard a good deal of her. They say that she is queer."

"The very queen of crazy women, but with an exquisite perfume of modernness. Come and let me present you to her." Taking him by the arm he led him toward a young woman who was always compared to a doll, a pale and charming little blond doll, invented and created by the devil himself for the damnation of those larger children who wear beards on their faces. She had long, narrow eyes, slightly turned up toward the temples, apparently like the eyes of the Chinese; their soft blue glances stole out between lids that were seldom opened to their full extent, heavy, slowly-moving lids, designed to veil and hide this creature's mysterious nature.

Her hair, very light in color, shone with silky, silvery reflections, and her delicate mouth, with its thin lips, seemed to have been cut by the light hand of a sculptor from the design of a miniature-painter. The voice that issued from it had bell-like intonations, and the audacity of her ideas, of a biting quality that was peculiar to herself, smacking of wickedness and drollery, their destructive charm, their cold, corrupting seductiveness, all the complicated nature of this full-grown, mentally diseased child acted upon those who were brought in contact with her in such a way as to produce in them violent passions and disturbances.

She was known all over Paris as being the most extravagant of the mondaines of the real monde, and also the wittiest, but no one could say exactly what she was, what were her ideas, what she did. She exercised an irresistible sway over mankind in general. Her husband, also, was quite as much of an enigma as she. Courteous and affable and a great nobleman, he seemed quite unconscious of what was going on. Was he indifferent, or complaisant, or was he simply blind? Perhaps, after all, there was nothing in it more than those little eccentricities which doubtless amused him as much as they did her. All sorts of opinions, however, were prevalent in regard to him, and some very ugly reports were circulated. Rumor even went so far as to insinuate that his wife's secret vices were not unprofitable to him.

Between her and Mme de Burne there were natural attractions and fierce jealousies, spells of friendship succeeded by crises of furious enmity. They liked and feared each other and mutually sought each other's society, like professional duelists, who appreciate at the same time that they would be glad to kill each other.

It was the Baronne de Frémines who was having the upper hand at this moment. She had just scored a victory, an important victory: she had conquered Lamarthe, had taken him from her rival and borne him away ostentatiously to domesticate him in her flock of acknowledged followers. The novelist seemed to be all at once smitten, puzzled, charmed, and stupefied by the discoveries he had made in this creature sui generis, and he could not help talking about her to everybody that he met, a fact which had already given rise to much gossip.

Just as he was presenting Mariolle he encountered Mme de Burne's look from the other end of the room; he smiled and whispered in his friend's ear: "See, the mistress of the house is angry."

André raised his eyes, but Madame had turned to meet Massival, who just then made his appearance beneath the raised portière. He was followed almost immediately by the Marquise de Bratiane, which elicited from Lamarthe: "Ah! we shall only have a second rendition of 'Dido'; the first has just been given in the Marquise's coupé."

Mme de Frémines added: "Really, our friend De Burne's collection is losing some of its finest jewels."

Mariolle felt a sudden impulse of anger rising in his heart, a kind of hatred against this woman, and a brusque sensation of irritation against these people, their way of life, their ideas, their tastes, their aimless inclinations, their childish amusements. Then, as Lamarthe bent over the young woman to whisper something in her ear, he profited by the opportunity to slip away.

Handsome Mme le Prieur was sitting by herself only a few steps away; he went up to her to make his bow. According to Lamarthe she stood for the old guard among all this irruption of modernism. Young, tall, handsome, with very regular features and chestnut hair through which ran threads of gold, extremely affable, captivating by reason of her tranquil, kindly charm of manner, by reason also of a calm, well-studied coquetry and a great desire to please that lay concealed beneath an outward appearance of simple and sincere affection, she had many firm partisans, whom she took good care should never be exposed to dangerous rivalries. Her house had the reputation of being a little gathering of intimate friends, where all the habitués, moreover, concurred in extolling the merits of the husband.

She and Mariolle now entered into conversation. She held in high esteem this intelligent and reserved man, who gave people so little cause to talk about him and who was perhaps of more account than all the rest.

The remaining guests came dropping in: big Fresnel, puffing and giving a last wipe with his handkerchief to his shining and perspiring forehead, the philosophic George de Maltry, finally the Baron de Gravil accompanied by the Comte de Marantin. M. de Pradon assisted his daughter in doing the honors of the house; he was extremely attractive to Mariolle.

But Mariolle, with a heavy heart, saw her going and coming and bestowing her attentions on everyone there more than on him.

Twice, it is true, she had thrown him a swift look from a distance which seemed to say, "I am not forgetting you," but they were so fleeting that perhaps he had failed to catch their meaning. And then he could not be unconscious to the fact that Lamarthe's aggressive assiduities to Mme de Frémines were displeasing to Mme de Burne. "That is only her coquettish feeling of spite," he said to himself, "a woman's irritation from whose salon some valuable trinket has been spirited away." Still it made him suffer, and his suffering was the greater since he saw that she was constantly watching them in a furtive, concealed kind of way, while she did not seem to trouble herself a bit at seeing him sitting beside Mme le Prieur.

The reason was that she had him in her power, she was sure of him, while the other was escaping her. What, then, could be to her that love of theirs, that love which was born but yesterday, and which in him had banished and killed every other idea?

M. de Pradon had called for silence, and Massival was opening the piano, which Mme de Bratiane was approaching, removing her gloves meanwhile, for she was to sing the woes of "Dido," when the door again opened and a young man appeared upon whom every eye was immediately fixed. He was tall and slender, with curling side-whiskers, short, blond, curly hair, and an air that was altogether aristocratic. Even Mme le Prieur seemed to feel his influence.

"Who is it?" Mariolle asked her.

"What! is it possible that you do not know him?"

"No, I do not."

"It is Comte Rudolph de Bernhaus."

"Ah! the man who fought a duel with Sigismond Fabre."

"Yes."

The story had made a great noise at the time. The Comte de Bernhaus, attached to the Austrian embassy and a diplomat of the highest promise, an elegant Bismarck, so it was said, having heard some words spoken in derogation of his sovereign at an official reception, had fought the next day with the man who uttered them, a celebrated fencer, and killed him. After this duel, in respect to which public opinion had been divided, the Comte acquired between one day and the next a notoriety after the manner of Sarah Bernhardt, but with this difference, that his name appeared in an aureole of poetic chivalry. He was in addition a man of great charm, an agreeable conversationalist, a man of distinction in every respect. Lamarthe used to say of him: "He is the one to tame our pretty wild beasts."

He took his seat beside Mme de Burne with a very gallant air, and Massival sat down before the keyboard and allowed his fingers to run over the keys for a few moments.

Nearly all the audience changed their places and drew their chairs nearer so as to hear better and at the same time have a better view of the singer. Thus Mariolle and Lamarthe found themselves side by side.

There was a great silence of expectation and respectful attention; then the musician began with a slow, a very slow succession of notes, something like a musical recitative. There were pauses, then the air would be lightly caught up in a series of little phrases, now languishing and dying away, now breaking out in nervous strength, indicative, it would seem, of distressful emotion, but always characterized by originality of invention. Mariolle gave way to reverie. He beheld a woman, a woman in the fullness of her mature youth and ripened beauty, walking slowly upon a shore that was bathed by the waves of the sea. He knew that she was suffering, that she bore a great sorrow in her soul, and he looked at Mme de Bratiane.

Motionless, pale beneath her wealth of thick black hair that seemed to have been dipped in the shades of night, the Italian stood waiting, her glance directed straight before her. On her strongly marked, rather stern features, against which her eyes and eyebrows stood out like spots of ink, in all her dark, powerful, and passionate beauty, there was something that struck one, something like the threat of the coming storm that we read in the blackening sky.

Massival, slightly nodding his head with its long hair in cadence with the rhythm, kept on relating the affecting tale that he was drawing from the resonant keys of ivory.

A shiver all at once ran through the singer; she partially opened her mouth, and from it there proceeded a long-drawn, heartrending wail of agony. It was not one of those outbursts of tragic despair that divas give utterance to upon the stage, with dramatic gestures, neither was it one of those pitiful laments for love betrayed that bring a storm of bravos from an audience; it was a cry of supreme passion, coming from the body and not from the soul, wrung from her like the roar of a wounded animal, the cry of the feminine animal betrayed. Then she was silent, and Massival again began to relate, more animatedly, more stormily, the moving story of the miserable queen who was abandoned by the man she loved. Then the woman's voice made itself heard again. She used articulate language now; she told of the intolerable torture of solitude, of her unquenchable thirst for the caresses that were hers no more, and of the grief of knowing that he was gone from her forever.

Her warm, ringing voice made the hearts of her audience beat beneath the spell. This somber Italian, with hair like the darkness of the night, seemed to be suffering all the sorrows that she was telling, she seemed to love, or to have the capacity of loving, with furious ardor. When she ceased her eyes were full of tears, and she slowly wiped them away. Lamarthe leaned over toward Mariolle and said to him in a quiver of artistic enthusiasm: "Good heavens! how beautiful she is just now! She is a woman, the only one in the room." Then he added, after a moment of reflection: "After all, who can tell? Perhaps there is nothing there but the mirage of the music, for nothing has real existence except our illusions. But what an art to produce illusions is that of hers!"

There was a short intermission between the first and the second parts of the musical poem, and warm congratulations were extended to the composer and his interpreter. Lamarthe in particular was very earnest in his felicitations, and he was really sincere, for he was endowed with the capacity to feel and comprehend, and beauty of all kinds appealed strongly to his nature, under whatever form expressed. The manner in which he told Mme de Bratiane what his feelings had been while listening to her was so flattering that it brought a slight blush to her face and excited a little spiteful feeling among the other women who heard it. Perhaps he was not altogether unaware of the feeling that he had produced.

When he turned around to resume his chair, he perceived Comte de Bernhaus just in the act of seating himself beside Mme de Frémines. She seemed at once to be on confidential terms with him, and they smiled at each other as if this close conversation was particularly agreeable to them both. Mariolle, whose gloom was momentarily increasing, stood leaning against a door; the novelist came and stationed himself at his side. Big Fresnel, George de Maltry, the Baron de Gravil and the Comte de Marantin formed a circle about Mme de Burne, who was going about offering tea. She seemed imprisoned in a crown of adorers. Lamarthe ironically called his friend's attention to it and added: "A crown without jewels, however, and I am sure that she would be glad to give all those rhinestones for the brilliant that she would like to see there."

"What brilliant do you mean?" inquired Mariolle. "Why, Bernhaus, handsome, irresistible, incomparable Bernhaus, he in whose honor this fête is given, for whom the miracle was performed of inducing Massival to bring out his 'Dido' here."

André, though incredulous, was conscious of a pang of regret as he heard these words. "Has she known him long?" he asked.

"Oh, no; ten days at most. But she put her best foot foremost during this brief campaign, and her tactics have been those of a conqueror. If you had been here you would have had a good laugh."

"How so?"

"She met him for the first time at Mme de Frémines's; I happened to be dining there that evening. Bernhaus stands very well in the good graces of the lady of that house, as you may see for yourself; all that you have to do is to look at them at the present moment; and behold, in the very minute that succeeded the first salutation that they ever made each other, there is our pretty friend De Burne taking the field to effect the conquest of the Austrian phoenix. And she is succeeding, and will succeed, although the little Frémines is more than a match for her in coquetry, real indifference, and perhaps perversity. But our friend De Burne uses her weapons more scientifically, she is more of a woman, by which I mean a modern woman, that is to say, irresistible by reason of that artificial seductiveness which takes the place in the modern woman of the old-fashioned natural charm of manner. And it is not her artificiality alone that is to be taken into account, but her æstheticism, her profound comprehension of feminine aesthetics; all her strength lies therein. She knows herself thoroughly, because she takes more delight in herself than in anything else, and she is never at fault as to the best means of subjugating a man and making the best use of her gifts in order to captivate men."

Mariolle took exception to this. "I think that you put it too strongly," he said. "She has always been very simple with me."

"Because simplicity is the right thing to meet the requirements of your case. I do not wish to speak ill of her, however. I think that she is better than most of her set. But they are not women."

Massival, striking a few chords on the piano, here reduced them to silence, and Mme de Bratiane proceeded to sing the second part of the poem, in which her delineation of the title-role was a magnificent study of physical passion and sensual regret.

Lamarthe, however, never once took his eyes from Mme de Frémines and the Comte de Bernhaus, where they were enjoying their tête-à-tête, and as soon as the last vibrations of the piano were lost in the murmurs of applause, he again took up his theme as if in continuation of an argument, or as if he were replying to an adversary: "No, they are not women. The most honest of them are coquettes without being aware of it. The more I know them the less do I find in them that sensation of mild exhilaration that it is the part of a true woman to inspire in us. They intoxicate, it is true, but the process wears upon our nerves, for they are too sophisticated. Oh, it is very good as a liqueur to sip now and then, but it is a poor substitute for the good wine that we used to have. You see, my dear fellow, woman was created and sent to dwell on earth for two objects only, and it is these two objects alone that can avail to bring out her true, great, and noble qualities — love and the family. I am talking like M. Prudhomme. Now the women of to-day are incapable of loving, and they will not bear children. When they are so inexpert as to have them, it is a misfortune in their eyes; then a burden. Truly, they are not women; they are monsters."

Astonished by the writer's violent manner and by the angry look that glistened in his eye, Mariolle asked him: "Why, then, do you spend half your time hanging to their skirts?"

Lamarthe hotly replied: "Why? Why? Because it interests me — parbleu! And then — and then — Would you prevent a physician from going to the hospitals to watch the cases? Those women constitute my clinic."

This reflection seemed to quiet him a little: he proceeded: "Then, too, I adore them for the very reason that they are so modern. At bottom I am really no more a man than they are women. When I am at the point of becoming attached to one of them, I amuse myself by investigating and analyzing all the resulting sensations and emotions, just like a chemist who experiments upon himself with a poison in order to ascertain its properties." After an interval of silence, he continued: "In this way they will never succeed in getting me into their clutches. can play their game as well as they play it themselves, perhaps even better, and that is of use to me for my books, while their proceedings are not of the slightest bit of use to them. What fools they are! Failures, every one of them — charming failures, who will be ready to die of spite as they grow older and see the mistake that they have made."

Mariolle, as he listened, felt himself sinking into one of those fits of depression that are like the humid gloom with which a long-continued rain darkens everything about us. He was well aware that the man of letters, as a general thing, was not apt to be very far out of the way, but he could not bring himself to admit that he was altogether right in the present case. With a slight appearance of irritation, he argued, not so much in defense of women as to show the causes of the position that they occupy in contemporary literature. "In the days when poets and novelists exalted them, and endowed them with poetic attributes," he said, "they looked for in life, and seemed to find, that which their heart had discovered in their reading. Nowadays you persist in suppressing everything that has any savor of sentiment and poetry, and in its stead give them only naked, undeceiving realities. Now, my dear sir, the more love there is in books, the more love there is in life. When you invented the ideal and laid it before them, they believed in the truth of your inventions. Now that you give them nothing but stern, unadorned realism, they follow in your footsteps and have come to measure everything by that standard of vulgarity."

Lamarthe, who was always ready for a literary discussion, was about to commence a dissertation when Mme de Burne came up to them. It was one of the days when she looked at her best, with a toilette that delighted the eye and with that aggressive and alluring air that denoted that she was ready to try conclusions with anyone. She took a chair. "That is what I like," she said; "to come upon two men and find that they are not talking about me. And then you are the only men here that one can listen to with any interest. What was the subject that you were discussing?"

Lamarthe, quite without embarrassment and in terms of elegant raillery, placed before her the question that had arisen between himself and Mariolle. Then he resumed his reasoning with a spirit that was inflamed by that desire of applause which, in the presence of women, always excites men who like to intoxicate themselves with glory.

She at once interested herself in the discussion, and, warming to the subject, took part in it in defense of the women of our day with a good deal of wit and ingenuity. Some remarks upon the faithfulness and the attachment that even those who were looked on with most suspicion might be capable of, incomprehensible to the novelist, made Mariolle's heart beat more rapidly, and when she left them to take a seat beside Mme de Frémines, who had persistently kept the Comte de Bernhaus near her, Lamarthe and Mariolle, completely vanquished by her display of feminine tact and grace, were united in declaring that, beyond all question, she was exquisite.

"And just look at them!" said the writer.

The grand duel was on. What were they talking about now, the Austrian and those two women?

Mme de Burne had come up just at the right moment to interrupt a tête-à-tête which, however agreeable the two persons engaged in it might be to each other, was becoming monotonous from being too long protracted, and she broke it up by relating with an indignant air the expressions that she had heard from Lamarthe's lips. To be sure, it was all applicable to Mme de Frémines, it all resulted from her most recent conquest, and it was all related in the hearing of an intelligent man who was capable of understanding it in all its bearings. The match was applied, and again the everlasting question of love blazed up, and the mistress of the house beckoned to Mariolle and Lamarthe to come to them; then, as their voices grew loud in debate, she summoned the remainder of the company.

A general discussion ensued, bright and animated, in which everyone had something to say. Mme de Burne was witty and entertaining beyond all the rest, shifting her ground from sentiment, which might have been factitious, to droll paradox. The day was a triumphant one for her, and she was prettier, brighter, and more animated than she had ever been.

VII

WHEN André Mariolle had parted from Mme de Burne and the penetrating charm of her presence had faded away, he felt within him and all about him, in his flesh, in his heart, in the air, and in all the surrounding world a sensation as if the delight of life which had been his support and animating principle for some time past had been taken from him.

What had happened? Nothing, or almost nothing. Toward the close of the reception she had been very charming in her manner toward him, saying to him more than once: "I am not conscious of anyone's presence here but yours." And yet he felt that she had revealed something to him of which he would have preferred always to remain ignorant. That, too, was nothing, or almost nothing; still he was stupefied, as a man might be upon hearing of some unworthy action of his father or his mother, to learn that during those twenty days which he had believed were absolutely and entirely devoted by her as well as by him, every minute of them, to the sentiment of their newborn love, so recent and so intense, she had resumed her former mode of life, had made many visits, formed many plans, recommenced those odious flirtations, had run after men and disputed them with her rivals, received compliments, and showed off all her graces.

So soon! All this she had done so soon! Had it happened later he would not have been surprised. He knew the world, he knew women and their ways of looking at things, he was sufficiently intelligent to understand it all, and would never have been unduly exacting or offensively jealous. She was beautiful; she was born — it was her allotted destiny — to receive the homage of men and listen to their soft nothings. She had selected him from among them all, and had bestowed herself upon him courageously, royally. It was his part to remain, he would remain in any event, a grateful slave to her caprices and a resigned spectator of her triumphs as a pretty woman. But it was hard on him; something suffered within him, in that obscure cavern down at the bottom of the heart where the delicate sensibilities have their dwelling.

No doubt he had been in the wrong; he had always been in the wrong since he first came to know himself. He carried too much sentimental prudence into his commerce with the world; his feelings were too thin-skinned. This was the cause of the isolated life that he had always led, through his dread of contact with the world and of wounded susceptibilities. He had been wrong, for this supersensitiveness is almost always the result of our not admitting the existence of a nature essentially different from our own, or else not tolerating it. He knew this, having often observed it in himself, but it was too late to modify the constitution of his being.

He certainly had no right to reproach Mme de Burne, for if she had forbidden him her salon and kept him in hiding during those days of happiness that she had afforded him, she had done it to blind prying eyes and be more fully his in the end. Why, then, this trouble that had settled in his heart? Ah! why? It was because he had believed her to be wholly his, and now it had been made clear to him that he could never expect to seize and hold this woman of a many-sided nature who belonged to all the world.

He was well aware, moreover, that all our life is made up of successes relative in degree to the "almost," and up to the present time he had borne this with philosophic resignation, dissembling his dissatisfaction and his unsatisfied yearnings under the mask of an assumed unsociability. This time he had thought that he was about to obtain an absolute success — the "entirely" that he had been waiting and hoping for all his life. The "entirely" is not to be attained in this world.

His evening was a dismal one, spent in analyzing the painful impression that he had received. When he was in bed this impression, instead of growing weaker, took stronger hold of him, and as he desired to leave nothing unexplored, he ransacked his mind to ascertain the remotest causes of his new troubles — they went, and came, and returned again like little breaths of frosty air, exciting in his love a suffering that was as yet weak and indistinct, like those vague neuralgic pains that we get by sitting in a draft, presages of the horrible agonies that are to come.

He understood in the first place that he was jealous, no longer as the ardent lover only but as one who had the right to call her his own. As long as he had not seen her surrounded by men, her men, he had not allowed himself to dwell upon this sensation, at the same time having a faint prevision of it, but supposing that it would be different, very different, from what it actually was. To find the mistress whom he believed had cared for none but him during those days of secret and frequent meetings — during that early period that should have been entirely devoted to isolation and tender emotion — to find her as much, and even more, interested and wrapped up in her former and frivolous flirtations than she was before she yielded herself to him, always ready to fritter away her time and attention on any chance comer, thus leaving but little of herself to him whom she had designated as the man of her choice, caused him a jealousy that was more of the flesh than of the feelings, not an undefined jealousy, like a fever that lies latent in the system, but a jealousy precise and well defined, for he was doubtful of her.

At first his doubts were instinctive, arising in a sensation of distrust that had intruded itself into his veins rather than into his thoughts, in that sense of dissatisfaction, almost physical, of the man who is not sure of his mate. Then, having doubted, he began to suspect.

What was his position toward her after all? Was he her first lover, or was he the tenth? Was he the successor of M. de Burne, or was he the successor of Lamarthe, Massival, George de Maltry, and the predecessor as well, perhaps, of the Comte de Bernhaus? What did he know of her? That she was surprisingly beautiful, stylish beyond all others, intelligent, discriminating, witty, but at the same time fickle, quick to weary, readily fatigued and disgusted with anyone or anything, and, above all else, in love with herself and an insatiable coquette. Had she had a lover — or lovers — before him? If not, would she have offered herself to him as she did? Where could she have got the audacity that made her come and open his bedroom door, at night, in a public inn? And then after that, would she have shown such readiness to visit the house at Auteuil? Before going there she had merely asked him a few questions, such questions as an experienced and prudent woman would naturally ask. He had answered like a man of circumspection, not unaccustomed to such interviews, and immediately she had confidingly said "Yes," entirely reassured, probably benefiting by her previous experiences.

And then her knock at that little door, behind which he was waiting, with a beating heart, almost ready to faint, how discreetly authoritative it had been! And how she had entered without any visible display of emotion, careful only to observe whether she might be recognized from the adjacent houses! And the way that she had made herself at home at once in that doubtful lodging that he had hired and furnished for her! Would a woman who was a novice, how daring soever she might be, how superior to considerations of morality and regardless of social prejudices, have penetrated thus calmly the mystery of a first rendezvous? There is a trouble of the mind, a hesitation of the body, an instinctive fear in the very feet, which know not whither they are tending; would she not have felt all that unless she had had some experience in these excursions of love and unless the practice of these things had dulled her native sense of modesty?

Burning with this persistent, irritating fever, which the warmth of his bed seemed to render still more unendurable, Mariolle tossed beneath the coverings, constantly drawn on by his chain of doubts and suppositions; like a man that feels himself irrecoverably sliding down the steep descent of a precipice. At times he tried to call a halt and break the current of his thoughts; he sought and found, and was glad to find, reflections that were more just to her and reassuring to him, but the seeds of distrust had been sown in him and he could not help their growing.

And yet, with what had he to reproach her? Nothing, except that her nature was not entirely similar to his own, that she did not look upon life in the same way that he did and that she had not in her heart an instrument of sensibility attuned to the same key as his.

Immediately upon awaking next morning the longing to see her and to reenforce his confidence in her developed itself within him like a ravening hunger, and he awaited the proper moment to go and pay her the visit demanded by custom. The instant that she saw him at the door of the little drawingroom devoted to her special intimates, where she was sitting alone occupied with her correspondence, she came to him with her two hands outstretched.

"Ah! Good day, dear friend!" she said, with so pleased and frank an air that all his odious suspicions, which were still floating indeterminately in his brain, melted away beneath the warmth of her reception.

He seated himself at her side and at once began to tell her of the manner in which he loved her, for their love was now no longer what it had been. He gently gave her to understand that there are two species of the race of lovers upon earth: those whose desire is that of madmen and whose ardor disappears when once they have achieved a triumph, and those whom possession serves to subjugate and capture, in whom the love of the senses, blending with the inarticulate and ineffable appeals that the heart of man at times sends forth toward a woman, gives rise to the servitude of a complete and torturing love.

Torturing it is, certainly, and forever so, however happy it may be, for nothing, even in the moments of closest communion, ever sates the need of her that rules our being.

Mme de Burne was charmed and gratified as she listened, carried away, as one is carried away at the theater when an actor gives a powerful interpretation of his rôle and moves us by awaking some slumbering echo in our own life. It was indeed an echo, the disturbing echo of a real passion; but it was not from her bosom that this passion sent forth its cry. Still, she felt such satisfaction that she was the object of so keen a sentiment, she was so pleased that it existed in a man who was capable of expressing it in such terms, in a man of whom she was really very fond, for whom she was really beginning to feel an attachment and whose presence was becoming more and more a necessity to her — not for her physical being but for that mysterious feminine nature which is so greedy of tenderness, devotion, and subjection — that she felt like embracing him, like offering him her mouth, her whole being, only that he might keep on worshiping her in this way.

She answered him frankly and without prudery, with that profound artfulness that certain women are endowed with, making it clear to him that he too had made great progress in her affections, and they remained tête-à-tête in the little drawingroom, where it so happened that no one came that day until twilight, talking always upon the same theme and caressing each other with words that to them did not have the common significance.

The servants had just brought in the lamps, when Mme de Bratiane appeared. Mariolle withdrew, and as Mme de Burne was accompanying him to the door through the main drawingroom, he asked her: "When shall I see you down yonder?"

"Will Friday suit you?"

"Certainly. At what hour?"

"The same, three o'clock."

"Until Friday, then. Adieu. I adore you!" During the two days that passed before this interview, he experienced a sensation of loneliness that he had never felt before in the same way. A woman was wanting in his life — she was the only existent object for him in the world, and as this woman was not far away and he was prevented by social conventions alone from going to her, and from passing a lifetime with her, he chafed in his solitude, in the interminable lapse of the moments that seemed at times to pass so slowly, at the absolute impossibility of a thing that was so easy.

He arrived at the rendezvous on Friday three hours before the time, but it was pleasing to him — it comforted his anxiety — to wait there where she was soon to come, after having already suffered so much in awaiting her mentally in places where she was not to come.

He stationed himself near the door long before the clock had struck the three strokes that he was expecting so eagerly, and when at last he heard them he began to tremble with impatience. The quarter struck. He looked out into the street, cautiously protruding his head between the door and the casing; it was deserted from one end to the other. The minutes seemed to stretch out in aggravating slowness. He was constantly drawing his watch from his pocket, and at last when the hand marked the halfhour it appeared to him that he had been standing there for an incalculable length of time. Suddenly he heard a faint sound upon the pavement outside, and the summons upon the door of the little gloved hand quickly made him forget his disappointment and inspired in him a feeling of gratitude toward her.

She seemed a little out of breath as she asked: "I am very late, am I not?"

"No, not very."

"Just imagine, I was near not being able to come at all. I had a houseful, and I was at my wits' end to know what to do to get rid of all those people. Tell me, do you go under your own name here?"

"No. Why do you ask?"

"So that I may send you a telegram if I should ever be prevented from coming."

"I am known as M. Nicolle."

"Very well; I won't forget. My! how nice it is here in this garden!"

There were five great splashes of perfumed, many-hued brightness upon the grassplots of the flowers, which were carefully tended and constantly renewed, for the gardener had a customer who paid liberally.

Halting at a bench in front of a bed of heliotrope: "Let us sit here for a while," she said; "I have something funny to tell you."

She proceeded to relate a bit of scandal that was quite fresh, and from the effect of which she had not yet recovered. The story was that *Mme.* Massival, the ex-mistress whom the artist had married, had come to Mme de Bratiane's, furious with jealousy, right in the midst of an entertainment in which the Marquise was singing to the composer's accompaniment, and had made a frightful scene: results, rage of the fair Italian, astonishment and laughter of the guests. Massival, quite beside himself, tried to take away his wife, who kept striking him in the face, pulling his hair and beard, biting him and tearing his clothes, but she clung to him with all her strength and held him so that he could not stir, while Lamarthe and two servants, who had hurried to them at the noise, did what they could to release him from the teeth and claws of this fury.

Tranquillity was not restored until after the pair had taken their departure. Since then the musician had remained invisible, and the novelist, witness of the scene, had been repeating it everywhere in a very witty and amusing manner. The affair had produced a deep impression upon Mme de Burne; it preoccupied her thoughts to such an extent that she hardly knew what she was doing. The constant recurrence of the names of Massival and Lamarthe upon her lips annoyed Mariolle.

"You just heard of this?" he said.

"Yes, hardly an hour ago."

"And that is the reason why she was late," he said to himself with bitterness. Then he asked aloud, "Shall we go in?"

"Yes," she absently murmured.

When, an hour later, she had left him, for she was greatly hurried that day, he returned alone to the quiet little house and seated himself on a low chair in their apartment. The feeling that she had been no more his than if she had not come there left a sort of black cavern in his heart, in all his being, that he tried to probe to the bottom. He could see nothing there, he could not understand; he was no longer capable of understanding. If she had not abstracted herself from his kisses, she had at all events escaped from the immaterial embraces of his tenderness by a mysterious absence of the will of being his. She had not refused herself to him, but it seemed as if she had not brought her heart there with her; it had remained somewhere else, very far away, idly occupied, distracted by some trifle.

Then he saw that he already loved her with his senses as much as with his feelings, even more perhaps. The deprivation of her soulless caresses inspired him with a mad desire to run after her and bring her back, to again possess himself of her. But why? What was the use — since the thoughts of that fickle mind were occupied elsewhere that day? So he must await the days and the hours when, to this elusive mistress of his, there should come the caprice, like her other caprices, of being in love with him.

He returned wearily to his house, with heavy footsteps, his eyes fixed on the sidewalk, tired of life, and it occurred to him that he had made no appointment with her for the future, either at her house or elsewhere.

VIII

UNTIL the setting in of winter she was pretty faithful to their appointments; faithful, but not punctual. During the first three months her tardiness on these occasions ranged between three-quarters of an hour and two hours. As the autumnal rains compelled Mariolle to await her behind the garden gate with an umbrella over his head, shivering, with his feet in the mud, he caused a sort of little summer-house to be built, a covered and inclosed vestibule behind the gate, so that he might not take cold every time they met.

The trees had lost their verdure, and in the place of the roses and other flowers the beds were now filled with great masses of white, pink, violet, purple, and yellow chrysanthemums, exhaling their penetrating, balsamic perfume — the saddening perfume by which these noble flowers remind us of the dying year — upon the moist atmosphere, heavy with the odor of the rain upon the decaying leaves. In front of the door of the little house the inventive genius of the gardener had devised a great Maltese cross, composed of rarer plants arranged in delicate combinations of color, and Mariolle could never pass this bed, bright with new and constantly changing varieties, without the melancholy reflection that this flowery cross was very like a grave.

He was well acquainted now with those long watches in the little summer-house behind the gate. The rain would fall sullenly upon the thatch with which he had had it roofed and trickle down the board siding, and while waiting in this receiving-vault he would give way to the same unvarying reflections, go through the same process of reasoning, be swayed in turn by the same hopes, the same fears, the same discouragements. It was an incessant battle that he had to fight; a fierce, exhausting mental struggle with an elusive force, a force that perhaps had no real existence: the tenderness of that woman's heart.

What strange things they were, those interviews of theirs! Sometimes she would come in with a smile upon her face, full to overflowing with the desire of conversation, and would take a seat without removing her hat and gloves, without raising her veil, often without so much as giving him a kiss. It never occurred to her to kiss him on such occasions; her head was full of a host of captivating little preoccupations, each of them more captivating to her than the idea of putting up her lips to the kiss of her despairing lover. He would take a seat beside her, heart and mouth overrunning with burning words which could find no way of utterance; he would listen to her and answer, and while apparently deeply interested in what she was saying would furtively take her hand, which she would yield to him calmly, amicably, without an extra pulsation in her veins.

At other times she would appear more tender, more wholly his; but he, who was watching her with anxious and clear-sighted eyes, with the eyes of a lover powerless to achieve her entire conquest, could see and divine that this relative degree of affection was owing to the fact that nothing had occurred on such occasions of sufficient importance to divert her thoughts from him.

Her persistent unpunctuality, moreover, proved to Mariolle with how little eagerness she looked forward to these interviews. When we love, when anything pleases and attracts us, we hasten to the anticipated meeting, but once the charm has ceased to work, the appointed time seems to come too quickly and everything serves as a pretext to delay our loitering steps and put off the moment that has become indefinably distasteful to us. An odd comparison with a habit of his own kept incessantly returning to his mind. In summer-time the anticipation of his morning bath always made him hasten his toilette and his visit to the bathing establishment, while in the frosty days of winter he always found so many little things to attend to at home before going out that he was invariably an hour behind his usual time. The meetings at Auteuil were to her like so many winter shower-baths.

For some time past, moreover, she had been making these interviews more infrequent, sending telegrams at the last hour, putting them off until the following day and apparently seeking for excuses for dispensing with them. She always succeeded in discovering excuses of a nature to satisfy herself, but they caused him mental and physical worries and anxieties that were intolerable. If she had manifested any coolness, if she had shown that she was tiring of this passion of his that she felt and knew was constantly increasing in violence, he might at first have been irritated and then in turn offended, discouraged, and resigned, but on the contrary she manifested more affection for him than ever, she seemed more flattered by his love, more desirous of retaining it, while not responding to it otherwise than by friendly marks of preference which were beginning to make all her other admirers jealous.

She could never see enough of him in her own house, and the same telegram that would announce to André that she could not come to Auteuil would convey to him her urgent request to dine with her or come and spend an hour in the evening. At first he had taken these invitations as her way of making amends to him, but afterward he came to understand that she liked to have him near her and that she really experienced the need of him, more so than of the others. She had need of him as an idol needs prayers and faith in order to make it a god; standing in the empty shrine it is but a bit of carved wood, but let a believer enter the sanctuary, and kneel and prostrate himself and worship with fervent prayers, drunk with religion, it becomes the equal of Brahma or of Allah, for every loved being is a kind of god. Mme de Burne felt that she was adapted beyond all others to play this rôle of fetich, to fill woman's mission, bestowed on her by nature, of being sought after and adored, and of vanquishing men by the arms of her beauty, grace, and coquetry.

In the meantime she took no pains to conceal her affection and her strong liking for Mariolle, careless of what folks might say about it, possibly with the secret desire of irritating and inflaming the others. They could hardly ever come to her house without finding him there, generally installed in the great easy-chair that Lamarthe had come to call the "pulpit of the officiating priest," and it afforded her sincere pleasure to remain alone in his company for an entire evening, talking and listening to him. She had taken a liking to this kind of family life that he had revealed to her, to this constant contact with an agreeable, well-stored mind, which was hers and at her command just as much as were the little trinkets that littered her dressing-table. In like manner she gradually came to yield to him much of herself, of her thoughts, of her deeper mental personality, in the course of those affectionate confidences that are as pleasant in the giving as in the receiving. She felt herself more at ease, more frank and familiar with him than with the others, and she loved him the more for it. She also experienced the sensation, dear to womankind, that she was really bestowing something, that she was confiding to some one all that she had to give, a thing that she had never done before.

In her eyes this was much, in his it was very little. He was still waiting and hoping for the great final breaking up of her being which should give him her soul beneath his caresses.

Caresses she seemed to regard as useless, annoying, rather a nuisance than otherwise. She submitted to them, not without returning them, but tired of them quickly, and this feeling doubtless engendered in her a shade of dislike to them. The slightest and most insignificant of them seemed to be irksome to her. When in the course of conversation he would take her hand and carry it to his lips and hold it there a little, she always seemed desirous of withdrawing it, and he could feel the movement of the muscles in her arm preparatory to taking it away.

He felt these things like so many thrusts of a knife, and he carried away from her presence wounds that bled unintermittently in the solitude of his love. How was it that she had not that period of unreasoning attraction toward him that almost every woman has when once she has made the entire surrender of her being? It may be of short duration, frequently it is followed quickly by weariness and disgust, but it is seldom that it is not there at all, for a day, for an hour! This mistress of his had made of him, not a lover, but a sort of intelligent companion of her life.

Of what was he complaining? Those who yield themselves entirely perhaps have less to give than she!

He was not complaining; he was afraid. He was afraid of that other one, the man who would spring up unexpectedly whenever she might chance to fall in with him, tomorrow, may be, or the day after, whoever he might be, artist, actor, soldier, or man of the world, it mattered not what, born to find favor in her woman's eyes and securing her favor for no other reason, because he was the man, the one destined to implant in her for the first time the imperious desire of opening her arms to him.

He was now jealous of the future as before he had at times been jealous of her unknown past, and all the young woman's intimates were beginning to be jealous of him. He was the subject of much conversation among them; they even made dark and mysterious allusions to the subject in her presence. Some said that he was her lover, while others, guided by Lamarthe's opinion, decided that she was only making a fool of him in order to irritate and exasperate them, as it was her habit to do, and that this was all there was to it. Her father took the matter up and made some remarks to her which she did not receive with good grace, and the more conscious she became of the reports that were circulating among her acquaintance, the more, by an odd contradiction to the prudence that had ruled her life, did she persist in making an open display of the preference that she felt for Mariolle.

He, however, was somewhat disturbed by these suspicious mutterings. He spoke to her of it.

"What do I care?" she said.

"If you only loved me, as a lover!"

"Do I not love you, my friend?"

"Yes and no; you love me well enough in your own house, but very badly elsewhere. I should prefer it to be just the opposite, for my sake, and even, indeed, for your own."

She laughed and murmured: "We can't do more than we can."

"If you only knew the mental trouble that I experience in trying to animate your love. At times I seem to be trying to grasp the intangible, to be clasping an iceberg in my arms that chills me and melts away within my embrace."

She made no answer, not fancying the subject, and assumed the absent manner that she often wore at Auteuil. He did not venture to press the matter further. He looked upon her a good deal as amateurs look upon the precious objects in a museum that tempt them so strongly and that they know they cannot carry away with them.

His days and nights were made up of hours of suffering, for he was living in the fixed idea, and still more in the sentiment than in the idea, that she was his and yet not his, that she was conquered and still at liberty, captured and yet impregnable. He was living at her side, as near her as could be, without ever reaching her, and he loved her with all the unsatiated longings of his body and his soul. He began to write to her again, as he had done at the commencement of their liaison. Once before with ink he had vanquished her early scruples; once again with ink he might be victorious over this later and obstinate resistance. Putting longer intervals between his visits to her, he told her in almost daily letters of the fruitlessness of his love. Now and then, when he had been very eloquent and impassioned and had evinced great sorrow, she answered him. Her letters, dated for effect midnight, or one, two, or three o'clock in the morning, were clear and precise, well considered, encouraging, and afflicting. She reasoned well, and they were not destitute of wit and even fancy, but it was in vain that he read them and reread them, it was in vain that he admitted that they were to the point, well turned, intelligent, graceful, and satisfactory to his masculine vanity; they had in them nothing of her heart, they satisfied him no more than did the kisses that she gave him in the house at Auteuil.

He asked himself why this was so, and when he had learned them by heart he came to know them so well that he discovered the reason, for a person's writings always afford the surest clue to his nature. Spoken words dazzle and deceive, for lips are pleasing and eyes seductive, but black characters set down upon white paper expose the soul in all its nakedness.

Man, thanks to the artifices of rhetoric, to his professional address and his habit of using the pen to discuss all the affairs of life, often succeeds in disguising his own nature by his impersonal prose style, literary or business, but woman never writes unless it is of herself and something of her being goes into her every word. She knows nothing of the subtilities of style and surrenders herself unreservedly in her ignorance of the scope and value of words. Mariolle called to mind the memoirs and correspondence of celebrated women that he had read; how distinctly their characters were all set forth there, the précieuses, the witty, and the sensible! What struck him most in Mme de Burne's letters was that no trace of sensibility was to be discovered in them. This woman had the faculty of thought but not of feeling. He called to mind letters that he had received from other persons; he had had many of them. A little bourgeoise that he had met while traveling and who had loved him for the space of three months had written delicious, thrilling notes, abounding in fresh and unexpected terms of sentiment; he had been surprised by the flexibility, the elegant coloring, and the variety of her style. Whence had she obtained this gift? From the fact that she was a woman of sensibility; there could be no other answer. A woman does not elaborate her phrases; they come to her intelligence straight from her emotions; she does not rummage the dictionary for fine words. What she feels strongly she expresses justly, without long and labored consideration, in the adaptive sincerity of her nature.

He tried to test the sincerity of his mistress's nature by means of the lines which she wrote him. They were well written and full of amiability, but how was it that she could find nothing better for him? Ah! for her he had found words that burned as living coals!

When his valet brought in his mail he would look for an envelope bearing the longed-for handwriting, and when he recognized it an involuntary emotion would arise in him, succeeded by a beating of the heart. He would extend his hand and grasp the bit of paper; again he would scrutinize the address, then tear it open. What had she to say to him? Would he find the word "love" there? She had never written or uttered this word without qualifying it by the adverb "well": "I love you well"; "I love you much"; "Do I not love you?" He knew all these formulas, which are inexpressive by reason of what is tacked on to them. Can there be such a thing as a comparison between the degrees of love when one is in its toils? Can one decide whether he loves well or ill? "To love much," what a dearth of love that expression manifests! One loves, nothing more, nothing less; nothing can be said, nothing expressed, nothing imagined that means more than that one simple sentence. It is brief, it is everything. It becomes body, soul, life, the whole of our being. We feel it as we feel the warm blood in our veins, we inhale it as we do the air, we carry it within us as we carry our thoughts, for it becomes the atmosphere of the mind. Nothing has existence beside it. It is not a word, it is an inexpressible state of being, represented by a few letters. All the conditions of life are changed by it; whatever we do, there is nothing done or seen or tasted or enjoyed or suffered just as it was before. Mariolle had become the victim of this small verb, and his eye would run rapidly over the lines, seeking there a tenderness answering to his own. He did in fact find there sufficient to warrant him in saying to himself: "She loves me very well," but never to make him exclaim: "She loves me!" She was continuing in her correspondence the pretty, poetical romance that had had its inception at Mont Saint-Michel. It was the literature of love, not of the love.

When he had finished reading and rereading them, he would lock the precious and disappointing sheets in a drawer and seat himself in his easy-chair. He had passed many a bitter hour in it before this.

After a while her answers to his letters became less frequent; doubtless she was somewhat weary of manufacturing phrases and ringing the changes on the same stale theme. And then, besides, she was passing through a period of unwonted fashionable excitement, of which André had presaged the approach with that increment of suffering that such insignificant, disagreeable incidents can bring to troubled hearts.

It was a winter of great gaiety. A mad intoxication had taken possession of Paris and shaken the city to its depths; all night long cabs and coupés were rolling through the streets and through the windows were visible white apparitions of women in evening toilette. Everyone was having a good time; all the conversation was on plays and balls, matinées and soirées. The contagion, an epidemic of pleasure, as it were, had quickly extended to all classes of society, and Mme de Burne also was attacked by it.

It had all been brought about by the effect that her beauty had produced at a dance at the Austrian embassy. The Comte de Bernhaus had made her acquainted with the ambassadress, the Princess de Malten, who had been immediately and entirely delighted with Mme de Burne. Within a very short time she became the Princess's very intimate friend and thereby extended with great rapidity her relations among the most select diplomatic and aristocratic circles. Her grace, her elegance, her charming manners, her intelligence and wit quickly achieved a triumph for her and made her la mode, and many of the highest titles among the women of France sought to be presented to her. Every Monday would witness a long line of coupés with arms on their panels drawn up along the curb of the Rue du Général-Foy, and the footmen would lose their heads and make sad havoc with the high-sounding names that they bellowed into the drawingroom, confounding duchesses with marquises, countesses with baronnes.

She was entirely carried off her feet. The incense of compliments and invitations, the feeling that she was become one of the elect to whom Paris bends the knee in worship as long as the fancy lasts, the delight of being thus admired, made much of, and run after, were too much for her and gave rise within her soul to an acute attack of snobbishness.

Her artistic following did not submit to this condition of affairs without a struggle, and the revolution produced a close alliance among her old friends. Fresnel, even, was accepted by them, enrolled on the regimental muster and became a power in the league, while Mariolle was its acknowledged head, for they were all aware of the ascendency that he had over her and her friendship for him. He, however, watched her as she was whirled away in this flattering popularity as a child watches the vanishing of his red balloon when he has let go the string. It seemed to him that she was eluding him in the midst of this elegant, motley, dancing throng and flying far, far away from that secret happiness that he had so ardently desired for both of them, and he was jealous of everybody and everything, men, women, and inanimate objects alike. He conceived a fierce detestation for the life that she was leading, for all the people that she associated with, all the fêtes that she frequented, balls, theaters, music, for they were all in a league to take her from him by bits and absorb her days and nights, and only a few scant hours were now accorded to their intimacy. His indulgence of this unreasoning spite came near causing him a fit of sickness, and when he visited her he brought with him such a wan face that she said to him:

"What ails you? You have changed of late, and are very thin."

"I have been loving you too much," he replied. She gave him a grateful look: "No one ever loves too much, my friend."

"Can you say such a thing as that?"

"Why, yes."

"And you do not see that I am dying of my vain love for you."

"In the first place it is not true that you love in vain; then no one ever dies of that complaint, and finally all our friends are jealous of you, which proves pretty conclusively that 1 am not treating you badly, all things considered."

He took her hand: "You do not understand me!"

"Yes, I understand very well."

"You hear the despairing appeal that I am incessantly making to your heart?"

"Yes, I have heard it."

"And — "

"And it gives me much pain, for I love you enormously."

"And then?"

"Then you say to me: 'Be like me; think, feel, express yourself as I do.' But, my poor friend, I can't. I am what I am. You must take me as God made me, since I gave myself thus to you, since I have no regrets for having done so and no desire to withdraw from the bargain, since there is no one among all my acquaintance that is dearer to me than you are."

"You do not love me!"

"I love you with all the power of loving that exists in me. If it is not different or greater, is that my fault?"

"If I was certain of that I might content myself with it."

"What do you mean by that?"

"I mean that I believe you capable of loving otherwise, but that I do not believe that it lies in me to inspire you with a genuine passion."

"My friend, you are mistaken. You are more to me than anyone has ever been hitherto, more than anyone will ever be in the future; at least that is my honest conviction. I may lay claim to this great merit: that I do not wear two faces with you, I do not feign to be what you so ardently desire me to be, when many women would act quite differently. Be a little grateful to me for this, and do not allow yourself to be agitated and unstrung; trust in my affection, which is yours, sincerely and unreservedly."

He saw how wide the difference was that parted them. "Ah!" he murmured, "how strangely you look at love and speak of it! To you, I am some one that you like to see now and then, whom you like to have beside you, but to me, you fill the universe: in it I know but you, feel but you, need but you."

She smiled with satisfaction and replied: "I know that; I understand. I am delighted to have it so, and I say to you: Love me always like that if you can, for it gives me great happiness, but do not force me to act a part before you that would be distressing to me and unworthy of us both. I have been aware for some time of the approach of this crisis; it is the cause of much suffering to me, for I am deeply attached to you, but I cannot bend my nature or shape it in conformity with yours. Take me as I am."

Suddenly he asked her: "Have you ever thought, have you ever believed, if only for a day, only for an hour, either before or after, that you might be able to love me otherwise?"

She was at a loss for an answer and reflected for a few seconds. He waited anxiously for her to speak, and continued: "You see, don't you, that you have had other dreams as well?"

"I may have been momentarily deceived in myself," she murmured, thoughtfully.

"Oh! how ingenious you are!" he exclaimed; "how psychological! No one ever reasons thus from the impulse of the heart."

She was reflecting still, interested in her thoughts, in this self-investigation; finally she said: "Before I came to love you as I love you now, I may indeed have thought that I might come to be more — more — more captivated with you, but then I certainly should not have been so frank and simple with you. Perhaps later on I should have been less sincere."

"Why less sincere later on?"

"Because all of love, according to your idea, lies in this formula: 'Everything or nothing,' and this 'everything or nothing' as far as I can see means: 'Everything at first, nothing afterward.' It is when the reign of nothing commences that women begin to be deceitful." —

He replied in great distress: "But you do not see how wretched I am — how I am tortured by the thought that you might have loved me otherwise. You have felt that thought: therefore it is some other one that you will love in that manner."

She unhesitatingly replied: "I do not believe it."

"And why? Yes, why, I ask you? Since you have had the foreknowledge of love, since you have felt in anticipation the fleeting and torturing hope of confounding soul and body with the soul and body of another, of losing your being in his and taking his being to be portion of your own, since you have perceived the possibility of this ineffable emotion, the day will come, sooner or later, when you will experience it."

"No; my imagination deceived me, and deceived itself. I am giving you all that I have to give you. I have reflected deeply on this subject since I have been your mistress. Observe that I do not mince matters, not even my words. Really and truly, I am convinced that I cannot love you more or better than I do at this moment. You see that I talk to you just as I talk to myself. I do that because you are very intelligent, because you understand and can read me like a book, and the best way is to conceal nothing from you; it is the only way to keep us long and closely united. And that is what I hope for, my friend."

He listened to her as a man drinks when he is thirsty, then kneeled before her and laid his head in her lap. He took her little hands and pressed them to his lips, murmuring: "Thanks! thanks!" When he raised his eyes to look at her, he saw that there were tears standing in hers; then placing her arms in turn about André's neck, she gently drew him toward her, bent over and kissed him upon the eyelids.

"Take a chair," she said; "it is not prudent to be kneeling before me here."

He seated himself, and when they had contemplated each other in silence for a few moments, she asked him if he would take her some day to visit the exhibition that the sculptor Prédolé, of whom everyone was talking enthusiastically, was then giving of his works. She had in her dressing-room a bronze Love of his, a charming figure pouring water into her bath-tub, and she had a great desire to see the complete collection of the eminent artist's works which had been delighting all Paris for a week past at the Varin gallery. They fixed upon a date and then Mariolle arose to take leave.

"Will you be at Auteuil tomorrow?" she asked him in a whisper.

"Oh! Yes!"

He was very joyful on his way homeward, intoxicated by that "Perhaps?" which never dies in the heart of a lover.

IX

Mme de Burne's coupé was proceeding at a quick trot along the Rue de Grenelle. It was early April, and the hailstones of a belated storm beat noisily against the glasses of the carriage and rattled off upon the roadway which was already whitened by the falling particles. Men on foot were hurrying along the sidewalk beneath their umbrellas, with coat-collars turned up to protect their necks and ears. After two weeks of fine weather a detestable cold spell had set in, the farewell of winter, freezing up everything and bringing chapped hands and chilblains.

With her feet resting upon a vessel filled with hot water and her form enveloped in soft furs that warmed her through her dress with a velvety caress that was so deliciously agreeable to her sensitive skin, the young woman was sadly reflecting that in an hour at farthest she would have to take a cab to go and meet Mariolle at Auteuil. She was seized by a strong desire to send him a telegram, but she had promised herself more than two months ago that she would not again have recourse to this expedient unless compelled to, for she had been making a great effort to love him in the same manner that he loved her. She had seen how he suffered, and had commiserated him, and after that conversation when she had kissed him upon the eyes in an outburst of genuine tenderness, her sincere affection for him had, in fact, assumed a warmer and more expansive character. In her surprise at her involuntary coldness she had asked herself why, after all, she could not love him as other women love their lovers, since she knew that she was deeply attached to him and that he was more pleasing to her than any other man. This indifference of her love could only proceed from a sluggish action of the heart, which could be cured like any other sluggishness.

She tried it. She endeavored to arouse her feelings by thoughts of him, to be more demonstrative in his presence. She was successful now and then, just as one excites his fears at night by thinking of ghosts or robbers. Fired a little herself by this pretense of passion, she even forced herself to be more caressing; she succeeded very well at first, and delighted him to the point of intoxication.

She thought that this was the beginning in her of a fever somewhat similar to that with which she knew that he was consuming. Her old intermittent hopes of love, that she had dimly seen the possibility of realizing the night that she had dreamed her dreams among the white mists of Saint-Michel's Bay, took form and shape again, not so seductive as then, less wrapped in clouds of poetry and idealism, but more clearly defined, more human, stripped of illusion after the experience of her liaison. Then she had summoned up and watched for that irresistible impulse of all the being toward another being that arises, she had heard, when the emotions of the soul act upon two physical natures. She had watched in vain; it had never come.

She persisted, however, in feigning ardor, in making their interviews more frequent, in saying to him: "I feel that I am coming to love you more and more." But she became weary of it at last, and was powerless longer to impose upon herself or deceive him. She was astonished to find that the kisses that he gave her were becoming distasteful to her after a while, although she was not by any means entirely insensible to them.

This was made manifest to her by the vague lassitude that took possession of her from the early morning of those days when she had an appointment with him. Why was it that on those mornings she did not feel, as other women feel, all her nature troubled by the desire and anticipation of his embraces? She endured them, indeed she accepted them, with tender resignation, but as a woman conquered, brutally subjugated, responding contrary to her own will, never voluntarily and with pleasure. Could it be that her nature, so delicate, so exceptionally aristocratic and refined, had in it depths of modesty, the modesty of a superior and sacred animality, that were as yet unfathomed by modern perceptions?

Mariolle gradually came to understand this; he saw her factitious ardor growing less and less. He divined the nature of her love-inspired attempt, and a mortal, inconsolable sorrow took possession of his soul.

She knew now, as he knew, that the attempt had been made and that all hope was gone. The proof of this was that this very day, wrapped as she was in her warm furs and with her feet on her hot-water bottle, glowing with a feeling of physical comfort as she watched the hail beating against the windows of her coupé, she could not find in her the courage to leave this luxurious warmth to get into an ice-cold cab to go and meet the poor fellow.

The idea of breaking with him, of avoiding his caresses, certainly never occurred to her for a moment. She was well aware that to completely captivate a man who is in love and keep him as one's own peculiar private property in the midst of feminine rivalries, a woman must surrender herself to him body and soul. That she knew, for it is logical, fated, indisputable. It is even the loyal course to pursue, and she wanted to be loyal to him in all the uprightness of her nature as his mistress. She would go to him then, she would go to him always; but why so often? Would not their interviews even assume a greater charm for him, an attraction of novelty, if they were granted more charily, like rare and inestimable gifts presented to him by her and not to be used too prodigally?

Whenever she had gone to Auteuil she had had the impression that she was bearing to him a priceless gift, the most precious of offerings. In giving in this way, the pleasure of giving is inseparable from a certain sensation of sacrifice; it is the pride that one feels in being generous, the satisfaction of conferring happiness, not the transports of a mutual passion.

She even calculated that Andre's love would be more likely to be enduring if she abated somewhat of her familiarity with him, for hunger always increases by fasting, and desire is but an appetite. Immediately that this resolution was formed she made up her mind that she would go to Auteuil that day, but would feign indisposition. The journey, which a minute ago had seemed to her so difficult through the inclement weather, now appeared to her quite easy, and she understood, with a smile at her own expense and at this sudden revelation, why she made such a difficulty about a thing that was quite natural. But a moment ago she would not, now she would. The reason why she would not a moment ago was that she was anticipating the thousand petty disagreeable details of the rendezvous! She would prick her fingers with pins that she handled very awkwardly, she would be unable to find the articles that she had thrown at random upon the bedroom floor as she disrobed in haste, already looking forward to the hateful task of having to dress without an attendant.

She paused at this reflection, dwelling upon it and weighing it carefully for the first time. After all, was it not rather repugnant, rather vulgarizing, this idea of a rendezvous for a stated time, settled upon a day or two days in advance, just like a business appointment or a consultation with your doctor? There is nothing more natural, after a long and charming tête-à-tête, than that the lips which have been uttering warm, seductive words should meet in a passionate kiss; but how different that was from the premeditated kiss that she went there to receive, watch in hand, once a week. There was so much truth in this that on those days when she was not to see André she had frequently felt a vague desire of being with him, while this desire was scarcely perceptible at all when she had to go to him in foul cabs, through squalid streets, with the cunning of a hunted thief, all her feelings toward him quenched and deadened by these considerations.

Ah! that appointment at Auteuil! She had calculated the time on all the clocks of all her friends; she had watched the minutes that brought her nearer to it slip away at Mme de Frémines's, at Mme de Bratiane's, at pretty Mme le Prieur's, on those afternoons when she killed time by roaming about Paris so as not to remain in her own house, where she might be detained by an inopportune visit or some other unforeseen obstacle.

She suddenly said to herself: "I will make today a day of rest; I will go there very late." Then she opened a little cupboard in the front of the carriage, concealed among the folds of black silk that lined the coupé, which was fitted up as luxuriously as a pretty woman's boudoir. The first thing that presented itself when she had thrown open the doors of this secret receptacle was a mirror playing on hinges that she moved so that it was on a level with her face. Behind the mirror, in their satin-lined niches, were various small objects in silver: a box for her rice-powder, a pencil for her lips, two crystal scent-bottles, an inkstand and penholder, scissors, a pretty paper-cutter to tear the leaves of the last novel with which she amused herself as she rolled along the streets. The exquisite clock, of the size and shape of a walnut, told her that it was four o'clock. Mme de Burne reflected: "I have an hour yet, at all events," and she touched a spring that had the effect of making the footman who was seated beside the coachman stoop and take up the speaking-tube to receive her order. She pulled out the other end from where it was concealed in the lining of the carriage, and applying her lips to the mouthpiece of rock-crystal: "To the Austrian embassy!" she said.

Then she inspected herself in the mirror. The look that she gave herself expressed, as it always did, the delight that one feels in looking upon one's best beloved; then she threw back her furs to judge of the effect of her corsage. It was a toilette adapted to the chill days of the end of winter. The neck was trimmed with a bordering of very fine white down that shaded off into a delicate gray as it fell over the shoulders, like the wing of a bird. Upon her hat — it was a kind of toque — there towered an aigret of more brightly colored feathers, and the general effect that her costume inspired was to make one think that she had got herself up in this manner in preparation for a flight through the hail and the gray sky in company with Mother Carey's chickens.

She was still complacently contemplating herself when the carriage suddenly wheeled into the great court of the embassy.

Thereupon she arranged her wrap, lowered the mirror to its place, closed the doors of the little cupboard, and when the coupé had come to a halt said to her coachman: "You may go home; I shall not need you any more." Then she asked the footman who came forward from the entrance of the hotel: "Is the Princess at home?"

"Yes, Madame."

She entered and ascended the stairs and came to a small drawingroom where the Princess de Malten was writing letters.

The ambassadress arose with an appearance of much satisfaction when she perceived her friend, and they kissed each other twice in succession upon the cheek, close to the corner of the lips. Then they seated themselves side by side upon two low chairs in front of the fire. They were very fond of each other, took great delight in each other's society and understood each other thoroughly, for they were almost counterparts in nature and disposition, belonging to the same race of femininity, brought up in the same atmosphere and endowed with the same sensations, although Mme de Malten was a Swede and had married an Austrian. They had a strange and mysterious attraction for each other, from which resulted a profound feeling of unmixed well-being and contentment whenever they were together. Their babble would run on for half a day on end, without once stopping, trivial, futile talk, interesting to them both by reason of their similarity of tastes.

"You see how I love you!" said Mme de Burne. "You are to dine with me this evening, and still I could not help coming to see you. It is a real passion, my dear."

"A passion that I share," the Swede replied with a smile.

Following the habit of their profession, they put each her best foot foremost for the benefit of the other; coquettish as if they had been dealing with a man, but with a different style of coquetry, for the strife was different, and they had not before them the adversary, but the rival.

Madame de Burne had kept looking at the clock during the conversation. It was on the point of striking five. He had been waiting there an hour. "That is long enough," she said to herself as she arose.

"So soon?" said the Princess.

"Yes," the other unblushingly replied. "I am in a hurry; there is some one waiting for me. I would a great deal rather stay here with you."

They exchanged kisses again, and Mme de Burne, having requested the footman to call a cab for her, drove away.

The horse was lame and dragged the cab after him wearily, and the animal's halting and fatigue seemed to have infected the young woman. Like the broken-winded beast, she found the journey long and difficult. At one moment she was comforted by the pleasure of seeing André, at the next she was in despair at the thought of the discomforts of the interview.

She found him waiting for her behind the gate, shivering. The biting blasts roared through the branches of the trees, the hailstones rattled on their umbrella as they made their way to the house, their feet sank deep into the mud. The garden was dead, dismal, miry, melancholy, and André was very pale. He was enduring terrible suffering.

When they were in the house: "Gracious, how cold it is!" she exclaimed.

And yet a great fire was blazing in each of the two rooms, but they had not been lighted until past noon and had not had time to dry the damp walls, and shivers ran through her frame. "I think that I will not take off my furs just yet," she added. She only unbuttoned her outer garment and threw it open, disclosing her warm costume and her plume-decked corsage, like a bird of passage that never remains long in one place.

He seated himself beside her.

"There is to be a delightful dinner at my house tonight," she said, "and I am enjoying it in anticipation."

"Who are to be there?"

"Why, you, in the first place; then Prédolé, whom I have so long wanted to know."

"Ah! Prédolé is to be there?"

"Yes; Lamarthe is to bring him."

"But Prédolé is not the kind of a man to suit you, not a bit! Sculptors in general are not so constituted as to please pretty women, and Prédolé less so than any of them."

"Oh, my friend, that cannot be. I have such an admiration for him!"

The sculptor Prédolé had gained a great success and had captivated all Paris some two months before by his exhibition at the Varin gallery. Even before that he had been highly appreciated;

people had said of him, "His figurines are delicious"; but when the world of artists and connoisseurs had assembled to pass judgment upon his collected works in the rooms of the Rue Varin, the outburst of enthusiasm had been explosive. They seemed to afford the revelation of such an unlooked-for charm, they displayed such a peculiar gift in the translation of elegance and grace, that it seemed as if a new manner of expressing the beauty of form had been born to the world. His specialty was statuettes in extremely abbreviated costumes, in which his genius displayed an unimaginable delicacy of form and airy lightness. His dancing girls, especially, of which he had made many studies, displayed in the highest perfection, in their pose and the harmony of their attitude and motion, the ideal of female beauty and suppleness.

For a month past Mme de Burne had been unceasing in her efforts to attract him to her house, but the artist was unsociable, even something of a bear, so the report ran. At last she had succeeded, thanks to the intervention of Lamarthe, who had made a touching, almost frantic appeal to the grateful sculptor.

"Whom have you besides?" Mariolle inquired. "The Princess de Malten."

He was displeased; he did not fancy that woman. " Who else?"

"Massival, Bernhaus, and George de Maltry. That is all: only my select circle. You are acquainted with Prédolé, are you not?"

"Yes, slightly."

"How do you like him?"

"He is delightful; I never met a man so enamored of his art and so interesting when he holds forth on it." She was delighted and again said: 'It will be charming."

He had taken her hand under her fur cloak; he gave it a little squeeze, then kissed it. Then all at once it came to her mind that she had forgotten to tell him that she was ill, and casting about on the spur of the moment for another reason, she murmured: "Gracious! how cold it is!"

"Do you think so?"

"I am chilled to my very marrow."

He arose to take a look at the thermometer, which was, in fact, pretty low; then he resumed his seat at her side.

She had said: "Gracious! how cold it is!" and he believed that he understood her. For three weeks, now, at every one of their interviews, he had noticed that her attempt to feign tenderness was gradually becoming fainter and fainter. He saw that she was weary of wearing this mask, so weary that she could continue it no longer, and he himself was so exasperated by the little power that he had over her, so stung by his vain and unreasoning desire of this woman, that he was beginning to say to himself in his despairing moments of solitude: "It will be better to break with her than to continue to live like this."

He asked her, by way of fathoming her intentions: "Won't you take off your cloak now?"

"Oh, no," she said; "I have been coughing all the morning; this fearful weather has given me a sore throat. I am afraid that I may be ill." She was silent a moment, then added: "If I had not wanted to see you very much indeed I would not have come to-day." As he did not reply, in his grief and anger, she went on: "This return of cold weather is very dangerous, coming as it does after the fine days of the past two weeks."

She looked out into the garden, where the trees were already almost green despite the clouds of snow that were driving among their branches. He looked at her and thought: "So that is the kind of love that she feels for me!" and for the first time he began to feel a sort of jealous hatred of her, of her face, of her elusive affection, of her form, so long pursued, so subtle to escape him. "She pretends that she is cold," he said to himself. "She is cold only because I am here. If it were a question of some party of pleasure, some of those idiotic caprices that go to make up the useless existence of these frivolous creatures, she would brave everything and risk her life. Does she not ride about in an open carriage on the coldest days to show her fine clothes? Ah! that is the way with them all nowadays!"

He looked at her as she sat there facing him so calmly, and he knew that in that head, that dear little head that he adored so, there was one wish paramount, the wish that their tête-à-tête might not be protracted; it was becoming painful to her.

Was it true that there had ever existed, that there existed now, women capable of passion, of emotion, who weep, suffer, and bestow themselves in a transport, loving with heart and soul and body, with mouth that speaks and eyes that gaze, with heart that beats and hand that caresses; women ready to brave all for the sake of their love, and to go, by day or by night, regardless of menaces and watchful eyes, fearlessly, tremorously, to him who stands with open arms waiting to receive them, mad, ready to sink with their happiness?

Oh, that horrible love that which now held him in its fetters! — love without issue, without end, joyless and triumphless, eating away his strength and devouring him with its anxieties; love in which there was no charm and no delight, cause to him only of suffering, sorrow, and bitter tears, where he was constantly pursued by the intolerable regret of the impossibility of awaking responsive kisses upon lips that are as cold and dry and sterile as dead trees!

He looked at her as she sat there, so charming in her feathery dress. Were not her dresses the great enemy that he had to contend against, more than the woman herself, jealous guardians, coquettish and costly barriers, that kept him from his mistress?

"Your toilette is charming," he said, not caring to speak of the subject that was torturing him so cruelly.

She replied with a smile: "You must see the one that I shall wear tonight." Then she coughed several times in succession and said: "I am really taking cold. Let me go, my friend. The sun will show himself again shortly, and I will follow his example."

He made no effort to detain her, for he was discouraged, seeing that nothing could now avail to overcome the inertia of this sluggish nature, that his romance was ended, ended forever, and that it was useless to hope for ardent words from those tranquil lips, or a kindling glance from those calm eyes. All at once he felt rising with gathering strength within him the stern determination to end this torturing subserviency. She had nailed him upon a cross; he was bleeding from every limb, and she watched his agony without feeling for his suffering, even rejoicing that she had had it in her power to effect so much. But he would tear himself from his deathly gibbet, leaving there bits of his body, strips of his flesh, and all his mangled heart. He would flee like a wild animal that the hunters have wounded almost unto death, he would go and hide himself in some lonely place where his wounds might heal and where he might feel only those dull pangs that remain with the mutilated until they are released by death.

"Farewell, then," he said.

She was struck by the sadness of his voice and rejoined: "Until this evening, my friend."

"Until this evening," he re-echoed. "Farewell." He saw her to the garden gate, and came back and seated himself, alone, before the fire.

Alonel How cold it was; how cold, indeed! How sad he was, how lonely! It was all ended! Ah, what a horrible thought! There was an end of hoping and waiting for her, dreaming of her, with that fierce blazing of the heart that at times brings out our existence upon this somber earth with the vividness of fireworks displayed against the blackness of the night. Farewell those nights of solitary emotion when, almost until the dawn, he paced his chamber thinking of her; farewell those wakings when, upon opening his eyes, he said to himself: "Soon I shall see her at our little house."

How he loved her! how he loved her! What a long, hard task it would be to him to forget her! She had left him because it was cold! He saw her before him as but now, looking at him and bewitching him, bewitching him the better to break his heart. Ah, how well she had done her work! With one single stroke, the first and last, she had cleft it asunder. He felt the old gaping wound begin to open, the wound that she had dressed and now had made incurable by plunging into it the knife of death-dealing indifference. He even felt that from this broken heart there was something distilling itself through his frame, mounting to his throat and choking him; then, covering his eyes with his hands, as if to conceal this weakness even from himself, he wept.

She had left him because it was cold! He would have walked naked through the driving snow to meet her, no matter where; he would have cast himself from the house top, only to fall at her feet. An old tale came to his mind, that has been made into a legend: that of the Côte des Deux Amans, a spot which the traveler may behold as he journeys toward Rouen. A maiden, obedient to her father's cruel caprice, which prohibited her from marrying the man of her choice unless she accomplished the task of carrying him, unassisted, to the summit of the steep mountain, succeeded in dragging him up there on her hands and knees, and died as she reached the top. Love, then, is but a legend, made to be sung in verse or told in lying romances!

Had not his mistress herself, in one of their earliest interviews, made use of an expression that he had never forgotten: "Men nowadays do not love women so as really to harm themselves by it. You may believe me, for I know them both" She had been wrong in his case, but not in her own, for on another occasion she had said: "In any event, I give you fair warning that I am incapable of being really smitten with anyone, be he who he may."

Be he who he may? Was that quite a sure thing? Of him, no; of that he was quite well assured now, but of another?

Of him? She could not love him. Why not?

Then the feeling that his life had been a wasted one, which had haunted him for a long time past, fell upon him as if it would crush him. He had done nothing, obtained nothing, conquered nothing, succeeded in nothing. When he had felt an attraction toward the arts he had not found in himself the courage that is required to devote one's self exclusively to one of them, nor the persistent determination that they demand as the price of success. There had been no triumph to cheer him; no elevated taste for some noble career to ennoble and aggrandize his mind. The only strenuous effort that he had ever put forth, the attempt to conquer a woman's heart, had proved ineffectual like all the rest. Take him all in all, he was only a miserable failure.

He was weeping still beneath his hands which he held pressed to his eyes. The tears, trickling down his cheeks, wet his mustache and left a salty taste upon his lips, and their bitterness increased his wretchedness and his despair.

When he raised his head at last he saw that it was night. He had only just sufficient time to go home and dress for her dinner.

X

ANDRÉ MARIOLLE was the first to arrive at Mme de Burne's. He took a seat and gazed about him upon the walls, the furniture, the hangings, at all the small objects and fa trinkets that were so dear to him from their association with her — at the familiar apartment where he had first known her, where he had come to her so many times since then, and where he had discovered in himself the germs of that ill-starred passion that had kept on growing, day by day, until the hour of his barren victory. With what eagerness had he many a time awaited her coming in this charming spot which seemed to have been made for no one but her, an exquisite setting for an exquisite creature! How well he knew the pervading odor of this salon and its hangings; a subdued odor of iris, so simple and aristocratic. He grasped the arms of the great armchair, from which he had so often watched her smile and listened to her talk, as if they had been the hands of some friend that he was part-

ing with forever. It would have pleased him if she could not come, if no one could come, and if he could remain there alone, all night, dreaming of his love, as people watch beside a dead man. Then at daylight he could go away for a long time, perhaps forever.

The door opened, and she appeared and came forward to him with outstretched hand. He was master of himself, and showed nothing of his agitation. She was not a woman, but a living bouquet — an indescribable bouquet of flowers.

A girdle of pinks enclasped her waist and fell about her in cascades, reaching to her feet. About her bare arms and shoulders ran a garland of mingled myosotis and lilies-of-the-valley, while three fairylike orchids seemed to be growing from her breast and caressing the milk-white flesh with the rosy and red flesh of their supernal blooms. Her blond hair was studded with violets in enamel, in which minute diamonds glistened, and other diamonds, trembling upon golden pins, sparkled like dewdrops among the odorous trimming of her corsage.

"I shall have a headache," she said, "but I don't care; my dress is becoming."

Delicious odors emanated from her, like spring among the gardens. She was more fresh than the garlands that she wore. André was dazzled as he looked at her, reflecting that it would be no less brutal and barbarous to take her in his arms at that moment than it would be to trample upon a blossoming flowerbed. So their bodies were no longer objects to inspire love; they were objects to be adorned, simply frames on which to hang fine clothes. They were like birds, they were like flowers, they were like a thousand other things as much as they were like women. Their mothers, all women of past and gone generations, had used coquettish arts to enhance their natural beauties, but it had been their aim to please in the first place by their direct physical seductiveness, by the charm of native grace, by the irresistible attraction that the female form exercises over the heart of the males. At the present day coquetry was everything. Artifice was now the great means, and not only the means, but the end as well, for they employed it even more frequently to dazzle the eyes of rivals and excite barren jealousy than to subjugate men.

What end, then, was this toilette designed to serve, the gratification of the eyes of him, the lover, or the humiliation of the Princess de Malten?

The door opened, and the lady whose name was in his thoughts was announced.

Mme de Burne moved quickly forward to meet her and gave her a kiss, not unmindful of the orchids during the operation, her lips slightly parted, with a little grimace of tenderness. It was a pretty kiss, an extremely desirable kiss, given and returned from the heart by those two pairs of lips.

Mariolle gave a start of pain. Never once had she run to meet him with that joyful eagerness, never had she kissed him like that, and with a sudden change of ideas he said to himself: "Women are no longer made to fulfill our requirements."

Massival made his appearance, then M. de Pradon and the Comte de Bernhaus, then George de Maltry, resplendent with English "chic."

Lamarthe and Prédolé were now the only ones missing. The sculptor's name was mentioned, and every voice was at once raised in praise of him. "He had restored to life the grace of form, he had recovered the lost traditions of the Renaissance, with something additional: the sincerity of modern art!" M. de Maltry maintained that he was the exquisite revealer of the suppleness of the human form. Such phrases as these had been current in the salons for the last two months, where they had been bandied about from mouth to mouth.

At last the great man appeared. Everyone was surprised. He was a large man of uncertain age, with the shoulders of a coal-heaver, a powerful face with strongly-marked features, surrounded by hair and beard that were beginning to turn white, a prominent nose, thick full lips, wearing a timid and embarrassed air. He held his arms away from his body in an awkward sort of way that was doubtless to be attributed to the immense hands that protruded from his sleeves. They were broad and thick, with hairy and muscular fingers; the hands of a Hercules or a butcher, and they seemed to be conscious of being in the way, embarrassed at finding themselves there and looking vainly for some convenient place to hide themselves. Upon looking more closely at his face, however, it was seen to be illuminated by clear, piercing, gray eyes of extreme expressiveness, and these alone served to impart some degree of life to the man's heavy and torpid expression. They were constantly searching, inquiring, scrutinizing, darting their rapid, shifting glances here, there, and everywhere, and it was plainly to be seen that these eager, inquisitive looks were the animating principle of a deep and comprehensive intellect.

Mme de Burne was somewhat disappointed; she politely led the artist to a chair which he took and where he remained seated, apparently disconcerted by this introduction to a strange house.

Lamarthe, master of the situation, approached his friend with the intention of breaking the ice and relieving him from the awkwardness of his position. "My dear fellow," he said, "let me make for you a little map to let you know where you are. You have seen our divine hostess; now look at her surroundings." He showed him upon the mantelpiece a bust, authenticated in due form, by Houdon, then upon a cabinet in buhl a group representing two women dancing, with arms about each other's waists, by Clodion, and finally four Tanagra statuettes upon an étagère, selected for their perfection of finish and detail.

Then all at once Prédolé's face brightened as if he had found his children in the desert. He arose and went to the four little earthen figures, and when Mme de Burne saw him grasp two of them at once in his great hands that seemed made to slaughter oxen, she trembled for her treasures. When he laid hands on them, however, it appeared that it was only for the purpose of caressing them, for he handled them with wonderful delicacy and dexterity, turning them about in his thick fingers which somehow seemed all at once to have become as supple as a juggler's. It was evident by the gentle way the big man had of looking at and handling them that he had in his soul and his very finger-ends an ideal and delicate tenderness for such small elegancies.

"Are they not pretty?" Lamarthe asked him.

The sculptor went on to extol them as if they had been his own, and he spoke of some others, the most remarkable that he had met with, briefly and in a voice that was rather low but confident and calm, the expression of a clearly defined thought that was not ignorant of the value of words and their uses.

Still under the guidance of the author, he next inspected the other rare bric-à-brac that Mme de Burne had collected, thanks to the counsels of her friends. He looked with astonishment and delight at the various articles, apparently agreeably disappointed to find them there, and in every case he took them up and turned them lightly over in his hands, as if to place himself in direct personal contact with them. There was a statuette of bronze, heavy as a cannonball, hidden away in a dark corner; he took it up with one hand, carried it to the lamp, examined it at length, and replaced jt where it belonged without visible effort. Lamarthe exclaimed: "The great, strong fellow! he is built expressly to wrestle with stone and marble!" while the ladies looked at him approvingly.

Dinner was now announced. The mistress of the house took the sculptor's arm to pass to the diningroom, and when she had seated him in the place of honor at her right hand, she asked him out of courtesy, just as she would have questioned a scion of some great family as to the exact origin of his name: "Your art, Monsieur, has also the additional honor, has it not, of being the most ancient of all?"

He replied in his calm deep voice: "Mon Dieu, Madame, the shepherds in the Bible play upon the flute, therefore music would seem to be the more ancient — although true music, as we understand it, does not go very far back, while true sculpture dates from remote antiquity."

"You are fond of music?"

"I love all the arts," he replied with grave earnestness.

"Is it known who was the inventor of your art?" He reflected a moment, then replied in tender accents, as if he had been relating some touching tale: "According to Grecian tradition it was Dædalus the Athenian. The most attractive legend, however, is that which attributes the invention to a Sicyonian potter named Dibutades. His daughter Kora having traced her betrothed's profile with the assistance of an arrow, her father filled in the rude sketch with clay and modeled it. It was then that my art was born."

"Charming!" murmured Lamarthe. Then turning to Mme de Burne, he said: "You cannot imagine, Madame, how interesting this man becomes when he talks of what he loves; what power he has to express and explain it and make people adore it."

But the sculptor did not seem disposed either to pose for the admiration of the guests or to perorate. He had tucked a corner of his napkin between his shirt-collar and his neck and was reverentially eating his soup, with that appearance of respect that peasants manifest for that portion of the meal. Then he drank a glass of wine and drew himself up with an air of greater ease, of making himself more at home. Now and then he made a movement as if to turn around, for he had perceived the reflection in a mirror of a modern group that stood on the mantelshelf behind him. He did not recognize it and was seeking to divine the author. At last, unable longer to resist the impulse, he asked: "It is by Falguière, is it not?"

Mme de Burne laughed. "Yes, it is by Falguière. How could you tell, in a glass?"

He smiled in turn. "Ah, Madame, I can't explain how it is done, but I can tell at a glance the sculpture of those men who are painters as well, and the painting of those who also practice sculpture. It is not a bit like the work of a man who devotes himself to one art exclusively."

Lamarthe, wishing to show off his friend, called for explanations, and Prédolé proceeded to give them. In his slow, precise manner of speech he defined and illustrated the painting of sculptors and the sculpture of painters in such a clear and original way that he was listened to as much with eyes as with ears. Commencing his demonstration at the earliest period and pursuing it through the history of art and gathering examples from epoch to epoch, he came down to the time of the early Italian masters who were painters and sculptors at the same time, Nicolas and John of Pisa, Donatello, Lorenzo Ghiberti. He spoke of Diderot's interesting remarks upon the same subject, and in conclusion mentioned Ghiberti's bronze gates of the baptistry of Saint John at Florence, such living and dramatically forceful bas-reliefs that they seem more like paintings upon canvas. He waved his great hands before him as if he were modeling, with such ease and grace of motion as to delight every eye, calling up above the plates and glasses the pictures that his tongue told of, and reconstructing the work that he mentioned with such conviction that everyone followed the motions of his fingers with breathless attention. Then some dishes that he fancied were placed before him and he ceased talking and began eating.

He scarcely spoke during the remainder of the dinner, not troubling himself to follow the conversation, which ranged from some bit of theatrical gossip to a political rumor; from a ball to a wedding; from an article in the "Revue des Deux Mondes" to the horse-show that had just opened. His appetite was good, and he drank a good deal, without being at all affected by it, having a sound, hard head that good wine could not easily upset.

When they had returned to the drawingroom, Lamarthe, who had not drawn the sculptor out to the extent that he wished to do, drew him over to a glass case to show him a priceless object, a classic, historic gem: a silver inkstand carved by Benvenuto Cellini. The men listened with extreme interest to his long and eloquent rhapsody as they stood grouped about him, while the two women, seated in front of the fire and rather disgusted to see so much enthusiasm wasted upon the form of inanimate objects, appeared to be a little bored and chatted together in a low voice from time to time. After that conversation became general, but not animated, for it had been somewhat damped by the ideas that had passed into the atmosphere of this pretty room, with its furnishing of precious objects.

Prédolé left early, assigning as a reason that he had to be at work at daybreak every morning. When he was gone Lamarthe enthusiastically asked Mme, de Burne: "Well, how did you like him?"

She replied, hesitatingly and with something of an air of ill nature: "He is quite interesting, but prosy."

The novelist smiled and said to himself: "Parbleu, that is because he did not admire your toilette; and you are the only one of all your pretty things that he hardly condescended to look at." He exchanged a few pleasant remarks with her and went over and took a seat by Mme de Malten, to whom he began to be very attentive. The Comte de Bernhaus approached the mistress of the house, and taking a small footstool, appeared sunk in devotion at her feet. Mariolle, Massival, Maltry, and M. de Pradon continued to talk of the sculptor, who had made a deep impression on their minds. M. de Maltry was comparing him to the old masters, for whom life was embellished and illuminated by an exclusive and consuming love of the manifestations of beauty, and he philosophized upon his theme with many very subtle and very tiresome observations.

Massival, quickly tiring of a conversation which made no reference to his own art, crossed the room to Mme de Malten and seated himself beside Lamarthe, who soon yielded his place to him and went and rejoined the men.

"Shall we go?" he said to Mariolle.

"Yes, by all means!"

The novelist liked to walk the streets at night with some friend and talk, when the incisive, peremptory tones of his voice seemed to lay hold of the walls of the houses and climb up them. He had an impression that he was very eloquent, witty, and sagacious during these nocturnal tête-à-têtes, which were monologues rather than conversations so far as his part in them was concerned. The approbation that he thus gained for himself sufficed his needs, and the gentle fatigue of legs and lungs assured him a good night's rest.

Mariolle, for his part, had reached the limit of his endurance. The moment that he was outside her door all his wretchedness and sorrow, all his irremediable disappointment, boiled up and overflowed his heart. He could stand it no longer; he would have no more of it. He would go away and never return.

The two men found themselves alone with each other in the street. The wind had changed and the cold that had prevailed during the day had yielded; it was warm and pleasant, as it almost always is two hours after a snowstorm in spring. The sky was vibrating with the light of innumerable stars, as if a breath of summer in the immensity of space had lighted up the heavenly bodies and set them twinkling. The sidewalks were gray and dry again, while in the roadway pools of water reflected the light of the gas-lamps.

Lamarthe said: "What a fortunate man he is, that Prédolé! He lives only for one thing, his art; thinks but of that, loves but that; it occupies all his being; consoles and cheers him, and affords him a life of happiness and comfort. He is really a great artist of the old stock. Ah! he doesn't let women trouble his head, not much, our women of to-day with their frills and furbelows and fantastic disguises! Did you remark how little attention he paid to our two pretty dames? And yet they were rather seductive. But what he is looking for is the plastic — the plastic pure and simple; he has no use for the artificial. It is true that our divine hostess put him down in her books as an insupportable fool. In her estimation a bust by Houdon, Tanagra statuettes, and an inkstand by Cellini are but so many unconsidered trifles that go to the adornment and the rich and natural setting of a masterpiece, which is Herself; she and her dress, for dress is part and parcel of Herself; it is the fresh accentuation that she places on her beauty day by day. What a trivial, personal thing is woman!"

He stopped and gave the sidewalk a great thump with his cane, so that the noise resounded through the quiet street, then he went on.

"They have a very clear and exact perception of what adds to their attractions: the toilette and the ornaments in which there is an entire change of fashion every ten years; but they are heedless of that attribute which involves rare and constant power of selection, which demands from them keen and delicate artistic penetration and a purely aesthetic exercise of their senses. Their senses, moreover, are extremely rudimentary, incapable of high development, inaccessible to whatever does not touch directly the feminine egotism that absorbs everything in them. Their acuteness is the stratagem of the savage, of the red Indian; of war and ambush. They are even almost incapable of enjoying the material pleasures of the lower order, which require a physical education and the intelligent exercise of an organ, such as good living. When, as they do in exceptional cases, they come to have some respect for decent cookery, they still remain incapable of appreciating our great wines, which speak to masculine palates only, for wine does speak."

He again thumped the pavement with his cane, accenting his last dictum and punctuating the sentence, and continued.

"It won't do, however, to expect too much from them, but this want of taste and appreciation that so frequently clouds their intellectual vision when higher considerations are at stake often serves to blind them still more when our interests are in question. A man may have heart, feeling, intelligence, exceptional merits, and qualities of all kinds, they will all be unavailing to secure their favor as in bygone days when a man was valued for his worth and his courage. The women of to-day are actresses, second-rate actresses at that, who are merely playing for effect a part that has been handed down to them and in which they have no belief. They have to have actors of the same stamp to act up to them and lie through the rôle just as they do; and these actors are the coxcombs that we see hanging around them; from the fashionable world, or elsewhere.”

They walked along in silence for a few moments, side by side. Mariolle had listened attentively to the words of his companion, repeating them in his mind and approving of his sentiments under the influence of his sorrow. He was aware also that a sort of Italian adventurer who was then in Paris giving lessons in swordsmanship, Prince Epilati by name, a gentleman of the fencing-schools, of considerable celebrity for his elegance and graceful vigor that he was in the habit of exhibiting in black-silk tights before the upper ten and the select few of the demimonde, was just then in full enjoyment of the attentions and coquetries of the pretty little Baronne de Frémines.

As Lamarthe said nothing further, he remarked to him:

“It is all our own fault; we make our selections badly; there are other women besides those.”

The novelist replied: “The only ones now that are capable of real attachment are the shopgirls and some sentimental little bourgeoises, poor and unhappily married. I have before now carried consolation to one of those distressed souls. They are overflowing with sentiment, but such cheap, vulgar sentiment that to exchange ours against it is like throwing your money to a beggar. Now I assert that in our young, wealthy society, where the women feel no needs and no desires, where all that they require is some mild distraction to enable them to kill time, and where the men regulate their pleasures as scrupulously as they regulate their daily labors, I assert that under such conditions the old natural attraction, charming and powerful as it was, that used to bring the sexes toward each other, has disappeared.”

“You are right,” Mariolle murmured.

He felt an increasing desire to fly, to put a’ great distance between himself and these people, these puppets who in their empty idleness mimicked the beautiful, impassioned, and tender life of other days and were incapable of savoring its lost delights.

“Good night,” he said; “I am going to bed.” He went home and seated himself at his table and wrote:

“Farewell, Madame. Do you remember my first letter? In it too I said farewell, but I did not go. What a mistake that was!

When you receive this I shall have left Paris; need I tell you why? Men like me ought never to meet with women like you. Were I an artist and were my emotions capable of expression in such manner as to afford me consolation, you would have perhaps inspired me with talent, but I am only a poor fellow who was so unfortunate as to be seized with love for you, and with it its accompanying bitter, unendurable sorrow.

“When I met you for the first time I could not have deemed myself capable of feeling and suffering as I have done. Another in your place would have filled my heart with divine joy in bidding it wake and live, but you could do nothing but torture it. It was not your fault, I know; I reproach you with nothing and I bear you no hard feeling; I have not even the right to send you these lines. Pardon me. You are so constituted that you cannot feel as I feel; you cannot even divine what passes in my breast when I am with you, when you speak to me and I look on you.

“Yes, I know; you have accepted me and offered me a rational and tranquil happiness, for which I ought to thank you on my knees all my life long, but I will not have it. Ah, what a horrible, agonizing love is that which is constantly craving a tender word, a warm caress, without ever receiving them! My heart is empty, empty as the stomach of a beggar who has long followed your carriage with outstretched hand and to whom you have thrown out pretty toys, but no bread. It was bread, it was love, that I hungered for. I am about to go away wretched and in need, in sore need of your love, a few crumbs of which would have saved me.

I have nothing left in the world but a cruel memory that clings and will not leave me, and that I must try to kill.

"Adieu, Madame. Thanks, and pardon me. I love you still, this evening, with all the strength of my soul. Adieu.

"ANDRE MARIOLLE."

XI

THE city lay basking in the brightness of a sunny morning. Mariolle climbed into the carriage that stood waiting at his door with a traveling bag and two trunks on top. He had made his valet the night before pack the linen and other necessaries for a long absence, and now he was going away, leaving as his temporary address Fontainebleau post-office. He was taking no one with him, it being his wish to see no face that might remind him of Paris and to hear no voice that he had heard while brooding over certain matters.

He told the driver to go to the Lyons station and the cab started. Then he thought of that other trip of his, last spring, to Mont Saint-Michel; it was a year ago now lacking three months. He looked out into the street to drive the recollection from his mind.

The vehicle turned into the Avenue des Champs-Elysées, which was flooded with the light of the sun of early spring. The green leaves, summoned forth by the grateful warmth that had prevailed for a couple of weeks and not materially retarded by the cold storm of the last two days, were opening so rapidly on this bright morning that they seemed to impregnate the air with an odor of fresh verdure and of sap evaporating on the way to its work of building up new growths. It was one of those growing mornings when one feels that the dome-topped chestnut-trees in the public gardens and all along the avenues will burst into bloom in a single day through the length and breadth of Paris, like chandeliers that are lighted simultaneously. The earth was thrilling with the movement preparatory to the full life of summer, and the very street was silently stirred beneath its paving of bitumen as the roots ate their way through the soil. He said to himself as he jolted along in his cab: "At last I shall be able to enjoy a little peace of mind. I will witness the birth of spring in solitude deep in the forest."

The journey seemed long to him. The few hours of sleeplessness that he had spent in bemoaning his fate had broken him down as if he had passed ten nights at the bedside of a dying man. When he reached the village of Fontainebleau he went to a notary to see if there was a small house to be had furnished in the neighborhood of the forest. He was told of several. In looking over the photographs the one that pleased him most was a cottage that had just been given up by a young couple, man and wife, who had resided for almost the entire winter in the village of Montigny-sur-Loing. The notary smiled, notwithstanding that he was a man of serious aspect; he probably scented a love story.

"You are alone, Monsieur!" he inquired.

"I am alone."

"No servants, even?"

"No servants, even; I left them at Paris. I wish to engage some of the residents here. I am coming here to work in complete seclusion."

"You will have no difficulty in finding that, at this season of the year."

A few minutes afterward an open landau was whirling Mariolle and his trunks away to Montigny.

The forest was beginning to awake. The copses at the foot of the great trees, whose heads were covered with a light veil of foliage, were beginning to assume a denser aspect. The early birches, with their silvery trunks, were the only trees that seemed completely attired for the summer, while the great oaks only displayed small tremulous splashes of green at the ends of their branches and the beeches, more quick to open their pointed buds, were just shedding the dead leaves of the past year.

The grass by the roadside, unobscured as yet by the thick shade of the tree-tops, was growing lush and bright with the influx of new sap, and the odor of new growth that Mariolle had already remarked in the Avenue des Champs-Elysées, now wrapped him about and immersed him in a great bath of green life budding in the sunshine of the early season. He inhaled it greedily, like one just liberated from prison, and with the sensation of a man whose fetters have just been broken he luxuriously extended his arms along the two sides of the landau and let his hands hang down over the two wheels.

He passed through Marlotte, where the driver called his attention to the Hotel Corot, then just opened, of the original design of which there was much talk. Then the road continued, with the forest on the left hand and on the right a wide plain with trees here and there and hills bounding the horizon. To this succeeded a long village street, a blinding white street lying between two endless rows of little tile-roofed houses. Here and there an enormous lilac bush displayed its flowers over the top of a wall.

This street followed the course of a narrow valley along which ran a little stream. It was a narrow, rapid, twisting, nimble little stream, on one of its banks laving the foundations of the houses and the garden-walls and on the other bathing the meadows where the small trees were just beginning to put forth their scanty foliage. The sight of it inspired Mariolle with a sensation of delight.

He had no difficulty in finding his house and was greatly pleased with it. It was an old house that had been restored by a painter, who had tired of it after living there five years and offered it for rent. It was directly on the water, separated from the stream only by a pretty garden that ended in a terrace of lindens. The Loing, which just above this point had a picturesque fall of a foot or two over a dam erected there, ran rapidly by this terrace, whirling in great eddies. From the front windows of the house the meadows on the other bank were visible.

"I shall get well here," Mariolle thought.

Everything had been arranged with the notary in case the house should prove suitable. The driver carried back his acceptance of it. Then the housekeeping details had to be attended to, which did not take much time, the" mayor's clerk having provided two women, one to do the cooking, the other to wash and attend to the chamber-work.

Downstairs there were a parlor, diningroom, kitchen, and two small rooms; on the floor above a handsome bedroom and a large apartment that the artist owner had fitted up as a studio. The furniture had all been selected with loving care, as people always furnish when they are enamored of a place, but now it had lost a little of its freshness and was in some disorder, with the air of desolation that is noticeable in dwellings that have been abandoned by their master. A pleasant odor of verbena, however, still lingered in the air, showing that the little house had not been long uninhabited. "Ah!" thought Mariolle, "verbena, that indicates simplicity of taste. The woman that preceded me could not have been one of those complex, mystifying natures. Happy man!"

It was getting toward evening, all these occupations having made the day pass rapidly. He took a seat by an open window, drinking in the agreeable coolness that exhaled from the surrounding vegetation and watching the setting sun as it cast long shadows across the meadows.

The two servants were talking while getting the dinner ready and the sound of their voices ascended to him faintly by the stairway, while through the window came the mingled sounds of the lowing of cows, the barking of dogs, and the cries of men bringing home the cattle or conversing with their companions on the other bank of the stream. Everything was peaceful and restful.

For the thousandth time since the snorning Mariolle; asked himself: "What did she think when she received my letter? What will she do?" Then he said to himself: "I wonder what she is doing now?" He looked at his watch; it was half past six. "She has come in from the street. She is receiving."

There rose before his mental vision a picture of the drawingroom, and the young woman chatting with the Princess de Malten, Mme de Frémines, Massival, and the Comte de Bernhaus.

His soul was suddenly moved with an impulse that was something like anger. He wished that he was there. It was the hour of his accustomed visit to her, almost every day, and he felt within him a feeling of discomfort, not of regret. His will was firm, but a sort of physical suffering afflicted him akin to that of one who is denied his morphine at the accustomed time. He no longer beheld the meadows, nor the sun sinking behind the hills of the horizon; all that he could see was her, among her friends, given over to those cares of the world that had robbed him of her. "I will think of her no more," he said to himself.

He arose, went down to the garden and passed on to the terrace. There was a cool mist there rising from the water that had been agitated in its fall over the dam, and this sensation of chilliness, striking to a heart already sad, caused him to retrace his steps. His dinner was awaiting him in the diningroom. He ate it quickly; then, having nothing to occupy him, and feeling that distress of mind and body, of which he had had the presage, now increasing on him, he went to bed and closed his eyes in an attempt to slumber, but it was to no purpose. His thoughts refused to leave that woman; he beheld her in his thought and he suffered.

On whom would she bestow her favor now? On the Comte de Bernhaus, doubtless! He was just the man, elegant, conspicuous, sought after, to suit that creature of display. He had found favor with her, for had she not employed all her arts to conquer him even at a time when she was mistress to another man?

Notwithstanding that his mind was beset by these haunting thoughts, it would still keep wandering off into that misty condition of semi-somnolence in which the man and woman were constantly reappearing to his eyes. Of true sleep he got none, and all night long he saw them at his bedside, braving and mocking him, now retiring as if they would at last permit him to snatch a little sleep, then returning as soon as oblivion had begun to creep over him and awaking him with a spasm of jealous agony in his heart. He left his bed at earliest break of day and went away into the forest with a cane in his hand, a stout serviceable stick that the last occupant of the house had left behind him.

The rays of the newly risen sun were falling through the tops of the oaks, almost leafless as yet, upon the ground, which was carpeted in spots by patches of verdant grass, here by a carpet of dead leaves and there by heather reddened by the frosts of winter. Yellow butterflies were fluttering along the road like little dancing flames. To the right of the road was a hill, almost large enough to be called a mountain. Mariolle ascended it leisurely, and when he reached the top seated himself on a great stone, for he was quite out of breath. His legs were overcome with weakness and refused to support him; all his system seemed to be yielding to a sudden breaking down. He was well aware that this languor did not proceed from fatigue; it came from her, from the love that weighed him down like an intolerable burden, and he murmured: "What wretchedness! why does it possess me thus, me, a man who has always taken from existence only that which would enable him to enjoy it without suffering afterward?"

His attention was awakened by the fear of this malady that might prove so hard to cure, and he probed his feelings, went down to the very depths of his nature, endeavoring to know and understand it better, and make clear to his own eyes the reason of this inexplicable crisis. He said to himself: "I have never yielded to any undue attraction. I am not enthusiastic or passionate by nature; my judgment is more powerful than my instinct, my curiosity than my appetite, my fancy than my perseverance.

I am essentially nothing more than a man that is delicate, intelligent, and hard to please in his enjoyments.

I have loved the things of this life without ever allowing myself to become greatly attached to them, with the perceptions of an expert who sips and does not suffer himself to become surfeited, who knows better than to lose his head. I submit everything to the test of reason, and generally I analyze my likings too severely to submit to them blindly. That is even my great defect, the only cause of my weakness.

"And now that woman has taken possession of me, in spite of myself, in spite of my fears and of my knowledge of her, and she retains her hold as if she had plucked away one by one all the different aspirations that existed in me. That may be the case. Those aspirations of mine went out toward inanimate objects, toward nature, that entices and softens me, toward music, which is a sort of ideal caress, toward reflection, which is the delicate feasting of the mind, toward everything on earth that is beautiful and agreeable.

"Then I met a creature who collected and concentrated all my somewhat fickle and fluctuating likings, and directing them toward herself, converted them into love. Charming and beautiful, she pleased my eyes; bright, intelligent, and witty, she pleased my mind, and she pleased my heart by the mysterious charm of her contact and her presence and by the secret and irresistible emanation from her personality, until all these things enslaved me as the perfume of certain flowers intoxicates. She has taken the place of everything for me, for I no longer have any aspirations, I no longer wish or care for anything."

"In other days how my feelings would have thrilled and started in this forest that is putting forth its new life! To-day I see nothing of it, I am regardless of it; I am still at that woman's side, whom I desire to love no more.

"Come! I must kill these ideas by physical fatigue; unless I do I shall never get well."

He arose, descended the rocky hillside and resumed his walk with long strides, but still the haunting presence crushed him as if it had been a burden that he was bearing on his back. He went on, constantly increasing his speed, now and then encountering a brief sensation of comfort at the sight of the sunlight piercing through the foliage or at a breath of perfumed air from some grove of resinous pine-trees, which inspired in him a presentiment of distant consolation.

Suddenly he came to a halt. "I am not walking any longer," he said, "I am flying from something!" Indeed, he was flying, straight ahead, he cared not where, pursued by the agony of his love.

Then he started on again at a more reasonable speed. The appearance of the forest was undergoing a change. The growth was denser and the shadows deeper, for he was coming to the warmer portions of it, to the beautiful region of the beeches. No sensation of winter lingered there. It was wondrous spring, that seemed to have been the birth of a night, so young and fresh was everything.

Mariolle made his way among the thickets, beneath the gigantic trees that towered above him higher and higher still, and in this way he went on for a long time, an hour, two hours, pushing his way through the branches, through the countless multitudes of little shining leaves, bright with their varnish of new sap. The heavens were quite concealed by the immense dome of verdure, supported on its lofty columns, now perpendicular, now leaning, now of a whitish hue, now dark beneath the black moss that drew its nourishment from the bark.

Thus they towered, stretching away indefinitely in the distance, one behind the other, lording it over the bushy young copses that grew in confused tangles at their feet and wrapping them in dense shadow through which in places poured floods of vivid sunlight. The golden rain streamed down through all this luxuriant growth until the wood no longer remained a wood, but became a brilliant sea of verdure illumined by yellow rays. Mariolle stopped, seized with an ineffable surprise. Where was he? Was he in a forest, or had he descended to the bottom of a sea, a sea of leaves and light, an ocean of green resplendency?

He felt better — more tranquil; more remote, more hidden from his misery, and he threw himself down upon the red carpet of dead leaves that these trees do not cast until they are ready to put on their new garments. Rejoicing in the cool contact of the earth and the pure sweetness of the air, he was soon conscious of a wish, vague at first but soon becoming more defined, not to be alone in this charming spot, and he said to himself: "Ah! if she were only here, at my side!"

He suddenly remembered Mont Saint-Michel, and recollecting how different she had been down there to what she was in Paris, how her affection had blossomed out in the open air before the yellow sands, he thought that on that day she had surely loved him a little for a few hours. Yes, surely, on the road where they had watched the receding tide, in the cloisters where, murmuring his name: "André," she had seemed to say, "I am yours," and on the "Madman's

Path," where he had almost borne her through space, she had felt an impulsion toward him that had never returned since she placed her foot, the foot of a coquette, on the pavement of Paris.

He continued to yield himself to his mournful reveries, still stretched at length upon his back, his look lost among the gold and green of the tree-tops, and little by little his eyes closed, weighed down with sleep and the tranquillity that reigned among the trees. When he awoke he saw that it was past two o'clock of the afternoon.

When he arose and proceeded on his way he felt less sad, less ailing. At length he emerged from the thickness of the wood and came to a great open space where six broad avenues converged and then stretched away and lost themselves in the leafy, transparent distance. A sign-board told him that the name of the locality was "Le Bouquet-du-Roi." It was indeed the capital of this royal country of the beeches.

A carriage passed, and as it was empty and disengaged Mariolle took it and ordered the driver to take him to Marlotte, whence he could make his way to Montigny after getting something to eat at the inn, for he was beginning to be hungry.

He remembered that he had seen this establishment, which was only recently opened, the day before: the Hotel Corot, it was called, an artistic public-house in middle-age style of decoration, modeled on the Chat Noir in Paris. His driver set him down there and he passed through an open door into a vast room where old-fashioned tables and uncomfortable benches seemed to be awaiting drinkers of a past century. At the far end a woman, a young waitress, no doubt, was standing on top of a little folding ladder, fastening some old plates to nails that were driven in the wall and seemed nearly beyond her reach. Now raising herself on tiptoe on both feet, now on one, supporting herself with one hand against the wall while the other held the plate, she reached up with pretty and adroit movements; for her figure was pleasing and the undulating lines from wrist to ankle assumed changing forms of grace at every fresh posture. As her back was toward him she had been unaware of Mariolle's entrance, who stopped to watch her. He thought of Prédolé and his figurines; "It is a pretty picture, though!" he said to himself. "She is very graceful, that little girl."

He gave a little cough. She was so startled that she came near falling, but as soon as she had recovered her self-possession, she jumped down from her ladder as lightly as a rope dancer, and came to him with a pleasant smile on her face. "What will Monsieur have?" she inquired.

"Breakfast, Mademoiselle."

She ventured to say: "It should be dinner, rather, for it is half past three o'clock."

"We will call it dinner if you like. I lost myself in the forest."

Then she told him what dishes there were ready; he made his selection and took a seat. She went away to give the order, returning shortly to set the table for him. He watched her closely as she bustled around the table; she was pretty and very neat in her attire. She had a spry little air that was very pleasant to behold, in her working dress with skirt pinned up, sleeves rolled back, and neck exposed; and her corset fitted closely to her pretty form, of which she had no reason to be ashamed.

Her face was rather red painted by exposure to me open air, and it seemed somewhat too fat and puffy, but it was as fresh as a new-blown rose, with fine, bright, brown eyes, a large mouth with its complement of handsome teeth, and chestnut hair that revealed by its abundance the healthy vigor of this strong young frame.

She brought radishes and bread and butter and he began to eat, ceasing to pay attention to the attendant. He called for a bottle of champagne and drank the whole of it, as he did two glasses of kummel after his coffee, and as his stomach was empty — he had taken nothing before he left his house but a little bread and cold meat — he soon felt a comforting feeling of tipsiness stealing over him that he mistook for oblivion. His griefs and sorrows were diluted and tempered by the sparkling wine which, in so short a time, had transformed the torments of his heart into insensibility. He walked slowly back to Montigny, and being very tired and sleepy went to bed as soon as it was dark, falling asleep as soon as his head touched the pillow.

He awoke after a while, however, in the dense darkness, ill at ease and disquieted as if a night-man that had left him for an hour or two had furtively reappeared at his bedside to murder sleep. She was there, she, Mme de Burne, back again, roaming about his bed, and accompanied still by M. de Bernhaus. "Come!" he said, "it must be that I am jealous. What is the reason of it?"

Why was he jealous? He quickly told himself why. Notwithstanding all his doubts and fears he knew that as long as he had been her lover she had been faithful to him — faithful, indeed, without tenderness and without transports, but with a loyal strength of resolution. Now, however, he had broken it all off, and it was ended; he had restored her freedom to her. Would she remain without a liaison? Yes, doubtless, for a while. And then? This very fidelity that she had observed toward him up to the present moment, a fidelity beyond the reach of suspicion, was it not due to the feeling that if she left him, Mariolle, because she was tired of him, she would some day, sooner or later, have to take some one to fill his place, not from passion, but from weariness of being alone?

Is it not true that lovers often owe their long lease of favor simply to the dread of an unknown successor? And then to dismiss one lover and take up with another would not have seemed the right thing to such a woman — she was too intelligent, indeed, to bow to social prejudices, but was gifted with a delicate sense of moral purity that kept her from real indelicacies. She was a worldly philosopher and not a prudish bourgeoise, and while she would not have quailed at the idea of a secret attachment, her nature would have revolted at the thought of a succession of lovers.

He had given her her freedom — and now? Now most certainly she would take up with someone else, and that some one would be the Comte de Bernhaus. He was sure of it, and the thought was now affording him inexpressible suffering. Why had he left her? She had been faithful, a good friend to him, charming in every way. Why? Was it because he was a brutal sensualist who could not separate true love from its physical transports? Was that it? Yes — — but there was something besides. He had fled from the pain of not being loved as he loved, from the cruel feeling that he did not receive an equivalent return for the warmth of his kisses, an incurable affliction from which his heart, grievously smitten, would perhaps never recover. He looked forward with dread to the prospect of enduring for years the torments that he had been anticipating for a few months and suffering for a few weeks. In accordance with his nature he had weakly recoiled before this prospect, just as he had recoiled all his life long before any effort that called for resolution. It followed that he was incapable of carrying anything to its conclusion, of throwing himself heart and soul into such a passion as one develops for a science or an art, for it is impossible, perhaps, to have loved greatly without having suffered greatly.

Until daylight he pursued this train of thought, which tore him like wild horses; then he got up and went down to the bank of the little stream. A fisherman was casting his net near the little dam, and when he withdrew it from the water that flashed and eddied in the sunlight and spread it on the deck of his small boat, the little fishes danced among the meshes like animated silver.

Mariolle's agitation subsided little by little in the balmy freshness of the early morning air. The cool mist that rose from the miniature waterfall, about which faint rainbows fluttered, and the stream that ran at his feet in rapid and ceaseless current, carried off with them a portion of his sorrow. He said to himself: "Truly, I have done the right thing; I should have been too unhappy otherwise!" Then he returned to the house, and taking possession of a hammock that he had noticed in the vestibule, he made it fast between two of the lindens and throwing himself into it, endeavored to drive away reflection by fixing his eyes and thoughts upon the flowing stream.

Thus he idled away the time until the hour of breakfast, in an agreeable torpor, a physical sensation of well-being that communicated itself to the mind, and he protracted the meal as much as possible that he might have some occupation for the dragging minutes. There was one thing, however, that he looked forward to with eager expectation, and that was his mail. He had telegraphed to Paris and written to Fontainebleau to have his letters forwarded, but had received nothing, and the sensation of being entirely abandoned was beginning to be oppressive. Why? He had no reason to expect that there would be anything particularly pleasing or comforting for him in the little black box that the carrier bore slung at his side, nothing beyond useless invitations and unmeaning communications. Why, then, should he long for letters of whose contents he knew nothing as if the salvation of his soul depended on them? Was it not that there lay concealed in his heart the vainglorious expectation that she would write to him?

He asked one of his old women: "At what time does the mail arrive?"

"At noon, Monsieur."

It was just midday, and he listened with increased attention to the noises that reached him from outdoors. A knock at the outer door brought him to his feet; the messenger brought him only the newspapers and three unimportant letters. Mariolle glanced over the journals until he was tired, and went out.

What should he do? He went to the hammock and lay down in it, but after half an hour of that he experienced an uncontrollable desire to go somewhere else. The forest? Yes, the forest was very pleasant, but then the solitude there was even deeper than it was in his house, much deeper than it was in the village, where there were at least some signs of life now and then. And the silence and loneliness of all those trees and leaves filled his mind with sadness and regrets, steeping him more deeply still in wretchedness. He mentally reviewed his long walk of the day before, and when he came to the wideawake little waitress of the Hotel Corot, he said to himself: "I have it! I will go and dine there." The idea did him good; it was something to occupy him, a means of killing two or three hours, and he set out forthwith.

The long village street stretched straight away in the middle of the valley between two rows of low, white, tile-roofed houses, some of them standing boldly up with their fronts close to the road, others, more retiring, situated in a garden where there was a lilac-bush in bloom and chickens scratching over manure-heaps, where wooden stairways in the open air climbed to doors cut in the wall. Peasants were at work before their dwellings, lazily fulfilling their domestic duties. An old woman, bent with age and with threads of gray in her yellow hair, for country folk rarely have white hair, passed close to him, a ragged jacket upon her shoulders and her lean and sinewy legs covered by a woolen petticoat that failed to conceal the angles and protuberances of her frame. She was looking aimlessly before her with expressionless eyes, eyes that had never looked on other objects than those that might be of use to her in her poor existence.

Another woman, younger than this one, was hanging out the family wash before her door. The lifting of her skirt as she raised her arms aloft disclosed to view thick, coarse ankles incased in blue knitted stockings, with great, projecting, fleshless bones, while the breast and shoulders, flat and broad as those of a man, told of a body whose form must have been horrible to behold.

Mariolle thought: "They are women! Those scarecrows are women!" The vision of Mme de Burne arose before his eyes. He beheld her in all her elegance and beauty, the perfection of the human female form, coquettish and adorned to meet the looks of man, and again he smarted with the sorrow of an irreparable loss; then he walked on more quickly to shake himself free of this impression.

When he reached the inn at Marlotte the little waitress - recognized him immediately, and accosted him almost familiarly: "Good day, Monsieur."

"Good day, Mademoiselle."

"Do you wish something to drink?"

"Yes, to begin with; then I will have dinner." They discussed the question of what he should drink in the first place and what he should eat subsequently. He asked her advice for the pleasure of hearing her talk, for she had a nice way of expressing herself. She had a short little Parisian accent, and her speech was as unconstrained as was her movements. He thought as he listened: "The little girl is quite agreeable; she seems to me to have a bit of the cocotte about her."

"Are you a Parisian?" he inquired.

"Yes, sir."

"Have you been here long?"

"Two weeks, sir."

"And do you like it?"

"Not very well so far, but it is too soon to tell, and then I was tired of the air of Paris, and the country has done me good; that is why I made up my mind to come here. Then I shall bring you a vermouth, Monsieur?"

"Yes, Mademoiselle, and tell the cook to be careful and pay attention to my dinner."

"Never fear, Monsieur."

After she had gone away he went into the garden of the hotel, and took a seat in an arbor, where his vermouth was served. He remained there all the rest of the day, listening to a blackbird whistling in its cage, and watching the little waitress in her goings and comings. She played the coquette, and put on her sweetest looks for the gentleman, for she had not failed to observe that he found her to his liking.

He went away as he had done the day before after drinking a bottle of champagne to dispel gloom, but the darkness of the way and the coolness of the night air quickly dissipated his incipient tipsiness, and sorrow again took possession of his devoted soul. He thought: "What am I to do? Shall I remain here? Shall I be condemned for long to drag out this desolate way of living?" It was very late when he got to sleep.

The next morning he again installed himself in the hammock, and all at once the sight of a man casting his net inspired him with the idea of going fishing. The grocer from whom he bought his lines gave him some instructions upon the soothing sport, and even offered to go with him and act as his guide upon his first attempt. The offer was accepted, and between nine o'clock and noon Mariolle succeeded, by dint of vigorous exertion and unintermitting patience, in capturing three small fish.

When he had dispatched his breakfast he took up his march again for Mariotte. Why? To kill time, of course.

The little waitress began to laugh when she saw him coming. Amused by her recognition of him, he smiled back at her, and tried to engage her in conversation. She was more familiar than she had been the preceding day, and met him halfway.

Her name was Elisabeth Ledru. Her mother, who took in dressmaking, had died the year before; then the husband, an accountant by profession, always drunk and out of work, who had lived on the little earnings of his wife and daughter, disappeared, for the girl could not support two persons, though she shut herself up in her garret room and sewed all day long. Tiring of her lonely occupation after a while, she got a position as waitress in a cook-shop, remained there a year, and as the hard work had worn her down, the proprietor of the Hotel Corot at Mariotte, upon whom she had waited at times, engaged her for the summer with two other girls who were to come down a little later on. It was evident that the proprietor knew how to attract customers.

Her little story pleased Mariolle, and by treating her with respect and asking her a few discriminating questions, he succeeded in eliciting from her many interesting details of this poor dismal home that had been laid in ruins by a drunken father. She, poor, homeless, wandering creature that she was, gay and cheerful because she could not help it, being young, and feeling that the interest that this stranger took in her was unfeigned, talked to him with confidence, with that expansiveness of soul that she could no more restrain than she could restrain the agile movements of her limbs.

When she had finished he asked her: "And — do you expect to be a waitress all your life?"

"I could not answer that question, Monsieur. How can I tell what may happen to me tomorrow?" "And yet it is necessary to think of the future." She had assumed a thoughtful air that did not linger long upon her features, then she replied: "I suppose that I shall have to take whatever comes to me. So much the worse!"

They parted very good friends. After a few days he returned, then again, and soon he began to go there frequently, finding a vague distraction in the girl's conversation, and that her artless prattle helped him somewhat to forget his grief.

When he returned on foot to Montigny in the evening, however, he had terrible fits of despair as he thought of Mme de Burne. His heart became a little lighter with the morning sun, but with the night his bitter regrets and fierce jealousy closed in on him again. He had no intelligence; he had written to no one and had received letters from no one.

Then, alone with his thoughts upon the dark road, his imagination would picture the progress of the approaching liaison that he had foreseen between his quondam mistress and the Comte de Bernhaus. This had now become a settled idea with him and fixed itself more firmly in his mind every day. That man, he thought, will be to her just what she requires; a distinguished, assiduous, unexacting lover, contented and happy to be the chosen one of this superlatively delicious coquette. He compared him with himself. The other most certainly would not behave as he had, would not be guilty of that tiresome impatience and of that insatiable thirst for a return of his affection that had been the destruction of their amorous understanding. He was a very discreet, pliant, and well-posted man of the world, and would manage to get along and content himself with but little, for he did not seem to belong to the class of impassioned mortals.

On one of André Mariolle's visits to Marlotte one day, he beheld two bearded young fellows in the other arbor of the Hotel Corot, smoking pipes and wearing Scotch caps on their heads. The proprietor, a big, broad-faced man, came forward to pay his respects as soon as he saw him, for he had an interested liking for this faithful patron of his dinner-table, and said to him: "I have two new customers since yesterday, two painters."

"Those gentlemen sitting there?"

"Yes. They are beginning to be heard of. One of them got a second-class medal last year." And having told all that he knew about the embryo artists, he asked: "What will you take to-day, Monsieur Mariolle?"

"You may send me out a vermouth, as usual." The proprietor went away, and soon Elisabeth appeared, bringing the salver, the glass, the carafe, and the bottle. Whereupon one of the painters called to her: "Well! little one, are we angry still?"

She did not answer and when she approached Mariolle he saw that her eyes were red.

"You have been crying," he said.

"Yes, a little," she simply replied.

"What was the matter?"

"Those two gentlemen there behaved rudely to me."

"What did they do to you?"

"They took me for a bad character."

"Did you complain to the proprietor?"

She gave a sorrowful shrug of the shoulders, "Oh! Monsieur — the proprietor. I know what he is now — — the proprietor!"

Mariolle was touched, and a little angry; he said to her: "Tell me what it was all about."

She told him of the brutal conduct of the two painters immediately upon their arrival the night before, and then began to cry again, asking what she was to do, alone in the country and without friends or relatives, money or protection.

Mariolle suddenly said to her: "Will you enter my service? You shall be well treated in my house, and when I return to Paris you will be free to do what you please."

She looked him in the face with questioning eyes, and then quickly replied: "I will, Monsieur.

"How much are you earning here?"

"Sixty francs a month," she added, rather uneasily, "and I have my share of the pourboires besides; that makes it about seventy."

"I will pay you a hundred."

She repeated in astonishment: "A hundred francs a month?"

"Yes. Is that enough?"

"I should think that it was enough!"

"All that you will have to do will be to wait on me, take care of my clothes and linen, and attend to my room."

"It is a bargain, Monsieur."

"When will you come?"

"Tomorrow, if you wish. After what has happened here I will go to the mayor and will leave whether they are willing or not."

Mariolle took two louis from his pocket and handed them to her. "There's the money to bind our bargain."

A look of joy flashed across her face and she said in a tone of decision: "I will be at your house before midday tomorrow, Monsieur."

XII

ELISABETH came to Montigny next day, attended by a countryman with her trunk on a wheelbarrow. Mariolle had made a generous settlement with one of his old women and got rid of her, and the newcomer took possession of a small room on the top floor adjoining that of the cook. She was quite different from what she had been at Marlotte, when she presented herself before her new master, less effusive, more respectful, more self-contained; she was now the servant of the gentleman to whom she had been almost an humble friend beneath the arbor of the inn. He told her in a few words what she would have to do. She listened attentively, went and took possession of her room, and then entered upon her new service.

A week passed and brought no noticeable change in the state of Mariolle's feelings. The only difference was that he remained at home more than he had been accustomed to do, for he had nothing to attract him to Mariotte, and his house seemed less dismal to him than at first. The bitterness of his grief was subsiding a little, as all storms subside after a while; but in place of this aching wound there was arising in him a settled melancholy, one of those deep-seated sorrows that are like chronic and lingering maladies, and sometimes end in death. His former liveliness of mind and body, his mental activity, his interests in the pursuits that had served to occupy and amuse him hitherto were all dead, and their place had been taken by a universal disgust and an invincible torpor, that left him without even strength of will to get up and go out of doors. He no longer left his house, passing from the salon to the hammock and from the hammock to the salon, and his chief distraction consisted in watching the current of the Loing as it flowed by the terrace and the fisherman casting his net.

When the reserve of the first few days had begun to wear off, Elisabeth gradually grew a little bolder, and remarking with her keen feminine instinct the constant dejection of her employer, she would say to him when the other servant was not by: "Monsieur finds his time hang heavy on his hands?"

He would answer resignedly: "Yes, pretty heavy."

"Monsieur should go for a walk."

"That would not do me any good."

She quietly did many little unassuming things for his pleasure and comfort. Every morning when he came into his drawingroom, he found it filled with flowers and smelling as sweetly as a conservatory. Elisabeth must surely have enlisted all the boys in the village to bring her primroses, violets, and buttercups from the forest, as well as putting under contribution the small gardens where the peasant girls tended their few plants at evening. In his loneliness and distress he was grateful for her kind thoughtfulness and her unobtrusive desire to please him in these small ways.

It also seemed to him that she was growing prettier, more refined in her appearance, and that she devoted more attention to the care of her person. One day when she was handing him a cup of tea, he noticed that her hands were no longer the hands of a servant, but of a lady, with well-trimmed, clean nails, quite irreproachable. On another occasion he observed that the shoes that she wore were almost elegant in shape and material. Then she had gone up to her room one afternoon and come down wearing a delightful little gray dress, quite simple and in perfect taste. "Hallo!" he exclaimed, as he saw her, "how dressy you are getting to be, Elisabeth!" She blushed up to the whites of her eyes. "What, I, Monsieur? Why, no. I dress a little better because I have more money."

"Where did you buy that dress that you have on?"

"I made it myself, Monsieur."

"You made it? When? I always see you busy at work about the house during the day."

"Why, during my evenings, Monsieur."

"But where did you get the stuff? and who cut it for you?"

She told him that the shopkeeper at Montigny had brought her some samples from Fontainebleau, that she had made her selection from them, and paid for the goods out of the two louis that he had paid her as advanced wages. The cutting and fitting had not troubled her at all, for she and her mother had worked four years for a readymade clothing house. He could not resist telling her: "It is very becoming to you. You look very pretty in it." And she had to blush again, this time to the roots of her hair.

When she had left the room he said to himself: "I wonder if she is beginning to fall in love with me?" He reflected on it, hesitated, doubted, and finally came to the conclusion that after all it might be possible. He had been kind and compassionate toward her, had assisted her, and been almost her friend; there would be nothing very surprising in this little girl being smitten with the master, who had been so good to her. The idea did not strike him very disagreeably, moreover, for she was really very presentable, and retained nothing of the appearance of a servant about her. He experienced a flattering feeling of consolation, and his masculine vanity, that had been so cruelly wounded and trampled on and crushed by another woman, felt comforted. It was a compensation — trivial and unnoteworthy though it might be, it was a compensation — for when love comes to a man unsought, no matter whence it comes, it is because that man possesses the capacity of inspiring it. His unconscious selfishness was also gratified by it; it would occupy his attention and do him a little good, perhaps, to watch this young heart opening and beating for him. The thought never occurred to him of sending the child away, of rescuing her from the peril from which he himself was suffering so cruelly, of having more pity for her than others had showed toward him, for compassion is never an ingredient that enters into sentimental conquests.

So he continued his observations, and soon saw that he had not been mistaken. Petty details revealed it to him more clearly day by day. As she came near him one morning while waiting on him at table, he smelled on her clothing an odor of perfumery — villainous, cheap perfumery, from the village shopkeeper's, doubtless, or the druggist's — so he presented her with a bottle of Cyprus toilette-water that he had been in the habit of using for a long time, and of which he always carried a supply about with him. He also gave her fine soaps, tooth-washes, and rice-powder. He thus lent his assistance to the transformation that was becoming more apparent every day, watching it meantime with a pleased and curious eye. While remaining his faithful and respectful servant, she was thus becoming a woman in whom the coquettish instincts of her sex were artlessly developing themselves.

He, on his part, was imperceptibly becoming attached to her. She inspired him at the same time with amusement and gratitude. He trifled with this dawning tenderness as one trifles in his hours of melancholy with anything that can divert his mind. He was conscious of no other emotion toward her than that undefined desire which impels every man toward a prepossessing woman, even if she be a pretty servant, or a peasant maiden with the form of a goddess — a sort of rustic Venus. He felt himself drawn to her more than all else by the womanliness that he now found in her. He felt the need of that — an undefined and irresistible need, bequeathed to him by that other one, the woman whom he loved, who had first awakened in him that invincible and mysterious fondness for the nature, the companionship, the contact of women, for the subtle aroma, ideal or sensual, that every beautiful creature, whether of the people or of the upper class, whether a lethargic, sensual native of the Orient with great black eyes, or a blue-eyed, keen-witted daughter of the North, inspires in men in whom still survives the immemorial attraction of femininity.

These gentle, loving, and unceasing attentions that were felt rather than seen, wrapped his wound in a sort of soft, protecting envelope that shielded it to some extent from its recurrent attacks of suffering, which did return, nevertheless, like flies to a raw sore. He was made especially impatient by the absence of all news, for his friends had religiously respected his request not to divulge his address. Now and then he would see Massival's or Lamarthe's name in the newspapers among those who had been present at some great dinner or ceremonial, and one day he saw Mme de Burne's, who was mentioned as being one of the most elegant, the prettiest, and best dressed of the women who were at the ball at the Austrian embassy. It sent a trembling through him from head to foot. The name of the Comte de Bernhaus appeared a few lines further down, and that day Mariolle's jealousy returned and wrung his heart until night. The suspected liaison was no longer subject for doubt for him now. It was one of those imaginary convictions that are even more torturing than reality, for there is no getting rid of them and they leave a wound that hardly ever heals.

No longer able to endure this state of ignorance and uncertainty, he determined to write to Lamarthe, who was sufficiently well acquainted with him to divine the wretchedness of his soul, and would be likely to afford him some clew as to the justice of his suspicions, even without being directly questioned on the subject. One evening, therefore, he sat down and by the light of his lamp concocted a long, artful letter, full of vague sadness and poetical allusions to the delights of early spring in the country and veiled requests for information. When he got his mail four days later he recognized at the very first glance the novelist's firm, upright handwriting.

Lamarthe sent him a thousand items of news that were of great importance to his jealous eyes. Without laying more stress upon Mme de Burne and Bernhaus than upon any other of the crowd of people whom he mentioned, he seemed to place them in the foreground by one of those tricks of style characteristic of him, which led the attention to just the point where he wished to lead it without revealing his design. The impression that this letter, taken as a whole, left upon Mariolle was that his suspicions were at least not destitute of foundation. His fears would be realized tomorrow, if they had not been yesterday. His former mistress was always the same, leading the same busy, brilliant, fashionable life. He had been the subject of some talk after his disappearance, as the world always talks of people who have disappeared, with lukewarm curiosity.

After the receipt of this letter he remained in his hammock until nightfall; then he could eat no dinner, and after that he could get no sleep; he was feverish through the night. The next morning he felt so tired, so discouraged, so disgusted with his weary, monotonous life, between the deep silent forest that was now dark with verdure on the one hand and the tiresome little stream that flowed beneath his windows on the other, that he did not leave his bed.

When Elisabeth came to his room in response to the summons of his bell, she stood in the doorway pale with surprise and asked him: "Is Monsieur ill?"

"Yes, a little."

"Shall I send for the doctor?"

"No. I am subject to these slight indispositions."

"What can I do for Monsieur?"

He ordered his bath to be got ready, a breakfast of eggs alone, and tea at intervals during the day.

About one o'clock, however, he became so restless that he determined to get up. Elisabeth, whom he had rung for repeatedly during the morning with the fretful irresolution of a man who imagines himself ill and who had always come up to him with a deep desire of being of assistance, now, beholding him so nervous and restless, with a blush for her own boldness, offered to read to him.

He asked her: "Do you read well?"

"Yes, Monsieur; I gained all the prizes for reading when I was at school in the city, and I have read so many novels to mamma that I can't begin to remember the names of them."

He was curious to see how she would do, and he sent her into the studio to look among the books that he had packed up for the one that he liked best of all, "Manon Lescaut."

When she returned she helped him to settle himself in bed, arranged two pillows behind his back, took a chair, and began to read. She read well, very well indeed, intelligently and with a pleasing accent that seemed a special gift. She evinced her interest in the story from the commencement and showed so much feeling as she advanced in it that he stopped her now and then to ask her a question and have a little conversation about the plot and the characters.

Through the open windows, on the warm breeze loaded with the sweet odors of growing things, came the trills and roulades of the nightingales among the trees saluting their mates with their amorous ditties in this season of awakening love. The young girl, too, was moved beneath André's gaze as she followed with bright eyes the plot unwinding page by page.

She answered the questions that he put to her with an innate appreciation of the things connected with tenderness and passion, an appreciation that was just, but, owing to the ignorance natural to her position, sometimes crude. He thought: "This girl would be very intelligent and bright if she had a little teaching."

Her womanly charm had already begun to make itself felt in him, and really did him good that warm, still, spring afternoon, mingling strangely with that other charm, so powerful and so mysterious, of "Manon," the strangest conception of woman ever evoked by human ingenuity.

When it became dark after this day of inactivity Mariolle sank into a kind of dreaming, dozing state, in which confused visions of Mme de Burne and Elisabeth and the mistress of Des Grieux rose before his eyes. As he had not left his room since the day before and had taken no exercise to fatigue him he slept lightly and was disturbed by an unusual noise that he heard about the house.

Once or twice before he had thought that he heard faint sounds and footsteps at night coming from the ground floor, not directly underneath his room, but from the laundry and bathroom, small rooms that adjoined the kitchen. He had given the matter no attention, however.

This evening, tired of lying in bed and knowing that he had a long period of wakefulness before him, he listened and distinguished something that sounded like the rustling of a woman's garments and the splashing of water. He decided that he would go and investigate, lighted a candle and looked at his watch; it was barely ten o'clock. He dressed himself, and having slipped a revolver into his pocket, made his way down the stairs on tiptoe with the stealthiness of a cat.

When he reached the kitchen, he was surprised to see that there was a fire burning in the furnace. There was not a sound to be heard, but presently he was conscious of something stirring in the bathroom, a small, whitewashed apartment that opened off the kitchen and contained nothing but the tub. He went noiselessly to the door and threw it open with a quick movement; there, extended in the tub, he beheld the most beautiful form that he had ever seen in his life.

It was Elisabeth.

XIII

WHEN she appeared before him next morning bringing him his tea and toast, and their eyes met, she began to tremble so that the cup and sugar-bowl rattled on the salver. Mariolle went to her and relieved her of her burden and placed it on the table; then, as she still kept her eyes fastened on the floor, he said to her: "Look at me, little one."

She raised her eyes to him; they were full of tears.

"You must not cry," he continued. As he held her in his arms, she murmured: "Oh! mon Dieu!" He knew that it was not regret, nor sorrow, nor remorse that had elicited from her those three agitated words, but happiness, true happiness. It gave him a strange, selfish feeling of delight, physical rather than moral, to feel this small person resting against his heart, to feel there at last the presence of a woman who loved him. He thanked her for it, as a wounded man lying by the roadside would thank a woman who had stopped to succor him; he thanked her with all his lacerated heart, and he pitied her a little, too, in the depths of his soul. As he watched her thus, pale and tearful, with eyes alight with love, he suddenly said to himself: "Why, she is beautiful! How quickly a woman changes, becomes what she ought to be, under the influence of the desires of her feelings and the necessities of her existence!"

"Sit down," he said to her. He took her hands in his, her poor toiling hands that she had made white and pretty for his sake, and very gently, in carefully chosen phrases, he spoke to her of the attitude that they should maintain toward each other. She was no longer his servant, but she would preserve the appearance of being so for a while yet, so as not to create a scandal in the village. She would live with him as his housekeeper and would read to him frequently, and that would serve to account for the change in the situation. He would have her eat at his table after a little, as soon as she should be permanently installed in her position as his reader.

When he had finished she simply replied: "No, Monsieur, I am your servant, and I will continue to be so. I do not wish to have people learn what has taken place and talk about it."

He could not shake her determination, although he urged her strenuously, and when he had drunk his tea she carried away the salver while he followed her with a softened look.

When she was gone he reflected. "She is a woman," he thought, "and all women are equal when they are pleasing in our eyes. I have made my waitress my mistress. She is pretty, she will be charming! At all events she is younger and fresher than the mondaines and the cocottes. What difference does it make, after all? How many celebrated actresses have been daughters of concierges! And yet they are received as ladies, they are adored like heroines of romance, and princes bow before them as if they were queens. Is this to be accounted for on the score of their talent, which is often doubtful, or of their beauty, which is often questionable? Not at all. But a woman, in truth, always holds the place that she is able to create for herself by the illusion that she is capable of inspiring."

He took a long walk that day, and although he still felt the same distress at the bottom of his heart and his legs were heavy under him, as if his suffering had loosened all the springs of his energy, there was a feeling of gladness within him like the song of a little bird. He was not so lonely, he felt himself less utterly abandoned; the forest appeared to him less silent and less void.

He returned to his house with the glad thought that Elisabeth would come out to meet him with a smile upon her lips and a look of tenderness in her eyes.

The life that he now led for about a month on the bank of the little stream was a real idyl. Mariolle was loved as perhaps very few men have ever been, as a child is loved by its mother, as the hunter is loved by his dog. He was all in all to her, her Heaven and earth, her charm and delight. He responded to all her ardent and artless womanly advances, giving her in a kiss her fill of ecstasy. In her eyes and in her soul, in her heart and in her flesh there was no object but him; her intoxication was like that of a young man who tastes wine for the first time. Surprised and delighted, he reveled in the bliss of this absolute selfsurrender, and he felt that this was drinking of love at its fountain-head, at the very lips of nature.

Nevertheless he continued to be sad, sad, and haunted by his deep, unyielding disenchantment. His little mistress was agreeable, but he always felt the absence of another, and when he walked in the meadows or on the banks of the Loing and asked himself: "Why does this lingering care stay by me so?" such an intolerable feeling of desolation rose within him as the recollection of Paris crossed his mind that he had to return to the house so as not to be alone.

Then he would swing in the hammock, while Elisabeth, seated on a camp-chair, would read to him. As he watched her and listened to her he would recall to mind conversations in the drawingroom of Michèle, in the days when he passed whole evenings alone with her. Then tears would start to his eyes, and such bitter regret would tear his heart that he felt that he must start at once for Paris or else leave the country forever.

Elisabeth, seeing his gloom and melancholy, asked him: "Are you suffering? Your eyes are full of tears."

"Give me a kiss, little one," he replied; "you could not understand."

She kissed him, anxiously, with a foreboding of some tragedy that was beyond her knowledge. He, forgetting his woes for a moment beneath her caresses, thought: "Oh! for a woman who could be these two in one, who might have the affection of the one and the charm of the other! Why is it that we never encounter the object of our dreams, that we always meet with something that is only approximately like them?"

He continued his vague reflections, soothed by the monotonous sound of the voice that fell unheeded on his ear, upon all the charms that had combined to seduce and vanquish him in the mistress whom he had abandoned. In the besetment of her memory, of her imaginary presence, by which he was haunted as a visionary by a phantom, he asked himself: "Am I condemned to carry her image with me to all eternity?"

He again applied himself to taking long walks, to roaming through the thicknesses of the forest, with the vague hope that he might lose her somewhere, in the depths of a ravine, behind a rock, in a thicket, as a man who wishes to rid himself of an animal that he does not care to kill sometimes takes it away a long distance so that it may not find its way home.

In the course of one of these walks he one day came again to the spot where the beeches grew. It was now a gloomy forest, almost as black as night, with impenetrable foliage. He passed along beneath the immense, deep vault in the damp, sultry air, thinking regretfully of his earlier visit when the little half-opened leaves resembled a verdant, sunshiny mist, and as he was following a narrow path, he suddenly stopped in astonishment before two trees that had grown together. It was a sturdy beech embracing with two of its branches a tall, slender oak; and there could have been no picture of his love that would have appealed more forcibly and more touchingly to his imagination. Mariolle seated himself to contemplate them at his ease. To his diseased mind, as they stood there in their motionless strife, they became splendid and terrible symbols, telling to him, and to all who might pass that way the everlasting story of his love.

Then he went on his way again, sadder than before, and as he walked along, slowly and with eyes downcast, he all at once perceived, half hidden by the grass and stained by mud and rain, an old telegram that had been lost or thrown there by some wayfarer. He stopped. What was the message of joy or sorrow that the bit of blue paper that lay there at his feet had brought to some expectant soul?

He could not help picking it up and opening it with a mingled feeling of curiosity and disgust. The words "Come — me — four o'clock — "were still legible; the names had been obliterated by the moisture.

Memories, at once cruel and delightful, thronged upon his mind of all the messages that he had received from her, now to appoint the hour for a rendezvous, now to tell him that she could not come to him. Never had anything caused him such emotion, nor startled him so violently, nor so stopped his poor heart and then set it thumping again as had the sight of those messages, burning or freezing him as the case might be. The thought that he should never receive more of them filled him with unutterable sorrow.

Again he asked himself what her thoughts had been since he left her. Had she suffered, had she regretted the friend whom her coldness had driven from her, or had she merely experienced a feeling of wounded vanity and thought nothing more of his abandonment? His desire to learn the truth was so strong and so persistent that a strange and audacious, yet only half-formed resolve, came into his head. He took the road to Fontainebleau, and when he reached the city went to the telegraph office, his mind in a fluctuating state of unrest and indecision; but an irresistible force proceeding from his heart seemed to urge him on. With a trembling hand, then, he took from the desk a printed blank and beneath the name and address of Mme de Burne wrote this dispatch:

"I would so much like to know what you think of me! For my part I can forget nothing. — André Mariolle."

Then he went out, engaged a carriage, and returned to Montigny, disturbed in mind by what he had done and regretting it already.

He had calculated that in case she condescended \o answer him he would receive a letter from her two days later, but the fear and the hope that she might send him a dispatch kept him in his house all the following day. He was in his hammock under the lindens on the terrace, when, about three o'clock, Elisabeth came to tell him that there was a lady at the house who wanted to see him.

The shock was so great that his breath failed him for a moment and his legs bent under him, and his heart beat violently as he went toward the house. And yet he could not dare hope that it was she.

When he appeared at the drawingroom door Mme de Burne arose from the sofa where she was sitting and came forward to shake hands with a rather reserved smile upon her face, with a slight constraint of manner and attitude, saying: "I came to see how you are, as your message did not give me much information on the subject."

He had become so pale that a flash of delight rose to her eyes, and his emotion was so great that he could not speak, could only hold his lips glued to the hand that she had given him.

"Dieu! how kind of you!" he said at last.

"No; but I do not forget my friends, and I was anxious about you."

She looked him in the face with that rapid, searching woman's look that reads everything, fathoms one's thoughts to their very roots, and unmasks every artifice. She was satisfied, apparently, for her face brightened with a smile. "You have a pretty hermitage here," she continued. "Does happiness reside in it?"

"No, Madame."

"Is it possible? In this fine country, at the side of this beautiful forest, on the banks of this pretty stream? Why, you ought to be at rest and quite contented here."

"I am not, Madame."

"Why not, then?"

"Because I cannot forget."

"Is it indispensable to your happiness that you should forget something?"

"Yes, Madame."

"May one know what?"

"You know."

"And then?"

"And then I am very wretched."

She said to him with mingled fatuity and commiseration: "I thought that was the case when I received your telegram, and that was the reason that I came, with the resolve that I would go back again at once if I found that I had made a mistake." She was silent a moment and then went on: "Since I am not going back immediately, may I go and look around your place? That little alley of lindens yonder has a very charming appearance; it looks as if it might be cooler out there than here in this drawingroom."

They went out. She had on a mauve dress that harmonized so well with the verdure of the trees and the blue of the sky that she appeared to him like some amazing apparition, of an entirely new style of beauty and seductiveness. Her tall and willowy form, her bright, clean-cut features, the little blaze of blond hair beneath a hat that was mauve, like the dress, and lightly crowned by a long plume of ostrich-feathers rolled about it, her tapering arms with the two hands holding the closed sunshade crosswise before her, the loftiness of her carriage, and the directness of her step seemed to introduce into the humble little garden something exotic, something that was foreign to it. It was a figure from one of Watteau's pictures, or from some fairy-tale or dream, the imagination of a poet's or an artist's fancy, which had been seized by the whim of coming away to the country to show how beautiful it was. As Mariolle looked at her, all trembling with his newly lighted passion, he recalled to mind the two peasant women that he had seen in Montigny village.

"Who is the little person who opened the door for me?" she inquired.

"She is my servant."

"She does not look like a waitress."

"No; she is very good looking."

"Where did you secure her?"

"Quite near here; in an inn frequented by painters, where her innocence was in danger from the customers."

"And you preserved it?"

He blushed and replied: "Yes, I preserved it."

"To your own advantage, perhaps."

"Certainly, to my own advantage, for I would rather have a pretty face about me than an ugly one."

"Is that the only feeling that she inspires in you?"

"Perhaps it was she who inspired in me the irresistible desire of seeing you again, for every woman when she attracts my eyes, even if it is only for the duration of a second, carries my thoughts back to you."

"That was a very pretty piece of special pleading! And does she love her preserver?"

He blushed more deeply than before. Quick as lightning the thought flashed through his mind that jealousy is always efficacious as a stimulant to a woman's feelings, and decided him to tell only half a lie, so he answered, hesitatingly: "I don't know how that is; it may be so. She is very attentive to me."

Rather pettishly, Mme de Burne murmured: And you?"

He fastened upon her his eyes that were aflame with love, and replied: "Nothing could ever distract my thoughts from you."

This was also a very shrewd answer, but the phrase seemed to her so much the expression of an indisputable truth, that she let it pass without noticing it. Could a woman such as she have any doubts about a thing like that? So she was satisfied, in fact, and had no further doubts upon the subject of Elisabeth.

They took two canvas chairs and seated themselves in the shade of the lindens over the running stream. He asked her: "What did you think of me?"

"That you must have been very wretched."

"Was it through my fault or yours?"

"Through the fault of us both."

"And then?"

"And then, knowing how beside yourself you were, I reflected that it would be best to give you a little time to cool down. So I waited."

"What were you waiting for?"

"For a word from you. I received it, and here I am. Now we are going to talk like people of sense. So you love me still? I do not ask you this as a coquette — I ask it as your friend."

"I love you still."

"And what is it that you wish?"

"How can I answer that? I am in your power."

"Oh! my ideas are very clear, but I will not tell you them without first knowing what yours are. Tell me of yourself, of what has been passing in your heart and in your mind since you ran away from me."

"I have been thinking of you; I have had no other occupation." He told her of his resolution to forget her, his flight, his coming to the great forest in which he had found nothing but her image, of his days filled with memories of her, and his long nights of consuming jealousy; he told her everything, with entire truthfulness, always excepting his love for Elisabeth, whose name he did not mention.

She listened, well assured that he was not lying, convinced by her inner consciousness of her power over him, even more than by the sincerity of his manner, and delighted with her victory, glad that she was about to regain him, for she loved him still.

Then he bemoaned himself over this situation that seemed to have no end, and warming up as he told of all that he had suffered after having carried it so long in his thoughts, he again reproached her, but without anger, without bitterness, in terms of impassioned poetry, with that impotency of loving of which she was the victim. He told her over and over: "Others have not the gift of pleasing; you have not the gift of loving."

She interrupted him, speaking warmly, full of arguments and illustrations. "At least I have the gift of being faithful," she said. "Suppose I had adored you for ten months, and then fallen in love with another man, would you be less unhappy than you are?"

He exclaimed: "Is it, then, impossible for a woman to love only one man?"

But she had her answer ready for him: "No one can keep on loving forever; all that one can do is to be constant. Do you believe that that exalted delirium of the senses can last for years? No, no. As for the most of those women who are addicted to passions, to violent caprices of greater or less duration, they simply transform life into a novel. Their heroes are different, the events and circumstances are unforeseen and constantly changing, the dénouement varies. I admit that for them it is amusing and diverting, for with every change they have a new set of emotions, but for him — when it is ended, that is the last of it. Do you understand me?"

"Yes; what you say has some truth in it. But I do not see what you are getting at."

"It is this: there is no passion that endures a very long time; by that I mean a burning, torturing passion like that from which you are suffering now. It is a crisis that I have made hard, very hard for you to bear — I know it, and I feel it — by — by the aridity of my tenderness and the paralysis of my emotional nature. This crisis will pass away, however, for it cannot last forever."

"And then?" he asked with anxiety.

"Then I think that to a woman who is as reasonable and calm as I am you can make yourself a lover who will be pleasing in every way, for you have a great deal of tact. On the other hand you would make a terrible husband. But there is no such thing as a good husband, there never can be."

He was surprised and a little offended. "Why," he asked, "do you wish to keep a lover that you do not love?"

She answered, impetuously: "I do love him, my friend, after my fashion. I do not love ardently, but I love."

"You require above everything else to be loved and to have your lovers make a show of their love."

"It is true. That is what I like. But beyond that my heart requires a companion apart from the others. My vainglorious passion for public homage does not interfere with my capacity for being faithful and devoted; it does not destroy my belief that I have something of myself that I could bestow upon a lover that no other man should have: my loyal affection, the sincere attachment of my heart, the entire and secret trustfulness of my soul; in exchange for which I should receive from him, together with all the tenderness of a lover, the sensation, so sweet and so rare, of not being entirely alone upon the earth. That is not love from the way you look at it, but it is not entirely valueless, either."

He bent over toward her, trembling with emotion, and stammered: "Will you let me be that man?"

"Yes, after a little, when you are more yourself. In the meantime, resign yourself to a little suffering once in a while, for my sake. Since you have to suffer in any event, isn't it better to endure it at my side rather than somewhere far from me?" Her smile seemed to say to him: "Why can you not have confidence in me?" and as she eyed him there, his whole frame quivering with passion, she experienced through every fiber of her being a feeling of satisfied well-being that made her happy in her way, in the way that the bird of prey is happy when he sees his quarry lying fascinated beneath him and awaiting the fatal talons.

"When do you return to Paris?" she asked.

"Why — tomorrow!"

"Tomorrow be it. You will come and dine with me?"

"Yes, Madame."

"And now I must be going," said she, looking at the watch set in the handle of her parasol.

"Oh! why so soon?"

"Because I must catch the five o'clock train. I have company to dinner to-day, several persons: the Princess de Malten, Bernhaus, Lamarthe, Massival, De Maltry, and a stranger, M. de Charlaine, the explorer, who is just back from upper Cambodia, after a wonderful journey. He is all the talk just now."

Mariolle's spirits fell; it hurt him to hear these names mentioned one after the other, as if he had been stung by so many wasps. They were poison to him.

"Will you go now?" he said, "and we can drive through the forest and see something of it."

"I shall be very glad to. First give me a cup of tea and some toast."

When the tea was served, Elisabeth was not to be found. The cook said that she had gone out to make some purchases. This did not surprise Mme de Burne, for what had she to fear now from this servant? Then they got into the landau that was standing before the door, and Mariolle made the coachman take them to the station by a roundabout way which took them past the Gorge-aux-Loups. As they rolled along beneath the shade of the great trees where the nightingales were singing, she was seized by the ineffable sensation that the mysterious and allpowerful charm of nature impresses on the heart of man. "Dieu!" she said, "how beautiful it is, how calm and restful!"

He accompanied her to the station, and as they were about to part she said to him: "I shall see you tomorrow at eight o'clock, then?"

"Tomorrow at eight o'clock, Madame."

She, radiant with happiness, went her way, and he returned to his house in the landau, happy and contented, but uneasy withal, for he knew that this was not the end.

Why should he resist? He felt that he could not. She held him by a charm that he could not understand, that was stronger than all. Flight would not deliver him, would not sever him from her, but would be an intolerable privation, while if he could only succeed in showing a little resignation, he would obtain from her at least as much as she had promised, for she was a woman who always kept her word.

The horses trotted along under the trees and he reflected that not once during that interview had she put up her lips to him for a kiss. She was ever the same; nothing in her would ever change and he would always, perhaps, have to suffer at her hands in just that same way. The remembrance of the bitter hours that he had already passed, with the intolerable certainty that he would never succeed in rousing her to passion, laid heavy on his heart, and gave him a clear foresight of struggles to come and of similar distress in the future. Still, he was content to suffer everything rather than lose her again, resigned even to that everlasting, ever unappeased desire that rioted in his veins and burned into his flesh.

The raging thoughts that had so often possessed him on his way back alone from Auteuil were now setting in again. They began to agitate his frame as the landau rolled smoothly along in the cool shadows of the great trees, when all at once the thought of Elisabeth awaiting him there at his door, she, too, young and fresh and pretty, her heart full of love and her mouth full of kisses, brought peace to his soul. Presently he would be holding her in his arms, and, closing his eyes and deceiving himself as men deceive others, confounding in the intoxication of the embrace her whom he loved and her by whom he was loved, he would possess them both at once. Even now it was certain that he had a liking for her, that grateful attachment of soul and body that always pervades the human animal as the result of love inspired and pleasure shared in common. This child whom he had made his own, would she not be to his dry and wasting love the little spring that bubbles up at the evening halting place, the promise of the cool draught that sustains our energy as wearily we traverse the burning desert?

When he regained the house, however, the girl had not come in. He was frightened and uneasy and said to the other servant: "You are sure that she went out?"

"Yes, Monsieur."

Thereupon he also went out in the hope of finding her. When he had taken a few steps and was about to turn into the long street that runs up the valley, he beheld before him the old, low church, surmounted by its square tower, seated upon a little knoll and watching the houses of its small village as a hen watches over her chicks. A presentiment that she was there impelled him to enter. Who can tell the strange glimpses of the truth that a woman's heart is capable of perceiving? What had she thought, how much had she understood? Where could she have fled for refuge but there, if the shadow of the truth had passed before her eyes?

The church was very dark, for night was closing in. The dim lamp, hanging from its chain, suggested in the tabernacle the ideal presence of the divine Consoler. With hushed footsteps Mariolle passed up along the lines of benches. When he reached the choir he saw a woman on her knees, her face hidden in her hands. He approached, recognized her, and touched her on the shoulder. They were alone.

She gave a great start as she turned her head. She was weeping.

"What is the matter?" he said.

She murmured: "I see it all. You cams here because she had caused you to suffer. She came to take you away."

He spoke in broken accents, touched by the grief that he in turn had caused: "You are mistaken, little one. I am going back to Paris, indeed, but I shall take you with me."

She repeated, incredulously: "It can't be true, it can't be true."

"I swear to you that it is true."

"When?"

"Tomorrow."

She began again to sob and groan: "My God! My God!"

Then he raised her to her feet and led her down the hill through the thick blackness of the night, but when they came to the river-bank he made her sit down upon the grass and placed himself beside her. He heard the beating of her heart and her quick breathing, and clasping her to his heart, troubled by his remorse, he whispered to her gentle words that he had never used before. Softened by pity and burning with desire, every word that he uttered was true; he did not endeavor to deceive her, and surprised himself at what he said and what he felt, he wondered how it was that, thrilling yet with the presence of that other one whose slave he was always to be, he could tremble thus with longing and emotion while consoling this love-stricken heart.

He promised that he would love her, — he did not say simply "love" — , that he would give her a nice little house near his own and pretty furniture to put in it and a servant to wait on her. She was reassured as she listened to him, and gradually grew calmer, for she could not believe that he was capable of deceiving her, and besides his tone and manner told her that he was sincere. Convinced at length and dazzled by the vision of being a lady, by the prospect — so undreamed of by the poor girl, the servant of the inn — of becoming the "good friend" of such a rich, nice gentleman, she was carried away in a whirl of pride, covetousness, and gratitude that mingled with her fondness for André. Throwing her arms about his neck and covering his face with kisses, she stammered: "Oh! I love you so! You are all in all to me!"

He was touched and returned her caresses. "Darling! My little darling!" he murmured.

Already she had almost forgotten the appearance of the stranger who but now had caused her so much sorrow. There must have been some vague feeling of doubt floating in her mind, however, for presently she asked him in a tremulous voice: "Really and truly, you will love me as you love me now?"

And unhesitatingly he replied: "I will love you as I love you now."

THE END

Pierre and Jean

Le Roman – 'The Novel'

I do not intend in these pages to put in a plea for this little novel. On the contrary, the ideas I shall try to set forth will rather involve a criticism of the class of psychological analysis which I have undertaken in Pierre et Jean. I propose to treat of novels in general.

I am not the only writer who finds himself taken to task in the same terms each time he brings out a new book. Among many laudatory phrases, I invariably meet with this observation, penned by the same critics: "The greatest fault of this book is that it is not, strictly speaking, a novel."

The same form might be adopted in reply:

"The greatest fault of the writer who does me the honor to review me is that he is not a critic."

For what are, in fact, the essential characteristics of a critic?

It is necessary that, without preconceived notions, prejudices of "School," or partisanship for any class of artists, he should appreciate, distinguish, and explain the most antagonistic tendencies and the most dissimilar temperaments, recognizing and accepting the most varied efforts of art.

Now the Critic who, after reading Manon Lescaut, Paul and Virginia, Don Quixote, Les Liaisons dangereuses, Werther, Elective Affinities (Wahlverwandschaften), Clarissa Harlowe, Émile, Candide, Cinq-Mars, René, Les Trois Mousquetaires, Mauprat, Le Père Goriot, La Cousine Bette, Colomba, Le Rouge et le Noir, Mademoiselle de Maupin, Notre-Dame de Paris, Salammbo, Madame Bovary, Adolphe, M. de Camors, l'Assommoir, Sapho, etc., still can be so bold as to write "This or that is, or is not, a novel," seems to me to be gifted with a perspicacity strangely akin to incompetence. Such a critic commonly understands by a novel a more or less improbable narrative of adventure, elaborated after the fashion of a piece for the stage, in three acts, of which the first contains the exposition, the second the action, and the third the catastrophe or dénouement.

And this method of construction is perfectly admissible, but on condition that all others are accepted on equal terms.

Are there any rules for the making of a novel, which, if we neglect, the tale must be called by another name? If Don Quixote is a novel, then is Le Rouge et le Noir a novel? If Monte Christo is a novel, is l'Assommoir? Can any conclusive comparison be drawn between Goethe's Elective Affinities, The Three Mousqueteers, by Dumas, Flaubert's Madame Bovary, M. de Camors by Octave Feuillet, and Germinal, by Zola? Which of them all is The Novel? What are these famous rules? Where did they originate? Who laid them down? And in virtue of what principle, of whose authority, and of what reasoning?

And yet, as it would appear, these critics know in some positive and indisputable way what constitutes a novel, and what distinguishes it from other tales which are not novels. What this amounts to is that without being producers themselves they are enrolled under a School, and that, like the writers of novels, they reject all work which is conceived and executed outside the pale of their esthetics. An intelligent critic ought, on the contrary, to seek out everything which least resembles the novels already written, and urge young authors as much as possible to try fresh paths.

All writers, Victor Hugo as much as M. Zola, have insistently claimed the absolute and incontrovertible right to compose — that is to say, to imagine or observe — in accordance with their individual conception of originality, and that is a special manner of thinking, seeing, understanding, and judging. Now the critic who assumes that "the novel" can be defined in conformity with the ideas he has based on the novels he prefers, and that certain immutable rules of construction can be laid down, will always find himself at war with the artistic temperament of a writer who introduces a new manner of work. A critic really worthy of the name ought to be an analyst, devoid of preferences or passions; like an expert in pictures, he should simply estimate the artistic value of the object of art submitted to him. His intelligence, open to everything, must so far supersede his individuality as to leave him free to discover and praise books which as a man he may not like, but which as a judge he must duly appreciate.

But critics, for the most part, are only readers; whence it comes that they almost always find fault with us on wrong grounds, or compliment us without reserve or measure.

The reader, who looks for no more in a book than that it should satisfy the natural tendencies of his own mind, wants the writer to respond to his predominant taste, and he invariably praises a work or a passage which appeals to his imagination, whether idealistic, gay, licentious, melancholy, dreamy, or positive, as "striking" or "well written."

The public as a whole is composed of various groups, whose cry to us writers is:

"Comfort me."

"Amuse me."

"Touch me."

"Make me dream."

"Make me laugh."

"Make me shudder."

"Make me weep."

"Make me think."

And only a few chosen spirits say to the artist:

"Give me something fine in any form which may suit you best, according to your own temperament."

The artist makes the attempt; succeeds or fails.

The critic ought to judge the result only in relation to the nature of the attempt; he has no right to concern himself about tendencies. This has been said a thousand times already; it will always need repeating.

Thus, after a succession of literary schools which have given us deformed, superhuman, poetical, pathetic, charming or magnificent pictures of life, a realistic or naturalistic school has arisen, which asserts that it shows us the truth, the whole truth, and nothing but the truth.

All these theories of art must be recognized as of equal interest, and we must judge the works which are their outcome solely from the point of view of artistic value, with an a priori acceptance of the general notions which gave birth to each. To dispute the author's right to produce a poetical work or a realistic work, is to endeavor to coerce his temperament, to take exception to his originality, to forbid his using the eyes and wits bestowed on him by Nature. To blame him for seeing things as beautiful or ugly, as mean or epic, as gracious or sinister, is to reproach him for not being made on this or that pattern, and for having eyes which do not see exactly as ours see.

Let him be free by all means to conceive of things as he pleases, provided he is an artist. Let us rise to poetic heights to judge an idealist, and then prove to him that his dream is commonplace, ordinary, not mad or magnificent enough. But if we judge a materialistic writer, let us show him wherein the truth of life differs from the truth in his book.

It is self-evident that schools so widely different must have adopted diametrically opposite processes in composition.

The novelist who transforms truth — immutable, uncompromising, and displeasing as it is — to extract from it an exceptional and delightful plot, must necessarily manipulate events without an exaggerated respect for probability, molding them to his will, dressing and arranging them so as to attract, excite, or affect the reader. The scheme of his romance is no more than a series of ingenious combinations, skillfully leading to the issue. The incidents are planned and graduated up to the culminating point and effect of the conclusion, which is the crowning and fatal result, satisfying the curiosity aroused from the first, closing the interest, and ending the story so completely that we have no further wish to know what happened on the morrow to the most engaging actors in it.

The novelist who, on the other hand, proposes to give us an accurate picture of life, must carefully eschew any concatenation of events which might seem exceptional. His aim is not to tell a story to amuse us, or to appeal to our feelings, but to compel us to reflect, and to understand the occult and deeper meaning of events. By dint of seeing and meditating he has come to regard the world, facts, men, and things in a way peculiar to himself, which is the outcome of the sum total of his studious observation. It is this personal view of the world which he strives to communicate to us by reproducing it in a book. To make the spectacle of life as moving to us as it has been to him, he must bring it before our eyes with scrupulous exactitude. Hence he must construct his work with such skill, it must be so artful under so simple a guise, that it is impossible to detect and sketch the plan, or discern the writer's purpose.

Instead of manipulating an adventure and working it out in such a way as to make it interesting to the last, he will take his actor or actors at a certain period of their lives, and lead them by natural stages to the next. In this way he will show either how men's minds are modified by the influence of their environment, or how their passions and sentiments are evolved; how they love or hate, how they struggle in every sphere of society, and how their interests clash — social interests, pecuniary interests, family interests, political interests. The skill of his plan will not consist in emotional power or charm, in an attractive opening or a stirring catastrophe, but in the happy grouping of small but constant facts from which the final purpose of the work may be discerned. If within three hundred pages he depicts ten years of a life so as to show what its individual and characteristic significance may have been in the midst of all the other human beings which surrounded it, he ought to know how to eliminate from among the numberless trivial incidents of daily life all which do not serve his end, and how to set in a special light all those which might have remained invisible to less clear-sighted observers, and which give his book caliber and value as a whole.

It is intelligible that this method of construction, so unlike the old manner which was patent to all, must often mislead the critics, and that they will not all detect the subtle and secret wires — almost invisibly fine — which certain modern artists use instead of the one string formerly known as the "plot."

In a word, while the novelist of yesterday preferred to relate the crises of life, the acute phases of the mind and heart, the novelist of to-day writes the history of the heart, soul, and intellect in their normal condition. To achieve the effects he aims at — that is to say, the sense of simple reality, and to point the artistic lesson he endeavors to draw from it — that is to say, a revelation of what his contemporary man is before his very eyes, he must bring forward no facts that are not irrefragible and invariable.

But even when we place ourselves at the same point of view as these realistic artists, we may discuss and dispute their theory, which seems to be comprehensively stated in these words: "The whole Truth and nothing but the Truth." Since the end they have in view is to bring out the philosophy of certain constant and current facts, they must often correct events in favor of probability and to the detriment of truth; for

"Le vrai peut quelquefois, n'être pas le vraisemblable." (Truth may sometimes not seem probable.)

The realist, if he is an artist, will endeavor not to show us a commonplace photograph of life, but to give us a presentment of it which shall be more complete, more striking, more cogent than reality itself. To tell everything is out of the question; it would require at least a volume for each day to enumerate the endless, insignificant incidents which crowd our existence. A choice must be made — and this is the first blow to the theory of "the whole truth."

Life, moreover, is composed of the most dissimilar things, the most unforeseen, the most contradictory, the most incongruous; it is merciless, without sequence or connection, full of inexplicable, illogical, and contradictory catastrophes, such as can only be classed as miscellaneous facts. This is why the artist, having chosen his subject, can only select such characteristic details as are of use to it, from this life overladen with chances and trifles, and reject everything else, everything by the way.

To give an instance from among a thousand. The number of persons who, every day, meet with an accidental death, all over the world, is very considerable. But how can we bring a tile onto the head of an important character, or fling him under the wheels of a vehicle in the middle of a story, under the pretext that accident must have its due?

Again, in life there is no difference of foreground and distance, and events are sometimes hurried on, sometimes left to linger indefinitely. Art, on the contrary, consists in the employment of foresight, and elaboration in arranging skillful and ingenious transitions, in setting essential events in a strong light, simply by the craft of composition, and giving all else the degree of relief, in proportion to their importance, requisite to produce a convincing sense of the special truth to be conveyed.

"Truth" in such work consists in producing a complete illusion by following the common logic of facts and not by transcribing them pellmell, as they succeed each other.

Whence I conclude that the higher order of Realists should rather call themselves Illusionists.

How childish it is, indeed, to believe in this reality, since to each of us the truth is in his own mind, his own organs. Our own eyes and ears, taste and smell, create as many different truths as there are human beings on earth. And our brains, duly and differently informed by those organs, apprehend, analyze, and decide as differently as if each of us were a being of an alien race. Each of us, then, has simply his own illusion of the world — poetical, sentimental, cheerful, melancholy, foul, or gloomy, according to his nature. And the writer has no other mission than faithfully to reproduce this illusion, with all the elaborations of art which he may have learnt and have at his command. The illusion of beauty — which is merely a conventional term invented by man! The illusion of ugliness — which is a matter of varying opinion! The illusion of truth — never immutable! The illusion of depravity — which fascinates so many minds! All the great artists are those who can make other men see their own particular illusion.

Then we must not be wroth with any theory, since each is simply the outcome, in generalizations, of a special temperament analyzing itself.

Two of these theories have more particularly been the subject of discussion, and set up in opposition to each other instead of being admitted on an equal footing: that of the purely analytical novel, and that of the objective novel.

The partisans of analysis require the writer to devote himself to indicating the smallest evolutions of a soul, and all the most secret motives of our every action, giving but a quite secondary importance to the act and fact in itself. It is but the goal, a simple milestone, the excuse for the book. According to them, these works, at once exact and visionary, in which imagination merges into observation, are to be written after the fashion in which a philosopher composes a treatise on psychology, seeking out causes in their remotest origin, telling the why and wherefore of every impulse, and detecting every reaction of the soul's movements under the promptings of interest, passion, or instinct.

The partisans of objectivity — odious word — aiming, on the contrary, at giving us an exact presentment of all that happens in life, carefully avoid all complicated explanations, all disquisitions on motive, and confine themselves to let persons and events pass before our eyes. In their opinion, psychology should be concealed in the book, as it is in reality, under the facts of existence.

The novel as conceived of on these lines gains in interest; there is more movement in the narrative, more color, more of the stir of life.

Hence, instead of giving long explanations of the state of mind of an actor in the tale, the objective writer tries to discover the action or gesture which that state of mind must inevitably lead to in that personage, under certain given circumstances. And he makes him so demean himself from one end of the volume to the other, that all his actions, all his movements shall be the expression of his inmost nature, of all his thoughts, and all his impulses or hesitancies. Thus they conceal psychology instead of flaunting it; they use it as the skeleton of the work, just as the invisible bony framework is the skeleton of the human body. The artist who paints our portrait does not display our bones.

To me it seems that the novel executed on this principle gains also in sincerity. It is, in the first place, more probable, for the persons we see moving about us do not divulge to us the motives from which they act.

We must also take into account the fact that, even if by close observation of men and women we can so exactly ascertain their characters as to predict their behavior under almost any circumstances, if we can say decisively: "Such a man, of such a temperament, in such a case, will do this or that"; yet it does not follow that we could lay a finger, one by one, on all the secret evolutions of his mind — which is not our own; all the mysterious pleadings of his instincts — which are not the same as ours; all the mingled promptings of his nature — in which the organs, nerves, blood, and flesh are different from ours.

However great the genius of a gentle, delicate man, guileless of passions and devoted to science and work, he never can so completely transfuse himself into the body of a dashing, sensual, and violent man, of exuberant vitality, torn by every desire or even by every vice, as to understand and delineate the inmost impulses and sensations of a being so unlike himself, even though he may very adequately foresee and relate all the actions of his life.

In short, the man who writes pure psychology can do no more than put himself in the place of all his puppets in the various situations in which he places them. It is impossible that he should change his organs, which are the sole intermediary between external life and ourselves, which constrain us by their perceptions, circumscribe our sensibilities, and create in each of us a soul essentially dissimilar to all those about us. Our purview and knowledge of the world, and our ideas of life, are acquired by the aid of our senses, and we cannot help transferring them, in some degree, to all the personages whose secret and unknown nature we propose to reveal. Thus, it is always ourselves that we disclose in the body of a king or an assassin, a robber or an honest man, a courtesan, a nun, a young girl, or a coarse market woman; for we are compelled to put the problem in this personal form: "If I were a king, a murderer, a prostitute, a nun, or a market woman, what should I do, what should I think, how should I act?" We can only vary our characters by altering the age, the sex, the social position, and all the circumstances of life, of that ego which nature has in fact inclosed in an insurmountable barrier of organs of sense. Skill consists in not betraying this ego to the reader, under the various masks which we employ to cover it.

Still, though on the point of absolute exactitude, pure psychological analysis is impregnable, it can nevertheless produce works of art as fine as any other method of work.

Here, for instance we have the Symbolists. And why not? Their artistic dream is a worthy one; and they have this especially interesting feature: that they know and proclaim the extreme difficulty of art.

And, indeed, a man must be very daring or foolish to write at all nowadays. And so many and such various masters of the craft, of such multifarious genius, what remains to be done that has not been done, or what to say that has not been said? Which of us all can boast of having written a page, a phrase, which is not to be found — or something very like it — in some other book? When we read, we who are so soaked in (French) literature that our whole body seems as it were a mere compound of words, do we ever light on a line, a thought, which is not familiar to us, or of which we have not had at least some vague forecast?

The man who only tries to amuse his public by familiar methods, writes confidently, in his candid mediocrity, works intended only for the ignorant and idle crowd. But those who are conscious of the weight of centuries of past literature, whom nothing satisfies, whom everything disgusts because they dream of something better, to whom the bloom is off everything, and who always are impressed with the uselessness, the commonness of their own achievements — these come to regard literary art as a thing unattainable and mysterious, scarcely to be detected save in a few pages by the greatest masters.

A score of phrases suddenly discovered thrill us to the heart like a startling revelation; but the lines which follow are just like all other verse, the further flow of prose is like all other prose.

Men of genius, no doubt, escape this anguish and torment because they bear within themselves an irresistible creative power. They do not sit in judgment on themselves. The rest of us, who are no more than persevering and conscientious workers, can only contend against invincible discouragement by unremitting effort.

Two men by their simple and lucid teaching gave me the strength to try again and again: Louis Bouilhet and Gustave Flaubert.

If I here speak of myself in connection with them, it is because their counsels, as summed up in a few lines, may prove useful to some young writers who may be less self-confident than most are when they make their début in print. Bouilhet, whom I first came to know somewhat intimately about two years before I gained the friendship of Flaubert, by dint of telling me that a hundred lines — or less — if they are without a flaw and contain the very essence of the talent and originality of even a second-rate man, are enough to establish an artist's reputation, made me understand that persistent toil and a thorough knowledge of the craft, might, in some happy hour of lucidity, power, and enthusiasm, by the fortunate occurrence of a subject in perfect concord with the tendency of our mind, lead to the production of a single work, short but as perfect as we can make it. Then I learned to see that the best-known writers have hardly ever left us more than one such volume; and that needful above all else is the good fortune which leads us to hit upon and discern, amid the multifarious matter which offers itself for selection, the subject which will absorb all our faculties, all that is of worth in us, all our artistic powers.

At a later date, Flaubert, whom I had occasionally met, took a fancy to me. I ventured to show him a few attempts. He read them kindly and replied: "I cannot tell whether you will have any talent. What you have brought me proves a certain intelligence; but never forget this, young man: talent — as Chateaubriand says — is nothing but long patience. Go and work."

The idea did not originate with Chateaubriand.

I worked; and I often went to see him, feeling that he liked me, for he had taken to calling me, in jest, his disciple. For seven years I wrote verses, I wrote tales, I even wrote a villainous play. Nothing of all this remains. The master read it all; then, the next Sunday while we breakfasted together, he would give me his criticisms, driving into me by degrees two or three principles which sum up the drift of his long and patient exhortations: "If you have any originality," said he, "you must above all things bring it out; if you have not you must acquire it."

Talent is long patience.

Everything you want to express must be considered so long, and so attentively, as to enable you to find some aspect of it which no one has yet seen and expressed. There is an unexplored side to everything, because we are wont never to use our eyes but with the memory of what others before us have thought of the things we see. The smallest thing has something unknown in it; we must find it. To describe a blazing fire, a tree in a plain, we must stand face to face with that fire or that tree, till to us they are wholly unlike any other fire or tree. Thus we may become original.

Then, having established the truth that there are not in the whole world two grains of sand, two flies, two hands, or two noses absolutely alike, he would make me describe in a few sentences some person or object, in such a way as to define it exactly, and distinguish it from every other of the same race or species.

"When you pass a grocer sitting in his doorway," he would say, "a porter smoking his pipe, or a cab stand, show me that grocer and that porter, their attitude and their whole physical aspect, including, as indicated by the skill of the portrait, their whole moral nature, in such a way that I could never mistake them for any other grocer or porter; and by a single word give me to understand wherein one cab horse differs from fifty others before or behind it."

I have explained his notions of style at greater length in another place; they bear a marked relation to the theory of observation I have just laid down. Whatever the thing we wish to say, there is but one word to express it, but one verb to give it movement, but one adjective to qualify it. We must seek till we find this noun, this verb, and this adjective, and never be content with getting very near it, never allow ourselves to play tricks, even happy ones, or have recourse to sleights of language to avoid a difficulty. The subtlest things may be rendered and suggested by applying the hint conveyed in Boileau's line:

"D'un mot mis en sa place enseigna le pouvoir." "He taught the power of a word put in the right place."

There is no need for an eccentric vocabulary to formulate every shade of thought — the complicated, multifarious, and outlandish words which are put upon us nowadays in the name of artistic writing; but every modification of the value of a word by the place it fills must be distinguished with extreme clearness. Give us fewer nouns, verbs, and adjectives, with almost inscrutable shades of meaning, and let us have a greater variety of phrases, more variously constructed, ingeniously divided, full of sonority and learned rhythm. Let us strive to be admirable in style, rather than curious in collecting rare words.

It is in fact more difficult to bend a sentence to one's will and make it express everything — even what it does not say, to fill it full of implications of covert and inexplicit suggestions, than to invent new expressions, or seek out in old and forgotten books all those which have fallen into disuse and lost their meaning, so that to us they are as a dead language.

The French tongue, to be sure, is a pure stream, which affected writers never have and never can trouble. Each age has flung into the limpid waters its pretentious archaisms and euphuisms, but nothing has remained on the surface to perpetuate these futile attempts and impotent efforts. It is the nature of the language to be clear, logical, and vigorous. It does not lend itself to weakness, obscurity, or corruption.

Those who describe without duly heeding abstract terms, those who make rain and hail fall on the cleanliness of the window panes, may throw stones at the simplicity of their brothers of the pen. The stones may indeed hit their brothers, who have a body, but will never hurt simplicity — which has none.

Guy de Maupassant.
La Guillette, Etretat, September, 1887.

I

"Tschah!" exclaimed old Roland suddenly, after he had remained motionless for a quarter of an hour, his eyes fixed on the water, while now and again he very slightly lifted his line sunk in the sea.

Mme. Roland, dozing in the stern by the side of *Mme.* Rosemilly, who had been invited to join the fishing-party, woke up, and turning her head to look at her husband, said:

"Well, well! Gerome."

And the old fellow replied in a fury:

"They do not bite at all. I have taken nothing since noon. Only men should ever go fishing. Women always delay the start till it is too late."

His two sons, Pierre and Jean, who each held a line twisted round his forefinger, one to port and one to starboard, both began to laugh, and Jean remarked:

"You are not very polite to our guest, father."

M. Roland was abashed, and apologized.

"I beg your pardon, *Mme.* Rosemilly, but that is just like me. I invite ladies because I like to be with them, and then, as soon as I feel the water beneath me, I think of nothing but the fish."

Mme. Roland was now quite awake, and gazing with a softened look at the wide horizon of cliff and sea.

"You have had good sport, all the same," she murmured.

But her husband shook his head in denial, though at the same time he glanced complacently at the basket where the fish caught by the three men were still breathing spasmodically, with a low rustle of clammy scales and struggling fins, and dull, ineffectual efforts, gasping in the fatal air. Old Roland took the basket between his knees and tilted it up, making the silver heap of creatures slide to the edge that he might see those lying at the bottom, and their death-throes became more convulsive, while the strong smell of their bodies, a wholesome reek of brine, came up from the full depths of the creel. The old fisherman sniffed it eagerly, as we smell at roses, and exclaimed:

"Cristi! But they are fresh enough!" and he went on: "How many did you pull out, doctor?"

His eldest son, Pierre, a man of thirty, with black whiskers trimmed square like a lawyer's, his mustache and beard shaved away, replied:

"Oh, not many; three or four."

The father turned to the younger. "And you, Jean?" said he.

Jean, a tall fellow, much younger than his brother, fair, with a full beard, smiled and murmured:

"Much the same as Pierre — four or five."

Every time they told the same fib, which delighted father Roland. He had hitched his line round a row-lock, and folding his arms he announced:

"I will never again try to fish after noon. After ten in the morning it is all over. The lazy brutes will not bite; they are taking their siesta in the sun." And he looked round at the sea on all sides, with the satisfied air of a proprietor.

He was a retired jeweller who had been led by an inordinate love of seafaring and fishing to fly from the shop as soon as he had made enough money to live in modest comfort on the interest of his savings. He retired to le Havre, bought a boat, and became an amateur skipper. His two sons, Pierre and Jean, had remained at Paris to continue their studies, and came for the holidays from time to time to share their father's amusements.

On leaving school, Pierre, the elder, five years older than Jean, had felt a vocation to various professions and had tried half a dozen in succession, but, soon disgusted with each in turn, he started afresh with new hopes. Medicine had been his last fancy, and he had set to work with so much ardour that he had just qualified after an unusually short course of study, by a special remission of time from the minister. He was enthusiastic, intelligent, fickle, but obstinate, full of Utopias and philosophical notions.

Jean, who was as fair as his brother was dark, as deliberate as his brother was vehement, as gentle as his brother was unforgiving, had quietly gone through his studies for the law and had just taken his diploma as a licentiate, at the time when Pierre had taken his in medicine. So they were now having a little rest at home, and both looked forward to settling in Havre if they could find a satisfactory opening.

But a vague jealousy, one of those dormant jealousies which grow up between brothers or sisters and slowly ripen till they burst, on the occasion of a marriage perhaps, or of some good fortune happening to one of them, kept them on the alert in a sort of brotherly and non-aggressive animosity. They were fond of each other, it is true, but they watched each other. Pierre, five years old when Jean was born, had looked with the eyes of a little petted animal at that other little animal which had suddenly come to lie in his father's and mother's arms and to be loved and fondled by them. Jean, from his birth, had always been a pattern of sweetness, gentleness, and good temper, and Pierre had by degrees begun to chafe at everlastingly hearing the praises of this great lad, whose sweetness in his eyes was indolence, whose gentleness was stupidity, and whose kindliness was blindness. His parents, whose dream for their sons was some respectable and undistinguished calling, blamed him for so often changing his mind, for his fits of enthusiasm, his abortive beginnings, and all his ineffectual impulses towards generous ideas and the liberal professions.

Since he had grown to manhood they no longer said in so many words: "Look at Jean and follow his example," but every time he heard them say "Jean did this — Jean does that," he understood their meaning and the hint the words conveyed.

Their mother, an orderly person, a thrifty and rather sentimental woman of the middle class, with the soul of a soft-hearted bookkeeper, was constantly quenching the little rivalries between her two big sons to which the petty events of their life constantly gave rise. Another little circumstance, too, just now disturbed her peace of mind, and she was in fear of some complications; for in the course of the winter, while her boys were finishing their studies, each in his own line, she had made the acquaintance of a neighbour, *Mme.* Rosemilly, the widow of a captain of a merchantman who had died at sea two years before. The young widow — quite young, only three-and-twenty — a woman of strong intellect who knew life by instinct as the free animals do, as though she had seen, gone through, understood, and weighted every conceivable contingency, and judged them with a wholesome, strict, and benevolent mind, had fallen into the habit of calling to work or chat for an hour in the evening with these friendly neighbours, who would give her a cup of tea.

Father Roland, always goaded on by his seafaring craze, would question their new friend about the departed captain; and she would talk of him, and his voyages, and his old-world tales, without hesitation, like a resigned and reasonable woman who loves life and respects death.

The two sons on their return, finding the pretty widow quite at home in the house, forthwith began to court her, less from any wish to charm her than from the desire to cut each other out.

Their mother, being practical and prudent, sincerely hoped that one of them might win the young widow, for she was rich; but then she would have liked that the other should not be grieved.

Mme. Rosemilly was fair, with blue eyes, a mass of light waving hair, fluttering at the least breath of wind, and an alert, daring, pugnacious little way with her, which did not in the least answer to the sober method of her mind.

She already seemed to like Jean best, attracted, no doubt, by an affinity of nature. This preference, however, she betrayed only by an almost imperceptible difference of voice and look and also by occasionally asking his opinion. She seemed to guess that Jean's views would support her own, while those of Pierre must inevitably be different. When she spoke of the doctor's ideas on politics, art, philosophy, or morals, she would sometimes say: "Your crotchets." Then he would look at her with the cold gleam of an accuser drawing up an indictment against women — all women, poor weak things.

Never till his sons came home had M. Roland invited her to join his fishing expeditions, nor had he ever taken his wife; for he liked to put off before daybreak, with his ally, Captain Beausire, a master mariner retired, whom he had first met on the quay at high tides and with whom he had struck up an intimacy, and the old sailor Papagris, known as Jean Bart, in whose charge the boat was left.

But one evening of the week before, *Mme.* Rosemilly, who had been dining with them, remarked, "It must be great fun to go out fishing." The jeweller, flattered by her interest and suddenly fired with the wish to share his favourite sport with her, and to make a convert after the manner of priests, exclaimed: "Would you like to come?"

"To be sure I should."

"Next Tuesday?"

"Yes, next Tuesday."

"Are you the woman to be ready to start at five in the morning?"

She exclaimed in horror:

"No, indeed: that is too much."

He was disappointed and chilled, suddenly doubting her true vocation. However, he said:

"At what hour can you be ready?"

"Well — at nine?"

"Not before?"

"No, not before. Even that is very early."

The old fellow hesitated; he certainly would catch nothing, for when the sun has warmed the sea the fish bite no more; but the two brothers had eagerly pressed the scheme, and organized and arranged everything there and then.

So on the following Tuesday the Pearl had dropped anchor under the white rocks of Cape la Heve; they had fished till midday, then they had slept awhile, and then fished again without catching anything; and then it was that father Roland, perceiving, rather late, that all that *Mme.* Rosemilly really enjoyed and cared for was the sail on the sea, and seeing that his lines hung motionless, had uttered in a spirit of unreasonable annoyance, that vehement "Tschah!" which applied as much to the pathetic widow as to the creatures he could not catch.

Now he contemplated the spoil — his fish — with the joyful thrill of a miser; seeing as he looked up at the sky that the sun was getting low: "Well, boys," said he, "suppose we turn homeward."

The young men hauled in their lines, coiled them up, cleaned the hooks and stuck them into corks, and sat waiting.

Roland stood up to look out like a captain.

"No wind," said he. "You will have to pull, young 'uns."

And suddenly extending one arm to the northward, he exclaimed:

"Here comes the packet from Southampton."

Away over the level sea, spread out like a blue sheet, vast and sheeny and shot with flame and gold, an inky cloud was visible against the rosy sky in the quarter to which he pointed, and below it they could make out the hull of the steamer, which looked tiny at such a distance. And to southward other wreaths of smoke, numbers of them, could be seen, all converging towards the Havre pier, now scarcely visible as a white streak with the lighthouse, upright, like a horn, at the end of it.

Roland asked: "Is not the Normandie due to-day?" And Jean replied:

"Yes, to-day."

"Give me my glass. I fancy I see her out there."

The father pulled out the copper tube, adjusted it to his eye, sought the speck, and then, delighted to have seen it, exclaimed:

"Yes, yes, there she is. I know her two funnels. Would you like to look, *Mme.* Rosemilly?"

She took the telescope and directed it towards the Atlantic horizon, without being able, however, to find the vessel, for she could distinguish nothing — nothing but blue, with a coloured halo round it, a circular rainbow — and then all manner of queer things, winking eclipses which made her feel sick.

She said as she returned the glass:

"I never could see with that thing. It used to put my husband in quite a rage; he would stand for hours at the windows watching the ships pass."

Old Roland, much put out, retorted:

"Then it must be some defect in your eye, for my glass is a very good one."

Then he offered it to his wife.

"Would you like to look?"

"No, thank you. I know before hand that I could not see through it."

Mme. Roland, a woman of eight-and-forty but who did not look it, seemed to be enjoying this excursion and this waning day more than any of the party.

Her chestnut hair was only just beginning to show streaks of white. She had a calm, reasonable face, a kind and happy way with her which it was a pleasure to see. Her son Pierre was wont to say that she knew the value of money, but this did not hinder her from enjoying the delights of dreaming. She was fond of reading, of novels, and poetry, not for their value as works of art, but for the sake of the tender melancholy mood they would induce in her. A line of poetry, often but a poor one, often a bad one, would touch the little chord, as she expressed it, and give her the sense of some mysterious desire almost realized. And she delighted in these faint emotions which brought a little flutter to her soul, otherwise as strictly kept as a ledger.

Since settling at Havre she had become perceptibly stouter, and her figure, which had been very supple and slight, had grown heavier.

This day on the sea had been delightful to her. Her husband, without being brutal, was rough with her, as a man who is the despot of his shop is apt to be rough, without anger or hatred; to such men to give an order is to swear. He controlled himself in the presence of strangers, but in private he let loose and gave himself terrible vent, though he was himself afraid of every one. She, in sheer horror of the turmoil, of scenes, of useless explanations, always gave way and never asked for anything; for a very long time she had not ventured to ask Roland to take her out in the boat. So she had joyfully hailed this opportunity, and was keenly enjoying the rare and new pleasure.

From the moment when they started she surrendered herself completely, body and soul, to the soft, gliding motion over the waves. She was not thinking; her mind was not wandering through either memories or hopes; it seemed to her as though her heart, like her body, was floating on something soft and liquid and delicious which rocked and lulled it.

When their father gave the word to return, "Come, take your places at the oars!" she smiled to see her sons, her two great boys, take off their jackets and roll up their shirtsleeves on their bare arms.

Pierre, who was nearest to the two women, took the stroke oar, Jean the other, and they sat waiting till the skipper should say: "Give way!" For he insisted on everything being done according to strict rule.

Simultaneously, as if by a single effort, they dipped the oars, and lying back, pulling with all their might, began a struggle to display their strength. They had come out easily, under sail, but the breeze had died away, and the masculine pride of the two brothers was suddenly aroused by the prospect of measuring their powers. When they went out alone with their father they plied the oars without any steering, for Roland would be busy getting the lines ready, while he kept a lookout in the boat's course, guiding it by a sign or a word: "Easy, Jean, and you, Pierre, put your back into it." Or he would say, "Now, then, number one; come, number two — a little elbow grease." Then the one who had been dreaming pulled harder, the one who had got excited eased down, and the boat's head came round.

But to-day they meant to display their biceps. Pierre's arms were hairy, somewhat lean but sinewy; Jean's were round and white and rosy, and the knot of muscles moved under the skin.

At first Pierre had the advantage. With his teeth set, his brow knit, his legs rigid, his hands clinched on the oar, he made it bend from end to end at every stroke, and the Pearl was veering landward. Father Roland, sitting in the bows, so as to leave the stern seat to the two women, wasted his breath shouting, "Easy, number one; pull harder, number two!" Pierre pulled harder in his frenzy, and "number two" could not keep time with his wild stroke.

At last the skipper cried: "Stop her!" The two oars were lifted simultaneously, and then by his father's orders Jean pulled alone for a few minutes. But from that moment he had it all his own way; he grew eager and warmed to his work, while Pierre, out of breath and exhausted by his first vigorous spurt, was lax and panting. Four times running father Roland made them stop while the elder took breath, so as to get the boat into her right course again. Then the doctor, humiliated and fuming, his forehead dropping with sweat, his cheeks white, stammered out:

"I cannot think what has come over me; I have a stitch in my side. I started very well, but it has pulled me up."

Jean asked: "Shall I pull alone with both oars for a time?"

"No, thanks, it will go off."

And their mother, somewhat vexed, said:

"Why, Pierre, what rhyme or reason is there in getting into such a state. You are not a child."

And he shrugged his shoulders and set to once more.

Mme. Rosemilly pretended not to see, not to understand, not to hear. Her fair head went back with an engaging little jerk every time the boat moved forward, making the fine wayward hairs flutter about her temples.

But father Roland presently called out:

"Look, the Prince Albert is catching us up!"

They all looked round. Long and low in the water, with her two raking funnels and two yellow paddle-boxes like two round cheeks, the Southampton packet came ploughing on at full steam, crowded with passengers under open parasols. Its hurrying, noisy paddle-wheels beating up the water which fell again in foam, gave it an appearance of haste as of a courier pressed for time, and the upright stem cut through the water, throwing up two thin translucent waves which glided off along the hull.

When it had come quite near the Pearl, father Roland lifted his hat, the ladies shook their handkerchiefs, and half a dozen parasols eagerly waved on board the steamboat responded to this salute as she went on her way, leaving behind her a few broad undulations on the still and glassy surface of the sea.

There were other vessels, each with its smoky cap, coming in from every part of the horizon towards the short white jetty, which swallowed them up, one after another, like a mouth. And the fishing barks and lighter craft with broad sails and slender masts, stealing across the sky in tow of inconspicuous tugs, were coming in, faster and slower, towards the devouring ogre, who from time to time seemed to have had a surfeit, and spewed out to the open sea another fleet of steamers, brigs, schooners, and three-masted vessels with their tangled mass of rigging. The hurrying steamships flew off to the right and left over the smooth bosom of the ocean, while sailing vessels, cast off by the pilot-tugs which had hauled them out, lay motionless, dressing themselves from the main-mast to the fore-tops in canvas, white or brown, and ruddy in the setting sun.

Mme. Roland, with her eyes half-shut, murmured: "Good heavens, how beautiful the sea is!"

And *Mme.* Rosemilly replied with a long sigh, which, however, had no sadness in it:

"Yes, but it is sometimes very cruel, all the same."

Roland exclaimed:

"Look, there is the Normandie just going in. A big ship, isn't she?"

Then he described the coast opposite, far, far away, on the other side of the mouth of the Seine — that mouth extended over twenty kilometres, said he. He pointed out Villerville, Trouville, Houlgate, Luc, Arromanches, the little river of Caen, and the rocks of Calvados which make the coast unsafe as far as Cherbourg. Then he enlarged on the question of the sandbanks in the Seine, which shift at every tide so that even the pilots of Quilleboeuf are at fault if they do not survey the channel every day. He bid them notice how the town of Havre divided Upper from Lower Normandy. In Lower Normandy the shore sloped down to the sea in pasture-lands, fields, and meadows. The coast of Upper Normandy, on the contrary, was steep, a high cliff, ravined, cleft and towering, forming an immense white rampart all the way to Dunkirk, while in each hollow a village or a port lay hidden: Etretat, Fecamp, Saint-Valery, Treport, Dieppe, and the rest.

The two women did not listen. Torpid with comfort and impressed by the sight of the ocean covered with vessels rushing to and fro like wild beasts about their den, they sat speechless, somewhat awed by the soothing and gorgeous sunset. Roland alone talked on without end; he was one of those whom nothing can disturb. Women, whose nerves are more sensitive, sometimes feel, without knowing why, that the sound of useless speech is as irritating as an insult.

Pierre and Jean, who had calmed down, were rowing slowly, and the Pearl was making for the harbour, a tiny thing among those huge vessels.

When they came alongside of the quay, Papagris, who was waiting there, gave his hand to the ladies to help them out, and they took the way into the town. A large crowd, the crowd which haunts the pier every day at high tide — was also drifting homeward. *Mme.* Roland and *Mme.* Rosemilly led the way, followed by the three men. As they went up the Rue de Paris they stopped now and then in front of a milliner's or a jeweller's shop, to look at a bonnet or an ornament; then after making their comments they went on again. In front of the Place de la Bourse Roland paused, as he did every day, to gaze at the docks full of vessels — the Bassin du

Commerce, with other docks beyond, where the huge hulls lay side by side, closely packed in rows, four or five deep. And masts innumerable; along several kilometres of quays the endless masts, with their yards, poles, and rigging, gave this great gap in the heart of the town the look of a dead forest. Above this leafless forest the gulls were wheeling, and watching to pounce, like a falling stone, on any scraps flung overboard; a sailor boy, fixing a pulley to a cross-beam, looked as if he had gone up there bird's-nesting.

"Will you dine with us without any sort of ceremony, just that we may end the day together?" said *Mme.* Roland to her friend.

"To be sure I will, with pleasure; I accept equally without ceremony. It would be dismal to go home and be alone this evening."

Pierre, who had heard, and who was beginning to be restless under the young woman's indifference, muttered to himself: "Well, the widow is taking root now, it would seem." For some days past he had spoken of her as "the widow." The word, harmless in itself, irritated Jean merely by the tone given to it, which to him seemed spiteful and offensive.

The three men spoke not another word till they reached the threshold of their own house. It was a narrow one, consisting of a ground-floor and two floors above, in the Rue Belle-Normande. The maid, Josephine, a girl of nineteen, a rustic servant-of-all-work at low wages, gifted to excess with the startled animal expression of a peasant, opened the door, went up stairs at her master's heels to the drawingroom, which was on the first floor, and then said:

"A gentleman called — three times."

Old Roland, who never spoke to her without shouting and swearing, cried out:

"Who do you say called, in the devil's name?"

She never winced at her master's roaring voice, and replied:

"A gentleman from the lawyer's."

"What lawyer?"

"Why, M'sieu 'Canu — who else?"

"And what did this gentleman say?"

"That M'sieu 'Canu will call in himself in the course of the evening."

Maitre Lecanu was M. Roland's lawyer, and in a way his friend, managing his business for him. For him to send word that he would call in the evening, something urgent and important must be in the wind; and the four Rolands looked at each other, disturbed by the announcement as folks of small fortune are wont to be at any intervention of a lawyer, with its suggestions of contracts, inheritance, lawsuits — all sorts of desirable or formidable contingencies. The father, after a few moments of silence, muttered:

"What on earth can it mean?"

Mme. Rosemilly began to laugh.

"Why, a legacy, of course. I am sure of it. I bring good luck."

But they did not expect the death of any one who might leave them anything.

Mme. Roland, who had a good memory for relationships, began to think over all their connections on her husband's side and on her own, to trace up pedigrees and the ramifications of cousin-ship.

Before even taking off her bonnet she said:

"I say, father" (she called her husband "father" at home, and sometimes "Monsieur Roland" before strangers), "tell me, do you remember who it was that Joseph Lebru married for the second time?"

"Yes — a little girl named Dumenil, a stationer's daughter."

"Had they any children?"

"I should think so! four or five at least."

"Not from that quarter, then."

She was quite eager already in her search; she caught at the hope of some added ease dropping from the sky. But Pierre, who was very fond of his mother, who knew her to be somewhat visionary and feared she might be disappointed, a little grieved, a little saddened if the news were bad instead of good, checked her:

"Do not get excited, mother; there is no rich American uncle. For my part, I should sooner fancy that it is about a marriage for Jean."

Every one was surprised at the suggestion, and Jean was a little ruffled by his brother's having spoken of it before *Mme.* Rosemilly.

"And why for me rather than for you? The hypothesis is very disputable. You are the elder; you, therefore, would be the first to be thought of. Besides, I do not wish to marry."

Pierre smiled sneeringly:

"Are you in love, then?"

And the other, much put out, retorted: "Is it necessary that a man should be in love because he does not care to marry yet?"

"Ah, there you are! That 'yet' sets it right; you are waiting."

"Granted that I am waiting, if you will have it so."

But old Roland, who had been listening and cogitating, suddenly hit upon the most probable solution.

"Bless me! what fools we are to be racking our brains. Maitre Lecanu is our very good friend; he knows that Pierre is looking out for a medical partnership and Jean for a lawyer's office, and he has found something to suit one of you."

This was so obvious and likely that every one accepted it.

"Dinner is ready," said the maid. And they all hurried off to their rooms to wash their hands before sitting down to table.

Ten minutes later they were at dinner in the little diningroom on the ground-floor.

At first they were silent; but presently Roland began again in amazement at this lawyer's visit.

"For after all, why did he not write? Why should he have sent his clerk three times? Why is he coming himself?"

Pierre thought it quite natural.

"An immediate decision is required, no doubt; and perhaps there are certain confidential conditions which it does not do to put into writing."

Still, they were all puzzled, and all four a little annoyed at having invited a stranger, who would be in the way of their discussing and deciding on what should be done.

They had just gone upstairs again when the lawyer was announced. Roland flew to meet him.

"Good-evening, my dear Maitre," said he, giving his visitor the title which in France is the official prefix to the name of every lawyer.

Mme. Rosemilly rose.

"I am going," she said. "I am very tired."

A faint attempt was made to detain her; but she would not consent, and went home without either of the three men offering to escort her, as they always had done.

Mme. Roland did the honours eagerly to their visitor.

"A cup of coffee, monsieur?"

"No, thank you. I have just had dinner."

"A cup of tea, then?"

"Thank you, I will accept one later. First we must attend to business."

The deep silence which succeeded this remark was broken only by the regular ticking of the clock, and below stairs the clatter of saucepans which the girl was cleaning — too stupid even to listen at the door.

The lawyer went on:

"Did you, in Paris, know a certain M. Marechal — Leon Marechal?"

M. and *Mme.* Roland both exclaimed at once: "I should think so!"

"He was a friend of yours?"

Roland replied: "Our best friend, monsieur, but a fanatic for Paris; never to be got away from the boulevard. He was a head clerk in the exchequer office. I have never seen him since

I left the capital, and latterly we had ceased writing to each other. When people are far apart
you know — — "

The lawyer gravely put in:

"M. Marechal is deceased."

Both man and wife responded with the little movement of pained surprise, genuine or false,
but always ready, with which such news is received.

Maitre Lecanu went on:

"My colleague in Paris has just communicated to me the main item of his will, by which he
makes your son Jean — Monsieur Jean Roland — his sole legatee."

They were all too much amazed to utter a single word. *Mme.* Roland was the first to control
her emotion and stammered out:

"Good heavens! Poor Leon — our poor friend! Dear me! Dear me! Dead!"

The tears started to her eyes, a woman's silent tears, drops of grief from her very soul, which
trickle down her cheeks and seem so very sad, being so clear. But Roland was thinking less of
the loss than of the prospect announced. Still, he dared not at once inquire into the clauses of
the will and the amount of the fortune, so to work round to these interesting facts he asked:

"And what did he die of, poor Marechal?"

Maitre Lecanu did not know in the least.

"All I know is," said he, "that dying without any direct heirs, he has left the whole of his
fortune — about twenty thousand francs a year ($3,840) in three per cents — to your second
son, whom he has known from his birth up, and judges worthy of the legacy. If M. Jean should
refuse the money, it is to go to the foundling hospitals."

Old Roland could not conceal his delight and exclaimed:

"Sacristi! It is the thought of a kind heart. And if I had had no heir I would not have
forgotten him; he was a true friend."

The lawyer smiled.

"I was very glad," he said, "to announce the event to you myself. It is always a pleasure to
be the bearer of good news."

It had not struck him that this good news was that of the death of a friend, of Roland's best
friend; and the old man himself had suddenly forgotten the intimacy he had but just spoken
of with so much conviction.

Only *Mme.* Roland and her sons still looked mournful. She, indeed, was still shedding a
few tears, wiping her eyes with her handkerchief, which she then pressed to her lips to smother
her deep sobs.

The doctor murmured:

"He was a good fellow, very affectionate. He often invited us to dine with him — my brother
and me."

Jean, with wide-open, glittering eyes, laid his hand on his handsome fair beard, a familiar
gesture with him, and drew his fingers down it to the tip of the last hairs, as if to pull it longer
and thinner. Twice his lips parted to utter some decent remark, but after long meditation he
could only say this:

"Yes, he was certainly fond of me. He would always embrace me when I went to see him."

But his father's thoughts had set off at a gallop — galloping round this inheritance to come;
nay, already in hand; this money lurking behind the door, which would walk in quite soon,
tomorrow, at a word of consent.

"And there is no possible difficulty in the way?" he asked. "No lawsuit — no one to dispute
it?"

Maitre Lecanu seemed quite easy.

"No; my Paris correspondent states that everything is quite clear. M. Jean has only to sign
his acceptance."

"Good. Then — then the fortune is quite clear?"

"Perfectly clear."

"All the necessary formalities have been gone through?"

"All."

Suddenly the old jeweller had an impulse of shame — obscure, instinctive, and fleeting; shame of his eagerness to be informed, and he added:

"You understand that I ask all these questions immediately so as to save my son unpleasant consequences which he might not foresee. Sometimes there are debts, embarrassing liabilities, what not! And a legatee finds himself in an inextricable thorn-bush. After all, I am not the heir — but I think first of the little 'un."

They were accustomed to speak of Jean among themselves as the "little one," though he was much bigger than Pierre.

Suddenly *Mme.* Roland seemed to wake from a dream, to recall some remote fact, a thing almost forgotten that she had heard long ago, and of which she was not altogether sure. She inquired doubtingly:

"Were you not saying that our poor friend Marechal had left his fortune to my little Jean?"

"Yes, madame."

And she went on simply:

"I am much pleased to hear it; it proves that he was attached to us."

Roland had risen.

"And would you wish, my dear sir, that my son should at once sign his acceptance?"

"No — no, M. Roland. Tomorrow, at my office tomorrow, at two o'clock, if that suits you."

"Yes, to be sure — yes, indeed. I should think so."

Then *Mme.* Roland, who had also risen and who was smiling after her tears, went up to the lawyer, and laying her hand on the back of his chair while she looked at him with the pathetic eyes of a grateful mother, she said:

"And now for that cup of tea, Monsieur Lecanu?"

"Now I will accept it with pleasure, madame."

The maid, on being summoned, brought in first some dry biscuits in deep tin boxes, those crisp, insipid English cakes which seem to have been made for a parrot's beak, and soldered into metal cases for a voyage round the world. Next she fetched some little gray linen doilies, folded square, those tea-napkins which in thrifty families never get washed. A third time she came in with the sugar-basin and cups; then she departed to heat the water. They sat waiting.

No one could talk; they had too much to think about and nothing to say. *Mme.* Roland alone attempted a few commonplace remarks. She gave an account of the fishing excursion, and sang the praises of the Pearl and of *Mme.* Rosemilly.

"Charming, charming!" the lawyer said again and again.

Roland, leaning against the marble mantelshelf as if it were winter and the fire burning, with his hands in his pockets and his lips puckered for a whistle, could not keep still, tortured by the invincible desire to give vent to his delight. The two brothers, in two armchairs that matched, one on each side of the centre-table, stared in front of them, in similar attitudes full of dissimilar expressions.

At last the tea appeared. The lawyer took a cup, sugared it, and drank it, after having crumbled into it a little cake which was too hard to crunch. Then he rose, shook hands, and departed.

"Then it is understood," repeated Roland. "Tomorrow, at your place, at two?"

"Quite so. Tomorrow, at two."

Jean had not spoken a word.

When their guest had gone, silence fell again till father Roland clapped his two hands on his younger son's shoulders, crying:

"Well, you devilish lucky dog! You don't embrace me!"

Then Jean smiled. He embraced his father, saying:

"It had not struck me as indispensable."

The old man was beside himself with glee. He walked about the room, strummed on the furniture with his clumsy nails, turned about on his heels, and kept saying:

"What luck! What luck! Now, that is really what I call luck!"

Pierre asked:

"Then you used to know this Marechal well?"

And his father replied:

"I believe! Why, he used to spend every evening at our house. Surely you remember he used to fetch you from school on half-holidays, and often took you back again after dinner. Why, the very day when Jean was born it was he who went for the doctor. He had been breakfasting with us when your mother was taken ill. Of course we knew at once what it meant, and he set off post-haste. In his hurry he took my hat instead of his own. I remember that because we had a good laugh over it afterward. It is very likely that he may have thought of that when he was dying, and as he had no heir he may have said to himself: 'I remember helping to bring that youngster into the world, so I will leave him my savings.'"

Mme. Roland, sunk in a deep chair, seemed lost in reminiscences once more. She murmured, as though she were thinking aloud:

"Ah, he was a good friend, very devoted, very faithful, a rare soul in these days."

Jean got up.

"I shall go out for a little walk," he said.

His father was surprised and tried to keep him; they had much to talk about, plans to be made, decisions to be formed. But the young man insisted, declaring that he had an engagement. Besides, there would be time enough for settling everything before he came into possession of his inheritance. So he went away, for he wished to be alone to reflect. Pierre, on his part, said that he too was going out, and after a few minutes followed his brother.

As soon as he was alone with his wife, father Roland took her in his arms, kissed her a dozen times on each cheek, and, replying to a reproach she had often brought against him, said:

"You see, my dearest, that it would have been no good to stay any longer in Paris and work for the children till I dropped, instead of coming here to recruit my health, since fortune drops on us from the skies."

She was quite serious.

"It drops from the skies on Jean," she said. "But Pierre?"

"Pierre? But he is a doctor; he will make plenty of money; besides, his brother will surely do something for him."

"No, he would not take it. Besides, this legacy is for Jean, only for Jean. Pierre will find himself at a great disadvantage."

The old fellow seemed perplexed: "Well, then, we will leave him rather more in our will."

"No; that again would not be quite just."

"Drat it all!" he exclaimed. "What do you want me to do in the matter? You always hit on a whole heap of disagreeable ideas. You must spoil all my pleasures. Well, I am going to bed. Goodnight. All the same, I call it good luck, jolly good luck!"

And he went off, delighted in spite of everything, and without a word of regret for the friend so generous in his death.

Mme. Roland sat thinking again in front of the lamp which was burning out.

II

As soon as he got out, Pierre made his way to the Rue de Paris, the high-street of Havre, brightly lighted up, lively and noisy. The rather sharp air of the seacoast kissed his face, and he walked slowly, his stick under his arm and his hands behind his back. He was ill at ease, oppressed, out of heart, as one is after hearing unpleasant tidings. He was not distressed by any definite thought, and he would have been puzzled to account, on the spur of the moment, for this dejection of spirit and heaviness of limb. He was hurt somewhere, without knowing where; somewhere within him there was a pin-point of pain —one of those almost imperceptible wounds which we cannot lay a finger on, but which incommode us, tire us, depress us, irritate us — a slight and occult pang, as it were a small seed of distress.

When he reached the square in front of the theatre, he was attracted by the lights in the Cafe Tortoni, and slowly bent his steps to the dazzling facade; but just as he was going in he reflected that he would meet friends there and acquaintances — people he would be obliged to talk to; and fierce repugnance surged up in him for this commonplace good-fellowship over coffee cups and liqueur glasses. So, retracing his steps, he went back to the high-street leading to the harbour.

"Where shall I go?" he asked himself, trying to think of a spot he liked which would agree with his frame of mind. He could not think of one, for being alone made him feel fractious, yet he could not bear to meet any one. As he came out on the Grand Quay he hesitated once more; then he turned towards the pier; he had chosen solitude.

Going close by a bench on the breakwater he sat down, tired already of walking and out of humour with his stroll before he had taken it.

He said to himself: "What is the matter with me this evening?" And he began to search in his memory for what vexation had crossed him, as we question a sick man to discover the cause of his fever.

His mind was at once irritable and sober; he got excited, then he reasoned, approving or blaming his impulses; but in time primitive nature at last proved the stronger; the sensitive man always had the upper hand over the intellectual man. So he tried to discover what had induced this irascible mood, this craving to be moving without wanting anything, this desire to meet some one for the sake of differing from him, and at the same time this aversion for the people he might see and the things they might say to him.

And then he put the question to himself, "Can it be Jean's inheritance?"

Yes, it was certainly possible. When the lawyer had announced the news he had felt his heart beat a little faster. For, indeed, one is not always master of one's self; there are sudden and pertinacious emotions against which a man struggles in vain.

He fell into meditation on the physiological problem of the impression produced on the instinctive element in man, and giving rise to a current of painful or pleasurable sensations diametrically opposed to those which the thinking man desires, aims at, and regards as right and wholesome, when he has risen superior to himself by the cultivation of his intellect. He tried to picture to himself the frame of mind of a son who had inherited a vast fortune, and who, thanks to that wealth, may now know many long-wished-for delights, which the avarice of his father had prohibited — a father, nevertheless, beloved and regretted.

He got up and walked on to the end of the pier. He felt better, and glad to have understood, to have detected himself, to have unmasked the other which lurks in us.

"Then I was jealous of Jean," thought he. "That is really vilely mean. And I am sure of it now, for the first idea which came into my head was that he would marry *Mme.* Rosemilly. And yet I am not in love myself with that priggish little goose, who is just the woman to disgust a man with good sense and good conduct. So it is the most gratuitous jealousy, the very essence of jealousy, which is merely because it is! I must keep an eye on that!"

By this time he was in front of the flagstaff, whence the depth of water in the harbour is signalled, and he struck a match to read the list of vessels signalled in the roadstead and coming in with the next high tide. Ships were due from Brazil, from La Plata, from Chili and Japan, two Danish brigs, a Norwegian schooner, and a Turkish steamship — which startled Pierre as much as if it had read a Swiss steamship; and in a whimsical vision he pictured a great vessel crowded with men in turbans climbing the shrouds in loose trousers.

"How absurd!" thought he. "But the Turks are a maritime people, too."

A few steps further on he stopped again, looking out at the roads. On the right, above Sainte-Adresse, the two electric lights of Cape la Heve, like monstrous twin Cyclops, shot their long and powerful beams across the sea. Starting from two neighbouring centres, the two parallel shafts of light, like the colossal tails of two comets, fell in a straight and endless slope from the top of the cliff to the uttermost horizon. Then, on the two piers, two more lights, the children of these giants, marked the entrance to the harbour; and far away on the other side of the Seine others were in sight, many others, steady or winking, flashing or revolving, opening and shutting like eyes — the eyes of the ports — yellow, red, and green, watching the night-wrapped sea covered with ships; the living eyes of the hospitable shore saying, merely by the mechanical and regular movement of their eyelids: "I am here. I am Trouville; I am Honfleur; I am the Andemer River." And high above all the rest, so high that from this distance it might be taken for a planet, the airy lighthouse of Etouville showed the way to Rouen across the sand banks at the mouth of the great river.

Out on the deep water, the limitless water, darker than the sky, stars seemed to have fallen here and there. They twinkled in the night haze, small, close to shore or far away — white, red, and green, too. Most of them were motionless; some, however, seemed to be scudding onward. These were the lights of the ships at anchor or moving about in search of moorings.

Just at this moment the moon rose behind the town; and it, too, looked like some huge, divine pharos lighted up in the heavens to guide the countless fleet of stars in the sky. Pierre murmured, almost speaking aloud: "Look at that! And we let our bile rise for twopence!"

On a sudden, close to him, in the wide, dark ditch between the two piers, a shadow stole up, a large shadow of fantastic shape. Leaning over the granite parapet, he saw that a fishing-boat had glided in, without the sound of a voice or the splash of a ripple, or the plunge of an oar, softly borne in by its broad, tawny sail spread to the breeze from the open sea.

He thought to himself: "If one could but live on board that boat, what peace it would be — perhaps!"

And then again a few steps beyond, he saw a man sitting at the very end of the breakwater.

A dreamer, a lover, a sage — a happy or a desperate man? Who was it? He went forward, curious to see the face of this lonely individual, and he recognised his brother.

"What, is it you, Jean?"

"Pierre! You! What has brought you here?"

"I came out to get some fresh air. And you?"

Jean began to laugh.

"I too came out for fresh air." And Pierre sat down by his brother's side.

"Lovely — isn't it?"

"Oh, yes, lovely."

He understood from the tone of voice that Jean had not looked at anything. He went on:

"For my part, whenever I come here I am seized with a wild desire to be off with all those boats, to the north or the south. Only to think that all those little sparks out there have just come from the uttermost ends of the earth, from the lands of great flowers and beautiful olive or copper coloured girls, the lands of humming-birds, of elephants, of roaming lions, of negro kings, from all the lands which are like fairy-tales to us who no longer believe in the White Cat or the Sleeping Beauty. It would be awfully jolly to be able to treat one's self to an excursion out there; but, then, it would cost a great deal of money, no end — "

He broke off abruptly, remembering that his brother had that money now; and released from care, released from labouring for his daily bread, free, unfettered, happy, and lighthearted, he might go whither he listed, to find the fairhaired Swedes or the brown damsels of Havana. And then one of those involuntary flashes which were common with him, so sudden and swift that he could neither anticipate them, nor stop them, nor qualify them, communicated, as it seemed to him, from some second, independent, and violent soul, shot through his brain.

"Bah! He is too great a simpleton; he will marry that little Rosemilly." He was standing up now. "I will leave you to dream of the future. I want to be moving." He grasped his brother's hand and added in a heavy tone:

"Well, my dear old boy, you are a rich man. I am very glad to have come upon you this evening to tell you how pleased I am about it, how truly I congratulate you, and how much I care for you."

Jean, tender and soft-hearted, was deeply touched.

"Thank you, my good brother — thank you!" he stammered.

And Pierre turned away with his slow step, his stick under his arm, and his hands behind his back.

Back in the town again, he once more wondered what he should do, being disappointed of his walk and deprived of the company of the sea by his brother's presence. He had an inspiration. "I will go and take a glass of liqueur with old Marowsko," and he went off towards the quarter of the town known as Ingouville.

He had known old Marowsko-le pere Marowsko, he called him — in the hospitals in Paris. He was a Pole, an old refugee, it was said, who had gone through terrible things out there, and who had come to ply his calling as a chemist and druggist in France after passing a fresh examination. Nothing was known of his early life, and all sorts of legends had been current among the indoor and outdoor patients and afterward among his neighbours. This reputation as a terrible conspirator, a nihilist, a regicide, a patriot ready for anything and everything, who had escaped death by a miracle, had bewitched Pierre Roland's lively and bold imagination; he had made friends with the old Pole, without, however, having ever extracted from him any revelation as to his former career. It was owing to the young doctor that this worthy had come to settle at Havre, counting on the large custom which the rising practitioner would secure him. Meanwhile he lived very poorly in his little shop, selling medicines to the small tradesmen and workmen in his part of the town.

Pierre often went to see him and chat with him for an hour after dinner, for he liked Marowsko's calm look and rare speech, and attributed great depth to his long spells of silence.

A simple gas-burner was alight over the counter crowded with phials. Those in the window were not lighted, from motives of economy. Behind the counter, sitting on a chair with his legs stretched out and crossed, an old man, quite bald, with a large beak of a nose which, as a prolongation of his hairless forehead, gave him a melancholy likeness to a parrot, was sleeping soundly, his chin resting on his breast. He woke at the sound of the shop-bell, and recognising the doctor, came forward to meet him, holding out both hands.

His black frock-coat, streaked with stains of acids and sirups, was much too wide for his lean little person, and looked like a shabby old cassock; and the man spoke with a strong Polish accent which gave the childlike character to his thin voice, the lisping note and intonations of a young thing learning to speak.

Pierre sat down, and Marowsko asked him: "What news, dear doctor?"

"None. Everything as usual, everywhere."

"You do not look very gay this evening."

"I am not often gay."

"Come, come, you must shake that off. Will you try a glass of liqueur?"

"Yes, I do not mind."

"Then I will give you something new to try. For these two months I have been trying to extract something from currants, of which only a sirup has been made hitherto — well, and I have done it. I have invented a very good liqueur — very good indeed; very good."

And quite delighted, he went to a cupboard, opened it, and picked out a bottle which he brought forth. He moved and did everything in jerky gestures, always incomplete; he never quite stretched out his arm, nor quite put out his legs; nor made any broad and definite movements. His ideas seemed to be like his actions; he suggested them, promised them, sketched them, hinted at them, but never fully uttered them.

And, indeed, his great end in life seemed to be the concoction of sirups and liqueurs. "A good sirup or a good liqueur is enough to make a fortune," he would often say.

He had compounded hundreds of these sweet mixtures without ever succeeding in floating one of them. Pierre declared that Marowsko always reminded him of Marat.

Two little glasses were fetched out of the back shop and placed on the mixing-board. Then the two men scrutinized the colour of the fluid by holding it up to the gas.

"A fine ruby," Pierre declared.

"Isn't it?" Marowsko's old parrot-face beamed with satisfaction.

The doctor tasted, smacked his lips, meditated, tasted again, meditated again, and spoke:

"Very good — capital; and quite new in flavour. It is a find, my dear fellow."

"Ah, really? Well, I am very glad."

Then Marowsko took counsel as to baptizing the new liqueur. He wanted to call it "Extract of currants," or else "Fine Groseille" or "Groselia," or again "Groseline." Pierre did not approve of either of these names.

Then the old man had an idea:

"What you said just now would be very good, very good: 'Fine Ruby.'" But the doctor disputed the merit of this name, though it had originated with him. He recommended simply "Groseillette," which Marowsko thought admirable.

Then they were silent, and sat for some minutes without a word under the solitary gas-lamp. At last Pierre began, almost in spite of himself:

"A queer thing has happened at home this evening. A friend of my father's, who is lately dead, has left his fortune to my brother."

The druggist did not at first seem to understand, but after thinking it over he hoped that the doctor had half the inheritance. When the matter was clearly explained to him he appeared surprised and vexed; and to express his dissatisfaction at finding that his young friend had been sacrificed, he said several times over:

"It will not look well."

Pierre, who was relapsing into nervous irritation, wanted to know what Marowsko meant by this phrase.

Why would it not look well? What was there to look badly in the fact that his brother had come into the money of a friend of the family?

But the cautious old man would not explain further.

"In such a case the money is left equally to the two brothers, and I tell you, it will not look well."

And the doctor, out of all patience, went away, returned to his father's house, and went to bed. For some time afterward he heard Jean moving softly about the adjoining room, and then, after drinking two glasses of water, he fell asleep.

III

The doctor awoke next morning firmly resolved to make his fortune. Several times already he had come to the same determination without following up the reality. At the outset of all his trials of some new career the hopes of rapidly acquired riches kept up his efforts and confidence, till the first obstacle, the first check, threw him into a fresh path. Snug in bed between the warm sheets, he lay meditating. How many medical men had become wealthy in quite a short time! All that was needed was a little knowledge of the world; for in the course of his studies he had learned to estimate the most famous physicians, and he judged them all to be asses. He was certainly as good as they, if not better. If by any means he could secure a practice among the wealth and fashion of Havre, he could easily make a hundred thousand francs a year. And he calculated with great exactitude what his certain profits must be. He would go out in the morning to visit his patients; at the very moderate average of ten a day, at twenty francs each, that would mount up to seventy-two thousand francs a year at least, or even seventy-five thousand; for ten patients was certainly below the mark. In the afternoon he would be at home to, say, another ten patients, at ten francs each — thirty-six thousand francs. Here, then, in round numbers was an income of twenty thousand francs. Old patients, or friends whom he would charge only ten francs for a visit, or see at home for five, would perhaps make a slight reduction on this sum total, but consultations with other physicians and various incidental fees would make up for that.

Nothing could be easier than to achieve this by skilful advertising remarks in the Figaro to the effect that the scientific faculty of Paris had their eye on him, and were interested in the cures effected by the modest young practitioner of Havre! And he would be richer than his brother, richer and more famous; and satisfied with himself, for he would owe his fortune solely to his own exertions; and liberal to his old parents, who would be justly proud of his fame. He would not marry, would not burden his life with a wife who would be in his way, but he would choose his mistress from the most beautiful of his patients. He felt so sure of success that he sprang out of bed as though to grasp it on the spot, and he dressed to go and search through the town for rooms to suit him.

Then, as he wandered about the streets, he reflected how slight are the causes which determine our actions. Any time these three weeks he might and ought to have come to this decision, which, beyond a doubt, the news of his brother's inheritance had abruptly given rise to.

He stopped before every door where a placard proclaimed that "fine apartments" or "handsome rooms" were to be let; announcements without an adjective he turned from with scorn. Then he inspected them with a lofty air, measuring the height of the rooms, sketching the plan in his notebook, with the passages, the arrangement of the exits, explaining that he was a medical man and had many visitors. He must have a broad and well-kept staircase; nor could he be any higher up than the first floor.

After having written down seven or eight addresses and scribbled two hundred notes, he got home to breakfast a quarter of an hour too late.

In the hall he heard the clatter of plates. Then they had begun without him! Why? They were never wont to be so punctual. He was nettled and put out, for he was somewhat thin-skinned. As he went in Roland said to him:

"Come, Pierre, make haste, devil take you! You know we have to be at the lawyer's at two o'clock. This is not the day to be dawdling."

Pierre sat down without replying, after kissing his mother and shaking hands with his father and brother; and he helped himself from the deep dish in the middle of the table to the cutlet which had been kept for him. It was cold and dry, probably the least tempting of them all. He thought that they might have left it on the hot plate till he came in, and not lose their heads so completely as to have forgotten their other son, their eldest.

The conversation, which his entrance had interrupted, was taken up again at the point where it had ceased.

"In your place," *Mme.* Roland was saying to Jean, "I will tell you what I should do at once. I should settle in handsome rooms so as to attract attention; I should ride on horseback and select one or two interesting cases to defend and make a mark in court. I would be a sort of amateur lawyer, and very select. Thank God you are out of all danger of want, and if you pursue a profession, it is, after all, only that you may not lose the benefit of your studies, and because a man ought never to sit idle."

Old Roland, who was peeling a pear, exclaimed:

"Christi! In your place I should buy a nice yacht, a cutter on the build of our pilot-boats. I would sail as far as Senegal in such a boat as that."

Pierre, in his turn, spoke his views. After all, said he, it was not his wealth which made the moral worth, the intellectual worth of a man. To a man of inferior mind it was only a means of degradation, while in the hands of a strong man it was a powerful lever. They, to be sure, were rare. If Jean were a really superior man, now that he could never want he might prove it. But then he must work a hundred times harder than he would have done in other circumstances. His business now must be not to argue for or against the widow and the orphan, and pocket his fees for every case he gained, but to become a really eminent legal authority, a luminary of the law. And he added in conclusion:

"If I were rich wouldn't I dissect no end of bodies!"

Father Roland shrugged his shoulders.

"That is all very fine," he said. "But the wisest way of life is to take it easy. We are not beasts of burden, but men. If you are born poor you must work; well, so much the worse; and you do work. But where you have dividends! You must be a flat if you grind yourself to death."

Pierre replied haughtily:

"Our notions differ. For my part, I respect nothing on earth but learning and intellect; everything else is beneath contempt."

Mme. Roland always tried to deaden the constant shocks between father and son; she turned the conversation, and began talking of a murder committed the week before at Bolbec Nointot. Their minds were immediately full of the circumstances under which the crime had been committed, and absorbed by the interesting horror, the attractive mystery of crime, which, however commonplace, shameful, and disgusting, exercises a strange and universal fascination over the curiosity of mankind. Now and again, however, old Roland looked at his watch. "Come," said he, "it is time to be going."

Pierre sneered.

"It is not yet one o'clock," he said. "It really was hardly worth while to condemn me to eat a cold cutlet."

"Are you coming to the lawyer's?" his mother asked.

"I? No. What for?" he replied dryly. "My presence is quite unnecessary."

Jean sat silent, as though he had no concern in the matter. When they were discussing the murder at Bolbec he, as a legal authority, had put forward some opinions and uttered some reflections on crime and criminals. Now he spoke no more; but the sparkle in his eye, the bright colour in his cheeks, the very gloss of his beard seemed to proclaim his happiness.

When the family had gone, Pierre, alone once more, resumed his investigations in the apartments to let. After two or three hours spent in going up and down stairs, he at last found, in the Boulevard Francois, a pretty set of rooms; a spacious entresol with two doors on two different streets, two drawingrooms, a glass corridor, where his patients while they waited, might walk among flowers, and a delightful diningroom with a bow-window looking out over the sea.

When it came to taking it, the terms — three thousand francs — pulled him up; the first quarter must be paid in advance, and he had nothing, not a penny to call his own.

The little fortune his father had saved brought him in about eight thousand francs a year, and Pierre had often blamed himself for having placed his parents in difficulties by his long delay in deciding on a profession, by forfeiting his attempts and beginning fresh courses of study. So he went away, promising to send his answer within two days, and it occurred to him to ask Jean to lend him the amount of this quarter's rent, or even of a half-year, fifteen hundred francs, as soon as Jean should have come into possession.

"It will be a loan for a few months at most," he thought. "I shall repay him, very likely before the end of the year. It is a simple matter, and he will be glad to do so much for me."

As it was not yet four o'clock, and he had nothing to do, absolutely nothing, he went to sit in the public gardens; and he remained a long time on a bench, without an idea in his brain, his eyes fixed on the ground, crushed by weariness amounting to distress.

And yet this was how he had been living all these days since his return home, without suffering so acutely from the vacuity of his existence and from inaction. How had he spent his time from rising in the morning till bedtime?

He had loafed on the pier at high tide, loafed in the streets, loafed in the cafes, loafed at Marowsko's, loafed everywhere. And on a sudden this life, which he had endured till now, had become odious, intolerable. If he had had any pocket-money, he would have taken a carriage for a long drive in the country, along by the farm-ditches shaded by beech and elm trees; but he had to think twice of the cost of a glass of beer or a postage-stamp, and such an indulgence was out of his ken. It suddenly struck him how hard it was for a man of past thirty to be reduced to ask his mother, with a blush for a twenty-franc piece every now and then; and he muttered, as he scored the gravel with the ferule of his stick:

"Christi, if I only had money!"

And again the thought of his brother's legacy came into his head like the sting of a wasp; but he drove it out indignantly, not choosing to allow himself to slip down that descent to jealousy.

Some children were playing about in the dusty paths. They were fair little things with long hair, and they were making little mounds of sand with the greatest gravity and careful attention, to crush them at once by stamping on them.

It was one of those gloomy days with Pierre when we pry into every corner of our souls and shake out every crease.

"All our endeavours are like the labours of those babies," thought he. And then he wondered whether the wisest thing in life were not to beget two or three of these little creatures and watch them grow up with complacent curiosity. A longing for marriage breathed on his soul. A man is not so lost when he is not alone. At any rate, he has some one stirring at his side in hours of trouble or of uncertainty; and it is something only to be able to speak on equal terms to a woman when one is suffering.

Then he began thinking of women. He knew very little of them, never having had any but very transient connections as a medical student, broken off as soon as the month's allowance was spent, and renewed or replaced by another the following month. And yet there must be some very kind, gentle, and comforting creatures among them. Had not his mother been the good sense and saving grace of his own home? How glad he would be to know a woman, a true woman!

He started up with a sudden determination to go and call on *Mme.* Rosemilly. But he promptly sat down again. He did not like that woman. Why not? She had too much vulgar and sordid common sense; besides, did she not seem to prefer Jean? Without confessing it to himself too bluntly, this preference had a great deal to do with his low opinion of the widow's intellect; for, though he loved his brother, he could not help thinking him somewhat mediocre and believing himself the superior. However, he was not going to sit there till nightfall; and as he had done on the previous evening, he anxiously asked himself: "What am I going to do?"

At this moment he felt in his soul the need of a melting mood, of being embraced and comforted. Comforted — for what? He could not have put it into words; but he was in one of these hours of weakness and exhaustion when a woman's presence, a woman's kiss, the touch of a hand, the rustle of a petticoat, a soft look out of black or blue eyes, seem the one thing needful, there and then, to our heart. And the memory flashed upon him of a little barmaid at a beer-house, whom he had walked home with one evening, and seen again from time to time.

So once more he rose, to go and drink a bock with the girl. What should he say to her? What would she say to him? Nothing, probably. But what did that matter? He would hold her hand for a few seconds. She seemed to have a fancy for him. Why, then, did he not go to see her oftener?

He found her dozing on a chair in the beer-shop, which was almost deserted. Three men were drinking and smoking with their elbows on the oak tables; the bookkeeper in her desk was reading a novel, while the master, in his shirtsleeves, lay sound asleep on a bench.

As soon as she saw him the girl rose eagerly, and coming to meet him, said:

"Good-day, monsieur — how are you?"

"Pretty well; and you?"

"I — oh, very well. How scarce you make yourself!"

"Yes. I have very little time to myself. I am a doctor, you know."

"Indeed! You never told me. If I had known that — I was out of sorts last week and I would have sent for you. What will you take?"

"A bock. And you?"

"I will have a bock, too, since you are willing to treat me."

She had addressed him with the familiar tu, and continued to use it, as if the offer of a drink had tacitly conveyed permission. Then, sitting down opposite each other, they talked for a while. Every now and then she took his hand with the light familiarity of girls whose kisses are for sale, and looking at him with inviting eyes she said:

"Why don't you come here oftener? I like you very much, sweetheart."

He was already disgusted with her; he saw how stupid she was, and common, smacking of low life. A woman, he told himself, should appear to us in dreams, or such a glory as may poetize her vulgarity.

Next she asked him:

"You went by the other morning with a handsome fair man, wearing a big beard. Is he your brother?"

"Yes, he is my brother."

"Awfully good-looking."

"Do you think so?"

"Yes, indeed; and he looks like a man who enjoys life, too."

What strange craving impelled him on a sudden to tell this tavern-wench about Jean's legacy? Why should this thing, which he kept at arm's length when he was alone, which he drove from him for fear of the torment it brought upon his soul, rise to his lips at this moment? And why did he allow it to overflow them as if he needed once more to empty out his heart to some one, gorged as it was with bitterness?

He crossed his legs and said:

"He has wonderful luck, that brother of mine. He had just come into a legacy of twenty thousand francs a year."

She opened those covetous blue eyes of hers very wide.

"Oh! and who left him that? His grandmother or his aunt?"

"No. An old friend of my parents'."

"Only a friend! Impossible! And you — did he leave you nothing?"

"No. I knew him very slightly."

She sat thinking some minutes; then, with an odd smile on her lips, she said:

"Well, he is a lucky dog, that brother of yours, to have friends of this pattern. My word! and no wonder he is so unlike you."

He longed to slap her, without knowing why; and he asked with pinched lips: "And what do you mean by saying that?"

She had put on a stolid, innocent face.

"O — h, nothing. I mean he has better luck than you."

He tossed a franc piece on the table and went out.

Now he kept repeating the phrase: "No wonder he is so unlike you."

What had her thought been, what had been her meaning under those words? There was certainly some malice, some spite, something shameful in it. Yes, that hussy must have fancied, no doubt, that Jean was Marechal's son. The agitation which came over him at the notion of this suspicion cast at his mother was so violent that he stood still, looking about him for some place where he might sit down. In front of him was another cafe. He went in, took a chair, and as the waiter came up, "A bock," he said.

He felt his heart beating, his skin was gooseflesh. And then the recollection flashed upon him of what Marowsko had said the evening before. "It will not look well." Had he had the same thought, the same suspicion as this baggage? Hanging his head over the glass, he watched the white froth as the bubbles rose and burst, asking himself: "Is it possible that such a thing should be believed?"

But the reasons which might give rise to this horrible doubt in other men's minds now struck him, one after another, as plain, obvious, and exasperating. That a childless old bachelor should leave his fortune to a friend's two sons was the most simple and natural thing in the world; but that he should leave the whole of it to one alone — of course people would wonder, and whisper, and end by smiling. How was it that he had not foreseen this, that his father had not felt it? How was it that his mother had not guessed it? No; they had been too delighted at this unhoped-for wealth for the idea to come near them. And besides, how should these worthy souls have ever dreamed of anything so ignominious?

But the public — their neighbours, the shopkeepers, their own tradesmen, all who knew them — would not they repeat the abominable thing, laugh at it, enjoy it, make game of his father and despise his mother?

And the barmaid's remark that Jean was fair and he dark, that they were not in the least alike in face, manner, figure, or intelligence, would now strike every eye and every mind. When any one spoke of Roland's son, the question would be: "Which, the real or the false?"

He rose, firmly resolved to warn Jean, and put him on his guard against the frightful danger which threatened their mother's honour.

But what could Jean do? The simplest thing no doubt, would be to refuse the inheritance, which would then go to the poor, and to tell all friends or acquaintances who had heard of the bequest that the will contained clauses and conditions impossible to subscribe to, which would have made Jean not inheritor but merely a trustee.

As he made his way home he was thinking that he must see his brother alone, so as not to speak of such a matter in the presence of his parents. On reaching the door he heard a great noise of voices and laughter in the drawingroom, and when he went in he found Captain Beausire and *Mme.* Rosemilly, whom his father had brought home and engaged to dine with them in honour of the good news. Vermouth and absinthe had been served to whet their appetites, and every one had been at once put into good spirits. Captain Beausire, a funny little man who had become quite round by dint of being rolled about at sea, and whose ideas also seemed to have been worn round, like the pebbles of a beach, while he laughed with his throat full of r's, looked upon life as a capital thing, in which everything that might turn up was good to take. He clinked his glass against father Roland's, while Jean was offering two freshly filled glasses to the ladies. *Mme.* Rosemilly refused, till Captain Beausire, who had known her husband, cried:

"Come, come, madame, bis repetita placent, as we say in the lingo, which is as much as to say two glasses of vermouth never hurt any one. Look at me; since I have left the sea, in this way I give myself an artificial roll or two every day before dinner; I add a little pitching after my coffee, and that keeps things lively for the rest of the evening. I never rise to a hurricane, mind you, never, never. I am too much afraid of damage."

Roland, whose nautical mania was humoured by the old mariner, laughed heartily, his face flushed already and his eye watery from the absinthe. He had a burly shopkeeping stomach — nothing but stomach — in which the rest of his body seemed to have got stowed away; the flabby paunch of men who spend their lives sitting, and who have neither thighs, nor chest, nor arms, nor neck; the seat of their chairs having accumulated all their substance in one spot. Beausire, on the contrary, though short and stout, was as tight as an egg and as hard as a cannonball.

Mme. Roland had not emptied her glass and was gazing at her son Jean with sparkling eyes; happiness had brought a colour to her cheeks.

In him, too, the fulness of joy had now blazed out. It was a settled thing, signed and sealed; he had twenty thousand francs a year. In the sound of his laugh, in the fuller voice with which he spoke, in his way of looking at the others, his more positive manners, his greater confidence, the assurance given by money was at once perceptible.

Dinner was announced, and as the old man was about to offer his arm to *Mme.* Rosemilly, his wife exclaimed:

"No, no, father. Everything is for Jean to-day."

Unwonted luxury graced the table. In front of Jean, who sat in his father's place, an enormous bouquet of flowers — a bouquet for a really great occasion — stood up like a cupola dressed with flags, and was flanked by four high dishes, one containing a pyramid of splendid peaches; the second, a monumental cake gorged with whipped cream and covered with pinnacles of sugar — a cathedral in confectionery; the third, slices of pine-apple floating in clear sirup; and the fourth — unheard-of lavishness — black grapes brought from the warmer south.

"The devil!" exclaimed Pierre as he sat down. "We are celebrating the accession of Jean the rich."

After the soup, Madeira was passed round, and already every one was talking at once. Beausire was giving the history of a dinner he had eaten at San Domingo at the table of a negro general. Old Roland was listening, and at the same time trying to get in, between the sentences, his account of another dinner, given by a friend of his at Mendon, after which every guest was ill for a fortnight. *Mme.* Rosemilly, Jean, and his mother were planning an excursion to breakfast at Saint Jouin, from which they promised themselves the greatest pleasure; and Pierre was only sorry that he had not dined alone in some pothouse by the sea, so as to escape all this noise and laughter and glee which fretted him. He was wondering how he could now set to work to confide his fears to his brother, and induce him to renounce the fortune he had already accepted and of which he was enjoying the intoxicating foretaste. It would be hard on him, no doubt; but it must be done; he could not hesitate; their mother's reputation was at stake.

The appearance of an enormous shade-fish threw Roland back on fishing stories. Beausire told some wonderful tales of adventure on the Gaboon, at Sainte-Marie, in Madagascar, and above all, off the coasts of China and Japan, where the fish are as queer-looking as the natives. And he described the appearance of these fishes — their goggle gold eyes, their blue or red bellies, their fantastic fins like fans, their eccentric crescent-shaped tails — with such droll gesticulation that they all laughed till they cried as they listened.

Pierre alone seemed incredulous, muttering to himself: "True enough, the Normans are the Gascons of the north!"

After the fish came a vol-au-vent, then a roast fowl, a salad, French beans with a Pithiviers lark-pie. *Mme.* Rosemilly's maid helped to wait on them, and the fun rose with the number of glasses of wine they drank. When the cork of the first champagne-bottle was drawn with a pop, father Roland, highly excited, imitated the noise with his tongue and then declared: "I like that noise better than a pistol-shot."

Pierre, more and more fractious every moment, retorted with a sneer:

"And yet it is perhaps a greater danger for you."

Roland, who was on the point of drinking, set his full glass down on the table again, and asked:

"Why?"

He had for some time been complaining of his health, of heaviness, giddiness, frequent and unaccountable discomfort. The doctor replied:

"Because the bullet might very possibly miss you, while the glass of wine is dead certain to hit you in the stomach."

"And what then?"

"Then it scorches your inside, upsets your nervous system, makes the circulation sluggish, and leads the way to the apoplectic fit which always threatens a man of your build."

The jeweller's incipient intoxication had vanished like smoke before the wind. He looked at his son with fixed, uneasy eyes, trying to discover whether he was making game of him.

But Beausire exclaimed:

"Oh, these confounded doctors! They all sing the same tune — eat nothing, drink nothing, never make love or enjoy yourself; it all plays the devil with your precious health. Well, all I can say is, I have done all these things, sir, in every quarter of the globe, wherever and as often as I have had the chance, and I am none the worse."

Pierre answered with some asperity:

"In the first place, captain, you are a stronger man than my father; and in the next, all free livers talk as you do till the day when — when they come back no more to say to the cautious doctor: 'You were right.' When I see my father doing what is worst and most dangerous for him, it is but natural that I should warn him. I should be a bad son if I did otherwise."

Mme. Roland, much distressed, now put in her word: "Come, Pierre, what ails you? For once it cannot hurt him. Think of what an occasion it is for him, for all of us. You will spoil his pleasure and make us all unhappy. It is too bad of you to do such a thing."

He muttered, as he shrugged his shoulders.

"He can do as he pleases. I have warned him."

But father Roland did not drink. He sat looking at his glass full of the clear and luminous liquor while its light soul, its intoxicating soul, flew off in tiny bubbles mounting from its depths in hurried succession to die on the surface. He looked at it with the suspicious eye of a fox smelling at a dead hen and suspecting a trap. He asked doubtfully: "Do you think it will really do me much harm?" Pierre had a pang of remorse and blamed himself for letting his ill-humour punish the rest.

"No," said he. "Just for once you may drink it; but do not take too much, or get into the habit of it."

Then old Roland raised his glass, but still he could not make up his mind to put it to his lips. He contemplated it regretfully, with longing and with fear; then he smelt it, tasted it, drank it in sips, swallowing them slowly, his heart full of terrors, of weakness and greediness; and then, when he had drained the last drop, of regret.

Pierre's eye suddenly met that of *Mme.* Rosemilly; it rested on him clear and blue, farseeing and hard. And he read, he knew, the precise thought which lurked in that look, the indignant thought of this simple and right-minded little woman; for the look said: "You are jealous — that is what you are. Shameful!"

He bent his head and went on with his dinner.

He was not hungry and found nothing nice. A longing to be off harassed him, a craving to be away from these people, to hear no more of their talking, jests, and laughter.

Father Roland meanwhile, to whose head the fumes of the wine were rising once more, had already forgotten his son's advice and was eyeing a champagne-bottle with a tender leer as it stood, still nearly full, by the side of his plate. He dared not touch it for fear of being lectured again, and he was wondering by what device or trick he could possess himself of it without exciting Pierre's remark. A ruse occurred to him, the simplest possible. He took up the bottle with an air of indifference, and holding it by the neck, stretched his arm across the table to fill the doctor's glass, which was empty; then he filled up all the other glasses, and when he came to his own he began talking very loud, so that if he poured anything into it they might have sworn it was done inadvertently. And in fact no one took any notice.

Pierre, without observing it, was drinking a good deal. Nervous and fretted, he every minute raised to his lips the tall crystal funnel where the bubbles were dancing in the living, translucent fluid. He let the wine slip very slowly over his tongue, that he might feel the little sugary sting of the fixed air as it evaporated.

Gradually a pleasant warmth glowed in his frame. Starting from the stomach as a centre, it spread to his chest, took possession of his limbs, and diffused itself throughout his flesh, like a warm and comforting tide, bringing pleasure with it. He felt better now, less impatient, less annoyed, and his determination to speak to his brother that very evening faded away; not that he thought for a moment of giving it up, but simply not to disturb the happy mood in which he found himself.

Beausire presently rose to propose a toast. Having bowed to the company, he began:

"Most gracious ladies and gentlemen, we have met to do honour to a happy event which has befallen one of our friends. It used to be said that Fortune was blind, but I believe that she is only shortsighted or tricksy, and that she has lately bought a good pair of glasses which enabled her to discover in the town of Havre the son of our worthy friend Roland, skipper of the Pearl."

Every one cried bravo and clapped their hands, and the elder Roland rose to reply. After clearing his throat, for it felt thick and his tongue was heavy, he stammered out:

"Thank you, captain, thank you — for myself and my son. I shall never forget your behaviour on this occasion. Here's good luck to you!"

His eyes and nose were full of tears, and he sat down, finding nothing more to say.

Jean, who was laughing, spoke in his turn:

"It is I," said he, "who ought to thank my friends here, my excellent friends," and he glanced at *Mme.* Rosemilly, "who have given me such a touching evidence of their affection. But it is not by words that I can prove my gratitude. I will prove it tomorrow, every hour of my life, always, for our friendship is not one of those which fade away."

His mother, deeply moved, murmured: "Well said, my boy."

But Beausire cried out:

"Come, *Mme.* Rosemilly, speak on behalf of the fair sex."

She raised her glass, and in a pretty voice, slightly touched with sadness, she said: "I will pledge you to the memory of M. Marechal."

There was a few moments' lull, a pause for decent meditation, as after prayer. Beausire, who always had a flow of compliment, remarked:

"Only a woman ever thinks of these refinements." Then turning to Father Roland: "And who was this Marechal, after all? You must have been very intimate with him."

The old man, emotional with drink, began to whimper, and in a broken voice he said:

"Like a brother, you know. Such a friend as one does not make twice — we were always together — he dined with us every evening — and would treat us to the play — I need say no more — no more — no more. A true friend — a real true friend — wasn't he, Louise?"

His wife merely answered: "Yes; he was a faithful friend."

Pierre looked at his father and then at his mother, then, as the subject changed he drank some more wine. He scarcely remembered the remainder of the evening. They had coffee, then liqueurs, and they laughed and joked a great deal. At about midnight he went to bed, his mind confused and his head heavy; and he slept like a brute till nine next morning.

IV

These slumbers, lapped in Champagne and Chartreuse, had soothed and calmed him, no doubt, for he awoke in a very benevolent frame of mind. While he was dressing he appraised, weighed, and summed up the agitations of the past day, trying to bring out quite clearly and fully their real and occult causes, those personal to himself as well as those from outside.

It was, in fact, possible that the girl at the beer-shop had had an evil suspicion — a suspicion worthy of such a hussy — on hearing that only one of the Roland brothers had been made heir to a stranger; but have not such natures as she always similar notions, without a shadow of foundation, about every honest woman? Do they not, whenever they speak, vilify, calumniate, and abuse all whom they believe to be blameless? Whenever a woman who is above imputation is mentioned in their presence, they are as angry as if they were being insulted, and exclaim: "Ah, yes, I know your married women; a pretty sort they are! Why, they have more lovers than we have, only they conceal it because they are such hypocrites. Oh, yes, a pretty sort, indeed!"

Under any other circumstances he would certainly not have understood, not have imagined the possibility of such an insinuation against his poor mother, who was so kind, so simple, so excellent. But his spirit seethed with the leaven of jealousy that was fermenting within him. His own excited mind, on the scent, as it were, in spite of himself, for all that could damage his brother, had even perhaps attributed to the tavern barmaid an odious intention of which she was innocent. It was possible that his imagination had, unaided, invented this dreadful doubt — his imagination, which he never controlled, which constantly evaded his will and went off, unfettered, audacious, adventurous, and stealthy, into the infinite world of ideas, bringing back now and then some which were shameless and repulsive, and which it buried in him, in the depths of his soul, in its most fathomless recesses, like something stolen. His heart, most certainly, his own heart had secrets from him; and had not that wounded heart discerned in this atrocious doubt a means of depriving his brother of the inheritance of which he was jealous?

He suspected himself now, cross-examining all the mysteries of his mind as bigots search their consciences.

Mme. Rosemilly, though her intelligence was limited, had certainly a woman's instinct, scent, and subtle intuitions. And this notion had never entered her head, since she had, with perfect simplicity, drunk to the blessed memory of the deceased Marechal. She was not the woman to have done this if she had had the faintest suspicion. Now he doubted no longer; his involuntary displeasure at his brother's windfall of fortune and his religious affection for his mother had magnified his scruples — very pious and respectable scruples, but exaggerated. As he put this conclusion into words in his own mind he felt happy, as at the doing of a good action; and he resolved to be nice to every one, beginning with his father, whose manias, and silly statements, and vulgar opinions, and too conspicuous mediocrity were a constant irritation to him.

He came in not late for breakfast, and amused all the family by his fun and good humour.

His mother, quite delighted, said to him:

"My little Pierre, you have no notion how humorous and clever you can be when you choose."

And he talked, putting things in a witty way, and making them laugh by ingenious hits at their friends. Beausire was his butt, and *Mme.* Rosemilly a little, but in a very judicious way, not too spiteful. And he thought as he looked at his brother: "Stand up for her, you muff. You may be as rich as you please, I can always eclipse you when I take the trouble."

As they drank their coffee he said to his father:

"Are you going out in the Pearl to-day?"

"No, my boy."

"May I have her with Jean Bart?"

"To be sure, as long as you like."

He bought a good cigar at the first tobacconist's and went down to the quay with a light step. He glanced up at the sky, which was clear and luminous, of a pale blue, freshly swept by the sea-breeze.

Papagris, the boatman, commonly called Jean Bart, was dozing in the bottom of the boat, which he was required to have in readiness every day at noon when they had not been out fishing in the morning.

"You and I together, mate," cried Pierre. He went down the iron ladder of the quay and leaped into the vessel.

"Which way is the wind?" he asked.

"Due east still, M'sieu Pierre. A fine breeze out at sea."

"Well, then, old man, off we go!"

They hoisted the foresail and weighed anchor; and the boat, feeling herself free, glided slowly down towards the jetty on the still water of the harbour. The breath of wind that came down the streets caught the top of the sail so lightly as to be imperceptible, and the Pearl seemed endowed with life — the life of a vessel driven on by a mysterious latent power. Pierre took the tiller, and, holding his cigar between his teeth, he stretched his legs on the bunk, and with his eyes half-shut in the blinding sunshine, he watched the great tarred timbers of the breakwater as they glided past.

When they reached the open sea, round the nose of the north pier which had sheltered them, the fresher breeze puffed in the doctor's face and on his hands, like a somewhat icy caress, filled his chest, which rose with a long sigh to drink it in, and swelling the tawny sail, tilted the Pearl on her beam and made her more lively. Jean Bart hastily hauled up the jib, and the triangle of canvas, full of wind, looked like a wing; then, with two strides to the stern, he let out the spinnaker, which was close-reefed against his mast.

Then, along the hull of the boat, which suddenly heeled over and was running at top speed, there was a soft, crisp sound of water hissing and rushing past. The prow ripped up the sea like the share of a plough gone mad, and the yielding water it turned up curled over and fell white with foam, as the ploughed soil, heavy and brown, rolls and falls in a ridge. At each wave they met — and there was a short, chopping sea — the Pearl shivered from the point of the bowsprit to the rudder, which trembled under Pierre's hand; when the wind blew harder in gusts, the swell rose to the gunwale as if it would overflow into the boat. A coal brig from Liverpool was lying at anchor, waiting for the tide; they made a sweep round her stern and went to look at each of the vessels in the roads one after another; then they put further out to look at the unfolding line of coast.

For three hours Pierre, easy, calm, and happy, wandered to and fro over the dancing waters, guiding the thing of wood and canvas, which came and went at his will, under the pressure of his hand, as if it were a swift and docile winged creature.

He was lost in daydreams, the dreams one has on horseback or on the deck of a boat; thinking of his future, which should be brilliant, and the joys of living intelligently. On the morrow he would ask his brother to lend him fifteen hundred francs for three months, that he might settle at once in the pretty rooms on the Boulevard Francois.

Suddenly the sailor said: "The fog is coming up, M'sieu Pierre. We must go in."

He looked up and saw to the northward a gray shade, filmy but dense, blotting out the sky and covering the sea; it was sweeping down on them like a cloud fallen from above. He tacked for land and made for the pier, scudding before the wind and followed by the flying fog, which gained upon them. When it reached the Pearl, wrapping her in its intangible density, a cold shudder ran over Pierre's limbs, and a smell of smoke and mould, the peculiar smell of a sea-fog, made him close his mouth that he might not taste the cold, wet vapour. By the time the boat was at her usual moorings in the harbour the whole town was buried in this fine mist, which did not fall but yet wetted everything like rain, and glided and rolled along the roofs and streets like the flow of a river. Pierre, with his hands and feet frozen, made haste home and threw himself on his bed to take a nap till dinnertime. When he made his appearance in the diningroom his mother was saying to Jean:

"The glass corridor will be lovely. We will fill it with flowers. You will see. I will undertake to care for them and renew them. When you give a party the effect will be quite fairylike."

"What in the world are you talking about?" the doctor asked.

"Of a delightful apartment I have just taken for your brother. It is quite a find; an entresol looking out on two streets. There are two drawingrooms, a glass passage, and a little circular diningroom, perfectly charming for a bachelor's quarters."

Pierre turned pale. His anger seemed to press on his heart.

"Where is it?" he asked.

"Boulevard Francois."

There was no possibility for doubt. He took his seat in such a state of exasperation that he longed to exclaim: "This is really too much! Is there nothing for any one but him?"

His mother, beaming, went on talking: "And only fancy, I got it for two thousand eight hundred francs a year. They asked three thousand, but I got a reduction of two hundred francs on taking for three, six, or nine years. Your brother will be delightfully housed there. An elegant home is enough to make the fortune of a lawyer. It attracts clients, charms them, holds them fast, commands respect, and shows them that a man who lives in such good style expects a good price for his words."

She was silent for a few seconds and then went on:

"We must look out for something suitable for you; much less pretentious, since you have nothing, but nice and pretty all the same. I assure you it will be to your advantage."

Pierre replied contemptuously:

"For me! Oh, I shall make my way by hard work and learning."

But his mother insisted: "Yes, but I assure you that to be well lodged will be of use to you nevertheless."

About halfway through the meal he suddenly asked:

"How did you first come to know this man Marechal?"

Old Roland looked up and racked his memory:

"Wait a bit; I scarcely recollect. It is such an old story now. Ah, yes, I remember. It was your mother who made the acquaintance with him in the shop, was it not, Louise? He first came to order something, and then he called frequently. We knew him as a customer before we knew him as a friend."

Pierre, who was eating beans, sticking his fork into them one by one as if he were spitting them, went on:

"And when was it that you made his acquaintance?"

Again Roland sat thinking, but he could remember no more and appealed to his wife's better memory.

"In what year was it, Louise? You surely have not forgotten, you who remember everything. Let me see — it was in — in — in fifty-five or fifty-six? Try to remember. You ought to know better than I."

She did in fact think it over for some minutes, and then replied in a steady voice and with calm decision:

"It was in fifty-eight, old man. Pierre was three years old. I am quite sure that I am not mistaken, for it was in that year that the child had scarlet fever, and Marechal, whom we knew then but very little, was of the greatest service to us."

Roland exclaimed:

"To be sure — very true; he was really invaluable. When your mother was half-dead with fatigue and I had to attend to the shop, he would go to the chemist's to fetch your medicine. He really had the kindest heart! And when you were well again, you cannot think how glad he was and how he petted you. It was from that time that we became such great friends."

And this thought rushed into Pierre's soul, as abrupt and violent as a cannonball rending and piercing it: "Since he knew me first, since he was so devoted to me, since he was so fond of me and petted me so much, since I — I was the cause of his great intimacy with my parents, why did he leave all his money to my brother and nothing to me?"

He asked no more questions and remained gloomy; absentminded rather than thoughtful, feeling in his soul a new anxiety as yet undefined, the secret germ of a new pain.

He went out early, wandering about the streets once more. They were shrouded in the fog which made the night heavy, opaque, and nauseous. It was like a pestilential cloud dropped on the earth. It could be seen swirling past the gaslights, which it seemed to put out at intervals. The pavement was as slippery as on a frosty night after rain, and all sorts of evil smells seemed to come up from the bowels of the houses — the stench of cellars, drains, sewers, squalid kitchens — to mingle with the horrible savour of this wandering fog.

Pierre, with his shoulders up and his hands in his pockets, not caring to remain out of doors in the cold, turned into Marowsko's. The druggist was asleep as usual under the gaslight, which kept watch. On recognising Pierre for whom he had the affection of a faithful dog, he shook off his drowsiness, went for two glasses, and brought out the Groseillette.

"Well," said the doctor, "how is the liqueur getting on?"

The Pole explained that four of the chief cafes in the town had agreed to have it on sale, and that two papers, the Northcoast Pharos and the Havre Semaphore, would advertise it, in return for certain chemical preparations to be supplied to the editors.

After a long silence Marowsko asked whether Jean had come definitely into possession of his fortune; and then he put two or three other questions vaguely referring to the same subject. His jealous devotion to Pierre rebelled against this preference. And Pierre felt as though he could hear him thinking; he guessed and understood, read in his averted eyes and in the hesitancy of his tone, the words which rose to his lips but were not spoken — which the druggist was too timid or too prudent and cautious to utter.

At this moment, he felt sure, the old man was thinking: "You ought not to have suffered him to accept this inheritance which will make people speak ill of your mother."

Perhaps, indeed, Marowsko believed that Jean was Marechal's son. Of course he believed it! How could he help believing it when the thing must seem so possible, so probable, self-evident?

Why, he himself, Pierre, her son — had not he been for these three days past fighting with all the subtlety at his command to cheat his reason, fighting against this hideous suspicion?

And suddenly the need to be alone, to reflect, to discuss the matter with himself — to face boldly, without scruple or weakness, this possible but monstrous thing — came upon him anew, and so imperative that he rose without even drinking his glass of Groseillette, shook hands with the astounded druggist, and plunged out into the foggy streets again.

He asked himself: "What made this Marechal leave all his fortune to Jean?"

It was not jealousy now which made him dwell on this question, not the rather mean but natural envy which he knew lurked within him, and with which he had been struggling these three days, but the dread of an overpowering horror; the dread that he himself should believe that Jean, his brother, was that man's son.

No. He did not believe it, he could not even ask himself the question which was a crime! Meanwhile he must get rid of this faint suspicion, improbable as it was, utterly and forever. He craved for light, for certainty — he must win absolute security in his heart, for he loved no one in the world but his mother. And as he wandered alone through the darkness he would rack his memory and his reason with a minute search that should bring out the blazing truth. Then there would be an end to the matter; he would not think of it again — never. He would go and sleep.

He argued thus: "Let me see: first to examine the facts; then I will recall all I know about him, his behaviour to my brother and to me. I will seek out the causes which might have given rise to the preference. He knew Jean from his birth? Yes, but he had known me first. If he had loved my mother silently, unselfishly, he would surely have chosen me, since it was through me, through my scarlet fever, that he became so intimate with my parents. Logically, then, he ought to have preferred me, to have had a keener affection for me — unless it were that he felt an instinctive attraction and predilection for my brother as he watched him grow up."

Then, with desperate tension of brain and of all the powers of his intellect, he strove to reconstitute from memory the image of this Marechal, to see him, to know him, to penetrate the man whom he had seen pass by him, indifferent to his heart during all those years in Paris.

But he perceived that the slight exertion of walking somewhat disturbed his ideas, dislocated their continuity, weakened their precision, clouded his recollection. To enable him to look at the past and at unknown events with so keen an eye that nothing should escape it, he must be motionless in a vast and empty space. And he made up his mind to go and sit on the jetty as he had done that other night. As he approached the harbour he heard, out at sea, a lugubrious and sinister wail like the bellowing of a bull, but more long-drawn and steady. It was the roar of a fog-horn, the cry of a ship lost in the fog. A shiver ran through him, chilling his heart; so deeply did this cry of distress thrill his soul and nerves that he felt as if he had uttered it himself. Another and a similar voice answered with such another moan, but farther away; then, close by, the fog-horn on the pier gave out a fearful sound in answer. Pierre made for the jetty with long steps, thinking no more of anything, content to walk on into this ominous and bellowing darkness.

When he had seated himself at the end of the breakwater he closed his eyes, that he might not see the two electric lights, now blurred by the fog, which make the harbour accessible at night, and the red glare of the light on the south pier, which was, however, scarcely visible. Turning half-round, he rested his elbows on the granite and hid his face in his hands.

Though he did not pronounce the words with his lips, his mind kept repeating: "Marechal — Marechal," as if to raise and challenge the shade. And on the black background of his closed eyelids, he suddenly saw him as he had known him: a man of about sixty, with a white beard cut in a point and very thick eyebrows, also white. He was neither tall nor short, his manner was pleasant, his eyes gray and soft, his movements gentle, his whole appearance that of a good fellow, simple and kindly. He called Pierre and Jean "my dear children," and had never seemed to prefer either, asking them both together to dine with him. And then Pierre, with the pertinacity of a dog seeking a lost scent, tried to recall the words, gestures, tones, looks, of this man who had vanished from the world. By degrees he saw him quite clearly in his rooms in the Rue Tronchet, where he received his brother and himself at dinner.

He was waited on by two maids, both old women who had been in the habit — a very old one, no doubt — of saying "Monsieur Pierre" and "Monsieur Jean." Marechal would hold out both hands, the right hand to one of the young men, the left to the other, as they happened to come in.

"How are you, my children?" he would say. "Have you any news of your parents? As for me, they never write to me."

The talk was quiet and intimate, of commonplace matters. There was nothing remarkable in the man's mind, but much that was winning, charming, and gracious. He had certainly been a good friend to them, one of those good friends of whom we think the less because we feel sure of them.

Now, reminiscences came readily to Pierre's mind. Having seen him anxious from time to time, and suspecting his student's impecuniousness, Marechal had of his own accord offered and lent him money, a few hundred francs perhaps, forgotten by both, and never repaid. Then this man must always have been fond of him, always have taken an interest in him, since he thought of his needs. Well then — well then — why leave his whole fortune to Jean? No, he had never shown more marked affection for the younger than for the elder, had never been more interested in one than in the other, or seemed to care more tenderly for this one or that one. Well then — well then — he must have had some strong secret reason for leaving everything to Jean — everything — and nothing to Pierre.

The more he thought, the more he recalled the past few years, the more extraordinary, the more incredible was it that he should have made such a difference between them. And an agonizing pang of unspeakable anguish piercing his bosom made his heart beat like a fluttering rag. Its springs seemed broken, and the blood rushed through in a flood, unchecked, tossing it with wild surges.

Then in an undertone, as a man speaks in a nightmare, he muttered: "I must know. My God! I must know."

He looked further back now, to an earlier time, when his parents had lived in Paris. But the faces escaped him, and this confused his recollections. He struggled above all to see Marechal, with light, or brown, or black hair. But he could not; the later image, his face as an old man, blotted out all others. However, he remembered that he had been slighter, and had a soft hand, and that he often brought flowers. Very often — for his father would constantly say: "What, another bouquet! But this is madness, my dear fellow; you will ruin yourself in roses." And Marechal would say: "No matter; I like it."

And suddenly his mother's voice and accent, his mother's as she smiled and said: "Thank you, my kind friend," flashed on his brain, so clearly that he could have believed he heard her. She must have spoken those words very often that they should remain thus graven on her son's memory.

So Marechal brought flowers; he, the gentleman, the rich man, the customer, to the humble shopkeeper, the jeweller's wife. Had he loved her? Why should he have made friends with these tradespeople if he had not been in love with the wife? He was a man of education and fairly refined tastes. How many a time had he discussed poets and poetry with Pierre. He did not appreciate these writers from an artistic point of view, but with sympathetic and responsive feeling. The doctor had often smiled at his emotions which had struck him as rather silly, now he plainly saw that this sentimental soul could never, never have been the friend of his father, who was so matter-of-fact, so narrow, so heavy, to whom the word "Poetry" meant idiocy.

This Marechal then, being young, free, rich, ready for any form of tenderness, went by chance into the shop one day, having perhaps observed its pretty mistress. He had bought something, had come again, had chatted, more intimately each time, paying by frequent purchases for the right of a seat in the family, of smiling at the young wife and shaking hands with the husband.

And what next — what next — good God — what next?

He had loved and petted the first child, the jeweller's child, till the second was born; then, till death, he had remained impenetrable; and when his grave was closed, his flesh dust, his name erased from the list of the living, when he himself was quiet and forever gone, having nothing to scheme for, to dread or to hide, he had given his whole fortune to the second child! Why?

The man had all his wits; he must have understood and foreseen that he might, that he almost infallibly must, give grounds for the supposition that the child was his. He was casting obloquy on a woman. How could he have done this if Jean were not his son?

And suddenly a clear and fearful recollection shot through his brain. Marechal was fair — fair like Jean. He now remembered a little miniature portrait he had seen formerly in Paris, on the drawingroom chimney-shelf, and which had since disappeared. Where was it? Lost, or hidden away? Oh, if he could but have it in his hand for one minute! His mother kept it perhaps in the unconfessed drawer where love-tokens were treasured.

His misery in this thought was so intense that he uttered a groan, one of those brief moans wrung from the breast by a too intolerable pang. And immediately, as if it had heard him, as if it had understood and answered him, the fog-horn on the pier bellowed out close to him. Its voice, like that of a fiendish monster, more resonant than thunder — a savage and appalling roar contrived to drown the clamour of the wind and waves — spread through the darkness, across the sea, which was invisible under its shroud of fog. And again, through the mist, far and near, responsive cries went up to the night. They were terrifying, these calls given forth by the great blind steamships.

Then all was silent once more.

Pierre had opened his eyes and was looking about him, startled to find himself here, roused from his nightmare.

"I am mad," thought he, "I suspect my mother." And a surge of love and emotion, of repentance, and prayer, and grief, welled up in his heart. His mother! Knowing her as he knew her, how could he ever have suspected her? Was not the soul, was not the life of this simple-minded, chaste, and loyal woman clearer than water? Could any one who had seen and known her ever think of her but as above suspicion? And he, her son, had doubted her! Oh, if he could but have taken her in his arms at that moment, how he would have kissed and caressed her, and gone on his knees to crave pardon.

Would she have deceived his father — she?

His father! — A very worthy man, no doubt, upright and honest in business, but with a mind which had never gone beyond the horizon of his shop. How was it that this woman, who must have been very pretty — as he knew, and it could still be seen — gifted, too, with a delicate, tender emotional soul, could have accepted a man so unlike herself as a suitor and a husband? Why inquire? She had married, as young French girls do marry, the youth with a little fortune proposed to her by their relations. They had settled at once in their shop in the Rue Montmartre; and the young wife, ruling over the desk, inspired by the feeling of a new home, and the subtle and sacred sense of interests in common which fills the place of love, and even of regard, by the domestic hearth of most of the commercial houses of Paris, had set to work, with all her superior and active intelligence, to make the fortune they hoped for. And so her life had flowed on, uniform, peaceful and respectable, but loveless.

Loveless? — was it possible then that a woman should not love? That a young and pretty woman, living in Paris, reading books, applauding actresses for dying of passion on the stage, could live from youth to old age without once feeling her heart touched? He would not believe it of any one else; why should she be different from all others, though she was his mother?

She had been young, with all the poetic weaknesses which agitate the heart of a young creature. Shut up, imprisoned in the shop, by the side of a vulgar husband who always talked of trade, she had dreamed of moonlight nights, of voyages, of kisses exchanged in the shades of evening. And then, one day a man had come in, as lovers do in books, and had talked as they talk.

She had loved him. Why not? She was his mother. What then? Must a man be blind and stupid to the point of rejecting evidence because it concerns his mother? But did she give herself to him? Why yes, since this man had had no other love, since he had remained faithful to her when she was far away and growing old. Why yes, since he had left all his fortune to his son — their son!

And Pierre started to his feet, quivering with such rage that he longed to kill some one. With his arm outstretched, his hand wide open, he wanted to hit, to bruise, to smash, to strangle! Whom? Every one; his father, his brother, the dead man, his mother!

He hurried off homeward. What was he going to do?

As he passed a turret close to the signal mast the strident howl of the fog-horn went off in his very face. He was so startled that he nearly fell and shrank back as far as the granite parapet. He sat down half-stunned by the sudden shock. The steamer which was the first to reply seemed to be quite near and was already at the entrance, the tide having risen.

Pierre turned round and could discern its red eye dim through the fog. Then, in the broad light of the electric lanterns, a huge black shadow crept up between the piers. Behind him the voice of the lookout man, the hoarse voice of an old retired sea-captain, shouted:

"What ship?" And out of the fog the voice of the pilot standing on deck — not less hoarse — replied:

"The Santa Lucia."

"Where from?"

"Italy."

"What port?"

"Naples."

And before Pierre's bewildered eyes rose, as he fancied, the fiery pennon of Vesuvius, while, at the foot of the volcano, fireflies danced in the orange-groves of Sorrento or Castellamare. How often had he dreamed of these familiar names as if he knew the scenery. Oh, if he might but go away, now at once, never mind whither, and never come back, never write, never let any one know what had become of him! But no, he must go home — home to his father's house, and go to bed.

He would not. Come what might he would not go in; he would stay there till daybreak. He liked the roar of the fog-horns. He pulled himself together and began to walk up and down like an officer on watch.

Another vessel was coming in behind the other, huge and mysterious. An English Indiaman, homeward bound.

He saw several more come in, one after another, out of the impenetrable vapour. Then, as the damp became quite intolerable, Pierre set out towards the town. He was so cold that he went into a sailors' tavern to drink a glass of grog, and when the hot and pungent liquor had scorched his mouth and throat he felt a hope revive within him.

Perhaps he was mistaken. He knew his own vagabond unreason so well! No doubt he was mistaken. He had piled up the evidence as a charge is drawn up against an innocent person, whom it is always so easy to convict when we wish to think him guilty. When he should have slept he would think differently.

Then he went in and to bed, and by sheer force of will he at last dropped asleep.

V

But the doctor's frame lay scarcely more than an hour or two in the torpor of troubled slumbers. When he awoke in the darkness of his warm, closed room he was aware, even before thought was awake in him, of the painful oppression, the sickness of heart which the sorrow we have slept on leaves behind it. It is as though the disaster of which the shock merely jarred us at first, had, during sleep, stolen into our very flesh, bruising and exhausting it like a fever. Memory returned to him like a blow, and he sat up in bed. Then slowly, one by one, he again went through all the arguments which had wrung his heart on the jetty while the fog-horns were bellowing. The more he thought the less he doubted. He felt himself dragged along by his logic to the inevitable certainty, as by a clutching, strangling hand.

He was thirsty and hot, his heart beat wildly. He got up to open his window and breathe the fresh air, and as he stood there a low sound fell on his ear through the wall. Jean was sleeping peacefully, and gently snoring. He could sleep! He had no presentiment, no suspicions! A man who had known their mother had left him all his fortune; he took the money and thought it quite fair and natural! He was sleeping, rich and contented, not knowing that his brother was gasping with anguish and distress. And rage boiled up in him against this heedless and happy sleeper.

Only yesterday he would have knocked at his door, have gone in, and sitting by the bed, would have said to Jean, scared by the sudden waking:

"Jean you must not keep this legacy which by tomorrow may have brought suspicion and dishonour on our mother."

But to-day he could say nothing; he could not tell Jean that he did not believe him to be their father's son. Now he must guard, must bury the shame he had discovered, hide from every eye the stain which he had detected and which no one must perceive, not even his brother — especially not his brother.

He no longer thought about the vain respect of public opinion. He would have been glad that all the world should accuse his mother if only he, he alone, knew her to be innocent! How could he bear to live with her every day, believing as he looked at her that his brother was the child of a stranger's love?

And how calm and serene she was, nevertheless, how sure of herself she always seemed! Was it possible that such a woman as she, pure of soul and upright in heart, should fall, dragged astray by passion, and yet nothing ever appear afterward of her remorse and the stings of a troubled conscience? Ah, but remorse must have tortured her, long ago in the earlier days, and then have faded out, as everything fades. She had surely bewailed her sin, and then, little by little, had almost forgotten it. Have not all women, all, this fault of prodigious forgetfulness which enables them, after a few years, hardly to recognise the man to whose kisses they have given their lips? The kiss strikes like a thunderbolt, the love passes away like a storm, and then life, like the sky, is calm once more, and begins again as it was before. Do we ever remember a cloud?

Pierre could no longer endure to stay in the room! This house, his father's house, crushed him. He felt the roof weigh on his head, and the walls suffocate him. And as he was very thirsty he lighted his candle to go to drink a glass of fresh water from the filter in the kitchen.

He went down the two flights of stairs; then, as he was coming up again with the water-bottle filled, he sat down, in his nightshirt, on a step of the stairs where there was a draught, and drank, without a tumbler, in long pulls like a runner who is out of breath. When he ceased to move the silence of the house touched his feelings; then, one by one, he could distinguish the faintest sounds. First there was the ticking of the clock in the diningroom which seemed to grow louder every second. Then he heard another snore, an old man's snore, short, laboured, and hard, his father beyond doubt; and he writhed at the idea, as if it had but this moment sprung upon him, that these two men, sleeping under the same room — father and son — were nothing to each other! Not a tie, not the very slightest, bound them together, and they did not know it! They spoke to each other affectionately, they embraced each other, they rejoiced and lamented together over the same things, just as if the same blood flowed in their veins. And two men born at opposite ends of the earth could not be more alien to each other than this father and son. They believed they loved each other, because a lie had grown up between them. This paternal love, this filial love, were the outcome of a lie — a lie which could not be unmasked, and which no one would ever know but he, the true son.

But yet, but yet — if he were mistaken? How could he make sure? Oh, if only some like-ness, however slight, could be traced between his father and Jean, one of those mysterious resemblances which run from an ancestor to the great-great-grandson, showing that the whole race are the offspring of the same embrace. To him, a medical man, so little would suffice to enable him to discern this — the curve of a nostril, the space between the eyes, the character of the teeth or hair; nay less — a gesture, a trick, a habit, an inherited taste, any mark or token which a practised eye might recognise as characteristic.

He thought long, but could remember nothing; no, nothing. But he had looked carelessly, observed badly, having no reason for spying such imperceptible indications.

He got up to go back to his room and mounted the stairs with a slow step, still lost in thought. As he passed the door of his brother's room he stood stock still, his hand put out to open it. An imperative need had just come over him to see Jean at once, to look at him at his leisure, to surprise him in his sleep, while the calm countenance and relaxed features were at rest and all the grimace of life put off. Thus he might catch the dormant secret of his physiognomy, and if any appreciable likeness existed it would not escape him.

But supposing Jean were to wake, what could he say? How could he explain this intrusion?

He stood still, his fingers clinched on the door-handle, trying to devise a reason, an excuse. Then he remembered that a week ago he had lent his brother a phial of laudanum to relieve a fit of toothache. He might himself have been in pain this night and have come to find the drug. So he went in with a stealthy step, like a robber. Jean, his mouth open, was sunk in deep, animal slumbers. His beard and fair hair made a golden patch on the white linen; he did not wake, but he ceased snoring.

Pierre, leaning over him, gazed at him with hungry eagerness. No, this youngster was not in the least like Roland; and for the second time the recollection of the little portrait of Marechal, which had vanished, recurred to his mind. He must find it! When he should see it perhaps he should cease to doubt!

His brother stirred, conscious no doubt of a presence, or disturbed by the light of the taper on his eyelids. The doctor retired on tip-toe to the door which he noiselessly closed; then he went back to his room, but not to bed again.

Day was long in coming. The hours struck one after another on the diningroom clock, and its tone was a deep and solemn one, as though the little piece of clockwork had swallowed a cathedral-bell. The sound rose through the empty staircase, penetrating through walls and doors, and dying away in the rooms where it fell on the torpid ears of the sleeping household. Pierre had taken to walking to and fro between his bed and the window. What was he going to do? He was too much upset to spend this day at home. He wanted still to be alone, at any rate till the next day, to reflect, to compose himself, to strengthen himself for the common everyday life which he must take up again.

Well, he would go over to Trouville to see the swarming crowd on the sands. That would amuse him, change the air of his thoughts, and give him time to inure himself to the horrible thing he had discovered. As soon as morning dawned he made his toilet and dressed. The fog had vanished and it was fine, very fine. As the boat for Trouville did not start till nine, it struck the doctor that he must greet his mother before starting.

He waited till the hour at which she was accustomed to get up, and then went downstairs. His heart beat so violently as he touched her door that he paused for breath. His hand as it lay on the lock was limp and tremulous, almost incapable of the slight effort of turning the handle to open it. He knocked. His mother's voice inquired:

"Who is there?"

"I — Pierre."

"What do you want?"

"Only to say good-morning, because I am going to spend the day at Trouville with some friends."

"But I am still in bed."

"Very well, do not disturb yourself. I shall see you this evening, when I come in."

He hoped to get off without seeing her, without pressing on her cheek the false kiss which it made his heart sick to think of. But she replied:

"No. Wait a moment. I will let you in. Wait till I get into bed again."

He heard her bare feet on the floor and the sound of the bolt drawn back. Then she called out:

"Come in."

He went in. She was sitting up in bed, while, by her side, Roland, with a silk handkerchief by way of nightcap and his face to the wall, still lay sleeping. Nothing ever woke him but a shaking hard enough to pull his arm off. On the days when he went fishing it was Josephine, rung up by Papagris at the hour fixed, who roused her master from his stubborn slumbers.

Pierre, as he went towards his mother, looked at her with a sudden sense of never having seen her before. She held up her face, he kissed each cheek, and then sat down in a low chair.

"It was last evening that you decided on this excursion?" she asked.

"Yes, last evening."

"Will you return to dinner?"

"I do not know. At any rate do not wait for me."

He looked at her with stupefied curiosity. This woman was his mother! All those features, seen daily from childhood, from the time when his eye could first distinguish things, that smile, that voice — so well known, so familiar — abruptly struck him as new, different from what they had always been to him hitherto. He understood now that, loving her, he had never looked at her. All the same it was very really she, and he knew every little detail of her face; still, it was the first time he clearly identified them all. His anxious attention, scrutinizing her face which he loved, recalled a difference, a physiognomy he had never before discerned.

He rose to go; then, suddenly yielding to the invincible longing to know which had been gnawing at him since yesterday, he said:

"By the way, I fancy I remember that you used to have, in Paris, a little portrait of Marechal, in the drawingroom."

She hesitated for a second or two, or at least he fancied she hesitated; then she said:

"To be sure."

"What has become of the portrait?"

She might have replied more readily:

"That portrait — stay; I don't exactly know — perhaps it is in my desk."

"It would be kind of you to find it."

"Yes, I will look for it. What do you want it for?"

"Oh, it is not for myself. I thought it would be a natural thing to give it to Jean, and that he would be pleased to have it."

"Yes, you are right; that is a good idea. I will look for it, as soon as I am up."

And he went out.

It was a blue day without a breath of wind. The folks in the streets seemed in good spirits, the merchants going to business, the clerks going to their office, the girls going to their shop. Some sang as they went, exhilarated by the bright weather.

The passengers were already going on board the Trouville boat; Pierre took a seat aft on a wooden bench.

He asked himself:

"Now was she uneasy at my asking for the portrait or only surprised? Has she mislaid it, or has she hidden it? Does she know where it is, or does she not? If she had hidden it — why?"

And his mind, still following up the same line of thought from one deduction to another, came to this conclusion:

That portrait — of a friend, of a lover, had remained in the drawingroom in a conspicuous place, till one day when the wife and mother perceived, first of all and before any one else, that it bore a likeness to her son. Without doubt she had for a long time been on the watch for this resemblance; then, having detected it, having noticed its beginnings, and understanding that any one might, any day, observe it too, she had one evening removed the perilous little picture and had hidden it, not daring to destroy it.

Pierre recollected quite clearly now that it was long, long before they left Paris that the miniature had vanished. It had disappeared, he thought, about the time that Jean's beard was beginning to grow, which had made him suddenly and wonderfully like the fair young man who smiled from the picture-frame.

The motion of the boat as it put off disturbed and dissipated his meditations. He stood up and looked at the sea. The little steamer, once outside the piers, turned to the left, and puffing and snorting and quivering, made for a distant point visible through the morning haze. The red sail of a heavy fishing-bark, lying motionless on the level waters, looked like a large rock standing up out of the sea. And the Seine, rolling down from Rouen, seemed a wide inlet dividing two neighbouring lands. They reached the harbour of Trouville in less than an hour, and as it was the time of day when the world was bathing, Pierre went to the shore.

From a distance it looked like a garden full of gaudy flowers. All along the stretch of yellow sand, from the pier as far as the Roches Noires, sunshades of every hue, hats of every shape, dresses of every colour, in groups outside the bathing huts, in long rows by the margin of the waves, or scattered here and there, really looked like immense bouquets on a vast meadow. And the Babel of sounds — voices near and far ringing thin in the light atmosphere, shouts and cries of children being bathed, clear laughter of women — all made a pleasant, continuous din, mingling with the unheeding breeze, and breathed with the air itself.

Pierre walked among all this throng, more lost, more remote from them, more isolated, more drowned in his torturing thoughts, than if he had been flung overboard from the deck of a ship a hundred miles from shore. He passed by them and heard a few sentences without listening; and he saw, without looking, how the men spoke to the women, and the women smiled at the men. Then, suddenly, as if he had awoke, he perceived them all; and hatred of them all surged up in his soul, for they seemed happy and content.

Now, as he went, he studied the groups, wandering round them full of a fresh set of ideas. All these many-hued dresses which covered the sands like nosegays, these pretty stuffs, those showy parasols, the fictitious grace of tightened waists, all the ingenious devices of fashion from the smart little shoe to the extravagant hat, the seductive charm of gesture, voice, and smile, all the coquettish airs in short displayed on this seashore, suddenly struck him as stupendous efflorescences of female depravity. All these bedizened women aimed at pleasing, bewitching, and deluding some man. They had dressed themselves out for men — for all men — all excepting the husband whom they no longer needed to conquer. They had dressed themselves out for the lover of yesterday and the lover of tomorrow, for the stranger they might meet and notice or were perhaps on the lookout for.

And these men sitting close to them, eye to eye and mouth to mouth, invited them, desired them, hunted them like game, coy and elusive notwithstanding that it seemed so near and so easy to capture. This wide shore was, then, no more than a love-market where some sold, others gave themselves — some drove a hard bargain for their kisses while others promised them for love. All these women thought only of one thing, to make their bodies desirable — bodies already given, sold, or promised to other men. And he reflected that it was everywhere the same, all the world over.

His mother had done what others did — that was all. Others? These women he saw about him, rich, giddy, love-seeking, belonged on the whole to the class of fashionable and showy women of the world, some indeed to the less respectable sisterhood, for on these sands, trampled by the legion of idlers, the tribe of virtuous, home-keeping women were not to be seen.

The tide was rising, driving the foremost rank of visitors gradually landward. He saw the various groups jump up and fly, carrying their chairs with them, before the yellow waves as they rolled up edged with a lace-like frill of foam. The bathing-machines too were being pulled up by horses, and along the planked way which formed the promenade running along the shore from end to end, there was now an increasing flow, slow and dense, of well-dressed people in two opposite streams elbowing and mingling. Pierre, made nervous and exasperated by this bustle, made his escape into the town, and went to get his breakfast at a modest tavern on the skirts of the fields.

When he had finished with coffee, he stretched his legs on a couple of chairs under a lime-tree in front of the house, and as he had hardly slept the night before, he presently fell into a doze. After resting for some hours he shook himself, and finding that it was time to go on board again he set out, tormented by a sudden stiffness which had come upon him during his long nap. Now he was eager to be at home again; to know whether his mother had found the portrait of Marechal. Would she be the first to speak of it, or would he be obliged to ask for it again? If she waited to be questioned further it must be because she had some secret reason for not showing the miniature.

But when he was at home again, and in his room, he hesitated about going down to dinner. He was too wretched. His revolted soul had not yet time to calm down. However, he made up his mind to it, and appeared in the diningroom just as they were sitting down.

All their faces were beaming.

"Well," said Roland, "are you getting on with your purchases? I do not want to see anything till it is all in its place."

And his wife replied: "Oh, yes. We are getting on. But it takes much consideration to avoid buying things that do not match. The furniture question is an absorbing one."

She had spent the day in going with Jean to cabinetmakers and upholsterers. Her fancy was for rich materials, rather splendid to strike the eye at once. Her son, on the contrary, wished for something simple and elegant. So in front of everything put before them they had each repeated their arguments. She declared that a client, a defendant, must be impressed; that as soon as he is shown into his counsel's waiting-room he should have a sense of wealth.

Jean, on the other hand, wishing to attract only an elegant and opulent class, was anxious to captivate persons of refinement by his quiet and perfect taste.

And this discussion, which had gone on all day, began again with the soup.

Roland had no opinion. He repeated: "I do not want to hear anything about it. I will go and see it when it is all finished."

Mme. Roland appealed to the judgment of her elder son.

"And you, Pierre, what do you think of the matter?"

His nerves were in a state of such intense excitement that he would have liked to reply with an oath. However, he only answered in a dry tone quivering with annoyance.

"Oh, I am quite of Jean's mind. I like nothing so well as simplicity, which, in matters of taste, is equivalent to rectitude in matters of conduct."

His mother went on:

"You must remember that we live in a city of commercial men, where good taste is not to be met with at every turn."

Pierre replied:

"What does that matter? Is that a reason for living as fools do? If my fellow-townsmen are stupid and ill-bred, need I follow their example? A woman does not misconduct herself because her neighbour has a lover."

Jean began to laugh.

"You argue by comparisons which seem to have been borrowed from the maxims of a moralist."

Pierre made no reply. His mother and his brother reverted to the question of stuffs and armchairs.

He sat looking at them as he had looked at his mother in the morning before starting for Trouville; looking at them as a stranger who would study them, and he felt as though he had really suddenly come into a family of which he knew nothing.

His father, above all, amazed his eyes and his mind. That flabby, burly man, happy and besotted, was his own father! No, no; Jean was not in the least like him.

His family!

Within these two days an unknown and malignant hand, the hand of a dead man, had torn asunder and broken, one by one, all the ties which had held these four human beings together. It was all over, all ruined. He had now no mother — for he could no longer love her now that he could not revere her with that perfect, tender, and pious respect which a son's love demands; no brother — since his brother was the child of a stranger; nothing was left him but his father, that coarse man whom he could not love in spite of himself.

And he suddenly broke out:

"I say, mother, have you found that portrait?"

She opened her eyes in surprise.

"What portrait?"

"The portrait of Marechal."

"No — that is to say — yes — I have not found it, but I think I know where it is."

"What is that?" asked Roland. And Pierre answered:

"A little likeness of Marechal which used to be in the diningroom in Paris. I thought that Jean might be glad to have it."

Roland exclaimed:

"Why, yes, to be sure; I remember it perfectly. I saw it again last week. Your mother found it in her desk when she was tidying the papers. It was on Thursday or Friday. Do you remember, Louise? I was shaving myself when you took it out and laid in on a chair by your side with a pile of letters of which you burned half. Strange, isn't it, that you should have come across the portrait only two or three days before Jean heard of his legacy? If I believed in presentiments I should think that this was one."

Mme. Roland calmly replied:

"Yes, I know where it is. I will fetch it presently."

Then she had lied! When she had said that very morning to her son who had asked her what had become of the miniature: "I don't exactly know — perhaps it is in my desk" — it was a lie! She had seen it, touched it, handled it, gazed at it but a few days since; and then she had hidden it away again in the secret drawer with those letters — his letters.

Pierre looked at the mother who had lied to him; looked at her with the concentrated fury of a son who had been cheated, robbed of his most sacred affection, and with the jealous wrath of a man who, after long being blind, at last discovers a disgraceful betrayal. If he had been that woman's husband — and not her child — he would have gripped her by the wrists, seized her by the shoulders or the hair, have flung her on the ground, have hit her, hurt her, crushed her! And he might say nothing, do nothing, show nothing, reveal nothing. He was her son; he had no vengeance to take. And he had not been deceived.

Nay, but she had deceived his tenderness, his pious respect. She owed to him to be without reproach, as all mothers owe it to their children. If the fury that boiled within him verged on hatred it was that he felt her to be even more guilty towards him than toward his father.

The love of man and wife is a voluntary compact in which the one who proves weak is guilty only of perfidy; but when the wife is a mother her duty is a higher one, since nature has intrusted her with a race. If she fails, then she is cowardly, worthless, infamous.

"I do not care," said Roland suddenly, stretching out his legs under the table, as he did every evening while he sipped his glass of black-currant brandy. "You may do worse than live idle when you have a snug little income. I hope Jean will have us to dinner in style now. Hang it all! If I have indigestion now and then I cannot help it."

Then turning to his wife he added:

"Go and fetch that portrait, little woman, as you have done your dinner. I should like to see it again myself."

She rose, took a taper, and went. Then, after an absence which Pierre thought long, though she was not away more than three minutes, *Mme.* Roland returned smiling, and holding an old-fashioned gilt frame by the ring.

"Here it is," said she, "I found it at once."

The doctor was the first to put forth his hand; he took the picture, and holding it a little away from him, he examined it. Then, fully aware that his mother was looking at him, he slowly raised his eyes and fixed them on his brother to compare the faces. He could hardly refrain, in his violence, from saying: "Dear me! How like Jean!" And though he dared not utter the terrible words, he betrayed his thought by his manner of comparing the living face with the painted one.

They had, no doubt, details in common; the same beard, the same brow; but nothing sufficiently marked to justify the assertion: "This is the father and that the son." It was rather a family likeness, a relationship of physiognomies in which the same blood courses. But what to Pierre was far more decisive than the common aspect of the faces, was that his mother had risen, had turned her back, and was pretending, too deliberately, to be putting the sugar basin and the liqueur bottle away in a cupboard. She understood that he knew, or at any rate had his suspicions.

"Hand it on to me," said Roland.

Pierre held out the miniature and his father drew the candle towards him to see it better; then, he murmured in a pathetic tone:

"Poor fellow! To think that he was like that when we first knew him! Cristi! How time flies! He was a good-looking man, too, in those days, and with such a pleasant manner — was not he, Louise?"

As his wife made no answer he went on:

"And what an even temper! I never saw him put out. And now it is all at an end — nothing left of him — but what he bequeathed to Jean. Well, at any rate you may take your oath that that man was a good and faithful friend to the last. Even on his deathbed he did not forget us."

Jean, in his turn, held out his hand for the picture. He gazed at it for a few minutes and then said regretfully:

"I do not recognise it at all. I only remember him with white hair."

He returned the miniature to his mother. She cast a hasty glance at it, looking away as if she were frightened; then in her usual voice she said:

"It belongs to you now, my little Jean, as you are his heir. We will take it to your new rooms." And when they went into the drawingroom she placed the picture on the chimney-shelf by the clock, where it had formerly stood.

Roland filled his pipe; Pierre and Jean lighted cigarettes. They commonly smoked them, Pierre while he paced the room, Jean, sunk in a deep armchair, with his legs crossed. Their father always sat astride a chair and spat from afar into the fireplace.

Mme. Roland, on a low seat by a little table on which the lamp stood, embroidered, or knitted, or marked linen.

This evening she was beginning a piece of worsted work, intended for Jean's lodgings. It was a difficult and complicated pattern, and required all her attention. Still, now and again, her eye, which was counting the stitches, glanced up swiftly and furtively at the little portrait of the dead as it leaned against the clock. And the doctor, who was striding to and fro across the little room in four or five steps, met his mother's look at each turn.

It was as though they were spying on each other; and acute uneasiness, intolerable to be borne, clutched at Pierre's heart. He was saying to himself — at once tortured and glad:

"She must be in misery at this moment if she knows that I guess!" And each time he reached the fireplace he stopped for a few seconds to look at Marechal's fair hair, and show quite plainly that he was haunted by a fixed idea. So that this little portrait, smaller than an opened palm, was like a living being, malignant and threatening, suddenly brought into this house and this family.

Presently the street-door bell rang. *Mme.* Roland, always so self-possessed, started violently, betraying to her doctor son the anguish of her nerves. Then she said: "It must be *Mme.* Rosemilly;" and her eye again anxiously turned to the mantelshelf.

Pierre understood, or thought he understood, her fears and misery. A woman's eye is keen, a woman's wit is nimble, and her instincts suspicious. When this woman who was coming in should see the miniature of a man she did not know, she might perhaps at the first glance discover the likeness between this face and Jean. Then she would know and understand everything.

He was seized with dread, a sudden and horrible dread of this shame being unveiled, and, turning about just as the door opened, he took the little painting and slipped it under the clock without being seen by his father and brother.

When he met his mother's eyes again they seemed to him altered, dim, and haggard.

"Good evening," said *Mme.* Rosemilly. "I have come to ask you for a cup of tea."

But while they were bustling about her and asking after her health, Pierre made off, the door having been left open.

When his absence was perceived they were all surprised. Jean, annoyed for the young widow, who, he thought, would be hurt, muttered: "What a bear!"

Mme. Roland replied: "You must not be vexed with him; he is not very well to-day and tired with his excursion to Trouville."

"Never mind," said Roland, "that is no reason for taking himself off like a savage."

Mme. Rosemilly tried to smooth matters by saying: "Not at all, not at all. He has gone away in the English fashion; people always disappear in that way in fashionable circles if they want to leave early."

"Oh, in fashionable circles, I dare say," replied Jean. "But a man does not treat his family a l'Anglaise, and my brother has done nothing else for some time past."

VI

For a week or two nothing occurred. The father went fishing; Jean, with his mother's help, was furnishing and settling himself; Pierre, very gloomy, never was seen excepting at mealtimes.

His father having asked him one evening: "Why the deuce do you always com in with a face as cheerful as a funeral? This is not the first time I have remarked it."

The doctor replied: "The fact is I am terribly conscious of the burden of life."

The old man did not have a notion what he meant, and with an aggrieved look he went on: "It really is too bad. Ever since we had the good luck to come into this legacy, every one seems unhappy. It is as though some accident had befallen us, as if we were in mourning for some one."

"I am in mourning for some one," said Pierre.

"You are? For whom?"

"For some one you never knew, and of whom I was too fond."

Roland imagined that his son alluded to some girl with whom he had had some love passages, and he said:

"A woman, I suppose."

"Yes, a woman."

"Dead?"

"No. Worse. Ruined!"

"Ah!"

Though he was startled by this unexpected confidence, in his wife's presence too, and by his son's strange tone about it, the old man made no further inquiries, for in his opinion such affairs did not concern a third person.

Mme. Roland affected not to hear; she seemed ill and was very pale. Several times already her husband, surprised to see her sit down as if she were dropping into her chair, and to hear her gasp as if she could not draw her breath, had said:

"Really, Louise, you look very ill; you tire yourself too much with helping Jean. Give yourself a little rest. Sacristi! The rascal is in no hurry, as he is a rich man."

She shook her head without a word.

But to-day her pallor was so great that Roland remarked on it again.

"Come, come," said he, "this will not do at all, my dear old woman. You must take care of yourself." Then, addressing his son, "You surely must see that your mother is ill. Have you questioned her, at any rate?"

Pierre replied: "No; I had not noticed that there was anything the matter with her."

At this Roland was angry.

"But it stares you in the face, confound you! What on earth is the good of your being a doctor if you cannot even see that your mother is out of sorts? Why, look at her, just look at her. Really, a man might die under his very eyes and this doctor would never think there was anything the matter!"

Mme. Roland was panting for breath, and so white that her husband exclaimed:

"She is going to faint."

"No, no, it is nothing — I shall get better directly — it is nothing."

Pierre had gone up to her and was looking at her steadily.

"What ails you?" he said. And she repeated in an undertone:

"Nothing, nothing — I assure you, nothing."

Roland had gone to fetch some vinegar; he now returned, and handing the bottle to his son he said:

"Here — do something to ease her. Have you felt her heart?"

As Pierre bent over her to feel her pulse she pulled away her hand so vehemently that she struck it against a chair which was standing by.

"Come," said he in icy tones, "let me see what I can do for you, as you are ill."

Then she raised her arm and held it out to him. Her skin was burning, the blood throbbing in short irregular leaps.

"You are certainly ill," he murmured. "You must take something to quiet you. I will write you a prescription." And as he wrote, stooping over the paper, a low sound of choked sighs, smothered, quick breathing and suppressed sobs made him suddenly look round at her. She was weeping, her hands covering her face.

Roland, quite distracted, asked her:

"Louise, Louise, what is the mater with you? What on earth ails you?"

She did not answer, but seemed racked by some deep and dreadful grief. Her husband tried to take her hands from her face, but she resisted him, repeating:

"No, no, no."

He appealed to his son.

"But what is the matter with her? I never saw her like this."

"It is nothing," said Pierre, "she is a little hysterical."

And he felt as if it were a comfort to him to see her suffering thus, as if this anguish mitigated his resentment and diminished his mother's load of opprobrium. He looked at her as a judge satisfied with his day's work.

Suddenly she rose, rushed to the door with such a swift impulse that it was impossible to forestall or to stop her, and ran off to lock herself into her room.

Roland and the doctor were left face to face.

"Can you make head or tail of it?" said the father.

"Oh, yes," said the other. "It is a little nervous disturbance, not alarming or surprising; such attacks may very likely recur from time to time."

They did in fact recur, almost every day; and Pierre seemed to bring them on with a word, as if he had the clew to her strange and new disorder. He would discern in her face a lucid interval of peace and with the willingness of a torturer would, with a word, revive the anguish that had been lulled for a moment.

But he, too, was suffering as cruelly as she. It was dreadful pain to him that he could no longer love her nor respect her, that he must put her on the rack. When he had laid bare the bleeding wound which he had opened in her woman's, her mother's heart, when he felt how wretched and desperate she was, he would go out alone, wander about the town, so torn by remorse, so broken by pity, so grieved to have thus hammered her with his scorn as her son, that he longed to fling himself into the sea and put an end to it all by drowning himself.

Ah! How gladly now would he have forgiven her. But he could not, for he was incapable of forgetting. If only he could have desisted from making her suffer; but this again he could not, suffering as he did himself. He went home to his meals, full of relenting resolutions; then, as soon as he saw her, as soon as he met her eye — formerly so clear and frank, now so evasive, frightened, and bewildered — he struck at her in spite of himself, unable to suppress the treacherous words which would rise to his lips.

This disgraceful secret, known to them alone, goaded him up against her. It was as a poison flowing in his veins and giving him an impulse to bite like a mad dog.

And there was no one in the way now to hinder his reading her; Jean lived almost entirely in his new apartments, and only came home to dinner and to sleep every night at his father's.

He frequently observed his brother's bitterness and violence, and attributed them to jealousy. He promised himself that some day he would teach him his place and give him a lesson, for life at home was becoming very painful as a result of these constant scenes. But as he now lived apart he suffered less from this brutal conduct, and his love of peace prompted him to patience. His good fortune, too, had turned his head, and he scarcely paused to think of anything which had no direct interest for himself. He would come in full of fresh little anxieties, full of the cut of a morning-coat, of the shape of a felt hat, of the proper size for his visiting-cards. And he talked incessantly of all the details of his house — the shelves fixed in his bedroom cupboard to keep linen on, the pegs to be put up in the entrance hall, the electric bells contrived to prevent illicit visitors to his lodgings.

It had been settled that on the day when he should take up his abode there they should make an excursion to Saint Jouin, and return after dining there, to drink tea in his rooms. Roland wanted to go by water, but the distance and the uncertainty of reaching it in a sailing boat if there should be a head-wind, made them reject his plan, and a break was hired for the day.

They set out at ten to get there to breakfast. The dusty high road lay across the plain of Normandy, which, by its gentle undulations, dotted with farms embowered in trees, wears the aspect of an endless park. In the vehicle, as it jogged on at the slow trot of a pair of heavy horses, sat the four Rolands, *Mme.* Rosemilly, and Captain Beausire, all silent, deafened by the rumble of the wheels, and with their eyes shut to keep out the clouds of dust.

It was harvest-time. Alternating with the dark hue of clover and the raw green of beetroot, the yellow corn lighted up the landscape with gleams of pale gold; the fields looked as if they had drunk in the sunshine which poured down on them. Here and there the reapers were at work, and in the plots where the scythe had been put in the men might be seen seesawing as they swept the level soil with the broad, wing-shaped blade.

After a two-hours' drive the break turned off to the left, past a windmill at work — a melancholy, gray wreck, half rotten and doomed, the last survivor of its ancient race; then it went into a pretty inn yard, and drew up at the door of a smart little house, a hostelry famous in those parts.

The mistress, well known as "La belle Alphonsine," came smiling to the threshold, and held out her hand to the two ladies who hesitated to take the high step.

Some strangers were already at breakfast under a tent by a grassplot shaded by apple trees — Parisians, who had come from Etretat; and from the house came sounds of voices, laughter, and the clatter of plates and pans.

They were to eat in a room, as the outer dining-halls were all full. Roland suddenly caught sight of some shrimping nets hanging against the wall.

"Ah! ha!" cried he, "you catch prawns here?"

"Yes," replied Beausire. "Indeed it is the place on all the coast where most are taken."

"First-rate! Suppose we try to catch some after breakfast."

As it happened it would be low tide at three o'clock, so it was settled that they should all spend the afternoon among the rocks, hunting prawns.

They made a light breakfast, as a precaution against the tendency of blood to the head when they should have their feet in the water. They also wished to reserve an appetite for dinner, which had been ordered on a grand scale and to be ready at six o'clock when they came in.

Roland could not sit still for impatience. He wanted to buy the nets specially constructed for fishing prawns, not unlike those used for catching butterflies in the country. Their name on the French coast is lanets; they are netted bags on a circular wooden frame, at the end of a long pole. Alphonsine, still smiling, was happy to lend them. Then she helped the two ladies to make an impromptu change of toilet, so as not to spoil their dresses. She offered them skirts, coarse worsted stockings and hemp shoes. The men took off their socks and went to the shoemaker's to buy wooden shoes instead.

Then they set out, the nets over their shoulders and creels on their backs. *Mme.* Rosemilly was very sweet in this costume, with an unexpected charm of countrified audacity. The skirt which Alphonsine had lent her, coquettishly tucked up and firmly stitched so as to allow of her running and jumping fearlessly on the rocks, displayed her ankle and lower calf — the firm calf of a strong and agile little woman. Her dress was loose to give freedom to her movements, and to cover her head she had found an enormous garden hat of coarse yellow straw with an extravagantly broad brim; and to this, a bunch of tamarisk pinned in to cock it on one side, gave a very dashing and military effect.

Jean, since he had come into his fortune, had asked himself every day whether or no he should marry her. Each time he saw her he made up his mind to ask her to be his wife, and then, as soon as he was alone again, he considered that by waiting he would have time to reflect. She was now less rich than he, for she had but twelve thousand francs a year; but it was in real estate, in farms and lands near the docks in Havre; and this by-and-bye might be worth a great deal. Their fortunes were thus approximately equal, and certainly the young widow attracted him greatly.

As he watched her walking in front of him that day he said to himself:

"I must really decide; I cannot do better, I am sure."

They went down a little ravine, sloping from the village to the cliff, and the cliff, at the end of this comb, rose about eighty metres above the sea. Framed between the green slopes to the right and left, a great triangle of silvery blue water could be seen in the distance, and a sail, scarcely visible, looked like an insect out there. The sky, pale with light, was so merged into one with the water that it was impossible to see where one ended and the other began; and the two women, walking in front of the men, stood out against the bright background, their shapes clearly defined in their closely-fitting dresses.

Jean, with a sparkle in his eye, watched the smart ankle, the neat leg, the supple waist, and the coquettish broad hat of *Mme.* Rosemilly as they fled away from him. And this flight fired his ardour, urging him on to the sudden determination which comes to hesitating and timid natures. The warm air, fragrant with seacoast odours — gorse, clover, and thyme, mingling with the salt smell of the rocks at low tide — excited him still more, mounting to his brain; and every moment he felt a little more determined, at every step, at every glance he cast at the alert figure; he made up his mind to delay no longer, to tell her that he loved her and hoped to marry her. The prawn-fishing would favour him by affording him an opportunity; and it would be a pretty scene too, a pretty spot for love-making — their feet in a pool of limpid water while they watched the long feelers of the shrimps lurking under the wrack.

When they had reached the end of the comb and the edge of the cliff, they saw a little footpath slanting down the face of it; and below them, about halfway between the sea and the foot of the precipice, an amazing chaos of enormous boulders tumbled over and piled one above the other on a sort of grassy and undulating plain which extended as far as they could see to the southward, formed by an ancient landslip. On this long shelf of brushwood and grass, disrupted, as it seemed, by the shocks of a volcano, the fallen rocks seemed the wreck of a great ruined city which had once looked out on the ocean, sheltered by the long white wall of the overhanging cliff.

"That is fine!" exclaimed *Mme.* Rosemilly, standing still. Jean had come up with her, and with a beating heart offered his hand to help her down the narrow steps cut in the rock.

They went on in front, while Beausire, squaring himself on his little legs, gave his arm to *Mme.* Roland, who felt giddy at the gulf before her.

Roland and Pierre came last, and the doctor had to drag his father down, for his brain reeled so that he could only slip down sitting, from step to step.

The two young people who led the way went fast till on a sudden they saw, by the side of a wooden bench which afforded a resting-place about halfway down the slope, a thread of clear water, springing from a crevice in the cliff. It fell into a hollow as large as a washing basin which it had worn in the stone; then, falling in a cascade, hardly two feet high, it trickled across the footpath which it had carpeted with cresses, and was lost among the briers and grass on the raised shelf where the boulders were piled.

"Oh, I am so thirsty!" cried *Mme.* Rosemilly.

But how could she drink? She tried to catch the water in her hand, but it slipped away between her fingers. Jean had an idea; he placed a stone on the path and on this she knelt down to put her lips to the spring itself, which was thus on the same level.

When she raised her head, covered with myriads of tiny drops, sprinkled all over her face, her hair, her eyelashes, and her dress, Jean bent over her and murmured: "How pretty you look!"

She answered in the tone in which she might have scolded a child:

"Will you be quiet?"

These were the first words of flirtation they had ever exchanged.

"Come," said Jean, much agitated. "Let us go on before they come up with us."

For in fact they could see quite near them now Captain Beausire as he came down, backward, so as to give both hands to *Mme.* Roland; and further up, further off, Roland still letting himself slip, lowering himself on his hams and clinging on with his hands and elbows at the speed of a tortoise, Pierre keeping in front of him to watch his movements.

The path, now less steep, was here almost a road, zigzagging between the huge rocks which had at some former time rolled from the hilltop. *Mme.* Rosemilly and Jean set off at a run and they were soon on the beach. They crossed it and reached the rocks, which stretched in a long and flat expanse covered with seaweed, and broken by endless gleaming pools. The ebbed waters lay beyond, very far away, across this plain of slimy weed, of a black and shining olive green.

Jean rolled up his trousers above his calf, and his sleeves to his elbows, that he might get wet without caring; then saying: "Forward!" he leaped boldly into the first tide-pool they came to.

The lady, more cautious, though fully intending to go in too, presently, made her way round the little pond, stepping timidly, for she slipped on the grassy weed.

"Do you see anything?" she asked.

"Yes, I see your face reflected in the water."

"If that is all you see, you will not have good fishing."

He murmured tenderly in reply:

"Of all fishing it is that I should like best to succeed in."

She laughed: "Try; you will see how it will slip through your net."

"But yet — if you will?"

"I will see you catch prawns — and nothing else — for the moment."

"You are cruel — let us go a little farther, there are none here."

He gave her his hand to steady her on the slippery rocks. She leaned on him rather timidly, and he suddenly felt himself overpowered by love and insurgent with passion, as if the fever that had been incubating in him had waited till to-day to declare its presence.

They soon came to a deeper rift, in which long slender weeds, fantastically tinted, like floating green and rose-coloured hair, were swaying under the quivering water as it trickled off to the distant sea through some invisible crevice.

Mme. Rosemilly cried out: "Look, look, I see one, a big one. A very big one, just there!" He saw it too, and stepped boldly into the pool, though he got wet up to the waist. But the creature, waving its long whiskers, gently retired in front of the net. Jean drove it towards the seaweed, making sure of his prey. When it found itself blockaded it rose with a dart over the net, shot across the mere, and was gone. The young woman, who was watching the chase in great excitement, could not help exclaiming: "Oh! Clumsy!"

He was vexed, and without a moment's thought dragged his net over a hole full of weed. As he brought it to the surface again he saw in it three large transparent prawns, caught blindfold in their hiding-place.

He offered them in triumph to *Mme.* Rosemilly, who was afraid to touch them, for fear of the sharp, serrated crest which arms their heads. However, she made up her mind to it, and taking them up by the tip of their long whiskers she dropped them one by one into her creel, with a little seaweed to keep them alive. Then, having found a shallower pool of water, she stepped in with some hesitation, for the cold plunge of her feet took her breath away, and began to fish on her own account. She was dextrous and artful, with the light hand and the hunter's instinct which are indispensable. At almost every dip she brought up some prawns, beguiled and surprised by her ingeniously gentle pursuit.

Jean now caught nothing; but he followed her, step by step, touched her now and again, bent over her, pretended great distress at his own awkwardness, and besought her to teach him.

"Show me," he kept saying. "Show me how."

And then, as their two faces were reflected side by side in water so clear that the black weeds at the bottom made a mirror, Jean smiled at the face which looked up at him from the depth, and now and then from his finger-tips blew it a kiss which seemed to light upon it.

"Oh! how tiresome you are!" she exclaimed. "My dear fellow, you should never do two things at once."

He replied: "I am only doing one — loving you."

She drew herself up and said gravely:

"What has come over you these ten minutes; have you lost your wits?"

"No, I have not lost my wits. I love you, and at last I dare to tell you so."

They were at this moment both standing in the salt pool wet halfway up to their knees and with dripping hands, holding their nets. They looked into each other's eyes.

She went on in a tone of amused annoyance.

"How very ill-advised to tell me here and now! Could you not wait till another day instead of spoiling my fishing?"

"Forgive me," he murmured, "but I could not longer hold my peace. I have loved you a long time. To-day you have intoxicated me and I lost my reason."

Then suddenly she seemed to have resigned herself to talk business and think no more of pleasure.

"Let us sit down on that stone," said she, "we can talk more comfortably." They scrambled up a rather high boulder, and when they had settled themselves side by side in the bright sunshine, she began again:

"My good friend, you are no longer a child, and I am not a young girl. we both know perfectly well what we are about and we can weigh the consequences of our actions. If you have made up your mind to make love to me to-day I must naturally infer that you wish to marry me."

He was not prepared for this matter-of-fact statement of the case, and he answered blandly: "Why, yes."

"Have you mentioned it to your father and mother?"

"No, I wanted to know first whether you would accept me."

She held out her hand, which was still wet, and as he eagerly clasped it:

"I am ready and willing," she said. "I believe you to be kind and true-hearted. But remember, I should not like to displease your parents."

"Oh, do you think that my mother has never foreseen it, or that she would not be as fond of you as she is if she did not hope that you and I should marry?"

"That is true. I am a little disturbed."

They said no more. He, for his part, was amazed at her being so little disturbed, so rational. He had expected pretty little flirting ways, refusals which meant yes, a whole coquettish comedy of love chequered by prawn-fishing in the splashing water. And it was all over; he was pledged, married with twenty words. They had no more to say about it since they were agreed, and they now sat, both somewhat embarrassed by what had so swiftly passed between them; a little perplexed, indeed, not daring to speak, not daring to fish, not knowing what to do.

Roland's voice rescued them.

"This way, this way, children. Come and watch Beausire. The fellow is positively clearing out the sea!"

The captain had, in fact, had a wonderful haul. Wet above his hips he waded from pool to pool, recognizing the likeliest spots at a glance, and searching all the hollows hidden under seaweed, with a steady slow sweep of his net. And the beautiful transparent, sandy-gray prawns skipped in his palm as he picked them out of the net with a dry jerk and put them into his creel. *Mme.* Rosemilly, surprised and delighted, remained at his side, almost forgetful of her promise to Jean, who followed them in a dream, giving herself up entirely to the childish enjoyment of pulling the creatures out from among the waving sea-grasses.

Roland suddenly exclaimed:

"Ah, here comes *Mme.* Roland to join us."

She had remained at first on the beach with Pierre, for they had neither of them any wish to play at running about among the rocks and paddling in the tide-pools; and yet they had felt doubtful about staying together. She was afraid of him, and her son was afraid of her and of himself; afraid of his own cruelty which he could not control. But they sat down side by side on the stones. And both of them, under the heat of the sun, mitigated by the sea-breeze, gazing at the wide, fair horizon of blue water streaked and shot with silver, thought as if in unison: "How delightful this would have been — once."

She did not venture to speak to Pierre, knowing that he would return some hard answer; and he dared not address his mother, knowing that in spite of himself he should speak violently. He sat twitching the water-worn pebbles with the end of his cane, switching them and turning them over. She, with a vague look in her eyes, had picked up three or four little stones and was slowly and mechanically dropping them from one hand into the other. Then her unsettled gaze, wandering over the scene before her, discerned, among the weedy rocks, her son Jean fishing with *Mme.* Rosemilly. She looked at them, watching their movements, dimly understanding, with motherly instinct, that they were talking as they did not talk every day. She saw them leaning over side by side when they looked into the water, standing face to face when they questioned their hearts, then scrambled up the rock and seated themselves to come to an understanding. Their figures stood out very sharply, looking as if they were alone in the middle of the wide horizon, and assuming a sort of symbolic dignity in that vast expanse of sky and sea and cliff.

Pierre, too, was looking at them, and a harsh laugh suddenly broke form his lips. Without turning to him *Mme.* Roland said:

"What is it?"

He spoke with a sneer.

"I am learning. Learning how a man lays himself out to be cozened by his wife."

She flushed with rage, exasperated by the insinuation she believed was intended.

"In whose name do you say that?"

"In Jean's, by Heaven! It is immensely funny to see those two."

She murmured in a low voice, tremulous with feeling: "O Pierre, how cruel you are! That woman is honesty itself. Your brother could not find a better."

He laughed aloud, a hard, satirical laugh:

"Ha! hah! Hah! Honesty itself! All wives are honesty itself — and all husbands are — betrayed." And he shouted with laughter.

She made no reply, but rose, hastily went down the sloping beach, and at the risk of tumbling into one of the rifts hidden by the seaweed, of breaking a leg or an arm, she hastened, almost running, plunging through the pools without looking, straight to her other son.

Seeing her approach, Jean called out:

"Well, mother? So you have made the effort?"

Without a word she seized him by the arm, as if to say: "Save me, protect me!"

He saw her agitation, and greatly surprised he said:

"How pale you are! What is the matter?"

She stammered out:

"I was nearly falling; I was frightened at the rocks."

So then Jean guided her, supported her, explained the sport to her that she might take an interest in it. But as she scarcely heeded him, and as he was bursting with the desire to confide in some one, he led her away and in a low voice said to her:

"Guess what I have done!"

"But — what — I don't know."

"Guess."

"I cannot. I don't know."

"Well, I have told *Mme.* Rosemilly that I wish to marry her."

She did not answer, for her brain was buzzing, her mind in such distress that she could scarcely take it in. She echoed: "Marry her?"

"Yes. Have I done well? She is charming, do not you think?"

"Yes, charming. You have done very well."

"Then you approve?"

"Yes, I approve."

"But how strangely you say so! I could fancy that — that you were not glad."

"Yes, indeed, I am — very glad."

"Really and truly?"

"Really and truly."

And to prove it she threw her arms round him and kissed him heartily, with warm motherly kisses. Then, when she had wiped her eyes, which were full of tears, she observed upon the beach a man lying flat at full length like a dead body, his face hidden against the stones; it was the other one, Pierre, sunk in thought and desperation.

At this she led her little Jean farther away, quite to the edge of the waves, and there they talked for a long time of this marriage on which he had set his heart.

The rising tide drove them back to rejoin the fishers, and then they all made their way to the shore. They roused Pierre, who pretended to be sleeping; and then came a long dinner washed down with many kinds of wine.

VII

In the break, on their way home, all the men dozed excepting Jean. Beausire and Roland dropped every five minutes on to a neighbour's shoulder which repelled them with a shove. Then they sat up, ceased to snore, opened their eyes, muttered, "A lovely evening!" and almost immediately fell over on the other side.

By the time they reached Havre their drowsiness was so heavy that they had great difficulty in shaking it off, and Beausire even refused to go to Jean's rooms where tea was waiting for them. He had to be set down at his own door.

The young lawyer was to sleep in his new abode for the first time; and he was full of rather puerile glee which had suddenly come over him, at being able, that very evening, to show his betrothed the rooms she was so soon to inhabit.

The maid had gone to bed, *Mme.* Roland having declared that she herself would boil the water and make the tea, for she did not like the servants to be kept up for fear of fire.

No one had yet been into the lodgings but herself, Jean, and the workmen, that the surprise might be the greater at their being so pretty.

Jean begged them all to wait a moment in the anteroom. He wanted to light the lamps and candles, and he left *Mme.* Rosemilly in the dark with his father and brother; then he cried: "Come in!" opening the double door to its full width.

The glass gallery, lighted by a chandelier and little coloured lamps hidden among palms, india-rubber plants, and flowers, was first seen like a scene on the stage. There was a spasm of surprise. Roland, dazzled by such luxury, muttered an oath, and felt inclined to clap his hands as if it were a pantomime scene. They then went into the first drawingroom, a small room hung with dead gold and furnished to match. The larger drawingroom — the lawyer's consulting-room, very simple, hung with light salmon-colour — was dignified in style.

Jean sat down in his armchair in front of his writing-table loaded with books, and in a solemn, rather stilted tone, he began:

"Yes, madame, the letter of the law is explicit, and, assuming the consent I promised you, it affords me absolute certainty that the matter we discussed will come to a happy conclusion within three months."

He looked at *Mme.* Rosemilly, who began to smile and glanced at *Mme.* Roland. *Mme.* Roland took her hand and pressed it. Jean, in high spirits, cut a caper like a schoolboy, exclaiming: "Hah! How well the voice carries in this room; it would be capital for speaking in."

And he declaimed:

"If humanity alone, if the instinct of natural benevolence which we feel towards all who suffer, were the motive of the acquittal we expect of you, I should appeal to your compassion, gentlemen of the jury, to your hearts as fathers and as men; but we have law on our side, and it is the point of law only which we shall submit to your judgment."

Pierre was looking at this home which might have been his, and he was restive under his brother's frolics, thinking him really too silly and witless.

Mme. Roland opened a door on the right.

"This is the bedroom," said she.

She had devoted herself to its decoration with all her mother's love. The hangings were of Rouen cretonne imitating old Normandy chintz, and the Louis XV. design — a shepherdess, in a medallion held in the beaks of a pair of doves — gave the walls, curtains, bed, and armchairs a festive, rustic style that was extremely pretty!

"Oh, how charming!" *Mme.* Rosemilly exclaimed, becoming a little serious as they entered the room.

"Do you like it?" asked Jean.

"Immensely."

"You cannot imagine how glad I am."

They looked at each other for a second, with confiding tenderness in the depths of their eyes.

She had felt a little awkward, however, a little abashed, in this room which was to be hers. She noticed as she went in that the bed was a large one, quite a family bed, chosen by *Mme.* Roland, who had no doubt foreseen and hoped that her son should soon marry; and this motherly foresight pleased her, for it seemed to tell her that she was expected in the family.

When they had returned to the drawingroom Jean abruptly threw open the door to the left, showing the circular diningroom with three windows, and decorated to imitate a Chinese lantern. Mother and son had here lavished all the fancy of which they were capable, and the room, with its bamboo furniture, its mandarins, jars, silk hangings glistening with gold, transparent blinds threaded with beads looking like drops of water, fans nailed to the wall to drape the hangings on, screens, swords, masks, cranes made of real feathers, and a myriad trifles in china, wood, paper, ivory, mother-of-pearl, and bronze, had the pretentious and extravagant aspect which unpractised hands and uneducated eyes inevitably stamp on things which need the utmost tact, taste, and artistic education. Nevertheless it was the most admired; only Pierre made some observations with rather bitter irony which hurt his brother's feelings.

Pyramids of fruit stood on the table and monuments of cakes. No one was hungry; they picked at the fruit and nibbled at the cakes rather than ate them. Then, at the end of about an hour, *Mme.* Rosemilly begged to take leave. It was decided that old Roland should accompany her home and set out with her forthwith; while *Mme.* Roland, in the maid's absence, should cast a maternal eye over the house and see that her son had all he needed.

"Shall I come back for you?" asked Roland.

She hesitated a moment and then said: "No, dear old man; go to bed. Pierre will see me home."

As soon as they were gone she blew out the candles, locked up the cakes, the sugar, and liqueurs in a cupboard of which she gave the key to Jean; then she went into the bedroom, turned down the bed, saw that there was fresh water in the water-bottle, and that the window was properly closed.

Pierre and Jean had remained in the little outer drawingroom; the younger still sore under the criticism passed on his taste, and the elder chafing more and more at seeing his brother in this abode. They both sat smoking without a word. Pierre suddenly started to his feet.

"Cristi!" he exclaimed. "The widow looked very jaded this evening. Long excursions do not improve her."

Jean felt his spirit rising with one of those sudden and furious rages which boil up in easy-going natures when they are wounded to the quick. He could hardly find breath to speak, so fierce was his excitement, and he stammered out:

"I forbid you ever again to say 'the widow' when you speak of *Mme.* Rosemilly."

Pierre turned on him haughtily:

"You are giving me an order, I believe. Are you gone mad by any chance?"

Jean had pulled himself up.

"I am not gone mad, but I have had enough of your manners to me."

Pierre sneered: "To you? And are you any part of *Mme.* Rosemilly?"

"You are to know that *Mme.* Rosemilly is about to become my wife."

Pierre laughed the louder.

"Ah! ha! very good. I understand now why I should no longer speak of her as 'the widow.' But you have taken a strange way of announcing your engagement."

"I forbid any jesting about it. Do you hear? I forbid it."

Jean had come close up to him, pale, and his voice quivering with exasperation at this irony levelled at the woman he loved and had chosen.

But on a sudden Pierre turned equally furious. All the accumulation of impotent rage, of suppressed malignity, of rebellion choked down for so long past, all his unspoken despair mounted to his brain, bewildering it like a fit.

"How dare you? How dare you? I order you to hold your tongue — do you hear? I order you."

Jean, startled by his violence, was silent for a few seconds, trying in the confusion of mind which comes of rage to hit on the thing, the phrase, the word, which might stab his brother to the heart. He went on, with an effort to control himself that he might aim true, and to speak slowly that the words might hit more keenly:

"I have known for a long time that you were jealous of me, ever since the day when you first began to talk of 'the widow' because you knew it annoyed me."

Pierre broke into one of those strident and scornful laughs which were common with him.

"Ah! ah! Good Heavens! Jealous of you! I? I? And of what? Good God! Of your person or your mind?"

But Jean knew full well that he had touched the wound in his soul.

"Yes, jealous of me — jealous from your childhood up. And it became fury when you saw that this woman liked me best and would have nothing to say to you."

Pierre, stung to the quick by this assumption, stuttered out:

"I? I? Jealous of you? And for the sake of that goose, that gaby, that simpleton?"

Jean, seeing that he was aiming true, went on:

"And how about the day when you tried to pull me round in the Pearl? And all you said in her presence to show off? Why, you are bursting with jealousy! And when this money was left to me you were maddened, you hated me, you showed it in every possible way, and made every one suffer for it; not an hour passes that you do not spit out the bile that is choking you."

Pierre clenched his fist in his fury with an almost irresistible impulse to fly at his brother and seize him by the throat.

"Hold your tongue," he cried. "At least say nothing about that money."

Jean went on:

"Why your jealousy oozes out at every pore. You never say a word to my father, my mother, or me that does not declare it plainly. You pretend to despise me because you are jealous. You try to pick a quarrel with every one because you are jealous. And now that I am rich you can no longer contain yourself; you have become venomous, you torture our poor mother as if she were to blame!"

Pierre had retired step by step as far as the fireplace, his mouth half open, his eyes glaring, a prey to one of those mad fits of passion in which a crime is committed.

He said again in a lower tone, gasping for breath: "Hold your tongue — for God's sake hold your tongue!"

"No! For a long time I have been wanting to give you my whole mind! You have given me an opening — so much the worse for you. I love the woman; you know it, and laugh her to scorn in my presence — so much the worse for you. But I will break your viper's fangs, I tell you. I will make you treat me with respect."

"With respect — you?"

"Yes — me."

"Respect you? You who have brought shame on us all by your greed."

"You say — ? Say it again — again."

"I say that it does not do to accept one man's fortune when another is reputed to be your father."

Jean stood rigid, not understanding, dazed by the insinuation he scented.

"What? Repeat that once more."

"I say — what everybody is muttering, what every gossip is blabbing — that you are the son of the man who left you his fortune. Well, then — a decent man does not take the money which brings dishonour on his mother."

"Pierre! Pierre! Pierre! Think what you are saying. You? Is it you who give utterance to this infamous thing?"

"Yes, I. It is I. Have you not seen me crushed with woe this month past, spending my nights without sleep and my days in lurking out of sight like an animal? I hardly know what I am doing or what will become of me, so miserable am I, so crazed with shame and grief; for first I guessed — and now I know it."

"Pierre! Be silent. Mother is in the next room. Remember she may hear — she must hear."

But Pierre felt that he must unburden his heart. He told Jean all his suspicions, his arguments, his struggles, his assurance, and the history of the portrait — which had again disappeared. He spoke in short broken sentences almost without coherence — the language of a sleep-walker.

He seemed to have quite forgotten Jean, and his mother in the adjoining room. He talked as if no one were listening, because he must talk, because he had suffered too much and smothered and closed the wound too tightly. It had festered like an abscess and the abscess had burst, splashing every one. He was pacing the room in the way he almost always did, his eyes fixed on vacancy, gesticulating in a frenzy of despair, his voice choked with tearless sobs and revulsions of self-loathing; he spoke as if he were making a confession of his own misery and that of his nearest kin, as though he were casting his woes to the deaf, invisible winds which bore away his words.

Jean, distracted and almost convinced on a sudden by his brother's blind vehemence, was leaning against the door behind which, as he guessed, their mother had heard them.

She could not get out, she must come through his room. She had not come; then it was because she dare not.

Suddenly Pierre stamped his foot.

"I am a brute," he cried, "to have told you this."

And he fled, bareheaded, down the stairs.

The noise of the front-door closing with a slam roused Jean from the deep stupor into which he had fallen. Some seconds had elapsed, longer than hours, and his spirit had sunk into the numb torpor of idiocy. He was conscious, indeed, that he must presently think and act, but he would wait, refusing to understand, to know, to remember, out of fear, weakness, cowardice. He was one of those procrastinators who put everything off till tomorrow; and when he was compelled to come to a decision then and there, still he instinctively tried to gain a few minutes.

But the perfect silence which now reigned, after Pierre's vociferations, the sudden stillness of walls and furniture, with the bright light of six wax candles and two lamps, terrified him so greatly that he suddenly longed to make his escape too.

Then he roused his brain, roused his heart, and tried to reflect.

Never in his life had he had to face a difficulty. There are men who let themselves glide onward like running water. He had been duteous over his tasks for fear of punishment, and had got through his legal studies with credit because his existence was tranquil. Everything in the world seemed to him quite natural and never aroused his particular attention. He loved order, steadiness, and peace, by temperament, his nature having no complications; and face to face with this catastrophe, he found himself like a man who has fallen into the water and cannot swim.

At first he tried to be incredulous. His brother had told a lie, out of hatred and jealousy. But yet, how could he have been so vile as to say such a thing of their mother if he had not himself been distraught by despair? Besides, stamped on Jean's ear, on his sight, on his nerves, on the in-most fibres of his flesh, were certain words, certain tones of anguish, certain gestures of Pierre's, so full of suffering that they were irresistibly convincing; as incontrovertible as certainty itself.

He was too much crushed to stir or even to will. His distress became unbearable; and he knew that behind the door was his mother who had heard everything and was waiting.

What was she doing? Not a movement, not a shudder, not a breath, not a sigh revealed the presence of a living creature behind that panel. Could she have run away? But how? If she had run away — she must have jumped out of the window into the street. A shock of terror roused him — so violent and imperious that he drove the door in rather than opened it, and flung himself into the bedroom.

It was apparently empty, lighted by a single candle standing on the chest of drawers.

Jean flew to the window; it was shut and the shutters bolted. He looked about him, peering into the dark corners with anxious eyes, and he then noticed that the bed-curtains were drawn. He ran forward and opened them. His mother was lying on the bed, her face buried in the pillow which she had pulled up over her ears that she might hear no more.

At first he thought she had smothered herself. Then, taking her by the shoulders, he turned her over without her leaving go of the pillow, which covered her face, and in which she had set her teeth to keep herself from crying out.

But the mere touch of this rigid form, of those arms so convulsively clinched, communicated to him the shock of her unspeakable torture. The strength and determination with which she clutched the linen case full of feathers with her hands and teeth, over her mouth and eyes and ears, that he might neither see her nor speak to her, gave him an idea, by the turmoil it roused in him, of the pitch suffering may rise to, and his heart, his simple heart, was torn with pity. He was no judge, not he; not even a merciful judge; he was a man full of weakness and a son full of love. He remembered nothing of what his brother had told him; he neither reasoned nor argued, he merely laid his two hands on his mother's inert body, and not being able to pull the pillow away, he exclaimed, kissing her dress:

"Mother, mother, my poor mother, look at me!"

She would have seemed to be dead but that an almost imperceptible shudder ran through all her limbs, the vibration of a strained cord. And he repeated:

"Mother, mother, listen to me. It is not true. I know that it is not true."

A spasm seemed to come over her, a fit of suffocation; then she suddenly began to sob into the pillow. Her sinews relaxed, her rigid muscles yielded, her fingers gave way and left go of the linen; and he uncovered her face.

She was pale, quite colourless; and from under her closed lids tears were stealing. He threw his arms round her neck and kissed her eyes, slowly, with long heartbroken kisses, wet with her tears; and he said again and again:

"Mother, my dear mother, I know it is not true. Do not cry; I know it. It is not true."

She raised herself, she sat up, looked in his face, and with an effort of courage such as it must cost in some cases to kill one's self, she said:

"No, my child; it is true."

And they remained speechless, each in the presence of the other. For some minutes she seemed again to be suffocating, craning her throat and throwing back her head to get breath; then she once more mastered herself and went on:

"It is true, my child. Why lie about it? It is true. You would not believe me if I denied it."

She looked like a crazy creature. Overcome by alarm, he fell on his knees by the bedside, murmuring:

"Hush, mother, be silent." She stood up with terrible determination and energy.

"I have nothing more to say, my child. Goodbye." And she went towards the door.

He threw his arms about her exclaiming:

"What are you doing, mother; where are you going?"

"I do not know. How should I know — There is nothing left for me to do, now that I am alone."

She struggled to be released. Holding her firmly, he could find only words to say again and again:

"Mother, mother, mother!" And through all her efforts to free herself she was saying:

"No, no. I am not your mother now, poor boy — goodbye."

It struck him clearly that if he let her go now he should never see her again; lifting her up in his arms he carried her to an armchair, forced her into it, and kneeling down in front of her barred her in with his arms.

"You shall not quit this spot, mother. I love you and I will keep you! I will keep you always — I love you and you are mine."

She murmured in a dejected tone:

"No, my poor boy, it is impossible. You weep tonight, but tomorrow you would turn me out of the house. You, even you, could not forgive me."

He replied: "I? I? How little you know me!" with such a burst of genuine affection that, with a cry, she seized his head by the hair with both hands, and dragging him violently to her kissed him distractedly all over his face.

Then she sat still, her cheek against his, feeling the warmth of his skin through his beard, and she whispered in his ear: "No, my little Jean, you would not forgive me tomorrow. You think so, but you deceive yourself. You have forgiven me this evening, and that forgiveness has saved my life; but you must never see me again."

And he repeated, clasping her in his arms:

"Mother, do not say that."

"Yes, my child, I must go away. I do not know where, nor how I shall set about it, nor what I shall do; but it must be done. I could never look at you, nor kiss you, do you understand?"

Then he in his turn spoke into her ear:

"My little mother, you are to stay, because I insist, because I want you. And you must pledge your word to obey me, now, at once."

"No, my child."

"Yes, mother, you must; do you hear? You must."

"No, my child, it is impossible. It would be condemning us all to the tortures of hell. I know what that torment is; I have known it this month past. Your feelings are touched now, but when that is over, when you look on me as Pierre does, when you remember what I have told you — oh, my Jean, think — think — I am your mother!"

"I will not let you leave me, mother. I have no one but you."

"But think, my son, we can never see each other again without both of us blushing, without my feeling that I must die of shame, without my eyes falling before yours."

"But it is not so, mother."

"Yes, yes, yes, it is so! Oh, I have understood all your poor brother's struggles, believe me! All — from the very first day. Now, when I hear his step in the house my heart beats as if it would burst, when I hear his voice I am ready to faint. I still had you; now I have you no longer. Oh, my little Jean! Do you think I could live between you two?"

"Yes, I should love you so much that you would cease to think of it."

"As if that were possible!"

"But it is possible."

"How do you suppose that I could cease to think of it, with your brother and you on each hand? Would you cease to think of it, I ask you?"

"I? I swear I should."

"Why you would think of it at every hour of the day."

"No, I swear it. Besides, listen, if you go away I will enlist and get killed."

This boyish threat quite overcame her; she clasped Jean in a passionate and tender embrace. He went on:

"I love you more than you think — ah, much more, much more. Come, be reasonable. Try to stay for only one week. Will you promise me one week? You cannot refuse me that?"

She laid her two hands on Jean's shoulders, and holding him at arm's length she said:

"My child, let us try and be calm and not give way to emotions. First, listen to me. If I were ever to hear from your lips what I have heard for this month past from your brother, if I were once to see in your eyes what I read in his, if I could fancy from a word or a look that I was as odious to you as I am to him — within one hour, mark me — within one hour I should be gone forever."

"Mother, I swear to you — "

"Let me speak. For a month past I have suffered all that any creature can suffer. From the moment when I perceived that your brother, my other son, suspected me, that as the minutes went by, he guessed the truth, every moment of my life has been a martyrdom which no words could tell you."

Her voice was so full of woe that the contagion of her misery brought the tears to Jean's eyes. He tried to kiss her, but she held him off.

"Leave me — listen; I still have so much to say to make you understand. But you never can understand. You see, if I stayed — I must — no, no. I cannot."

"Speak on, mother, speak."

"Yes, indeed, for at least I shall not have deceived you. You want me to stay with you? For what — for us to be able to see each other, speak to each other, meet at any hour of the day at home, for I no longer dare open a door for fear of finding your brother behind it. If we are to do that, you must not forgive me — nothing is so wounding as forgiveness — but you must owe me no grudge for what I have done. You must feel yourself strong enough, and so far unlike the rest of the world, as to be able to say to yourself that you are not Roland's son without blushing for the fact or despising me. I have suffered enough — I have suffered too much; I can bear no more, no indeed, no more! And it is not a thing of yesterday, mind you, but of long, long years. But you could never understand that; how should you! If you and I are to live together and kiss each other, my little Jean, you must believe that though I was your father's mistress I was yet more truly his wife, his real wife; that, at the bottom of my heart, I cannot be ashamed of it; that I have no regrets; that I love him still even in death; that I shall always love him and never loved any other man; that he was my life, my joy, my hope, my comfort, everything — everything in the world to me for so long! Listen, my boy, before God, who hears me, I should never have had a joy in my existence if I had not met him; never anything — not a touch of tenderness or kindness, not one of those hours which make us regret growing old — nothing. I owe everything to him! I had but him in the world, and you two boys, your brother and you. But for you, all would have been empty, dark, and void as the night. I should never have loved, or known, or cared for anything — I should not even have wept — for I have wept, my little Jean; oh, yes, and bitter tears, since we came to Havre. I was his wholly and forever; for ten years I was as much his wife as he was my husband before God who created us for each other. And then I began to see that he loved me less. He was always kind and courteous, but I was not what I had been to him. It was all over! Oh, how I have cried! How dreadful and delusive life is! Nothing lasts. Then we came here — I never saw him again; he never came. He promised it in every letter. I was always expecting him, and I never saw him again — and now he is dead! But he still cared for us since he remembered you. I shall love him to my latest breath, and I never will deny him, and I love you because you are his child, and I could never be ashamed of him before you. Do you understand? I could not. So if you wish me to remain you must accept the situation as his son, and we will talk of him sometimes; and you must love him a little and we must think of him when we look at each other. If you will not do this — if you cannot — then goodbye, my child; it is impossible that we should live together. Now, I will act by your decision."

Jean replied gently:

"Stay, mother."

She clasped him in her arms, and her tears flowed again; then, with her face against his, she went on:

"Well, but Pierre. What can we do about Pierre?"

Jean answered:

"We will find some plan! You cannot live with him any longer."

At the thought of her elder son she was convulsed with terror.

"No, I cannot; no, no!" And throwing herself on Jean's breast she cried in distress of mind:

"Save me from him, you, my little one. Save me; do something — I don't know what. Think of something. Save me."

"Yes, mother, I will think of something."

"And at once. You must, this minute. Do not leave me. I am so afraid of him — so afraid."

"Yes, yes; I will hit on some plan. I promise you I will."

"But at once; quick, quick! You cannot imagine what I feel when I see him."

Then she murmured softly in his ear: "Keep me here, with you."

He paused, reflected, and with his blunt good-sense saw at once the dangers of such an arrangement. But he had to argue for a long time, combating her scared, terror-stricken insistence.

"Only for tonight," she said. "Only for tonight. And tomorrow morning you can send word to Roland that I was taken ill."

"That is out of the question, as Pierre left you here. Come, take courage. I will arrange everything, I promise you, tomorrow; I will be with you by nine o'clock. Come, put on your bonnet. I will take you home."

"I will do just what you desire," she said with a childlike impulse of timidity and gratitude.

She tried to rise, but the shock had been too much for her; she could not stand.

He made her drink some sugared water and smell at some salts, while he bathed her temples with vinegar. She let him do what he would, exhausted, but comforted, as after the pains of childbirth. At last she could walk and she took his arm. The town hall struck three as they went past.

Outside their own door Jean kissed her, saying:

"Goodnight, mother, keep up your courage."

She stealthily crept up the silent stairs, and into her room, undressed quickly, and slipped into bed with a reawakened sense of that long-forgotten sin. Roland was snoring. In all the house Pierre alone was awake, and had heard her come in.

VIII

When he got back to his lodgings Jean dropped on a sofa; for the sorrows and anxieties which made his brother long to be moving, and to flee like a hunted prey, acted differently on his torpid nature and broke the strength of his arms and legs. He felt too limp to stir a finger, even to get to bed; limp body and soul, crushed and heartbroken. He had not been hit, as Pierre had been, in the purity of filial love, in the secret dignity which is the refuge of a proud heart; he was overwhelmed by a stroke of fate which, at the same time, threatened his own nearest interests.

When at last his spirit was calmer, when his thoughts had settled like water that has been stirred and lashed, he could contemplate the situation which had come before him. If he had learned the secret of his birth through any other channel he would assuredly have been very wroth and very deeply pained, but after his quarrel with his brother, after the violent and brutal betrayal which had shaken his nerves, the agonizing emotion of his mother's confession had so bereft him of energy that he could not rebel. The shock to his feeling had been so great as to sweep away in an irresistible tide of pathos, all prejudice, and all the sacred delicacy of natural morality. Besides, he was not a man made for resistance. He did not like contending against any one, least of all against himself, so he resigned himself at once; and by instinctive tendency, a congenital love of peace, and of an easy and tranquil life, he began to anticipate the agitations which must surge up around him and at once be his ruin. He foresaw that they were inevitable, and to avert them he made up his mind to superhuman efforts of energy and activity. The knot must be cut immediately, this very day; for even he had fits of that imperious demand for a swift solution which is the only strength of weak natures, incapable of a prolonged effort of will. His lawyer's mind, accustomed as it was to disentangling and studying complicated situations and questions of domestic difficulties in families that had got out of gear, at once foresaw the more immediate consequences of his brother's state of mind. In spite of himself, he looked at the issue from an almost professional point of view, as though he had to legislate for the future relations of certain clients after a moral disaster. Constant friction against Pierre had certainly become unendurable. He could easily evade it, no doubt, by living in his own lodgings; but even then it was not possible that their mother should live under the same roof with her elder son. For a long time he sat meditating, motionless, on the cushions, devising and rejecting various possibilities, and finding nothing that satisfied him.

But suddenly an idea took him by storm. This fortune which had come to him. Would an honest man keep it?

"No," was the first immediate answer, and he made up his mind that it must go to the poor. It was hard, but it could not be helped. He would sell his furniture and work like any other man, like any other beginner. This manful and painful resolution spurred his courage; he rose and went to the window, leaning his forehead against the pane. He had been poor; he could become poor again. After all he should not die of it. His eyes were fixed on the gas lamp burning at the opposite side of the street. A woman, much belated, happened to pass; suddenly he thought of *Mme.* Rosemilly with a pang at his heart, the shock of deep feeling which comes of a cruel suggestion. All the dire results of his decision rose up before him together. He would have to renounce his marriage, renounce happiness, renounce everything. Could he do such a thing after having pledged himself to her? She had accepted him knowing him to be rich. She would take him still if he were poor; but had he any right to demand such a sacrifice? Would it not be better to keep this money in trust, to be restored to the poor at some future date.

And in his soul, where selfishness put on a guise of honesty, all these specious interests were struggling and contending. His first scruples yielded to ingenious reasoning, then came to the top again, and again disappeared.

He sat down again, seeking some decisive motive, some all-sufficient pretext to solve his hesitancy and convince his natural rectitude. Twenty times over had he asked himself this question: "Since I am this man's son, since I know and acknowledge it, is it not natural that I should also accept the inheritance?"

But even this argument could not suppress the "No" murmured by his inmost conscience.

Then came the thought: "Since I am not the son of the man I always believed to be my father, I can take nothing from him, neither during his lifetime nor after his death. It would be neither dignified nor equitable. It would be robbing my brother."

This new view of the matter having relieved him and quieted his conscience, he went to the window again.

"Yes," he said to himself, "I must give up my share of the family inheritance. I must let Pierre have the whole of it, since I am not his father's son. That is but just. Then is it not just that I should keep my father's money?"

Having discerned that he could take nothing of Roland's savings, having decided on giving up the whole of this money, he agreed; he resigned himself to keeping Marechal's; for if he rejected both he would find himself reduced to beggary.

This delicate question being thus disposed of he came back to that of Pierre's presence in the family. How was he to be got rid of? He was giving up his search for any practical solution when the whistle of a steam-vessel coming into port seemed to blow him an answer by suggesting a scheme.

Then he threw himself on his bed without undressing, and dozed and dreamed till daybreak.

At a little before nine he went out to ascertain whether his plans were feasible. Then, after making sundry inquiries and calls, he went to his old home. His mother was waiting for him in her room.

"If you had not come," she said, "I should never have dared to go down."

In a minute Roland's voice was heard on the stairs: "Are we to have nothing to eat to-day, hang it all?"

There was no answer, and he roared out, with a thundering oath this time: "Josephine, what the devil are you about?"

The girl's voice came up from the depths of the basement.

"Yes, M'sieu — what is it?"

"Where is your Miss'es?"

"Madame is upstairs with M'sieu Jean."

Then he shouted, looking up at the higher floor: "Louise!"

Mme. Roland half opened her door and answered:

"What is it, my dear?"

"Are we to have nothing to eat to-day, hang it all?"

"Yes, my dear, I am coming."

And she went down, followed by Jean.

Roland, as soon as he saw him, exclaimed:

"Hallo! There you are! Sick of your home already?"

"No, father, but I had something to talk over with mother this morning."

Jean went forward holding out his hand, and when he felt his fingers in the old man's fatherly clasp, a strange, unforeseen emotion thrilled through him, and a sense as of parting and farewell without return.

Mme. Roland asked:

"Pierre is not come down?"

Her husband shrugged his shoulders.

"No, but never mind him; he is always behindhand. We will begin without him."

She turned to Jean:

"You had better go to call him, my child; it hurts his feelings if we do not wait for him."

"Yes, mother. I will go."

And the young man went. He mounted the stairs with the fevered determination of a man who is about to fight a duel and who is in a fright. When he knocked at the door Pierre said:

"Come in."

He went in. The elder was writing, leaning over his table.

"Good-morning," said Jean.

Pierre rose.

"Good-morning!" and they shook hands as if nothing had occurred.

"Are you not coming down to breakfast?"

"Well — you see — I have a good deal to do." The elder brother's voice was tremulous, and his anxious eye asked his younger brother what he meant to do.

"They are waiting for you."

"Oh! There is — is my mother down?"

"Yes, it was she who sent me to fetch you."

"Ah, very well; then I will come."

At the door of the diningroom he paused, doubtful about going in first; then he abruptly opened the door and saw his father and mother seated at the table opposite each other.

He went straight up to her without looking at her or saying a word, and bending over her, offered his forehead for her to kiss, as he had done for some time past, instead of kissing her on both cheeks as of old. He supposed that she put her lips near but he did not feel them on his brow, and he straightened himself with a throbbing heart after this feint of a caress. And he wondered:

"What did they say to each other after I had left?"

Jean constantly addressed her tenderly as "mother," or "dear mother," took care of her, waited on her, and poured out her wine.

Then Pierre understood that they had wept together, but he could not read their minds. Did Jean believe in his mother's guilt, or think his brother a base wretch?

And all his self-reproach for having uttered the horrible thing came upon him again, choking his throat and his tongue, and preventing his either eating or speaking.

He was now a prey to an intolerable desire to fly, to leave the house which was his home no longer, and these persons who were bound to him by such imperceptible ties. He would gladly have been off that moment, no matter whither, feeling that everything was over, that he could not endure to stay with them, that his presence was torture to them, and that they would bring on him incessant suffering too great to endure. Jean was talking, chatting with Roland. Pierre, as he did not listen, did not hear. But he presently was aware of a pointed tone in his brother's voice and paid more attention to his words. Jean was saying:

"She will be the finest ship in their fleet. They say she is of 6,500 tons. She is to make her first trip next month."

Roland was amazed.

"So soon? I thought she was not to be ready for sea this summer."

"Yes. The work has been pushed forward very vigorously, to get her through her first voyage before the autumn. I looked in at the Company's office this morning, and was talking to one of the directors."

"Indeed! Which of them?"

"M. Marchand, who is a great friend of the Chairman of the Board."

"Oh! Do you know him?"

"Yes. And I wanted to ask him a favour."

"Then you will get me leave to go over every part of the Lorraine as soon as she comes into port?"

"To be sure; nothing could be easier."

Then Jean seemed to hesitate, to be weighing his words, and to want to lead up to a difficult subject. He went on:

"On the whole, life is very endurable on board those great Transatlantic liners. More than half the time is spent on shore in two splendid cities — New York and Havre; and the remainder at sea with delightful company. In fact, very pleasant acquaintances are sometimes made among the passengers, and very useful in after-life — yes, really very useful. Only think, the captain, with his perquisites on coal, can make as much as twenty-five thousand francs a year or more."

Roland muttered an oath followed by a whistle, which testified to his deep respect for the sum and the captain.

Jean went on:

"The purser makes as much as ten thousand, and the doctor has a fixed salary of five thousand, with lodgings, keep, light, firing, service, and everything, which makes it up to ten thousand at least. That is very good pay."

Pierre raising his eyes met his brother's and understood.

Then, after some hesitation, he asked:

"Is it very hard to get a place as medical man on board a Transatlantic liner?"

"Yes — and no. It all depends on circumstances and recommendation."

There was a long pause; then the doctor began again.

"Next month, you say, the Lorraine is to sail?"

"Yes. On the 7th."

And they said nothing more.

Pierre was considering. It certainly would be a way out of many difficulties if he could embark as medical officer on board the steamship. By-and-by he could see; he might perhaps give it up. Meanwhile he would be gaining a living, and asking for nothing from his parents. Only two days since he had been forced to sell his watch, for he would no longer hold out his hand to beg of his mother. So he had no other resource left, no opening to enable him to eat the bread of any house but this which had become uninhabitable, or sleep in any other bed, or under any other roof. He presently said, with some little hesitation:

"If I could, I would very gladly sail in her."

Jean asked:

"What should hinder you?"

"I know no one in the Transatlantic Shipping Company."

Roland was astounded.

"And what has become of all your fine schemes for getting on?"

Pierre replied in a low voice:

"There are times when we must bring ourselves to sacrifice everything and renounce our fondest hopes. And after all it is only to make a beginning, a way of saving a few thousand francs to start fair with afterward."

His father was promptly convinced.

"That is very true. In a couple of years you can put by six or seven thousand francs, and that well laid out, will go a long way. What do you think of the matter, Louise?"

She replied in a voice so low as to be scarcely audible:

"I think Pierre is right."

Roland exclaimed:

"I will go and talk it over with M. Poulin: I know him very well. He is assessor of the Chamber of Commerce and takes an interest in the affairs of the Company. There is M. Lenient, too, the shipowner, who is intimate with one of the vice-chairmen."

Jean asked his brother:

"Would you like me to feel my way with M. Marchand at once?"

"Yes, I should be very glad."

After thinking a few minutes Pierre added:

"The best thing I can do, perhaps, will be to write to my professors at the college of Medicine, who had a great regard for me. Very inferior men are sometimes shipped on board those vessels. Letters of strong recommendation from such professors as Mas-Roussel, Remusot, Flanche, and Borriquel would do more for me in an hour than all the doubtful introductions in the world. It would be enough if your friend M. Marchand would lay them before the board."

Jean approved heartily.

"Your idea is really capital." And he smiled, quite reassured, almost happy, sure of success and incapable of allowing himself to be unhappy for long.

"You will write to-day?" he said.

"Directly. Now; at once. I will go and do so. I do not care for any coffee this morning; I am too nervous."

He rose and left the room.

Then Jean turned to his mother:

"And you, mother, what are you going to do?"

"Nothing. I do not know."

"Will you come with me to call on *Mme.* Rosemilly?"

"Why, yes — yes."

"You know I must positively go to see her to-day."

"Yes, yes. To be sure."

"Why must you positively?" asked Roland, whose habit it was never to understand what was said in his presence.

"Because I promised her I would."

"Oh, very well. That alters the case." And he began to fill his pipe, while the mother and son went upstairs to make ready.

When they were in the street Jean said:

"Will you take my arm, mother?"

He was never accustomed to offer it, for they were in the habit of walking side by side. She accepted and leaned on him.

For some time they did not speak; then he said:

"You see that Pierre is quite ready and willing to go away."

She murmured:

"Poor boy!"

"But why 'poor boy'? He will not be in the least unhappy on board the Lorraine."

"No — I know. But I was thinking of so many things."

And she thought for a long time, her head bent, accommodating her step to her son's; then, in the peculiar voice in which we sometimes give utterance to the conclusion of long and secret meditations, she exclaimed:

"How horrible life is! If by any chance we come across any sweetness in it, we sin in letting ourselves be happy, and pay dearly for it afterward."

He said in a whisper:

"Do not speak of that any more, mother."

"Is that possible? I think of nothing else."

"You will forget it."

Again she was silent; then with deep regret she said:

"How happy I might have been, married to another man!"

She was visiting it on Roland now, throwing all the responsibility of her sin on his ugliness, his stupidity, his clumsiness, the heaviness of his intellect, and the vulgarity of his person. It was to this that it was owing that she had betrayed him, had driven one son to desperation, and had been forced to utter to the other the most agonizing confession that can make a mother's heart bleed. She muttered: "It is so frightful for a young girl to have to marry such a husband as mine."

Jean made no reply. He was thinking of the man he had hitherto believed to be his father; and possibly the vague notion he had long since conceived, of that father's inferiority, with his brother's constant irony, the scornful indifference of others, and the very maidservant's contempt for Roland, had somewhat prepared his mind for his mother's terrible avowal. It had all made it less dreadful to him to find that he was another man's son; and if, after the great shock and agitation of the previous evening, he had not suffered the reaction of rage, indignation, and rebellion which *Mme.* Roland had feared, it was because he had long been unconsciously chafing under the sense of being the child of this well-meaning lout.

They had now reached the dwelling of *Mme.* Rosemilly.

She lived on the road to Sainte-Adresse, on the second floor of a large tenement which she owned. The windows commanded a view of the whole roadstead.

On seeing *Mme.* Roland, who entered first, instead of merely holding out her hands as usual, she put her arms round her and kissed her, for she divined the purpose of her visit.

The furniture of this drawingroom, all in stamped velvet, was always shrouded in chair-covers. The walls, hung with flowered paper, were graced by four engravings, the purchase of her late husband, the captain. They represented sentimental scenes of seafaring life. In the first a fisherman's wife was seen, waving a handkerchief on shore, while the vessel which bore away her husband vanished on the horizon. In the second the same woman, on her knees on the same shore, under a sky shot with lightning, wrung her arms as she gazed into the distance at her husband's boat which was going to the bottom amid impossible waves.

The others represented similar scenes in a higher rank of society. A young lady with fair hair, resting her elbows on the ledge of a large steamship quitting the shore, gazed at the already distant coast with eyes full of tears and regret. Whom is she leaving behind?

Then the same young lady sitting by an open widow with a view of the sea, had fainted in an armchair; a letter she had dropped lay at her feet. So he is dead! What despair!

Visitors were generally much moved and charmed by the commonplace pathos of these obvious and sentimental works. They were at once intelligible without question or explanation, and the poor women were to be pitied, though the nature of the grief of the more elegant of the two was not precisely known. But this very doubt contributed to the sentiment. She had, no doubt, lost her lover. On entering the room the eye was immediately attracted to these four pictures, and riveted as if fascinated. If it wandered it was only to return and contemplate the four expressions on the faces of the two women, who were as like each other as two sisters. And the very style of these works, in their shining frames, crisp, sharp, and highly finished, with the elegance of a fashion plate, suggested a sense of cleanliness and propriety which was confirmed by the rest of the fittings. The seats were always in precisely the same order, some against the wall and some round the circular centre-table. The immaculately white curtains hung in such straight and regular pleats that one longed to crumple them a little; and never did a grain of dust rest on the shade under which the gilt clock, in the taste of the first empire — a terrestrial globe supported by Atlas on his knees — looked like a melon left there to ripen.

The two women as they sat down somewhat altered the normal position of their chairs.

"You have not been out this morning?" asked *Mme.* Roland.

"No. I must own to being rather tired."

And she spoke as if in gratitude to Jean and his mother, of all the pleasure she had derived from the expedition and the prawn-fishing.

"I ate my prawns this morning," she added, "and they were excellent. If you felt inclined we might go again one of these days."

The young man interrupted her:

"Before we start on a second fishing excursion, suppose we complete the first?"

"Complete it? It seems to me quite finished."

"Nay, madame, I, for my part, caught something on the rocks of Saint Jouain which I am anxious to carry home with me."

She put on an innocent and knowing look.

"You? What can it be? What can you have found?"

"A wife. And my mother and I have come to ask you whether she had changed her mind this morning."

She smiled: "No, monsieur. I never change my mind."

And then he held out his hand, wide open, and she put hers into it with a quick, determined movement. Then he said: "As soon as possible, I hope."

"As soon as you like."

"In six weeks?"

"I have no opinion. What does my future motherin-law say?"

Mme. Roland replied with a rather melancholy smile:

"I? Oh, I can say nothing. I can only thank you for having accepted Jean, for you will make him very happy."

"We will do our best, mamma."

Somewhat overcome, for the first time, *Mme.* Rosemilly rose, and throwing her arms round *Mme.* Roland, kissed her a long time as a child of her own might have done; and under this new embrace the poor woman's sick heart swelled with deep emotion. She could not have expressed the feeling; it was at once sad and sweet. She had lost her son, her big boy, but in return she had found a daughter, a grown-up daughter.

When they faced each other again, and were seated, they took hands and remained so, looking at each and smiling, while they seemed to have forgotten Jean.

Then they discussed a number of things which had to be thought of in view of an early marriage, and when everything was settled and decided *Mme.* Rosemilly seemed suddenly to remember a further detail and asked: "You have consulted M. Roland, I suppose?"

A flush of colour mounted at the same instant on the face of both mother and son. It was the mother who replied:

"Oh, no, it is quite unnecessary!" Then she hesitated, feeling that some explanation was needed, and added: "We do everything without saying anything to him. It is enough to tell him what we have decided on."

Mme. Rosemilly, not in the least surprised, only smiled, taking it as a matter of course, for the good man counted for so little.

When *Mme.* Roland was in the street again with her son she said:

"Suppose we go to your rooms for a little while. I should be glad to rest."

She felt herself homeless, shelterless, her own house being a terror to her.

They went into Jean's apartments.

As soon as the door was closed upon her she heaved a deep sigh, as if that bolt had placed her in safety, but then, instead of resting as she had said, she began to open the cupboards, to count the piles of linen, the pocket-handkerchiefs, and socks. She changed the arrangement to place them in more harmonious order, more pleasing to her housekeeper's eye; and when she had put everything to her mind, laying out the towels, the shirts, and the drawers on their several shelves and dividing all the linen into three principal classes, body-linen, household-linen, and table-linen, she drew back and contemplated the results, and called out:

"Come here, Jean, and see how nice it looks."

He went and admired it to please her.

On a sudden, when he had sat down again, she came softly up behind his armchair, and putting her right arm round his neck she kissed him, while she laid on the chimney-shelf a small packet wrapped in white paper which she held in the other hand.

"What is that?" he asked. Then, as she made no reply, he understood, recognising the shape of the frame.

"Give it me!" he said.

She pretended not to hear him, and went back to the linen cupboards. He got up hastily, took the melancholy relic, and going across the room, put it in the drawer of his writing-table, which he locked and double locked. She wiped away a tear with the tip of her finger, and said in a rather quavering voice: "Now I am going to see whether your new servant keeps the kitchen in good order. As she is out I can look into everything and make sure."

IX

Letters of recommendation from Professors Mas-Roussel, Remusot, Flache, and Borriquel, written in the most flattering terms with regard to Dr. Pierre Roland, their pupil, had been submitted by M. Marchand to the directors of the Transatlantic Shipping Co., seconded by M. Poulin, judge of the Chamber of Commerce, M. Lenient, a great shipowner, and Mr. Marival, deputy to the Mayor of Havre, and a particular friend of Captain Beausires's. It proved that no medical officer had yet been appointed to the Lorraine, and Pierre was lucky enough to be nominated within a few days.

The letter announcing it was handed to him one morning by Josephine, just as he was dressed. His first feeling was that of a man condemned to death who is told that his sentence is commuted; he had an immediate sense of relief at the thought of his early departure and of the peaceful life on board, cradled by the rolling waves, always wandering, always moving. His life under his father's roof was now that of a stranger, silent and reserved. Ever since the evening when he allowed the shameful secret he had discovered to escape him in his brother's presence, he had felt that the last ties to his kindred were broken. He was harassed by remorse for having told this thing to Jean. He felt that it was odious, indecent, and brutal, and yet it was a relief to him to have uttered it.

He never met the eyes either of his mother or his brother; to avoid his gaze theirs had become surprisingly alert, with the cunning of foes who fear to cross each other. He was always wondering: "What can she have said to Jean? Did she confess or deny it? What does my brother believe? What does he think of her — what does he think of me?" He could not guess, and it drove him to frenzy. And he scarcely ever spoke to them, excepting when Roland was by, to avoid his questioning.

As soon as he received the letter announcing his appointment he showed it at once to his family. His father, who was prone to rejoicing over everything, clapped his hands. Jean spoke seriously, though his heart was full of gladness: "I congratulate you with all my heart, for I know there were several other candidates. You certainly owe it to your professors' letters."

His mother bent her head and murmured:

"I am very glad you have been successful."

After breakfast he went to the Company's offices to obtain information on various particulars, and he asked the name of the doctor on board the Picardie, which was to sail next day, to inquire of him as to the details of his new life and any details he might think useful.

Dr. Pirette having gone on board, Pierre went to the ship, where he was received in a little state-room by a young man with a fair beard, not unlike his brother. They talked together a long time.

In the hollow depths of the huge ship they could hear a confused and continuous commotion; the noise of bales and cases pitched down into the hold mingling with footsteps, voices, the creaking of the machinery lowering the freight, the boatswain's whistle, and the clatter of chains dragged or wound on to capstans by the snorting and panting engine which sent a slight vibration from end to end of the great vessel.

But when Pierre had left his colleague and found himself in the street once more, a new form of melancholy came down on him, enveloping him like the fogs which roll over the sea, coming up from the ends of the world and holding in their intangible density something mysteriously impure, as it were the pestilential breath of a far-away, unhealthy land.

In his hours of greatest suffering he had never felt himself so sunk in a foul pit of misery. It was as though he had given the last wrench; there was no fibre of attachment left. In tearing up the roots of every affection he had not hitherto had the distressful feeling which now came over him, like that of a lost dog. It was no longer a torturing mortal pain, but the frenzy of a forlorn and homeless animal, the physical anguish of a vagabond creature without a roof for shelter, lashed by the rain, the wind, the storm, all the brutal forces of the universe. As he set foot on the vessel, as he went into the cabin rocked by the waves, the very flesh of the man, who had always slept in a motionless and steady bed, had risen up against the insecurity henceforth of all his morrows. Till now that flesh had been protected by a solid wall built into the earth which held it, by the certainty of resting in the same spot, under a roof which could resist the gale. Now all that, which it was a pleasure to defy in the warmth of home, must become a peril and a constant discomfort. No earth under foot, only the greedy, heaving, complaining sea; no space around for walking, running, losing the way, only a few yards of planks to pace like a convict among other prisoners; no trees, no gardens, no streets, no houses; nothing but water and clouds. And the ceaseless motion of the ship beneath his feet. On stormy days he must lean against the wainscot, hold on to the doors, cling to the edge of the narrow berth to save himself from rolling out. On calm days he would hear the snorting throb of the screw, and feel the swift flight of the ship, bearing him on in its unpausing, regular, exasperating race.

And he was condemned to this vagabond convict's life solely because his mother had yielded to a man's caresses.

He walked on, his heart sinking with the despairing sorrow of those who are doomed to exile. He no longer felt a haughty disdain and scornful hatred of the strangers he met, but a woeful impulse to speak to them, to tell them all that he had to quit France, to be listened to and comforted. There was in the very depths of his heart the shamefaced need of a beggar who would fain hold out his hand — a timid but urgent need to feel that some one would grieve at his departing.

He thought of Marowsko. The old Pole was the only person who loved him well enough to feel true and keen emotion, and the doctor at once determined to go and see him.

When he entered the shop, the druggist, who was pounding powders in a marble mortar, started and left his work.

"You are never to be seen nowadays," said he.

Pierre explained that he had had a great many serious matters to attend to, but without giving the reason, and he took a seat, asking:

"Well, and how is business doing?"

Business was not doing at all. Competition was fearful, and rich folks rare in that workmen's quarter. Nothing would sell but cheap drugs, and the doctors did not prescribe the costlier and more complicated remedies on which a profit is made of five hundred per cent. The old fellow ended by saying: "If this goes on for three months I shall shut up shop. If I did not count on you, dear good doctor, I should have turned shoeblack by this time."

Pierre felt a pang, and made up his mind to deal the blow at once, since it must be done.

"I — oh, I cannot be of any use to you. I am leaving Havre early next month."

Marowsko took off his spectacles, so great was his agitation.

"You! You! What are you saying?"

"I say that I am going away, my poor friend."

The old man was stricken, feeling his last hope slipping from under him, and he suddenly turned against this man, whom he had followed, whom he loved, whom he had so implicitly trusted, and who forsook him thus.

He stammered out:

"You are surely not going to play me false — you?"

Pierre was so deeply touched that he felt inclined to embrace the old fellow.

"I am not playing you false. I have not found anything to do here, and I am going as medical officer on board a Transatlantic passenger boat."

"O Monsieur Pierre! And you always promised you would help me to make a living!"

"What can I do? I must make my own living. I have not a farthing in the world."

Marowsko said: "It is wrong; what you are doing is very wrong. There is nothing for me but to die of hunger. At my age this is the end of all things. It is wrong. You are forsaking a poor old man who came here to be with you. It is wrong."

Pierre tried to explain, to protest, to give reasons, to prove that he could not have done otherwise; the Pole, enraged by his desertion, would not listen to him, and he ended by saying, with an allusion no doubt to political events:

"You French — you never keep your word!"

At this Pierre rose, offended on his part, and taking rather a high tone he said:

"You are unjust, pere Marowsko; a man must have very strong motives to act as I have done and you ought to understand that. Au revoir — I hope I may find you more reasonable." And he went away.

"Well, well," he thought, "not a soul will feel a sincere regret for me."

His mind sought through all the people he knew or had known, and among the faces which crossed his memory he saw that of the girl at the tavern who had led him to doubt his mother.

He hesitated, having still an instinctive grudge against her, then suddenly reflected on the other hand: "After all, she was right." And he looked about him to find the turning.

The beer-shop, as it happened, was full of people, and also full of smoke. The customers, tradesmen, and labourers, for it was a holiday, were shouting, calling, laughing, and the master himself was waiting on them, running from table to table, carrying away empty glasses and returning them crowned with froth.

When Pierre had found a seat not far from the desk he waited, hoping that the girl would see him and recognise him. But she passed him again and again as she went to and fro, pattering her feet under her skirts with a smart little strut. At last he rapped a coin on the table, and she hurried up.

"What will you take, sir?"

She did not look at him; her mind was absorbed in calculations of the liquor she had served.

"Well," said he, "this is a pretty way of greeting a friend."

She fixed her eyes on his face. "Ah!" said she hurriedly. "Is it you? You are pretty well? But I have not a minute to-day. A bock did you wish for?"

"Yes, a bock!"

When she brought it he said:

"I have come to say goodbye. I am going away."

And she replied indifferently:

"Indeed. Where are you going?"

"To America."

"A very find country, they say."

And that was all!

Really, he was very ill-advised to address her on such a busy day; there were too many people in the cafe.

Pierre went down to the sea. As he reached the jetty he descried the Pearl; his father and Beausire were coming in. Papagris was pulling, and the two men, seated in the stern, smoked their pipes with a look of perfect happiness. As they went past the doctor said to himself: "Blessed are the simple-minded!" And he sat down on one of the benches on the breakwater, to try to lull himself in animal drowsiness.

When he went home in the evening his mother said, without daring to lift her eyes to his face:

"You will want a heap of things to take with you. I have ordered your under-linen, and I went into the tailor's shop about cloth clothes; but is there nothing else you need — things which I, perhaps, know nothing about?"

His lips parted to say, "No, nothing." But he reflected that he must accept the means of getting a decent outfit, and he replied in a very calm voice: "I hardly know myself, yet. I will make inquiries at the office."

He inquired, and they gave him a list of indispensable necessaries. His mother, as she took it from his hand, looked up at him for the first time for very long, and in the depths of her eyes there was the humble expression, gentle, sad, and beseeching, of a dog that has been beaten and begs forgiveness.

On the 1st of October the Lorraine from Saint-Nazaire, came into the harbour of Havre to sail on the 7th, bound for New York, and Pierre Roland was to take possession of the little floating cabin in which henceforth his life was to be confined.

Next day as he was going out, he met his mother on the stairs waiting for him, to murmur in an almost inaudible voice:

"You would not like me to help you to put things to rights on board?"

"No, thank you. Everything is done."

Then she said:

"I should have liked to see your cabin."

"There is nothing to see. It is very small and very ugly."

And he went downstairs, leaving her stricken, leaning against the wall with a wan face.

Now Roland, who had gone over the Lorraine that very day, could talk of nothing all dinnertime but this splendid vessel, and wondered that his wife should not care to see it as their son was to sail on board.

Pierre had scarcely any intercourse with his family during the days which followed. He was nervous, irritable, hard, and his rough speech seemed to lash every one indiscriminately. But the day before he left he was suddenly quite changed, and much softened. As he embraced his parents before going to sleep on board for the first time he said:

"You will come to say goodbye to me on board, will you not?"

Roland exclaimed:

"Why, yes, of course — of course, Louise?"

"Certainly, certainly," she said in a low voice.

Pierre went on: "We sail at eleven precisely. You must be there by halfpast nine at the latest."

"Hah!" cried his father. "A good idea! As soon as we have bid you goodbye, we will make haste on board the Pearl, and look out for you beyond the jetty, so as to see you once more. What do you say, Louise?"

"Certainly."

Roland went on: "And in that way you will not lose sight of us among the crowd which throngs the breakwater when the great liners sail. It is impossible to distinguish your own friends in the mob. Does that meet your views?"

"Yes, to be sure; that is settled."

An hour later he was lying in his berth — a little crib as long and narrow as a coffin. There he remained with his eyes wide open for a long time, thinking over all that had happened during the last two months of his life, especially in his own soul. By dint of suffering and making others suffer, his aggressive and revengeful anguish had lost its edge, like a blunted sword. He scarcely had the heart left in him to owe any one or anything a grudge; he let his rebellious wrath float away down stream, as his life must. He was so weary of wrestling, weary of fighting, weary of hating, weary of everything, that he was quite worn out, and tried to stupefy his heart with forgetfulness as he dropped asleep. He heard vaguely, all about him, the unwonted noises of the ship, slight noises, and scarcely audible on this calm night in port; and he felt no more of the dreadful wound which had tortured him hitherto, but the discomfort and strain of its healing.

He had been sleeping soundly when the stir of the crew roused him. It was day; the tidal train had come down to the pier bringing the passengers from Paris. Then he wandered about the vessel among all these busy, bustling folks inquiring for their cabins, questioning and answering each other at random, in the scare and fuss of a voyage already begun. After greeting the Captain and shaking hands with his comrade the purser, he went into the saloon where some Englishmen were already asleep in the corners. The large low room, with its white marble panels framed in gilt beading, was furnished with looking-glasses, which prolonged, in endless perspective, the long tables, flanked by pivot-seats covered with red velvet. It was fit, indeed, to be the vast floating cosmopolitan dining-hall, where the rich natives of two continents might eat in common. Its magnificent luxury was that of great hotels, and theatres, and public rooms; the imposing and commonplace luxury which appeals to the eye of the millionaire.

The doctor was on the point of turning into the second-class saloon, when he remembered that a large cargo of emigrants had come on board the night before, and he went down to the lower deck. He was met by a sickening smell of dirty, poverty-stricken humanity, an at-mosphere of naked flesh (far more revolting than the odour of fur or the skin of wild beasts). There, in a sort of basement, low and dark, like a gallery in a mine, Pierre could discern some hundreds of men, women, and children, stretched on shelves fixed one above another, or lying on the floor in heaps. He could not see their faces, but could dimly make out this squalid, ragged crowd of wretches, beaten in the struggle for life, worn out and crushed, setting forth, each with a starving wife and weakly children, for an unknown land where they hoped, perhaps, not to die of hunger. And as he thought of their past labour — wasted labour, and barren effort — of the mortal struggle taken up afresh and in vain each day, of the energy expended by this tattered crew who were going to begin again, not knowing where, this life of hideous misery, he longed to cry out to them:

"Tumble yourselves overboard, rather, with your women and your little ones." And his heart ached so with pity that he went away unable to endure the sight.

He found his father, his mother, Jean, and *Mme.* Rosemilly waiting for him in his cabin.

"So early!" he exclaimed.

"Yes," said *Mme.* Roland in a trembling voice. "We wanted to have a little time to see you."

He looked at her. She was dressed all in black as if she were in mourning, and he noticed that her hair, which only a month ago had been gray, was now almost white. It was very difficult to find space for four persons to sit down in the little room, and he himself got on to his bed. The door was left open, and they could see a great crowd hurrying by, as if it were a street on a holiday, for all the friends of the passengers and a host of inquisitive visitors had invaded the huge vessel. They pervaded the passages, the saloons, every corner of the ship; and heads peered in at the doorway while a voice murmured outside: "That is the doctor's cabin."

Then Pierre shut the door; but no sooner was he shut in with his own party than he longed to open it again, for the bustle outside covered their agitation and want of words.

Mme. Rosemilly at last felt she must speak.

"Very little air comes in through those little windows."

"Portholes," said Pierre. He showed her how thick the glass was, to enable it to resist the most violent shocks, and took a long time explaining the fastening. Roland presently asked: "And you have your doctor's shop here?"

The doctor opened a cupboard and displayed an array of phials ticketed with Latin names on white paper labels. He took one out and enumerated the properties of its contents; then a second and a third, a perfect lecture on therapeutics, to which they all listened with great attention. Roland, shaking his head, said again and again: "How very interesting!" There was a tap at the door.

"Come in," said Pierre, and Captain Beausire appeared.

"I am late," he said as he shook hands, "I did not want to be in the way." He, too, sat down on the bed and silence fell once more.

Suddenly the Captain pricked his ears. He could hear the orders being given, and he said:

"It is time for us to be off if we mean to get on board the Pearl to see you once more outside, and bid you goodbye out on the open sea."

Old Roland was very eager about this, to impress the voyagers on board the Lorraine, no doubt, and he rose in haste.

"Goodbye, my boy." He kissed Pierre on the whiskers and then opened the door.

Mme. Roland had not stirred, but sat with downcast eyes, very pale. Her husband touched her arm.

"Come," he said, "we must make haste, we have not a minute to spare."

She pulled herself up, went to her son and offered him first one and then another cheek of white wax which he kissed without saying a word. Then he shook hands with *Mme.* Rosemilly and his brother, asking:

"And when is the wedding to be?"

"I do not know yet exactly. We will make it fit in with one of your return voyages."

At last they were all out of the cabin, and up on deck among the crowd of visitors, porters, and sailors. The steam was snorting in the huge belly of the vessel, which seemed to quiver with impatience.

"Goodbye," said Roland in a great bustle.

"Goodbye," replied Pierre, standing on one of the landing-planks lying between the deck of the Lorraine and the quay. He shook hands all round once more, and they were gone.

"Make haste, jump into the carriage," cried the father.

A fly was waiting for them and took them to the outer harbour, where Papagris had the Pearl in readiness to put out to sea.

There was not a breath of air; it was one of those crisp, still autumn days, when the sheeny sea looks as cold and hard as polished steel.

Jean took one oar, the sailor seized the other and they pulled off. On the breakwater, on the piers, even on the granite parapets, a crowd stood packed, hustling, and noisy, to see the Lorraine come out. The Pearl glided down between these two waves of humanity and was soon outside the mole.

Captain Beausire, seated between the two women, held the tiller, and he said:

"You will see, we shall be close in her way — close."

And the two oarsmen pulled with all their might to get out as far as possible. Suddenly Roland cried out:

"Here she comes! I see her masts and her two funnels! She is coming out of the inner harbour."

"Cheerily, lads!" cried Beausire.

Mme. Roland took out her handkerchief and held it to her eyes.

Roland stood up, clinging to the mast, and answered:

"At this moment she is working round in the outer harbour. She is standing still — now she moves again! She is taking the tow-rope on board no doubt. There she goes. Bravo! She is between the piers! Do you hear the crowd shouting? Bravo! The Neptune has her in tow. Now I see her bows — here she comes — here she is! Gracious Heavens, what a ship! Look! Look!"

Mme. Rosemilly and Beausire looked behind them, the oarsmen ceased pulling; only *Mme.* Roland did not stir.

The immense steamship, towed by a powerful tug, which, in front of her, looked like a caterpillar, came slowly and majestically out of the harbour. And the good people of Havre, who crowded the piers, the beach, and the windows, carried away by a burst of patriotic enthusiasm, cried: "Vive la Lorraine!" with acclamations and applause for this magnificent beginning, this birth of the beautiful daughter given to the sea by the great maritime town.

She, as soon as she had passed beyond the narrow channel between the two granite walls, feeling herself free at last, cast off the tow-ropes and went off alone, like a monstrous creature walking on the waters.

"Here she is — here she comes, straight down on us!" Roland kept shouting; and Beausire, beaming, exclaimed: "What did I promise you! Heh! Do I know the way?"

Jean in a low tone said to his mother: "Look, mother, she is close upon us!" And *Mme.* Roland uncovered her eyes, blinded with tears.

The Lorraine came on, still under the impetus of her swift exit from the harbour, in the brilliant, calm weather. Beausire, with his glass to his eye, called out:

"Look out! M. Pierre is at the stern, all alone, plainly to be seen! Look out!"

The ship was almost touching the Pearl now, as tall as a mountain and as swift as a train. *Mme.* Roland, distraught and desperate, held out her arms towards it; and she saw her son, her Pierre, with his officer's cap on, throwing kisses to her with both hands.

But he was going away, flying, vanishing, a tiny speck already, no more than an imperceptible spot on the enormous vessel. She tried still to distinguish him, but she could not.

Jean took her hand.

"You saw?" he said.

"Yes, I saw. How good he is!"

And they turned to go home.

"Cristi! How fast she goes!" exclaimed Roland with enthusiastic conviction.

The steamer, in fact, was shrinking every second, as though she were melting away in the ocean. *Mme.* Roland, turning back to look at her, watched her disappearing on the horizon, on her way to an unknown land at the other side of the world.

In that vessel which nothing could stay, that vessel which she soon would see no more, was her son, her poor son. And she felt as though half her heart had gone with him; she felt, too, as if her life were ended; yes, and she felt as though she would never see the child again.

"Why are you crying?" asked her husband, "when you know he will be back again within a month."

She stammered out: "I don't know; I cry because I am hurt."

When they had landed, Beausire at once took leave of them to go to breakfast with a friend. Then Jean led the way with *Mme.* Rosemilly, and Roland said to his wife:

"A very fine fellow, all the same, is our Jean."

"Yes," replied the mother.

And her mind being too much bewildered to think of what she was saying, she went on:

"I am very glad that he is to marry *Mme.* Rosemilly."

The worthy man was astounded.

"Heh? What? He is to marry *Mme.* Rosemilly?"

"Yes, we meant to ask your opinion about it this very day."

"Bless me! And has this engagement been long in the wind?"

"Oh, no, only a very few days. Jean wished to make sure that she would accept him before consulting you."

Roland rubbed his hands.

"Very good. Very good. It is capital. I entirely approve."

As they were about to turn off from the quay down the Boulevard Francois, his wife once more looked back to cast a last look at the high seas, but she could see nothing now but a puff of gray smoke, so far away, so faint that it looked like a film of haze.

Strong as Death

Part I

Broad daylight streamed down into the vast studio through a skylight in the ceiling, which showed a large square of dazzling blue, a bright vista of limitless heights of azure, across which passed flocks of birds in rapid flight. But the glad light of heaven hardly entered this severe room, with high ceilings and draped walls, before it began to grow soft and dim, to slumber among the hangings and die in the portieres, hardly penetrating to the dark corners where the gilded frames of portraits gleamed like flame. Peace and sleep seemed imprisoned there, the peace characteristic of an artist's dwelling, where the human soul has toiled. Within these walls, where thought abides, struggles, and becomes exhausted in its violent efforts, everything appears weary and overcome as soon as the energy of action is abated; all seems dead after the great crises of life, and the furniture, the hangings, and the portraits of great personages still unfinished on the canvases, all seem to rest as if the whole place had suffered the master's fatigue and had toiled with him, taking part in the daily renewal of his struggle. A vague, heavy odor of paint, turpentine, and tobacco was in the air, clinging to the rugs and chairs; and no sound broke the deep silence save the sharp short cries of the swallows that flitted above the open skylight, and the dull, ceaseless roar of Paris, hardly heard above the roofs. Nothing moved except a little cloud of smoke that rose intermittently toward the ceiling with every puff that Olivier Bertin, lying upon his divan, blew slowly from a cigarette between his lips.

With gaze lost in the distant sky, he tried to think of a new subject for a painting. What should he do? As yet he did not know. He was by no means resolute and sure of himself as an artist, but was of an uncertain, uneasy spirit, whose undecided inspiration ever hesitated among all the manifestations of art. Rich, illustrious, the gainer of all honors, he nevertheless remained, in these his later years, a man who did not know exactly toward what ideal he had been aiming. He had won the Prix of Rome, had been the defender of traditions, and had evoked, like so many others, the great scenes of history; then, modernizing his tendencies, he had painted living men, but in a way that showed the influence of classic memories. Intelligent, enthusiastic, a worker that clung to his changing dreams, in love with his art, which he knew to perfection, he had acquired, by reason of the delicacy of his mind, remarkable executive ability and great versatility, due in some degree to his hesitations and his experiments in all styles of his art. Perhaps, too, the sudden admiration of the world for his works, elegant, correct, and full of distinctions, influenced his nature and prevented him from becoming what he naturally might have been. Since the triumph of his first success, the desire to please always made him anxious, without his being conscious of it; it influenced his actions and weakened his convictions. This desire to please was apparent in him in many ways, and had contributed much to his glory.

His grace of manner, all his habits of life, the care he devoted to his person, his long-standing reputation for strength and agility as a swordsman and an equestrian, had added further attractions to his steadily growing fame. After his Cleopatra, the first picture that had made him illustrious, Paris suddenly became enamored of him, adopted him, made a pet of him; and all at once he became one of those brilliant, fashionable artists one meets in the Bois, for whose presence hostesses maneuver, and whom the Institute welcomes thenceforth. He had entered it as a conqueror, with the approval of all Paris.

Thus Fortune had led him to the beginning of old age, coddling and caressing him.

Under the influence of the beautiful day, which he knew was glowing without, Bertin sought a poetic subject. He felt somewhat dreamy, however, after his breakfast and his cigarette; he pondered awhile, gazing into space, in fancy sketching rapidly against the blue sky the figures of graceful women in the Bois or on the sidewalk of a street, lovers by the water — all the pleasing fancies in which his thoughts reveled. The changing images stood out against the bright sky, vague and fleeting in the hallucination of his eye, while the swallows, darting through space in ceaseless flight, seemed trying to efface them as if with strokes of a pen.

He found nothing. All these half-seen visions resembled things that he had already done; all the women appeared to be the daughters or the sisters of those that had already been born of his artistic fancy; and the vague fear, that had haunted him for a year, that he had lost the power to create, had made the round of all subjects and exhausted his inspiration, outlined itself distinctly before this review of his work — this lack of power to dream anew, to discover the unknown.

He arose quietly to look among his unfinished sketches, hoping to find something that would inspire him with a new idea.

Still puffing at his cigarette, he proceeded to turn over the sketches, drawings, and rough drafts that he kept in a large old closet; but, soon becoming disgusted with this vain quest, and feeling depressed by the lassitude of his spirits, he tossed away his cigarette, whistled a popular street-song, bent down and picked up a heavy dumb-bell that lay under a chair. Having raised with the other hand a curtain that draped a mirror, which served him in judging the accuracy of a pose, in verifying his perspectives and testing the truth, he placed himself in front of it and began to swing the dumb-bell, meanwhile looking intently at himself.

He had been celebrated in the studios for his strength; then, in the gay world, for his good looks. But now the weight of years was making him heavy. Tall, with broad shoulders and full chest, he had acquired the protruding stomach of an old wrestler, although he kept up his fencing every day and rode his horse with assiduity. His head was still remarkable and as handsome as ever, although in a style different from that of his earlier days. His thick and short white hair set off the black eyes beneath heavy gray eyebrows, while his luxuriant moustache — the moustache of an old soldier — had remained quite dark, and it gave to his countenance a rare characteristic of energy and pride.

Standing before the mirror, with heels together and body erect, he went through the usual movements with the two iron balls, which he held out at the end of his muscular arm, watching with a complacent expression its evidence of quiet power.

But suddenly, in the glass, which reflected the whole studio, he saw one of the portieres move; then appeared a woman's head — only a head, peeping in. A voice behind him asked:

"Anyone here?"

"Present!" he responded promptly, turning around. Then, throwing his dumb-bell on the floor, he hastened toward the door with an appearance of youthful agility that was slightly affected.

A woman entered attired in a light summer costume. They shook hands.

"You were exercising, I see," said the lady.

"Yes," he replied; "I was playing peacock, and allowed myself to be surprised."

The lady laughed, and continued:

"Your concierge's lodge was vacant, and as I know you are always alone at this hour I came up without being announced."

He looked at her.

"Heavens, how beautiful you are! What chic!"

"Yes, I have a new frock. Do you think it pretty?"

"Charming, and perfectly harmonious. We can certainly say that nowadays it is possible to give expression to the lightest textiles."

He walked around her, gently touching the material of the gown, adjusting its folds with the tips of his fingers, like a man that knows a woman's toilet as the modiste knows it, having all his life employed his artist's taste and his athlete's muscles in depicting with slender brush changing and delicate fashions, in revealing feminine grace enclosed within a prison of velvet and silk, or hidden by snowy laces. He finished his scrutiny by declaring: "It is a great success, and it becomes you perfectly!"

The lady allowed herself to be admired, quite content to be pretty and to please him.

No longer in her first youth, but still beautiful, not very tall, somewhat plump, but with that freshness which lends to a woman of forty an appearance of having only just reached full maturity, she seemed like one of those roses that flourish for an indefinite time up to the moment when, in too full a bloom, they fall in an hour.

Beneath her blonde hair she possessed the shrewdness to preserve all the alert and youthful grace of those Parisian women who never grow old; who carry within themselves a surprising vital force, an indomitable power of resistance, and who remain for twenty years triumphant and indestructible, careful above all things of their bodies and ever watchful of their health.

She raised her veil and murmured:

"Well, you do not kiss me!"

"I have been smoking."

"Pooh!" said the lady. Then, holding up her face, she added, "So much the worse!"

Their lips met.

He took her parasol and divested her of her spring jacket with the prompt, swift movement indicating familiarity with this service. As she seated herself on the divan, he asked with an air of interest:

"Is all going well with your husband?"

"Very well; he must be making a speech in the House at this very moment."

"Ah! On what, pray?"

"Oh — no doubt on beets or on rape-seed oil, as usual!"

Her husband, the Comte de Guilleroy, deputy from the Eure, made a special study of all questions of agricultural interest.

Perceiving in one corner a sketch that she did not recognize, the lady walked across the studio, asking, "What is that?"

"A pastel that I have just begun — the portrait of the Princesse de Ponteve."

"You know," said the lady gravely, "that if you go back to painting portraits of women I shall close your studio. I know only too well to what that sort of thing leads!"

"Oh, but I do not make twice a portrait of Any!" was the answer.

"I hope not, indeed!"

She examined the newly begun pastel sketch with the air of a woman that understands the technic of art. She stepped back, advanced, made a shade of her hand, sought the place where the best light fell on the sketch, and finally expressed her satisfaction.

"It is very good. You succeed admirably with pastel work."

"Do you think so?" murmured the flattered artist.

"Yes; it is a most delicate art, needing great distinction of style. It cannot be handled by masons in the art of painting."

For twelve years the Countess had encouraged the painter's leaning toward the distinguished in art, opposing his occasional return to the simplicity of realism; and, in consideration of the demands of fashionable modern elegance, she had tenderly urged him toward an ideal of grace that was slightly affected and artificial.

"What is the Princess like?" she asked.

He was compelled to give her all sorts of details — those minute details in which the jealous and subtle curiosity of women delights, passing from remarks upon her toilet to criticisms of her intelligence.

Suddenly she inquired: "Does she flirt with you?"

He laughed, and declared that she did not.

Then, putting both hands on the shoulders of the painter, the Countess gazed fixedly at him. The ardor of her questioning look caused a quiver in the pupils of her blue eyes, flecked with almost imperceptible black points, like tiny ink-spots.

Again she murmured: "Truly, now, she is not a flirt?"

"No, indeed, I assure you!"

"Well, I am quite reassured on another account," said the Countess. "You never will love anyone but me now. It is all over for the others. It is too late, my poor dear!"

The painter experienced that slight painful emotion which touches the heart of middle-aged men when some one mentions their age; and he murmured: "To-day and tomorrow, as yesterday, there never has been in my life, and never will be, anyone but you, Any."

She took him by the arm, and turning again toward the divan made him sit beside her.

"Of what were you thinking?" she asked.

"I am looking for a subject to paint."

"What, pray?"

"I don't know, you see, since I am still seeking it."

"What have you been doing lately?"

He was obliged to tell her of all the visits he had received, about all the dinners and soirees he had attended, and to repeat all the conversations and chit-chat. Both were really interested in all these futile and familiar details of fashionable life. The little rivalries, the flirtations, either well known or suspected, the judgments, a thousand times heard and repeated, upon the same persons, the same events and opinions, were bearing away and drowning both their minds in that troubled and agitated stream called Parisian life. Knowing everyone in all classes of society, he as an artist to whom all doors were open, she as the elegant wife of a Conservative deputy, they were experts in that sport of brilliant French chatter, amiably satirical, banal, brilliant but futile, with a certain shibboleth which gives a particular and greatly envied reputation to those whose tongues have become supple in this sort of malicious small talk.

"When are you coming to dine?" she asked suddenly.

"Whenever you wish. Name your day."

"Friday. I shall have the Duchesse de Mortemain, the Corbelles, and Musadieu, in honor of my daughter's return — she is coming this evening. But do not speak of it, my friend. It is a secret."

"Oh, yes, I accept. I shall be charmed to see Annette again. I have not seen her in three years."

"Yes, that is true. Three years!"

Though Annette, in her earliest years, had been brought up in Paris in her parents' home, she had become the object of the last and passionate affection of her grandmother, Madame Paradin, who, almost blind, lived all the year round on her son-in-law's estate at the castle of Roncieres, on the Eure. Little by little, the old lady had kept the child with her more and more, and as the De Guilleroys passed almost half their time in this domain, to which a variety of interests, agricultural and political, called them frequently, it ended in taking the little girl to Paris on occasional visits, for she herself preferred the free and active life of the country to the cloistered life of the city.

For three years she had not visited Paris even once, the Countess having preferred to keep her entirely away from it, in order that a new taste for its gaieties should not be awakened in her before the day fixed for her debut in society. Madame de Guilleroy had given her in the country two governesses, with unexceptionable diplomas, and had visited her mother and her daughter more frequently than before. Moreover, Annette's sojourn at the castle was rendered almost necessary by the presence of the old lady.

Formerly, Olivier Bertin had passed six weeks or two months at Roncieres every year; but in the past three years rheumatism had sent him to watering-places at some distance, which had so much revived his love for Paris that after his return he could not bring himself to leave it.

As a matter of custom, the young girl should not have returned home until autumn, but her father had suddenly conceived a plan for her marriage, and sent for her that she might meet immediately the Marquis de Farandal, to whom he wished her to be betrothed. But this plan was kept quite secret, and Madame de Guilleroy had told only Olivier Bertin of it, in strict confidence.

"Then your husband's idea is quite decided upon?" said he at last.

"Yes; I even think it a very happy idea."

Then they talked of other things.

She returned to the subject of painting, and wished to make him decide to paint a Christ. He opposed the suggestion, thinking that there was already enough of them in the world; but she persisted, and grew impatient in her argument.

"Oh, if I knew how to draw I would show you my thought: it should be very new, very bold. They are taking him down from the cross, and the man who has detached the hands has let drop the whole upper part of the body. It has fallen upon the crowd below, and they lift up their arms to receive and sustain it. Do you understand?"

Yes, he understood; he even thought the conception quite original; but he held himself as belonging to the modern style, and as his fair friend reclined upon the divan, with one daintily-shod foot peeping out, giving to the eye the sensation of flesh gleaming through the almost transparent stocking, he said: "Ah, that is what I should paint! That is life — a woman's foot at the edge of her skirt! Into that subject one may put everything — truth, desire, poetry. Nothing is more graceful or more charming than a woman's foot; and what mystery it suggests: the hidden limb, lost yet imagined beneath its veiling folds of drapery!"

Sitting on the floor, a la Turque, he seized her shoe and drew it off, and the foot, coming out of its leather sheath, moved about quickly, like a little animal surprised at being set free.

"Isn't that elegant, distinguished, and material — more material than the hand? Show me your hand, Any!"

She wore long gloves reaching to the elbow. In order to remove one she took it by the upper edge and slipped it down quickly, turning it inside out, as one would skin a snake. The arm appeared, white, plump, round, so suddenly bared as to produce an idea of complete and bold nudity.

She gave him her hand, which drooped from her wrist. The rings sparkled on her white fingers, and the narrow pink nails seemed like amorous claws protruding at the tips of that little feminine paw.

Olivier Bertin handled it tenderly and admiringly. He played with the fingers as if they were live toys, while saying:

"What a strange thing! What a strange thing! What a pretty little member, intelligent and adroit, which executes whatever one wills — books, laces, houses, pyramids, locomotives, pastry, or caresses, which last is its pleasantest function."

He drew off the rings one by one, and as the wedding-ring fell in its turn, he murmured smilingly:

"The law! Let us salute it!"

"Nonsense!" said the Countess, slightly wounded.

Bertin had always been inclined to satirical banter, that tendency of the French to mingle irony with the most serious sentiments, and he had often unintentionally made her sad, without knowing how to understand the subtle distinctions of women, or to discern the border of sacred ground, as he himself said. Above all things it vexed her whenever he alluded with a touch of familiar lightness to their attachment, which was an affair of such long standing that he declared it the most beautiful example of love in the nineteenth century. After a silence, she inquired:

"Will you take Annette and me to the varnishing-day reception?"

"Certainly."

Then she asked him about the best pictures to be shown in the next exposition, which was to open in a fortnight.

Suddenly, however, she appeared to recollect something she had forgotten.

"Come, give me my shoe," she said. "I am going now."

He was playing dreamily with the light shoe, turning it over abstractedly in his hands. He leaned over, kissed the foot, which appeared to float between the skirt and the rug, and which, a little chilled by the air, no longer moved restlessly about; then he slipped on the shoe, and Madame de Guilleroy, rising, approached the table, on which were scattered papers, open letters, old and recent, beside a painter's inkstand, in which the ink had dried. She looked at it all with curiosity, touched the papers, and lifted them to look underneath.

Bertin approached her, saying:

"You will disarrange my disorder."

Without replying to this, she inquired:

"Who is the gentleman that wishes to buy your Baigneuses?"

"An American whom I do not know."

"Have you come to an agreement about the Chanteuse des rues?"

"Yes. Ten thousand."

"You did well. It was pretty, but not exceptional. Good-by, dear."

She presented her cheek, which he brushed with a calm kiss; then she disappeared through the portieres, saying in an undertone:

"Friday — eight o'clock. I do not wish you to go with me to the door — you know that very well. Good-by!"

When she had gone he first lighted another cigarette, then he began to pace slowly to and fro in his studio. All the past of this liaison unrolled itself before him. He recalled all its details, now long remote, sought them and put them together, interested in this solitary pursuit of reminiscences.

It was at the moment when he had just risen like a star on the horizon of artistic Paris, when the painters were monopolizing the favor of the public, and had built up a quarter with magnificent dwellings, earned by a few strokes of the brush.

After his return from Rome, in 1864, he had lived for some years without success or renown; then suddenly, in 1868, he exhibited his Cleopatra, and in a few days was being praised to the skies by both critics and public.

In 1872, after the war, and after the death of Henri Regnault had made for all his brethren, a sort of pedestal of glory, a Jocaste a bold subject, classed Bertin among the daring, although his wisely original execution made him acceptable even to the Academicians. In 1873 his first medal placed him beyond competition with his Juive d'Alger, which he exhibited on his return from a trip to Africa, and a portrait of the Princesse de Salia, in 1874, made him considered by the fashionable world the first portrait painter of his day. From that time he became the favorite painter of Parisian women of that class, the most skilful and ingenious interpreter of their grace, their bearing, and their nature. In a few months all the distinguished women in Paris solicited the favor of being reproduced by his brush. He was hard to please, and made them pay well for that favor.

After he had become the rage, and was received everywhere as a man of the world he saw one day, at the Duchesse de Mortemain's house, a young woman in deep mourning, who was just leaving as he entered, and who, in this chance meeting in a doorway, dazzled him with a charming vision of grace and elegance.

On inquiring her name, he learned that she was the Comtesse de Guilleroy, wife of a Normandy country squire, agriculturist and deputy; that she was in mourning for her husband's father; and that she was very intellectual, greatly admired, and much sought after.

Struck by the apparition that had delighted his artist's eye, he said:

"Ah, there is some one whose portrait I should paint willingly!"

This remark was repeated to the young Countess the next day; and that evening Bertin received a little blue-tinted note, delicately perfumed, in a small, regular handwriting, slanting a little from left to right, which said:

"MONSIEUR:

"The Duchesse de Mortemain, who has just left my house, has assured me that you would be disposed to make, from my poor face, one of your masterpieces. I would entrust it to you willingly if I were certain that you did not speak idly, and that you really see in me something that you could reproduce and idealize.

"Accept, Monsieur, my sincere regards.

"ANNE DE GUILLEROY."

He answered this note, asking when he might present himself at the Countess's house, and was very simply invited to breakfast on the following Monday.

It was on the first floor of a large and luxurious modern house in the Boulevard Malesherbes. Traversing a large salon with blue silk walls, framed in white and gold, the painter was shown into a sort of boudoir hung with tapestries of the last century, light and coquettish, those tapestries a la Watteau, with their dainty coloring and graceful figures, which seem to have been designed and executed by workmen dreaming of love.

He had just seated himself when the Countess appeared. She walked so lightly that he had not heard her coming through the next room, and was surprised when he saw her. She extended her hand in graceful welcome.

"And so it is true," said she, "that you really wish to paint my portrait?"

"I shall be very happy to do so, Madame."

Her close-fitting black gown made her look very slender and gave her a youthful appearance though a grave air, which was belied, however, by her smiling face, lighted up by her bright golden hair. The Count entered, leading by the hand a little six-year-old girl.

Madame de Guilleroy presented him, saying, "My husband."

The Count was rather short, and wore no moustache; his cheeks were hollow, darkened under the skin by his close-shaven beard. He had somewhat the appearance of a priest or an actor; his hair was long and was tossed back carelessly; his manner was polished, and around the mouth two large circular lines extended from the cheeks to the chin, seeming to have been acquired from the habit of speaking in public.

He thanked the painter with a flourish of phrases that betrayed the orator. He had wished for a long time to have a portrait of his wife, and certainly he would have chosen M. Olivier Bertin, had he not feared a refusal, for he well knew that the painter was overwhelmed with orders.

It was arranged, then, with much ceremony on both sides, that the Count should accompany the Countess to the studio the next day. He asked, however, whether it would not be better to wait, because of the Countess's deep mourning; but the painter declared that he wished to translate the first impression she had made upon him, and the striking contrast of her animated, delicate head, luminous under the golden hair, with the austere black of her garments.

She came, then, the following day, with her husband, and afterward with her daughter, whom the artist seated before a table covered with picture-books.

Olivier Bertin, following his usual custom, showed himself very reserved. Fashionable women made him a little uneasy, for he hardly knew them. He supposed them to be at once immoral and shallow, hypocritical and dangerous, futile and embarrassing. Among the women of the demimonde he had had some passing adventures due to his renown, his lively wit, his elegant and athletic figure, and his dark and animated face. He preferred them, too; he liked their free ways and frank speech, accustomed as he was to the gay and easy manners of the studios and green-rooms he frequented. He went into the fashionable world for the glory of it, but his heart was not in it; he enjoyed it through his vanity, received congratulations and commissions, and played the gallant before charming ladies who flattered him, but never paid court to any. As he did not allow himself to indulge in daring pleasantries and spicy jests in their society, he thought them all prudes, and himself was considered as having good taste. Whenever one of them came to pose at his studio, he felt, in spite of any advances she might make to please him, that disparity of rank which prevents any real unity between artists and fashionable people, no matter how much they may be thrown together. Behind the smiles and the admiration which among women are always a little artificial, he felt the indefinable mental reserve of the being that judges itself of superior essence. This brought about in him an abnormal feeling of pride, which showed itself in a bearing of haughty respect, dissembling the vanity of the parvenu who is treated as an equal by princes and princesses, who owes to his talent the honor accorded to others by their birth. It was said of him with slight surprise: "He is really very well bred!" This surprise, although it flattered him, also wounded him, for it indicated a certain social barrier.

The admirable and ceremonious gravity of the painter a little annoyed Madame de Guilleroy, who could find nothing to say to this man, so cold, yet with a reputation for cleverness.

After settling her little daughter, she would come and sit in an armchair near the newly begun sketch, and tried, according to the artist's recommendation, to give some expression to her physiognomy.

In the midst of the fourth sitting, he suddenly ceased painting and inquired:

"What amuses you more than anything else in life?"

She appeared somewhat embarrassed.

"Why, I hardly know. Why this question?"

"I need a happy thought in those eyes, and I have not seen it yet."

"Well, try to make me talk; I like very much to chat."

"Are you gay?"

"Very gay."

"Well, then, let us chat, Madame."

He had said "Let us chat, Madame," in a very grave tone; then, resuming his painting, he touched upon a variety of subjects, seeking something on which their minds could meet. They began by exchanging observations on the people that both knew; then they talked of themselves —always the most agreeable and fascinating subject for a chat.

When they met again the next day they felt more at ease, and Bertin, noting that he pleased and amused her, began to relate some of the details of his artist life, allowing himself to give free scope to his reminiscences, in a fanciful way that was peculiar to him.

Accustomed to the dignified presence of the literary lights of the salons, the Countess was surprised by this almost wild gaiety, which said unusual things quite frankly, enlivening them with irony; and presently she began to answer in the same way, with a grace at once daring and delicate.

In a week's time she had conquered and charmed him by her good humor, frankness, and simplicity. He had entirely forgotten his prejudices against fashionable women, and would willingly have declared that they alone had charm and fascination. As he painted, standing before his canvas, advancing and retreating, with the movements of a man fighting, he allowed his fancy to flow freely, as if he had known for a long time this pretty woman, blond and black, made of sunlight and mourning, seated before him, laughing and listening, answering him gaily with so much animation that she lost her pose every moment.

Sometimes he would move far away from her, closing one eye, leaning over for a searching study of his model's pose; then he would draw very near to her to note the slightest shadows of her face, to catch the most fleeting expression, to seize and reproduce that which is in a woman's face beyond its more outward appearance; that emanation of ideal beauty, that reflection of something indescribable, that personal and intimate charm peculiar to each, which causes her to be loved to distraction by one and not by another.

One afternoon the little girl advanced, and, planting herself before the canvas, inquired with childish gravity:

"That is mamma, isn't it?"

The artist took her in his arms to kiss her, flattered by that naïve homage to the resemblance of his work.

Another day, when she had been very quiet, they suddenly heard her say, in a sad little voice:

"Mamma, I am so tired of this!"

The painter was so touched by this first complaint that he ordered a shopful of toys to be brought to the studio the following day.

Little Annette, astonished, pleased, and always thoughtful, put them in order with great care, that she might play with them one after another, according to the desire of the moment. From the date of this gift, she loved the painter as little children love, with that caressing, animal-like affection which makes them so sweet and captivating.

Madame de Guilleroy began to take pleasure in the sittings. She was almost without amusement or occupation that winter, as she was in mourning; so that, for lack of society and entertainments, her chief interest was within the walls of Bertin's studio.

She was the daughter of a rich and hospitable Parisian merchant, who had died several years earlier, and of his ailing wife, whose lack of health kept her in bed six months out of the twelve, and while still very young she had become a perfect hostess, knowing how to receive, to smile, to chat, to estimate character, and how to adapt herself to everyone; thus she early became quite at her ease in society, and was always farseeing and compliant. When the Count de Guilleroy was presented to her as her betrothed, she understood at once the advantages to be gained by such a marriage, and, like a sensible girl, admitted them without constraint, knowing well that one cannot have everything and that in every situation we must strike a balance between good and bad.

Launched in the world, much sought because of her beauty and brilliance, she was admired and courted by many men without ever feeling the least quickening of her heart, which was as reasonable as her mind.

She possessed a touch of coquetry, however, which was nevertheless prudent and aggressive enough never to allow an affair to go too far. Compliments pleased her, awakened desires, fed her vanity, provided she might seem to ignore them; and when she had received for a whole evening the incense of this sort of homage, she slept quietly, as a woman who has accomplished her mission on earth. This existence, which lasted seven years, did not weary her nor seem monotonous, for she adored the incessant excitement of society, but sometimes she felt that she desired something different. The men of her world, political advocates, financiers, or wealthy idlers, amused her as actors might; she did not take them too seriously, although she appreciated their functions, their stations, and their titles.

The painter pleased her at first because such a man was entirely a novelty to her. She found the studio a very amusing place, laughed gaily, felt that she, too, was clever, and felt grateful to him for the pleasure she took in the sittings. He pleased her, too, because he was handsome, strong, and famous, no woman, whatever she may pretend, being indifferent to physical beauty and glory. Flattered at having been admired by this expert, and disposed, on her side, to think well of him, she had discovered in him an alert and cultivated mind, delicacy, fancy, the true charm of intelligence, and an eloquence of expression that seemed to illumine whatever he said.

A rapid friendship sprang up between them, and the hand-clasp exchanged every day as she entered seemed more and more to express something of the feeling in their hearts.

Then, without deliberate design, with no definite determination, she felt within her heart a growing desire to fascinate him, and yielded to it. She had foreseen nothing, planned nothing; she was only coquettish with added grace, as a woman always is toward a man who pleases her more than all others; and in her manner with him, in her glances and smiles, was that seductive charm that diffuses itself around a woman in whose breast has awakened a need of being loved.

She said flattering things to him which meant "I find you very agreeable, Monsieur;" and she made him talk at length in order to show him, by her attention, how much he aroused her interest. He would cease to paint and sit beside her; and in that mental exaltation due to an intense desire to please, he had crises of poetry, of gaiety or of philosophy, according to his state of mind that day.

She was merry when he was gay; when he became profound she tried to follow his discourse, though she did not always succeed; and when her mind wandered to other things, she appeared to listen with so perfect an air of comprehension and such apparent enjoyment of this initiation, that he felt his spirit exalted in noting her attention to his words, and was touched to have discovered a soul so delicate, open, and docile, into which thought fell like a seed.

The portrait progressed, and was likely to be good, for the painter had reached the state of emotion that is necessary in order to discover all the qualities of the model, and to express them with that convincing ardor which is the inspiration of true artists.

Leaning toward her, watching every movement of her face, all the tints of her flesh, every shadow of her skin, all the expression and the translucence of her eyes, every secret of her physiognomy, he had become saturated with her personality as a sponge absorbs water; and, in transferring to canvas that emanation of disturbing charm which his eye seized, and which flowed like a wave from his thought to his brush, he was overcome and intoxicated by it, as if he had drunk deep of the beauty of woman.

She felt that he was drawn toward her, and was amused by this game, this victory that was becoming more and more certain, animating even her own heart.

A new feeling gave fresh piquancy to her existence, awaking in her a mysterious joy. When she heard him spoken of her heart throbbed faster, and she longed to say — a longing that never passed her lips — "He is in love with me!" She was glad when people praised his talent, and perhaps was even more pleased when she heard him called handsome. When she was alone, thinking of him, with no indiscreet babble to annoy her, she really imagined that in him she had found merely a good friend, one that would always remain content with a cordial hand-clasp.

Often, in the midst of a sitting, he would suddenly put down his palette on the stool and take little Annette in his arms, kissing her tenderly on her hair, and his eyes, while gazing at the mother, said, "It is you, not the child, that I kiss in this way."

Occasionally Madame de Guilleroy did not bring her daughter, but came alone. On these days he worked very little, and the time was spent in talking.

One afternoon she was late. It was a cold day toward the end of February. Olivier had come in early, as was now his habit whenever she had an appointment with him, for he always hoped she would arrive before the usual hour. While waiting he paced to and fro, smoking, and asking himself the question that he was surprised to find himself asking for the hundredth time that week: "Am I in love?" He did not know, never having been really in love. He had had his caprices, certainly, some of which had lasted a long time, but never had he mistaken them for love. To-day he was astonished at the emotion that possessed him.

Did he love her? He hardly desired her, certainly, never having dreamed of the possibility of possessing her. Heretofore, as soon as a woman attracted him he had desired to make a conquest of her, and had held out his hand toward her as if to gather fruit, but without feeling his heart affected profoundly by either her presence or her absence.

Desire for Madame de Guilleroy hardly occurred to him; it seemed to be hidden, crouching behind another and more powerful feeling, which was still uncertain and hardly awakened. Olivier had believed that love began with reveries and with poetic exaltations. But his feeling, on the contrary, seemed to come from an indefinable emotion, more physical than mental. He was nervous and restless, as if under the shadow of threatening illness, though nothing painful entered into this fever of the blood which by contagion stirred his mind also. He was quite aware that Madame de Guilleroy was the cause of his agitation; that it was due to the memories she left him and to the expectation of her return. He did not feel drawn to her by an impulse of his whole being, but he felt her always near him, as if she never had left him; she left to him something of herself when she departed — something subtle and inexpressible. What was it? Was it love? He probed deep in his heart in order to see, to understand. He thought her charming, but she was not at all the type of ideal woman that his blind hope had created. Whoever calls upon love has foreseen the moral traits and physical charms of her who will enslave him; and Madame de Guilleroy, although she pleased him infinitely, did not appear to him to be that woman.

But why did she thus occupy his thought, above all others, in a way so different, so unceasing? Had he simply fallen into the trap set by her coquetry, which he had long before understood, and, circumvented by his own methods, was he now under the influence of that special fascination which gives to women the desire to please?

He paced here and there, sat down, sprang up, lighted cigarettes and threw them away, and his eyes every instant looked at the clock, whose hands moved toward the usual hour in slow, unhurried fashion.

Several times already he had almost raised the convex glass over the two golden arrows turning so slowly, in order to push the larger one on toward the figure it was approaching so lazily. It seemed to him that this would suffice to make the door open, and that the expected one would appear, deceived and brought to him by this ruse. Then he smiled at this childish, persistent, and unreasonable desire.

At last he asked himself this question: "Could I become her lover?" This idea seemed strange to him, indeed hardly to be realized or even pursued, because of the complications it might bring into his life. Yet she pleased him very much, and he concluded: "Decidedly I am in a very strange state of mind."

The clock struck, and this reminder of the hour made him start, striking on his nerves rather than his soul. He awaited her with that impatience which delay increases from second to second. She was always prompt, so that before ten minutes should pass he would see her enter. When the ten minutes had elapsed, he felt anxious, as at the approach of some grief, then irritated because she had made him lose time; finally, he realized that if she failed to come it would cause him actual suffering. What should he do? Should he wait for her? No; he would go out, so that if, by chance, she should arrive very late, she would find the studio empty.

He would go out, but when? What latitude should he allow her? Would it not be better to remain and to make her comprehend, by a few coldly polite words, that he was not one to be kept waiting. And suppose she did not come? Then he would receive a despatch, a card, a servant or a messenger. If she did not come, what should he do? It would be a day lost; he could not work. Then? Well, then he would go to seek news of her, for see her he must!

It was quite true; he felt a profound, tormenting, harassing necessity for seeing her. What did it mean? Was it love? But he felt no mental exaltation, no intoxication of the senses; it awakened no reverie of the soul, when he realized that if she did not come that day he should suffer keenly.

The doorbell rang on the stairway of the little hotel, and Olivier Bertin suddenly found himself somewhat breathless, then so joyous that he executed a pirouette and flung his cigarette high in the air.

She entered; she was alone! Immediately he was seized with a great audacity.

"Do you know what I asked myself while waiting for you?"

"No, indeed, I do not."

"I asked myself whether I were not in love with you?"

"In love with me? You must be mad!"

But she smiled, and her smile said: That is very pretty; I am glad to hear it! However, she said: "You are not serious, of course; why do you make such a jest?"

"On the contrary, I am absolutely serious," he replied. "I do not declare that I am in love with you; but I ask myself whether I am not well on the way to become so."

"What has made you think so?"

"My emotion when you are not here; my happiness when you arrive."

She seated herself.

"Oh, don't disturb yourself over anything so trifling! As long as you sleep well and have an appetite for dinner, there will be no danger!"

He began to laugh.

"And if I lose my sleep and no longer eat?"

"Let me know of it."

"And then?"

"I will allow you to recover yourself in peace."

"A thousand thanks!"

And on the theme of this uncertain love they spun theories and fancies all the afternoon. The same thing occurred on several successive days. Accepting his statement as a sort of jest, of no real importance, she would say gaily on entering: "Well, how goes your love to-day?"

He would reply lightly, yet with perfect seriousness, telling her of the progress of his malady, in all its intimate details, and of the depth of the tenderness that had been born and was daily increasing. He analyzed himself minutely before her, hour by hour, since their separation the evening before, with the air of a professor giving a lecture; and she listened with interest, a little moved, and somewhat disturbed by this story which seemed that in a book of which she was the heroine. When he had enumerated, in his gallant and easy manner, all the anxieties of which he had become the prey, his voice sometimes trembled in expressing by a word, or only by an intonation, the tender aching of his heart.

And she persisted in questioning him, vibrating with curiosity, her eyes fixed upon him, her ear eager for those things that are disturbing to know but charming to hear.

Sometimes when he approached her to alter a pose he would seize her hand and try to kiss it. With a swift movement she would draw away her fingers from his lips, saying, with a slight frown:

"Come, come — work!"

He would begin his work again, but within five minutes she would ask some adroit question that led him back to the sole topic that interested them.

By this time she began to feel some fear deep in her heart. She longed to be loved — but not too much! Sure of not being led away, she yet feared to allow him to venture too far, thereby losing him, since then she would be compelled to drive him to despair after seeming to encourage him. Yet, should it become necessary to renounce this tender and delicate friendship, this stream of pleasant converse which rippled along bearing nuggets of love like a river whose sand is full of gold, it would cause her great sorrow — a grief that would be heartbreaking.

When she set out from her own home to go to the painter's studio, a wave of joy, warm and penetrating, overflowed her spirit, making it light and happy. As she laid her hand on Olivier's bell, her breast throbbed with impatience, and the stair-carpet seemed the softest her feet ever had pressed. But Bertin became gloomy, a little nervous, often irritable. He had his moments of impatience, soon repressed, but frequently recurring.

One day, when she had just entered, he sat down beside her instead of beginning to paint, saying:

"Madame, you can no longer ignore the fact that what I have said is not a jest, and that I love you madly."

Troubled by this beginning and seeing that the dreaded crisis had arrived, she tried to stop him, but he listened to her no longer. Emotion overflowed his heart, and she must hear him, pale, trembling, and anxious as she listened. He spoke a long time, demanding nothing, tenderly, sadly, with despairing resignation; and she allowed him to take her hands, which he kept in his. He was kneeling before her without her taking any notice of his attitude, and with a far-away look upon his face he begged her not to work him any harm. What harm? She did not understand nor try to understand, overcome by the cruel grief of seeing him suffer, yet that grief was almost happiness. Suddenly she saw tears in his eyes and was so deeply moved that she exclaimed: "Oh!" — ready to embrace him as one embraces a crying child. He repeated in a very soft tone: "There, there! I suffer too much;" then, suddenly, won by his sorrow, by the contagion of tears, she sobbed, her nerves quivering, her arms trembling, ready to open.

When she felt herself suddenly clasped in his embrace and kissed passionately on the lips, she wished to cry out, to struggle, to repulse him; but she judged herself lost, for she consented while resisting, she yielded even while she struggled, pressing him to her as she cried: "No, no, I will not!"

Then she was overcome with the emotion of that moment; she hid her face in her hands, then she suddenly sprang to her feet, caught up her hat which had fallen to the floor, put it on her head and rushed away, in spite of the supplications of Olivier, who held a fold of her skirt.

As soon as she was in the street, she had a desire to sit down on the curbstone, her limbs were so exhausted and powerless. A cab was passing; she called to it and said to the driver: "Drive slowly, and take me wherever you like." She threw herself into the carriage, closed the door, sank back in one corner, feeling herself alone behind the raised windows — alone to think.

For some minutes she heard only the sound of the wheels and the jarring of the cab. She looked at the houses, the pedestrians, people in cabs and omnibuses, with a blank gaze that saw nothing; she thought of nothing, as if she were giving herself time, granting herself a respite before daring to reflect upon what had happened.

Then, as she had a practical mind and was not lacking in courage, she said to herself: "I am a lost woman!" For some time she remained under that feeling of certainty that irreparable misfortune had befallen her, horror-struck, like a man fallen from a roof, knowing that his legs are broken but dreading to prove it to himself.

But, instead of feeling overwhelmed by the anticipation of suffering, her heart remained calm and peaceful after this catastrophe; it beat slowly, softly, after the fall that had terrified her soul, and seemed to take no part in the perturbation of her mind.

She repeated aloud, as if to understand and convince herself: "Yes, I am a lost woman." No echo of suffering responded from her heart to this cry of her conscience.

She allowed herself to be soothed for some time by the movement of the carriage, putting off a little longer the necessity of facing this cruel situation. No, she did not suffer. She was afraid to think, that was all; she feared to know, to comprehend, and to reflect; on the contrary, in that mysterious and impenetrable being created within us by the incessant struggle between our desires and our will, she felt an indescribable peace.

After perhaps half an hour of this strange repose, understanding at last that the despair she had invoked would not come, she shook off her torpor and murmured: "It is strange: I am hardly sorry even!"

Then she began to reproach herself. Anger awakened within her against her own blindness and her weakness. How had she not foreseen this, not comprehended that the hour for that struggle must come; that this man was so dear to her as to render her cowardly, and that sometimes in the purest hearts desire arises like a gust of wind, carrying the will before it?

But, after she had judged and reprimanded herself severely, she asked herself what would happen next?

Her first resolve was to break with the painter and never to see him again. Hardly had she formed this resolution before a thousand reasons sprang up as quickly to combat it. How could she explain such a break? What should she say to her husband? Would not the suspected truth be whispered, then spread abroad?

Would it not be better, for the sake of appearances, to act, with Olivier Bertin himself, the hypocritical comedy of indifference and forgetfulness, to show him that she had effaced that moment from her memory and from her life?

But could she do it? Would she have the audacity to appear to recollect nothing, to assume a look of indignant astonishment in saying: "What would you with me?" to the man with whom she had actually shared that swift and ardent emotion?

She reflected a long time, and decided that any other solution was impossible.

She would go to him courageously the next day, and make him understand as soon as she could what she desired him to do. She must not use a word, an allusion, a look, that could recall to him that moment of shame.

After he had suffered — for assuredly he would have his share of suffering, as a loyal and upright man — he would remain in future that which he had been up to the present.

As soon as this new resolution was formed, she gave her address to the coachman and returned home, profoundly depressed, with a desire to take to her bed, to see no one, to sleep and forget. Having shut herself up in her room, she remained there until the dinner hour, lying on a couch, benumbed, not wishing to agitate herself longer with that thought so full of danger.

She descended at the exact hour, astonished to find herself so calm, and awaited her husband with her ordinary demeanor. He appeared, carrying their little one in his arms; she pressed his hand and kissed the child, and felt no pang of anguish.

Monsieur de Guilleroy inquired what she had been doing. She replied indifferently that she had been posing, as usual.

"And the portrait — is it good?" he asked.

"It is coming on very well."

He spoke of his own affairs, in his turn; he enjoyed talking, while dining, of the sitting of the Chamber, and of the discussion of the proposed law on the adulteration of food-stuffs.

This rather tiresome talk, which she usually endured amiably, now irritated her, and made her look with closer attention at the man who was vulgarly loquacious in his interest in such things; but she smiled as she listened, and replied pleasantly, more gracious even than usual, more indulgent toward these banalities. As she looked at him she thought: "I have deceived him! He is my husband, and I have deceived him! How strange it is! Nothing can change that fact, nothing can obliterate it! I closed my eyes. I submitted for a few seconds, a few seconds only, to a man's kisses, and I am no longer a virtuous woman. A few seconds in my life — seconds that never can be effaced — have brought into it that little irreparable fact, so grave, so short, a crime, the most shameful one for a woman — and yet I feel no despair! If anyone had told me that yesterday, I should not have believed it. If anyone had convinced me that it would indeed come to pass, I should have thought instantly of the terrible remorse that would fill my heart to-day."

Monsieur de Guilleroy went out after dinner, as he did almost every evening. Then the Countess took her little daughter on her lap, weeping over her and kissing her; the tears she shed were sincere, coming from her conscience, not from her heart.

But she slept very little. Amid the darkness of her room, she tormented herself afresh as to the dangers of the attitude toward the painter that she purposed to assume; she dreaded the interview that must take place the following day, and the things that he must say to her, looking her in the face meanwhile.

She arose early, but remained lying on her couch all the morning, forcing herself to foresee what it was she had to fear and what she must say in reply, in order to be ready for any surprise.

She went out early, that she might yet think while walking.

He hardly expected her, and had been asking himself, since the evening before, what he should do when he met her.

After her hasty departure — that flight which he had not dared to oppose — he had remained alone, still listening, although she was already far away, for the sound of her step, the rustle of her skirt, and the closing of the door, touched by the timid hand of his goddess.

He remained standing, full of deep, ardent, intoxicating joy. He had won her, her! That had passed between them! Was it possible? After the surprise of this triumph, he gloated over it, and, to realize it more keenly, he sat down and almost lay at full length on the divan where he had made her yield to him.

He remained there a long time, full of the thought that she was his mistress, and that between them, between the woman he had so much desired and himself, had been tied in a few moments that mysterious bond which secretly links two beings to each other. He retained in his still quivering body the piercingly sweet remembrance of that wild, fleeting moment when their lips had met, when their beings had united and mingled, thrilling together with the deepest emotion of life.

He did not go out that evening, in order to live over again that rapturous moment; he retired early, his heart vibrating with happiness. He had hardly awakened the next morning before he asked himself what he should do. To a cocotte or an actress he would have sent flowers or even a jewel; but he was tortured with perplexity before this new situation.

He wished to express, in delicate and charming terms, the gratitude of his soul, his ecstasy of mad tenderness, his offer of a devotion that should be eternal; but in order to intimate all these passionate and high-souled thoughts he could find only set phrases, commonplace expressions, vulgar and puerile.

Assuredly, he must write — but what? He scribbled, erased, tore up and began anew twenty letters, all of which seemed to him insulting, odious, ridiculous.

He gave up the idea of writing, therefore, and decided to go to see her, as soon as the hour for the sitting had passed, for he felt very sure that she would not come.

Shutting himself up in his studio, he stood in mental exaltation before the portrait, his lips longing to press themselves on the painting, whereon something of herself was fixed; and again and again he looked out of the window into the street. Every gown he saw in the distance made his heart throb quickly. Twenty times he believed that he saw her; then when the approaching woman had passed he sat down again, as if overcome by a deception.

Suddenly he saw her, doubted, then took his opera-glass, recognized her, and, dizzy with violent emotion, sat down once more to await her.

When she entered he threw himself on his knees and tried to take her hands, but she drew them away abruptly, and, as he remained at her feet, filled with anguish, his eyes raised to hers, she said haughtily:

"What are you doing, Monsieur? I do not understand that attitude."

"Oh, Madame, I entreat you — "

She interrupted him harshly:

"Rise! You are ridiculous!"

He rose, dazed, and murmured:

"What is the matter? Do not treat me in this way — I love you!"

Then, in a few short, dry phrases, she signified her wishes, and decreed the situation.

"I do not understand what you wish to say. Never speak to me of your love, or I shall leave this studio never to return. If you forget for a single moment this condition of my presence here, you never will see me again."

He looked at her, crushed by this unexpected harshness; then he understood, and murmured:

"I shall obey, Madame."

"Very well," she rejoined; "I expected that of you! Now work, for you are long in finishing that portrait."

He took up his palette and began to paint, but his hand trembled, his troubled eyes looked without seeing; he felt a desire to weep, so deeply wounded was his heart.

He tried to talk to her; she barely answered him. When he attempted to pay her some little compliment on her color, she cut him short in a tone so brusque that he felt suddenly one of those furies of a lover that change tenderness to hatred. Through soul and body he felt a nervous shock, and in a moment he detested her. Yes, yes, that was, indeed, woman! She, too, was like all the others! Why not? She, too, was false, changeable, and weak, like all of them. She had attracted him, seduced him with girlish ruses, trying to overcome him without intending to give him anything in return, enticing him only to refuse him, employing toward him all the tricks of cowardly coquettes who seem always on the point of yielding so long as the man who cringes like a dog before them dares not carry out his desire.

But the situation was the worse for her, after all; he had taken her, he had overcome her. She might try to wash away that fact and answer him insolently; she could efface nothing, and he — he would forget it! Indeed, it would have been a fine bit of folly to embarrass himself with this sort of mistress, who would eat into his artist life with the capricious teeth of a pretty woman.

He felt a desire to whistle, as he did in the presence of his models, but realized that his nerve was giving way and feared to commit some stupidity. He cut short the sitting under pretense of having an appointment. When they bowed at parting they felt themselves farther apart than the day they first met at the Duchesse de Mortemain's.

As soon as she had gone, he took his hat and topcoat and went out. A cold sun, in a misty blue sky, threw over the city a pale, depressing, unreal light.

After he had walked a long time, with rapid and irritated step, elbowing the passersby that he need not deviate from a straight line, his great fury against her began to change into sadness and regret. After he had repeated to himself all the reproaches he had poured upon her, he remembered, as he looked at the women that passed him, how pretty and charming she was. Like many others who do not admit it, he had always been waiting to meet the "impossible she," to find the rare, unique, poetic and passionate being, the dream of whom hovers over our hearts. Had he not almost found it? Was it not she who might have given him this almost impossible happiness? Why, then, is it true that nothing is realized? Why can one seize nothing of that which he pursues, or can succeed only in grasping a phantom, which renders still more grievous this pursuit of illusions?

He was no longer resentful toward her; it was life itself that made him bitter. Now that he was able to reason, he asked himself what cause for anger he had against her? With what could he reproach her, after all? — with being amiable, kind, and gracious toward him, while she herself might well reproach him for having behaved like a villain!

He returned home full of sadness. He would have liked to ask her pardon, to devote himself to her, to make her forget; and he pondered as to how he might enable her to comprehend that henceforth, until death, he would be obedient to all her wishes.

The next day she arrived, accompanied by her daughter, with a smile so sad, an expression so pathetic, that the painter fancied he could see in those poor blue eyes, that had always been so merry, all the pain, all the remorse, all the desolation of that womanly heart. He was moved to pity, and, in order that she might forget, he showed toward her with delicate reserve the most thoughtful attentions. She acknowledged them with gentleness and kindness, with the weary and languid manner of a woman who suffers.

And he, looking at her, seized again with a mad dream of loving and of being loved, asked himself why she was not more indignant at his conduct, how she could still come to his studio, listen to him and answer him, with that memory between them.

Since she could bear to see him again, however, could endure to hear his voice, having always in her mind the one thought which she could not escape, it must be that this thought had not become intolerable to her. When a woman hates the man who has conquered her thus, she cannot remain in his presence without showing her hatred, but that man never can remain wholly indifferent to her. She must either detest him or pardon him. And when she pardons that transgression, she is not far from love!

While he painted slowly, he arrived at this conclusion by small arguments, precise, clear, and sure; he now felt himself strong, steady, and master of the situation. He had only to be prudent, patient, devoted, and one day or another she would again be his.

He knew how to wait. In order to reassure her and to conquer her once more, he practised ruses in his turn; he assumed a tenderness restrained by apparent remorse, hesitating attentions, and indifferent attitudes. Tranquil in the certainty of approaching happiness, what did it matter whether it arrived a little sooner, a little later? He even experienced a strange, subtle pleasure in delay, in watching her, and saying to himself, "She is afraid!" as he saw her coming always with her child.

He felt that between them a slow work of reconciliation was going on, and thought that in the Countess's eyes was something strange: constraint, a sweet sadness, that appeal of a struggling soul, of a faltering will, which seems to say: "But — conquer me, then!"

After a while she came alone once more, reassured by his reserve. Then he treated her as a friend, a comrade; he talked to her of his life, his plans, his art, as to a brother.

Deluded by this attitude, she assumed joyfully the part of counselor, flattered that he distinguished her thus above other women, and convinced that his talent would gain in delicacy through this intellectual intimacy. But, from consulting her and showing deference to her, he caused her to pass naturally from the functions of a counselor to the sacred office of inspirer. She found it charming to use her influence thus over the great man, and almost consented that he should love her as an artist, since it was she that gave him inspiration for his work!

It was one evening, after a long talk about the loves of illustrious painters, that she let herself glide into his arms. She rested there this time, without trying to escape, and gave him back his kisses.

She felt no remorse now, only the vague consciousness of a fall; and to stifle the reproaches of her reason she attributed it to fatality.

Drawn toward him by her virgin heart and her empty soul, the flesh overcome by the slow domination of caresses, little by little she attached herself to him, as do all tender women who love for the first time.

With Olivier it was a crisis of acute love, sensuous and poetic. It seemed to him sometimes that one day he had taken flight, with hands extended, and that he had been able to clasp in full embrace that winged and magnificent dream which is always hovering over our hopes.

He had finished the Countess's portrait, the best, certainly, that he ever had painted, for he had discovered and crystallized that inexpressible something which a painter seldom succeeds in unveiling — that reflection, that mystery, that physiognomy of the soul, which passes intangibly across a face.

Months rolled by, then years, which hardly loosened the tie that united the Comtesse de Guilleroy and the painter, Olivier Bertin. With him it was no longer the exaltation of the beginning, but a calm, deep affection, a sort of loving friendship that had become a habit.

With her, on the contrary, the passionate, persistent attachment of certain women who give themselves to a man wholly and forever was always growing. Honest and straight in adulterous love as they might have been in marriage, they devote themselves to a single object with a tenderness from which nothing can turn them. Not only do they love the lover, but they wish to love him, and, with eyes on him alone, they so fill their hearts with thoughts of him that nothing strange can thenceforth enter there. They have bound their lives resolutely, as one who knows how to swim, yet wishes to die, ties his hands together before leaping from a high bridge into the water.

But from the moment when the Countess had yielded, she was assailed by fears for Bertin's constancy. Nothing held him but his masculine will, his caprice, his passing fancy for a woman he had met one day just as he had already met so many others! She realized that he was so free, so susceptible to temptation — he who lived without duties, habits, or scruples, like all men! He was handsome, celebrated, much sought after, having, to respond to his easily awakened desires, fashionable women, whose modesty is so fragile, women of the demimonde of the theater, prodigal of their favors with such men as he. One of them, some evening after supper, might follow him and please him, take him and keep him.

Thus she lived in terror of losing him, watching his manner, his attitudes, startled by a word, full of anguish when he admired another woman, praised the charm of her countenance or her grace of bearing. All of which she was ignorant in his life made her tremble, and all of which she was cognizant alarmed her. At each of their meetings she questioned him ingeniously, without his perceiving it, in order to make him express his opinion on the people he had seen, the houses where he had dined, in short, the lightest expression of his mind. As soon as she fancied she detected the influence of some other person, she combated it with prodigious astuteness and innumerable resources.

Oh, how often did she suspect those brief intrigues, without depth, lasting perhaps a week or two, from time to time, which come into the life of every prominent artist!

She had, as it were, an intuition of danger, even before she detected the awakening of a new desire in Olivier, by the look of triumph in his eyes, the expression of a man when swayed by a gallant fancy.

Then she would suffer; her sleep would be tortured by doubts. In order to surprise him, she would appear suddenly in his studio, without giving him notice of her coming, put questions that seemed naïve, tested his tenderness while listening to his thoughts, as we test while listening to detect hidden illness in the body. She would weep as soon as she found herself sure that some one would take him from her this time, robbing her of that love to which she clung so passionately because she had staked upon it all her will, her strength of affection, all her hopes and dreams.

Then, when she saw that he came back to her, after these brief diversions, she experienced, as she drew close to him again, took possession of him as of something lost and found, a deep, silent happiness which sometimes, when she passed a church, urged her go in and thank God.

Her preoccupation in ever making herself pleasing to him above all others, and of guarding him against all others, had made her whole life become a combat interrupted by coquetry. She had ceaselessly struggled for him, and before him, with her grace, her beauty and elegance. She wished that wherever he went he should hear her praised for her charm, her taste, her wit, and her toilets. She wished to please others for his sake, and to attract them so that he should be both proud and jealous of her. And every time that she succeeded in arousing his jealousy, after making him suffer a little, she allowed him the triumph of winning her back, which revived his love in exciting his vanity. Then, realizing that it was always possible for a man to meet in society a woman whose physical charm would be greater than her own, being a novelty, she resorted to other means: she flattered and spoiled him. Discreetly but continuously she heaped praises upon him; she soothed him with admiration and enveloped him in flattery, so that he might find all other friendship, all other love, even, a little cold and incomplete, and that if others also loved him he would perceive at last that she alone of them all understood him.

She made the two drawingrooms in her house, which he entered so often, a place as attractive to the pride of the artist as to the heart of the man, the place in all Paris where he liked best to come, because there all his cravings were satisfied at the same time.

Not only did she learn to discover all his tastes, in order that, while gratifying them in her own house, she might give him a feeling of well-being that nothing could replace, but she knew how to create new tastes, to arouse appetites of all kinds, material and intellectual, habits of little attentions, of affections, of adoration and flattery! She tried to charm his eye with elegance, his sense of smell with perfumes, and his taste with delicate food.

But when she had planted in the soul and in the senses of a selfish bachelor a multitude of petty, tyrannical needs, when she had become quite certain that no mistress would trouble herself as she did to watch over and maintain them, in order to surround him with all the little pleasures of life, she suddenly feared, as she saw him disgusted with his own home, always complaining of his solitary life, and, being unable to come into her home except under all the restraints imposed by society, going to the club, seeking every means to soften his lonely lot — she feared lest he thought of marriage.

On some days she suffered so much from all these anxieties that she longed for old age, to have an end of this anguish and rest in a cooler and calmer affection.

Years passed, however, without disuniting them. The chain wherewith she had attached him to her was heavy, and she made new links as the old ones wore away. But, always solicitous, she watched over the painter's heart as one guards a child crossing a street full of vehicles, and day by day she lived in expectation of the unknown danger, the dread of which always hung over her.

The Count, without suspicion or jealousy, found this intimacy of his wife with a famous and popular artist a perfectly natural thing. Through continually meeting, the two men, becoming accustomed to each other, finally became excellent friends.

II

When Bertin entered, on Friday evening, the house of his friend, where he was to dine in honor of the return of Antoinette de Guilleroy, he found in the little Louis XV salon only Monsieur de Musadieu, who had just arrived.

He was a clever old man, who perhaps might have become of some importance, and who now could not console himself for not having attained to something worth while.

He had once been a commissioner of the imperial museums, and had found means to get himself reappointed Inspector of Fine Arts under the Republic, which did not prevent him from being, above all else, the friend of princes, of all the princes, princesses, and duchesses of

European aristocracy, and the sworn protector of artists of all sorts. He was endowed with an alert mind and quick perceptions, with great facility of speech that enabled him to say agreeably the most ordinary things, with a suppleness of thought that put him at ease in any society, and a subtle diplomatic scent that gave him the power to judge men at first sight; and he strolled from salon to salon, morning and evening, with his enlightened, useless, and gossiping activity.

Apt at everything, as he appeared, he would talk on any subject with an air of convincing competence and familiarity that made him greatly appreciated by fashionable women, whom he served as a sort of traveling bazaar of erudition. As a matter of fact, he knew many things without ever having read any but the most indispensable books; but he stood very well with the five Academies, with all the savants, writers, and learned specialists, to whom he listened with clever discernment. He knew how to forget at once explanations that were too technical or were useless to him, remembered the others very well, and lent to the information thus gleaned an easy, clear, and good-natured rendering that made them as readily comprehensible as the popular presentation of scientific facts. He gave the impression of being a veritable storehouse of ideas, one of those vast places wherein one never finds rare objects but discovers a multiplicity of cheap productions of all kinds and from all sources, from household utensils to the popular instruments for physical culture or for domestic surgery.

The painters, with whom his official functions brought him in continual contact, made sport of him but feared him. He rendered them some services, however, helped them to sell pictures, brought them in contact with fashionable persons, and enjoyed presenting them, protecting them, launching them. He seemed to devote himself to a mysterious function of fusing the fashionable and the artistic worlds, pluming himself on his intimate acquaintance with these, and of his familiar footing with those, on breakfasting with the Prince of Wales, on his way through Paris, or dining, the same evening, with Paul Adelmant, Olivier Bertin, and Amaury Maldant.

Bertin, who liked him well enough, found him amusing, and said of him: "He is the encyclopedia of Jules Verne, bound in ass's skin!"

The two men shook hands and began to talk of the political situation and the rumors of war, which Musadieu thought alarming, for evident reasons which he explained very well, Germany having every interest in crushing us and in hastening that moment for which M. de Bismarck had been waiting eighteen years; while Olivier Bertin proved by irrefutable argument that these fears were chimerical, it being impossible for Germany to be foolish enough to risk her conquest in an always doubtful venture, or for the Chancelor to be imprudent enough to risk, in the latter years of his life, his achievements and his glory at a single blow.

M. de Musadieu, however, seemed to know something of which he did not wish to speak. Furthermore, he had seen a Minister that morning and had met the Grand Duke Vladimir, returning from Cannes, the evening before.

The artist was unconvinced by this, and with quiet irony expressed doubt of the knowledge of even the best informed. Behind all these rumors was the influence of the Bourse! Bismarck alone might have a settled opinion on the subject.

M. de Guilleroy entered, shook hands warmly, excusing himself in unctuous words for having left them alone.

"And you, my dear Deputy," asked the painter, "what do you think of these rumors of war?"

M. de Guilleroy launched into a discourse. As a member of the Chamber, he knew more of the subject than anyone else, though he held an opinion differing from that of most of his colleagues. No, he did not believe in the probability of an approaching conflict, unless it should be provoked by French turbulence and by the rodomontades of the self-styled patriots of the League. And he painted Bismarck's portrait in striking colors, a portrait a la Saint-Simon. The man Bismarck was one that no one wished to understand, because one always lends to others his own ways of thinking, and credits them with a readiness to do that which he would do were he placed in their situation. M. de Bismarck was not a false and lying diplomatist, but frank and brutal, always loudly proclaiming the truth and announcing his intentions. "I want peace!"

said he. That was true; he wanted peace, nothing but peace, and everything had proved it in a blinding fashion for eighteen years; everything — his arguments, his alliances, that union of peoples banded together against our impetuosity. M. de Guilleroy concluded in a tone of profound conviction: "He is a great man, a very great man, who desires peace, but who has faith only in menaces and violent means as the way to obtain it. In short, gentlemen, a great barbarian."

"He that wishes the end must take the means," M. de Musadieu replied. "I will grant you willingly that he adores peace if you will concede to me that he always wishes to make war in order to obtain it. But that is an indisputable and phenomenal truth: In this world war is made only to obtain peace!"

A servant announced: "Madame la Duchesse de Mortemain."

Between the folding-doors appeared a tall, large woman, who entered with an air of authority. Guilleroy hastened to meet her, and kissed her hand, saying:

"How do you do, Duchess?"

The other two men saluted her with a certain distinguished familiarity, for the Duchess's manner was both cordial and abrupt.

She was the widow of General the Duc de Mortemain, mother of an only daughter married to the Prince de Salia; daughter of the Marquis de Farandal, of high family and royally rich, and received at her mansion in the Rue de Varenne all the celebrities of the world, who met and complimented one another there. No Highness passed through Paris without dining at her table; no man could attract public attention that she did not immediately wish to know him. She must see him, make him talk to her, form her own judgment of him. This amused her greatly, lent interest to life, and fed the flame of imperious yet kindly curiosity that burned within her.

She had hardly seated herself when the same servant announced:

"Monsieur le Baron and Madame la Baronne de Corbelle."

They were young; the Baron was bald and fat, the Baroness was slender, elegant, and very dark.

This couple occupied a peculiar situation in the French aristocracy due solely to a scrupulous choice of connections. Belonging to the polite world, but without value or talent, moved in all their actions by an immoderate love of that which is select, correct, and distinguished; by dint of visiting only the most princely houses, of professing their royalist sentiments, pious and correct to a supreme degree; by respecting all that should be respected, by condemning all that should be condemned, by never being mistaken on a point of worldly dogma or hesitating over a detail of etiquette, they had succeeded in passing in the eyes of many for the finest flower of high life. Their opinion formed a sort of code of correct form and their presence in a house gave it a true title of distinction.

The Corbelles were relatives of the Comte de Guilleroy.

"Well," said the Duchess in astonishment, "and your wife?"

"One instant, one little instant," pleaded the Count. "There is a surprise: she is just about to come."

When Madame de Guilleroy, as the bride of a month, had entered society, she was presented to the Duchesse de Mortemain, who loved her immediately, adopted her, and patronized her.

For twenty years this friendship never had diminished, and when the Duchess said, "Ma petite," one still heard in her voice the tenderness of that sudden and persistent affection. It was at her house that the painter and the Countess had happened to meet.

Musadieu approached the group. "Has the Duchess been to see the exposition of the In-temperates?" he inquired.

"No; what is that?"

"A group of new artists, impressionists in a state of intoxication. Two of them are very fine."

The great lady murmured, with disdain: "I do not like the jests of those gentlemen."

Authoritative, brusque, barely tolerating any other opinion than her own, and founding hers solely on the consciousness of her social station, considering, without being able to give a good reason for it, that artists and learned men were merely intelligent mercenaries charged by God to amuse society or to render service to it, she had no other basis for her judgments than the degree of astonishment or of pleasure she experienced at the sight of a thing, the reading of a book, or the recital of a discovery.

Tall, stout, heavy, red, with a loud voice, she passed as having the air of a great lady because nothing embarrassed her; she dared to say anything and patronized the whole world, including dethroned princes, with her receptions in their honor, and even the Almighty by her generosity to the clergy and her gifts to the churches.

"Does the Duchess know," Musadieu continued, "that they say the assassin of Marie Lambourg has been arrested?"

Her interest was awakened at once.

"No, tell me about it," she replied.

He narrated the details. Musadieu was tall and very thin; he wore a white waistcoat and little diamond shirt-studs; he spoke without gestures, with a correct air which allowed him to say the daring things which he took delight in uttering. He was very near-sighted, and appeared, notwithstanding his eyeglass, never to see anyone; and when he sat down his whole frame seemed to accommodate itself to the shape of the chair. His figure seemed to shrink into folds, as if his spinal column were made of rubber; his legs, crossed one over the other, looked like two rolled ribbons, and his long arms, resting on the arms of the chair, allowed to droop his pale hands with interminable fingers. His hair and moustache, artistically dyed, with a few white locks cleverly forgotten, were a subject of frequent jests.

While he was explaining to the Duchess that the jewels of the murdered prostitute had been given as a present by the suspected murderer to another girl of the same stamp, the door of the large drawingroom opened wide once more, and two blond women in white lace, a creamy Mechlin, resembling each other like two sisters of different ages, the one a little too mature, the other a little too young, one a trifle too plump, the other a shade too slender, advanced, clasping each other round the waist and smiling.

The guests exclaimed and applauded. No one, except Olivier Bertin, knew of Annette de Guilleroy's return, and the appearance of the young girl beside her mother, who at a little distance seemed almost as fresh and even more beautiful — for, like a flower in full bloom, she had not ceased to be brilliant, while the child, hardly budding, was only beginning to be pretty — made both appear charming.

The Duchess, delighted, clapped her hands, exclaiming: "Heavens! How charming and amusing they are, standing beside each other! Look, Monsieur de Musadieu, how much they resemble each other!"

The two were compared, and two opinions were formed. According to Musadieu, the Corbelles, and the Comte de Guilleroy, the Countess and her daughter resembled each other only in coloring, in the hair, and above all in the eyes, which were exactly alike, both showing tiny black points, like minute drops of ink, on the blue iris. But it was their opinion that when the young girl should have become a woman they would no longer resemble each other.

According to the Duchess, on the contrary, and also Olivier Bertin, they were similar in all respects, and only the difference in age made them appear unlike.

"How much she has changed in three years!" said the painter. "I should not have recognized her, and I don't dare to tutoyer the young lady!"

The Countess laughed. "The idea! I should like to hear you say 'you' to Annette!"

The young girl, whose future gay audacity was already apparent under an air of timid playfulness, replied: "It is I who shall not dare to say 'thou' to Monsieur Bertin."

Her mother smiled.

"Yes, continue the old habit — I will allow you to do so," she said. "You will soon renew your acquaintance with him."

But Annette shook her head.

"No, no, it would embarrass me," she said.

The Duchess embraced her, and examined her with all the interest of a connoisseur.

"Look me in the face, my child," she said. "Yes, you have exactly the same expression as your mother; you won't be so bad by-and-by, when you have acquired more polish. And you must grow a little plumper — not very much, but a little. You are very thin."

"Oh, don't say that!" exclaimed the Countess.

"Why not?"

"It is so nice to be slender. I intend to reduce myself at once."

But Madame de Mortemain took offense, forgetting in her anger the presence of a young girl.

"Oh, of course, you are all in favor of bones, because you can dress them better than flesh. For my part, I belong to the generation of fat women! To-day is the day of thin ones. They make me think of the lean kine of Egypt. I cannot understand how men can admire your skeletons. In my time they demanded more!"

She subsided amid the smiles of the company, but added, turning to Annette:

"Look at your mamma, little one; she does very well; she has attained the happy medium — imitate her."

They passed into the diningroom. After they were seated, Musadieu resumed the discussion.

"For my part, I say that men should be thin, because they are formed for exercises that require address and agility, incompatible with corpulency. But the women's case is a little different. Don't you think so, Corbelle?"

Corbelle was perplexed, the Duchess being stout and his own wife more than slender. But the Baroness came to the rescue of her husband, and resolutely declared herself in favor of slimness. The year before that, she declared, she had been obliged to struggle with the beginning of embonpoint, over which she soon triumphed.

"Tell us how you did it," demanded Madame de Guilleroy.

The Baroness explained the method employed by all the fashionable women of the day. One must never drink while eating; but an hour after the repast a cup of tea may be taken, boiling hot. This method succeeded with everyone. She cited astonishing cases of fat women who in three months had become more slender than the blade of a knife. The Duchess exclaimed in exasperation:

"Good gracious, how stupid to torture oneself like that! You like nothing any more — nothing — not even champagne. Bertin, as an artist, what do you think of this folly?"

"Mon Dieu, Madame, I am a painter and I simply arrange the drapery, so it is all the same to me. If I were a sculptor I might complain."

"But as a man, which do you prefer?"

"I? Oh, a certain rounded slimness — what my cook calls a nice little cornfed chicken. It is not fat, but plump and delicate."

The comparison caused a laugh; but the incredulous Countess looked at her daughter and murmured:

"No, it is very much better to be thin; slender women never grow old."

This point also was discussed by the company; and all agreed that a very fat person should not grow thin too rapidly.

This observation gave place to a review of women known in society and to new discussions on their grace, their chic and beauty. Musadieu pronounced the blonde Marquise de Lochrist incomparably charming, while Bertin esteemed as a beauty Madame Mandeliere, with her brunette complexion, low brow, her dusky eyes and somewhat large mouth, in which her teeth seemed to sparkle.

He was seated beside the young girl, and said suddenly, turning to her:

"Listen to me, Nanette. Everything that we have just been saying you will hear repeated at least once a week until you are old. In a week you will know all that society thinks about politics, women, plays, and all the rest of it. Only an occasional change of names will be necessary —

names of persons and titles of works. When you have heard us all express and defend our opinions, you will quietly choose your own among those that one must have, and then you need never trouble yourself to think of anything more, never. You will only have to rest in that opinion."

The young girl, without replying, turned upon him her mischievous eyes, wherein sparkled youthful intelligence, restrained, but ready to escape.

But the Duchess and Musadieu, who played with ideas as one tosses a ball, without perceiving that they continually exchanged the same ones, protested in the name of thought and of human activity.

Then Bertin attempted to show how the intelligence of fashionable people, even the brightest of them, is without value, foundation, or weight; how slight is the basis of their beliefs, how feeble and indifferent is their interest in intellectual things, how fickle and questionable are their tastes.

Warmed by one of those spasms of indignation, half real, half assumed, aroused at first by a desire to be eloquent, and urged on by the sudden prompting of a clear judgment, ordinarily obscured by an easygoing nature, he showed how those persons whose sole occupation in life is to pay visits and dine in town find themselves becoming, by an irresistible fatality, light and graceful but utterly trivial beings, vaguely agitated by superficial cares, beliefs, and appetites.

He showed that none of that class has either depth, ardor, or sincerity; that, their intellectual culture being slight and their erudition a simple varnish, they must remain, in short, manikins who produce the effect and make the gesture of the enlightened beings that they are not. He proved that, the frail roots of their instincts having been nourished on conventionalities instead of realities, they love nothing sincerely, that even the luxury of their existence is a satisfaction of vanity and not the gratification of a refined bodily necessity, for usually their table is indifferent, their wines are bad and very dear.

They live, as he said, beside everything, but see nothing and study nothing; they are near science, of which they are ignorant; nature, at which they do not know how to look; outside of true happiness, for they are powerless to enjoy it; outside of the beauty of the world and the beauty of art, of which they chatter without having really discovered it, or even believing in it, for they are ignorant of the intoxication of tasting the joys of life and of intelligence. They are incapable of attaching themselves in anything to that degree that existence is illumined by the happiness of comprehending it.

The Baron de Corbelle thought that it was his duty to come to the defense of society. This he did with inconsistent and irrefutable arguments, which melt before reason as snow before the fire, yet which cannot be disproved — the absurd and triumphant arguments of a country curate who would demonstrate the existence of God. In concluding, he compared fashionable people to race-horses, which, in truth, are good for nothing, but which are the glory of the equine race.

Bertin, irritated by this adversary, preserved a politely disdainful silence. But suddenly the Baron's imbecilities exasperated him, and, interrupting him adroitly, he recounted the life of a man of fashion from his rising to his going to rest, without omitting anything. All the details, cleverly described, made up an irresistibly amusing silhouette. Once could see the fine gentleman dressed by his valet, first expressing a few general ideas to the hairdresser that came to shave him; then, when taking his morning stroll, inquiring of the grooms about the health of the horses; then trotting through the avenues of the Bois, caring only about saluting and being saluted; then breakfasting opposite his wife, who in her turn had been out in her coupe, speaking to her only to enumerate the names of the persons he had met that morning; then passing from drawingroom to drawingroom until evening, refreshing his intelligence by contact with others of his circle, dining with a prince, where the affairs of Europe were discussed, and finishing the evening behind the scenes at the Opera, where his timid pretensions at being a gay dog were innocently satisfied by the appearance of being surrounded by naughtiness.

The picture was so true, although its satire wounded no one present, that laughter ran around the table.

The Duchess, shaken by the suppressed merriment of fat persons, relieved herself by discreet chuckles.

"Really, you are too funny!" she said at last; "you will make me die of laughter."

Bertin replied, with some excitement:

"Oh, Madame, in the polite world one does not die of laughter! One hardly laughs, even. We have sufficient amiability, as a matter of good taste, to pretend to be amused and appear to laugh. The grimace is imitated well enough, but the real thing is never done. Go to the theaters of the common people — there you will see laughter. Go among the bourgeoisie, when they are amusing themselves; you will see them laugh to suffocation. Go to the soldiers' quarters, you will see men choking, their eyes full of tears, doubled up on their beds over the jokes of some funny fellow. But in our drawingrooms we never laugh. I tell you that we simulate everything, even laughter."

Musadieu interrupted him:

"Permit me to say that you are very severe. It seems to me that you yourself, my dear fellow, do not wholly despise this society at which you rail so bitterly."

Bertin smiled.

"I? I love it!" he declared.

"But then — — "

"I despise myself a little, as a mongrel of doubtful race."

"All that sort of talk is nothing but a pose," said the Duchess.

And, as he denied having any intention of posing, she cut short the discussion by declaring that all artists try to make people believe that chalk is cheese.

The conversation then became general, touching upon everything, ordinary and pleasant, friendly and critical, and, as the dinner was drawing toward its end, the Countess suddenly exclaimed, pointing to the full glasses of wine that were ranged before her plate:

"Well, you see that I have drunk nothing, nothing, not a drop! We shall see whether I shall not grow thin!"

The Duchess, furious, tried to make her swallow some mineral water, but in vain; then she exclaimed:

"Oh, the little simpleton! That daughter of hers will turn her head. I beg of you, Guilleroy, prevent your wife from committing this folly."

The Count, who was explaining to Musadieu the system of a threshing-machine invented in America, had not been listening.

"What folly, Duchess?"

"The folly of wishing to grow thin."

The Count looked at his wife with an expression of kindly indifference.

"I never have formed the habit of opposing her," he replied.

The Countess had risen, taking the arm of her neighbor; the Count offered his to the Duchess, and they passed into the large drawingroom, the boudoir at the end being reserved for use in the daytime.

It was a vast and well lighted room. On the four walls the large and beautiful panels of pale blue silk, of antique pattern, framed in white and gold, took on under the light of the lamps and the chandelier a moonlight softness and brightness. In the center of the principal one, the portrait of the Countess by Olivier Bertin seemed to inhabit, to animate the apartment. It had a look of being at home there, mingling with the air of the salon its youthful smile, the grace of its pose, the bright charm of its golden hair. It had become almost a custom, a sort of polite ceremony, like making the sign of the cross on entering a church, to compliment the model on the work of the painter whenever anyone stood before it.

Musadieu never failed to do this. His opinion as a connoisseur commissioned by the State having the value of that of an official expert, he regarded it as his duty to affirm often, with conviction, the superiority of that painting.

"Indeed," said he, "that is the most beautiful modern portrait I know. There is prodigious life in it."

The Comte de Guilleroy, who, through hearing this portrait continually praised, had acquired a rooted conviction that he possessed a masterpiece, approached to join him, and for a minute or two they lavished upon the portrait all the art technicalities of the day in praise of the apparent qualities of the work, and also of those that were suggested.

All eyes were lifted toward the portrait, apparently in a rapture of admiration, and Olivier Bertin, accustomed to these eulogies, to which he paid hardly more attention than to questions about his health when meeting some one in the street, nevertheless adjusted the reflector lamp placed before the portrait in order to illumine it, the servant having carelessly set it a little on one side.

Then they seated themselves, and as the Count approached the Duchess, she said to him:

"I believe that my nephew is coming here for me, and to ask you for a cup of tea."

Their wishes, for some time, had been mutually understood and agreed, without either side ever having exchanged confidences or even hints.

The Marquis de Farandal, who was the brother of the Duchesse de Mortemain, after almost ruining himself at the gaming table, had died of the effects of a fall from his horse, leaving a widow and a son. This young man, now nearly twenty-eight years of age, was one of the most popular leaders of the cotillion in Europe, for he was sometimes requested to go to Vienna or to London to crown in the waltz some princely ball. Although possessing very small means, he remained, through his social station, his family, his name, and his almost royal connections, one of the most popular and envied men in Paris.

It was necessary to give a solid foundation to this glory of his youth, and after a rich, a very rich marriage, to replace social triumphs by political success. As soon as the Marquis should become a deputy, he would become also, by that attainment alone, one of the props of the future throne, one of the counselors of the King, one of the leaders of the party.

The Duchess, who was well informed, knew the amount of the enormous fortune of the Comte de Guilleroy, a prudent hoarder of money, who lived in a simple apartment when he was quite able to live like a great lord in one of the handsomest mansions of Paris. She knew about his always successful speculations, his subtle scent as a financier, his share in the most fruitful schemes of the past ten years, and she had cherished the idea of marrying her nephew to the daughter of the Norman deputy, to whom this marriage would give an immense influence in the aristocratic society of the princely circle. Guilleroy, who had made a rich marriage, and had thereby increased a large personal fortune, now nursed other ambitions.

He had faith in the return of the King, and wished, when that event should come, to be so situated as to derive from it the largest personal profit.

As a simple deputy, he did not cut a prominent figure. As a father-in-law of the Marquis of Farandal, whose ancestors had been the faithful and chosen familiars of the royal house of France, he might rise to the first rank.

The friendship of the Duchess for his wife lent to this union an element of intimacy that was very precious; and, for fear some other young girl might appear who would please the Marquis, he had brought about the return of his own daughter in order to hasten events.

Madame de Mortemain, foreseeing and divining his plans, lent him her silent complicity; and on that very day, although she had not been informed of the sudden return of the young girl, she had made an appointment with her nephew to meet her at the Guilleroys, so that he might gradually become accustomed to visit that house frequently.

For the first time, the Count and the Duchess spoke of their mutual desires in veiled terms; and when they parted, a treaty of alliance had been concluded.

At the other end of the room everyone was laughing at a story M. de Musadieu was telling to the Baroness de Corbelle about the presentation of a negro ambassador to the President of the Republic, when the Marquis de Farandal was announced.

He appeared in the doorway and paused. With a quick and familiar gesture, he placed a monocle on his right eye and left it there, as if to reconnoiter the room he was about to enter, but perhaps to give those that were already there the time to see him and to observe his entrance. Then by an imperceptible movement of cheek and eyebrow, he allowed to drop the bit of glass at the end of a black silk hair, and advanced quickly toward Madame de Guilleroy, whose extended hand he kissed, bowing very low. He saluted his aunt likewise, then shook hands with the rest of the company, going from one to another with easy elegance of manner.

He was a tall fellow, with a red moustache, and was already slightly bald, with the figure of an officer and the gait of an English sportsman. It was evident, at first sight of him, that all his limbs were better exercised than his head, and that he cared only for such occupations as developed strength and physical activity. He had some education, however, for he had learned, and was learning every day, by much mental effort, a great deal that would be useful to him to know later: history, studying dates unweariedly, but mistaking the lesson to be learned from facts and the elementary notions of political economy necessary to a deputy, the A B C of sociology for the use of the ruling classes.

Musadieu esteemed him, saying: "He will be a valuable man." Bertin appreciated his skill and his vigor. They went to the same fencing-hall, often hunted together, and met while riding in the avenues of the Bois. Between them, therefore, had been formed a sympathy of similar tastes, that instinctive freemasonry which creates between two men a subject of conversation, as agreeable to one as to the other.

When the Marquis was presented to Annette de Guilleroy, he immediately had a suspicion of his aunt's designs, and after saluting her he ran his eyes over her, with the rapid glance of a connoisseur.

He decided that she was graceful, and above all full of promise, for he had led so many cotillions that he knew young girls well, and could predict almost to a certainty the future of their beauty, as an expert who tastes a wine as yet too new.

He exchanged only a few unimportant words with her, then seated himself near the Baroness de Corbelle, so that he could chat with her in an undertone.

Everyone took leave at an early hour, and when all had gone, when the child was in her bed, the lamps were extinguished, the servants gone to their own quarters, the Comte de Guilleroy, walking across the drawingroom, lighted now by only two candles, detained for a long time the Countess, who was half asleep in an armchair, to tell her of his hopes, to suggest the attitude for themselves to assume, to forecast all combinations, the chances and the precautions to be taken.

It was late when he retired, charmed, however, with this evening, and murmuring, "I believe that that affair is a certainty."

III

"When will you come, my friend? I have not seen you for three days, and that seems a long time to me. My daughter occupies much of my time, but you know that I can no longer do without you."

The painter, who was drawing sketches, ever seeking a new subject re-read the Countess's note, then, opening the drawer of a writing-desk, he deposited it on a heap of other letters, which had been accumulating there since the beginning of their love-affair.

Thanks to the opportunities given them by the customs of fashionable society, they had grown used to seeing each other almost every day. Now and then she visited him, and sat for an hour or two in the armchair in which she had posed, while he worked. But, as she had some fear of the criticisms of the servants, she preferred to receive him at her own house, or to meet him elsewhere, for that daily interview, that small change of love.

These meetings would be agreed upon beforehand, and always seemed perfectly natural to M. de Guilleroy.

Twice a week at least the painter dined at the Countess's house, with a few friends; on Monday nights he visited her in her box at the Opera; then they would agree upon a meeting at such or such a house, to which chance led them at the same hour. He knew the evenings that she did not go out, and would call then to have a cup of tea with her, feeling himself very much at home even near the folds of her robe, so tenderly and so surely settled in that ripe affection, so fixed in the habit of finding her somewhere, of passing some time by her side, or exchanging a few words with her and of mingling a few thoughts, that he felt, although the glow of his passion had long since faded, an incessant need of seeing her.

The desire for family life, for a full and animated household, for the family table, for those evenings when one talks without fatigue with old friends, that desire for contact, for familiarity, for human intercourse, which dwells dormant in every human heart, and which every old bachelor carries from door to door to his friends, where he installs something of himself, added a strain of egoism to his sentiments of affection. In that house, where he was loved and spoiled, where he found everything, he could still rest and nurse his solitude.

For three days he had not seen his friends, who must be very much occupied by the return of the daughter of the house; and he was already feeling bored, and even a little offended because they had not sent for him sooner, but not wishing, as a matter of discretion, to be the first to make an approach.

The Countess's letter aroused him like the stroke of a whip. It was three o'clock in the afternoon. He decided to go immediately to her house, that he might find her before she went out.

The valet appeared, summoned by the sound of Olivier's bell.

"What sort of weather is it, Joseph?"

"Very fine, Monsieur."

"Warm?"

"Yes, Monsieur."

"White waistcoat, blue jacket, gray hat."

He always dressed with elegance, but although his tailor turned him out in correct styles, the very way in which he wore his clothes, his manner of walking, his comfortable proportions encased in a white waistcoat, his high gray felt hat, tilted a little toward the back of his head, seemed to reveal at once that he was both an artist and a bachelor.

When he reached the Countess's house, he was told that she was dressing for a drive in the Bois. He was a little vexed at this, and waited.

According to his habit, he began to pace to and fro in the drawingroom, going from one seat to another, or from the windows to the wall, in the large drawingroom darkened by the curtains. On the light tables with gilded feet, trifles of various kinds, useless, pretty, and costly, lay scattered about in studied disorder. There were little antique boxes of chased gold, miniature snuffboxes, ivory statuettes, objects in dull silver, quite modern, of an exaggerated severity, in which English taste appeared: a diminutive kitchen stove, and upon it a cat drinking from a pan, a cigarette-case simulating a loaf of bread, a coffee-pot to hold matches, and in a casket a complete set of doll's jewelry — necklaces, bracelets, rings, brooches, earrings set with diamonds, sapphires, rubies, emeralds, a microscopic fantasy that seemed to have been executed by Lilliputian jewelers.

From time to time he touched some object, given by himself on some anniversary; he lifted it, handled it, examining it with dreamy indifference, then put it back in its place.

In one corner some books that were luxuriously bound but seldom opened lay within easy reach on a round table with a single leg for a foundation, which stood before a little curved sofa. The Revue des Deux Mondes lay there also, somewhat worn, with turned-down pages, as if it had been read and re-read many times; other publications lay near it, some of them uncut: the Arts modernes, which is bought only because of its cost, the subscription price being four hundred francs a year; and the Feuille libre, a thin volume between blue covers, in which appear the more recent poets, called "les enerves."

Between the windows stood the Countess's writing-desk, a coquettish piece of furniture of the last century, on which she wrote replies to those hurried questions handed to her during her receptions. A few books were on that, also, familiar books, index to the heart and mind of a woman: Musset, Manon Lescaut, Werther; and, to show that she was not a stranger to the complicated sensations and mysteries of psychology, Les Fleurs du Mal, Le Rouge et le Noir, La Femme au XVIII Siecle, Adolphe.

Beside the books lay a charming hand-mirror, a masterpiece of the silversmith's art, the glass being turned down upon a square of embroidered velvet, in order to allow one to admire the curious gold and silver workmanship on the back. Bertin took it up and looked at his own reflection. For some years he had been growing terribly old in appearance, and although he thought that his face showed more originality than when he was younger, the sight of his heavy cheeks and increasing wrinkles saddened him.

A door opened behind him.

"Good morning, Monsieur Bertin," said Annette.

"Good morning, little one; are you well?"

"Very well; and you?"

"What, are you not saying 'thou' to me, then, after all?"

"No, indeed! It would really embarrass me."

"Nonsense!"

"Yes, it would. You make me feel timid."

"And why, pray?"

"Because — because you are neither young enough nor old enough — "

The painter laughed.

"After such a reason as that I will insist no more."

She blushed suddenly, up to the white brow, where the waves of hair began to ripple, and resumed, with an air of slight confusion:

"Mamma told me to say to you that she will be down immediately, and to ask you whether you will go to the Bois de Boulogne with us."

"Yes, certainly. You are alone?"

"No; with the Duchesse de Mortemain."

"Very well; I will go."

"Then will you allow me to go and put on my hat?"

"Yes, go, my child."

As Annette left the room the Countess entered, veiled, ready to set forth. She extended her hands cordially.

"We never see you any more. What are you doing?" she inquired.

"I did not wish to trouble you just at this time," said Bertin.

In the tone with which she spoke the word "Olivier!" she expressed all her reproaches and all her attachment.

"You are the best woman in the world," he said, touched by the tender intonation of his name.

This little love-quarrel being finished and settled, the Countess resumed her light, society tone.

"We shall pick up the Duchess at her hotel and then make a tour of the Bois. We must show all that sort of thing to Nanette, you know."

The landau awaited them under the porte-cochere.

Bertin seated himself facing the two ladies, and the carriage departed, the pawing of the horses making a resonant sound against the over-arching roof of the porte-cochere.

Along the grand boulevard descending toward the Madeleine all the gaiety of the springtime seemed to have fallen upon the tide of humanity.

The soft air and the sunshine lent to the men a festive air, to the women a suggestion of love; the bakers' boys deposited their baskets on the benches to run and play with their brethren, the street urchins; the dogs appeared in a great hurry to go somewhere; the canaries hanging in the boxes of the concierges trilled loudly; only the ancient cab-horses kept their usual sedate pace.

"Oh, what a beautiful day! How good it is to live!" murmured the Countess.

The painter contemplated both mother and daughter in the dazzling light. Certainly, they were different, but at the same time so much alike that the latter was veritably a continuation of the former, made of the same blood, the same flesh, animated by the same life. Their eyes, above all, those blue eyes flecked with tiny black drops, of such a brilliant blue in the daughter, a little faded in the mother, fixed upon him a look so similar that he expected to hear them make the same replies. And he was surprised to discover, as he made them laugh and talk, that before him were two very distinct women, one who had lived and one who was about to live. No, he did not foresee what would become of that child when her young mind, influenced by tastes and instincts that were as yet dormant, should have expanded and developed amid the life of the world. This was a pretty little new person, ready for chances and for love, ignored and ignorant, who was sailing out of port like a vessel, while her mother was returning, having traversed life and having loved!

He was touched at the thought that she had chosen himself, and that she preferred him still, this woman who had remained so pretty, rocked in that landau, in the warm air of springtime.

As he expressed his gratitude to her in a glance, she divined it, and he thought he could feel her thanks in the rustle of her robe.

In his turn he murmured: "Oh, yes, what a beautiful day!"

When they had taken up the Duchess, in the Rue de Varenne, they spun along at a swift pace toward the Invalides, crossed the Seine, and reached the Avenue des Champs-Elysees, going up toward the Arc de triomphe de l'Etoile in the midst of a sea of carriages.

The young girl was seated beside Olivier, riding backward, and she opened upon this stream of equipages wide and wondering eager eyes. Occasionally, when the Duchess and the Countess acknowledged a salutation with a short movement of the head, she would ask "Who is that?" Bertin answered: "The Pontaiglin," "the Puicelci," "the Comtesse de Lochrist," or "the beautiful Madame Mandeliere."

Now they were following the Avenue of the Bois de Boulogne, amid the noise and the rattling of wheels. The carriages, a little less crowded than below the Arc de Triomphe, seemed to struggle in an endless race. The cabs, the heavy landaus, the solemn eight-spring vehicles, passed one another over and over again, distanced suddenly by a rapid victoria, drawn by a single trotter, bearing along at a reckless pace, through all that rolling throng, bourgeois and aristocratic, through all societies, all classes, all hierarchies, an indolent young woman, whose bright and striking toilette diffused among the carriages it touched in passing a strange perfume of some unknown flower.

"Who is that lady?" Annette inquired.

"I don't know," said Bertin, at which reply the Duchess and the Countess exchanged a smile.

The leaves were opening, the familiar nightingales of that Parisian garden were singing already among the tender verdure, and when, as the carriage approached the lake, it joined the long file of other vehicles at a walk, there was an incessant exchange of salutations, smiles, and friendly words, as the wheels touched. The procession seemed now like the gliding of a flotilla in which were seated very well-bred ladies and gentlemen. The Duchess, who was bowing every moment before raised hats or inclined heads, appeared to be passing them in review, calling to mind what she knew, thought, or supposed of these people, as they defiled before her.

"Look, dearest, there is the lovely Madame Mandeliere again — the beauty of the Republic."

In a light and dashing carriage, the beauty of the Republic allowed to be admired, under an apparent indifference to this indisputable glory, her large dark eyes, her low brow beneath a veil of dusky hair, and her mouth, which was a shade too obstinate in its lines.

"Very beautiful, all the same," said Bertin.

The Countess did not like to hear him praise other women. She shrugged her shoulders slightly, but said nothing.

But the young girl, in whom the instinct of rivalry suddenly awoke, ventured to say: "I do not find her beautiful at all."

"What! You do not think her beautiful?" said the painter.

"No; she looks as if she had been dipped in ink."

The Duchess, delighted, burst into laughter.

"Bravo, little one!" she cried. "For the last six years half the men in Paris have been swooning at the feet of that negress! I believe that they sneer at us. Look at the Comtesse de Lochrist instead."

Alone, in a landau with a white poodle, the Countess, delicate as a miniature, a blond with brown eyes, whose grace and beauty had served for five or six years as the theme for the admiration of her partisans, bowed to the ladies, with a fixed smile on her lips.

But Nanette exhibited no greater enthusiasm than before.

"Oh," she said, "she is no longer young!"

Bertin, who usually did not at all agree with the Countess in the daily discussions of these two rivals, felt a sudden irritation at the stupid intolerance of this little simpleton.

"Nonsense!" he said. "Whether one likes her or not, she is charming; and I only hope that you may become as pretty as she."

"Pooh! pooh!" said the Duchess. "You notice women only after they have passed the thirtieth year. The child is right. You admire only passee beauty."

"Pardon me!" he exclaimed; "a woman is really beautiful only after maturing, when the expression of her face and eyes has become fully developed!"

He enlarged upon this idea that the first youthful freshness is only the gloss of riper beauty; he demonstrated that men of the world were wise in paying but little attention to young girls in their first season, and that they were right in proclaiming them beautiful only when they passed into their later period of bloom.

The Countess, flattered, murmured: "He is right; he speaks as an artist. The youthful countenance is very charming, but it is always a trifle commonplace."

The painter continued to urge his point, indicating at what moment a face that was losing, little by little, the undecided grace of youth, really assumed its definite form, its true character and physiognomy.

At each word the Countess said "Yes," with a little nod of conviction; and the more he affirmed, with all the heat of a lawyer making a plea, with the animation of the accused pleading his own cause, the more she approved, by glance and gesture, as if they two were allied against some danger, and must defend themselves against some false and menacing opinion. Annette hardly heard them, she was so engrossed in looking about her. Her usually smiling face had become grave, and she said no more, carried away by the pleasure of the rapid driving. The sunlight, the trees, the carriage, this delightful life, so rich and gay — all this was for her!

Every day she might come here, recognized in her turn, saluted and envied; and perhaps the men, in pointing her out to one another, would say that she was beautiful. She noticed all those that appeared to her distinguished among the throng and inquired their names, without thinking of anything beyond the mere sound of the syllables, though sometimes they awoke in her an echo of respect and admiration, when she realized that she had seen them often in the newspapers or heard stories concerning them. She could not become accustomed to this long procession of celebrities; it seemed unreal to her, as if she were a part of some stage spectacle. The cabs filled her with disdain mingled with disgust; they annoyed and irritated her, and suddenly she said:

"I think they should not allow anything but private carriages to come here."

"Indeed, Mademoiselle!" said Bertin; "and then what becomes of our equality, liberty and fraternity?"

Annette made a moue that signified "Don't talk about that!" and continued:

"They should have a separate drive for cabs — that of Vincennes, for instance."

"You are behind the times, little one, and evidently do not know that we are swimming in the full tide of democracy. But, if you wish to see this place free from any mingling of the middle class, come in the morning, and then you will find only the fine flower of society."

He proceeded to describe graphically, as he knew well how to do, the Bois in the morning hours with its gay cavaliers and fair Amazons, that club where everyone knows everyone else by their Christian names, their pet names, their family connections, titles, qualities, and vices, as if they all lived in the same neighborhood or in the same small town.

"Do you come here often at that hour?" Annette inquired.

"Very often; there is no more charming place in Paris."

"Do you come on horseback in the mornings?"

"Yes."

"And in the afternoon you pay visits?"

"Yes."

"Then, when do you work?"

"Oh, I work — sometimes; and besides, you see, I have chosen a special entertainment suited to my tastes. As I paint the portraits of beautiful women, it is necessary that I should see them and follow them everywhere."

"On foot and on horseback!" murmured Annette, with a perfectly serious face.

He threw her a sidelong glance of appreciation, which seemed to say: "Ah! you are witty, even now! You will do very well."

A breath of cold air from far away, from the country that was hardly awake as yet, swept over the park, and the whole Bois, coquettish, frivolous, and fashionable, shivered under its chill. For some seconds it caused the tender leaves to tremble on the trees, and garments on shoulders. All the women, with a movement almost simultaneous, drew up over their arms and chests their wraps lying behind them; and the horses began to trot, from one end of the avenue to the other, as if the keen wind had flicked them like a whip.

The Countess's party returned quickly, to the silvery jingle of the harness, under the slanting red rays of the setting sun.

"Shall you go home?" inquired the Countess of Bertin, with whose habits she was familiar.

"No, I am going to the club."

"Then, shall we set you down there in passing?"

"Thank you, that will be very convenient."

"And when shall you invite us to breakfast with the Duchess?"

"Name your day."

This painter in ordinary to the fair Parisians, whom his admirers christened "a Watteau realist" and his detractors a "photographer of gowns and mantles," often received at breakfast or at dinner the beautiful persons whose feature he had reproduced, as well as the celebrated and the well known, who found very amusing these little entertainments in a bachelor's establishment.

"The day after tomorrow, then. Will the day after tomorrow suit you, my dear Duchess?" asked Madame de Guilleroy.

"Yes, indeed; you are charming! Monsieur Bertin never thinks of me when he has his little parties. It is quite evident that I am no longer young."

The Countess, accustomed to consider the artist's home almost the same as her own, replied:

"Only we four, the four of the landau — the Duchess, Annette, you and I, eh, great artist?"

"Only ourselves," said he, alighting from the carriage, "and I will have prepared for you some crabs a l'alsacienne."

"Oh, you will awaken a desire for luxury in the little one!"

He bowed to them, standing beside the carriage door, then entered quickly the vestibule of the main entrance to the club, threw his topcoat and cane to a group of footmen, who had risen like soldiers at the passing of an officer; mounted the broad stairway, meeting another brigade of servants in knee-breeches, pushed open a door, feeling himself suddenly as alert as a young man, as he heard at the end of the corridor a continuous clash of foils, the sound of stamping feet, and loud exclamations: "Touche!" "A moi." "Passe!" "J'en ai!" "Touche!" "A vous!"

In the fencing-hall the swordsmen, dressed in gray linen, with leather vests, their trousers tight around the ankles, a sort of apron falling over the front of the body, one arm in the air, with the hand thrown backward, and in the other hand, enormous in a large fencing-glove, the thin, flexible foil, extended and recovered with the agile swiftness of mechanical jumping-jacks.

Others rested and chatted, still out of breath, red and perspiring, with handkerchief in hand to wipe off faces and necks; others, seated on a square divan that ran along the four sides of the hall, watched the fencing — Liverdy against Landa, and the master of the club, Taillade, against the tall Rocdiane.

Bertin, smiling, quite at home, shook hands with several men.

"I choose you!" cried the Baron de Baverie.

"I am with you, my dear fellow," said Bertin, passing into the dressing-room to prepare himself.

He had not felt so agile and vigorous for a long time, and, guessing that he should fence well that day, he hurried as impatiently as a schoolboy ready for play. As soon as he stood before his adversary he attacked him with great ardor, and in ten minutes he had touched him eleven times and had so fatigued him that the Baron cried for quarter. Then he fenced with Punisimont, and with his colleague, Amaury Maldant.

The cold douche that followed, freezing his palpitating flesh, reminded him of the baths of his twentieth year, when he used to plunge head first into the Seine from the bridges in the suburbs, in order to amaze the bourgeois passersby.

"Shall you dine here?" inquired Maldant.

"Yes."

"We have a table with Liverdy, Rocdiane, and Landa; make haste; it is a quarter past seven."

The diningroom was full, and there was a continuous hum of men's voices.

There were all the nocturnal vagabonds of Paris, idlers and workers, all those who from seven o'clock in the evening know not what to do and dine at the club, ready to catch at anything or anybody that chance may offer to amuse them.

When the five friends were seated the banker Liverdy, a vigorous and hearty man of forty, said to Bertin:

"You were in fine form this evening."

"Yes, I could have done surprising things to-day," Bertin replied.

The others smiled, and the landscape painter, Amaury Maldant, a thin little bald-headed man with a gray beard, said, with a sly expression:

"I, too, always feel the rising of the sap in April; it makes me bring forth a few leaves — half a dozen at most — then it runs into sentiment; there never is any fruit."

The Marquis de Rocdiane and the Comte Landa sympathized with him. Both were older than he, though even a keen eye could not guess their age; clubmen, horsemen, swordsmen, whose incessant exercise had given them bodies of steel, they boasted of being younger in every way than the enervated good-for-nothings of the new generation.

Rocdiane, of good family, with the entree to all salons, though suspected of financial intrigues of many kinds (which, according to Bertin, was not surprising, since he had lived so much in the gaming-houses), married, but separated from his wife, who paid him an annuity, a director of Belgian and Portuguese banks, carried boldly upon his energetic, Don Quixote-like face the somewhat tarnished honor of a gentleman, which was occasionally brightened by the blood from a thrust in a duel.

The Comte de Landa, a good-natured colossus, proud of his figure and his shoulders, although married and the father of two children, found it difficult to dine at home three times a week; he remained at the club on the other days, with his friends, after the session in the fencing-hall.

"The club is a family," he said, "the family of those who as yet have none, of those who never will have one, and of those who are bored by their own."

The conversation branched off on the subject of women, glided from anecdotes to reminiscences, from reminiscences to boasts, and then to indiscreet confidences.

The Marquis de Rocdiane allowed the names of his inamoratas to be guessed by unmistakable hints — society women whose names he did not utter, so that their identity might be the better surmised. The banker Liverdy indicated his flames by their first names. He would say: "I was at that time the best of friends with the wife of a diplomat. Now, one evening when I was leaving her, I said to her, 'My little Marguerite'" — then he checked himself, amid the smiles of his fellows, adding "Ha! I let something slip. One should form a habit of calling all women Sophie."

Olivier Bertin, very reserved, was accustomed to declare, when questioned:

"For my part, I content myself with my models."

They pretended to believe him, and Landa, who was frankly a libertine, grew quite excited at the idea of all the pretty creatures that walked the streets and all the young persons who posed undraped before the painter at ten francs an hour.

As the bottle became empty, all these graybeards, as the younger members of the club called them, acquired red faces, and their kindling ardor awakened new desires.

Rocdiane, after the coffee, became still more indiscreet, and forgot the society women to celebrate the charms of simple cocottes.

"Paris!" said he, a glass of kummel in his hand, "The only city where a man never grows old, the only one where, at fifty, if he is sound and well preserved, he will always find a young girl, as pretty as an angel, to love him."

Landa, finding again his Rocdiane after the liqueurs, applauded him enthusiastically, and mentioned the young girls who still adored him every day.

But Liverdy, more skeptical, and pretending to know exactly what women were worth, murmured: "Yes, they tell you that they adore you!"

"They prove it to me, my dear fellow," exclaimed Landa.

"Such proofs don't count."

"They suffice me!"

"But, sacrebleu! they do mean it," cried Rocdiane. "Do you believe that a pretty little creature of twenty, who has been going the rounds in Paris for five or six years already, where all our moustaches have taught her kisses and spoiled her taste for them, still knows how to distinguish a man of thirty from a man of sixty? Pshaw! what nonsense! She has seen and known too many of them. Now, I'll wager that, down in the bottom of her heart, she actually prefers an old banker to a young stripling. Does she know or reflect upon that? Have men any age here? Oh, my dear fellow, we grow young as we grow gray, and the whiter our hair becomes the more they tell us they love us, the more they show it, and the more they believe it."

They rose from the table, their blood warmed and lashed by alcohol, ready to make any conquest; and they began to deliberate how to spend the evening, Bertin mentioning the Cirque, Rocdiane the Hippodrome, Maldant the Eden, and Landa the Folies-Bergere, when a light and distant sound of the tuning of violins reached their ears.

"Ah, there is music at the club to-day, it seems," said Rocdiane.

"Yes," Bertin replied. "Shall we listen for ten minutes before going out?"

"Agreed."

They crossed a salon, a billiard-room, a card-room, and finally reached a sort of box over the gallery of the musicians. Four gentlemen, ensconced in armchairs, were waiting there already, in easy attitudes, while below, among rows of empty seats, a dozen others were chatting, sitting or standing.

The conductor tapped his desk with his bow; the music began.

Olivier adored music as an opium-eater adores opium. It made him dream.

As soon as the sonorous wave from the instruments reached him he felt himself borne away in a sort of nervous intoxication, which thrilled body and mind indescribably. His imagination ran riot, made drunk by melody, and carried him along through sweet dreams and charming reveries. With closed eyes, legs crossed, and folded arms, he listened to the strains, and gave himself up to the visions that passed before his eyes and into his mind.

The orchestra was playing one of Haydn's symphonies, and when Bertin's eyelids drooped over his eyes, he saw again the Bois, the crowd of carriages around him, and facing him in the landau the Countess and her daughter. He heard their voices, followed their words, felt the movement of the carriage, inhaled the air, filled with the odor of young leaves.

Three times, his neighbor, speaking to him, interrupted this vision, which three times he began again, as the rolling of the vessel seems to continue when, after crossing the ocean, one lies motionless in bed.

Then it extended itself to a long voyage, with the two women always seated before him, sometimes on the railway, again at the table of strange hotels. During the whole execution of the symphony they accompanied him, as if, while driving with him in the sunshine, they had left the image of their two faces imprinted on his vision.

Silence followed; then came a noise of seats being moved and chattering of voices, which dispelled this vapor of a dream, and he perceived, dozing around him, his four friends, relaxed from a listening attitude to the comfortable posture of sleep.

"Well, what shall we do now?" he asked, after he had roused them.

"I should like to sleep here a little longer," replied Rocdiane frankly.

"And I, too," said Landa.

Bertin rose.

"Well, I shall go home," he said. "I am rather tired."

He felt very animated, on the contrary, but he wished to go, fearing the end of the evening around the baccarat-table of the club, which unfortunately he knew so well.

He went home, therefore, and the following day, after a nervous night, one of those nights that put artists in that condition of cerebral activity called inspiration, he decided not to go out, but to work until evening.

It was an excellent day, one of those days of facile production, when ideas seem to descend into the hands and fix themselves upon the canvas.

With doors shut, far from the world, in the quiet of his own dwelling, closed to everyone, in the friendly peace of his studio, with clear eye, lucid mind, enthusiastic, alert, he tasted that happiness given only to artists, the happiness of bringing forth their work in joy. Nothing existed any more for him in such hours of work except the piece of canvas on which was born an image under the caress of his brush; and he experienced, in these crises of productiveness, a strange and delicious sensation of abounding life which intoxicated him. When evening came he was exhausted as by healthful fatigue, and went to sleep with agreeable anticipation of his breakfast the next morning.

The table was covered with flowers, the menu was carefully chosen, for Madame de Guilleroy's sake, as she was a refined epicure; and in spite of strong but brief resistance, the painter compelled his guests to drink champagne.

"The little one will get intoxicated," protested the Countess.

"Dear me! there must be a first time," replied the indulgent Duchess.

Everyone, as the party returned to the studio, felt stirred by that light gaiety which lifts one as if the feet had wings.

The Duchess and the Countess, having an engagement at a meeting of the Committee of French Mothers, were to take Annette home before going to the meeting; but Bertin offered to take her for a walk, and then to the Boulevard Malesherbes; so both ladies left them.

"Let us take the longest way," said Annette.

"Would you like to stroll about the Monceau Park?" asked Bertin. "It is a very pretty place; we will look at the babies and nurses."

"Yes, I should like that."

They passed through the Avenue Velasquez and entered the gilded and monumental gate that serves as a sign and an entrance to that exquisite jewel of a park, displaying in the heart of Paris its verdant and artificial beauty, surrounded by a belt of princely mansions.

Along the wide walks, which unroll their massive and artistic curves through grassy lawns, throngs of people, sitting on iron chairs, watch the passers; while in the little paths, deep in shade and winding like streams, groups of children crawl in the sand, run about, or jump the rope under the indolent eyes of nurses or the anxious watchfulness of mothers. Two enormous trees, rounded into domes, like monuments of leaves, the gigantic horse-chestnuts, whose heavy verdure is lighted up by red and white clusters, the showy sycamores, the graceful plane-trees with their trunks designedly polished, set off in a charming perspective the tall, undulating grass.

The weather was warm, the turtledoves were cooing among the branches, and flying to meet one another from the tree-tops, while the sparrows bathed in the rainbow formed by the sunshine and the spray thrown over the smooth turf. White statues on their pedestals seemed happy in the midst of the green freshness. A little marble boy was drawing from his foot an invisible thorn, as if he had just pricked himself in running after the Diana fleeing toward the little lake, imprisoned by the woods that screened the ruins of a temple.

Other statues, amorous and cold, embraced one another on the borders of the groves, or dreamed there, holding one knee in the hand. A cascade foamed and rolled over the pretty rocks; a tree, truncated like a column, supported an ivy; a tombstone bore an inscription. The stone shafts erected on the lawns hardly suggest better the Acropolis than this elegant little park recalled wild forests. It is the charming and artificial place where city people go to look at flowers grown in hothouses, and to admire, as one admires the spectacle of life at the theater, that agreeable representation of the beauties of nature given in the heart of Paris.

Olivier Bertin had come almost every day for years to this favorite spot to look at the fair Parisians moving in their appropriate setting. "It is a park made for toilettes," he would say; "Badly dressed people are horrible in it." He would rove about there for hours, knowing all the plants and all the habitual visitors.

He now strolled beside Annette along the avenues, his eye distracted by the motley and animated crowd in the gardens.

"Oh, the little love!" exclaimed Annette. She was gazing at a tiny boy with blond curls, who was looking at her with his blue eyes full of surprise and delight.

Then she passed all the children in review, and the pleasure she felt in seeing those living dolls, decked out in their dainty ribbons, made her talkative and communicative.

She walked slowly, chatting to Bertin, giving him her reflections on the children, the nurses, and the mothers. The larger children drew from her little exclamations of joy, while the little pale ones touched her sympathy.

Bertin listened, more amused by her than by the little ones, and, always remembering his work, he murmured, "That is delicious!" thinking that he must make an exquisite picture, with one corner of this park and a bouquet of nurses, mothers and children. Why had he never thought of it before?

"You like those little ones?" he inquired.

"I adore them!"

He felt, from her manner of looking at them, that she longed to take them in her arms, to hug and kiss them — the natural and tender longing of a future mother; and he was surprised at this secret instinct hidden in this little woman.

As she appeared ready to talk, he questioned her about her tastes. She admitted, with pretty naivete, that she had hopes of social success and glory, and that she desired to have fine horses, which she knew almost as well as a horse-dealer, for a part of the farm at Roncieres was devoted to breeding; but she appeared to trouble her head no more about a fiance than one is concerned about an apartment, which is always to be found among the multitude of houses to rent.

They approached the lake, where two swans and six ducks were quietly floating, as clean and calm as porcelain birds, and they passed before a young woman sitting in a chair, with an open book lying on her knees, her eyes gazing upward, her soul having apparently taken flight in a dream.

She was as motionless as a wax figure. Plain, humble, dressed as a modest girl who has no thought of pleasing, she had gone to the land of Dreams, carried away by a phrase or a word that had bewitched her heart. Undoubtedly she was continuing, according to the impulse of her hopes, the adventure begun in the book.

Bertin paused, surprised. "How beautiful to dream like that!" said he.

They had passed before her; now they turned and passed her again without her perceiving them, so attentively did she follow the distant flight of her thought.

"Tell me, little one," said the painter to Annette, "would it bore you very much to pose for me once or twice?"

"No, indeed! Quite the contrary."

"Look well at that young lady who is roaming in the world of fancy."

"The lady there, in that chair?"

"Yes. Well, you, too, will sit on a chair, you will have an open book on your knee, and you will try to do as she does. Have you ever had daydreams?"

"Yes, indeed."

"Of what?"

He tried to confess her as to her aerial flights, but she would make no reply, evaded his questions, looked at the ducks swimming after some bread thrown to them by a lady, and seemed embarrassed, as if he had touched upon a subject that was a sensitive point with her.

Then, to change the conversation, she talked about her life at Roncieres, spoke of her grandmother, to whom she read aloud a long time every day, and who must now feel very lonely and sad.

As he listened, the painter felt as gay as a bird, gay as he never had been. All that she had said, all the doings, the trifling everyday details of the simple life of a young girl, amused and interested him.

"Let us sit down," he said.

They seated themselves near the water, and the two swans came floating toward them, expecting some fresh dainty.

Bertin felt recollections awakening within him — those faded remembrances that are drowned in forgetfulness, and which suddenly return, one knows not why. They surged up rapidly, of all sorts, and so numerous at the same time that it seemed to him a hand was stirring the miry depths of his memory.

He tried to guess the reasons of this rising up of his former life which several times already, though never so insistently as to-day, he had felt and remarked. A cause always existed for these sudden evocations — a natural and simple cause, an odor, perhaps, often a perfume. How many times a woman's draperies had thrown to him in passing, with the evaporating breath of some essence, a host of forgotten events. At the bottom of old perfume-bottles he had often found bits of his former existence; and all wandering odors — of streets, fields, houses, furniture, sweet or unsavory, the warm odors of summer evenings, the cold breath of winter nights, revived within him far-off reminiscences, as if odors kept embalmed within him these dead-and-gone memories, as aromatics preserve mummies.

Was it the damp grass or the chestnut blossoms that thus reanimated the past? No. What, then?

Was it his eye to which he owed this alertness? What had he seen? Nothing. Among the persons he had met, perhaps one might have resembled some one he had known, and, although he had not recognized it, it might have rung in his heart all the chords of the past.

Was it not a sound, rather? Very often he had heard by chance a piano, an unknown voice, even a hand-organ in the street playing some old air, which had suddenly made him feel twenty years younger, filling his breast with tender recollections, long buried.

But this appeal, continued, incessant, intangible, almost irritating! What was there near him to revive thus his extinct emotions?

"It is growing a little cool; we must go home," he said.

They rose, and resumed their walk.

He looked at the poor people sitting on benches, for whom a chair was too great an expense.

Annette also observed them, and felt disturbed at the thought of their lives, their occupations, surprised that they should come to lounge in this beautiful public garden, when their own appearance was so forlorn.

More than ever was Olivier now dreaming over past years. It seemed to him that a fly was humming in his ear, filling it with a buzzing song of bygone days.

The young girl, observing his dreamy air, asked:

"What is the matter? You seem sad."

His heart thrilled within him. Who had said that? She or her mother? Not her mother with her present voice but with her voice of long ago, so changed that he had only just recognized it.

"Nothing," he replied, smiling. "You entertain me very much; you are very charming, and you remind me of your mother."

How was it that he had not sooner remarked this strange echo of a voice once so familiar, now coming from these fresh lips?

"Go on talking," he said.

"Of what?"

"Tell me what your teachers have taught you. Did you like them?"

She began again to chat pleasantly. He listened, stirred by a growing anxiety; he watched and waited to detect, among the phrases of this young girl, almost a stranger to his heart, a word, a sound, a laugh, that seemed to have been imprisoned in her throat since her mother's youth. Certain intonations made him tremble with astonishment. Of course there were differences in their tones, the resemblance of which he had not remarked immediately, and which were in some ways so dissimilar that he had not confounded them at all; but these differences rendered all the more striking this sudden reproduction of the maternal speech. He had noted their facial resemblance with a friendly and curious eye, but now the mystery of this resuscitated voice mingled them in such a way that, turning away his head that he might no longer see the young girl, he asked himself whether it were not the Countess who was speaking thus to him, twelve years earlier.

Then when he had woven this hallucination, he turned toward her again, and found, as their eyes met, a little of the shy hesitation with which the mother's gaze had met his in the first days of their love.

They had already walked three times around the park, passing always before the same persons, the same nurses and children.

Annette was now inspecting the buildings surrounding the garden, inquiring the names of their owners. She wished to know all about them, asked questions with eager curiosity, seeming to fill her feminine mind with these details, and, with interested face, listening with her eyes as much as with her ears.

But when they arrived at the pavilion that separates the two gates of the outer boulevard, Bertin perceived that it was almost four o'clock.

"Oh," he said, "we must go home."

They walked slowly toward the Boulevard Malesherbes.

After the painter had left Annette at her home he proceeded toward the Place de la Concorde.

He sang to himself softly, longed to run, and would have been glad to jump over the benches, so agile did he feel. Paris seemed radiant to him, more beautiful than ever. "Decidedly the springtime revarnishes the whole world," was his reflection.

He was in one of those periods of mental excitement when one understands everything with more pleasure, when the vision is clearer and more comprehensive, when one feels a keener joy in seeing and feeling, as if an allpowerful hand had brightened all the colors of earth, reanimated all living creatures, and had wound up in us, as in a watch that has stopped, the activity of sensation.

He thought, as his glance took in a thousand amusing things: "And I said that there were moments when I could no longer find subjects to paint!"

He felt such a sensation of freedom and clear-sightedness that all his artistic work seemed commonplace to him, and he conceived a new way of expressing life, truer and more original; and suddenly he was seized with a desire to return home and work, so he retraced his steps and shut himself up in his studio.

But as soon as he was alone, before a newly begun picture, the ardor that had burned in his blood began to cool. He felt tired, sat down on his divan, and again gave himself up to dreaming.

The sort of happy indifference in which he lived, that carelessness of the satisfied man whose almost every need is gratified, was leaving his heart by degrees, as if something were still lacking. He realized that his house was empty and his studio deserted. Then, looking around him, he fancied he saw pass by him the shadow of a woman whose presence was sweet. For a long time he had forgotten the sensation of impatience that a lover feels when awaiting the coming of his mistress, and now he suddenly felt that she was far away, and he longed, with the ardor of a young man, to have her near him.

He was moved in thinking how much they had loved each other; and in that vast apartment he found once more, where she had come so often, innumerable reminders of her, her gestures, words, and kisses. He recalled certain days, certain hours, certain moments, and he felt around him the sweetness of her early caresses.

He got up, unable to sit quietly any longer, and began to walk, thinking again that, in spite of this intimacy that had so filled his life, he still remained alone, always alone. After the long hours of work, when he looked around him, dazed by the reawakening of the man who returns to life, he saw and felt only walls within reach of his hand and voice. Not having any woman in his home, and not being able to meet the one he loved except with the precautions of a thief, he had been compelled to spend his leisure time in public places where one finds or purchases the means of killing time. He was accustomed to going to the club, to the Cirque and the Hippodrome, on fixed days, to the Opera, and to all sorts of places, so that he should not be compelled to go home, where no doubt he would have lived in perfect happiness had he only had her beside him.

Long before, in certain hours of tender abandon, he had suffered cruelly because he could not take her and keep her with him; then, as his ardor cooled, he had accepted quietly their separation and his own liberty; now he regretted them once more, as if he were again beginning to love her. And this return of tenderness invaded his heart so suddenly, almost without reason, because the weather was fine, and possibly because a little while ago he had recognized the rejuvenated voice of that woman! How slight a thing it takes to move a man's heart, a man who is growing old, with whom remembrance turns into regret!

As in former days, the need of seeing her again came to him, entering body and mind, like a fever; and he began to think after the fashion of a young lover, exalting her in his heart, and feeling himself exalted in his desire for her; then he decided, although he had seen her only that morning, to go and ask for a cup of tea that same evening.

The hours seemed long to him, and as he set out for the Boulevard Malesherbes he was seized with a fear of not finding her, which would force him still to pass the evening alone, as he had passed so many others.

To his query: "Is the Countess at home?" the servant's answer, "Yes, Monsieur," filled him with joy.

He said, with a radiant air: "It is I again!" as he appeared at the threshold of the smaller drawingroom where the two ladies were working, under the pink shade of a double lamp of English metal, on a high and slender standard.

"What, is it you? How fortunate!" exclaimed the Countess.

"Well, yes. I feel very lonely, so I came."

"How nice of you!"

"You are expecting someone?"

"No — perhaps — I never know."

He had seated himself and now looked scornfully at the gray knitting-work that mother and daughter were swiftly making from heavy wool, working at it with long needles.

"What is that?" he asked.

"Coverlets."

"For the poor?"

"Yes, of course."

"It is very ugly."

"It is very warm."

"Possibly, but it is very ugly, especially in a Louis Fifteenth apartment, where everything else charms the eye. If not for your poor, you really ought to make your charities more elegant, for the sake of your friends."

"Oh, heavens, these men!" said the Countess, with a shrug of her shoulders. "Why, everyone is making this kind of coverlets just now."

"I know that; I know it only too well! Once cannot make an evening call now without seeing that frightful gray stuff dragged over the prettiest gowns and the most elegant furniture. Bad taste seems to be the fashion this spring."

To judge whether he spoke the truth, the Countess spread out her knitting on a silk-covered chair beside her; then she assented indifferently:

"Yes, you are right — it is ugly."

Then she resumed her work. Upon the two bent heads fell a stream of light; a rosy radiance from the lamp illumined their hair and complexions, extending to their skirts and their moving fingers. They watched their work with that attention, light but continuous, given by women to this labor of the fingers which the eye follows without a thought.

At the four corners of the room four other lamps of Chinese porcelain, borne by ancient columns of gilded wood, shed upon the hangings a soft, even light, modified by lace shades thrown over the globes.

Bertin took a very low seat, a dwarf armchair, in which he could barely seat himself, but which he had always preferred when talking with the Countess because it brought him almost at her feet.

"You took a long walk with Nane this afternoon in the park," said the Countess.

"Yes. We chatted like old friends. I like your daughter very much. She resembles you very strongly. When she pronounces certain phrases, one would believe that you had left your voice in her mouth."

"My husband has already said that very often."

He watched the two women work, bathed in the lamplight, and the thought that had often made him suffer, which had given him suffering that day, even — the recollection of his desolate home, still, silent, and cold, whatever the weather, whatever fire might be lighted in chimney or furnace — saddened him as if he now understood his bachelor's isolation for the first time.

Oh, how deeply he longed to be the husband of this woman, and not her lover! Once he had desired to carry her away, to take her from that man, to steal her altogether. To-day he was jealous of him, that deceived husband who was installed beside her forever, in the habits of her household and under the sweet influence of her presence. In looking at her he felt his heart full of old things revived, of which he wished to speak. Certainly, he still loved her very much, even a little more to-day than he had for some time; and the desire to tell her of this return of youthful feeling, which would be sure to delight her, made him wish that she would send the young girl to bed as soon as possible.

Obsessed by this strong desire to be alone with her, to sit near her and lay his head on her knee, to take the hands from which would slip the quilt for the poor, the needles, and the ball of wool, which would roll under a sofa at the end of a long, unwound thread, he looked at the time, relapsed into almost complete silence, and thought that it was a great mistake to allow young girls to pass the evening with grown-up persons.

Presently a sound of footsteps was heard in the next room, and a servant appeared at the door announcing:

"Monsieur de Musadieu."

Olivier Bertin felt a spasm of anger, and when he shook hands with the Inspector of Fine Arts he had a great desire to take him by the shoulders and throw him into the street.

Musadieu was full of news; the ministry was about to fall, and there was a whisper of scandal about the Marquis de Rocdiane. He looked at the young girl, adding: "I will tell you about that a little later."

The Countess raised her eyes to the clock and saw that it was about to strike ten.

"It is time to go to bed, my child," she said to her daughter.

Without replying, Annette folded her knitting-work, rolled up her ball of wool, kissed her mother on the cheeks, gave her hand to the two gentlemen, and departed quickly, as if she glided away without disturbing the air as she went.

"Well, what is your scandal?" her mother demanded, as soon as she had gone.

It appeared that rumor said that the Marquis de Rocdiane, amicably separated from his wife, who paid to him an allowance that he considered insufficient, had discovered a sure if singular means to double it. The Marquise, whom he had had watched, had been surprised in flagrante delictu, and was compelled to buy off, with an increased allowance, the legal proceedings instituted by the police commissioner.

The Countess listened with curious gaze, her idle hands holding the interrupted needlework on her knee.

Bertin, who was still more exasperated by Musadieu's presence since Annette had gone, was incensed at this recital, and declared, with the indignation of one who had known of the scandal but did not wish to speak of it to anyone, that the story was an odious falsehood, one of those shameful lies which people of their world ought neither to listen to nor repeat. He appeared greatly wrought up over the matter, as he stood leaning against the mantelpiece and speaking with the excited manner of a man disposed to make a personal question of the subject under discussion.

Rocdiane was his friend, he said; and, though he might be criticised for frivolity in certain respects, no one could justly accuse him or even suspect him of any really unworthy action. Musadieu, surprised and embarrassed, defended himself, tried to explain and to excuse himself.

"Allow me to say," he remarked at last, "that I heard this story just before I came here, in the drawingroom of the Duchesse de Mortemain."

"Who told it to you? A woman, no doubt," said Bertin.

"No, not at all; it was the Marquis de Farandal."

The painter, irritated still further, retorted: "That does not astonish me — from him!"

There was a brief silence. The Countess took up her work again. Presently Olivier said in a calmer voice: "I know for a fact that that story is false."

In reality, he knew nothing whatever about it, having heard it mentioned then for the first time.

Musadieu thought it wise to prepare the way for his retreat, feeling the situation rather dangerous; and he was just beginning to say that he must pay a visit at the Corbelles' that evening when the Comte de Guilleroy appeared, returning from dining in the city.

Bertin sat down again, overcome, and despairing now of getting rid of the husband.

"You haven't heard, have you, of the great scandal that is running all over town this evening?" inquired the Count pleasantly.

As no one answered, he continued: "It seems that Rocdiane surprised his wife in a criminal situation, and has made her pay dearly for her indiscretion."

Then Bertin, with his melancholy air, with grief in voice and gesture, placing one hand on Guilleroy's shoulder, repeated in a gentle and amicable manner all that he had just said so roughly to Musadieu.

The Count, half convinced, annoyed to have allowed himself to repeat so lightly a doubtful and possibly compromising thing, pleaded his ignorance and his innocence. The gossips said so many false and wicked things!

Suddenly, all agreed upon this statement: the world certainly accused, suspected, and calumniated with deplorable facility! All four appeared to be convinced, during the next five minutes, that all the whispered scandals were lies; that the women did not have the lovers ascribed to them; that the men never committed the sins they were accused of; and, in short, that the outward appearance of things was usually much worse than the real situation.

Bertin, who no longer felt vexed with Musadieu since De Guilleroy's arrival, was now very pleasant to him, led him to talk on his favorite subjects, and opened the sluices of his eloquence. The Count wore the contented air of a man who carries everywhere with him an atmosphere of peace and cordiality.

Two servants noiselessly entered the drawingroom, bearing the tea-table, on which the boiling water steamed in a pretty, shining kettle over the blue flame of an alcohol lamp.

The Countess rose, prepared the hot beverage with the care and precaution we have learned from the Russians, then offered a cup to Musadieu, another to Bertin, following this with plates containing sandwiches of pate de foies gras and little English and Austrian cakes.

The Count approached the portable table, where was also an assortment of syrups, liqueurs, and glasses; he mixed himself a drink, then discreetly disappeared into the next room.

Bertin found himself again facing Musadieu, and felt once more the sudden desire to thrust outside this bore, who, now put on his mettle, talked at great length, told stories, repeated jests, and made some himself. The painter glanced continually at the clock, the hands of which approached midnight. The Countess noticed his glances, understood that he wished to speak to her alone, and, with that ability of a clever woman of the world to change by indescribable shades of tone the whole atmosphere of a drawingroom, to make it understood, without saying anything, whether one is to remain or to go, she diffused about her, by her attitude alone, by the bored expression of her face and eyes, a chill as if she had just opened a window.

Musadieu felt this chilly current freezing his flow of ideas; and, without asking himself the reason, he felt a sudden desire to rise and depart.

Bertin, as a matter of discretion, followed his example. The two men passed through both drawingrooms together, followed by the Countess, who talked to the painter all the while. She detained him at the threshold of the antechamber to make some trifling explanation, while Musadieu, assisted by a footman, put on his topcoat. As Madame de Guilleroy continued to talk to Bertin, the Inspector of Fine Arts, having waited some seconds before the front door, held open by another servant, decided to depart himself rather than stand there facing the footman any longer.

The door was closed softly behind him, and the Countess said to the artist in a perfectly easy tone:

"Why do you go so soon? It is not yet midnight. Stay a little longer."

They reentered the smaller drawingroom together and seated themselves.

"My God! how that animal set my teeth on edge!" said Bertin.

"Why, pray?"

"He took you away from me a little."

"Oh, not very much."

"Perhaps not, but he irritated me."

"Are you jealous?"

"It is not being jealous to find a man a bore."

He had taken his accustomed armchair, and seated close beside her now he smoothed the folds of her robe with his fingers as he told her of the warm breath of tenderness that had passed through his heart that day.

The Countess listened, surprised, charmed, and gently laid her hand on his white locks, which she caressed tenderly, as if to thank him.

"I should like so much to live always near you!" he sighed.

He was thinking of her husband, who had retired to rest, asleep, no doubt, in some neighboring chamber, and he continued:

"It is undoubtedly true that marriage is the only thing that really unites two lives."

"My poor friend!" she murmured, full of pity for him and also for herself.

He had laid his cheek against the Countess's knees, and he looked up at her with a tenderness touched with sadness, less ardently than a short time before, when he had been separated from her by her daughter, her husband, and Musadieu.

"Heavens! how white your hair has grown!" said the Countess with a smile, running her fingers lightly over Olivier's head. "Your last black hairs have disappeared."

"Alas! I know it. Everything goes so soon!"

She was concerned lest she had made him sad.

"Oh, but your hair turned gray very early, you know," she said. "I have always known you with pepper-and-salt locks."

"Yes, that is true."

In order to dispel altogether the slight cloud of regret she had evoked, she leaned over him and, taking his head between her hands, kissed him slowly and tenderly on the forehead, with long kisses that seemed as if they never would end. Then they gazed into each other's eyes, seeking therein the reflection of their mutual fondness.

"I should like so much to pass a whole day with you," Bertin continued. He felt himself tormented obscurely by an inexpressible necessity for close intimacy. He had believed, only a short time ago, that the departure of those who had been present would suffice to realize the desire that had possessed him since morning; and now that he was alone with his mistress, now that he felt on his brow the touch of her hands, and, against his cheek, through the folds of her skirt, the warmth of her body, he felt the same agitation reawakened, the same longing for a love hitherto unknown and ever fleeing him. He now fancied that, away from that house — perhaps in the woods where they would be absolutely alone — this deep yearning of his heart would be calmed and satisfied.

"What a boy you are!" said the Countess. "Why, we see each other almost every day."

He begged her to devise a plan whereby she might breakfast with him, in some suburb of Paris, as she had already done four or five times.

The Countess was astonished at his caprice, so difficult to realize now that her daughter had returned. She assured him that she would try to do it as soon as her husband should go to Ronces; but that it would be impossible before the varnishing-day reception, which would take place the following Saturday.

"And until then when shall I see you?" he asked.

"Tomorrow evening at the Corbelles'. Come over here Thursday, at three o'clock, if you are free; and I believe that we are to dine together with the Duchess on Friday."

"Yes, exactly."

He arose.

"Good-by!"

"Good-by, my friend."

He remained standing, unable to decide to go, for he had said almost nothing of all that he had come to say, and his mind was still full of unsaid things, his heart still swelled with vague desires which he could not express.

"Goodbye!" he repeated, taking her hands.

"Good-by, my friend!"

"I love you!"

She gave him one of those smiles with which a woman shows a man, in a single instant, all that she has given him.

With a throbbing heart he repeated for the third time, "Good-by!" and departed.

IV

One would have said that all the carriages in Paris were making a pilgrimage to the Palais de l'Industrie that day. As early as nine o'clock in the morning they began to drive, by way of all streets, avenues, and bridges, toward that hall of the fine arts where all artistic Paris invites all fashionable Paris to be present at the pretended varnishing of three thousand four hundred pictures.

A long procession of visitors pressed through the doors, and, disdaining the exhibition of sculpture, hastened upstairs to the picture gallery. Even while mounting the steps they raised their eyes to the canvases displayed on the walls of the staircase, where they hang the special category of decorative painters who have sent canvases of unusual proportions or works that the committee dare not refuse.

In the square salon a great crowd surged and rustled. The artists, who were in evidence until evening, were easily recognized by their activity, the sonorousness of their voices, and the authority of their gestures. They drew their friends by the sleeve toward the pictures, which they pointed out with exclamations and mimicry of a connoisseur's energy. All types of artists were to be seen — tall men with long hair, wearing hats of mouse-gray or black and of indescribable shapes, large and round like roofs, with their turned-down brims shadowing the wearer's whole chest. Others were short, active, slight or stocky, wearing foulard cravats and round jackets, or the sack-like garment of the singular costume peculiar to this class of painters.

There was the clan of the fashionables, of the curious, and of artists of the boulevard; the clan of Academicians, correct, and decorated with red rosettes, enormous or microscopic, according to individual conception of elegance and good form; the clan of bourgeois painters, assisted by the family surrounding the father like a triumphal chorus.

On the four great walls the canvases admitted to the honor of the square salon dazzled one at the very entrance by their brilliant tones, glittering frames, the crudity of new color, vivified by fresh varnish, blinding under the pitiless light poured from above.

The portrait of the President of the Republic faced the entrance; while on another wall a general bedizened with gold lace, sporting a hat decorated with ostrich plumes, and wearing red cloth breeches, hung in pleasant proximity to some naked nymphs under a willow-tree, and near by was a vessel in distress almost engulfed by a great wave. A bishop of the early Church excommunicating a barbarian king, an Oriental street full of dead victims of the plague, and the Shade of Dante in Hell, seized and captivated the eye with irresistible fascination.

Other paintings in the immense room were a charge of cavalry; sharpshooters in a wood; cows in a pasture; two noblemen of the eighteenth century fighting a duel on a street corner; a madwoman sitting on a wall; a priest administering the last rites to a dying man; harvesters, rivers, a sunset, a moonlight effect — in short, samples of everything that artists paint, have painted, and will paint until the end of the world.

Olivier, in the midst of a group of celebrated brother painters, members of the Institute and of the jury, exchanged opinions with them. He was oppressed by a certain uneasiness, a dissatisfaction with his own exhibited work, of the success of which he was very doubtful, in spite of the warm congratulations he had received.

Suddenly he sprang forward; the Duchesse de Mortemain had appeared at the main entrance.

"Hasn't the Countess arrived yet?" she inquired of Bertin.

"I have not seen her."

"And Monsieur de Musadieu?"

"I have not seen him either."

"He promised me to be here at ten o'clock, at the top of the stairs, to show me around the principal galleries."

"Will you permit me to take his place, Duchess?"

"No, no. Your friends need you. We shall see each other again very soon, for I shall expect you to lunch with us."

Musadieu hastened toward them. He had been detained for some minutes in the hall of sculpture, and excused himself, breathless already.

"This way, Duchess, this way," said he. "Let us begin at the right."

They were just disappearing among the throng when the Comtesse de Guilleroy, leaning on her daughter's arm, entered and looked around in search of Olivier Bertin.

He saw them and hastened to meet them. As he greeted the two ladies, he said:

"How charming you look to-day. Really, Nanette has improved very much. She has actually changed in a week."

He regarded her with the eye of a close observer, adding: "The lines of her face are softer, yet more expressive; her complexion is clearer. She is already something less of a little girl and somewhat more of a Parisian."

Suddenly he bethought himself of the grand affair of the day.

"Let us begin at the right," said he, "and we shall soon overtake the Duchess."

The Countess, well informed on all matters connected with painting, and as preoccupied as if she were herself on exhibition, inquired: "What do they say of the exposition?"

"A fine one," Bertin replied. "There is a remarkable Bonnat, two excellent things by Carolus Duran, an admirable Puvis de Chavannes, a very new and astonishing Roll, an exquisite Gervex, and many others, by Beraud, Cazin, Duez — in short, a heap of good things."

"And you?" said the Countess.

"Oh, they compliment me, but I am not satisfied."

"You never are satisfied."

"Yes, sometimes. But to-day I really feel that I am right."

"Why?"

"I do not know."

"Let us go to see it."

When they arrived before Bertin's picture — two little peasant-girls taking a bath in a brook — they found a group admiring it. The Countess was delighted, and whispered: "It is simply a delicious bit — a jewel! You never have done anything better."

Bertin pressed close to her, loving her and thanking her for every word that calmed his suffering and healed his aching heart. Through his mind ran arguments to convince him that she was right, that she must judge accurately with the intelligent observation of an experienced Parisian. He forgot, so desirous was he to reassure himself, that for at least twelve years he had justly reproached her for too much admiring the dainty trifles, the elegant nothings, the sentimentalities and nameless trivialities of the passing fancy of the day, and never art, art alone, art detached from the popular ideas, tendencies, and prejudices.

"Let us go on," said he, drawing them away from his picture. He led them for a long time from gallery to gallery, showing them notable canvases and explaining their subjects, happy to be with them.

"What time is it?" the Countess asked suddenly.

"Half after twelve."

"Oh, let us hasten to luncheon then. The Duchess must be waiting for us at Ledoyen's, where she charged me to bring you, in case we should not meet her in the galleries."

The restaurant, in the midst of a little island of trees and shrubs, seemed like an overflowing hive. A confused hum of voices, calls, the rattling of plates and glasses came from the open windows and large doors. The tables, set close together and filled with people eating, extended in long rows right and left of a narrow passage, up and down which ran the distracted waiters, holding along their arms dishes filled with meats, fish, or fruit.

Under the circular gallery there was such a throng of men and women as to suggest a living pate. Everyone there laughed, called out, drank and ate, enlivened by the wines and inundated by one of those waves of joy that sweep over Paris, on certain days, with the sunshine.

An attendant showed the Countess, Annette, and Bertin upstairs into a reserved room, where the Duchess awaited them. As they entered, the painter observed, beside his aunt, the Marquis de Farandal, attentive and smiling, and extending his hand to receive the parasols and wraps of the Countess and her daughter. He felt again so much displeasure that he suddenly desired to say rude and irritating things.

The Duchess explained the meeting of her nephew and the departure of Musadieu, who had been carried off by the Minister of the Fine Arts, and Bertin, at the thought that this insipidly good-looking Marquis might marry Annette, that he had come there only to see her, and that he regarded her already as destined to share his bed, unnerved and revolted him, as if some one had ignored his own rights — sacred and mysterious rights.

As soon as they were at table, the Marquis, who sat beside the young girl, occupied himself in talking to her with the devoted air of a man authorized to pay his addresses.

He assumed a curious manner, which seemed to the painter bold and searching; his smiles were satisfied and almost tender, his gallantry was familiar and officious. In manner and word appeared already something of decision, as if he were about to announce that he had won the prize.

The Duchess and the Countess seemed to protect and approve this attitude of a pretender, and exchanged glances of complicity.

As soon as the luncheon was finished the party returned to the Exposition. There was such a dense crowd in the galleries, it seemed impossible to penetrate it. An odor of perspiring humanity, a stale smell of old gowns and coats, made an atmosphere at once heavy and sickening. No one looked at the pictures any more, but at faces and toilets, seeking out well-known persons; and at times came a great jostling of the crowd as it was forced to give way before the high double ladder of the varnishers, who cried: "Make way, Messieurs! Make way, Mesdames!"

At the end of ten minutes, the Countess and Olivier found themselves separated from the others. He wished to find them immediately, but, leaning upon him, the Countess said: "Are we not very well off as it is? Let them go, since it is quite natural that we should lose sight of them; we will meet them again in the buffet at four o'clock."

"That is true," he replied.

But he was absorbed by the idea that the Marquis was accompanying Annette and continuing his attempts to please her by his fatuous and affected gallantry.

"You love me always, then?" murmured the Countess.

"Yes, certainly," he replied, with a preoccupied air, trying to catch a glimpse of the Marquis's gray hat over the heads of the crowd.

Feeling that he was abstracted, and wishing to lead him back to her own train of thought, the Countess continued:

"If you only knew how I adore your picture of this year! It is certainly your chef-d'oeuvre."

He smiled, suddenly, forgetting the young people in remembering his anxiety of the morning.

"Do you really think so?" he asked.

"Yes, I prefer it above all others."

With artful wheedling, she crowned him anew, having known well for a long time that nothing has a stronger effect on an artist than tender and continuous flattery. Captivated, reanimated, cheered by her sweet words, he began again to chat gaily, seeing and hearing only her in that tumultuous throng.

By way of expressing his thanks, he murmured in her ear: "I have a mad desire to embrace you!"

A warm wave of emotion swept over her, and, raising her shining eyes to his, she repeated her question: "You love me always, then?"

He replied, with the intonation she wished to hear, and which she had not heard before:

"Yes, I love you, my dear Any."

"Come often to see me in the evenings," she said. "Now that I have my daughter I shall not go out very much."

Since she had recognized in him this unexpected reawakening of tenderness, her heart was stirred with great happiness. In view of Olivier's silvery hair, and the calming touch of time, she had not suspected that he was fascinated by another woman, but she was terribly afraid that, from pure dread of loneliness, he might marry. This fear, which was of long standing, increased constantly, and set her wits to contriving plans whereby she might have him near her as much as possible, and to see that he should not pass long evenings alone in the chill silence of his empty rooms. Not being always able to hold and keep him, she would suggest amusements for him, sent him to the theater, forced him to go into society, being better pleased to know that he was mingling with many other women than alone in his gloomy house.

She resumed, answering his secret thought: "Ah, if I could only have you always with me, how I should spoil you! Promise me to come often, since I hardly go out at all now."

"I promise it."

At that moment a voice murmured "Mamma!" in her ear.

The Countess started and turned. Annette, the Duchess, and the Marquis had just rejoined them.

"It is four o'clock," said the Duchess. "I am very tired and I wish to go now."

"I will go, too; I have had enough of it," said the Countess.

They reached the interior stairway which divides the galleries where the drawings and water-colors are hung, overlooking the immense garden inclosed in glass, where the works of sculpture are exhibited.

From the platform of this stairway they could see from one end to the other of this great conservatory, filled with statues set up along the pathway around large green shrubs, and below was the crowd which covered the paths like a moving black wave. The marbles rose from this mass of dark hats and shoulders, piercing it in a thousand places, and seeming almost luminous in their dazzling whiteness.

As Bertin took leave of the ladies at the door of exit, Madame de Guilleroy whispered:

"Then — will you come this evening?"

"Yes, certainly."

Bertin reentered the Exposition, to talk with the artists over the impressions of the day.

Painters and sculptors stood talking in groups around the statues and in front of the buffet, upholding or attacking the same ideas that were discussed every year, using the same arguments over works almost exactly similar. Olivier, who usually took a lively share in these disputes, being quick in repartee and clever in disconcerting attacks, besides having a reputation as an ingenious theorist of which he was proud, tried to urge himself to take an active part in the debates, but the things he said interested him no more than those he heard, and he longed to go away, to listen no more, to understand no more, knowing beforehand as he did all that anyone could say on those ancient questions of art, of which he knew all sides.

He loved these things, however, and had loved them until now in an almost exclusive way; but to-day he was distracted by one of those slight but persistent preoccupations, one of those petty anxieties which are so small we ought not to allow ourselves to be troubled by them, but which, in spite of all we do or say, prick through our thoughts like an invisible thorn buried in the flesh.

He had even forgotten his anxiety over his little peasant bathers in the remembrance of the displeasing idea of the Marquis approaching Annette. What did it matter to him, after all?

Had he any right? Why should he wish to prevent this precious marriage, already arranged, and suitable from every point of view? But no reasoning could efface that impression of uneasiness and discontent which had seized him when he had beheld Farandal talking and smiling like an accepted suitor, caressing with his glances the fair face of the young girl.

When he entered the Countess's drawingroom that evening, and found her alone with her daughter, continuing by the lamplight their knitting for the poor, he had great difficulty in preventing himself from saying sneering things about the Marquis, and from revealing to Annette his real banality, veiled by a mask of elegance and good form.

For a long time, during these after-dinner evening visits, he had often allowed himself to lapse into occasional silence that was slightly somnolent, and was accustomed to fall into the easy attitudes of an old friend who does not stand on ceremony. But now he seemed suddenly to rouse himself and to show the alertness of men who do their best to be agreeable, who take thought as to what they wish to say, and who, before certain persons, seek for the best phrases in which to express their ideas and render them attractive. No longer did he allow the conversation to lag, but did his best to keep it bright and interesting; and when he had made the Countess and her daughter laugh gaily, when he felt that he had touched their emotions, or when they ceased to work in order to listen to him, he felt a thrill of pleasure, an assurance of success, which rewarded him for his efforts.

He came now every time that he knew they were alone, and never, perhaps, had he passed such delightful evenings.

Madame de Guilleroy, whose continual fears were soothed by this assiduity, made fresh efforts to attract him and to keep him near her. She refused invitations to dinners in the city, she did not go to balls, nor to the theaters, in order to have the joy of throwing into the telegraph-box, on going out at three o'clock, a little blue despatch which said: "Come tonight." At first, wishing to give him earlier the tete-a-tete that he desired, she had sent her daughter to bed as soon as it was ten o'clock. Then after one occasion when he had appeared surprised at this and had begged laughingly that Annette should not be treated any longer like a naughty little girl, she had allowed her daughter a quarter of an hour's grace, then half an hour, and finally a whole hour. Bertin never remained long after the young girl had retired; it was as if half the charm that held him there had departed with her. He would soon take the little low seat that he preferred beside the Countess and lay his cheek against her knee with a caressing movement. She would give him one of her hands, which he clasped in his, and the fever of his spirit would suddenly be abated; he ceased to talk, and appeared to find repose in tender silence from the effort he had made.

Little by little the Countess, with the keenness of feminine instinct, comprehended that Annette attracted him almost as much as she herself. This did not anger her; she was glad that between them he could find something of that domestic happiness which he lacked; and she imprisoned him between them, as it were, playing the part of tender mother in such a way that he might almost believe himself the young girl's father; and a new bond of tenderness was added to that which had always held him to this household.

Her personal vanity, always alert, but disturbed since she had felt in several ways, like almost invisible pin-pricks, the innumerable attacks of advancing age, took on a new allurement. In order to become as slender as Annette, she continued to drink nothing, and the real slimness of her figure gave her the appearance of a young girl. When her back was turned one could hardly distinguish her from Annette; but her face showed the effect of this regime. The plump flesh began to be wrinkled and took on a yellowish tint which rendered more dazzling by contrast the superb freshness of the young girl's complexion. Then the Countess began to make up her face with theatrical art, and, though in broad daylight she produced an effect that was slightly artificial, in the evening her complexion had that charmingly soft tint obtained by women who know how to make up well.

The realization of her fading beauty, and the employment of artificial aid to restore it, somewhat changed her habits. As much as possible, she avoided comparison with her daughter in the full light of day, but rather sought it by lamplight, which, if anything, showed herself to greater advantage. When she was fatigued, pale, and felt that she looked older than usual, she had convenient headaches by reason of which she excused herself from going to balls and theaters; but on days when she knew she looked well she triumphed again and played the elder sister with the grave modesty of a little mother. In order always to wear gowns like those of her daughter, she made Annette wear toilettes suitable for a fully-grown young woman, a trifle too old for her; and Annette who showed more and more plainly her joyous and laughing disposition, wore them with sparkling vivacity that rendered her still more attractive. She lent herself with all her heart to the coquettish arts of her mother, acting with her, as if by instinct, graceful little domestic scenes; she knew when to embrace her at the effective moment, how to clasp her tenderly round the waist, and to show by a movement, a caress, or some ingenious pose, how pretty both were and how much they resembled each other.

From seeing the two so much together, and from continually comparing them, Olivier Bertin sometimes actually confused them in his own mind. Sometimes, when Annette spoke, and he happened to be looking elsewhere, he was compelled to ask: "Which of you said that?" He often amused himself by playing this game of confusion when all three were alone in the drawingroom with the Louis XV tapestries. He would close his eyes and beg them to ask him the same question, the one after the other, and then change the order of the interrogations, so that he might recognize their voices. They did this with so much cleverness in imitating each other's intonations, in saying the same phrases with the same accents, that often he could not tell which spoke. In fact, they had come to speak so much alike that the servants answered "Yes, Madame" to the daughter and "Yes, Mademoiselle" to the mother.

From imitating each other's voices and movements for amusement, they acquired such a similarity of gait and gesture that Monsieur de Guilleroy himself, when he saw one or the other pass through the shadowy end of the drawingroom, confounded them for an instant and asked: "Is that you, Annette, or is it your mamma?"

From this resemblance, natural and assumed, was engendered in the mind and heart of the painter a strange impression of a double entity, old and young, wise yet ignorant, two bodies made, the one after the other, with the same flesh; in fact, the same woman continued, but rejuvenated, having become once more what she was formerly. Thus he lived near them, shared between them, uneasy, troubled, feeling for the mother his old ardor awakened, and for the daughter an indefinable tenderness.

Part II

I

"Paris, July 20, 11 P. M.

"MY FRIEND: My mother has just died at Roncieres. We shall leave here at midnight. Do not come, for we have told no one. But pity me and think of me. YOUR ANY."

"July 21, 12 M.

"MY POOR FRIEND: I should have gone, notwithstanding what you wrote, if I had not become used to regarding all your wishes as commands. I have thought of you with poignant grief ever since last night. I think of that silent journey you made, sitting opposite your daughter and your husband, in that dimly-lighted carriage, which bore you toward your dead. I could see all three of you under the oil lamp, you weeping and Annette sobbing. I saw your arrival at the station, the entrance of the castle in the midst of a group of servants, your rush up the stairs toward that room, toward that bed where she lies, your first look at her, and your kiss on her thin, motionless face. And I thought of your heart, your poor heart — that poor heart, of which half belongs to me and which is breaking, which suffers so much, which stifles you, making me suffer also at this moment.

"With profound pity, I kiss your eyes filled with tears.

"OLIVIER."

"Roncieres, July 24.

"Your letter would have done me good, my friend, if anything could do me good in the horrible situation into which I have fallen. We buried her yesterday, and since her poor lifeless body has gone out of this house it seems to me that I am alone in the world. We love our mothers almost without knowing or feeling it, for such love is as natural as it is to live, and we do not realize how deep-rooted is that love until the moment of final separation. No other affection is comparable to that, for all others come by chance, while this begins at birth; all the others are brought to us later by the accidents of life, while this has lived in our very blood since our first day on earth. And then, and there, we have lost not only a mother but our childhood itself, which half disappears, for our little life of girlhood belonged to her as much as to ourselves. She alone knew it as we knew it; she knew about innumerable things, remote, insignificant and dear, which are and which were the first sweet emotions of our heart. To her alone I could still say: 'Do you remember, mother, the day when — ? Do you remember, mother, the china doll that grandmother gave me?' Both of us murmured to each other a long, sweet chapter of trifling childish memories, which no one on earth now knows of but me. So it is a part of myself that is dead — the older, the better. I have lost the poor heart wherein the little girl I was once still lived. Now no one knows her any more; no one remembers the little Anne, her short skirts, her laughter and her faces.

"And a day will come — and perhaps it is not far away — when in my turn I too shall go, leaving my dear Annette alone in the world, as mamma has left me to-day. How sad all this is, how hard, and cruel! Yet one never thinks about it; we never look about us to see death take someone every instant, as it will soon take us. If we should look at it, if we should think of it, if we were not distracted, rejoiced, or blinded by all that passes before us, we could no longer live, for the sight of this endless massacre would drive us mad.

"I am so crushed, so despairing, that I have no longer strength to do anything. Day and night I think of my poor mamma, nailed in that box, buried beneath that earth, in that field, under the rain, whose old face, which I used to kiss with so much happiness, is now only a mass of frightful decay! Oh, what horror!

"When I lost papa, I was just married, and I did not feel all these things as I do to-day. Yes, pity me, think of me, write to me. I need you so much just now.

"ANNE."

"Paris, July 25.

"MY POOR FRIEND: Your grief gives me horrible pain, and life no longer seems rosy to me. Since your departure I am lost, abandoned, without ties or refuge. Everything fatigues me, bores me and irritates me. I am ceaselessly thinking of you and Annette; I feel that you are both far, far away when I need you near me so much.

"It is extraordinary how far away from me you seem to be, and how I miss you. Never, even in my younger days, have you been my all, as you are at this moment. I have foreseen for some time that I should reach this crisis, which must be a sunstroke in Indian summer. What I feel is so very strange that I wish to tell you about it. Just fancy that since your absence I cannot take walks any more! Formerly, and even during the last few months, I liked very much to set out alone and stroll along the street, amusing myself by looking at people and things, and enjoying the mere sight of everything and the exercise of walking. I used to walk along without knowing where I was going, simply to walk, to breathe, to dream. Now, I can no longer do this. As soon as I reach the street I am oppressed by anguish, like the fear of a blind man that has lost his dog. I become uneasy, exactly like a traveler that has lost his way in the wood, and I am compelled to return home. Paris seems empty, frightful, alarming. I ask myself: 'Where am I going?' I answer myself: 'Nowhere, since I am still walking.' Well, I cannot, for I can no longer walk without some aim. The bare thought of walking straight before me wearies and bores me inexpressibly. Then I drag my melancholy to the club.

"And do you know why? Only because you are no longer here. I am certain of this. When I know that you are in Paris, my walks are no longer useless, for it is possible that I may meet you in the first street I turn into. I can go anywhere because you may go anywhere. If I do not see you, I may at least find Annette, who is an emanation of yourself. You and she fill the streets full of hope for me — the hope of recognizing you, whether you approach me from a distance, or whether I divine your identity in following you. And then the city becomes charming to me, and the women whose figures resemble yours stir my heart with all the liveliness of the streets, hold my attention, occupy my eyes, and give me a sort of hunger to see you.

"You will consider me very selfish, my poor friend, to speak to you in this way of the solitude of an old cooing pigeon when you are shedding such bitter tears. Pardon me! I am so used to being spoiled by you that I cry 'Help! Help!' when I have you no longer.

"I kiss your feet so that you may have pity on me.

"OLIVIER."

"Roncieres, July 30.

"MY FRIEND: Thanks for your letter. I need so much to know that you love me! I have just passed some frightful days. Indeed, I believed that grief would kill me in my turn.

"It was like a block of suffering in my breast, growing larger and larger, stifling me, strangling me. The physician that was called to treat me for the nervous crisis I was enduring, which recurred four or five times a day, injected morphine, which made me almost wild, and the great heat we have had aggravated my condition and threw me into a state of overexcitement that was almost delirium. I am a little more calm since the great storm of Friday. I must tell you that since the day of the funeral I could weep no more, but during the storm, the approach of which upset me, I suddenly felt the tears beginning to flow from my eyes, slow, small, burning. Oh, those first tears, how they hurt me! They seemed to tear me, as if they had claws, and my throat was so choked that I could hardly breathe. Then the tears came faster, larger, cooler. They ran from my eyes as from a spring, and came so fast that my handkerchief was saturated and I had to take another. The great block of grief seemed to soften and to flow away through my eyes.

"From that moment I have been weeping from morning till night, and that is saving me. One would really end by going mad or dying, if one could not weep. I am all alone, too. My husband is making some little trips around the country, and I insisted that he should take Annette with him, to distract and console her a little. They go in the carriage or on horseback as far as eight or ten leagues from Roncieres, and she returns to me rosy with youth, in spite of her sadness, her eyes shining with life, animated by the country air and the excursion she has had. How beautiful it is to be at that age! I think that we shall remain here a fortnight or three weeks longer; then, although it will be August, we shall return to Paris for the reason you know.

"I send to you all that remains to me of my heart.

"ANY."

"Paris, August 4th.

"I can bear this no longer, my dear friend; you must come back, for something is certainly going to happen to me. I ask myself whether I am not already ill, so great a dislike have I for everything I used to take pleasure in doing, or did with indifferent resignation. For one thing, it is so warm in Paris that every night means a Turkish bath of eight or nine hours. I get up overcome by the fatigue of this sleep in a hot bath, and for an hour or two I walk about before a white canvas, with the intention to draw something. But mind, eye, and hand are all empty. I am no longer a painter! This futile effort to work is exasperating. I summon my models; I place them, and they give me poses, movements, and expressions that I have painted to satiety. I make them dress again and let them go. Indeed, I can no longer see anything new, and I suffer from this as if I were blind. What is it? Is it fatigue of the eye or of the brain, exhaustion of the artistic faculty or of the optic nerve? Who knows? It seems to me that I have ceased to discover anything in the unexplored corner that I have been permitted to visit. I no longer perceive anything but that which all the world knows; I do the things that all poor painters have done; I have only one subject now, and only the observation of a vulgar pedant. Once upon a time, and not so very long ago, either, the number of new subjects seemed to me unlimited, and in order to express them I had such a variety of means the difficulty of making a choice made me hesitate. But now, alas! Suddenly the world of half-seen subjects has become depopulated, my study has become powerless and useless. The people that pass have no more sense for me. I no longer find in every human being the character and savor which once I liked so much to discern and reveal. I believe, however, that I could make a very pretty portrait of your daughter. Is it because she resembles you so much that I confound you both in my mind? Yes, perhaps.

"Well, then, after forcing myself to sketch a man or a woman who does not resemble any of the familiar models, I decide to go and breakfast somewhere, for I no longer have the courage to sit down alone in my own diningroom. The Boulevard Malesherbes seems like a forest path imprisoned in a dead city. All the houses smell empty. On the street the sprinklers throw showers of white rain, splashing the wooden pavement whence rises the vapor of damp tar and stable refuse; and from one end to the other of the long descent from the Parc Monceau to Saint Augustin, one sees five or six black forms, unimportant passers, tradesmen or domestics. The shade of the plane-trees spreads over the burning sidewalks, making a curious spot, looking almost like liquid, as if water spilled there were drying. The stillness of the leaves on the branches, and of their gray silhouettes on the asphalt, expresses the fatigue of the roasted city, slumbering and perspiring like a workman asleep on a bench in the sun. Yes, she perspires, the beggar, and she smells frightfully through her sewer mouths, the vent-holes of sinks and kitchens, the streams through which the filth of her streets is running. Then I think of those summer mornings in your orchard full of little wild-flowers that flavor the air with a suggestion of honey. Then I enter, sickened already, the restaurant where bald, fat, tired-looking men are eating, with half-opened waistcoats and moist, shining foreheads. The food shows the effect of heat — the melon growing soft under the ice, the soft bread, the flabby filet, the warmed-over vegetables, the purulent cheese, the fruits ripened on the premises. I go out, nauseated, and go home to try to sleep a little until the hour for dinner, which I take at the club.

"There I always find Adelmans, Maldant, Rocdiane, Landa, and many others, who bore and weary me as much as hand-organs. Each one has his own little tune, or tunes, which I have heard for fifteen years, and they play them all together every evening in that club, which is apparently a place where one goes to be entertained. Someone should change my own generation for my benefit, for my eyes, my ears, and my mind have had enough of it. They still make conquests, however, they boast of them and congratulate one another on them!

"After yawning as many times as there are minutes between eight o'clock and midnight, I go home and go to bed, and while I undress I think that the same thing will begin over again the next day.

"Yes, my dear friend, I am at the age when a bachelor's life becomes intolerable, because there is nothing new for me under the sun. An unmarried man should be young, curious, eager. When one is no longer all that, it becomes dangerous to remain free. Heavens! how I loved my liberty, long ago, before I loved you more! How burdensome it is to me to-day! For an old bachelor like me, liberty is an empty thing, empty everywhere; it is the path to death, with nothing in himself to prevent him from seeing the end; it is the ceaseless query: 'What shall I do? Whom can I go to see, so that I shall not be alone?' And I go from one friend to another, from one handshake to the next, begging for a little friendship. I gather up my crumbs, but they do not make a loaf. You, I have You, my friend, but you do not belong to me. Perhaps it is because of you that I suffer this anguish, for it is the desire for contact with you, for your presence, for the same roof over our heads, for the same walls inclosing our lives, the same interests binding our hearts together, the need of that community of hopes, griefs, pleasures, joys, sadness, and also of material things, that fills me with so much yearning. You do belong to me — that is to say, I steal a little of you from time to time. But I long to breathe forever the same air that you breathe, to share everything with you, to possess nothing that does not belong to both of us, to feel that all which makes up my own life belongs to you as much as to me — the glass from which I drink, the chair on which I sit, the bread I eat and the fire that warms me.

"Adieu! Return soon. I suffer too much when you are far away.

"OLIVIER."

"Roncieres, August 8th.

"MY FRIEND: I am ill, and so fatigued that you would not recognize me at all. I believe that I have wept too much. I must rest a little before I return, for I do not wish you to see me as I am. My husband sets out for Paris the day after tomorrow, and will give you news of us. He expects to take you to dinner somewhere, and charges me to ask you to wait for him at your house about seven o'clock.

"As for me, as soon as I feel a little better, as soon as I have no more this corpse-like face which frightens me, I will return to be near you. In all the world, I have only Annette and you, and I wish to offer to each of you all that I can give without robbing the other.

"I hold out my eyes, which have wept so much, so that you may kiss them.

"ANY."

When he received this letter announcing the still delayed return, Olivier was seized with an immoderate desire to take a carriage for the railway station to catch a train for Roncieres; then, thinking that M. de Guilleroy must return the next day, he resigned himself, and even began to wish for the arrival of the husband with almost as much impatience as if it were that of the wife herself.

Never had he liked Guilleroy as during those twenty-four hours of waiting. When he saw him enter, he rushed toward him, with hands extended, exclaiming:

"Ah, dear friend! how happy I am to see you!"

The other also seemed very glad, delighted above all things to return to Paris, for life was not gay in Normandy during the three weeks he had passed there.

The two men sat down on a little two-seated sofa in a corner of the studio, under a canopy of Oriental stuffs, and again shook hands with mutual sympathy.

"And the Countess?" asked Bertin, "how is she?"

"Not very well. She has been very much affected, and is recovering too slowly. I must confess that I am a little anxious about her."

"But why does she not return?"

"I know nothing about it. It was impossible for me to induce her to return here."

"What does she do all day?"

"Oh, heavens! She weeps, and thinks of her mother. That is not good for her. I should like very much to have her decide to have a change of air, to leave the place where that happened, you understand?"

"And Annette?"

"Oh, she is a blooming flower."

Olivier smiled with joy.

"Was she very much grieved?" he asked again.

"Yes, very much, very much, but you know that the grief of eighteen years does not last long."

After a silence Guilleroy resumed:

"Where shall we dine, my dear fellow? I need to be cheered up, to hear some noise and see some movement."

"Well, at this season, it seems to me that the Cafe des Ambassadeurs is the right place."

So they set out, arm in arm, toward the Champs-Elysees. Guilleroy, filled with the gaiety of Parisians when they return, to whom the city, after every absence, seems rejuvenated and full of possible surprises, questioned the painter about a thousand details of what people had been doing and saying; and Olivier, after indifferent replies which betrayed all the boredom of his solitude, spoke of Roncieres, tried to capture from this man, in order to gather round him that almost tangible something left with us by persons with whom we have recently been associated, that subtle emanation of being one carries away when leaving them, which remains with us a few hours and evaporates amid new surroundings.

The heavy sky of a summer evening hung over the city and over the great avenue where, under the trees, the gay refrains of open-air concerts were beginning to sound. The two men, seated on the balcony of the Cafe des Ambassadeurs, looked down upon the still empty benches and chairs of the inclosure up to the little stage, where the singers, in the mingled light of electric globes and fading day, displayed their striking costumes and their rosy complexions. Odors of frying, of sauces, of hot food, floated in the slight breezes from the chestnut-trees, and when a woman passed, seeing her reserved chair, followed by a man in a black coat, she diffused on her way the fresh perfume of her dress and her person.

Guilleroy, who was radiant, murmured:

"Oh, I like to be here much better than in the country!"

"And I," Bertin replied, "should like it much better to be there than here."

"Nonsense!"

"Heavens, yes! I find Paris tainted this summer."

"Oh, well, my dear fellow, it is always Paris, after all."

The Deputy seemed to be enjoying his day, one of those rare days of effervescence and gaiety in which grave men do foolish things. He looked at two cocottes dining at a neighboring table with three thin young men, superlatively correct, and he slyly questioned Olivier about all the well-known girls, whose names were heard every day. Then he murmured in a tone of deep regret:

"You were lucky to have remained a bachelor. You can do and see many things."

But the painter did not agree with him, and, as a man will do when haunted by a persistent idea, he took Guilleroy into his confidence on the subject of his sadness and isolation. When he had said everything, had recited to the end of his litany of melancholy, and, urged by the longing to relieve his heart, had confessed naively how much he would have enjoyed the love and companionship of a woman installed in his home, the Count, in his turn, admitted that marriage had its advantages. Recovering his parliamentary eloquence in order to sing the praises of his domestic happiness, he eulogized the Countess in the highest terms, to which Olivier listened gravely with frequent nods of approval.

Happy to hear her spoken of, but jealous of that intimate happiness which Guilleroy praised as a matter of duty, the painter finally murmured, with sincere conviction:

"Yes, indeed, you were the lucky one!"

The Deputy, flattered, assented to this; then he resumed:

"I should like very much to see her return; indeed, I am a little anxious about her just now. Wait — since you are bored in Paris, you might go to Roncieres and bring her back. She will listen to you, for you are her best friend; while a husband — you know — — "

Delighted, Olivier replied: "I ask nothing better. But do you think it would not annoy her to see me arriving in that abrupt way?"

"No, not at all. Go, by all means, my dear fellow."

"Well, then, I will. I will leave tomorrow by the one o'clock train. Shall I send her a telegram?"

"No, I will attend to that. I will telegraph, so that you will find a carriage at the station."

As they had finished dinner, they strolled again up the Boulevard, but in half an hour the Count suddenly left the painter, under the pretext of an urgent affair that he had quite forgotten.

II

The Countess and her daughter, dressed in black crape, had just seated themselves opposite each other, for breakfast, in the large diningroom at Roncieres. The portraits of many ancestors, crudely painted, one in a cuirass, another in a tight-fitting coat, this a powdered officer of the French Guards, that a colonel of the Restoration, hung in line on the walls, a collection of deceased Guilleroys, in old frames from which the gilding was peeling. Two servants, stepping softly, began to serve the two silent women, and the flies made a little cloud of black specks, dancing and buzzing around the crystal chandelier that hung over the center of the table.

"Open the windows," said the Countess, "It is a little cool here."

The three long windows, reaching from the floor to the ceiling, and large as bay-windows, were opened wide. A breath of soft air, bearing the odor of warm grass and the distant sounds of the country, swept in immediately through these openings, mingling with the slightly damp air of the room, inclosed by the thick walls of the castle.

"Ah, that is good!" said Annette, taking a full breath.

The eyes of the two women had turned toward the outside and now gazed, beneath the blue sky, lightly veiled by the midday haze which was reflected on the meadows impregnated with sunshine, at the long and verdant lawns of the park, with its groups of trees here and there, and its perspective opening to the yellow fields, illuminated as far as the eye could see by the golden gleam of ripe grain.

"We will take a long walk after breakfast," said the Countess. "We might walk as far as Berville, following the river, for it will be too warm on the plain."

"Yes, mamma, and let us take Julio to scare up some partridges."

"You know that your father forbids it."

"Oh, but since papa is in Paris! — it is so amusing to see Julio pointing after them. There he is now, worrying the cows! Oh, how funny he is, the dear fellow!"

Pushing back her chair, she jumped up and ran to the window, calling out: "Go on, Julio! After them!"

Upon the lawn three heavy cows, gorged with grass and overcome with heat, lay on their sides, their bellies protruding from the pressure of the earth. Rushing from one to another, barking and bounding wildly, in a sort of mad abandon, partly real, partly feigned, a hunting spaniel, slender, white and red, whose curly ears flapped at every bound, was trying to rouse the three big beasts, which did not wish to get up. It was evidently the dog's favorite sport, with which he amused himself whenever he saw the cows lying down. Irritated, but not frightened, they gazed at him with their large, moist eyes, turning their heads to watch him.

Annette, from her window, cried:

"Fetch them, Julio, fetch them!"

The excited spaniel, growing bolder, barked louder and ventured as far as their cruppers, feigning to be about to bite them. They began to grow uneasy, and the nervous twitching of their skin, to get rid of the flies, became more frequent and protracted.

Suddenly the dog, carried along by the impetus of a rush that he could not check in time, bounced so close to one cow that, in order not to fall against her, he was obliged to jump over her. Startled by the bound, the heavy animal took fright, and first raising her head she finally raised herself slowly on her four legs, sniffing loudly. Seeing her erect, the other two immediately got up also, and Julio began to prance around them in a dance of triumph, while Annette praised him.

"Bravo, Julio, bravo!"

"Come," said the Countess, "come to breakfast, my child."

But the young girl, shading her eyes with one hand, announced:

"There comes a telegraph messenger!"

Along the invisible path among the wheat and the oats a blue blouse appeared to be gliding along the top of the grain, and it came toward the castle with the firm step of a man.

"Oh, heavens!" murmured the Countess; "I hope he does not bring bad news!"

She was still shaken with that terror which remains with us a long time after the death of some loved one has been announced by a telegram. Now she could not remove the gummed band to open the little blue paper without feeling her fingers tremble and her soul agitated, believing that from those folds which it took so long to open would come a grief that would cause her tears to flow afresh.

Annette, on the contrary, full of girlish curiosity, was delighted to meet with the unknown mystery that comes to all of us at times. Her heart, which life had just saddened for the first time, could anticipate only something joyful from that black and ominous bag hanging from the side of the mail-carrier, who saw so many emotions through the city streets and the country lanes.

The Countess ceased to eat, concentrating her thoughts on the man who was approaching, bearer of a few written words that might wound her as if a knife had been thrust in her throat. The anguish of having known that experience made her breathless, and she tried to guess what this hurried message might be. About what? From whom? The thought of Olivier flashed through her mind. Was he ill? Dead, perhaps, too!

The ten minutes she had to wait seemed interminable to her; then, when she had torn open the despatch and recognized the name of her husband, she read: "I telegraph to tell you that our friend Bertin leaves for Roncieres on the one o'clock train. Send Phaeton station. Love."

"Well, mamma?" said Annette.

"Monsieur Olivier Bertin is coming to see us."

"Ah, how lucky! When?"

"Very soon."

"At four o'clock?"

"Yes."

"Oh, how kind he is!"

But the Countess had turned pale, for a new anxiety had lately troubled her, and the sudden arrival of the painter seemed to her as painful a menace as anything she might have been able to foresee.

"You will go to meet him with the carriage," she said to her daughter.

"And will you not come, too, mamma?"

"No, I will wait for you here."

"Why? That will hurt him."

"I do not feel very well."

"You wished to walk as far as Berville just now."

"Yes, but my breakfast has made me feel ill."

"You will feel better between now and the time to go."

"No, I am going up to my room. Let me know as soon as you arrive."

"Yes, mamma."

After giving orders that the phaeton should be ready at the proper hour, and that a room be prepared, the Countess returned to her own room, and shut herself in.

Up to this time her life had passed almost without suffering, affected only by Olivier's love and concerned only by her anxiety to retain it. She had succeeded, always victorious in that struggle. Her heart, soothed by success and by flattery, had become the exacting heart of a beautiful worldly woman to whom are due all the good things of earth, and, after consenting to a brilliant marriage, with which affection had nothing to do, after accepting love later as the complement of a happy existence, after taking her part in a guilty intimacy, largely from inclination, a little from a leaning toward sentiment itself as a compensation for the prosaic hum-drum of daily life, had barricaded itself in the happiness that chance had offered her, with no other desire than to defend it against the surprises of each day. She had therefore accepted with the complacency of a pretty woman the agreeable events that occurred; and, though she ventured little, and was troubled little by new necessities and desires for the unknown; though she was tender, tenacious, and farseeing, content with the present, but naturally anxious about the morrow, she had known how to enjoy the elements that Destiny had furnished her with wise and economical prudence.

Now, little by little, without daring to acknowledge it even to herself, the vague preoccupation of passing time, of advancing age, had glided into her soul. In her consciousness it had the effect of a gnawing trouble that never ceased. But, knowing well that this descent of life was without an end, that once begun it never could be stopped, and yielding to the instinct of danger, she closed her eyes in letting herself glide along, that she might retain her dream, that she might not be seized with dizziness at sight of the abyss or be made desperate by her impotence.

She lived, then, smiling, with a sort of factitious pride in remaining beautiful so long, and when Annette appeared at her side with the freshness of her eighteen years, instead of suffering from this contrast, she was proud, on the contrary, of being able to command preference, in the ripe grace of her womanhood, over that blooming young girl in the radiant beauty of first youth.

She had even believed that she had entered upon the beginning of a happy, tranquil period when the death of her mother struck a blow at her heart. During the first few days she was filled with that profound despair that leaves no room for any other thought. She remained from morning until night buried in grief, trying to recall a thousand things of the dead, her familiar words, her face in earlier days, the gowns she used to wear, as if she had stored her memory with relics; and from the now buried past she gathered all the intimate and trivial recollections with which to feed her cruel reveries. Then, when she had arrived at such paroxysms of despair that she fell into hysterics and swooned, all her accumulated grief broke forth in tears, flowing from her eyes by day and by night.

One morning, when her maid entered, and opened the shutters after raising the shades, asking: "How does Madame feel to-day?" she answered, feeling exhausted from having wept so much: "Oh, not at all well! Indeed, I can bear no more."

The servant, who was holding a tea-tray, looked at her mistress, and, touched to see her lying so pale amide the whiteness of the bed, she stammered, in a tone of genuine sadness: "Madame really looks very ill. Madame would do well to take care of herself."

The tone in which this was said pierced the Countess's heart like a sharp needle, and as soon as the maid had gone she rose to go and look at her face in her large dressing-mirror.

She was stupefied at the sight of herself, frightened by her hollow cheeks, her red eyes, the ravages produced in her by these days of suffering. Her face, which she knew so well, which she had often looked at in so many different mirrors, of which she knew all the expressions, all the smiles, the pallor which she had already corrected so many times, smoothing away the marks of fatigue, and the tiny wrinkles at the corners of the eyes, visible in too strong a light — her face suddenly seemed to her that of another woman, a new face that was distorted and irreparably ill.

In order to see herself better, to be surer with regard to this unexpected misfortune, she approached near enough to the mirror to touch it with her forehead, so that her breath, spreading a light mist over the glass, almost obscured the pale image she was contemplating. She was compelled to take a handkerchief to wipe away this mist, and, trembling with a strange emotion, she made a long and patient examination of the alterations in her face. With a light finger she stretched the skin of her cheeks, smoothed her forehead, pushed back her hair, and turned the eyelids to look at the whites of her eyes. Then she opened her mouth and examined her teeth which were a little tarnished where the gold fillings shone, and she was disturbed to note the livid gums and the yellow tint of the flesh above the cheeks and at the temples.

She was so lost in this examination of her fading beauty that she did not hear the door open, and was startled when her maid, standing behind her, said:

"Madame has forgotten to take her tea."

The Countess turned, confused, surprised, ashamed, and the servant, guessing her thoughts continued:

"Madame has wept too much; there is nothing worse to spoil the skin. One's blood turns to water."

And as the Countess added sadly: "There is age also," the maid exclaimed: "Oh, but Madame has not reached that time yet! With a few days of rest not a trace will be left. But Madame must go to walk, and take great care not to weep."

As soon as she was dressed the Countess descended to the park, and for the first time since her mother's death she visited the little orchard where long ago she had liked to cultivate and gather flowers; then she went to the river and strolled beside the stream until the hour for breakfast.

She sat down at the table opposite her husband, and beside her daughter, and remarked, that she might know what they thought: "I feel better today. I must be less pale."

"Oh, you still look very ill," said the Count.

Her heart contracted and she felt like weeping, for she had fallen into the habit of it.

Until evening, and the next day, and all the following days, whether she thought of her mother or of herself, every moment she felt her throat swelling with sobs and her eyes filling with tears, but to prevent them from overflowing and furrowing her cheeks she repressed them, and by a superhuman effort of will turned her thoughts in other directions, mastered them, ruled them, separated them from her sorrow, forced herself to feel consoled, tried to amuse herself and to think of sad things no more, in order to regain the hue of health.

Above all, she did not wish to return to Paris and to receive Olivier Bertin until she had become more like her former self. Realizing that she had grown too thin, that the flesh of women of her age needs to be full in order to keep fresh, she sought to create appetite by walking in the woods and along the roads; and though she returned weary and not hungry she forced herself to eat a great deal.

The Count, who wished to go away, could not understand her obstinacy. Finally, as her resistance seemed invincible, he declared that he would go alone, leaving the Countess free to return when she might feel so disposed.

The next day she received the telegram announcing Olivier's arrival.

A desire to flee seized her, so much did she fear his first look. She would have preferred to wait another week or two. In a week, with care one may change the face completely, since women, even when young and in good health, under the least change of influence become unrecognizable from one day to another. But the idea of appearing in broad daylight before Olivier, in the open fields, in the heat of August, beside Annette, so fresh and blooming, disturbed her so much that she decided immediately not to go to the station, but to await him in the half-darkened drawingroom.

She went up to her room and fell into a dream. Breaths of warm air stirred the curtains from time to time; the song of the crickets filled the air. Never before had she felt so sad. It was no more the great grief that had shattered her heart, overwhelming her before the soulless body of her beloved old mother. That grief, which she had believed incurable, had in a few days become softened, and was now but a sorrow of the memory; but now she felt herself swept away on a deep wave of melancholy into which she had entered gradually, and from which she never would emerge.

She had an almost irresistible desire to weep — and would not. Every time she felt her eyelids grow moist she wiped them away quickly, rose, paced about the room, looked out into the park and gazed at the tall trees, watched the slow, black flight of the crows against the background of blue sky. Then she passed before her mirror, judged her appearance with one glance, effaced the trace of a tear by touching the corner of her eye with rice powder, and looked at the clock, trying to guess at what point of the route he must have reached.

Like all women who are carried away by a distress of soul, whether real or unreasonable, she clung to her lover with a sort of frenzy. Was he not her all — all, everything, more than life, all that anyone must be who has come to be the sole affection of one who feels the approach of age?

Suddenly she heard in the distance the crack of a whip; she ran to the window and saw the phaeton as it made the turn round the lawn, drawn by two horses. Seated beside Annette, in the back seat of the carriage, Olivier waved his handkerchief as he saw the Countess, to which she responded by waving him a salutation from the window. Then she went down stairs with a heart throbbing fast but happy now, thrilled with joy at knowing him so near, of speaking to him and seeing him.

They met in the antechamber, before the drawingroom door.

He opened his arms to her with an irresistible impulse, and in a voice warmed by real emotion, exclaimed: "Ah, my poor Countess, let me embrace you!"

She closed her eyes, leaned toward him and pressed against him, lifted her cheek to him, and as he pressed his lips upon it, she murmured in his ear: "I love thee!"

Then Olivier, without dropping the hands he clasped in his own, looked at her, saying: "Let us see that sad face."

She felt ready to faint.

"Yes, a little pale," said he, "but that is nothing."

To thank him for saying that, she said brokenly,

"Ah, dear friend, dear friend!" finding nothing else to say.

But he turned, looking behind her in search of Annette, who had disappeared.

"Is it not strange," he said abruptly, "to see your daughter in mourning?"

"Why?" inquired the Countess.

"What? You ask why?" he exclaimed, with extraordinary animation. "Why, it is your own portrait painted by me — it is my portrait. It is yourself, such as you were when I met you long ago when I entered the Duchess's house! Ah, do you remember that door where you passed under my gaze, as a frigate passes under a cannon of a fort? Good heavens! when I saw the little one, just now, at the railway station, standing on the platform, all in black, with the sun shining on her hair massed around her face, the blood rushed to my head. I thought I should weep. I tell you, it is enough to drive one mad, when one has known you as I have, who has studied you as no one else has, and reproduced you in painting, Madame. Ah, I thought that you had sent her alone to meet me at the station in order to give me that surprise. My God! but I was surprised, indeed! I tell you, it is enough to drive one mad."

He called: "Annette! Nane!"

The young girl's voice replied from outside, where she was giving sugar to the horses:

"Yes, yes, I am here!"

"Come in here!"

She entered quickly.

"Here, stand close beside your mother."

She obeyed, and he compared the two, but repeated mechanically, "Yes, it is astonishing, astonishing!" for they resembled each other less when side by side than they did before leaving Paris, the young girl having acquired a new expression of luminous youth in her black attire, while the mother had for a long time lost that radiance of hair and complexion that had dazzled and entranced the painter when they met for the first time.

Then the Countess and Olivier entered the drawingroom. He seemed in high spirits.

"Ah, what a good plan it was to come here!" he said. "But it was your husband's idea that I should come, you know. He charged me to take you back with me. And I — do you know what I propose? You have no idea, have you? Well, I propose, on the contrary, to remain here! Paris is odious in this heat, while the country is delicious. Heavens! how sweet it is here!"

The dews of evening impregnated the park with freshness, the soft breeze made the trees tremble, and the earth exhaled imperceptible vapors which threw a light, transparent veil over the horizon. The three cows, standing with drooping heads, cropped the grass with avidity, and four peacocks, with a loud rustling of wings, flew up into their accustomed perch in a cedar-tree under the windows of the castle. The barking of dogs in the distance came to the ear, and in the quiet air of the close of day the calls of human voices were heard, in phrases shouted across the fields, from one meadow to another, and in those short, guttural cries used in driving animals.

The painter, with bared head and shining eyes, breathed deeply, and, as he met the Countess's look, he said:

"This is happiness!"

"It never lasts," she answered, approaching nearer.

"Let us take it when it comes," said he.

"You never used to like the country until now," the Countess replied, smiling.

"I like it to-day because I find you here. I do not know how to live any more where you are not. When one is young, he may be in love though far away, through letters, thoughts, or dreams, perhaps because he feels that life is all before him, perhaps too because passion is stronger than pure affection; at my age, on the contrary, love has become like the habit of an invalid; it is a binding up of the soul, which flies now with only one wing, and mounts less frequently into the ideal. The heart knows no more ecstasy, only selfish wants. And then I know quite well that I have no time to lose to enjoy what remains for me."

"Oh, old!" she remonstrated, taking his hand tenderly.

"Yes, yes, I am old," he repeated. "Everything shows it, my hair, my changing character, the coming sadness. Alas! that is something I never have known till now — sadness. If someone had told me when I was thirty that a time would come when I should be sad without cause, uneasy, discontented with everything, I should not have believed it. That proves that my heart also has grown old."

The Countess replied with an air of profound certainty:

"Oh, as for me, my heart is still young. It never has changed. Yes, it has grown younger, perhaps. Once it was twenty; now it is only sixteen!"

They remained a long while thus, talking in the open window, mingled with the spirit of evening, very near each other, nearer than they ever had been, in this hour of tenderness, this twilight of love, like that of the day.

A servant entered, announcing:

"Madame la Comtesse is served."

"Have you called my daughter?" the Countess asked.

"Mademoiselle is in the diningroom."

All three sat down at the table. The shutters were closed, and two large candelabra with six candles each illumined Annette's face and seemed to powder her hair with gold dust. Bertin, smiling, looked at her continually.

"Heavens, now pretty she is in black!" he said.

And he turned toward the Countess while admiring the daughter, as if to thank the mother for having given him this pleasure.

When they returned to the drawingroom the moon had risen above the trees in the park. Their somber mass appeared like a great island, and the country round about like a sea hidden under the light mist that floated over the plains.

"Oh, mamma, let us take a walk," said Annette.

The Countess consented.

"I will take Julio."

"Very well, if you wish."

They set out. The young girl walked in front, amusing herself with the dog. When they crossed the lawn they heard the breathing of the cows, which, awake and scenting their enemy, raised their heads to look. Under the trees, farther away, the moon was pouring among the branches a shower of fine rays that fell to earth, seeming to wet the leaves that were spread out on the path in little patches of yellow light. Annette and Julio ran along, each seeming to have on this serene night, the same joyful and unburdened hearts, the gaiety of which expressed itself in graceful gambols.

In the little openings, where the wave of moonlight descended as into a well, the young girl looked like a spirit, and the painter called her back, marveling at this dark vision with its clear and brilliant face. Then when she darted away again, he took the Countess's hand and pressed it, often seeking her lips as they traversed the deeper shadows, as if the sight of Annette had revived the impatience of his heart.

At last they reached the edge of the plain, where they could just discern, afar, here and there, the groups of trees belonging to the farms. Through the milky mist that bathed the fields the horizon appeared illimitable, and the soft silence, the living silence of that vast space, so warm and luminous, was full of inexpressible hope, of that indefinable expectancy which makes summer nights so sweet. Far up in the heavens a few long slender clouds looked like silver shells. Standing still for a few seconds, one could hear in that nocturnal peace a confused, continuous murmur of life, a thousand slight sounds, the harmony of which seemed like silence.

A quail in a neighboring field uttered her double cry, and Julio, his ears erect, glided furtively toward the two flute-like notes of the bird, Annette following, as softly as he, holding her breath and crouching low.

"Ah," said the Countess, standing alone with the painter, "why do moments like this pass so quickly? We can hold nothing, keep nothing. We have not even time to taste what is good. It is over already."

Olivier kissed her hand, and replied, smiling:

"Oh, I cannot philosophize this evening! I belong to the present hour entirely."

"You do not love me as I love you," she murmured.

"Ah, do not — "

"No," she interrupted, "in me you love, as you said very truly before dinner, a woman who satisfies the needs of your heart, a woman who never has caused you a pain, and who has put a little happiness into your life. I know that; I feel it. Yes, I have the good consciousness, the ardent joy of having been good, useful, and helpful to you. You have loved, you still love all that you find agreeable in me, my attentions to you, my admiration, my wish to please you, my passion, the complete gift I made to you of my whole being. But it is not I you really love, do you know? Oh, I feel that as one feels a cold current of air. You love a thousand things about me — my beauty, which is fast leaving me, my devotion, the wit they say I possess, the opinion the world has of me, and that which I have of you in my heart; but it is not I — I, nothing but myself — do you understand?"

He laughed in a soft and friendly way.

"No, I do not understand you very well. You make a reproachful attack which is quite un-expected."

"Oh, my God! I wish I could make you understand how I love you! I am always seeking, but cannot find a means. When I think of you — and I am always thinking of you — I feel in the depths of my being an unspeakable intoxication of longing to be yours, an irresistible need of giving myself to you even more completely. I should like to sacrifice myself in some absolute way, for there is nothing better, when one loves, than to give, to give always, all, all, life, thought, body, all that one has, to feel that one is giving, to be ready to risk anything to give still more. I love you so much that I love to suffer for you, I love even my anxieties, my torments, my jealousies, the pain I feel when I realize that you are not longer tender toward me. I love in you a someone that only I have discovered, a you which is not the you of the world that is admired and known, a you which is mine, which cannot change nor grow old, which I cannot cease to love, for I have, to look at it, eyes that see it alone. But one cannot say these things. There are no words to express them."

He repeated softly, over and over:

"Dear, dear, dear Any!"

Julio came back, bounding toward them, without having found the quail, which had kept still at his approach; Annette followed him, breathless from running.

"I can't run any more," said she. "I will prop myself up with you, Monsieur painter!"

She leaned on Olivier's free arm, and they returned, walking thus, he between them, under the shadow of the trees. They spoke no more. He walked on, possessed by them, penetrated by a sort of feminine essence with which their contact filled him. He did not try to see them, since he had them near him; he even closed his eyes that he might feel their proximity the better. They guided him, conducted him, and he walked straight before him, fascinated by them, with the one on the left as well as the one on the right, without knowing, indeed, which was on the left or which on the right, which was mother, which was daughter. He abandoned himself willingly to the pleasure of unpremeditated and exquisite sensuous delight. He even tried to mingle them in his heart, not to distinguish them in his thought, and quieted desire with the charm of this confusion. Was it not only one woman beside him, composed of this mother and daughter, so much alike? And did not the daughter seem to have come to earth only for the purpose of reanimating his former love for the mother?

When he opened his eyes on entering the castle, it seemed to him that he had just passed through the most delicious moments of his life; that he had experienced the strangest, the most puzzling, yet complete emotion a man might feel, intoxicated with the same love by the seductiveness emanating from two women.

"Ah, what an exquisite evening!" said he, as soon as he found himself between them in the lamplight.

"I am not at all sleepy," said Annette; "I could pass the whole night walking when the weather is fine."

The Countess looked at the clock.

"Oh, it is half after eleven. You must go to bed, my child."

They separated, and went to their own apartments. The young girl who did not wish to go to bed was the only one that went to sleep at once.

The next morning, at the usual hour, when the maid, after opening the curtains and the shutters, brought the tea and looked at her mistress, who was still drowsy, she said:

"Madame looks better to-day, already."

"Do you think so?"

"Oh, yes. Madame's face looks more rested."

Though she had not yet looked at herself, the Countess knew that this was true. Her heart was light, she did not feel it throb, and she felt once more as if she lived. The blood flowing in her veins was no longer coursing so rapidly as on the day before, hot and feverish, sending nervousness and restlessness through all her body, but gave her a sense of well-being and happy confidence.

When the maid had gone she went to look at herself in the mirror. She was a little surprised, for she felt so much better that she expected to find herself rejuvenated by several years in a single night. Then she realized the childishness of such a hope, and, after another glance, resigned herself to the knowledge that her complexion was only clearer, her eyes less fatigued, her lips a little redder than on the day before. As her soul was content, she could not feel sad, and she smiled, thinking: "Yes, in a few days I shall be quite myself again. I have gone through too much to recover so quickly."

But she remained seated a very long time before her toilet-table, upon which were laid out in graceful order on a muslin scarf bordered with lace, before a beautiful mirror of cut crystal, all her little ivory-handled instruments of coquetry, bearing her arms surmounted by a coronet. There they were, innumerable, pretty, all different, destined for delicate and secret use, some of steel, fine and sharp, of strange shapes, like surgical instruments for operations on children, others round and soft, of feathers, of down, of the skins of unknown animals, made to lay upon the tender skin the caresses of fragrant powders or of powerful liquid perfumes.

She handled them a long time with practised fingers, carrying them from her lips to her temples with touches softer than a kiss, correcting imperfections, underlining the eyes, beautifying the eyelashes. At last, when she went down stairs, she felt almost sure that the first glance cast upon her would not be too unfavorable.

"Where is Monsieur Bertin?" she inquired of a servant she met in the vestibule.

"Monsieur Bertin is in the orchard, playing tennis with Mademoiselle," the man replied.

She heard them from a distance counting the points. One after the other, the deep voice of the painter and the light one of the young girl, called: "Fifteen, thirty, forty, vantage, deuce, vantage, game!"

The orchard, where a space had been leveled for a tennis-court, was a great, square grassplot, planted with apple-trees, inclosed by the park, the vegetable-garden, and the farms belonging to the castle. Along the slope that formed a boundary on three sides, like the defenses of an intrenched camp, grew borders of various kinds of flowers, wild and cultivated, roses in masses, pinks, heliotrope, fuchsias, mignonnette, and many more, which as Bertin said gave the air a taste of honey. Besides this, the bees, whose hives, thatched with straw, lined the wall of the vegetable-garden, covered the flowery field in their yellow, buzzing flight.

In the exact center of this orchard a few apple-trees had been cut down, in order to make a good court for tennis, and a tarry net, stretched across this space, separated it into two camps.

Annette, on one side, with bare head, her black skirt caught up, showing her ankles and half way up to her knee when she ran to catch a ball, dashed to and fro, with sparkling eyes and flushed cheeks, tired, out of breath with the sure and practised play of her adversary.

He, in white flannels, fitting tightly over the hips, a white shirt, and a white tennis cap, his abdomen somewhat prominent in that costume, awaited the ball coolly, judged its fall with precision, received and returned it without haste, without running, with the elegant pose, the passionate attention, and professional skill which he displayed in all athletic sports.

It was Annette that spied her mother first.

"Good morning, mamma!" she cried, "wait till we have finished this play."

That second's distraction lost her the game. The ball passed against her, almost rolling, touched the ground and went out of the game.

Bertin shouted "Won!" and the young girl, surprised, accused him of having profited by her inattention. Julio, trained to seek and find the lost balls, as if they were partridges fallen among the bushes, sprang behind her to get the ball rolling in the grass, seized it in his jaws, and brought it back, wagging his tail.

The painter now saluted the Countess, but, urged to resume the game, animated by the contest, pleased to find himself so agile, he threw only a short, preoccupied glance at the face prepared so carefully for him, asking:

"Will you allow me, dear Countess? I am afraid of taking cold and having neuralgia."

"Oh, yes," the Countess replied.

She sat down on a haystack, mowed that morning in order to give a clear field to the players, and, her heart suddenly touched with sadness, looked on at the game.

Her daughter, irritated at losing continually, grew more animated, excited, uttered cries of vexation or of triumph, and flew impetuously from one end of the court to the other. Often, in her swift movements, little locks of hair were loosened, rolled down and fell upon her shoulders. She seized them with impatient movements, and, holding the racket between her knees, fastened them up in place, thrusting hairpins into the golden mass.

And Bertin, from his position, cried to the Countess:

"Isn't she pretty like that, and fresh as the day?"

Yes, she was young, she could run, grow warm, become red, let her hair fly, brave anything, dare everything, for all that only made her more beautiful.

Then, when they resumed their play with ardor, the Countess, more and more melancholy, felt that Olivier preferred that game, that childish sport, like the play of kittens jumping after paper balls, to the sweetness of sitting beside her that warm morning, and feeling her loving pressure against him.

When the bell, far away, rang the first signal for breakfast, it seemed to her that someone had freed her, that a weight had been lifted from her heart. But as she returned, leaning on his arm, he said to her:

"I have been amusing myself like a boy. It is a great thing to be, or to feel oneself, young. Ah, yes, there is nothing like that. When we do not like to run any more, it is all over with us."

When they left the table the Countess, who on the preceding day had for the first time omitted her daily visit to the cemetery, proposed that they should go there together; so all three set out for the village.

They were obliged to go through some woods, through which ran a stream called "La Rainette," no doubt because of the frogs that peopled it; then they had to cross the end of a plain before arriving at the church, situated in the midst of a group of houses that sheltered the grocer, the baker, the butcher, the wine-merchant, and several other modest tradesmen who supplied the needs of the peasants.

The walk was made in thoughtful silence, the recollection of the dead weighing on their spirits. Arrived at the grave, the women knelt and prayed a long time. The Countess, motionless, bent low, her handkerchief at her eyes, for she feared to weep lest her tears run down her cheeks. She prayed, but not as she had prayed before this day, in a sort of invocation to her mother, a despairing appeal penetrating under the marble of the tomb until she seemed to feel by the poignancy of her own anguish that the dead must hear her, listen to her, but a simple, hesitating, and earnest utterance of the consecrated words of the Pater Noster and the Ave Maria. She would not have had that day sufficient strength and steadiness of nerve necessary for that cruel communion that brought no response with what remained of that being who had disappeared in the tomb where all that was left of her was concealed. Other anxieties had penetrated her woman's heart, had agitated, wounded, and distracted her; and her fervent prayer rose to Heaven, full of vague supplications. She offered her adoration to God, the inexorable God who has made all poor creatures on the earth, and begged Him to take pity on her as well as on the one He had recalled to Himself.

She could not have told what she had asked of God, so vague and confused were her fears still; but she felt the need of Divine aid, of a superhuman support against approaching dangers and inevitable sorrows.

Annette, with closed eyes, having also murmured the formulas, sank into a reverie, for she did not wish to rise before her mother.

Olivier Bertin looked at them, thinking that he never had seen a more ravishing picture, and somewhat regretful that it was out of the question for him to be permitted to make a sketch of the scene.

On their way back they talked of human life, softly stirring those bitter and poetic ideas of a tender but pessimistic philosophy, which is a frequent subject of conversation between men and women whom life has wounded a little, and whose hearts mingle as they sympathize with each other's grief.

Annette, who was not ripe for such thoughts, left them frequently to gather wild flowers beside the road.

But Olivier, desiring to keep her near him, nervous at seeing her continually darting away, never removed his eyes from her. He was irritated that she should show more interest in the colors of the plants than in the words he spoke. He experienced an inexpressible dissatisfaction at not being able to charm her, to dominate her, as he had captivated her mother; and he felt a desire to hold out his hand and seize her, hold her, forbid her to go away. He felt that she was too alert, too young, too indifferent, too free — free as a bird, or like a little dog that will not come back, will not obey, which has independence in its veins, that sweet instinct of liberty which neither voice nor whip has yet vanquished.

In order to attract her he talked of gayer things, and at times he questioned her, trying to awaken her feminine curiosity so that she would listen; but one would think that the capricious wind of heaven was blowing through Annette's head that day, as it blew across the undulating grain, carrying away and dispersing her attention into space, for she hardly uttered even the commonplace replies expected of her, between her short digressions, and made them with an absent air, then returned to her flowers. Finally he became exasperated, filled with a childish impatience, and as she ran up to beg her mother to carry her first bouquet so that she could gather another, he caught her by the elbow and pressed her arm, so that she could not escape again. She struggled, laughing, pulling with all her strength to get away from him; then, moved by masculine instinct, he tried gentler means, and, not being able to win her attention he tried to purchase it by tempting her coquetry.

"Tell me," said he, "what flower you prefer, and I will have a brooch made of it for you."

She hesitated, surprised.

"What, a brooch?"

"In stones of the same color; in rubies if it is the poppy; in sapphires if it is the cornflower, with a little leaf in emeralds."

Annette's face lighted up with that affectionate joy with which promises and presents animate a woman's countenance.

"The cornflower," said she, "it is so pretty."

"The cornflower it shall be. We will go to order it as soon as we return to Paris."

She no longer tried to leave him, attracted by the thought of the jewel she already tried to see, to imagine.

"Does it take very long to make a thing like that?" she asked.

He laughed, feeling that he had caught her.

"I don't know; it depends upon the difficulties. We will make the jeweler do it quickly."

A dismal thought suddenly crossed her mind.

"But I cannot wear it since I am in deep mourning!"

He had passed his arm under that of the young girl, and pressed it against him.

"Well, you will keep the brooch until you cease to wear mourning," said he; "that will not prevent you from looking at it."

As on the preceding evening, he was walking between them, held captive between their shoulders, and in order to see their eyes, of a similar blue dotted with tiny black spots, raised to his, he spoke to them in turn, moving his head first toward the one, then toward the other. As the bright sunlight now shone on them, he did not so fully confound the Countess with Annette, but he did more and more associate the daughter with the newborn remembrances of what the mother had been. He had a strong desire to embrace both, the one to find again upon cheek and neck a little of that pink and white freshness which he had already tasted, and which he saw now reproduced as by a miracle; the other because he loved her as he always had, and felt that from her came the powerful appeal of long habit. He even realized at that moment that his desire and affection for her, which for some time had been waning, had revived at the sight of her resuscitated youth.

Annette went away again to gather more flowers. This time Olivier did not call her back; it was as if the contact of her arm and the satisfaction of knowing that he had given her pleasure had quieted him; but he followed all her movements with the pleasure one feels in seeing the persons or things that captivate and intoxicate our eyes. When she returned, with a large cluster of flowers, he drew a deep breath, seeking unconsciously to inhale something of her, a little of her breath or the warmth of her skin in the air stirred by her running. He looked at her, enraptured, as one watches the dawn, or listens to music, with thrills of delight when she bent, rose again, or raised her arms to arrange her hair. And then, more and more, hour by hour, she evoked in him the memory of the past! Her laughter, her pretty ways, her motions, brought back to his lips the savor of former kisses given and returned; she made of the far-off past, of which he had forgotten the precise sensation, something like a dream in the present; she confused epochs, dates, the ages of his heart, and rekindling the embers of cooled emotions, she mingled, without his realizing it, yesterday with tomorrow, recollection with hope.

He asked himself as he questioned his memory whether the Countess in her brightest bloom had had that fawn-like, supple grace, that bold, capricious, irresistible charm, like the grace of a running, leaping animal. No. She had had a riper bloom but was less untamed. First, a child of the city, then a woman, never having imbibed the air of the fields and lived in the grass, she had grown pretty under the shade of the walls and not in the sunlight of heaven.

When they reentered the castle the Countess began to write letters at her little low table in the bay-window; Annette went up to her own room, and the painter went out again to walk slowly, cigar in mouth, hands clasped behind him, through the winding paths of the park. But he did not go away so far that he lost sight of the white facade or the pointed roof of the castle. As soon as it disappeared behind groups of trees or clusters of shrubbery, a shadow seemed to fall over his heart, as when a cloud hides the sun; and when it reappeared through the apertures in the foliage he paused a few seconds to contemplate the two rows of tall windows. Then he resumed his walk. He felt agitated, but content. Content with what? With everything.

The air seemed pure to him, life was good that day. His body felt once more the liveliness of a small boy, a desire to run, to catch the yellow butterflies fluttering over the lawn, as if they were suspended at the end of elastic threads. He sang little airs from the opera. Several times he repeated the celebrated phrase by Gounod: "Laisse-moi contempler ton visage," discovering in it a profoundly tender expression which never before he had felt in the same way.

Suddenly he asked himself how it was that he had so soon become different from his usual self. Yesterday, in Paris, dissatisfied with everything, disgusted, irritated; to-day calm, satisfied with everything — one would say that some benevolent god had changed his soul. "That same kind god," he thought, "might well have changed my body at the same time, and rejuvenated me a little." Suddenly he saw Julio hunting among the bushes. He called him, and when the dog ran up to put his finely formed head, with its curly ears, under his hand, he sat down on the grass to pet him more comfortably, spoke gentle words to him, laid him on his knees, and growing tender as he caressed the animal, he kissed it, after the fashion of women whose hearts are easily moved to demonstration.

After dinner, instead of going out as on the evening before, they spent the hours in the drawingroom.

Suddenly the Countess said: "We must leave here soon."

"Oh, don't speak of that yet!" Olivier exclaimed. "You would not leave Roncieres when I was not here; now what I have come, you think only of going away."

"But, my dear friend," said she, "we three cannot remain here indefinitely."

"It does not necessarily follow that we need stay indefinitely, but just a few days. How many times have I stayed at your house for whole weeks?"

"Yes, but in different circumstances, when the house was open to everyone."

"Oh, mamma," said Annette, coaxingly, "let us stay a few days more, just two or three. He teaches me so well how to play tennis. It annoys me to lose, but afterward I am glad to have made such progress."

Only that morning the Countess had been planning to make this mysterious visit of her friend's last until Sunday, and now she wished to go away, without knowing why. That day which she had hoped would be such a happy one had left in her soul an inexpressible but poignant sadness, a causeless apprehension, as tenacious and confused as a presentiment.

When she was once more alone in her room she even sought to define this new access of melancholy.

Had she experienced one of those imperceptible emotions whose touch has been so slight that reason does not remember it, but whose vibrations still stir the most sensitive chords of the heart? Perhaps? Which? She recalled, certainly, some little annoyances, in the thousand degrees of sentiment through which she had passed, each minute having its own. But they were too petty to have thus disheartened her. "I am exacting," she thought. "I have no right to torment myself in this way."

She opened her window, to breathe the night air, and leaned on the windowsill, gazing at the moon.

A slight noise made her look down. Olivier was pacing before the castle. "Why did he say that he was going to his room?" she thought; "why did he not tell me he was going out again? Why did he not ask me to come with him? He knows very well that it would have made me so happy. What is he thinking of now?"

This idea that he had not wished to have her with him on his walk, that he had preferred to go out alone this beautiful night, alone, with a cigar in his mouth, for she could see its fiery-red point — alone, when he might have given her the joy of taking her with him; this idea that he had not continual need of her, that he did not desire her always, created within her soul a new fermentation of bitterness.

She was about to close the window, that she might not see him or be tempted to call to him, when he raised his eyes and saw her.

"Well, are you star-gazing, Countess?"

"Yes," she answered. "You also, as it appears."

"Oh, I am simply smoking."

She could not resist the desire to ask: "Why did you not tell me you were going out?"

"I only wanted to smoke a cigar. I am coming in now."

"Then goodnight, my friend."

"Goodnight, Countess."

She retired as far as her low chair, sat down in it and wept; and her maid, who was called to assist her to bed, seeing her red eyes said with compassion:

"Ah, Madame is going to make a sad face for herself again tomorrow."

The Countess slept badly; she was feverish and had nightmare. As soon as she awoke she opened her window and her curtains to look at herself in the mirror. Her features were drawn, her eyelids swollen, her skin looked yellow; and she felt such violent grief because of this that she wished to say she was ill and to keep her bed, so that she need not appear until evening.

Then, suddenly, the necessity to go away entered her mind, to depart immediately, by the first train, to quit the country, where one could see too clearly by the broad light of the fields the ineffaceable marks of sorrow and of life itself. In Paris one lives in the half shadow of apartments, where heavy curtains, even at noontime, admit only a softened light. She would herself become beautiful again there, with the pallor one should have in that discreetly softened light. Then Annette's face rose before her eyes — so fresh and pink, with slightly disheveled hair, as when she was playing tennis. She understood then the unknown anxiety from which her soul had suffered. She was not jealous of her daughter's beauty! No, certainly not; but she felt, she acknowledged for the first time that she must never again show herself by Annette's side in the bright sunlight.

She rang, and before drinking her tea she gave orders for departure, wrote some telegrams, even ordering her dinner for that evening by telegraph, settled her bills in the country, gave her final instructions, arranged everything in less than an hour, a prey to feverish and increasing impatience.

When she went down stairs, Annette and Olivier, who had been told of her decision, questioned her with surprise. Then, seeing that she would not give any precise reason for this sudden departure, they grumbled a little and expressed their dissatisfaction until they separated at the station in Paris.

The Countess, holding out her hand to the painter, said: "Will you dine with us tomorrow?"

"Certainly, I will come," he replied, rather sulkily. "All the same, what you have done was not nice. We were so happy down there, all three of us."

III

As soon as the Countess was alone with her daughter in her carriage, which was taking her back to her home, she suddenly felt tranquil and quieted, as if she had just passed through a serious crisis. She breathed easier, smiled at the houses, recognized with joy the look of the city, whose details all true Parisians seem to carry in their eyes and hearts. Each shop she passed suggested the ones beyond, on a line along the Boulevard, and the tradesman's face so often seen behind his showcase. She felt saved. From what? Reassured. Why? Confident. Of what?

When the carriage stopped under the arch of the porte-cochere, she alighted quickly and entered, as if flying, the shadow of the stairway; then passed to the shadow of her drawingroom, then to that of her bedroom. There she remained standing a few moments, glad to be at home, in security, in the dim and misty daylight of Paris, which, hardly brightening, compels one to guess as well as to see, where one may show what he pleases and hide what he will; and the unreasoning memory of the dazzling glare that bathed the country remained in her like an impression of past suffering.

When she went down to dinner, her husband, who had just arrived at home, embraced her affectionately, and said, smiling: "Ah, ha! I knew very well that our friend Bertin would bring you back. It was very clever of me to send him after you."

Annette responded gravely, in the peculiar tone she affected when she said something in jest without smiling:

"Oh, he had a great deal of trouble. Mamma could not decide for herself."

The Countess said nothing, but felt a little confused.

The doors being closed to visitors, no one called that evening. Madame de Guilleroy passed the whole of the following day in different shops, choosing or ordering what she needed. She had loved, from her youth, almost from her infancy, those long sittings before the mirrors of the great shops. From the moment of entering one, she took delight in thinking of all the details of that minute rehearsal in the green-room of Parisian life. She adored the rustle of the dresses worn by the salesgirls, who hastened forward to meet her, all smiles, with their offers, their queries; and Madame the dressmaker, the milliner, or corset-maker, was to her a person of consequence, whom she treated as an artist when she expressed an opinion in asking advice. She enjoyed even more to feel herself in the skilful hands of the young girls who undressed her and dressed her again, causing her to turn gently around before her own gracious reflection. The little shiver that the touch of their fingers produced on her skin, her neck, or in her hair, was one of the best and sweetest little pleasures that belonged to her life of an elegant woman.

This day, however, she passed before those candid mirrors, without her veil or hat, feeling a certain anxiety. Her first visit, at the milliner's, reassured her. The three hats which she chose were wonderfully becoming; she could not doubt it, and when the milliner said, with an air of conviction, "Oh, Madame la Comtesse, blondes should never leave off mourning" she went away much pleased, and entered other shops with a heart full of confidence.

Then she found at home a note from the Duchess, who had come to see her, saying that she would return in the evening; then she wrote some letters; then she fell into dreamy reverie for some time, surprised that this simple change of place had caused to recede into a past that already seemed far away the great misfortune that had overwhelmed her. She could not even convince herself that her return from Roncieres dated only from the day before, so much was the condition of her soul modified since her return to Paris, as if that little change had healed her wounds.

Bertin, arriving at dinnertime, exclaimed on seeing her:

"You are dazzling this evening!"

And this exclamation sent a warm wave of happiness through her being.

When they were leaving the table, the Count, who had a passion for billiards, offered to play a game with Bertin, and the two ladies accompanied them to the billiard-room, where the coffee was served.

The men were still playing when the Duchess was announced, and they all returned to the drawingroom. Madame de Corbelle and her husband presented themselves at the same time, their voices full of tears. For some minutes it seemed, from the doleful tones, that everyone was about to weep; but little by little, after a few tender words and inquiries, another current of thought set in; the voices took on a more cheerful tone, and everyone began to talk naturally, as if the shadow of the misfortune that had saddened them had suddenly been dissipated.

Then Bertin rose, took Annette by the hand, led her under the portrait of her mother, in the ray of light from the reflector, and said:

"Isn't this stupefying?"

The Duchess was so greatly surprised that she seemed dazed; she repeated many times: "Heavens! is it possible? Heavens! is it possible? It is like someone raised from the dead. To think that I did not see that when I came in! Oh, my little Any, I find you again, I, who knew you so well then in your first mourning as a woman — no, in your second, for you had already lost your father. Oh, that Annette, in black like that — why, it is her mother come back to earth! What a miracle! Without that portrait we never should have perceived it. Your daughter resembles you very much, but she resembles that portrait much more."

Musadieu now appeared, having heard of Madame de Guilleroy's return, as he wished to be one of the first to offer her the "homage of his sorrowful sympathy."

He interrupted his first speech on perceiving the young girl standing against the frame, illumined by the same ray of light, appearing like the living sister of the painting.

"Ah, that is certainly one of the most astonishing things I ever have seen," he exclaimed.

The Corbelles, whose convictions always followed established opinions, marveled in their turn with a little less exuberant ardor.

The Countess's heart seemed to contract, little by little, as if all these exclamations of astonishment had hurt it. Without speaking, she looked at her daughter standing by the image of herself, and a sudden feeling of weakness came over her. She longed to cry out: "Say no more! I know very well that she resembles me!"

Until the end of the evening she remained in a melancholy mood, having lost once more the confidence she had felt the day before.

Bertin was chatting with her when the Marquis de Farandal was announced. As soon as the painter saw him enter and approach the hostess he rose and glided behind her armchair, murmuring: "This is delightful! There comes that great animal now." Then, making a detour of the apartment, he reached the door and departed.

After receiving the salutations of the newcomer, the Countess looked around to find Olivier, to resume with him the talk in which she had been interested. Not seeing him, she asked:

"What, has the great man gone?"

"I believe so, my dear," her husband answered; "I just saw him going away in the English fashion."

She was surprised, reflected a few moments, and then began to talk to the Marquis.

Her intimate friends, however, discreetly took their leave early, for, so soon after her affliction, she had only half-opened her door, as it were.

When she found herself again lying on her bed, all the griefs that had assailed her in the country reappeared. They took a more distinct form; she felt them more keenly. She realized that she was growing old!

That evening, for the first time, she had understood that, in her own drawingroom, where until now she alone had been admired, complimented, flattered, loved, another, her daughter, was taking her place. She had comprehended this suddenly, when feeling that everyone's homage was paid to Annette. In that kingdom, the house of a pretty woman, where she will permit no one to overshadow her, where she eliminated with discreet and unceasing care all disadvantageous comparisons, where she allows the entrance of her equals only to attempt to make them her vassals, she saw plainly that her daughter was about to become the sovereign. How strange had been that contraction of her heart when all eyes were turned upon Annette as Bertin held her by the hand standing before the portrait! She herself felt as if she had suddenly disappeared, dispossessed, dethroned. Everyone looked at Annette; no one had a glance for her any more! She was so accustomed to hear compliments and flattery, whenever her portrait was admired, she was so sure of eulogistic phrases, which she had little regarded but which pleased her nevertheless, that this desertion of herself, this unexpected defection, this admiration intended wholly for her daughter, had moved, astonished, and hurt her more than if it had been a question of no matter what rivalry under any kind of conditions.

But, as she had one of those natures which, in all crises, after the first blow, react, struggle, and find arguments for consolation, she reasoned that, once her dear little daughter should be married, when they should no longer live under the same roof, she herself would no longer be compelled to endure that incessant comparison which was beginning to be too painful for her under the eyes of her friend Olivier.

But the shock had been too much for her that evening. She was feverish and hardly slept at all. In the morning she awoke weary and overcome by extreme lassitude, and then within her surged up an irresistible longing to be comforted again, to be succored, to ask help from someone who could cure all her ills, all her moral and physical ailments.

Indeed, she felt so ill at ease and weak that she had an idea of consulting her physician. Perhaps she was about to be seriously affected, for it was not natural that in a few hours she should pass through those successive phases of suffering and relief. So she sent him a telegram, and awaited his coming.

He arrived about eleven o'clock. He was one of those dignified, fashionable physicians whose decorations and titles guarantee their ability, whose tact at least equals mere skill, and who have, above all, when treating women, an adroitness that is surer than medicines.

He entered, bowed, looked at his patient, and said with a smile: "Come, this is not a very grave case. With eyes like yours one is never very ill."

She felt immediate gratitude to him for this beginning, and told him of her troubles, her weakness, her nervousness and melancholy; then she mentioned, without laying too much stress on the matter, her alarmingly ill appearance. After listening to her with an attentive air, though asking no questions except as to her appetite, as if he knew well the secret nature of this feminine ailment, he sounded her, examined her, felt of her shoulders with the tips of his fingers, lifted her arms, having undoubtedly met her thought and understood with the shrewdness of a practitioner who lifts all veils that she was consulting him more for her beauty than for her health. Then he said:

"Yes, we are a little anemic, and have some nervous troubles. That is not surprising, since you have experienced such a great affliction. I will write you a little prescription that will set you right again. But above all, you must eat strengthening food, take beef-tea, no water, but drink beer. I will indicate an excellent brand. Do not tire yourself by late hours, but walk as much as you can. Sleep a good deal and grow a little plumper. This is all that I can advise you, my fair patient."

She had listened to him with deep interest, trying to guess at what his words implied. She caught at the last word.

"Yes, I am too thin," said she. "I was a little too stout at one time, and perhaps I weakened myself by dieting."

"Without any doubt. There is no harm in remaining thin when one has always been so; but when one grows thin on principle it is always at the expense of something else. Happily, that can be soon remedied. Goodbye, Madame."

She felt better already, more alert; and she wished to send for the prescribed beer for her breakfast, at its headquarters, in order to obtain it quite fresh.

She was just leaving the table when Bertin was announced.

"It is I, again," said he, "always I. I have come to ask you something. Have you anything particular to do this afternoon?"

"No, nothing. Why?"

"And Annette?"

"Nothing, also."

"Then, can you come to the studio about four o'clock?"

"Yes, but for what purpose?"

"I am sketching the face of my Reverie, of which I spoke to you when I asked you whether Annette might pose for me a few moments. It would render me a great service if I could have her for only an hour to-day. Will you?"

The Countess hesitated, annoyed, without knowing the reason why. But she replied:

"Very well, my friend; we shall be with you at four o'clock."

"Thank you! You are goodness itself!"

He went away to prepare his canvas and study his subject, so that he need not tire his model too much.

Then the Countess went out alone, on foot, to finish her shopping. She went down to the great central streets, then walked slowly up the Boulevard Malesherbes, for she felt as if her limbs were breaking. As she passed Saint Augustin's, she was seized with a desire to enter the church and rest. She pushed open the door, sighed with satisfaction in breathing the cool air of the vast nave, took a chair and sat down.

She was religious as very many Parisians are religious. She believed in God without a doubt, not being able to admit the existence of the universe without the existence of a creator. But associating, as does everyone, the attributes of divinity with the nature of the created matter that she beheld with her own eyes, she almost personified the Eternal God with what she knew of His work, without having a very clear idea as to what this mysterious Maker might really be.

She believed in Him firmly, adored Him theoretically, feared Him very vaguely, for she did not profess to understand His intentions or His will, having a very limited confidence in the priests, whom she regarded merely as the sons of peasants revolting from military service. Her father, a middle-class Parisian, never had imposed upon her any particular principles of devotion, and she had lived on thinking little about religious matters until her marriage. Then, her new station in life indicating more strictly her apparent duties toward the Church, she had conformed punctiliously to this light servitude, as do so many of her station.

She was lady patroness to numerous and very well known infant asylums, never failed to attend mass at one o'clock on Sundays, gave alms for herself directly, and for the world by means of an abbe, the vicar of her parish.

She had often prayed, from a sense of duty, as a soldier mounts guard at a general's door. Sometimes she had prayed because her heart was sad, especially when she suspected Olivier of infidelity to her. At such times, without confiding to Heaven the cause for her appeal, treating God with the same naïve hypocrisy that is shown to a husband, she asked Him to succor her. When her father died, long before, and again quite recently, at her mother's death, she had had violent crises of religious fervor, and had passionately implored Him who watches over us and consoles us.

And, now behold! to-day, in that church where she had entered by chance, she suddenly felt a profound need to pray, not for some one nor for some thing, but for herself, for herself alone, as she had already prayed the other day at her mother's grave. She must have help from some source, and she called on God now as she had summoned the physician that very morning.

She remained a long time on her knees, in the deep silence of the church, broken only by the sound of footsteps. Then suddenly, as if a clock had struck in her heart, she awoke from her memories, drew out her watch and started to see that it was already four o'clock. She hastened away to take her daughter to the studio, where Olivier must already be expecting them.

They found the artist in his studio, studying upon the canvas the pose of his Reverie. He wished to reproduce exactly what he had seen in the Parc Monceau while walking with Annette: a young girl, dreaming, with an open book upon her knees. He had hesitated as to whether he should make her plain or pretty. If she were ugly she would have more character, would arouse more thought and emotion, would contain more philosophy. If pretty, she would be more seductive, would diffuse more charm, and would please better.

The desire to make a study after his little friend decided him. The Reveuse should be pretty, and therefore might realize her poetic vision one day or other; whereas if ugly she would remain condemned to a dream without hope and without end.

As soon as the two ladies entered Olivier said, rubbing his hands:

"Well, Mademoiselle Nane, we are going to work together, it seems!"

The Countess seemed anxious. She sat in an armchair, and watched Olivier as he placed an iron garden-chair in the right light. He opened his bookcase to get a book, then asked, hesitating:

"What does your daughter read?"

"Dear me! anything you like! Give her a volume of Victor Hugo."

"'La Legende des Siecles?'"

"That will do."

"Little one, sit down here," he continued, "and take this volume of verse. Look for page — page 336, where you will find a poem entitled 'Les Pauvres Gens.' Absorb it, as one drinks the best wines, slowly, word by word, and let it intoxicate you and move you. Then close the book, raise your eyes, think and dream. Now I will go and prepare my brushes."

He went into a corner to put the colors on his palette, but while emptying on the thin board the leaden tubes whence issued slender, twisting snakes of color, he turned from time to time to look at the young girl absorbed in her reading.

His heart was oppressed, his fingers trembled; he no longer knew what he was doing, and he mingled the tones as he mixed the little piles of paste, so strongly did he feel once more before this apparition, before that resurrection, in that same place, after twelve years, an irresistible flood of emotion overwhelming his heart.

Now Annette had finished her reading and was looking straight before her. Approaching her, Olivier saw in her eyes two bright drops which, breaking forth, ran down her cheeks. He was startled by one of those shocks that make a man forget himself, and turning toward the Countess he murmured:

"God! how beautiful she is!"

But he remained stupefied before the livid and convulsed face of Madame de Guilleroy. Her large eyes, full of a sort of terror, gazed at her daughter and the painter. He approached her, suddenly touched with anxiety.

"What is the matter?" he asked.

"I wish to speak to you."

Rising, she said quickly to Annette; "Wait a moment, my child; I have a word to say to Monsieur Bertin."

She passed swiftly into the little drawingroom near by, where he often made his visitors wait. He followed her, his head confused, understanding nothing. As soon as they were alone, she seized his hands and stammered:

"Olivier! Olivier, I beg you not to make her pose for you!"

"But why?" he murmured, disturbed.

"Why? Why?" she said precipitately. "He asks it! You do not feel it, then yourself? Why? Oh, I should have guessed it sooner myself, but I only discovered it this moment. I cannot tell you anything now. Go and find my daughter. Tell her that I am ill; fetch a cab, and come to see me in an hour. I will receive you alone."

"But, really, what is the matter with you?"

She seemed on the verge of hysterics.

"Leave me! I cannot speak here. Get my daughter and call a cab."

He had to obey and reentered the studio. Annette, unsuspicious, had resumed her reading, her heart overflowing with sadness by the poetic and lamentable story.

"Your mother is indisposed," said Olivier. "She became very ill when she went into the other room. I will take some ether to her."

He went out, ran to get a flask from his room and returned.

He found them weeping in each other's arms. Annette, moved by "Les Pauvres Gens," allowed her feelings full sway, and the Countess was somewhat solaced by blending her grief with that sweet sorrow, in mingling her tears with those of her daughter.

He waited for some time, not daring to speak; he looked at them, his own heart oppressed with an incomprehensible melancholy.

"Well," said he at last. "Are you better?"

"Yes, a little," the Countess replied. "It was nothing. Have you ordered a carriage?"

"Yes, it will come directly."

"Thank you, my friend — it is nothing. I have had too much grief for a long time."

"The carriage is here," a servant announced.

And Bertin, full of secret anguish, escorted his friend, pale and almost swooning, to the door, feeling her heart throb against his arm.

When he was alone he asked himself what was the matter with her, and why had she made this scene. And he began to seek a reason, wandering around the truth without deciding to discover it. Finally, he began to suspect. "Well," he said to himself, "is it possible she believes that I am making love to her daughter? No, that would be too much!" And, combating with ingenious and loyal arguments that supposititious conviction, he felt indignant that she had lent for an instant to this healthy and almost paternal affection any suspicion of gallantry. He became more and more irritated against the Countess, utterly unwilling to concede that she had dared suspect him of such villainy, of an infamy so unqualifiable; and he resolved, when the time should come for him to answer her, that he would not soften the expression of his resentment.

He soon left his studio to go to her house, impatient for an explanation. All along the way he prepared, with a growing irritation, the arguments and phrases that must justify him and avenge him for such a suspicion.

He found her on her lounge, her face changed by suffering.

"Well," said he, drily, "explain to me, my dear friend, the strange scene that has just occurred."

"What, you have not yet understood it?" she said, in a broken voice.

"No, I confess I have not."

"Come, Olivier, search your own heart well."

"My heart?"

"Yes, at the bottom of your heart."

"I don't understand. Explain yourself better."

"Look well into the depths of your heart, and see whether you find nothing there that is dangerous for you and for me."

"I repeat that I do not comprehend you. I guess that there is something in your imagination, but in my own conscience I see nothing."

"I am not speaking of your conscience, but of your heart."

"I cannot guess enigmas. I entreat you to be more clear."

Then, slowing raising her hands, she took the hands of the painter and held them; then, as if each word broke her heart, she said:

"Take care, my friend, or you will fall in love with my daughter!"

He withdrew his hands abruptly, and with the vivacity of innocence which combats a shameful accusation, with animated gesture and increasing excitement, he defended himself, accusing her in her turn of having suspected him unjustly.

She let him talk for some time, obstinately incredulous, sure of what she had said. Then she resumed:

"But I do not suspect you, my friend. You were ignorant of what was passing within you, as I was ignorant of it until this morning. You treat me as if I had accused you of wishing to seduce Annette. Oh, no, no! I know how loyal you are, worthy of all esteem and of every confidence. I only beg you, I entreat you to look into the depths of your heart and see whether the affection which, in spite of yourself, you are beginning to have for my daughter, has not a characteristic a little different from simple friendship."

Now he was offended, and, growing still more excited, he began once more to plead his loyalty, just as he argued all alone in the street.

She waited until he had finished his defense; then, without anger, but without being shaken in her conviction, though frightfully pale, she murmured:

"Olivier, I know very well all that you have just said to me, and I think as you do. But I am sure that I do not deceive myself. Listen, reflect, understand. My daughter resembles me too much, she is too much what I was once when you began to love me, that you should not begin to love her, too."

"Then," he exclaimed, "you dare to throw in my face such a thing as that on this simple supposition and ridiculous reasoning: 'He loves me; my daughter resembles me; therefore he will love her'!"

But seeing the Countess's face changing more and more, he continued in a softer tone:

"Now, my dear Any, it is precisely because I do find you once more in her that this young girl pleases me so much. It is you, you alone, that I love when I look at her."

"Yes, and it is just that from which I begin to suffer, and which makes me so anxious. You are not yet aware of what you feel, but by and by you will no longer be able to deceive yourself regarding it."

"Any, I assure you that you are mad."

"Do you wish proofs?"

"Yes."

"You had not come to Roncieres for three years, in spite of my desire to have you come. But you rushed down there when it was proposed that you should come to fetch us."

"Oh, indeed! You reproach me for not leaving you alone down there, knowing that you were ill, after your mother's death!"

"So be it! I do not insist. But look: the desire to see Annette again is so imperious with you that you could not pass this day without asking me to take her to your studio, under the pretext of posing her."

"And do you not suppose it was you I wished to see?"

"At this moment you are arguing against yourself, trying to convince yourself — but you do not deceive me. Listen again: Why did you leave abruptly, the night before last, when the Marquis de Farandal entered? Do you know why?"

He hesitated, very much surprised, disturbed, disarmed by this observation. Then he said slowly:

"But — I hardly know — I was tired, and then, to be candid, that imbecile makes me nervous."

"Since when?"

"Always."

"Pardon me, I have heard you sing his praises. You liked him once. Be quite sincere, Olivier."

He reflected a few moments; then, choosing his words, he said:

"Yes, it is possible that the great love I have for you makes me love so much everything that belongs to you as to modify my opinion of that bore, whom I might meet occasionally with indifference, but whom I should not like to see in your house almost every day."

"My daughter's house will not be mine. But this is sufficient. I know the uprightness of your heart. I know that you will reflect deeply on what I have just said to you. When you have reflected you will understand that I have pointed out a great danger to you, while yet there is time to escape it. And you will beware. Now let us talk of something else, will you?"

He did not insist, but he was much disturbed; he no longer knew what to think, though indeed he had need for reflection. He went away after a quarter of an hour of unimportant conversation.

IV

With slow steps, Olivier returned to his own house, troubled as if he had just learned some shameful family secret. He tried to sound his heart, to see clearly within himself, to read those intimate pages of the inner book which seemed glued together, and which sometimes only a strange hand can turn over by separating them. Certainly he did not believe himself in love with Annette. The Countess, whose watchful jealousy never slept, had foreseen this danger from afar, and had signaled it before it even existed. But might that peril exist tomorrow, the day after, in a month? It was the frank question that he tried to answer sincerely. It was true that the child stirred his instincts of tenderness, but these instincts in men are so numerous that the dangerous ones should not be confounded with the inoffensive. Thus he adored animals, especially cats, and could not see their silky fur without being seized with an irresistible sensuous desire to caress their soft, undulating backs and kiss their electric fur.

The attraction that impelled him toward this girl a little resembled those obscure yet innocent desires that go to make up part of all the ceaseless and unappeasable vibrations of human nerves. His eye of the artist, as well as that of the man, was captivated by her freshness, by that springing of beautiful clear life, by that essence of youth that glowed in her; and his heart, full of memories of his long intimacy with the Countess, finding in the extraordinary resemblance of Annette to her mother a reawakening of old feelings, of emotions sleeping since the beginning of his love, had been startled perhaps by the sensation of an awakening. An awakening? Yes. Was it that? This idea illumined his mind. He felt that he had awakened after years of sleep. If he had loved the young girl without being aware of it, he should have experienced near her that rejuvenation of his whole being which creates a different man as soon as the flame of a new desire is kindled within him. No, the child had only breathed upon the former fire. It had always been the mother that he loved, but now a little more than recently, no doubt, because of her daughter, this reincarnation of herself. And he formulated this decision with the reassuring sophism: "One loves but once! The heart may often be affected at meeting some other being, for everyone exercises on others either attractions or repulsions. All these influences create friendship, caprices, desire for possession, quick and fleeting ardors, but not real love. That this love may exist it is necessary that two beings should be so truly born for each other, should be linked together in so many different ways, by so many similar tastes, by so many affinities of body, of mind, and of character, and so many ties of all kinds that the whole shall form a union of bonds. That which we love, in short, is not so much Madame X. or Monsieur Z.; it is a women or a man, a creature without a name, something sprung from Nature, that great female, with organs, a form, a heart, a mind, a combination of attributes which like a magnet attract our organs, our eyes, our lips, our hearts, our thoughts, all our appetites, sensual as well as intellectual. We love a type, that is, the reunion in one single person of all the human qualities that may separately attract us in others."

For him, the Comtesse de Guilleroy had been this type, and their long-standing liaison, of which he had not wearied, proved it to him beyond doubt. Now, Annette so much resembled physically what her mother had been as to deceive the eye; so there was nothing astonishing in the fact that this man's heart had been surprised, if even it had not been wholly captured. He had adored one woman! Another woman was born of her, almost her counterpart. He could not prevent himself from bestowing on the latter a little tender remnant of the passionate attachment he had had for the former. There was no harm nor danger in that. Only his eyes and his memory allowed themselves to be deluded by this appearance of resurrection; but his instinct never had been affected, for never had he felt the least stirring of desire for the young girl.

However, the Countess had reproached him with being jealous of the Marquis! Was it true? Again he examined his conscience severely, and decided that as a matter of fact he was indeed a little jealous. What was there astonishing in that, after all? Are we not always being jealous of men who pay court to no matter what woman? Does not one experience in the street, at a restaurant, or a theater, a little feeling of enmity toward the gentleman who is passing or who enters with a lovely girl on his arm? Every possessor of a woman is a rival, a triumphant male, a conqueror envied by all the other males. And then, without considering these physiological reasons, if it was natural that he should have for Annette a sympathy a little excessive because of his love for her mother, was it not natural also that he should feel in his heart a little masculine hatred of the future husband? He could conquer this unworthy feeling without much trouble.

But in the depths of his heart he still felt a sort of bitter discontent with himself and with the Countess. Would not their daily intercourse be made disagreeable by the suspicion that he would be aware of in her? Should he not be compelled to watch with tiresome and scrupulous attention all that he said and did, his very looks, his slightest approach toward the young girl? for all that he might do or say would appear suspicious to the mother. He reached his home in a gloomy mood and began to smoke cigarettes, with the vehemence of an irritated man who uses ten matches to light his tobacco. He tried in vain to work. His hand, his eye, and his brain seemed to have lost the knack of painting, as if they had forgotten it, or never had known and practised the art. He had taken up to finish a little sketch on canvas — a street corner, at which a blind man stood singing — and he looked at it with unconquerable indifference, with such a lack of power to continue it that he sat down before it, palette in hand, and forgot it, though continuing to gaze at it with attention and abstracted fixity.

Then, suddenly, impatience at the slowness of time, at the interminable minutes, began to gnaw him with its intolerable fever. What should he do until he could go to the club for dinner, since he could not work at home? The thought of the streets tired him only to think of, filled him with disgust for the sidewalks, the pedestrians, the carriages and shops; and the idea of paying visits that day, to no matter whom, aroused in him an instantaneous hatred for everyone he knew.

Then, what should he do? Should he pace to and fro in his studio, looking at the clock at every turn, watching the displacement of the long hand every few seconds? Ah, he well knew those walks from the door to the cabinet, covered with ornaments. In his hours of excitement, impulse, ambition, of fruitful and facile execution, these pacings had been delicious recreation — these goings and comings across the large room, brightened, animated, and warmed by work; but now, in his hours of powerlessness and nausea, the miserable hours, when nothing seemed worth the trouble of an effort or a movement, it was like the terrible tramping of a prisoner in his cell. If only he could have slept, even for an hour, on his divan! But no, he should not sleep; he should only agitate himself until he trembled with exasperation. Whence came this sudden attack of bad temper? He thought: "I am becoming excessively nervous to have worked myself into such a state for so insignificant a cause."

Then he thought he would take a book. The volume of La Legende des Siecles had remained on the iron chair where Annette had laid it. He opened it and read two pages of verse without understanding them. He understood them no more than if they had been written in a foreign tongue. He was determined, however, and began again, only to find that what he read had not really penetrated to his mind. "Well," said he to himself, "it appears that I am becoming imbecile!" But a sudden inspiration reassured him as to how he should fill the two hours that must elapse before dinnertime. He had a hot bath prepared, and there he remained stretched out, relaxed and soothed by the warm water, until his valet, bringing his clothes, roused him from a doze. Then he went to the club, where he found the usual companions. He was received with open arms and exclamations, for they had not seen him for several days.

"I have just returned from the country," he explained.

All those men, except Musadieu, the landscape painter, professed a profound contempt for the fields. Rocdiane and Landa, to be sure, went hunting there, but among plains or woods they only enjoyed the pleasure of seeing pheasants, quail, or partridges falling like handfuls of feathers under their bullets, or little rabbits riddled with shot, turning somersaults like clowns, going heels over head four or five times, showing their white bellies and tails at every bound. Except for these sports of autumn and winter, they thought the country a bore. As Rocdiane would say: "I prefer little women to little peas!"

The dinner was lively and jovial as usual, animated by discussions wherein nothing unforeseen occurs. Bertin, to arouse himself, talked a great deal. They found him amusing, but as soon as he had had coffee, and a sixty-point game of billiards with the banker Liverdy, he went out, rambling from the Madeleine to the Rue Taitbout; after passing three times before the Vaudeville, he asked himself whether he should enter; almost called a cab to take him to the Hippodrome; changed his mind and turned toward the Nouveau Cirque, then made an abrupt half turn, without motive, design, or pretext, went up the Boulevard Malesherbes, and walked more slowly as he approached the dwelling of the Comtesse de Guilleroy. "Perhaps she will think it strange to see me again this evening," he thought. But he reassured himself in reflecting that there was nothing astonishing in his coming a second time to inquire how she felt.

She was alone with Annette, in the little back drawingroom, and was still working on her coverlets for the poor.

She said simply, on seeing him enter: "Ah, is it you, my friend?"

"Yes, I felt anxious; I wished to see you. How are you?"

"Thank you, very well."

She paused a moment, then added, significantly:

"And you?"

He began to laugh unconcernedly, as he replied: "Oh. I am very well, very well. Your fears were entirely without foundation."

She raised her eyes, pausing in her work, and fixed her gaze upon him, a gaze full of doubt and entreaty.

"It is true," said he.

"So much the better," she replied, with a smile that was slightly forced.

He sat down, and for the first time in that house he was seized with irresistible uneasiness, a sort of paralysis of ideas, still greater than that which had seized him that day as he sat before his canvas.

"You may go on, my child; it will not annoy him," said the Countess to her daughter.

"What was she doing?"

"She was studying a fantaisie."

Annette rose to go to the piano. He followed her with his eyes, unconsciously, as he always did, finding her pretty. Then he felt the mother's eye upon him, and turned his head abruptly, as if he were seeking something in the shadowy corner of the drawingroom.

The Countess took from her work-table a little gold case that he had given her, opened it, and offered him some cigarettes.

"Pray smoke, my friend," said she; "you know I like it when we are alone here."

He obeyed, and the music began. It was the music of the distant past, graceful and light, one of those compositions that seem to have inspired the artist on a soft moonlight evening in springtime.

"Who is the composer of that?" asked Bertin.

"Schumann," the Countess replied. "It is little known and charming."

A desire to look at Annette grew stronger within him, but he did not dare. He would have to make only a slight movement, merely a turn of the neck, for he could see out of the corner of his eye the two candles lighting the score; but he guessed so well, read so clearly, the watchful gaze of the Countess that he remained motionless, his eyes looking straight before him, interested apparently in the gray thread of smoke from his cigarette.

"Was that all you had to say to me?" Madame de Guilleroy murmured to him.

He smiled.

"Don't be vexed with me. You know that music hypnotizes me; it drinks my thoughts. I will talk soon."

"I must tell you," said the Countess, "that I had studied something for you before mamma's death. I never had you hear it, but I will play it for you immediately, as soon as the little one has finished; you shall see how odd it is."

She had real talent, and a subtle comprehension of the emotion that flows through sounds. It was indeed one of her surest powers over the painter's sensibility.

As soon as Annette had finished the pastoral symphony by Mehul, the Countess rose, took her place, and awakened a strange melody with her fingers, a melody of which all the phrases seemed complaints, divers complaints, changing, numerous, interrupted by a single note, beginning again, falling into the midst of the strains, cutting them short, scanning them, crashing into them, like a monotonous, incessant, persecuting cry, an unappeasable call of obsession.

But Olivier was looking at Annette, who had sat down facing him, and he heard nothing, comprehended nothing.

He looked at her, without thinking, indulging himself with the sight of her, as a good and habitual possession of which he had been deprived, drinking her youthful beauty wholesomely, as we drink water when thirsty.

"Well," said the Countess, "was not that beautiful?"

"Admirable! Superb!" he said, aroused. "By whom?"

"You do not know it?"

"No."

"What, really, you do not know it?"

"No, indeed."

"By Schubert."

"That does not astonish me at all," he said, with an air of profound conviction. "It is superb! You would be delightful if you would play it over again."

She began once more, and he, turning his head, began again to contemplate Annette, but listened also to the music, that he might taste two pleasures at the same time.

When Madame de Guilleroy had returned to her chair, in simple obedience to the natural duplicity of man he did not allow his gaze to rest longer on the fair profile of the young girl, who knitted opposite her mother, on the other side of the lamp.

But, though he did not see her, he tasted the sweetness of her presence, as one feels the proximity of a fire on the hearth; and the desire to cast upon her swift glances only to transfer them immediately to the Countess, tormented him — the desire of the schoolboy who climbs up to the window looking into the street as soon as the master's back is turned.

He went away early, for his power of speech was as paralyzed as his mind, and his persistent silence might be interpreted.

As soon as he found himself in the street a desire to wander took possession of him, for whenever he heard music it remained in his brain a long time, threw him into reveries that seemed the music itself in a dream, but in a clearer sequel. The sound of the notes returned, intermittent and fugitive, bringing separate measures, weakened, and far off as an echo; then, sinking into silence, appeared to leave it to the mind to give a meaning to the themes, and to seek a sort of tender and harmonious ideal. He turned to the left on reaching the outer Boulevard, perceiving the fairylike illumination of the Parc Monceau, and entered its central avenue, curving under the electric moons. A policeman was slowly strolling along; now and then a belated cab passed; a man, sitting on a bench in a bluish bath of electric light, was reading a newspaper, at the foot of a bronze mast that bore the dazzling globe. Other lights on the broad lawns, scattered among the trees, shed their cold and powerful rays into the foliage and on the grass, animating this great city garden with a pale life.

Bertin, with hands behind his back, paced the sidewalk, thinking of his walk with Annette in this same park when he had recognized in her the voice of her mother.

He let himself fall upon a bench, and, breathing in the cool freshness of the dewy lawns, he felt himself assailed by all the passionate expectancy that transforms the soul of youth into the incoherent canvas of an unfinished romance of love. Long ago he had known such evenings, those evenings of errant fancy, when he had allowed his caprice to roam through imaginary adventures, and he was astonished to feel a return of sensations that did not now belong to his age.

But, like the persistent note in the Schubert melody, the thought of Annette, the vision of her face bent beside the lamp, and the strange suspicion of the Countess, recurred to him at every instant. He continued, in spite of himself, to occupy his heart with this question, to sound the impenetrable depths where human feelings germinate before being born. This obstinate research agitated him; this constant preoccupation regarding the young girl seemed to open to his soul the way to tender reveries. He could not drive her from his mind; he bore within himself a sort of evocation of her image, as once he had borne the image of the Countess after she had left him; he often had the strange sensation of her presence in the studio.

Suddenly, impatient at being dominated by a memory, he arose, muttering: "Any was stupid to say that to me. Now she will make me think of the little one!"

He went home, disturbed about himself. After he had gone to bed he felt that sleep would not come to him, for a fever coursed in his veins, and a desire for reverie fermented in his heart. Dreading a wakeful night, one of those enervating attacks of insomnia brought about by agitation of the spirit, he thought he would try to read. How many times had a short reading served him as a narcotic! So he got up and went into his library to choose a good and soporific work; but his mind, aroused in spite of himself, eager for any emotion it could find, sought among the shelves for the name of some author that would respond to his state of exaltation and expectancy. Balzac, whom he loved, said nothing to him; he disdained Hugo, scorned Lamartine, who usually touched his emotions, and fell eagerly upon Musset, the poet of youth. He took the volume and carried it to bed, to read whatever he might chance to find.

When he had settled himself in bed, he began to drink, as with the thirst of a drunkard, those flowing verses of an inspired being who sang, like a bird, of the dawn of existence, and having breath only for the morning, was silent in the arid light of day; those verses of a poet who above all mankind was intoxicated with life, expressing his intoxication in fanfares of frank and triumphant love, the echo of all young hearts bewildered with desires.

Never had Bertin so perfectly comprehended the physical charm of those poems, which move the senses but hardly touch the intelligence. With his eyes on those vibrating stanzas, he felt that his soul was but twenty years old, radiant with hopes, and he read the volume through in a state of youthful intoxication. Three o'clock struck, and he was astonished to find that he had not yet grown sleepy. He rose to shut his window and to carry his book to a table in the middle of the room; but at the contact of the cold air a pain, of which several seasons at Aix had not cured him, ran through his loins, like a warning or a recall; and he threw aside the poet with an impatient movement, muttering: "Old fool!" Then he returned to bed and blew out his light.

He did not go to see the Countess the next day, and he even made the energetic resolution not to return there for two days. But whatever he did, whether he tried to paint or to walk, whether he bore his melancholy mood with him from house to house, his mind was everywhere harassed by the preoccupation of those two women, who would not be banished.

Having forbidden himself to go to see them, he solaced himself by thinking of them, and he allowed both mind and heart to give themselves up to memories of both. It happened often that in that species of hallucination in which he lulled his isolation the two faces approached each other, different, such as he knew them; then, passing one before the other, mingled, blended together, forming only one face, a little confused, a face that was no longer the mother's, not altogether that of the daughter, but the face of a woman loved madly, long ago, in the present, and forever.

Then he felt remorse at having abandoned himself to the influence of these emotions, which he knew were powerful and dangerous. To escape them, to drive them away, to deliver his soul from this sweet and captivating dream, he directed his mind toward all imaginable ideas, all possible subjects of reflection and meditation. Vain efforts! All the paths of distraction that he took led him back to the same point, where he met a fair young face that seemed to be lying in wait for him. It was a vague and inevitable obsession that floated round him, recalling him, stopping him, no matter what detour he might make in order to fly from it.

The confusion of these two beings, which had so troubled him on the evening of their walk at Roncieres, rose again in his memory as soon as he evoked them, after ceasing to reflect and reason, and he attempted to comprehend what strange emotion was this that stirred his being. He said to himself: "Now, have I for Annette a more tender feeling than I should have?" Then, probing his heart, he felt it burning with affection for a woman who was certainly young, who had Annette's features, but who was not she. And he reassured himself in a cowardly way by thinking: "No, I do not love the little one; I am the victim of a resemblance."

However, those two days at Roncieres remained in his soul like a source of heat, of happiness, of intoxication; and the least details of those days returned to him, one by one, with precision, sweeter even than at the time they occurred. Suddenly, while reviewing the course of these memories, he saw once more the road they had followed on leaving the cemetery, the young girl plucking flowers, and he recollected that he had promised her a cornflower in sapphires as soon as they returned to Paris.

All his resolutions took flight, and without struggling longer he took his hat and went out, rejoiced at the thought of the pleasure he was about to give her.

The footman answered him, when he presented himself:

"Madame is out, but Mademoiselle is at home."

Again he felt a thrill of joy.

"Tell her that I should like to speak to her."

Annette appeared very soon.

"Good-day, dear master," said she gravely.

He began to laugh, shook hands with her, and sitting near her, said:

"Guess why I have come."

She thought a few seconds.

"I don't know."

"To take you and your mother to the jeweler's to choose the sapphire cornflower I promised you at Roncieres."

The young girl's face was illumined with delight.

"Oh, and mamma has gone out," said she. "But she will return soon. You will wait for her, won't you?"

"Yes, if she is not too long."

"Oh, how insolent! Too long, with me! You treat me like a child."

"No, not so much as you think," he replied.

He felt in his heart a longing to please her, to be gallant and witty, as in the most successful days of his youth, one of those instinctive desires that excite all the faculties of charming, that make the peacock spread its tail and the poet write verses. Quick and vivacious phrases rose to his lips, and he talked as he knew how to talk when he was at his best. The young girl, animated by his vivacity, answered him with all the mischief and playful shrewdness that were in her.

Suddenly, while he was discussing an opinion, he exclaimed: "But you have already said that to me often, and I answered you — "

She interrupted him with a burst of laughter.

"Ah, you don't say 'tu' to me any more! You take me for mamma!"

He blushed and was silent, then he stammered:

"Your mother has already sustained that opinion with me a hundred times."

His eloquence was extinguished; he knew no more what to say, and he now felt afraid, incomprehensibly afraid, of this little girl.

"Here is mamma," said she.

She had heard the door open in the outer drawingroom, and Olivier, disturbed as if some one had caught him in a fault, explained how he had suddenly bethought him of his promise, and had come for them to take them to the jeweler's.

"I have a coupe," said he. "I will take the bracket seat."

They set out, and a little later they entered Montara's.

Having passed all his life in the intimacy, observation, study, and affection of women, having always occupied his mind with them, having been obliged to sound and discover their tastes, to know the details of dress and fashion as they knew them, being familiar with the minute details of their private life, he had arrived at a point that enabled him often to share certain of their sensations, and he always experienced, when entering one of the great shops where the charming and delicate accessories of their beauty are to be found, an emotion of pleasure that almost equaled that which stirred their hearts. He interested himself as they did in those coquettish trifles with which they set forth their beauty; the stuffs pleased his eyes; the laces attracted his hands; the most insignificant furbelows held his attention. In jewelers' shops he felt for the showcases a sort of religious respect, as if before a sanctuary of opulent seduction; and the counter, covered with dark cloth, upon which the supple fingers of the goldsmith make the jewels roll, displaying their precious reflections, filled him with a certain esteem.

When he had seated the Countess and her daughter before this severe piece of furniture, on which each, with a natural movement, placed one hand, he indicated what he wanted, and they showed him models of little flowers.

Then they spread sapphires before him, from which it was necessary to choose four. This took a long time. The two women turned them over on the cloth with the tips of their fingers, then lifted them carefully, looked through them at the light, studying them with knowing and passionate attention. When they had laid aside those they had chosen, three emeralds had to be selected to make the leaves, then a tiny diamond that would tremble in the center like a drop of dew.

Then Olivier, intoxicated with the joy of giving, said to the Countess:

"Will you do me the favor to choose two rings?"

"I?"

"Yes. One for you, one for Annette. Let me make you these little presents in memory of the two days I passed at Roncieres."

She refused. He insisted. A long discussion followed, a struggle of words and arguments, which ended, not without difficulty, in his triumph.

Rings were brought, some, the rarest, alone in special cases; others arranged in similar groups in large square boxes, wherein all the fancifulness of their settings were displayed in alignment on the velvet. The painter was seated between the two women, and began, with the same ardent curiosity, to take up the gold rings, one by one, from the narrow slits that held them. He deposited them before him on the cloth-covered counter where they were massed in two groups, those that had been rejected at first sight and those from which a choice would be made.

Time was passing, insensibly and sweetly, in this pretty work of selection, more captivating than all the pleasures of the world, distracting and varied as a play, stirring also an exquisite and almost sensuous pleasure in a woman's heart.

Then they compared, grew animated, and, after some hesitation, the choice of the three judges settled upon a little golden serpent holding a beautiful ruby between his thin jaws and his twisted tail.

Olivier, radiant, now arose.

"I will leave you my carriage," said he; "I have something to look after, and I must go."

But Annette begged her mother to walk home, since the weather was so fine. The Countess consented, and, having thanked Bertin, went out into the street with her daughter.

They walked for some time in silence, enjoying the sweet realization of presents received; then they began to talk of all the jewels they had seen and handled. Within their minds still lingered a sort of glittering and jingling, an echo of gaiety. They walked quickly through the crowd which fills the street about five o'clock on a summer evening. Men turned to look at Annette, and murmured in distinct words of admiration as they passed. It was the first time since her mourning, since black attire had added brilliancy to her daughter's beauty, that the Countess had gone out with her in the streets of Paris; and the sensation of that street success, that awakened attention, those whispered compliments, that little wake of flattering emotion which the passing of a pretty woman leaves in a crowd of men, contracted her heart little by little with the same painful feeling she had had the other evening in her drawingroom, when her guests had compared the little one with her own portrait. In spite of herself, she watched for those glances that Annette attracted; she felt them coming from a distance, pass over her own face without stopping and suddenly settle upon the fair face beside her own. She guessed, she saw in the eyes the rapid and silent homage to this blooming youth, to the powerful charm of that radiant freshness, and she thought: "I was as pretty as she, if not prettier." Suddenly the thought of Olivier flashed across her mind, and she was seized, as at Roncieres, with a longing to flee.

She did not wish to feel herself any longer in this bright light, amid this stream of people, seen by all those men who yet did not look at her. Those days seemed far away, though in reality quite recent, when she had sought and provoked comparison with her daughter. Who, to-day, among the passers, thought of comparing them? Only one person had thought of it, perhaps, a little while ago, in the jeweler's shop. He? Oh, what suffering! Could it be that he was thinking continually of that comparison? Certainly he could not see them together without thinking of it, and without remembering the time when she herself had entered his house, so fresh, so pretty, so sure of being loved!

"I feel ill," said she. "We will take a cab, my child."

Annette was uneasy.

"What is the matter, mamma?" she asked.

"It is nothing; you know that since your grandmother's death I often have these moments of weakness."

V

Fixed ideas have the tenacity of incurable maladies. Once entered in the soul they devour it, leaving it no longer free to think of anything, or to have a taste for the least thing. Whatever she did, or wherever she was, alone or surrounded by friends, she could no longer rid herself of the thought that had seized her in coming home side by side with her daughter. Could it be that Olivier, seeing them together almost every day, thought continually of the comparison between them?

Surely he must do it in spite of himself, incessantly, himself haunted by that unforgettable resemblance, accentuated still further by the imitation of tone and gesture they had tried to produce. Every time he entered she thought of that comparison; she read it in his eyes, guessed it and pondered over it in her heart and in her mind. Then she was tortured by a desire to hide herself, to disappear, never to show herself again beside her daughter.

She suffered, too, in all ways, not feeling at home any more in her own house. That pained feeling of dispossession which she had had one evening, when all eyes were fixed on Annette under her portrait, continued, stronger and more exasperating than before. She reproached herself unceasingly for feeling that yearning need for deliverance, that unspeakable desire to send her daughter away from her, like a troublesome and tenacious guest; and she labored against it with unconscious skill, convinced of the necessity of struggling to retain, in spite of everything, the man she loved.

Unable to hasten Annette's marriage too urgently, because of their recent mourning, she feared, with a confused yet dominating fear, anything that might defeat that plan; and she sought, almost in spite of herself, to awaken in her daughter's heart some feeling of tenderness for the Marquis.

All the resourceful diplomacy she had employed so long to hold Olivier now took with her a new form, shrewder, more secret, exerting itself to kindle affection between the young people, and to keep the two men from meeting.

As the painter, who kept regular hours of work, never breakfasted away from home, and usually gave only his evenings to his friends, she often invited the Marquis to breakfast. He would arrive, spreading around him the animation of his ride, a sort of breath of morning air. And he talked gaily of all those worldly things that seem to float every day upon the autumnal awakening of brilliant and horse-loving Paris in the avenues of the Bois. Annette was amused in listening to him, acquired some taste for those topics of the days that he recounted to her, fresh and piquant as they were. An intimacy of youth sprang up between them, a pleasant companionship which a common and passionate love for horses naturally fostered. When he had gone the Countess and the Count would artfully praise him, saying everything necessary to let the young girl know that it depended only upon herself to marry him if he pleased her.

She had understood very quickly, however, and reasoning frankly with herself, judged it a very simple thing to take for a husband this handsome fellow, who would give her, besides other satisfactions, that which she preferred above all others, the pleasure of galloping beside him every morning on a thoroughbred.

They found themselves betrothed one day, quite naturally, after a clasp of the hand and a smile, and the marriage was spoken of as something long decided. Then the Marquis began to bring gifts, and the Duchess treated Annette like her own daughter. The whole affair, then, had been fostered by common accord, warmed over the fire of a little intimacy, during the quiet hours of the day; and the Marquis, having many other occupations, relatives, obligations and duties, rarely came in the evening.

That was Olivier's time. He dined regularly every week with his friends, and also continued to appear without appointment to ask for a cup of tea between ten o'clock and midnight.

As soon as he entered the Countess watched him, devoured by a desire to know what was passing in his heart. He gave no glance, made no gesture that she did not immediately interpret, and she was tortured by this thought: "It is impossible that he is not in love with her, seeing us so close together."

He, too, brought gifts. Not a week passed that he did not appear bearing two little packages in his hands, offering one to the mother, the other to the daughter; and the Countess, opening the boxes, which often held valuable objects, felt again that contraction of the heart. She knew so well that desire to give which, as a woman, she never had been able to satisfy — that desire to bring something that would give pleasure, to purchase for someone, to find in the shops some trifle that would please.

The painter had already been through this phase, and she had seen him come in many times with that same smile, that same gesture, a little packet in his hand. That habit had ceased after awhile, and now it had begun again. For whom? She had no matter of doubt. It was not for her!

He appeared fatigued and thin. She concluded that he was suffering. She compared his entrances, his manner, his bearing with the attitude of the Marquis, who was also beginning to be attracted by Annette's grace. It was not at all the same thing: Monsieur de Farandal admired her, Olivier Bertin loved! She believed this at least during her hours of torture; then, in quieter moments she still hoped that she had deceived herself.

Oh, often she could hardly restrain herself from questioning him when she was alone with him, praying, entreating him to speak, to confess all, to hide nothing! She preferred to know and to weep under certainty than to suffer thus under doubt, not able to read that closed heart, wherein she felt another love was growing.

That heart, which she prized more highly than her life, over which she had watched, and which she had warmed and animated with her love for twelve years, of which she had believed herself sure, which she had hoped was definitely hers, conquered, submissive, passionately devoted for the rest of their lives, behold! now that heart was escaping her by an inconceivable, horrible, and monstrous fatality! Yes, it had suddenly closed itself, upon a secret. She could no longer penetrate it by a familiar word, or hide therein her own affection as in a faithful retreat open for herself alone. What is the use of loving, of giving oneself without reserve, if suddenly he to whom one has offered her whole being, her entire existence, all, everything she had in the world, is to escape thus because another face has pleased him, transforming him in a few days almost into a stranger?

A stranger! He, Olivier? He spoke to her, as always, with the same words, the same voice, the same tone. And yet there was something between them, something inexplicable, intangible, invincible, almost nothing — that almost nothing that causes a sail to float away when the wind turns.

He was drifting, in fact, drifting away from her a little more each day, by all the glances he cast upon Annette. He himself did not attempt to see clearly into the depths of his heart. He felt, indeed, that fermentation of love, that irresistible attraction; but he would not understand, he trusted to events, to the unforeseen chances of life.

He had no longer any other interest than that of his dinners and his evenings between those two women, separated from the gay world by their mourning. Meeting only indifferent faces at their house — those of the Corbelles, and Musadieu oftener — he fancied himself almost alone in the world with them; and as he now seldom saw the Duchess and the Marquis, for whom the morning and noontimes were reserved, he wished to forget them, suspecting that the marriage had been indefinitely postponed.

Besides, Annette never spoke of Monsieur de Farandal before him. Was this because of a sort of instinctive modesty, or was it perhaps from one of those secret intuitions of the feminine heart which enable them to foretell that of which they are ignorant?

Weeks followed weeks, without changing this manner of life, and autumn came, bringing the reopening of the Chamber, earlier than usual because of certain political dangers.

On the day of the reopening, the Comte de Guilleroy was to take to the meeting of Parliament Madame de Mortemain, the Marquis, and Annette, after a breakfast at his own house. The Countess alone, isolated in her sorrow, which was steadily increasing, had declared that she would remain at home.

They had left the table and were drinking coffee in the large drawingroom, in a merry mood. The Count, happy to resume parliamentary work, his only pleasure, talked very well concerning the existing situation and of the embarrassments of the Republic; the Marquis, unmistakably in love, answered him brightly, while gazing at Annette; and the Duchess was almost equally pleased with the emotion of her nephew and the distress of the government. The air of the drawingroom was warm with that first concentrated heat of newly-lighted furnaces, the heat of draperies, carpets, and walls, in which the perfumes of asphyxiated flowers was evaporating. There was in this closely shut room, filled with the aroma of coffee, an air of comfort, intimate, familiar, and satisfied, when the door was opened before Olivier Bertin.

He paused at the threshold, so surprised that he hesitated to enter, surprised as a deceived husband who beholds his wife's crime. A confusion of anger and mingled emotion suffocated him, revealing to him the fact that his heart was worm-eaten with love! All that they had hidden from him, and all that he had concealed from himself appeared before him as he perceived the Marquis installed in the house, as a betrothed lover!

He understood, in a transport of exasperation, all that which he would rather not have known and all that the Countess had not dared to tell him. He did not ask himself why all those preparations for marriage had been concealed from him. He guessed it, and his eyes, growing hard, met those of the Countess, who blushed. They understood each other.

When he was seated, everyone was silent for a few seconds, his unexpected entrance having paralyzed their flow of spirits; then the Duchess began to speak to him, and he replied in a brief manner, his voice suddenly changed.

He looked around at these people who were now chatting again, and said to himself: "They are making game of me. They shall pay for it." He was especially vexed with the Countess and Annette, whose innocent dissimulation he suddenly understood.

"Oh, oh! it is time to go," exclaimed the Count, looking at the clock. Turning to the painter, he added: "We are going to the opening of Parliament. My wife will remain here, however. Will you accompany us? It would give me great pleasure."

"No, thanks," replied Olivier drily. "Your Chamber does not tempt me."

Annette approached in a playful way, saying: "Oh, do come, dear master! I am sure that you would amuse us much more than the deputies."

"No, indeed. You will amuse yourself very well without me."

Seeing him discontented and chagrined, she insisted, to show that she felt kindly toward him.

"Yes, come, sir painter! I assure you that as for myself I cannot do without you."

His next words escaped him so quickly that he could nether check them as he spoke nor soften their tone:

"Bah! You do well enough without me, just as everyone else does!"

A little surprised at his tone, she exclaimed: "Come, now! Here he is beginning again to leave off his 'tu' to me!"

His lips were curled in one of those smiles that reveal the suffering of a soul, and he said with a slight bow: "It will be necessary for me to accustom myself to it one day or another."

"Why, pray?"

"Because you will marry, and your husband, whoever he may be, would have the right to find that word rather out of place coming from me."

"It will be time enough then to think about that," the Countess hastened to say. "But I trust that Annette will not marry a man so susceptible as to object to such familiarity from so old a friend."

"Come, come!" cried the Count; "let us go. We shall be late."

Those who were to accompany him, having risen, went out after him, after the usual handshakes and kisses which the Duchess, the Countess, and her daughter exchanged at every meeting as at every parting.

They remained alone, She and He, standing, behind the draperies over the closed door.

"Sit down, my friend," said she softly.

But he answered, almost violently: "No, thanks! I am going, too."

"Oh, why?" she murmured, entreatingly.

"Because this is not my hour, it appears. I ask pardon for having come without warning."

"Olivier, what is the matter with you?"

"Nothing. I only regret having disturbed an organized pleasure party."

She seized his hand.

"What do you mean?" she asked. "They were just about to set out, since they were going to be present at the opening of the session. I intended to stay at home. Contrary to what you said just now, you were really inspired in coming to-day when I am alone."

He sneered.

"Inspired? Yes, I was inspired!"

She seized his wrists, and looking deep into his eyes she murmured very low:

"Confess to me that you love her!"

He withdrew his hands, unable to control his impatience any longer.

"But you are simply insane with that idea!"

She seized him again by the arm and, tightening her hold on his sleeve, she implored:

"Olivier! Confess, confess! I would rather know. I am certain of it, but I would rather know. I would rather — Oh, you do not comprehend what my life has become!"

He shrugged his shoulders.

"What would you have me do? Is it my fault if you lose your head?"

She held him, drawing him toward the other salon at the back, where they could not be heard. She drew him by his coat, clinging to him and panting. When she had led him as far as the little circular divan, she made him let himself fall upon it; then she sat down beside him.

"Olivier, my friend, my only friend, I pray you to tell me that you love her. I know it, I feel it from all that you do. I cannot doubt it. I am dying of it, but I wish to know it from your own lips."

As he still resisted, she fell on her knees at his feet. Her voice shook.

"Oh, my friend, my only friend! Is it true that you love her?"

"No, no, no!" he exclaimed, as he tried to make her rise. "I swear to you that I do not."

She reached up her hand to his mouth and pressed it there tight, stammering: "Oh, do not lie! I suffer too much!"

Then, letting her head fall on this man's knees, she sobbed.

He could see only the back of her neck, a mass of blond hair, mingled with many white threads, and he was filled with immense pity, immense grief.

Seizing that heavy hair in both hands he raised her head violently, turning toward himself two bewildered eyes, from which tears were flowing. And then on those tearful eyes he pressed his lips many times, repeating:

"Any! Any! My dear, my dear Any!"

Then she, attempting to smile, and speaking in that hesitating voice of children when choking with grief, said:

"Oh, my friend, only tell me that you still love me a little."

He embraced her again, even more tenderly than before.

"Yes, I love you, my dear Any."

She arose, sat down beside him again, seized his hands, looked at him, and said tenderly:

"It is such a long time that we have loved each other. It should not end like this."

He pressed her close to him, asking:

"Why should it end?"

"Because I am old, and because Annette resembles too much what I was when you first knew me."

Now it was his turn to close her sad lips with his fingers, saying:

"Again! I beg that you will speak no more of that. I swear to you that you deceive yourself."

"Oh, if you will only love me a little," she repeated.

"Yes, I love you," he said again.

They remained a long time without speaking, hands clasped in hands, deeply moved and very sad. At last she broke the silence, murmuring:

"Oh, the hours that remain for me to live will not be gay!"

"I will try to make them sweet to you."

The shadow of the clouded sky that precedes the twilight by two hours was darkening the drawingroom, burying them little by little in the gray dimness of an autumn evening.

The clock struck.

"It is a long time since we came in here," said she. "You must go, for someone might come, and we are not calm."

He arose, clasped her close, kissing her half-open lips, as he used to do; then they crossed the two drawingrooms, arm in arm, like a newly-married pair.

"Good-by, my friend."

"Good-by, my friend."

And the portiere fell behind him.

He went downstairs, turned toward the Madeleine, and began to walk without knowing what he was doing, dazed as if from a blow, his legs weak, his heart hot and palpitating as if something burning shook within his breast. For two or three hours, perhaps four, he walked straight before him, in a sort of moral stupor and physical prostration which left him only just strength enough to put one foot before the other. Then he went home to reflect.

He loved this little girl, then. He comprehended now all that he had felt near her since that walk in the Parc Monceau, when he found in her mouth the call from a voice hardly recognized, the voice that long ago had awakened his heart; then all that slow, irresistible renewal of a love not yet extinct, not yet frozen, which he persisted in not acknowledging to himself.

What should he do? But what could he do? When she was married he would avoid seeing her often, that was all. Meantime, he would continue to return to the house, so that no one should suspect anything, and he would hide his secret from everyone.

He dined at home, which he very seldom did. Then he had a fire made in the large stove in his studio, for the night promised to be very cold. He even ordered the chandeliers to be lighted, as if he disliked the dark corners, and then he shut himself in. What strange emotion, profound, physical, frightfully sad, had seized him! He felt it in his throat, in his breast, in all his relaxed muscles as well as in his fainting soul. The walls of the apartment oppressed him; all his life was inclosed therein — his life as an artist, his life as a man. Every painted study hanging there recalled a success, each piece of furniture spoke of some memory. But successes and memories were things of the past. His life? How short, how empty it seemed to him, yet full. He had made pictures, and more pictures, and always pictures, and had loved one woman. He recalled the evenings of exaltation, after their meetings, in this same studio. He had walked whole nights with his being on fire with fever. The joy of happy love, the joy of worldly success, the unique intoxication of glory, had caused him to taste unforgettable hours of inward triumph.

He had loved a woman, and that woman had loved him. Through her he had received that baptism which reveals to man the mysterious world of emotions and of love. She had opened his heart almost by force, and now he could no longer close it. Another love had entered, in spite of him, through this opening — another, or rather the same relighted by a new face; the same, stronger by all the force which this need to adore takes on in old age. So he loved this little girl! He need no longer struggle, resist, or deny; he loved her with the despairing knowledge that he should not even gain a little pity from her, that she would always be ignorant of his terrible torment, and that another would marry her! At this thought constantly recurring, impossible to drive away, he was seized with an animal-like desire to howl like chained dogs, for like them he felt powerless, enslaved, imprisoned. Becoming more and more nervous, the longer he thought, he walked with long strides through the vast room, lighted up as if for a celebration. At last, unable to tolerate longer the pain of that reopened wound, he wished to try to calm it with the recollection of his early love, to drown it in evoking his first and great passion. From the closet where he kept it he took the copy of the Countess's portrait that he had made formerly for himself, then he put it on his easel, and sitting down in front of it, gazed at it. He tried to see her again, to find her living again, such as he had loved her before. But it was always Annette that rose upon the canvas. The mother had disappeared, vanished, leaving in her place that other face which resembled hers so strangely. It was the little one, with her hair a little lighter, her smile a little more mischievous, her air a little more mocking; and he felt that he belonged body and soul to that young being, as he never had belonged to the other, as a sinking vessel belongs to the waves!

Then he arose, and in order to see this apparition no more he turned the painting around; then, as he felt his heart full of sadness, he went to his chamber to bring into the studio the drawer of his desk, wherein were sleeping all the letters of the mistress of his heart. There they lay, as if in a bed, one upon the other, forming a thick layer of little thin papers. He thrust his hands among the mass, among all that which spoke of both of them, deep into that bath of their long intimacy. He looked at that narrow board coffin in which lay the mass of piled-up envelopes, on which his name, his name alone, was always written. He reflected that the love, the tender attachment of two beings, one for the other, were recounted therein, among that yellowish wave of papers spotted by red seals, and he inhaled, in bending over it, the old melancholy odor of letters that have been packed away.

He wished to re-read them, and feeling in the bottom of the drawer, he drew out a handful of the earlier ones. As soon as he opened them vivid memories emerged from them, which stirred his soul. He recognized many that he had carried about on his person for whole weeks, and found again, throughout the delicate handwriting that said such sweet things to him, the forgotten emotions of early days. Suddenly he found under his fingers a fine embroidered handkerchief. What was that? He pondered a few minutes, then he remembered! One day, at his house, she had wept because she was a little jealous, and he had stolen and kept her handkerchief, moist with her tears!

Ah, what sad things! What sad things! The poor woman!

From the depths of that drawer, from the depths of his past, all these reminiscences rose like a vapor, but it was only the impalpable vapor of a reality now dead. Nevertheless, he suffered and wept over the letters, as one weeps over the dead because they are no more.

But the remembrance of all his early love awakened in him a new and youthful ardor, a wave of irresistible tenderness which called up in his mind the radiant face of Annette. He had loved the mother, through a passionate impulse of voluntary servitude; he was beginning to love this little girl like a slave, a trembling old slave on whom fetters are riveted that he never can break. He felt this in the depths of his being, and was terrified. He tried to understand how and why she possessed him thus. He knew her so little! She was hardly a woman as yet; her heart and soul still slept with the sleep of youth.

He, on the other hand, was now almost at the end of his life. How, then, had this child been able to capture him with a few smiles and locks of her hair? Ah, the smiles, the hair of that little blonde maiden made him long to fall on his knees and strike the dust with his head!

Does one know, does one ever know why a woman's face has suddenly the power of poison upon us? It seems as if one had been drinking her with the eyes, that she had become one's mind and body. We are intoxicated with her, mad over her; we live of that absorbed image and would die of it!

How one suffers sometimes from this ferocious and incomprehensible power of a certain face on a man's heart!

Olivier Bertin began to pace his room again; night was advancing, his fire had gone out. Through the windowpanes the cold air penetrated from outside. Then he went back to bed, where he continued to think and suffer until daylight.

He rose early, without knowing why, nor what he was going to do, agitated by his nervousness, irresolute as a whirling weather-vane.

In seeking some distraction for his mind, some occupation for his body, he recollected that on that particular day of the week certain members of his club had the habit of meeting regularly at the Moorish Baths, where they breakfasted after the massage. So he dressed quickly, hoping that the hot room and the shower would calm him, and he went out.

As soon as he found himself in the street, he felt the cold air, that first crisp cold of the early frost, which destroys in a single night the last trances of summer.

All along the Boulevards fell a thick shower of large yellow leaves which rustled down with a dry sound. As far as could be seen, they fell from one end of the broad avenue to the other, between the facades of the houses, as if all their stems had just been cut from the branches by a thin blade of ice. The road and the sidewalks were already covered with them, resembling for a few hours the paths in the woods at the beginning of winter. All that dead foliage crackled under the feet, and massed itself, from time to time, in light waves under the gusts of wind.

This was one of those days of transition which mark the end of one season and the beginning of another, which have a savor or a special sadness — the sadness of the death-struggle or the savor of rising sap.

In crossing the threshold of the Moorish Baths, the thought of the heat that would soon penetrate his flesh after his walk in the cold air gave a feeling of satisfaction to Olivier's sad heart.

He undressed quickly, wrapping around his body the light scarf the attendant handed to him, and disappeared behind the padded door open before him.

A warm, oppressive breath, which seemed to come from a distant furnace, made him pant as if he needed air while traversing a Moorish gallery lighted by two Oriental lanterns. Then a negro with woolly head, attired only in a girdle, with shining body and muscular limbs, ran before him to raise a curtain at the other end; and Bertin entered the large hot-air room, round, high-studded, silent, almost as mystic as a temple. Daylight fell from above through a cupola and through trefoils of colored glass into the immense circular room, with paved floor and walls covered with pottery decorated after the Arab fashion.

Men of all ages, almost naked, walked slowly about, grave and silent; others were seated on marble benches, with arms crossed; others still chatted in low tones.

The burning air made one pant at the very entrance. There was, within that stifling and decorated circular room, where human flesh was heated, where black and yellow attendants with copper-colored legs moved about, something antique and mysterious.

The first face the painter saw was that of the Comte de Landa. He was promenading around like a Roman wrestler, proud of his enormous chest and of his great arms crossed over it. A frequenter of the hot baths, he felt when there like an admired actor on the stage, and he criticised like an expert the muscles of all the strong men in Paris.

"Good-morning, Bertin," said he.

They shook hands; then Landa continued: "Splendid weather for sweating!"

"Yes, magnificent."

"Have you seen Rocdiane? He is down there. I was at his house just as he was getting out of bed. Oh, look at that anatomy!"

A little gentleman was passing, bow-legged, with thin arms and flanks, the sight of whom caused the two old models of human vigor to smile disdainfully.

Rocdiane approached them, having perceived the painter. They sat down on a long marble table and began to chat quite as if they were in a drawingroom. The attendants moved about, offering drinks. One could hear the clapping of the masseurs' hands on bare flesh and the sudden flow of the shower-baths. A continuous pattering of water, coming from all corners of the great amphitheater, filled it also with a sound like rain.

At every instant some newcomer saluted the three friends, or approached them to shake hands. Among them were the big Duke of Harrison, the little Prince Epilati, Baron Flach, and others.

Suddenly Rocdiane said: "How are you, Farandal?"

The Marquis entered, his hands on his hips, with the easy air of well-made men, who never feel embarrassed at anything.

"He is a gladiator, that chap!" Landa murmured.

Rocdiane resumed, turning toward Bertin: "Is it true that he is to marry the daughter of your friend?"

"I think so," said the painter.

But the question, before that man, in that place, gave to Olivier's heart a frightful shock of despair and revolt. The horror of all the realities he had foreseen appeared to him for a second with such acuteness that he struggled an instant or so against an animal-like desire to fling himself on Farandal.

He arose.

"I am tired," said he. "I am going to the massage now."

An Arab was passing.

"Ahmed, are you at liberty?"

"Yes, Monsieur Bertin."

And he went away quickly in order to avoid shaking hands with Farandal, who was approaching slowly in making the rounds of the Hammam.

He remained barely a quarter of an hour in the large quiet resting-room, in the center of a row of cells containing the beds, with a parterre of African plants and a little fountain in the center. He had a feeling of being pursued, menaced, that the Marquis would join him, and that he should be compelled, with extended hand, to treat him as a friend, when he longed to kill him.

He soon found himself again on the Boulevard, covered with dead leaves. They fell no more, the last ones having been detached by a long blast of wind. Their red and yellow carpet shivered, stirred, undulated from one sidewalk to another, blown by puffs of the rising wind.

Suddenly a sort of roaring noise glided over the roofs, the animal-like sound of a passing tempest, and at the same time a furious gust of wind that seemed to come from the Madeleine swept through the Boulevard.

All the fallen leaves, which appeared to have been waiting for it, rose at its approach. They ran before it, massing themselves, whirling, and rising in spirals up to the tops of the buildings. The wind chased them like a flock, a mad flock that fled before it, flying toward the gates of Paris and the free sky of the suburbs. And when the great cloud of leaves and dust had disappeared on the heights of the Quartier Malesherbes, the sidewalks and roads remained bare, strangely clean and swept.

Bertin was thinking: "What will become of me? What shall I do? Where shall I go?" And he returned home, unable to think of anything.

A news-stand attracted his eye. He bought seven or eight newspapers, hoping that he might find in them something to read for an hour or two.

"I will breakfast here," said he, as he entered, and went up to his studio.

But as he sat down he felt that he could not stay there, for throughout his body surged the excitement of an angry beast.

The newspapers, which he glanced through, could not distract his mind for a minute, and the news he read met his eye without reaching his brain. In the midst of an article which he was not trying to comprehend, the name of Guilleroy made him start. It was about the session of the Chamber, where the Count had spoken a few words.

His attention, aroused by that call, was now arrested by the name of the celebrated tenor Montrose, who was to give, about the end of December, a single performance at the Opera. This would be, the newspaper stated, a magnificent musical solemnity, for the tenor Montrose, who had been absent six years from Paris, had just won, throughout Europe and America, a success without precedent; moreover, he would be supported by the illustrious Swedish singer, Helsson, who had not been heard in Paris for five years.

Suddenly Olivier had an idea, which seemed to spring from the depths of his heart — he would give Annette the pleasure of seeing this performance. Then he remembered that the Countess's mourning might be an obstacle to this scheme, and he sought some way to realize it in spite of the difficulty. Only one method presented itself. He must take a stage-box where one may be almost invisible, and if the Countess should still not wish to go, he would have Annette accompanied by her father and the Duchess. In that case, he would have to offer his box to the Duchess. But then he would be obliged to invite the Marquis!

He hesitated and reflected a long time.

Certainly, the marriage was decided upon; no doubt the date was settled. He guessed the reason for his friend's haste in having it finished soon; he understood that in the shortest time possible she would give her daughter to Farandal. He could not help it. He could neither prevent, nor modify, nor delay this frightful thing. Since he must bear it, would it not be better for him to try to master his soul, to hide his suffering, to appear content, and no longer allow himself to be carried away by his rage, as he had done?

Yes, he would invite the Marquis, and so allay the Countess's suspicions, and keep for himself a friendly door in the new establishment.

As soon as he had breakfasted, he went down to the Opera to engage one of the boxes hidden by the curtain. It was promised to him. Then he hastened to the Guilleroys'.

The Countess appeared almost immediately, apparently still a little moved by their tender interview of the day before.

"How kind of you to come again to-day!" said she.

"I am bringing you something," he faltered.

"What is it?"

"A stage-box at the Opera for the single performance of Helsson and Montrose."

"Oh, my friend, what a pity! And my mourning?"

"Your mourning has lasted for almost four months."

"I assure you that I cannot."

"And Annette? Remember that she may never have such an opportunity again."

"With whom could she go?"

"With her father and the Duchess, whom I am about to invite. I intend also to offer a seat to the Marquis."

She gazed deep into his eyes, and a wild desire to kiss him rose to her lips. Hardly believing her ears, she repeated: "To the Marquis?"

"Why, yes."

She consented at once to this arrangement.

He continued, in an indifferent tone: "Have you fixed the date of their marriage?"

"Oh, yes, almost. We have reasons for hastening it very much, especially as it was decided upon before my mother's death. You remember that?"

"Yes, perfectly. And when will it take place?"

"About the beginning of January. I ask your pardon for not having told you of it sooner."

Annette entered. He felt his heart leap within him as if on springs, and all the tenderness that drew him toward her suddenly became bitter, arousing in his heart that strange, passionate animosity into which love changes when lashed by jealousy.

"I have brought you something," he said.

"So we have decided to say 'you'?" she replied.

He assumed a paternal tone.

"Listen, my child, I know all about the event that is soon to occur. I assure you that then it will be indispensable. Better say 'you' now than later."

She shrugged her shoulders with an air of discontent, while the Countess remained silent, looking afar off, her thoughts preoccupied.

"Well, what have you brought me?" inquired Annette.

He told her about the performance, and the invitations he intended to give. She was delighted, and, throwing her arms around his neck with the manner of a little girl, she kissed him on both cheeks.

He felt ready to sink, and understood, when he felt the light caresses of that little mouth with its sweet breath, that he never should be cured of his passion.

The Countess, annoyed, said to her daughter: "You know that your father is waiting for you."

"Yes, mamma, I am going."

She ran away, still throwing kisses from the tips of her fingers.

As soon as she had gone, Olivier asked: "Will they travel?"

"Yes, for three months."

"So much the better," he murmured in spite of himself.

"We will resume our former life," said the Countess.

"Yes, I hope so," said he, hesitatingly.

"But do not neglect me meanwhile."

"No, my friend."

The impulse he had shown the evening before, when seeing her weep, and the intention which he had just expressed of inviting the Marquis to the performance at the Opera, had given new hope to the Countess.

But it was short. A week had not passed ere she was again following the expression of this man's face with tortured and jealous attention, watching every stage of his suffering. She could ignore nothing, herself enduring all the pain that she guessed at in him; and Annette's constant presence reminded her at every moment of the day of the hopelessness of her efforts.

Everything oppressed her at the same time — her age and her mourning. Her active, intelligent, and ingenious coquetry, which all her life had given her triumph, found itself paralyzed by that black uniform which marked her pallor and the change in her features, while it rendered the adolescence of her daughter absolutely dazzling. The time seemed far away, though it was quite recent, when, on Annette's return to Paris, she had proudly sought similar toilets which at that time were favorable to her. Now she had a furious longing to tear from her body those vestments of death which made her ugly and tortured her.

If she had felt that all the resources of elegance were at her service, if she had been able to choose and use delicately shaded stuffs, in harmony with her coloring, which would have lent a studied power to her fading charms, as captivating as the inert grace of her daughter, she would no doubt have known how to remain still the more charming.

She knew so well the influences of the fever-giving costume of evening, and the soft sensuousness of morning attire, of the disturbing deshabille worn at breakfast with intimate friends, which lend to a woman until noontime a sort of reminiscence of her rising, the material and warm impression of the bed and of her perfumed room!

But what could she attempt under that sepulchral robe, that convict's dress, which must cover her for a whole year? A year! She must remain a year imprisoned in that black attire, inactive and vanquished. For a whole year she would feel herself growing old, day by day, hour by hour, minute by minute, under that sheath of crape! What would she be in a year if her poor ailing body continued to alter thus under the anguish of her soul?

These thoughts never left her, and spoiled for her everything she might have enjoyed, turned into sadness things that would have given her joy, leaving her not a pleasure, a contentment, or a gaiety intact. She was agitated incessantly by an exasperating need to shake off this weight of misery that crushed her, for without this tormenting obsession she would still have been so happy, alert, and healthy! She felt that her soul was still fresh and bright, her heart still young, the ardor of a being that is beginning to live, an insatiable appetite for happiness, more voracious even than before, and a devouring desire to love.

And now, all good things, all things sweet, delicious and poetic, which embellish life and make it enjoyable, were withdrawing from her, because she was growing old! It was all finished! Yet she still found within her the tenderness of the young girl and the passionate impulses of the young woman. Nothing had grown old but her body, that miserable skin, that stuff over the bones, fading little by little like the covering of a piece of furniture. The curse of this decay had attached itself to her, and had become almost a physical suffering. This fixed idea had created a sensation of the epidermis, the sensation of growing old, continuous and imperceptible, like that of cold or of heat. She really believed that she felt an indescribable sort of itching, the slow march of wrinkles upon her forehead, the weakening of the tissues of the cheeks and throat, and the multiplication of those innumerable little marks that wear out the tired skin. Like some one afflicted with a consuming disease, whom a continual prurience induces to scratch himself, the perception and terror of that abominable, swift and secret work of time filled her soul with an irresistible need of verifying it in her mirrors. They called her, drew her, forced her to come, with fixed eyes, to see, to look again, to recognize incessantly, to touch with her finger, as if to assure herself, the indelible mark of the years. At first this was an intermittent thought, returning whenever she saw the polished surface of the dreaded crystal, at home or abroad. She paused in the street to gaze at herself in the shop-windows, hanging as if by one hand to all the glass plates with which merchants ornament their facades. It became a disease, an obsession. She carried in her pocket a dainty little ivory powder-box, as large as a nut, the interior of which contained a tiny mirror; and often, while walking, she held it open in her hand and raised it to her eyes.

When she sat down to read or write in the tapestried drawingroom, her mind, distracted for the time by a new occupation, would soon return to its obsession. She struggled, tried to amuse herself, to have other ideas, to continue her work. It was in vain; the prick of desire tormented her, and soon dropping her book or her pen, her hand would steal out, by an irresistible impulse, toward the little hand-glass mounted in antique silver that lay upon her desk. In this oval, chiseled frame her whole face was inclosed, like a face of days gone by, a portrait of the last century, or a once fresh pastel now tarnished by the sun. Then after gazing at herself a long time, she laid, with a weary movement, the little glass upon the desk and tried to resume her work; but ere she had read two pages or written twenty lines, she was again seized with the invincible and torturing need of looking at herself, and once more would extend her hand to take up the mirror.

She now handled it like an irritating and familiar toy that the hand cannot let alone, used it continually even when receiving her friends, and made herself nervous enough to cry out, hating it as if it were a sentient thing while turning it in her fingers.

One day, exasperated by this struggle between herself and this bit of glass, she threw it against the wall, where it was broken to pieces.

But after a time her husband, who had it repaired, brought it back to her, clearer than ever; and she was compelled to take it, to thank him, and resign herself to keep it.

Every evening, too, and every morning, shut up in her own room, she resumed, in spite of herself, that minute and patient examination of the quiet, odious havoc.

When she was in bed she could not sleep; she would light a candle again and lie, wide-eyed, thinking how insomnia and grief hasten irremediably the horrible work of fleeting time. She listened in the silence of the night to the ticking of the clock, which seemed to murmur, in its monotonous and regular tic-tac: "It goes, it goes, it goes!" and her heart shrank with such suffering that, with the sheet gripped between her teeth, she groaned in despair.

Once, like everyone else, she had some notion of the passing years and of the changes they bring. Like everyone else, she had said to herself every winter, every spring, and every summer, "I have changed very much since last year." But, always beautiful, with a changing beauty, she was never uneasy about it. Now, however, suddenly, instead of admitting peacefully the slow march of the seasons, she had just discovered and understood the formidable flight of the minutes. She had had a sudden revelation of the gliding of the hour, of that imperceptible race, maddening when we think of it — of that infinite defile of little hurrying seconds, which nibble at the body and the life of men.

After these miserable nights, she had long periods of somnolence that made her more tranquil, in the warmth of her bed, when her maid had opened the curtains and lighted the morning fire. She lay there tired, drowsy, neither awake nor asleep, in the torpor of thought which brings about the revival of that instinctive and providential hope which gives light and life to the hearts of men up to their last days.

Every morning now, as soon as she had risen from her bed, she felt moved by a powerful desire to pray to God, to obtain from Him a little relief and consolation.

She would kneel, then, before a large figure of Christ carved in oak, a gift from Olivier, a rare work he had discovered; and, with lips closed, but imploring with that voice of the soul with which we speak to ourselves, she lifted toward the Divine martyr a sorrowful supplication. Distracted by the need of being heard and succored, naïve in her distress, as are all faithful ones on their knees, she could not doubt that He heard her, that He was attentive to her request, and was perhaps touched at her grief. She did not ask Him to do for her that which He never had done for anyone — to leave her until death all her charm, her freshness and grace; she begged only a little repose, a little respite. She must grow old, of course, just as she must die. But why so soon? Some women remain beautiful so long! Could He not grant that she should be one of these? How good He would be, He who had also suffered so much, if only He would let her keep for two or three years still the little charm she needed in order to be pleasing.

She did not say these things to Him, of course, but she sighed them forth, in the confused plaint of her being.

Then, having risen, she would sit before her toilet-table, and with a tension of thought as ardent as in her prayer, she would handle the powders, the pastes, the pencils, the puffs and brushes, which gave her once more a plaster-like beauty, fragile, lasting only for a day.

VI

On the Boulevard two names were heard from all lips: "Emma Helsson" and "Montrose." The nearer one approached the Opera, the oftener he heard those names repeated. Immense posters, too, affixed to the Morris columns, announced them in the eyes of passers, and in the evening air could be felt the excitement of an approaching event.

That heavy monument called the National Academy of Music, squatted under the black sky, exhibited to the crowd before its doors the pompous, whitish facade and marble colonnade of its balcony, illuminated like a stage setting by invisible electric lights.

In the square the mounted Republican guards directed the movement of the crowds, and the innumerable carriages coming from all parts of Paris allowed glimpses of creamy light stuff and fair faces behind their lowered windows.

The coupes and landaus formed in line under the reserved arcades, and stopped for a moment, and from them alighted fashionable and other women, in their opera-cloaks, trimmed with fur, feathers, and rare laces — precious bodies, divinely set forth!

All the way along the celebrated stairway was a sort of fairy flight, an uninterrupted mounting of ladies dressed like queens, whose throats and ears scattered flashing rays from their diamonds, and whose long trains swept the stairs.

The theater was filling early, for no one wished to lose a note of the two illustrious artists; and throughout the vast amphitheater, under the dazzling electric light from the great chandelier, a throng of people were seating themselves amid an uproar of voices.

From the stage-box, already occupied by the Duchess, Annette, the Count, the Marquis, Bertin and Musadieu, one could see nothing but the wings, where men were talking, running about, and shouting, machinists in blouses, gentlemen in evening dress, actors in costume. But behind the great curtain one heard the deep sound of the crowd, one felt the presence of a mass of moving, overexcited beings, whose agitation seemed to penetrate the curtain, and to extend even to the decorations.

They were about to present Faust.

Musadieu was relating anecdotes about the first representatives of this work at the Theatre Lyrique, of its half success in the beginning followed by brilliant triumph, of the original cast, and their manner of singing each aria. Annette, half turned toward him, listened with that eager, youthful curiosity with which she regarded the whole world; and at times she cast a tender glance at her fiance, who in a few days would be her husband. She loved him, now, as innocent hearts love; that is to say she loved in him all the hopes she had for the future. The intoxication of the first feasts of life, and the ardent longing to be happy, made her tremble with joy and expectation.

And Olivier, who saw all, and knew all, who had sounded all the depths of secret, helpless, and jealous love, down in the furnace of human suffering, where the heart seems to crackle like flesh over hot coals, stood in the back of the box looking at them with eyes that betrayed his torture.

The three blows were struck, and suddenly the sharp little tap of a bow on the leader's desk stopped short all movement, all coughing and whispering; then, after a brief and profound silence, the first measure of the introduction arose, filling the house with the invisible and irresistible mystery of the music that penetrates our bodies, thrills our nerves and souls with a poetic and sensuous fever, mingling with the limpid air we breathe a wave of sound to which we listen.

Olivier took a seat at the back of the box, painfully affected, as if his heart's wounds had been touched by those accents. But when the curtain rose he stood up again, and saw Doctor Faust, lost in sorrowful meditation, seated in his alchemist's laboratory.

He had already heard the opera twenty times, and almost knew it by heart, and his attention soon wandered from the stage to the audience. He could see only a small part of it behind the frame of the stage which concealed their box, but the angle that was visible, extending from the orchestra to the top gallery, showed him a portion of the audience in which he recognized many faces. In the orchestra rows, the men in white cravats, sitting side by side, seemed a museum of familiar countenances, society men, artists, journalists, the whole category of those that never fail to go where everyone else goes. In the balcony and in the boxes he noted and named to himself the women he recognized. The Comtesse de Lochrist, in a proscenium box, was absolutely ravishing, while a little farther on a bride, the Marquise d'Ebelin, was already looking through her lorgnette. "That is a pretty debut," said Bertin to himself.

The audience listened with deep attention and evident sympathy to the tenor Montrose, who was lamenting over his waning life.

Olivier thought: "What a farce! There is Faust, the mysterious and sublime Faust who sings the horrible disgust and nothingness of everything; and this crowd are asking themselves anxiously whether Montrose's voice has not changed!" Then he listened, like the others, and behind the trivial words of the libretto, through that music which awakens profound perception in the soul, he had a sort of revelation as to how Goethe had been able to conceive the heart of Faust.

He had read the poem some time before, and thought it very beautiful without being moved by it, but now he suddenly realized its unfathomable depth, for it seemed to him that on that evening he himself had become a Faust.

Leaning lightly upon the railing of the box, Annette was listening with all her ears; and murmurs of satisfaction were beginning to be heard from the audience, for Montrose's voice was better and richer than ever!

Bertin had closed his eyes. For a whole month, all that he had seen, all that he had felt, everything that he had encountered in life he had immediately transformed into a sort of accessory to his passion. He threw the world and himself as nourishment to this fixed idea. All that he saw that was beautiful or rare, all that he imagined that was charming, he mentally offered to his little friend; and he had no longer an idea that he did not in some way connect with his love.

Now he listened from the depths of his soul to the echo of Faust's lamentations, and the desire to die surged up within him, the desire to have done with all his grief, with all the misery of his hopeless love. He looked at Annette's delicate profile, and saw the Marquis de Farandal, seated behind her, also looking at it. He felt old, lost, despairing. Ah, never to await anything more, never to hope for anything more, no longer to have even the right to desire, to feel himself outside of everything, in the evening of life, like a superannuated functionary whose career is ended — what intolerable torture!

Applause burst forth; Montrose had triumphed already. And Labarriere as Mephistopheles sprang up from the earth.

Olivier, who never had heard him in this role, listened with renewed attention. The remembrance of Aubin, so dramatic with his bass voice, then of Faure, so seductive with his baritone, distracted him a short time.

But suddenly a phrase sung by Montrose with irresistible power stirred him to the heart. Faust was saying to Satan:

"Je veux un tresor qui les contient tous —
Je veux la jeunesse."

And the tenor appeared in silken doublet, a sword by his side, a plumed cap on his head, elegant, young, and handsome, with the affectations of a handsome singer.

A murmur arose. He was very attractive and the women were pleased with him. But Olivier felt some disappointment, for the poignant evocation of Goethe's dramatic poem disappeared in this metamorphosis. Thenceforth he saw before him only a fairy spectacle, filled with pretty little songs, and actors of talent whose voices were all he listened to. That man in a doublet, that pretty youth with his roulades, who showed his thighs and displayed his voice, displeased him. This was not the real, irresistible, and sinister Chevalier Faust, who was about to seduce the fair Marguerite.

He sat down again, and the phrase he had just heard returned to his mind:

"I would have a treasure that embraces all — Youth!"

He murmured it between his teeth, sang it sadly in the depths of his soul, and, with eyes fixed always upon Annette's blonde head, which rose in the square opening of the box, he felt all the bitterness of that desire that never could be realized.

But Montrose had just finished the first act with such perfection that enthusiasm broke forth. For several minutes, the noise of clapping, stamping, and bravos swept like a storm through the theater. In all the boxes the women clapped their gloved hands, while the men standing behind them shouted as they applauded.

The curtain fell, but it was raised twice before the applause subsided. Then, when the curtain had fallen for the third time, separating the stage and the interior boxes from the audience, the Duchess and Annette continued their applause a few moments, and were specially thanked by a discreet bow from the tenor.

"Oh, he looked at us!" said Annette.

"What an admirable artist!" said the Duchess.

And Bertin, who had been leaning over, looked with a mingled feeling of irritation and disdain at the admired actor as he disappeared between two wings, waddling a little, his legs stiff, one hand on his hip, in the affected pose of a theatrical hero.

They began to talk of him. His social successes had made him as famous as his talent. He had visited every capital, in the midst of feminine ecstasies of those who, hearing before he appeared that he was irresistible, had felt their hearts throb as he appeared upon the stage. But it was said that he appeared to care very little for all this sentimental delirium, and contented himself with his musical triumphs. Musadieu related, in veiled language because of Annette's presence, details of the life of this handsome singer, and the Duchess, quite carried away, understood and approved all the follies that he was able to create, so seductive, elegant, and distinguished did she consider this exceptional musician! She concluded, laughing: "And how can anyone resist that voice!"

Olivier felt angry and bitter. He did not understand how anyone could really care for a mere actor, for that perpetual representation of human types which never resembled himself in the least; that illusory personification of imaginary men, that nocturnal and painted manikin who plays all his characters at so much a night.

"You are jealous of them!" said the Duchess. "You men of the world and artists all have a grudge against actors because they are more successful than you." Turning to Annette, she added: "Come, little one, you who are entering life and look at it with healthy eyes, what do you think of this tenor?"

"I think he is very good indeed," Annette replied, with an air of conviction.

The three strokes sounded for the second act, and the curtain rose on the Kermesse.

Helsson's passage was superb. She seemed to have more voice than formerly, and to have acquired more certainty of method. She had, indeed, become the great, excellent, exquisite singer, whose worldly fame equaled that of Bismarck or De Lesseps.

When Faust rushed toward her, when he sang in his bewitching voice phrases so full of charm and when the pretty blonde Marguerite replied so touchingly the whole house was moved with a thrill of pleasure.

When the curtain fell, the applause was tremendous, and Annette applauded so long that Bertin wished to seize her hands to make her stop. His heart was stung by a new torment.

He did not speak between the acts, for he was pursuing into the wings, his fixed thought now become absolute hatred, following to his box, where he saw, putting more white powder on his cheeks, the odious singer who was thus overexciting this child!

Then the curtain rose on the garden scene. Immediately a sort of fever of love seemed to spread through the house, for never had that music, which seems like the breath of kisses, been rendered by two such interpreters. It was no longer two illustrious actors, Montrose and Helsson; they became two beings from the ideal world, hardly two beings, indeed, but two voices: the eternal voice of the man that loves, the eternal voice of the woman that yields; and together they sighed forth all the poetry of human tenderness.

When Faust sang:

"Laisse-moi, laisse-moi contempler ton visage,"

in the notes that soared from his mouth there was such an accent of adoration, of transport and supplication that for a moment a desire to love filled every heart.

Olivier remembered that he had murmured that phrase himself in the park at Roncieres, under the castle windows.

Until then he had thought it rather ordinary; but now it rose to his lips like a last cry of passion, a last prayer, the last hope and the last favor he might expect in this life.

Then he listened no more, heard nothing more. A sharp pang of jealousy tore his heart, for he had just seen Annette carry her handkerchief to her eyes.

She wept! Then her heart was awakening, becoming animated and moved, her little woman's heart which as yet knew nothing! There, very near him, without giving a thought to him, she had a revelation of the way in which love may overwhelm a human being; and this revelation, this initiation had come to her from that miserable strolling singer!

Ah, he felt very little anger now toward the Marquis de Farandal, that stupid creature who saw nothing, who did not know, did not understand! But how he execrated that man in tights, who was illuminating the soul of that young girl!

He longed to throw himself upon her, as one throws himself upon a person in danger of being run over by a fractious horse, to seize her by the arm and drag her away, and say to her: "Let us go! let us go! I entreat you!"

How she listened, how she palpitated! And how he suffered. He had suffered thus before, but less cruelly. He remembered it, for the stings of jealousy smart afresh like reopened wounds. He had first felt it at Roncieres, in returning from the cemetery, when he felt for the first time that she was escaping from him, that he could not control her, that young girl as independent as a young animal. But down there, when she had irritated him by leaving him to pluck flowers, he had experienced chiefly a brutal desire to check her playful flights, to compel her person to remain beside him; to-day it was her fleeting, intangible soul that was escaping. Ah, that gnawing irritation which he had just recognized, how often he had experienced it by the indescribable little wounds which seem to be always bruising a loving heart. He recalled all the painful impressions of petty jealousy that he had endured, in little stings, day after day. Every time that she had remarked, admired, liked, desired something, he had been jealous of it; jealous in an imperceptible but continuous fashion, jealous of all that absorbed the time, the looks, the attention, the gaiety, the astonishment or affection of Annette, for all that took a little of her away from him. He had been jealous of all that she did without him, of all that he did not know, of her going about, her reading, of everything that seemed to please her, jealous even of a heroic officer wounded in Africa, of whom Paris talked for a week, of the author of a much praised romance, of a young unknown poet she never had seen, but whose verses Musadieu had recited; in short, of all men that anyone praised before her, even carelessly, for when one loves a woman one cannot tolerate without anguish that she should even think of another with an appearance of interest. In one's heart is felt the imperious need of being for her the only being in the world. One wishes her to see, to know, to appreciate no one else. So soon as she shows an indication of turning to look at or recognize some person, one throws himself before her, and if one cannot turn aside or absorb her interest he suffers to the bottom of his heart.

Olivier suffered thus in the presence of this singer, who seemed to scatter and to gather love in that opera-house, and he felt vexed with everyone because of the tenor's triumph, with the women whom he saw applauding him from their boxes, with the men, those idiots who were giving a sort of apotheosis to that coxcomb!

An artist! They called him a artist, a great artist! And he had successes, this paid actor, interpreter of another's thought, such as no creator had ever known! Ah, that was like the justice and the intelligence of the fashionable world, those ignorant and pretentious amateurs for whom the masters of human art work until death. He looked at them, applauding, shouting, going into ecstasies; and the ancient hostility that had always seethed at the bottom of his proud heart of a parvenu became a furious anger against those imbeciles, allpowerful only by right of birth and wealth.

Until the end of the performance he remained silent, a prey to thought; then when the storm of enthusiasm had at last subsided he offered his arm to the Duchess, while the Marquis took Annette's. They descended the grand stairway again, in the midst of a stream of men and women, in a sort of slow and magnificent cascade of bare shoulders, sumptuous gowns, and black coats. Then the Duchess, the young girl, her father, and the Marquis entered the same landau, and Olivier Bertin remained alone with Musadieu in the Place de l'Opera.

Suddenly he felt a sort of affection for this man, or rather that natural attraction one feels for a fellow-countryman met in a distant land, for he now felt lost in that strange, indifferent crowd, whereas with Musadieu he might still speak of her.

So he took his arm.

"You are not going home now?" said he. "It is a fine night; let us take a walk."

"Willingly."

They went toward the Madeleine, in the mist of the nocturnal crowd possessed by that short and violent midnight excitement which stirs the Boulevards when the theaters are being emptied.

Musadieu had a thousand things in his mind, all his subjects for conversation from the moment when Bertin should name his preference; and he let his eloquence loose upon the two or three topics that interested him most. The painter allowed him to run on without listening to him, and holding him by the arm, sure of being able soon to lead him to talk of Annette, he walked along without noticing his surroundings, imprisoned within his love. He walked, exhausted by that fit of jealousy which had bruised him like a fall, overcome by the conviction that he had nothing more to do in the world.

He should go on suffering thus, more and more, without expecting anything. He should pass empty days, one after another, seeing her from afar, living, happy, loved and loving, without doubt. A lover! Perhaps she would have a lover, as her mother had had one! He felt within him sources of suffering so numerous, diverse, and complicated, such an afflux of miseries, such inevitable tortures, he felt so lost, so far overwhelmed, from this moment, by a wave of unimaginable agony that he could not suppose anyone ever had suffered as he did. And he suddenly thought of the puerility of poets who have invented the useless labor of Sisyphus, the material thirst of Tantalus, the devoured heart of Prometheus! Oh, if they had foreseen, if they had experienced the mad love of an elderly man for a young girl, how would they had expressed the painful and secret effort of a being who can no longer inspire love, the tortures of fruitless desire, and, more terrible than a vulture's beak, a little blonde face rending a heart!

Musadieu talked without stopping, and Bertin interrupted him, murmuring almost in spite of himself, under the impulse of his fixed idea:

"Annette was charming this evening."

"Yes, delicious!"

The painter added, to prevent Musadieu from taking up the broken thread of his ideas: "She is prettier than her mother ever was."

To this the other agreed absentmindedly, repeating "Yes, yes, yes!" several times in succession, without his mind having yet settled itself on this new idea.

Olivier endeavored to continue the subject, and in order to attract his attention by one of Musadieu's own favorite fads, he continued:

"She will have one of the first salons in Paris after her marriage."

That was enough, and, the man of fashion being convinced, as well as the Inspector of Fine Arts, he began to talk wisely of the social footing on which the Marquise de Farandal would stand in French society.

Bertin listened to him, and fancied Annette in a large salon full of light, surrounded by men and women. This vision, too, made him jealous.

They were now going up the Boulevard Malesherbes. As they passed the Guilleroys' house the painter looked up. Lights seemed to be shining through the windows, among the openings in the curtains. He suspected that the Duchess and the Marquis had been invited to come and have a cup of tea. And a burning rage made him suffer terribly.

He still held Musadieu by the arm, and once or twice attempted to continue, by contradicting Musadieu's opinions, the talk about the future Marquise. Even that commonplace voice in speaking of her caused her charming image to flit beside them in the night.

When they arrived at the painter's door, in the Avenue de Villiers, Bertin asked: "Will you come in?"

"No, thank you. It is late, and I am going to bed."

"Oh, come up for half an hour, and we'll have a little more talk."

"No, really. It is too late."

The thought of staying there alone, after the anguish he had just endured, filled Olivier's soul with horror. He had someone with him; he would keep him.

"Do come up; I want you to choose a study that I have intended for a long time to offer you."

The other, knowing that painters are not always in a giving mood, and that the remembrance of promises is short, seized the opportunity. In his capacity as Inspector of Fine Arts, he possessed a gallery that had been furnished with skill.

"I am with you," said he.

They entered.

The valet was aroused and soon brought some grog; and the talk was for some time all about painting. Bertin showed some studies, and begged Musadieu to take the one that pleased him best; Musadieu hesitated, disturbed by the gaslight, which deceived him as to tones. At last he chose a group of little girls jumping the rope on a sidewalk; and almost at once he wished to depart, and to take his present with him.

"I will have it taken to your house," said the painter.

"No; I should like better to have it this very evening, so that I may admire it while I am going to bed," said Musadieu.

Nothing could keep him, and Olivier Bertin found himself again alone in his house, that prison of his memories and his painful agitation.

When the servant entered the next morning, bringing tea and the newspapers, he found his master sitting up in bed, so pale and shaken that he was alarmed.

"Is Monsieur indisposed?" he inquired.

"It is nothing — only a little headache."

"Does not Monsieur wish me to bring him something?"

"No. What sort of weather is it?"

"It rains, Monsieur."

"Very well. That is all."

The man withdrew, having placed on the little table the tea-tray and the newspapers.

Olivier took up the Figaro and opened it. The leading article was entitled "Modern Painting." It was a dithyrambic eulogy on four or five young painters who, gifted with real ability as colorists, and exaggerating them for effect, now pretended to be revolutionists and renovators of genius.

As did all the older painters, Bertin sneered at these newcomers, was irritated at their assumption of exclusiveness, and disputed their doctrines. He began to read the article, then, with the rising anger so quickly felt by a nervous person; at last, glancing a little further down, he saw his own name, and these words at the end of a sentence struck him like a blow of the fist full in the chest: "The old-fashioned art of Olivier Bertin."

He had always been sensitive to either criticism or praise, but, at the bottom of his heart, in spite of his legitimate vanity, he suffered more from being criticised than he enjoyed being praised, because of the uneasiness concerning himself which his hesitations had always encouraged. Formerly, however, at the time of his triumphs, the incense offered was so frequent that it made him forget the pin-pricks. To-day, before the ceaseless influx of new artists and new admirers, congratulations were more rare and criticism was more marked. He felt that he had been enrolled in the battalion of old painters of talent, whom the younger ones do not treat as masters; and as he was as intelligent as he was perspicacious he suffered now from the least insinuations as much as from direct attacks.

But never had any wound to his pride as an artist hurt him like this. He remained gasping, and reread the article in order to grasp its every meaning. He and his equals were thrown aside with outrageous disrespect; and he arose murmuring those words, which remained on his lips: "The old-fashioned art of Olivier Bertin."

Never had such sadness, such discouragement, such a sensation of having reached the end of everything, the end of his mental and physical being, thrown him into such desperate distress of soul. He sat until two o'clock in his armchair, before the fireplace, his legs extended toward the fire, not having strength to move, or to do anything. Then the need of being consoled rose within him, the need to clasp devoted hands, to see faithful eyes, to be pitied, succored, caressed with friendly words. So he went, as usual, to the Countess.

When he entered Annette was alone in the drawingroom, standing with her back toward him, hastily writing the address on a letter. On a table beside her lay a copy of Figaro. Bertin saw the journal at the moment that he saw the young girl and was bewildered, not daring to advance! Oh, if she had read it! She turned, and in a preoccupied, hurried way, her mind haunted with feminine cares, she said to him:

"Ah, good-morning, sir painter! You will excuse me if I leave you? I have a dressmaker upstairs who claims me. You understand that a dressmaker, at the time of a wedding, is very important. I will lend you mamma, who is talking and arguing with my artist. If I need her I will call her for a few minutes."

And she hastened away, running a little, to show how much she was hurried.

This abrupt departure, without a word of affection, without a tender look for him who loved her so much — so much! — quite upset him. His eyes rested again on the Figaro, and he thought: "She has read it! They laugh at me, they deny me. She no longer believes in me. I am nothing to her any more."

He took two steps toward the journal, as one walks toward a man to strike him. Then he said to himself: "Perhaps she has not read it, after all. She is so preoccupied to-day. But someone will undoubtedly speak of it before her, perhaps this evening, at dinner, and that will make her curious to read it."

With a spontaneous, almost unthinking, movement he took the copy, closed it, folded it, and slipped it into his pocket with the swiftness of a thief.

The Countess entered. As soon as she saw Olivier's convulsed and livid face, she guessed that he had reached the limit of suffering.

She hastened toward him, with an impulse from all her poor soul, so agonized also, and from her poor body, that was itself so wounded. Throwing her hands upon his shoulders, and plunging her glance into the depths of his eyes, she said:

"Oh, how unhappy you are!"

This time he did not deny it; his throat swelled with a spasm of pain, and he stammered:

"Yes — yes — yes!"

She felt that he was near weeping, and led him into the darkest corner of the drawingroom, toward two armchairs hidden by a small screen of antique silk. They sat down behind this slight embroidered wall, veiled also by the gray shadow of a rainy day.

She resumed, pitying him, deeply moved by his grief:

"My poor Olivier, how you suffer!"

He leaned his white head on the shoulder of his friend.

"More than you believe!" he said.

"Oh, I knew it! I have felt it all. I saw it from the beginning and watched it grow."

He answered as if she had accused him: "It is not my faulty, Any."

"I know it well; I do not reproach you for it."

And softly, turning a little, she laid her lips on one of Olivier's eyes, where she found a bitter tear.

She started, as if she had just tasted a drop of despair, and repeated several times:

"Ah, poor friend — poor friend — poor friend!"

Then after a moment of silence she added: "It is the fault of our hearts, which never have grown old. I feel that my own is full of life!"

He tried to speak but could not, for now his sobs choked him. She listened, as he leaned against her, to the struggle in his breast. Then, seized by the selfish anguish of love, which had gnawed at her heart so long, she said in the agonized tone in which one realizes a horrible misfortune:

"God! how you love her!"

Again he confessed: "Ah, yes! I love her!"

She reflected a few moments, then continued: "You never have loved me thus?"

He did not deny it, for he was passing through one of those periods in which one speaks with absolute truth, and he murmured:

"No, I was too young then."

She was surprised.

"Too young? Why?"

"Because life was too sweet. It is only at our age that one loves despairingly."

"Does the love you feel for her resemble that which you felt for me?" the Countess asked.

"Yes and no — and yet it is almost the same thing. I have loved you as much as anyone can love a woman. As for her, I love her just as I loved you, since she is yourself; but this love has become something irresistible, destroying, stronger than death. I belong to it as a burning house belongs to the fire."

She felt her sympathy wither up under a breath of jealousy; but, assuming a consoling tone, she said:

"My poor friend! In a few days she will be married and gone. When you see her no more no doubt you will be cured of this fancy."

He shook his head.

"Oh, I am lost, lost, lost!"

"No, no, I say! It will be three months before you see her again. That will be sufficient. Three months were quite enough for you to love her more than you love me, whom you have known for twelve years!"

Then, in his infinite distress, he implored: "Any, do not abandon me!"

"What can I do, my friend?"

"Do not leave me alone."

"I will go to see you as often as you wish."

"No. Keep me here as much as possible."

"But then you would be near her."

"And near you!"

"You must not see her any more before her marriage."

"Oh, Any!"

"Well, at least, not often."

"May I stay here this evening?"

"No, not in your present condition. You must divert your mind; go to the club, or the theater — no matter where, but do not stay here."

"I entreat you — "

"No, Olivier, it is impossible. And, besides, I have guests coming to dinner whose presence would agitate you still more."

"The Duchess and — he!"

"Yes."

"But I spent last evening with them."

"And you speak of it! You are in a fine state to-day."

"I promise you to be calm."

"No, it is impossible."

"Then I am going away."

"Why do you hurry now?"

"I must walk."

"That is right! Walk a great deal, walk until evening, kill yourself with fatigue and then go to bed."

He had risen.

"Good-by, Any!"

"Good-by, dear friend. I will come to see you tomorrow morning. Would you like me to do something very imprudent, as I used to do — pretend to breakfast here at noon, and then go and have breakfast with you at a quarter past one?"

"Yes, I should like it very much. You are so good!"

"It is because I love you."

"And I love you, too."

"Oh, don't speak of that any more!"

"Good-by, Any."

"Good-by, dear friend, till tomorrow."

"Good-by!"

He kissed her hands many times, then he kissed her brow, then the corner of her lips. His eyes were dry now, his bearing resolute. Just as he was about to go, he seized her, clasped her close in both arms, and pressing his lips to her forehead, he seemed to drink in, to inhale from her all the love she had for him.

Then he departed quickly, without turning toward her again.

When she was alone she let herself sink, sobbing, upon a chair. She would have remained there till night if Annette had not suddenly appeared in search of her. In order to gain time to dry her red eyelids, the Countess answered: "I have a little note to write, my child. Go upstairs, and I will join you in a few seconds."

She was compelled to occupy herself with the great affair of the trousseau until evening.

The Duchess and her nephew dined with the Guilleroys, as a family party. They had just seated themselves at table, and were speaking of the opera of the night before, when the butler appeared, carrying three enormous bouquets.

Madame de Mortemain was surprised.

"Good gracious! What is that?"

"Oh, how lovely they are!" exclaimed Annette; "who can have sent them?"

"Olivier Bertin, no doubt," replied her mother.

She had been thinking of him since his departure. He had seemed so gloomy, so tragic, she understood so clearly his hopeless sorrow, she felt so keenly the counter-stroke of that grief, she loved him so much, so entirely, so tenderly, that her heart was weighed down by sad presentiments.

In the three bouquets were found three of the painter's cards. He had written on them in pencil, respectively, the names of the Countess, the Duchess, and Annette.

"Is he ill, your friend Bertin?" the Duchess inquired. "I thought he looked rather bad last night."

"Yes, I am a little anxious about him, although he does not complain," Madame de Guilleroy answered.

"Oh, he is growing old, like all the rest of us," her husband interposed. "He is growing old quite fast, indeed. I believe, however, that bachelors usually go to pieces suddenly. Their breaking-up comes more abruptly than ours. He really is very much changed."

"Ah, yes!" sighed the Countess.

Farandal suddenly stopped his whispering to Annette to say: "The Figaro has a very disagreeable article about him this morning."

Any attack, any criticism or allusion unfavorable to her friend's talent always threw the Countess into a passion.

"Oh," said she, "men of Bertin's importance need not mind such rudeness."

Guilleroy was astonished.

"What!" he exclaimed, "a disagreeable article about Olivier! But I have not read it. On what page?"

The Marquis informed him: "The first page, at the top, with the title, 'Modern Painting.'"

And the deputy ceased to be astonished. "Oh, exactly! I did not read it because it was about painting."

Everyone smiled, knowing that apart from politics and agriculture M. de Guilleroy was interested in very few things.

The conversation turned upon other subjects until they entered the drawingroom to take coffee. The Countess was not listening and hardly answered, being pursued by anxiety as to what Olivier might be doing. Where was he? Where had he dined? Where had he taken his hopeless heart at that moment? She now felt a burning regret at having let him go, not to have kept him; and she fancied him roving the streets, so sad and lonely, fleeing under his burden of woe.

Up to the time of the departure of the Duchess and her nephew she had hardly spoken, lashed by vague and superstitious fears; then she went to bed and lay there long, her eyes wide open in the darkness, thinking of him!

A very long time had passed when she thought she heard the bell of her apartment ring. She started, sat up and listened. A second time the vibrating tinkle broke the stillness of the night.

She leaped out of bed, and with all her strength pressed the electric button that summoned her maid. Then, candle in hand, she ran to the vestibule.

Through the door she asked: "Who is there?"

"It is a letter," an unknown voice replied.

"A letter! From whom?"

"From a physician."

"What physician?"

"I do not know; it is about some accident."

Hesitating no more, she opened the door, and found herself facing a cabdriver in an oilskin cap. He held a paper in his hand, which he presented to her. She read: "Very urgent — Monsieur le Comte de Guilleroy."

The writing was unknown.

"Enter, my good man," said she; "sit down, and wait for me."

When she reached her husband's door her heart was beating so violently that she could not call him. She pounded on the wood with her metal candlestick. The Count was asleep and did not hear.

Then, impatient, nervous, she kicked the door, and heard a sleepy voice asking: "Who is there? What time is it?"

"It is I," she called. "I have an urgent letter for you, brought by a cabman. There has been some accident."

"Wait! I am getting up. I'll be there," he stammered from behind his bed-curtains.

In another minute he appeared in his dressing-gown. At the same time two servants came running, aroused by the ringing of the bell. They were alarmed and bewildered, having seen a stranger sitting on a chair in the diningroom.

The Count had taken the letter and was turning it over in his fingers, murmuring: "What is that? I cannot imagine."

"Well, read it, then!" said the Countess, in a fever.

He tore off the envelope, unfolded the paper, uttered an exclamation of amazement, then looked at his wife with frightened eyes.

"My God! what is it?" said she.

He stammered, hardly able to speak, so great was his emotion: "Oh, a great misfortune — a great misfortune! Bertin has fallen under a carriage!"

"Dead?" she cried.

"No, no!" said he; "read for yourself."

She snatched from his hand the letter he held out and read:

"MONSIEUR: A great misfortune has just happened. Your friend, the eminent artist, M. Olivier Bertin, has been run over by an omnibus, the wheel of which passed over his body. I cannot as yet say anything decisive as to the probable result of this accident, which may not be serious, although it may have an immediate and fatal result. M. Bertin begs you earnestly and entreats Madame la Comtesse de Guilleroy to come to him at once. I hope, Monsieur, that Madame la Comtesse and yourself will grant the desire of our friend in common, who before daylight may have ceased to live.

"DR. DE RIVIL."

The Countess stared at her husband with great, fixed eyes, full of terror. Then suddenly she experienced, like an electric shock, an awakening of that courage which comes to women at times, which makes them in moments of terror the most valiant of creatures.

Turning to her maid she said: "Quick! I am going to dress."

"What will Madame wear?" asked the servant.

"Never mind that. Anything you like. James," she added, "be ready in five minutes."

Returning toward her room, her soul overwhelmed, she noticed the cabman, still waiting, and said to him: "You have your carriage?"

"Yes, Madame."

"That is well; we will take that."

Wildly, with precipitate haste, she threw on her clothes, hooking, clasping, tying, and fastening at haphazard; then, before the mirror, she lifted and twisted her hair without a semblance of order, gazing without thinking of what she was doing at the reflection of her pale face and haggard eyes.

When her cloak was over her shoulders, she rushed to her husband's room, but he was not yet ready. She dragged him along.

"Come, come!" said she; "remember, he may die!"

The Count, dazed, followed her stumblingly, feeling his way with his feet on the dark stairs, trying to distinguish the steps, so that he should not fall.

The drive was short and silent. The Countess trembled so violently that her teeth rattled, and through the window she saw the flying gas-jets, veiled by the falling rain. The sidewalks gleamed, the Boulevard was deserted, the night was sinister. On arriving, they found that the painter's door was open, and that the concierge's lodge was lighted but empty.

At the top of the stairs the physician, Dr. de Rivil, a little gray man, short, round, very well dressed, extremely polite, came to meet them. He bowed low to the Countess and held out his hand to the Count.

She asked him, breathing rapidly as if climbing the stairs had exhausted her and put her out of breath:

"Well, doctor?"

"Well, Madame, I hope that it will be less serious than I thought at first."

"He will not die?" she exclaimed.

"No. At least, I do not believe so."

"Will you answer for that?"

"No. I only say that I hope to find only a simple abdominal contusion without internal lesions."

"What do you call lesions?"

"Lacerations."

"How do you know that there are none?"

"I suppose it."

"And if there are?"

"Oh, then it would be serious."

"He might die of them?"

"Yes."

"Very soon?"

"Very soon. In a few minutes or even seconds. But reassure yourself, Madame; I am convinced that he will be quite well again in two weeks."

She had listened, with profound attention, to know all and understand all.

"What laceration might he have?"

"A laceration of the liver, for instance."

"That would be very dangerous?"

"Yes — but I should be surprised to find any complication now. Let us go to him. It will do him good, for he awaits you with great impatience."

On entering the room she saw first a pale face on a white pillow. Some candles and the firelight illumined it, defined the profile, deepened the shadows; and in that pale face the Countess saw two eyes that watched her coming.

All her courage, energy, and resolution fell, so much did those hollow and altered features resemble those of a dying man. He, whom she had seen only a little while ago, had become this thing, this specter! "Oh, my God!" she murmured between her teeth, and she approached him, palpitating with horror.

He tried to smile, to reassure her, and the grimace of that attempt was frightful.

When she was beside the bed, she put both hands gently on one of Olivier's, which lay along his body, and stammered: "Oh, my poor friend!"

"It is nothing," said he, in a low tone, without moving his head.

She now looked at him closely, frightened at the change in him. He was so pale that he seemed no longer to have a drop of blood under his skin. His hollow cheeks seemed to have been sucked in from the interior of his face, and his eyes were sunken as if drawn by a string from within.

He saw the terror of his friend, and sighed: "Here I am in a fine state!"

"How did it happen?" she asked, looking at him with fixed gaze.

He was making a great effort to speak, and his whole face twitched with pain.

"I was not looking about me — I was thinking of something else — something very different — oh, yes! — and an omnibus knocked me down and ran over my abdomen."

As she listened she saw the accident, and shaking with terror, she asked: "Did you bleed?"

"No. I am only a little bruised — a little crushed."

"Where did it happen?" she inquired.

"I do not know exactly," he answered in a very low voice; "it was far away from here."

The physician rolled up an armchair, and the Countess sank into it. The Count remained standing at the foot of the bed, repeating between his teeth: "Oh, my poor friend! my poor friend! What a frightful misfortune!"

And he was indeed deeply grieved, for he loved Olivier very much.

"But where did it happen?" the Countess repeated.

"I know hardly anything about it myself, or rather I do not understand it at all," the physician replied. "It was at the Gobelins, almost outside of Paris! At least, the cabman that brought him home declared to me that he took him in at a pharmacy of that quarter, to which someone had carried him, at nine o'clock in the evening!" Then, leaning toward Olivier, he asked: "Did the accident really happen near the Gobelins?"

Bertin closed his eyes, as if to recollect; then murmured: "I do not know."

"But where were you going?"

"I do not remember now. I was walking straight before me."

A groan that she could not stifle came from the Countess's lips; then oppressed with a choking that stopped her breathing a few seconds, she drew out her handkerchief, covered her eyes, and wept bitterly.

She knew — she guessed! Something intolerable, overwhelming had just fallen on her heart — remorse for not keeping Olivier near her, for driving him away, for throwing him into the street, where, stupefied with grief, he had fallen under the omnibus.

He said in that colorless voice he now had: "Do not weep. It distresses me."

By a tremendous effort of will, she ceased to sob, uncovered her eyes and fixed them, wide open, upon him, without a quiver of her face, whereon the tears continued slowly to roll down.

They looked at each other, both motionless, their hands clasped under the coverlet. They gazed at each other, no longer knowing that any other person was in the room; and that gaze carried a superhuman emotion from one heart to the other.

They gazed upon each other, and the need of talking, unheard, of hearing the thousand intimate things, so sad, which they had still to say, rose irresistibly to their lips. She felt that she must at any price send away the two men that stood behind her; she must find a way, some ruse, some inspiration, she, the woman, fruitful in resources! She began to reflect, her eyes always fixed on Olivier.

Her husband and the doctor were talking in undertones, discussing the care to be given. Turning her head the Countess said to the doctor: "Have you brought a nurse?"

"No, I prefer to send a hospital surgeon, who will keep a better watch over the case."

"Send both. One never can be too careful. Can you still get them tonight, for I do not suppose you will stay here till morning?"

"Indeed, I was just about to go home. I have been here four hours already."

"But on your way back you will send us the nurse and the surgeon?"

"It will be difficult in the middle of the night. But I shall try."

"You must!"

"They may promise, but will they come?"

"My husband will accompany you and will bring them back either willingly or by force."

"You cannot remain here alone, Madame!"

"I?" she exclaimed with a sort of cry of defiance, of indignant protest against any resistance to her will. Then she pointed out, in that authoritative tone to which no one ventures a reply, the necessities of the situation. It was necessary that the nurse and the surgeon should be there within an hour, to forestall all accident. To insure this, someone must get out of bed and bring them. Her husband alone could do that. During this time she would remain near the injured man, she, for whom it was a duty and a right. She would thereby simply fulfil her role of friend, her role of woman. Besides, this was her will, and no one should dissuade her from it.

Her reasoning was sensible. They could only agree upon that, and they decided to obey her.

She had risen, full of the thought of their departure, impatient to know that they were off and that she was left alone. Now, in order that she should commit no error during their absence, she listened, trying to understand perfectly, to remember everything, to forget nothing of the physician's directions. The painter's valet, standing near her, listened also, and behind him his wife, the cook, who had helped in the first binding of the patient, indicated by nods of the head that she too understood. When the Countess had recited all the instructions like a lesson, she urged the two men to go, repeating to her husband:

"Return soon, above all things, return soon!"

"I will take you in my coupe," said the doctor to the Count. "It will bring you back quicker. You will be here again in an hour."

Before leaving, the doctor again carefully examined the wounded man, to assure himself that his condition remained satisfactory.

Guilleroy still hesitated.

"You do not think that we are doing anything imprudent?" he asked.

"No," said the doctor. "He needs only rest and quiet. Madame de Guilleroy will see that he does not talk, and will speak to him as little as possible."

The Countess was startled, and said:

"Then I must not talk to him?"

"Oh, no, Madame! Take an armchair and sit beside him. He will not feel that he is alone and will be quite content; but no fatigue of words, or even of thoughts. I will call about nine o'clock tomorrow morning. Goodbye, Madame. I salute you!"

He left the room with a low bow, followed by the Count who repeated:

"Do not worry yourself, my dear. Within an hour I shall return, and then you can go home."

When they were gone, she listened for the sound of the door below being closed, then to the rolling wheels of the coupe in the street.

The valet and the cook still stood there, awaiting orders. The Countess dismissed them.

"You may go now," said she; "I will ring if I need anything."

They too withdrew, and she remained alone with him.

She had drawn quite near to the bed, and putting her hands on the two edges of the pillow, on both sides of that dear face, she leaned over to look upon it. Then, with her face so close to his that she seemed to breathe her words upon it, she whispered:

"Did you throw yourself under that carriage?"

He tried to smile still, saying: "No, it was that which threw itself upon me."

"That is not true; it was you."

"No, I swear to you it was it!"

After a few moments of silence, those instants when souls seem mingled in glances, she murmured: "Oh, my dear, dear Olivier, to think that I let you go, that I did not keep you with me!"

"It would have happened just the same, some day or another," he replied with conviction.

They still gazed at each other, seeking to read each other's inmost thoughts.

"I do not believe that I shall recover," he said at last. "I suffer too much."

"Do you suffer very much?" she murmured.

"Oh, yes!"

Bending a little lower, she brushed his forehead, then his eyes, then his cheeks with slow kisses, light, delicate as her care for him. She barely touched him with her lips, with that soft little breath that children give when they kiss. This lasted a long time, a very long time. He let that sweet rain of caresses fall on him, and they seemed to soothe and refresh him, for his drawn face twitched less than before.

"Any!" he said finally.

She ceased her kissing to listen to him.

"What, my friend?"

"You must make me a promise."

"I will promise anything you wish."

"If I am not dead before morning, swear to me that you will bring Annette to me, just once, only once! I cannot bear to die without seeing her again... . Think that...tomorrow...at this time perhaps I shall have...shall surely have closed my eyes forever and that I never shall see you again. I...nor you...nor her!"

She stopped him; her heart was breaking.

"Oh, hush...hush! Yes, I promise you to bring her!"

"You swear it?"

"I swear it, my friend. But hush, do not talk any more. You hurt me frightfully — hush!"

A quick convulsion passed over his face; when it had passed he said:

"Since we have only a few minutes more to remain together, do not let us lose them; let us seize them to bid each other good-by. I have loved you so much — — "

"And I," she sighed, "how I still love you!"

He spoke again:

"I never have had real happiness except through you. Only these last days have been hard... . It was not your fault... . Ah, my poor Any, how sad life is!...and how hard it is to die!"

"Hush, Olivier, I implore you!"

He continued, without listening to her: "I should have been a happy man if you had not had your daughter... ."

"Hush! My God! Hush!..."

He seemed to dream rather than speak.

"Ah, he that invented this existence and made men was either blind or very wicked...."

"Olivier, I entreat you...if you ever have loved me, be quiet, do not talk like that any more!"

He looked at her, leaning over him, she herself so pale that she looked as if she were dying, too; and he was silent.

Then she seated herself in the armchair, close to the bed, and again took the hand on the coverlet.

"Now I forbid you to speak," said she. "Do not stir, and think of me as I think of you."

Again they looked at each other, motionless, joined together by the burning contact of their hands. She pressed, with gentle movement, the feverish hand she clasped, and he answered these calls by tightening his fingers a little. Each pressure said something to them, evoked some period of their finished past, revived in their memory the stagnant recollections of their love. Each was a secret question, each was a mysterious reply, sad questions and sad replies, those "do you remembers?" of a bygone love.

Their minds, in this agonizing meeting, which might be the last, traveled back through the years, through the whole history of their passion; and nothing was audible in the room save the crackling of the fire.

Suddenly, as if awakening from a dream, he said, with a start of terror:

"Your letters!"

"What? My letters?" she queried.

"I might have died without destroying them!"

"Oh, what does that matter to me? That is of no consequence now. Let them find them and read them — I don't care!"

"I will not have that," he said. "Get up, Any; open the lowest drawer of my desk, the large one; they are all there, all. You must take them and throw them into the fire."

She did not move at all, but remained crouching, as if he had counseled her to do something cowardly.

"Any, I entreat you!" he continued; "if you do not do this, you will torture me, unnerve me, drive me mad. Think — they may fall into anyone's hands, a notary, a servant, or even your husband... . I do not wish...."

She rose, still hesitating, and repeating:

"No, that is too hard, too cruel! I feel as if you were compelling me to burn both our hearts!"

He supplicated her, his face drawn with pain.

Seeing him suffer thus, she resigned herself and walked toward the desk. On opening the drawer, she found it filled to the edge with a thick packet of letters, piled one on top of another, and she recognized on all the envelopes the two lines of the address she had written so often. She knew them — those two lines — a man's name, the name of a street — as well as she knew her own name, as well as one can know the few words that have represented to us in life all hope and all happiness. She looked at them, those little square things that contained all she had known how to express of her love, all that she could take of herself to give to him, with a little ink on a bit of white paper.

He had tried to turn his head on the pillow that he might watch her, and again he said: "Burn them, quick!"

Then she took two handfuls, holding them a few seconds in her grasp. They seemed heavy to her, painful, living, at the same time dead, so many different things were in them, so many things that were now over — so sweet to feel, to dream! It was the soul of her soul, the heart of her heart, the essence of her loving self that she was holding there; and she remembered with what delirium she had scribbled some of them, with what exaltation, what intoxication of living and of adoring some one, and of expressing it.

"Burn them! Burn them, Any!" Olivier repeated.

With the same movement of both hands, she cast into the fireplace the two packets of papers, which became scattered as they fell upon the wood. Then she seized those that remained in the desk and threw them on top of the others, then another handful, with swift movements, stooping and rising again quickly, to finish as soon as might be this terrible task.

When the fireplace was full and the drawer empty, she remained standing, waiting, watching the almost smothered flames as they crept up from all sides on that mountain of envelopes. They attacked them first at the edges, gnawed at the corners, ran along the edge of the paper, went out, sprang up again, and went creeping on and on. Soon, all around that white pyramid glowed a vivid girdle of clear fire which filled the room with light; and this light, illuminating the woman standing and the man dying, was their burning love, their love turned to ashes.

The Countess turned, and in the dazzling light of that fire she beheld her friend leaning with a haggard face on the edge of the bed.

"Are they all there?" he demanded.

"Yes, all."

But before returning to him she cast a last look upon that destruction, and on that mass of papers, already half consumed, twisting and turning black, and she saw something red flowing. It looked like drops of blood, and seemed to come out of the very heart of the letters, as from a wound; it ran slowly toward the flames, leaving a purple train.

The Countess received in her soul the shock of supernatural terror, and recoiled as if she had seen the assassination of a human being; then she suddenly understood that she had seen simply the melting of the wax seals.

She returned to the wounded man, and lifting his head tenderly laid it back in the center of the pillow. But he had moved, and his pain increased. He was panting now, his face drawn by fearful suffering, and he no longer seemed to know that she was there.

She waited for him to become a little calmer, to open his eyes, which remained closed, to be able to say one word more to her.

Presently she asked: "Do you suffer much?"

He did not reply.

She bent over him and laid a finger on his forehead to make him look at her. He opened his eyes then, but they were wild and dazed.

Terrified, she repeated: "Do you suffer? Olivier! Answer me! Shall I call? Make an effort! Say something to me!"

She thought she heard him murmur: "Bring her...you swore to me."

Then he writhed under the bedclothes, his body grew rigid, his face convulsed with awful grimaces.

"Olivier! My God! Olivier!" she cried. "What is the matter? Shall I call?"

This time he heard her, for he replied, "No...it is nothing."

He appeared to grow easier, in fact, to suffer less, to fall suddenly into a sort of drowsy stupor. Hoping that he would sleep, she sat down again beside the bed, took his hand, and waited. He moved no more, his chin had dropped to his breast, his mouth was half opened by his short breath, which seemed to rasp his throat in passing. Only his fingers moved involuntarily now and then, with slight tremors which the Countess felt to the roots of her hair, making her long to cry out. They were no more the tender little meaning pressures which, in place of the weary lips, told of all the sadness of their hearts; they were spasms of pain which spoke only of the torture of the body.

Now she was frightened, terribly frightened, and had a wild desire to run away, to ring, to call, but she dared not move, lest she might disturb his repose.

The far-off sound of vehicles in the streets penetrated the walls; and she listened to hear whether that rolling of wheels did not stop before the door, whether her husband were not coming to deliver her, to tear her away at last from this sad tete-a-tete.

As she tried to draw her hand from Olivier's, he pressed it, uttering a deep sigh! Then she resigned herself to wait, so that she should not trouble him.

The fire was dying out on the hearth, under the black ashes of the letters; two candles went out; some pieces of furniture cracked.

All was silent in the house; everything seemed dead except a tall Flemish clock on the stairs, which regularly chimed the hour, the half hour, and the quarter, singing the march of time in the night, modulating it in divers tones.

The Countess, motionless, felt an intolerable terror rising in her soul. Nightmare assailed her; fearful thoughts filled her mind; and she thought she could feel that Olivier's fingers were growing cold within her own. Was that true? No, certainly not. But whence had come that sensation of inexpressible, frozen contact? She roused herself, wild with terror, to look at his face. It was relaxed, impassive, inanimate, indifferent to all misery, suddenly soothed by the Eternal Oblivion.

THE END

www.ingramcontent.com/pod-product-compliance
Lightning Source LLC
Chambersburg PA
CBHW070148310726
48976CB00001B/26